D1199134

The Letters of

SYLVIA PLATH

VOLUME I

1940–1956

By Sylvia Plath

poetry

ARIEL

THE COLOSSUS

CROSSING THE WATER

WINTER TREES

COLLECTED POEMS
(edited by Ted Hughes)

SELECTED POEMS
(edited by Ted Hughes)

ARIEL: THE RESTORED EDITION
(Foreword by Frieda Hughes)

POEMS
(chosen by Carol Ann Duffy)

fiction

THE BELL JAR

JOHNNY PANIC AND THE BIBLE OF DREAMS

non-fiction

LETTERS HOME: CORRESPONDENCE 1950–1963
(edited by Aurelia Schober Plath)

THE JOURNALS OF SYLVIA PLATH
(edited by Karen V. Kukil)

SYLVIA PLATH: DRAWINGS
(edited by Frieda Hughes)

for children

THE BED BOOK
(illustrated by Quentin Blake)

THE IT-DOESN'T-MATTER SUIT
(illustrated by Rotraut Susanne Berner)

COLLECTED CHILDREN'S STORIES
(illustrated by David Roberts)

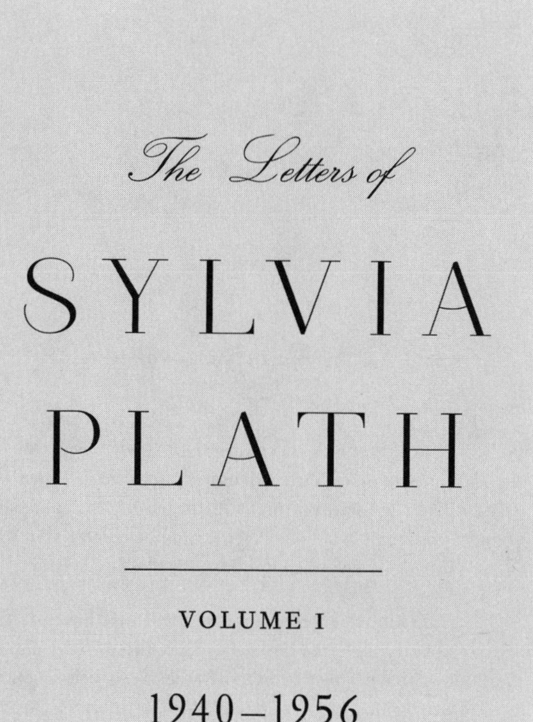

EDITED BY

PETER K. STEINBERG AND

KAREN V. KUKIL

HARPER

An Imprint of HarperCollins*Publishers*

HarperCollins books may be purchased for educational, business, or sales promotional use. For information, please email the Special Markets Department at SPsales@harpercollins.com.

Originally published in the United Kingdom in 2017 by Faber & Faber Ltd.

FIRST U.S. EDITION

Library of Congress Cataloging-in-Publication Data has been applied for.

ISBN 978-0-06-274043-4

17 18 19 20 21 LSC 10 9 8 7 6 5 4 3 2 1

CONTENTS

ACKNOWLEDGEMENTS

A remarkable collaboration produced this edition of *The Letters of Sylvia Plath*. We have many people to thank. Editing Sylvia Plath's letters began as an academic inter-term course taught at Smith College by Karen V. Kukil for the Archives Concentration program. Students in Editing Sylvia Plath's Correspondence learned the art of exact and accurate transcription, proofreading, and emendation based upon primary resources. A few years before the class began, Rebecca Rosenthal, class of 2007, processed the correspondence in the Sylvia Plath Collection held by the Mortimer Rare Book Room at Smith College. Over a three-year period from January 2011 to January 2013, students transcribed all the letters at Smith College. In January 2012 Plath scholar Peter K. Steinberg co-taught the course and then proceeded to locate, transcribe, and annotate all the extant Sylvia Plath letters in other collections. This edition of Sylvia Plath's letters is the product of our partnership with many students at Smith College, including Robin Whitham Acker '12; Sylvia L. Altreuter '12; Taylor A. Barrett '15; Taylor M. Bayer '12; Rachel E. Brenner '14; Ingrid Brioso-Rieumont '15; Virginia Choi '11; Melanie S. Colvin '13; Emily Cook '11; Ellen Cormier '11; Kristen L. De Lancey '15; Caroline F. T. Doenmez '09; Amanda P. Ferrara '13; Hope C. Fried '14; Alexandra Ghiz '12; Noa R. Gutterman '14; Kristen F. Haseney '04; Catherine Hatas '13; Victoria K. Henry '13; Cheryl R. Holmes '11; Katherine M. Horning '13; Angelica Huertas '10; Eve N. Hunter '12; Salma Hussain '14; Esra Karamehmet '12; Jinjin Lu '13; Emerson M. Lynch '15; Taylor A. Marks '15; Grace K. Martin '13; Katherine A. Nelson '12; Rebecca L. O'Leary '13; Lois Jenkins Peters '09; Emma Ramsay '12; Anne M. Re '13; Maris E. Schwarz '15; Chelsea A. Seamon '13; Joyce P. Shalaby '13; Jihyun J. Shim '14; Naomi Sinnathamby '14; Gabrielle E. Termuehlen '16; Dior Vargas '09; Alexandra B. von Mering '14; Drew L. Wagner '11; Genevieve C. Ward-Wernet '13; Erin M. Whelchel '09; Kaidi Williams '11; and Alison R. Winger '14. Professor Adrianne Andrews and other faculty members at Smith College also participated in the project.

A number of family, friends, and professional contacts of Sylvia Plath provided information reflected in the footnotes. In addition to Frieda Hughes, we would like to thank Warren Plath and his daughters Susan

Plath Winston and Jennifer Plath. We also appreciate the information received from Jane Baltzell-Kopp, Joan Cantor Barnes, Sarah Christie Bellwood, James B. Biery, Janet Burroway, Jonathan Christie, Susan Stetson Clarke, David Compton, Liadin Cooke, Blair Cruickshank, Ann Davidow-Goodman Hayes, Dena Dincauze, Jacquie Dincauze, Ruth Fainlight, Aidan Foster, Marian Foster, Johannes B. Frankfort, Nicholas Frankfort, Michael Frayn, Cary Plumer Frye, Charles S. Gardner, Ruth P. Geissler, Leo A. Goodman, Carol Hughes, Daniel Huws, Judy Kahrl, David N. Keightley, Elinor Friedman Klein, Lynne Lawner, Philip E. McCurdy, James McNeely, Eugene L. Mark, Doug Miller, Jane Nalieri, Kenneth Neville-Davies, Dr Richard Newell, Dr Perry Norton, Dr Richard A. Norton, Judith Raymo, Simon Sidamon-Eristoff, Elizabeth and William Sigmund, Robert Truslow, Louise Giesey White, Rosemary Wilson, and Nicolette Zeeman.

Professor Linda Wagner-Martin first articulated the need for a full edition of Sylvia Plath's letters during her plenary lecture at the Sylvia Plath 75th Year Symposium at Oxford University in 2007. A number of other scholars later contributed their insights and expertise as well. We would particularly like to thank professors Lynda K. Bundtzen (Williams College), Anita Helle (Oregon State University), Dianne Hunter (Trinity College), and Susan Van Dyne (Smith College) for their guidance. In addition, we would like to thank Dr Amanda Golden (New York Institute of Technology) for sharing her expansive knowledge of Plath's and Hughes's pedagogy, marginalia, poetry, and literary influence. Dr Gail Crowther provided invaluable research and information, as well as immeasurable support during the project. Gail was a vital contributor in building the notes to add context to Plath's activities. Gail located the two late letters to Gilbert and Marian Foster, which in addition to being fascinating documents add a new dimension to Plath's late interpersonal relationships. Her friendship, advice, and expertise helped to make this book possible. Likewise, without the dedication, passion, and camaraderie of David Trinidad, this book would be a shell of itself. David compiled an initial list of known letters, believed in the project since its inception, shared tireless thoughts with us in Plath-like 'bull sessions', located letters, and provided information for the notes. The amount of credit Golden, Crowther, and Trinidad deserve is unquantifiable.

The archivists, librarians, and curators responsible for photocopies and scans of Plath's letters, as well as for research assistance, who must be thanked for their tireless and important work are: Christine Barber and Peter Nelson at Amherst College; Elizabeth Maisey at Assumption College;

Louise North at the BBC Written Archives Centre; Andrew Gough and Helen Melody at the British Library; James Maynard at the University of Buffalo; Jacqueline Cox, Patricia McGuire, and Anne Thomson at the University of Cambridge; Rochelle Rubinstein at the Central Zionist Archives; Christine Colburn and Barbara Gilbert at the University of Chicago; James Merrick at Colby College; Tara C. Craig and Brigette C. Kamsler at Columbia University; Rebecca Parmer at Connecticut College; Allyson Glazier, Barbara L. Krieger, and Morgan R. Swan at Dartmouth College; Emily Erwin Jones at Delta State University; Claudia Frazer at Drake University; Seamus Helferty at University College, Dublin; Sara J. Logue and Kathy Shoemaker at Emory University; Robert Brown, archivist at Faber & Faber; Allison Haack at Grinnell College; the reference staff at Harvard University; Cara Bertram and Anna Chen at the University of Illinois at Urbana-Champaign; Zachary T. Downy, David Kim Frasier, Sarah McElroy Mitchell, Cherry Dunham Williams, and the staff of the Lilly Library, Indiana University at Bloomington; Karen Cook at the University of Kansas; Alexander Koch at Kenyon College; Anne L. Moore and Caroline White at the University of Massachusetts at Amherst; Renu Barrett at McMaster University; Katie Wood at the University of Melbourne; James Moske at the Metropolitan Museum of Art; Erin George at the University of Minnesota; Melina Baron-Deutsch and Deborah Richards at Mount Holyoke College; Michelle Harvey at The Museum of Modern Art, New York; Lyndsi Barnes, Isaac Gewirtz, Tal Nadan, Lee Spilberg, Weatherly Stephan, and Kyle R. Triplett at the New York Public Library; Connor Gaudet at New York University; Brooke Guthrie at the University of North Carolina at Chapel Hill; Susan Liberator and Lindy M. Smith at Ohio State University; Sylvie Merian and Maria Isabel Molestina-Kurlat at Pierpont Morgan Library; AnnaLee Pauls and Gabriel Swift at Princeton University; Ellen Shea at the Radcliffe Institute; Natalie Ford and Jean Rose at the Random House Group Archive & Library; Jenifer Monger at Rensselaer Polytechnic Institute; Blair A. Benson at the University of Rochester; Matthew Reynolds at Sewanee: The University of the South; Jason Wood at Simmons College; Kevin Auer, Jean Cannon, Susan C. Floyd, Kurt Johnson, Jordan P. Mitchell, Marian Oman, Emily Roehl, Richard B. Watson, and Richard Workman at the University of Texas at Austin; Milissa Burkart and Kristina Rosenthal at the University of Tulsa; Amanda Leinberger at the United Nations Archives; Lisa Jonsson and Lotta Sundberg at Uppsala University; Molly Dohrmann and Teresa Gray at Vanderbilt University; Victoria Platt at the Archive of Art and Design, Victoria and Albert Museum Archives; Sarah Schnuriger at Washington

University, St Louis; Chery Kinnick and Carla Rickerson at the University of Washington; Sue Hamilos at the Wellesley Free Library; Kathleen Fahey at the Wellesley Historical Society; Linda L. Hall at Williams College; and Heather Abbott, Jessica Becker, Michael Frost, Nancy F. Lyon, and William Massa at Yale University. Smith College colleagues and former colleagues who deserve special thanks include Martin Antonetti, Barbara Blumenthal, Mary Irwin and her student assistant Erinn Summers '16, Dr Meg Meiman, Christina Ryan, and Nanci Young.

The following array of scholars and friends have also provided assistance that in various ways greatly benefited this book: Anna Arays, Sir Jonathan Bate, Carol Bere, Laura Joy Broom, Sarah Funke Butler, Ruby Butler-Weeks, Heather Clark, Rosemary Clark; Vanessa Cook, Diane Demko, Suzanne Demko, Joseph J. Feeney, SJ, Gunnar Fernlund, Amanda Ferrara, Susan France, Peter Fydler, Andre Gailani, Sarah George-Waterfield, Sara Georgini, Jonathan Glover, Alix de Gramont, Kelly Holbert, Eric Homberger, Richard Honan, Shaun Kelly, An Kieu, Jocelyne Kolb, Barbara F. Kozash, Arthur Languirand, Richard Larschan, Jane Lawrence, Carol Lewis, Maria R. Lichtmann, Annika J. Lindskog, Kim Maddever, Ann Safford Mandel, Sherry Marker, Laura Anderson Martino, Lisa Matchett, Gesa Matthies, Aubrey Menard, Mark Morford, Catherine Morgan, Maeve O'Brien, Kevin O'Donnell, Laura de la Paz Rico, Cornelia Pearsall, Hannah Piercy, Neil Roberts, Carl Rollyson, Angelyn Singer, Ann Skea, Tristine Skyler, Nick Smart, Jeffrey Summers, Angélique Thomine, Angeline Wang, Louise Watson, Reverend Nick Weldon, Ian Widdicks, Dianne Wieland, Lydia K. Wilkins, Andrew Wilson, Elizabeth Winder, and Mark Wormald.

For permission to quote from published material, we gratefully acknowledge David Higham Associates Limited, New Directions Publishing Corporation, and Oberon Books Ltd.

Our gratitude must extend to those at Faber & Faber who were instrumental in parts of this project, including Erica Brown, Emma Cheshire, Pauline Collingridge, Matthew Hollis, Hamish Ironside, Lavinia Singer, Camilla Smallwood, Donald Sommerville, and Martha Sprackland. The commitment of Matthew Hollis and his team at Faber & Faber to publish a complete edition of Sylvia Plath's letters is greatly appreciated. We also thank Terry Karten and her colleagues at HarperCollins: Robin Bilardello, Tina Andreadis, Tom Hopke, Cindy Achar, and Laura Brown.

Personally, Karen is grateful to Sylvia Plath's friends who recognized her talent, preserved her letters, and donated them to Smith College where they are cherished. Generous support from former president Ruth

Simmons and alumnae, including Rachael Bartels, also added select letters to the collection. Karen also thanks Beth Myers, Director of Special Collections, and Christopher Loring, former Director of Libraries, who extended all the resources of the Smith College Libraries for the duration of this independent project. In addition to former curator and mentor Ruth Mortimer, who collected the papers of Sylvia Plath for Smith College with the support of president Jill Ker Conway, Karen would like to recognize her first professional mentor, Wilmarth S. Lewis, who edited the *Yale Edition of Horace Walpole's Correspondence* and taught her the exacting art of editing letters. Karen is particularly indebted to her brilliant co-editor, Peter K. Steinberg, who completed the lion's share of work on this edition with superior erudition and dedication. Most profoundly, Karen wishes to thank her extended Valuckas and Kukil families, especially her husband, Bohdan Kukil, for his humour and unwavering love and support during this intense editing project.

Peter would like to thank his wife Courtney for her love, extraordinary patience, and support for the duration of this project. The love and understanding of the families Steinberg, Levine, Little, and Plocinski at home and during vacations over the last five years must be recognized. Peter would not have pursued his interest in Sylvia Plath were it not for the initial encouragement from Andrea Holland and Jamie Wasserman. Since meeting Karen V. Kukil in 1998, she has always been a mentor and inspiration, helping both personally and professionally. Peter would like to thank Karen for her complete belief and trust in him, which made his contribution to this project possible.

ILLUSTRATIONS

17. Self-portrait holding a book, from SP to Marcia B. Stern, 1 July 1951.
18. Sylvia Plath standing beside a bicycle, Marblehead, Massachusetts, 24 July 1951.

19. Drawing of a female on crutches in a high wind with hands reaching through ice, from SP to Myron Lotz, 9 January 1953.
20. Drawings of jackets, dresses, and a shoe, from SP to Aurelia Plath, 28 April 1953.
21. Drawing of a female wearing a robe, on a pillow, holding a pen, from SP to Gordon Lameyer, 22 June 1954.
22. Drawing of streets, houses, and ocean in Winthrop, Massachusetts, from SP to Gordon Lameyer, 22 June 1954.
23. Drawing of soup on a table, from SP to Gordon Lameyer, 22 June 1954.
24. Sylvia Plath at Chatham, Massachusetts, *c.* 24 July 1954.
25. Sylvia Plath and Ruth (Freeman) Geissler on Ruth's wedding day, Winthrop, Massachusetts, 11 June 1955.
26. Drawing of SP's room at Whitstead, from SP to Aurelia Plath, 2 October 1955.
27. Drawing of a coffee table with a plant, a *New Yorker*, and other items on back of an envelope, from SP to J. Mallory Wober, 16 November 1955.
28. Drawing of a female figure in dressing room looking in mirror holding a pen, from SP to J. Mallory Wober, 24 November 1955.
29. Drawing of a bouquet of daffodils on back of an envelope, from SP to Aurelia Schober, 2 February 1956.
30. Sylvia Plath atop Torre dell'Orologio, Venice, 8 April 1956.
31. Sylvia Plath at Fontana Muta, Rampa Caffarelli, Rome, 10 April 1956.
32. Sylvia Plath sitting on stone wall with typewriter, on Yorkshire moors, September 1956.

Items 3, 5, 9, 10, 14, 19, 20, 21, 22, 23, 24, 26, 29, 30, 31 are reproduced by courtesy of the Lilly Library, Indiana University, Bloomington, Indiana. No. 3 © Unknown; Nos 24, 30, 31 © Estate of Gordon Lameyer.

Items 4 and 8 are reproduced by courtesy of the Estate of Margot Loungway Drekmeier; No. 4 © Estate of Margot Loungway Drekmeier.

Items 27 and 28 are reproduced by courtesy of the King's College Archives, Cambridge University.

FOREWORD

My mother, Sylvia Plath, wrote an enormous number of letters during her all-too-short lifetime: letters to family and friends about family and friends; about work, to promote work, to submit work; as well as writing her *Journals* (published by Faber, UK, and Anchor Books, US.) I am in awe of her output, and the way in which she recorded so much of her life so that it was not lost to us. Through publication of her poems, prose, diaries, and now her collected letters, my mother continues to exist; she is best explained in her own words, capturing a real sense of the era at the time, and her passion for literature and life – and for my father, Ted Hughes.

It has always been my conviction that the reason my mother should be of interest to readers at all is due to my father, because, irrespective of the way their marriage ended, he honoured my mother's work and her memory by publishing *Ariel*, the collection of poems that launched her into the public consciousness, after her death. He, perhaps more than anyone, recognised and acknowledged her talent as extraordinary. Without *Ariel*, my mother's literary genius might have gone unremarked forever. Although, by ensuring her work got the attention it surely deserved, my father also initiated the castigation that was to hound him for the rest of his life.

It seems to me that, as a result of their profound belief in each other's literary abilities, my parents are as married in death as they once were in life.

Frieda Hughes
2017

PREFACE

This complete and unabridged edition of Sylvia Plath's letters, prepared in two volumes, finally allows the author to fully narrate her own autobiography through correspondence with a combination of family, friends and professional contacts. Plath's epistolary style is as vivid, powerful, and complex as her poetry, prose and journal writing. While her journal entries were frequently exercises in composition, her letters often dig out the caves behind each character and situation in her life. Plath kept the interests of her addressees in mind as she crafted her letters. As a result, her voice is as varied as the more than 1,390 letters in these volumes to her more than 140 correspondents.

Plath's first letters to her parents were written in pencil in a cursive script. She often illustrated her early letters with drawings and flourishes in colour. Later letters were either written in black ink or typed on a variety of coloured papers, greeting cards and memorandum sheets.

Most of the original letters are held by the Lilly Library, Indiana University, Bloomington, Indiana, and the William Allan Neilson Library, Smith College, Northampton, Massachusetts. Additional letters are dispersed among more than forty libraries and archives. Some letters are still in private collections.

Sylvia Plath was extremely well read and curious about all aspects of culture in the mid-twentieth century. As a result, the topics of her letters were wide-ranging, from the atomic bomb to W. B. Yeats. All phases of her development are documented in her correspondence. The most intimate details of her daily life were candidly described in letters to her mother from 1940 to 1963. (This correspondence, originally published in an abridged form by Aurelia Schober Plath as *Letters Home*, appears here in a complete transcription for the first time.) Plath wrote about early hobbies, such as stamp collecting, to one of her childhood friends, Margot Loungway Drekmeier. During high school, she explained the intricacies of American popular culture to a German pen pal, Hans-Joachim Neupert. There were many men in Plath's life. To an early boyfriend, Philip McCurdy, she wrote about friendship as their romance waned. Later to some of her former Smith College roommates, such as Marcia Brown Plumer Stern, she wrote about her travels in Europe, marital relationships, motherhood, and domestic crafts. In the sixteen letters written to Ted Hughes shortly after their marriage and honeymoon, Plath described her courses and life in Cambridge. Her discussion of their poetry documents their extraordinary creative partnership. Plath's business-related letters show a different side. Readers familiar with her journals will know she long sought publication in the *New Yorker*. Plath's correspondence with several editors of the *New Yorker* demonstrates her efforts to satisfy concerns they had about lines, imagery, punctuation, and titles. Her submissions were not always accepted, but what arises is a healthy working relationship that routinely brought her poetry to publication. In addition to her literary development, the genesis of many poems, short stories, and novels is fully revealed in her letters. Her primary focus was always on her poetry, thrusting up from her 'psychic ground root'.

Some memorable incidents from Plath's life were recounted and enhanced multiple times in her letters and often found their way into her prose and poetry. She was so conscious of her audience that even when her experiences were repeated there were subtle variations of emphasis aimed to achieve a maximum response or reaction.

When Plath's *Letters Home* was published in the United States in 1975 (and in the United Kingdom the following year), the edition was highly selected with unmarked editorial omissions, changes to Plath's words, and incorrect dates assigned to some letters. Only 383 of 856 letters to her mother and family were partially published in *Letters Home*. By contrast, the goal of this edition of Plath's letters is to present a complete and historically accurate text of all the known, existing letters to a full range of her correspondents. The transcriptions of the letters are as faithful to the author's originals as possible. Plath's final revisions are preserved and her substantive deletions and corrections are discussed in the footnotes. Plath's spelling, capitalization, punctuation, and grammar, as well as her errors, have been carefully transcribed and are presented without editorial comment. Original layout and page breaks, however, are not duplicated. Incredibly frugal and conscientious of the limited space available to her, Plath wrote and typed to the very edges of her paper. This was especially the case when she wrote from England on blue aerogrammes. Occasionally, punctuation marks are not present in the original letters, but are implied by the start of a new sentence or paragraph. As a result, when Plath's intention was clear, punctuation has been added to the letter without editorial comment.

Dates for undated letters were assigned from postmarks and/or internal and external evidence and are identified with a *circa* date (for example, to

Ann Davidow-Goodman, *c.* Friday 12 January 1951). In some instances where dating a letter exactly proved too difficult or uncertain, we have offered either a range of days or simply the month or the year (for example, to *Mademoiselle*, *c.* February 1955 and to Edith & William Hughes, *c.* 1957). Locations of the original manuscripts are also included in the introductory header for each letter. Scans of selected drawings included in letters by Plath and photographs of her life are gathered together in the plates. Enclosures of early poems have been transcribed and included with the appropriate letter. Many of these photographs and poems have never been published.

Comprehensive factual and supporting footnotes are provided. These annotations aim to bring context to Plath's life; her experiences, her publication history and that of Ted Hughes, cultural events, and her education and interests. Significant places, family, friends and professional contacts are identified at their first mention. Where possible, the footnotes supply referential information about the letters to which Plath was responding, as well as the locations for books from her personal library and papers written for her university courses. We made use of Plath's early diaries, adult journals, scrapbooks, and personal calendars to offer additional biographical information in order to supply, for instance, dates of production for her creative writing.

An extensive index completes the publication and serves as an additional reference guide. The adult names of Plath's female friends and acquaintances are used, but the index also includes cross references to their birth names and other married names.

As we read, edited, and annotated the letters initially available to us, we kept a running list of all the other letters Plath mentioned writing, which number more than 700. Some letters were destroyed, lost or not retained, such as those to Eddie Cohen and to boyfriends Richard Sassoon and Richard Norton. Other letters are presumed to remain in private hands, such as a postcard sent from McLean Hospital in December 1953, which was offered for sale at Sotheby's in 1982. Plath wrote letters and notes to many other acquaintances, Smith classmates, publishers, teachers, and mentors, as well as to family friends. We attempted to contact many of these recipients; a majority of these requests went unanswered. Those who did respond yielded some positive results. After this edition of *The Letters of Sylvia Plath* is published, additional letters that are discovered may be gathered for subsequent publication.

INTRODUCTION

Sylvia Plath was many things to many people: daughter, niece, sister, student, journalist, poet, friend, artist, girlfriend, wife, novelist, peer, and mother; but perhaps the most overlooked feature of her life was that she was human, and therefore fallible. She misspelled words, punctuated incorrectly, lied, misquoted texts, exaggerated, was sarcastic, and sometimes brutally honest. All, and more, are aspects of the *Letters of Sylvia Plath*.

The first letters collected in this volume are to Sylvia Plath's parents, written in February 1940. They were found in the attic of the Plath family home at 92 Johnson Avenue, Winthrop, Massachusetts. Plath was seven and a quarter years old and staying temporarily with her grandparents nearby at 892 Shirley Street when her correspondence begins. Written in pencil on 19 February, the letter to her father, Otto, includes a heart-shaped enclosure in which she expresses concern for his health, 'I hope you are better' and is signed 'With love / from / Sylvia'. Plath's readers may recognize the same imagery in 'Daddy', when the speaker claims her father had 'bit my pretty red heart in two'. Otto Plath died later that year. On 20 February, Plath wrote to her mother, the first of more than 700 letters sent over the next twenty-three years, adding a crayon drawing to illustrate the text. Throughout her life, Sylvia Plath would express herself in the medium of drawing, as well as the literary arts, often combining the two in her correspondence.

Between 1943 and 1948, Plath spent her summers away from the family home at camps in New Hampshire and Massachusetts. She wrote nearly every day to her mother, less frequently to her brother and maternal relatives. These letters show from the start the importance afforded to correspondence in the Plath household. We may take for granted today the ease and instantaneousness of communication, but in the 1940s replies were slower. On 18 July 1943, Plath wrote 'I didn't get a letter from you yesterday, I hope you are all right . . . Are you well? I worry when I don't receive letters from you.' These letters tender a catalogue of quintessential activities from swimming and hiking to arts and crafts and eating. The young Plath had a voracious appetite as evidenced by this meal in July 1945: 'For lunch I had a bird's feed of <u>6</u> plates of casserole

& sauce containing potatos, peas, onions, carrots, chicken (yum, yum); five cups of punch and a scoop of vanilla, coffee, and orange ice cream.' Here, Plath's sense of humour shines through: 'If you're hard up on ration points when I come home you can have Joe slaughter me and you can eat me for pork.' In time, Plath became competent and energetic about food preparation. She hosted a large party while attending Harvard Summer School, serving 'a huge bouffet, with delectable varieties of meat, fish, hors d'ouvres, desserts' (5 August 1954). She made the most of limited resources on 'a single gas ring' as a Fulbright student at Newnham College by managing 'to create a steak dinner complete with sherry, hors d'oeuvres, salad, etc. in rebellion versus English cooking' (14 December 1955).

The earlier letters also include Plath's youthful verse and some of these poems appear here in print for the first time. In a letter dated 20 March 1943, Plath sent her mother the following quatrain:

> Plant a little seedling
> Mix with rain and showers,
> Stir them with some sun-shine,
> And up come some flowers.

The predominant themes of fairies and nature that appeared in these poems were acknowledged by Plath much later when she was asked 'What sort of thing did you write about when you began?' She replied:

> Nature, I think: birds, bees, spring, fall, all those subjects which are absolute gifts to the person who doesn't have any interior experience to write about. I think the coming of spring, the stars overhead, the first snowfall and so on are gifts for a child, a young poet.

In their focus upon her immediate surroundings, the poems by the young writer composed at summer camp established a practice that she continued until the end. In 'Camp Helen Storrow', the speaker observes 'The trees are swaying in the wind / The night is dark & still' (7 July 1945); likewise in Plath's late poem 'Mystic', the speaker's memories allude to her time at summer camp, 'I remember / The dead smell of sun on wood cabins'. Plath had success writing about places. For example, her poems about Cape Cod, Massachusetts ('Mussel Hunter at Rock Harbor'), Grantchester, England ('Watercolour of Grantchester Meadows'), and Benidorm, Spain ('The Net Menders') were each accepted for publication by the *New Yorker*. Similarly, she regularly published travel articles in the *Christian Science Monitor*.

Plath's non-familial letters begin with a friend Margot Loungway Drekmeier (seventeen letters, 1945–7); her best friend's mother Marion Freeman (twelve letters, 1946–62); and a German pen-pal Hans-Joachim Neupert (eighteen letters, 1947–52). In these we learn of Plath's little-known interest in philately; her sincerity and graciousness to a woman she considered a 'second mother'; and her ability to relate to a foreign pen-pal and convey what it was like growing up in America. What readers will see here is Plath's empathetic attention to her recipients and how, like writing a poem or short story for a specific market, she was able to craft a letter concentrating solely on her relationship to the addressee. There are often inside jokes and other content that will be above our heads, but Plath's letter writing is a serious art form.

Following the appearance of her short story 'And Summer Will Not Come Again' (*Seventeen*, August 1950) and weeks from matriculating at Smith College, Plath received her first fan letter from Edward Cohen of Chicago. In one of her replies, Plath provided a self-portrait as a nearly eighteen-year-old:

> Maybe you don't know how it is not to be accepted in a group of kids because you're just a little too individual. Shyness, in their terminology is conceit, good marks signify the horror of horrors . . . a brain. No doubt this all sounds oozingly pathetic, but it's one of the reasons that I'm the way I am. I'm sarcastic, skeptical and sometimes callous because I'm still afraid of letting myself be hurt. There's that very vulnerable core in me which every egoist has . . . and I try rather desperately not to let it show.
>
> (11 August 1950)

Of the eighty-five collected letters written during her first semester at Smith College, all but two are to her mother. An additional sixty-six letters were sent to Wellesley between January and May of 1951. The result is a nearly uninterrupted narrative of her first year away from home. That spring, Plath also sent eight letters to her good friend Ann Davidow-Goodman Hayes, who did not return to Smith after the first semester. These letters to Ann, as well as to her other lifelong friend Marcia Brown Stern, span both volumes and provide a glimpse of the strong bonds Plath made with her classmates.

Many of Plath's journal entries at the start of her college years are undated. To the contrary, Plath's letters were either meticulously dated by her or have been assigned dates by the present editors. This may allow those journal passages with no dates to be identified. For example, Plath's undated journal entry 45 recounts 'Another blind date. This one is older.' She provided a more staid version of the evening in a letter written to her mother on 3 December 1950. Journal entry 64 contains 'Notes on an experimental film', which was *Un Chien Andalou* directed by Luis Buñuel and Salvador Dali. Plath wrote to her mother on the night of 10 April 1951: 'Saw a brief Dali shock movie – my one free act for the rest of the year.' This exercise may lead to a ripple effect, forwards and backwards, of being able to date additional journal entries.

There are no journals from autumn 1953 to autumn 1955. Publishing Plath's letters from this period fills an autobiographical void and offers first-hand accounts of her life from readmission to Smith College in 1954 to her departure for Britain in September 1955. The letters to Gordon Lameyer, Philip McCurdy, her mother, Richard Sassoon, and Jon Rosenthal, for example, establish her successful re-immersion in both academic and social life. Plath always took her studies and writing seriously, but she regularly travelled to Boston, New York, and New Haven for dates and cultural events. Hungry for new experiences because they encourage 'personality adjustments', she challenged her own comfort in numerous ways such as taking a two-seater plane flight and adjudicating a high-school writing contest. In her last semester at Smith, Plath enrolled in a special studies course, 'The Theory and Practice of Poetics', and produced 'a "batch" of poems weekly', amounting to more than fifty new works (9 January 1955).

While her goal was still to appear in the *New Yorker*, by the time she graduated Smith on 6 June 1955 Plath's poetry was appearing in major American publications such as *Harper's* and the *Atlantic Monthly*. She had made the acquaintance of famous writers and poets, too, among them Elizabeth Bowen, and W. H. Auden, and Marianne Moore, who offered advice and support. With nearly a decade of experience to this point, Plath was practical in her approach to submitting her work and handling either acceptance or rejection. When she arrived in Britain she was presented with a new market of periodicals to which to offer her work and a different audience of readers. While still submitting poems to American journals, Plath quickly tried magazines based in London, Oxford, and Cambridge. She maximized exposure by publishing her work in Britain and America. For example, 'Epitaph for Fire and Flower' was published simultaneously in Cambridge's *Chequer* (Winter 1956–7) and Chicago's *Poetry* (January 1957).

In her first term at Newnham College, Cambridge, Plath joined the Amateur Dramatics Club, performing in a small 'nursery' production and in the big autumn performance of *Bartholomew Fair*. To Marcia Brown Stern, Plath wrote about the many possible groups and activities open to students: 'there are clubs for everything from puppetry to piloting, communists to heretics, wine tasters to beaglers! Indifference is the cardinal sin' (*c.* 14 December 1955).

Plath spent her Christmas 1955 break from Newnham on the continent, in Paris and Nice, with Richard Sassoon. Upon her return to Cambridge, Sassoon abruptly ended their relationship. Plath was not short of male attention (she wrote to her mother that there were '10 men to each woman!'), but Sassoon's departure disturbed her. She sent Sassoon a number of letters that winter and thoughtfully transcribed excerpts into her journals. Although printed in the *Journals of Sylvia Plath* (Faber, 2000), these excerpts appear in this volume to lend documentary force and context in the storyline of her spring 1956 correspondence.

On 25 February 1956, Plath wrote to her mother that 'it is a new day: bright, with sun, and a milder aspect' and notified her that she was 'going to a party celebrating the publication of a new literary review'. The following week, Plath wrote again to her mother:

> Met, by the way, a brilliant ex-Cambridge poet at the wild St. Botolph's Review party last week; will probably never see him again (he works for J. Arthur Rank in London) but wrote my best poem about him afterwards: the only man I've met yet here who'd be strong enough to be equal with; such is life; will send a few poems in my next letter so you can see what I'm doing.
>
> (3 March 1956)

True to her word, on 9 March Plath sent her mother 'Pursuit' with a full explication. It is not until 19 April, however, that Plath formally introduces 'this poet, this Ted Hughes' by name. 'He is tall, hulking, with a large-cut face, shocks of dark brown hair and blazing green & blue flecked eyes; he wears the same old clothes all the time: a thick black sweater & wine-stained khaki pants.'

The courtship and marriage of Plath and Hughes has been well documented in the past by biographers, but never before in Plath's own, unedited words. Their marriage was kept secret, as Plath feared she would lose her Fulbright scholarship if the authorities discovered she was married. On their honeymoon in Spain, the couple resumed a routine established in Cambridge of reading and writing verse. As noted earlier, Plath relished preparing meals under somewhat rustic conditions. Thus, in Benidorm, she had the time and opportunity to 'cook on a fickle one-ring petrol burner, and write and write. We are happy as hell, writing stories, poems, books, fables' (10 August 1956).

The happiness continued through a September spent with the Hughes family at the Beacon in Heptonstall. In addition to writing while in Yorkshire, they made frequent excursions on the surrounding moors. Plath returned to Cambridge, alone, on 1 October. Once back in her room at Whitstead, she wrote the first of sixteen letters to Hughes over the next twenty-two days. The journey 'was hell', but she returned to news that 'POETRY has accepted SIX of my poems!!!!!!!!!! Like we dreamed of.'

As the month progressed the separation became unbearable. In the first of two letters to Hughes on 21 October, Plath writes 'I feel so mere and fractional without you.' In the second letter that day she admits 'I am terribly lonely for you.' The next day, Plath imparted the results of some research, 'I looked up the fulbright lists and found three married women on it; so singleness is not a condition of a fulbright for ladies' (22 October 1956).

This volume closes with two letters written on 23 October 1956, four days prior to Plath's twenty-fourth birthday. To Peter Davison, an editor at the *Atlantic Monthly* and former boyfriend, Plath submitted her husband's manuscript of children's fables and caught up on general news and acceptances. She concludes optimistically, 'I look most forward to coming back home next June. I feel somehow like a feminine Samson with hair cut, if such is possible---being so far away from editors & publishing houses!' To her mother she exuberates:

> ted is coming to live & work in cambridge for the rest of the year; in the next two weeks we are going on a rigorous campaign of making our marriage public to first my philosophy supervisor, next the fulbright, next newnham; we are married and it is ridiculous and impossible for either of us to be whole or healthy apart.

Peter K Steinberg and Karen V. Kukil
2017

CHRONOLOGY

1932

27 October — Sylvia Plath born in Boston, Massachusetts, to Otto Emil and Aurelia Schober Plath; the family lives at 24 Prince Street, Jamaica Plain, a neighbourhood in Boston.

1935

27 April — Warren Joseph Plath born.

1936

Autumn — The Plaths move to 92 Johnson Avenue in Winthrop, Massachusetts.

1937

September — Enrols in the Sunshine School, Winthrop.

1938

September — Enters Annie F. Warren Grammar School, Winthrop.

1940

February — Writes first letters to her parents.
September — Enters E. B. Newton School, Winthrop.
October — Otto Plath admitted to the New England Deaconess Hospital, Boston; his left, gangrenous leg amputated.
5 November — Otto Plath dies from an embolus in his lung.

1941

10 August — 'Poem' appears in the *Boston Herald*; her first publication.

1942

October — Moves with her mother, brother, and grandparents, Frank and Aurelia Schober, to 26 Elmwood Road, Wellesley, Massachusetts. Enters the Marshall Perrin Grammar School.

1943/4	
Summers	Attends Camp Weetamoe in Center Ossipee, New Hampshire.
1944	
January	Begins writing in a journal.
September	Enters Alice L. Phillips Junior High School, publishes in school paper.
1945/6	
Summers	Attends Camp Helen Storrow in Plymouth, Massachusetts.
1947/8	
Summers	Attends Vineyard Sailing Camp at Oak Bluffs, Martha's Vineyard.
September	Enters Gamaliel Bradford Senior High School, Wellesley.
1948	
June	Named co-editor of school newspaper, *The Bradford*.
1949	
March	Publishes poem 'Sea Symphony' in *Student Life*.
Summer	Attends Unitarian conference at Star Island, New Hampshire.
1950	
March	Publishes article 'Youth's Plea for World Peace' in the *Christian Science Monitor*.
May	Accepted into Class of 1954 at Smith College, Northampton, Massachusetts. Receives Olive Higgins Prouty scholarship.
Summer	Works at Lookout Farm with Warren Plath in Natick, Massachusetts.
August	Publishes short story 'And Summer Will Not Come Again' in *Seventeen*.
Autumn	Enters Smith College, resides at Haven House. Meets Prouty.

1951

February	Begins dating Richard 'Dick' Norton, a senior at Yale University and Wellesley resident.
March	Attends Yale Junior Prom with Norton. Meets Eddie Cohen.
Summer	Works as nanny for Mayo family in Swampscott, Massachusetts. Her friend Marcia Brown nannies nearby.
Autumn	Writes articles for local newspapers as Press Board correspondent for Smith College.

1952

Summer	Waitresses at the Belmont Hotel in West Harwich, Massachusetts. 'Sunday at the Mintons'' wins *Mademoiselle* short fiction contest. Works as nanny for the Cantor family in Chatham, Massachusetts.
September	Moves to Lawrence House, a cooperative house, at Smith College.
Autumn	Continues writing for Press Board. Dick Norton treated for exposure to tuberculosis in New York.
November	Meets Yale student Myron Lotz; relationship with Norton strained.
December	Visits Norton at Ray Brook, New York; breaks leg in skiing accident.

1953

February	Dates Lotz and Gordon Lameyer, a senior at Amherst College. Writes villanelle 'Mad Girl's Love Song'.
April–May	*Harper's* accepts three poems; wins Guest Editor competition at *Mademoiselle* in New York City.
June	Lives at Barbizon Hotel in New York; works at *Mademoiselle*.
July–August	Treated for insomnia and exhaustion; counselled by psychiatrist; given poorly administered outpatient electro-convulsive shock treatments.
24–26 August	Attempts suicide in the basement of her house by taking an overdose of sleeping pills. When found, admitted to Newton-Wellesley Hospital.
September	Transfers first to Massachusetts General Hospital, Boston, then to McLean Hospital, Belmont, Massachusetts. Begins treatment with Dr Ruth Beuscher.

1954

January	Re-enters Smith College; repeats second semester of her junior year.
April	Meets Richard Sassoon, a Yale student.
Summer	Attends Harvard Summer School and lives in Cambridge, Massachusetts.
Autumn	Senior year at Smith College on full scholarship; writes thesis on Dostoevsky.

1955

February	Accepted by Newnham College, University of Cambridge.
April	Competes in Glascock Poetry Contest, Mount Holyoke College, Hadley, Massachusetts.
May	Wins Fulbright scholarship to University of Cambridge.
6 June	Graduates Smith College, *summa cum laude*.
September	Sails on the *Queen Elizabeth* to UK.
October	Begins courses at Newnham College.
Winter	Travels to Paris and the south of France with Sassoon.

1956

25 February	Attends party at Falcon Yard, meets Edward 'Ted' James Hughes.
March–April	Travels through France, Germany, and Italy with Gordon Lameyer.
16 June	Marries Ted Hughes at St George-the-Martyr, Queen Square, London.
Summer	Honeymoons in Alicante and Benidorm; meets Warren Plath in Paris; lives at the Hughes home, The Beacon, in Heptonstall, Yorkshire.
Autumn	Begins second year at Newnham College; keeps marriage a secret.
December	Moves to 55 Eltisley Avenue, Cambridge, UK.

1957

23 February	Hughes's poetry collection *The Hawk in the Rain* wins *Harper's* poetry prize.
12 March	Smith College offers Plath teaching position on English faculty.

June	Finishes programme at Newnham; sails on *Queen Elizabeth* to New York.
Summer	Vacations in Eastham, Massachusetts.
September	Moves to 337 Elm Street, Northampton, Massachusetts; begins teaching at Smith College.

1958

June	Leaves position at Smith College. Records poems for Woodberry Poetry Room, Harvard. Receives first *New Yorker* acceptances for 'Mussel Hunter at Rock Harbor' and 'Nocturne' ['Hardcastle Crags'].
9 August	'Mussel Hunter at Rock Harbor' appears in *The New Yorker*.
September	Moves to 9 Willow Street, Beacon Hill, Boston.
10 December	Resumes seeing Dr Beuscher, records details in her journals.

1959

February	Records more poems for Woodberry Poetry Room. Attends Robert Lowell's poetry course at Boston University, meets Anne Sexton.
8 March	Visits father's grave in Winthrop.
July–August	Travels across North America; becomes pregnant.
Autumn	Spends two months at the writer's colony Yaddo, Saratoga Springs, New York. Has creative writing breakthrough.
December	Sails on the *United States* to UK.

1960

January	Rents flat at 3 Chalcot Square, Primrose Hill, London.
10 February	Signs contract with Heinemann in London to publish her first collection of poetry, *The Colossus and Other Poems*.
1 April	Daughter, Frieda Rebecca Hughes born.
31 October	*The Colossus* published in Britain.

1961

February	Suffers a miscarriage.
March	Has an appendectomy.
Spring	Begins writing *The Bell Jar*.

June	Records poems for BBC series *The Living Poet*.
July	Travels to France; reads 'Tulips' at the Poetry at the Mermaid festival in London.
August	Purchases Court Green in North Tawton, Devonshire; sublets London flat to David and Assia Wevill.
1 September	Moves to Court Green.

1962

17 January	Son, Nicholas Farrar Hughes born.
May	Visits from Ruth Fainlight and Alan Sillitoe, as well as the Wevills.
Summer	Assia Wevill and Hughes begin an affair. Aurelia Plath visits Court Green.
September	Visits Irish poet Richard Murphy in Cleggan, Ireland; Hughes abruptly leaves.
October	Writes twenty-five poems; records 'Berck-Plage' for BBC and fifteen poems for British Council/Woodberry Poetry Room.
November	Rents flat at 23 Fitzroy Road, London, formerly a residence of W. B. Yeats.
10 December	Moves with Frieda and Nicholas into Fitzroy Road flat.

1963

January	Dubbed the 'Big Freeze of 1963', London experiences its coldest winter of the century.
10 January	Records review of Donald Hall's *Contemporary American Poetry* for BBC.
14 January	Heinemann publishes *The Bell Jar* under the pseudonym Victoria Lucas.
4 February	Writes last known letters.
4–5 February	Writes last known poems.
7–10 February	Stays with Jillian and Gerry Becker at nearby 5 Mountfort Crescent, Islington.
11 February	Protects children then commits suicide by gas poisoning.
18 February	Laid to rest in Heptonstall.

ABBREVIATIONS AND SYMBOLS

AL	autograph letter (unsigned)
ALS	autograph letter signed
ASP	Aurelia Schober Plath
Lilly Library	Lilly Library, Indiana University at Bloomington
SP	Sylvia Plath
TH	Ted Hughes
TL	typed letter (unsigned)
TLS	typed letter signed
< >	editorial intervention – where ( ) and [ ] are printed in letters these are as used by SP

THE LETTERS
1940–1956

1940

TO *Otto Emil Plath*[1]

Monday 19 February 1940 — ALS with envelope and heart-shaped enclosure, Smith College

<envelope>

Mr. O. E. Plath
92 Johnson Ave.
Winthrop Mass.

<letter>

Feb. 19. 1940

Dear Father

I am coming home soon. Are you as glad as I am?

Over in Frank's[2] work room I got some ink on my fingers which never comes of! I had to rub them with a stone. And the stone took it of.

I wrote a letter to Mother[3] and Warren[4] to. If you want to you may ask them to read it to you.

My letter is not very long.

Warren likes me to wright in orange.[5] Mummy likes me to wright in red. But nearly everybody likes me to wright in blue or black.

1–Otto Emil Plath (1885–1940); German instructor and biology professor at Boston University, 1922–40; SP's father. SP was visiting her maternal grandparents at 892 Shirley Street, Winthrop, Massachusetts, when she wrote this letter. Their phone number was OCEan 1212-W.

2–Frank Richard Schober (1919–2009); SP's uncle.

3–Aurelia Schober Plath (1906–94); associate professor, College of Practical Arts and Letters, Boston University, 1942–71; SP's mother.

4–Warren Joseph Plath (1935–); educated at Phillips Exeter Academy, Exeter, New Hampshire; A.B. 1957, Harvard College; Fulbright student at the University of Bonn, 1957–8; Ph.D. 1964, Harvard University; SP's brother.

5–The names of colours mentioned in this and the next letter are written with a corresponding coloured pencil.

As I told you my letter is not very long. So good by now. I'll be home soon.

With Love,
from
Sylvia

<enclosure>

Dear Father,

I hope you are better. Over grandma's[1] there were many ice-cakes and on every one sat a Seagull! Isn't that funny (Ha Ha).

With Love
from
Sylvia

TO *Aurelia Schober Plath*

Tuesday 20 February 1940 — ALS with envelope, Smith College

February 20. 1940

Dear Mother

I liked your letter. The waves were up to our front steps they were as high as the window!

And I wrote a letter to Aunt Dot.[2] The letter said how delightful it is to fly! And showed a picture of aunt dot flying with a wand (which grandpa[3] said was an ice-cream cone or a flower.) (Ha Ha)

(My letter is short.) The only colors I may use are yellow purple orange red blue. The light that is glass is rainbow colors! bye now.

from Sylvia
With Love

<self-portrait of SP holding a flower next to her Aunt Dorothy holding a wand>

1–Aurelia Greenwood Schober (1887–1956); SP's maternal grandmother.

2–Dorothy Schober Benotti (1911–81); SP's aunt; married to Joseph Benotti (1911–96) on 19 April 1941; SP served as flower girl. They lived at 49 Silver Hill Road, Weston, Mass.

3–Frank Schober (1880–1965); *maître d'hôtel* at Brookline Country Club; SP's maternal grandfather.

1943

TO *Aurelia Schober Plath*

January 1943[1] ALS, Indiana University

January 1943

Dearest Mother,

I have some thing for you on the sideboard where the blue Christmas tree used to be. It is now quater past seven. I have done three quarters of an hour music, and Warren and I have been very good there were no mishaps at tall. I played with Marcia[2] till fivo clock.

In music I did the fingering just like you told me to. And I kept saying to myself "This is what mother would want me to do" so I got along very well. I ate all my breakfast very well and did not tease Warren, I went to school with him and defended him. And O by the way Miss Denway loaned mee the book of poetry which I have in school.

I must now get ready for Bed.

I am all reddy now it is 25 of eight

Love
Sylvia
grandma's signature
Aurelia R Schober

PS. Carl Ludwig called & will call some other time or come over going to send Warrens XMAS gIFT.

1–Date supplied by ASP.

2–Probably Marcia Egan, a friend and classmate who lived at 9 Mayo Road, Wellesley, Mass.

TO *Aurelia Schober Plath*

Saturday 20 March 1943[1] TLS with envelope, Indiana University

March 20, 1942

Dear Mother,

Today is Saturday and this morning I got up and had a good breakfast. Then I went upstairs with Grammy, and had a bath and shampoo.

I have made up some poems, here they are:

Plant a little seedling
Mix with rain and showers,
Stir them with some sun-shine,
And up come some flowers.

I have a little fairy
Two kittens and a mouse
We all live together,
In one tiny little house.
The fairy rides the kittins
And pats the mousies fur,
When we want a lullaby
Both the kittens pur.

You have to have my fairy ears[2]
To here the bluebells ring
Among the[3] green, green grassy fields,
Where all the flowers sing.

--

You have to have my fairy eyes
To see the pot of gold,
That lies beyond the rainbow;
Amongst treasures all untold.
You have to have my fairy wings
To flutter in the sky,

1–Letter misdated 1942 by SP.
2–Sylvia Plath, 'Fairy Wonders'.
3–Added in pen in an unknown hand, possibly ASP's.

And pass a conversation with
A friendly butterfly.

--

Some day when theres nothing much to do
And you want to see and hear
These magic wonders loud and clear
I'll lend these things to you.

I would like to give all these things to you but I know I can make it up by being good. Mrs. Acker[1] has given me a piece called the "Merry Farmer" by Schuman.[2] I have fallen in love with it.

I have read the nicest book I have ever read, the name was "A Fairy to Stay.[3] The story of a motherless little girl whose father was in East Africa so she lived with two aunts who did not like mordern children or any children for that matter. The little girls dream was to go to school, and be a Brownie with a brown mushroom hat and to have bobbed hair as hers was always in a straight pigtail.

One day when her aunts came to give her her lessons they found her reading a Fairy Book. Demanding what silly nonsense she had been reading, she replied that she wanted to go to school, she told them all her her dreams and that Fairys wernt "silly nonsense". The aunts were shocked and sent her up to bed. She felt that she was living in a horrid dream all of a sudden a dreadful thought came into her mind siezing up her aunts sisors she started to cut her hair then the braid came of in her temper. When the aunts came in her room and found out they were horrified and told her to look in the mirror. Her hair was all straight and long on one side and short on the other, for punishment she would have to go like that for one week. Sending her out in the garden they decided that disipline was the best thing they could do. Out side the little girl rubbed her eyes and looked about what did she see but a fairy! The fairy asked her what was the matter, Pamela (for that was her name) poured out her story. The fairy told her to shut her eyes and she would dry clean her, she touched Pamelas hair, it began to curl, she touched her dirty tearstained face it grew pink and clean she touched her wrinkled dress, it grew clean and white. The fairy went into the house unseen by everyone except the

1–Possibly Marion Acker, who lived nearby at 398 Weston Road, Wellesley.

2–'The Merry Farmer' by German composer Robert Schumann (1810–56).

3–Margaret Beatrice Lodge, *A Fairy to Stay* (New York: Oxford University Press, 1929); with illustrations by A. H. [Alice Helena] Watson.

little girl. The fairy said to her-self that she would try to "disipline" the aunts. The whole book is about the fairy and the little girl trying (comicly) trying to disipline the aunts.

Here is another poem I made up:

I found a little fairy
Sleeping in a rose,
As I picked her up
She rubbed her tiny nose.

--

I took her in the house
And made a tiny bed,
Lined with softest thistle down
And rose petals for her head.

--

This little fairy
(I named her Rosie)
Grew and grew and grew,
And many was the posie
She picked me under skies so blue.
I like my little fairy
Wouldn't you like one too?

Love
Sylvia

P. S. Write soon. I am going to enclose papers from school.

<Two enclosures not transcribed. The first is a list of nineteen words. The second contains mathematical problems (fractions).>

TO *Aurelia Schober Plath*

Monday 28 June 1943[1] ALS, Indiana University

Monday

Dear Mother,

I received your letter and enjoyed it. We will send you some paper to write on. We are going to Wellesley to pack my duffle bag. I am going to make a note of what I take and check it of when I pack it to go home. I am enclosing the daffodil. (The stitches are awful) The chickens laid 4 eggs.

Loads of love,
Sylvia
XXXXXXXXXXXXXXX***X

<drawing of chicken with eggs, with caption 'A proud mother'>

TO *Aurelia Schober Plath*

Tuesday 29 June 1943[2] ALS, Indiana University

To Mother

<drawing of daffodil with caption 'How did you like your daffodil?'>
<drawing of flower>
<drawing of heart>

Tuesday

Dear Mother,

We sent my duffle bag by express today. It is raining as though it will never stop, the temprature is 66!

Yesterday Dottie and I, (going to my health examination) found a quarter and a nickel. She let me spend it as I wanted. I spent 20¢ on 2 paper doll books, Rita Hayworth and Hedy Lamar.[3] The rest I will spend on a defense stamp.

Dot and I went haying today with the wheelbarrow and got it all under cover before it rained.

Loads of Love
Sylvia
XXXXX XXXXXX***

<drawing of pitchfork with caption 'Pitch fork we used'>

1–Date supplied from internal evidence.
2–Date supplied from internal evidence.
3–American actors Rita Hayworth (1918–87) and Hedy Lamarr (1914–2000).

TO *Aurelia Schober Plath*

c. Friday 2 July 1943 ALS, Indiana University

To Mother
Friday

Dear Mother,

How are you? I miss you alot. I hope you will get better so you will be with us over the weekend.

I will miss Dot, Joe and all my little chicken and bird friends too.

I helped Dot with the wash today.

I am making a jar full of rose and other petals. I have learned the secret is to dry them in the sun. Sofar the smell almost knocks you out.

Loads of love
Sylvia.

P.S. I also saw Warren last night, he does not miss us at all. I have my train ticket already.

<drawing of a jar with rose petals; SP identifies each component: 'knocking out smell', 'wax paper', 'rose petals' and the 'JAR'>

TO *Aurelia Schober Plath*

Monday 5 July 1943 ALS (postcard), Indiana University

July 5 <drawing of heart>

Dear Mother,

We came on the train from North Station to Mountainview NH. The journey started with a jerk and ended with a jerk. When we got there it was pouring rain, instead of riding to camp in a haywagon we crowded in cars. When we got there we sang songs around a fireplace, then we had the lunch we brought with hot coco. Mine was: kheese & balonae sandwich, 5 Tollhouse cookies and a cup of coco. Then we got organized in our tents & units. My unit was Oehda, my tent, 3. There were 6 cots in each tent. For supper I had 2 bowls of vegetable soup, 2 cups of milk, 1 orange & 1 peanut-butter sandwich. My friends are: Joan Farrell, Joan Patchett, Jean Patchett, Jean Steck, Marge Taylor, Jody Davenport, Gretchen McGoun, Cinthia Sellman, Emily Pitts. Fun here.

Love
Sylvia

TO *Aurelia Schober Plath*

Tuesday 6 July 1943 ALS (postcard), Indiana University

July 6,

Dear Mother,

This morning we woke up before the bugle and really got aquainted. For breakfast I had 1 orange, a bowl of rice crispies, acup of milk and a cup of coco. We we went in swimming before lunch for a half an hour. I was in the advanced swimmers group that swims a little over my head. My bathing cap is yellow and cost 15¢, it was a good cap too. For lunch I had two helpings of corn, ham and beans a glass of water and the biggest helping of raspberry jello. Am I going to camp for a month? For supper I had 2 pieces of bread with chopped beef, salad, prunes & milk. We are being read the House at Pooh Corner[1] before going to sleep. Send me some 1¢ stamps.

Love
Sylvia

TO *Aurelia Schober Plath*

Tuesday 6 July 1943 ALS (postcard), Indiana University

Tuesday

Dear Mother,

Today they voted for new reporters. I was sad because I liked my job. But what do you think! I was one of the two, all the girls wanted me to be one of them.

I received Mowglis[2] letter? and yours. Thank you for the two comic strips I wish you'd send some more. I got every question in the quiz save the last.

Loads of Love
Sylvia

1–A. A. Milne, *The House at Pooh Corner* (1928).
2–Mowgli was the Plath family cat.

TO *Aurelia Schober Plath*

Wednesday 7 July 1943 ALS (postcard), Indiana University

July 7 <drawing of heart>

Dear Mother,

I can't describe what a wonderful time I'm having. From my tent flap I can see across Lake Ossipee to the beautiful Green Mountain. We had a high tide. We go in swiming at ten o'clock for a half an hour then an hour after lunch for another half an hour. For breakfast I had a bowl of Ralston two doughnuts a cup of milk a cup of apple juice. Please send me a pillow & case.

Love
Sylvia

TO *Aurelia Schober Plath*

Friday 9 July 1943 ALS (postcard), Indiana University

July 9

Dear Mother,

How are you? I have received all your letters, Including Warrens lovely drawing. I was one of two newspaper reporters[1] selected from our unit. I have made up two poems. I have written every day to you. I spent 95¢ I need a little more money about 2 dollar I found my pillow & case, received all stamps.

xxxxxx****
Sylvia

TO *Aurelia Schober Plath*

Saturday 10 July 1943 ALS (postcard), Indiana University

Saturday

Dear Mother,

I miss you an awful lot. I received your letter with the 2 dollars and deposited them immediatly. We went for a ride on the hay-rack. My letters

1–In the Oehda unit, SP was made a reporter along with Louise Anthony. SP, 'Hike to Lovell River' (report) and 'Camping' (poem), *Weetamoe Megpahone* (18 July 1943).

have not been neat so most of them are dead letters. For I have been writing every day. Found pillow & case. got stamps.

Loads of love,
Sylvia

TO *Aurelia Schober Plath*

Monday 12 July 1943 ALS (postcard), Indiana University

Monday

Dear Mother,

How are you? I am having loads of fun one girl has gone home and another is crying all the time. One day I tried a hand at comfroting her. I told her about lots of things, finally she said "I'll try not to cry any more you're nice." So I am tring my best to make her happy. We have a bath every week and a shampoo every 2 weeks.

Love
Sylvia

received stamps, found pillow & case

TO *Aurelia Schober Plath*

Friday 16 July 1943[1] ALS (postcard), Indiana University

Dear Mother,

I received your letter. I miss you terribly, I do almost wish I could go home in two weeks, I have put arrid under arm. For lunch I had: one potato, spinich an egg, beets, a cup of water, and a cocktail dessert. Our mail has not been collected yet you will get it all soon. We are going on a hay ride to climb a mountain and some night we are going to have a picnic campfire. Write soon. I received your check for rest of month.

xxxxx*****
Love
Sylvia

1–Date supplied from postmark.

TO *Aurelia Schober Plath*

Saturday 17 July 1943[1] ALS (postcard), Indiana University

Dear Mother,

I love you so much. I miss you an awful lot. I wonder how I will get my duffle bag home. If I send it home the day before I go where will I sleep? I hope you will get the rest of my letters. I write every day and received all your letters and Warrens lovely drawing.

<drawing of tent with caption 'Tent'>

<drawing of heart>

Loads of love,
Sylvia

TO *Aurelia Schober Plath*

Sunday 18 July 1943 ALS (postcard), Indiana University

Sunday

Dearest Mother,

<u>All</u> the girls in my tent are going home tomorrow so I feel left out. I didn't get a letter from you yesterday, I hope you are all right. There are some pretty pictures of secenery around they are quite expensive but I bought a few.

I wonder if I should have my picture taken 6 for 35¢. I have seen lots of pictures to draw. I will have lots of things to show you. Are you well? I worry when I don't receive letters from you. I am having a bath and shampoo today we have a bath every week and a shampoo every two. My letters are likely dead. I write daily but my addressed are not clear.

xxx
Sylvia

1 – Date supplied from postmark.

TO *Aurelia Schober Plath*

Tuesday 20 July 1943[1] ALS (postcard) Indiana University

Tuesday

Dear Mother

The two new girls in my tent are not well brought up. Luckily the other 3 are lovely, one of them is so funny. The new girls say "ain't" "youse" kids, "guys" "horsebackin." It just hurts my ears. I long for my familys soft, sweet talk. Did Warren get my card? We had honeydew melon and hot blue berry muffins this morning. The temprature was below 40! I am so happy here. I miss you but your letters keep me from being homsick. I will see you in two weeks.

xxxxxxxSylvia***

TO *Aurelia Schober Plath*

Wednesday 21 July 1943[2] ALS on Camp Weetamoe letterhead, Indiana University

I have some drawin
Wednesday

Dear Mother,

How are you? I will see you in less than 2 weeks. I am lucky to be staying for a month. In case you did not receive my cards, I found my pillow & case. I received your money and deposited it. We have gone on the hay ride. You should have had the blueberry muffins and sweet-as-honey-dew melon we had. We have gone boating several times and I am trying to pass my rookie test.

All the girls have gone from my tent There are two new campers and three old, the new ones are awful and the old ones are splendid.[3]

I have washed: 2 pairs of socks, 1 face cloth, 1 jersey and 1 pr. of pants I have spent about 45¢ on laundry about 20¢ on fruit, 1.50 on nessities and 20¢ on unnessities. About 2.40 in all. I will not need to spend much more, just on laundry and fruit. I have received all your letters, Mowgli's card, and, do thank Grammy for my sneakers.

1–Date supplied from internal evidence. The postcard was not postmarked.
2–Date supplied from internal evidence.
3–This paragraph added by SP in the top margin of the second page of the letter.

If you have any more stamps please send them to me. I have bought 2 10¢ defense stamps.

xxxxxxxx Extra Love xxxxxxx
xxxxxxx Sylvia xxxxxx
xxxxxxxx**********
****

TO *Aurelia Schober Plath*

Saturday 24 July 1943 ALS (postcard), Indiana University

<drawing of blueberry> Saturday

Dear Mother

Just think, I will be home in less than 2 weeks. We went on another hayride today and to night we are going to pick blueberries. I am very glad Mowgli got that chicken leg he deserves it. I have made something for you in arts & crafts. The view across the lake is beautiful. The sun and clouds cast shadows on it from time to time. The camp paper is 2¢ and comes out every 2 weeks. I will have 2 copies to take home.

xxxxxxx *****
xxxxxxx Love – Sylvia ****
****

Did you get my letter?

TO *Aurelia Schober Plath*

Wednesday 28 July 1943[4] ALS (postcard), Indiana University

Dear Mother,

Today was a red letter day for I got 3 letters one from you, one from Ruthie[5] (she received my card) and one from Mrs. Freeman.[6] Ruth sent me some lovely green embroidered shoelacings and her mother sent some blue. I will see you in one week. I will send my dufflebag by express so

4–Date supplied from postmark.

5–Ruth Freeman Geissler (1933–); B.A. 1955, University of Massachusetts at Amherst; SP's childhood friend from Winthrop, Massachusetts; married Arthur Geissler, Jr (1932–2013); degree in Business Administration 1954, University of Massachusetts at Amherst; SP was maid of honour at their wedding on 11 June 1955.

6–Marion Saunders Freeman (1908–98), lived at 8 Somerset Terrace, Winthrop, Mass. The Freemans were neighbours of the Plath family.

it will get home a little after I do. I wrote the first 2 days at camp in my diary but then I stopped.

<drawing of shoelaces with caption 'My shoelaces'>

Love
Sylvia

TO *Aurelia Schober Plath*

Thursday 29 July 1943 — ALS (postcard), Indiana University

July 29

Dear Mother,

I received the suitcase, and have devoured the funnies eagerly.

I had 2.20 in trading post before you sent me a dollar. (Thanks loads)

I will leave here on the train, Monday 3.08 and get to North Station at 6.31. (Unless the train is late,) we were spposed to climb Whitter[1] today but we got caught in the rain.

Love
Sylvia

TO *Aurelia Schober Plath*

Saturday 31 July 1943 — ALS on Camp Weetamoe letterhead, Indiana University

July 31,

Dear Mother,

Just think! When you receive this letter I will be on my way home. The days have sped by on wings. I have made two things at Arts & Crafts which are to be surprises for you and Grammy both. A girl gave me a strip of oil cloth so I cut it into 3 pieces and made a change purse for Grammy with flowers here and there.

<drawing of change purse>

I have bougt 6 beautiful pictures of scenery for →	1.50
and my pictures for →	.35
Laundry →	.75
nessities →	.50

1 – Mount Whittier, West Ossipee, New Hampshire.

Unnessities →   .30
3.40
5.50
3.40
about 2.10 left

When I get home maybe you will go to bed when I do some nights and I will tell you every detail about camp. It seems like a happy dream.

Love
Sylvia

P.S. When I come home you will see a great difference in my caracter. Give my love to every body. I am enclosing drawings.

<drawing of bed with captions ‘my bed’, ‘DUFFLE BAG’, ‘JOE’S SUITCASE’, ‘SMALL SUITCASE’>

1944

TO *Aurelia Schober Plath*

Friday 14 July 1944 ALS (postcard), Indiana University

9[1]
July 14,

Dear Mother,

See if you can guess by my pictures what I am giving Dot & Grammy for an Xmas <drawing of present>. Dot <drawing of a coaster and two potholders> – Grammy <drawing of a coaster and two potholders>. I will show them to you when I come <drawing of house>. I will see you at <drawing of clock> (6:31) at No. Station. I have spent 1.25 so far (80¢ in Arts in Crafts)

$4.75
1.25
3.50 left.

I will come home with $3.25 at least. I have not worn 1 <drawing of shirt>, or blouse. I am going to try to look <drawing of eyes> neat coming home. We have <drawings of an ice cube and a jug of cream> every other day. I swam 100 yds. side stroke (over my head without stopping!). I never thought I could do it!! see you. Monday at 6.31.

Love,
Sylvia

1–Letter numbered 9 by SP; letters one through eight not present. SP's diary indicates that by this day she had written fourteen letters. Those named include her mother, grandparents, and Betsy Powley.

TO *Aurelia Schober Plath*

Saturday 15 July 1944 ALS (postcard), Indiana University

10

July 15,

Dear Mother,

Today was our patriotic day <drawing of flag>. I wore a red <drawing of barrette>, red <drawing of bow>, white <drawing of shirt>, blue <drawing of shorts> (borrowed). Our tent <drawing of tent> (4) won inspection this week as well as last. In inspection for no papers our <drawing of house> in Neyati won!! All the <drawing of table> tables were decorated, Neyati were like this. <drawing of boats; boats designated 'red' and the sails 'white' on 'blue paper water'>. All of the units had to sang a song. Neyati was said to be by the judges "A jump ahead of the others." Are we proud <drawing of woman (mother)>.

Love <drawing of heart>
Sylvia

TO *Aurelia Schober Plath*

Monday 17 July 1944 ALS (postcard), Indiana University

11

July 17,

Dear Mother <drawing of heart (around Dear)>,

I have packed all of my <drawing of bag>. I received the <drawing of tag-label> tags. I have written to Ruthie. I have spent 1.40! Is that bad? Only $.70 on Art's & Crafts. We are going on a <drawing of boat> trip for winning inspection! I have gotten 20 <drawing of letters>. I am so glad Frank & Louise[1] are home <drawing of house>. I'll see you Monday! I will be happy <drawing of smiling face> to come home! The only thing wrong with me is that <drawing of eye> bit my <drawing of face with tongue sticking out> & there is a blister <drawing of tongue with blister> on it.

Love
Sylvia

1–Louise Bowman Schober (1920–2002); married SP's uncle Frank Schober on 27 June 1942; SP was flower girl at the wedding.

TO *Frieda Heinrichs*[1]

Tuesday 26 December 1944 ALS, Indiana University

26 Elmwood Road
Wellesley 81, Mass.
December 26, 1944

Dear Aunt Frieda,

I can't thank you enough for the lovely tooled leather diary you sent me. I kept my diary every day last year, but it was not as beautiful as this new one.

I do enjoy writing in it, because it helps me to use complete sentences. I read over my last year's diary and found that it was full of spelling mistakes.

Even though you do live in California, I hope that you will come to visit us soon. The fall is the most colorful time of the year in New England, and I'm sure you will take delight in the brilliant foliage.

Your loving niece,
Sylvia

1–Frieda Plath Heinrichs (1897–1970). Otto Plath's sister.

1945

TO *Aurelia Schober Plath*

Monday 2 July 1945 ALS (postcard), Indiana University

July 2, 1945

Dear Mother,

My bed is so cosy and I am all unpacked and every thing is neatly put away. We had an invigorating swim after you left Sunday at 4:30. The dock is shaped like this <drawing of dock and beach> and we (our unit swam in here <arrow pointing to enclosed space within dock>) for today. The water was very cold at first but once I ducked in it was so comfortable. The water was the most beautiful color that I have ever seen! The pure white sand gleamed through its crystal, pale, blue-green depths. The only thing I missed at supper was butter! I ate: fresh spinach, sliced turkey, 2 baked potatos, brick (vanilla, strawberry, chocolate) icecream, and four cups of milk! I am well and overwhelmingly happy. <drawing of heart>

Love,
Sylvia

TO *Warren Plath*

Monday 2 July 1945 ALS (postcard), Indiana University

July 2,

Dearest Warren, <flourish>

I hope that you had a nice time over at Dotties. I love Camp. Betsy[1] and I are in cabin 3 (only two in a cabin) in the Ridge Unit. Our Unit Leader is "Flash", her assistant is "Dash" (I mean its vice versa) and the one in charge of the waterfront is "Splash." They are the "Ash" trio. You would love to be here. There are trees every where; and at night the fireflies are countless, and they light up the earth and sky. The birds, at about 5:00 in

1–Betsy Powley Wallingford (1932–), SP's friend from Wellesley.

the morning, sing so sweetly. Will you ask mummy to send that little bird book in your book case on the left of the 2nd shelf?

Love,
Sylvia

TO *Aurelia Schober Plath*

Tuesday 3 July 1945 ALS (postcard), Indiana University

July 3, 1945

Dearest Mother,

Last evening (Monday) our unit invited Unit "Cove" to a night of folk-dancing, in the unit house. A rain storm was raging outside as we danced by the fireplace. We had a beautiful time and sang songs around the campfire before going to bed. We have "Trading Post" every other day. So far I've spent: bathing cap – $.25, tie – $.35, KLEENEX – $.15. If you want me to buy an extra box please tell me. (If I still can get it). The food is wonderful! For instance I had for lunch: 3 bowls tomato-soup, cream cheese and olives on rolls, cupcakes, 3 cups milk. Write soon. I'm fine! xxx

Love,
Sylvia

TO *Aurelia Schober Plath*

Tuesday–Wednesday 3–4 July 1945 ALS (postcard), Indiana University

July 3 & 4, 1945

Dear Mummy,

I am just preparing to go for a swim after rest hour. It is now about quarter past three. Our cabin is so nice and cosy.

<flourish>

July 4, 1945

Dear Mummy,

I am disappointed in either you or the mail for I haven't even one letter and this is Wednesday! We went "nail picking" today and are having a contest to see who of our unit and another could pick the most nails at where the barn fell down. I am about 3rd or, 4th with 327 nails in ½ (half) hour. Write soon. Send music MB Murmering Brook.[1]

Love
Sylvia.

TO *Aurelia Schober Plath & Warren Plath*

Thursday 5 July 1945

ALS on Camp Helen Storrow letterhead, Indiana University

Remember to say Long Pond
on my Address!

Dearest Mother, and Warren

Today is Thursday the 5th of July and we haven't received any mail yet so I hope I'll at least get one letter or card. Last night we had Retreat. One music loving girl named "Chopin", played some music on- her accordian. (She made up the music too!) After flag lowering we sat on the beach (the whole camp) and watched the perfect tawny-red ball of sun sink slowly out of sight in the West. I read my part of the ceremony and was complimented on it by "Dash." You know how I used to adore Miss Chadwick?[2] Well, now my ideal is our unit leader, "Dash." <drawing of heart> We went boating today in the row boats. I met a girl from "Four Winds" out on the lake and asked her if she knew Ruthie Freeman. She did, so I sent my regards (by way of water) to Ruthie. I am now basking on my bed in the sun during rest hour. It is so perfectly warm and comfortable! Can you tell me what-these signs in shorthand mean? <drawing of shorthand character> and <drawing of shorthand character> (< drawing of shorthand character>). Thanks. Yesterday night Betsy and I saw a firefly settle on our window for a half hour and he kept blinking his light off and on. How're these menus:[3] Lunch- two bowls of vegetable soup, loads of peanut butter, four pieces of coffee cake, chocolate cake and marsh mellow sauce, three cups of milk. Supper- Haddock, nineteen carrots, lettuce and tomatoes, cucumber, punch, two potatoes, four slices of water mellon! Boy! My stomach could hardly hold those two amounts of food. I have, next to Betsy a special friend named Joan Beales. She is the sweetest girl. She can play piano and violin, tapdance, and sings on the

1–SP's diary indicates this was German composer Carl Bohm's 'Murmuring Brook'.

2–Ruth Chadwick, SP's social studies teacher at the Alice L. Phillips Junior High School, Wellesley, Mass.

3–'~~How's~~ How're these menus:' appears in the original.

radio, and best of all is really frankly modest. My one consolation is that she's my second best friend and she can't draw. I'm tanned and perfectly happy.

xxxxxx and ****
Sylvia

TO *Aurelia Schober Plath*

Friday 6 July 1945 ALS (postcard), Indiana University

July 6, 1945

Dear Mother,

You know, in swimming we have three classes starting with the lowest red, next-white, highest-blue. For three days I was a red cap but today I was promoted to a white cap! I am quite happy. "Dash" complimented me on braiding my hair so neatly and so often! I love camp, and it is near enough to you so that I never feel homesick. Yahoo! I got that big fat letter from you tonight and was showing the beautiful drawings to the whole unit! If any one says I can draw I'll know I inherited it from you.

Love xxxx
Sylvia

P.S. I have a reputation with my unit leader for eating more than any one!

TO *Aurelia Schober Plath*

Friday 6 July 1945 ALS (postcard), Indiana University

July 6, 1945

Dearest Mummy,

Today is so beautiful! As a rule all days have been sunshiny save about one. Every time you write me a card I wish you would illustrate it as you did the first one. I will always treasure it. I was able to get my whole arm in the waist of my shorts before breakfast but after the following two meals I couldn't even get my finger in! Shredded wheat, two muffins and crabapple jelly, four cups milk, and 40 raw cherries. Lunch three whole egg & lettuce sandwiches, three whole jelly sandwiches, five cups milk. I'm healthy and happy. Give my love to Warren.

Love, <drawing of heart>
<drawing of heart> Sylvia

TO *Aurelia Schober Plath*

Saturday 7 July 1945 — ALS (postcard), Indiana University

July 7, 1945

Dear Mother,

I have written to Grammy and Grampy and "Hayzee."[1] My other friends can wait. I hope that you and Warrie got my big letter.[2] I made up a poem starting like this:

> At night I watch the stars above[3]
> Twinkling in the sky
> While on the silent world below
> Deepening shadows lie.
> The trees are swaying in the wind
> The night is dark & still,
> The grass is whispering to the moon
> Which shines above the hill.

I love you loads!
Sylvia

TO *Aurelia Schober Plath*

Sunday 8 July 1945 — ALS (postcard), Indiana University

July 8, 1945

Dear Mother,

Today (in my opinion is the most beautiful day I spent at camp! We had a wonderful time swimming – and boating in the morning. For lunch I had a bird's feed of 6 plates of casserole & sauce containing potatos, peas, onions, carrots, chicken (yum, yum); five cups of punch and a scoop of vanilla, coffee, and orange ice cream. (If you're hard up on ration points when I come home you can have Joe slaughter me and you can eat me for

1 – Possibly Mrs Eleanor Hayes of 12 Durant Road, Wellesley, Mass. In SP's camp diary, held by Lilly Library, there is an entry for 'Mrs. Wentworth L. Hayes, R.F.D. #2 – c/o Benson, Division Road, East Greenwich, R.I'.

2 – See SP to Warren and Aurelia Schober Plath, 5 July 1945, above.

3 – Sylvia Plath, 'Camp Helen Storrow'.

pork. We had crafts today (nothing like Weetamoe though.) I making prints to decorate stationary. xxxx

Love,
S.

TO *Aurelia Schober Plath*

Monday 9 July 1945 ALS (postcard), Indiana University

July 9, 1945

Dear Mother,

Has the apron I ordered come yet? Did anyone get honorable mention on the good sport page?[1] Have I any mail? Betsy and I have just finished a blanket roll for our unit has the fun of sleeping on the beach tonight!! I have the second verse to the poem I sent you:

Camp Helen Storrow

At night I watch the tiny lights
Of fireflies flitting near
And gleaming in the frosty air
Above Long Pond so clear.
This is our camp beside the lake-
The one we all do love,
And over us God's light will shine
From the vast heaven above.

Give my love to Warrie
Sylvia

1–A feature in the children's section of the *Sunday Boston Herald*. SP's first poem ('Poem', first line 'Hear the crickets chirping') and drawing ('Funny Faces') were featured in this section on 10 August 1941 and 2 August 1942 respectively.

TO *Aurelia Schober Plath*

Wednesday 11 July 1945 ALS (postcard), Indiana University

July 11

Dear Mother,

We had a minstrel show last night. I was dressed as a little girl pickininy and had my face charcoaled. It was a great success. I got your big fat letter with the map. Everybody envies me – receiving such meaty letters! I am leaving with Betsy – Saturday though we'll really stay[1] overnight with the Powley's friends. Betsy says that their friends have room and to spare. I received dear Warren's letter and thought it one of the loveliest I've received.

Love to all
Sylvia

TO *Aurelia Greenwood Schober & Frank Schober*

Friday 13 July 1945[2] ALS (postcard), Indiana University

Dear Grammy and Grampy

Thank you so much for the cards you sent me! I am leaving camp tomorrow (Saturday) and will sleep over Theils[3] and come home Sunday. Our unit took a five mile hike over a dirt road to fisherman's cove which is right on the salty ocean! We stayed for the whole day! I had to laugh at some of the girls because I was the only one who dared to go in first for the waves were strong and cold until you ducked. I love camp.

Love,
Sylvia

TO *Aurelia Schober Plath*

Friday 13 July 1945 ALS (postcard), Indiana University

July 13, 1945

Dear Mother,

I had the most wonderful day at camp yesterday! Our unit hiked five miles over a dirt road (averaging 1 mile in 20 min!) to the really salty

1–'we'll ~~probably~~ really stay' appears in the original.
2–Date supplied from postmark.
3–The Thiel family of Parker Road, Wellesley, Mass.

ocean at fisherman's cove. We stayed the whole day. We swam on a sand bar that had not a pebble on it. I had the best time riding the waves we were completely hidden in the large cove (I drew it) and a huge sand cliff in back of us had the homes of BELTED KINGFISHERS (Warrie might be interested) <drawing of cliff and kingfishers>. We were driven home. I will even be campsick for camp.

Love,
Sylvia.

TO *Margot Loungway Drekmeier*[1]

Wednesday 9 August 1945 — ALS with envelope, Estate of Margot Drekmeier

August 9, 1945

Dear Margot,

Thank you ever so much for the perfect time I had at Innisfree in the past seventeen days.[2] I have never felt better and I have gained two pounds. (Must be due to those five potatoes I consumed one night for supper.)

We had a lovely trainride home. We passed through two pelting rainstorms, but they both only lasted a few minutes as we were traveling express from Portland.

We arrived in Boston at seven-twenty and, as my grandmother called for us at North Station in the car, we were home by eight-thirty.

I awoke this morning and started with horror for a moment, but then sighed with relief as I saw the moose head at the foot of my bed rapidly dwindle into a bedpost! You see, your imaginative influence still clings to my mind.

Last night all I dreamed about was a rainstorm soaking all the valuable stamps in the world from albums and washing them up to my doorstep sorted out and in perfect condition. Isn't that an ideal way to accumulate stamps?

By the way, I am enclosing three stamps.[3] I believe they are Swedish. These are the only duplicates that I have come across so far, but if I find any in the future I will send them to you immediately. If you already

1–Margot Loungway Drekmeier (1932–2008). The Loungways were family friends who lived in Oxford, Maine. In April or May 1946 the Loungways moved to 4 Agassiz Park, Jamaica Plain, Mass.

2–SP visited the Loungways in Oxford, Maine, from 23 July to 8 August 1945.

3–The stamps are no longer with the letter.

have these stamps please stick them in one of your letters to me because my dearest little brother has set his eyes on them longingly, already. I am going to Boston in the near future and will then buy a much longed for stamp album!!! I hardly can wait to mount my stamps in it. I have just received my "American Girl" magazine and have seen an offer to buy stamps "on approval" from the Jamestown Stamp Company.[1] I am going to send in as you advised me to, after I finish mounting stamps in my promised album.

Have you recovered your laundry bag yet? If I see any of the ghosts which inhabit our storeroom, I'll be sure to see if the sheets are marked Innisfree and send them to you, ghost and all.

love to all,
Sylvia

<drawing of a moose head with caption 'THE MOOSE' on back of envelope>

TO *Margot Loungway Drekmeier*

Saturday 18 August 1945

ALS with envelope, Estate of Margot Drekmeier

August 18, 1945

Dear Margot,

I just received your nice long letter this morning. It's wonderful to at last have found someone that writes really worthwhile letters.

Thank you for those seventeen stamps you sent me. I'm returning the four which I have already. Enclosed also is a stamp from Chile which I hope you don't have yet. However, if you do have it, please return it. Let's adopt that plan. Is that allright with you?

On Monday, August 13, Mother took me to Boston with the purpose in mind of shopping and buying me a stamp album. We went to the Harris Stamp Company[2] to get my album the first thing. I got an album which is the exact duplicate of yours (price and all). As the album was heavy and the day was humid we decided to go to a movie instead of shopping. We saw "The Valley of Decision"[3] starring Gregory Peck and Greer Garson.

1–Founded in 1939, Jamestown Stamp Company began as a mail order company located in Jamestown, NY. The advertisement appeared in *American Girl*, August 1945, 34.

2–H. E. Harris & Co. was located at 108 Massachusetts Avenue, Boston, Mass.

3–*The Valley of Decision* was showing at both the Loew's State Theatre, then located at 205 Massachusetts Avenue, and Loew's Orpheum, then located at 1 Hamilton Place, Boston, Mass.

Have you ever read the book? The acting was suburbly done and we enjoyed the afternoon thoroughly.

On Tuesday I hinged all my United States Stamps in my album and by Thursday I had all of the stamps you gave me pasted in. Recently I have been trading stamps with Warren who has quite a nice set. I have on the average of 300 different stamps now. In the Agust issue of the American Girl an offer was made by the Jamestown Stamp Company. Here it is: To Serious approval applicants only (that means you, Margot,) we make this biggest offer in Stampdom – for ten cents in coin we will send you a packet of five hundred stamps from missions over all the world!

<flourish>

In case you are interested you know their address.

Mother bought my stamp album for me in exchange for a play she promised me (both about the same cost – $6.00.)

Warren is now saving up for his album. We are both searching avidly for stamps (this is one interest that will never die down.)

How, may I ask, is dearest Ellen? Has she invited you to supper yet? By the way, did you continue going to Bible School the two mornings after I left? If so how is Dunstan[1] <drawing of male head with glasses> and the bad side of Christianity? Has him's darlin' 'ittle Lois got herself any songs to sing beside "B-I-B-L-E, le Bible?"

How is your hand made <drawing of book with the word "DIARY" on cover> coming along. I have persuaded my mater to get me a small one year diary for Christmas and also an unmarked journal for special events.

We all rejoiced in hearing the good news about the recovering of your laundry.

All of us are joyful that the end of the war with Japan has occured at last so we have sent up a little box to make the news sweeter for the family.

Do not tell John,[2] but I am glad (for you) that part of his sprayer was lost and hope (again from me in concern for you) that it is never recovered, considering the terrible purpose for which he used it.

How are the two kittens, Patch and yours? (Have you named yours yet?) Upon returning home I was very sadly upset to find my only and most beloved son, Mowgli, gone, <drawing of cat> (for good it seems), so I erected his memorial shaft in my little lower bed <flourish> <drawing of memorial post in a flower garden with printing "Here lies my <illegible>">

1–According to SP's diary, this was Reverend Dunstan. SP and Margot Loungway attended bible school from 30 July to 3 August 1945 while the Plaths were in Oxford, Maine.

2–John Loungway (1935–2009).

Maybe I should be given a gold star to put in his cemetary because he was a brave cat and maybe he lost his life as a general in the war between the Tiger and Bob cats in our neighborhood. (He was always a loyal Tiger!)

Has the sex of your cats been determined yet? Some morning you may wake up and find a dozen little apatchies or gray and white kittens climbing all over your bed and still more peeping down from the bats roost <arrow pointing at drawing of bedroom> in your room. I hope for your Mother's sake that this will never happen in such quantity.

Love to all from – your friend,
<drawing>
Sylvia
(alias Moosie-Moose)

P.S. Warren plans to write to John but don't be surprised if he receives the letter after John has started to shave. <drawing of a boy>

TO *Margot Loungway Drekmeier*

Thursday 30 August 1945 — ALS with envelope, Estate of Margot Drekmeier

August 30, 1945

Dear Margot,

Thank you for the Christmas present. Warren and I are waiting in great excitement until we open the package on December the twenty-fifth. We thought, at first, that we had been unfortunate victims of some cruel practical joker (you, of course) until we came across the Christmas wrapping paper and then we reluctantly decided that we had better not open it 'till Christmastime to humor your caustic wit. (Remember – "He who laughs best laughs last!") (Heh! Heh! Heh!)

In the envelope I'm enclosing a few so-called stamp hinges.[1] I usually get the kind of hinges that you do, but as I ran out of them I had to resort to the enclosed specimens. (Ugh!) If, up to this time, you have been licking your hinges – please – of all things, DON'T LICK THESE !!!!!!!!! To me they taste (when licked) like decayed bread pudding garnished with alcohol! I have warned you – do now what you will.

I heartily agree with you concerning Mr. (I won't disgrace churches or ministers by associating him (or his name) with "Reverend) "Morbid

1 – '~~Enclosed~~ In the envelope' appears in the original. The enclosed stamp hinges are no longer with the letter.

Religious Drible" Dunstan. Here are two sketches to show the only things I remember of him <flourish>

this <drawing of arrow pointed at bubble gum wrapper with caption 'CHOMPING GUM'> and this <drawing of arrow pointed at a grotesque caricature of the reverend with caption 'MORBID CHRISTMAS RELIGIOUS TALES' and 'BLOOD' dripping from his hands>

How I shudder to think of your mothers wrath when you have a few countless batches of caterwauling kittens under-foot. Probably (not if I know her though) she (pardon the crossed "h"), will take advantage of the name "Disappearing Cat from Saturn"[1] and make them all disappear with a few doses of potomaine poison. (Perish the thought!)

Speaking of stamp offers, I just received that packet of 500 stamps. I had to divvy half and half with Warren as he paid half of the cost. I did this with my eyes closed so all would be fair. I only got one or two duplicates beside some red Canadian friends and about 40 green English friends. I received about fifty large stamps that were all beautiful pictures and various colors.

I enjoy buying stamps on approval. Do you usually send the money in cash? I had none of the stamps you sent me so I put them all in my album. I'm enclosing[2] in a little transparent envelope in which are a few of my best duplicates. I hope you will be able to use some of them. Let's use the envelope for trading purposes. All right?

I have had my haircut and really I think it looked quite presentable!! <drawings of SP with hair cut showing 'Back View' and 'Front View'> By the way I am wearing one of the dresses which you so kindly bequeathed me. Everybody had nice remarks about my favorite – that light blue flowered one. <drawing of SP wearing light blue flowered dress> I have had a picture taken and if it comes out I'll send it to you so you can see how I've changed (to the worse.)

To day has been very busy for me. First we went to Boston to the dentists, then we rushed home and in about five minutes were on our way at 55 miles an hour to have luncheon at the Wayside Inn in Sudbury[3] (with three friends[4]). On the way home after an interesting tour of the spot of

1–Probably a reference to Enid Blyton, *The Mystery of a Disappearing Cat* (1944).

2–The enclosure is no longer with the letter.

3–The Wayside Inn, Sudbury, Mass.

4–SP's diary notes that she went to the Wayside Inn with Reverend Max Gaebler (1921–), his wife Carolyn Farr Gaebler (1922–2009), and Max's brother Ralph Gaebler (1926–), and that she signed the guestbook.

Longfellow's historic poem[1] I remembered that I had a viola lesson in 15 minutes and so the friend who was driving obliging screeched around corners at the tortoise pace of 60 mi. per hr. (I saw the speedometer, mind you!) I was not surprised to be at my lesson 5 min. early!!!

Love,
Sylvia

<on back of envelope>

HA! Don't laugh at the one who knows. HA!

NO N S EN SE[2]

Is your kitten Disky-Disky the Disappearing cat from Mars?

Pardon the waylaid-letter

TO *Margot Loungway Drekmeier*

Tuesday 18 September 1945 — ALS with envelope, Estate of Margot Drekmeier

September 18, 1945
<drawing of a moose>

Dear Margot,

Are you giving up hope of ever getting a letter from me? Hold on!! Here it is:

I enjoyed receiving your dignified letter and looked over the stamp sheets carefully. At first I wondered how you printed the sheet but figured you used carbon paper. (Is that so?) As school has begun I did not have much spare time and that was swamped with homework. Several times I have sat down to write you but only got as far as the date or making stamp sheets. I verily believe that your brother's idea is good but as I don't have much allowance left over after dues, church, lunch money, and such, have been deducted, I have only a few cents with which to purchase stamps but will do the best I can. I hope that you will need some of my stamps that I'm sending on two different sheets.

I am receiving a few nice stamps from Great Britain and I'm enclosing one as a special gift in case you don't already have it. <stamp pasted to letter[3]>

Do you have any other people besides us three (you, John, & me) in your impressive stamp circle?

1 – Henry Wadsworth Longfellow, *Tales of a Wayside Inn* (1863).
2 – Each of these letter clusters, spelling 'Nonsense' is encircled.
3 – 6d purple stamp depicting King George VI.

I am in assembly tomorrow and so is Betsy Powley. When she was rehearsing her song on stage I ran my finger over my mouth in an imitation of a moronic relapse (she knows the joke) and she began to burst out laughing, only the Music teacher hushed her with a fierce "Shhhh!!!!!" One that afternoon we were crowed on a packed bus after two and one-half hours rehearsal and I dropped my ticket and as I was on my knees hunting for it Betsy sat on my head. Everybody around us was laughing fit to kill.

No, I have never tried writing to anyone in foreign countries although I have often wanted to. How do you obtain the addressesses and how many different languages do you have to know?

By the way, in Darien, did you know a blonde girl in your division by the name of Patty[4] who was rather pretty, self-centered, and, shall we say, "pleasantly plump" in the upper regions? Was she nice to you? Smart in school? and so on. I want to know because she is now living in Wellesley and is in love with my friends' no-good brother and I want to know if you liked Patty huh?

I have seen countless babies since I have been in Maine, but, I feel pangs of regret in my heart when I remember how I didn't take "Dunkie"[5] and Susie[6] home with me as no other child can compare with them.

How do you like school now? Mater starts teaching tomorrow.

Love,
Sylvia

<with a heart above the i in Sylvia >

P.S. Yawn <drawing of a person yawning>
PP.SS. Time is passing. Almost 11:00 (And ½ hr.)
PP.P.SSS. Mater's calling
P.P.P.P.SSSS. I have written to you!!!!!!!!!!!
PPPPP.SSSSS. – Goodnight!!!!
PPPPPPSSSSSS – z-z-z-z-zz-zz-zz-zzzzzzz
Eureka! (or something of the sort)

4–Patricia May Thomson; 1949, Wellesley High School; moved from Darien, Connecticut, in the summer of 1945; lived at 97 Audubon Road, Wellesley.
5–Duncan Peck Loungway (1944–).
6–Susan Kent Loungway (1943–2007).

TO *Margot Loungway Drekmeier*

Monday 5 November 1945 ALS with envelope,
Estate of Margot Drekmeier

November 5, 1945

Dearest Margot,

I received your nice birthday card and incoherent postcard some time ago and have been too busy since to answer them.

I have, in the meanwhile, received a whole pile of lovely stamps – three of which are alone worth $2.50! The Harris Company sent them as a special birthday gift and they're from Cape Juby. I have 51 Austrian Stamps and would like more on approval. Have you any special sets or countries that you want stamps from?

On October the 26th I went to Boston and played my viola in the orchestra for the Teachers' Convention.[1] It was my first public appearance and it was fun!

How is school going with you? I am going through grueling (sp?) rehearsals for P.T.A. night. I am "Social Studies" in an epilogue.

By the way, I'm writing this letter from the old jail itself! (It's the only time I can find to write to you this week in my nightmares I can see your face, which is pretty bad!!)

(For my birthday I got two kerchief, money, books, stamps, mittens and a whole lot of everything mentioned.) Every minute I'm doing something – I even enjoy going to bed! (Strange as it may seem.)

In gym we're learning to play field hockey. Of course it won't count, but I thought of not going out for sports and when I tried it out it was so much fun that I continued. I really think that it is relaxing.

We have already had a snowfall that spread everything with a lacy veil and even though it was yesterday (Sunday) – it still lasts in places.

Oh-Oh! (As Susie says) There goes the bell. Write soon, please.

Love,
Sylvia

Give love to Duncan & <drawing of heart> Susie especially, and also to everyone else.

S.

1 – The Norfolk County Teachers' Convention and concert was held at the Tremont Temple, 88 Tremont Street, Boston, Mass.

TO *Margot Loungway Drekmeier*

Saturday 17 November 1945[1] ALS with envelope, Smith College

December 25, 1945
(is coming soon)

Dearest Margot,

How are you old top? I am fine also.

The address you wanted is: <drawing of two buildings and a street>

H. E. Harris Company
108 Massachusetts Ave.
Boston 17, Massachusetts.

The so-called company knew the date of my birthday because they asked for it on an approval sheet.

I'm enclosing my favorite picture of me with my little brown jug.[2]

We had a lovely P.T.A night[3] up at the Junior High School. I was in a tableau as you probably know. There was an exibition of all our work in all of the rooms and in the hall.

Could you name some specific stamps you want? Maybe I have it. How many stamps do you have in your album. What countries do you have most in? I would like basic information about the stamp circle. Are the stamps all your duplicates? I have bought quite a few nice stamps from the Jamestown Company already and I find that their offers are quite reasonable. How Do you go about getting so many good duplicates?

Its astounding about Susie saying such things! The "old top" sounds sort of fishy though. I would love to know what Duncan looks like <drawing of a head with a '?' where the face would be>

For over a week now, we've been having cold gray weather with stinging rain almost unceasingly. Speaking of poetry I just began a notebook of my poems and already have about 5 real ones, and have about 5 medium and about 15 jingles.

Have you many Stamps from Southern Rhodesia? You certainly were prompt in answering my letter.

After I saw the "return within 10 days" underlined I resolved to do so.

What are your latest stories about, by the way? I would love to have a copy of a few of them.

I recently looked through a magazine and I found all of the various stages in eye making pictured. This is the finished model. <SP glued the

1–Date supplied from postmark and other evidence.

2–The photograph is no longer with the letter.

3–The Parent–Teachers' Association night was held on 15 November 1945.

image of an eye, cut-out from the magazine with the caption: ‘Ah! To see within the inner eye. (Owner of eye’s has not claimed this yet’> Its a beautiful specimin.[1]

This is definitely a true experience of mine:[2] “About a few months ago I went to the Art Museum[3] with Priscilla[4] and Patty D.[5] (two friends of mine.) We were studying about Egypt and so went up to the mummy room. In a showcase on the wall there were various Egyptian relics being displayed. A queer old man came up silently and said, “O ho! You girls must be interested in my treasures. I’m keeper here and I have something in my other pants that may be of interest to you.” Off he went into a dark corridor. I immediately wanted to go home for my feet hurt, but the two others were interested and I had, evidently, been reading too many “Nancy Drew” stories. I, of course, stayed on with them. In a few minutes the old man walked back with a new suit on! Out of his pocket he took a tiny, queer shaped sort of magnifying glass. This, the funny (or shall I say peculiar) man took, and lead us over to the showcase. In the case there were various types of Indian jewelry and Egyptian jewelry. (Do you know the story of the Mummy’s foot.[6] Ask your mother[7] if she does.) One little box contained an agate eye! It looked, (to shivering me) like the real thing. The man cackled when he saw my terror and held out the glass –

He held the glass over the eye and, as though it were jelly, the eye wriggled and the pupil contracted as the man tipped the glass!! He laughed once more and asked us to come down the dark corridor to see some more relics.

All of a sudden I felt very ill and grabbed the girls by the hand. Muttering with relief I dragged them to the front entry. The man started after us calling, “I’ve something else to show you”. I rushed out, not caring to see any more eyes which he said were genuine Egyptian.

The girls, evidently, had not seen the eye wiggle and would have gone back had I not reminded them that it was past lunch time!

When I got home safely with no eyes following me I immediately said to Priscilla, “My that Egyptian exhibit was certainly wonderful.” She

1–SP drew lines around this paragraph.

2–SP based her short story ‘The Mummy’s Tomb’ (17 May 1946) on this experience.

3–The Museum of Fine Arts, Boston, Mass.

4–Priscilla Steele (1933–), SP’s classmate, who lived at 5 Boulder Brook Road, Wellesley, Mass.

5–Possibly Patricia Ann Dunne, who lived at 32 Beverly Road, Wellesley, Mass.

6–Théophile Gauthier, ‘The Mummy’s Foot’ (1840). According to SP’s diary, she finished reading this on 6 June 1945.

7–Margaret Neall Peck Loungway (1907–63).

whispered back, "I wish I really felt that way too. The eye was terrible." I told her conscendingly, "Oh! That's only natural for someone who hasn't had as much experience as I have."

So you see what influence such things have on peoples lives. Sometimes when I go to sleep I see in my dreams eyes coming toward me at a terrific rate and whizzing past just in time. When I work with stamps too much this happens too. Take my advice – never take eyes too lightly. They really are supernatural sometimes.

I am very glad for you that your father[1] is coming home. I hope also that Susie knows him.

With love,
Sylvia

<on back of envelope>

Read inner flap.

<on inner flap of envelope>

I did not send you some of my stamps this time but will probably be up in about ten days if you will wait.

TO *Margot Loungway Drekmeier*

Sunday 16 December 1945 — ALS with envelope, Estate of Margot Drekmeier

December 16

<drawing of a sparkling star with two eyes and a mouth>

Dearest Margot,

I am writing this letter to you from bed. I have a cold as well as an itchy rash over my face and arms for I picked some poison sumach berries. I thought that they were bayberries but was sadly mistaken.

I have explained to you why I was not able to buy any of your stamps on the reply sheet.

How is the weather up there in Maine? Our town is a frosty cold point of snow on the map. We get out of school on December 21st. and go back on January 2nd. How long a vacation do you have?

How are the kittens? I'm in a dither for I have to prepare two oral reports, a test, and two homework papers for tomorrow.

1–Ferdinand John Loungway (1903–89). Loungway was a chaplain and commander in the US Navy during World War II.

I followed your advice and sent a selection of stamps to Joyce Martin.[1] As you said, she was not able to buy them but wants the offer later. Evidently she gets in the same predicaments that I do.

I am so glad that your father has come home. Duncan must be growing up quickly like babies inevitably do. I miss Susie alot as well as everyone else. In Wellesley there is no inkling of seeing even a baby <drawing of a moose with caption 'Moose!'> I often remember the perfect time we had at your house this summer.

Love to all,
Sylvia

P.S. I'll write a longer letter when I'm better.

s.

TO *Margot Loungway Drekmeier*

c. 1945 ALS, Estate of Margot Drekmeier

<in each of the four corners of the letter a word, each underlined with a flourish, spelling For | Get | Me | Not>

Dear Margot –

These are gold ships ~ <drawing of two ships>
These are silver ships ~ <drawing of two ships>
But there is no ship
Like our friendship.

<flourish>

True friends are like diamonds,
Precious and rare. <drawing of a sparkling diamond>
False friends are like leaves –
Found everywhere. <drawing of a leaf>

Love from
Sylvia Plath

<flourish>

1 – Possibly Joyce Martin of Otisfield, Maine.

1946

TO *Margot Loungway Drekmeier*

Sunday 13 January 1946 | ALS with envelope, Estate of Margot Drekmeier

January 13, 1946

<drawing of postage stamp with caption 'United States 1¢'>

Dearest Margot,

Do you notice any difference in my printing. I have a new $10 fountain pen[1] that will last me a lifetime. It is green and gold and very ultra-modern. In my new diary <drawing of diary cover with caption 'Diary 1946'> (alas, it's much smaller than my previous one[2]) I am keeping account of my stamp expenditures and – income! I have only spent 35¢ this year and have received 10¢ from my sheets that I send out.

Do you know of anyone else that hasn't a super stamp collection like yours? I want to send to some more in your stamp Circle if there's any one who hasn't too many stamps. (Besides Joyce Martin.) <drawing of a heart over the 'i' in 'Martin'>

For Christmas I received some very nice stamps. Do you have any United States stamps on the first Page? I have two there. <drawing of stamp album> How many U.S. stamps d'you have in all? I am enclosing a special offer of 50 different stamps for 10¢. You may have all – in that case please return to me, Bub. Are you collecting much money from the stamp Circle? I sent in for an offer from the Owen's Stamp Co.[3] that did not mention approvals and what did I receive!! Approvals! (and a measly free envelope of duplicates) You should have seen the thank-you refusal I wrote back – I praised their low prices, valuable stamps and a whole pile of other things.

We have had cold weather this winter and the ground is covered with a film of frozen snow. What is the weather like up there?

1–SP was given the fountain pen by her grandfather on 6 January 1946. From her diary: 'Grampy bought me a new fountainpen with my name in gold on it! It's beautiful.'

2–SP's 1945 diary measured 21 cm × 14.5 cm (h × w); her 1946 diary measured 15 cm × 9 cm.

3–Owens Stamp Company was located in Bay City, Michigan.

Have you read any of Richard Halliburton's books? ("Royal Road to Romance," "Flying Carpet," "Glorious Adventure", and "New Worlds to Conquer."[1]) If you haven't you should. They're full of lovely expressions and descriptions.

I hope you noticed the envelope,[2] Bub. (Ha-Ha) (One good turn deserves another, Maggot) <drawing of a maggot, a spider, and a worm[3]> Don't feel wormy, just remember – Sylvia A. Plath (S.A.P.)

<drawing of an arm, with caption 'from', and hand with finger pointed to SP's signature>

Regards and consolations,
Sylvia Artimis Platovksy

TO *Frank Schober*

Wednesday 16 January 1946 ALS, Indiana University

<drawing of a heart with the word 'Love' in it>

Jan. 16, 1946

Dearest Grampy,

As I was walking home from my piano lesson this evening I saw this beautiful picture of the earth.

Enclosed is an original poem about it.

Special love,
Sylvia

<drawing of smiling female>
<drawing of a winter scene with moon>

A WINTER SUNSET
by Sylvia Plath

Over the earth's dark rim
 The daylight softly fades,
The sky from orange to gold
 And then to copen shades.

1–Richard Halliburton, *The Royal Road to Romance*, *The Flying Carpet*, *The Glorious Adventure*, *New Worlds to Conquer* (Indianapolis: Bobbs-Merrill, 1925, 1932, 1927, 1929).
2–SP addressed the letter to 'Miss Maggot Loungway'.
3–A very similar drawing appears in SP's diary entry for 12 January 1946.

The moon hangs, a globe of iridescent light
In a frosty winter sky,
While against the western glow one sees
The bare, black skeleton of the trees.

The stars come out and one by one
Survey the world with lofty stare;
But, from the last turn in the road
A cosy home beckons to me there.

TO *Margot Loungway Drekmeier*

Friday 22 February 1946 — ALS with envelope, Estate of Margot Drekmeier

February 22, '46

<drawing of stamp with caption: 'How many 1940 stamps of famous poets, artists etc.[1] do you have? (1940) United States'>

Dear Margot,

Happy George Washington's Birthday. How are you all? What is this I hear about you moving somewhere in the vicinity of Wellesley? Goodie!!!!! It will be easier for me to kidnap dear Duncan and sweet Susie! I can't wait.

Enclosed is one dime for your offer. Warren bought it. What are the numbers of the stamps on the first page of the United States in your album? The stamps that you have on the first page.[2]

So far this year I have kept a record[3] of the stamps cost that I've bought along with my income. My expenditures are high (for me) this past two months and my income only covers one-fourth of it.

Have you any spare snapshots of you? I'd like one to pin up in my Chamber of Horrors. <drawing of a girl in checkered skirt, biting her fingers with hair raised looking at a picture>

1–The American Poets stamps issued in 1940 included Henry Wadsworth Longfellow, John Greenleaf Whittier, James Russell Lowell, Walt Whitman, and James Whitcomb Riley. The artists were Gilbert Stuart, James McNeill Whistler, Augustus Saint-Gaudens, Daniel Chester French, and Frederic Remington. Additional stamps were issued for American composers, scientists, educators, and inventors.

2–This sentence added and bracketed in the margin.

3–See SP's 1946 diary, particularly the 'Memoranda' section in the back; held by Lilly Library.

I, too, have received 20¢ from Joyce Martin. She sounds like a lovely person only evidently doesn't like to write much!

My diary is very punk. The pages measure 3½" × 6" and there are only 18 lines for writing. Most of the time I write double lines. At the beginning of the year I illustrated each page but now only have time for a sketch here and there.

I'm still taking piano, viola, and dancing lessons, am in the shool's Friday orchestra and belong to an active scout troop. <drawing of SP in Girl Scout uniform and hat with a halo overhead> How is Ellen? What are you doing in school? Have I told you how the Jamestown Stamp Company spells my name. I sent in for a packet a second time and sent back the approvals. They utterly thought I was two different people – Sylivia and Sulvia. I thought Sulvia was really the worst as I printed very plainly. (sniff-sniff!)

Please tell me a little more coherently about the Stamp circle members you sent my name to about free offers mixed up with something else. I'd like some addresses of gullible people (If you can find any in your intelligent vicinity.) I can't wait until summer comes with camp and such. The three weeks I spent in Maine last summer (believe it or not) were the most fun I've ever had. I will never forget it.

Warren and I have had a wonderful time coasting. Have I told you? The hill was made with bulldozers and I've never seen anything so steep. The weather was damp for one day and the hill froze solid to ice. When Warren and I pulled the sled up it was like the legendary glass hill. Our sled is very streamlined. We went down the hill like this: <drawing of a steep hill with two people on a sled at the bottom by a labelled 'Brook'> Last night I dreamed that I was over your house and was looking at your stamp album. I can't wait to see it and to compare some of your spaces with mine.

Please write soon. I received a letter from you containing eight pennies. If this was to pay for my offer that I last sent you it is fine for that was the price. I don't know if the pennies were lucky or not.

Love,
The Stamp

TO *Marion Freeman*

Tuesday 16 April 1946 ALS with envelope, Smith College

April 16, 1946

Dear Mrs. Freeman,

I've so much to write now that I've come from Winthrop. This weekend has been so full that I've had to write double lines in my diary. But I can never write enough to fully express the super-wonderful time I had at 8 Somerset Terrace (and vicinity).

The minute I got up at 11:45 this morning, the telephone rang; – Prissy. She was aching for me to describe the details of my visit, (especially about Dave.[1]) Betsy called up this evening and spent the time listening to my story. I did not exaggerate one tiny bit and they believed me implicitly.

When I told about the blouse, however, they were rather doubtful. They know how I loved to sew (read this sarcastically <arrow pointing to the word 'loved'>) and found it hard to believe when I told them how wonderful it was and how I enjoyed it.

<drawing of blouse and hat on a female head>

This afternoon Prissy and I rode our bikes to Wellesley College and climbed the well-known tower[2] alone. The first 250 feet of steps (after the elevator took us four flights) were very bare and breathtaking. They went around the dark walls and you could look through the stairs to the bottom everywhere. This was not very comforting. Then the fun began – the stairs were all of a sudden very small and triangular and went around and around – up and up – for I don't know how long. We could hardly squeeze through the conical structure. <drawing of winding stairwell> Then the ever-resourceful Prissy opened a tiny door – the wind rushed by in torrents of force (that mightn't sound right but thats the way it felt.) We walked out of a flat square of brick with a wall (very low) all around and four lacy turrets at the corners. Way, way down below us the countryside lay, seemingly flat. The miniature green fields were dotted with tiny white houses, gleaming blue lakes, small spots of little trees. The ribbons of road that criss-crossed the land were speckled with shiny cars. Two ant-like girls strolled chummily on the walk below. (I do hope that they don't mind the comparison.) Prissy and I reluctantly made our way down. We both mentioned to each other afterward that our knees were beginning to feel stronger.

1–David C. Freeman (1932–2007), Ruth Freeman's brother.
2–The Galen Stone Tower, which stands 182 feet tall and is a focal point of the campus.

I must thank you once more for being so wonderful to me – helping me make the blouse, supplying me with a new Easter dress and all the other wonderful things.

If it won't be much to a bother, I'd like to tell the following people the following things:

Mr. Freeman[1] – I do hope that I may see your finished painting. In my estimation it should be in the Art Museum along with Winslow Homer and the rest.

<drawing of a framed painting>

Dave – Prissy is very anxious to meet you – likewise Betsy. I do appreciate your following the bus – especially popping out by East Boston. <drawing of bicycle>

Ruthie – The hat is adorable. Mum loves it. I do hope you will have a nice time in Saugus. (Did you sleep last night?) <arrow pointing to the word 'Saugus'>

Wayne[2] – My bike feels so uncomfortable and strange. I always used to like it but now I think that I should loosen the front wheel and paint it orange.

<drawing of a girl holding a piece of paper sitting at a desk with an inkwell on it>

Give my love to the family,
Love,
Sylvia

TO *Margot Loungway Drekmeier*

Sunday 26 May 1946 — ALS with envelope, Estate of Margot Drekmeier

May 26, 1946

Dear Margot,

My mother is shocked and horrified at the fact that it is over a week since I have written to you! There is so much time that I have spent writing stories when I should have been writing to thank you for the perfectly wonderful time that I had over your house! The week has flashed by with a snap of the tail, and yet it seems like years since I have last seen you.

1–William H. Freeman (1884–1954).

2–W. Wayne Sterling (1932–), a friend from Winthrop, who lived at 7 Enfield Road, Winthrop, Mass.

Before I tell you the things I have been doing, I must thank the whole family for the beautiful time I had visiting. We never need to plan entertainment for each other, because there is always so much to do with stamps and stories that we can never get it all in. I am enclosing a rather expensive, but very good, offer.[1] Please – please get rid of it. Maybe to Elsa. I do hope that you will be able to sell my other two offers, because my expenses are soaring. I wonder if there is such a thing as a blind stamp collector!

I finished writing "On the Penthouse Roof" but it came out mushily. My best girl friend (for going to the movies) read both "In the Mummy's Tomb" and the other one. Since she is exceedingly romantic, she thought that the penthouse roof was the better of the two. I have not yet typed it up, as I did the others. I have, so far, completed three stories and begun a fourth.

The are something like this, according to subject.

The Mummy's Tomb – Murder Mystery
On the Penthouse Roof Terrible smuggler mystery
A May Morning – Descriptive
Stardust A Fairy tale

I am very anxious to receive a copy of "Feathers." I mean the story. Remember the five types we're going to send each other copies of:

(Love) – (I don't want that type)
True-life
Fairy Tale
Mystery
Murder
Descriptive

This must be a very short note, because if I wrote a longer letter, it would not get in the mail soon enough. How is Dunkie? and Susie? and the rest of the family? I had a lovely time attending a Rainbow installation[2] on Friday night. It was beautiful. I talked to one of my family, my brother, in fact, about your "sedentary work" story, or whatever it was. I told it to him, word for word. The only place I added anything to was where you heard the last earthly cries of the victims in the unsealed coffins. After mentioning those burning specimins I just said, "The delicious smell of frying flesh reached my nostrils!" I hope you don't mind. Do drop me a

1 – The enclosure is no longer with the letter.

2 – Per SP's diary, the Rainbow installation is part of the Masonic youth organization and took place at the Masonic Temple in Natick, Mass.

letter. My uncle and aunt are dropping in for this weekend (seems that a lot of things are dropping.) I'll write a real <u>letter</u> soon.

Love
Sylvia.

P.S. My name for the stamp offer is Laurice Anduoir – Like your P. P. Lane.

TO *Margot Loungway Drekmeier*

Friday 28 June 1946 — ALS with envelope, Estate of Margot Drekmeier

June 28, 1946

Dear "Muscles,"

My mother has just received your exciting letter. She tore it open with shaking hands, and, after finishing reading the contents, she collapsed. I hope that your parents enjoyed that bit of a note as much as the W. B. did. The approving things that you called me were also enjoyed by W. B. since you can translate such difficult languages as the sternal Coopnagle language, I hope that you know who W. B. is.

Now, to leave that gruesome subject of acknowledging your thank-you "note," I will ask you – was Elsa sweet enough to buy my stupendously marvelous bargain offers which you so kindly meddled with???

I had the thrilling experience of going to the dentist on Wednesday. On the way to the bus stop I managed to wriggle out of my mothers commanding grasp, and be absorbed in a huge, awed crowd in the middle of one of Boston's most trafficy streets. I soon crawled up to the inner edge of the group of people. There, lying in the street I saw a frenzied criminal, being handcuffed by two grim police men. A man whispered in my hearing device, "That's what you get for resisting the LAW!"

A little shiver ran up my spine as I thought how it easily <u>might</u> have been you. My thoughts were interrupted by the paddy wagon screaming around the corner. It had six policeman inside. My mother dragged me away from the scene, fearful that It might have some influence on me.

I was quite surprised to received a letter addressed to me from Austria yesterday. It was from my grandfather's half-sister's granddaughter[1] (figure that out for me.) She is also thirteen, and just learning to write English, and so wanted someone to correspond with. She also sent some very interesting photos of her family.

1 – According to SP's diary, this was Mary Hillbrand.

How are you coming on your stories. Remember to send me copies of them, please. I will gladly send you a penciled copy of "The Mummie's Tomb"[1] in exchange for one of "A Fateful Night," or what ever you call it. On the day after you left I finished typing the second chapter of "Stardust,"[2] which you were so derisive of, "Fairy Tales," you know.

My doctor examined my for health a few days ago. Looking at me rather doubtfully, he gave me the knee-test (which, mind you, was not required on my camp card.) I grew rather worried, and so when he hit my floating cartilige, I kicked my leg out a bit, just to do away with any suspicions that he might have. Mother was hovering about nervously, and looked anxiously at the doctor, who looked queerly puzzled after having completed my examination.

By the way, my address until July 27 will be:

Camp Helen Storrow
Buzzard's Bay, Route #2
Cape Cod, Mass.

So in your next letter (I hope it will be a letter) to me, you had better write there. Also, shall I next write to you at Innisfree?

I hope that we will get together for the tiniest part of the summer! (Hint! Hint!) Can't you just see us lying on soft pine needles and writing best-sellers in the quiet serenity of the woods? Maybe the picture is a bit exaggerated, but even so ---

In the meantime, give my love to the family.

Sincerely,
"Toothpick Bean

TO *Aurelia Schober Plath*

Saturday 29 June 1946 ALS (postcard), Indiana University

June 29

Dearest Mother,

Oh! Camp certainly is wonderful. On Sunday afternoon we had ham and cheese just to start off the season with. I had two helpings along with four cups of milk. The sky is gray, and clouds are skudding across it. The

1–Sylvia Plath, 'The Mummy's Tomb'.
2–Sylvia Plath, 'Stardust'.

wind is wonderful, too. It blows so hard and sighs through the pine trees breathing a delicious piny smell. We went in for a short dip before supper. I have never seen such water. It is like liquid crystal. The sand is so white, that the water is a translucent green. Out farther it was a lovely blue, although sometimes it reflected the moods of the sky by turning gray. Bets and I got the cabin fixed before taps blew at nine. We didn't go to sleep for a while because of listening to the wind and watching fireflies.

xxxx
Sylvia

TO *Aurelia Schober Plath*

Monday 1 July 1946 ALS (postcard), Indiana University

July 1, 1946

Dear Mummy,

Today was sort of damp and cloudy. The wind keeps blowing and blowing. Today is Monday. The sun came out three times, but went in before we could run out to see the miracle. In swimming we had our tests to see what group we would be in. I was so happy to get to be a white cap, where I left off last year. The beginners are red caps, intermediates are white caps, and accomplished are blue. Bets is also a white cap, but will soon get to be a blue cap. I had such fun with her underwater (with nose plugs of course) playing and doing surface dives. We had a barn dance in our unit house[1] with another unit. Oh! It certainly was fun. Our Arts and Crafts Program is swell.

Love,
Siv

Remember to save the funnies

TO *Aurelia Schober Plath*

Tuesday 2 July 1946 ALS (postcard), Indiana University

Tuesday
July 2, 1946

Dear Mother,

Yesterday we had canteen. I spent a quarter for another sketch pad. There are lots of projects, and so I am very happy with arts and crafts.

1–SP was in Cove Unit.

Today is miserable, all it does is rain and RAIN. It is so terribly boring. We are sitting in our cabin together, and looking out into the damp, gray world. Last night we got to sleep soon after taps and had to be woken up before reville. Time sometimes flies and sometimes drags. I have not gotten a card from you as yet, but we only have had one mail in which two letters were given out. I am having such fun. I have begun to sketch one of the cabins. Our art teacher is eccentric – named Rosamond French, or something like that. Until I have more to write.

lots of love –
sylvia

TO *Aurelia Greenwood Schober*

Tuesday 2 July 1946 — ALS, Indiana University

July 2, 1946

Dear Grammy

I hope this gets to you in time to wish you a very Happy BIRTHDAY!

<drawing of floral bouquet>

With love,
From Sylvia

TO *Aurelia Schober Plath*

Wed.–Thurs. 3–4 July 1946 — ALS on Wellesley, Mass.[1] letterhead, Indiana University

July 3, 1946

Dear Mother,

Last night I received your lovely letter in the second mail. I also appreciated Warren's little bit of humor. Do send me some ribbons; the one and only black one that I brought has disappeared. I also would like my nailnipper, for my fingers have disgracefully long nails.

Betsy is having a swell time too, and I have made a lot of paintings, but have given them all away. However, I am going to save the rest of them.

We had quite a time in our unit last night. The fish we had the day before disagreed with them, and so five people threw-up. The councilors were up all night. About thirty people, or over one-fourth of the camp,

1 – Above the printed text on the letterhead, SP had written 'To'.

were ill. We have had so much soup that I am floating around inside. Do not bother to send my tennis racket now. I do not need it as yet. I have made a lot of friends, but none compare with Joan Beals. We have had two cookouts. I am stuffing myself with bread, potatoes, and cereal, but they all float around in the everlasting soup. Well! At last the sun has come out. I sure hope that it dries up all the moisture. We had loads of fun in boating. Both of our councilors are young, pretty, and loads fun. In swimming we had loads of fun, Gayle Greenough[1] and Marilyn[2] and I had loads of fun under water. We danced around on the floor of the lake and had a swell time.

I am eating all I can, but do not have an opportunity to get weighed. The food we have is almost as bad as Uncle Frank's dog biscuits.

Tonight the oddest thing happened. Gayle saw the bandage on my so-called "tumor", and said she'd pull it off for me. She did; but the back half of the growth ripped off, and I filled up two hankies with blood. Everyone was in our cabin and they gaped at me so. One girl cried out in a terrified tone, "Get to the nurse, quick! or you'll get cancer."

I laughed so hard that I began to have tears roll down my cheeks, because I was half-scared myself. They "hearded" (<u>herded</u>, I mean) me to the nurse's office. Skipper, the head of the camp was there. "Doc" told me that it was very simple, just a pimple (trying to not alarm me.) Skipper shooed the rest of the kids out "doc" stopped the breathing (I mean <u>bleeding</u>) and put some orange stuff on. I laughed so hard when Skipper pulled me over to look at the sunset. My appreciation of "nature's beauty", you know.

Doc put on some orange stuff, and my dried up "tumor" clung to my nose unnoticibly. I had such fun with Betsy and Gayle, because they thought I was sort of hysterical.

Please do send my nailnipper, for I have "tingrown-oenails."

<u>June 4</u>[3]
<u>Thursday</u>

Today is really beautiful. The sun is shining brightly and we played badminton in the tennis court. My stroke is really atrocious, and Betsy won, two to three. At lunch I stuffed myself like a hog. – two bowls of vegetable soup, one piece of bread, two helpings of raisin and carrot salad, two helpings of potatoes and cabbage, a piece of cake, and seven

1 – Wellesley friend and classmate Gayle Greenough (1932–).
2 – Marilyn Fraser, who lived at 20 Dover Road, Wellesley, Mass.
3 – Misdated by SP, should be 4 July.

cups of milk. I try so hard to drink water, but it doesn't work out so well. I have enough liquid, though. I have loads of pals here. Tomorrow we're having the last rehearsal for the minstrel show we're having on Saturday, for another unit. I almost died, for I was unanimously elected the "guest star," Frank Sinatra. I have, so they say, the perfect build. However I have the voice of a lovesick horse, and can you imagine me getting out on the floor wailing "Prisoner of Love"[1] off key! I can't get out of it and still be a good sport, so I just guess I'll dooo it. I really think Gayle is swell. She is so sweet, and is a wonderful sport. I am having such fun, and have good ideas for two poems. I do hope you will like them. In my next card (or letter) I will describe the most beautiful morning I have ever seen, and then I will describe the sunset. We had the most beautiful cobweb almost bigger than me, out in front of our cabin between two trees. All the cobwebs were dew spangled, and were draped about in misty beauty all over the place.

Love,
"Siv"

TO *Aurelia Schober Plath*

Thursday 4 July 1946 ALS (postcard), Indiana University

July 4, 1946

Dear Mother,

I do hope that the mail you get from me does not come too unevenly. The cards you get are collected at 4:00, and no mail is collected today or on Sunday, and sometimes I don't finish them on time, so you see how it is. I hope you got my letter.

In swimming we began to do dives from the dock. Doris Toabe[2] and I had a terrible time. She jumped this afternoon, but I tried to dive. I ended up in doing a couple of belly-flops. I washed my hair today, as well as washing my socks that I have (you said to) so far used. It was really good to get it over with, (washing, I mean).

Lots of love,
"Siv"

1–A 1931 song, popularized in 1945 by Billy Eckstine, Art Blakey, and Duke Ellington. Perry Como also sang a version released in 1945.
2–Doris A. Toabe (1932–2003), from Marshfield, Mass.

TO *Aurelia Schober Plath*

Friday 5 July 1946 ALS (postcard), Indiana University

July 5, 1946

Dear Mother,

Could you please tell me when to start writing to you at the Isle of Shoals. Last night we had a nice formal retreat and a lovely campfire on the beach. We sang songs, and the art leader told us a nice story. After we had watched the sun sink in a fold of gold and red behind the purple hills, we went in the mess hall and had some wonderful icecream. Even though I am having a horrid time diving, I was very happy today to hear Splash say that I had a <u>very</u> good side stroke. I am now lying in the field sunbathing. I had a beautiful time in boating, for I love to row, and can, if I say so myself, row quite well. Check up on my scheaffer pen to see that its still there!

Siv

TO *Aurelia Schober Plath*

Friday 5 July 1946 ALS (postcard), Indiana University

July 5, 1946

Dear Mater,

I am in a very good mood today, which is rather odd, because my caper was to clean out the latrines. I hope that you aren't discouraged, but I sunbathed out in the field today, and I got a slight burn, but I was rubbing toothpaste on it, so it didn't hurt at all. I <u>should</u> be gaining weight! Just listen to what I had for lunch:

Two bowls of noodle soup
One slice of bread
Two helpings of potatoes and cabbage
Two helpings of salad (including lettuce, cheese, peas, eggs)
Three bowls of custard
One cup of milk – two of cocoa.

I'm eating so much, no matter what, or how horrible it is, that I can hardly walk after each meal.

Love,
Sylvia

TO *Aurelia Schober Plath*

Sunday 7 July 1946

ALS on Wellesley, Mass. letterhead,[1] Indiana University

July 7, 1946

Dear Mother,

I do hope that you are getting all of my mail. So far, and this is Sunday morning, I have gotten three letters[2] and a postcard from you, and a nice letter from Grammy, Grampy, Frank and Louise

I do not like to tell you, but I have come down with a miserable cold. I am so mad! Betsy had a slight one, and I caught it from her, only mine is much worse. As I have no temperature, the nurse does not think that it is much. The only relief I get is when she puts nose drops up in the night. My nose is stuffed, and I feel so badly that I won't be able to go swimming for a long time.

I also had the cold yesterday. Yesterday was a miserably cold, rainy day, and all we did was rehearse for the variety show we gave to the Ridge Unit last night. It made quite a hit.

I was dressed in a white men's shirt, gray slacks, bow tie, and jacket with my hair pulled back for Frankie. I leaned against the piano for my microphone was a broom with a cup on top. <drawing of broom topped by a cup> The funny part about it was that Betsy sang and played the piano, while made gestures, and opend my mouth to silently form the words. The people who did not know Betsy's voice <u>actually</u> believed that I was singing. It made quite a hit since I stopped to blow my nose once at the end, while Betsy kept on singing.

I was also in "Casey at the Bat" – the umpire. I wore an old sweatshirt and my handy green visor cap back wards. For both acts my hair was tightly skinned back in the way you dislike so much. <drawing of SP as Casey with caption 'Strrrike Oone!'> Casey was such a riot that we had to do it over again. It was really fun, but, to tell the truth, I'm glad to have it over with. This morning, Ricky, my unit leader (oh! is she super!) did not make me get up for breakfast, but I stayed in my own cosy cabin bed, which I had just changed, and I was <u>not</u> made to go to the infirmary. Ricky is certainly sweet.

By the way, on the next visiting day (<u>next</u> Sunday) if you are not coming, there is the slight, <u>very</u> slight in fact, possibility of my being

1 – Above the printed text on the letterhead, SP had written 'To'.

2 – '~~two~~ three letters' appears in the original.

taken across the lake by one certain Anne Brown. That is, if her aunt is home. If I am asked, will you mind my going? I am ready to jump at the opportunity, but if you would rather have me not go, it will be all right. This Anne has taken a fancy to Betsy and me, but Betsy can't go for her parents are coming. I like Anne somewhat, but truthfully, she is spoiled and sometimes stupidly unresponsive.

I had an awful sunburn, but as sunburns are not supposed to be had, I kept quiet. Gloria,[1] however, rubbed some cream on it so it doesn't hurt any more.

Friday night Gayle slept in the same bed, and so did Sally[2] and I. We slept quite well and I do not think the counsellors found out, for we were quiet and slept quite well. I sort of wish they had, for I get a better sleep alone, and don't want them to think I'm a sissy and get mad. So--- I'm using diplomacy. A good case of imaginary cramps and three tablespoons of "medicine" (magnesia) convinced Betsy. I'm using my cold for an excuse not to have anyone sleep in my bed, and I'll think up something better later.

Last night we put on our pajamas and our Cove Unit went down to Skipper's cabin and listened to the radio after taps while having delicious punch and cookies. Having a wonderful time. Write soon.

Loads of love,
Sylvia
XXXX

TO *Aurelia Schober Plath*

Monday 8 July 1946

ALS with envelope, on Wellesley, Mass. letterhead, Indiana University

Monday
July 8, 1946

Dear, Dear Mother,

I do hope that you are at the Isle of Shoals now, and that you get my letters. Yesterday was Sunday, so we got no mail. I have got letters and a card from you dated Sunday – June 30, Monday – July 1, Tuesday – July 2 and Wednesday – July 3. Grammy's letter was written July 5. Tonight, however, I hope to get alot of letters.

1–Gloria Marie Caouette (1933–), from Lexington, Mass.
2–Probably Sally Howard, a fellow Girl Scout and Unitarian, who lived at 25 Highgate, Wellesley, Mass.

Last night, Sunday, we had a lovely Scouts' Own on the beach. The unit that was giving it sang lovely prayers and songs, and read some beautiful poetry. We sat and watched the firey ball of sun sink over the misty purple hills before leaving. By the way, yesterday we had the following for Sunday dinner: chicken, fluffy white mashed potatoes, peas, icecream and cupcakes. Boy! was it good.

Yesterday "Frenchie," our Arts and Crafts teacher took eight girls from different units on a two hour sketching trip. I was the only one from our unit that went. The other seven girls evidently had taken lessons, for they looked experienced. I gaily started out, feeling somewhat inexperienced and inferior. We hiked along the dusty road until we came to the quaintest little old house nestled in the trees. We sat down across the road and began to draw. I used broad pencils, and they are swell. I was eager to see the work of the others, and was surprised to see that it was not at all much better than mine. In fact, only one came up to mine. When the girl-next to me showed my drawing to Frenchie, she asked me if I was taking art lessons. When I said no, she snapped, "Why not! You should lap up all the instruction you can get!" I do think that I will take viola with Mrs. Bates next year, and try to save up toward art (preferably sketching) lessons, for I love it so. In crafts I am making a tiny tinish nut spoon for $.35!!!! It is fat and crooked, and looks like this <two drawings of spoons> If it comes out nice enough I intend to give it to Dot for Christmas, so don't tell her. Arts is wonderful, there are so many grand things to do. Last night the whole unit was supposed to sleep on the beach for preparation for the overnight hike on Thursday. I most likely could have gone if I had insisted, but Rikki said I had better not, since I had a nasty cold. I had the cold only Saturday and Sunday. To tell the truth, I really was glad not to go, for I would probably not be well enough to go on the hike to fisherman's cove Tuesday, and that I will not miss. I moved my quilt into Anne Brown's cabin, for we were the only two not going. I fell into a comfortable sleep at 9:15 and woke up at 7:15 and went back to my cabin. I felt rested and my cold was all gone. I was doubly glad that I didn't sleep out because the girls got no more than a meager five hrs sleep, and were awfully cold.

I felt fine and wide awake. Our unit cooked out on the beach (twelve girls). The other half had breakfast in the hall. Bets and I made the best fire, even though It did not start right away, we beat the others. We had three crisp, delicious pieces of bacon and an egg apiece cooked on our own private tin can stove. We also had milk, oranges, and I ate five muffins. I enjoyed it so. While we went to crafts, Skipper cut my clothesline down and took it away, saying, "Hmph! Clotheslines are unheard of at camp!"

Boy, I sure was mad! Betsy, Gloria, and I made an agreement never to do something, and if we did, we bought each of the others something worth 5¢ at canteen. Now I owe Gloria 5¢, but she owes me 10¢ and Betsy 10¢, so I really gain 5¢! Do send the nailnipper, for my ingrown toenail is infected and awfully swollen. Every time I touch it pus comes out. Now that my cold is over, I really feel wonderful. We're not supposed to get sun on us, but because "to finish up my cold" Rikki gave me permission to lie out in the field for a couple of minutes. My aim is to get very tan (in secret, if possible.)

Lots of love,
Sylvia

<drawing of two hearts on back of envelope>

TO *Aurelia Greenwood Schober & Frank Schober*

Tuesday 9 July 1946 — ALS on Wellesley, Mass. letterhead, Indiana University

Tuesday, July 9

Dear Dear Grammy and Grampy,

In case I have not already told you, I was really very happy to get your nice letters all in one. I have already written a card to Frank and Louise. I have been having quite a time with my cold, on Saturday and Sunday. Sunday night we were supposed to go with our unit to sleep on the beach in preparation for our overnight hike the next week. I slept alone in the unit with another girl who couldn't sleep out. We slept soundly from nine to seven o'clock. I was so glad that I didn't go out, for when the girls came back they said they had been very cold and had no more than five hours sleep! I had woken up in my cosy cabin feeling wonderful, my cold all gone, whereupon it would have been worse.

Yesterday, "Frenchie", our art teacher, took eight girls on a two hour sketching trip. We stopped opposite the sweetest little house and sat down to sketch it. I thought that I would probably be inexperienced compared to the others, for they looked professional. When I had almost finished my drawing with pencil, Frenchie asked to see it. To my surprise I only liked one as well as mine. When Frenchie asked if I took art lessons, and I said no, she seemed rather angry and told me that I should "lap up all the instruction I can get." I really hope that I can take art lessons next year.

Last night we took the boats and rowed across the lake to have supper. The distance was one mile, and I rowed one of the boats going over. We sat on the sandy beach and had cheese sandwiches (two) tomatoes (three, we're only supposed to have one) carrots crackers, and six cups of milk. We really have quite good food, only we aren't allowed to fill up on bread and potatoes, which I try to do.

Just now Betsy and I are preparing for the masquerade tonight. We are going as mother and daughter of the 1890's. I am wearing a stiff white gathered mosquito netting skirt, a long sleeved black blouse, mosquito netting also, a white top, and my hair up with a flower in it. Betsy is wearing a short white shirt and a long skirt, her hair in braids. I do hope we get one of the prizes.

<drawing of two females in costume>

Just at this moment we were interrupted by mail call. I was so pleased to get a nice card from you. It's very sweet of you to take time out to write.

I wrote a nice long letter to mother on Star Island, but did not address it to the Oceanic Hotel, so I don't know if it ever got there. I also have received my jersey and sheet, thanks loads. The weather here has not been really hot as yet. This one week has whizzed by so quickly, I don't know where all my time goes.

I am always plenty warm enough. So far I have gotten mail every day. I'm so happy you and Grammy are taking it easy – you certainly deserve that, and more. I, also am having a lovely time. The water is really wonderful, too.

I will write as soon as I have another spare moment,

Lots of love,
Sylvia

<drawing of smiling female>

TO *Aurelia Schober Plath*

Tuesday 9 July 1946

ALS with envelope,
Indiana University

Tuesday, July 9

Dear Mummie,

This is the third letter that I have written to you on Star Island. I doubt if the first two will ever get to you, for I so brilliantly addressed them to plain "Star Island", no address at the hotel!!!

In case you haven't heard the good news, my cold is all gone. I have written to Grampy and Grammy at the Whistling Whale,[1] to Warren at Benotti's, to Frank and Louise. I still am writting (writing, that is!) a lot. I also sent a card to Dot, Joe, and Bobby.[2]

I sure am making, as well as losing money. The money I "get rid of" is only in crafts. So far I have spent 75¢ in all (35¢ for crafts, 3 for book, 7¢ for postcards, 25¢ for sketch pad, 5¢ for Gloria.)

I have gained 5¢ from Betsy, 5¢ from Gloria, and 10¢ as a prize, which I'll tell about soon. Gloria, Betsy, and I have a little agreement, out of which I have made 10¢.

Tonight Betsy and I hurried to the cabin after supper to dress for the masquerade. I just had deposited my $3 in the office, and requested that Ruthie be in cove when she comes. She probably won't be, but – nevertheless.

Betsy and I dressed as a mother and daughter of the 1890's. We did Hope to get one of the prizes. Betsy dressed in a ruffly white blouse, a gathered long white skirt, and a white bonnet. <drawing of Betsy> She wore her hair in short pigtails. By the way, Betsy used one of my sheets for the skirt. She only cut it in half. You see when I gaily hopped in bed one night, My long shovel of a toenail caught where it was sewed down the middle and made an unmendable (?) rent. I decided to let it go, but one night some ink fell in little patterns on the old rag, so I sadly tore it up. I did not want to disgrace you by bringing it home!!!!! I do hope you will forgive me, "mater" dear. (Ha Ha) (Balmy) Betsy sweetly sewed my exclusive costume on me. (Very Ritzy.) I had used my black mosquito netting for a long full-sleeved blouse over my white t-shirt. I had 5 yds. of someones white mosquito netting for a peplum skirt with a tight white belt (mine) around the waist. My hair was tied up and drooped down and decorated with my white flower. I had a black velvet choker. Everybody was aghast that Betsy and I had actually made such a finished product in a few hours. <drawing of SP in costume>

Very many people had similar ideas. There were about 50 people. (2 units) one unit staged a wedding. Four people from each unit dressed as bathing beauties and were surprised and dismayed to see each other, for they had thought their idea original. Gayle was perfect as 1925. She wore an exact copy of the period. She looked so cute! One girl dressed as a sultan, and another as an arab, another as a pirate, darkies, husbands and

1–A guesthouse located on Main Street, Chatham, Mass.

2–SP's cousin Robert J. Benotti (1945–   ).

wives, were some other ideas. <drawing of pirate with caption 'Something like this'> When we had the grande Marche the bride got one prize, a "horse" got another, and "Miss 1960" got one. To my surprise I got second prize for the best old-fashion'd, and well made costume! It was a package of 25 Storrow stickers like the one you see on the outside of this letter (worth 10¢) that's the prize I told you about. The night before we rowed across the lake (one mile). I rowed one boat (the leading boat) over. It was such fun! We had a nosebag supper, I had two cheese sandwhiches, three tomatoes, crackers, carrots, an orange, and six cups of milk. (We seldom get that good a meal.) We then rowed back in the path of the setting sun. Please tell me if this letter and a postcard with a sticker[1] on it reach U at the same time.

Siv

TO *Aurelia Schober Plath*

Wednesday 10 July 1946 ALS (postcard), Indiana University

Wedy
July 10, 46

Dear Mother,

Did this card get to you at the same time as the letter did? Last night Betsy and I woke up similtaneously (or how ever you spell it) at the same thunder clap. She was quite scared and with a flying leap jumped into my bed. For the first time in my life I was really frightened. I kept worrying about grammy and grampy. The thunder tumbled over the lightning which crackled all about us. Finally the storm passed over, but the lightning contented it self with glowering at us from the distance. It rained so hard, that Betsy and I thought the roof would cave in! At last we fell asleep. I woke up this morning feeling fine.

Love,
Siv

1–SP to ASP, 10 July 1946.

TO *Aurelia Schober Plath*

Wed.–Thurs. 10–11 July 1946

ALS with envelope on Wellesley, Mass. letterhead, Indiana University

Wednesday
July 10
NO. ONE

Dear Mother,

The stamps on this letter are part of my payment from Gloria. I got her mad enough to swear again!!!!!!! I now have made 10¢ cents clear from her. Today was a rather hasty aftermath of the thunder storm last night.

The mail just arrived, and I got your post card. I felt almost like crying to hear you had not gotten a letter from me for a week! I have written at least a card a day, and this is about my fifth letter! From now on I am going to number my letters and cards so you will know if you get them. The mails are very queer. This is message No. I. I last wrote you about the masquerade and the thunderstorm.

I am quite healthy, save for my ingrown toenail. We have good meals once in a while. The rotten ones always come before the yummy ones. For instance, this noon we had just "fish chowder" (fish floating in water) dry cabbage, and cold, leftover cocoa that tasted like polluted coffee. Now for supper tonight we had turkey, potatoes, carrots, bread, jam, and icecream. I guess the cook thought she had better make up for the "lunch".

We have not had a crowded schedule lately, but all of a sudden things have piled up on us. We're making a shado-graph of "The Sleeping Beauty", and I am in charge of the proceedings. We are also starting work on the newspaper. I only hope that I can make up something good enough to live up to my rather super reputation of last year. I haven't gone in swimming for five days because of my cold, but plan to go in the next time.

Thursday
July 11

Today we were planning to hike to fisherman's cove, but instead we have to hike around the lake because the darn weather is so cold and nasty. Last night Betsy and I received the worst scare of our lives! We were both in my bed writing. Taps had just blown. I really didn't want her to sleep with me in the same bed, but just as we were putting our things away for the night, we heard the most pitiful, and yet terrible cry, I have ever, or probably will ever hear. It was long and drawn out, and sounded partly like a tortured cat, and partly like a little child being murdered.

Betsy and I were both petrified. We lay taut and tense on our backs, holding together for dear life. How glad we were that we had locked our door and put most of the flaps up. Nothing would pay Betsy to cross that cabin floor and get back to bed, and nothing would pay me to let her go. We stayed still for about 20 minutes, and then tryed to tell funny jokes to get our minds of the howl, when we heard the horrible sound once more, even longer this time. We prayed fervently for sleep to come, which it did, but not with its merciful oblivion. My whole night was a waking dream. I dreamed that people were frozen corpses, that the Cooper Boy had died, and that Margot had killed Duncan and Susie. Isn't it awful! Somewhere in the pit where my mind was wandering I heard my name called, and with difficulty I jerked my self out of sleep and found a gray day, and Jean Baker saying that Betsy and I had only ten minutes to dress before breakfast. Not once have we been woken up by reville! Almost anything can happen here. I wouldn't be surprised to hear superman knocking at the door.

I have a lot of wash to do, but today is a rotten day to do it in. I am really having a wonderful time. I only wish the mails were better. My next message will be number two.

Love,
Sylvia

TO *Aurelia Schober Plath*

Thursday–Friday 11–12 July 1946 ALS with envelope, Indiana University

Message #2 No. 2

<u>Thursday</u>
July 11

Dear Mummie,

Oh! My aching feet! I just got back from a long hike with half the unit. Fourteen girls and two councilors. We went all the way around Long Pond on a five mile hike, but we took the wrong road and ended up in taking at least an eight mile hike. By the time we sat down to eat our lunch I had finished mine. I was very hungry, so I ate some salt. We sat down on the edge of the Miles Standish reservation. As we were settling down, Rikki and I saw a beautiful deer bounding away from us. It was very close, and it was so graceful that it took my breath away. We evidently took the wrong road, for we had left the pond long ago. We hiked for miles along a yellow dirt road straggling between endless hills of scrub pines. Around every new bend or hill we'd think "there *must* be some sign of man," but there were only more bends and *more* hills. After we were almost collapsing in the glaring sun, which had miraculously come out, one girl called that she saw another road not far ahead. Sure enough, our eyes were greeted by the welcome sight of a paved road and cars whizzing by.

<drawing of map with captions
'Route we should have taken' and 'Route we did take'>

This is a *very* rough map of what happened when we had hiked a couple of miles down the road and stopped at the first farmhouse we saw. They willingly gave us a pitcher of water and we poured[1] the punch in it that we had been carrying all the time. Oh! Never had anything tasted so good. We all had three graham crackers. At last we had hit the road to camp. My feet were covered with big blisters when we at long last reached our unit. I flopped down on my bed and rested my aching muscles. As soon as I hit the pillow I went to sleep until suppertime. An example of the fact we got off the path is that it took us 4½ hours to get around the pond, where it took the other unit, 1½ hours (3 hours difference).

Friday- July 12

Oh! This morning I had the most wonderful experience! An "Education Van" came to camp, and two young men opened up the back. Inside it was a huge wonderland of nature's works. On the far end were two folding bed, that went up against the wall during the day. On the ceiling was a map of the stars. There were airy screened windows, and a table on which was a file full of hundreds of pamphlets, some of which were distributed among us. A great stuffed owl glared at us with his glassy eyes. There were several neat screened cages. In one was a small, garter snake, three turtles, and a beautifully marked frog. The small turtle was one of the variety that grows the largest. The middle sized turtle had red irises and was beautifully marked with red. The man took out the tiny garter snake. Most of the girls screamed and backed away, but I looked so interested that he let me hold it. It felt so nice slithering through my hands, all slippery. Next he took out a pair of water moccasins that had just shed their skins. You could see remnants of the old skin left over their eyes. He turned them over, and showed us their beautiful dull red markings. My! I certainly like snakes, there's something about them that fascinates me.

The man (Elmer, but very strong and nice even for his name) showed us some books, and cases of butterflies and moths. I was able to identify the

1 – 'pourde' appears in the original.

luna and Polyphemus moth. They were in rather poor condition because the owl (that had died only a few days before) had crashed through the glass, broken in, and torn up most of the mounted insects. I am sending Warren some pamphlets in a separate envelope, because he wouldn't get half the excitement in finding them in your letter.

Last night we went on another short sketching trip. I hobbled along as best I could, but was so tired that I did not draw well at all. We went to a very interesting family graveyard[1] that we passed coming up. I was so interested in the names and dates on the old stones, that I felt quite subdued and rather filled with the tragedy that pervaded the air. There were three stones together. A man between two wives,[2] one wife died at the age of 40, the other did die a year after the man – 72 years. Another tiny stone was for a little girl who died at the age of two years[3] the saddest stone was so small that it was over grown by witch grass. It was for such a little child that it only had room for Lovell on it. There were several rather showy and decorative stones, with lovely designs on them.

The call for delivering mail has come, so I must get this letter in on time.

With love,
Sylvia

TO *Aurelia Schober Plath*

Sat.–Sun. 13–14 July 1946 ALS, Indiana University

Message 3
Saturday
July 13

Dearest Mother,

I will probably not have time to mail this letter today, as I have spent all rest hour and such washing out twelve pairs of socks, three pairs of pants, and an undershirt. It was the first decent day for washing, for the rest have been very nasty. Today was my idea of a perfect day. The wind was blowing and the sky was that heavenly blue with clouds sailing across it in big white puffs, and the lake was blue as blue, with big choppy waves, It reminded me so much of the ocean. It was just bubbling over with joy and enthusiasm. RUTH FREEMAN IS COMING TO COVE AND

1–The Bassett Cemetery is located on Herring Way, Plymouth, Mass.

2–Calvin Raymond (*c.* 1795–1867) and his two wives, Polly Cahoon Raymond (1800–40) and Sarah Douglas Raymond (1811–84).

3–Tirzah Raymond (1828–30), daughter of Calvin and Polly Raymond.

IS BEING IN MY CABIN WHEN SHE COMES ON SUNDAY!!!!!!!! Rikki did not put Gayle and Betsy together, and It could so easily have been done. I want them to be together as much as I wanted Ruthie and me to be together. I only hope Rikki changes her mind, though she says its final. Today to my relief, I finished my nutspoon. It came out so much better than I expected. Frenchie actually says that she loves it!!!!!! I have decided to give it to grammy and grampy, for Christmas maybe, with a little copper dish I'm making. The spoon is a darling squat little tiny thing, all shiny. It is designed something like this: <drawing of spoon with caption 'Hammered bowl and border and Initial S for Schober'>

The copper dish is going to follow the same design. They each cost about thirtyfive cents. Guess what?!! Grampy and Grammy have sent me two more dollars! So far I have spent only eighty cents out of my first book yet! I have not recklessly spent my money on Storrow hats either ($1.60!) but am yet enjoying myself and going to town in crafts. How I love metal work! When I get home I'll have a least $5 left for my darling bank account. Please do send me some hairbands and try to send the nailnippers for just my finger nails. (metacarpus nails????) I wrote Warren about the nature van and hope that he got the letter. Evidently you and grammy and grampy have been having pretty nasty weather. Skipper says it is O.K. for grammy and grampy to drop in on Saturday the 20th, so I'm dropping them a letter[1] also. I hope that they bring fruit if they can, for that we get here is mainly sour and hard. We had some gooey apple pan doughy, and I don't mean doughty for dessert tonight. All the two week campers left today, and boy! am I glad I'm not going home. I love camp so, for all its faults that I dread July 27th. Betsy received some gum and life-savers, but I wouldn't want any candy sent to me. Fruit is allright to bring I am quite sure, and I asked Skipper if it would be alright if Grammy and Grampy dropped in, and she said yes, even though it is on the twentieth, a Saturday. My first ingrown toenail is all better, but I have one on my left toe that is much worse, and is swollen alot more. The nurse stuffed cotton under the corner, it hurts so that I can hardly walk. I have to hobble along, and it is very annoying. As I have probabably told you, I am dropping Grammy a card. I am so glad that Ruthie is going to be in my cabin, Betsy probably will get with Gayle. On this day (Sunday, now) Rikki clamped down on us, and made one girl (poor thing) clean all the latrines by herself, and I had to sweep my cabin four or five times before I went to crafts. Betsy and I thought that the next two weeks would

1 – See SP to Aurelia and Frank Schober, 15 July 1946.

be torture, but now that the new campers are coming things seem to be brightening up.

Love
"Siv"

P.S. I am going to Maine, too, whether I'm invited or not! I am so sad that they evidently did not want me.

TO *Aurelia Greenwood Schober & Frank Schober*

Monday 15 July 1946 — ALS on Wellesley, Mass. letterhead, Indiana University

Monday
July 15

Dear Grammy and Grampy,

You don't know how happy I was to receive the two dollars you sent me! I never expected anything like it. I have spent only a little as yet, and am putting the main part of the money towards crafts.

It would be perfectly alright for you to drop by at camp when you come by on the 20th, as mother said you would. I'd love it if you could bring a little fruit, because the fruit we get here is usually all green and unripened. Lots of the girls have candy, but I wouldn't want any of that. Do you suppose you could bring the nail nipper if you have it. My fingernails are really too terribly long. If you can find the camp, I would like to know about what time you will come, so I can go up to the office or the parking lot to meet you. Do write a card and tell me If and when you're coming.

I am so happy, because, in answer to my many requests, Ruth Freeman had been put in my unit and is in my very same cabin! We are going to have such fun together. Oh! Grampy, for the rest of my life I will cut my toenails straight across. Now that I have no nipper to dig the corners out with, the nails on both my big toes have grown in and become infected and swollen with pus. I made a beeling for the nurse, and she stuck cotton under the corners and way under my toe nail. This morning she actually soaked them in boiling sulfo-naphthol, or something like that, my feet were all raw and red when I took them out, but I am really glad that she is doing something to help.

Betsy got stung by a bumble bee when getting wood, and her lips and whole left cheek are swollen. She looked so funny, like Mortimer Snurd[1]

1–Mortimer Snerd, a radio and comic strip character as well as a ventriloquist dummy developed by Edgar Bergen in the 1930s and 1940s.

would probably look, that I couldn't help laughing after I got out of her hearing! She is in the same cabin with Gayle Greenough in Cabin 13, and Ruthie and I are right next to them in cabin 9. The cabins run in a pattern, which is quite odd until you figure it out.

<drawing of camp map with numbered cabins>

I only have time for a short letter before the mails go out, so Goodbye for now.

Love,
Sylvia

TO *Aurelia Schober Plath*

Tues.–Wed. 16–17 July 1946

ALS with envelope,[1]
Indiana University

July 16, 1946

Dearest, Most-Revered, Twice Honored Mater,

Last night was a red-letter night because I got two postcards and two nice big fat letters from you including those thrilling snaps of me. Why you sent that glamorous one of me hunched over, and snoring under the maple tree, I will never know. I have missed getting this letter in the mail, so naturally It will arrive late. This wonderful month at camp is certainly speeding by fast. Grammy and Grampy are coming on Saturday at about three o'clock. That just happens to be the day we are hiking to Fisherman's Cove, so I won't be able to go on the hike I looked forward to for so many weeks. I only wish it could be arranged that I go. Today I continued to work on my copper mint dish, which is rather small, but which I hope you will appreciate. I am very busy finding ideas for poems for the newspaper. Do you like this one about the lake:

The lake is a creature,[2]
Quiet, yet wild.
Rough, and yet gentle, –
An untamed child.
Tranquil and blue
Where the boats slip by,

1–Letter addressed to ASP c/o Loungway, Innisfree, Oxford, Maine, and forwarded to Wellesley, Mass.
2–Sylvia Plath, 'The Lake'.

Whirlpools of silver
Were the oars dip nigh.
Emerald Green
When the clouds scud across,
And before the wind
Gay white caps toss.
The lake is really
The earth's clear eye
Where are mirrored the moods
Of the wind and the sky.

<flourish>

July 17, 1946
Wednesday

Today I had the most fun I've yet had while at camp! Our unit hiked two miles to work as pickers on a blueberry farm! We were to be paid 10¢ for every quart box we picked and the blueberry bushes were taller than I was. Never have I seen such blueberries. I don't know if even the country club can beat them! They come in clusters like small grapes. They were the most wonderful things I had ever seen – rows and rows of laden bushes! Ruthie and I each took a box that held six quart baskets and began to pick at one of the choicest spots. We both cooperated with each other and picked with the thought of the payment ahead of us. We had worked almost two hours, when we stopped for lunch. Ruth had just begun her fifth basket and I had just finished my fifth. However, I dropped the box, and the tops of the baskets fell off, so I used up half of the fifth basket in filling the others after lunch and rest hour we were eager to continue picking. Ruthie and I finished our fifth, sixth, and seventh baskets with ease. The eighth baskets were slightly harder. When Ruth had begun her ninth quart, and I my tenth (!) she filled my box up, so that I had earned $1.00 and I filled up her last boxes with her so that she also had earned $1.00. We turned in our boxes joyfully with no mishaps. We both received checks for $1.00 to be added to our camp fund. That covers what I paid for my stamp offer and also my nutspoon!!!! I really felt rich. Only one girl picked nine quarts, but she earned $1.10 for packing some boxes also. I am so happy that I could earn some money, even though it is not much, it helps! We came home rather tired, but joyous. I had received a slight burn, but it looked more like a tan. Ruthie and I certainly slept well.

With love
Sylvia

TO *Margot Loungway Drekmeier*

Thursday 18 July 1946[1] ALS with envelope, Estate of Margot Drekmeier

Dear Margot,

It pains me to use up this valuable three cent stamp on you, but my offer is enclosed. Do not open the inner envelope unless you wish to buy, which you won't. It was very good thinking on your part to invite Mater and Warren up while I'm away, so I won't have to come. I do hope you show this newsy letter to my Mater so I won't have to bother to write her.

From
Sylvia
<drawing of smiling female>

TO *Aurelia Schober Plath*

Friday 19 July 1946 ALS with envelope, Indiana University

July 19
Friday

Dear Mother,

Today is a beautiful day, save that it is very hot and humid. I would much rather have cool weather at camp. I turned in my two poems to the newspaper. The editor, who evidently did not think too much of me, went as far as to say they were excellent! The second one which I made up is not as good as the first, and is called

<flourish>

Mornings of Mist

Frail cobwebs of lacy filigree
Clutched by gnarled fingers
Of a tree.
Where mornings lips have kissed
The grassy meadow, there are
Fields of mist.
Between the trees twine
Trails of silver fog like a

1–Date supplied from postmark.

Misty vine
Now the sky is a tinted rose
As the first pale little
Sunbeam shows.
Dimpling and blue the lake is won
By the golden beams of the
Morning sun.

<flourish>

I am receiving your daily cards joyfully. Your latest one sounded like a lovely poem in blank verse. I really will always treasure it. I regret to say that I will not have time to make dear grampy an ashtray, and besides, they are dinky little copper ones. So I'm giving him the nut spoon and grammy the mint dish. Do you think I could give it to them for Christmas, or maybe for grampy's Birthday. I have something that I made, or am making rather to show them, so I hope that they won't suspect. Everything I am making in crafts seems to be of metal. Last night was rather hectic. Some men in canoes were seen in the cove, and word got around among the campers that the councilors were going to meet them. So, after taps, a whole brigade headed for the Cove beach. I was out filling a pail of water from the tap, and so did hear lots of whistles and noises. Ruthie and I climbed out of our back window, leaving the front door locked, and went down to Betsy and Gayle's cabin. We stayed there a short while with them, but were horrified to here Skees, (on taps duty) pounding on the locked door of our cabin, and shining her light on the empty beds. I ran out of the other cabin with Ruth. She had to climb in the back window under Skees' glare, and meekly unlock the front door for me, who stood there innocently and mumbled something about "What's all the noise!" Skees said sternly that I was contributing my part to the racket, and watched until Ruth and I had got in bed. I like everyone in general, (by the way, Gayle, Betsy, Ruth, and I pal around together alot and have such fun doing things in fours. That's the way true friends should be I think, not coveting every minute of each others time. I do hope Warrie wasn't hurt badly when playing "Murder." The weather here has been lovely the last few days. Tonight I went on another sketching trip. This time I did quite a good job. Frenchie said, as well as some others, when judging drawings, that mine had such depth that they could almost step into it! Frenchie also says I'll be foolish if I don't take art lessons, for I've an "interesting technique."

<drawing of heart>
"Siv"

TO *Aurelia Schober Plath*

Saturday 20 July 1946

ALS with envelope,
Indiana University

July 20, 1946

Dear Mother,

How do you like this stationary? Rather gaudy, don't you think! However a girl at camp gave this piece to me so I might as well use it. At least there is plenty of room to write on it, so it will probably take a long time to fill all the space. Ruthie is only a red cap, and she has not been able to go in swimming and work up to a white cap. I am spending almost all my spare time in crafts trying to finish up a rather tremendous project. It just happens to cost 50¢ fifty cents, that is. But seeing that I have not quite spent three dollars yet, I hope that you won't mind. I am really quite saving when it comes to spending money.

Well, grammy and grampy are supposed to be coming in a few hours. To my joy, the unit did not go on the hike to Fisherman's Cove, so I will be able to go if we do go in the coming week. The end of camp is drawing to a close so speedily, that I'm afraid that I'll wake up some morning soon, and find Grammy saying, "Better get up! Time for school." I am having a perfectly beautiful time being in the same cabin with Ruthie. She is really so much fun. She also wrote an excellent article for the camp newspaper about blueberrying. Today is another perfect day. The sun is shining, and a cool breeze is swishing through the trees and rippling up the lake. There is also a fresh, piny odor in the air.

I am going on another sketching trip tomorrow with "Frenchie."

I have plenty of clothes left now that Ruthie's here, and probably will not need to wear one or two of my new jerseys at all. I am now dressed in my blue shorts, white belt, socks, jersey, and saddle shoes, writing this to you during rest hour while waiting for grammy and grampy to arrive. My hair is full of dandruff, and rather oily. It does no good to wash our hair here in the icy water, because it never even gets clean the least bit. I do enjoy boating, especially rowing. I am in no great hurry to get out in a canoe after taking my tippy test. I always wear my bathing suit top when rowing, and there are two white splotches in the exact shape of my ribbon that hang down. <drawing of SP in a boat showing ribbons> That is where I have not gotten tan. My face is no perfect example of a peaches and cream complexion by any means. I am regularly taking magnesia, although I'm drinking all the water I can get, I'm still not drinking enough. Our diet is mainly a startchy one – potatoes and bread,

bread and potatoes with mayhap a sickly leaf of cooked cabbage thrown in. On the last page I will give you an example of my expenditures, as well as my deposits

	Deposits	Spent	Reason
	$3	$1.20	Crafts
(you sent)	$3	.10	Postcards
(Grampy grammy)	$2	.60	Stamps (etc.)
blueberries	$1	.33	Stamps
Total	$9 (nine dollars)	$2.23	
		.05	Gloria
		.25	Sketch pad
		2.53	

So far I have spent two dollars and 53 cents. Imagining that by the time I come home I will have spent three dollars at the most, it seems I have a balance of about six dollars. I only hope that my figuring is correct.

Our food prospects are brighter, for on Sunday we always have good meat and ice cream. Our soups and cocoa, however, are made with water, and are terribly thin or much too thick. Having a perfect time.

Love,
"Siv"

TO *Aurelia Schober Plath*

Sunday 21 July 1946 — ALS with envelope, Indiana University

<drawing of fleur-de-lis>

July 21, 1946
Sunday

Dear Mother,

Oh! Poor grammy and grampy! The time they had in finding this camp! Dear grammy thought that it was Four Winds, and for some strange reason kept insisting that this was Four Winds. Our unit and Ridge were playing a softball game, and Ruth and I were not on the team, so when Grammy and Grampy at last drove up at 4:00, we ran to meet them, and showed them the way to the guest house so they drove up. As they got up, Skipper came out to meet them. I do not think the Skipper was especially overjoyed at their visit, but she welcomed them graciously, and Ruth and led them to our unit, after they unloaded the car for us. When they were cosily seated in our comfy little cabin, they displayed what they had bought for us. Ruthie and I were goggle-eyed! All the fresh fruit we could possibly divide between us two – six oranges, ten peaches, eleven plums, two pounds of cherries, and, to cap it all, a bag of Ritz crackers and cheese complete to the little spoon with which to spread the cheese on the crackers. Ruthie and I had never seen such a piece of wonder! Grammy and grampy sat watching contentedly as we carefully devoured one lb. of the ripe red-black cherries. Ah! What utter delight. I put the oranges and peaches in Ruthie's tiny, empty, suitcase. We were so happy, because it was really exciting to get so much stuff. Out of the kindness of his heart grampy slipped me another two dollars!!!!!!!!!! I just had to give them my little nut spoon. It has "S" for "Schober" on it. We walked back to the car with them, and, after putting into the trunk my dirty clothes, we saw them off. Tears fill my eyes at the though of having such wonderfully grand grand parents!

After taps it was very muggy. Ruth and I kept dozing off and waking up. With our stomachs rolling, growling, and complaining. We just had to finish our cherries. We awoke again in the middle of the night in the midst of a wonderful thunderstorm. The lightning was magnificent, but when I looked I was blinded, and only could see black, so---I drifted back into a fitful slumber.

When we awoke this morning, the out-of-doors looked as if it had come from one of Arthur Rackham's[1] pictures. The black, gnarled trees were dark and forbidding. There was a thick fog, and the air was cold and nasty.

I was one of the few who went swimming. The water was like a warm bath. To make it happier, Ruthie was moved from red cap (lowest) to white cap (middle) group. She was beaming happily when she jumped down off the dock. We had a royal dinner this noon. We had chicken, boiled potatoes, gravy, butter, cranberry sauce, carrots, beets, pickled egg (no greens!) cupcakes and icecream. The weather is the type that really makes me long for home and my stampcollection. I will be rather sad to get away from camp, but I will be very glad to get to my own little mummie's house.

Well, rest hour's over, and I must prepare for another sketching trip.

Love,
Siv

1 – 'from one of ~~authur~~ Arthur Rackham's' appears in the original. English book illustrator Arthur Rackham (1867–1939).

TO *Aurelia Schober Plath*

Monday 22 July 1946 — ALS with envelope, Indiana University

July 22, 1946

Dear Mother,

Oh! I'm so happy. I am all done with my crafts projects! Now I won't have to go any more.

In swimming the only things I have to pass to be a bluecap are my standing front dive and my crawl. "Skees" taught me how to "fall in" yesterday morning, and in the afternoon Rikki taught me how to spring off the dock. <drawing of girl diving> My legs still bend a little, but I'm very glad that I am learning how to dive. That was the one cloud on my horizon, even though I was not conscious of it. I have done my twelve lengths of sidestroke, and yesterday afternoon I took my "tippy test." I paddled a canoe out on the lake, stowed the paddle, stood up on the gunners and tipped the canoe over on top of me. I then righted it, and jumped in. It was full of water, and I had to paddle back to shore with my hands.

By the way, my oldest middy is ruined. I wore it down to the beach over my bathing suit and left it down there by mistake. It must have been long ago, because it was full of bugs, worms, cocoons and slime. It is so far gone that I never could wear it, so I'll not bother bringing it home.

We have had two cracker jacks of thunderstorms and alot of wind and rain. Today was a wonderful day for washing – sunny, and oh! what a marvelous wind!

I am going home with the Powleys. They are coming at about 3:00-4:00. I am having a perfectly beautiful time. In our scouts own we (Gloria, Betsy, and I) sang "Nearer my God to Thee."[1]

Ruthie and I had a perfectly wonderful time dividing up the fruit. We have been practically living on a fresh fruit diet. <u>Saturday</u> one pound of cherries. <u>Sunday</u>. One pound of cherries two and a half plums[2] (a piece) <u>Monday</u> – two plums, four peaches, eight crackers.

Last night when it was raining, Betsy and Ruth went around the units waking up people in the cabins. The councilors were at a party saying farewell to Skees, so while Gayle and I slept soundly in our Beds, Ruth

1–A nineteenth-century Christian hymn by Sarah Flower Adams based on Genesis 28: 11–19.

2–'two and a half ~~peaches~~ plums' appears in the original.

and Betsy slept together in Betsy's bed. I kept my screen door locked so that they wouldn't come in and wake me up after I got to sleep. One of the councilors asked me to draw some ideas for the cover of the paper, so I did. I can't wait to go swimming again this afternoon so that I can dive again. Do not be worried if you do not get a letter from me for quite a short while because I am next going to write a nice long letter to Margot. We are not going to have an overnight hike, but I do hope we will go to fisherman's Cove some time. Have you been getting much mail from me? I have been writing every day.

I hope you are having nice weather in Wellesley. Is the grass beyond recovery, or can it be watered and brought back to its beautiful soft green stage. I will be glad to get back to our own white house in Wellesley. Do have Ruthie over soon so I can go back to her house to visit. The food we get now is about the best a camp could get, only I miss the fresh vegetables.

Love,
"Siv"

TO *Aurelia Schober Plath*

Thursday 25 July 1946 — ALS with envelope, Indiana University

July 25, 1946

Dear Mother,

I have been overwhelmingly busy the past few days. On Wednesday we at last took the long awaited hike to Fishermans Cove. Only nine of us went, and Rikki made the tenth. We hiked the five miles without even noticing it. The sun had come out and it had become a glorious day, the first for almost a week. When we arrived we sat down on the familiar white sand and had our nosebag lunches, and then made our barefoot way tediously over the barnacled rocks, until we at last reached the sandy golden strip where the low tide was. We fell all over ourselves in the icy, exhilarating salt waves. How I love the ocean! We then hunted for sea creatures in the shallow, warm pools between the rocks. I got quite a tan, and so did Ruthie. Betsy didn't come, because she doesn't especially like hikes like I do. Bunny called for us in the truck, and we rode back, singing gaily. I had a perfect time, and everything was so much nicer than last year.

Quiz

<u>Do you know that:</u>

I was chosen to make the cover of the camp newspaper?

I was elected unanamously to write a report about Cove[1] and read it at the banquet last night?

<flourish>

Last night I was at the first banquet that I had ever experienced. Formal too. The tables were arranged in a U. Skipper sat at the head table, and so did the five girls who were going to make unit or news reports. I had a placecard and everything. I was so excited that I was going to make a "speech". The first one too. Everything worked out perfectly. After everybody had scraped up the last of the yummy ice cream dessert, I was announced. I stood up and began to read of my rather long report. Slowly and clearly. I was never so happy. Everyone laughed at the right places, and I got loads of praise and applause. Evidently everyone thought that It was the best report given, or so they all told me. The other ones didn't have so much expression – (as I have learned so well from you and Mrs. Warren[2]) that is very necessary to give a speech the interesting quality.

I had a perfect night. Did you also know that I am a blue cap. I passed up from the white, and will now be classified as an intermediate swimmer. The caps go like this:

Advanced (only a few)
Blue
White
Red

I am now a blue! Three cheers. I enjoyed three safety movies that were given the evening of our hike to fisherman's cove. They were excellent. The first was about floods, and how one fire can cause a terrible loss of life, and awful floods. The second was an MGM film about Our Gang.[3] It was really cute. I learned alot about traffic rules, even though the picture was rather youngish. The third was a darling one in Technicolor. – titled "Once Upon a Time."[4] It worked in Pandora's box, with Cinderella, simple Simon, the Giant, Georgie Porgie, and a few others. It told about

1 – Sylvia Plath, 'Cove Unit Report'; held by Lilly Library.

2 – Rose Smith Warren; SP's English teacher at the Alice L. Phillips Junior High School, then at 324 Washington Street, Wellesley, Mass.

3 – Probably MGM's 1941 release *1-2-3 Go*, a road safety short film featuring characters from the *Our Gang* series (also known as *The Little Rascals*).

4 – A 1937 car safety film by Radio and Television Packagers, Inc.

how the two bad ghosts[1] flew out of the box and induced the drivers of various cars to speed. The accidents that were caused, and how they were remedied makes a sweet little story. I am having a perfectly beautiful time with Ruthie. She is such a wonderful, staunch friend. We both think the same way about so many things. I hope that this gets to you before you leave tomorrow for coming here.

Love,
Sylvia

TO *Margot Loungway Drekmeier*

Mon.–Fri. 29 July–2 Aug. 1946[2] ALS with envelope,
Estate of Margot Drekmeier

July 29, 1946

Dear Margot,

I am very sorry that I have not written for such a long time. Surprisingly enough, at camp I was terribly busy making up contributions for the camp newspaper. I made the cover of it, and sent in two poems which were published.

We had a super banquet which brought a thrill-packed month to a close. The tables were arranged in a U <drawing of table arrangement>, and I sat with the head of the camp, and a few others, at the head table. After a wonderful meal of roast beef, corn on the cob, fluffy mounds of mashed potatoes (with gravy and butter) apple salad, grapefruit, and icecream, I was asked to read the report of my units' activities, which I had written before hand. It was evidently quite a hit. Everyone laughed in just the right places, and I received loads of applause. I was very excited, for it was my first real banquet, and It was quite an honor to be seated at the head table. I had a perfectly beautiful time, and enjoyed every minute of it.

Camp is really beautiful. The first impression that you get is of the deep green pines against the clear blue sky, and the puffy white of the clouds floating lazily by. The lake water is always changing. It is more or less translucent and the white sand beneath its depths gives a rather odd color effect. Sometimes it is mirrored and blue, and on other times a wild emerald green, with tossing sprays of foam and rough white caps. I had a beautiful time swimming. I learned how to dive for the first time in my life, and had such fun doing it. I advanced to the blue cap group, which

1–'the two (~~the two~~) bad ghosts' appears in the original.
2–Date supplied by internal evidence and postmark.

is just below the highest, or advanced swimmer. In other words, a junior lifesaver. I enjoyed rowing so much, that I had perfected my different turns and strokes, before I took my tippy test, which enabled me to go out in a canoe. We took two trips by boat across the lake, and one was made especially exciting by the fact that one girl broke her oar. Our counselor had to row in and then row out again in another boat with an extra oar. She just got to the crippled boat before it began to be blown out into the lake. It was really quite exciting, considering that I was in the counselors boat.

We went on a "five" mile hike around the lake with ten girls and our favorite counselors. However, we got off the right road, and walked for miles along a sand road, flanked by seemingly endless pine hills. No sign of life save that of a deer bounding gracefully off into the woods. After long last we came out on a paved road, and hiked the remaining miles back to Storrow. All in all, the hike took over eight weary miles. However, Rikki, the counselor, made almost every minute of it enjoyable.

We also hiked with nine girls and Rikki, the five miles to Fisherman's Cove. I have never seen such a glorious place. The sand stretched a golden arm out into the green waters of the ocean. A steep sandcliff curved protectingly around the beach. As the tide was out, we walked way out to the water's edge, and after getting thoroughly soaked in its icy waves, we dabbled around in the warm, sandy, rock pools, and found all types of sea creatures. I had a beautiful time, and came back with a nice brown tan. I really had a very exciting time at camp. I made loads of friends, and renewed acquaintances with my old ones.

However, it is good to be home once again in my own cosy little "matchbox." I really love my house – it has such a charming personality.

Mother is starting me on typing lessons now. I have begun my third, and she says that I am progressing admirably. I do have some hope that by next summer I will be able to type stories once more. My "Stardust" has come to a standstill for the time-being as I have had a great deal to do, what with typing and helping with the housework. I am doing a great deal more of this. Oddly enough, I rather enjoy it. Especially the canning part – as I am new to this, it still holds quite a novelty for me. Getting back to my story – I have only done about ten pages. As yet, the first chapter needs some revision, which the second chapter is complete to the last detail. I do think that it came out very well – better than any of my last ones.

To my great amazement, mother took me in town yesterday, and let me buy my first set of oil paints (out of my own money, of course.) She supplied me with four canvases of different sizes. So far I have made two rather amateurish paintings. Alot of things came out wrong, but I had fun in doing them that I never have had in anything else. One was a still life of some zinnias in a blue bowl <drawing of zinnias in a bowl> and another larger one of three birch trees with some icecream cone mountains in the background <drawing of birch trees and mountains>.

Oh, by the way, how is your diary coming along? Sometimes mine is rather tiresome, but on the whole I really enjoy it. This letter has been in the making for so many days that the dates are most likely all slightly mixed.[1]

Speaking of stamp offers, I have been having a great deal of trouble with the Gray Stamp Company, Toronto Canada. I told them to please stop sending approvals, because when I sent for their offer, approvals were not mentioned. I expressed my refusal sweetly and appreciatively, but when I got them the next time, I grew a good deal firmer in my statements. However, when I received them for the third time, I sent them back unopened, saying that I would not be responsible the next time I received approvals from them. I think that is only fair, because I have to waste four cents postage on them every time I send back an offer. If they do persist in sending approvals again, I will not return them, as I said to them the last time. Are all of your approvals that you do not want, effectively stopped at last? I do hope they are, for I now realize how annoying these stubborn stamp companies can be. I can just imagine how harried you must have been with a whole flock of them sweetly persisting on sending you offers.

<SP added a note here: 'NOTE This is page seven not six, which is [arrow to page six] this other page. Strangely enough'>

When do you start school? I believe we go back to the old antique shop on September the third. Next year it will probably begin in the middle of August.

I enjoyed reading the letter which you pointedly sent to just about everything in the house except me. It was quite thrilling. I especially enjoyed the one message that you wrote to the eighty-first key on the piano.

I do love wearing that darling dress I got from you last summer. It is my favorite – the flowered one with the rickrack on it I mean. <drawing of dress> By the way, did you receive the offer I sent you with my long epistle from camp. I believe that it was the one 20 beautiful, extraordinary stamps for only fifteen cents?

1 – The letter was postmarked on 2 August 1946; based on the contents of SP's diary, many of the events mentioned took place between 29 July 1946 and that date.

My mother is now dramatically plowing through the "Tale of Two Cities" – reading aloud to my brother – who sits wide-eyed in bed, gnawing anxiously on the sheet waiting for her to go on. <drawing of wide-eyed boy and woman> Even through the wall which separates his bedroom from the livingroom I can hear my mother droning nasally through her teeth in what she imagines is the sinister manner of the Marquee, or whoever she happens to be reading about. The periodic shakings of the floor are when my brother gets so excited that he cannot control his feelings, and so bounces all over the bed. It really is an interesting bit of emotional reactions. I know you're not supposed to pardon anything in a letter, but please forgive any too queer mistakes I've made in composition as its late, and mother's too absorbed in her reading to notice the time.

from her mother's daughter
From her mother's daughter –
Sylvia Artemis Platowsky

"Drive him fast to his tomb"---frill of paper – stone face – too many

TO *Margot Loungway Drekmeier*

Tues.–Wed. 27–28 August[1] 1946 ALS with envelope,
Estate of Margot Drekmeier

August 29

<drawing of flower>

Dear Margot,
Can't you take a hint? – a very broad one? First I wrote you a long eight page letter. Then after waiting for a whole pile of weeks (almost three) I sent you a business letter. All I got in reply was an uninformative typewritten letter in return for my painstaking efforts.

I do hope my stamp offers do not give you too much trouble when you try to get rid of them.

Here is the Harris envelope dressed up as a rainbow offer. Will it pass? Enclosed are some other things. Approvals or <drawing of eight small circles> something for you to sell. (If you can.) I'm sort of hazy about it, as it's almost ten-thirty. You see, mother would be shocked if I was not soundly snoring at nine o'clock, and she would have fits of worry. She is now having a gay time with Warren visiting in Connecticut. She has left Grammy home with me (I have a bad sore throat) and she (Grammy,

1 – Letter misdated by SP; date supplied from internal evidence.

I mean) is now in the next town taking care of my Aunt Dot's two year old boy. It is sort of lonely here alone (strangely enough) and queer footsteps keep stealthily hopping around. Unluckily I have three windows and four doors to keep my eyes on.

𝄞 I am now listening to Sousa's inspiring "Stars and Stripes Forever"[1] march over the radio. I have listened (in succession) to scatterbrained Judy on "Date with Judy",[2] "The Marquis,"[3] an excellent radio theatre. (Now Sigmund Romberg[4] (how do you spell it?) is playing ♪ the lilting, immortal blue Danube.[5]) How I love it!

I heard just about the best program I've ever heard over WEEI at 10:00, I believe. It was titled "Disputed Passage."[6] It was the moving story of two doctors, one old – one young – only a delightful speck of romance to give it more human flavor. I guess its hard to live without if you want to be a success. (Or so they say)

Now they are playing my favorite song in the popular world "Wanting You"[7] – You know:

♪ ♪ "Wanting you, wanting you

Noone else in this world will do!" I love the tune. The singers aren't that washday blues kind, but a real woman's clear soprano and a man's lovely harmony.

Now Romberg (that's near enough the spelling.) is playing a delightful composition by his son Donald[8] – "Sunset in Seville." It's the first time played on the air, and it is truly lovely, and characteristic to the title.

Now they end it then: sotto voce "Science truth positive Raleigh[9] – the only leading cigarette that gives you less nicotine etc. – etc." What a let down!

But he builds it up again with the powerful, manly song from "Strong Men"[10] which is blended with the lovely soprano singing "We Have Been

1–American composer John Philip Sousa, 'The Stars and Stripes Forever' (1897).
2–Radio serial *A Date with Judy*; the role of Judy performed by Louise Erickson 1944–9; aired at 8:30 p.m. on WBZ, 27 August 1946.
3–The romantic radio serial *The Grand Marquee*; aired at 9:00 p.m. on WBZ, 27 August 1946.
4–Austro-Hungarian composer Sigmund Romberg (1887–1951), his *Evening with Romberg* aired at 10:30 on WBZ, 27 August 1946.
5–Johann Strauss, 'The Blue Danube' (1866).
6–*Disputed Passage* aired at 9:30 p.m. on WEEI, 27 August 1946.
7–Sigmund Romberg and Oscar Hammerstein II, 'Wanting You', *The New Moon* (1927).
8–Possibly American composer Don Gillis (1912–78).
9–Raleigh cigarettes.
10–Possibly Sigmund Romberg and Oscar Hammerstein II, 'Stout-Hearted Men', *The New Moon* (1927).

Young"[1] – 𝄞 ♩♩ When I grow too old to dream, I'll remember you." ♪♪

Just as they are beginning "Sweethearts,"[2] I (Here we go) hear the pleasant crunching of Grammy's car wheels on the Gravel driveway. I better hurry up with this letter before she comes upstairs with a bedtime snack for me (snack, not shake!)

Goodnight for now!

<drawing of window, bed, and bedside table, and a music note and thirteen stars>

<drawing of smiling face> Now it is moring once again. I have just woken up. It is rather late, after eleven o'clock. So you see I slept around the clock, you may find this "letter" a bit hard to read, but I sincerely hope not. Have you found a good brick-laying job yet. I've thought and thought but I can't find one. (a job, not a thought.) ☆ There is a little man digging in my throat with a pitchfork, boy! he must be trying to get to China and promote friendly foreign relations!

The most fun in writing a letter to you is ending it. So I am hurrying to get to that pleasant point. This letter is sort of warped because I spilled a jug of water on it will you help me keep track of my offers that I send you by noting names and prices, and sending them to me? The P.S. especially pertains to you. I knew that you would take this to heart (if you have such an odd thing)

See if you can decipher this. <drawing of toothpick>

As always
From your own:
TOOTHPICK BEAN
With love

P.S. Remember! Crime doesn't pay[3] (well enough)

<on back of envelope>

From 26 Elmwood Boulevard
Wellesley 81, Massachusetts
United States of America
The World – Planet Earth
Solar System No. 1
Universe <drawing of an open book>
How 'bout writing.

1 – Sigmund Romberg and Oscar Hammerstein II, 'When I Grow Too Old to Dream' (1934).
2 – Possibly Sigmund Romberg, 'Will You Remember (Sweetheart)?', *Maytime* (1917).
3 – A tagline from the radio serial *The Shadow*.

Drop me a line huh!
Don't you think that you could drop me a line!
To My most esteemed (very)
Margot Loungway
How about writing me old
Sender – Miss Sylvia Artemis Platouski
My letters to you would fill a book

TO *Marion Freeman*

Monday 4 November 1946 ALS, Smith College

November 4, 1946

Dear "Marion,"

I still have a left-over glow from the lovely time I had at your house. It is a weekend I will never forget. The movie[1] is one that I had wanted to see, and the evening dinner was like a happy dream. Ruthie was a peach <drawing of a peach on a leafed branch> to entertain me as she did, although everybody helped. It was so thoughtful of you to invite Wayne over, too. You will always be like a second mother to me, you know, and even though it was "precipitating" outside it was so sun-shiny inside that I hardly noticed.

I do hope that the next time I come I will be able to see Mr. Freeman at "work" on his oil painting. I know that I need to learn everything possible about oil painting if I ever intend to use it as a worthwhile hobby.

Now that Ruthie and I "know our way around Boston", I hope that I will see her out here very soon.

Love,
Sylvia

1–According to SP's diary, she and Ruth Freeman saw *Janie Gets Married* (1946), which played at the State Theatre, then at 415 Shirley Street, Winthrop, Mass.

1947

TO *Margot Loungway Drekmeier*

Saturday 11 January 1947[1] ALS with envelope, Estate of Margot Drekmeier

January 11, 1946

Dear Margot,

Do not disturb yourself over wondering what prompted me to use this shade of delicate blue ink. I feel just fine! One of my favorite weaknesses is colored ink, and, having received a few bottles, (of colored ink) don't be surprised if my next letter is written in bright pink on green paper. (I've tried green on blue paper, but It just doesn't seem to work!)

The party I went to on the night you left[2] was just wonderful! There were four (4 that is) boys and two girls.[3] We sat around a cosy fire and played loads of games, mostly guessing games. Since two boys were in the twelfth grade, that made the games harder, but more fun. For refreshments we had oatmeal cookies and gingerale. It was strictly a sporty party – no dancing, for which I was slightly greatly grateful, because of my dilapidated shoes! However, the other girl wore shoes even "dilapidateder" than mine. I got home at twelve o'clock and slept late Sunday morning.

On the Tuesday after you left[4] I helped clean the house from top to bottom, in preparation for the coming of my dear friends. Wayne, David, and Ruthie arrived at 11:30. After a delicious lunch we all went tobogganning! Oh! What fun! When we came home we played games and pulled molasses candy. After dinner we played forfeits. Wayne happened to get the old one "Bow to the wittiest, kneel to the prettiest, and kiss the one you love the best!" Oh, brother! He sure was funny – his attempts, you know. The two boys left at nine o'clock, and Ruthie stayed until the next day. It was partly due to Ruthie that I am off on this colored ink spree, for she brought me a pale green, a pale pink, and a pale blue bottle,

1 – Letter misdated by SP; date supplied from postmark.

2 – Margot Loungway visited on 27–8 December 1946.

3 – According to SP's diary, the party was held by Perry and Richard Norton; also present were John Hoag, Dick Thornton, and Marilyn Buell.

4 – Tuesday 31 December 1946.

in addition to the navy blue, black, and red ink that I have already. To add to my collection I need brown, yellow, orange, deep purple, and fuschia!

We're going to have our senior class elections this week, and as you probably know I'm running for secretary.[1] There really is no chance of my winning, because I'm running against the most popular boy in school. I've had loads of fun campaigning, though! I have four posters (that were made for me) hanging up in school, as well as 130 campaign tags in circulation. I am giving my speech in assembly with all the rest. Prissy spent all afternoon helping me with the stunt I'm giving in assembly also. My whole campaign is on the Indian-sailing motif, so we took a huge clothes basket and covered by tacking white cloth over it. Then we made a sail by tacking a triangular piece of white cloth over some poles. We printed "Sylvia for" on the sail, and "Secretary" on the basket in huge black ink letters. To give you an idea of the size of the "sailboat," the sail stands a good 5 feet high. Some of my friends will pull it across the stage, while Prissy is inside the basket holding the sail. I only hope the sail doesn't collapse in the middle of the stage!

<drawing of a sailboat with 'SYLVIA FOR SECRETARY' written on the sail and port side>

Priscilla has kept rather silent about the whole incident of your little skating trip. I guess that she just didn't appreciate your suttle humor – or something!

The next time I write to you that will be after I receive the next long letter to you, I will send you some valuable stamps to sell and get enough money to set me on Easy Street with. Perhaps I will even quote my latest masterpiece of poetry that appeared in our school magazine,[2] and was approved by an eminent author. Until our next meeting or your next letter.

Au revoir,
Sylvia Artemis Platowsky

1–According to SP's diary, she ran against classmates Sarah Bond, Ted Edson, and Ted Short. Speeches were given in an assembly on 15 January; elections were held on 16 January, and the results announced on 17 January. Sarah Bond was declared the winner.

2–SP's most recent publications were: 'To Miss Cox' and 'October', *The Phillipian*, November 1946, 3–4. The issue also featured a short report on the book lovers and recreational reading club on page 14. SP's poem 'To Miss Cox' was written on 13 October 1946, in memory of Miss Catherine A. Cox, a business and mathematics teacher at the Alice L. Phillips junior high school, who passed away on 12 September 1946.

TO *Hans-Joachim Neupert*[1]

Sunday 13 April 1947 ALS (photocopy), Smith College

April 13, 1947

Dear Hans,

I received your letter today, saying that you wished to correspond with an American high-school pupil so – here I am.

It will be so enjoyable to write to each other, and discuss our interests, ideas and ambitions.

We American students do not know about your personal lives, although we study your country in our history classes, so I would be interested to find out how you live – how you eat.

First, I will tell you about myself. I am almost sixteen years old, tall, brown hair and eyes. I am a girl in the tenth grade, that is, tenth year altogether, of high-school. My interests are many. I like to draw, write stories, play piano, go sailing in the summer and play basketball in the winter. Do you have games like football and baseball in your gym classes? In school, now, I am studying English (creative writing, mostly), French (first year), Latin (second year), Geometry and Art. This not seem like a very hard program, does it? But, oh! we spent a great deal of time doing home-lessons. Do you take either Latin or French? Or only English?

I, personally, do not know what war is like. I have heard sad stories, it is true, but I have never experienced the horror of being bombed. I hope I never will. Does it not seem strange that young people, such as you and I, can correspond and be friends at distant corners of the earth, while countries wage war and murder each other's young, most promising men?!

You are, perhaps, under the impression that American youth is frivolous – caring only for parties and luxuries. Well, most of us are not that spoiled.

Do you know a great deal about America? In your reply to this do tell me what you would like to know – what you are interested in. In this way I will be better able to write to you.

In your letter to Washington you indicated no preference as to whether a boy or girl should write. I trust you do not mind my being a girl.

In Germany, do you have much leisure time? I get up about 6:30 each morning and go to bed by ten o'clock. I have lunch at school. The school day lasts from 8:30 to 2:30, and we go home to work, play, or do home-lessons. We have school five days a week – Montag, Dienstag, Mittwoch, Donnerstag and Freitag I believe you call them. I do not know German or study it, but my mother does know the language very well.

1 – Hans-Joachim Neupert; from Grebenhain, West Germany, corresponded with SP, 1947–52.

Do you have difficulty obtaining supplies? I mean, like clothes, food, paper, utensils and tools. Our costs for food are very high, but if one is rich one can buy almost anything. I, of course, am far from rich. We have a huge middle class in America, and comparatively few very-rich and very-poor.

We want so much to have peace – we students. We love our land of woods, fields and free citizens, and wish to aid the countries ravished by war. We have had many discussions about war, and believe that another world war would be fatal. Do you not feel as I do – that war is futile in the end?

What is the land like where you live? In Wellesley there are rolling green hills, shady woodlands, blue lakes and little white houses. Do you read much? I like to read quite a lot. Are you mechanical-minded? I await your next letter with greatest interest.

When I "grow-up" I hope to be a foreign correspondant, a newspaper reporter, or an author or artist. Are you able to choose your own occupations?

As I write at my desk, I wonder what you are doing. I am enclosing two pictures of me and my house, hoping you will get a little idea as to what my surroundings are like. The arrow in the winter picture indicates the window of the room in which I write.

Please send me

<rest of the letter missing>

TO *Aurelia Schober Plath*

Friday 27 June 1947[1] AL (postcard), Indiana University

Epistle 2
June 27, 1947

2

Dear Mother,

The weather is heavenly and it is so wonderful to have the smell of salt in the air! The water is a beautiful shade of briny green. One girl in my tent, June Smith, reminds me lots of Betsy – she's 4'9" and talks with a cute little lisp. Do write me cheery letters. I felt a wave of homesickness pass over me at breakfast – we just had cold wheat sparkies, and I missed the squiggles in my eggnog! The girls are so nice that it's hard to feel

1 – Dated and ordered by Plath's date on postcard, not her numbering as 2 in the sequence.

badly, and June takes the place of Betsy (a little bit) and Ann[1] takes the place of Ruthie (a little bit, too.) It will be better when we start doing things, so far we've just slept and ate. I've just come back from our first swim. We had to swim 100 yds. and tread water for 1 min. in order to go sailing on Monday. I thought I'd never make it, But I did. Water is cold but refreshing. No arts & crafts at all.

TO *Aurelia Schober Plath*

Saturday 28 June 1947 ALS (postcard), Indiana University

Epistle 1
June 28, 1947

1

Saturday

Dear Mummy,

I am fine. All my baggage is here, including my bike. I am in a tent with three other girls – two of whom are simply loads of fun. The other one doesn't talk much. We three go around together. Friday supper was very good – hot fish, beets, and salads. The boatride over was delicious. I sat on the top deck and drank a bottle of milk that I bought down in the boat's lunchroom. I ate my sandwiches on the train and on the ship. Boy! Were they good! I was very glad to have them cause we had a long wait for the boat and didn't have supper until about 7. The bedtime, by the way, is 9:30. We didn't get to bed until late last night, but I slept well, after we three got through talking. Now that you have got all the essentials, pulease send me a packet of about 4 or 5 bobpins and a flashlight. I found 1 facecloth!

Love,
Sherry

Sherry is my new name.

1–Probably Ann Bowker.

TO *Aurelia Schober Plath*

Sunday 29 June 1947[1] ALS (postcard), Indiana University

3

June 28, 1947
Sunday

Dear Mother,

We got our coupon books today. I put in $9 for spending money and got a $3 book with only $.97 in it, $1 for the boat trip, $1 for the camp truck ride (all both ways) and $.03 for the book were taken out! Remember to send me the directions for sending my stuff home. Today is Sunday, and this morning it was damp and foggy, but now the sun is out. So I hope I can go sailing tomorrow! I could never even think of being homesick with June and Ann around. Ann is so funny, and June is more like Betsy all the time. It's so surprising! I'm wearing my good blue slacks today, and one of my new white shortsleeved shirts. June is wonderful. She practices fixing my hair and I massage her back just like Betsy and I used to do. I feel so lazy. My bottle of magn. is supposed to be turned in to the nurse, of all things, but I haven't yet as I haven't had to use it. Do <u>write</u> & send those things I wrote about – flashlight & hair bobpins.

Love,
Sivvy

TO *Aurelia Schober Plath*

Sunday–Monday 29–30 June 1947 ALS (postcard), Indiana University

Sunday and a little bit of Monday

4

Dear Mummy,

The weather has cleared and is nice and warm now. As you can see, I'm numbering all my postcards to you. I have written a few cards to Betsy and hope to get mail when it comes tomorrow. June is wonderful. She likes to do everything Betsy does, and doesn't eat much candy and feels the way I do about a lot of things. I just had sunday dinner. I eat all I possibly can get, which isn't overmuch. I had: a chicken bone, 2 helpings of rice, peas, a little salad of spinach & carrots, vanilla icecream, and 2 cups of milk. I feel fine, only a little tired once in a while. I was only 114

1 – Letter misdated by SP.

pounds when they weighed me here and 5'8" tall, but I don't feel too bad cause one thin girl here is 5'11" and Ann, in my tent, is 5'8", too. Ooh! My bed is so comfy. There is something – an atmosphere – about camp that just can't be got at home. I love it.

xxx
Sivvy

TO *Aurelia Schober Plath*

Monday 30 June 1947 ALS (postcard), Indiana University

Monday June 30

5

Dear Mummy,

Shame on you! No letters today. It is glorious out – the sky is blue and there is cool east wind although the day is warm. I went sailing this morning for the first time. It was just heavenly. We have six boats and I went out for 3 hours in the "corallina" with another girl and an instructor. I had alternate turns at the jib halyards and the tiller. I'm getting really nautical in my vocabulary am I not?! It was lots of fun when we keeled way over. I got my pants splashed and I guess I turned a little green the first time, but now I really love it. I can't wait until we go on one of our bike trips, which we haven't as yet since all the bikes haven't come (mine has tho'.) Now I'm getting used to the morning fogs and the clearing weather. I have plenty of warm clothes, so don't worry! My toe had swelled up and I had to limp yesterday, but now it's down again and doesn't hurt so much. Do remember to wish grammy a Happy Birthday for me.

xxx
sivvy

TO *Aurelia Schober Plath*

Monday 30 June 1947 ALS (postcard), Indiana University

Monday

6

Dear Mummy,

I am eating all I possibly can. For our Sunday nite picnic supper I ate six slices of bread with lettuce & mayonnaise, peanut butter, olives, and egg fillings respectively. I topped this with one apricot, half a pear, two cookies and 2 cups of milk. Water is a little awkward to get a lot of, but I make it up almost with milk. I have a nice sunburn on my face from sailing, and if I do say so, it makes me look lots better – not so pale you know. Also my thighs are red from the position I sat in while sailing. I'm sorry I claimed I had no mail. I got your 2 page letter and package just this evening. My toe has stopped hurting. Do save my postcards so I can write in my diary when I get home – I haven't much time here. I do want to stay here a month next year – I'm having such a <u>swell</u> time (and I mean wonderful). June and I explored the bluffs at our picnic supper. We found sand & oak trees (that's all). Our crew came in 3rd in a scavenger hunt for things from A to Z.

xxx
Sherry

TO *Aurelia Schober Plath*

Tuesday–Thursday 1–3 July 1947 ALS with envelope, Indiana University

July 1, 1947
Tuesday

Dear Mummy,

Oh! I am pooped! I've just come back from our unit's first bicycle ride. We left this morning after a refreshing ½ hour swim. It was about 10:15 and the sun was out, but a cool breeze was blowing in from the sea. We started out and rode for about ¼ mile over a dirt road, and I suddenly realized that I had not used my leg muscles as much as I thought I had! We quickly got on a paved road and the going was much easier. We passed little country farms and gardens on the way, luxuriant with placid spotted cows and bright yellow daisies. The warm, sweet moist smell of the wayside grass was wafted to our nostrils as we rounded a bend and came smack against the blue curve of the ocean, blowing a salty breeze in our faces. The ride along the flat shore road was pleasant. The houses were built in an odd manner – quaint little gables and turrets crowding in at every possible angle of the roofs. The shingle were silvered and gray by the sea air, and roses and daisies and petunias bloomed in profusion in all the gardens. After panting and pumping furiously up a hill we reached a small water tower, and down below lay East Chop. Because of the private homes obstructing the view we were not able to go near the swirling waters or to get a close view of them, but I looked out into the misty blue ocean and took in the land of West Chop opposite me, remembering the foggy horizon and the bright sunny sky, with the brilliant glossy white clouds blowing by. That will always be my picture of east Chop. Tomorrow (If everything goes as planned) our unit will bike to West Chop and watch the sailboat races! On the way home we stopped at a public beach and took pictures of each other. I so want to bring a camera next year – It means so much to have pictures, and the scenery around these parts is lovely. At last we reached camp again and collapsed on our beds before lunch. I had a big lunch and lay on my cot propped up comfortably by my white duffel bag, and wrote cards for most of rest hour. I've just got to gain weight – I eat ever so much, only I use alot of it up in exercise.

Last night tent two (my tent) was visited by tent three after taps for about 10 minutes. They got in our beds and divided two chocolate bars between the 8 of us, as well as some of Andy's salt water taffy. I was not in a very receptive mood since I was tired and wanted to go to sleep, but what can one do and not be unpopular? So – I entered in to the fun. I had previously made up my mind to put the chocolate under my pillow and eat only one piece of taffy to be sociable, thus imagine my enjoyment when June said, "Sherry and I don't want any chocolate; we've sworn it off for the summer." She is the one who looks like Betsy and is very popular, so the girls didn't say anything adverse and they were really quite glad cause they got more chocolate.

I fell to sleep immediately after they left and slept soundly from about 10:30 P.M. to 7:00 A.M. This afternoon we went sailing again, and though I wore a shirt I got more of a burn on my arms and thighs. The nurse put calamine lotion or milk of magnetia lotion, but it soon began to burn again. I then washed it off and Lois put some Noxema on, which made it feel much better

<drawing of a girl with sunburnt face, arms, and thighs>

Wednesday, July 2[1]

We left early this morning right after capers on our bike trip to West Chop. We carried along our lunch, for we were going to stay away all day and watch the sailboat races. The weather was clear and glorious. We had a long ride, and by the time we got to West Chop we were all quite tired. I climbed up into the lighthouse with most of the other girls and looked out over the water through the big, transparent glass windows. The water was so cooling, and we went wading after we had lunch on the beach. I have about three shells that I picked up on the beach as souvenirs. We

1 – 'Wednesday, Jun~~e~~ly 2' appears in the original.

were not allowed to buy anything in the stores except drinks to go with our lunch, so I got Orangeade when we passed though Vineyard Haven. I don't know whether it's any better for complexion than Coke – but then I can't die of thirst. I would appreciate it if you would send me a little map of Martha's Vineyard with the chops and gayhead and the cities labeled so I could see the directions where we go on trips. I'm glad I have a nickname, because now everybody calls me "Sherry" and I feel like a different person without any old restrictions. If someone says something mean about me (which no one does, thank goodness) I can just go back home and start being "sylvia" again. In case you do not know where I got my nickname, remember "School Girl Allies"?[1] Well I just took Sheridan's nickname for my own, and I like it alot better than "Tibi." I am having a lovely time. The girls are all so nice. I weighed myself after supper tonight and also last night and I have gained 4 lbs. (I now weight 118 lbs.) I only hope I don't loose them with all the exercise I'm getting! There is always something to do around here. I'm wearing my hair parted on the side and braided over my head – one of the ways June tried. I hope you realize that I have been writing this letter for two days now, and since this is Thursday the Third I hope that you will let the length of this epistle make up for the two post cards I did not write. I am very busy, but not too much to write regularly to you. Of course on some-days I write more postcards than on others, but then, you know how it is. Will you meet me at South Station when I come home? I will probably bring $6 of my spending money back since I have $.50 left out of my 1st three $ book (most of it was spent for car fare!) Last night I had three big helpings of potatoes (mashed) and carrots for supper and a scant helping of meatloaf as well as 2 pieces of bread & butter, 2 apricots & a glass of milk. I eat at least 2 slices of bread at every meal, more often 3. I love you very, very much & do miss you just a little.

xxx

sivvy

<on back of envelope>

One of our Menemshas came in second in the race, and the others followed in close succession!

I hope you get this by Saturday!

I have written to Warren at camp and sent two fat postcards to Betsy.

Do write me lots of letters if you're not too busy.

1–Rebecca M. Samson, *Schoolgirl Allies* (Boston: Lothrop, Lee & Shepard, 1917). According to SP's diaries, she read *Schoolgirl Allies* in 1944, 1945 and 1946.

I have alredy received one letter and a card from you and a package (facecloth etc.) also a card from Warren (which was rather extraordinary!

<drawing of heart>

Lots of Love

TO *Aurelia Schober Plath*

Thursday 3 July 1947 ALS (postcard), Indiana University

July 3, 1947

Dear Mummy,

If I write this to you now I can do something else in rest hour. I have written 2 fat postcards to Warren and 3 to Betsy. Tues. we went 7 miles on our bikes, and yesterday we went 12 miles. When I come home I am going to be very hungry. I would like a chicken salad dinner with all the tomato, bacon and cheese sandwiches I can eat. Also mashed potatoes, pie and icecream. If you please – yum, yum. Do buy me a copy of the July SEVENTEEN which is now out on the newsstands. Don't send it here, but save it for me when I get home. We're having a talent auction on Saturday. The counselors offer various things for auction such as shoe shines or breakfast in bed. Then the girls do stunts and the one who finishes and gets the most applause has the counselor do the favor for her. Well! There goes the warning bell for lunch.

Lots of love,
Sylvia

TO *Aurelia Schober Plath*

Friday 4 July 1947[1] ALS (postcard), Indiana University

June 4, 1947

<drawing of a pink fire cracker exploding in half with caption 'Bang'>

Dear Mummy,

How are you celebrating the glorious fourth? Remember to save my cards and letters so that I can catch up in my Diary when I get back home. I have caught up to Tuesday June 2, but I still do not have much time. Yesterday I went sailing with my favorite counselor (Web.) I just love her. I was sort of dumb when it came to jibing and almost broke the mast and

1 – Letter misdated by SP.

boom on her precious ‘sea horse’, but she just grabbed in time. Did I have fun! This morning we had to get up early to be hoppers – 6:45. Isn’t that awful. I slept like a log all night, falling asleep at 10:00 P.M. & waking up at 6:45. I dreampt that I was driving to Radio City with June in the camp truck. The counselor wouldn’t let us out to get a sundae, so we sneaked into the theatre and saw Ingrid Bergman in ‘Joan of Lorraine.’[1] I’m writing this just before lunch. It is dark, cloudy, and raw. I’m warm tho’ – wearing my blue & pink plaid jacket over Macey’s[2] navy sweater over my peach wool shirt over my underwear. At breakfast we had 4 people at our table, so I at a whole serving dish of apricots ’cause no one else liked ’em. I’m always hungry from exercise.

Love,
Sylvia

TO *Aurelia Schober Plath*

Saturday 5 July 1947 ALS (postcard), Indiana University

July 5, 1947

Dear Mummy,

Well! I got that other post card to you off just in time for the day’s mails, so I’ll take more time on this to describe the occurrences of the 4th. The costume ball was most hilarious. I couldn’t think of anything much to wear, so I dressed up as Saturday Night in my pajamas (rolled up), a beach coat, and my hair pinned up on top of my head. I carried a tooth brush, soap, a facecloth & a towel, etc. as well as wearing galoshes. <drawing of SP with caption ‘ME’> I won no prize, as I did last year, but I never laughed so hard in my whole life. Some of the costumes were: an ice cream cone <drawing of ice cream cone>, mosquitoes <drawing of a person with a mosquito head with caption ‘MOSQUITO’>, old sailors in an impromptu boat, Santa Claus, take offs on the councilors, a sandpiper, a mock wedding and funniest of all – two of my favorite councilors dressed up so that they really looked like sailors, and escorted in the substansial camp nurse dressed in a very scanty costume and supposedly being French

1–A 1946 play by Maxwell Anderson performed at the Alvin Theatre, 18 November 1946–10 May 1947.

2–Macey Gerson Feingold (1925–); B.S. 1948, Massachusetts Institute of Technology; a friend of the Plath family.

or English as the occasion demanded. Words can't describe the riotous combination of these 3. Icecream cones on the beach were heavenly.

xx
Siv

TO *Aurelia Schober Plath*

Saturday 5 July 1947 ALS (postcard), Indiana University

July 5, 1947

Dear Mummy,

I am starting this just before leaving for another bike hike at 9:00, so I doubt if I will have time to finish it before the mails go out. I just got your letter with the 4 bobbiepins on July 4th. That does make 6 messages, and by now you probably received my card stating that I was getting mail. I wrote a long letter to Ruthie (almost as long as the one I wrote you) in return for a surprisingly long letter (3 pages) which she wrote me. From what I read between the lines, she must be awfully homesick. She got in a unit where one of the gangs from Wellesley. I know them, and they are very close and snubbish, and of course since Betsy and I aren't there she doesn't know hardly anyone. I guess camp isn't as nice as last year, so I thought that a long letter would cheer her up. Last night we had a lovely 4th of July celebration – we had a wienie roast on the beach and then a costume ball. At twilight we changed back to our pajamas and had a bonfire on the beach with 2 icecream cones each. We sang songs and watched fireworks across the lagoon til taps. Wonderful!

xxx
Siv

Will write more on next card

TO *Aurelia Schober Plath*

Saturday 5 July 1947 ALS (postcard), Indiana University

<drawing of the beach, houses, and the ocean>

July 5,

Dear Mummy,

This is a very quick sketch of the beach we biked to this morning. We totaled only 13 miles, and we left at about 9:30 A.M. and came back at 12:00 after spending 45 min. in swimming and resting on the warm white sands. Hardly any people were there, so we were left more or less to ourselves. The waters were a light, salty blue and a sandy, smooth bar stretched out into the ocean. The water was free from crabs and seaweed, and I went swimming with Sally Haven,[1] an adorable girl who lives in Newton. She has soft light hair and lovely dark eyes – almost as tall as I am, and still has a little girl charm about her since she does not act <u>old</u>, and yet does not seem in the least silly. I just love her. We had loads of fun swimming under water and sitting on the smooth sandy bottom pretending to comb our hair. When I come home please do not expect me to have a very dark tan since I don't. How long does it take my cards to get to Wellesley?

xxxxxx
Sivvy

TO *Aurelia Schober Plath*

Sunday 6 July 1947 — ALS (postcard), Indiana University

July 6, 1947[2]

Got package with light and pins, thanks

Dear Mummy,

This is Sunday morning, about 8:00 A.M., and I am now comfortably propped up in bed <still in pajamas), waiting to be served breakfast by Honica, one of my favorite counsellors, who just came over from Holland. No! I haven't broken my neck or half-drowned by falling off Menemsha, I just won breakfast-in-bed in the talent Auction last night. What is it? Well! The councilors get up one by one, and offer things to auction – such as a bedtime snack – "Do I hear any bidders?" The a camper or so gets up and sings or dances etc. and the judges decide the winner by the amount of applause. "Going once, going twice, GONE." You're probably dying to know what your untalented li'l daughter did. I recited "I'm Alone in the House" with exaggerated gestures, and when I first started it I knew it would go over, because they laughed in all the right places and clapped very hard. The only other contestant was Margie Jones who did a wonderful take-off on Al Jolson and California.

1 – Sally Ann Haven (1934–), who lived at 58 Greylock Road, Newtonville, Mass.
2 – 'Ju~~ne~~ly 6, 1947' appears in the original.

I thought she'd win surely, but the judges could not decide, so we both get the breakfast.

xxx
Siv

TO *Aurelia Schober Plath*

Sunday 6 July 1947 ALS, Indiana University

July 6, 1947

Dear Mother,

How do you like my ingenious way of using up envelope-less letter paper? I do hope that this makeshift gets to you! By now you have probably received that happy little post card describing my wait for the little breakfast that never came! How could I make such an awful mistake! The breakfast-in-bed is tomorrow morning! It better come! I waited and waited, and then suddenly broke my resolution to stay in bed until Honica came by jumping up and dashing down to the dining hall. My mind was filled with the horrible picture of sardonic, implacable councilors locking the doors of the camp hall in my face and leaving me outside to die of slow starvation from having had nothing for breakfast. The first part of my imaginings were true – they were just beginning to clear away the meals, but I had just chance to eat a little. I had one big hot roll, an orange, a little box of rice crispies and a cup of milk when the food at the tables were gone, so I gathered up my courage and wandered out to the kitchen and begged sweetly for a little piece of butter to go on my bread, so when the kindly cook heard my sad story of waiting in bed for breakfast she gave me two extra big pats of butter and I filled up on four good pieces of bread, butter, and jam which satisfied me for the time. I then peeled carrots, radishes and just hundreds of potatoes with my crew for camp capers and spent the morning cleaning up my tent and relaxing for a change. Today is visiting day, so I caught up to this Sunday in my diary while waiting eagerly for dinner. Ahh! I sat with two of my favorite councilors and all my tentmates and ate a most delicious meal. Each table of eight had a whole roast duck to eat. I have gained five pounds (am now 119 lbs.) and think I keep it (I hope) because for dinner I ate three big helpings of duck and delicious mashed potatoes and two helpings of carrots and also radish salad. I garnished this with only one piece of bread and butter, two cups of milk, and one great scoop of strawberry icecream. Yummy!!!!! I am now very hungry again an am waiting eagerly for supper! I am having a heavenly time here. I just did "I'm Alone in the House" over again for the kids in our tents. We're in one tent, all nine of us, and the girls have been teasing Ann and telling her that they're going to send her home Thursday and keep me here instead. Tonight we had a delicious picnic supper. I had six slices of bread filled with strawberry jam, ham, mustard and egg and olive filling respectively. Also two cups of milk. I sat on the bluffs with the girls and had a little talent show. After supper we had a treasure hunt, and though we did not find it first or get a prize (toll house cookies) we had fun. I wouldn't have eaten the cookies anyway, because my complexion, which has kept very clear for the past week, just broke out. I am going on an even stricter diet = no sweets (as before) as much sleep as possible (which amounts to a good 9 hrs.) as much water (I just drank three cups) and also keeping regular. I just had a big soft you-know-what this morning, so I feel a lot better. When I come home I have my schedule all planned. I want a shampoo and hot bath as soon as I arrive If I am not too tired, which I hope not to be. After that I want a nice cool salad and a big dinner (tomato, bacon and cheese sandwiches) If possible! Oh! Boy! I'll be glad to see you again, but I feel awful about leaving camp. I had a very pretty, but sad, dream last night. I dreampt that I was leaving camp on our bicycles, only a few of us, and we were going the long way home. I remember that I was crying as I looked back and saw Andy and Ann still playing in the water. All of a sudden I came to a beautiful palace. Fascinated, I walked inside, leaving the rest to go on their long way. As-soon as the great ebony doors clanged behind me I knew that I could never go home or back to camp again. I was really glad to wake up to hear the 7:15 bell clanging loudly in my ears. We have had simply gorgeous weather – not one little drop of rain! We are going to leave for Chapaquidick,[1] a large island off the coast. We're going in a few minutes, so I doubt if I will mail this today. I will tell you all about our long trip when I get home. This will probably be the last epistle that I write to you while at camp, mummy dear, because I'll tell you everything we do from now on first hand when I get home! I love you so! I'm really glad we're going to the island on our bikes because they charge the other units a dollar each when they go in the camp truck – what a racket. They charge for every little piece[2] of transportation here – even 25¢ to and from church each Sunday. I'll insure my baggage if possible. I haven't worn quite a few of my clothes, and I'm filling up both

1 – Chappaquiddick Island is an island off Edgartown, Martha's Vineyard, Mass.
2 – '~~letter~~ little piece' appears in the original.

of my duffle bags full so I won't have so much to carry in my suitcase. I'll be seeing you on Thursday afternoon. Will you meet me at the station (I hope)? I have three more nights and three and a half days before I see you. I am going to be glad to be home Thursday and I can't wait to begin my PIANO LESSONS! I love you! I will miss camp, but I'll be glad to see you all again.

xxxxxxxxxxxxxxxxxxxxxxx
Sivvy

TO *Aurelia Schober Plath*

Monday 7 July 1947 ALS (postcard), Indiana University

July 7, 1947

Dearest Mummy,

It's just a matter of hours now before I see you. I don't know as yet when I will arrive at the station. We made a twenty mile round bike trip to the island of Chappaquiddick. We passed through quaint, crooked-streeted, darling little Edgartown, for which I was very glad, because I wanted so badly to see it even if I couldn't get Gay Head! We crossed over to the island on the funniest little "ferry boat", which was honestly just a chunky little float of wood no bigger than our cabin floor! It cost 10¢ cents for a round trip of about 20 yards both ways, what a racket, we practically could jump across. However, it was lots of fun. When we crossed over to the island we walked along the sandy beach which was decorated with many lovely shells some of which I am bringing home, labeled with their name and date. We went swimming on a lovely, hard sand bar and then started back after eating a lunch of sandwiches and gingerale. The ride back was lots easier than the ride over, although I have had some appendicitis cramps during the past days.

xxx. I love you.
Sivvy xxx

TO *Aurelia Schober Plath*

Tuesday 8 July 1947 ALS (postcard), Indiana University

July 8, 1947

Dear Mummy,

I do hope you get this postcard in time. Our boat leaves on Thursday morning at 8:25 A.M. and, according to schedule, the train arrives in South Station at 11:40 A.M. Of course we may be a little late if the train is delayed. I do hope someone will meet me. If no one is there I will wait on the track we come in on for some someone to arrive.

Lots of love,
Sivvy

TO *Aurelia Schober Plath*

Tuesday 8 July 1947 ALS (postcard), Indiana University

July 8, 1947

Dearest Mummy,

This is truly the last card I'm going to write to you while I'm at camp (I think) because I'll get there before the mails will. This morning I really had breakfast-in-bed. I had a delicious time eating it and I was so comfortable! First I had an orange, then a huge soup plate of hot oatmeal (just like home), three pieces of delectable cinnamon toast, and some milk to top it off! Oh! Heavenly bliss! The sky was overcast with a cloudy fog when we went sailing this morning for the first time since the fourth of July. It cleared up this noon, though, which made it very nice for the photographer to take our pictures. Imagine! They chose my tent to take all the campers pictures in front of, so if I buy any pictures (which I probably won't since I'll leave before they're developed) there will be familiar ground in each. We have had glorious weather here all the time, and I have made a vow to bring my children up in sailboats – I'm so awfully dumb about them, but I love them more every time I go out.

xx
Siv

TO *Margot Loungway Drekmeier*

Sunday 3 August 1947

ALS with envelope,
Estate of Margot Drekmeier

August 3, 1947

Dear Margot,

I was very glad to receive your last letter. It truly would be heart-breakingly sad to destroy our correspondence while it was so steadfast and blooming. I really feel quite virtuous as I write this letter, since I have completed two solid hours of piano practicing and a few letters to some of my more important acquaintances (no offence intended), among whom is William Dana Orcutt,[1] who has recently presented with a set of five art books and two personally autographed books of his own. Perhaps you have read his "Dagger and Jewels" or "Escape to Laughter"? Both of these I highly reccommend for excellent reading pleasure.

Besides, it is so warm and comfortable here in our backyard in the warm sunshine and cool breezes, that I am strongly tempted to fall asleep and add, if possible, to my already dark tan. Instead, I write to you, which should raise your-self-esteem. (Again I add, "if possible!")

By the time I finish writing this epistle, I'm sure that the paper will have a considerable sunburn!

I have not been reading much lately, but have been devoting the bulk of my time to outdoor sports. I go swimming regularly down at the nearby lake and have been taking bike trips recently.

Yesterday, Ruthie[2] and I started out on a bike trip at 12 noon and didn't get back until seven P.M. We rode along a winding country road, shaded by a leafy, interlacing canopy of tree branches, until we arrived at my aunt's home in Weston. We climbed up on a hill in her back yard and ate our delectable picnic lunch. We relaxed and chatted a bit before starting back. While we were riding along beside each other, two boys (about 20 yrs. old,) passed us, going in the opposite direction on a motorcycle. Although they stared rudely at us, we payed them no attention, but speeded up our bikes. I had already broken two of my spokes, and was

1–American author, writer, and book and typeface designer, William Dana Orcutt (1870–1953). Author of *Dagger and Jewels: The Gorgeous Adventures of Benvenuto Cellini, A Romantic Novel* (New York: Dodd, Mead and Co., 1931); and *Escape to Laughter* (Norwood, Mass.: Plimpton Press, 1942). According to SP's diary, she received these books on 27 July 1947.

2–According to SP's diary, this was Ruth Geisel (1932–); friend of SP; attended Wellesley High School and Dana Hall School; B.A. 1953, English, Wellesley College; lived at 5 Durant Road, Wellesley, Mass.

just dismounting to walk the rest of the way, when I chanced to glance behind us. The motorcycle had turned around and the boys were chasing us. Naturally we were no match for their speed, although we pedalled fast and furiously. Luckily we reached Weston village by the time they caught up with us, and when we ignored them when they asked if we wanted to come for a ride, they rode back where they had come from. Ruthie and I were so relieved and exhausted that we just went in the drugstore, practically collapsed on the counter, and ordered a drink of ice water. We quickly recovered our strength, and continued our journey, making a 5 mile detour to drop in on Betsy Powley, who has her leg in a cast. When we at last arrived home, seat-sore and weary (but very elated) we figured accurately that we had ridden over 20 miles!

In case I did not write to you from camp, I had a perfectly unexcelled time, saw all the interesting sights and towns on Martha's Vineyard, learned how to sail a menemsha, accomplished over a 50 mile total in bike trips, and gained 5 pounds in weight.

Since I have been home I have: visited the Freeman's, where I went swimming in the ocean and attended movie[1] with 15 yr. old David; went to an Esplanade evening concert[2] with a very nice boy[3] who held my hand all evening; saw the movies "Cynthia" and "The Great Waltz"[4] with mother and dined at the Old France[5] afterwards; saw the two plays "The First Mr. Fraser" and "Dear Ruth" at the Wellesley Summer Theater.[6] These are only a few highlights of my thrill-packed summer, which are condensed for lack of space. Write soon –

Love,
Sylvia

P.S. Let's keep up a quick correspondence? Hmmmn? I just had a steak dinner – Yumm. I am so full!

1 – According to SP's diary, she and David Freeman saw *Vacation Days* and *Calcutta* at the Winthrop State Theatre on 23 July 1947.

2 – The concert included selections from *Eugene Onegin* by Peter Tchaikovsky, *The Merry Wives of Windsor* by Otto Nicolai, *King Christian* by Jean Sibelius, *Les Preludes* by Franz Liszt, *Aida* by Giuseppe Verdi, *Dreams* by Richard Wagner, *Voices of Spring* by Johann Strauss, and *The Snow Maiden* by Nikolay Rimsky-Korsakov.

3 – According to SP's diary, this was Redmond Sheets (1931–).

4 – A double feature SP and her mother saw on 12 July 1947 at the Loew's State Theatre.

5 – Old France was a restaurant then at 258 Huntington Avenue, Boston, Mass.

6 – According to SP's diary, she saw *The First Mr Fraser* on 18 July 1947 and *Dear Ruth* on 31 July 1947.

TO *Aurelia Schober Plath*

Monday 8 September 1947 ALS with envelope,[1] Indiana University

Monday, September 8

xxxxxx

Dearest mummy,

Guess what I did the first thing upon arriving home at 3 P.M.? Missed you, of course! Really, though, I drank two big glasses of water, washed my face with soap and water and changed into my shorts. I then took my homework out in the sunny, breezy back yard and commenced to write this note to you, knowing that youre wondering how my version of dear old Matt Arnold[2] came out. Well, I'll keep you in "Suzpenze" for a few minutes more.

Ruthie left at 20 of 5 yesterday, and we played cards all afternoon (at her express request – I didn't even mention the stuff!).

I did my homework from five to eight: fifteen (taking time out for supper) and then gladly packed up my books and was in bed & asleep by 9:30 after having treated and done up my hair and cleaned up my face and put goo on.

This morning I looked in the mirror before washing. Ugh! The grease made me look as white as syntrogyl pill! I looked in the mirror after washing. A miracle – a stupendous miracle had taken place. My skin, save for a few large pimples, was free of all cluttering blackheads, whiteheads, et cetera (Latin outbreak)! Of course as the day wore on it didn't look as wonderful. After a sleep I always look better – anyway, it's a sign of hope! <drawing of SP looking in handheld mirror with item captioned 'Rose Laird Kit'[3]>

I worked up my Arnold theme to one & one-half sides of a paper – including Palestine and all. With some misgivings I took the paper to English. We took the paragraph apart for most of the period and during the latter part of the class we read our papers. Where most received only a nod and a "Thank you" from Mr. Crockett,[4] he said "very well said"

1 – Letter addressed to ASP c/o Carney Hospital, One Harbor Road, South Boston, Mass.

2 – British poet Matthew Arnold (1822–88).

3 – A cosmetic company.

4 – Wilbury A. Crockett (1913–94); SP's English teacher at Wellesley High School (formerly Gamaliel Bradford Senior High School), 1947–50; lived at 82 Forest Street, Wellesley, Mass., with his wife Vera M. Crockett, and their children Deborah L. Crockett and Stephen Crockett.

for mine. I just about burst with pride. I don't even think Perry's[1] was quite as good as mine. We weren't quite able to finish all of them in the hour period, but I think, as far as we went, that only three or four were as good, or better than mine. Mary Ventura[2] was the only one beside me who received more than an "uhHuh" beside me!

By the way, almost half the class dropped out today and took a lower class instead. Mr. Crockett smiled to himself when he said "It seems we've had quite a desertion," as he took the attendance. Now we have only nineteen in our group, which makes it nice. I just love English – specially Mr. Crockett who thinks we're "a likely lot" with "a knack for our subject."

I had art today, and like my teacher[3] more and more as time goes on. I've done three rough charcoals and two new ones today. He thinks that the composition and lifelike action in my pictures is very good. I have drawn various pictures – all have people as a main interest.

Today my subjects, in order, were as follows:

Latin – read reading lesson – a few mistakes but pretty well done – will review

Math – Homework correct – class progressing slowly so far

Study – Here I enjoyed Orchestra instead

Study – By the time we got seated and all I only had time to do my math homework

Lunch – Yum!

English – Discussion of Arnold's paragraph

Art – charcoal sketches

No French today. This is all I have time for now. I have to write in a hurry. Will be in bed early tonight. Medium amt. of H.work. Lot of (groan) Latin!!!

From your very own Sylvia-girl
With love and best wishes.

<enclosed with this letter, sent to ASP c/o Carney Hospital,
are a letter from Aurelia Schober to ASP
and the following illustrated poem by SP>

1 – Charles Perry Norton (1932–), B.S. 1954, Yale College; M.D. 1957, Boston University School of Medicine; SP's friend from Wellesley. SP dated Perry Norton in high school and later dated his older brother Richard Norton.

2 – Mary Ventura, high school classmate of SP.

3 – Joseph Coletta (1919–98); SP's art teacher.

<drawing of flowers in left corner; drawing of house in right with caption 'Home Sweet Home'>

Missing Mother
by Sylvia
When mother goes away from me
I miss her as much as much can be.
And when I go away from mother
She misses me, and so does brother.

TO *Aurelia Schober Plath*

Tuesday 9 September 1947 ALS, Indiana University

September 9, 1947
Tuesday
7:30 P.M.

<drawing of four illustrated faces with captions 'BEFORE' / 'POOR COMPLEXION'; '1ST STEP' / 'SOAP, GREASE, LOTION/; '2ND' / 'THOROUGH WASHING'; and 'AFTER' / 'GLAMOROUS SKIN!'>

Dearest Mother,

I regret to say that I have not as much time to write to you tonight as I did on Monday, but I will make the most of what I have.

No more news about last evening, save that I did my piano, and put up my hair so that it came out just perfectly today.

My complexion is showing signs of improvement daily. Just this morning I saw that a few of my big red spots were drying up. Every night I send a little prayer of thankfulness to darling Rose Laird.

Well, about todays happenings. Here is my schedule of periods again today:

1 Latin: Read homework of last night. Was mainly successful in oral contributions.

2 French: "J'entre dans la sale de classe." We just went over our homework orally. No signs of starring individuals, yet!

3 Study <drawing of heart> Did all of Latin H. Work save review of declensions.

P. Education Weighed – 119¼ lbs.
Height – 5'8"
Eyesight – Perfectly Super

Arden[1] is 5'9" and weighs 147 lbs

Signed up for beginner tennis and basketball

<drawing of female face smiling with hearts>

English 21 Here is the class I just love. I could sit and listen to Mr. Crockett all day. We finished reading our paraphrases and, after we were through, Mr. Crockett said "Now, after we've gone through the whole bunch, whose paper do you think was the best?"

John Pollard[2] raised his hand immediately and said, "Sylvia's", whereupon dear old Davy (Mr. Crockett) replied, "I decidedly think so." He also praised about 5 others, not Perry, either!

Well! Our combination (your suggestion and my effort, of course) worked nicely in this case, didn't it?

Art We worked in using masses of mixed color on paper. Not too interesting, as you may imagine!

Miscellaneous Remarks:

1 Prissy[3] isn't so bad afterall, although you'd wince, too, if you saw her in that lurid patch-worky dress.

2 My English Class has so stimulated me that I'm chock-full of ideas for new poems. I can't wait to get time to write them down. I can't let Shakespeare get too far ahead of me, you know.

3 I have ideas for lots of paintings, too.

I like to write these notes to you in my spare moments because its second best to talking, at least I know you're hearing and understanding what I'm doing. I must have someone understanding to talk to.

Warren is quite noncommittal about his school events, except that he has been elected to two offices. I guess he misses you more than I do, not having so much work to do. Of course I'm just smart. I fool myself into not having time to miss you by planning what I'm going to do in every minute of my time so I'll never have any moment left to "be lonesome" in.

I've done all my homework, sitting outdoors from four to six since this is an easier night.

I know you like to read about the little "homely things" I do if your anything like "me is." (Did dishes tonight.) Warren's been going to bed exceptionally early.

1–Arden Tapley Ramrath (1932–82), SP's classmate who lived at 1 Audubon Road, Wellesley, Mass.

2–Possibly John Albert Pollard (1932–); dated SP 1947–9; SP's high school classmate who lived at several addresses in Newton and Wellesley, Mass.

3–Priscilla Steele.

That's all I have time for now. Am anxious to know how you are. I pray for you every night.

Lots of love,
Sylvia

P.S. Got "Frost's Poems"[1] at Hathaway House for 25¢.[2]

Time now – 8:00 P.M.

Will get ready for bed right away.

Thanks for sweet little postcard.

Love, S.

JOKE TO BE READ IN TIMES of Great Sadness!

Mr Crockett told us this:

"One of my pupils, in a written examination, wrote the title of the poem, "Intimations of Mortality" with two mistakes. He got it mixed and wrote "Imitations of Immorality" instead!! (appreciative LAUGHTER)

Or have you heard that one before?!!

<drawing of two figures, one in profile and the other in full view>

Love,
Me, ---

a bear of very little brain! A great big nothing – like a jar!

<drawing of three doctors and two nurses with caption
'From your card – here are three doctors and two nurses!'>

<drawing of female face with halo with caption
'YOU! (In my eyes)' and ' Sorry! THE PEN BLURRED!';
drawing of a heart>

1–Probably *The Pocket Poems of Robert Frost* (New York: Pocket Poems, 1946).

2–Hathaway House Bookshop, 103 Central Street, Wellesley, Mass.

1948

TO *Hans-Joachim Neupert*

Monday 14 June 1948 ALS (photocopy), Smith College

June 14, 1948

Dear Hans-Joachim,

This afternoon I found your letter in the mail box, so you see that it takes about a month for mail to cross the ocean.

As for your writing, I think that it is remarkably nice. I can imagine how difficult it must be for you to learn english – there are so many idioms and exceptions to every rule. Your printing is very neat and readable. If only you could see the printing of a few of my classmates – yours is so much better by comparison!

I wish that you could visit me some time, or that I could visit you! You must work very hard in school. If we want to go to a college (or a university) we must study hard and get good marks. However, a great part of American youth is carefree and jolly, thinking only of parties and fun. Perhaps you have been told this already. But, all in all, many of us have serious aims. Do you know that we have special magazines for young people? There are magazines for both girls and boys, and they sponser contests in art, writing and music. (Do send me a sample of your drawing!) These competitions are nation-wide, and give us the opportunity to exchange ideas and win recognition if we are skilled enough. Perhaps you would like me to send you an example of one of these magazines?

As for school, – this week we have final examinations. We have a 1½ hour examination in each subject. These tests cover the whole year's work, so we have to review all the books in every subject.

Have I told you that my Father was born in Germany? He came to America as a boy and worked until he became a professor of German and Biology at Boston University. He even wrote a book on the history of the bumblebee.[1] My father is dead now, so my mother teaches instead.

What you call desk-tennis must be what we call "ping-pong" or "paddle tennis." We play with a table, a net and "paddles." <drawing of a ping-

1 – Otto Emil Plath, *Bumblebees and Their Ways* (New York: Macmillan, 1934).

pong table with paddle and ball> We also read alot in school. I have heard about the writers which you mention, but I have not been so fortunate as to read their works. Of course we have read a great deal of Shakespeare – he is considered of the greatest dramatists of all time.

I have to buy my own supplies and pay for my own expenses, so how do you think I earn money?! I go baby-sitting! In case you have not heard of this leisure-time occupation, I will describe it. No, I do not sit <u>on</u> the babies – it is like this – when parents wish to go visiting with friends in the evening, they pay a girl or boy (our age) a certain amount of money an hour to take care of their child until they get home. This is very profitable for us.

At this time of year, all children are looking forward to the summer vacation – we have no school all during July and August. What type of stories and poems do you like to read? If you will let me know, I will attempt to send you a copy of the work of some of our American authors. I think that it would help your study of English.

I will like very much to hear about Germany in your next letter. Would you like to compare some of our ideas about religion, war, or life or science? I hope so, because I'd enjoy finding out what you think concerning such things.

As I write this, I am out in our back yard. The sun is very hot, and this is the first day of nice weather we have had for weeks. Everyone is glad, because we got so tired of the dull gray skies and the continuous rain.

You say that Film (that is the English word – they are very similar) cannot be purchased? It is not difficult to get here, but it is tremendously expensive.

Well that is all that I have room to write now, but I feel that I'll get to know you better as we continue our correspondance.

As always,
Sylvia

P.S. I cut the corner off my picture because it was torn.

<drawing of map of the Massachusetts coastline with sea creatures and a boat; major cities and Plath's hometown are labelled>

To give you, too, an idea of where I live, here is a little map of part of Massachusetts around Boston. Have you heard of Boston in your History or Geography courses? I assume that you have, but you can never be sure. Wellesley is a residential town – very "country-like", and yet with all the shops and stores there are in the city. The streets are shaded with large maples and elms, while the houses are small and the lawns are large and green.

Thank you for your beautifully drawn map. I was able to find Grebenhain just by following the course of the Rhine – I mean I found it on a big map of Germany that we have in an encyclopedia. I have Grebenhain marked with a star to show that you live there.

Your picture of yourself was very enjoyable – was it taken a few years ago as mine were?

I look so forward to your next letter! I will write you the day I receive it.

Until then –
Best wishes,
Sylvia

TO *Aurelia Schober Plath*

Friday 2 July 1948 ALS, Indiana University

July 2, 1948

Dear Mother,

Well! I'm not in the Biking Unit – I got Pre-Counselor instead. Ruth and Betsy got Biking and Anne and I got Pre-c., so, after slight confusion and indignation, Anne and another girl traded with Betsy and Ruth (who wanted to be with me)! So, now everybody is happy – especially me! I'm in the same Pre-Counselor tent with Bets, Ruth, and another girl, who is 18, fat homely, and a pain – she won't even write home to her mother! We three musketeers have the best tent in the unit – nearest the dining hall, the toilets, and the beach.

The trip down yesterday was fun – I had none of that waiting around that I did last year because, although we arrived early, I met Ann, and joined her and her mother and 3 girls I didn't know. We went on a drive to Falmouth where Mrs. Bowker treated us to a pile of creamy ice-cream. When we came back, the train had come in and I met Ruthy and Bets again. The boat-ride was fun, only foggy. Before we started, Betsy, Ruth and I had a last conversation with three sailors in another boat. They had spy glasses and a megaphone, so we progressed nicely. Last night (the boat left the dock at 5:30!) we had a late supper at 9:00 PM and then unpacked by flashlight. You can imagine how comfortable that was in the soggy, wet air! We got in late, and no one got to sleep till much later, what with talking and foghorns. Today, however, was simply gorgeous – cool, clear, sunny. Right after breakfast we peeled potatoes and then went down to pass our swimming tests. I thought I'd drown, but I didn't. We're going sailing this afternoon, and we can't wait.

I found that guests to camp come after noon & before 4:30 on Sundays, and get taxis to and from camp. Usually you find someone who is going to camp too, and split the round trip cost, which is $2 (yow!). The way they grab money around here is scandalous – $1 for transportation from Oak Bluffs to camp $1.20 for boat trip $.50 for "bike expenses." By the way, Warren's bike got a flat tire while waiting here on a hot day, so I'll have to pay for that. After I get through I'll be bankrupt, but don't send any more money – I'll manage.

The food isn't too much, but I fill up on bread and margerine. If you feel like it – send me an old pack of cards just for fun. We three are going to try to go biking any way, as soon as I get Warren's tire fixed. Our councilors are very nice and understanding.

The morning swim in the cool green water was invigorating, and washed away all my tiredness, leaving only a mild sensation of laziness. As always, the first night is hardest – when you're so tired – now we're in the routine, and we love it. I haven't much rest hour time left now, because I've just gotten comfortably settled and arranged. Do send me Wayne's address – Ruthy says he asks for me alot, so I might as well drop him a line. If you can, forward mail and find out Marianne's (the French girl's)[1] address from the Norton's quickly, because I must write her very soon.

I'll never get homesick – I love it here – It's so nice to be in with Bets & Ruth – I don't miss Anne too much.

That's all for now – Don't expect more than a post card each day,

Love,
Sherry.

TO *Aurelia Schober Plath*

Saturday 3 July 1948 ALS (postcard), Indiana University

July 3, 1948
Saturday

What's Warren's address!

Dear Mother,

I got those two packages yesterday – the mosquito netting is wonderful – I don't have one single mosquito inside it. I don't need the wind-breaker at all, 'cause Betsy's red jacket is so nice and warm. Betsy & Ruth slept

1 – Probably Marianne Lévy, a pen pal of SP according to her high school scrapbook (p. 14); held by Lilly Library.

in the same cot last night and talked and laughed from 3 to 5 – of course I couldn't sleep – Ruthie wasn't so noisy, but Betsy!! and she knows how I love to sleep, too, darn her. So I feel quite sleepy this morning. If she wakes me up again – I'll conk her with my suit case. I went sailing yesterday and had the most wonderful time – everything I learned last year is slowly coming back. Betsy and Ruth are dissatisfied with the counselling unit, but I'm going to try to get a good reputation in case I'm ever a counselor.

Love
Sherry

TO *Aurelia Schober Plath*

Saturday 3 July 1948 — ALS (postcard), Indiana University

July 3, 1948
Sat. afternoon

Dear Mum,

Boy, do I feel wonderful! Bets, Ruthy and I have been laying out on the beach after our swim and we all feel so refreshed. The counsellor has gone down to get my bike from the repair shop so that I can bike to the races at Vineyard Haven today. The things I like most are biking and sailing, and I live to go sailing! I feel a sort of thrill go through me when I'm at the tiller thinking "This is me sailing the boat." I hope we can wangle more bike-trips for our unit. The salt air is very invigorating and I love it down here – I'd die if I couldn't stay a month. Do send me Warren's address – I forgot it. I'm going to start learning that monologue. Give my love to Grammy and grampy. When I tried to swim the crawl today, I almost swallowed the whole lagoon.

Love,
Sherry

TO *Aurelia Schober Plath*

Saturday 3 July 1948 — ALS (postcard), Indiana University

July 3, 1948
Sat. evening

Dear Mum,

Here I am again. At this rate I'll use all my post cards up in a week. Well, my bike got back in time for me to go to see the races with the rest of the camp. It was such fun biking! I only weighed 122 when I came, but I'm starved at meals and eat and eat! I'm starved for people, and it's such fun to wave to all the cars – the boys (the few there are 'on the island) are so good looking! I'm probably going to bike to church tomorrow – they changed the front tire on the bike, and I thought that they were new just a short while ago! I have company, because Ruthy's bike broke down on the trip today and will have to be repaired. I don't dare ask what the price will be for my job on my bike! I've just begun to learn my monologue – I've got one of the four pages learned.

Love,
Sherry

TO *Aurelia Schober Plath*

Sunday 4 July 1948 ALS (postcard), Indiana University

July 4, 1948
Sunday noon

Dear Mum,

This morning I biked about 4 miles to church at Oak bluffs. We went to an open-air Methodist Trinity Church[1] which has a lovely dome for the roof and open-sides. Birds kept flying in and out the huge room during the service, which was dull and hot. The singing was nice though. We're going on a bike hike (all except the bike unit) to South beach where we'll go swimming. We don't go sailing again till Tuesday. My bike repairs cost $5! I thought I'd die! I have hardly anything left – especially for pottery. I have about $3 already taken off my account for transportation expenses! Do come visit me on the 11th – maybe you could bring a little fruit – if that tire I had changed was just new, maybe you could take it back with you.

love
siv.

1–The Trinity United Methodist Church, Trinity Park, Oak Bluffs, Mass.

TO *Aurelia Schober Plath*

Monday 5 July 1948 ALS (postcard), Indiana University

July 5, 1948

Dear Mummy,

We're going to have a swimming meet this afternoon, and I'm so sleepy that I'll probably drown. It'll be so nice to have you come to visit me. We're riding our bikes down to a pottery demonstration – I hope I can scrape together enough to take it if I like it. Things are so gypsy here – $1 to go anywhere in the camp truck – $2.50 to go to Nantucket – I'd hate to get left out. I hope that you have a wonderful vacation. We only go sailing 8 times this month, and we have nothing much besides swimming and an occasional bike trip now and then – sometimes things get so dull. – I don't see Ann much. I hope we have a talent show sometime – I'm trying to finish learning that "thing."

Love,
"Sherry"

TO *Aurelia Schober Plath*

Tuesday 6 July 1948 ALS (postcard), Indiana University

July 6, 1948

Dear Mum,

Could you please send me your address at Falmouth.

Honestly, you should see how grasping they are with money. If I take pottery for 2 weeks, I can't go to Nantucket or anything. We biked to Vineyard Haven for the pottery demonstration and it looks simply fascinating! 3 dollars takes care of 4 lessons in which one can make a small article or two. I went sailing this morning with my favorite counsellor – she's adorable, but very indomitable about sailing. She's daring, too, and the boat heeled so much that I practically went on my face in the water – the boat was perpendicular to the waves and these pictures are no exaggeration! <drawing of two sailboats> My hair is so caked with salt that it won't curl, and I'm going to wash it this afternoon.

Love,
Me

TO *Aurelia Schober Plath*

Tuesday 6 July 1948 ALS (postcard), Indiana University

July 6, 1948
Tuesday

Dear Mum,

I can't wait to see you Sunday – don't spend too much money coming over, now. I miss you a little, and it will be nice when you come. I want to gain weight, and I eat enough, only we have so much exercise that it's hard to. When you come, do bring a few express tags. Tonight we had a terrible thunderstorm, and the rain was blown over the lagoon in silvery sheets. I'm hoping my bike holds out – if we go on any more trips. I washed my hair this afternoon, but it won't stay clean long with all our sailing (only 14 hours a month) and swimming. My Docks (the old ones) are getting so holey that it's impossible to mend them! The overnight hike is what I really dread – sleeping on the cooold cold ground! They seem so stupid to me, but then I miss my inbetween meal snacks.

Love
Sherry

TO *Aurelia Schober Plath*

Wednesday 7 July 1948 ALS (postcard), Indiana University

July 7, 1948
Wednesday

Dear Mum,

Today it was Only 50° in the morning, so I wore about three layers of clothes to be comfortable. The diet here is very skimpy. We have only had <u>meat</u> twice (and only minute servings) and eggs not at all – mostly salads and odd soups with mixtures of obscure vegetables, so we have to fill up on what there is of bread and butter – Just at present I'd like a chicken dinner – my stomach is shrunken before lunch! Let's hope I can get my skit memorized. I doubt if it's good enough to be the representative from our group. I've written to you every day, once, at least, so I hope you get my mail regularly. I'm so proud – I've got more mail from home than anyone else in my tent – Keep up the good work! This is really the most scenic place that I've seen for ages. I've never had such a comfortable bed in my life. I hate to get up at 7:00! I'll try drawing the kids in my tent, too, If I have time

Love,
me

TO *Aurelia Schober Plath*

Thursday 8 July 1948

ALS with envelope,
Indiana University

July 8, 1948
Thursday

Dear Mummy,

As I write, I'm sitting on the beach with the sun warm on my back. I couldn't go swimming because I have a sore throat and backache, and the nurse won't let me. The thing that bothered me was that I began to spit up rusty phlegm this morning. I know it sounds sort of bad – the kids say I no doubt have T.B. (cheery thought) but the nurse says it's probably just a few little capillaries breaking. Betsy wants to go home alot, and we're always trying to cheer her up, and just beginning to succeed. Of course, when you're sick at camp you miss home most. We're going on an overnight Friday, and I just hope I don't get pneumonia!

We have begun arts and crafts, but the awful thing is that we have to make (and pay for) ties out of cheap white cloth! I wanted to draw, but we have to cut and sew the darn old ties.

The more I'm in this old unit, the less I want to be a counsellor. For one thing, the counsellors don't like our tent because we are always late, and talking together and everyone (except me) doesn't want to be a counsellor. Every bit of time we have to ourselves, we get together and talk and laugh and play cards. We're the five musketeers – Bets, Ruthie, the girl from our tent, and Marilyn (a darling girl from our unit) and me. Yesterday we all had a laughing fit and I laughed so hard that I thought my sides would burst – we all were literally rolling on the floor! You see, we'd just had a game of hearts, and Ruthy had just fallen out of the cabin when the bed she was sitting on slipped over the edge of the floor. Since the drop was about 5 feet, it was very hilarious. We're going sailing this afternoon, and I can't wait.

I wear my flannels every night, and am very grateful for them. My mosquito netting is just marvelous. Have you changed your address yet? I am only 123 lbs. in weight.

One unit went deepsea fishing today (price $1) and they caught 60 fish or so. As I have said before, our meals our very skimpy – last night we actually had hotdogs!

Be glad you don't have to take the car over on the boat – it costs $15! I know an easy way to get bankrupt – come to Vineyard for a month – remember come over between 12 noon and 4:30! We all look forward to seeing you this Sunday. I'll probably feel better by then, I hope.

Give my special love to grammy and grampy, and do send me Warren's and Wayne's and that French girl. Gee, I wish grammy had asked who the strange "male" was. It might have been John, as you suggest. If anyone else calls, give them my address, please.

I think I'm really too old to go to camp anymore, except as a counsellor, which I probably won't because of my councellor's dislike for our whole tent. So far I've done a pencil crayon picture of bets, but I'm so used to pastels that it doesn't look at all like her.

If I haven't told you already, the cookout last night was delectable. We hope to do more of the same.

Love to all, from your very own me
Sherry
<drawing of smiling girl in sailboat>

<on back of envelope>

Having a wonderful time here! Just about to go sailing now!

TO *Aurelia Schober Plath*

Sunday–Monday 11–12 July 1948[1] ALS with envelope, Indiana University

After you left

Naughty, naughty mother,

Honestly, I simply could die when I think of you running up and down that damn old hill. I just wish you would have called to me and let me do it! I only hope you're all right! – making me worry so! I went right up and drank 3 glasses of water and shed some more tears and then I was all through for the rest of the month. I feel better already, and I hope you can write honestly that you are fine and rested and suffer no ill effects from your silly run! I don't know how you'd get along without me, really. The

1–Date supplied from internal evidence.

water really made me feel a lot better, and I won't be homesick any more, I know.

Don't join the "rocking chair" brigade anymore, will you! I have so much to look forward to here, and when I go home, I'm sure I'll write more poems and stories like I did last summer. You know, I started thinking of the main idea of "Alone and Alone"[1] last summer at camp!

The aftermath of your visit was pleasant. I feel like I've had an emotional purge – all my pent up feelings let go when I cried, and I feel so much better.

"Jo", our tentmate (who is 40 years old) came in second in the race. I've never seen anyone so dazed. Let's hope the counsellors don't find out about our private grocery store! This afternoon we took some funny pictures of each other on Betsy's camera. Give my love to everyone.

Honestly, now, instead of going around with a hungry pain, I just take a bite of cooky and think of you with love.

We had a nice scout's own tonight – singing hymns around the campfire. Somehow there's nothing so comforting as singing with a group.

<u>Monday Morning</u>

Oh, am I dead! Last night two of the girls were missing from our unit, and of course we were all nervous after taps. It was about eleven when we learned that they had been found hiding in another tent. By that time we were starved, so we ate some cherries and peanut butter crackers. By that time we were so tired we were dizzy. This morning we had fun sailing, but I don't know if I'll <u>ever</u> get to crew in a race – there is <u>so</u> much I don't know.

Well, mail's going out now, so I'll have to skimp on my three cent stamp and close.

Love
Sherry

TO *Aurelia Schober Plath*

Tuesday 13 July 1948 ALS (postcard), Indiana University

July 13, 1948

Dear Mummy,

It is just rest hour, and we've spent the morning sailing (2 hours.) In the lunch period our unit divided up into 3 groups, and, one went into

1–Sylvia Plath, 'Alone and Alone in the Woods Was I', written c. 11 September 1947.

each unit, and each girl had some special activity to supervise in the preparing of the meal I had fire builders in the pioneer unit, and it was so much fun. I got to know so many more kids and it was nice to have the responsibility. We had a cookout because our water supply is on the blink. I have no more sore throat or phlegm, but one of my eyes is all bloodshot and watery – it's probably from the salt water, but it is very annoying. It is cloudy and looks like rain and my face is all broken out and Ruthy is a pain in the neck sometimes – always bragging about you-know-what and saying I'm jealous – At times like this I long for my very own mummy. I miss our piano, too, but I'll cheer up.

Love,
me

TO *Aurelia Schober Plath*

Wednesday 14 July 1948 ALS (postcard), Indiana University

I

July 14, 1948 (noon)

Dear Mum,

In spite of being dead tired after 6 hours of sleep last night (Jo was talking all the time because it was her last night), I feel much better. My eye is clearing up, and the nurse put arguol[1] in it. Betsy is going to be in a harbor race today, and I only wish that I was going, too. We had loads of fun at the camp house last night. Each unit dramatized a story – ours was "Snow White". Right away, Betsy said to me "I'll be Snow White and you be Prince Charming." (You know how she always is the star.) Well, she almost had conniption's when the kids elected me as Snow White. She was "Grumpy." I had such fun – Ruthy was the wicked queen, and looked stunning in a draped rose bathrobe – I wore a lacy white blouse and a blue silk skirt. Of course my eye was worse then, and my skin a mess, but I enjoyed every minute!

Love,
Me.

1 – The treatment was probably Argyrol, an antiseptic compound.

TO *Aurelia Schober Plath*

Wednesday 14 July 1948 ALS (postcard), Indiana University

2

July 14, 1948
(rest hour)

Dear Mum,

This afternoon I think we'll have pottery this afternoon, and Ruthy and I are going to be the only ones from our unit – (of course there are others from other units) – and it promises to be lots of fun. Our craft teacher has an adhesion of the intestine, so – no more ties for a while! You have no idea how relieved I was to receive your card that you were well and happy after your little run. My little spat of jealousy at Betsy's racing has passed, and during her absence Marilyn & Ruth and I consumed the rest of the bananas and a tin of molasses Cookies (we left 3 for Betsy.) A stomach full of food puts me in a very contented mood! That should put on the weight my lack of sleep takes off! From your very happy, acneyed daughter

Love,
Sylvia

TO *Aurelia Schober Plath*

Wednesday 14 July 1948 ALS (postcard), Indiana University

July 14, 1948

3

Dearest Mum,

Honestly, the way I keep writing to you today I'll use up all my postcards – I keep leaving out some news, so I write a new card. About the food – it's delicious. We've eaten the raisins, all the cookies and bananas and Betsy's saltines and made quite a dent in the jar of peanut butter. We are having a wonderful time. Ruthy is so sweet when she's by herself – I like her more than Betsy sometimes, even though she's like a wound-up clock when she talks at night. It's dark and damp and chilly today, and the sky is filled with rain. My eye is almost all cleared up, and my mosquito netting admits not one mosquito. We have rearranged our tent so it is much cosier

– I like Marilyn ten times more than Jo! Jo was so sloppy and legarthic. I am so happy here, I'll cry when I come home.

Lots of love,
me

TO *Aurelia Schober Plath*

Thursday 15 July 1948 ALS (postcard), Indiana University

July 15, 1948

Dear Mum,

Last night we had interest groups, and I went out rowing. It was such fun – I'm meeting new friends all the time and I would love to work at a camp with young children. I can see how counsellors have favorites – I like a few of the younger girls here (by that I mean 14 years old) very much! I'm going to send you two pictures of me taken by Betsy. They'll give you an example of how much fun we have. Well, It's only 2 weeks now till I'll see you – I'm so glad you're having such fun at Falmouth. How long does it take my cards to reach you? I'm mailing this at 3:00 P.M. I'm just curious.

Love,
Sylvia

TO *Aurelia Schober Plath*

Thursday–Friday 15–16 July 1948 ALS with envelope, Indiana University

July 15, 1948

Don't I look nice in the group photo?

Dear Mummy,

Please return the enclosed pictures after you look at them, as they are Betsy's. We took them after you left Sunday, and I think that they came out quite well, all except that one of me on the profile side where my mouth appears sort of funny.

This morning we had an outdoor cookout for breakfast and had blueberry pancakes. I know it sounds good, but after we had turned them over and gotten them all crumbly, they tasted like dough, half burnt, half raw.

I think I'll mail this tomorrow so I can write more news.

I'm going up to wash my hair now – the water is working again.

Later in the afternoon

I've been lying out on the beach all afternoon with Betsy, drying our hair – it feels so nice and soft, after the salt caked on it has been scrubbed off. As of July 14th, you say you haven't received any cards – I don't know why – I wrote every day except Sunday. I hope that this letter makes up for those cards you've missed.

Camp is really in full swing now!

July 16th

Last night as we stood in a circle outside the camp house and sang songs, I looked across the dark lake, mirroring the yellow lights of Vineyard Haven. Honestly, I felt just like crying when I thought of leaving this heavenly place! The weather is perfect! The sky is like a clear blue bowl, and the water is blue, blue, and invigorating. The air is dry and comfortable, with cooling breezes and bright sunlight. Every day has been like this except for three rainy evenings during the first week.

We're really beginning our counsellor training – planning meals and unit programs as if we were counsellors. I'm a very lucky girl – wait till I tell you! Mary, the crafts teacher, was flown to the hospital with her adhesion, so there was no one left to take her place. Of course this meant I couldn't take over crafts on the day we counsel in the units, because we have to have a staff supervisor. But Happy (she was awed by you, I think – yak! yak!) knew how much I wanted to do it, so she said I could take over the biking unit at Crafts this morning! I did, and was it fun! Ann was in the unit, too. I just went around showing the girls how to mix paint and advising them how to draw designs etc. etc. It was easy, because I knew how to mix all the stuff, and the kids aren't too fussy about results – In my way of thinking just about the whole camp is getting to know me! In addition to my morning Of (ahem!) craft instruction all by myself, I'm to have tomorrow and Monday with the rest of the unit. We go in twos into the jobs of our choice and see how they are done. Bets and I have the biking unit tomorrow and we're going on an all day trip with them (hurrah!) Monday we have store, so we'll have a lot of free time to sunbathe on the beach in. These last two weeks are so crowded that they'll just fly by. I'm having such fun. Marilyn is nicer than Joe, and I can manage Ruthy's occasional nasty cracks very well.

We've started pottery, if you could call it that. They said they were going to have a wheel to mold on, but no! All we can do is tiles and funny shaped ashtrays! I've already begun the course, so I'll have to make the best of it. The tiles can only be done in two colors, and it's cheap clay also. I started a fruit spray on my tile, and the woman (not very artistic) did say that I had an inborn sense of balance and design. The only thing I wouldn't like about teaching crafts is that you have to be indoors. I'd love to have outdoor classes, in the sun, but It doesn't seem possible.

We're going sailing this afternoon. I do hope I can crew in one of the races, but I doubt it. Betsy is <u>in</u> now (sailing I mean) but Ruthy keeps me company.

At night it is cool, and the moon is getting fuller. I have never seen such bright, iridescent moonlight before.[1] It is like a clear, silver wash over the trees and it shines through the leaves and into our tent, touching everything with a quiet, hushed radiance. I'm drinking as much water I am able, so that my skin will be clearer by the time I come home. Thanks for those three clippings, by the way, especially the tips of teens! I have not had to use my Magnesia yet, except once.

I haven't done much swimming here because of my throat a week ago and my eye more recently. Both have given me no trouble as of the last few days.

The days here slip by so fast that it's hard to remember all that we've done. We have eaten up every thing except the peanut butter, the jam, the cheese, and the surprise package which we won't open till the last few nights. We're waiting eagerly for the crackers Betsy's mother's supposedly sending us. Tell me if the surprise package contains cheese crackers, so we can save some of Betsy's upon which to spread the chicken (It is chicken, isn't it?) That's all for now. I hope this makes up for the poopy delay of those poopy old cards from me!

love,
sylvia

TO *Aurelia Schober Plath*

Saturday 17 July 1948 ALS (postcard), Indiana University

July 17

Dear Mum –

I have hardly a minute in my tent before we leave for our all day bike hike. We're going a mere 30 miles, (heh! heh!) Bets and I have been dashing thru our morning chores and we have just finished making up our beds. Please send me a clean facecloth if possible. Mine are filthy dirty and I haven't had time to wash them out. I have decided that my pusy eye is due to that fact. My emotional thermometer is stationed permanently at

1 – 'moonlight ~~ever~~ before' appears in the original.

the "Highly Happy" mark. I'll write you in more detail tomorrow – this is just so you'd get a card –

All love,
me

TO *Aurelia Schober Plath*

Sunday 18 July 1948 ALS (postcard), Indiana University

July 18, 1948

Dear mummy

I was going to write you a long letter, but I just haven't the strength. The bike hike yesterday was wonderful, yet a times I wondered if I'd get back to camp! We ate on Indian Hill, the highest point on the island. The road that led up to it was a two rut dirt lane, and it was extremely steep. We had a delicious meal, only there was nothing to drink. On the way back we stopped by the road and picked cupfuls of large, sun ripened blueberries. I rode Ruthy's bike and I had a super time, (and got even tanner). Last night we had a masquerade and went as advertisements. I went as the chinese girl of Chen Yu nail polish. Oh, some bad news – the chain on Warren's bike broke in two – of course I can't ride it. I don't think I should have it repaired here, do you? I won't need it.

Love
me

TO *Aurelia Schober Plath*

Monday 19 July 1948 ALS (postcard), Indiana University

July 19, 1948

Dear mum,

You know, my bloodshot eyes were caused by too much sun. I'd gone sailing and biking without sun glasses too much. Now I'm wearing Betsy's sunglasses because she doesn't wear them. Yesterday I went to church, and the sermon was dull as usual. It was called "The Rod of the Almond Tree." Even so, I found a little message in it. The only thing I don't like is mouthing adorations to "the Trinity," when I believe in no such thing – at least nothing so didactic. I'm so happy here. I've seen more of Anne Bowker, and we like each other alot, I think. She's staying in N. Falmouth for August. I don't have much time to write, but of course you'll get a card each day. Give my special love to Grammy & grampy. These two weeks are flying by on wings of jam and cheese.

Love
me.

TO *Aurelia Schober Plath*

Monday 19 July 1948 ALS (postcard), Indiana University

July 19, 1948

Dearest Mum,

Today is the second and last pre-counselor day we have. It's such fun to walk into meals ahead of the campers! Bets and I had store today, so we also had alot of extra jobs to go with it. After breakfast we went to the (ugh!) garbage dump and emptied barrel after barrel: P.U. Then we had to lug heavy rocks up the hill for our john drain! At last we went down the beach and used up our "free time" in lying about in the sun. We then went in for a free swim and I never had such fun. The water felt deliciously cool on my tanned skin, and we'd swim about and lie on the raft until we dried off and then we'd take another dip. My e thermometer is rising a little more even.

Lots of hugs & kisses,
me

TO *Aurelia Schober Plath*

Monday 19 July 1948 ALS (postcard), Indiana University

3

July 19, 1948

Dear Mum,

One of the few camp fixtures that I <u>won't</u> miss is the menu. I have a least 2 pieces of bread at every meal, and last night (we always have sandwiches for Sun. nite supper) I had <u>six</u> pieces. That may help me gain weight, but all that starch and positively <u>no</u> greens is rather bad. We had the loveliest campfire last night out on the bluffs. A gray evening fog shut off the view of the sea, so we appeared to be on the extreme brink of empty gray space. The glowing red coals and sparks of the fire appeared so beautiful against the hazy background! Pardon me while I drink two cups of water!

Lots of Love!
"Sherry"

TO *Aurelia Schober Plath*

Tuesday 20 July 1948 ALS (postcard), Indiana University

1

July 20

Dearest Mum,

Honestly, this is one of those rare moments when I just could cry! Both Bets and Ruth have gone sailing in the harbor race, and I haven't yet. I'm glad I can be alone in my tent for a few minutes so I won't have to go through the torture of gay talk while I feel so sad inside. Ruth & Bets have passed more of their requirements as a result – I was up to Ruth until I had to take over crafts one night while she took land-sailing. Well, my first wave sadness has left me – If only I wasn't so easily hurt and so darn sensitive! I take pottery for the second time this afternoon – all we make is an ash tray – isn't that disgusting? Well, I'll cheer up and do some sketching this rest hour. I'm getting tanner – so watch out.

Love
me

TO *Aurelia Schober Plath*

Tuesday 20 July 1948 ALS (postcard), Indiana University

2

July 20

Dear mummy,

I hope you get the two cards I wrote today at the same time – I just had to blow off steam to someone, and now I feel much better. I'm going to draw designs for the camp book with a couple of other girls, so life is brighter. The mail you send is quite irregular – I got none from you last night, but three cards the night before! We have had meat about 5 times since we've been here. Listen to these two outrageous menus and be rightfully indignant! Supper bread soaked in water with a sprinkling of tomato sauce, potatoes and bread and jam: chocolate pudding for dessert!

Lunch Mere scalloped potatoes and bread & jam. Half a canned peach for dessert. Starches! Starches! Of course our "store" has diminished to spreads, with only bread snitched from the table to put it on!

Loads of love from a happier
me

TO *Aurelia Schober Plath*

Tuesday 20 July 1948 ALS (postcard), Indiana University

3

July 20

Dear Mum,

Here I am again for the third time today, and feeling even better! Do you know an odd coincidence? One girl in my unit came up to me and asked if I knew Wayne Sterling! It seems that her little brother wrote her from the Y camp where Wayne is counsellor, and Wayne wanted to know if I went to his sister's camp! We had a girl scout troop from V. Haven come to visit us for a day & night, and they left this morning. They were all cute except for one freak who scared Bets & me & looked like this: <drawing of a 'freak' girl scout> I pitied her, but she was so utterly horribly slovenly that we kept away from her. I'm not so homely after all.

Lots of love
– me

TO *Aurelia Schober Plath*

Tuesday 20 July 1948[1] ALS (postcard), Indiana University

<drawing of four hearts throughout letter>

June 20th

P.S. I'll write more tomorrow

Dear Mummy,

I had about the most fun today as I have had yet. The morning was very calm, and we sailed across down the lagoon to a boat-building place where we were to leave them to be tuned up for the big race this week. It was so calm that it took us two hours to get over to the place in Vineyard Haven, and we had to wait around for the camp truck to take us back.

1 – Letter misdated by SP.

I was in the 2nd load, and the truck got a flat while taking back the 1st group, so about 5 of us waited around in V. Haven till the truck returned at long last. I was out in the sun from 9:30 until one, and I have a dark burn over my tan. Have you been getting all my cards? I've written quite a few. It's so nice to hear from you every day.

Love,
Sherry

TO *Aurelia Schober Plath*

Wednesday 21 July 1948 ALS (postcard), Indiana University

July 21
Late afternoon & early evening

Dear Mum,

I am so happy it bubbles over! My "thermometer" is back to it's high normal again. Nothing special has happened except that I have, in the midst of my petty jealousies, found myself. I am filled with complete serenity and love for you and your cheery little cards which have arrived so faithfully! Tonite was wonderful! I got a card from you and Mrs. Freeman and a letter from Wayne! I gave my skit to our unit but they didn't pick it for the talent show! – It was too frivolous, I think. Today I had two pottery lessons, while Ruth raced, so my thoughts were happily absorbed. I can only make two things – a tile and (I persuaded the man instructor) a little pot with a cover. It's very simple 'cause I had to make it by hand – without a wheel.

Love,
Me – Sherry – <drawing of pot with cover> sivvy

TO *Aurelia Schober Plath*

Thursday 22 July 1948 ALS (postcard), Indiana University

July 22

Dear Mum,

Here I am again! About the pottery – I have made a tile, but it will have to be fired and then glazed with colors before it's ready. I won't be able to take it home with me, but it will be sent when finished (more expense!) My jam pot is a little lopsided since I had to round it out by hand, but as long as nothing breaks in the firing I will be satisfied. I won't be sorry

I spent $3 if everything comes out all right! Don't expect too much, though. Ruthy missed two lessons while racing, so the potter left clay, and I'm teaching her how to make a jam pot! I have had more experience in crafts instructing since the counsellor got her adhesion – I know as much as anyone in camp and the head of camp likes me to be at the craft house alot!

Love
Me

TO *Aurelia Schober Plath*

Friday 23 July 1948 ALS (postcard), Indiana University

July 23, 1948

Dear Mummy,

How I love my little lopsided jam pot! It looks an ugly clay-color just now because I have just finished modeling it. Pottery takes an awful long time to complete! It takes days and days to dry out after modeling, and then it must be fired. Then it must be soaked, then glazed (painted with colors) and then heated again! I did three hundred yards of swimming today without stopping once – 50 crawl, 50 inverted breast stroke, 50 elem. backstroke, 50 sidestroke, 50 brest stroke, 50 dogpaddle. By the time I got through, my noseplugs broke and I got a noseful of salt water – a little sniffle resulted, and I'll have to mend my plugs somehow. I am drawing portraits for just about the whole camp – one girl saw the sketch I did of Bets, and so I went on from there. I've done about 6 so far and my drawing papers all gone.

Love
me

TO *Aurelia Schober Plath*

Friday 23 July 1948 ALS (postcard), Indiana University

July 23

Dearest Mummy,

Boy, this morning was surely cold and raw! I wore my heavy navy sweater until we went down to the beach and it was so hot in the sun that I put on a halter. Now, in rest hour, it's cold and cloudy again. At night I'm warm with my flannels – I don't use my netting any more because my dear little tent-mates broke off all my netting poles – didn't look nice, they said. I told you what a demand there was for pictures! That's where everyone's vanity crops up! – They all want self-portraits! They don't like us to lie out in the sun much, so that's another thing I'll enjoy when I get home. I'll be seeing you at Woods Hole in 5 days – I'll be glad to see your face again! I love you so much!

Love,
me

TO *Aurelia Schober Plath*

Saturday 24 July 1948 ALS, Indiana University

July 24, 1948

Dear Mum,

Boy! Do I have an earful to tell you! I was up in the infirmary to get some nosedrops to clear up a sinus headache, when the assistant cook came in the adjoining room. I was lying on the bed for a few minutes to let the drops soak up and what I didn't hear! "Buddy," the nurse was talking to her and trying to soothe her, for she was obviously hysterical – she talked in a choked voice and laughed queerly now and then. She talked so loudly that I could hear every word. This, in brief is what she said:

"This camp has the oddest set-up I've ever seen. When I hired out as assistant cook I expected to help buy and plan menus – but Monty (the head of camp) does all that. Mrs. Lamb (the head cook) has nothing to say about the diet. Why, when she had to make cocoa for the whole camp at the beginning of the month she said "I don't know how to make cocoa!' She doesn't even know how to make a pie. If she's that bad why is she head cook?!! I can't make a pie myself – don't know the knack of rolling out the crust. That stew this noon was nothing but garbage left over. The counsellors around here are so fussy that they won't eat leftovers. When the kids come back from the Regatta (sail boat races) tonight they'll be starved, and you know what there is to eat? 15 hotdogs for each 25 people and a potatoe salad! Why can't someone besides Monty prepare meals! The cook did last year!"

Hereupon the nurse interrupted, saying that the helpings had to be very small to go around a table of eight. The nurse then gave the assistant cook some medicine and came into the room where I was lying with my mouth open waiting for the drops to clear my sinuses. She said laughingly. "Can you keep your mouth shut while I'm gone? I know you can't really, but you know what I mean."

As you can imagine, the cook's little outburst shocked me no end, but I pretended to be dumb about it. Later on in the day she tossed me a hard red plum after asking whether I wanted one, and said "It's not very ripe, but it's the ripest we have."

I hope no one knows I've written this letter, but I just had to tell you!

Well, now that's off my chest I can feel better! I hope my cold clears up by the time I see you on Wednesday. Yesterday our island, too, was shrouded in fog. Isn't it fun to watch the tattered gray mists blow in from the sea!

I'll write more later,
Love and more love,
Sylvia

TO *Aurelia Schober Plath*

Tuesday 10 August 1948 — ALS (postcard), Indiana University[1]

Tuesday
Sailed till sunset yesterday!

Dear Mum,

I will be in South Station at noon (12:00) on Thursday, not Wednesday. The train leaves here at 10:15. I have had a wonderful appetite and eaten like a queen – had corn-on-the-cob for the 1st time this year. Yesterday we had the most wonderful time! Three of ann's friends & ann's parents & us took an all day cruise in the Bowker's big big sailboat. We went by motor about 10 miles across the ocean to Marion,[2] had a picnic lunch there and then jaunted back! It was a treat for me, as you can guess! When Ann & I got back, about 4 P.M, we took her small sail boat and sailed in the harbor till supper. I got my fill of sun for the day & a nice tan on my face (and lots of midge bites.) I was glad to get your letter! I am lucky!! I love you lots & realize how lucky I am to have you for a mother. "Having a wonderful time."

Me xx
xx
Love
x

1 – Date supplied from postmark.
2 – Marion, Mass., on Buzzard's Bay in Plymouth County.

TO *Hans-Joachim Neupert*

Friday 24 September 1948 ALS (photocopy), Smith College

September 24

Dear Hans-Joachim,

How glad I was to find your letter waiting for me when I came home from school. While I was walking down my street, I hurried a little because I kept thinking, "Perhaps, perhaps I will find a letter from Bahnhof waiting for me!" And so it was!

Time and again I have thought how lucky I was to have found such an entertaining correspondant. Have I told you that I chose your letter from a large ammount of others, almost by chance? You see, I read all the letters, and then thought that yours sounded more interesting than all the rest. And I was right!

Truly, you seem to have a good understanding of English. Of course Idioms are difficult to master, but that will come to you in time. I know that when I attempt to write in French my phrasing is awkward, and I do not say what I mean always. You, however, write as nicely as many of my friends do.

Your school begins early. Our first day was the ninth of September. Our vacation lasted from June 20th until September 9th.

What a good time you must have had in the Alps! As for myself, I spent most of the summer by the seashore. Somehow I have a special place in my heart for the ocean. I like the way the water changes from one mood to another – from high waves on dark, stormy days, to tranquil ripples on sunny days. I still remember a night that I spent on a lonely beach with a few other girls. We brought blankets along and cooked our supper of tomato soup, bread, cheese and milk, over a driftwood fire. Then we curled up in our blankets for the night. It was strange and peaceful to be on that Island beach, far from the rest of humanity. The only sound was the damp night wind sighing in the eelgrass and the waves thundering on the flat, unbroken shore. I could not sleep for a long while, because I felt compelled to watch the procession of twinkling stars across the black night sky. I felt, somehow, very small and inconsequential in comparison to the endless space of sky, sand and sea. It is an inspiring feeling to be on the edge of the land. I think that the greatness of Nature is somehow healing to the spirit. After dealing with so many problems in world affairs it is comforting to think, for a change, that this world amounts to little more than a speck of dust in the unbelievably huge universe.

How right you are when you say one can not fully understand the seriousness of life when one lives in good conditions! From our snug, sunny little homes, from our complacent little towns it is so difficult to imagine that somewhere in the world, people are starving, somewhere people are homeless. Our main worry is about the high price of food, about a new car! I do not mean to be quite as sarcastic as I sound. It is only that history seems to flow past my door without affecting me, as a person. Perhaps when I get out of school and into the business world, that will change.

Take the last war, for instance. To me, it was as unreal as a fairytale. Food was scarer, to be sure, and the headlines in the newspapers gave daily accounts of the battles, but beyond a vague, cold fear that my home might be bombed or that someone I loved might be killed, I felt nothing. The newspapers and the radio bring the urgent matters of today to my attention, but since I do not see them or experience them, they are not real. When one has lived in a comfortable home all one's life it is hard to comprehend that other people live much differently. Of course we young people think seriously and with concern about present-day issues. I would like to plunge into the vital world, if I could, but I am young still, and I suppose that there will be time.

About our school system, I imagine that it is a great deal like yours, except that we have books. Education is compulsory for both boys and girls until the age of sixteen. One begins school at the age of five years, usually. Then one is in the First Grade. The first and earliest branch of school is called <u>Elementary</u>, and it includes from the first to sixth grades (a grade is a year of school.) Then comes <u>Junior High</u>, containing seventh to ninth grades. Then <u>Senior High School</u>, (where I am now) which runs from the tenth to twelfth grades. I am in the eleventh grade, which means my 11th year of schooling. After one graduates from High School, one is usually about seventeen years of age. Then one is free to begin the job of ones choosing, or to go on to a college or university for four years. This is what I hope to do. After college I will enter a job in the field of work in which I am most interested. I am not sure whether that will be commercial art or journalism (writing.)

A college education is a great advantage when one is searching for a job. Men and women are preferred if they have this background.

I, too, think that the religion is important for a civilization. If we would only follow some Christian precepts there would be no wars, I think. If only our churches would forget their small, technical differences and band together into a united faith, allowing for the differences in beliefs, I think that we would be a stronger nation. At present, we have in our hands the atom bomb, the weapon which could blow man from the face of the earth. Shall we use it for war or peace. When one considers the dread results of such a weapon, there can be but one answer. Why can't the nations forget their differences and work toward a common goal?! Why must we always distrust our neighbors?! If our faith in the goodness of mankind was sufficiently powerful, I believe that we could answer these questions.

There are so many things I want to ask you! How are your lives in your part of Germany directed? Do you live much as you did before the war? (I mean, aside from physical changes.) Have you any plans for your life after school? Is their much future for your youth? Do tell me about your home-town, as you said you would! What is the general (that is a very indefinite word, I'm afraid) opinion of America held by the people around you? Do you "worry" about Russia as many of us do?

I had not intended to write such a lengthy letter, but once I started it was difficult to stop. I await your next letter eagerly.

Bravo for your understanding of English. (If there is anything you do not understand in my writing, let me know so I may explain it.)

Sincerely,
Sylvia

TO *Hans-Joachim Neupert*

Monday 20 December 1948 ALS (photocopy) Smith College

Dec. 20, 1948

Dear Hans,

When your first letter arrived, I was on my Thanksgiving vacation, and when I saw it, I said "Ah, I must write Hans a long letter and tell him a lot!" But I did not sit down to write until today. Your second letter came in the mail this afternoon, and I was sad that you were so worried.

Of course you have said nothing to displease me! You could not displease me if you tried! As for your English, it is excellent. It is easy for me to write to you in my own language, but I admire you for doing so well in a foreign tongue.

Forgive me for not answering you so promptly. I will send this letter by airmail also so that you will receive it without delay.

I wish that I could give you a clearer detailed picture of our life. I imagine that it is, for the most part, similar to yours. Do you have any special dishes of food to eat? For breakfast most people eat eggs or oatmeal or cold cereal. In Germany do you have the same type of cold cereal? It is called by various silly names such as "Rice Krispies" and "Cheery Oats" and it always tastes the same – like little pieces of pressed hay or sawdust. When I read about the old-fashioned breakfasts I get a longing for them. The people had fish & potatoes and gravy as at a regular dinner, so you can imagine how much more they ate at a main meal. While a great deal of cooking here is tasteless, I am very fortunate to have an Austrian grandmother who cooks good European dishes for us. School is over now for the Christmas vacation, and a light, powdery snow has covered the earth. Already one may see the first Christmas trees light up with red, green, yellow, and blue bulbs and shining silver ornaments.

Down in the shopping district, all the stores are all aglow with brilliant lights, and at night I love to walk by and "window-shop." That is, to gaze in and pretend I could buy all that I would like.

Out of a loud-speaker, carols of Christmas pour forth into the cold night air, and the frosty little stars themselves seem to twinkle with delight. All over the country wide-eyed little children are eagerly awaiting the arrival of "Santa Claus" and his eight reindeer. On Christmas Eve the young ones hang up stockings on the mantlepiece of the fireplace and the next morning they awake to find them bulging with presents, fruit and candies.

<drawing of two stockings on a fireplace>

For myself, as the Christmas bells ring out across the moonlit snow, my thoughts will be with you, although my letter may not reach you for a while.

We call "snow-boots-driving" "skiing" in America. All through the winter people ski on the hillsides, and almost everyone enjoys this sport.

Our school vacations end on January 3rd, and then we begin to prepare seriously for the mid-year examinations. I only have exams in four subjects – English, third year Latin, second year French and third year math. The tests each last 1½ hours and are quite difficult.

You have no idea how much I enjoyed your picture. It was so nice of you to send me such a good one of you.

Everywhere I go babysitting, now, the children demand some stories of Santa Claus. Their child-like faith is really touching.

When I am through with college, I hope to get a job either on the staff of a newspaper or a magazine, as a correspondant, or in fashion design or book-illustrating or even as the secretary to some foreign dealer. Who knows – perhaps I may save enough to sail to Europe some day. Only this is one of my far off dreams!

The days of vacation speed by oh! so quickly. And then there is the long, drab winter with the steel-gray skies and deep snow, but at last spring will come, and that is something to look forward to in the long, dark winter days.

I moved to Wellesley when I was 10 years old, and have lived here for six years. Before this I lived at the sea side, and my childhood memories of that place are pleasant. Have you any brothers or sisters? I have one younger brother, as I have no doubt mentioned before.

I hope again that you will forgive me for replying so late. I am sending a small book of verse which has given me much pleasure, and I hope you will enjoy it.

Best wishes,
Sylvia

1949

TO *Hans-Joachim Neupert*

Sat. 29 Jan.–Sun. 6 Feb. 1949[1] ALS (photocopy), Smith College

Jan. 29, 1949

Dear Hans,

How entertaining your letters are! I enjoy reading them so much! I am very glad that you liked the little book. Have you read any of Stephen Vincent Bénet's stories or poems.[2] He is, I think, one of our greatest American writers, and certainly, one of my favorites!

The Christmas tree has been in American homes for over a century, now, and is a beloved custom at Christmas time. Many years ago, the early settlers in our nation did not know the symbol of the tree, and thought it a barbaric custom. But when one man cut down a pine tree and decorated it in spite of the angry citizens, the townspeople saw how beautiful the glowing candles and the fresh green boughs were, so they adopted the custom and it has been with us since then.

When I wrote of "Thanksgiving" I did not think to explain to you the origin of this American Holiday. If you are studying American History you probably know about the landing of the pilgrims at Plymouth rock in 1620. It was then winter, and the cold, barren, snow-swept land of America, the unknown continent, seemed strange and unfriendly. However, though a great part of the little band died of cold, a few friendly Indians taught the new settlers how to plant crops, and in that wintery season, about November, the "redskins" brought food – corn and meat for the hungry white-men. It was then that the settlers realized their good fortune, and bowed their heads to give thanks to God for their blessings. It is this day we set aside as a day of thanks-giving, and we celebrate by a holiday and a big meal, in remembrance of the food brought by the Indians.

Your weather in Germany is much like ours in America – we have had little snow, and the climate has been unseasonably warm. I have probably

1 – Dates supplied from internal evidence.
2 – American poet and writer Stephen Vincent Bénet (1898–1943).

told you that I have no skis, but I think that skiing is one of the most graceful sports. I have seen pictures of the skier, like a swooping bird, skimming down the snowy slopes.

I am in sympathy with you about "The German Italian Experience" paper, for I have just finished writing a twenty-five page thesis on "Mormonism,"[1] one of the unique religious sects in the United States. I am so glad you are studying American history! There are many parts which are colorful & fascinating!

I do not know the Jamesbourg Highschool. Do you know what state it is in?

How is it that you are so familiar with American terms for music? Even I am not too well acquainted with "Be-Bop." I like most classical music, especially the dreamy pieces of Chopin and Débussy. In fact I like music in general. Like you, I have not had much time to play the piano lately. I enjoy popular music – but I like slow dance tunes better than jazz. I can play a little Boogie-Woogie on the piano. Do you have that in Germany? It is a type of jazz, and yet it has a classical touch.

A third world war! How I dread the thought of it. Almost all my class mates are against all war, and hope only to promote peace all over the world. It is my belief that wars are disastrous & unnecessary, if only mankind would forget its petty struggles for wealth, land and power and devote its energies, not to scientific massacre but to the promotion of brotherhood the whole world over. I am in favor of encouraging a reverence for life. Life is sacred to me, and if only we could resolve our struggles & military combat in a peaceful discussion! A third world war would be a disaster from which humanity would never recover! Those few left (it would no doubt be an atomic war) would never be able to rebuild the world again, and our civilization (if we may presume to call it that) would be degraded and destroyed also.

Berlin – ah! I am not too well equipped to answer that question. Perhaps if all Europe could forgo sovereignty and combine into an European bloc, there would be more chance for peace. Switzerland, I think, is an example to follow. She has combined varied nationalities into a neutral state. Why could not Europe, & eventually the world, do the same thing? If nationalities mingled, French, German, American, Oriental, etc., in the process of a few million years we would have <u>one</u> human race – united under a just power of government . . . . But that is too idealistic, I'm afraid, and has a great many flaws.

1 – Probably Sylvia Plath, 'The Latter-Day Saints'; held by Lilly Library.

Anyway, American youth does not want to sacrifice its fittest young people on the bloody alters of another war. We have had enough of that. War is so irrational. The youngest, the strongest, the fittest are sent to be slaughtered, while the aged & crippled remain at home. If only more young people, aware of the vital hopes and the glowing promise of their lives, if only more of these could control our politics, then we might be in a better world. For instance, I think that corresponding, the way we are doing, is a great help toward peace. I consider you as a special friend, and I do not think of Germany as a cold, impersonal nation, but rather I think of Germany as made up of a lot of Hans-Joachims, all willing to be friends if only we will get to know them better.

You are so right about hope. It would be impossible to exist with out it. I know that I would be very unhappy if I had nothing to look forward to when I was feeling depressed.

I do like to dance very much, in fact we just had our class dance in-school last night.[1] It was formal and all the girls wore evening dresses & the boys wore tuxedos. I was at school all afternoon with some classmates putting up all the painted decorations which we'd done up around the gym. At night, with colored lights, balloons and ferns the school gym really looked charming.

I am enclosing a little folder that tells about a World Federalist Group which seems to have the right idea of world peace.

Write soon!
Sylvia.

TO *Irwin Edman*[2]

Tuesday 15 March 1949 TLS, Columbia University

March 15, 1949

Professor Irwin Edman
Columbia University
New York City, New York

Dear Professor Edman:

We the members of English 31, have read your article entitled "A Reasonable Life in a Mad World,"[3] which appeared in the March issue

1 – The Junior Prom was held on Sat. 5 February 1949; SP was on the Decorations Committee.
2 – American philosopher Irwin Edman (1896–1954).
3 – Edman, 'A Reasonable Life in a Mad World', *Atlantic Monthly* 183 (March 1949), 60–2.

of the Atlantic Monthly. Although yours is a logical analysis of modern man's dilemma, we do not feel that the solution which you offer is wholly adequate. In the hope that you will consider and evaluate our opinions, we should like to challenge a few of your statements.

Undeniably, part of the life of reason is the contemplation of the unchanged and the unchangeable in nature, for there is a healing, uplifting calm to be derived from nature. Indeed, there is a stability and an inexplicable order to the universe, but the point is man cannot by himself create a corresponding order in his own civilization.

Essentially, we human beings are limited. Our environment does not permit us to visualize the universal pattern of the world; the mind of no man is creative enough to comprehend the significance of the universe. Therefore, how can we rely on man alone?

Granted, you have wisely advocated the combination of stoicism, the pleasure principle, and hope. But what about the spiritual element? By this we mean the inner compulsion of every man to seek beyond himself for guidance. You mentioned nature; that is only part of the solution. We do not intend, by any means, to suggest that we encourage escape or oblivion in another world; nor do we uphold a blind beatific faith. No, none of these, but rather the recognition of a force, a creative intelligence, above mankind. By recognizing this omniscient power, man may view his problems and his goals in a less distorted relationship with the rest of the universe.

In order to reach a more perfect, a more reasonable, understanding of life, we must have an insight, an awareness of relative values. However, we cannot attain this state of discernment by using our narrow intellects alone, for we are not sufficient unto ourselves. When we acknowledge the divinity, of which we are a minute part, we may elevate ourselves spiritually, just as we do by observing nature. Then, and only then, will we attain that excellent philosophy: "a brave contemplation of what things are discoverably like and a resolute attempt to improve the lot of man in the conditions into which he finds himself born."

Sincerely yours,
Jeanne Woods[1]
Sylvia Plath

1 – Jeanne Woods Haile (1932–); B.A. 1954, Wellesley College; friend of SP from Wellesley.

TO *Hans-Joachim Neupert*

Thursday 14 April 1949 ALS (photocopy), Smith College

April 14, 1949

Dear Hans,

Thank you so much for the lovely Easter card which you sent me! I appreciated it so much.

It must be extremely difficult for you to study without any books – I find it hard enough to study with them! Today is our first afternoon of Easter vacation, and the whole lovely week stretches before me. I will practice tennis (I'm a terrible player, but I love the sport,) write some stories, and find more time to practice piano.

Speaking of music, I enjoy all of your German musicians' works. They are so well-liked here in America that we think of Beethoven, Handel, Mozart, and the rest, as old friends in music. I like the power of Beethoven – one of my favorites is the famous "Moonlight Sonata." Do you enjoy Débussy? He is one of my ideal composers – his music is so clear-cut and dreamy – Have you heard "La Mer," "La Fille aux Cheveaux de Lin," "Deux Arabesques," or "Claire de Lune"?

The talk about the end of the world reminds me of the stories of the revivals in America about one hundred years ago. Then, about fifty little religious sects sprang up throughout the states. The people were superstitious and believed in the deceit practiced by the leaders of these groups. Most of the factions lasted only a short time, but it was an era of emotion and "spiritual revelations." The head of one group claimed to know that the world would end in some days. His followers became so excited that they bought ascension robes and climbed upon the nearest hill to await Judgment Day, which, of course, never came!

Your class dances sound like fun. I, too, love to dance. About classes with boy and girls, I think that is by far the best, don't you? After all, we will be men and women together in the world when we grow up, so why not become accustomed to getting along with each other now?

Today is really the first day that spring has come. It is such a relief to see the faint sprouts of green leaves against the dark trees. The daffodils are all in bloom in our yard, and the air is sweet and earthy-smelling.

I can imagine how unsure you must feel, writing in English. I feel the same way about writing in French. It is like piecing together strange words and hoping that they will mean what you want to say. Of course there are a few expressions that are difficult to master, but I find your letters extremely interesting – and quite natural. Since you wish, I will point out a few phrases that we say a bit differently. Instead of "before some weeks," meaning past time, we are more likely to say "some weeks ago." And rather than "But it is here . . . we have no books," we might begin "But here." Instead of "the most of," just "most of" – instead of "in some days" = "in a few days." I had to try very hard to find any errors in your letter, and these small changes are the only ones that I can suggest. They will, perhaps, help your writing to sound even more natural.

What American writings do you especially like? I'm glad that the library has been opened up.

One of my special friends and I have decided to take advantage of the vacation and go on a painting trip together for one whole day. We will be loaded down with papers, paints, easels, water-jars and plates (to mix paint on) as well as a picnic lunch, but what does that matter? It's all for the sake of Art! (I might add that neither of us are very good artists, but we have such good times in spite of that fact!)

There is so much I want to know about Germany! Let's pretend I am going to come to visit you, and in your next letter, describe where you would meet me at the railway station, and what the country is like that we would travel over to get to your house, and then all the things we could do – like take hikes or swim, etc!

I would also know what your friends and classmates are like. Would you tell me about some of them, too?

I hope that Easter brings you happiness. Do write soon!

Best of luck,
Sylvia

P.S. Do you have big fat robins that come in the spring? There is one bold fellow eating a worm on our lawn right this minute!!!

S.

TO *Aurelia Schober Plath*

Monday 27 June 1949[1]

ALS with envelope on Oceanic Hotel, Isles of Shoals, letterhead, Indiana University

<u>Monday</u>

Dear Maman,

Obviously, the first thing you'll want to know is I'm fine! (No fever, because things go too fast to think about it.) I just <u>love</u> it here,[2] and I think everyone's heavenly, naturally. Nothing like a little salt air and the sort of guy who's sitting beside me to cure sunstroke, you know. I wrote to John[3] at 7:30 this A.M., but was too sleepy to be very witty. Time? What is the stuff, anyhow? I had a date arranged by dear old Ginny last night (Nick Safford[4] – a bellhop from Wellesley) but he's gone today and I've spent my day with a boy from Kentucky[5] – eating at noon & going to chapel & on walks & watching the baseball game. I don't think I would have met him unless we'd had a fire this A.M & part of the roof burned. Luckily no one was hurt, only scared. Hope <u>this</u> one lasts a day or so, but you meet so many new people every day. I'll write again. Send up some water – there's none to drink around here.

Love,
Sylvia

1–Date supplied from postmark.

2–SP was at the Star Island Unitarian Youth Conference.

3–John Suffern Hodges (1930–); dated SP 1949 and lived at 106 Dover Road, Wellesley, Mass. Hodges was a 1948 graduate of Phillips Academy in Andover, Mass., and had just completed his freshman year at Denison University in Granville, Ohio. After serving two years in the Army, Hodges graduated with a B.A. 1955, Denison University.

4–Nicholas Heath Safford (1932–), a classmate of SP's from Wellesley High School; B.A. 1954, Amherst College.

5–Dick Gilbert.

TO *Aurelia Schober Plath*

Tuesday 28 June 1949[1]

ALS with envelope on Oceanic Hotel, Isles of Shoals, letterhead, Indiana University

Tuesday

Dear Mum,

I hate to waste another 3¢ stamp on you, but I haven't time to go upstairs to get postcards. I just can't tell you all we've done (I played tennis today – (feeling perfect)) we had another dance tonite – a costume ball, and my darling roommate & a girl I "double-date" with (both Judys – and both sweet) dressed up as poison ivy & won 3rd prize or thereabouts – I'm so proud! We all dressed in green with wreathes of leaves in our hair – and we scratched – Tell me something personal in your postcards – I don't care about book reviews as much as you & the family. Today we went on cook's tour – it's such fun when you have someone (male, naturally) to go places with. Kentucky is still a constant state and I've got my fingers crossed. The girls are at least 2 to 1 boy, so you see it's pretty bad. – But I'm not worried yet. John Pollard is here – what an odd thing he is – my date was telling me a lot about him I didn't know.

I am on two wonderful workshops – the leaders matter alot and I've got Joe Gunde[2] for Personal Problems & a nice vivacious young thing for Recreation. I love everyone – but go mostly with the 2 Judys and Dick Gilbert (Kentucky) and a nice friendly guy[3] who sits at my table. I really don't need any sleeping pills by the time the day is over. The food is nothing to brag about. There goes the bell – more when we have time. –

Love
Me.

TO *Hans-Joachim Neupert*

Monday 4 July 1949

ALS (photocopy), Smith College

July 4, 1949

Dear Hans,

I think that in the future I will send my letters by "Luftpost" as you do, for then they will fly back and forth a great deal faster. I always

1 – Date supplied from postmark.
2 – In SP's 1949 diary, she spells his last name Giunta.
3 – According to SP's record of summer dates, 2 June–2 August 1949, this was Eddie Mason.

await your mail very eagerly, and read your letters with great delight.

How I enjoyed that little booklet you sent me! I have formed a picture of your Germany in my mind. The country must be so beautiful! Just so is our America.

I agree with you that one really must live in the foreign land to learn all the sounds and idioms. I feel I could learn French so much faster if I were surrounded by French-speaking people who could understand me only if I spoke their language.

We have completed final examinations and school is closed at last for the two summer months of July and August. How I look forward to the long days stretching ahead, even though I know they will fleet past too quickly. I am taking painting lessons this summer, so I go out driving every Wednesday morning with my teacher[1] in search of a suitable spot. Last week it was a group of houses reflected in a river. My watercolor sketches still look pretty messy, but I'm learning bit by bit. Someday when I'm better I will make one for you especially.

This is the first summer that I have not gone to camp. It is also the last summer I will have free – without a job, I mean. So I am going to make the most of it. Next school year is my last year in high school, so I will have to study very hard to get good marks for college. I will also be co-editor of our school newspaper,[2] which is a great deal of work. Therefore, I plan to have a real vacation at home these two months. This evening I went with a date to watch fireworks which celebrate our 4th of July holiday – our Independence Day as you probably know already. Everyone gathers in the town park to watch the colorful display after dark. We took a blanket and lay on our backs to watch the noisy explosions of rockets, bursting into red, green, blue and gold stars overhead. It was really breathtaking! There were fiery comets and blazing pinwheels of sizzling light, and firecrackers went off periodically with a series of sharp "pops!" There was ice-cream covered with chocolate to eat on sticks, and everybody was laughing together. Whenever an especially beautiful rocket went off against the black sky, blossoming out into burning bouquets of light, a huge sigh of awe would rise from the crowd of thousands as if it came from one throat. This is one of our favorite American holidays.

1–During the summer of 1949, SP studied watercolour painting with American painter Sophia Lewis Morrill (1889–1970); B.A. 1911, Vassar College; member of the Wellesley Society of Artists; instructor at Wellesley College.

2–*The Bradford*, student newspaper of Wellesley High School. Sylvia Plath and Frank Irish were co-editors, 1949–50.

Last week I had just about the most wonderful experience of my life – I went to a Unitarian religious conference on a small island[1] off the coast of Maine (perhaps you already know a bit about this one of the New England states.) There were 100 girls & sixty boys as well as numerous speakers attending the conference. Picture a small, rocky island in the middle of the ocean (well, almost the middle). There are no trees, only jutting expanses of stone cliffs where the surf dashes in ever changing shades of blue and green. The horizon is a circle of water all around. Everywhere you look, your eyes lift to the glorious blue sky – cloudless by day, star-studded by night. What a place! I came away even more determined that there is a magnificent power above us all – call it nature, or call it God – which is responsible for the vast beauty of heaven and earth. The view of land and sky is open to us all – no matter where we live or what we do. I have been very cynical, at times, but I cannot help but be awed by the huge glory of the painted sunsets, or the first rosy light of dawn across the ocean. In the morning we spent two hours out on the rocks in the sunlight listening to a speaker and discussing the topics we had chosen. There were about 10 different groups. Mine was called "Personal Problems," and here we talked over our troubles, and tried to help each other out. There was time for swimming before lunch, and afterwards we had another discussion group in the afternoon. After supper there was something planned for every evening – square dancing, a costume party (my roommate & I won 3rd prize – we came all dressed in green crowned with leaves as "poison ivy") stunt night. We also had movies. The last night was the gala occasion – we could stay up until two in the morning dancing, or singing, or sitting on the wide verandah of the old building and talking. By this time, everyone had made special friends, and so as the fated hour drew near, I felt a little touch of sadness. The boy I was with lived in New Jersey (quite far away) so we knew that we would probably never meet soon again.[2] We sat out on the porch and watched the moon sink lower and lower until it was time to go in. Everyone was going on the early boat the next day so there were many sad farewells. I must confess that I shed a few tears.

But here I am at home again and my friends here are once more taking the place of those I will never see again.

1 – Star Island, Isles of Shoals, off Portsmouth, New Hampshire. SP attended the American Unitarian Youth Conference, 25 June–2 July 1949 held at the Oceanic Hotel owned by the Star Island Corporation.

2 – According to SP's record of summer dates, 2 June–2 August 1949, this was Hank Glover.

You asked about high school – there are 600 people in our building (a very modern, beautiful place, with broadcasting systems from room to room) and about 150 in my grade – boys and girls.

Your trip sounds lovely – I would very much like to come by bike – it's just about the best way to see a beautiful country.

As for me, I have not yet been to Yellowstone, but it is one of the best spots of natural beauty here. What are your projects for this summer? And for your next school year? Write soon!

Best wishes,
Sylvia

TO *Hans-Joachim Neupert*

Wednesday 24 August 1949 — ALS in greeting card[1] (photocopy), Smith College

August 24, 1949

Dear Hans,

I am sitting in my back yard, and as I write to you, a dry yellow leaf drifts down from the trees above my head. This has been a perfect summer, but ever since our last rainfall there has been a sharpness in the air that fortells autumn. (Here, in New England we have had an abnormally dry season. The grass is all dry and brown and the flowers wilt and die on the stems.)

As always, in the few weeks before school starts (September 8), I feel wistful and nostalgic. It is a bit sad to be caught between two worlds. When school begins, life will be entirely different. All the good friends that I have made this summer will go back to their respective homes, and I will miss them in spite of my school-friends.

This has been my last summer of really carefree youth – next summer I will get some sort of job and earn money in preparation for college. I would like to be able to live on the college campus but unless some miracle happens, I will consider myself fortunate if I win a scholarship, although I have to live at home. Wellesley has a very wealthy class of people dwelling here, and in my school life almost all my acquaintances come from well-to-do homes. Naturally, their only worry is to get good

1–Printed by White & Wyckoff, Holyoke, Massachusetts; entitled *Scenic Notes* (206–9), featuring a sketch by Stephen Hamilton of rolling hills with two pine trees and a white house in the foreground.

marks so their parents can send them any where. With me it is the other way – I have the high marks, but a sad lack of funds. In this land of wonderful, unbelievable opportunities, however, I can work for the money-awards set up to aid school-children. If a person has talent and ability, there are many situations open to him.

I have tried to improve my health and gain weight in these last two months, because I work so hard in the winter that I am usually run-down by the end of the year. I have biked regularly to and from the tennis courts almost every day. This is my first season at tennis and already it is my favorite sport. Of course I am not very good, yet, but several excellent young men have played with me, and under their instruction I have rapidly improved. I live outdoors as much as I can, taking hikes, canoeing and swimming. (Unfortunately the dry season has made our lakes stagnant and scummy, so I have not swum too often.) Yesterday I was driven out into the country with a very good friend of mine. We climbed a water tower[1] and stood up on top, looking over a sea of green leaves to the hills beyond, melting away bluer & bluer into the distance. The wind blew the clouds over our heads and the sunlight was clean and warm. Nestled in the valleys we could see the roof tops of neighboring towns. (like the view on the front.)

<drawing of a water tower> In order to reach the top of the tower, it was necessary to clamber up a leg of it, crossed with zig-zagging metal, and then to worm one's way to the ladder through a treacherous maze of iron bands. I am unreasonably afraid of falling or letting go in high places where I can look way down, but I would not admit this fear to John,[2] who made his way easily & swiftly to the top. By some good fortune I reached the observation walk without giving voice to my fears. If I once conquered them, I would never be afraid of heights again. Well, that was all right, but when we had looked our fill at the view, I stared down at the narrow metal bars and my knees turned to jelly – they refused to move. I could never bring myself to climb down. I just closed my eyes and wished in vain to be on "terra firma" once more. After reasoning firmly with me, John persuaded me to put my foot over the rail and swing down to the girders by my hands. Once I did this, the rest was easy. I ran lightly down with a feeling of great exhilaration, for I had conquered myself.

1–According to SP's diary and scrapbook, this was Dean's Tower.

2–John Arthur Hall (1930–   ); B.A. 1953, Williams College; dated SP in 1949.

I have written a few stories and poems this summer and sent them to various magazines. As usual, they all come back home again with a rejection slip attached. Sometimes, if I am lucky, I get a note of encouragement from the editor. Still, in spite of my continual failures, I will keep trying.

This evening I am playing a tennis match at the courts. I was a bit silly to enter the annual summer tournament[1] since this is my first season playing. The girls that I have played and beaten are really not too good, but this one is small, well-built, and about 21. I expect to lose but I hope I can lose by a respectable score – and give her a fight. There will be people watching, and I have to overcome my nervousness of an audience but quickly! I am really scared – of what exactly I do not know – it's only a game after all! I must talk firmly to myself and be convinced that it is not a matter of life and death or lifelong disgrace if I lose! By the time you get this letter I will be involved in something else and tennis will be far behind me – but the six long hours until I play that game! Ah – it seems eternity. I can't wait till this time tomorrow when it will be all over.

Sometimes, when you are by yourself for a while, do you ever wonder little things? Like why you are you and not someone else . . . it sounds silly to say it, but it is absorbing when you think of it. I mean, why couldn't I have been born into the body of a cripple, instead of my own . . . or into a family in another country? I wonder, too, what makes us like certain things and fear others? Is it our environment that accustoms us to our surroundings, or some inherited partiality that comes down from our parents?? I think that many of our opinions are not really our own, but rather ideas that we have unconsciously borrowed from other people. For instance, when I meet someone here who has a German background, I immediately say to myself inside, "Hmmm, must be a nice person." I have a partiality – for no good reason except that I, too, have a german background. Then, also, I do not think I got my fear of high places just all by myself. I have often heard my mother speak of her fright of heights, so probably I unconsciously cultivated that fright in myself. What I am trying to say is – I do not believe that children are naturally afraid or full of hate. I think that they can be trained to love. Naturally, all of us have a few inherent animal instincts – self-preservation, for example, but we are not born with hatred or killing instinct . . . are we?? That is one of the reasons I think wars are totally against the principle of humanity. It is entirely against reason to kill the best and the healthiest – why not

1–SP participated in the 1949 Tennis Tournament at the Hunnewell Playfield courts, Wellesley. SP lost the semi-final match to Florence Santospago (1927–).

the aged cripples, if we must kill . . .? enough for fumblings in a wide darkness . . .

Do write soon, your friend,
Sylvia
BEST WISHES –

TO *Hans-Joachim Neupert*

Tuesday 10 October 1949 ALS (photocopy), Smith College

Tuesday
October 10, 1949

Dear Hans –

How nice to get your letter once again! That trip you took with your class sounds simply fascinating! And what a beautiful description you gave me of the river-side at night. We saw some colored slides of the ruins in large German towns last Sunday, and they were a sad contrast to the jolly story in your letters. Is it true that many bodies are still buried under the crumbled rubble of the large buildings?

My English teacher (a very intelligent and thoroughly remarkable man) plans to take a group of young people to Europe this summer – not on a "conducted tour" which jumps from the most obvious highlights of one country to another, but rather on a bike trip through the countries themselves whereby the students will gain an understanding of the way the people really live. Unfortunately, all my small savings must be hoarded toward college expenses, so I can not afford to make this wonderful journey.

I know just how you feel about going to a dance during school time. The boy whom I "go around" with,[1] as we say over here, is away at college, but he did not leave until after I had started school. Although he is nice to be with, it was a rather difficult time for me, because he expected me to stay up at night and spend all my hours with him rather than on my studies! But I survived, and it is so much more convenient to write to him!

As to my poems and stories, I am quite at a loss about what to send you. I wish I could be there when you read anything I send you to explain just what I was trying to express. The poems are all very different, expressing various moods, many of which I no longer can feel, but I have selected

1–Robert George Riedeman (1930–2014); B.A. 1952, M.S. 1954, botany, University of New Hampshire; dated SP, 1949–50.

a few for you – every one is written in traditional rhyme except "City Streets." Perhaps if you read them aloud you will get more from them. I do not know what they will mean to you – which you like & which you don't, but I'll give you a brief idea of what "inspired" each one:

White Phlox – Here I tried to express the feeling that one moment could last forever which I experienced while sitting before a vase of flowers in a quiet house.

Gone is the River – a contrast between the frenzied heat of the hurried city and the timeless peace of summer in the country.

The Farewell – a feeling of nostalgia just as the last snows were melting into spring – a vague lonesomeness.

The Stranger – A feeling that I was near to the answer of some question, but that the truth (the Stranger) was never found through my own inability to grasp it.

City Streets – The dull finality of a rainy day in the city –

I do hope you will evaluate these attempts of mine!

My birthday, in case you do not know, will probably be over by the time you receive this. It is October 27th, and I will be 17. I accept your congratulations in advance with many thanks!

I feel a strong kinship for anything German. I think that it is the most beautiful language in the world, and whenever I meet anyone with a German name or German traits, I have a sudden secret warmth. Austria too, I love! Johann Strauss waltzes always make me feel like shedding happy tears.

Here are some books you might enjoy!

Boston East The Late George Apley – John Marquand
Main Street / Arrow Smith – Sinclair Lewis
West My Antonia – Willa Cather
Poems of Robert Frost
Plays by Eugene O'Neill: Strange Interlude, Great God Brown, Emperor Jones
Civil War Gone With The Wind – Margaret Mitchell

All these are very worthwhile – expressive of various sections & eras of American culture.

Write soon!
All my best wishes –
your good friend
Sylvia

<enclosures>

Sylvia Plath
Age 16
Wellesley, Mass.

White Phlox

From the silver vase
White phlox petals fall;
Silence floods the parlor
And fills the narrow hall.
The only sound's a clock,
Ticking on the wall.

Is there naught to measure thought
Save the ticking of the clock,
And the fitful drift of white
Petals from a withered stalk?

Is the house asleep?
Are the tenants gone?
That the clock and I
Keep our watch alone?
Are we the only ones to mark
The petals falling in the dark?

The present moment seems
That it will ever be;
Can the fall of a blossom
Take eternity?

Sylvia Plath
Age 16
Wellesley, Mass.

Gone is the River

The heat of the noonday
Lies heavy upon the city.
It rises in waves from the sidewalks;
From the sweltering steel and the sunbaked brick.
The buildings are steeped in the merciless glare.
It is hot, hot everywhere.

(The earth is soft with wet green moss;
Blue dragonflies dart where the sunbeams quiver;
A breeze murmurs drowsily through the tall grass,
And willows flaunt their leafy parasols
All along the river.
A blackbird twitters, low and sweet,
And the water is cool on my dusty feet.
Oh, I could stay in the shade by the river
And listen to the song of the water forever.)

But the river is gone that was once so pretty,
And the heat of the noonday blankets the city.

Sylvia Plath
Age 16
Wellesley, Mass.

The Farewell

Oh, the sun beats down on the dusty town,
And a little breeze is sighing;
But in the street there's the patter of feet
        And the sound of someone crying.

Oh, the tulips blow in a crimson row,
And it's spring, there's no denying;

But in the lane there's the rustle of rain
And the sound of someone crying.

Oh, the woods are green, and April's queen,
And the tattered clouds are flying;
But in the shade where the snow has stayed
There's the sound of someone crying.

Sylvia Plath
Age 16
Wellesley, Mass.

The Stranger

He tapped upon my pane last night
As he went by,
But, being proud, I did not heed.
Not I.

He passed again when snows lay deep
Beneath the moon;
I heard him whistle to himself
A tune.

Once yet, a third time, he drew near
My bolted door.
He called my name and waited as
Before.

It was so late when I arose
He'd gone away.
And oh, I wish I'd asked him if
He'd stay!

Sylvia Plath
Age 15
Wellesley, Mass.

CITY STREETS

The dreary wetness of the rainy streets;
The doleful drops that fall forlornly from the shingled roofs;
The slim, black slipperiness of a tree
Gleams chill and cold as the wind whines by.

A yellow fog slinks low along the ground
And clings to the dingy brick walls of the tenements
that crowd by the gutter.
A damp newspaper somersaults along with the wind
And then succumbs on the flat pavement, lonely, left behind.

Blue spirals of smoke curl out of the sooty factory chimneys.
A lean gray cat sulks around a rubbish heap,
Seeking food, yet finding none.

These are the wan, gray shreds of the tattered day.

TO *Hans-Joachim Neupert*

c. Saturday 26 November 1949[1] ALS in greeting card (photocopy),[2] Smith College

Dear Hans,

Hello! How are you? I thought I'd send you a note of greeting and wish you a Merry Christmas and a Happy New Year!

Much has happened since I last wrote you. I am in the midst of my last year in high school and my life is very happy. I am writing this card during the Thanksgiving vacations . . . you know, celebrating the good fortunes of the Pilgrims so many years ago. I have to study especially hard this year, as we have our long exams next spring which determine whether or not

1–Date supplied by ASP.
2–This letter is written on a Fravessi-Lamont card with the printed greeting 'May the real Happiness of Christmas / be with you always.'

we get into college. I wish you could see my room now – I have hung up on the walls all the best drawings I have done, and it looks quite nice now. This year I am editor of our high school newspaper (4 big pages) which comes out six times a year. No sooner do we get one issue published, then there is another to start working on.

You may be interested to know that I have another 30 page term paper to do for English this year, and I have chosen as my subject Thomas Mann! Any advice you could give me about this great German writer would be a big help. Our English teacher, as I have no doubt often told you, is an extraordinary man. I like him so – he does not try to indoctrinate us with ideas whatsoever, but is continually striving to get us to speak for ourselves and think also for ourselves. This summer he is conducting a European tour for 15 students from high school. I would have given anything to sign up – but $800 was too much to pay – I could not afford it. So I am very wistful, thinking that perhaps I could have seen you as the group passed through Germany. They are going to see the passion play, visit the music festival at Salzburg, cruise down the Rhine, and do all sorts of other wonderful things.

Let me hear from you soon –
Best wishes,
your friend, Sylvia

1950

TO *Hans-Joachim Neupert*

Monday 2 January 1950 ALS (photocopy), Smith College

January 2, 1950

Dear Hans,

How I admire you for writing so well in English! I wish I could do the same in your language, but alas, I must fumble along in my own. At these times I wish that there were ways of transmitting ideas to you by a purer method instead of just words. How much easier it would be to understand someone's thoughts without having first to transpose them into a language! I think that then there would be less misunderstanding.

We have read in our magazines about the government in West Germany. I would like to discuss it further with you in my next letter.

Over the holidays, which today come to a close, I have gone to many dances with a friend of mine who is home from the university. I told him about you, for he, too, is one of these rare people who likes to exchange ideas. I am so tired of all the young girls here who think of nothing but party dresses and of boys who care for nothing but money and pretty faces. It is a relief to find someone who will talk about ideas of life and religion with one. I think that spiritual companionship is very necessary in a world where so much is superficial – and so few attractions are genuine.

If you could attend some of the parties! Of course, in a community where most boys use the "family car" to take girls places (movies, dances, etc.) there is much more opportunity for social gatherings. But after awhile such parties become so meaningless! There is always loud laughter and gay chatter and cigarette smoke filling the room. And always the same empty faces with painted smiles. And all the noise and music can not cover up the emptiness that lies beneath. Why must people try to fool themselves by thinking that money, clothes and cars are so important? Are they afraid of facing their souls? Perhaps they unconsciously realize that they can never reach spiritual perfection and must try to get something they can reach . . . something concrete and material.

But every day the inner world of our minds and souls is being invaded. Every home usually has a radio. True, it keeps us in contact with the world . . . but there is so much worthless drama and poor music that comes over the airwaves to hypnotize those who are too lazy to think for themselves. And television! It has become the goal of the poorest family to own a television set . . . to sit around a screen and watch crude vaudeville shows and baseball and football which are a national craze. It is so easy to shut off thought . . . to be lulled into a dreamy, semiconscious state to these entertainments which numb our creative intelligence. I would much rather read a book and have the pictures and images made in my own mind than to have someone else think for me. I believe that everyone must think for himself – and imagine for himself. Why live if we are just an echo and a reflection?

Forgive me for being so vehement! I wander on and on. But there are so many things which disturb me. I can't just sit back and take them calmly. I must cry out against them. And I take advantage of your patience by doing so. I wish you would also reveal to me your joys and your angers.

Today it rains. Yesterday it rained. We have had no snow all winter, except once in November. How I long for spring! But now I must work for my college exams and my term paper . . . . I await your next letter eagerly –

Best wishes,
Sylvia

TO *Hans-Joachim Neupert*

Monday 20 February 1950 ALS (photocopy), Smith College

February 20, 1950
Monday

Dear Hans,

How thoughtful of you to send me all that writing about Thomas Mann! It will be very helpful to me since I don't have to turn in my paper until April. Your letter gets to me in about 10 days when you send it "via air mail" . . . I think it is quite wonderful that my thoughts can go to you across sea and land in such a short time, don't you?

I will write you later about the dates that my student friends will visit Oberammergau. I don't know it just now.

This week we have vacation. But for me, it will mean more studying, for I have college Board exams in less than a month, and I must read many History, French and English books before then. Those are the important exams which tell whether or not we get accepted into college. I have to get good marks if I am to get a scholarship.

Last week we had our first big snowstorm of the year, and today I am sitting downstairs in the dining room, writing to you. Outside the sun is shining brightly on the blinding white snow, and the sky is a brilliant windswept blue. Oh, how cold it is! The wind is shrieking and wailing around the corners of the house, and the floorboards are creaking. It is good to be warm inside the house. However, I think that after I finish writing you I shall put on my winter jacket and mittens and walk into the woods for a little while. I like to battle the cold winds.

Tell me, what do you think of the U.S. producing hydrogen bombs? Have you heard anything about it? If so, do let me know your ideas. A friend of mine and I wrote a letter of protest to a newspaper concerning the new bomb.[1]

This is my first day home for three days. Last Friday I packed my suitcase to go to a winter carnival at the University of New Hampshire. Perhaps you can find it on a map of the United States. It is one of the states above Massachusetts.

On Friday evening there was a formal dance,[2] with colored streamers and balloons for decorations. Saturday we went to watch ski and toboggan events, while in the evening we went out to diner with two other couples, and then to a dance hall called the "Stardust" in Maine.[3] I took the train home on Sunday with another girl. We were both very sleepy, so as she dozed, I stared out of the window at the countryside speeding past. The afternoon was shading into twilight, and in the west hung a red ball of sun in a smoky gray sky. The dirty, sooty houses along the railroad track had a bleak, ugly, cheerless look, and the dingy, snowy fields were very bare and lonely. In spite of this, the barren sadness of the landscape had a strange fascination for me. Do you understand what I mean? Sometimes cheerless places have more appeal to the heart than a scene of all pretty sunshine and flowers.

At any rate, I was soon in Boston, carrying my heavy suitcase, which seemed to get heavier every minute. On the way home in the bus I watched the bright lights sparkling in the frosty air – and here I am, with only memories of a lovely time. It is as if it were a dream, now, and I begin to wonder if I imagined that I went away.

1 – Sylvia Plath and Perry Norton, 'Youth's Plea for World Peace', *Christian Science Monitor*, 16 March 1950, 19.

2 – The 29th Carnival Ball.

3 – Warren's Stardust Inn was in Kittery, Maine.

Sometimes I wish there were one universal language, so that everyone would understand everyone else. How many new friends we would have! . . . across the world!

I will say "good-bye" until your next letter –

Your friend,
Sylvia

TO *Hans-Joachim Neupert*

Tuesday 30 May 1950 ALS (photocopy), Smith College

May 30, 1950

Dear Hans,

How impatient you must be with me for not writing until now – but so much has happened in the last month – and I have so much to tell you.

Our high school days end in a week with our graduation ceremony. I cannot believe that I have arrived at the end of 12 years of school! But the most wonderful thing has happened---after months of suspense and exams I was notified that I was accepted at Smith College at Northampton, in the northern corner of Massachusetts. Naturally I could not go unless I got a large scholarship, but the college voted me a sufficient amount---so next fall I'll be able to pack my things and be off to another four years of school. Of course I'll have to resist the temptation of college parties in order to keep my marks up! But, even so, the thought of it is delightful.

My Thomas Mann paper went over well. Our teacher of English decided to have each of us give an hour's oral report instead of doing a paper so that the whole class could benefit by our research. I enjoyed my reading in Thomas Mann very much, and plan to do more this summer. My two favorite books were <u>Buddenbrooks</u> and <u>Der Zauberberg</u> (where the two brothers are named Hans and Joachim!) Perhaps you would be interested to know that I read to the class the part of your letter about Mann's last visit to Germany---and the students enjoyed it very much!

Of all the luck, I have a job this summer to help me with my college expenses this year. I didn't especially want to work indoors (I love the sunshine and the country air), and jobs were scarce. But finally I obtained one after my own heart. It is working on a farm in a nearby town.[1] I will be working in the fields and in the greenhouses---rain or shine. I imagine that the first few weeks will be hard on my poor muscles, but I hope to get

1–Lookout Farm, South Natick, Mass. SP worked there in the summer of 1950.

accustomed to the work soon and end the season tan and healthy. I will bike over and back every day. How does this sound to you?

I would appreciate it very much if you'd send me a photo of you again – you mentioned that you'd had some taken. I'm not sure if I sent you the last photo of me – it's small, of just my head. If I did not already send it, let me know, and I will enclose it in my next letter! <drawing of SP's head>[1]

As I write, I am seated in the back yard in the hot sun. This is the first nice day we've had this spring. May has been a cold, rainy month. Now the air is thick with heat, and no breeze comes to relieve the humid rays of the sun.

You may be amused to know that I feel my German background very strongly. I noticed a sort of patriotic pride when I read Mann.

We've been hearing much about the F.D.J.[2] In fact pages in our news magazines were devoted to pictures of them. Did you see them? I was amazed to see how like regular children---my own school mates---they looked. What a pity that youth cannot unite. We're all working for the same thing – peace & prosperity, but we don't seem to be able to work together.

That's all for now, my friend. Write soon –

Best wishes,
Sylvia

TO *Edward Cohen*[3]

Sunday 6 August 1950 TLS, Indiana University

August 6

Dear Eddie

My first sneaking suspicion on receiving your letter was that you spend you spare time sending out scintillating notes to all "Seventeen"

1–This self-portrait is similar to the photograph SP submitted to the Smith College publication *Who's Who in 1954*.

2–Freie Deutsche Jugend (Free German Youth), then an official youth organization in East Germany.

3–Edward M. Cohen (1928–2008); SP's correspondent from Chicago, Illinois. Cohen and SP corresponded from 1950 until 1954 and met during SP's spring vacations in 1951 and 1952. There are very few letters from SP to Cohen. The few there are may have been typed by Cohen and sent to SP while he retained the originals. One of Cohen's wives destroyed SP's letters. There are many letters from Cohen to SP held by Lilly Library.

contributors[1] while chuckling, "MY, what a thrill I'll give the little darlings." However, brushing this nagging thought aside, I decided to be honest and admit that your letted did appeal to me, or rather to my ego. So, accepting the adequate chaperonage of 1500 miles, here I am.

You asked for particulars. I live in a six room white house in what would be called a suburban environment. My father is dead; my mother teaches. I have a kid brother. I am going to enter college as a prospective English major this fall. Since I am surprisingly bad at describing myself, I think you have enough integrity to read between the lines. English majors are noted for their integrity.

I don't know just what you would like to learn about me, so I shall just sprinkle this with anything that comes to mind. You see, all I know about you is that you are impulsive, extremely entertaining and that you have a writing technique. As for me, I like to write. And I am determined to write well. After receiving over fifty rejection slips from various magazines, I finally got an acceptance from "Seventeen". Other stories which I considered better, less trite, less syrupy, came home with those horribly polite little slips. I would be delighted to have a critic. Corresponding with an English major interests me. So if you will let down your little wall of polished humor and permit me to know you, I will be glad to reciprocate.

This summer I am working on a truck farm in a neighboring town. It is My First Job, and I'm firmly convinced I couldn't have done better. A ten mile bike trip plus an eight hour day picking beans, loading radish crates and weeding corn six days a week is hardly relaxation, but the people I work with---Negroes, Displaced Persons, and boys and girls my own age---are worth the low pay. I'm up at six, in bed by nine, and very grimy in between. But I just smile when my white collar acquaintances look at me with unbelievable dismay as I tell them about soaking my hands in bleach to get them clean.

I would like very much to read some of your stories, so if you will send me samples of your writing I will do the same.

I too will be peering into the mailbox during the next few weeks.

One last shot . . . how in the name of heaven did you know I live at 26 Elmwood Road?

Sincerely
Sylvia Plath

P.S. On considering your letter more carefully I am even more skeptical than I was at first. I consider my story not far from the usual "Seventeen"

1–Sylvia Plath, 'And Summer Will Not Come Again', *Seventeen* 9 (August 1950), 191, 275–6.

drivel. Why is it that my particular brand of drivel rates such subtle flattery? Have you a long standing bet with Ernest Hemingway on the gullibility of would-be female writers? At least I deserve a commission or something. Please set me straight. I was about to send you some of my writing, but have decided to reserve it until I see some of yours. Now you know that my nature is far from sweet and trusting.

Another thing . . . what college are you an English major at?

S.

TO *Edward Cohen*

Friday 11 August 1950 — TLS (incomplete), Indiana University

August 11,

Dear Eddie,

Hello again! You guessed it, I'm back for more. And indeed, after your last--er--shall we say epistle, I should find it rather difficult to resist such a magnetic correspondant. Ah, yes, it's amazing what 1500 miles, a writing technique and long eyelashes can do. Seriously, though, I wasn't aware that anyone quite like you existed. Oh, I've known my share of intellectuals who were fascinating when it came to discussing evolution and destiny, but who didn't know the left foot from the right on a dance floor . . . and then the big brawny lettermen who used one word to describe every conceivable situation. But never, in my seventeen (almost eighteen) short years of experience, have I come across such an absorbing combination of characteristics rolled into one. (By now you are probably hiding modestly in your waste basket, so I'll look the other way while you crawl out. In fact I'll even begin another paragraph.)

It appears that you like frankness. Well, I can serve up plenty of that little commodity. I was just about to follow your lead and start off by plungiing into a list of external characteristics when I remembered that you have already had the profound misfortune to see a picture of me. I have enough vanity to believe that I have changed considerably since that was taken. How about a few statistics not visible? I'M tall, tipping the yardstick at five feet eight; slender (this morning's breakfast of steak, fried potatoes and apple pie not adding an ounce); tan enough so that women tap my shoulder on the beach: "Podden me, miss, but what sun tan oil do you use?" None, lady, but forty eight hours in the blazing sun per week does wonders. I have light brown hair, on the blondish side in the summer, and dark brown eyes. Top this off by a mercurial disposition and there I am. A red-blooded American girl. (Do I hear strains of the national anthem in the background?)

Ice cream and pickles are my dish. Perhaps it's because that concoction describes my own character rather well. I like to think of myself as original and unconventional. (Unfortunately, several thousand other girls in the United States like to think the same thing.) At any rate, I didn't emerge from the awkward stage until a couple of years ago . . . a lot later than the average girl, and during that period when my little pals were trying out their first formals, I was reading Brave New World, by Huxley and doing self-portraits in pencils. Noble as that may sound, it didn't compensate . . . then. Now, as I look back, I'm darn glad I had a hard time. Maybe you don't know how it is not to be accepted in a group of kids because you're just a little too individual. Shyness, in their terminology is conceit, good marks signify the horror of horrors . . . a brain. No doubt this all sounds oozingly pathetic, but it's one of the reasons that I'm the way I am. I'm sarcastic, skeptical and sometimes callous because I'm still afraid of letting myself be hurt. There's that very vulnerable core in me which every egoist has . . . and I try rather desperately[1] not to let it show.

Then I grew up, and just like it says in Seventeen,[2] You Too Can Be A Party Girl. So there were boys all of a sudden, and I've forgotten what it was like not to have some guy in the kitchen[3] eating mother's cookies and discussing the World Series with my brother. (I've gone babysitting of Bob Elliot,[4] but I wouldn't know a batting average if I saw one.) My biggest trouble is that fellows look at me[5] and think that no serious thought has ever troubled my little head. They seldom realize the chaos that seethes behind my exterior. As for the who am I? what am I? angle . . . that will preoccupy me till the day I die.

If I tried to describe my personality I'd start to gush about living by the ocean half of my life, being brought up on Alice in Wonderland, and believing in magic, for years and years. Maybe a little bit about my background would shed a ray of light on the subject. I'm of German-Austrian descent. My late father was a college professor. Even wrote a book on Bumblebees (MacMillan, 1934) and countless scientific articles.

1 – 'I try rather ~~hard~~ desperately' appears in the original.

2 – 'just like ~~Cinderella~~ it says in *Seventeen*' appears in the original.

3 – 'some ~~fellow~~ guy in the kitchen' appears in the original.

4 – Robert Irving Elliott (1916–66), played Major League Baseball for the Boston Braves, 1947–51.

5 – 'is that ~~people~~ fellows look at me' appears in the original.

My brother, a scholarship boy at Exeter, takes after him. I'm more subjective than objective, and take after my mother. By the way, I'll be starting my freshman year on scholarship at Smith this fall. I

I've touched on the social and statistical side. Now for religion. I don't go to church much, because I'm a firm believer that the individual has to figure out his own purpose, his own destiny. I don't like the idea of salvation being spooned out to those too spineless to think for themselves. I suppose I could be labeled an atheist, but I've a great respect for life and for the potentialities of man. Sounds flowery, doesn't it. But I am pretty much disgusted with human behavior most of the time. I too could write satirical little essays on such subjects as the Unknown Soldier, Christmas and polygamy. One last note, I'm Unitarian by choice.

There are so many incidents I could tell you about, so many people I would like you to meet. Up at the farm there's Ilo,[1] a good-looking blonde from Estonia who wants to go to New York to be an artist. He's studied in Europe and just came over here this spring . . . and tries so hard to catch on to all our american expressions. Out in the strawberry field we were talking about German writers, and he suddenly burst out You like Frank Sinatra, ja? He is so sendimendal, so romandic, so moonlight night." And then there's Robert, the negroe who ran away with his wife's pay and came haome from Bost n the next mornig at five with a taxi bill of $8 and very v ry inebrieated

<the rest of the letter is missing>

TO *Hans-Joachim Neupert*

Saturday 12 August 1950 ALS (photocopy), Smith College

August 12, 1950

Dear Hans-Joachim,

How thoughtful of you to send me the lovely postal card from the Passion Play. And then the nice letter. I hope that we will always be able to keep writing to each other. Perhaps when both of us are old and gray we shall still be sending letters. But I would like so much to see you some day. We get letters from our group in Europe, and I feel very sad that I had not money enough to go with them. They are having such wonderful times.

1–Ilo Pill (1917–2012), an Estonian refugee; dated and corresponded with SP, 1950–4. Pill immigrated in March 1950.

My only secret hope is that I shall do well enough in college to be sent to spend my third year in Europe.

My job this summer is quite hard for one who is used to sitting and studying all year instead of doing heavy physical work. I like being out in the sun, though, and the farm is on a hill where you can see the blue distance from the fields. It is good to be working with the earth. The pay is not much, but the people I work with are very interesting. There are several displaced persons. One from Estonia who wishes to be an artist, and one from Poland. They came over here this spring and speak English quite well, considering the short time they have been here.

Then there is the old, weather-beaten farm worker who tells us funny stories. Only most of them are not at all humorous, but one must laugh, and he is pleased.

I pick strawberries, beans, radishes, spinach, peas, and I weed other vegetables. The summer has gone so fast. I work six days a week, am up at six in the morning and so tired that I go to bed about nine. I have no time or energies for the gay parties I attended last summer when I did not work. I wish sometime that one did not have to think of money but could do all the wonderful things, like traveling, without it.

As for the Korean situation, I feel ill every time I read about it. On the farm they are always talking about war, and I look at the sunny blue sky, the green leaves, the tan young boys working, and I think, what fools are men to fight when there is so much in nature to live for already. We are using our own men to fight for Korea, a little piece of land, and the whole thing seems so futile. Of course the leaders say that once we let Russia advance a little she will feel she can run over the world, and that must not happen. But there was a picture in the newspaper of a young Marine, crying as his train left, for he was being sent over. There is nothing brave or heroic about this war. What are we fighting for? For nothing. Against communism. That word, communism, is blinding. No one knows exactly what it means, and yet they hate everything associated with it. One thing I am convinced of: you can't kill an idea. You can kill men, but an idea springs up in people's minds and grows there unseen, and you can't get rid of it. Another thing: war isn't "human nature", not if you're fed and clothed and peace-loving. When I think of my younger brother, with his love of life, even in small animals, I would hate the government that put a gun in his hands and told him to kill men. Yet that is what is happening. My only hope is that the great horror of the atom bomb will be great enough to prevent such a terrible war. That the A-bomb was ever dropped seems like a sin to me. Perhaps you smile and say, what a silly girl. She does not know how a boy feels about fighting. But I think of you, of my brother, of my school friends, strong and healthy. I cannot picture any of you, crippled, maimed, dead. I like people, everybody. And war to me seems so terrible that it is absurd. Like little children playing with fire crackers. But the American children who have never seen the effects of war, they are the dangerous ones, too. They are not aware of what it means, they do not take it seriously. Oh, there is so much I could say, but I will leave it for another letter.

I do feel, Hans, that we are good friends, and feel alike about many things. If you and I, so many miles apart, can get along, I feel that there can be no war against a Race, or a Country that is right. For every nation has those who are good, those who are bad.

Have you ever heard this poem by Thomas Hardy:

"The man he killed"

"Had he and I but met
By some old ancient inn,
We should have sat us down to wet
Right many a nipperkin!

—

But ranged as infantry,
And staring face to face,
I shot at him as he at me,
And killed him in his place.

—

Yes; quaint and curious war is!
You shoot a fellow down
You'd treat if met where any bar is,
Or help to half a crown."

Enough for now. Do write me your ideas on the subject, and write me as soon as you have time.

Best wishes, always,
your friend
Sylvia

P.S. Don't forget the picture!

TO *Edward Cohen*

c. Monday 11 September 1950 TL (copy),[1] Indiana University

Dear Ed,

Your letter[2] came just now . . . the one about your walk in the city, about war. You don't know quite what it did to me. My mental fear which can be, at times, forced into the background, reared up and caught me in the pit of my stomach; it became a physical nausea which wouldn't let me eat breakfast. So I thought I'd type a few lines back.

Let's face it: I'm scared too, scared and frozen. Animals, at least, don't experience fear until it's upon them, immediate. But our nerve reactions can convey worry about the future, until the fear insinuates itself into the present, into everything. So I'm sick, and I'm trying to figure out just what I'm afraid of.

First, I guess I'm afraid for myself . . . the old primitive urge for survival. At times like this you get your blind urges shot into strong relief. I want to escape . . . to get off into a dimension where I'll be safe. It's getting so I live every moment with terrible intensity. Last night, driving back from Boston, I lay back in the car and let the colored lights come at me, the music from the radio, and the reflection of the guy driving. It all flowed over me with a screaming ache of pain . . . remember, remember, this is now, and now and now. Live it, feel it, cling to it. I don't want to blot the fear out, and blur the edges of living now. I want to become acutely aware of all that I've taken for granted. When you feel that this is the good bye, the last time, it hits you harder.

Another thing. If this is It, the great ultimate destruction, I've got to transfer my egoistic dreams of a leisurely, expressive life for me to something else. After the insane thing is over, if I'm left, there'll be the job of building on chaos, on nothing, on quicksand. May be your kids could pick up where you left off. The crazy thing about the first two wars being made to clear the world for unborn generations is that we generations don't seem to have a chance. Who are the fat prosperous movie producers that said: "we may be weary of war, but it's better to fight. One steady lock at the Politburo makes it obvious to any American that he could not endure existence in that vast concentration camp which

1 – Typed by Eddie Cohen from the original and enclosed with Eddie Cohen to SP, 14 May 1951; held by Lilly Library. SP excerpted this letter as entry 20 in her journals, see Karen V. Kukil, ed., *The Journals of Sylvia Plath* (London: Faber & Faber, 2000), 19.
2 – Eddie Cohen to SP, [8 September 1950]; held by Lilly Library.

is Russia and her satellites."[1] Will they have to put on a uniform? Hell, no. The movie intake will just rise as more and more try to escape for an hour, an evening.

And all the guys. Maybe the ones who never would have made anything of themselves would like a purpose shoved at them: God, what a noble thing, to fight for my country. In the papers you can read quoted statements, "When I'm called I'll go." "Sure I'll go." They don't print your letters, or your feelings. What about all the fellows who think, who don't need Harry Truman to tell them when twenty years of living are going to end? And what about girls like me, who want to live and love on solid ground? who want time to mature, to grow up? Oh, Ed, don't laugh at me . . . I'm so pathetically intense. I just can't be any other way. But I love all the guys who are like your friend who was going to Paris, and the one about to get his Ph. D. They'll never know me, but I'm with them, thinking of them. And you, you're someone to cling to . . . one of those human associations . . . a voice, a listener. It's crazy, but somehow I feel it's good to have you there. I never realized how much associations meant. How much a tangible object can mean in a time when your life, your ideas, face obliteration. The very three-dimensional feel of this typewriter has a calming effect. It says: I'm here; you can still hold to me.

I've got to have something. I want to stop it all, the monumental grotesque joke. But writing letters and poems doesn't seem to do much good. The big men are all deaf; they don't want to hear the little squeaking as they walk across the street in cleated boots. Ed, maybe all this sounds a little frantic. I guess I am. When you catch your mother, the childhood symbol of security and rightness, crying desperately in the kitchen; when you look at your tall dreamy eyed kid brother and think that all his potentialities in the line of science are going to be cut off before he gets a chance . . . it kind of gets you.

There's much more to say. I could tell you how insane men are; how simple peaceful living can be had if only they'll stop before it's too late. I'd rather have half the world enslaved than have the whole world a radio active junk heap. The promise of a War To End Wars is slightly frayed around the edges. It is not human nature to kill; I'm human, and I have

1–'The Chips', *Time*, 11 September 1950, 102. SP slightly misquotes from the article: 'But one steady look at the Politburo makes it obvious to any American that he could not endure existence in that vast concentration camp which is Russia and her satellites . . . Weary of war though we are, it's better to fight.' The movie producers credited for the text are Cecil B. DeMille, Sam Goldwyn, Darryl Zanuck, Joseph M. Schenk, Warner Bros. and Louis B. Mayer.

a great reverence for life, for the integrity of the individual, as you would say. But I guess you're a Communist nowadays if you sign peace appeals. Ed, people don't seem to see that this negative Anti-communist attitude is destroying all the freedom of thought we've ever had. They don't see that in the hate of Russia, they're transferring all the hate they've ever had. Do you realize that if you stated your views, you'd no doubt be labeled a Communist? That's because everything they don't agree with is communist. Even if you're for Pacifism, you're a communist. They are so small-minded that they can't give anyone credit for wanting life and peace even more than world-domination. I get stared at in horror when I suggest that we are as guilty in this as Russia is; that we are war-mongers too.

That is all for now. You know; you understand. And get this, I'm with you. Don't stop talking to me, please. It's as important as if we were the only people alive . . . .

. . . . Two weeks and I'll be off to college. Funny how hard it is to study when you don't see how much value French verbs will be to you, when you realize that studying philosophies of life won't help you when you're dead.

TO *Aurelia Schober Plath*

Sunday 24 September 1950[1] ALS, Indiana University

Sunday night

Dearest Mummy,

Well, only five minutes till midnight, so I thought I'd spend them writing my first letter to my favorite person. If my printing's crooked, it's only because I drank too much apple cider tonight.

Even though I don't have much finery adorning my room yet, it seems that it's pretty much home. Tangible things can be awfully friendly at times. Even though I've only been here since three, an awful lot seems to have happened. I kind of like getting a quiet first acquaintance with my room and the girls.

I feel that I've wandered into a New York apartment by mistake . . . The maple on my desk feels like velvet. I love my room, and am going to have a terrific time decorating it.

I lay down for half-an-hour, and listened to the clock. I think I'm going to like it . . . The ticking is so rhythmic and self-assured that it's

1 – Date supplied from internal evidence.

like the beat of someone's heart. Sooo . . . it stays on the bureau.

I wandered downstairs and saw Ann Bennett[1] (the Wellesley soph) and our House Pres. for a while. We chatted, and then at 9:15 to 10:15 had an informal cider party in the Pres.' room. The girls are all pretty wonderful. Of course as we live through social and school work, personalities and character traits will no doubt crop up, rather obviously. Just now it's nice not to have any serious thoughts. After our little get-to-gether, at which a delightful extrovert freshman from Kansas[2] kept us in hysterics, we three freshmen sat and talked. After which I left them in their room on the first floor, drifted into conversation with Ann on the second, and finally arrived here at 11:30. Girls are a new world for me. I should have some fascinating times learning about the creatures. Gosh, to live in a house with 48 kids my own age---what a life! There are (don't faint) 600 in my class . . . Mrs. Shakespeare[3] is very sweet. In fact I like everything.

Tomorrow – up at 7 -- shopping etc. with people – hygiene – tea registration -- class meeting. My next letter, I hope, will be more coherent . . .

Love
Sivvy.

TO *Aurelia Schober Plath*

Monday 25 September 1950[4] ALS (postcard), Indiana University

Monday morn

Dear Mum . . .

Woke up early this morning and went to Freshman breakfast . . . rather overwhelming to wonder what's behind the various faces. So many . . . many. I put $180 in the bank this morning in a savings acc. (They prefer you get a checking acc.) and think it will help me save by not ripping off checks every minute. Lunch in an hour here – then exam, tea supper, frosh meeting . . . I'll catch a nap sometime. Bought the dearest table at the exchange for $4 . . . my little luxury. Bedspreads are, in general, horrible. Bates[5] come in insipid colors, and I saw my dream one . . . slightly higher,

1–Anne Bennett Vernon (1931–); B.A. 1953, music, Smith College; SP's friend from Wellesley, and housemate at Haven House.

2–Probably Nancy Teed Shears (1932–2014) withdrew from Smith College, July 1952; B.A. 1954, business management and administration, University of Kansas; SP's housemate at Haven House.

3–Margaret Pratt Shakespeare (1886–1968), Head of Haven and Wesley Houses, 1944–52.

4–Date supplied from postmark.

5–Bates Manufacturing Company is a maker of bedding.

which I may decide to buy---deep wine . . . plain which is rare. Can't wait to get mail – – even Eddie C. would do.

Love
Sivvy

TO *Aurelia Schober Plath*

Tuesday 26 September 1950[1] ALS (postcard), Indiana University

Tuesday

Dear Mother,

I just thought I'd drop you a line before I left for a 5 minute chat with my faculty advisor.[2] Yesterday I dropped in at the tea at the president's house . . . Mr. Wright is a doll.[3] My mind is rather a blank, as I can't quite remember what I did after that. Am drinking water like mad. Food is good . . . and I'm bound to eat & eat. I am the Freshman in a floor with Juniors and Seniors . . . you should hear them "Deah me, I must go to the Yale-Cornell game, I'll call up Bill . . ." or "She didn't marry him . . . Oh, God!" Life, when it settles down, may be rather fascinating. Our class is immense. M. Schnieders[4] is a dear---reminds me of you.

Love –
your sivvy

TO *Aurelia Schober Plath*

Tuesday 26 September 1950[5] ALS, Indiana University

Tuesday noon

Dear Mother,

Well, after being deluged with 604 new faces, voices, screams and individual attitudes, I am slowly finding one or two "landmarks." My first impression was that the whole house was a medley of party girls,

1 – Date supplied from postmark.

2 – Kenneth E. Wright (1902–88); botany professor, Smith College, 1946–67; SP's faculty adviser and professor of general botany course (Botany 11) completed by SP, 1950–1; SP's colleague, 1957–8.

3 – Benjamin Fletcher Wright (1900–76); president of Smith College, 1949–59; lived at 8 Paradise Road, Northampton, Mass.

4 – Marie Schnieders (1906–73), German professor, Smith College, 1937–71; 1954 class dean, SP's colleague, 1957–8.

5 – Date supplied from internal evidence.

but one Freshman (a Smith granddaughter . . . with two sisters here) saw my Bénet[1] poetry book . . . seems she likes him too. Of course, classes just aren't discussed much under the flurry of getting rooms arranged. Anyhow two SCAN[2] representatives just walked out, and told me to drop around second semester if I want to get on . . . of course I was glad to have that homey touch . . . I love reporting because I forget myself and get to know other people. I think if I worked up from a freshman it would be fun . . . even if I only dusted desks this first year. And I've subscribed to the Sunday Tribune[3] for the first semester. ($3.20) Is that the one you recommended over the Times? I got to talking with a girl . . . a sophomore from Lawrence House . . . about the money situation, and she said she'd love me to drop over and see what co-op house living is like.

My faculty advisor---Mr. Kenneth Wright, a Botany instructor, is a darling. What with half the class to advise, I don't imagine I meant too much to him, but he said that people had written nice things about me, and Smith could expect alot. (I'm so curious . . . I'd love to read my recommendations.) He said two things "Keep liking all your courses" and "have a good social life." Well!

Ilo wrote the dearest letter to me. If I save enough money this year, I'm going to New York for a weekend with a {some} girl friend . . . he said he's entering an art exhibit this spring, and knows a lot of young men that would like to meet me. So . . . if I save, who knows? His mother[4] is slim, young-looking, very intelligent---speaks French, Russian and German.

The hygiene exam was peculiar. I would not be surprised if I did not pass. Technical questions were few and far between, and even K. Frances-Scott[5] didn't say whether the best way to stop a dormitory cold epedemic was to sterilize all dishes or to isolate the victims. Both look pretty sensible to me. If I do get those slightly more expensive drapes, I'll no doubt want three bright pillows and a bureau scarf in flowered pattern – gray & royal blue, or gray & maroon---but we shall see . . . Boy, adjustment is frustrating . . . but fascinating.

Love
Sivvy

1–Possibly *Stephen Vincent Bénet Pocket Book* (Pocket Books, 1946), which SP received as a Christmas gift in 1947.

2–*Smith College Associated News*, the college newspaper that ran from 1945 to 1952. Continued by *The Sophian* in 1952.

3–The Sunday edition of the *New York Herald Tribune*.

4–Hilda Pill (1896–1989). The Pills lived at 2023 Lexington Avenue, Apartment 4, New York.

5–Kate Francis Scott (1890–1971); author of *A College Course in Hygiene* (Ann Arbor: Edwards Brothers, 1937). Associate professor in hygiene, Smith College, 1927–55.

TO *Aurelia Schober Plath*

Tuesday 26 September 1950[1] ALS (postcard), Indiana University

Tuesday night

Dear Mummy,

I don't know just how much I've written you, but I'm sure you won't complain about an extra postcard here & there. So much to ask you---so much to say. I haven't had a minute alone so far. Now I'm sitting on the second floor, music playing, and four other frosh in various attitudes around me. Got the curtains & spread – BATES for $17.95. Sounds awful, doesn't it? But my room will be terrific if I get 3 gray & maroon or gray & royal blue flowered pillows Will do wonders! Think you could make up a bureau scarf of the same material for me – 30" × 15"?? How about a gray patterned scatter rug? Or is that out of the question. 25¢ bought me a wastebasket – and that was that. For a long time! I have firmly resolved to buy no clothes. Wonder how much my lab fee will be. Lisa[2] is very sweet . . . very friendly--red haired. Girls are fascinating creatures.

Love,
Sivvy

30 × 15

TO *Aurelia Schober Plath*

Tuesday 26 September 1950[3] ALS (postcard), Indiana University

Tues. night

Dear Mummy,

Another card before I drop off to bed. My time is improving---it's only quarter of 12 now. Lisa and I had a lovely talk for a while. I think I'm going to like being in my room an awful lot. It's terrifically homey, and the whole house is just the friendliest conglomeration of people imagineable. "Gerry"[4] – – one gorgeous creature just got a picture & write up in Flair as representative of eastern women's colleges. People are always talking

1 – Date supplied from postmark.

2 – Elizabeth Powell Dempsey (1931–2012); B.A. 1952, economics, Smith College; SP's housemate at Haven House. Elected Phi Beta Kappa in 1951.

3 – Date supplied from postmark.

4 – Marjorie Clarke Coxe (1929–); B.A. 1951, English, Smith College; SP's housemate at Haven House. Coxe was featured in the article 'Four BWOC', *Flair*, August 1950, 48–9. 'BWOC' stands for 'Big Woman on Campus'.

about Europe & N.Y. Lisa told me about how good it is not to work too hard, but to allot time for "playing" with kids in the house. Seems she's done a neat job of adjusting. I hope I can really get to know her some time. She has quite a friendly attitude, and I could talk to her about almost anything. She mentions almost nothing about herself, though. But I'm crazy about her.

Love---
me.

Someone's already borrowed my short story book!

TO *Aurelia Schober Plath*

Wednesday 27 September 1950[1] ALS, Indiana University

Wednesday 9 PM

Dear Mother,

I've been going so steady for these past days that I decided to take the evening off and go to bed early. If my plans work out, I'll do so in a few minutes . . . that is, if no one drops in to visit me. I've taken a bath, washed my hair, and feel infinitely more at home. My room looks so homey, and if I get homemade cookies now & then, it will help. (That hint dropped like lead, I'm afraid.)

The food here is better than at the country club. One freshman has a crate of apples, so we're always munching those between meals. And bed time snacks are a usual thing. Thank God I'm trying to gain weight. My belt is already quite snug. The eggs in the morning are done to perfection. We go out to the kitchen and wait to catch it hot from the griddle on our toast. Roast beef & Yorkshire pudding were on tonight's menu.

Girls are sweet. The freshmen are dears. One girl in our annex house is from Indiana or Ohio (I forget which), and if we have room I'd like to have her up for Thanksgiving. So many Western girls can't go home, and I'd love to have at least one stay over.

Most of the frosh are out tonight at the student center, but I thought I'd turn in. Music drifts down the hall. How could I ever be homesick? There are so many openings---so many groups, so many girls. Lisa is a dear. She doesn't smoke, she knits, plays bridge, and is evidently the most brilliant girl in her class. She doesn't do her studying obtrusively, and she seems very steady & self-willed. She also doesn't stay up past 11 ever.

1–Date supplied from internal evidence.

I feel kind of good knowing she got through by being so sensible. It's sure a challenge to me. Evidently you can be good in studies and have fun in the evenings too.

Our house,[1] I'm sure, is the friendliest. A homely maternal Jewish Girl from Boston Latin school offered to start me off knitting a simple sweater, and I'm going to get some of the freshmen to teach me how to play Bridge. Mr. Loungway was oh, so right about – "The little things."

In fact, so far, I've gotten along with everyone in the house. It's good to see more faces familiar to me. I love my room, my location, and am firmly convinced that the whole episode here is up to me. I have no excuse for not getting along in all respects. Just to find a balance is the first problem.

We had our college assembly this morning. I never came so close to crying since I've been here when I saw the professors, resplendent with colors, medals & emblems, march across the stage and heard the adorable Mr. Wrights stimulating adress. I still can't believe I'm a Smith Girl!

Love,
Sivvy

TO *Aurelia Schober Plath*

Thursday 28 September 1950[2] ALS (postcard), Indiana University

Thursday

Dear Mummy,

Well, another chair has been added to my room free of charge by some generous senior. I now have three. Clothes up here are strictly informal. If I get a white cardigan for some such occasion as Birthday or Xmas, I can wear it over my white dress and not have to worry about the WHITE UNIFORM.

For spring, Bermuda wool plaid shorts are the rage. Dungarees will be my garb for week days the rest of the fall – with pedal pushers for special occasions. I could use a few warm sweaters come Xmas. But nothing is

1 – Haven House, 96 Elm Street, Northampton, Mass.; residence of SP during her first two years at Smith College, 1950–2. During her freshman year, SP had a single room on the third floor. During her sophomore year, SP roomed with Marcia Brown Stern; they occupied room 6 on the second floor.

2 – Date supplied from postmark.

necessary now---I have everything. Most girls are even more careful than I with money so far. I shall do my best to keep a tight budget.

Love,
Sivvy

PS. Have you mailed my baby – Den of Lions?[1]

TO *Aurelia Schober Plath*

Thursday 28 September 1950[2] ALS (postcard), Indiana University

Thursday
3:30 P.M.

Dear Mother . . .

Well, I passed the hygiene exam! Patsy[3] did not, but Louise[4] did. So that nasty little requirement is off. I'm switching to French 16 . . . I'm not sure just how wise that is, but Patsy & Lou are taking it, and the 13 course, judging from my 1st period today seems deceptively easy. This Junior year abroad sounds terrific; but I don't know whether or not I should think of it. Now that I've switched, I'm almost tempted to turn back to 13. Botany, the only other class I've had as yet, should not only prove to be fun, but interesting. I bought the textbook for $2 less from a girl in the house. I can't wait till classes[5] get underway, I also can't wait till Who's Who[6] comes out---Maybe I'll get a date then---not that boys interest me in the least.

Love,
Sivvy

1–Sylvia Plath, 'Den of Lions', *Seventeen* 10 (May 1951), 127, 144–5.

2–Date supplied from postmark.

3–Patricia O'Neil Pratson (1932–); B.A. 1954, English, Smith College; SP's friend from Wellesley.

4–Louise Giesey White (1932–); B.A. 1954, government, Smith College. Resident of Hopkins B House. Classmate of SP in high school in Wellesley, class of 1950.

5–During her first year at Smith College, SP completed Art 13 (basic design) taught by Mervin Jules; Botany 11 (general botany) taught by Kenneth E. Wright; English 11 (Freshman English) directed by Mary Ellen Chase and Edna Rees Williams; French 16 (introduction to French literature) taught by members of the department; History 11 (general European) taught by Elisabeth Ahlgrimm Koffka; and Physical Education 1 (body mechanics, dance, and sports).

6–Mary McBreen, ed., *Who's Who in 1954* (Northampton, Mass.: Smith College, 1950). SP's annotated copy held by Lilly Library.

TO *Aurelia Schober Plath*

Thursday 28 September 1950[1] ALS (postcard), Indiana University

Thurs. night

Dear Mummy,

The most utterly divine thing has happened to me. I was standing innocently in the parlor having coffee after supper when a senior said sotto voce in my ear "I have a man all picked out for you." I just stood there with that "Who me?" expression, and she proceeded to explain. Seems she met this young guy who lives in Mass. but went to Culver Military Acad. He is a freshman at Amherst this year, tall, cute and – get this – HE WRITES POETRY. I just sat there burbling inarticulately into my coffee. She said he should be around in a few weeks. God, am I thrilled. The hope, even, of getting to know a sensitive guy who isn't a roughneck, makes the whole world swim in pink mist. The food is fabulous. I've had two helpings of everything since I got here, and should gain alot. I love everybody. If only I can unobtrusively do well in all my courses and get enough sleep, I should be tops. I'm so happy. This anticipation makes everything super. I keep muttering I'M A SMITH GIRL NOW.

me

TO *Aurelia Schober Plath*

Saturday 30 September 1950[2] ALS, Indiana University

Friday night midnight

Dear Mother,

Don't be disturbed by the late hour – I'm planning to sleep late Sunday morning. Circumstances call for a letter at the present moment, however.

I just took a warm bath, and now feel greatly relaxed. Today has been the fullest yet. After hauling myself out of bed at 7:15, I had breakfast – which is usually coffee, fruit juice, rolls (sometimes stale) and cereal (dry) plus eggs three times a week. I then picked up my room and headed for my physical exam. This consisted of getting swathed in a sheet and passing from one room to another in nudity. I'm so used to hearing "Drop your sheet," that I have to watch myself now lest I forget to dress. My height is an even five nine, my weight a solid 137, my posture – good,

1 – Date supplied from postmark.
2 – Date supplied from postmark.

although when my posture picture was taken I took such pains to get my ears & heels in a straight line that I forgot to tilt up straight. The result was something like this. <drawing of female leaning forward> "You have good alignment," she said, "but you are in constant danger of falling on your face." Well!

Then to the registrar to change my French course to 16. A long wait here. Then quickly back to the house to pick up the much awaited mail. There was that lovely letter from you and <u>two</u> from Eddie.[1] Bob has written also. I'm so pleased with your news. It's all so happy---especially about Exeter.

As for me, I then dashed to my first French 16 class at 11. Patsy is in it! About 25 girls, and am I glad I changed. The teacher[2] is a second Mrs. Gorton – short, black haired with a terrific humorous twinkle. She's so different from that other wishy-washy grammar teacher. I'd much rather have a stimulating course that one all peaches & cream. I just hope I stay in, I should have a terrific time if we always have her. Botany at 12. It promises to be fascinating too. Then lunch. Friday lunch is always poor – fish, ugh. But I have such an appetite that I always eat 2 helpings of everything.

Then to the library for the first time with Pat. We studied from 2-5, and I can see that I'll spend all the hours I can during the day there. The atmosphere is very quiet and refreshing.

Went to my first little chapel last night & witnessed my first communion. Beautiful ceremony, but nothing I could ever believe in.

After supper, we gathered around the piano and sang for a good hour. Never have I felt so happy, standing with a group of girls with piano, Lisa's accordion, and two ukeles, singing my favorite popular songs. It was such a warm feeling. No home life could make up for the "cameraderie" of living with a group of girls. I like them all.

After singing, two girls from our annex house came up to my room for the purpose of studying. However, we got in the process of learning the Charleston, and I am afraid the noise of our shrieks carried over the whole house. After our usual bedtime snack (left over desert & milk---tonight it was peach shortcake) one girl left, and Anne Davidow[3] stayed

1–Probably Eddie Cohen to SP, two letters dated [28 September 1950]; held by Lilly Library.
2–Probably Madeleine Guilloton.
3–Children's book author and illustrator Ann Davidow-Goodman (1932–); daughter of Leonard and Claire Sondheim Davidow of Highland Park, Illinois; SP's friend. Ann Davidow withdrew from Smith College in January 1951 following her first semester; earned B.A. 1954, University of Chicago; married Leo Goodman 1960 (divorced 1976); married Russell Hayes 1983. Corresponded with SP, 1951–62.

to do her Religion homework. We drifted into discussion, and she is the closest girl yet that I've wanted for a friend. She is a free thinker---we discussed God and religion and men---and her parents are Jewish. I find her very attractive---almost as tall as I, freckle-faced, short brown hair and twinkling blue eyes. She likes to draw horses, and has a palimino named Sylvia. Needless to say, I was much flattered. She might even get me a date tomorrow night. My first real blind one. I kinda hope it comes thru. Once I get started, I'm sure I'll have no trouble. This sensitive guy I told you about in the card has not yet matured. should it be "materialized"?[1] I'll give him a month. I've fallen for him already merely because of the poetry angle.

Ann read some of Eddie's letters and thinks he's wonderfully socially conscious.

My room is lovely. Did I tell you another small table has been added by the generosity of some senior? All I need now is pillows and pictures, big ones, little ones, loads. Could you have Ilo's framed? I've got to get a bulletin board some how to fill wall space. But I love my "den."

If I can get enough sleep & do well in my studies, I ask for nothing more. Girls are so sweet here. There are so many different ones. When I get used to the routine, I'll no doubt be more rested.

I love this place so much. Of course I haven't been here long, but I'm very happy so far. The campus is utterly lovely.

My bike is in the racks outside the house along with 101 others. Come winter, I'll store it in the cellar.

Till later,
Love,
Sivvy

<on back of envelope>

Sat PS. No date after all.

1–This sentence added by SP in the left margin.

TO *Aurelia Schober Plath*

Sunday 1 October 1950[1]

ALS with envelope,
Indiana University

Sunday afternoon

Dear Mother,

Here I sit, barefoot on a blanket by Paradise pond, preparing to plunge into my homework. Jo Stocklan,[2] a sophomore girl in my house, is here with me, and the sun is hotter than on a late spring day. All around it is quiet, only a low murmur of voices and crickets. I wish they let us wear halters, it's so warm. The trees are yellow-green, and the grass is buttery with light. Paradise lies at our feet, calm and clear as a black marble table top.

I slept until ten thirty this morning, and then Jo and I went downtown to get coffee and hamburg for breakfast. I then went upstairs to do my "laundry" and to clean my room before dinner.

Last night I had my first blind date (after all the indecision it finally came through.) Ann Davidow, the lovely Jewish girl I told you about, got me a date from Amherst. During the morning I went to the library and to my one saturday class – French. Then to the first half of freshman day---sports demonstration. I missed out on supper and the step sing, because Ann and I went back at four to get dressed for our "dinner date." I wore my navy blue bolero suit with my wide red belt. With some misgivings, I trotted over to our annex house to wait with Ann. It was a triple date, and when the boys came, I was relieved to see that mine was 6 feet tall, and slender & cleancut. Turns out that he lives in West Newton! I don't know just what chance of fate threw us together, but my first "blind date" sure was lucky. At first there was nothing extraordinary. We all had a steak dinner, cafeteria style, at the Amherst dining hall. Then on to the Chi Phi house. We sat around and talked upstairs in one of the rooms, music blaring, and I felt I didn't even know the guy I was with at all, which was rather frustrating after not really knowing <u>anybody</u> at all well. Somehow the noise got louder, and Bill[3] and I separated from the crowd & went down the hall to his room. It was lovely – a fireplace, records, big leather chairs. And some how we got to talking very frankly. He surprised me by hitting rather well on a few points of my personality which I usually keep hidden. But there was a sensitivity about him which appealed to me in comparison

1 – Date supplied from postmark.

2 – Joyce Stocklan Goldberg (1932–); B.A. 1953, American studies, Smith College; SP's housemate at Haven House.

3 – William Albert Gallup, Jr (1929–2005); B.A. 1951, Amherst College; dated SP in 1950.

to the hearty, rough-neck drinking crowd, so I talked quite openly. His manner is somewhat reminiscent of Warren. He has dark brown eyes, is very slender (150) pounds and (this struck me with awe) he's a senior and will be 22 on April 26! He didn't even approach me which is another thing in his favor. After we discussed several important things which I don't exactly recall---something about ego and religious belief---he got up abruptly and we went to another house to dance. After a few dances, he led me equally abruptly out of the house and by mutual consent we walked around the campus. Nothing is as beautiful as a campus at night. Music drifted out from the houses, fog blurred the lights, and from the hill, it looked as if we could step over the edge into nothingness. It seemed that in his room he was suddenly overwhelmed with his inability to think the situation over clearly, and at the dance he suddenly realized that he enjoyed talking to me in quiet.

Never, since I have come here, have I been in such an island of inner calm. I like people, but to learn about one individual always appeals to me more than anything. We sat and talked out in the cool dark of the steps, and I told him how I felt about being at ease---seems he felt the same way. So we went home at 12:30 with the others, and I felt very happy. To think that I didn't have to torture myself by sitting in a smoke-filled room with a painted party smile watching my date get drunk! This guy was very gentle and sweet---not one of those old Casanovas. He goes out for crew, so I told him all about Warren.

I do think he liked me a little, though. He said he wasn't a "wheel with women," which made me feel glad. I had a very real time. Nothing at all superficial about it.

Back at Haven, we stood for a while outside; the other couples were all coming up the walk, kissing each other regardless of onlookers. So he just smiled and looked at me saying "some people just don't have any inhibitions" and kissed the tip of my nose briefly.

So that was that. I hope I see him again. He made no definite date but said he was glad he knew I lived at Haven, so he wouldn't have to go scouting the campus for me.

Among his various observations: I lived "hard," am dramatic in my manner, talk sometimes like a school girl reporting a theme, and have a southern accent!

Don't mind my rambling. The first college date is a big thing, and I really feel a part of life now.

Love,
Sivvy

TO *Aurelia Schober Plath*

Monday 2 October 1950[1] ALS (postcard), Indiana University

Monday 3 PM

1

Dear Mother,

Today has been utterly hell-hot, sunny, and I had 4 hours of classes this morning & one this afternoon. My desk is loaded with books, all the classrooms are on the third floor, and I am physically & mentally exhausted. I went to bed at 10 last night, yet early sleep always makes me more tired at first. So I'm going to try to keep good hours all this week. History will be my hardest course, English & Art the most enjoyable. French quite tough, and Botany elaborately difficult. Thank God I have a single room. Patsy saw me for a minute today & is almost hysterical. Her roommate is a party girl, and their room is the gathering place for the whole floor. Since I'm on a floor with srs & Jrs. I can come & go at will. The only consolation is that I remember how overwhelmed I was my first week at the farm, maybe I'll get rested and balanced in a month. Just now Thanksgiving seems awfully far away.

Love,
Sylvia

TO *Aurelia Schober Plath*

Monday 2 October 1950[2] ALS (postcard), Indiana University

Mon night

2

Dear Mother

Well, wrapped deep in the midst of my studies I was visited by my senior girl friend who knew the poetry-writing boy. The angel got me a date with him for this Saturday – football game at Amherst, dinner & evening. Just now the phone rang -- my blind date last Saturday wanting date for this Fr. & Sat. I accepted for Fri. So it seems I'm not going to be a social flop after all! Even a senior at Amherst comes back for more of my scintillating peculiarities. God, this homework fazes me.

Love,
Sylvia

1–Date supplied from postmark.
2–Date supplied from postmark.

TO *Aurelia Schober Plath*

Tuesday 3 October 1950[1]

ALS with envelope,
Indiana University

Tuesday
3. P.M.

Dear Mother . . .

Just got your Sunday letter this morning, so I thought I'd drop you a line. Your letters are utterly fascinating, and they mean so much since I don't get much mail or have too much time to write coherently. I've heard once from Bob & Ilo, twice from Eddie, and thrice from you. That's all.

I wish I really did have only 18 hours of classes. With 24, I find myself hard pressed. I am enclosing a copy of my schedule[2] which may serve to enlighten you somewhat. You see, I have six hours in both Art and Botany which fills it in rather heavily.

History is the course which floors me. There are over 600 in our lecture hall, and in the two periods of actual class, I find I have no background whatsoever. I find reading and comprehending 40 pages a night a bit taxing. Botany requires a lot of work. English, French and Art at least have a keen interest for me which makes up for the labor involved. English is strictly critical, no creative writing. French is mostly literature, under a fascinating teacher. Pronunciation & conversation are part of it.

I don't have much chance to admire the lovely foliage, although I wish I could. As you see, I don't get through classes until three, and often four o'clock.

Patsy declined an invitation to double date with me to Saturday's game and dance since she has so much work to do. I feel almost guilty going out twice this weekend, but shall try to forget it and work hard now, and forget work & enjoy myself then.

I do think it's too bad that they have to keep Freshmen so "busy" according to the schedule.

I don't dare think of marks. If I fail History I shall not be amazed. It is notoriously the most difficult Freshmen course, and there are Sophs & Juniors who find it hard.

Well, off to the libe for an hour or two of trying futiley to get a day's work done.

Love,
Sivvy

1–Date supplied from postmark.
2–No longer with the letter.

TO *Aurelia Schober Plath*

Wednesday 4 October 1950[1] ALS (postcard), Indiana University

1

Wednesday 1 PM

Dear Mother,

Today is my "easiest day". I spent three hours in the libe this morning trying to din 30 more pages of history in my head. Your letters are such treats – even the advice. Don't worry about my bedtime. I've been in by 10:15 the last three nights. I get up at 7. I am nowhere near as physically exhausted as I was at first. In fact I see a little order in the chaos already. Wait for a few weeks till I build up study habits and sleep habits, and I'll have more time to breath. Just now I can't look ahead more than a few hours at a time. But that, I tell myself, is as it should be. Rome was not built in a day, & If I accept confusion as a normal consequence of being uprooted from home environment, I should be able to cope with my problems better. Today should have been Mountain day.[2] The tree outside my window is pure shining gold. Oh, what joy to have no studies & to bike to the mountains.

Love,
Sivvy

TO *Aurelia Schober Plath*

Wednesday 4 October 1950[3] ALS (postcard), Indiana University

2

Dear Mother,

Just a few questions, requests and answers – please send wool socks as soon as possible – I only brought up 2 pairs. Another bulletin board would be fine. I'll send the stories off when I come home on Thanksgiving. Shall I send my P.J.'s and starched sport shirts home when dirty? I've written Warren, Ilo, Bob and Eddie.

Do send up the Nov. Seventeen[4] when it comes. And <u>don't</u> worry about me. I'm gradually getting used to this, and will sleep before 10:30 or 11 every week night. Weekends (heh heh) is another matter.

1 – Date supplied from postmark.
2 – A day when classes are cancelled by the president of the college; a tradition since 1877.
3 – Date supplied from postmark.
4 – Sylvia Plath, 'Ode to a Bitten Plum', *Seventeen* 9 (November 1950), 104.

If <u>only</u> I don't appear as stupid to my profs as I do to myself!

Love,
Sivvy

TO *Aurelia Schober Plath*

Wednesday 4 October 1950[1] ALS (postcard), Indiana University

3

Wednesday night
10:15

Dear Mum –

Don't worry that I'm sacrificing valuable time. These cards take only a sec. Just before I hop to bed, thought I'd send you a snatch of verse:

Gold leaves shiver
In this crack of time;
Yellow flickers
In the shrill clear sun;
Light skips and dances,
Pirouettes;
While blue above
Leaps the sheer sky.

— —

Gold leaves dangle
In the wind.
Gold threads snap.

— —

In giddy whirls
And sweeps of fancy
Sunlit leaves plane down.

— —

Lisping along the street
In dry and deathless dance,
The leaves on slipshod feet
Advance and swirl
frisk,
dip,

1–Date supplied from postmark.

spiral,
circle
twirl.
Brief gold glitters
In the gutters;
Flares and flashes
Husky rushes;
Brisk wind hushes
hushes
hushes.
And in that moment, silent, cold,
across the lawn – dull pools of gold.

S.

TO *Aurelia Schober Plath*

Friday 6 October 1950[1] ALS (postcard), Indiana University

Dear Mother,

Do you suppose by any chance you could send me all my old Seventeen's? Don't laugh – I actually need them for my art course. We have to make a scrapbook of texture, line, color, etc. so magazines, unusual photos and adds, are indespensable. The cost of sending them would no doubt be less than buying new ones. Another thing: I just realized how important long sleeved sweaters are. All I have for co-o-old winter days are 1 Bob's sweatshirt 2 my plaid wool shirt (new) and 3 my gray cardigan. Blouses, pants, skirts aplenty, but no warm sweaters.

Everyone of my teachers is extremely good. French and History (my Waterloo) are fascinating. English and Botany are two sweet men, and Art is a nice man too (Fr & Hist are females.)[2]

Love,
Sivvy

1–Date supplied from postmark.
2–'(~~Eng~~ Fr & Hist are females.)' appears in the original.

TO *Aurelia Schober Plath*

Sunday 8 October 1950[1] ALS, Indiana University

Sunday

Dear Mother,

At last I have a moment to write you. It is Sunday morning, 11 o'clock, and I sit curled up in one of my easy chairs in pajamas and bath robe and wool socks (must not get draft on feet) and slippers. Sunday mornings are always lackadaisacal (sp?) One sleeps late, or eats breakfast in p.j.'s, or drifts aimlessly from room to room discussing last night's date.

As for me, my weekend has been rather unique. Everybody in the house has colds. Coughing and sneezing echoes up and down the halls. So Thursday I went to bed early with the prophetic sore throat. Friday morning, feeling very hot and miserable, I got up, dressed, and went to the Doctor's Office. Nothing like getting initiated into the procedure early, I always say. She told me I had post nasal drip, to gargle with salt, sniff Salt water up my nose, take 2 cold pills 3 times a day, take troches etc. So I went home with all my directions and crawled into bed. The day is rather a blank. I got a yellow slip which excused me from classes, and in the process I called Bill Gallup who was very understanding. He refused my gallant offer to get him a blind date and said he would come over to see me if I could get up for a little. So in the evening I donned my red jersey & black velvet skirt and went down to the front room for a while. I was amazed to find that my first enthusiasm for him had cooled completely. As Eddie Cohen analyzed my sentiments![2] I had confided so openly in him because I was rather terrified at being in a world indifferent to me and I wanted quite desperately to find security some where. Eddie, as he often does, hit the nail on the head. I looked at Bill in a different light, and realized that he had served his purpose. Any sensitive quiet boy would have done. So I accepted tentatively a date for next Saturday, and doubt very much if I will go. However, I enjoyed myself. I went to bed at 10. Yesterday I was at my worst. I woke up early after a horrible nightmarish sleep, and my morning class stared me in the face. I had slept through breakfast. I couldn't face the thought of a football game. Ugh! And yet I wanted so to meet this boy. So when my senior acquaintance who had arranged the date came in with two of my freshman friends, I burst into tears (Dear me, how pathetic can we get.) Before I knew what was happening, I was undressed, back in bed, sipping a pot of hot tea and

1–Date supplied from internal evidence.

2–See Eddie Cohen to SP, [5 October 1950]; held by Lilly Library.

eating an apple, listening to conversation and feeling much less homesick. The girls were simply dear – I had two meals in bed. The girl with whom I was to double-date went to the game, and Austin[1] had decided not to go and was going to stay with Monte[2] (the senior) and talk. So Monte told me if I felt well enough to come down and meet him. By this time life looked almost rosy. I felt better with two meals in my stomach and nosedrops up my nose, so I donned my red skirt and the gray sweater ensemble and made my way down.

If you could meet Austin Kenefick your heart would be lost. He is the dearest boy – just eighteen, very unspoiled and quite delightful. He reminds me very strongly of Perry. Of course he is nowhere as good-looking – he's tall, with a raw-boned freckled face, brown hair, ugly in his youthful awkwardness at times, but at other times beautiful in his sincerity. I was enchanted by his open-ness. We got started talking under the supervision of Monte, who then thoughtfully disappeared. For the whole afternoon – 1-6, we talked, sometimes joining in with other couples in the room, sometimes being by ourselves. I listened to him tell me about Dorothy (why do I inspire boys to tell me their stories?) and I told him about the story in Seventeen. That impressed him. He said he knew alot of girls who gushed about writing, but to get something published – well! He also was familiar with Margot MacDonald.[3] He enjoys sketching. He told me about The Blue something[4] – that restaurant on the wharf in Boston with the bottle candles? and he went to Culver, knew John Hall's two roommates who went their and was very friendly with two of Perry's roommates who were in his class.

Like Perry, he is quite articulate, but more poetically so. Nothing suave or polished about him – just a delighfully gangling innocent boy, which is so refreshing. Evidently this Dorothy still hurts him some, and he was quite amazed to find that I liked trees with sun shining through and clouds and water. He wanted to go for a walk because we could talk better, but good girl that I was, I stayed in the house. He stayed for dinner, and then he & Monte wanted me to see "The Titan"[5] with them. I wanted so to go,

1–Austin Walsh Kenefick, Jr (1932–); B.A. 1954, Amherst College; dated SP 1950–1.

2–Elizabeth Carlo Day (1928–2010); B.A. 1951, art history, Smith College; SP's housemate at Haven House.

3–Margot Macdonald, editor of the 'It's All Yours' section of *Seventeen*.

4–The Blue Ship Tea Room, then located on T Wharf. See SP's journals, 5 September 1958 for her description of eating there.

5–*The Titan: Story of Michelangelo* (1950); a film about the artist directed by Robert J. Flaherty and Richard Lydford. Played at Sage Hall, 7 October 1950, at 7:30 p.m. and 9:30 p.m.

but decided to go to bed early. So he said goodbye, leaving me a play by Christopher Fry[1] to read. I don't know just how I impressed him, but I'd love to see him again. I would very much like to find someone with whom I could escape the party whirl & glitter.

So I went to bed, rather tired from my day, the cold pills making me feel queer. All the other freshmen had gone to the big acquaintance dance between the big 4 men's colleges. Damn. But since Austin was here I wouldn't have gone anyway. And Austin was so thoughtful to stay with me all afternoon. He has none of Perry's stiffness – I wish you could see him.

So today, my head stuffed and very hard, I will try to do homework. Someday I think I'll have my sinuses drained, they're so packed.

Another thing – how do you take off those typewriter ribbon caps? The ribbon is all tangled up. The heat here is awfully dry. Should I get one of those containers of water to hang behind the radiator?

Love,
Sivvy

TO *Aurelia Schober Plath*

Monday 9 October 1950[2] ALS, Indiana University

Monday

Dear Mummy,

No doubt you are wondering about my present condition. As nasty as it is to have a sinus cold at the present moment, I have become philosophical and decided that it is a challenge. As comforting as it would be to crawl sniffily into your arms and have you tell me what to do, relieving me of all responsibility, I realize that now is the time for me to learn to be master of myself.

Today is mountain day. In a way I'm sorry. In a way I'm glad. I didn't feel like facing 5 hours of classes. I wanted very much to go to mountain climbing. All my friends have either gotten dressed to kill and headed to Yale & Dartmouth, or packed a picnic & headed off on a bike trip. I decided I was well enough for neither. Rather than stay in my lonely bed, I have taken a chair and footstool out on our 3rd floor piazza and am

1–English poet and playwright Christopher Fry (1907–2005); his *The Lady's Not For Burning* (1948). SP's copy, with Kenefick's ownership inscription on the front pastedown, held by Lilly Library. See SP to ASP, 4 November 1950.

2–Date supplied from internal evidence.

basking in the sun. It is an Indian summer day – blue-skied, leaves golden, falling. Some girls are studying – some few. So I sit here, sheltered, the sun warming me inside. And life is good. Out of misery comes joy, clear and sweet. I feel that I am learning. I will rest today, take a nap perhaps. Go to bed early. I was in at 9 last night. I almost welcome this quiet solitude, since I feel still too shaky for much energetic work.

I am making the most of the day that I can in my circumstances. What sense to mourn and spoil these lovely sunny hours? I can't do everything.

As for nylon sweaters – I do love them. A pull-over would be lovely. Of course a white cardigan would complete my white piqué dress for that WHITE Dress ensemble. Thanks for the pictures and the spray. Did I tell you Ilo promised to send some of his paintings to brighten my room?

Another thing – wool undershirts would be very sensible & welcome. (My, how I've swallowed my pride.) I've dropped Warren a letter, but haven't heard from him yet. How I love that boy!

Your cards are so sweet & sunny. Eddie and Ilo are writing very encouragingly and sustainingly. I love them both. I've gotten two notes from Bob, too.

This Austin was a sweet boy, but he evidently likes short blondes, so I fear I must either cut my self in two, or be sweet to Bill Gallup, who evidently has taken quite a fancy to me. He was talking to some girls over at Amherst about me this Sat., and one of them said later, "My deah, you made a great impression on him." Naturally I blushed modestly.

God, today is lovely. My cold is still runny, but with plenty of sleep & nosedrops I should be well rid of it soon. By the way, do you suck those buffered penicillin, or swallow with water? Next time I'm ill I don't want to kill myself by taking them the wrong way!

Cheerio!
sivvy

TO *Aurelia Schober Plath*

Tuesday 10 October 1950[1] ALS, Indiana University

Tuesday,

Dear Mother,

Well today it poured – a fitting follow-up to mountain day. I went from class to class quite dry – bundled up in raincoat, raindana, overshoes

1–Date supplied from internal evidence.

and umbrella (loaned by a housemate.) Tomorrow I intend to purchase a slicker, which I can probably get under $10. Did I tell you that my art supplies cost $10 and that the art lab fee is the same?

Your two packages arrived today, for which I thank you.

As for my cold, it has dried up, leaving me a bit tired. I intend to be in bed early every night, though, I went to the D.O. again today, and had her paint my throat. They took a slide of a blister they thought might be (ugh!) Trenchmouth. Of course it wasn't, but at least I gave them a scare.

You say you might come up on a Saturday. Nothing would give me more pleasure. At a time when the pace of college life was a little too strong & swift for my rundown constitution, I thought of coming home for a day of enjoyable calm.

However, I don't know just how wise you think that is. Perhaps the travel would be too long to make a Saturday night & Sunday at home worthwhile? But I'd love to take off.

I could always come on a bus after my 1:00 class Sat. and leave after supper Sunday evening. Perhaps you could send me a bus schedule.

On the other hand, it might be wiser for you to come here – yet in my present state, I might be even more likely to miss you after you'd gone.

History is going to require a lifetime of study. My schedule now is study = sleep; study, sleep. Perhaps you could send me a few A & D vitamins. <u>Everyone</u> has colds, coughs etc. In class, in the dorm, we are constantly exposed. I certainly can't afford another siege. After all, I want to be a bit more sociable with the girls here. It's getting so they ask where I keep myself. But I've got to spend every available minute (and there aren't too many of those–) studying. Tell me if you can see – my coming home for a day – or what day you can come up. I really could do with a day of sleep & study that home could offer. But since I'm on the mend and doing all I can to take care of my self, don't worry about me.

Love,
Sivvy

TO *Aurelia Schober Plath*

Tuesday 10 October 1950[1] ALS (postcard), Indiana University

Tuesday night

1

Dear Mother–

If you could see me – curled up in my cosy room, the light bringing out the rich maroons and blues and light maples – my throat is the only reminder of my cold. And as I munch cookies I forget even that. It's warm, cosy, and homey. A soph just dropped in and gave me a few hints about my first Eng. paper. Botany & English I hope to do well in. I would like to know a good weekend to come home on – I could rest, visit with you & study history. Just now the school work seems endless. Perhaps history goes on forever. I don't see how girls can play bridge in the livingroom all night . . . For these first months I'm going to study every chance I get. I'll have enough chance to be "seen around" more, once I see how my 1st semester grades pan out. I'll be amazed if I get one A.

Love,
Sivvy

TO *Aurelia Schober Plath*

Tuesday 10 October 1950[2] ALS (postcard), Indiana University

Tuesday night

2

Dear Mum –

These postcards are getting to be a habit. How about my dropping home Sat. October 21? Monday, October 30, is our first hour history written, & I could go to bed early Sat. the 21 (which I couldn't do here – dates you know – noise till 1 AM.) and study & organize notes most of Sunday in peace and family surroundings. It sounds ideal to me. I think it might help me make order out of the chaos of barbarian civilization, plus seeing that favorite person of mine for a while (You, of course)

Love,
Sivvy

1–Date supplied from postmark.
2–Date supplied from postmark.

TO *Aurelia Schober Plath*

Thursday 12 October 1950[1] ALS (postcard), Indiana University

Thursday

Dear Mother–

How nice to get your cheerful letter! I was so sorry to hear about your cold – do be good & rest – don't work at those "jobs around the house" too hard. As for me, I have a throat canker & a slight temp. I have run into a nice doctor at the D.O. She's painting & spraying me up in fine shape. So I hope I can still go to classes, tho', and not get stuck in the infirmary.[2] I have decided to cut my Fr. class Sat. Oct 21 and come home Fri night. The bus I want to take should get to W. Hills by 9 PM Fri. Oct 20. I'd love to see you, and whereas if you came up here I'd be seeing you all the time & not working, if I come home I can work & rest and see you. Sounds fine, huh? Your letters, just now, are a sustaining life force. It poured again today, so for $11.60 I bought a red slicker & a big black waterproof hat. I will take back an umbrella when I come home. We're reading short stories in Eng– they're terrific – can't wait to see you – only 9 more days –

Love,
Sivvy

TO *Aurelia Schober Plath*

Sunday 15 October 1950[3] ALS (postcard), Indiana University

Sunday

Dear Mum–

Well, they let me out of the institution for dinner at the house today. I sleep at the infirm tonight, and should be discharged for good tomorrow A.M. I plan to have a dentist look at my tooth which hurts when I breath cold air on it. I don't want to have it decayed by Thanksgiving. Gosh, it's nice to get a glimpse of my room again. Can't wait to come back for good. Got a letter from that brother of mine today. Very sweet. I probably won't come home till Thanksgiving. $5 could well be saved till this winter, when I plan to make a few trips back. So many girls here like to write. One frosh

1–Date supplied from postmark.
2–The Elizabeth Mason Infirmary, 69 Paradise Road, Northampton, Mass.
3–Date supplied from postmark.

sends out piles of stuff. I'm dying to know if she gets much in print. Save dear old Den of Lions till Thanksgiving. I'd love to get it in. Just to prove I'm really competition. Typed my brief 4 pg. Eng. theme[1] in bed last night while waiting for the ENEM to take effect

– Love –
Syl

TO *Aurelia Schober Plath*

Monday 16 October 1950[2] ALS (postcard), Indiana University

Mon. 8:30 A.M.

Dear Mum–

Gosh, life is wonderful. I signed out of the infirmary just 20 minutes ago. As nice as it was to have my last breakfast in bed, I won't miss being waited on at all. It was so good to leave the sterilized hall, nurses pushing trays of nosedrops, gargles, etc. from door to door, and walk out into the early crisp October sunshine with my green suitcase. Striding down the street, I passed a young, handsome Phillipino boy walking books in hand, obviously luxuriating in the morning. We exchanged smiles of complete and happy understanding. I can't wait to catch up on my work. It's really too bad there isn't more time to get out-of-doors, but I make the most of what I have. Smith is the most beautiful college on earth. I'm sure that in some months I will cease to see only the trees instead of the forest. As yet I'm not settled enough to pass judgement on my wonderful surroundings. Everything is here. It's up to me to discover & choose.

Love,
Sivvy

TO *Aurelia Schober Plath*

Monday 16 October 1950[3] ALS (postcard), Indiana University

Monday 1 PM

Dear Mum–

Can't seem to stop dropping my favorite person postcards. Although the work piled up on me this week is fabulous, at least my "rest cure" has

1–Sylvia Plath, 'The Golden Season'; held by Lilly Library.
2–Date supplied from postmark.
3–Date supplied from postmark.

made me vigorous to face it. Botany test Thurs. History continually piling – My first Eng. theme should come back graded next week. Needless to say, English is my favorite course. And today, as I was bemoaning my fate of staying indoors, I learned that we were – joy of joys – taking a field trip in Botany lab. So for two hours we walked around in the glorious sunlight examining trees. Even though I find it tough going to learn technical names, I've got a curiosity about plant life which should help me over the rough spots. Life seems very rich on a day like this – especially because I'm rested & healthy. I'm dying to see my poem in 17. Two other girls in the neighboring house like to write and are always sending things out to Cosmopolitan, Coronet[1] & Children's magazines. If I had time now, I'd love to do the same. But I'll have to wait till vacations

Love,
Sivvy

TO *Aurelia Schober Plath*

Tuesday 17 October 1950[2] ALS (postcard), Indiana University

Tuesday 8 AM

Dear Mum–

And so dawns another day. Yesterday, for the sum of $3 I went to the dentist and had my tooth, which hurt when cold air got on it, smoothed and painted with fluorine (sp??). Now it's fine, and I won't have to think about it. Is it my imagination, or is the air in my room almost dewey because of the lovely water holder? I have a Botany test, an art assignment and 40 pages of French translation due Thursday, plus regular Eng & Hist. assignments. However, when I look at the tired faces of some of my friends, I'm even more determined never to go to bed after 10:30. Got my gray sweater ensemble on now with my blue pedal pushers – very warm, very stylish. I don't see how I ever considered coming home before Thanksgiving. I've so much work to do. There is nothing compared to living at college. I walked downtown to get some books yesterday – it's really my home. It's such fun to know what girl goes with whom and where – things you'd never know if you commuted. I love eating with a crowd & chatting at meals. In fact I love the whole place.

Your
Sivvy

1–A general interest magazine published 1936–71.
2–Date supplied from postmark.

TO *Aurelia Schober Plath*

Wednesday 18 October 1950[1] AL (postcard), Indiana University

Wednesday
6 PM

Dear Mum–

Another mild orange-gold October day. Just to think, I'm almost 18! I get a little frightened when I think of life slipping through my fingers like water – so fast that I have little time to stop running. I have to keep on like the White Queen, to stay in the same place.

Today I have experienced the pin-point arranging of time. I painted my first art assignment after English. I did it hurriedly – a splashed color impression of Chapel meeting, but I got a thrill out of thinking how much I must improve. After History & Body Mechanics I got together with Pat, who's driven herself hard . . . That rest cure at the infirmary was a life saver. Life looks so bright when you're rested & well. Got a Botany test tomorrow, and 40 pages of make-up French to translate, so I must study very hard. This weekend I hope to devote to a summing up of what I've unthinkingly outlined in History. English is the one course that I don't have to work in. My teacher calls me "Syl"!! Of course the others have nicknames too!

Love—

TO *Aurelia Schober Plath*

Thursday 19 October 1950[2] ALS (postcard), Indiana University

Thurs.[3]

Dear Mum,

The fact that I'm writing another postcard reminds me of a few notes of minor necessities that would be nice for suggestions for inexpensive Xmas gifts. (Bermuda shorts are a luxury I'm not considering.) I've stationary galore, but could always use 1000 postcards & a million 3¢ stamps. A note on the more sensible side: knee socks in red, gray or navy. Here at least, warmth is a primary concern – no blue-goose-pimpled high school legs for me. Boraxo to wash my comb & brush, & raisins or something

1 – Date supplied from postmark.
2 – Date supplied from postmark.
3 – 'Thurs. ~~Tuesda~~' appears in the original.

rough to munch on while studying. Keep this card to remind me when I come home. My French teacher is utterly fascinating. Her voice can express anything. I'm going to slave for her. In tennis I met the most interesting girl – Enid Epstein[1] – She went to the high school of Music & art in New York and freelances drawings for 17! Think she's going to have something in the Nov. Ish, too. She loves art and writing. Maybe this could lead to a friendship – who knows? There is so much to discover here! Gosh, I wish the Norton males would get me a date to the Hvd.-Yale game. I'd give anything to go! Smith is the best place. How on earth did I get the luck to come! It's heaven!

Love,
Sivvy

TO *Aurelia Schober Plath*

Thursday 19 October 1950[2] ALS (postcard), Indiana University

Thursday night

Dear Mum,

It is ten o'clock, and I'm just going to turn in. I've been rushing around all week, and am going to try to rest from now till Monday. My end of the week courses are more of a pleasure to do. I have to prepare nothing for art lectures – just projects for studio. I have no preparation for Botany lab – just studying for tests in lecture period. So really art & French is all I have to worry about on Fri & Sat. I don't see how my schedule could be better. The only teacher I have who is poor is in art – he's a foggy bumbling man – says nothing definite, is always mumbling as if thru a cold. Our class[3] is really too huge. Went outdoor sketching today. I gasped when I saw some of the terrific work. At least of half the class is made up of Picassos, the other half is worse than I – some comfort. By the way my watch suddenly stopped. Shaking & tapping are to no avail. I can wind it down, but not up. Perhaps I over wound it. What'll I do; I need it a lot? Another thing, if you could get one of those history outlines on

1 – Enid Epstein Mark (1932–2008); B.A. 1954, English, Smith College; SP's classmate and friend, 1951–4. The High School of Music and Art was located at 443–65 W. 135th Street, New York.

2 – Date supplied from postmark.

3 – '~~His~~ Our class' appears in the original.

Feudal times – Med. History from fall of Rome on, do send it. I can't find any outlines up here. I love you –

XXXX
Love,
Sivvy

TO *Aurelia Schober Plath*

Friday 20 October 1950[1] ALS (postcard), Indiana University

Friday morning

Dear Mummy,

For me, this weather could last all year. This morning has been utter heaven. From 8:30-10 I sat out in the sun writing letters. At 10 I had another hour practicing backhand in my tennis class, which is really too big, but the exercise is something I look forward to every week. And now, wonder of wonders, our French teacher called a cut, so I have another hour of sunlight before Botany lecture. As you may imagine, days like this are rare indeed. You should see the view from my 3rd floor sunporch. The hills are rising over the gold trees and blue and red tile roofs in a smoky blue-purple haze. Paradise is reflecting russets & bronzes. Wellesley never had such hills! My bicycle & I are inseperable. I just coast from class to class. There is so much that is paintable here. Only with studying, I rarely find time to go out & cultivate new acquaintances. That must come later on.

Love –
Sivvy

TO *Aurelia Schober Plath*

Friday 20 October 1950[2] ALS (postcard), Indiana University

Friday night

Dear Mummy,

At the end of a strenuous week I feel rather exhausted. It is 9:30, so I am going to take a hot bath and be in bed at 10. Downstairs the piano is giving out with lovely jazzy tunes, as if for my special pleasure. Merci for

1–Date supplied from postmark.
2–Date supplied from postmark.

the vitamin pills. I drink water by the gallon. Today I had 2 helpings of fish for lunch, spinach, potatoes & two of Marie's special "black bottom pie."[1] I have lost no weight but actually gained one pound – 138, now. I spent 4 hours this afternoon 2-6, doing a problem for art – a black, white and gray study of my original color picture. Next week will be tough – a French & Botany test due Thursday, and an English paper and the (heaven help me) History written the following Monday. Toll house cookies will be most welcome. I'm too hungry to share many, so will eat them with my before-bed glass of milk. Do let me know what to do about the watch. There is so much to do all the time, I don't see how anyone could be unhappy or sad. One sure thing, I'll have to learn bridge & knitting during next summer. They are nice "small" ways of conforming. There is so much I "can't wait for" -- the Nov. Seventeen, the right boy (whoever he is, poor thing) for my Freshman year, my first English theme to come back. – Life here is lovely –

Love,
sivvy

TO *Aurelia Schober Plath*

Monday 23 October 1950[2] ALS, Indiana University

Monday mornings

Dear Mother–

Another Monday – another week. This one is going to be the toughest yet – a test in Botany and French on Thursday, and an English paper and history written a week from Monday. This weekend I went out Saturday with Bill. We doubled with Anne Davidow – that nice girl I told you about. We went over to Amherst as usual. Honestly, I have never seen anything so futile as their system of dating. The boys take their dates up to their rooms, usually to drink. After the first hour, the groups break up, and couples wander from fraternity to fraternity in search of a crowd into which they can merge, or a "party" which they can join. It is like wandering from one plush room to another and finding the remains of an evening scattered here and there. I can't say I give a damn about it. Bill, at least, is very sweet and thoughtful – nowhere as superficial as most of the boys I've run into over there. We were both quite tired and not in the

1 – Probably a Marie Callender pie.
2 – Date supplied from internal evidence.

mood for any party glitter, so we went to the suite, and I curled up on the red leather couch and dozed, while he stretched out in a chair. He had built a fire and put on some good records, so for about two hours I rested, and my eyes shut. We didn't even talk. At least both of us were tired at the same time. I almost have to laugh when I think back on it now. What would my housemates say if they knew what an entertaining evening I spent? I don't suppose they would realize that I had a better time under the circumstances than I could have had by straining to achieve a bright empty smile in a crowd all night. Sunday night I did the rather unwise thing of accepting a blind date to Alpha Delta (god, these Greek names are foolish.) Perhaps it wasn't so unwise after all. The other freshman from my house who doubled with me, really likes her date. Mine was tall dark, and more like John Hall than anyone I've ever met. He looked like Cary Grant and was a bit more suave, being a junior, but those were the only differences. The "sing" was lovely. We all sat by firelight in the living room and sang mellow college songs. The D Q[1] – Amherst singing group did a few numbers. There is something so hauntingly mellow about boys voices harmonizing.

Then we went down to the bar where I consumed three cokes. There seemed nothing very real about the occasion. The boys are all rather good-looking, the girls all rather lovely or pretty or cute, as the case may be. My date had pictures & scrapbooks of his girl – a Smith girl spending her Junior year abroad – around the room. So I was more or less just a date. It's funny, but the whole system of weekends seems more intent on saying "I went to Yale" or "Dartmouth." That's enough. You've gone somewhere. Why add: "I had a hell of a time. I hated my date." You see, I don't think people with ideals like our mutual friends the Nortons, frequent the bars where I have hitherto made my appearance. As for what I wore – my aqua dress Sat, and my red skirt & black jersey last night.

This next weekend I have vowed to stay home and sleep and study.

I wonder if I will ever meet a congenial boy. Oh, well–

Love,
Sivvy

1–The DQ is Amherst College's oldest secular, co-ed, *a cappella* singing group.

TO *Aurelia Schober Plath*

Monday 23 October 1950[1] ALS (postcard), Indiana University

Mon. afternoon

Dear Mum,

One rather pleasant note about this weekend which I neglected to mentioned – took a 10 mile bike trip with Betsy Whittemore[2] – a tall (5'11") quiet Freshman in my house. It was a glorious day, & we biked along the foot of the mountain range, munching winesaps we bought at a stand along the way. It was warm in the sun, and the fields were full of pumpkins & corn stalks. The countryside looked russet & gold – mellow enough to be done by Rembrandt – the red barns & white, clean-cut New England houses are so charming. We got lost eventually, and had to put our bikes in a farmer's car & be driven back to Hamp because it was too far to bike before dark. I had my medical today. Picked up athlete's foot from somewhere & am treating it. My hemoglobin is high – even after my cold, and I am 5'9" & 140 pounds heavy---perfect weight, said the nurse, according to my chart. I should have orthopedic & posture treatment, however – my feet are queerly lined. Oh, well, we all have our peculiarities –

Love,
Sivvy

P.S. Cookies are simply delectable.

TO *Aurelia Schober Plath*

Monday 23 October 1950[3] ALS (postcard), Indiana University

Mon. Afternoon

Dear Mum . . .

Since I feel rather drowsy today after two late nights (2 AM Sat – 1 AM Sun) I have resolved: No more Sun. night dating. I got a slight shock today – my first mark in English. After I worked so hard on my paper, to get a B- made me slightly sick. And another thing – <u>no</u> comments or corrections except one word underlined as trite – on the back, where other girls had paragraphs of criticism was written in tiny letters "Very

1 – Date supplied from postmark.

2 – Elizabeth ('Betsy') Whittemore MacArthur (1933–); B.A. 1954, botany, Smith College; SP's housemate at Haven House.

3 – Date supplied from postmark.

well put together." Now if I do my best and get B- in my "best" subject, what chance do I have in my tough courses? Most marks were from B- to C-. I saw none higher. I talked with a girl who had him last year, and she thinks he's a hard marker because he didn't give out any A's – thinks no-one's that good. I had to laugh at Warren's getting B- in English. His brilliant authoress of a sister is rather in the same boat. As the history written approaches, I get frozen, having slept away the weekend. I am going to devote most of my time after Thursday to shutting myself up & studying. One slight help – our eng. paper was postponed a week, so I won't be under pressure when I write it.

Love from your mediocre child.
Sivvy

TO *Aurelia Schober Plath*

Tuesday 24 October 1950[1] ALS (postcard), Indiana University

Tues. night

Dear Mum–

It is now 10 P.M., and I am drying my hair preparatory to going to bed. Today was another strenuous one – I'm still weary from my weekend, & classes never seem to let up. During my 2½ hours free time this afternoon, I propped my eyes open & did my immediate homework. I won't have time to start my history until Thursday. For supper, however, we broke the routine, and four advisors in the house took four of us advisees to dinner at Wiggin's.[2] Lisa is a terrific girl, and I feel I could go to her with any problem at all . . . only I don't have any serious ones yet. We had a lovely time stuffing ourselves (I had chicken, potatoes, beans, 5 rolls, cake, ice cream and coffee) in the delightful low, dark-paneled interior with black iron utensils on the wall. We didn't get back till 8:30, and I have been fixing my necessities like curlers & such & doing my hair & taking a bath since then. Time ticks by relentlessly. Am I queer, or is it normal that I am so snowed by being a microcosm here that I don't yet get the feeling of going to Smith? It's hard to explain, but I don't find myself able to pull away & evaluate my self in relation to my surroundings. Am I still numb

1–Date supplied from postmark.
2–Wiggins Tavern, in the Hotel Northampton, 36 King Street, Northampton, Mass.

from the shock of fighting 2,500 other individuals or what? I am content, thrilled, and yet feel inadequate to meet all that's offered me –

Love
Sivvy

TO *Aurelia Schober Plath*

Wednesday 25 October 1950[1] ALS (postcard), Indiana University

Wed. night

Dear Mum–

You have no idea how heroic I feel. I just refused a Friday night date and a weekend at Wesleyan both with faithful old Bill. I would have liked to go, but would have had a miserable time with the history written hanging over me. I thought that theoretical choice between a history written & a weekend was farfetched -- guess it isn't. Anyhow, I said I'd go to the game with him the weekend after. But this history thing scares me, so I'm devoting the whole weekend to it – no late nights to make me use up mornings sleeping. Tonight will be spent studying for the Botany and French quizzes. A note which hit me – one of the peppiest suavest freshmen in our house got called up by Ted Powell.[2] She asked me if I knew him because he was from Wellesley. So I said I did vaguely. Oh, dear will a nice freshman boy never give me a tumble? Pat got C- in her first English paper – and felt as sick as I did about mine. We had a mock Honor Board[3] trial today, and when I saw those faces in my Freshman Handbook materialize on stage, poised, lovely, assured, I wondered how so many people could devote all their energy to extra-curricular activities and still be brilliant, beautiful & popular. They are perfect Smith girls. I just hope I can contribute in some small way to this huge city.

Love
Sivvy

P.S. The History outline is a huge help to me – Thanks XXX

1–Date supplied from postmark.

2–Probably Ralph Dewey Powell, Jr (1932–); B.S. 1954, Amherst College. Powell lived at 8 Locust Road, Weston, Mass.

3–A student–faculty group that judged infringements of the academic honour system at Smith College. During the 1952–3 academic year, SP served as secretary of the Honor Board, under the direction of Helen Whitcomb Randall (1908–2000); English professor at Smith College, 1931–73; dean of the college, 1948–60; SP's colleague, 1957–8.

TO *Aurelia Schober Plath*

Thursday 26 October 1950[1] ALS (postcard), Indiana University

Thursday night

Dear Mum–

I couldn't wait another minute before writing you how touched I was to get my birthday package which just came. I walked into the house after my last class, & there it was – so I ran upstairs to open it. Who should be in my room but Pat, studying, so I opened the things in front of her – the maroon blouse is a dream (no wonder you're bankrupt) and the socks are warm & fit just right. I think I'll share the cake with freshmen in the house tomorrow. The dates are already half gone, & the bureau scarf just <u>makes</u> the room. This is my first birthday away from home, so I was rather overwhelmed by the packages. This morning I got 3 cards – one from Ilo, one from Aunt Hazel[2] (with a welcome $10) and my favorite gift of the day: a letter from & a picture of my brother! His snapshot now occupies a prominent place on my bulletin board. He is the handsomest, most wonderful boy in the world. I'm <u>so</u> proud of him. This morning I slept over an hour & got a 50¢ breakfast before going to class – 2 donuts, a hamburg, a glass of milk & a cup of coffee. My last vestige of makeup work will be a French test this Saturday, which sort of crowds things. Thanks for the lovely things.

XX
Sivvy

TO *Aurelia Schober Plath*

Friday 27 October 1950[3] ALS (postcard), Indiana University

Oct 27th 11:00

Dear Mum–

Well, your 18 year old (Gosh, hand me down my rocking chair) girl is just about to collapse into bed. At 10:00 tonight I disposed of half my cake in the kitchen with the aid of friends – yummy with milk. Tomorrow the rest will go even more rapidly. Even Mrs. Shakespeare joined us for a piece. Thinks you're a wonderful cook! I had to laugh – one of the girl's

1–Date supplied from postmark.
2–Probably Hazel M. Purmort (1883–1955), a professor of secretarial studies at Boston University. The Plaths used the term 'Aunt' quite loosely.
3–Date supplied from postmark.

was trying to persuade me to go dancing with a Dartmouth guy this Sat. Mrs. S. was horrified when I said no, I was staying home & turning in early. "But my dear, you mustn't let studying blot out your social life – it's so important to keep in circulation." I agreed with a smile, making a mental reservation (sleep, after 2 weeks of solid speed & tension, also is important.) She was relieved to hear I'm going out to a game next weekend. One of the girl's told me she is the most powerful house mother – can practically hand-pick her house! I agree with her when she says its the best-knit group of girls on campus. Today was an example of their sweetness. Today has been so full – I ate 2 pieces of apple pie à la mode at lunch & 6 pieces of cake at tea & supper combined. What a life –

Love to you all –
Sivvy

TO *Aurelia Schober Plath*

Saturday 28 October 1950[1] ALS (postcard), Indiana University

SAT morning

Dear Mum–

Just got back from taking my French quiz in the libe. I have 5 minutes before going to French, so I thought I'd drop you a line & let you know what I've been doing for the past month (haw). It was so good to talk to you last night! I can't describe in a card just how much this college experience away from home is doing for me. An amusing incident – 3 days ago my Botany prof & advisor walked into the coffee shop where I was having a late breakfast. I was so flustered when he sat beside me at the counter that I thought "He'll never know me among all his students," so I just sat and drank, while reading my mail. Of course I cursed myself for not saying anything afterwards as it dawned upon me that he might know who I was after all. So today, my pangs of conscience were rewarded when he walked in again. I greeted him with a cheery good morning, & he actually knew my name. so we conversed about mere nothings over coffee & he asked with a twinkle if I was "passing all my subjects." It all made me feel that there is a very personal side to this big impersonal organism. I love life – for the 1000th time – are there any colleges other than Smith?

Love,
me

1 – Date supplied from postmark.

TO *Aurelia Schober Plath*

Saturday 28 October 1950[1] ALS (postcard), Indiana University

Sat 3:00 PM

Dear Mum–

First, a few questions – what is Aunt Frieda's whole name – I want to write a Thank you note for the hanky? Second, I have an interview with Miss Mensel[2] Tuesday. What should I take for my policy of response to her? A horrible thought just occured to me. After falling so in love with my house & this special group of girls – how can I ask for a co-op house? It seems pitiful to get my roots growing down in fertile soil & have to rip them up & start all over somewhere else! It is now 3:00 & I am prepared to plunge into my history. All Satan's devil's were tempting me to put it off & stay out late tonight – not only Bill from Amherst, but a blind date from Dartmouth & one from Yale. God, I'm so noble I have to laugh! But my reward will come . . . in hell, if not here. Don't pity me – lots of kids are staying home & studying! To make up for my boyless weekend, I splurged 3.60 for a seat at the play "Streetcar named Desire"[3] this Thursday. Also bought "Vivid" lipstick – goes beautifully with my orange top. Everytime I see a girl on the street I can't help grinning broadly – "Isn't Smith heaven!" I think to myself. I can't rave enough over my French teacher. I look so forward to class. That woman is terrific – I wish you could come to hear her.

XXX
Sivvy

TO *Aurelia Schober Plath*

Sunday 29 October 1950[4] ALS (postcard), Indiana University

Sun Night

Dear Mum–

It is now the zero hour – 11 PM, just before I hop to bed. Tomorrow I have classes straight through till history – so no time to study then. It's

1–Date supplied from postmark.

2–Mary E. Mensel, Director of Scholarships and Student Aid (1946–64); 1918 graduate of Smith College; daughter of Ernest H. Mensel, professor of German at Smith College (1901–33) and Ann Mensel, associate professor of German at Smith College (1927–50).

3–*A Streetcar Named Desire* was performed at the Academy of Music, Northampton, Mass., at 8:30 p.m.

4–Date supplied from postmark.

just as well not to study the day of an exam, Lisa says. I spent all last evening and all today from 2-10 PM studying till my head was crammed full with a jumble of empires, centuries & trends. If I get D- I will only smile bravely & say "The Lord works in mysterious ways . . ." I have taken a hot bath & sleeping pill, & so should get 8 good hours of sleep in. Saw Pat in the carrels today. I was so shocked – she often skips supper & studies thru the noon till 10 PM. However she's met a sweet frosh at Amherst whom she's crazy about. I went to church this morning for the first time – a church date with a frosh from Dartmouth. He is very self-conscious of his face which shows scars of acne, but I felt sorry for him. The question is – should I go up to Dartmouth Sat Nov 14 – I'd not cut French, & the fare would be about $7 – so I can't decide if it's worth it. There's to be a dance, but I probably would be with this guy all the time. He's all right, but looks as if he'd shrink into the ground whenever anyone looks at his face. I am tempted to go for the hell of it & to make him feel confident – but I'd love you to sway me one way or the other. It's a gamble either way you look at it. I might have a good time – I might not. Hanover is supposed to be a nice town. What do you think?

Love
Sivvy

TO *Aurelia Schober Plath*

Monday 30 October 1950[1] ALS (postcard), Indiana University

Monday

Dear Mum,

Well, it's a known fact that post-mortems don't help. But at least the question was fair – "From the time of Constantine to the 11th cen there were frequent instances of close coöperation between secular rulers & the church. Discuss the principal instances, giving attention to reasons for cooperation & the consequences in each case." I made my little outline – & proceeded I thought I covered a lot, when coming back from the exam I encountered a fellow victim. "Oh," she said calmly, "I followed it thru to the conquering of England." Whereupon I felt slightly sick, realizing I had left out England completely. ⅓ of the important Empires missing! I can only pray for a C-. It's rather a shock to realize that here everyone studies, and often there are people more intelligent than I am . . . only too

1–Date supplied from postmark.

often. My only cause for rejoicing that my 3 small quiz grades in Botany have been A-, A, and A+. So if I study hard for our Bot. written next week, I should try to do well there. Another English paper is due Mon – on atmosphere.[1] If I get another B- I'll scream. At least our next history written is Dec. 4, so I can study over Thanksgiving. Oh well, I may not thoroughly appreciate the intracacy of Church & state, but I still love to draw ***

Your moronic offspring –
Sivvy

TO *Aurelia Schober Plath*

Tuesday 31 October 1950[2] — TLS with envelope, Indiana University

Tuesday

Dear Mother,

Well, I have just come from a half hour session with Miss Mensel. I was really foolish to ask you what I should say to her. It all poured out during the course of the conversation. Really, she is the dearest person . . . not beautiful . . . freckled and gray-haired, rather, . . . but with a keen vital twinkle in her blue eyes. She wants to meet all the scholarship girls in the freshman class and get to know them so she can describe them and their needs to the Board. In other words she is the personal medium through which the Board gets to know who we are and what we deserve. So I found myself telling her how stimulating my courses are . . . how French relates with History, and Art with Botany. How I want to take creative writing, and art courses. I even said how I love my house and the girls in it . . . the older ones too, who could give us a sort of perspective on college life. And about how nice it was to get dressed up and go out on weekends . . . or just go bike riding through the countryside. I had to keep myself from getting tears in my eyes as I told her how happy I was. I only hope I can live up to my courses and get good grades. The history does worry me a little. I was afraid I would be stiff and nervous at first, by my enthusiasm washed all that away, and I just flooded over and told her about how stimulating it was here. She agrees that I am in a superlative house, and also stressed the point about getting out on weekends so as not to go stale.

1 – Sylvia Plath, 'Atmosphere in the Short Story'; held by Lilly Library.
2 – Date supplied from postmark.

Now I come to the most thrilling part . . . about whose scholarship I have. The thing is, Miss Mensel likes the girls to establish contact with their benefactors so the people who give out the money are rewarded by a flesh-and-blood case. And whomshould my $850 come from but Olive Higgins Prouty!!![1] Miss Mensel said it was very seldom given to freshmen, but with my enjoyment of writing and my prize from the Atlantic Monthly (I'm afraid my Atlantic Monthly honorable mention has increased its prestige too much) Olive Higgins would be very pleased to hear from me and learn about my achievements and future plans, and also about the impact Smith has had on me. Now I will plunge into those darn critical English themes with renewed vigor. And go through my art exercises with that "means-to-an-end" gleam in my eye. If only I can meet all the opportunities. Just now I feel rather overwhelmed at the things Smith offers. Olive Higgins Prouty. Isn't she the one who dramatizes Stella Dallas? The fascinating thing is that she lives in Brookline, Mass.

Tonight we have a house party for Hallowe'en. Another girl--a gorgeous blonde freshman--wrote the dialogue for our freshmen skit and I wrote the words to the songs. The whole thing is rather foolish, but rather funny in rhyme. I hope it goes off all right. It's things like that that take up time in the evenings. I am still battling with history. I think I was left permanently in the dark ages. I can just see Louise Giesey getting Sophia Smith or something, while I come out with all B's and C's. I just can't stand the idea of being mediocre, yet I'll have to spend double time on history if I even hope to get an average mark. And even then I have so much to do in Botany to keep up . . . and in French. I'll be studying and sleeping all Thanksgiving, I fear. About the going out angle . . . I'll plan on going out Saturday night and staying home the others. After all, I can go out all the time here, but my family isn't seen so often. I can't understand the Freeman's . . . Mrs. F. sent me a love-and-best-wishes card with a dollar enclosed . . . no note from Ruth . . just a bit of cash. Not like her usual personal slant, I must say. As for Bob, all I got from him was one of those luxuriously gilded cards with violent purple and pink flowers and the usual sentimental birthday message. I don't know what's the matter with him. I think he's peeved because I told him I didn't know yet whether it would be wise for him to come down the weekend before thanksgiving or not as I didn't know how my work would pan out. I also mentioned that Thanksgiving wasn't very far away, which might have bothered him,

1–American novelist Olive Higgins Prouty (1882–1974). SP received the Olive Higgins Prouty scholarship as a student at Smith College. Corresponded with SP 1950–63.

as I no doubt should be languishing from loneliness and missing him no end. Frankly I hardly have time to give him a second thought. He is no part of my life here, and I am so busy finding out about Smith that I have no time to be either homesick or lovesick. Boys are strictly secondary in my present life. They can come and go or not come at all and I don't care too much. Of course I can see that this year for Bob is mere repetition . . . very little new except courses, and perhaps my absence makes him miss me or something. It's really too bad that the feeling isn't mutual. I find myself numb as far as feeling goes. All I'm trying to do is keep my head above water, and emotions are more or less absent or dormant for the while. It's a good thing to have one less distraction.

If only I'm good enough to deserve all this. I'm afraid the study of Pope Pompus the XXX and the Concordat of Worms is not subjective enough to fascinate me. I would be thrilled even to make some order out of the chaos of rising and falling powers, but I don't even seem to be able to see trends. It's so disheartening to read 20 pages of factual material and not understand the greater meaning behind the petty kings and popes . . . and see other girls give all the right answers. I really am going to work on it during my few days of respite in Thanksgiving . . . also on my art scrapbook which I haven't even begun. Our art lectures are fascinating . . . if not my studio teacher.

Oh, well, enough for now, I really must work. I am driving myself rather hard lately, and hope I can let up and go to bed and sleep at 9 tomorrow night . . . if I last that long.

Love,
Sivvy

TO *Aurelia Schober Plath*

Wednesday 1 November 1950[1] ALS (postcard), Indiana University

Wednesday –

Dear Mum–

Here I sit in the glorious morning sunshine. The sun is hot, there is no breeze – only crisp fresh air – and I can think of nothing nicer than to sit & bask on the porch while studying (heh heh) history.

Your letters are so interesting – Got a short impromptu English quiz back with a B and no comment. Perhaps the big (1200) (word) paper due

1 – Date supplied from postmark.

next Wednesday will rate a remark or two. We have to read All the King's Men[1] & Mayor of Castorbridge[2] very soon – both of which books I can buy or borrow for a mere pittance. Our little house costume party went off in great style – all the girls are so friendly. Ever since Miss Mensel told me about the Olive Higgins Prouty scholarship I've gone around with a lift in my heart. I have so much to live up to. I'll try to go easy on starches – but I'm so hungry all the time – I drink oodles of water & so have not had any of my chronic trouble (aren't I delicate.) I'm going to the Amherst-Tufts game with Bill this weekend – I'll tell you the results later on. Well – on to history –

Love,
Sivvy

TO *Aurelia Schober Plath*

Thursday 2 November 1950[3] ALS (postcard), Indiana University

Thurs.

Dear Mum–

Whew! Life is crowded. Mid-semesters are approaching – a 1200 wd. eng paper due Monday – Botany written Thurs, Art Notebook due Friday, 400 page novel a week from Monday – and a French mid-semester due the same week. I'm so happy – even cutting out pictures from magazines for art is fun. Have you seen 17?? There's rather a brilliant air about the magazine this issue . . . could it be that flattering picture of yours truly? Tonight I see StreetCar. I'll have to work extra hard this weekend, but it'll be worth it. History (ugh) doesn't come back for a week. I'm so happy about French. She doesn't mark the first test, but I had no corrections on the essay questions & "a very good paper" written on it. I got A on the little vocab quiz. If only I can make out as well on the written. P.S. If you find any examples of chinese brush drawing, sculpture pictures or pictures of lithographs & woodcuts, send 'em along so Ill get them before Friday. Our art book is examples of graphic art & line drawing.

Love
Sivvy

1–Robert Penn Warren, *All the King's Men* (New York: Modern Library, 1953); SP's copy held by Lilly Library.
2–Thomas Hardy, *The Mayor of Casterbridge* (New York: Modern Library, 1944); SP's copy held by Lilly Library.
3–Date supplied from postmark.

TO *Aurelia Schober Plath*

Friday 3 November 1950[1] ALS (postcard), Indiana University

Friday night

Dear Mum–

Well, tonight I'm staying home to start whacking away at my English paper. It's a nice night – wet and fresh after today's cold drizzle. Streetcar was dynamic. I haven't seen a play for so long. It was, I think, poetic bestiality. The scenery and lighting effects were superb – the feeling of dark wood rotting, and mouldy decay. The sister of the heroine – Blanche – reminded me a little of Mary MaGilura – a straight forward, honest simplicity in contrast to the taut, jagged nervousness of the heroine. I got in bed after midnight, but it was worth it. I am not going to Dartmouth. I'd rather stay home & study than spend money . . . on someone dull. Ruthie sent me 2 pretty scarves which I got today. House life is so cosy – I love dropping into the girls' rooms & sharing pieces of their lives. Costs are mounting, but I think I'll get along if I keep scrimping on luxuries.

Love,
Sivvy

a carrel is a metal enclosed study desk in the solitary quiet of the stacks in library

TO *Aurelia Schober Plath*

Saturday 4 November 1950[2] ALS (postcard), Indiana University

Saturday

Dear Mum–

Today my mail was wonderful – 4 letters and a postcard. My Hanover boy wrote a cute letter – but I'm so glad I decided to write him a refusal. House Dance[3] on Dec. 16 will cost me over $10, and I want to go – hope I find someone nice by then. As for "The Lady's Not For Burning"– by Fry, I believe – that's the book Austin left for me to read – never returning to get it back. I'll have to read it, now, you make it sound so delightful! Today it's cold & pouring rain. Instead of going to the game as so many

1–Date supplied from postmark.
2–Date supplied from postmark.
3–Each student residence at Smith College hosted its own winter and spring dances in the 1950s.

girls are, Bill & I are going to sit by the fire in his room & listen to it over the radio. I'd rather do my English paper, but so much time I will sacrifice to the collegiate spirit. The girls are sweet – dropping in & telling me to be sure to wear my raincoat and my overshoes . . . etc. * P.S. Just got back & am ready to hop into bed at 1 AM. Hardly got one drop of rain on me the whole time. Had a terrific steak dinner at Valentine Hall[1] – the Amherst eating place, and saw a vaudeville show put on by the boys afterwards. Amherst really is a "singing college."

Love,
Sivvy

TO *Aurelia Schober Plath*

Sunday 5 November 1950[2] ALS (postcard), Indiana University

Sunday 2 PM

Dear Mum–

Just a note before I at last settle down to my English paper. I slept till 10 this morning, had an apple and a few glasses of water, and sat in my bathrobe and chatted with another freshman till dinner. I like the drowsy quiet & leisurely morning on Sunday. Dinner was good – roast beef, potatoes & peas. I wore that lovely blue plaid Viyella blouse with my navy blue skirt today and it looks utterly rich! I love it! Did you see the write-up on Fry's play in the Trib?[3] My evening with Bill proved profitable in regard to my art assignment. A friend of his had an old photography book which he let me tear up, & I got pages of pictures which are just what I want – for now & future assignments. I am going to curl up in my easy chair and, slippers & wool socks on, make my self comfy while I hash out my little 1200 wd. treatise. Wish me luck on it. Love to my favorite person –

Your
Sivvy

1 – Valentine Hall, 59 College Street, Amherst, Mass.
2 – Date supplied from postmark.
3 – 'Christopher Fry Succeeded By Defying the Rules', *New York Herald Tribune*, 5 November 1950, Section 5, p. 1.

TO *Aurelia Schober Plath*

Monday 6 November 1950[1] ALS (postcard), Indiana University

Monday

Dear Mum—

Well – another week – gosh how they fly – it's like an obstacle race to the goal-line (Thanksgiving) when I can relax at the close of the race – & catch a breath before the next lap. Seriously, I am wary of these next two weeks. Very tight, they are. I did my Eng. Paper (6 pg.) all day yesterday & will hand it in Wed. He just better give me a good mark. One of the girls told him about my 17 story & poem – so he knows, but doesn't know I know he knows! I love that class – feel completely at ease in it. Ed sent me a lucid criticism[2] of my poem, which he grabbed on Nov. 1 (the loyal old thing.) Thinks I overdid the first part too lushly (which I did) but likes the second about the history inside the stone. Several girls have perused various of his letters. Conclusions: varied. Mainly envy & awe of him – "terrific writer–" "lots of drama in my life" etc. etc. Personally, I think he is a little too sure of his philosophy of life & his infallibility in analyzing others. Oh, heck – he's only 23 – give him time. It is now 11:15. My latest. But I can't afford to get sick now. Had supper at Louise's house tonight. You think you know Smith because your own house is so familiar – an then you plunge into another group of strange faces and again begin to wonder who you are.

Love,
Sivvy

TO *Aurelia Schober Plath*

Tuesday 7 November 1950[3] ALS (postcard), Indiana University

Tuesday night

Dear mum—

TSK TSK – 11 o'clock again. But I have had so much to do, and the time just whizzes. All afternoon I spent in the libe doing my daily homework. After supper Carol Pierson,[4] a friend from 1st floor, came up to the room

1–Date supplied from postmark.

2–See Eddie Cohen to SP, [5 November 1950]; held by Lilly Library.

3–Date supplied from postmark.

4–Carol Pierson Ryser (1932–2012); B.A. 1954, sociology, Smith College; SP's friend and housemate at Haven House.

to type a theme while I sat on the floor & worked on my art notebook. I have it about ⅓ done now. After doing a rather stilted job on the 1st 4 pages, I got into a real creative stride on the next ones. It is so mild out, now! I am sending some laundry home. My watch is in a little box wrapped in a green towel. The jeweler here took a piece of metal out of the works, but said it needed a thorough cleaning. I can't believe that in only two weeks I'll be going home!! Do see what shows are coming this Xmas. Our "family group" should take in a few good times while we're together. (This card is a masterpiece of incoherence.) I was rather embarassed in Eng today when my teacher said to let the rest of the class work at a story for a while – that I was explaining too much. It's so annoying to sit back & watch people fumble over a point you see so clearly. Eng. is not too challenging, I fear.

Love
Sivvy

TO *Aurelia Schober Plath*

Thursday 9 November 1950[1] ALS (postcard), Indiana University

Thursday 9 AM

Dear Mum—

I sure appreciate your scouring the stores for art magazines. They should arrive today, as I have to finish the book tonight. The etching by Rembrandt, the prints & especially Bellows[2] lithographs were a godsend, especially as I had none of the latter. Pat came over after supper last night, and we studied till 10 for the Botany written today. I am very sleepy, and hope to catch up on that rare commodity this weekend. As yet I haven't had time to write Mrs. Gorton or Mrs. Prouty, but I'll try to this weekend. Well, In less than two weeks I'll be home! Don't be surprised if I look a bit hollow-eyed – a good night's sleep will fix me up fine. I wrote Mr. Crockett a long letter about life up here – he's done so much for me that I felt he should share some of this experience too. Pat mentioned an advanced course in creative writing under Mrs. Chase[3] who marks papers according to the standards of Harper's & The New Yorker – that

1–Date supplied from postmark.

2–American realist painter and lithographer George Wesley Bellows (1882–1925).

3–American writer Mary Ellen Chase (1887–1973); professor of English, Smith College, 1926–55; SP completed English 11 (Freshman English), directed by Chase, 1950–1; SP's colleague 1957–8; Chase lived at 54 Prospect St., Northampton, Mass.

would be something to work for, wouldn't it? Wish me luck on my written today –

Love,
Sivvy

TO *Aurelia Schober Plath*

Thursday 9 November 1950[1] ALS (postcard), Indiana University

Thur. night

Dear Mum—

I'm writing this at "house meeting" while I dry my hair. Every other Thurs. night from 10:15-12 we all get together & hear reports from the house of Reps & vote on things – soo everybody knits, writes & otherwise is inattentive. My Botany written was the sort of thing you don't know how you did on. At least I passed!! Louise Giesey came over for supper (as my guest) & stayed all evening while I pasted up my art notebook. If I do say so, It's a pretty neat job – after the 1st 4 pages I really hit my stride – cutting out colored papers & shapes & arranging the pictures. I used all the graphic examples in those magazines which arrived this afternoon – and almost everything you sent. It's a big project, and I don't know what I'd have done without your help! I hope the old fool of a teacher realizes how brilliantly artistic I am – heh heh! I can't wait till tomorrow when at last I can go to bed early & relax for a while. My Eddie has been my most loyal correspondent (after you, of course) I've gotten at least 10 fat letters since I came here[2] – some people are so thoughtful –

Love
Sivvy

1–Date supplied from postmark.

2–In addition to previously cited letters, see Eddie Cohen to SP [12 Oct. 1950], [18 Oct. 1950], [24 Oct. 1950], [28 Oct. 1950], [5 Nov. 1950], and [7 Nov. 1950]; held by Lilly Library.

TO *Aurelia Schober Plath*

Friday 10 November 1950[1] ALS (postcard), Indiana University

Friday night

Dear Mum—

Well, it is 12:30 P.M. & I'm just crawling into bed. The amount of sleep I've had this week has been nil, so tonight I thought Id get my work done & hop in early. I was up in my room talking with a lovely girl in our annex (she's one of the people I really can tell things to.) And I was expounding on the misery & inferior feeling of being dateless this weekend. Bill had asked me out, but I had refused---he just isn't my sort – no spark. So nothing had turned up. I was saying how sad it was that my 3 blind dates here had fizzled so soon, when the phone rang. It was Louise Giesey – 3 boys had just dropped over & would I go out tonight. So I threw on my clothes – all the time ranting to dear Anne on how never to commit suicide because something unexpected always happens. Turned out that my date was a doll – Corby Johnson[2] – black hair – blue-eyes. His hobbies are sailing, drinking beer & playing bridge, but the 6 of us sat at Rahar's[3] & talked & laughed all evening. I had a good time – in fact I now feel terrific – what a man can do. Oh, well, I'll do my homework before class tomorrow

LOVE,
Sivvy

TO *Aurelia Schober Plath*

Saturday 11 November 1950[4] ALS handmade card with envelope, Indiana University

Saturday

Dear Mother –

Just for the sake of variety I thought I'd give you a demonstration of my "art work." This whole afternoon I spent in the art studio doing next week's art assignment. The little gem on the front page of this was run off in the press in a moment of frivolity. In reality it is not my real block print,

1–Date supplied from postmark.
2–Corbet Stephens Johnson, Jr (1932–94); B.A. 1953, Amherst College; briefly dated SP in 1950.
3–Rahar's Inn, a bar/restaurant at 7 Old South Street, Northampton, Mass., in the 1950s.
4–Date supplied from postmark.

but just a trial "scrap block." Even though I just used it to try out tools, I think it has a certain verve to it.

I am rather tired from standing on my feet for three hours – but I never had such fun. My block print was a gay informal design of three daisies. I ran it off 25 times on all sorts of material – colored paper, white paper, newspaper. The best effects were gotten when I put a cutout design of one color on a square of another & printed it. I thought that method out all by myself! The purpose is to understand the relief method of printing by doing it ourselves, & experimenting with all sorts of backgrounds. Some day I'll buy my own little press & print Xmas cards! I never had so much fun as standing in the big airy studio on the 4th floor of the art building & printing my gay little concoctions.

I am rather weary from my strenuous week and am oh! so glad I don't have to drag myself out tonight. I haven't even the energy to keep a smile pasted on my face. What could be nicer than to put on socks & slippers, curl up in another freshman's room downstairs & read "The Mayor of Castorbridge" while munching apples? Then a hot bath & to bed? I look so forward to relaxing.

It smells like Snow and Thanksgiving. It is just before supper, & music drifts up to my room. Oh, mumsy, I'm so happy here I could cry! I love every girl & every blade of grass. Even that adorable Amherst boy served his purpose & gave me an uproarious time last night! My lucky star brightens all the time. Ruth Giesel & I've been writing a lot.

Love you all – your happy girl –
Sivvy

TO *Aurelia Schober Plath*

Monday 13 November 1950[1] — ALS with envelope, Indiana University

Monday 1:30 P.M.

Dear Mother –

Well, another week begun. I have accumulated rather a large store of fatigue substances in my system, so that it will be a welcome respite to relax utterly & completely over Thanksgiving. The only trouble now is that I have to keep going till the last day – 9 Wed morning – when

1 – Date supplied from postmark.

I pass in my English paper on The Mayor of Casterbridge.[1] Have you any suggestions as to a definite topic? I had thought of doing it on fate or atmosphere or something like that.

Just now every hour is filled to the last minute. My French mid-semester looms up on Thursday. Unfortunately, all my studying for it must be done Wednesday – and then to start my paper.

Yesterday Mrs. Shakespeare mentioned to me that Mrs. Carle[2] called her. It was a clear bitter November day, so immediately after a delicious dinner I hied myself over to the library with my trusty copy of the "M. of. C." The browsing room is ideal for enjoyable reading assignments since it is sound proof, there is no danger of being disturbed by the telephone or by visitors, and yet there are all the comforts of home . . . good reading lamps & great cushioned easy chairs where you can take off your shoes & curl up in all sorts of odd positions. The chairs are all in front of windows, so you can put your feet up on the window seat, & look out across the campus to the Holyoke range, foggily purplish in the Sunday dusk. And all the while the carillon bells are chiming out hymns and college songs -- a lovely thing to hear.

Today was rather full – 4 hours of classes this am. – History lecture – then the libe till six where I struggled over history – reading, but not assimilating very easily. Perhaps you can correct my study habits if you see the book itself. The time I spend is hours above the actual things I learn. Tonight I just got back from another bout at the libe – it is now after nine. My letter to Mrs. Prouty will have to wait until Thanksgiving, I fear.

Oh, if you only could have seen how it was walking back from the libe tonight – that clear, crisp frosty air (perhaps like the night you walked to Wellesley College.) Lights from the dorms in square yellow dominos against the black. And hope, opportunity, capacity everywhere – Conversation overheard: "And in Zurich I took all my notes in German . . ." Gosh! This sure is international –

Love,
your old Sivvy

1–Sylvia Plath, 'Character is Fate'; held by Lilly Library.

2–Possibly Helen Carle of 30 Audubon Road, Wellesley, Mass.; Carle was a real estate agent and member of the Red Cross Gray Lady Service.

TO *Aurelia Schober Plath*

Tuesday 14 November 1950[1] ALS with envelope, Indiana University

Tuesday night–

Dear Mother–

There are times when schoolwork definitely should be put aside regardless. And tonight was one of them. I have been working pretty steadily, so I decided I owed it to myself to hear Peter Bertocci[2] of B.U. speak on "Sex Before Marriage." Naturally the title of the lecture drew hordes, and the browsing room was packed to the gills. I have to hand it to the man: he knows what a college crowd needs – none of this dodging the issue, either. I quickly lost my consciousness of the fact that he has an unpleasantly raspy voice and was lost in the sound maze of his contentions. Am I right in thinking that he's the one who lives on Pine Street in Wellesley? Or is that someone else?

As for the substance of his talk, it was not to dictate, but to set up a pattern of inquiry in our own minds. His lecture was phrased so that you could apply your own history & ideals with the case histories and questions which he brought out. Naturally my mind was receptive to clear cold logic – no Emile[3] around to make my emotions fight reason. In fact since I haven't really enjoyed myself with a boy since Emile, my emotional problems are vague and dormant. Maybe it's a good thing. I have thrown all my energy, physical and mental, into Smith – perhaps that would be a temporary sort of sublimation. The part that is hardest is this interregnum between boys. I need rather desperately to feel physically desirable at all times, and mentally desirable in cases where I admire a boy for his ideas too, but just now I am lacking any object of affection – no one to pour myself into except a close girl friend – Ann Davidow. And I talk to her only too rarely.

In other words, this is a period of sterility emotionally. Mentally it is a fertilization of the soil in my mind . . . who knows what may bloom in the fruitful season later on? Enough symbolism. I am happy – which is strange, as I realize myself socially & emotionally unfulfilled. But with my old resilient optimism I know deep down inside that when I find a

1–Date supplied from postmark.

2–Peter Anthony Bertocci (1910–89); professor of Philosophy at Boston University. His talk 'The Question of Sex Before Marriage' took place in the Browsing Room of the Neilson Library at 7:15 p.m. Bertocci lived at 30 Pine Street, Wellesley, Mass.

3–Emile George de Coen, III (1930–), who lived at 22 Grantland Road, Wellesley, Mass.

real companion in a boy, I will be only too glad I had this period of static waiting to increase my sense of pleasure. As to my subjects – I'm beginning to see light – I love them all. I'm being stretched, pulled, to delights & depths of thought I never dreamed possible . . . and what is most wonderful --- this is only a beginning. The future holds infinite hope and challenge. I somehow can't keep from singing to myself, no matter how weary I am – sunshine which I had when I was little seems to have been restored by Smith. And I know that in the cycle of joy and sorrow, there will always be an outlet for me – I can never lose everything – all at once. Once I get my scholarship firmly established, I may have time to turn my attention more thoroughly to art and creative writing. Even now I am greatly encouraged to find that the black, immovable wall of competition is not so formidable when broken down into small human units. I am finding myself still in upper brackets as far as marks go. Sure, I work hard – and so do hundreds of others. But my sane weekend life has kept me healthy & able to cope with most daily work. I'm getting study habits, keeping up. When I get that down to a science I can weekend with relative impunity.

Above all, I'm happy – knowing that from pain comes understanding, I rejoice in whatever happens. Strangely enough, I am rather well-adjusted, I think, and enjoying life more fully than I ever have.

If only I can weld now – where I'm living so hard I have no energy to produce – into art, writing later on. It's like animals storing up fat and then, in hibernation or relaxation, using it up. I have a feeling that my love of learning, of people, of wanting to perfect techniques of expression, may help me to reach the goals I choose to set. Can you make any sense out of this? Maybe you can analyze the ramblings of your child better than she can herself–

Love,
Sivvy

TO *Aurelia Schober Plath*

Thursday 16 November 1950[1] ALS (postcard), Indiana University

Thursday

Dear Mother–

Well, I had my French mid-semester today. It's one of those things that you don't know how you did in. I was so relieved to get your little $5

1 – Date supplied from postmark.

gift! I went right down and bought a round trip ticket for $5.12. The 10:30 bus is one of those connection affairs involving a 1 hour wait in between. Train is definitely out – too expensive & too awkward – So it looks like I'll be taking the one o'clock p.m. bus. I should be home by 5 P.M. unless I should unexpectedly get a ride, in which case I'll see you in the afternoon. I think I'll wash my hair the first thing so I'll be nice for the weekend. I'm afraid I'll have to bring a few books home as I have an Eng. novel to read & a History (ugh) written & Botany written the very next week.

See you soon–
Love,
Sivvy

TO *Aurelia Schober Plath*

Friday 17 November 1950[1] ALS (postcard), Indiana University

Friday night

1

Dear Mother –

It is now the scandalously late hour of 12:30, but I really don't use up much time writing to you – it takes so little effort to drop a line each day – and each day has it's own special assets & liabilities. Today was an asset day straight through. Two cards from you & a fat letter from Eddie.[2] And in Botany – <u>guess</u> what I got on my first hour exam!!! 96***!! I almost flopped! I'm going to study like mad for our next exam Friday, cause I've gotten far behind on my lab sheets. But so far my average in Botany is straight, pure, unadulterated A! I need that so much to balance my next history written. I will study for that, too, over Thanksgiving – but at least my Botany encourages me no end. I spent the afternoon in the art room. I had my little conference with the teacher – my notebook, I'm afraid, "leaves much to be desired."

Love,
Sivvy

1–Date supplied from postmark.
2–See Eddie Cohen to SP, [15 November 1950]; held by Lilly Library.

TO *Aurelia Schober Plath*

Friday 17 November 1950[1] ALS (postcard), Indiana University

Friday

2

continued –

Here I am again to finish up the account of the day. After coming back from Art, I had a cup of tea & some cake at our weekly Friday social hour. Then Anne Davidow and I headed nobly to the libe to spend an hour there before supper. Unfortunately the sun was setting in clear pink, mirrored in Paradise pond, so we looked at each other helplessly as our feet marched us down to the grassy banks – it was like a Chinese painting – with the lights of the boathouse reflecting in the glassy water & the lavendar-blue twilit hill in the distance – like that blue in the picture over your desk. So we talked – frankly about everything. She's a wonderful girl – I love her for her witty spontaneous temperament & evidently the feeling is mutual. After supper – to the libe in ernest with Anne, & then to a delightfully cosy Open House for a few of us at the Chaplains[2] – cider, gingerbread, a crackling fire, parlor games & lots of laughs –

XX
Sivvy

TO *Aurelia Schober Plath*

Saturday 18 November 1950[3] ALS (postcard), Indiana University

Saturday

Dear Mum –

Slept till nine this A.M. and awoke to find three letters waiting for me. I opened the one from Warren first – a four page epistle with humor that had me in stitches. Honestly, his letters are more entertaining than Bob's. Then a letter from Ruth Geisel who has arranged me a date with a gorgeous blond hunk of man from R.P.I. for heaven knows what night. I look so forward to seeing her again. (Remind me to get my stories off!) The third letter was from Bob. Seems he went down to Wellesley last weekend to the big N.H.-Tufts game & to a dance and party afterwards.

1–Date supplied from postmark.
2–William Graham Cole (1917–2011), chaplain and assistant professor of Religion and Biblical Literature, Smith College, 1947–52.
3–Date supplied from postmark.

I'm really glad. Wants me to see Streetcar again,[1] but I wouldn't sit through it twice! I look so forward to seeing you all in a few days. Just think! Four whole days home & then Xmas!!!

Love,
Sivvy

TO *Aurelia Schober Plath*

Sunday 19 November 1950[2] ALS (postcard), Indiana University

Sunday, am.

Dear Mum –

When you see me walk into the house Wednesday, don't be surprised if I don't speak to you, but instead march upstairs & fall into bed! I'm so sleepy, but I can thank my lucky stars that I haven't gotten sick again. If I make it till Wed., I think it will be O.K. Last night I got to bed at two. By the machinations of my friend Anne Davidow, I got a blind date to dinner & the Mardi Gras at Amherst. I went over on the traditional bus with two other girls – the ride was such fun! Luckily my date – a frosh – was 6'2" and very entertaining. I saw so many people I knew during the festivities that I had a warm glow of really being at home – saw Mrs. Powell[3] at dinner, Jeanne Woods, up from Wellesley, & Bob Blakesley[4] at the dance, good old Bill with his date (rather on my type – tall, long hair) and my sparkling soph date of last Friday – not to mention Pat's flame with a blonde & various of my housemates. I like going with freshmen (my first.) They plan things, & don't just sit & drink like the frat men do. Saw a super aqua show – such high dives – ! Guy[5] & I rode back on the bus which was packed with Smith & Amherst dates. Felt very collegiate.

Love
Sivvy

1–*A Streetcar Named Desire* was on its third Boston run on 13–25 November 1950 at the Plymouth Theatre, 131 Stuart Street, Boston, Mass.

2–Date supplied from postmark.

3–Eugenia Norris Powell (1899–1976), of 8 Locust Road, Weston, Mass.

4–Robert Blakesley (1932–); B.A. 1954, Amherst College; friend of SP from Wellesley.

5–Guy Wyman Wilbor (1932–); B.A. 1954, Amherst College; dated SP, 1950–1.

TO *Aurelia Schober Plath*

Monday 20 November 1950[1] ALS (postcard), Indiana University

Mon. morning

Dear Mumsy –

This is the nicest Monday yet. For once I feel wide-awake. I put aside all my work last night, took a hot bath, and was asleep by 9. As a result I feel quite ready to do my English theme. I had a delightfully leisurely breakfast to make up for the two I missed this weekend as a result of over-sleeping – tomato juice, egg, applesauce, milk, coffee, and three sweet rolls. I feel so good inside. I know that if I work I am capable of getting along well in my subjects – and that helps. I have a few good freshmen friends who confide their datelife to me. It's so nice to live a few other lives beside your own. I wonder how I deserve being so cosy and happy! Perhaps I have it inside me – nothing can keep me down for long – I always end up by laughing at myself and remembering how hopeful the future is. See you Wednesday afternoon –

Love,
Sivvy

TO *Aurelia Schober Plath*

Sunday 26 November 1950[2] ALS (postcard), Indiana University

Sun 8:30 PM.

Dear Mum –

Well, I didn't know just when the wave of homesickness would hit, but I guess it was when I walked in to my room – empty & bare. Only three or four girls were in the house – so I sat up there & unpacked and ate my "supper." Gosh, I felt lonely! I had so much work I should have done, and my schedule for the week looked so bleak & unsurmountable. But I have now snapped out of my great depression---the first real sad mood I've had since I've been here! I am now writing this in the cosy livingroom with a girl beside me & music coming out of the radio – what one human presence can mean! I realized that for all my brave bold talk of being self-sufficient---I realized how much you mean to me – you and Warren & my dear grampy and grammy! It is now 9:30 & I am hopping into bed. – My

1 – Date supplied from postmark.
2 – Date supplied from postmark.

loneliness perhaps springs from the fact that the busy routine I associate with life here is momentarily lifted & I am left spinning in a vacuum. I'm glad the rain is coming down hard. It's the way I feel inside. I love you so.

Your
Sivvy

TO *Aurelia Schober Plath*

Tuesday 28 November 1950[1] ALS (postcard), Indiana University

Tuesday

Dear Mother –

I guess I never told you that the ride back was calm & without event. It's a relief to have a routine to fall into – which keeps me from thinking too much about myself. Tell Grampy those delicious Apples sure are a treat! I am just now consuming the last with relish. I think I would go utterly & completely mad if I didn't have Xmas vacation[2] to look forward to – these last few days were just tantalizing. By the way, my spring vacation is from March 21 – Wed to April 5 – two weeks no less! My exams are on the 24th & 31st of Jan. & the 2nd of Feb. So I could, I think, come home Wednesday the 24th of Jan. & safely stay till the next Monday – I'd have a real chance to get to work. This basketball at 4 Mon & Tues really upsets my schedule – 6 hours of classes exhausts me, leaving no time to work till after supper – but as a consequence, the end of the week is easier, which is something. Basketball should prove good all around. It's terribly strenuous, but I love the exercise & it's fun playing with a group

XX
Sivvy

1 – Date supplied from postmark.
2 – 'if I didn't have Xmas ~~Thanksgiving~~ vacation' appears in the original.

TO *Aurelia Schober Plath*

Wednesday 29 November 1950[1] ALS (postcard), Indiana University

Wednesday –

Dear Mother –

Well, if wishes were fishes I would buy a few tall handsome males to squire me to House Dance. As it is, I drooled over those luscious clothes you described – the white sleeveless jersey sounds divine – it would be better than the black blouse (which would also be lovely) because it's a change from my old black velvet dress – (remember?) which I still hope to wear. <drawing of dress> Also the white jersey skirt sounds lovely. As much as I was fascinated by the idea of appearing in metal like Sir Launcelot, the white jersey ensemble, if it could be worn together as a dress, seems to be the most versatile – the white top could go with my black velvet or red cord-skirt, while my black jersey could go with the skirt – Yes, Bob Humphrey[2] is a thoughtful fellow – I'd like to see him again – but on the way up Tooky Sisson[3] (tra la la), told him to sit in front because someone short could sit in back with us better & she preoccupied him with a rapid discussion of old times & their trip to Arizona a year ago – leaving me slightly out in the cold – I have to admire her technique! As Ruth said, the boys all fall for it. I'm seriously considering inviting Warren or Clem[4] to House Dance – heh heh

XX
Sivvy

1 – Date supplied from postmark.

2 – Robert Hills Humphrey (1929–); B.Arch. 1952, Rensselaer Polytechnic Institute; dated SP, 1950–1.

3 – SP's classmate Lois Sisson Ames (1931–); B.A. 1952, English, Smith College; M.A. 1958, University of Chicago; married Robert Webb Ames (divorced 1969).

4 – Clement Moore Henry (1937–); Warren Plath's roommate at Phillips Exeter Academy; A.B. 1957, Ph.D.1963, Harvard University; M.B.A. 1981, University of Michigan.

TO *Aurelia Schober Plath*

Wednesday 29 November 1950[1] ALS (postcard), Indiana University

Wednesday night

Dear Mum –

This has been another one of those days that leaves a little glow inside. In chapel we heard a speaker from a Chinese college we support[2] tell about conditions there under the communist rule. Naturally we took up the discussion among ourselves – to support or not to support – It is such a relief to talk with girls who are thoughtful and idealistic and well-informed – none of this "Bomb them off the map" Business!! So many agree with my pacifistic ideas, and we had such fun talking at supper about it. When you look at the thing in perspective it seems almost amusing – and you wonder with impersonal curiosity what will happen after man runs out his little space in time. By the way, I'm almost famous . . . There is a bulletin board in College Hall (where the president & all the deans work) which has weekly clippings of Smith girls "in the news" – Yup! Some newshound dug up my poem and it & my face shine out – I had a strange experience in History today – as I always sit in the middle seat in the front row, it seems as if Mrs. Koffka[3] is talking directly to me. I felt the oddest thrill – History is becoming rather vital and fascinating – specially when she quotes german

XXX
Love
Sivvy

1–Date supplied from postmark.

2–The speaker in Chapel was Dr Florence King (1902–94) who taught at Ginling College in Nanjing, China, 1932–50.

3–Elisabeth Ahlgrimm Koffka (1896–1994); history professor, Smith College, 1929–61. Koffka taught general European history (History 11) completed by SP, 1950–1.

TO *Olive Higgins Prouty*

Wednesday 29 November 1950 TLS (carbon), Smith College Archives

November 29

Dear Mrs. Prouty,

When Miss Mensel told me that I had received the Olive Higgins Prouty scholarship this year, I resolved that I would try to tell you just what my experience at Smith means to me. The only difficulty is in knowing just where to begin, and just where to stop, for I could write on and on.

First of all, I am a Freshman, living at Haven House. I'll never forget the first day I saw my house and the campus. It was about a week before the college opened, and the streets were quiet in the thick summer afternoon. It is difficult for me to describe the sensations I felt as I walked up Observatory Hill and looked at the buildings, then strange and unfamiliar. I had the feeling of exhilaration that comes when you say to yourself – "This is it: The door is open; the reality is here. Everything I dreamed is here, in these buildings, and the people that will live in them."

And so I walked across the porch of Haven, my footsteps echoing in the silence. I looked for a long time at the window of my room on the third floor, knowing that in a week I would be on the other side of the wall, and that the view would become an accustomed sight.

Perhaps you will understand a little better my keen pleasure in finding Smith a tangible actuality when I tell you how unsure I was of my future a year ago. I was at Wellesley High School, and there was no possibility of my going anywhere unless I received a full scholarship. So I applied for a town scholarship at Wellesley and, under the encouragement of my English teacher, for a scholarship at Smith. At first I didn't want to let myself hope for Smith, because a disappointment would have been hard. But more and more I became aware of how much fuller my life would be if I were able to live away from home. There would be a beginning of independence, and then the stimulation of living with a group of girls my own age. After weeks of waiting and indecision, I heard from Smith that I was being awarded a scholarship. The Smith Club of Wellesley had agreed to help me out in meeting the balance, so I went about the house for days in a sort of trance, and not quite believing myself when I heard my voice saying, "Yes, I'm going to Smith."

And here I am! There are times when I find myself just letting the sights and impressions pour into me until the joy is so sharp that it almost hurts. I think it will always be this way. There is so much here, and it is up to me to find myself and make the person I will be. I still remember the first evening when we had our Freshman meeting. I was separated from the girls I knew in my house, and as I stood bewildered on the steps of Scott Gym, watching six hundred strange faces surge at me and pass by like a flood, I felt that I was drowning in a sea of personalities, each one as eager to be a whole individual as I was. I wondered then if I could ever get behind the faces and know what they were thinking, dreaming, and planning deep inside. I wondered if I would ever feel that I was more than a name typewritten on a card.

But even now I smile at myself. For with the studying, and with the ability to isolate and differentiate one person from another, and with the increasing sense of belonging, I find myself at the beginning of the most challenging experience I've ever had.

As for my courses, I have never felt such a sharp sense of stimulation and competition. I am especially fortunate in my instructors – all of whom are vital and alive with enthusiasm for their particular subjects. In art we sketch the same trees that we analyze in Botany. In French we follow the ideas of men who were influenced by the events and times we read about in History. And in English – which has always been my favorite subject – we read and do critical essays. (It's the usual Freshman course, and I am eagerly awaiting next year, when I will be able to take creative writing.) As you can see, my courses fit together like a picture puzzle, and life has suddenly taken on deeper perspective and meaning. I don't just see trees when I bike across the campus – I see shape and color outwardly, and then the cells and the microscopic mechanisms always working inside. No doubt all this sounds a bit incoherent, but it's just that excitement which comes when you are increasingly aware of the infinite suggestions and possibilities of the world you live in.

The people here are also another source of amazement and new discovery. I don't think I've ever been so conscious of the dignity and capacity of women. Why, even in my house there is a startling collection of intelligent, perceptive girls – each one fascinating in her own way. I enjoy knowing people well and learning about their thoughts and backgrounds. Although I have never been able to travel outside the New England states, I feel that the nation – and a good part of the world – is at my fingertips. My acquaintances come from all sorts of homes, all sorts of localities, and as I get to know them better, I learn about all varieties of past personal history.

This brings me, in a round-a-bout way, to be sure, to my interest in writing. Miss Mensel suggested, since yours is a scholarship for someone interested in creative writing, that I tell you about my little successes and failures in that field. I guess I have always been rather introspective, and when I began the teens I felt the need of expressing myself, so I naturally drifted into sketching and writing poems. I never thought much about it, for it was always so natural to put my feelings for a snowflake or a sunset into rhyme. In high school, however, I fell into the hands of a stimulating English teacher who encouraged me to write as much as I could. I never had any instruction, for he believed that an individual who needed to be pushed and coddled was not worth the effort, and one who was determined would work on her own anyway.

I began to take a new delight in recording my emotions. I would catch myself observing my own reactions from a distance and mentally taking notes: "She said this" or "She wondered . . ." – all in the third person. Always I wanted to say something, to twist out a chunk of my life and put it on paper in the most effective way possible. I never thought much about style, but I was influenced, naturally, by the authors I read. For instance, there was a time when Edna St. Vincent Millay seemed to voice all my agony and joy of adolescence. And then Sinclair Lewis dawned on my horizons, and then Stephen Vincent Benet. And Virginia Woolf. I guess it's like that with everybody – the thrill of "discovering" a new writer. So I began sending my stories and poems out to magazines about two years ago. There was a time when all I asked of life was to be accepted in "SEVENTEEN". It was not so much the idea of being in print, as the idea that my life and my observations were worth something in the eyes of others. Naturally I began to pile up rejection slips. I bombarded the poor editor of SEVENTEEN with manuscript after manuscript, and after about thirty failures, I had a story published in August in the "It's All Yours Section" of SEVENTEEN. This November a poem of mine was published there. I also sent in to the Atlantic Monthly contests, and one of my stories won a top paper award last year. This summer I worked on a farm in Dover, Massachusetts, and after a thoroughly delightful experience of "laboring" in the fields with negroes, displaced persons, and a unique assortment of other characters, I wrote a poem and a brief essay which appeared in the Christian Science Monitor in August and September respectively.[1] That is my story to date. Perhaps I have gone a bit overboard in telling you all these details, but that is a very vital part of

1 – Sylvia Plath, 'Bitter Strawberries', *Christian Science Monitor*, 11 August 1950, 17; Sylvia Plath, 'Rewards of a New England Summer', *Christian Science Monitor*, 12 September 1950, 15.

me, and perhaps you will be sympathetic even if I talk at too much length.

I don't know now where my interest in writing will lead me. Whether or not I am any good, I will keep on purely from necessity. Gradually, I think, I will evolve from recording my own experiences, to recording those of other lives. But now I best understand that which happens to me, which perhaps is too egotistical. However, I hope my grasp of range of subject matter will continue to broaden. And that is another reason why I love it here. There is the opportunity to learn, to improve, to be criticized.

Now that I have taken so much of your time talking about myself, I wonder if I have said anything worth while – or if I have revealed even a small part of my love for Smith. There are so many little details that are so wonderful – the lights of the houses against the night sky, the chapel bells on Sunday afternoon, the glimpse of Paradise from my window. All this and so much more.

No, I don't think I could ever express just what this opportunity means to me, for even I don't fully realize all that lies ahead. I just want you to understand that you are responsible, in a sense, for the formation of an individual. And I am fortunate enough to be that person.

Sincerely,
Sylvia Plath
Haven House

TO *Aurelia Schober Plath*

Thursday 30 November 1950[1] ALS (postcard), Indiana University

Thursday

Dear Mum –

Another one of our charming house meetings – and so I write little notes. My schedule of writtens and papers is rapidly building up into a horrible network – it's like steering a leaky boat (me: – note the symbolism) through rocky rapids. I was rather depressed that noone asked me out this weekend, but (something always turns up) Pat has gotten me a blind date with someone over at Amherst, so even if he isn't much, it should be fun doubling with her. I won't be able to study history till Friday night – but even so, I feel that I need the contrast of an evening out to relieve the intensive routine of studying. I went to a brief House of Representative

1 – Date supplied from postmark.

meeting tonight. All Freshmen are required to go sooner or later, and it was rather exciting to get behind the scenes of the college. I wrote a long letter to Mrs. Prouty last night – which took up a few hours of thought and time, but good heavens – she is responsible for all this. French gets progressively harder. I only got a B+ for my midsemester test and grade – but I guess that's not <u>too</u> bad.

Love,
Sivvy

TO *Aurelia Schober Plath*

Friday 1 December 1950[1] ALS (postcard), Indiana University

Friday night

Dear Mum –

It is now eight o'clock, so this will be a brief note before I hop off for a 2 hour stint of history at the library. We got our mid-semester marks today – understand that they are only tentative, and that surely History & possibly French may go down by midyears, they were: Botany: A, French A-, History A-, English B, and Art B-. I just hope I can keep up. The secretary who gave me my card told me I should by "very proud," Ah, well! Tonight I went to supper at Wiggins with Anne Davidow, her parents, and two other girls from the house. We had a lovely meal – all beautiful people – and Mrs. Davidow is a strikingly lovely woman – very lovely & intelligent. It developed that none of us four girls have got a date for House Dance, so we decided to get together & resolved to dig ourselves up four Amherst males by hook or crook. Well, four brains are better than one, so wish us luck –

Au revoir
Sivvy

1 – Date supplied from postmark.

TO *Aurelia Schober Plath*

Sunday 3 December 1950[1] — ALS with envelope, Indiana University

Sunday 3 P.M.

Dear Mother –

It was so nice to get your little card today – mail on Sundays is a treat. (I agree with your sentiments about Tooky completely!)

I am rather weary, as I didn't get to bed till 2:30 this morning, and as a result am rather groggy – sad state to study history in, I fear. But no matter how much I don't accomplish I'm going to take two little pills and be asleep by nine o'clock. I am convinced that even if you don't know quite all you should, a clear rested mind can put things together better and make the most of what you <u>do</u> know.

So I had to write you about everything before I began to work. I really think I should see Fran[2] about my periods when I come home at Christmas. I haven't had one yet, just a sort of watery secretion which is rather uncomfortable.

I am learning a lot. There is the sort of person who has problems and never tells them to anyone and thus no one ever knows them; there is the sort of person who has problems and tells them to one understanding person, and there is the sort of person who fools everyone, even herself, in to thinking there are no problems except those shallow material ones which can be overcome.

All this, as you may have gathered leads up to my date last night. As I said, I doubled with Patsy. It was ordinary enough driving over with the couples – my date[3] looked rather old – (in fact his hair was somewhat reminiscent of Mr. Crockett's) and he had a rather good-looking face. It developed that he and I liked English, and that he was majoring in Political Science. So as we all sat around the fire, I decided to stab in the dark and see if I could get to know him better. I told him how I liked to write and draw and know people more than just on the surface, and I said I'd like him to tell me all about the things that ever had hurt him or bothered him so I'd be able to understand him better. Well, it was just

1 – Date supplied from postmark.

2 – Dr Francesca M. Racioppi Benotti (1916–98); the Plaths' family doctor, who practised in Wellesley, Mass., under her maiden name Francesca M. Racioppi.

3 – William Deming Nichols (1924–2006); World War II marine in command of an anti-aircraft battery on the Pacific Island of Tinian; B.A. 1951, Amherst College; LL.B 1954, Harvard University; dated SP in 1950.

a try, but evidently he was rather overwhelmed by the fact that I could be so "intelligent" and yet not be ugly or something, and as we danced after cooking our supper over the fireplace in their room at the Fraternity House, he told me that he was twenty-five, disabled in the last war. Naturally that bowled me over, so I asked if he could tell me at all about it.

Pat said that his roommates don't really know him because he keeps everything to himself, so I was rather amazed that he would confide in me.

At his suggestion we went for a walk so we could talk better, and he told me a little about fighting in the Mariana's, and about what its like to have to kill someone or be killed. Then he asked when my father died, and when I told him, he said his died two weeks ago, and that he had been with him for the last days. It seems his father[1] was the best patent attorney in Missouri – clients from England even, and this guy idolized him rather a lot. So he told me how he felt about him, and said that the other girls he'd been out with since didn't give a damn, etc.

Naturally nothing like that had ever happened to me before – and I guess he was so overwhelmed with the idea that at last someone was interested in him as a person, not just as a date, that he seemed to think we should have intercourse. Of course, I was in rather a bad position having gaily gone on a walk but I told him quite forcibly that I wouldn't oblige. All of which made a scene, and I asked him how many other girls he had known, and he said he would tell me the truth, that the marine core wasn't the place to be a gentleman, and that ideals didn't quite matter when you slept and lived in the mud. So I learned about the girl in Hawaii and about the English nurse when he was in the hospital for two years.

Naturally I came back home in rather a fog. I don't know just how things will work out, or whether I should see him again. I am just beginning to realize that you can't ostracize a person for having relations with alot of others. That doesn't automatically cancel out their worth as a human being as I once thought. One thing – don't worry about me . . . I am able to take care of myself, but I would like your opinion on the matter, as I don't quite know what to make of it, never having run into anyone quite so determined before.

It's sickening to see all the uniforms on campus and hear that Amherst won't even be here next year – I am so tired, and I'm looking forward to being with the family this Christmas.

1 – Malcolm Parrott Nichols (1891–1950).

Keep smiling – (why do I always inspire males to pour out their life story on my shoulder? I guess I just ask for it.)

Love,
Sivvy

TO *Aurelia Schober Plath*

Monday 4 December 1950[1] ALS (postcard), Indiana University

Monday 3:30

Dear Mum –

I wish this card could have gotten off in the same mail as my rather thoughtless letter. I have to laugh at that situation on Sat. night which bothered me. I talked it over with some of the girls, and most of them had something similar happen to them. The general concensus was that my date needed security of some sort, and the idea that someone was sympathetic and would hear him out sort of threw him off balance. Well, we shall see. Your letter sure gave my ego a shot in the arm – when I think of what a skimpy basis they have to judge me on! But anyway, I think my talk with Miss Mensel may have had something to do with it! I'd love to go to John Hancock any time. Our history written was queer – the question was very superficial which annoyed me no end. Perhaps I was foolish, but I said in my exam how the question was only a half-truth. At any rate, I found out who got the other A- & invited her to supper tomorrow. Our section teacher told us in passing after the exam that she hated to give A- as a first mark because the second mark was usually a discouraging shock – but to realize that we could bring it up next time. Oh – well – on to basketball.

Love
Sivvy

1 – Date supplied from postmark.

TO *Aurelia Schober Plath*

Tuesday 5 December 1950[1] ALS (postcard), Indiana University

Tuesday A.M.

Dear Mum –

Well, another day has dawned, and I'm ready to face the world once more. I got a B+ on my third English paper, which is rather annoying – staying in the same spot. I'm determined to do a better paper for next Monday – even if I will only have the weekend to do it in. Last night was one of those rare nights that I stay up till after twelve . . . but I got talking with one of the girls and didn't start my history till rather late. I honestly hope the Wellesley Club doesn't take my marks as an indication of my future grades. I know I went down rather a lot in History – – my first grade was more a matter of luck than of understanding, I fear. Oh, well, I'll study like mad for midyears! Just think! In two short weeks from today I will be home at last – how time flies etc –

Love,
Sivvy

TO *Aurelia Schober Plath*

Tuesday 5 December 1950[2] ALS (postcard), Indiana University

Tuesday

Dear Mum –

Well my mail today had a nice little shot of diversion to it – a note from Charlie Sullivan,[3] Bradford Editor--- a shot in my ego about Mr. Crockett, which made me think again what a dear man he is. (We must drop over to see him this vacation.) The best, however, was a rather terse typewritten note from guess where – Troy, N.Y.!! Seems Bob Humphrey didn't have such a bad time after all, and amidst a discreet discussion of the weather, he mentioned that he looked forward to seeing me this Xmas! Tooky just doesn't happen to be tall enough to dance with a 6'4" male (hoh-hoh!) Nothing definite – understand, but even so! I feel that my appeal has not quite vanished completely. The girl I had over to supper tonight was lovely – she wants to be an actress and played "Emily" in "Our Town"[4] at

1 – Date supplied from postmark.
2 – Date supplied from postmark.
3 – Charles Sullivan (1933–); schoolmate of SP's from Wellesley, class of 1951.
4 – *Our Town* (1938), by American playwright and novelist Thornton Wilder (1897–1975).

a summer theater this summer – she's English, and very sweet, with long black hair and a shining face. Now that she's gone, I face a dull evening of homework.

XX
Sivvy

TO *Aurelia Schober Plath*

Thursday 7 December 1950[1]　　　ALS (postcard), Indiana University

Thursday

Dear Mum –

Your letter & one from Olive Higgins Prouty[2] came in the same mail. It was so nice to hear you "chat" with me about my last date – and remember that dream you had years ago about a tidal wave coming, and all of us watching from a hilltop and me being an old grandmother telling my children about it? Well, you may laugh, but there might have been something to it after all.

I was thrilled to see Mrs. Prouty's scratchy, almost illegible hand. Her letter is one I will always keep. -- She thinks I have "a gift for creative writing" and wants me to send her some of my poems and drop in to have a cup of tea when I come home on vacation. She even said she's having my letter typed up with carbons to send to some of her alumnae friends. It makes me feel so wonderful that I could even partly express to her how I felt about Smith -- and as Miss Mensel said, it's nice to have a scholarship mean more than a grant of money –

Love,
Sivvy

TO *Aurelia Schober Plath*

Thursday 7 December 1950[3]　　　ALS (postcard), Indiana University

Thursday

Dear Mum –

After four hours this afternoon trying vainly to carve a "hand sculpture" out of an obstinate block of wood which turned out very untouchable &

1–Date supplied from postmark.
2–See Olive Higgins Prouty to SP, 6 December 1950; held by Lilly Library.
3–Date supplied from postmark.

ugly, I have decided that my life has no purpose to it. So, in the midst of my black despair I decided to throw over all my nagging assignments for the evening and go to a life class – my first (tra la la.) She was a Smith girl (the model) and it was fun trying to sketch her – piles of talented art majors were there. So here I sit in house meeting, hoping that I can make it to Xmas vacation without going completely insane – you know that sort of morbid depression I sink into – Well, if I can only get through till my Botany written next Friday, I should be O.K.

Love
Sivvy

TO *Aurelia Schober Plath*

Friday 8 December 1950[1] ALS, Indiana University

Dear Mum –

It is now Friday night, 11:30, and I don't feel the least bit tired. Today has been one of the most peculiar since I have been to college. It all began this morning when I awoke to a dark, soggy, warm grey dawn and trudged sleepily down to breakfast. A girl at my table casually remarked that her room mate was sick and didn't want to come down. Well, that was natural enough, until another girl came up and mentioned the same thing. We put two & two together and arrived at the brilliant conclusion that something was wrong with Haven House food. But when we went to classes, we discovered that the whole college was hit. All through the day girls became siezed with violent vomiting & diarreha (sp?) spells, and even tonight they are still groaning and rushing back & forth from the John. It seems that the whole Connecticut Valley is seized with this germ – and it may either come from water or milk – I can't quite figure out how I was one of the very few to be spared – especially since I'm usually so susceptible. I've got my fingers crossed that I don't have a delayed reaction.

Naturally I didn't feel much like working this evening, so I talked with Lisa, who was feeling pretty miserable, and then with another girl. I then took a bath in the scummy brown water (they say it's too much rainfall) and here I am . . . feeling a bit queer – it's like the Black Plague or something----you wonder why <u>you</u> escape.

1–Date supplied from internal evidence.

Oh yes, Dot came for lunch. Although I only had an hour with her, I felt I got to know her better in that time than I have in all the years of my life. She's really the sweetest, most intelligent person. And thanks for the cake & apples. I'm sending home some party dresses via Dot which will make my packing easier come Xmas vac.

I was amused to get your note about Tony.[1] Although I have suspicions that he is plotting long-term revenge, I shall surely accept if I get his letter. How about shopping for a formal the day after I get back? The dance, I guess, is that Friday night. Also I have 2 history assignments, an English novel & an art notebook to do over vac. (ugh!)

By for now – here's hoping I don't drop dead in the next 12 hours –

Love,
Sivvy

TO *Aurelia Schober Plath*

Sunday 10 December 1950[2] — ALS with envelope, Indiana University

Sunday A.M.

Dear Mother –

It may amuse you to see how our class elections are held. Girls are elected from each house in proportion to the number in the house. Haven could put up three for each office, so getting to be one in a group of twelve out of eighteen was not in the least an honor. However, it is amusing to see how many Wellesley girls showed their faces as we marched across the stage. I have never been so impressed with our class. Clad in dungarees and shirts, about 400 paraded across – all of them appealing in individual ways. Some beautiful, some friendly, some too cocky, some shy – but without exception a fine group. I always feel so lucky to be a part of this wonderful place! Needless to say, I, (in fact none of us from Wellesley) was not among the finalists, but evenso, I had my fun.

I have not felt too much like working lately, and as today is a bright crisp sunfrozen day, I would like nothing better than to take a bike ride off into the mountains . . . but no, I shall work and work. At last the end is in sight---one more week, really.

1–John Anthony Stout (1933–98); B.A. 1955, Harvard College, MAT 1956, Harvard University; SP's friend from Wellesley.
2–Date supplied from postmark.

I have been rather worried about that friend of mine---Anne Davidow. Her usual gaiety has been getting brighter & more artificial as the days go by. So yesterday, after lunch, I made her come up to my room. At first she was very light & evasive, but at last her face gave way & melted. It seems that since Thanksgiving she hasn't been able to do her work, and now, having let it slide, she can only reiterate "I can never do it, never." She hasn't been getting enough sleep, but has been waking up early in the morning, obsessed by the feeling she has to do her work, even if she is in such a state that she can only go through the motions. She also is in our small annex house which is very cliquey, and the girls think she is insincere and ignore her, which of course makes things worse. She finally told me that she had realized she was not intelligent enough for Smith – that if she could do the work nothing would matter, but her parents were either deceiving her into thinking she was creative, or really didn't know how incapable she was. The girl was in such a state of numbness that she didn't feel any emotion, I guess, except this panic. I got scared when she told me how she had been saving sleeping pills and razor blades and could think of nothing better than to commit suicide. Oh, mother, you don't know how inadequate I felt! I talked to her all afternoon, but then some girls came & she went back to the house. If only I could make her sleep & personally supervise her for a few days! I can't say anything to Mrs. Shakespeare or anyone here, because Anne would only put up a mental barrier, thinking they wouldn't understand. But I have been thinking of writing a note to her parents – (she admitted that it would be more convenient if she took the car & killed herself at home in Chicago.) telling them a bit of how tired she is, & how she needs rest before she can do her work. For her mother kept telling her she was foolish & could do it all. But her mother really couldn't see how incapable the poor girl is of thinking in this state.

Oh, well. Maybe it's none of my business, but I love the girl, and feel very inadequate & responsible. If you were her mother, she would be all right.

Love,
Sivvy

TO *Aurelia Schober Plath*

Monday 11 December 1950[1] ALS with envelope, Indiana University

Dear Mother –

Another one of those broken fragments of monday afternoon from 5:15 to 6:00 when all I can do is wash up from basketball and drag myself down to supper. So I have a few letters to write. So I write them. I am just glad vacation is coming, because I am so saturated with work that I have no capacity to put anything more into my little head.

I am rather exhausted, having gone to bed late every night this weekend, contrary to my best resolutions. Friday, as I said, I stayed up and talked to various sick friends. Saturday afternoon I talked to Anne (who seems much better) and at four a girl came over to ask me out on a blind date. I have to hand it to myself how I handled a nasty situation. This girl was a lovely (bleached) blonde with shoulder length hair & black eyes – very sultry. Her date was a sweet Yale man who adored the ground she set her conquering foot on. My date was the perfect Joe College. When he was quiet, he looked a great deal like Dick Norton,[2] only much handsomer. But when he opened his foolish mouth the illusion was destroyed completely. –

After 20 beers or so, he finally realized I existed, and I had decided that when we all went back to change for the evening that I would ditch the conceited brainless ass completely. Fortunately, the blonde & her date started back early after supper, & he had nothing to do but realize that I was there. So I started talking to him & got him expounding on how life is hell and how some fools go to Yale to study (poor creatures) when we all should eat drink & be merry. I led him on merrily, agreeing that I hated being a girl ("all they do is wait for the phone to ring and worry about their reputations") and if I were a man I'd sow my wild oats – and oh, how I envied him! So he was in a good mood, and I decided it would be a challenge if I could keep him interested in me & thus save face. I managed to amuse myself at his expense all evening and make him think I agreed with his "toadish" boasting. Oh well, make the best of a bad thing. Yesterday, from 4-11 I went over to Amherst on a very legal "study date" with this Bill Nichols (the vet.) I read by a fire in his room (he was

1–Date supplied from postmark.

2–Richard Allen Norton (1929–); B.A. 1951, Yale, resident of Jonathan Edwards College; M.D. 1957, Harvard University; dated SP, 1951–3. There are very few letters from SP to Norton as they were not retained. There are many letters from Norton to SP held by Lilly Library.

deep in Elizabethan drama – also taking Honors in polit science.) He took me out to supper & we stayed at the house & studied & talked. You'll be pleased – though naturally my ego was pained – but "if he had a sister, he'd like her to be like me." (ugh.) In other words, he takes other girls out for a good time, but he just thinks of me as a youngster. Oh, well –

Love
Sivvy

TO *Aurelia Schober Plath*

Monday 11 December 1950[1] ALS (postcard), Indiana University

Mon. night

Dear Mum –

Gosh, I'm happy! Telling no one what I was doing, I rashly dropped one of my inimitable notes to that nice Freshman date Anne Davidow got me before Thanksgiving (that night the Powells saw me.) I invited him on the off chance that he hadn't called again because of shyness (rather than dislike.) I wasn't even hoping he would accept – but he at last called today during supper – & I was so happy I could hardly clear the table! He's a very promising fellow -- tall (6'2") nice-looking, doesn't smoke or drink, and is very conscientious (from what Anne says) about his work. The only other alternative I would have would be to call the vet – but as nice as he is, Guy Wilbor is on my own level – so I should have a nice time this Saturday! Will wear my white blouse & black velvet skirt. <drawing of outfit> Wish me luck!

(Haven't heard from Tony!)

Love,
Sivvy

1 – Date supplied from postmark.

TO *Guy Wilbor*

c. Monday 11 December 1950[1] ALS,[2] Indiana University

<card with handwriting on cover>

'HAVEN HOUSE cordially invites you to its Christmas Dance Weekend December 16th and 17th, 1950. Informal'

Dear Guy –

This is just to make things official – and to say how glad I am that the answer was yes –

Sincerely,
Sylvia

TO *Aurelia Schober Plath*

Tuesday 12 December 1950[3] ALS (postcard), Indiana University

Tuesday

Dear Mum –

Ah me – please help me out of an awkward situation! On the same day that Tony's invitation arrived, a mimeographed invitation to a class reunion dance on the same night came through (Fri. Dec –22.) It would be a gamble either way – as Tony is socially such a child, and would no doubt toss me off as a partner (it's the High School Cotillion[4]) to mere children. On the other hand, he's a fine (embryo) of a person. And then going to the high school reunion might re-introduce me to some of the members of my own senior class . . . I don't know if I would have to go with a date or not – but either way there are pros & cons – how about mailing me some of your own ideas on the subject as soon as you can?

Love
Sivvy

1–Date supplied from internal evidence.
2–SP pasted this letter into her high school scrapbook, p. 37; held by Lilly Library.
3–Date supplied from postmark.
4–The Christmas Cotillion was held at the Wellesley Country Club.

TO *Aurelia Schober Plath*

Wednesday 13 December 1950[1] ALS, Indiana University

Wednesday

Dear Mother –

Your two letters and a card arrived today – my, but you're prolific! As you may imagine, your last letter had me in hysterics! I shall be pleasantly vague about my weekend history---imagine, I've never been to either Harvard or Dartmouth! Oh well, I've made the impression and saved the car fare! Probably if I had gone no one would have seen me anyway.

My schedule looks quite crowded already . . . what with our English party the Wednesday after I get back, then the Norton's, then either the Class Reunion Dance or the Cotillion (as to the last, I'm eager to know your opinion – I'm leaning strongly toward the Class Reunion even if I go stag with some girls, because after all, that's a group I do want to keep in touch with. How about it? Or maybe I wouldn't have fun anyway.)

As for me – life doesn't look quite so grim now that I've gotten through the first three days of the week. By dint of cutting three classes I finished my English paper[2] (8 pages.) I think I did a pretty neat job & if I don't get more than a B+ I will have a talk with him asking how I can improve. If he can criticize, well & good. If he can't, why the hell can't he give me an A-???

Friday is my Botany written. After that, the rest of my stay here will be solid enjoyment (I hope.) I can really look forward to the weekend, now that I have a sweet date to House Dance & the supper beforehand. I'm so glad I'm not taking an out of town college boy 'cause rooms are so expensive. (Guy can pay his own bus fare.) Dinner & Dance are costing me $7.

Do you suppose you could scare up about 50 Brownie cards (different) for me? I'll have to get busy the day I get home – I have the addresses of all my friends here in the Register.

As for odd items to buy at home – remind me to get some more blue Calais Ripple Stationery (esp. envelopes), stamps, stockings (I have one pair left---Amherst is full of splinters) ink and vinegar. I never have much time to shop here.

What will I do for Xmas gifts? esp. for my little brother and my grandparents?

1 – Date supplied from internal evidence.

2 – Sylvia Plath, 'The Agony of Will'; held by Lilly Library.

Christmas is in the air, but I can't believe it! Everywhere we go we sing carols -- in art, in gym – all over. The weather is what I would like it to be all winter---dry, crisp & freezing cold! They have a tree in the Library even!

I am going to wash my hair tonight & try to be in bed by 9:00.) It's so nice to have plans for Christmas to anchor myself to. This will really be coming home – to all the people & places I love.

See you soon –
Love,
Sivvy

TO *Aurelia Schober Plath*

Friday 15 December 1950[1] ALS, Indiana University

Friday –

Dear Mum –

This, I fear, will be my last letter till I come home. It is eight o'clock on Friday night, and I am on watch for an hour, using it as an excuse to write a few last notes to answer cards & invitations, etc. You seemed rather sure that I had come down with "The Green Death" as it is so fondly called here. Not yet – I have been rather pasty-looking, but I hope I shall make it home all right. Warren should be home tonight – give him my love.

Today we had just the right amount of snow to make things Christmassy and white. There are all sorts of parties & affairs tonight, but I'm going to take a hot bath & turn in early as I've got a strenuous week ahead. Tomorrow, Guy is coming at about 5 – and we're all going to an Inn in Williamsburg for dinner – after which is an hour sleigh ride up and over a mountain, and then House Dance! I'll tell you all about it when I come home. We have our Xmas tree set up in the hall already.

Sunday afternoon and evening I will probably spend at Amherst again at a faculty egg nog party with Bill Nichols, who is social chairman of Theta Delt. I didn't expect him to ask me out again because of this big-brother feeling which he has built up toward me. But since he seems to still want to see me now and then, I feel rather glad, because it's on my terms.

It's nice hearing a few masculine voices in the house---already males have begun to arrive. Tomorrow will be the real influx, though.

1 – Date supplied from internal evidence.

I'm so glad I won't have any more tests after today, because I have reached the saturation point when it comes to studying. I did rather badly on my Botany written today – and may even have failed – but don't get panicked. My average so far is about 95 – so if I do well on the midyears, my blank spot today shouldn't be too disastrous. –

I don't know just when I'll be home as yet – any time Tuesday night. Can't wait to see you all! I'm fine (and (unless I get double pneumonia between now & Tuesday) I hope to stay that way.

Love to the best mummy in the world –

Your,
Sivvy

TO *Hans-Joachim Neupert*

Sunday 24 December 1950 ALS (photocopy), Smith College

December 24, 1950

Dear Hans –

How nice it was to hear from you again, and to get your wonderful picture! I appreciated it very much. Do not think I am cross at your not writing for a while. I understand how busy and crowded life is, and I know that often it is hard to put aside a piece of time to write to far-off friends across the Atlantic.

I am now home from Christmas to New Year's – and it is a rest from college life. I finished working on the farm in September and then packed my suitcases to head for Smith College in Northampton, Mass., which is only 100 miles away from home. I am very fortunate, for I would not have been able to go had I not received a scholarship which paid most of my expenses. Smith is a large place (2500 women students) and although I feel lost at times among such a great number of talented, intelligent girls, I am beginning to love the place with all my heart. There is such a wonderful opportunity for a good education here – and I always have to work hard to keep up my grades, so I can renew my scholarship next year.

I am studying French literature, Botany, European History, Art, English, with gym thrown in as a requirement. It is a new experience living away from home with a group of girls. The only unfortunate thing is that studies keep us so busy that we never have enough time for all the conversations about life that we'd like to have.

Of course there are dances and parties on weekends, but this war-scare bothers me so much that I can never completely forget myself in artificial gaiety. Always in the background there is the fear that I will never be able to live in peace and love for the rest of my life with my friends & my family. Many feel the way I do – and would sacrifice much for peace. But then there are those fools who think the only thing to do is to have a war to end the Communist threat. I don't see how anyone can believe that the A-Bomb would cure us of evils. Surely democracy and freedom would mean little in a world of rubble and radioactive rays. If only some Americans could see what war would mean – and realize how impossible it would be for our juicy million-dollar land to survive bombing & invasion. I think of us as of the Roman Empire and feel that this is the fall, perhaps, of our new and bright civilization. At times like this, I wish I were living in Sweden, or Africa, anywhere so that this threat would not be so horrible. I think so much as you do about war. I'm sure many others do, also. But still men are driven by a nameless force to fight & kill and destroy all that is beautiful and good.

Oh, well, perhaps we should cease worrying too much about the future, and enjoy each present moment to the fullest! We have had no snow yet, and it is Christmas eve. I'd love to see some of the pictures you take with your new camera. I've always wished that I could learn to ski – but equipment is so expensive, and there are no really good hills around here. Perhaps when I am old and independent I shall learn.

Best of luck in your work at the university – and I think it would be wonderful if you could get a position in South America later on!

Let me know how life is turning out for you – and don't worry if you don't find time to write for a while. I'll understand!

So here's to a Happy New Year for you Hans – I wish you the best of everything–

Sincerely,
your friend –
Sylvia

1951

TO *Aurelia Schober Plath*

Thursday 4 January 1951[1] ALS (postcard), Indiana University

Thursday night

Dear Mum –

Well, I thought I'd write as soon as I could to let you know how things are. I got up here at 12:30, and didn't have a chance to say goodbye to grammy as I wanted to. Some girls helped me carry my suitcases in, and she had gone when I came out. I was a bit groggy from the ride, but felt better after lunch, and so went to art. Even 2 hours can help. After that I came back & unpacked till 5, I then lay down for ½ hour before supper. Pat came over after supper to tell me about the work I missed. Don't worry about me! I am on the mend---Tired, sure, but I'm going to bed right now (8:30!) and will for the next 3 nights, I wish I had the energy to really work, but I'm going to take life easy while convalescing – I'll see the D.O. & registrar tomorrow. So don't be anxious – I'm taking all my pills & will be tubby once more when you see me in 3 weeks.

LOVE
Sivvy

TO *Aurelia Schober Plath*

Friday 5 January 1951[2] ALS (postcard), Indiana University

Friday

Dear Mum –

I went to the D.O.'s today and had the college physician check me over. She took down the medecin I'm taking & told me to get alot of rest and report next Wednesday. So you needn't worry about my being under supervision. I got a 91 in that Botany test I was so sure I failed! I still don't see how I did it. So my average there is still A. And it will be, too,

1 – Date supplied from postmark.
2 – Date supplied from postmark.

If I have any thing to say about it. I'm only glad I don't have any other exam except French midyears before I come home. I do have a Botany quiz and an English source theme and piles of work – and I can't work as fast or do as much as I feel still weary. My head is still stuffy, but that will pass, I trust. I worked on art all this evening & still have 2 assignments of back work to do. Tomorrow I'm determined to sleep. I'm eating as much as I can.

Love,
Sivvy

TO *Aurelia Schober Plath*

Sunday 7 January 1951[1] ALS (postcard), Indiana University

Sunday A.M.

Dear Mumsy –

Today at last I begin to feel much better. I slept 9 hours last night and the night before, and although I'm still not the peppiest creature in the world, I'm on the upgrade. I stopped taking penicillin yesterday, but am still taking nosedrops because my nose is still stuffy – not badly so, but it does get clogged up. Yesterday it was lovely & clear, but today it is snowing like mad. I'm so glad I don't have to go out in it. I do love Sunday mornings when I get up. I go downstairs in my pajamas for breakfast, and then come back to my room and do odds & ends of work and letters and don't get dressed till dinner. It's so restful not to go out or see anyone for a while. I spent all yesterday afternoon at the library catching up on back history – an unpleasant task, to be sure. Well, I'll be seeing you again in only 18 days!

Love,
Sivvy

1 – Date supplied from postmark.

TO *Aurelia Schober Plath*

Sunday 7 January 1951[1] ALS (postcard), Indiana University

Sunday

Dear Mother –

Today was a lovely lazy day. I finished translating that French play, and by dint of spending a few hours on "warping the surface" of a paper with pen & ink and organizing squares into constellations of tension, I got through with all my art up to date. Tomorrow I will spend solely on history, I guess. This week's going to take a wee bit of tight planning – but I am going to bed now – 9:30. My nose is still stuffed, but I feel able to cope with classes once more. Most of the freshmen went to supper & the movies tonight, but as it was snowing I regretfully stayed in. I did get to talking with an adorable Freshman girl, however for an hour or so. This house has the nicest, most intelligent group of girls imagineable. Guy Wilbor called tonight (my house dance date) just to chat – his exams are before mine, so he won't have time to date till after he's studied, when mine are, so we set a tentative date somewhere in Feb. Did I tell you Ann Davidow didn't come back??

Love,
Sivvy

TO *Ann Davidow-Goodman*

Sunday 7 January 1951[2] ALS, Smith College

Sunday

Dear Davy,

By the time you get this you'll probably be convalescing from whatever strange virus has attacked you! I didn't come back to Smith until later either, because I caught a sinus infection the day before New Year's (from too much partying and late hours---mother warned me: she always does) and saw the year in while struggling to get a sniff of O_2 (or whatever air is made of) through my block-head. They wouldn't let me up till the week-end, so here I am, sort of wobbly, with work left over from before vacation grinning me in the face.

It's Sunday a.m., and after nose-drops, penicillin and my morning swig of cough medecin (I swear the stuff is half alcohol) I feel a bit more

1–Date supplied from postmark.
2–Dated 'Jan 51' by Ann Davidow-Goodman.

chipper. The only thing is, I feel sort of lost without you around. The place seems horribly empty without anyone to be confidential with, and I am getting an increasingly bad complex about not knowing how to skate or play bridge. I really have to have some link with Haven House humanity, and I am damn sick of being told I don't come downstairs enough and being looked at oddly when I come into the living room. I really need you around to tell me how silly I'm being letting stupid things like that bother me. I also miss having a close friend – I hope you know that's the label I give you!

Eddie wrote me a letter[1] answering my last one about how his immoral ways were responsible for his unhappiness. I was in a careless mood when I wrote to him, & evidently hurt the poor guy's masculine pride, because his last letter was definitely chilly – e.g. "I still think you're a great girl, but far from perfect. If you were perfect you wouldn't be writing me!" Oh, well, maybe I wouldn't.

It's snowing now for the first time in weeks, and I feel sort of odd – a little homesick, I guess. It was such a relief to go back and feel the responsibility slide off my shoulders on to my family's. I realize now, though, that mother can't be the refuge that she was before, and that hit me hard. The reason why I hate the idea of growing up, I guess, is subconsciously (how Eddie would love this!) because I want to remain a child and be sheltered from accepting the responsibility of things like earning a living, cooking, and taking care of myself. I'm so scatterbrained in that regard that it is a mental effort to remember to wash my underwear – to bring in a practical note. I also shy away from making decisions and thinking about what I'm good for – which I am convinced, isn't much. Oh, well, enough of that!

I'm sure that when spring comes life will again brighten! After all, you can't do more than make the most of what you've got. The shock I got when I went home was mainly this: My mother's purpose in life is to see me & my brother "happy and fulfilled." And I can't cry on her shoulder any more when things go wrong. I've got to pretend to her that I am all right & doing what I've always wanted . . . and she'll feel her slaving at work has been worthwhile. But it's an awful job to drag myself back here when I don't give a damn about dates, or much else right now. I went through an awfully black mood during vacation, but now that I am in the routine again, having to do my notebook, etc., I'm not quite so close to

1 – Eddie Cohen to SP, [3 January 1951]; held by Lilly Library. SP slightly misquotes Cohen, who wrote, 'I still think you are a teriffic (sp) gal, but fortunately, you are not perfect. If you were, you couldn't be bothered with me.'

going utterly and completely mad. I am convinced that if you face yourself and admit what's wrong, you can gradually build up a philosophy of life, or your purpose in it, or something, and be reasonably jolly. It's worth trying, even if you think no one is capable of understanding your problem or anything.

Oh, Davy, if only I knew what's happened to you and gone on in your head since I left you, I'd be able to say something that might possibly reach you. If you're sick, I hope you're better. If you're even thinking or rationalizing about not bothering to make the trip East again, you know what you want, but gosh, it sure hurts me to believe you would desert this damn place – me included. Because I think you're one of the most admirable characters I've ever met.

Do let me know how things are.
I've got my fingers crossed.
Love,
Sylvy

TO *Aurelia Schober Plath*

Tuesday 9 January 1951[1] ALS (postcard), Indiana University

<u>Tuesday</u>

Dear Mother –

Well, the two hardest days in the week are over, and I am so glad I didn't have to take gym today & yesterday. It was a welcome relief. I really was not trying to reassure you (you suspicious thing!) in my last letter, but I <u>am</u> much better. My head is at last clear, and I am taking vitamins regularly. I did my self the favor of washing my hair tonight, as it has hung in black, greasy little ringlets on my neck for the past few days. Did I ever tell you what I got on that 4th Eng. paper I vowed I'd put my heart & soul on? A-! It must have killed the man to give it to me, but I would have made a fuss if he hadn't. I sure deserved at least that. I hardly can believe that my first exam is in only two weeks! Ugh! I went over to supper with Sydney Webber[2] – a lovely girl in my history class who is extremely talented in dramatics. She's a sweet person.

See you soon,
Love,
Sivvy

1 – Date supplied from postmark.
2 – Sydney Webber Eddison (1932–); B.A. 1954, theatre, Smith College.

TO *Aurelia Schober Plath*

Wednesday 10 January 1951[1] ALS (postcard), Indiana University

Wednesday

Dear Mum –

Another day draws to a close. I had my "check-up" today & was pronounced in good condition – which I am. I am once more eating like a pig. I have a 15 page source theme[2] due in English before exams, and consequently feel rather frustrated. I'm doing T. Mann, as we had to take someone we knew quite well, and feel so hopeless when I realize how much reading I should do & want to do to really understand him, and how much reading I actually can do with my other subjects also clamoring for attention. I agree completely with Mrs. Koffka (hist.) who says there is no time for pleasure reading which is all-important. I hate skimming the surface, but would like leisure to delve into my favorite subjects. I got a sweet scrawly letter from Bob Humphrey today in answer to my apology for New Years Eve. I really don't know what I'd do if I had more than three exams. I just hope I can swing these all right.

Love to you & grammy –
Sivvy

TO *Aurelia Schober Plath*

Thursday 11 January 1951[3] ALS (postcard), Indiana University

Thursday –

Dear Mum –

Well, in two weeks from today I'll be home, studying madly for exams. I think the change of scenery will do me good. Almost everyone is going home the weekend after exams, but I'm just glad I'll be here to rest up and enjoy the House for those two precious days between semesters. I spent from 2-5 in the art lab again today just doing the days assignments. It's amazing how fast the time flies by when I'm up there. As for health, I'm doing fine. We have house meeting again tonight – and it usually runs till twelve, so I will sleep till ten tomorrow morning. (I hope.) It's really wonderful to be able to do that at the end of the week, when I am feeling

1 – Date supplied from postmark.
2 – Sylvia Plath, 'The Dualism of Thomas Mann'; held by Lilly Library.
3 – Date supplied from postmark.

a bit weary. I hope you are really resting now – and I do like your cards. I wrote Ann but haven't heard a word from her. I miss her terribly.

Love
Sivvy

TO *Ann Davidow-Goodman*

c. Friday 12 January 1951[1] ALS, Smith College

Friday night 8:30 pm

Dear Ann –

I have just finished catching up on my letter-writing, and I wanted to save you till the last, so I could take my time. I am alone in my room at the desk, and I have been having a good little cry and feeling very sorry for myself. You – damn it, are the cause. I got your letter today and Eddie can go to blazes! I never read anything that hit me so hard. There is a moon out – (I've got the blind up as usual) and I keep saying "Oh, Davy" and feeling sorrier & sorrier for me, selfish kid that I am.

The thing is, you will probably have a hell of a good time at home in art school (are you living there, and where is it?) seeing Jim[2] (Helène[3] told me you were pinned[4] – trust you to keep me in the dark!) You probably will get so damn happy living there that you wouldn't come back here come hell or high water. And that's it. I should be Christian & say "She'll be O.K. What more do I want?" But no. I sit here with my life going up in smoke. Dust & ashes. I feel like someone just yanked the life-preserver out from under me & left me treading water in the middle of the Atlantic. I am so lonely. I really haven't got a close friend now that you're gone. Diana,[5] Reggie[6] & Maureen[7] are off in their superior little gathering, laughing sugarily and making little insinuating remarks which get under

1–Letter misdated 'Wellesley Sep 14, 51' by Ann Davidow-Goodman. Date suplied from internal evidence.

2–James Nathan Schaffner (1931–2010). After being stationed in the Philippines during the Korean War, Schaffner earned a B.A. in philosophy from the University of Colorado.

3–Possibly Hélène Cattanès (1894–1977), professor of French, Smith College, 1921–63; launched the Junior Year Abroad programme in 1925.

4–Being 'pinned' meant that a couple was in a serious, exclusive relationship. The typical progression was dating, being pinned, getting engaged, and then marriage. Often the man would give the woman his fraternity pin to wear.

5–Diana Yates Lycette (1932–2008) withdrew from Smith College, June 1952.

6–Rosamond Horton Lownes (1932–); B.A. 1954, history, Smith College.

7–Maureen Buckley O'Reilly (1933–64); B.A. 1954, history, Smith College.

my skin now that you're not around. Blanton[1] is getting to be a socialite and in with the upperclassmen. Bobby Michelsen[2] & Betsy Whittemore are O.K. but one never says a word and the other is hopelessly juvenile. Callie[3] is as popular as ever, and so is Teedie – but I'm not strong enough to match their ever-present wit without someone to help me. Carol is sweet, and Brownie is even nicer,[4] but they'll be rooming together till kingdom comes. And that leaves me – high & dry. I almost wish I'd never met you – so I wouldn't feel so empty. What made me sparky & giddy was the friction of us two banging together & giving off electricity. Now I feel so horribly lonely. No one can balance me emotionally except you – no one else can make my heavy end of the seesaw come up into position. And this single room is so lonely. If only you could have roomed with me next year I would have had something to look forward to. But now I feel only a let-down. It is so awful to have found someone (I'm the type who has only a few close friends – if any) and then lost them. I wish you everything – but I'm not going to pretend to be jolly about your depriving me of the one thing that made this house worthwhile. There is no one, now. No one at all. I think more of you than anyone, Davy. So does Hèlene. It was so terrific having you there to spill over to.

Your letter came with a letter from SEVENTEEN saying I had won 3rd prize in the short story contest, $100. Maybe I'm silly, but if I'd had you to scream to about it, it would have been something. You know how much it could mean. But now I'm not even proud. I have no one to share it with – who understands. It is almost ironic that it should have come with your letter. The editor wished me "success." What the hell do I care about artificial black & white "success" if I haven't got a soul but my own perplexed self to talk to? God, Davy, I can't say how I miss you. I'm even beginning to bawl again. So few people really care. So many would draw back with a polite "How nice." And that's what kills me. They really are mad that anything nice has happened, and can't take it. So I keep it, to myself – and it hurts. I can't go around telling people how terrific I am,

1–Elizabeth Blanton McGrath (1932–); B.A. 1954, religion, Smith College; SP's housemate at Haven House.

2–Barbara Ingeborg Michelsen (1934–2000); B.A. 1954, education, Smith College.

3–Caroline White Fenn (1932–2004); B.A. 1954, chemistry, Smith College; SP's housemate at Haven House.

4–Early education specialist Marcia Brown Stern (1932–2012); B.A. 1954, sociology, Smith College; M.A., early childhood education, Lesley University; SP's friend and roommate at Haven House during her sophomore year. Only child of Archibald L. and Carol Taylor Brown. Marcia Brown married Davenport Plumer III in 1954 (divorced 1969) and later married Ernest Stern in 1971. Corresponded with SP, 1951–63.

because I can't believe it. Blanton has talked herself into thinking she's pretty & popular. It took a while & a lot of talk, but now, damn it, she is. But I don't believe I'm any good. You made me think I might have something.

This letter is the sweariest one I've ever written. I need so to love a person – be it girl or boy, friend or enemy. And without being able to, I sort of dry up.

Heck, don't start feeling sorry for me, even if this letter <u>has</u> been awfully pitiful. I'll write news, & you do the same. I love you, Davy. I love your mother. She's one of the finest, most beautiful women I've ever seen. Tell her hello for me.

Bye, baby,
your
Sylvy[1]

(not to be confused with <drawing of a horse's head>) (heck – I could never draw animals!)

TO *Aurelia Schober Plath*

Saturday 13 January 1951[2] ALS with envelope, Indiana University

Dear Mother –

Well, outside of your card, today's mail brought two shocks---one pleasant and one not so pleasant. Ann Davidow wrote me a letter that made me want to cry. She's not coming back – this year, anyway. She's going to art school at home for the rest of the time. You don't quite know what her letter did to me; I was sick. She was the one person in these two houses that I could have wholeheartedly roomed with; she is the one <u>real</u> friend I have yet run across up here. I love my single room, but it gets so lonely coming in and having no one to look up & greet me or to ask where I've been . . . no one to wash socks with or anything. And I was so looking forward to rooming with someone congenial---whom I could really admire and spill over to. I'm sure that would be a good thing for me. But as it is, I <u>like</u> the girls in the house (freshmen) but couldn't room with any of them, because I could never completely be myself . . . or write in that journal of mine without having to justify myself.

1 – Ann Davidow-Goodman owned a blonde-coated Palomino horse whose barn name was 'Sylvia' and nicknamed 'Sylvy'. Sylvy came to Smith with Davidow-Goodman.
2 – Date supplied from postmark.

I am a bit tired of having some upperclassmen say insinuatingly "I'd rather flunk out & be sociable than stick up in my room all the time." Of course I have to go to bed early (by 11) and I can't play bridge (which I must learn before next year – maybe the whole family can pick it up this summer.)

As Mr. Loungway said "Conform in the little things." I really have to, as I don't in other big things. But I've got to work---and I don't mind, but you see, if I had a roommate who liked to study we'd be "sticking in our room" together, and I wouldn't be quite so lonesome at times. You don't know how it is without Ann. I loved her so! I feel as if someone just yanked the life preserver out from under me, & I'm left treading water rather futiley.

I was so pleased to hear about your dress! I will approve of it when I come home during vacation between exams.

I got so preoccupied about bewailing Ann's deserting me, as it were, that I didn't have time to sprinkle on the best news. You no doubt wondered what that Special Delivery letter[1] from our favorite magazine was about. I can picture you feeling how thick it was and holding it up to the light. Well, don't get too excited, 'cause it's only a third prize, but it does mean $100 (one hundred) in cold cold cash. Seriously, I'm kind of dazed – I did love Den of Lions and Emile's name sure worked as a lucky piece. It seems my love affairs always get into print---only I doubt if anyone will recognize this one. This time I've got to get a good photograph---or snapshot. I'll bring home the documents to be signed when I come home in a week & ½. Could you have that old role of film developed? It would save expense if I had a good snapshot of myself on it.

Honestly, mother – can't you see it now? An illustration for it and everything? I'll show you the letter from the editor (very conventional and seventeenish & "hope you have a long, successful career," etc.) when I see you. I'm dying to see what got 1st & 2nd prize.[2] Oh, well, you can't always hit the top! But Clem's mother better watch out. I'll be Sarah-Elizabeth Rogering[3] her out of business in no time.

Love,
Your Sivvy

1–Alice Thompson (Editor-in-Chief, *Seventeen*) to SP, 5 January 1951; see SP's publications scrapbook, p. 9; held by Lilly Library.

2–First prize: Lynne McKelvey, 'The Threshold', *Seventeen* 10 (May 1951), 106, 146–7. Second Prize: Lois Duncan, 'The Corner', *Seventeen* 10 (May 1951), 112–13, 150–2.

3–American novelist and story writer Sarah-Elizabeth Rodger Moore (1909–85); B.A. 1931, Barnard College. Married Clement Sulivane Henry, Jr, 6 April 1933; divorced 1942. Married chemistry researcher Leonard Patrick Moore (1908–83) on 5 May 1945.

P.S. Am seriously thinking of spending a few days in New York this spring – la-de-dah!

TO *Aurelia Schober Plath*

Saturday 13 January 1951[1] ALS (postcard), Indiana University

Sat am

Dear Mum . . .

By rights this card should be read after my letter, although you probably are looking at it first as the most easily accessible source of news. At any rate, I feel much better now about things in general. I spent a while talking with Marcia Brown, a very nice freshman on the first floor, and after I came upstairs two girls dropped in. It's amazing how talking with people can make one feel easier. As for the news of my story – you probably wondered why I wasn't more exhilarated in the letter. The truth was that the realization didn't hit me till about 12 last night, as a result of which I couldn't sleep till after 2, but lay in bed giving little screams of joy – I'm rather grateful for being one of 3 3rd prizes![2] Guy called up, so I'm going to a movie with him tonight. I have to write a whole source theme this weekend & the 2 books I need I can only have Sunday morning till two – they're on reserve. Wish me luck –

Love,
your sivvy

TO *Aurelia Schober Plath*

Sunday 14 January 1951[3] ALS (postcard), Indiana University

Sun A.M.

Dear Mother –

It is 9:30, and I am spending the rest of the morning reading & taking hurried notes in the only 2 books on Mann the libe has, for by popular demand they will be due back in three hours. I spent all yesterday afternoon in the art studio doing a still life assignment. It's the first thing I've been

1 – Date supplied from postmark.
2 – The other third prize winners were: Patricia Cepress, 'For Angelica', *Seventeen* 10 (May 1951), 125, 153–4; and Claire Engelhard, 'The Long Day', *Seventeen* 10 (May 1951), 132, 140, 142, 165.
3 – Date supplied from postmark.

really excited about in that class. At last we had a chance to transpose some of our exercizes into real forms. Patsy was such a dear about my story & insisted on treating me to a dinner at Wiggins. I haven't had such a lovely supper for quite some time. She's the sweetest friend I know. Saw "All About Eve"[1] with Guy after I got back, & was in bed & asleep by 12:15, which is better than the usual 2 AM of most Saturday nights. Wish me luck on my source theme.

Love,
Sivvy

TO *Aurelia Schober Plath*

c. Sunday 14 January 1951[2] ALS, Indiana University

Dear Mum –

Here's the stuff about the insurance – better write right away!

Lovely warm crisp weather here now. I told Pat about my 100 dollar prize & realized the fruits of true friendship.

She made me feel so wonderful. Sharing is half the fun – if you know the answer isn't just politely envious enthusiasm!

Love you –
Sivvy

TO *Aurelia Schober Plath*

Monday 15 January 1951[3] ALS (postcard), Indiana University

Monday

Dear Mum –

Today is one of those Monday mornings when the weather is in complete accord. It snowed last night, and then rained. The result is that the air is thick with an unwholesome gray mist, and slush and brown water ooze all over the streets. Unfortunately I must take gym today – and the next – and the next, so my afternoons will be pretty well shot. And history will have to be done from 7-10 at night in the libe, leaving me little time for much else. By dint of taking hurried notes all yesterday morning,

1–*All About Eve* (1950) played at the Calvin Theatre, 19 King Street, Northampton, Mass.
2–Date supplied from internal evidence.
3–Date supplied from postmark.

of organizing them in the afternoon and writing like fury till eleven last night I finished writing the first draft of my source theme which, as you may imagine, is a load off my mind. The only thing is, it's mostly one big quote, so I'll have to pad it with my own mouthings, such as they are, to make it look more digested –

Love,
Sivvy

TO *Aurelia Schober Plath*

Tuesday 16 January 1951[1] ALS (postcard), Indiana University

Tuesday

Dear Mum –

It is now 12 P.M., and I have been working like fury since 7:30 typing my 11 page source theme. I am done at last, and if I do say so, it's a beautiful typewriting job. I think even you couldn't find too much fault with it! I am very happy, in spite of feeling tired, and in the midst of this chaos of work. I have made a schedule of my week till next Wed, mapping out studying very carefully. After my Botany test on Thursday, things should let up, since I can sleep Fri, Sat, & Sun. until 10 a.m., giving me time to get rested. I have four practically Free days till my Fr. exam & so will kick myself if I don't do all right. My average in Botany is: in the 2 exams 96 & 91 In quizzes, which count 50% of mark – a-, a, a+, a+, 100%. History I dread – map is important. Should see Bob Humphrey while home – so maybe could get ski pants as he wants to teach me how –

Love –
Your very own me!
So nice to talk with you!!!

TO *Aurelia Schober Plath*

Wednesday 17 January 1951[2] ALS (postcard), Indiana University

Wednesday night

Dear Mum—

Once again it is midnight as I go to bed. I passed in my source theme this morning & felt one of my many weights roll off my head. I only had

1–Date supplied from postmark.
2–Date supplied from postmark.

Eng & Gym this a.m. & did history the rest of the time. After section in Hist., about 3, I came up to my room & fell asleep from 3-5. As a result I felt a little more capable to read the 100 pages of Botany for a test tomorrow. I'm so glad I take Art. I would perish if I had another exam. As it is, I feel remarkably happy. Perhaps it is because the pressure & demand for my hours is so heavy that I can't afford to[1] think about it! I do enjoy life here, and feel so sorry for girls who live at home. They miss so much – you get to know people by living with them. I do love my art course – it is such an escape from routine. Did I tell you I did a still life of which I'm rather pleased? It's all transparent and done in flat areas of color. I just love experimenting. See you in a week.

Love,
Sivvy

TO *Aurelia Schober Plath*

Thursday 18 January 1951[2] ALS (postcard), Indiana University

Thurs.

Dear Mum –

Well, today the accumulation of this week's tiredness hit me full blast with the result that I can hardly hold my head up. However, tonight I am free to go to bed at 10 & sleep till ten tomorrow morning, so I feel pretty good about that, I am amazingly chipper, about life in general. Ann's departure might even be a good thing for me, considering I am now seeking out other freshmen more deeply than I ever would have if she had always been there for me to lean on. There are some lovely girls in this house, and I feel privileged to be one of them. I am probably going to the movies with two of my favorites this Sat. night. There is a lovely girl from Oklahoma[3] (won one of the regional scholarships) who paints all the time with me in art. She's a dear.

Love everybody. You specially! –
Sivvy

1–'that I can't ~~to~~ afford to' appears in the original.

2–Date supplied from postmark.

3–Bessie McAlpine Sullins (1932–55); B.A. 1954, government, Smith College; from Tulsa, Oklahoma.

TO *Aurelia Schober Plath*

Friday 19 January 1951[1] ALS (postcard), Indiana University

Friday –

Dear Mother –

It is now 11 and I have just taken a hot bath and am ready to turn in. I slept till about 10 this morning, and after French, Botany & lunch I spent from 2-6 and 7-10 in the art studio doing this week's work. Tonight it was really fun. There were about four or five of us, and Bessie (the girl from Okla.) brought her portable with her, so we had Strauss waltzes while we worked. I am doing a big painting in flat areas (like the one of mary) of two women sitting over a round table and eating. I am having the time of my life doing it. Tomorrow night I will probably go on a blind date[2] to the University of Massachusetts – Sunday, all of Monday except for 3 hours of classes, and all of Tuesday I will devote to studying French. Got a stiff little postcard from Warren in response to my news about the $100 – not even a word of congratulations!!!! Oh well –

XX
Sivvy

TO *Aurelia Schober Plath*

Sunday 21 January 1951[3] ALS (postcard), Indiana University

Sunday 10:30

Dear Mum –

Well, I am taking my usual Sunday morning relaxation period till lunch and sitting curled up in my room jotting down a few things in that notebook of mine – I don't write in it especially often, but when I do I go to town. Since August I've written about 60 pages (only 400 more to go.) It helps so much to see what you thought about a month ago – a year ago. For the memory is such a feeble thing – and blurs and distorts past impressions. It's one thing to reason out my reactions in the light of the present, and quite another to read how I felt then. Last night I went to a fraternity party at the U. of. Mass. It was amusing, for the enjoyment

1 – Date supplied from postmark.
2 – According to SP's calendar, the date was with David Gerard O'Brien (1932–); B.B.A. 1953; University of Massachusetts, Amherst.
3 – Date supplied from postmark.

of liquor & girls was present as at Amherst, of course, but on a bleaker and more obvious scale. It is one level of society to get plushily tight on highballs and maraschino cherries and another to get "stewed" on beer and greasy potato chips. Ruth will have fun there I hope. If you live there you can pick your own sort of person. I'll see you in three days. Love your letters

Love,
Sivvy

TO *Aurelia Schober Plath*

Sunday 21 January 1951[1] ALS (postcard), Indiana University

Sunday P.M.

Dear Mum –

This is certainly a January thaw.– After a sickish gray foggy morning the sun at last came out around noon and a viscious wind is whipping the sky into a white-and-blue froth and scraping clear lines of sun and shadow across the frozen campus. I took a walk before dinner with Marcia Brown – who is the dearest girl. She is so alive, and we were shouting out our opinions about life while striding along into the bitter wind and antiseptic sunlight. So I came back to a chicken & mashed potato dinner. Sat at Mrs. Shakespeare's table as she had a Unitarian minister for a guest – there are loads of Unitarians in the house. – We had a lovely meal, eating in the white-woodwork and white-linen atmosphere. I do love living here – On to French. – Bye for now

Love,
Sivvy

TO *Aurelia Schober Plath*

Monday 29 January 1951[2] ALS, Indiana University

Dear Mummy –

Thank you for putting up with me for 4 and a half days – for feeding me good meals, baking me my favorite desserts, buying me perfume and

1 – Date supplied from postmark.

2 – Date supplied from internal evidence.

stockings, letting me sleep late, keeping the house quiet and a hundred other thoughtful little favors –

Love –
Sivvy

TO *Aurelia Schober Plath*

Tuesday 30 January 1951[1] ALS with envelope, Indiana University

Tuesday AM

Dear Mum –

It is now 9 A.M., and after two donuts, orange juice, rhubarb, milk, and two cups of coffee, I am ready to face the world. I am going to the libe now, for four hours of history.

I really am glad that I stayed home for four days. I feel so rested and "ready for work". It is so lovely out that it makes my heart ache – I hate to shut myself up in a carrell. Let's hope it's nice this weekend.

The ride up was without event – Got here at 5 past 6, and luckily supper wasn't till 10 past. Hope you got the telegram all right. (taxi = 60¢ for a two minute ride.)

Don't forget to send up the pictures – I hope one is good, 'cause I forgot to take the one from my scrapbook – copied my expenses for you –

Love,
Sivvy

TO *Aurelia Schober Plath*

Wednesday 31 January 1951[2] ALS (postcard), Indiana University

Wednesday night

Dear Mum –

Got your cheerful letter this morning just before I left for my Botany exam along with a long letter from Ann Davidow. I will bring it home when I come in spring – and you will see from it what a dear friend I might have had. Already she is wishing that she had come back. I stayed in the library from 9-1 and 2-6 yesterday just outlining the french empire

1 – Date supplied from postmark.
2 – Date supplied from postmark.

– and I have so much more to learn & do. All I did for Botany was spend last evening and an hour this morning glancing over what I did at home. I didn't even need to do that. The questions were the same type as usual "why, when a cow is turned out in a fresh spring pasture, does it's butter become deeper yellow?" Now I ask you if that isn't laughable. I washed my hair tonight, as it's the only chance I'll have. As it has snowed all day I hope I will be going this weekend. I have been having trouble getting to sleep – my eyes are so sore from 10 hours solid reading a day! I guess I'll take sleeping pills till after exams are over

Love you
XX
Sivvy

TO *Aurelia Schober Plath*

Thursday 1 February 1951[1] ALS (postcard), Indiana University

Thurs. night

Dear Mum –

It is now just after supper, and in 24 short hours I will either have hung myself with typewriter ribbon or joined the A. Anonymous Society. I have a horrible feeling of tension and pressure, and as soon as I look at a general question, all the hundred Philips and Johns and Henries and Charlies of the various Empires promptly shuffle themselves around maliciously in my head, while dates and trends leak out like water from a seive. To top it off, Bob called tonight and said he couldn't get the car because of the weather, so he'll have to hitchhike to Brattleboro himself, since he has no way of getting me. I hadn't realized how much I had counted on a weekend out-of-doors until I felt the let down after hanging up. Oh, well, I will devote the weekend to rest and the charming company of females for which I have been starving so long. I hope I don't sound too bitter, but I would have liked to have something to frost the mudpie of this damn exam. I just know the questions will involve some obscure angle I never studied. Wish me luck.

XXXXX
Love,
Sivvy

1–Date supplied from postmark.

TO *Ann Davidow-Goodman*

Saturday 3 February 1951[1] ALS, Smith College

Dearest Ann –

After feeling rather bereft at not getting mail for days and days, your lovely plump letter arrived. Although the way you write brings home to me how much I've lost, I still love hearing from you and I love writing to you. It's funny – but the two people I spill over most to are now both writing irretrievably from Illinois.

There is so much to tell you, but I had to wait until exams were over before I really could feel the freedom necessary to write the way I want to.

Now about a few items of news you wanted. Eddie is still writing,[2] but as I told you perhaps, he has finally got another girl – Rita, is the name. I am afraid that the beloved Eddie I once adored is disintegrating. It's sad, but there are times when I have to smile a bit wistfully at some of his pearls of philosophy, because the hard edges of his environment and experience are beginning to show. For one thing, he has quit college (Roosevelt) to work selling shirts in Marshall Field. However, he is going back to RC the second semester to finish up last year's work which he threw up to live with the femme fatale – Bobbe. Although he blithely told me how fascinating it was to work at odd jobs (the four boys in the apartment had a total of twenty odd jobs in a six month period), I have a strong feeling that it is hard for him to toss it off so carelessly now that he is getting older. He also mentioned (you would love this) that he was afraid of the consequences of meeting me (i.e. going to Springfield) because "two people of such sensitive & emotional natures"[3] would no doubt get hopelessly involved – and he actually confessed he would fall for me and there was no solution since the three-date-a-week angle would be tantalizing and since marriage and any other reasonably fulfilling solution (hinting delicately that I would not live with him) were impossible at my tender age. You can imagine that made me feel rather good inside. It's pretty sad when a girl has to rely on typewritten words from a guy she's never met (and no doubt would not get along with if she did) to send a little shiver of excitement and tenderness up her spine. Shows how much she needs affection – or something.

1–Misdated 'Jan. 51' by Ann Davidow-Goodman. Midyear exams were held 24 January–2 February 1951.

2–See Eddie Cohen to SP, [17 January 1951] and [24 January 1951]; held by Lilly Library.

3–In Eddie Cohen to SP, [24 January 1951], Cohen wrote, 'With two people of our emotional sensitivities, it would, I fear, be a rather powerful, all-pervading love affair.'

As for my three dimensional males. For my own enlightenment, as well as yours, I shall review the situation concisely. (As if I could ever be concise!)

I had a date with Guy the 1st week I came back from Xmas. I had just got my notice from 17 (the story doesn't come out till May) and had had supper with Pat O'Neil to celebrate. Any dumb oaf could have seen I was walking on air, but all the way down to the movies in Hamp (we walked) Guy kept up a steady stream of chatter (maybe he's nervous & wants to make noise?) At any rate, I got more & more teed (sp?) off, and especially so when I found he didn't even look at me to see my reactions to his statements. (I am egotistical enough that I like to talk about me sometimes too.) So I amused myself by staring at him with exaggerated expressions of emotion as he rattled on oblivious to all my annoyance. (At least the movie was good – All About Eve.) I made the faux pas on the porch steps of telling him in no uncertain terms that I thought fraternities were demoralizing for a large number of reasons (which I made up, mostly.) I guess I was desperately determined to make him have some sort of reaction to me – unpleasant or not. He did. He was supposed to call me after exams. I never heard from him. Damn glad too, I must say.

As for Bill – the veteran. I haven't heard from him since before Xmas when under the influence of 20 eggnogs he vowed to show me New York on New Year's Eve. He is now going with a girl from Chapin. I don't expect to hear from him either.

I went on a blind date to the U. of M. with Sue Slye[1] after I came back, and met the saddest group of slobs I have yet run across. My date was supposedly the best-looking boy in his dorm – & he was attractive in a weak-dark hair-tonic sort of way. He was one of the those fool Americans who think of girls as a clotheshorse with convenient openings and curved structures for their own naive pleasure . . . no thoughts or anything else. Which illustrates one of my pet theories that I picked up from some essay or other: The American male does not think of woman as a friend and companion (the mature outlook) but childishly as a combination of mother and sweetheart.

While I'm throwing out bits of wisdom, get this: (I made it up myself – whee!) The difference between Amherst & the U. of M. is: at both places the boys go in for the same things in a big way (girls & gin) but at Amherst you get stoned on a cocktail with a cherry in it in a plush fraternity bedroom, while at the U. of M. you get klobbered on beer and

1–Susan Slye Taylor (1930–); B.A. 1952, English, Smith College; SP's housemate at Haven House.

greasy potato chips. (A small technical difference, to be sure, but all the space between the multimillionaire who becomes inebreated (sp?) in his libr'y under the moose-head to the bum who gets picked up from the gutter to spend the night in the town cell.)

I broke up with Bob (U. of N.H. – remember?) Rather finally at Xmas. He was sick – especially about the war – and thought he could make me bolster him up as usual. Unfortunately I like the bolstering to be mutual, and as I was feeling horribly low all Xmas vacation, I told him I hated everyone, didn't give a damn about anyone except myself, and had been attacked by a veteran, all of which was subconsciously calculated to make him sick. He was. And I didn't give a darn. I have not been emotionally involved for almost a year – since August & Emile. I am beginning to see how you can ignore sex if you aren't being excited by one of the opposite (sex.) I have a strange feeling I told you about Bob before?

So here I am. There is but one male on the horizon that hasn't run in the opposite direction or been sent packing. His name is Bob Humphrey & he goes to R.P.I. I like him for some obscure reason. I had a blind date with him Thanksgiving and was supposed to go out with him New Year's Eve. I went home last weekend for four days (supposedly to rest & study) and Bob came over & kept me in hysterics for three hours. That is a rather hard job, but his New England drawl & delightful sense of humor brought me up to a gay state I haven't been in for ages. As mother said afterwards, she hadn't heard me laugh for six months. He is 6'5" and rather rugged – loves to ski and can't write a letter for the life of him, so I am determined to learn to ski (you know how I can't do things other people do!) He's the sort of guy I'd like now – I'd never get emotionally involved, yet he's a nice man to have around the house.

After my rambling on for pages about my males (what is duller than another girl's love [ha!] life?) you are asleep, no doubt.

This letter is reaching huge proportions. – But one parting shot!

It's the funniest thing – remember how much you thought of Marcia Brown? Well I am now sitting in her aunt's cosy living room in Francestown, N.H., and writing while she does her History. I have somehow gotten to know her better, and find her one of the most thoroughly delightful people I've ever run across. I can only admire her hopelessly, feeling that as soon as she gets to know me better, she'll run too. – I don't feel I've anything to offer her in the way of personality or ideas. She is so adorably logical & intelligent – I just gape. So I will close now – write about life. (I wish to hell you'd get a tutor, or make up a course or two & come back. – We'd all love it if you would – and I know you could do it.)

Oh well – I'll shut my large and egocentric mouth.

All my love,
Sylvy

TO *Aurelia Schober Plath*

Saturday 3 February 1951[1]

ALS with envelope,
Indiana University

Saturday

Dear Mother –

No doubt you are wondering what I am doing with my little self during this free weekend after Bob escaped sans me to Brattleboro. Well, I am actually glad he did, because I am having one of the loveliest times I've had all year. I left right after the history exam yesterday with Marcia Brown and her mother for Francistown New Hampshire to visit "Aunt"[2] – one of the most delightful people I've met in a long time – with a history that involves marrying and divorcing a chilly old English naval commander, and then a seabee in Bermuda, and finally leaving him in Texas and establishing her self and her three children in a delightful white new England house up here. The only time that I could compare to it was the time I went up to Colerain with the Powleys[3] – the same snowy bleak views and cosy interior. All the way up it was like driving in the bleak wilds of Russia, still, black, with pines and stars and no light anywhere – just the headlights chiseling a tunnel in to the dry ice air ahead. We talked about everything from what we wrote in the exam to what is the line between heredity & environment to how horrible a fate television is for children. We stopped somewhere when a diner jumped out of the dark at us and brought back a little feeling in our numb veins with coffee and a club sandwich. On again, through Peterboro and finally we arrived at "Aunt's." She is a dear, and I love the way the house is decorated – one of those set ups that appeals to my Puritan nature – a very striking arrangement of dark gray floor, white-simple walls, yummy dusty green wood work, dusty rose curtains, very straight and clean-cut, and a lovely thick gray rug on the floor with dull pewter on the mantel

1 – Date supplied from postmark.

2 – Harriet Taylor Bosworth (1903–96). Bosworth lived at 47 2nd New Hampshire Turnpike South, Francestown, New Hampshire.

3 – SP visited Colrain, Mass., with Betsy Powley and family from 27 February to 2 March 1947.

– a low bookcase, cosy chairs, and portraits hung all around the simple walls. (Aunt Harriet can certainly catch the spirit of some of the new Englander's around here in her charcoal sketches.)

It was so lovely to walk into the warmth of a strange yet congenial room, and feel the delightful surge of relaxation as you realized that exams were over – and nothing was immediately demanding. Marcia whipped up the most delicious combination of scrambled eggs, melted cheese, garlic salt & pepper (and bacon) imagineable, and hot chocolate topped it off. We sat in the living room and ate a lovely pie and talked till we got so silly that we went upstairs and fell into the double bed. This morning we got up early and Marcia and I had a delightfully leisurely breakfast while chatting with her mother and aunt. Marcia & I then drove to Peterboro to go shopping – and browsed around the country stores. After lunch back home (tomato soup – liederkrantz cheese, applesauce – etc.) Aunt and Marcia and I went on a long hike. The roads are about a foot thick with solid ice, and the views are lovely. The sun was sort of vague in a gray cold sky, and I was grateful for my pajama bottoms under my ski pants and my navy sweater under my plaid shirt. After being out in the bitter air for an hour or two, I feel rather drowsy, and am working by turns on Monday's history assignment with Marcia.

I sort of hate the idea of going back to school tomorrow--- it is so nice up here, but I'll write more later.

Love
Sivvy –

PS Thanks for the pictures!

TO *Aurelia Schober Plath*

Sunday 4 February 1951[1] ALS, Kenneth W. Rendell Gallery[2]

Here are the pics, and thank you muchly. It is now midnight Sunday night and I have gotten back from the nicest weekend I ever had! I am no longer pale & pasty, but ruddy with windburn & sunburn from being out all day today and yesterday. Marcia and I got up at 10 and had a lovely liesurely breakfast in the front living room of the dear little house. Then

1 – Date supplied from internal evidence.

2 – Transcribed from the gallery's catalogue. The letter first sold via Sotheby's New York, Lot 105, on 6 April 1982. It then sold via Christie's New York, Lot 52, on 12 November 1997. Rendell offered the letter in 1999. Where Rendell's version has 'white-New-England', Sotheby's excerpt printed 'white-new-england'.

we went out into the most beautiful world imagineable! Snow had fallen in a fine powder last night, and the sun was out in a snow-blue sky. A white-New-England church is so lovely – and it was one of those heavenly dry-cold days, with blinding sun and snow and sharp blue shadows. The air was swimmingly blue. A kind neighbor loaned me a pair of skis and I 'skiid' for the first time in my life. We were off on a nice pasture lot in the heart of the snow-covered N.H. Hills, and I never have been so thrilled in my life! None of the wobbly-ankeled insecurity of skates! Of course the modest little gently rolling hill I learned on was not Sun Valley, but I would love to really learn. Marcia was a dear, telling me how to hold the poles, etc. Skiing, if you can do it well, must be pretty close to feeling like God. To bed & my six hour day tomorrow –

Your happy girl
Sylvia

TO *Aurelia Schober Plath*

Monday 5 February 1951[1] ALS (postcard), Indiana University

Monday night

Dear Mum –

It is now midnight, and I am about to collapse in bed. Tomorrow I have vowed to go to bed at nine, after washing my hair – but tonight I did no work – just had fun. It was rugged to sit through 6 hours today – and look forward to the same tomorrow. But right after supper tonight three of us dashed down to the movie to see "Harvey."[2] It was very whimsical, and I enjoyed crying in spots. After we came back we spent an hour reading aloud from Mary Poppins and Winnie the Pooh. It brought back such pleasant memories! No exams have come back yet – just my Eng. theme with another grudging A-. That should give me a B+ for midyears, & I'm determined to wring an A- out of him by finals! We must plan to have Marcia Brown down for a weekend or during spring vacation for a few days – she'd love to see Boston & plays. Is anything good coming? As she lives in N. Jersey I might see "Lady's not For Burning" with her spring vac. in New York! I hope it works out.

Love,
Sivvy.

1 – Date supplied from postmark.
2 – *Harvey* (1950) played at the Academy of Music Theatre, 274 Main Street, Northampton, Mass.

TO *Aurelia Schober Plath*

Thursday 8 February 1951[1] ALS with envelope, Indiana University

Thursday night

Dear Mother –

Well, I have just realized that I haven't written much mail lately, and that perhaps you were in on the short end. So I'll catch you up on news.

I still haven't got my history exam back yet, but got 91% in Botany and A- in French. I still find it hard for my tender ego to see other girls getting straight A with all sorts of wonderful comments. Pat O'Neil is doing wonderfully – she should, as she works so hard. A- in history! A- in French! A- in Greek. Now I ask you if that isn't marvelous for a friend of mine!

Oh yes – one encouraging thing! A girl came up to me from another art section & said "Oh, Sylvia, they showed your work in class today as an example of a promising Freshman." I just hope it's true! (I never believe anything good about myself.) But I do feel that those loving hours I spend in the studio may help. Keep your fingers crossed.

Bob Humphrey wrote about how they all missed me last weekend. The sweetest letter from Tony Stout came this afternoon. I really feel that my writing is an invaluable weapon. After not hearing from him since my refusal to his Christmas invitation (I invited him to drop in during vacation) I decided he was too promising to lose, and so last weekend while at Marcia's I composed a very strategic note – revealing my love for art & writing rather subtly and also my despisal (sp?) of superficial fraternity beer busts. The thing was calculated to reveal enough of myself to make him reply in one way or another. And the result was the dearest six page letter about our being "kindred spirits." His naivté is charming – and he said, Among other things that he has always had "a sort of wary, uneasy feeling about young females. This can be traced to a great shyness that I had years ago." Years ago! Don't you love that? I must let you read his letter – it is so trusting and self-revealing that I could cry. I am rather amazed that I can touch off the secret spring of confidence in someone I only knew casually – but I am rather touched by the consequences. He says "Am I correct in saying you are in love with Education?" A rather good perception, I think, for him to make.

1 – Date supplied from postmark.

This weekend, as lots of girls are going to the Dartmouth Winter Carnival, I'll spend two nights sleeping downstairs in Marcia's room – she got me a blind date for this Sat. I think you'd love her – she's adorably little (like Betsy) and logical & lovable & intelligent.

Love,
Sivvy

P.S. Thanks for the astrology. I like the part about choosing the eagle or scorpion.

<on back of envelope>

P.S. Saw "Harvey" Monday
Saw Pearl Primus[1] (African) dance Wednesday

TO *Aurelia Schober Plath*

Saturday 10 February 1951[2] ALS (postcard), Indiana University

Sat –

Dear Mum –

Well, it is a bright freezing day, and last night I slept with a sweater, bathrobe & wool socks on – and still my nose & toes had to be thawed back to shape. I am living downstairs for the weekend -- and as Marcia and I were doing our French last night, we both felt like groaning at the thought of dragging out the entertaining side of our personalities tonight on the date – so she telegrammed them that we are sick & the two of us stodgy females will take in a concert[3] by ourselves instead. Last night I went to supper at Jack August's "lobsterie"[4] with a party of 16 females – Pat & Louise had engineered a party for Jeannie Woods who is up visiting for the weekend. I wrote a note to grampy – the gift ($25.!!-) came just as I was reluctantly preparing to go down to the bank. See you in 5½ short weeks –

Love.
Sylvia

1–Dancer and choreographer Pearl Eileen Primus (1919–94); performed in John M. Greene Hall, Smith College.

2–Date supplied from postmark.

3–Probably the Cleveland Orchestra, directed by George Szell, which performed Brahms's First Symphony, Mozart's Posthorn Serenade, and Casella's 'Paganiniana' on 10 February 1951, at 8:30 p.m. in John M. Greene Hall.

4–Jack August's was a seafood restaurant and market then at 5 Bridge Street, Northampton, Mass.

TO *Aurelia Schober Plath*

Sunday 11 February 1951[1] ALS (postcard), Indiana University

Sunday

Dear Mum –

I am jotting you a little note as I sit in the libe this afternoon, ready to dig into work. Marty and I had a lovely day yesterday. In the afternoon we took our laundry to the Bendix – only 40¢ for a big load – and bought tea & cake and went for a 2 hour walk in the "country." One thing – we sure get enough fresh air – she's the only gal around here who takes looong walks. We had tea, and then supper, after which we went to the concert which was lovely. I'm so glad I decided not to go out. I could have gone with the U. of. M. boy, but Cupid that I am, I got him a date with Barb Michelsen – & they hit it off. I got Guy Wilbor a date with a girl's cousin next week & refused a date with him this Sat! Marty & I got in about 11 last night and sat & knit & listened to all sorts of records in our pj's till 12:30. We had a late breakfast & walk this A.M. and here I am, after a lovely weekend. Both of us hate women en masse. But individually they are nice. Love life – smiling all the time.

Happy Valentine's Day
Sivvy

<on address side of postcard>

P.S. Please send mittens – I've lost my old ones!

TO *Ann Davidow-Goodman*

Wednesday 14 February 1951 ALS, Smith College

Feb 14 –

<drawing of a heart>

Wed

Dearest Ann –

Honestly, I just love hearing from you. It's like getting a shot of personality in the arm & I never fail to feel much much better.

You've got the breeziest way of saying things – and I adore it. By now you've crawled into the wastebasket blushing, so I'll turn with effort to a more neutral subject – (Neutral, she says!) Eddie! I was in hysterics over your conversation with him (imaginary, of course.) Frankly, Ann, I would

1 – Date supplied from postmark.

give anything for you to meet him any time you had the chance – and you would know what to say. I mean if he had false teeth and three legs that didn't show in the picture he sent, you could sort of tell me gently. But – I don't think he's still at Marshall Fields. I last heard from him on January 24. That's just about the longest interval yet. I just got around to answering him last week, so he still has time to come through. But, he said in that letter that he was going back to Roosevelt College this semester after spending a week with Rita in Wisconsin to "shed a clearer light" on things.

So I don't know. Would he be married? Heaven forbid. I suppose it would be too much to ask you to track him down in his lair – 1422 Winona Ave. But someday if you are feeling adventurous – do look up the adress & walk by his apartment. Is it a tenement? Are women lurking by the lamposts? You've got me!

I liked your pep talk. I needed it but bad. As for the boy situation – it looks suddenly brighter. I stayed home with Marcia last Saturday night and slept in her room for two nights as Teed & Carol were at the Dartmouth Winter Carnival. I had the opportunity for three dates (it sounds wonderful when I say it numerically – but individually they're all sad-cases.) Marcia & I gave up our blind date plans. I got Guy a date with dodie's cousin and the U. of M. boy a date with Barb Michelson. A good time was had by all – especially Marcia & I.

As if by magic I got a completely unexpected letter a week or so ago. It was from the older brother of a boy I used to adore. Both are at Yale – the only people I know there. Out of the blue, Dick Norton (a senior) wrote[1] asking me down for this weekend. Nothing is "happening", but I don't give a damn. Ann, he is just the sort of boy I'd love to get to know better – a med student, good-looking, intelligent! Oh, I'll stop there. You see, our families have known each other for years, and he has always been very paternal & "older brother-ish" to me. So I thought he was asking me down just to give little sister a big thrill and a homey time of taking walks in the country (which I love) and tours of the campus. So I wrote a brief little letter as sparkly as I could, hoping he'd see I wasn't overawed (which I was.) So now, before he sees me, he asks me down for 2 days in March!![2] That was what tantalized me & got me wondering – what he was up to. Wish me luck! After one semester of sad blind dates, I hope at least to have these two weekends turn out right!

1–Richard Norton to SP, 30 January 1951; held by Lilly Library.
2–Richard Norton to SP, 7 February 1951; held by Lilly Library.

If you could be here now you would laugh. The past week has been the flare-up about rooms. I never have seen anything at once so sickening and so pathetically funny! The seniors have already chosen, and the juniors (this years sophs) are all moving over here. The only trouble is, they all want singles, and there are only a couple left – so roommates are either going to hate each other next year or lots of people are going to be miserable & move out. The Freshman picture is even more interesting. In Wesley, the pairs are Charlotte[1] & Joan,[2] Reggie & Maureen, Diana & Sarah,[3] with Sonia[4] the extra. Here, however, things have been very tense. Callie, Carol Pierson, and Nancy Teed evidently have been brewing a scheme for quite some time to room in a suite of three. It all burst out in the open on Monday when Marcia & Lola[5] were told the news by their respective roommates. Naturally it was a shock to both, who had sort of planned on a four year deal. Well, I was bowled over. I knew Barb Michelson would room with anyone. Betsy Blanton had planned on rooming with Teed – who never thought of it seriously. Betsy Whittemore would have roomed with Barb or me. Lola was miserable – not wanting to room with anyone. There were no single rooms. Everyone had to have a mate. So we all (with the exception of Carol, Teed & Marcia) got together and said we'd straighten things out openly (heh-heh) without any hurt feelings. Everybody sat there feeling very open-minded and giving with tense laughter. I felt in the position of utmost ease, as, aside from Callie, Carol & Teed, I had the best choice. I could keep my room and remain single – or wed myself to one of the pool. Needless to say, the only one I'd give up my freedom for would be Marcia. So I went down and talked to her, and amid stammers & blushes we agreed that we each either wanted to try our fate together or stay alone & not mix with the common herd. So I'm going to room with her next year, of all things. That left four people in the unique position of wanting roommates & having to have them – but not wanting each other at all. Four odd people without a match. Lola at last agreed to room with Bobby, as much as she was reluctant. Whittemore is thinking of moving to the German house, as she doesn't know if she can stand Blanton another year. And so we close our little intrigue. "Everyone lived happily ever after . . ." Marcia comes nowhere as close as you – so it's hard – a little. But I'll try. I need to learn

1–Charlotte Kennedy Ehrenhaft (1932–); B.A. 1954, religion, Smith College.
2–Joan Strong Buell (1932–); B.A. 1954, music, Smith College.
3–Sarah Frank Chaffin (1932–); B.A. 1954, sociology, Smith College.
4–Sonya Zelinkoff Simon (1932–); B.A. 1954, education, Smith College.
5–Eleanor Starr Darcy (1932–); B.A. 1954, history, Smith College.

to adjust to someone, & she's the only one I'd care to make the effort for after you've gone.

It is raining; & although the only thing wrong with me is lack of sleep, I've taken a yellow slip & am being pampered by staying in bed & catching up on all my back work. It got so I couldn't face it, so I took this way out.

Be good – Davy –
All my love,
Sylvy

P.S. The picture[1] is for laughs.

TO *Aurelia Schober Plath*

Wednesday 14 February 1951[2] ALS (postcard), Indiana University

Wednesday

Dear Mum –

I took a yellow slip & stayed in bed today, although I am fine. But in the last 2 days I haven't been to bed till after midnight, and have gotten no work done as there has been the stew over roommates which is so involved that no explanation would suffice. A least I am happy & sure, although many others are not. I'm just lucky. So I thought I'd catch up on sleep & work today as much as I hate to miss History section. Speaking of History – guess what!!! I got straight A on my midyear exam!!! I just don't see how my luck (that's what it is -- just chance that I reviewed the right thing) can hold out. I slept for two hours this morning & am really glad I decided not to go to classes because it is half snow-&-raining out, and I know I would have been "courting a cold." I want to be well & rested for this weekend. I hope I can steer away from colds till spring vacation. Louise G. is rather unhappy & wants to changes houses! I love you all –

XXX
Sivvy

1 – The enclosure is no longer with the letter.
2 – Date supplied from postmark.

TO *Aurelia Schober Plath*

Thursday 15 February 1951[1] ALS (postcard), Indiana University

Thursday

Dear Mum –

Got the cookies today & mittens – many thanks! I had my hair washed & set this morning & it sure was a luxury to feel someone else doing the job for a change. The charge was 1.75. The man didn't approve of the cut -- said it was too short for the page boy I wanted. So I gratefully said I'd let it grow & have him trim & set it some time in March. It seems I have hit a midwinter slump. Ever since I've come back from Francestown I haven't been able to work or study or get enthusiastic about much scholastically. I guess it's just a reaction from plugging so hard for those 2 exam weeks. You might be amused to hear I got a rather stiff letter from Bob Riedeman today. Still signs "Love", poor thing. You know just as well as I do where I'm going this weekend.[2] How did you find out?

Love
Sivvy

TO *Aurelia Schober Plath*

Monday 19 February 1951[3] ALS, Indiana University

Monday

Dear Mother –

I am enclosing my check from SEVENTEEN for deposit. And Grampy did send me $25 – incredible as it seems. I do hope he didn't do it by mistake.

As for my weekend – I thought I'd wait to tell you after it happened so you wouldn't spend half your days wondering & worrying about me. I left Sat. morning to go to Yale with Dick Norton – who wrote & asked me to drop down for a day or two for God knows what reason. I think he thought it would be a nice thing to do – show little cousin around the campus. But I did have a good time and learned a great deal. It rained all day Saturday, so we sat & talked in his room. He knows everything. I am so firmly convinced that knowledge comes through science that I would like to get some elementary books of physics or chemistry or math & study

1 – Date supplied from postmark.

2 – SP was making her first visit to Yale to see Richard Norton. See Richard Norton to SP, 7 February 1951; held by Lilly Library.

3 – Date supplied from internal evidence.

them this spring vacation and this summer. Perhaps Warren could help me. For I am the strange sort of person who believes in the impersonal laws of science as a God of sorts and yet does not know what any of those laws are. I don't care if I am not "mathematically minded." All that I write or paint is, to me, valueless if not evolved from a concrete basis of reasoning, however un-complex it must be. Now don't laugh & say that I must be content in my own little 2-dimensional world. Poetry & art may be the manifestations I'm best suited for, but there's no reason why I can't learn a few physical laws to hold me down to something nearer truth.

I came away last night feeling desperately eager to learn more and more. It's so easy to be satisfied with yourself if you aren't exposed to people farther advanced. I do feel a bit sorry for Dick, as I kept asking him to tell me about his interview results in sociology, and about what he met up with at the mental institution and all. It was a process of assimilation & taking on my part, and of necessity nothing reciprocal. But he has an amazing mind and a remarkable group of highly developed skills – dancing, skating, swimming & so on. So I felt a bit guilty to take up two days. You'll have to admit it was a rather unselfish gesture on his part.

An amusing thing was that I missed the last train last night (at 9:05) that would have gotten me in on time – so I got a later one & will have to report to Judicial Board[1] here & get some sort of penalty. I was rather glad to see Dick momentarily unnerved, although he didn't show it too visibly.

Another thing that interested me – I like the parts of his mother[2] I see in him – & do not like the parts of his father[3] (such as a hearty laugh) which crop out occasionally. All in all I had a lovely time.

I have piles of work to do this week & loads of back mail that requires long answers. So forgive me if I don't write for a few days.

Love,
Sivvy

P.S. We do get delivery on Sundays

1–Judicial Board held jurisdiction over all cases of infringement of the rules: curfew was midnight on Friday and Sunday and 1 a.m. on Saturday at Smith College.

2–Mildred Smith Norton (1905–2001). The Nortons lived at 47 Cypress Road, Wellesley Hills, Mass., and were friends of ASP.

3–William Bunnell Norton (1905–90).

TO *Aurelia Schober Plath*

Tuesday 20 February 1951[1] ALS with envelope, Indiana University

Tuesday night

Dear Mother –

At last Monday and Tuesday are over, leaving me breathing a bit easier, although I still have mountains of work to wade through, since I cut classes and slept yesterday morning, missed my classes Saturday, of course, and cut Wednesday, as I told you. I think if I get on Dean's list, which I will, that I can get free cuts for the rest of the semester! Neat, huh?

Luckily our English theme[2] was postponed till next Monday – and the first quiz I've taken this semester came back with an A+. Mendelian laws are coming a great deal easier! I am two weeks behind in art – and am looking forward to rally day[3] – (Thursday) since we have no classes. They planned it just at the right time – I'd be sunk otherwise. I look so forward to hearing Bunche![4] Friday night I will probably get a ticket & go to the traditional rally day show. Saturday they are having "The Rocking-Horse Winner"[5] at Smith movies – so I hope to dig up a few girl friends & go to that. This is our big formal Charity Ball weekend – but I didn't want to spend any money & I need the rest. Speaking of formals, would you send up <u>both</u> my white & black (clean) 'cause our freshman dance is coming up <u>soon</u> & I do hope to get a date for that!

Although you brushed with almost hysterical gaiety over your ulcer – I am only too aware that Fran's "demotion" was caused by trouble. I don't want you to worry about things, mummy. Is it money? or Warren? As for money, I have good news. Marcia and I got a double-decker on the second floor and that will be $50 less for the year. (I slept in one when I visited her, and managed quite well.)

Tonight I appear before Judicial Board because of my lateness. Did I tell you that Dick took me bicycling Sunday instead of church. I'll bet I'm one of the few girls who's walked through the New Haven streets in sneakers three sizes too big, a boy's dungarees & sweater & jacket,

1 – Date supplied from postmark.

2 – Sylvia Plath, 'Modern Tragedy in the Classic Tradition'; held by Lilly Library.

3 – In 1876 Rally Day began as a way to celebrate the birth of the first president of the United States, George Washington, but has since come to celebrate Smith College with special events and speakers around the campus.

4 – American political scientist, diplomat, and academic Ralph Johnson Bunche (1903/4–71); winner of Nobel Peace Prize in 1950. Bunche spoke at 10 a.m. on 22 February 1951, in John M. Greene Hall.

5 – A 1950 film version of D. H. Lawrence's short story, first published in 1926.

toting an old bike. <drawing of a person with bicycle> We took a leisurely ride & climbed a hill overlooking the whole town. Since we arrived back about three, we had a late dinner in a Chinese restaurant. Do tell the Nortons how I enjoyed looking over Dick's Sociology reports & hearing about his interviews. Also his roommates were dear. I especially liked the Jugoslavian[1] – brought up on Hitler's Nazi Youth Program. Perry's roommates' are all handsome, cleancut and brilliant. Do congratulate them on his 90% average.

Bob Humphrey called tonight to ask if I could come home for the weekend, but I said no – so he's probably coming up about 8 Sunday morning & we'll hunt up some snow. The U. of. M. boy also called – so I quickly thought up another excuse. He is a sad character. (No surprises anymore.)

I was amused at Dick. He regards me as an indulgent older cousin would. He even memorized some poetry & read aloud some – as much as he does not credit emotional expression as valuable without scientific knowledge . . . or something. But from a purely selfish point of view, I enjoyed walking around & being out in the open air for a few hours. Yale is lovely. – And even being an indulged younger cousin was very enjoyable.

Another thing. Dick remarked on my "practical gabardine coat." I enjoyed it – and would never feel quite at home in fur. Did I tell you that one girl loaned me a dear hat to wear down? My black one looked awfully out of place with the brown coat – too dressy & veiled for such a casual coat. So this hat was perfect in color & casualness – a sort of brown leopard spotted fur – quite nice & harmonizing.

<drawing of female head with leopard-spotted hat>

And now to my J. B. meeting! Don't forget the formals!

Love,
Sivvy

P.S. Watch out for those ulcers!

P.P.S. I'll be getting my marks tomorrow! Wish me luck.–!

<on back of envelope>

P.S. – See if you can get hold of the Feb. Smith Alumnae Quarterly[2] – part of my letter to Prouty got in anonymously![3]

1–Joze Kostelec (1930–2014) born in Šentrupert, Yugoslavia (now Slovenia), came to the United States in 1950, and became a citizen in 1955; B.A. 1952, Yale College; M.S. 1958, physics, New York University; Yale roommate of Richard Norton, 1950–1.

2–'Doors open to a New Life', *Smith Alumnae Quarterly*, February 1951, 77.

3–'part of my letter to Prouty got in anonymously! ~~A bit too personal for an "open sandwich" card~~!' appears in the original.

TO *Aurelia Schober Plath*

Thursday 22 February 1951[1] ALS (postcard), Indiana University

Dear Mother –

Just thought you might like to know I got a 6 page letter from my favorite man today.[2] He sure is developing a sense of humor. Also, got a note saying I'm on DEAN'S List. So is Pat. My marks at mid-term are:

Botany – A
History – A
French – A-
Art – A- !!!!!!!
Eng – (damn) B+

I am going to work & work & work to keep it up. I just hope I can. Especially in Art & HISTORY

Love,
Sivvy

TO *Aurelia Schober Plath*

Thursday 22 February 1951[3] ALS with envelope, Indiana University

Rally Day
Thursday

Dear Mother –

I had to laugh! The three letters I got in the mail today all involved Dick in some way. One was from the formost doctor-to-be-in-the-next-decades himself, saying how glad he was that I got back all right. The second was from Ann saying she had a feeling I'd have a successful time; the other was your little diatribe. I do feel I must scold you, mummy. You have the same weakness I have---getting cross at people who show up the inadequacies of someone we love. It is so easy for me to say "I'm so mad at him" and yet the one I'm really mad at is myself for not knowing how to skate, swim, charleston or cook and sew. You see, reason shows that I'm the one to blame anyway!

1 – Date supplied from postmark and internal evidence.
2 – Richard Norton to SP, 21 February 1951; held by Lilly Library.
3 – Date supplied from postmark.

As for my penalty---it is a very light sort of punishment – signing in the house at 9 PM from next Monday to Thursday! I won't even have to miss a weekend night – and I never go out on weekdays anyway.

Bunche was excellent – spoke about danger of fear & war-talk from within – of living by democracy as well as swearing by it – of putting all efforts into helping Africa and Asia medically, economically, etc. He also said they were working at the U.N. & through the Un – & to beware of hotheaded imperialism. He was a winning, encouraging speaker. It was indeed impressive to see the ranks of white and the diagonal colored class ribbons – and the procession of professors in their colored hoods and gowns.

Marcia & I took a walk in the country today for an hour or so & came back quite muddy. Tonight I'm going to see the rally day show.

If I sounded depressed in my last letters it might have been partially weariness & partially that I seem to be having my first regular period for five months. I just hope it keeps up.

Don't be a jealous mummy of other mummies' offspring, now!

Love,
Sivvy

TO *Aurelia Schober Plath*

Saturday 24 February 1951[1] ALS (postcard), Indiana University

SATURDAY

Dear Mum –

Just thought I'd tell you something that surprised me a bit. A senior said to me at lunch – "Congrats for being up on the College Hall Bulletin Board again". (Smith girls in the news, you know!) So, full of curiosity I hurried over. You should have seen it – I stood for a full 5 minutes laughing. It was one of those cartoon & personality write-ups titled "Teen-Triumphs." There was a sketch of a girl s'posed to be me – writing, also a cow. It said, & I quote: "BORN TO WRITE! Sylvia Plath, 17, really works at writing. To get atmosphere for a story about a farm she took a job as a farm hand. Now, she's working on a sea story." Then there's another sketch of me saying "And I'll get a job on a boat." Not only that: "A national magazine has published two of her brain children! The real test of being a writer. The little Wellesley, Mass blonde has won

1 – Date supplied from postmark.

a full scholarship to Smith College." All this effusive stuff appeared in the Peoria Illinois Star on Jan. 23.[1] Beats me where they got the sea stuff. I just laughed and laughed. Illinois – hmmm.

Love,
Sivvy

TO *Aurelia Schober Plath*

Wednesday 28 February 1951[2] ALS (postcard), Indiana University

Wednesday

Dear Mum –

Lord, I don't think I've written you for a month. Say bad correspondent, but I'm getting to be one! I was quite amused by that circular from that newspaper reporter. I am convinced people make too much of "youthful" "success." I am doubtful if I can say in all truthfulness "I was BORN TO WRITE!" I'd kind of like people to forget about it for a while. These next three weeks are to be the hardest all year, I think – what with papers, writtens and being a wee bit behind in art. But I shall probably go to Marcia's the weekend of March 31 – so could you tell me what plays are coming to Boston before & after said weekend? I have no way of knowing, and I'd like to show her a good time. (If she came after, she'd probably come back here with me Wednesday April 4.) Everyone around here has colds. I'm crossing my fingers that I escape the germs everyone's sneezing around. I suddenly seem to have no time at all – every-minute is taken up by trying to keep my head above water as far as my courses are concerned. I'd really love to take a few evenings out & just knit or suthing. Keep well –

Love,
Sivvy

1 – Stookie Allen, 'Teen-Age Triumphs', *Peoria Star*, 23 January 1951, A–9.
2 – Date supplied from postmark.

TO *Aurelia Schober Plath*

Thursday 1 March 1951 ALS (postcard), Indiana University

March 1–

Dear Mum—

And so we start March with a snowstorm – after the springlike weather at the beginning of the week. No sooner do I optimistically take my bicycle out of the cellar than I have to stow it away again. I think I shall start a new scrapbook about myself,[1] what with all my little attempts at writing being blown up rather out of proportion. Imagine one awestruck girl greeted me yesterday with "I hear you're writing a novel. I think that's just wonderful." Whereupon I felt like telling her I was my twin sister and never wrote a damn thing in my life. I've got to get to work if I'm going to live up to my "reputation." At least Olive Higgins can feel I really do write. Seems that scholarship was rather well chosen. Hope the dear thing is content.

XX
Sivvy

TO *Aurelia Schober Plath*

Saturday 3 March 1951[2] ALS with envelope, Indiana University

Saturday

Dear Mum –

Now really, I am not writing from the hospital or the morgue. In fact I am quite well, and have so far miraculously escaped the flu. I just got up this morning and got your postcard. Could I be as presumptuous to say you sounded a wee bit frantic? No news may be good news from Warren, but that doesn't mean that no news means I'm on my deathbed. If I were, I'd at least have time to drop you a postcard.

The dresses arrived all right, although the box was broken to pieces. Dick asked me down to a dance next weekend, and I am now sorry I accepted on two counts. First, I know he did it to salve his conscience about the train episode, and that he would just have loved me to refuse. Second, we have a big history written the Monday after I return. So I'm

1 – SP's Smith College scrapbook, held by Lilly Library.
2 – Date supplied from postmark.

petrefied. At least I'll bring a book along, but that can't compare to a solid weekend of review.

Just to let you know why you won't be hearing from me as often as usual – March 1 seems to be the sign for any teachers to clamp down. I've an English paper due every Monday from here till vacation, a Botany test every Thursday, a french written next Thursday, History written March 12 (⅓ of my semester grade) and art work I haven't even touched yet, which gobbles hours of my time up. So you see that I'm in a squirrel cage at present. Bob Humphrey couldn't come Sunday (was I mad!) because he had the flu. This weekend I'm not going out at all because I've got to catch up on sleep and work so that missing said commodities next weekend won't quite kill me.

I will probably wear my maroon coat over my white dress. Those gloves you sent had holes in them, but I have white ones of my own anyway. I just want to be sure I don't have to worry about hiding holes or spots.

It is lovely weather, and I am as yet fine. If I live till after March 12 I can face the atombomb with complete equanimity.

Forgive me if I don't write too often. What am I going to do about a job this summer – would like to wait on Cape. Is that impossible?

Love,
Sivvy

TO *Aurelia Schober Plath*

Sunday 4 March 1951[1] ALS (postcard), Indiana University

Sunday a.m.

Dear Mum –

Well, yesterday afternoon I finished writing and typing my English paper due this Monday. From 8-11 last night I went over to Pat's room and caught up on my art notebook. Today will be completely devoted to doing the week's reading in history, and hoping. Thereby to be able to set a few hours aside for review sometime during the all-too-crowded week. The weather is miserable – about five inches of snow last night and rain all day today. I just hope it clears for next weekend as the Nortons believe in walking. Taxis? God no! If I live thru the ordeal, I will have to congratulate myself. All I can see is exams, exams exams. No time for much but. Excuse the gloom, but I hope I live to see the first crocus

1 – Date supplied from postmark.

pop open. I shall burst into piteously grateful smiles. Did you hear that Christopher Robin got married? He is a toothy horribly weak young man. One more dream gone.

XXX
Sivvy

TO *Ann Davidow-Goodman,*

Monday 5 March 1951 ALS with envelope, Smith College

Dearest Davy –

It is 8:30 on Monday morning, and I'm gathering my forces (such as they are) for my good old six hour day. Do you realize why I have my desk facing the window? (I just figured out why this minute.) Hopkins house faces my room. Hopkins house is yellow. Yellow is a "morale-building" color. (Or so the higher-ups say in Art 13.) And there you have it.

The Yale weekend was fun, if you look at it in one way, and frightening, if you look at it in another. You see, the boy I went down with is a friend of the families and I've never gone out with him before. He is one of those people that you can't believe exist. Not only is he the traditionally handsome blue-eyed blonde, but he is the most intelligent creature I've ever run across. For example, he's got exempt from the draft to go to Harvard Medical School next year! He is very well built, and quite athletic (swims, skates, and does all the things I can't do.) He has had such exciting jobs as working at a mental hospital. He rooms with 3 fascinating characters – one of whom was a Jugoslavian brought up in the Hitler Nazi youth program. Dick (my date) even showed me the reports he did in sociology – which involved interviewing 25 married couples in New Haven (14 pages per each!) So you see, I can't even say he is just a brilliant student, because he has got such a damn outgoing personality. Did I rise to the occasion? Heh!

Oh, Ann, If you could have seen all the dumb brainless things I did all weekend! I just wished you were here when I came back to console me.

I hardly dared talk to him, because he could always reason me logically out of the stupid impressionable things I usually babble about. I just could feel him saying to himself "The poor child doesn't know much of the basic natural phenomena of life, so we'll just humor her along."

Don't get me wrong – he wasn't superior! If he had been I would have had the satisfaction of saying "Hell, he's too stuck-up for me." The thing was he was just perfect, and thought up the loveliest things for me to do.

Saturday night we watched the annual swimming meet. Sunday, instead of going to church, we put on old clothes and took a bike ride to a hill outside town where we could look all over New Haven. We came back late in the afternoon and had a delightfully unconventional dinner at 3:30 in a Chinese restaurant. The one flaw in his perfection was that he got me to the train one minute after the thing had pulled out of the station. So I got to Hamp at 1 o'clock, and had to appear before J. B. etc. etc.

All in all, I was grateful to the handsome old Einstein for taking me out, but God, Ann, I never felt so shallow in my whole life. I hate being patronized. When I came back, I tried and tried to rationalize, but couldn't say that one thought in my unlogical head was worthwhile.

The funny thing is, you know how I feel about drinking & necking – not unless you are "in love" (or something like that.) Well, if he'd kissed me <u>once</u>! Even cousinlyish. But no! And he wouldn't look at a girl who drank, yet I felt I needed a few cocktails rather badly before I was through.

Now you will try to cheer me up as you would have. But I'll stick in one last sentence. He knows life through physical & chemical laws & reason. Thus he has a sound basis for impressions and embroidery on his thoughts. I have only a slippery shifting basis of liberal arts, and all my expressions aren't worth too much without a foundation.

Now – something else. Do you know anyone in Peoria? Some old article came out about me, and I'm dying to know how they got hold of <u>my</u> name. You and Eddie (whom I haven't heard from for ages – sob, sob) are the only guilty beings I can think of. It was the Jan 23 Peoria, Ill., Star!

As for Brownie & me – I think both of us would have preferred you as a friend, rather than each other, but as you are gone, we can only make the best of a bad reality by putting up with each other. On my part, though, I do think she is a dear.

Merci for your picture – it occupies a prominent place on my bulletin board.

Speaking of Spring vacation, I loved your impulsive invitation to head Chicago-ward – but lack of funds prevents. Could <u>you</u> head east and me-wards? Or is that impossible for the same reason?

Love you, Davy,
yours,
Sylvy

TO *Aurelia Schober Plath*

Monday 5 March 1951[1] ALS (postcard), Indiana University

Monday

Dear Mum

When I got your letter yesterday my first, perhaps rather expensive, reaction was to jump to the phone and call you to apologize. I really was stupid not to tell you, since I have begun to realize just how talkative the Norton's are. The fact is, as I've said, I am worried about going before an exam, but since I'm going, I'll bring a book with me & study whenever I have the chance, trying to be "bright & cheerful" (la-de-dah) when I'm with people. If I sound a bit depressed, it's only because of mountanous weeks of exertion ahead of me. I really am thrilled to extinction to go to the Junior Prom. But really, as I said, I know he's just doing it to be nice. One question – what do you do when someone comes up to you & says "Oh, you're the one who's writing the book?" or "You're the one who got all A's in History?" It's too bad – because once one person knows, everybody does. The only quiet woman is a dead one.

Love,
Sivvy

TO *Aurelia Schober Plath*

Tuesday 6 March 1951[2] ALS (postcard), Indiana University

Tuesday

Dear Mum –

Just a note before I dash off to basketball at 4. I'll talk with Marty about the 21-24 & let you know as soon as possible. Thanks for working on the theater problem. As for eliminating everything except what must be done – all I could conceivably give up is eating & sleeping, & I propose to do neither. One nasty thing – I got a hideous B- on my first English paper which blasts hopes of bringing <u>that</u> mark up. He says I did a superficial job – and although he may be partly justified, I certainly am going to have a talk with him <u>if</u> I don't get a good mark on the paper I'll pass in

1 – Date supplied from postmark.
2 – Date supplied from postmark.

tomorrow. Feel fine. Weather beautiful so don't worry. Sorry to have missed <u>your</u> call – was at libe

XX
Sivvy

TO *Aurelia Schober Plath*

Tuesday 6 March 1951[1] ALS (postcard), Indiana University

Tuesday night

Dear Mum—

It is now 10 P.M., and although the work I have to do in the next two days is Herculean, I'm going to bed now to be more rested. Guess what? A dear junior girl said she'd loan me her old mouton coat to wear if it was cold. It's funny, but I hesitated just a bit before I said I'd wear it – Dick will be sure to ask where I picked up such a luxury – oh, well. I'll say Aunt Tillie willed it to me on one condition -- that I attend the Yale 1951 Prom. It's all settled about me. I will go to Marty's Friday March 30 till Sunday or Monday since they've got tickets for "darkness at Noon."[2] In order not to break up the vacation, she'll come home with me some weekend in April. Maybe we could go in for the Ballet Russe[3] or something later on. See you in two long long weeks.

Love,
Sivvy

TO *Aurelia Schober Plath*

Friday 9 March 1951[4] ALS, Indiana University

Friday 10 AM

Dear Mum –

After the fat yellow-stamped crowd of morale boosting letters you sent me all week, I thought that the least I could do would be to send you a note before I left. Of all things, it's <u>snowing</u> now – big white flakes. A lot

1–Date supplied from postmark.

2–Arthur Koestler, *Darkness at Noon* (1940). Performed at the Alvin Theatre (now the Neil Simon Theatre), 250 W. 52nd Street, New York.

3–The Ballet Russe de Monte Carlo performed at the Boston Opera House for six days beginning 23 April 1951.

4–Date supplied from internal evidence.

of it is melting, but I am pocketing those plastic overshoes in case it keeps up. I just called for a taxi to take me down to the train at 2:15. One of the maids pressed my evening dress for the fee of 50¢, and I will pack it in the box after lunch, with tissue paper in the folds to prevent wrinkling. It does look dreamy. I am cutting art studio today, and French tomorrow, but I hope it won't be too fatal. At least spring vacation is only about 13 (unlucky, hm?) days away.

I haven't even begun to look at my history, but will get back about 2 P.M. Sunday, in time for an afternoon and evening of work, and I plan to cut four hours of classes on Monday morning. So that's about 10 hours of studying, theoretically! I've just got to manage. Our French midsemester & Botany test are both on Friday, giving me a few days to recover, and my English paper[1] due Monday can be slaved on over the weekend.

I feel a bit like cinderella: a borrowed old fur coat, a borrowed black leather handbag, a borrowed crinoline, plus borrowed silver sandals, (I found mine here, but they are a speck too narrow and cut into my foot. Rather than dance in agony, I'm taking one girl's elastic-silver ones, which are comfortable as bedroom slippers.)

One request! Would you mind burrowing in my desk or yellow chest for a folder of old english papers & send as quickly as possible a printed one on the "Cherry Orchard"[2] – If you can find it. Don't worry about me catching cold. I've been in bed by eleven every night this week –

Love,
Sivvy

TO *Aurelia Schober Plath*

Saturday 10 March 1951 — ALS with envelope, Indiana University

New Haven, Conn.[3]
March 10, 1951

Hello Mother –

And don't say you never get much mail! This cooperative letter-writing affair is quite fun, but I don't know that I can add too much to Dick's

1–Probably Sylvia Plath, 'The Tragedy of Progress'; held by Lilly Library.

2–*The Cherry Orchard* (1904) is a play by Russian playwright Anton Chekhov (1860–1904).

3–In Richard Norton's hand; SP and Norton shared letter space. The first 2½ pages by Norton not transcribed.

account. I am still a speck concerned about reason two, but plan to douse myself in the subject tomorrow and Monday.

I managed packing neatly, and the dress accompanied me down on the train, reposing in its cardboard box without a wrinkle. I rode down with two girls from my house – both of whom I saw at the dance – in fact I saw five girls I knew from Smith at the dance, which gave me a rich sense of belonging.

Art will require a bit of extra time next week. If only you could hear the utter unassuming tone of our assignments. "This week we'll do a full painting in analytical cubism, employing advancing, receding and transparent planes and color and equivocal line." How's that for a mouthful? No Picasso's or Braque's have been produced by 13 yet, though.

I look quite forward to my stay at Marcia's during vacation. Did I tell you the dates? Probably from Friday March 30 to Sunday March or April (?). Mrs. Brown will no doubt write to you about the affair. She is a dear funny woman. I do hope you can stand her.

I'll write after I pass through this week. Either that, or you will receive a little ink bottle full of ashes. Please scatter them on the waters of the ocean I loved so well in infancy.

Love,
Sivvy.

TO *Ann Davidow-Goodman*

Thurs.–Fri. 15–16 March 1951[1] ALS with envelope, Smith College

Thursday night

Dearest Davy –

And now we shall see just how good I am at concentrating on important things. In other words, just how many sentences I can whip off during house meeting. I swear no guy would date a Smith gal if he could see the way we look – hair wet, or screwed up in pin curls, old pajamas, knitting needles clicking busily. But in spite of everything, the girls are a pretty sweet lot!

I appreciated more than anything your quotation from Marty's letter. You must know a little of how much it meant to me. I think one of my greatest faults is disbelief in my ability to attract anyone over a long period

1 – Date supplied from internal evidence.

of time. I felt that with you; I felt that with Marty; I felt that with Dick, this Yale boy. You see, I think it might be a carry-over from my days in junior high, and even the beginning of senior high. I probably told you that I was a gawky mess, with drab hair and a bad skin – an outcast of sorts, too, among the classmates of mine who were pretty and dateable. So, for five years of having my undesirability dinned rather forcibly into my head, you perhaps can see how I still have that basic skepticism left over. You see me as I am, without the awkward stage in the background. Maybe, too, one of the reasons I am so enthusiastic and emotional about everything is that, until these past two or three years I really never have felt that my hopes and dreams were being fulfilled at all. Then, suddenly, things began happening. A BOY liked me! I had an English teacher who encouraged my writing! I got to be editor of the school paper. Best of all, I got into Smith. And so I felt like, after years of being on the BEFORE side of the success add, I suddenly got shot over to the after half. And there you have it. My attempt at an explanation of some of my many vices.

But after getting letters from you, each full of a peculiar power which excites and encourages me! Letters aren't just on paper, but they can be, as I have discovered from reading yours and Eddie's, more of an emotional impact than anything else. And that is a wonderful thing to find out.

I am awfully proud of you, though, Ann, for telling me what you did about your feelings of leaving Smith. I've got to hand it to you – and I've always thought that your self-honesty was one of the most amazing and delightful thing about you. I can compare you and Eddie, I think, because both of you have stimulated me and been deep companions to me. Eddie has the horrible faults (I hate to admit it) of rationalizing and fooling himself that he is infallible and is living the best way he can. (At present,[1] he is going on the rocks with Rita . . . and he wouldn't ever admit that his stupid way of living for sex "before marriage" is time after time proving absurd.)

You, on the other hand, have done an act, courageous & decisive from one point of view, and yet frightening and fatal from another. But thank God you're being constructive about it. U. of Chi. is tremendous & has a great lot to offer in the way of subjects, teachers, and new ideas. (Eddie went there for two years, remember?) I envy you, in a way, and the new friends and new life you are making for yourself. I did so want to be a part of that – your circle of friends and the rest of your life. I hope, Ann, that somehow we will always remember what we might have had. I know I'll

1–Eddie Cohen to SP, [6 March 1951] and [13 March 1951]; held by Lilly Library.

always think of you will something like hurt and nostalgia---and a great deal of love.

I guess I'm getting sentimental again – but you and your letters mean an awful lot to me.

Eddie is on your trail, gal! He actually confessed that he had you looked up in the Hyde Park area. So I'll set him straight, and then, who knows! Maybe you can be me by proxy, or something.

I am in one of those spells where I think I won't live till vacation. I have two writtens tomorrow and a paper Monday. Fool that I am, I'm going out with Guy to some dance.[1] Each time I go out with him, I vow I'll never do it again because he is such a naïve kid (look who's talking!) But over the lapse of weeks I forget how dull the last time was and try over again.

I still haven't recovered from last week. Yale Junior prom! Honestly, that Dick practically floored me! Remember how cousinly I said he was last time? Well, I got dressed up to kill in my old white formal, and evidently things took a quick turn from the platonic to the . . . well, you know. As a result, I am still day-dreaming about dancing with him – and talking to him. The weather was divine all weekend – cold, clear and invigorating. As we walked up the hill to my "house" after the dance, we stopped for a minute and let the great windy silence come at us. It was dark, the streets were quiet and bare, and the stars were clear.

"It's like being in church," he said. And it was.

I will remember Saturday too, when we took a long bike-trip in through the countryside. God! I thought Id never live. Mile after mile we biked, up and down steep little woodland paths, and the wind got colder, and my legs got watery-er, and the sky got darker. Finally, after it seemed that I would freeze into a little mass of ice and stiff muscles, we sighted the welcome lights of New Haven. And that night we saw "Kiss the Boys Goodbye"[2] – and I said to myself: make the most of this kid, you may never see him again. After the show was over, we walked up onto a windy hill and watched the lights of the town below. Ann, I never have felt admiration for anyone as much as I have for him! He is going to Harvard Medical School next year, and will be a wonderful doctor, I know. And so I love him for giving part of himself to me, and will be quiet about my own inadequacies (see what a good influence you are!) All I want to do

1–The Amherst Freshman Prom.

2–The Yale Dramatic Association (Dramat) performed *Kiss the Boys Goodbye*, a musical comedy adaption of the play by Clare Booth Luce, in conjunction with the 95th Yale Junior Prom.

is work & work at making myself interesting & capable enough to make his time worthwhile.

And another thing; I am going to see the dear old thing again – when we both come home for Easter.

Friday a.m.

It is one of those typical gray days up here, but a softening and yellowing of the light indicates that the sun is breaking through, and spring may arrive any minute now.

I am doing what I always do before an exam – procrastinating about studying till the last minute, when I really manage to scare myself into it. French midsemester at 11 and Botany test after that. I have to learn all about ascomycetes & Napoleon, but here I am, allowing myself the luxury of writing to you. And the hands of the smug white-faced watch on my wrist are hopping quickly towards nine.

Mary Cronin[1] came into the kitchen last night as I was nibbling stale bread crusts. (She's one of the maids, remember.) She was very thrilled about something & told me with pride that she'd just won $15 dollars playing BINGO in Holyoke! What we don't know about the private lives of our maids! If I had the courage, I'd get to know them well enough so I could write about them – a lot more interesting subjects than the Smith college girl. I bet Marie's had quite a past!

And now, baby, I really must go. My letter paper is fast running out, too. Remember – we all love you, but 'specially me!

Love,
Sylvy

TO *Aurelia Schober Plath*

Monday 19 March 1951[2] ALS (postcard), Indiana University

Monday

Dear Mum –

These next three days are a slow, tedious process of gritting my teeth, and dragging my rebellious flesh through hour after hideous hour of classes which suddenly become weary-stale-flat-and-unprofitable. To add to this, we have to "spring-clean" our rooms – which involves washing, spraying & dusting the whole thing from top to bottom – a process which

1 – Miss Mary Cronin, parlour maid at Haven House, 1948–54, Smith College; lived at 24 Winter Street, Northampton, Mass.
2 – Date supplied from postmark.

will take about three precious hours. Also we've got a 50 page French assignment over vacation and a History assignment this week that would choke the Cyclops – 50 pages of small print per night. My two English marks this semester are a rip-roaring B- and B (I'm chatting with him tomorrow.) Also got my first B on a Botany quiz – but the lowest quiz mark doesn't count – so I'll work to get the rest all A's. Hope to have something lovely happen soon – in N. York, maybe. Saw Dick up here for the Soph prom this weekend with Jane A.[1] – pres. of her class. My date with Guy was terribly dull. On that boyant note I'll close – All I need is a shot of vitamins & a week's sleep.

XX

Sivvy

TO *Aurelia Schober Plath*

Monday 19 March 1951[2] ALS (postcard), Indiana University

Monday night

Dear Mum –

Excuse the 3" × 5½" piece of gloom that got sent your way earlier today! It is now midnight, and I have spent a delightful, if strenuous evening scrubbing the room from top to bottom with soap & water and moving out all furniture while Marty kept me company by typing a little sarcastic essay we wrote on boys.[3] That girl saves me from getting desperate at times – what human companionship won't do! Did you get my big suitcase? Olive Milne[4] offered to take me – and took the case instead. "Bobby" Michelsen will again drive me home, so, as my class gets out at 3, I should be home about 8 or 9 Wednesday night. I am bringing lots of clothes & work. Only 9 more hours of classes! Got tennis for gym at a good time – right before my Thurs & Friday a.m. classes! Life looks brighter. The life preserver has been caught & land sighted

XXX

Sivvy

1–Jane V. Anderson (1931–2010); B.A. 1955, art, Smith College; M.D. 1960, Boston University School of Medicine; SP's classmate from Wellesley; dated Richard Norton, 1950–1. Anderson matriculated at Smith College with the Class of 1953. However, as a result of hospitalization she graduated with the Class of 1955.

2–Date supplied from postmark.

3–Sylvia Plath and Marcia Brown, 'In Retrospect: A Plea for Moderation', *Princeton Tiger*, 4 May 1951, 14–15.

4–Olive Milne Smith Glaser (1929–); B.A. 1951, education and child studies, Smith College.

TO *Aurelia Schober Plath*

Friday 6 April 1951[1] ALS (postcard), Indiana University

Friday

Dear Mum . . .

Well, this afternoon I think will cut art studio and take a nap to make up for the night before I left . . . not sleeping till 2:30 a.m. It is strange to be back . . . and I hope I can rest this weekend so I can go unscathed through the next eight weeks. I have been shopping for all needed odds and ends & withdrawn some money from the bank. My aim will be to have an even $100 left by the end of the year. At present, all I can see ahead is work. I got my name on the list first for the BOOK which some teacher TOOK out just before I came. By dint of pleading, I think I can get it today, & just hope they'll let me keep it over the weekend. The one nice thing since I've been back was my semester conference with my art teacher who's very pleased with me. I'll see Miss Mensel sometime next week. PULEESE send my red jacket (ski) pronto! So I'll have it in case Dick comes up next weekend. NO sign of coat. Hope Eddie didn't sell it.

XXX
Sivvy

TO *Aurelia Schober Plath*

Sunday 8 April 1951[2] ALS (postcard), Indiana University

Sunday

Dear Mum . . .

Well, only 60 pages more to go, and then the endless job of trying to think out a lucid 5 page theme.[3] Even though I have to turn in the book Tuesday, Marty will let me borrow hers anytime. At present, I feel rather tired and disgusted with myself because I haven't done much of anything since I came back and I cannot look at the quiz schedule ahead of me with the proper exhilaration. It's a good thing my story is coming out so I'll have something to look forward to. Never have 8 weeks of work seemed SO monumental. History will sure need alot of studying before the exam. Art & English are pretty sure if I just keep going. Botany & French &

1–Date supplied from postmark.
2–Date supplied from postmark.
3–Probably Sylvia Plath, 'The Imagery in Patterns'; held by Lilly Library.

History require me to run like the white queen. At least I like playing tennis in gym. Honestly, I wonder when I can relax & read what I want & lie in the sun. It will be a long pull till June 2. Could you – if you have a minute – sort over "my cottons" (skirts & blouses) & whatever else & send them up sometime soon. No hurry really.

Love,
Sivvy

TO *Aurelia Schober Plath*

Tuesday 10 April 1951[1] ALS (postcard), Indiana University

Tuesday night

Dear Mum . . . . .

If you get cards from me with frightening irregularity just put it up to a sudden access of papers and meetings. I will be working on that damn history paper till doomsday – but I'll forget it for the three days when Dick is here. Speaking of that rather amazing blonde creature, your letter and his[2] arrived at the same time – so I sent his postcard telling him to come anyway and fear that I might have told him not to come if I hadn't been sure he was just giving me a choice to be his usual thoughtful self. I really can't see too much light ahead . . . because we've botany tests every week for the next two months, 2 eng papers, not to mention decorations for the prom . . . but I have to complain to someone, and I know that you will tell me I'll live . . . . I envy you taking a walk with Dick, and yet seeing as I have his company for the next weekend, I shall only say "aren't we females lucky". Saw a brief Dali shock movie[3] – my one free act for the rest of the year. Keep my morale up!

Love,
Sivvy

<on address side of postcard:>

P.S. Please send carbon of my application letter . . . I've got to re-send the Chatham deal to a new address

1–Date supplied from postmark.
2–Richard Norton to Sylvia Plath, 9 April 1951; held by Lilly Library.
3–*Un Chien Andalou* (1929) by Spanish director Luis Buñuel and artist Salvador Dali was shown at Graham Hall, Smith College.

TO *Aurelia Schober Plath*

Thursday 12 April 1951[1] ALS (postcard), Indiana University

Thursday

Dear Mother . . .

Barby Michelson and I are feeling quite proud of ourselves for having such illustrious advisors. Lisa just was elected one of the seven Junior Phi Beta's and her roommate was elected our house president. It's a lovely day out, and I'm glad I have tennis in the morning so I can spend at least one hour out of doors. I'm having my hair washed and set again this afternoon. I did a rather necessary thing & ordered a copy of that BOOK from the Hampshire bookshop,[2] for I fear I'll be writing the paper next weekend, while the rest study for the exam. Oh, well, at least I'll know what I'm writing about (I hope.) A friend and I had Mr. Madeira and his wife[3] over for supper last night – they are a lovely couple – and he's a good old father, if not, another Mr. Crockett. Only he's still giving me B's. Keep well.

Love,
Sivvy

TO *Aurelia Schober Plath*

Sunday 15 April 1951[4] ALS with envelope, Indiana University

Dear Mother –

It is sunday night, and I have never been so exhausted! Seems so much easier to take Dick's super-abundance of energy away from home. I suppose you are eager to know "what we did." Well, before I fall onto my bier, I'll give you an inkling.

Friday he came just before supper, so we went right over to Davis,[5] our student center & proceeded to talk until 10 about New York & Florida. By that time we got a hamburger & milk and took a long walk

1 – Date supplied from postmark.

2 – Edith Sitwell, *The Canticle of the Rose: Poems 1917–1949* (New York: Vanguard Press, 1949); SP's copy held by Smith College; used for her English 11b theme paper 'A New Idiom'; held by Lilly Library.

3 – Albert Pierpont Madeira (1911–64) and Beatrice vom Baur Madeira. Madeira was instructor in English, Smith College, 1948–51; taught SP's section of English 11, 1950–1.

4 – Date supplied from postmark.

5 – Davis Center, a student common room on the campus of Smith College.

around part of Paradise. I meant to eat breakfast Saturday, but I was just going downtown to get some before he came, but he came, and talked to everybody including Mrs. Shakespeare . . . so we just had time to get to French. I did have lunch here with him, & then he & Marcia & I took off for Look Park[1] on bikes. We hiked up a brook for a few miles, crossed a bridge & came back opposite where our bikes were. So since it was late, Dick brightly said "We'll wade across." <drawing of river, bikes, bridge> I shivered, but he & Marty were bravely taking off sneakers, so I did too. He took her across, and the current was awfully strong & she got soaked up to her hips. Luckily I have longer legs & only had wet dungarees to the knees. We took hot baths when we came home. Saturday night we again went to Davis before supper & made ourselves at home in the livingroom with books. All we had was milk & icecream, neither feeling like eating much. Marcia came over with some Greek boy she had gotten on a blind date, & we all played ping pong. Dick & I took another walk down to see the Junior prom from the outside, & by then I was feeling very queer & lightheaded. Whether from excitement or what I couldn't sleep late. So got up early this morning, hoping the dear man would come over. You can imagine how I felt when he called up & said very coolly "I've found some things to do over here & won't come until dinner & will hitchhike back right after." Marcia let me sob on her shoulder, and brought me breakfast she had saved . . . since food was among the many things I needed. So since I also needed an outlet for my sadness, she & her date took me down to the gym & taught me how to play badminton. That took my mind off the empty morning and I was endlessly grateful to them both. So Dick came to dinner & left & I am not going to the Prom & I have so horribly much work, but I had fun while it lasted, but certainly got the strong impression that something disturbed him a great deal at the end, because he wasn't too convincing about having a good time. Naturally I was sorry, but don't you be. Just tell the Norton's I was overjoyed to see the sweet wonder-man.

I won't be able to write for a week because of 2 papers & exams. So I'll tell you I'm still on my two feet, and you'll hear from me if I'm not.

Be good & don't worry. I'll live.
Love,
Sivvy

1–The Frank Newhall Look Memorial Park, Florence, Mass.

TO *Aurelia Schober Plath*

Wednesday 18 April 1951[1] ALS with envelope, Indiana University

Dear Mummy –

May I say I felt very guilty when you "thanked me in advance for the pleasant anticipation of a letter." I fear my epistle was the product of little sleep and less optimism. When I consider that there are but 45 days left to my Freshman year in college, I feel frightened. At the same time that I wish the tension and exams were over, so do I realize that I am thus wishing my life away. And as I look ahead I see only an accelerated work-pattern until the day I drop into the grave. One encouraging thing – we had a talk on taking honors this morning in chapel, and the 12 hour week appeals to me no end. This 24 hour schedule runs me, and I am sick of having to do work in isolated pieces with no time to follow through various absorbing facets of it.

I am extremely lost as to what courses to take next year. I must take a practical art & a creative writing course . . . but as I am still undecided as to my major, I should also take both an Eng. lit. and a History-of-Art course in case I choose one or the other. Also I should take science & government or sociology. Which leaves me in conflict. Sometimes I wonder whether or not I should "go into social work." If I did that, I could earn my own living . . . or if you could get me started secretarially next summer I might lay in summer experience for that "U.N. job". The question is – shall I plan for a career? (ugh! I hate the word.) Or should I major in Eng. & Art & have a "free-lance" career if I ever catch a man who can put up with the idea of having a wife who likes to be alone and working artistically now & then? I would like to start thinking about where I'll put the emphasis for the rest of my brief life.

If I get battered & discouraged in my creative course next year, I don't care. Olive Higgins Prouty (bless her withered Bostonian hide) said I "had something." Mr. Manzi[2] my art teacher spent an hour telling me how he liked what I was turning out in art (before supper, too, and he's a gourmet at that!)

One thing that bothers me: there are so many little cracks and crevices here to let your energies slip away in small endeavors. I speak of all the thousands of "organizations" on campus, which devour human

1 – Date supplied from postmark.

2 – Louis Manzi (1915–99); art instructor, Smith College, 1949–51.

woman-hours with amazing rapidity. I am not a "politician". I loved the president of student council who spoke on honors. Not only is she a brilliant personable student, but she has her hand on the pulse of the college. At the same time that I covet the feeling of "acting in an organization", I think I should conserve my time for a more personal and perhaps selfish line of development. I realize the importance of a "well-rounded" individual, but I cherish a few of my angles a bit too much to rub them off. So, with the overly inquisitive Smith Club in mind, I have joined Studio Club (Art) and plan to sacrifice the best part of my life next week painting decorations for a dance which I shall not attend (selfless service, you may call it.)

I have again run across Enid Epstein (the artistic girl who went to the High school of Music & Art in N.Y.) She's just won a prize in Springfield for an oil painting . . . so I am again grateful for the wealth of human gems this college offers . . . & hope to have her for supper next week.

As for jobs – I've been refused at Chatham, Crowleys & West Harwich. Have still got fingers crossed for Orleans. Marcia & I are seeing about a job for "two friends" baby-tending in Swampscott. Wish us luck!

Do send "all" my cottons. I haven't had a chance to go downtown to pick up a dress, but one girl here said she might help me make a brown skirt to replace the shiny skimpy one . . . If we have time. <u>Do</u> pick up that navy skirt & a <u>navy</u> <u>blouse</u>! I've got plenty of white ones, and all dresses here are <u>way</u> up in price. $85 is <u>nothing</u> for a date dress.

If you could see my schedule, you would shed a sympathetic tear. Decorating sure will kill me, but I have but one life to give for my country – let's hope I emerge with a slight residue of living protoplasm and a B average.

Louise Giesey is going around with Eddie White . . . bet they end up connubially![1] Pat is still crusading. I don't even have time to wash my hair or my clothes. Every minute is so valuable that I hate myself for not being able to get along on less sleep.

This letter (famous-last-words) will have to last you for a long time. My history paper must get written this weekend.

I already got a casual thank-you letter from Dick.[2] In response to all my friends queries "what did he say? Is he coming to the Prom," I had the reply "No" and a bright smile. I really don't care about the prom,

1–Edward Allen White (1932–); schoolmate of SP's in Wellesley, class of 1949. Giesey and White married on 25 June 1954.
2–Richard Norton to SP, 15 April 1951; held by Lilly Library.

but his offer to come up in the early & leave in the late afternoon of that Saturday did annoy me. I know he has piles of themes & other dates, but it would have been chivalrous to offer to stay over in Amherst that night, whether he wanted to go back to Yale at 6 am or not. Coming to say a brief hello on the day of our Freshman Dance and then leaving so he "can work Sunday" disgusted my housemates no end. They feel he could at least have sacrificed a precious evening (even if he didn't want to go to the dance) to take me to a movie or on a walk or something. I was dangerously tempted to take a blind date for the dance to salve my shattered ego. Luckily I will have a (hitherto) dateless Marcia to support me. Damn boys anyway.

And so I pass on to read 100 pages of Botany for a test tomorrow . . . and tomorrow . . and tomorrow.

Love,
Sivvy

TO *Aurelia Schober Plath*

Saturday 21 April 1951[1] ALS with envelope, Indiana University

Saturday

Dear Mother –

Got your cheerful letter this morning. Life sure is looking up. The story of the job goes like this: Marcia had applied to the vocational office which takes down your desires and capabilities and then sends you notices of all suitable requests for applicants that come in. So I was reading one of these mimeographed notices over Marty's shoulder and we both came to the phrase ". . . we would like two friends, since the houses are only two streets apart . . ." So we gulped and looked at each other with dawning enthusiasm. Marcia called and got us both an appointment with the woman at 2:15 Thursday. We made out data sheets to hand to her and walked in bravely. She impressed both of us right away, and we talked enthusiastically and handed her our sheets which she could read, so we wouldn't have to brag verbally. Incidentally, we were the first on a list of 22 people to be interviewed (Marcia had hoped to be last, because it would leave more of an impression.) Can you imagine our amazement when she said "As far as I'm concerned I'd take you two right away, but

1 – Date supplied from postmark.

I have to interview the others." So we walked out, fingers crossed. Sure enough, she called at suppertime and said she hadn't changed her mind.

After screaming and jumping up and down for several minutes we decided to play badminton to blow off steam.

Marcia will start work on Long Island & Join me in Swampscott at the beginning of July. Her children are 7, 9, 11. My job starts about Monday, June 18, and lasts till Labor Day. I will be taking care of Mrs. Fred Mayo's[1] three infants of 2, 4, 6. (Mrs. Aldrich[2] will let me try out on hers, I hope.) Also, in the 2 weeks I'll have at home, you can put me through a cooking schedule since we help with dinners on Sundays when the three families get together. One day off a week – $25 a week. I imagine life will not be a bed of roses, but my wish to have an incentive to learn to cook has come true. Also they have a private tennis court, and several boats including a yacht. That will be saved for "days-off." Child psychology will be a good thing to develop – I just hope they like me! Also, I'll brush up on fairy-tales. But unless they devise extra jobs, the littlest ones of mine should be in bed by eight. I think being a "mother" will be a new challenge. Also, she's a doctor's wife – and he'll be home on weekends – so it should prove informative, if nothing else.

I am awfully excited about the potentialities of the whole affair. I can't think of anything that I could have done would be more desirable.

Warren wrote me a delightful long letter in response to mine. He's the dearest boy I know! I am <u>so</u> happy! Marcia & I got up at 6:30 this morning and played tennis before breakfast because it was so beautiful! Not a soul was up or at the courts, and the day was so blue and fresh. Love this place. Anything is possible if you work.

Love
Sivvy

1–Anne Blodgett Mayo (1918–90) and Dr Frederic B. Mayo (1915–2000). During the summer of 1951, SP took care of their three children: Frederic (1944–), Esther ('Pinny') (1947–), and Joanne (1949–), at their home at 144 Beach Bluff Avenue, Swampscott, Mass.

2–Elizabeth ('Betty') Cannon Aldrich. Wife of C. Duane Aldrich, who lived across the street from the Plaths at 23 Elmwood Road, Wellesley. The Aldriches had nine children: Duane, Peter, Stephen, John, Mark, Elizabeth, Ann, Amy, and Sarah.

TO *Aurelia Schober Plath*

Monday 23 April 1951[1] ALS (postcard), Indiana University

Monday afternoon

Dear Mother –

Today has been utterly delightful – to begin with, I got my first A- this term on an Eng. paper I turned out in a tired depressed mood after Dick left last Sunday. Next, I found I got "A" in a Botany quiz I "failed." Mrs. Ford[2] took me to a scrumptious lunch at Wiggin's, & we had a lovely talk – she's a dear, really! I felt delightfully free as everyone trotted nervously off to the History written . . . and my paper was lying smugly on my desk! I went shopping, then, and bought some brown material for $3.95 for a skirt I'm going to make with this girl's help. Also, at supper I met a delightful Northampton girl resident who was a friend's guest . . . her father is a creative English professor here, and her mother writes for "slicks" like the Ladies Home Journal to help earn money!! Did I tell you that one of Dick's roommates is head of the Whiffenpoofs[3] next year?! I love reading over Dick's last letter[4] – complete with cartoons – that his roommate[5] brought me Sat. night. I'll probably be heading Yale-ward again on May 12 –

Love,
Sivvy

TO *Aurelia Schober Plath*

Wednesday 25 April 1951[6] ALS with envelope, Indiana University

Dear Mother –

I am so happy that I am taking time out of history to write to you. After 3 days of no mail, today's was delicious – a card from you and two

1–Date supplied from postmark.
2–Probably Clara Ford, who along with her husband Joseph F. Ford, was a scholarship fund donor at Smith College.
3–Founded in 1909, the Whiffenpoofs are an *a capella* group consisting of 14 Yale senior men.
4–Richard Norton to SP, 21 April 1951; held by Lilly Library.
5–Oliver Trull Carpenter (*c.* 1930–89); B.A. 1952, Yale College. Carpenter was a member of the Whiffenpoofs in 1952.
6–Date supplied from postmark.

wonderful letters from Dick[1] and Bob Humphrey. This weekend should be delectable! Dick will be here for the afternoon (and, if I can persuade him, dinner) Bob will arrive at about 9 p.m. & stay till Sunday. Bob has the most dear sense of humor – listen to what he wrote:

"I am all set to arrive at Haven House at 9:00 P.M. on the 28th. I will sit in a dark corner of the living room surrounded by a pile of back issues of Popular Mechanics, chewing Brownstone cigars, with a squirrel tail cap pulled down over my eyebrows. So you can come back to the house with your supper date and say goodbye to him without having to remark out of a clear sky 'Isn't that Bob Humphrey, my next date, sitting there?'"

Isn't that lovely?!! Also Bob says he hopes to see me this summer.

As for Dick, he invited me to come down on Friday May 11 to stay all weekend – seeing "Skin of Our Teeth"[2] and having a generally lovely time. I'm so excited over everything that I want to scream, shout and have everyone know how wonderful life is!

Ah, me – on to History! God, I've never been so joyous!

By the way, board & room is going up $50 – so I hope they consider that on my Smith Scholarship –

Love to the world –
even Stalin –
Love,
your own Sivvy

TO *Aurelia Schober Plath*

Friday 27 April 1951[3] ALS (postcard), Indiana University

Dear Mother . . .

It is Friday night, and I got your letter & postcards this morning. Dick's card was so thoughtful, original and adorable. Marcia and I took this beautiful afternoon to go shopping down town. In one brief hour of trying on a lot of pretty cottons we picked me out a beautiful Jonathan Logan[4] for only $8.95!! I am behind the dirndl skirt & frilly blouse stage. It is a dark black & aqua pincheck that looks dark blue, with tiny black buttons & a dear skirt: <drawing of dress> It is casual, simple, and yet lovely for an informal date dress. If you do get a butcher linen skirt -- please make

1–Probably Richard Norton to SP, 24 April 1951; held by Lilly Library.
2–Thornton Wilder, *The Skin of Our Teeth* (1942).
3–Date supplied from postmark.
4–A brand of women's clothing.

it black. We also ate out at Rahar's to celebrate our plans for the coming summer. I actually had a cocktail, and felt in quite a mellow mood as we sat and talked. I do hope you can come up in May!

Love,
Sivvy

TO *Aurelia Schober Plath*

Tuesday 1 May 1951 — ALS with envelope, Indiana University

May 1 –

Dear Mother . . .

I am really sorry that the old Infirmary is so conscientious about keeping you posted on all our minor aches and pains. The fact is, I came down with another one of my colds and decided to come up here to get the best possible care so I could get well in the least possible time. I know how you worry, so I wasn't going to tell you until I got out, forgetting that the D.O. notifies you anyway.

I hate the idea of missing three days of classes, especially as I have a written Friday and a big paper[1] Monday, but I knew if I stayed around the house that I'd never get enough sleep or the right food. You should see how pampered I am up here! Orange juice with icecubes three times a day, and steaming trays of delicious salads and broths. The nosedrops are wonderful, and I've had my head packed once (and Dick wonders where I got my fat nose!)

Today the runny part has stopped, and I feel fine, except for a little occasional mucous. So I'll be back at Haven tomorrow. Marcia has brought me mail and written me notes every day.

Got your dress, and must shed a tear as I send it back. Funny, but it is exactly the same material and color as the one Marcia and I bought for the same price, only mine has a much prettier style, as I drew, and doesn't emphasize flat collarbones as this one does. It is indeed ironic & tantalizing to be in bed on the first day "17" hits the newsstands!

Dick came on Saturday at 1:30 as I was feeling the first impact of my cold. Luckily I had tried to bake it in the sun that morning, so my face had a ruddy sunburnt glow. I really had fun exercising "mind over matter" and walking out in the hills with him. We had dinner at Wiggin's, as you

1–Sylvia Plath, 'A New Idiom'; held by Lilly Library.

suggested, only I had a huge fruit salad and sherbet, as that was all I could swallow. We walked back to Haven and Dick left on the 8 o'clock train after a delightful afternoon.

I told Bob Humphrey to come over anyway, and in a brief half hour before I left for the Infirmary, I tried to make him see how much I liked him and how sorry I was about spoiling Sunday. He asked me to a beach party in Gloucester this weekend, but I said no as I will be up to my ears in make-up work, not to mention the fact that I want to devote my all to making the last Yale weekend in my life the best one yet – which will demand a rested, care free spirit.

I really will miss Warren an awful lot this summer – it seems in this whirlwind of action there is no time left to savor the people who mean the most. All one can do as one races around the squirrel cage is write a note or two. I do hope that in the week during exams, and the two weeks after, I can see you and learn a little about babies. I wish I didn't have to work all summer just so I can work all the rest of the year. The Theory of the Leisure Class is fine only so long as you're a member of the aristocracy. When you aren't a member[1] of the nobility, you might as well revolt and institute a classless state. (Your reply, I suppose, will be to count my blessings.)

I am enclosing my watch with the dress. The band has frayed to bits and it has stopped again. The man I took it to down here said it runs very badly and unevenly, and that there is a big space between the case and the winder where dust and dirt can get in. <drawing of watch>

Do wish me luck on making up my various Botany labs and history classes. I'll have to study doubly hard between May 24 and May 31 to make up for all this forced leisure now.

I didn't have a chance to write Mrs. Ford, but I'll see Miss Mensel as soon as I get out of this place . . .

Be good to yourself, and don't worry about me – I've only a scant 33 more days to go –

Love,
Sivvy

P.S. Your news about Warren bothered me – I had sent him a silly Birthday card and letter, hoping to cheer him up, but I don't know if he cares about getting things from me or not. What time does he get out of school? Could you and I plan to go up there sometime after June 2? I'd like a chance to see Exeter and my bruvver again.

1 – 'When you aren't a ~~mememb~~ member' appears in the original.

Remind me to learn how to mend holes in socks & darn when I come home. I can't let Marcia show me up in everything domestic. Also, I don't want to be a slave to practicalities. If I'm going to have to do these things for myself when I get a job, I might as well learn how to do them efficiently in the least time possible.

Dick still has me baffled. He acts so queerly at times that I could swear he is two different people. I really wonder if his jovial heartiness and occasional annoying jolliness isn't a sort of cover-up for a certain uneasiness. Oh, well, you know him better than I do!

Love,
Sivvy

I hate the idea that I have to marry someone short so that my children won't be Gargantua's – Bob H. is such a lovely height for me – makes me feel so petite!

TO *Aurelia Schober Plath*

Wednesday 2 May 1951 ALS (postcard), Indiana University

Wednesday

Dear Mum . . .

Well, it sure is good to get back again! The leaves are beginning to come out, and the whole campus is just beautiful. I still "sound" nosy, but aside from feeling a little wobbly, I am fine – even got a slight tan from lying on the infirmary sundeck. I sneaked into a drugstore after my first class today and bought a copy of THE Magazine. Ghastly illustration, wot? However, I kind of like the raw, picasso-ish feeling. Wonder how tall the cute male artist[1] is? The sweetest thing happened – a gal I know in the cooperative house sent me a rose on my "publication day." I was just touched. Of course I am a week behind in all my subjects – but after the Botany exam Friday & the English paper I should be able to take it easy till exam time – see you Friday, May 25 –

Love,
Sivvy

1 – The illustration was by Floyd Johnson (1932–), from Topeka, Kansas.

TO *Aurelia Schober Plath*

Sunday 6 May 1951[1] — ALS with envelope, Indiana University

Dear Mum –

Say nice fat epistles – but your last one was (shades of John Hall!) I was quite amused to receive your comments on the story along with Eddie's and Dick's.[2] Dick, I think, was perhaps a bit impressed – and actually said he liked it. He is such a dear – I got a charming long letter from him all about it – saying how he showed the thing to various and sundry of his friends. Eddie was also surprisingly sweet and laudatory, and his criticisms were all extremely valid. It's funny, but he said some things that I had never thought of – about how he thought it should have gotten 1st, but 17 probably put it on a lower level because of the fuzzy characterization of Emile and the not-strong-enough explanation of Marcia's decision. He also thought the metaphors were "lovely writing" but too overdone – inhibiting straight action & dialogue. I can't say it as well as he did – but I can see his points completely. As for me, I think practice will help me grasp even larger situations. This new experience with children might prove writable, too.

I am guilty of making a few clothes purchases this am, but all of them are sensible, versatile, and very nice. I got a full navy cotton skirt which can be dressed up or down with all my blouses – a white tailored casual no sleeve blouse – a yellow tucked one of dressier proportions and a must for this summer – a neat two-piece white Jantzen bathing suit to alternate with my flowered one: prices:

white blouse	2.98
yellow blouse	2.98
navy skirt	5.95
bathing suit	8.95
	20.86

<drawing of 4 pieces of clothing>

I also am "making" a brown skirt (under the careful supervision of a friend) to take the place of the shiny skimpy one at home, so my mix-and-match separates have really proved quite economical. I have outgrown the frilly high school stage, tra la la.

1–Date supplied from postmark and internal evidence.

2–See Eddie Cohen to SP, 3 May 1951, and Richard Norton to SP, 3 May 1951; held by Lilly Library.

See you soon
Love,
Sivvy

<in left margin of page 1 of letter>

P.S. Got a lovely letter from Mrs. Mayo – who says the children are telling everyone proudly that "Sylvia is coming to stay with us this summer!"

TO *Aurelia Schober Plath*

Tuesday 8 May 1951[1]

ALS with envelope,
Indiana University

Tuesday

Dear Mother –

Sometimes I think the gods have it in for me – things have been much too smooth and placid so far. Anyhow, I'm over my cold, pretty well caught up in everything except Art, when bang!

I got my program pretty well settled for next year with my advisor (who is also my Botany teacher), when as I was striding cheerfully and skippingly out of his office I slipped on the smooth stone floor and fell on my ankle, which gave a nasty and protesting crunch. The train of events involved my throwing my arms about dear Mr. Wright's neck and getting him to half-carry me downstairs to his car. The doctor taped it, and I had it ex-rayed this morning for a possible break.

Needless to say, what with a huge Eng. paper due tomorrow and this divine weekend tottering in the balance, I feel all too close to tears. But self-pity isn't appreciated by people who have the use of their two feet, so I swallowed my salty sobs & grin bravely.

If it's a break, I'll have to have a cast. That would definitely finish the idea of my going anywhere. If it's only a bad sprain, I'll call dick and ask him if I can limp down. If he doesn't want me down, I'll ask him up, and if he doesn't want me either way, he's a bad doctor and a poor sport.

Seriously, I will ask for Mondays off – because there is nothing I'd rather do than see Dick. I really do think he's the most stimulating boy I've ever known, and I don't care much about anybody else anyway. I suppose I might be conservative and say that I adore him and worship his intellect and keen perceptions in almost every field. But I still think that if he ever

1 – Date supplied from postmark.

saw me with noseguards on, flailing impotently in the water or with skates on, standing on my ankles, that his enthusiasm in my direction might cool rapidly. I don't know why I let abnormal deficiencies like that bother me, but they do, and I can't see how any modern boy as athletic as Dick could bear a girl as uncoordinated as I am.

However, I have a rather odd feeling that the more I see Dick the more I like him and the more I like him the more I want to show him things and get his reactions on things. Of course I could always play safe and withdraw myself into a protective little shell so I won't feel too sad when he wearies of my company and browses in greener fields. Ah, me!

As for the 25th – I get out of my Botany exam at 5 pm. So If you could possibly drive up and take most of my things home, I could stay till the next Wednesday night or Thursday morning – Because my History exam is on Friday, June 1, and my French the next day. I'll have to study madly all the time I'm home, but out in the sun of our quiet backyard, I should think it would be rather pleasant – especially with my dear mummy around.

Dick said he might possibly say hello that weekend. But as he is going away with Perry from the 3rd to the 8th, I don't see how he could be languishing from the idea of a long absence & separation!

I'm seeing Miss Mensel this afternoon – wish me luck!

Pray it's not a break, dear mummy! And if so, I will keep my chin up!

If you ever want to call me, try between six and seven, as I am usually here for supper.

Love you very much,
Sivvy

TO *Ann Davidow-Goodman*

Wednesday 9 May 1951[1] ALS, Smith College

Dear Davy –

It is a bright blue Wednesday morning in May, and I am sitting in a halter on the Haven House porch, courting a tan. Speaking of bad correspondants---you're listening to one right this very minute. I do have one or two excuses – not that I want to burden you with my troubles, or anything. First, I spent a week in the infirmary with another one of my annual spring sinus colds. I had gone shopping with Marcia on a Friday,

1 – Date supplied from internal evidence. Dated 'May '51' by Ann Davidow-Goodman.

and Dick (THE man) was coming up for Saturday afternoon. (I had pulled a shrewd deal and got myself a date for Sat. night & Sunday, too, so when I began to feel queer Friday night, I went to bed, hopefully swallowing a handful of cold pills. No soap! Saturday I began to burn, but I bravely met Dick and pretended I was fine – so we tramped the hills all afternoon and I treated him to dinner at Wiggin's. By that time, all I could swallow was ice cream. When he left at eight, all my false energy suddenly left, too, and I collapsed with a slight fever. I met my next date, told him how nice he was, and left for the infirmary. Poor guy, I don't know what he did with himself for the rest of the weekend! Hope he picked up another girl!

So I came back from my sojurn last Wednesday, with make-up work piled shoulder high. But that was O.K. being I was dateless & could work this weekend & going to Yale with Dick on the 11th (Gosh, don't I sound popular! Heh-heh!) So what happens? I am in talking about next year's program with Mr. Wright, my advisor, and leaving his office very gaily, with a little skip. And what happens to the graceful little ox? Her slippery-soled loafers skid on the polished stone floor, and she falls with the loudest crash imagineable, her ankle crunching queerly as she sits on it. Now isn't that annoying – after making such a fashionable exit, to have your advisor have to rush out, pick you up off the floor and half carry you to the D.O.? I still am hoping the damn sprain will be walkable by this weekend so I can see Dick. Just when I wanted to look my best I have to have an ankle three times normal size!

<drawing of SP with a sprained ankle> It is broiling hot, now, and it is only 9:30. How much can a female suffer for her vanity? I'm determined to be golden brown, though. You should see the color Marcia is! (She's been lying out on every sunny day.)

Now to tell you how surprised and thrilled I was to get a letter from Boulder! Honey, you are so traveled! And it sounded like the divinest time. Jim is a cutie – and I hope everything stays as nice as it is.

By the way pu-lease let me know how your college applications came out. It would be heaven to have you back – whether you had a Freshman rate or whatever! Carol Pierson has left, too, and may have to come back the same way. Carol left way back at the beginning of April because she had a heart murmur or something. Anyhow, she's missed piles of exams & papers, and so I doubt if she'll be able to take finals or even catch up unless she goes to summer school or something. Do try to make it though! It would be so wonderful to see you again, baby!

I'm all at sea about money problems, as usual – not getting as much help financially as I did this year. I'll probably have to end up in a co-operative house in my junior or senior year. Oh, well! They say the best things in life are free! I'm not so sure.

Did I tell you that I ACTUALLY SAW EDDIE? I'll tell you how it happened anyway, just in case. I had just come back from my last class before spring vacation, & was all set to drive home with Barb Michelsen in an hour, when someone called "Oh, Syl. There's a boy to see you!" so I walked unsuspectingly into the livingroom, and there was this strange, dark-haired guy standing with a pipe gripped tightly between his teeth. "This is the third dimension," he said, just like in a play or something. So he said he'd come to drive me home. So, fool that I am, I threw all my suitcases in his father's nash, and we were off. The funny thing is, Ann, that even though he could talk to me about my private life more authentically than any of my friends, I just couldn't get used to the idea that this physical stranger was the guy I'd written such confidential letters to. I couldn't get rid of the impression that he was just some taxi driver off the street. So all during the three hour drive home I was very nervous – not quite sure whether or not I would ever reach my destination and petrified as to what my mother would say if she saw me coming up the walk with Eddie, who she never wanted me to meet. So I did a very stupid thing. I told him I was in love with a guy from home & couldn't go out with anyone else. Also I was very rude and didn't even invite him in because I was so scared about mother. Turned out she was cross – not at Ed, but at my "lack of hospitality." I <u>was</u> rather shaken and surprised by the whole unexpected encounter. The thing that makes me maddest at myself is that I just ignored the fact he'd driven night-and-day from Chi without stopping. So I just let him drive back. After which he wrote me a naughty letter[1] about how cold New Englanders were and how he'd slept with some doll in New York and cracked up the car in Ohio. However, we are now writing again just as if nothing had ever happened. C'est la vie! I am now convinced that the process of knowing a person should be a <u>combination</u> of getting used to their ideas at the same time as their physical looks and habits.

By the way (I am now dripping and melting up here on the porch.) Marcia & I have got a neat job this summer! Wait till you hear! Marcia applied to the Vocational Office for notices for summer jobs. Well this one came that wanted <u>two friends</u> to work two doors from each other in Swampscott taking care of kids – 3 each. So we got an interview – and got the job! $25 a week, room and board – a lot of work (my kids are 2, 4, 6)

1–Eddie Cohen to SP, [11 April 1951]; held by Lilly Library.

but I think we can make a good thing out of it! At least I'll have someone I know near me.

Say hello to Jim for me, baby, and let me know soon how things are & what's been happening –

Love, Syl

TO *Aurelia Schober Plath*

Wednesday 9 May 1951[1] ALS (postcard), Indiana University

Dear Mum –

Just a note to tell you that it is only a bad sprain – and whether Dick knows it or not, I'm coming down – I will call him, at least, and let him know that his date will have one very thick ankle and a slight hobble. Also she won't be able to run, jump or climb hills. Also I feel very good because I just finished my last English paper (9 pages) on Edith Sitwell. I finally relaxed & got the book, which I fondle lovingly from time to time – it's so beautiful. Talked w. Miss Mensel – who said she couldn't possibly give me co-op next year since I didn't need it badly enough. Oh, joy!

Love, your cripple –
Sylvia

TO *Aurelia Schober Plath*

Monday 14 May 1951[2] ALS with envelope, Indiana University

Dear Mother –

When I think that in a mere three weeks I will be free, I hardly can believe it! Of course the things I have to accomplish in that short time are unbelievable – and I have stacks of mail to answer – all long and demanding letters.

As for news – where can I begin? Remember that article on Blind Dates I wrote with Marcia? Well it got printed in the Princeton Tiger, no less. We haven't seen it yet, but the girls say it got a big spread. Also I was surprised to hear from John Hodges – a letter describing his wild travels and exploits in the army. I can't think of anything more suited to his

1–Date supplied from postmark.
2–Date supplied from internal evidence.

temperament – no responsibility – just taking orders & going wild on weekends. Ah, free spirit! Am I glad I never had more than a crush on him! At least he netted me $15. When I think, Emile netted my $100 prize! Any boy who asks me out, I fear, will be too wary now – Bob Humphrey is coming up the weekend of the 19th – and he wrote that he read my story, too. Probably his sister showed him. His gentleness is shown by what he said so cutely: "Have you ever met any guys so cruel in reality? I thought my god if I were sitting at the next table from them I would have come over and rescued that poor girl." Naive, but sweet, don't you think. Ilo's response was that he liked the story, and felt it was based on some fragments of personal "live-through". Only he said: "Only where did you get such a good natured 'lion' who gives away his meat so easily – without eating it–?"

I think I will make a collection of comments – they reflect my odd assortment of friends as well as their relationships with me. I feel that the people I know – Ilo, Eddie, Bob, Ann Davidow (<u>and</u> Dick) – are all conglomerate, yet fascinating in unique ways – and I love them all!

As for my weekend – I never have had such a heavenly out-of-door time. I rode down to New Haven Friday afternoon with Marcia, who was going home to New Jersey. Dick met me at the station & we dined at J. E.[1] (I notice that in his letter he carefully noted down every meal – just so you'd know we <u>did</u> eat.[2]) Friday night, as he said, we saw 'Skin of Our Teeth.'[3] Also delightful – loud & obvious, but fun. Saturday am I went to a class of his in Contemporary Events – enjoyed his stimulating instructor – then we browsed in a bookstore & headed back for lunch. Saturday was such fun – an afternoon at the J. E. picnic on a hotel overlooking my dear blue ocean – We played volleyball all afternoon, & then Dick & I took off & read Hemingway aloud on the rocky shore. Supper of hamburgs was good – we headed back then, & had a frappe with Perry (who is as lovable as ever) before turning in.

Sunday, however, was <u>the</u> best. Breakfast with Perry & then changing to dungarees & sweaters & hopping a bus to Lighthouse Point for a day in the sun on the beach. There was hardly anyone around, & I collected shells & smelled seaweed and mudflats, while Dick threw stones far out till the wind caught them & blew them up in twisted eddies of air. Then, after running, we lay on the rocks, warm & blue-skied – and talked & dozed, until my face was red and brown & Dick had turned his characteristic

1–Jonathan Edwards; a 'residential college' at Yale.
2–Richard Norton to ASP, 12 May 1951; held by Lilly Library.
3–See SP to ASP, 25 April 1951.

shade of pink. I think I am curing him of his jovial mask which made me so cross – because we had the loveliest airiest sunniest saltiest sort of day. It was 4:30 when we headed back for a huge gourmetish meal beginning with shrimp cocktail, minestrone soup, charcoal-crusted lamb chops, potatoes – and subsiding into milk & apple pie.

We had such fun – & I'll go up to Lucy Wheaton's[1] right after my first exam day – after you take me home – we'll leave Saturday and stay overnight – after which I must study – which I haven't been doing at all! Got a straight A (!) on the Sitwell paper – glad I bought the book.

Will write soon –
See you the 25th
Love
your Sivvy

TO *Aurelia Schober Plath*

Tuesday 15 May 1951[2] ALS with envelope, Indiana University

Tuesday

Dear Mother –

Couldn't seem to resist frittering away another few minutes by writing to you. If only you could be here today! I never have seen such lovely weather in my life! All the trees are out, shading the campus with a sort of green and fragrant liquidity – pink and white dogwood blooms everywhere, and the Botanical Gardens are in full bloom. As I write at my desk in front of the open window I can hear the subdued murmer of twilight birds – see leafy silhouettes of treetops, and one evening star.

I have been rather awfully lax as far as work is concerned – cutting classes right & left just to study out-of-doors. But I feel that I've worked so hard all year that I can enjoy myself now. We've had our last French class, and done our last paper for English. I'm running through the last History assignment of the year – a doubly long one to leave a bitter taste in our mouths. Botany is grinding out to the bitter end with a quiz tomorrow & two long labs next week. I have to do one more painting in Art – and work on the notebook over this weekend. But really, I can't get

1 – Probably Lucy S. Wheaton (1903–97) of 23 Rumford Street, Concord, New Hampshire. Married to public school principal Harvey H. Wheaton; mother of David S. Wheaton (1930–2001). SP and Richard Norton visited the Wheatons on Saturday–Sunday 26–7 May 1951.
2 – Date supplied from postmark.

too serious about these last bits of work. Exams is what I'll really have to study for. But I rationalize and say that taking the weekend off for going to Wheaton's will be a fine respite after Botany. As you probably know, I'm going to the Yale commencement and Dick will probably drive me home on the second of June after my last French exam.

So I hope I can leave all my furniture here & get all the rest carried home with you so I can be neat and just have a few things for Dick to tote back.

Today I cut four hours of morning classes to catch up on History – went to History section from 2-3, and sat in halter & shorts down by paradise with Marcia for the rest of the afternoon. We then had iced coffee & ice cream at Davis and went for a swim in the pool. I hope I can go every day to get some sort of stroke by this summer. I really am horrible and can't swim at all, but Marcia is "coaching" me to breathe with nose-plugs on. Really, I feel as if I were living at a landscaped country club. It just so happens that Haven House is the only one on campus with a sunporch, and it just happens to be right opposite my room – so I often put on sunglasses & lie out there. <drawing of girl sunbathing on deck>

By the way, Dick has the queer idea that daughters grow to be like their mothers. You better not be so capable and wonderful, because the poor boy doesn't know that I'm rather an awkward hybrid . . . I pointed out the discrepancy in our noses as an indication that like does not always breed like. He also thinks I have negroid features . . . say, we got compliments we ain't even used yet.

I'm definitely majoring in English. My schedule, tentative as it is, looks pretty good so far.

My black skirt is the most divinely versatile & wearable thing I've ever had. I just love it!

Have fun – good luck on your intersession, & give my love to Warren, Aunt Mildred & Mrs. Freeman –

Love,
Sivvy

TO *Aurelia Schober Plath*

Wednesday 16 May 1951[1] ALS (postcard), Indiana University

Wednesday –

Dear Mum –

A week from today at this time I will be through all my classes. The only ones I have left are Gym, Art, and Botany. I wonder if a girl on scholarship could go abroad Junior year? Could I find out from judicious inquiries into the Smith Club? Or should I meekly bow my head and hope they give me enough to stay here Jr. Year? I thought perhaps if I got a well-paid waitress job next summer I could slave joyfully if I had something so desirable to work for. But perhaps it's hopeless. I don't like to admit anything is hopeless, though. But I would take French next year if I thought I could go abroad. As my schedule stands, next year I'm taking Creative Writing, English lit., Art, Government & Religion. (Physical Sci. will wait till Jr. Year.) "Swam" again today & we all enjoyed our Botany prof. & advisor at dinner tonight. This getting-to-know your-professors deal sure is fun.

Love,
Sivvy

TO *Warren Plath*

Saturday 19 May 1951[2] ALS (photocopy), Indiana University

Dear Bruvver . . .

If it weren't for these damn old meetings you wouldn't be hearing from your sister atall-atall. As it is, I've got to keep awake somehow, so I thought I'd quote you part of a little pome that may be perverted but familiar.

I had my allowance
My next month's allowance,
I took my allowance
    to the Green Street sales.
I wanted some new clothes

1 – Date supplied from postmark.
2 – Date supplied from internal evidence.

And I looked for new clothes
    Most everywhere.

I went to the shop where they sold spring outfits
(It isn't spring without an outfit)
But my pocket wasn't equal to that outfit
I decided not to buy my new clothes there.

I had nuffin
No, I hadn't got nuffin
No I didn't go over
    to the Green Street sales.
But I went to my closet,
My <u>grungy</u> old closet,
And I saw my old blue jeans
    Just hanging there.

So I'm sorry for the people who sell smart sportswear
I'm sorry for the people who sell spring outfits,
I'm sorry for the people who sell pale organdy
'Cos this customer's got her blue jeans to wear!"

Not too hot, huh? But my favorite word was "grungy." I just <u>love</u> the word "grungy."

Haven't been to bed before midnight for the past week, so this staying up late deal tonight is just neat. I feel sort of in suspended animation . . . like a pickled pig.

I hear you lost a crew race by the hair of your chin? That's almost more maddening than missing by a mile, wot?

I have my first exam (Botany) next Friday – then I go home till my next & worst two – History & French (the <u>next</u> Friday & Saturday.) I really <u>should</u> study all the time, but told myself that exercise and sunshine are <u>sooo</u> much more important for my state of health.

You will be surprised how tan I am from slaving away in the library the way I do all the time! Truth is, I haven't done a lick of work for two solid weeks. I passed in my last English paper & art work for the year, so I cut all the rest of those classes. We have no more history or French – and I only have two more Botany labs next week, so guess wot I've been doing? Lying out in the sun wearing next to nuffin! Yup – the sunbathing laws around here are very strict because they don't want the campus to look like a nudist colony, so they just let people sunbathe on the gym roof – and not on weekends 'cause of visitors. So it just happens that Haven is the only house with a balcony, and that is outside the 3rd floor right across the hall from my little room. As you may imagine I haven't been studying too hard . . . don't want to strain my eyes glaring into the sun and all!

Last night I had a great time – the art club took the faculty (mostly nice men) on a picnic out to Look Park. This getting-to-know-your-professors-over-burnt-hamburgs idea is the best yet.

Well, I'll sign off now. Bob Humphrey is coming up to Float Night today, & I hope I have better luck & don't get malaria or St. Vitus Dance or anything –

See you soon –
Love,
Sivvy

TO *Ann Davidow-Goodman*

Sunday 20 May 1951[1] ALS, Smith College

Dear Davy –

Wow, that was a neat letter you sent me, kid! I take it out and read it over every time I want to get a warm glow inside. It is Sunday night, and I just got back from two hours of "playing" tennis. My sprained ankle still bothers on occasion, mostly after I have been running on the fool thing. So just now I am a mess – straight stringy hair, and wet sweatshirt – not a very savory morsel of femininity, I assure you. Today has been one of those sticky, cloudy, moist, muggy days, and I am just about to take my third cold bath. The only trouble is, the minute I step out of the tub I'm hot again.

I just finished my art assignments for the year and got one of life's little blows. I took my first painting together with my last one up to be criticized by Mr. Swinton.[2] (The last was a re-doing of the first, using all the "skills" we'd learned this year.) Mr. S.'s comment was hideously encouraging – thought the first was much better, more naive and free – that the last was artificial and gaudy as bad wallpaper. Made me feel I'd really accomplished something! (Now, Sylvia, don't be bitter!)

1 – Date supplied from internal evidence.
2 – George Swinton (1917–2002), art instructor, Smith College, 1950–3.

About your various irons in the fire as far as school is concerned. I shall try to say honestly what I think, hoping you'll take it all with a couple of grains of salt, as I don't know all the pros and cons – not by a long shot!

First, about Smith. Don't think that if you don't come back that means that you're beaten. You have no schedualed duel with Smith; your fight is with College as such, and the fact that you might go somewhere else and make a fresh start there only proves your victory – not that you're escaping from a conquering adversary. Also, coming back to Smith wouldn't be a fair test of your ability, because you'd have even more to overcome than at first – since you would have the disadvantage of knowing us, yet not knowing us – being a Freshman, yet not being a Freshman. I don't know if that's at all coherent, but you probably know what I mean. Only, from a purely personal and selfish point of view (the first part was an attempt at objectivity) I want you back very badly, and Marty & I would do anything to help you – because of a soft spot of admiration and, I guess, love, that we have for you. Smith is often Heaven, and sometimes Hell (especially for an overly-sensitive individual like yours truly.) But I'm sure that you could do it if you really wanted to. All you need to know is that getting to the end of the year takes occasional teeth-gritting and agony – the "I'll-never-be-able-to-get-up-tomorrow-morning-and-live-through-another-day" sort of thing.

So much for our dear and dog-fanged Alma Mater. I do think a "clean slate" would be better for you, as you said, but subjectively, I want you to return.

You know more about the U of Chi than I do – even though Eddie went there for two years.

What the hell (excuse please) if Northwestern's close to home. This breaking away from home deal is all very fine, but it shouldn't be an obsession. You can make just as much a mess of your life under the parental roof as 1500 miles away, (listen to the girl, she's getting to sound moralize-ish – TSK, TSK!)

Have you ever though of one of the other Eastern Women's Colleges – such as Wellesley? Northwestern does sound the most sensible – and you could always be having dentistry treatments – that's usually convincing.

Seriously, I would love to know just how the "old gal" in Chi works. What does she do and say? I'm awfully curious – such things interest me immensely. Of course I'd love the chance to go to one of those people and have them bring my various childhood persecution complexes to light. I would no doubt feel quite purged and clean again – spiritually, I mean.

Speaking of persecution complexes, let me tell you a few of the more unsavory sides of my life here which will show you that it all isn't quite the bed of roses it may seem. I am, in one nasty word, quite unpopular with our sweet Haven housemates. I have always been vaguely aware of the fact that I never go into the livingroom and never play bridge and never stay up late and gossip. But what goes on behind my back has been brought home to me by various little incidents which do manage to stab a sensitive spot in my hide. For one thing, when I grin "hello," I am greeted with a stony grudging stare, and followed by cold, calculating eyes that are obviously signaling each other – "what a sad sack!"

By now you are maybe laughing and saying that I exaggerate. I wish I were. Truth is, I'm paying the penalty for my individualistic ways of life. If you don't share a certain amount of your time and confidences with everyone, they either get the idea you're a snob or are very unfriendly, so there! Thus while people like Nancy Teed, Callie White, and Joan Strong get nominated for office after office . . . and can walk in the living room without seeing malicious and indifferent glances chill them from all sides, little me is suddenly aware of some great discrepancy between her way of life and that of the average Smith gal.

Funny thing is, except for sudden great twinges of doubt and misgiving (such as the time when Biz[1] came up and talked to me from 11 pm to 4 am about how one could be too selective with choosing friends [meaning Marcia] and how one should talk to people & share oneself with them like Rosie does) I have been rather happy. Is it rationalizing, Davy, when I say that I am the sort of person who has a very few deep and close and complete friends whom she devotes herself to – and not the gregarious sort of person who is loved by everyone all the time? Or am I making myself out to be too pure and a loof when I say that?

I do think that it is hard for me to share myself with everyone. My introspection and queer thoughts always make me feel no one will understand – except someone I love, like you, or Dick, or Eddie. When I love someone, I make myself increasingly vulnerable to them – and give them the power to hurt me by letting them know my sensitive spots. But by being confident in someone, I feel I can be my self with them at no great risk.

All this is getting very incoherent, because it is getting very late and I am very sleepy. But I did want to let you know that the few little outward

1–Elizabeth Storer Paynter (1929–); B.A. 1951, American Studies, Smith College, SP's housemate at Haven House.

successes I may seem to have, there are acres of misgiving and self-doubt in me.

It is almost a case of choosing between writing and loving a very few and living individualistically & often very painfully – or – rubbing off all my peculiar rough edges and becoming a nice neat round peg in a round hole. Luckily, perhaps, I'm too far gone to ever become the latter.

By the way, Hugh never wrote, but do remind him – next year I will be completely dateless – no contacts anywhere, since Dick is graduating from Yale. Even a Williams man would boost my old morale to eternity.

I falleth asleep . . . I drowseth –
Write, baby –
Love,
Sylvy

P.S. Love the snapshot – love my pregnant namesake – name the baby "Eddie", huh?

S.

TO *Aurelia Schober Plath*

Sunday 20 May 1951[1] ALS (postcard), Indiana University

Sunday
5 pm

Dear Mum –

Whew! Today was the hottest & muggiest yet! I've just taken a cold bath & feel much better. Yesterday was a day I wished you could have seen---even Nature seemed bound to display Smith-in-Spring to best advantage. All morning I wrote letters on the sunporch. All afternoon we meandered lazily over the sunny green athletic fields, watching the exhibition sports. Bob came in time for Float Night, which I so wanted you to see! All Paradise was lit up, and the leafy green island was the stage where the choirs sang while the spotlights picked out the painted floats gliding across the black waters. I had a driving lesson all evening – & the countryside was such fun to cruise through – moonlight on apple orchards! Today we took another drive, ate at Wiggin's, & went canoeing. I really hope I made up for that last time. Poor Bob! I do feel like a playgirl – this place is so country-clubish in spring –

Love,
Sivvy

1–Date supplied from postmark.

TO *Aurelia Schober Plath*

Wednesday 23 May 1951[1] ALS (postcard), Indiana University

Wednesday

Dear Mum –

One more class today and then I'm through (with classes, at least.) Will you be coming up Friday afternoon, and about what time? I think packing the car would be much easier if you brought up a few suitcases to hold all the things that you sent up in boxes during the year. I will take my bike and pillows home – and, in fact, everything except a change of clothes since I will only be coming back for two brief nights. Also, I would then only have a small suitcase to carry when Dick picks me up. This Botany exam doesn't worry me – if I study all tomorrow I should do well – but it's the French & History I'm going to have to slave for. Isn't this humid weather hideous? Hope going in town hasn't been too hard on you.

See you –
Love,
Sivvy

TO *Marcia B. Stern*

Tuesday 29 May 1951[2] ALS, Smith College

Tuesday

Angel Child –

Although I may even see your tan face before this missive reaches you, I couldn't resist telling about my Swampscott trip Saturday. (No, I didn't see them, but I did see The House.)

Well, after we left you on the back steps, we drove out to Look Park and picnicked. (sp?) Home was reached at the moderate hour of 10, and bed at 12.

Saturday, of course, the glorious specimen of Dick-hood arrived avec car and picnic. (Can't get away from sandwiches, it seems.) We planned to picnic in Swampscott on the way to Concord, N.H., and so we drove along the shore, asking all sorts of odd people directions to 144 Beach Bluff Avenue – where is located the domicile of the Mayos. Finally, after finding the right road, we drove along, noticing to our amazement that the

1 – Date supplied from postmark.
2 – Letter misdated '6/1' by Marcia Stern. Date supplied from internal evidence.

numbers seemed to begin with 142 and get smaller. I had a queer feeling that the house had been blown out to sea, and that we were out of a job. But, upon looking backward, we found we'd missed a sweeping driveway, hidden by a tall aristocratic hedge. That was "IT." Lord, Marty, if you could have seen! There was one huge and beautifully architectured (I am not sure about that last word) white house, and then two smaller ones, with all sorts of cars and shiny beach wagons parked carelessly about. Not only that – the landscaped green lawn had a few minor children's toys – such as a jungle gym – scattered around. Tennis court and yacht were modestly in hiding.

Methinks I shall arrive in a coach-in-four, with a diamond tiara tilted casually over one eye. Impressed? I'm still gasping.

See ya Thursday.
Love,
Syl

P.S. Home is <u>not</u> the place to study. Even administrations got psychology, darn 'em.

S.

TO *Hans-Joachim Neupert*

Wednesday 6 June 1951 ALS (photocopy), Smith College

June 6, 1951

Dear Hans-Joachim . . .

At last, at last exams are over for a few months, and I will not begin to take notes and read textbooks again until next September! My first of four years at college has whisked by so rapidly that I feel that I closed my eyes for a minute and someone played a cruel trick on me and made me a year older---just like that!

I have only a week and a half to rest at home now before I go down to Swampscott on the Massachusetts shore for my summer job. I will be taking care of three children, ages 2, 4 and 6, for a rather wealthy doctor's family. It will no doubt be a great deal of work, but I just hope the little ones will like me, as that will make the summer infinitely nicer.

My sympathies are with you in your job as "Practicant." Do you live all alone, with no other students nearby? It must be hard to manage away from home. Even though I am away at school I do not have to worry about meals and a room as I board there. So it is not too different from home in that respect.

And now again the summer is upon us. Even though college lets out early in June and begins late in September, it seems suddenly that the years accelerate and move faster and faster which is sad. The ice cream cart, painted with white enamel, is now driving slowly down the street, ringing its musical bell to call the children out from the houses and tempt them to buy the bright cold ices. And I know that it is truly summer once more.

By the way, I did enjoy your picture Hans! It was quite lovely; I showed it to my mother and she liked it too. Also, I certainly can read your handwriting, and in fact, find it quite easy to read. So don't bother to print . . . that takes so much time.

You mentioned that you were reading one of Upton Sinclair's works. I do know a little about him – but perhaps you know more than I. At any rate, his most famous work was perhaps "The Jungle" – a social work on the conditions in the Chicago stockyards. Most of his books have been about social issues in America; he dramatizes a situation in his powerful way, and thus calls the attention of the people to bad or unjust conditions through his dynamic writing. I am very interested to know what the "Voice of America" says. I hope they give a nearly-true picture of America – there are faults here, as everywhere, and there is a great easy class that owns maroon convertibles and swimming pools – but whatever people say, Money is not all America's God. There are a multitude of hard-working, sensible, idealistic, intelligent young people here, just as there are everywhere else.

And now it is getting late, and I must go to bed on time for once, as I still haven't caught up on sleep from all the nights I spent studying for exams.

My best to you in all your work, Hans. I know, as you do, that it is worth it to have to work in order to reach some of the important things in life.

Thanks again for your fine letter.
Sincerely,
Your friend
Sylvia

TO *Marcia B. Stern*

Wednesday 6 June 1951 | ALS with envelope on Smith College letterhead, Smith College[1]

Syl P.
26 Elmwood Rd.
Wellesley, Mass.

"She clasps the sun oil with hooked hands;
Close to the sun in backyard lands,
Ringed with azure halter, she stands,
—
The wrinkled rug beneath her crawls;
Her love for sunlight never palls,
Till with sunstroke down she falls . . ."

And now, after causing Tennyson[2] to writhe and mumble with insomnia in his tomb, we will commence by saying hello and it-was-so-nice-to-get-a-letter-at-home-from-you.

Seriously, though, it never quite feels like being home until after I've gotten that first letter . . . and yours was "it." Shall I get you caught up with past days?

Well, after you and votre mère pulled cheerily out of Hamp Friday, I swallowed various odd protuberances which had risen to my throat, shouldered the Books and headed once more over to the History seminar. Somehow I just couldn't get serious about the exam---I felt so washed out after History 11 that I kept expecting someone to give me a Purple Heart, pat me tenderly on my hard little head and send me home. No such luck, alas. 8 a.m. Saturday found me staring unbelievingly at the first French question which happened to be on history. Naturally I rewrote half of what I'd written for 11 and quoted symbolist poetry for the rest of the blue book. I hope to h— I answered some of the questions. (Having nagging suspicion I didn't.) Enough of such sordid details!

Spent all morning tying books in bundles, labeling things, and sitting on my suitcase, stuffing in that last towel. Afternoon spent thumbing with pathetic and frivolous nonchalance through Life. I felt so queer when Stobie said, "You lucky thing. I've got three more exams next week." I couldn't even comprehend . . . I was so stuffed.

1–Plath wrote the following footnote on the bottom of the first page: '1. Really not, I'm only-using-up-stationery, (Wellesley Press, June 6, 1951)'.
2–SP's poetic epigraph is a play on Alfred Tennyson's 'The Eagle'.

Suddenly, about 3:30 I looked up and there was a rather nice-looking guy in a white t-shirt and sneakers tiptoeing up behind me. "Hello," said I carelessly. Perry drove home, while Dick explained the intricacies (sp.?) of carboxyl and hydroxyl groups, to which I listened with not as much avidity as I should have.

The Yale men dropped me at home in time for supper. After which Dick biked over for a brief 15 minutes to show me the suave black paint job on his 2-wheeler & walk me quickly around the block. An intellectual pass on his part in the direction of the international situation was blocked on my part (with a mute resolve to read and memorize every issue of the Monitor this summer.) We parted . . . buddies, you might say.

He headed off with Perry for a week's trip in the wilds of Maine – around Jonesport – Sunday, so I will catch no glimpse of his pointed blond head till this Saturday leaving me a blissful week to "get things done in."

<drawing of SP mowing the lawn> Sunday I began with a will, got all unpacked, hung up, and drawers, bookcase, closet and trunk cleaned out and rearranged – a long task in itself. The lawn also awaited me – strictly a long-hair job saved up for a month. At last I plowed through it . . . only to have to begin again. Monday I went "downtown" to the Wellesley shopping district. I blew myself on a LP record of César Franck's symphony in D minor to give Dick for graduation. (What price culture?) Also swallowed conscience & bought 3 M. libe books –

Growth of the Soil, – Knut Hamsun[1]
In Dubious Battle – John Steinbeck[2]
As I Lay Dying / The Sound & the Fury – Faulkner[3]

Also picked up a few pocket books – Grapes of Wrath,[4] Native Son,[5] The Sun Also Rises,[6] Sanctuary,[7] The Good Earth.[8] Some of the covers are a bit lurid – but Hemingway & Faulkner aren't the coyest babies in the literary game, after all.

1–Knut Hamsun, *Growth of the Soil* (New York: Modern Library, 1921); SP's copy held by Lilly Library.
2–John Steinbeck, *In Dubious Battle* (New York: Modern Library, 1936); SP's copy held by Lilly Library.
3–William Faulkner, *The Sound and the Fury* and *As I Lay Dying* (New York: Modern Library, [1946]); SP's copy held by Smith College.
4–John Steinbeck, *The Grapes of Wrath* (New York: Bantam Books, 1946); SP's copy held by Lilly Library.
5–Richard Wright, *Native Son*; the location of SP's copy is unknown.
6–Ernest Hemingway, *The Sun Also Rises* (New York: Bantam Books, 1949); SP's copy held by Lilly Library.
7–William Faulkner, *Sanctuary* (New York: New American Library, 1950); SP's copy held by Lilly Library.
8–Pearl S. Buck, *The Good Earth*; the location of SP's copy is unknown.

On my way home I stopped at my old hunting ground – the town tennis courts. Ah, yes! Thereupon, while banging ball vs. backboard, I met my favorite young high school protegé[1] – a cutie who (with the addition of an inch or two) might have great possibilities. Honestly, I've never seen such a handsome, athletic and brilliant baby doll. He'll only be a senior next year, but is No. 1 on the tennis team and won 2nd prize in the U.N. contest this year. So I maternally patted him on the shoulder & told him to come up and see me some time.

As for yesterday – cold, nasty, wet, – I met mother in town and rambled through the Gardner Art Palace with her, browsing through old relics and letters to the Great Isabella from everybody from Dostoievsky to Hoover.

Spent all last night reading Dick's sociology papers which amounted to well over 100 pages – gosh, that boy! I often wonder how I can keep up with him.

Today, with the first ray of soleil I was out in the backyard in as little as possible . . . later this afternoon Pat O'Neil and I will head high school-ward to pay homage to our favorite Eng. prof. High School graduates tonight – such is life. I think I never mentally got over the chronological idea that I was just seventeen. 18 seems rather too old for me – I feel cheated.

Oh, well, if I meander much longer, I shall have no breath in my body.

Wrote Mayos – to ask about the Date of Arrival.

Let me know how life is working out . . .

Anon ---
Syl

TO *Marcia B. Stern*

Tuesday 12 June 1951[2] ALS with envelope, Smith College

Toosday

Postcard received, appreciated (and envied) in that order. Today is a Tuesday, and in a week from today I'll have spent one night already at my summer resort. This New England weather is driving me slowly insane. I sit out in the back yard with various "things to do" and strip to halter and shorts, apply sun oil, and settle back with a loud "Ah!" The sun beams brightly for all of five minutes, whereupon big glossy white clouds

1–Philip Emerald McCurdy (1935–); B.A. 1956, Harvard College; SP's friend from Wellesley.

2–Date supplied from internal evidence.

start charging up over the horizon and a cold wind springs up, leaving me shivering and muttering curses at the impersonal neutrality of nature in general. How I would love a month's vacation by the shore with naught to do but sun, read, and be unsociable.

That last adjective springs from this last weekend, which will be recounted shortly in proper order. All last week I lawnmowed, pianoed, tennised, read a little of "What Makes The Wheels Go Round"[1] – and rested in general – seeing Pat and a pal at Wellesley College. Friday Dick and Perry came back from a week of rough and evidently heavenly camping and fishing at Jonesport, Me. Dick called & asked me to join him babysitting Saturday night . . . and to stay over so I could leave early with the rest of the family Sunday a.m. Clad in my usual old skirt & blouse I went over about 6. Dick thoroughly embarrassed me by cooking and heating up a delightful and delicious dinner (damn boys anyway). We tucked David[2] (7 yr. old brother) in bed, and Dick told him a story. Whereupon we did dishes, listened to César Francks Symphony in D Minor (which I gave him for a commencement gift – at mother's suggestion – trust me not to think up things myself.) Parents came home early, and I went to bed – feeling only slightly strange appearing in p.j.'s before his somewhat conventional father (a History prof . . . at B.U. – graduated 1st in his class at Yale!) Mrs. Norton is my favorite – you would love her – very pretty in a mobile way – and terribly capable= keeps a house running and her four men well-fed, ironed, clothed and happy.

She got up at 5, Sunday a.m., and by the time I poked my lazy head out of the sack at 6, she had a picnic lunch packed, house cleaned, and huge breakfast of bacon, eggs, oatmeal – all sorts of yummy things – steaming on the table. The four of us set out for New Haven at 7 – "Aunt Mildred" and I sitting in back, and the two men in front – of P. K.'s[3] big beach wagon (loaned for the occasion.)

Never have I been dashed so madly from place to place and felt such an odd mixture of emotions. I stayed for the most part with Dick's parents – Baccalaureate (sp) occupied the morning – and the Pres. of Yale[4] gave

1–Probably Edward G. Huey, *What Makes the Wheels Go Round: A First-time Physics* (New York: Harcourt, Brace, 1940).

2–David William Norton (1944–); youngest brother of Richard Norton.

3–Probably Pamela Lewis Kent (1932–); SP's classmate from Wellesley High School; B.A. 1954, Connecticut College; resident of Chatham, Mass.

4–Alfred Whitney Griswold (1906–63); President of Yale, 1950–63. President Griswold delivered his first Baccalaureate Address in Woolsey Hall at 11 a.m. on Sunday, 10 June 1951. Senior Class Day Exercises followed in the afternoon. Yale University's 250th Commencement was held at 10:30 a.m. on Monday, 11 June 1951 in the Old Campus.

a neat speech which included delightfully pungent references about television, easy living and so on. After that, we picked up dick and drove miles out into the hills for a nice picnic spot, only to get there and find we'd left the lunch back at the room. Say, anticlimaxes!

Afternoon was Class Day – with dick always off with the class in cap & gown. Mildred & I had to smile at Mr. N. who is so much more serious about college spirit than Dick, who considers honorary societies, white handkerchief waving and "Bright College Years" so much nonsense. After Class Day, it was a two hour tea at the headmaster's house, and I got so damn sick of making small talk with mothers of boys and fiancées and young wives that I thought my sweet girlish smile had frozen to my face. I felt like drowning myself in the iced tea bowl, in a flurry of mint leaves. Dick and I weren't on speaking terms for a while . . . because I had refused to say I thought Class Day was trite in front of his boyishly enthusiastic father, and ad nauseam.

At last we freed ourselves and I welcomed Dick's invitation to "dress down". We all drove out to the beach, where it was cold and windy, and let the wind and quiet wash the gaiety off. Dick & I then got so excited at driving through Savin Rock[1] . . . a second Coney Island . . . that Mildred told us they'd watch the car while we joined the carnival crowd for a little. Had two rides on the merry-go-round and felt as excited as if I were eight years old. It's such fun to be able to put sophistication aside with hat & gloves and be a kid again. We had a late supper in New Haven, and they left Mildred & me at the "Y" where we were staying overnight. Before going to bed, Mr. Norton (a crack athlete for all his 46 years) tried to play ping pong with me, while Dick played songs on the piano . . . picture me in the "Y" game room, angel, hitting ping pong balls into bookcases and light bulbs!

Slept rawther little all night, as the trucks rumbled through on the street below for hours on end, and girls got up to go to work from 4 a.m. on. Breakfast with Mrs. N. – then Commencement – then lunch and drive home. Saw Dick in glimpses.

Fell into bed at 8 p.m., whereupon Dick called to inform me he's going off on a trip to Cape Ann with a family from Arizona that's visiting them for a week. Well, hell, didn't want to see him anyhow. Also, he's going west right after summer job to visit young married friends before school. Tra la la. Looks like glimpses is all we get, boy.

1 – An amusement park in West Haven, Connecticut.

Good lord, I'm cruel – rambling for pages about myself! Shush, you selfish creature, and let the gal hear something else than "I and Dick."

Say, but I hate dashing hither & yon . . . . I have packed and unpacked so many times in so many places that I begin to feel something like a transient. I love the idea of travel and so on, but there are times when I think I should have tuberculosis, just so I'd be justified to loaf in a sunny sanatorium and read and write and see nobody and make no small talk.

Speaking of corrupting the younger generation – I have descended to a new low. He's aiming at Harvard, but will only be a senior at high next year (16, sweet---etc.) He won 2nd prize in the U.N. contest and is 1st on our tennis team. Phil McCurdy is the name, and you should see the smug knowing looks of all the pretty, popular Wellesley High socialites. I can just hear the little beasts whispering, "There goes poor old Sylvia with that little baby – my, but her social contacts must be rusty." So I say cheerily "To Hell," pat my cute protegé on his boyish shoulder and ask him how to cut a tennis ball. Love life, and as long as people are interesting, who gives a damn about color, age or education! Be good and/or have fun.

Love,
Syl

TO *Aurelia Schober Plath*

Tuesday 19 June 1951[1]

ALS with envelope,
Indiana University

Tuesday

Dear Mother –

Say, but I feel that I'm cut off from all human kind. I don't even know how I can last one week – I feel like putting my head on your shoulder and weeping from sheer homesickness. They say not to let children be tyrants over you. Fine, but I'd like to know just how you get a thing done on your own if you are continually to "keep an eye" on them – while they play, when they want you to put them up on swings or play ball – or if I should maybe run after them all the time just so they'll think I'm on the job.

Last night I couldn't sleep & couldn't sleep, just because I wanted so badly to spill over to someone. My day begins at 6 or 6:30 with the first cry or bright face bursting in the door. Mr & Mrs. sleep downstairs with

1 – Date supplied from postmark.

the baby who is just a toddler and who "loves to get in to everything." The 4 year old girl is a "me-do", always doing death-defying leaps after big brother on the trapeeze. After I get the two oldest washed and dressed. I go down and help with breakfast, after which I do dishes, make beds, pick up and mop the kids rooms, do laundry in Bendix and hang it out, watch the children. There is no cook here, so a woman comes three days a week. I just hope she makes lunch for the kids and me on those days – she is very capable – and I don't know just whether I'll be in her way or not when I clumsily monkey about in the kitchen. But I'd love it if you could tell me how to cook some meats and vegetables – (like carrots, peas & beans) – in saucepans & frying pans. Do you always use water in the former & fat in the latter? Cause I cook our lunches when Helen (the lady) isn't here. (Hah!) After lunch the two youngest are supposed to have naps, while the boy plays around by himself. I hope to be able to rest in my room for an hour, then, although I will do the ironing whenever there's time – just for the kids who change clothes every day – so every day there's wash & ironing to do. I get the supper for myself and the children – and hope I feel more like eating as the days go by. After supper, I wash the baby & put her to bed. The two oldest play out till after seven, whereupon I call them in, bathe them & put them to bed. If I have my way, they'll all be out of the way by eight. By which time I shall probably be so dead that I can no more look at a book than anything. I can wash my laundry in the Bendix, though, so that saves money, I guess.

But after not a wink of sleep last night – being as I was just dropping off when Pinny started having a nightmare at two, and screamed till I got up and told her to be still in a gentle tone that amazes me even yet . . . I have to get used to just how much discipline I should use---and just to what subtle degree I should take over the role of boss.

Even now, as I write, I am so tired I can feel the tears coming to my eyes. In this state I can hardly be the bright and cheerful playmate and creative storyteller I would like to be if I had the energy. The oldest boy can be good if you interest him in a story or something, but oh, no, I can't devote myself to him . . . The little two year old, who can't understand a word I say, runs off, and I continually run after to bring her back to "play." All she does is stuff sand and grass in her mouth and either grin senselessly or bawl like a baby. Thank god she takes an hour's nap a day. As for Pinny, again, by herself, she would be alright . . . but incited by Freddie, or just out of plain ornariness, she does nasty things like throwing clean dishes on the water while I'm washing them. Freddy is all right when he has his way. Otherwise he's an unreasonable whining cuss. Excuse the language, but if you could see him shrieking on the top of his lungs, you'd agree. Am I quietly firm and insensible? Do I ignore their fights? Do I try to break them up? How do you inspire kids with awe & respect? By being decisive? By being ominously quiet.

Outside it is lovely. From my window I can see the beach. So I sit here exhausted, seeing no way out, seeing only slavery from 6 in the morning till eight at night, never knowing if or when I can completely relax. My nerves are always on edge. I can for see going to bed and lying awake every night dreading the next morning – and the interminable day . . . Fourteen hours . . . God! I almost wish I'd get the mumps so I could come home. I don't know what is wrong with me. I've completely lost my sense of humor. If they yell any more, I shall burst into tears of angry vexation.

Mrs. Mayo is just doing the wash and the hanging out with me so I can take over myself later, I guess. I don't know if I can life six whole days till whenever my "day off" comes. And what if it rains? Do I stay in my room and hear them squabbling downstairs? Do I come down for meals? Do I ignore the kids completely? I could just ask to make myself a sandwich for lunch & lie down the beach if it's nice, I guess.

One sure thing, I don't feel like traveling to Brewster. My face is a mess, all broken out, my tan is faded, my eyes are sunken. I look hideous. If I could be pretty, I wouldn't mind so much. But I shall do my best and try to keep the letters heading that way cheerful and light. If I die here, or get shot for letting the dog (yup – a nasty puppy who bites playfully – my leg still has the mark.)

By now you are either saying that I am a selfish creature to tell you my troubles, or "well, I thought it would be like this, but didn't want to tell her." However, I know I have no chance of seeing you till after the 6th – which is when Marcia is coming. I hope I don't take out my troubles on her – but I am rather sad that I drew the baby lot. I don't see how she can have a worse job with hers – who are old enough to know not to eat sand . . . & who can listen to stories. Maybe when you come down, you could make Bea's our headquarters, so I could lie on the beach, or rest, or be with you away from neighbors eyes.

Do write me now and then, but don't expect to hear from me too often . . . more than twice a week!

Your bewitched baby. –
Sivvy

<on back of envelope>

P.S. – c'est la vie!

TO *Marcia B. Stern*

Wednesday 20 June 1951 ALS[1] with envelope, Smith College

EXTRA! SWAMPSCOTT DAILY NEWS EXTRA!
HIRED GIRL RUNS WILD . . .

A shocking event took place today in the home of Swampscott's beloved & respected Doctor M. A hitherto outwardly normal teen-age girl was found chortling hysterically over the mangled bodies of three angelic children. Our reporters rushed to the scene and found her sobbing hysterically in the kitchen. When asked what she had done to the eldest, she cried, "I fed him down the chromium-plated disposal unit in the kitchen sink." The 4 year old girl was found broiling in the oven, cheerioats and jams sprinkled in her hair. The youngest was found percolating docilely in the coffee pot. The girl was sitting on the floor when the police wagons arrived, dociley feeding her fingers, one by one, to the Mayo's adorable three month old puppy, Abigail. "The can opener wouldn't open the special vitiminized dog-food," she said by way of explanation . . .

And so we trail off.

Seriously, Marty, I thought I would never live through my first day. I arrived Monday afternoon after four with Grammy and Mummy, after a brief sojurn at home with my brother over the weekend. I bade mother a fond farewell, with a little pang of sadness, and was escorted by three jubilant children to my quarters – a huge second floor room with adjoining bath – overlooking the ocean. Imagine, honey, I can hear the waves all night and see the big orange moon sail mistily up over the trees . . . say, lonesome, but I was last night! I know I'm living in the midst of affluence, but I betcha I don't lift a tennis racket or sail a yacht all summer long.

My Day began last night as I flopped into bed after unpacking and scrubbing Freddy and Pinny. I dozed uneasily till one, when I got up to shush Pinny who had been screaming for fifteen solid minutes over a nightmare. The baby, not yet two, began howling at five. As you may imagine, I was not too disposed to leap out of bed at six when Pinny barged in to be dressed, beaming, noisy & rested. The kids <u>look</u> adorable, but what woik! The toddler – Joanne – can't understand a word of English, and must be chased at frequent intervals, and Pinny is a daredevil who always wants to emulate brother Freddie. Alone, each would be a joy and quite manageable. Together, they nullify each others potentialities, if you see what I mean. Freddy can be read to and played with huskily – but

1 – The first page of this letter is formatted like a double-column newspaper article.

the two girls don't even listen to stories. Joanne can hardly pronounce the word "shoe" and is always doing silly things like eating gravel.

Picture Freddie striking Pinny and shouting and screaming, while the poor girl does the same for several eons, and all the while you're pulling them apart, Joanne has been squatting cheerily in the corner stuffing her rosebud mouth with sand. God!

Slight items like daily baths, helping with laundry and doing beds and such while keeping the three darlings alive – at the same time – challenge my homicidal tendencies no end, not to mention the heightened sensitivity given to my sadistic-masochistic temperament.

One parting shot before I literally crumble into bed – my one avenue for getting acquainted with Swampscott "young people" was opened today. It was my first venture "outside the swinging ivy hedges" – the beach with the kids & Mrs. M. As soon as Mrs. took Joanne back, a lean young male slicked back his hair & approached the three of us who were gaily building sand castles. "Say, I don't want you to think I'm fresh, but didn't I see you in Maine." Funny thing, but I could have hugged the old thing – the lanky dumb type if ever there was one. Demurely I blushed and refused the offer of a ride home, waved a nonchalant farewell to his "Anytime you want a tour of Swampscott, lemme know," and crossed the street to my domicile, warmed to the depths of my cold little heart. I think that made me decide to last another day at least.

Hope you are finding older ages more "playable." I hear chris[1] is usually off on his own anyhow. Bet he adores you by summer's end. Are they all cuties??

Your cohort,
Syl

1–During the summer of 1951, Marcia Brown (later Marcia B. Stern) took care of the children of Esther Blodgett Meyer (1916–2006); B.A. 1937, Smith College. Meyer's children were staying in Swampscott, Mass., with their grandparents John Henry Blodgett (1881–1971) and Ruth Sargent Paine Blodgett (1890–1967); B.A. 1912, Smith College. The Meyer children were G. Christian Meyer, Ann Meyer Wood, and Holly Meyer Humphrey.

TO *Aurelia Schober Plath*

Thursday 21 June 1951[1] ALS with envelope, Indiana University

Thursday

Dear mater –

Well, let's hope this sounds a bit more cheery than my last tear-stained missive. Life is looking up, and I think I'll live. Even got my sense of humor back. Funny, but the thing that gave me back my sense of proportion was a gawky boy. I took the kids down to the beach the day before yesterday, and after Mrs. Mayo took the youngest back, I saw a young blade slicking a comb through his hair and approaching. Hah, hah, said I. Just as I thought: "I don't want you to think I'm fresh," says he, "but didn't I know you in Maine?" "Sorry," says I. Turned out he goes to B.U. and works as a milkman in the summer. I politely grinned at the offer of a ride home and "a tour of Swampscott any time" and headed back to the maison with my charges, feeling that human kind still had the right attitude toward life. Probably he's the only male who will speak to me all summer, but at least <u>one</u> did.

This afternoon is Mr. Mayo's afternoon off, so he is playing with the kids, leaving me some spare time, thank goodness. Remember how beat I was after the farm job? Well, all I need is a few days to get used to the routine. I really don't work hard at all, and "variety is the spice of life" – each day has variations on the theme.

Dr. Mayo is here at odd times – a skinny, nice sort of man – and he has a nurse-secretary, who works in his office here five days a week. She takes all the phone calls, and there's an elaborate system of 1-2-3 buzzes, and an exchange which takes calls when he's out. If ever anyone says "No one's home" just tell them to "ring through."

Mrs. Mayo is very nice – and does a lot of the work with me, such as there is – and often minds one or another of the children while I take them off somewhere.

Only one thing bothers me a little, and that is as to how <u>closely</u> I should watch the children. For instance, this afternoon I felt that I was "tagging along" – and wondered just how much of that I should do when she or he plays with the kids. If I wander off, I feel that maybe I'm not doing my job, and yet I would like to sit out with a book if I could.

Well, I'll get up my courage and ask her sometime.

1 – Date supplied from postmark.

Be cheerful, and just hope they like me –

Love,
Sivvy

P.S. Just talked to you – hope no one overheard! Never can tell! But rest easy.

<on back of envelope>
Got package! Merci!

TO *Marcia B. Stern*

Thursday 21 June 1951 ALS with envelope, Smith College

Thursday – in the brief and only too elusive interval between 1:15 and 2:00, whilst infant sleeps, Pinny naps, and Freddy rebelliously "rests" downstairs.

From my airy and flowery suite I am overlooking sun and sea. Longing to be free and able to lie in sun on sand for hours in halters, I sit in my room where I could hear little ones should they yell, screech, or have appendicitis. Pinny is now calling me – "Marcia," she says or "Phyllis." I told her all about you, so she gets nomenclatures confused occasionally. By this time, I could use a nap, too. Back a wee bit weary from lugging almost-two-year-old Joanne over sand and sharp stones. Took Pinny and said Joanne to the beach for most of the morning. There are so <u>many</u> kids around here that I'm going to spend the summer getting names and poppas & mommas straight. Mr. Carey[1] (one of the many Blodgett relatives) came down to the beach this morning with two of his four infants (Bimbo and Lee Lee) and sat and made "nice conversation" with me. Seems he was wounded in the war – face looks grafted. Anyway he's a Yalie from Pierson (thinks J. E.'s dreadfully gloomy – at which I bit my lip and said "mmm.") Seems he didn't have high enough an average to go to Harvard med, so he went to graduate school for a year, then worked a year as he got married, and finally the war got him – so he never went through. As you may imagine, I felt very queer telling him about Dick's success when he asked.

1–Northeast Airlines pilot W. Peter Carey (1917–94); B.A. 1939, psychology, Yale, resident of Pierson College; married in 1941 to Madelyn Noyes Carey (1917–2012); pilot in the Air Transport Command during World War II; father of Tamsin (1942–), Pamela (1944–), Falda (1947–), Madelyn Leli (1949–), Amanda (1953–), Martha (1958–2005) and Peter Noyes Carey.

Feel a wee bit guilty about the cooking angle. Mrs. M. asked me if I could, so I confessed that about all I know how to do was make scrambled egg and cheese. I get "light suppers", but either she or a visiting made (maid!! sp!!) whip up hot lunches. Here's hoping I can take over before the summer's over. Funny, but I also feel guilty (yipes! what a guilt complex the girl has!) when I'm hitting a lull during the day. I'm tempted to carry a book along, but then again don't want to loaf under eyes which might possibly be disapproving. I sometimes feel I'd rather have a rule book of duties to consult than a dubious feeling that I shouldn't ever quite relax.

Upstairs is my province completely, including the picking up angle. Dishes also. Laundry too. I hear that there will be piles of college girls around this summer to help care for the 30 odd kids from about six houses right heah. Personally, as long as you come down, I don't give a d-a-m-n about socializing with all various and sundry females. All I want is someone to talk to – I suffer from silence, unfortunately. We can have our days off together, and I can't wait to pack up a picnic lunch with you and head to a quiet, readable place along the shore. If I could sleep late one a.m. a week, I should appreciate it no end – but I won't unless I get away.

Wait till you see my adorable charges. Joey, the youngest, is the cutest, and usually sweet tempered. Pinny and Freddy are dear (separately) and all right unless they fight, which always is holy hell, what with both kicking, screaming ferociously and sobbing. The one member of the family I don't care for is the little dog who has rawther sharp teeth. She actually bit me, yesterday, lightly on the leg, after being asked politely to stop hanging so viciously on to my dungarees, which she was gnawing, while growling ominously.

Saw your house today – only two white mansions and some rolling green lawns separate us – your room, I hear via the mouths of babes and sucklings, is on the 3rd floor – no doubt even more sumptuous than your present one.

Art coming Swampscott-ward about July 6?? J'espère . . . j'espère.

Letter from Dick[1] was waiting on arrival here, or did I tell you? Just a chatty note. I had the most hideously real nightmare about him last night . . . so ominous it actually frightened. Seems I broke a date (trivia, trivia) with him to go out with a rakish fly-by-night male. On returning from a vile time, I was greeted by mother and Dick, (who had taken Jane Anderson to the Prom.) It all ended by my holding my children (Freddy

1–Richard Norton to SP, 16 June 1951; held by Lilly Library.

& Pinny) in my arms, and seeing Dick recede step by step, never coming back, just shaking his head sadly and saying reproachfully as he faded off, "Oh, Syl." Night came, and I got into the car with my charges, saying "You fool, you fool" and knowing, like Scarlett O'Hara, that playing fast and loose had ruined me. (Hope I can get down to Brewster sometimes . . . just to keep an eye on him.) My, but there is a moral to that nightmare, huh! Twill be many a moon before I flirt with strange males with a clear conscience. Hope you meet Mrs. Mayo's brothers[1]. . . . The one I've seen is a doll, and I would feel quite smug if you captured his fancy! I felt like so much superfluous protoplasm in his presence – (looking very sloppy in my old dungarees and shirt . . . all I've worn since I got here.)

This letter has run wild. I'm sure you'll love it down here. And we can discuss our families together. I would enjoy seeing your good browned visage again.

Bon jour . . .
Syl

TO *Melvin Woody*[2]

Friday 22 June 1951 ALS, Smith College

Friday
June 20[3]
2:38 p.m.

Dear Mel . . .

Here I sit, like a bronze statue, to be galvanized into action only by the querulous cry of either of my two slumbering charges. At last I feel somewhat a master in my own domain. Brazenly I sit in the sun on my own big private porch overlooking the sea . . . and there is something about the achingly bright expanse of blue that makes me feel infinitely placid, infinitely calm, infinitely spacious. I must live by the sea, I think, for the immensity of it relegates man's absurdities to the stature of petty children's squabbles. Something there is about the ceaseless, unperturbed ebb and flow . . . about the vast masses of green-blue water . . . that heals all my uneasy questionings and self-searchings.

1–John H. Blodgett, Jr (1927–2002) and Donald W. Blodgett (1930–2002) were brothers of Esther Blodgett Meyer (1916–2006) and Anne Blodgett Mayo (1918–90).

2–J. Melvin Woody (1933–); B.A. 1956, Yale College; M.A. 1960, Ph.D. (philosophy) 1964, Yale University; dated SP, 1954.

3–The letter was misdated by SP.

Now . . . this letter is occasioned, not only by Marcia's vocal approval, but primarily as a result of her sharing several of your letters with me, notably the last one. So the mounting and unspoken admiration which I had already conceived for some of your previous writing (particularly for a poem called "Civilization") has come to the surface in the form of this note.

Next year you will be going to Yale. Popular college connotations would picture a good-looking blond guy in white bucks with an easy-to-please grin on his jovially ruddy features. But that's not it, not at all. That's just a type – one facet of a many-sided story. One great advantage about the bigness of the lovely Gothic place is that you can be any sort of an individual you want if you've got the strength of character and convictions. Lest this sound faintly moralistic in tone, let me hasten to say that I think you've made the best choice . . . and I'll echo with you that the easy way is to be avoided. Lord, how I despise the rosy path, which breeds only flabby, weak-minds slugs of individuals.

The part of your letter about "white-on-white" struck me with the most force . . . any guy who can write like that should have someone around to keep after him if he lets up or gets despondent. And Marty is the best person I could wish for you.

I also get seething mad at civilization, dogma, prejudice – and so on. Enough so that I've got to spill over on paper. Let me write a few lines of my latest rough sketch, and then I shall fold up my Sheaffer's Lifetime pen, and silently steal away . . .

> "We all know that we are created equal:[1]
> All conceived in the hot blood belly
> Of the twentieth century turbine;
> All born from the same sheet
> Of purple three-cent postage stamps;
> All spewed like bright green dollar bills
> From the same government press;
> All baptized with Chanel Number Five
> In the name of the Bendix, the Buick, and the Batting Average . . .
>
> —
>
> We all know that certain truths are self-evident:
> All of us freedom bent like the pink worm

1 – Sylvia Plath, 'I Am An American'. The first stanza matches a typescript copy held by the Lilly Library. The second stanza is a variation after the first line.

Crossing the street after rain . . .
All safe to spend an hour a Sunday
Meditating piously on the coming chicken dinner;
All made in god's image . . .
(Even Mrs. Maller with the double chin
And the slobbering village idiot
Jabbering senselessly on the corner.)

———

Enough, enough. Some people think of Yale as a great Gothic Martini. It isn't; I'm prejudiced, having gotten attached to the place through a rugged individualist.

Merci for writing the way you do.
Sincerely,
Sylvia

TO *Ann Davidow-Goodman*

Tuesday 26 June 1951 ALS, Smith College

Tuesday
June 26, 1951

<drawing of Joanne, Esther (Pinny), and Frederic Mayo>

Dear Davy –

I'm sure that you could draw the infants alot better than I can, but at least you get the general idea – two girls (2 and 4) and a boy (6). As you may imagine, that is just about the most wicked combination of ages possible!

But before I tell you about the situation here, I want you to know how thrilled I was to hear your voice over the phone the other night! I had the absurd feeling that you were in Lynn or Marblehead, just waiting to come over and say hello in person. Maybe you will, though, before the summer's over! I wish you could get down to Swampscott on my day off (any old time, in other words) and we could take a picnic and spend the whole time down on the beach. It's only about a half hour's trip from Boston!

Now for a little sketch of the place where I live and work and have my being (such as it is.) Well, it's a beautiful big white mansion on a big grassy green hill overlooking the water. My room is three times as big as the one back home, and it is a lovely sunny one, on the second floor, overlooking the ocean, too. There is a porch right outside it where I crawl out to lie in the sun, while the little angels (?) take their naps. The people who are employing me are beautifully rich (according to my standards.) It's a doctor's family, and he has his own beautiful five room office and labs downstairs, which gives you an idea of how big the house is.

Every one around here, in the series of big white houses, is related and the whole place is a part of a big family estate.

Sounds lovely, huh? Well, work consists of leaping cheerily out of bed in the morning when the faces of the two oldest (Freddy and Pinny) poke into my room. I dress them (after much fussiness as to which striped socks match which jersey – never knew kids could be so darn particular about what they wear!) and then bring them downstairs, where the youngest is usually howling in her room with a pair of soaking wet diapers clinging to her. There upon I feed the puppy, slice 7 oranges, squeeze them, toast about a loaf of bread, and, in general, help get breakfast underway. After which I do the dishes (for 6 of us), clean up the upstairs and make the kids beds, do the laundry in the Bendix (the washing sure piles up, as each little one gets a spandy clean outfit to dirty every day – and the baby wets through stacks of diapers.) After these little trifles, I usually do the ironing. In the rest of the morning I look after the kids, or take them down to the beach. Lunch is the hot meal. After which they all (thank God!) take a short nap. By this time I too need a nap, but good, and groan inwardly when I hear them clamoring to get up – the vivacious little darlings don't seem to appreciate the chance to sleep. But, I do, Boy! When little Joanne gets up, I don't have a minute's rest, but dog her wandering footsteps like a bloodhound. Supper I get myself, and by that time I have barely enough pep to slap myself up a sandwich. The baby gets a bath and bed. While I do dishes and get in the wash, the two older ones play act. Then I give them both a bath, and get them in bed by eight o'clock. Really, I could go to bed when they do – but I manage to read or write letters till about ten. I have one day off a week, in which I shall try to get as far from the sound of little pattering feet as possible. As you can imagine, for an undomestic, un-maternal creature like I am, this 14 hour day is a wee bit of a strain. However, I do think the children are adorable (except when they hit each other on the head with blocks, throw plates of hot soup on the floor and perform other such gentle antics.) Also, it's fun living with a doctor – and when his secretary isn't here I even take messages and make appointments.

The one funny and pathetic angle about this deal is the cooking part. When I came, Mrs. Mayo said casually – "I suppose you can cook meat and vegetables for the children." I gulped. "Me? Cook? Heh, heh. Well, no, I don't." Honestly, I told you all the many things I can't do. Well, cooking's another. Ann, I actually don't know how to cook eggs! I've never used an oven or a broiler in my life. Mother spoiled me by always being so capable and never making me work in the kitchen, and do I regret it now! It was horribly embarassing at first, as I scalded soup, tried to stuff a hotdog roll in the pop-up toaster (any half-brained fool would have cut it in half!) and burned the rolls in the oven. My hands are covered with cuts I got while trying clumsily to cut vegetables – only I would quickly run water over them to hide the dripping blood so she wouldn't laugh at me. Finally she realized that I was completely dumb and said she'd help me learn to cook a few things, for which I was piteously grateful. I thought she'd fire me on the spot.

In fact, the first day I worked here I was so homesick that I couldn't stop crying and feeling sorry for myself and wanting to go home. Another thing I miss is boys. Dick is way down the Cape working, and I don't know a soul else – especially down here. I'm around the house all day, and the only time I have to "meet people" is when I'm down the beach. But the sort of boys that will pick you up are pretty poor, pretty poor. So little Sylvia langishes, dateless, while the two handsome boys of the family take their girls to cocktail parties, yacht club dances and sailboat rides. I am a mess, by the end of the day, and feel most unattractive. Sex appeal---wow!

<annotated self-portrait with captions 'hair à la cereal – (the baby throws it)'; 'dishpan hands'; 'dog-chewed sock'>

Well, baby, I am about to fall willingly onto the sack after a full day.

About Jim – I don't like the idea of writing him. But if you say so, I'll drop him a postcard. I'll wait till I hear from you though . . .

Be good and come to see me!!!
Love,
Syl.

TO *Marcia B. Stern*

Sunday 1 July 1951[1] ALS with envelope, Smith College

Sunday

<self-portrait holding a book>

And here is a glamorized version of the psuedo-mater after a loooong day at the office. (Started out to be Pinny's face, but matured into a frowsy almost-adult.)

After Thursday and Friday off, I returned somewhat regretfully to my home at BB. I had worked over a week and a half without a rest, and so really slept at my domicile, which was startlingly silent and peaceful somehow. Best of all was sight of brother. When he walked in Thursday night after work (at farm), I gasped. Not only did he tower tanly above me, but he wasn't half bad looking, and his shoulders are getting broader by the minute. Seems he and his best pal (Rodney[2] – a skinny little guy with a cute sense of humor) have rented Rodney's brother's old jalopy for the summer, and so will toot back and forth from the old farm in style, now. Funny thing is, Rodney only got license yesterday – Warren is just learning. Had a lovely time listening to records and chatting with the two of them. Also managed to call up Dick's mother, who wanted to drive me down Capewards to see him. I was sooo tempted, but said no, next time – being as I wanted to rest and see home for a little. Do him good, too! He's the only man amidst billions of glamorous waitresses down there (last I heard, one from Arthur Murray's was teaching him a few new dance steps!) Absence makes the heart grow fonder ---- of someone else. (My, what platitudes the girl is lousing up.)

If you could see your home, deah! 100 Beach Bluff, I believe – has its own rose garden and garage opposite, wherein Grandma Blodgett picks posies and grandpa stores spare chauffeurs (respectively.) Say luxury, but we're living in the lap of it!

Feel not anxious re my un-domesticity. I'm managing better as days go by. I'll be glad to have you around, though, to answer certain questions which I've saved up. Even turned out a batch of Toll House Cookies today in absence of family and in spite of a fire in the oven, which caused me minor concern.

1–Date supplied from postmark.

2–Possibly Frederick Rodney Holt (1935–); B.Sc. 1961, Ohio State University; mathematician and one of the first employees of Apple Computers; Warren Plath's friend from Wellesley, 1947–53.

If I don't get mumps now, I never will. Freddy just got over them as I came here. When I got back yesterday, Pinny had 'em. She looks like a chipmunk. I myself have sore throat – no swelling though, so I keep silent and go about my daily labor.

One last shot – I had to laugh about Freddie's technique for getting food! He's smarter than I thought. He never gets anything to eat before bed – and is usually in by 8. If there is noise, I am firm – no bribes, either. He came back and said "Marcia gives us cookies. I'm hungry." I laughed uproariously as I remembered your letter.

See you Friday – la – de – dah
Syl

TO *Ann Davidow-Goodman*

c. Friday 6 July 1951[1] ALS, Smith College

Dear Ann,

God, you don't know how good it was to hear from you! I am months behind on writing letters to people, but I'm determined to answer yours first. I couldn't resist, after reading those dynamic pieces by your Boy. Seriously, Ann, I do think he's "got something" – a certain tough sensitivity, if there's any such thing. If he wanted to get down to business, I'm sure he could turn out some tight, neat stuff – but if he won't take criticism, he's really going to be his own worst enemy, as you say. First, he's got to stop thinking he's going to get away with messy and mistakenly typewritten manuscripts. By the way, that love letter was just glorious – I almost cried, because it was the most tender thing I have ever read. I think you're both wonderful people, and terribly lucky to have each other. I was almost tempted to keep that picture of the two of you and say that it got lost in the mail – but little Sylvia's got to be honest, if nothing else – so back it goes, after many admiring stares on my part. Gosh, but you-all look glamorous and wonderful, and lovely.

How I envy your going to art school this summer. I'd give anything to be there with you. I'm so glad that everything's worked out for the best as far as Smith's concerned. I am not only proud at your philosophy, but really pleased that life once again is lifting. I keep telling myself that you can bounce around on rock bottom just so long, until you get so used to the blackness that it begins to look lighter. That is all very fine to tell someone

1 – Date supplied from internal evidence.

else, but as far as I'm concerned, it's sometimes pretty awful to take your own advice and swallow it whole like a raw egg. I am so sick of drifting around after unruly children that I hardly can bear to grit my teeth every morning and trip gaily downstairs to get breakfast. I need someone to give me a good talking to, I fear. Of course, an added annoyance arises from the fact that I caught a cold, and have been bogged down by the usual sinus infection which always comes with it. If I weren't so darned proud, I'd quit and go crying home to mummy – but I've got to earn money this summer, and now that I've got stuck, I can only say "never again" and go bravely about my work, which comes in spurts from 7 am to 9 pm.

As for men, I am only a wee bit frustrated – seeing as I haven't spoken to one for a month. Dick is stashed away waiting (on tables, not for me, honey) down the Cape, and I write him long letters – to which he responds with accounts of how he misses not having more hours in the day so he could do all the wonderful things he wants to do down there. He is one of four waiters among about 50 gorgeous, talented waitresses. Dates, sports and visits fill his off-hours. Still the old dear says he hasn't found anyone quite like me. You have no ideas what that tidbit of information does for my collapsed ego. Eddie is long gone. I am completely to blame, since I didn't answer his last letter.[1] It was different last summer when I had oceans of weekends and evenings after farm work to write him long letters in. But now, sadly enough, I just don't have time. Up heah, I know not a male, although there are oodles of girls from college who are baby sitting around. But unfortunately, girls' company is greatly unsatisfying. Don't you agree that one has to see in other people's eyes that one is appreciated and loved in order to feel that one is worthwhile? I never realized that until now – when it is brought home to me that no one cares how I look or dress – no one says with a word, a gesture, "My, you're not so hard to look at." So after a while you don't believe in yourself any more. You consider yourself an unimportant nothing which is almost fatal. So I would like to get dressed up, to come downstairs and have a nice clean sharp guy waiting at the bottom to take my arm, as if I were an equal, not just a wee bit socially inferior.

Now more about Jim. Honestly, Ann, tell me more about him. I love you to feel you can confide in me without thinking I'll get fed up with a particular subject. When it's anything so special, I love to hear about it. He wrote me a short note which came a little after your letter – asking about getting things published and generally quite light and evasive . . .

1 – Probably Eddie Cohen to SP, [19 May 1951]; held by Lilly Library.

without coming out really frankly with opinions. But those I got from reading his letters to you. I really don't quite know what to write him, but I'll do my best to get acquainted, if you like. I still feel a little queer about it. I'd like it better if you and Jim could double with Dick and me, and get acquainted that way.

As soon as I have a spare minute, I shall look up this Marty Haskell of yours.[1] She sounds nice because <u>you</u> say so.

Wish me patience and fortitude on this business deal, baby, and pray I can turn those damn silver-plated clouds inside out somehow.

Love you – and want to know in details how things go with thou and Jimmy-boy.

Syl.

TO *Aurelia Schober Plath*

Friday 6 July 1951[2] — ALS with envelope, Indiana University

Friday noon

Dear Mummy –

Well, Marcia came yesterday, so I decided since she didn't know anything about when her next day off would be, that I'd take off today. Turned out to be a miserable cold gray day, which soured my independent beach plans. So I went over Marcia's instead and had a busman's holiday while listening to her talk and play the piano – she can play simply <u>any</u>thing. From what she says, I think she has a nice setup, and she loves her children – also has several hours off in the day while they play together or take swimming or sailing lessons. I have to struggle with myself not to be resentful, mad and jealous. Also, she has another young girl – 17 – staying at the same place as a waitress, so she should be kept company. Of course she can play with the older children and swim with them – which I can't do so well with my little ones. But I must control myself – to make the way for pleasant rooming next year.

Live and learn! I decided to stay in bed this morning in spite of children's noises. Freddy came in about 8:30 and said, "Mummy wants you to get up." So I did, and learned that I was expected to make beds, breakfast,

1–Possibly Susan Haskell (1932–2006) of Marblehead, Mass., who went to Bradford Junior College, 1950–2, and Smith College, 1952–3.
2–Date supplied from postmark.

and do dishes before going anywhere on my day off – to pay for my breakfast, no doubt. So I apologized. Not that I really mind. But the lunch and supper meals concern me a bit. I asked her what to do about them, and she said, "It's often more fun to eat out, and there are lots of stores where you can get picnic things." Which meandering I presume to mean that we are not welcomed to get sustenance here. Well, as it started to rain today, I couldn't see biking anywhere to eat out, so I curled up in my room with a pile of unanswered letters. About 1:30, Mrs. Mayo had gone out, so I went down and got myself, under Helen's friendly eye, a sandwich, a hardboiled egg, some cake and some milk – rather guiltily, I assure you. Do you think I have the right to do that? I don't think they care to have us hanging around on days off anyway.

I feel very sorry I don't write more often, mumsy, because your letters are great sustenance to me. I miss you and home and Warren, and wouldn't mind so much if I felt I was learning anything, or writing or drawing something worthwhile. As I said, when there is no one around to make you feel wanted and appreciated, it's sort of easy to talk yourself into feeling worthless. I haven't really thought about anything since I've been here. My reactions have been primarily blind and emotional---fear, insecurity, uncertainty, and anger at myself for making myself so stupid and miserable.

But now I realize that most of my sadness this past week has been due to a sore throat and hard cough which starts as soon as evening comes and lasts till noon. Of course my sinuses have been draining down constantly, but luckily they haven't turned into a cold. I got up courage to ask Mrs. Mayo today what I should do, and of course Dr. Mayo looked at me – but I am now much better, so he just gave me cough medicine and told me to gargle – that the throat would go away of its own accord. So I felt better and rather reassured. The idea of dying of tuberculosis in a doctor's house struck me as highly ironic. Naturally, my listless, headstuffed feeling contributed to my depression, but worry not, fair one, I am almost done with convalescing.

In fact, hard work never killed anyone – and I try to get at least 8 – often 9 – hours of sleep per night![1]

At last I have gotten "paid." Mrs. Mayo mentioned casually at breakfast "I guess I should be giving you some money," so I said that a check a week would be fine. Thus I now cherish a $50 check in my bureau

1–This paragraph is written up the left margin of the page with an arrow placed between the preceding and following paragraph.

drawer. Somehow I feel a little less like a minor under slave labor with that cashable piece of paper at hand.

I am glad you are heading Hampton beachward – would that I were with you! I am seriously thinking of ceasing labor on August 27 – a Monday – and saying I'm going to visit Dick or a friend on the Cape. I would have then earned $250, and think that the extra week would be worth more for getting rested up for school, than would be the $25. What do you think? Of course things might work out so that they'd make it desirable or that I'd really decide to work till September 3. But I doubt it. I want to get my four weeks of family and self-indulgence and health-building before I begin the old grind.

Seventeen sent two brief mimeographed copies of eulogistic letters[1] about my story. I laughed a bit sadistically, and take them out to read, whenever I think I'm a worthless, ungifted lummox – some gal by the name of Sylvia Plath sure has something – but who is she anyhow?

"My head is bloody, but unbowed
May children's bones bedeck my shroud."[2]

xx
Sivvy

P.S. I will grow up in jerks, it seems, so don't feel my growing pains too vicariously, dear.

Love you all heaps –
sivvy

1–Muriel Friedman (Reader Mail Editor, *Seventeen*) to SP, 28 June 1951, included two such letters dated 3 May and 7 May 1951, from readers in Rhode Island and Tennessee, respectively; see SP's publications scrapbook, Lilly Library, p. 13.

2–The first line is from the poem 'Invictus' by William Ernest Henley; the second is original to SP.

TO *Aurelia Schober Plath*

Thursday 12 July 1951[1] — ALS with envelope, Indiana University

Thursday

Mother dear –

A brief brief note to tell you and grammy just how much I love you both! I never got such strength out of an hour in my life. So I came back with renewed vigor, got supper, put the children to bed several times, and walked over to the Blodgett's to listen once to Beethoven's 9th (a choral symphony, and lovely, too.) The three of us girls were very weary, so I came back after ice cream and milk a little past ten. It is now going on eleven, but I feel that tomorrow night I can go to bed extra early.

You know, I really think if I get my numbed sensibilities back again that I can enjoy this even more. The beauty of Marblehead beckons – one day off I will surely consecrate to sketching – probably later in August, when Marcia will be seeing Mike.[2] It will be a treat if I can get some pastels – I am languishing for color. Also I should invest in new water colors – mine are dry and used almost up.

As for Monday, I'll call you probably as soon as I hear from that old boy. Saturday or Sunday.

One thing, I would like to drop in and see Fran for a 10 minute checkup, Dick wouldn't mind, I feel sure, and I'd love any suggestions about my throat – tis now two weeks of gargling and it drags on.

As you have seen, I eat well, and am far from the corpse I might be. So I'll carry on. How about sending me your sponge cake recipe? Mechanics bother me. Like how to get a layer cake right side up & together after cooling face down with out breaking or crumbling. Do you use a spatula? Hands?

<drawing of two pieces of a layer cake with caption:
'How to get this atop this' and arrows point to each layer>

Best love to you all,
Sivvy

1 – Date supplied from postmark.

2 – Davenport Plumer III (1932–); B.A. 1955, Dartmouth College; married SP's friend Marcia Brown on 15 June 1954 in Dartmouth, New Hampshire; SP served as bridesmaid; divorced 1969.

TO *Aurelia Schober Plath*

Wednesday 18 July 1951 — ALS with envelope, Indiana University

Wednesday
July 18

Dearest Mother . . .

Well, it is going on nine, and I am comfortably propped up in my big, comfortable bed, door to porch wide open, so that straight ahead of me I can see the bluegray of the twilit ocean, with the single point of streetlight. I can even now hear the waves above the whish of cars along the turnpike.

My room is so lovely, I luxuriate in it, as with the house. I feel a proprietary air about it now, and suddenly an intuition about many of the nebulous questions which at first buzzed around my head. Many of the housework items which at first seemed so staggering are now mere incidentals, even pleasant.

Really, when I went into the sweltering, sooty heat of Boston on Tuesday (I mean Monday) I felt infinitely sorry for the wet, harried, hot, wilted people plodding along the streets. When I think of going around in comfortable shorts and halters all day, and being visually exposed to glorious scenery, I laugh at my former moanings. I would get claustraphobia anywhere else.

Today I went down to the beach for an hour in the morning with Marcia and five of our charges. After lunch, Pinny and Joey were both very sleepy, so while they took an hour's nap, I lay out on My Porch in a halter and got a lovely placid rest and sunburn. Every now and then I would look across the green tree tops and swoop of lawn to the blue blue ocean beyond. If I lived by the sea I would never be <u>really</u> sad. I get an immense sense of eternity and peace from the ocean. I can lose myself in staring at it hour after hour.

Funny thing. I really don't want this summer to be over. I am really enjoying myself. I look wonderful, too, even tanner. Seems you can always be ruddy, no matter how tan you are.

Marcia brought her one over tonight and we all had supper together, after which we took her Holly and my Freddy and Pinny down to the beach for a twilight climb on the rocks. Marcia and I charlestoned on the sand and ran and played with them – much fun. Both of us are getting along fine. She let me read John Hodge's letter which was his usual impression-making sort. I feel no pangs about his quicksilver interest – or about the fact that he may come to see her this weekend. He isn't worth getting jealous over . . . scatterbrained goof that he is. However, any boy I really care about, will wait a long time before I start to rave about my "cute little blonde roommate." "Forewarned is for forearmed."

I had great fun driving back with the boys – hope the fan didn't break on the way back. I gather Rodney was much chagrined because of the noise the car was making – he is a sweet little guy.

Pinny responds well to much special love. Joey can now say "Syl". Freddy gave me four good-night-kisses – two for my neck, "because it's so long." So I am quite happy about life in general.

Could you please mail me your camera and a roll or two of film. I am looking my best, and would like to record it.

Love to you all,
your sivvy

TO *Aurelia Schober Plath*

Thursday 26 July 1951[1]

ALS with envelope,
Indiana University

Thursday

Dear Mother . . .

At present I am in a tired but amused state. It is 3 p.m., and after a rather breathless day, I have an hour to myself, which I am spending basking in the sun and letterwriting on the front porch off my room. Marcia, all children save Joanne, and the grownups, are going off for supper on the 'Mistral," the 66 foot yacht, so I have the dubious compensation of an hour now, and another one after Joanne goes to bed.

Saturday we all went for a day's cruise on the 'Mistral.' I was allowed to come on condition that I keep a hawk-like vigilance over Joanne. So I did. Never have I seen anything like that great schooner! A crew of three, including a young cook, mans the boat at all times. A comfortable cockpit, with room for a luncheon table and about 10 people is at the back, under the wheel. The under cabins can sleep twelve; there are two toilets; a neat galley, and great sails; plus a mahogany and brass ladder to let down to swim from. Imagine, if you can, clipping along over the blue waves in sun and wind, calmly chatting and drinking milk or cocktails. Of course I felt something like a puppet on a string, dashing after the slippery Joanne who

1 – Date supplied from postmark.

wanted to walk where she couldn't stand up by her self. Much time was spent marveling at the opulence which was so nonchalantly absorbed by the Blodgett's and their kin. I enjoyed chatting with the cook, by name of Warren, who goes to a school of drama design in Boston.

We moored at Gloucester and dove off into the icy water, swimming around the young children bobbing in their life preservers. Lunch -- a chicken salad ringed with olives,[1] tiny sandwiches, homemade cake pudding – with any drink from milk to gingerale to beer to iced coffee was served by a uniformed Warren.

Tan, sleepy, drunk with salt air, we headed home after being on the water from 11-6.

But, me dear, if you think that was an experience, listen to an account of Tuesday, our DAY OFF.[2] After chores, we packed a great picnic, books, bathing suits et al, and headed off on our Raleigh's to Marblehead. After an hour of biking up the sunny, narrow, antique hilly streets, with hollyhocks blooming from cracks between pavement and houses, we locked our bikes together on a dock, rented a rowboat, and set out for the high seas. Marcia squatted on the stern seat, reading aloud[3] while I pulled. God, it was good to feel my arms yank rhythmically, cutting oars through the great green swells. Objective: a deserted island[4] far off the coast – once a children's Hospital site. After two solid hours of rowing, we reached our objective. I must have been in great condition, for a side from a few callouses, I didn't feel a bit tired from my 2 hour stint. We explored the deserted houses, and the rotted buildings, eerie with the echoing mewing cries of wheeling gulls. After an hour we left, pulling back against a strong wind. A five hour journey cost us $1.25 apiece, and was more than worth it – exercise, sun, sea, and experience.

While Marcia was in buying us hamburg for a cookout supper, a young ruddy sunburnt fellow came up to me, looking a bit lost. "I say," quoth he, "can one buy a soda here?" "Sure," quoth I. I accepted his genial invitation to join him in a cooling float, and discovered that he was down from Canada for a week, resting from a series of 22 yacht races . . . staying at the Eastern.[5] Marcia joined us, and the ensuing gaiety prompted us to

1–'ringed with ~~lobsters~~ olives' appears in the original.
2–SP also wrote about this day in her later poem 'The Babysitters', written on 29 October 1961.
3–According to 'The Babysitters', the book read was Philip Wylie, *Generation of Vipers* (1942).
4–Children's Island, off Marblehead, Mass.
5–Eastern Yacht Club, 47 Foster Street, Marblehead.

ask him to come on our cookout and let us make supper for him. So he sportingly drove us out in his own ford to the Castle Rock Beach of our last day. A bracing half hour swim in the crystal salt water whetted our 3 respective appetites . . . after which the sizzle of hamburg and warmed up corn niblets and toasted marshmellows tasted delectable. At sunset we drove to watch a race in the Harbor. Marcia and I biked home, happy to have had such a rich day and a chance to practice American hospitality on a hungry Canadian. Arthur Gordon Stanway, was the name of the ruddy, snubnosed chap.

Yesterday he dropped over for a moment to sample my Molasses Cookies which he approved of. Last night found me sipping gingerale on the old verandah of the Eastern Yacht Club. Unfortunately Gordon got very drunk, as did the people we were with. So I made him stop his shiny Ford and let me drive, while he hung his head out of the window, clearing his head of fumes. I was as usual, annoyed and amused – he was so much fun when sober, but all my wit and clear thinking was lost on his soggy self.

So, I said, leaving him wavering unsteadily on the steps of 144 BB, I'll try anything once. At least the Mayo's could see I looked nice dressed up in my yellow dress. And I enjoyed getting a bit more driving in, also free gingerale, coffee and crackers and atmosphere.

Only casulty: a Manhattan spilt down the front of my white topper, which I shall send to the cleaners.

Dick, by the way, was as bewildered by my letter as I was by him. Couldn't see what bothered me. So all is peaceful on the Cape Coast.

Love you very much,
Your overworked minor,
Sylvia

TO *Aurelia Schober Plath*

Saturday 4 August 1951[1]

ALS with envelope,
Indiana University

Saturday

Dear Mum . . .

Today is what would be termed, in the materialistic jargon peculiar to Americans – a "million-dollar day." It is now eleven, and from the tennis

1 – Date supplied from postmark.

courts comes the enticing twang of ball smacking against racket. In my room sleeps a female weekend guest, still drowsing from a late night.

In spite of getting in at 2 o'clock this morning, I arose before eight and whipped up breakfast per usual – when I think of the langorous life some of these females must lead, and compare it to my working existence, I am moved to a wry smile.

The occasion last night was a double date for a "beach party" with Marcia. Through a guy she knows in Marblehead we both got blind dates. So, clad in dungarees and shirts we sat in Blodgett's living room listening to records from "The King and I." Donald Blodgett and two of his friends were the only ones in the big mansion, as all the rest of the family, including Marcia's two eldest – are off on a week's cruise. The boys were actually nice and civil for a change. They had cooked their own supper and sat in the living room and talked with us until our dates came.

I ended up with a junior at Dartmouth[1] who is a life guard for the Corinthian yacht club.[2] We all went down to the beach, where many other couples had congregated and it turned out that my date had a guitar and could strum out songs like nothing at all. I actually drank some cold beer which tasted pretty good. If it does me no harm, I can get along with a couple of cans in the course of an evening. What think you?

At any rate, rain chased us to the home of the hostess where Marcia made a big hit by jitterbugging impromptu-ishly with her date.

My boy liked skiing better than anything else in the world – but he was so gifted in all physical attributes – such as swimming, football, skiing . . . and Charlestoning, singing, pool playing – and so on, that I guess I bored him, perhaps. But I realized how much of the active life I've missed. Ski jumping must be a great religion. At least I had a great time being with a good-looking male again.

We adjourned to Blodgett's play room where three couples played records. Seems to me I'm relatively dumb about judging people – but an athletic boy like my date said "Oh, I know what you want. Security and someone to tell you adventure stories." Not a bad shot, either. A better judge of character than I by a long shot.

Yet I suddenly envied him very much – for the life he leads. Boys live so much harder than girls, and they know so much more about life. Learning the limitations of a woman's sphere is no fun at all.

1–According to SP's calendar, this was Bob Michael. Probably Robert Michael; B.A. 1953, Dartmouth College.
2–The Corinthian Yacht Club, 1 Nahant Street, Marblehead, Mass.

And so that was that. I really had a good time, and so did Marcia.

Marcia has a few days vacation this week, as her child is going off to join the family, so she'll be going up to Maine, and not coming home. Also, I won't come home Tuesday, as I'll probably be left with two children while Mrs. M. takes the eldest off. Probably I can get off Thursday night and come back Friday night. Thus I could sleep one morning, anyway. I'll call you about Tuesday night to tell you definitely. I could get a bus to Boston and come home at night if Grammy didn't want to call for me. Then, if Friday dawns nice, we could all head for a picnic and day at the beach around here – and drop me at the Mayo's after supper – thus killing two birds with one stone.

We'll see how it works out –
Love –
Sivvy

TO *Aurelia Schober Plath*

Thursday 9 August 1951[1] ALS with envelope, Indiana University

Thursday night

Dear Mummy –

I can't tell you how much our stay at 26 Elmwood meant to me this last Tuesday. You did a faultless job at having the house cleanswept and uncluttered. I love every corner of that dear place with all my heart. I was wondering if my stay in this mansion would sour or embitter me in regard to my relatively small lodgings. On the contrary – I associate home with all the self-possession and love which is an intrinsic part of my nature, and find a great overwhelming pleasure in coming back from my travels in the realm of adult independence to lay my head in blissful peace and security under my own hospitable roof. You and grammy and grampy and Warren are so lovely to be around after long months away from all companions save Marcia. Thanks again for being such a dear and understanding mummy. Marcia loves you too.

Here, I have talked over the end of my stay with Mrs. Mayo, and have agreed to keep on working till the end of the cruise – so I should be home on or before Sept. 1. The few days I can manage. After all, I couldn't walk out on her two days before she came back.

1 – Date supplied from postmark.

I am much more at home here than ever before. Yesterday it rained, and Marcia and I had Holly and Pinny help us make oatmeal cookies. Today, I worked all morning, figuring I might as well get pleasure out of completing tasks. This afternoon was the doctor's time off, so they took the children for a drive, leaving me time for a quick swim at the end of the street plus a chance to read an article on the Far East in the new issue of Mademoiselle.[1]

Hope to see you all on Tuesday morn. If it's not nice, call me up that morning and cancel our trip . . . no sense for you to come down when it rains.

Love,
Sivvy

<on back of envelope>

PS. – How about digging up the black & gold yarn in my closet – looking up the "Shining hour pattern" – and making me an Xmas present –?

TO *Aurelia Schober Plath*

Thursday 16 August 1951[2] ALS with envelope, Indiana University

Thursday

Dear Mum –

All is relatively silent on the home front. Just cooked some corn fresh out of the garden for the little ones – it's a cinch! Boil 20 minutes – c'est tout! Now, after much coaxing, Pinny naps, Joanne sleeps, and dishes are done. I really am enjoying myself – especially since I got those wonderful pastels. Already I've done a big full-sized self-portrait which came out sort of yellowish and sulky, but the face isn't bad at all. Quite traditional. Thought that when I get home I could cut it down. I love the hard pastels – much more precise than the soft – and cleaner cut. Only thing I've got to get over is the "rubbing" habit. I liken it to putting too much pedal on a sloppily played piano piece – it only serves to blur mistakes. Next subject: Freddie. He's the only one around here who can sit still.

Marcia is radiantly happy about Mike. Hope it lasts.

1–Probably 'The United States and Asia: *Mademoiselle*'s Eighth College Forum', *Mademoiselle*, August 1951, 276–9, 359–71.

2–Date supplied from postmark.

A short note from Dick says he may "drop in" Monday.[1] I am cross, because if he could have stayed for the supper hour, Marcia and I were planning a steak cook-out for our males. Oh, well!

You have no idea what a lovely relaxing evening I had after you left. I took a hot bath, and lay on my back in the tub, gazing out at the fog sifting whitely through the leaves. Read in bed, interrupted by Lane, whose dress hem I pinned, – and a small, serious Cupie-doll faced Freddie, who poked his head around the doorway, two large, abnormally pink ears sticking out at right angles from his head . . . cardboard, I later discovered, after emerging from a laughing fit he said gravely: "That was good driving you did. It's good practice for you."

And so, the job enhances itself day by day.

Love,
Sivvy

TO *Aurelia Schober Plath*

Monday 20 August 1951[2] ALS with envelope, Indiana University

Monday night

Dear Mum –

Dick has come and gone again, and this time our encounter was sane and rained-upon. All morning the sun shone, and I completed chores and marketed for hamburg and peaches. I had made date nut bars the previous evening, and so packed them, plus tomato sandwiches, oranges and eggs I stuffed this morning. All in all we made the picnic last through lunch and supper.

As soon as Dick came, before noon, a clap of thunder rent the sky and it began to pour. We ended up by cooking and eating at Lane's house. The afternoon was spent in biking to Castle Rock & Marblehead, getting soaked by another shower, and finishing our food by a roadside in the car. Not quite what I had planned. However.

Conversation was spasmodic, but evidently I will plan to spend a few days down the Cape after I come from work. Only a very few, as far as I'm concerned . . . to see a little of Dick and to get future employment

1–Richard Norton to SP, 14 August 1951; held by Lilly Library. SP slightly misquotes Norton, who wrote, 'No vital message this, but an affirmation of the plan to stop in at 144 B.B.A., S, M. on next Monday morning.'

2–Date supplied from postmark.

sounded out. I am not sold on waitressing. As a means to an end: money . . . it has it's points.

Dick left at seven, and I felt the sudden need for some vicious activity, no doubt to get rid of a few months of physically barren living. Even a regular cadence of weekend dating provides enough male friction or magnetism, taken in small doses, at a distance. And that system can cope with this emotional business. But after not being regarded approvingly by a boy in three months, I have to get rid of my twisted sensibilities by battering my head out on a stone wall. For a moment I wondered what on earth I could do, standing in my room alone. Finally I had it. I looked at the angry gray ocean, darkening in late twilight. So I put on my bathing suit, and ran barefoot down to the beach. It is a queer sensation to swim at night, but it was very warm after the rain. So I splashed and kicked, and the foam was strangely white in the dark. After I staggered out, I put on my sweatshirt and alternately ran and walked the length of the beach and back.

As I walked into the house, my purpose accomplished, I said good-night to the Mayo's who gaped, "You went swimming? Alone?"

They must all think I'm crazy, what with never having a date, reading every spare minute and going to bed early. But what the heck do I care. They leave on the cruise in three days, and I'll be on my own for the rest of my time here.

I expect grammy on Thursday the 30th to pick up my things. But, they have no idea when they'll be coming home on account of weather, so I shall no doubt not know definitely till the last minute.

Soo . . . only about 12 more days! My how trivial! There is so much I want to do, and so little time to do it in!

Love to Warren. How is his social life? I'll work on it when I get home.

xx

Sivvy

PS. Dick brought me a little wood picklefork he made – Also an oddly shaped thing that might be used for a paper knife. I didn't dare ask what it was for. Tell Mildred I was pleased.

TO *Aurelia Schober Plath*

Thursday 23 August 1951[1] ALS with envelope, Indiana University

Thursday

Dear Mum . . .

Only eleven more days and I'll be back home in the nest again. I finally know definitely that I will be home on Monday the 3rd of September . . . probably before lunch. I guess that they want to squeeze the last day of the week out of me. Anyway, I feel I owe myself a brief respite of leisure and no rushing around – heaven knows I have enough to do with the Cape job-hunting prospect, the driving appointment, the 10 minute speech,[2] and the few stories that I must write.

What do you think of the following merely descriptive lines:

> ". . . The acid gossip of the caustic wind,
> The wry pucker of the lemon-colored moon,
> And the sour blinking of the jaundiced stars . . ."[3]

———

Or have I degenerated horribly in my verbal expression?

Tomorrow is the day I have been waiting for for weeks. The Mayos, Meyers and Blodgett's are leaving for a week's cruise – and they are taking Freddie with them. Although he is my favorite, he is also the eldest and the ringleader. Pinny will be much more docile by herself, and will return to the babyish level of Joanne. Also, they will both be in bed by 7. Also they'll have naps. I'll see to it that we go to the beach and generally I'll feel wonderful without always feeling a supervisorly eye burning into my back.

Helen, the Irish maid, will be here too, and will take care of most of the cooking so that I shall feel quite a deal more master of the situation.

I received a ten-page epistle from Ann Davidow – saying she's coming east and wants to see me. She invited me to a great party in New York – said she'd provide me with a terrific date, too---but let alone the absurd money angle, I don't want to move from home.

1 – Date supplied from postmark.

2 – SP spoke at the Smith College Club meeting on 21 September 1951.

3 – SP used words and imagery from these lines in her poems 'Jilted' and 'Crossing the Equinox'.

Love to that courageous grammy – to dear grampy – and my special Warren – and you

xxx
your sivvy

<on back of envelope>

P.S. Yahoo! They drove off just a few minutes ago for a week – and Helen & I are planning for lambchop & steak dinners. Thusly I should learn a little about cooking meat. Joey & Pinny will be my babies, and this mansion my house for a week! Gracious, what a sense of importance and freedom! xxx

TO *Marcia B. Stern*

Tuesday 11 September 1951[1] TLS with envelope, Smith College

September 10,
Tuesday

A gray afternoon, hair just washed, three hours of futile shopping just completed with the awful realization that material things are so desirable and impossible to obtain. A really swish wool or knitted dress is fine, and I dearly enjoy all that I walk into . . . with an extremely sensuous appreciation of soft textures, graceful lines and rich sooty charcoal grays to leafy maroons. Malheureusement, my head is suddenly filled with visions of the coat, the shoes, the hat, the gloves, and the other properly simple, elegant, and accordingly expensive accessories that would really be the thing . . . and I kick myself where I deserve to be kicked for such horrible and mercenary afflictions of wishful thinking. Again I say that in twenty years I may have wrinkles and the physical charm of Eleanor Roosevelt, so what the hell, I work on my mental and invisible assets, such as they are. But that doesn't prevent me from being avaricious as far as money is concerned and wondering why the hell I wasn't born with a whole place setting of sterling silver in my mouth. Pardon the warped tone of this first and miserly paragraph.

To lift ourselves above the material plane: Cape Cod mission completed successfully inspite of 48 hours worth of misgivings. Last Wednesday, Mr. & Mrs. Norton picked mummy and me up and drove us down to our little tourist cabin in Brewster. On the way we picnicked on a typical Cape beach, and I got my dose of Pilgrim history at the Rock, under the

1–Letter misdated by SP.

guidance of "Uncle Bill" who is a History Prof and couldn't see my living in Mass. for all these years without bowing my head at the shrine. You know what that sort of commercialized patriotism does to me, but I really did enjoy seeing what they have done for the place; my self-control is no end strong . . . I didn't burst out laughing once.

My first encounter was Perry. The summer has done wonders for him . . . his hair is a fantastically delicious shade of sunbleached copper, and his tan is also great. From his towering height, he cast a very brotherly glance at me, and I felt that here was one guy I could really talk to. Funny thing, but I feel that if he were a girl or I were a boy, we would have the same Siamese-twin friendship that you and I experience in a way. As it is, our talks are few, intense, and always too brief. My love for him is purely intellectual, which amuses me. He is the first boy whom I can reason coldly and clearly about without any emotional surges. So his company did me great good. I hardly spoke to Dick all that first afternoon wherein the three of us went swimming with the three grownups. Something was definitely tense. It was Perry who ran all the way up the beach with me to get dry, and who pretended we were strangers and had to get acquainted, and who was terribly sweet and sat caressing my tan and making the sort of honest and healing remarks that I had been starving for all summer. That night we went for a long walk in the dark along roads smelling of the salt flats, and under the queer light of the stars. I wondered at random if there was any sense in falling or, more likely growing, in love with him. The outcome of the evening was that we kissed a few times, and both felt instant mental doubts. Perry is also a sort of alter ego of mine, on the male side . . . a very convenient thing to have. We discussed Dick, also Perry's girl, and came away, swearing like troopers to be lifelong comrades and confidants. An odd relationship . . . but.

As for Schmootzy, or however the heck you spell it. We spent the second evening with Uncle Bill, Rit (his handsome waiter roomie)[1] and Katherine, a forty-year-old professional waitress from Latham's . . . all of us visiting Joe Crowley . . . head of a little place (capacity 90) Dick had in mind for me next year. I laughed my head off . . . . Joe is the size of the fat cook on the side of the Sunshine Crackers box, and wears the traditional white bread loaf hat. God, the world is full of peculiar people!

1–During the summer of 1951, Perry Norton worked at Lathams, a restaurant in Brewster, Mass., with senior cook Joseph Crowley and Perry's roommate Richard Newell (1928–); B.A. 1951, Boston University; M.D. 1956, Boston University School of Medicine; 20 June 1953 'Rit' married Beverly L. Newell (1929–); B.S. 1950, education, Wheelock College.

But . . . as you may imagine, the evening was not just what I had in mind. So by the third afternoon, I managed to spend an hour down on a deserted beach with the dear man who came armed with a Physics Book. Somehow he couldn't concentrate, and kept asking me questions about what the summer had done to me. Unsatisfactory. Nothing actually said. For my money our dialogue could have been as decisive as John James Audubon trying to converse with a Dovetailed Kingfisher. So I decided, hell, old girl, speak out.

"I would like," I said suddenly and calmly, "to level your skull with this book; maybe you'd then say something."

"I know," he replies. "That's what worries me."

That night we plan to have a truth talk. He suggests it; two of his friends who are now married had one. All you do is ask questions; the other person answers them as truthfully and openly as possible. The answer to the answer is usually just "Oh . . ." with any number of possible inflections. So it is dark; there are a million stars, all falling or shooting or what ever they do on early autumn nights. There is great silence and tenseness. We hie ourselves to a great deserted open field and sit braced back to back. His voice comes from very far off. Sylvia learns that her letter made him feel she didn't particularly care about him any more. Hence the miffed attitude. Misinterpretations straightened out. Great scene of reconciliation in which terms as compromising as "Darling" were bandied about ferociously.

Hell, I can't keep talking that way. The fact is that he wishes I were three years older, and also feels a strange sense of longing . . . when he gets letters from his two married roommates . . . . We listed all the things we had in common . . . and also faults. The resultant proceedings were tender and quite wonderful. He came to the cabin the next morning at seven, before breakfast, and made mine for me. So that is all fine. Except I'm not sure yet that he is the temperamental mate for me. I wonder if I don't need someone a little less managing and positive . . . a little less uncompromising and more easy going. I don't know if I could keep up with him physically or not. But if I continue going out and meeting new men, I should soon find out.

At any rate, I drove all the way back from the Cape, and Uncle Bill and I got really acquainted, while Aunt Mildred and mother chatted in back like two schoolgirls. The results were that Bill would love dearly to have me for one of his daughter's-in-law . . . which fact made me feel a little like crying. I have told no one about the understanding between Dick and me . . . not even mother. I feel that if it works out, a lot of people will be happy. But there is a long time for me to make sure yet, and a life time isn't something you can swear away while wrapped in a rosy cloud of romance and fire. So I feel that a terrible lot depends on me and my attitudes in the next few years. All of which leaves me convinced of the awful and great implications of maturity and independence.

You know. And we will meet soon again, and chart our courses. I have a feeling that if we really decide what we want, we can work out a way to have it. You see, it is a sort of testimonial of our mutual relationship that makes me write things I could hardly describe to anyone else. I am proud enough to keep quiet, rather than make this business of growing love a prosaic, verbalized newspaper fact. You at least know what lies behind my inadequate statements.

The best with Mike during his visit.

Love,
Syl

TO *Ann Davidow-Goodman*

Wednesday 12 September 1951 ALS with envelope, Smith College

September 12, 1951
Wednesday

Dear Davy –

Boy, do I feel frustrated! The thought of you coming East and heading back without me having a chance to see you really threw me for a loop. You see, I have long since finished my job in Swampscott – your wonderful mammoth letter got there after I'd left. They forwarded it to 26 Elmwood, of course, but it waited unopened there for precious days while I stayed in a tourist cabin down the Cape, visiting Dick. The climax to this unhappy story is that when I came back from the Cape I opened your letter, only to find that it was in the middle of the dates you gave for coming East. Not knowing how the hell to reach you in N.Y.C., I slowly beat my head against the mailbox. Mother was equally disappointed at not being able to have you out – she has heard so much about you, and naturally looked forward to saying hello in person. Say something quick to stop me from kicking myself and muttering, "Damn, IF only I hadn't gone to the Cape. IF IF IF . . ."

And your letter! Glory, what a masterpiece. I was so proud, reading it, that I am going to read it aloud to Dick when he comes home, saying, "see, I knew her . . ." Honestly, I would like to have typed flyers made of that part about the "party system" and send them shooting down from an airplane into all the half-empty cocktail glasses of young socialites. Bravo! I can only admire your process of thinking, Ann, and you say things so cleanly and ferociously that it does my heart good – I think we both talk best when we need to blow off steam about something.

I can see just what you mean about the artificialities in party life, but everything is relative. As for me, I have had such a boyless summer, that I got to lusting for a handsome tall twelve year old who lived across the drive from the house where I was confined. Three dates in three months, all absurd, is not exactly the thing for a frustrated young college girl. When you knew me, I demanded a high powered combination of height, good looks and especially intelligence. After this summer of being a glorified child's companion, maid and babysitter, and washing up cocktail glasses while the husband and wife swished to one party after another, I got a terrible complex that the world was topsy-turvy, and that really the 30-year old couple should be knitting and sipping cocoa on the terrace, while gay young me went wild with the men. To put it bluntly, I need a good dose of tall young men cutting in on me at a few dances to bring me back to my old way of looking at life. It's bad enough to wander about and desire sex, when you are continually in the company of eligible men, but when you are in the company of children day and night you built up the idea of emotional passion to abnormal mental proportions – and get to wondering half-jokingly about just how people seduce husbands anyway.

The only thing that has kept me from going totally mad is Dick, working way way down the Cape, with only Monday off (I had Tuesday.) I lived, as I said, in a tourist cabin with his mother and father and my mother, for about a week. In the morning he would come over before work and cook my breakfast, and we'd go swimming in the afternoons. Nothing happened till the last night, when we both had been rather disturbed about our relationship. So we decided to have a truth talk . . . and get a lot of problems straightened out. So we walked a long way along the cape roads, smelling of the salt flats, under the queer light of a million stars – shooting all over the sky the way they do in autumn. At last we saw a big open field, where we sat, braced back to back, talking. It happened that he committed himself verbally to the extent that he wished I were three years older, and he'd like to marry me eventually, or someone like me. No proposal, requiring yes or no, but just a "let's wait and keep our fingers crossed deal."

Am I excited, blubbering, unable to eat? Hell, no. That's why I wish you were here, or were in some position in which you could judge me and the situation. I wonder very calmly and calculatingly – Do I love him? I know him and his family too well to experience the young romantic exhilaration that I did when I first dated him last spring. But I am afraid that if I eventually did settle down to be a Doctor's wife, I would be sinking deeper into the track I was born in, leaving the world untried, as it were. I mean, Ann, it's the same old thing. I realize in my head that a girl's period of attraction lasts only eight years or so, and that she better make out while the sun doesn't show up her wrinkles, but hell, I keep thinking of how long men can wait – till they're forty (and still handsome and eligible) before picking a young pretty female and settling down. I'm just not the type who wants a home and children of her own more than anything else in the world. I'm too selfish, maybe, to subordinate myself to one man's career – I want to share many and various ones, and yet I would kick myself afterwards, when I got old, and saw pretty young innocent things crowding in my place.

All this is no doubt an incoherent mess, Ann my girl, but it is a rather absorbing problem. After all, it's got to do with disposing of the rest of your life, and you just don't laugh that one off. What do you think about the whole thing?

Oh, I was aghast with delight at the person Ray Moore.[1] Ann, I knew something fascinating like that would walk in your front door! You are so cosmopolitan, now . . . I can just see you with this creature. Tell me how you met the boy – and more about him, including your physical, mental, and emotional relationships, if you care to. I get a vicarious excitement just hearing about him. I didn't know the world made such men!

By the way – if you know any young males who want a personally conducted tour of Smith, send 'em my way!

Give my best to Jim, and keep the home fires burning. That guy is really solid, and I love the way he speaks of you as "my Ann."

Oh, Davy, I die at the thought I missed your trip East. Do write and tell me about it!

Your admiring,
Sylvy

1 – Ray Moore, visual artist from the Deep South and friend of Ann Davidow-Goodman.

TO *Aurelia Schober Plath*

Thursday 27 September 1951[1]   ALS, Indiana University

Thursday

Dear Mother –

You should see our room now, mummy! Even though we haven't got our curtains and bedspreads, I would like to show it to you. After much to-do we finally got a desk – not the same size or color, but a desk, free to use for the year from a kindly upperclassman. As befits, Marcia has the pretty maple bureau, I have the good maple desk – we have Marcia's victrola, and Mrs. Brown is dying the old spreads dark green and getting some sort of white curtains. We've got white lampshades and blotters, and will maybe get a long narrow print of Georgia O'Keefe to point up the color scheme of the room -- green, blue, accented with white. We have colorfully filled bookcases and hope to get plants . . .

Yesterday we registered in chapel, heard Pres. Wright's address and got our schedules in sophomore meeting. In between I deposited $70 in the bank, making a total of $130 there, and bought some notebook paper at the Bookshop.

Patsy, Louey, and I all had our names read on Dean's list – a long, long list, by Miss Schnieders. After lunch, and another meeting, Marcia and I took a long walk across that beautiful countryside in the autumn afternoon, lay in the grass in the sun, listening to the cows mooing, and staring in a blissful collegiate stupor at the Holyoke range of hills.

Lisa Powell has a single room next to ours, and the second floor is so much more convenient.

Do please develop the negatives enclosed[2] & send them along – get two prints, if you please of the picture of me lying on the rocks and with the kiddies – the only ones I will have to prove I took care of infants . . . this summer.

I sincerely hope I will have something definite to tell you about the mental hospital[3] – I am hoping to join Press Board,[4] rather than a

1–Date supplied from internal evidence.

2–See Sylvia Plath's High School Scrapbook, p 57. The negatives are no longer with the letter.

3–Northampton State Hospital, Northampton, Mass., home to nearly 2,500 patients in the 1950s. SP was interested in working, in some capacity, at the hospital to gain experience for her writing. See SP to ASP, 12 December 1952.

4–SP wrote news releases about Smith College for local papers, including the *Springfield Daily News*, the *Springfield Union*, the *Springfield Sunday Republican*, and the *Daily Hampshire Gazette*, as a Press Board correspondent, 1951–4.

newspaper (perhaps also a newspaper if my schedule works out.) As for jobs, one rather unprofitable but hopeful thing just dropped in my lap. I am to represent a new section of the "Stocking Selling & Delivering" idea started by one of my friends on campus. At 10¢ a pair (10% commission) I don't know if I'll get rich, but I should earn a few dollars in the course of the year.

Courses[1] started today, with a Religion lecture at 10 am and a Religion section at 2 pm. It looks like a fascinating, but complicated course. Do send up a Bible from home as soon as you can. I'm using Marcia's in the meantime. We will visit synagogue's, attend masses, and end up the year by reading Schweitzer's "Out of My Life & Thought."[2] Got a paper due Saturday, plus reading.

I'm enclosing my schedule[3] so far . . . of course they can louse it up with gym – 3 hours worth, but my pride and joy is NO SATURDAY CLASSES. Got a lovely letter from Dick today,[4] you too. If all goes well, I shall come home early Friday evening, October 19 – to stay till the 21. See you then.

If you don't mind, I shall write you informatively at <u>least</u> twice a week – plus postcards, if I get time. I had forgotten how full a college day was, and how important every minute.

Do send me Mary Ventura's address, also Ruthie's. Also Warren's.

Marcia is also going to the party October 6 – a coming out party. Boys supplied, I guess. If <u>possible</u> beg Mrs. D.[5] to work on black dress – also send slip. Merci.

After your tea on Objectives for Stunted Students Growth, and a subsequent rest period – puleeze start pounding out more about your sordid friends & relations. Anna and her buddy Sandra will ennoble the Peters Clan yet!

See you soon – love –
your Smith Girl

1–During her second year at Smith College, SP completed Art 210 (drawing and painting) taught by H. George Cohen; English 211 (nineteenth- and twentieth-century literature) taught by Helen Whitcomb Randall and Elizabeth A. Drew; English 220 (practical writing) taught by Evelyn Page; Government 11 (introduction to politics) taught by Alan Burr Overstreet and Vera Micheles Dean; Physical Education 2 (dance and sports); and Religion 14 (introduction to religion) taught by Virginia Corwin and Stephen Trowbridge Crary.

2–German-born theologian, philosopher, and writer Albert Schweitzer (1875–1965); his *Out of My Life and Thought: An Autobiography* (London: George Allen and Unwin, 1933).

3–The schedule is no longer with the letter.

4–Richard Norton to Sylvia Plath, 25 September 1951; held by Lilly Library.

5–A note in ASP's hand identifies Mrs D as 'Mrs D – Ditiberio'. Probably Olga DiTiberio who lived at 144 Weston Road, Wellesley.

TO *Aurelia Schober Plath*

Monday 1 October 1951[1] ALS (postcard), Indiana University

Mon night.

Dear Mum . . .

What a hectic life! Friday afternoon Marcia and I biked out into the lovely pioneer valley, got dried corn to decorate our room. Saturday I took another bikeride with a transfer student[2] – a best friend of Ann Davidow's. The afternoon and early evening were devoted to freshman day – to which I conducted my advisee.[3] Saturday night I went to bed at 10 after talking with my actress pal Sydney Webber. Sunday I went to the unitarian church – found a good minister. I met a great guy[4] by chance Sun. night as I was innocently walking to supper. He's the most handsome thing I ever laid eyes on – a Junior & DEKE[5] at Wesleyan. So I had supper, conversation & a movie with him . . . The most amazing bit of chance fun I've had in years. He's an amazing creature – makes up his own lyric songs, has his own car, & sang his lyrics to me all night. Will never see him again no doubt, but loved every minute – classes gruelling, exciting – love Art $20 for supplies!

XXX
Sivvy

TO *Aurelia Schober Plath*

Monday 8 October 1951[6] ALS with envelope, Indiana University

monday a.m.

Dear Mother . . .

How can I ever ever tell you what a unique, dreamlike and astounding weekend I had! Never in my life, and perhaps never again will I live through such a fantastic twenty-four hours. Like years, it seems – so much of my life was involved.

1–Date supplied from postmark.
2–Edith Hirsch (1932–); transferred from the University of Colorado; married Edward M. Hull on 7 June 1953; withdrew from Smith College on 28 September 1953.
3–Joan Dutton Romig (1934–); B.A. 1955, government, Smith College.
4–According to SP's calendar, this was Donald Pogue Arrowsmith (1931–2012).
5–A DEKE is a member of the Delta Kappa Epsilon (DKE) fraternity.
6–Date supplied from postmark.

As it is, I'll start out with an attempt at time sequence. Saturday afternoon, at 2 p.m. about 15 girls from Smith started out for Sharon. Marcia and I drew a cream-colored convertible (with 3 other girls and a Dartmouth boy.) Picture me then, in my navy-blue bolero suit and versatile brown coat, snuggled in the back seat of an open car, whizzing for two sun-colored hours through the hilly Connecticut valley! The foliage was out in full tilt, and the hills of crimson sumach, yellow maples and scarlet oak that revolved past, the late afternoon sun on them, were almost more than I could bear.

At about 5 p.m. we rolled up the long drive to "The Elms." God! Compared to the Buckley's,[1] the Blodgett's are merely offensive & bourgeois. Great lawns and huge trees on a hill, with a view of the valley, distant green cow pastures, orange and yellow leaves, receding far into blue-purple distance. A cater's truck was unloading champagne at the back. We walked through the hall, greeted by a thousand living rooms, period pieces, rare objects of art everywhere. On the 3rd floor (every room was on a different level) most of the girls slept. Marcia & I and Joan Strong (a lovely girl, daughter of a former headmaster of Pomfret) had the best deal. We lived across the way at "Stone House", a similar mansion. Marcia & I had a big double bed & bath to ourselves in a room reminiscent of a period novel, with balconies, gold drapes, and another astounding view. We lay down under a big quilt for an hour, in the graypurple twilight, conjecturing about the exciting unknown evening fast coming. Joan, Marcia, & I were driven in a great black cadillac by one of the Buckley chauffeurs to the Sharon Inn where a lovely buffet supper was prepared for the 20-30 girls. After supper, Marcia, Joan, and I skipped and ran along the lovely dark moonlit road to our mansion. Another hour of lying down (reminding me of Scarlett O'Hara before the ball) and then the dressing. I struck up a delightful conversation (while ironing my black formal) with the Phillipino houseboy.

Again the chauffeur. Up the stone steps, under the white colonial columns of the Buckley home. Girls in beautiful gowns clustered by the stair. Everywhere there were swishes of taffeta, satin, silk. I looked at Marcia, lovely in a lilac moiré, and we winked at each other, walking out in the patio. Being early, we had a chance to look around. The Patio was in the center of the house, two stories high, with the elm treetops visible

1 – On 6 October 1951, Mr and Mrs William F. Buckley hosted a supper dance at their home in Sharon, Connecticut, in honour of their daughter Maureen Buckley O'Reilly.

through the glassed-in roof. Remember Mrs. Jack's patio?[1] The same: vines trailing from a balcony, fountains playing, blue glazed tiles set in mosaic on the floor. Pink walls, and plants growing everywhere. French doors led through a tented marquee built out on the lawn. There, on the grass, a great tent was erected. Two bars and the omnipresent waiters were serving champagne. Balloons, japanese lanterns, tables covered with white linen, leaves, covered ceiling & walls. A band platform was built up for dancing. I stood open mouthed, giddy, bubbling, wanting so much to show you. I am sure you would have been supremely happy if you had seen me. I know I looked beautiful. Even daughters of millionaires complimented my dress.

About 9:30 we were "announced" and received. There was a suspenseful time of standing in fluttering feminine groups, waiting for the dancing to begin, drinking the lilting bubbling, effervescent champagne. I began to wish I had brought a date, envying the initial security of the girls that had, wondering if I could compete with all the tall lovely girls there.

Let me tell you, by the end of the evening, I was <u>so</u> glad I hadn't hampered my style by a date and been obligated, like the girls who did.

I found myself standing next to a bespectacled Yale Senior. (The <u>whole</u> Senior class at Yale was there – it was just about All-Yale to All-Smith! Maureen's brother[2] is a senior. <u>10</u> children in the Catholic family, all brilliant, many writers!) I decided I might as well dance instead of waiting for a handsome man to come along. The boy was Carl Bradley,[3] a scholarship Philosophy major admitting a great inferiority complex. We got talking over champagne, and I had just about convinced him that he should be a teacher, when we went back to dance. Darn, I said. I can see me bolstering inferiority complexes all night.

At that point a lovely tall hook-nosed freshman named Eric Wilson[4] cut in. We cooled off on a terrace, sitting on a couch, staring up into leaves,

1–Probably a reference to the Isabella Stewart Gardner Museum in Boston, Mass. Isabella Stewart Gardner was married to John 'Jack' Lowell Gardner, and was referred to as 'Mrs. Jack'. SP visited the museum on 21 April 1945 and wrote in her diary: 'I cleaned most of the upstairs today to show my family I <u>could</u> do some work at home. I rode my bicycle to a fire later, and when I came home I had lunch and mother and I left for the Mrs Jack Gardener Art Palace! We were taken on a tour of the building and shown all the works of art. I saw the painting "The Dancer" by Sargeant in the special wing built just for it. I saw the beautiful flower court and climbing nastursiums trailed down the sides over two stories! . . .'

2–Fergus Reid Buckley (1930–2014); American writer, speaker, and educator; B.A. 1952, Yale College.

3–Carl Bradley; B.A. 1952, Yale College.

4–Probably Eric Lane Wilson (1932–2009); 1955, Yale College.

dramatically lighted. Turned out we both loved English. Great deal in common.

Back to floor with Carl, who asked me to Cornell weekend. I refused: nicely. Eric cut in.

Next I had a brief trot with the Editor of the Yale News. No possibilities there.

About then, the Yale Whiffenpoofs sang, among whom: one of Dick's old roommates, who grinned & chatted with me later.

NOW. Suddenly a lovely grinning darkhaired boy cut in. Name? I asked. The result was a sort of foreign gibberish. Upon a challenge, he produced a card bearing the engraved "Constantine Siedamon-Eristoff."[1] (sp?) I subsided. He was a wonderful dancer, and twirled so all I could see was a great cartwheel of colored lights, the one constant being his handsome face. Turned out his father[2] was general of the Georgian forces in the Russian Caucasus mts. He's a senior at Princeton.

I was interrupted in a wild Charleston (champaigne does wonders for my dancing prowess. I danced steps I never dreamed of . . . and my feet just flew with no propulsion of mine) by a tall homely boy who claimed his name was Plato. By that time, I was convinced that everyone was conspiring against me as far as names were concerned. Turned out he really <u>was</u> – Plato Sigouras (or Skouras)[3] whose father is a Greek[4]---head of 20th cen. FOX productions. Plato did the sweetest thing anyone has ever done. In the midst of dancing on the built-up platform, amid much gay music, he said, "I have a picture I want to show you." So we crossed through the cool, leaf-covered patio, the sound of the fountain dripping, and entered one of the many drawing rooms. Over the fireplace was a Boticelli Madonna.

"You remind me of her," he said.

I was really touched. Ugly, compelling, as he was – I enjoyed conversation infinitely. I learned later that he has traveled all over the world, speaks several languages, including Greek and a little Latin. A devout Catholic, I learned that he believes in the Divine Revelation of the Bible, and in Judgment Day, etc. You can imagine how much I would like

1 – Constantine Sidamon-Eristoff (1930–2011); B.S. 1952, geological engineering, Princeton University; 1st lieutenant artillery Army of the United States, 1952–4, Korea; LL.B. 1957, Columbia University; dated SP, 1951–2.

2 – Simon Sidamon-Eristoff (1891–1964); a Georgian aristocrat and soldier.

3 – Plato Alexander Skouras (1930–2004); B.A. 1952, Yale College.

4 – Spyros Panagiotis Skouras (1893–1971); motion picture pioneer and head of 20th Century Fox, 1942–62.

to have really gotten into an intense discussion with him. As it was, I had a lovely dialogue. Imagine meeting such fascinating, intelligent, versatile people! At a party, too.

From there followed a few more incidental people, and, saving best to last, my Constantine. Again he cut in, and we danced and danced. Finally we were so hot and breathless that we walked out on the lawn. The night was lovely, stars out, trees big and dark, so guess what we did – Strauss waltzes! You should have seen us swooping and whirling over the grass, with the music from inside faint and distant.

Constantine and I really talked. I found that I could say what I meant, use big words, say intelligent things to him.

Imagine, on a night like that, to have a handsome, perceptive male kiss your hand and tell you how beautiful you were and how lovely the skin was on your shoulders!

I would have taken it all with several grains of salt had we not gone farther. I came out with my old theory that all girls have lovely hair, nice eyes, attractive features – and that if beauty is the only criterion, I'd just as soon tell him to go and pick someone else and let me out.

He said he'd take me home, and so we drove and drove along in the beautiful night. I learned a great deal about him, and he said the most brilliant things. I learned about Jason & the Golden Fleece – the legend having been written about the Georgian peoples – who were a civilized culture, like China, while the Russians were "still monkeys". I learned about his ideas of love, childbirth, atomic energy, . . . and so much more.

I asked him what happened when a woman got old, and her physical beauty waned, and he said in his lovely liquid voice, "Why she will always be beautiful to the man she marries, we hope."

He told me that I was lovely inside, as well as outside, and when I asked him what I should call him, he told me three names.

"I like Constantine best," I said. "I like to say it, because of its good sound."

"I have a dear Grandmother who is ninety-two years old," he said, "and she always calls me Constantine. I do believe its because she likes the feeling of the name rolling from her tongue."

He sang for a while, and then the bells struck four o'clock in a church tower. So I asked if I could tell him my favorite poem. I did, and he loved it.

Oh, if you could have heard the wonderful way he talked about life and the world! That is what made me really enjoy the dear remarks he made about me.

Imagine! I told him teasingly not to suffocate in my long hair and he said, "What a divine way to die!" Probably all this sounds absurd, and very silly. But I never expressed myself so clearly and lucidly, never felt such warm, sympathetic response. There is a sudden glorying in womanhood when someone kisses your shoulder and says, "You are charming, beautiful, and, what is most important, intelligent."

When we drove into the drive at last, he made me wait until he opened the door on my side of the car, and helped me alight with a ceremonial "Milady . . ."

"Milord . . ." I replied, fancying myself a woman from a period novel, entering my castle.

It was striking five when I fell into bed beside Marcia, already asleep. I dreamed exquisite dreams all night, waking now and then to hear the wind wuthering outside the stone walls, and the rain splashing and dripping on the ivycovered eaves.

Brunch at Buckley's at 1 p.m. on a gray, rainy day. About 30-40 of the girls (and a few men) had the most amazing repast brought in by colored waiters in great copper tureens – scrambled eggs, bacon, sausages, rolls, preserves, a sort of white farina, coffee, orange juice! Lord, what luxury! Marcia and I left, went back to our mansion, and lay snuggled side by side in the great double bed under a warm quilt in the gray afternoon, talking and comparing experiences, glowing with happiness and love for each other & the world!

At 3 pm the chauffeur picked us up. Five girls drove back in the big cadillac. I sat up front, beside the driver, and wrapped myself in silence for two hours of driving through rain & yellow leaves.

Back here. I can't face the dead reality. I still lilt and twirl with Eric, Plato, and my wholly lovely Constantine under Japanese lanterns and a hundred moons twining in dark leaves, music spilling out and echoing yet inside my head.

To have you there in spirit! To have had you see me! I am sure you would have cried for joy. That is why I am spilling out at such a rate – to try to share as much as I can with you.

I wonder if I shall ever hear from Constantine again. I am almost afraid he was a dream – conjured up in a moment of wishful thinking. I really loved him that evening, for his sharing of part of his keen mind and delightful family, and for listening to me say poetry and for singing . . .

Ah, youth! Here is a fragmentary bit of free verse. What think you?

gold mouths cry with the green young
certainty of the bronze boy
remembering a thousand autumns
and how a hundred thousand leaves
came sliding down his shoulderblades.
persuaded by his bronze heroic reason
we ignore the coming doom of gold
and we are glad in this bright metal season.
even the dead laugh among the goldenrod.
the bronze boy stands kneedeep in centuries,
and never grieves,
remembering a thousand autumns,
with sunlight of a thousand years
upon his lips,
and his eyes gone blind with leaves.

Very rough. But I've got an evolving idea. Constantine is my bronze boy, although I didn't know him when I wrote it.

I've got to work & work! My courses are frightening. I can't keep up with them.

See you the 19th.

Love,
love,
love,
Sivvy

<on back of envelope>

Caution: To be read at leisure, sitting down . . . in a good light . . . slowly . . .

TO *Richard Norton*

Tuesday 9 October 1951 ALS (postcard), Indiana University

<postcard filled out and addressed by Plath; type in this font is handwritten by SP, who provided fill-in-the-blank boxes and underlines for RN's replies, which are in blue (reproduced here thus) and red (*reproduced thus*)>

Just check:

Concerning October 13

1. Sorry, can't come –
will take raincheck

. . . .

2. SEE You THEN –

a. Approximate
time: (of arrival)
1-4 p.m.
Possibly earlier.

b. Entertainment
desired:
Your presence. Visit to art gallery, tennis court, wildlife, Hamp's interior, or anything else, as weather and inclination direct. ¶ So glad to have your to-the-point ish letter. Lots of news for you . . . Including plans for October 20. Hi to Marcia.

Yours alone & best,
Dick

<signature: DN>

P.S. Textbooks will come along in the suitcase. Be assured.

TO *Aurelia Schober Plath*

Sunday 14 October 1951[1] ALS with envelope, Indiana University

Sunday 5:15

Dear Mother . . .

Well, I am now sitting on watch for an hour until suppertime. I felt quite weary after dinner today, so I sensibly put on my p.j.s and popped into bed from 2-4:30. I dozed and dreamed fitfully, and figured that now I can go on and face the rest of the week – which is gruelling. But I figure

1–Date supplied from postmark.

that this is just about the time I posted to the infirmary last year, so I am being extra careful. Next friday I have decided to cut my Religion class in the afternoon and take the 1 p.m. bus home. I should arrive, then, about 5 p.m., in time for supper, chatter, and early bedtime: a must, if I am to retain my health.

Dick came up at about 2:30 yesterday with his friend, Ken Warren;[1] happily I was able to fix him up with Carol Pierson, that lovely little longhaired creature you remarked upon on your arrival here this fall. It was quite a feat, at the end of the week, to get such a lovely creature, and I had a day of worry, as I asked about six other people before I hit on her. Everything went off well as far as the other couple was concerned, and Carol will be coming down to the dance at Med School[2] next Saturday. Could we possibly put her up Saturday night? It would only be for a short time, and no more than one or two meals. Let me know.

Dick and I went canoeing yesterday afternoon on Paradise Pond. Get him to tell you about our near spill, thanks to my getting up and falling over in the boat. We missed seeing the Modern Art exhibit[3] up here, but the four of us dressed up to kill and went to the "Yankee Peddlar"[4] for a big dinner. Came back and changed to sneakers, sweaters & twin skirts and went futiley in search of a square dance. We ended up at Joe's,[5] a noisy traditionally collegiate pizza & beer place. All in all, it was a hectic evening.

Dick & Ken went back from Amherst today, without coming back. It was so beautiful this morning, and Marcia & Mike were going for a bikeride, so I felt somewhat wistful, wishing I had someone to share the day with. So I asked Lisa Powell, last year's advisor, to come on a walk with me. (I only hope it's nice enough for you to take the same walk when you come down). Lisa & I talked about life, the dilemmas of womanhood, and the attraction of studies. I had a wonderful time, and drew much strength from her.

1–Probably Kenneth S. Warren (1929–96); B.A. 1950, Harvard College; M.D. 1955, Harvard Medical School.

2–Harvard Medical School, Boston, Mass.

3–*Six American Painters*, an exhibition at the Smith College Museum of Art, 24 September–22 October, 1951, featured works by Richard E. Baringer, Bessie Boris, William Congdon, Leonard Ruder, Richard Wilt, and Emerson Woelffer.

4–The Yankee Pedlar Inn, 1866 Northampton Street, Holyoke, Mass.

5–Joe's Spaghetti House, 33 Market Street, Northampton, Mass. A restaurant and bar owned and operated by Joseph Biondi.

By the way, Saturday morning, before Dick came, I bought a lovely short-sleeved white nylon sweater for $4.98. I can wear it with anything. It's versatile & becoming. Also, I had my hair trimmed & set. Looks nice.

Remind me to bring gray jacket home. Hope it passes inspection. Funny, but I had an intuition to send it back & say I didn't need it. As it was, I waited a few days before wearing it.

I finished one story for SEVENTEEN, at least, for my first English paper. The due date is again Dec. 15. I'll bring it home to be typed and notaried on Thanksgiving. I want to wait until she[1] criticizes it, so I can rework it. It's the one about the two babysitters – the Jewish affair.[2]

My first written is Thursday. How I dread it! Thank God I don't have exams in English and Art. My marks in those courses will have to be brought up by my test-courses, though.

See you on Friday evening.
Love,
Sylvia

P.S. I haven't yet heard from anyone at the party except one Yale freshman, Eric; he is hook-nosed and rather nice. Oh, well, I knew Constantine would melt away with the champagne anyway.

S.

TO *Aurelia Schober Plath*

Thursday 18 October 1951[3] ALS (postcard), Indiana University

1

Thursday 5 p.m.

Dear mum:

By tomorrow they should let me out of here for good. I feel much better, just a little shaky around the knees. Came down with heat waves and sneezes Monday – miserable by Tuesday. So I came up here for lunch & stayed. It's wonderful how comfortable strong nosedrops, hot compresses & penicillin & sleeping pills can make a sinus sufferer. I still suffered, but more unconsciously so. At least I am really resting, which I wouldn't be doing had I tried to stay at the house & endure classes. I've missed about a week's work, which I shall try to make up this weekend. Ugh. Also, if

1–Evelyn Page (1902–77), assistant professor of English, Smith College, 1949–56.
2–Sylvia Plath, 'The Perfect Set-Up', *Seventeen* 11 (October 1952), 76, 100–4.
3–Date supplied from postmark.

I have time, I'll try to send in an entry for that Mademoiselle contest. Had lunch at expense of magazine with 6 other maybe contestants. Veddy nice. They let me up today for a Religion written which I was too groggy to comprehend. Oh, well! Back to bed again. No need to say how I miss my Dick! <drawing of smiling face>

XXX
me

TO *Aurelia Schober Plath*

Thursday 18 October 1951[1] ALS (postcard), Indiana University

2

Dear Mum –

Hello again. I had to laugh. The head nurse just walked into my room & gazed on me with amazement "Why you look wonderful!" She gasped. She had last seen me this a.m., green, pale, swollen, dark greasy hair, smelly p.j.s. I came back from my exam bathed, dry shampooed, lipsticked, and happy. Some difference. I will no doubt be discharged tomorrow early. Thank God. Marcia is going to Yale Saturday and Sunday, so I'll be able to bury myself in work in my room. To hell with sociability. Eric wrote & asked me out Sat. night. I refused because I thought I was going home. I'm sorry about him, but it's all for the best. Late hours so soon after convalescence would be suicide. I may very probably come home the 26th if my work gets in hand all right. Got a letter from that boy in Canada I met this summer – who's working for Colgate-Palmolive – a Babitt if there ever was one – Also, a fan-letter from a girl named Olivia in Hong Kong about "Den of Lions." Old soldiers never die.

XX again,
me

1 – Date supplied from postmark.

TO *Aurelia Schober Plath*

Saturday 20 October 1951[1] ALS with envelope, Indiana University

date: Saturday
time: 8:30 a.m.
place: Browsing Room, library

Dear Mum . . .

As yet, not a soul has walked into the Browsing Room beside myself . . . it is my favorite place to study because of the combination of comfort & quiet. I shall probably spent the whole weekend here, trying to catch up on a mountain of backwork. Cheerful prospect, wot?

They let me out of the infirmary for good Friday a.m., and I marveled again at modern science. I was dosed with privine (a strong, allergy-creating nosedrop) and pyrobenzamine (which left me feeling terribly groggy and slow – now I know a little of Warren's trouble) and sleeping pills. I still have a headful of mucous, but it is past the painful stage, and I feel fine, just a little shaky . . . but really, all I have to do is wait a few days until the last remnants of tissue are shrunk to proper size. I really am glad I'm not coming home this weekend, for I am light years behind in work.

Health is my first problem; work comes next. Next weekend I may cut my religion section to get home in time for supper. I plan to go to bed early both Friday & Saturday, and will have to bring work back for perusal whenever I have a minute. Dick has been very understanding.

The two letters you forwarded were, as you no doubt guessed, from dear old Eddie[2] and a rather unceremonious return of poems from the SRL.[3] I guess I don't quite measure up to Edith yet, dear me! The blow was mitigated by the coincident arrival of the most beautiful[4] two page letter I've ever been written – yes, Constantine did not vanish like a leprechaun, with the bubbles in the champagne. I gave him "two weeks." I found myself writing schoolgirlishly in my notebook: "Dear Constantine, Ever since I danced with you on the lawn under the stars and elm leaves, and talked so intensely about the Georgian tribes, the purpose of life, and the possibility of the world's end, I have hope to see you again to renew the enchanting four hour acquaintance we had." I laughed at myself for

1–Date supplied from postmark.
2–Edward Cohen to SP, [16 October 1951]; held by Lilly Library.
3–The *Saturday Review of Literature*, a weekly magazine published from 1924 to 1982.
4–'arrival ~~for~~ of the most beautiful' appears in the original.

such foolishness, and felt that I would never hear from him, that all the delightful perceptive lyrical things we said were a dream – an ephemeral (sp?)[1] passing of two jaunty sloops in the night.

I'll bring his letter home when I come . . . the substance is that he has invited me to come to Princeton on November 3rd. After a first reaction of a loud scream and a sitting suddenly on the floor, I gathered myself together & thought of pros & cons.

Difficulties:

1. I'll be going away 2 weekends in a row. Bad policy for work. (Redeeming factor: This coming weekend at home will be partial rest & work. I am working every minute this weekend. If I do go, I won't go away again till after Thanksgiving.)

2. The trip is arduous and expensive. I would leave about 7 Sat. am. – takes 5 hours or more. (Rationalization: I have spent no money on social life. A prospect like Constantine is a potential. A trip like that is an experience, an emancipation, a new world.)

Now I am asking you, would you mind my going? I plan to build up into the lovely creature I really am during the next two weeks. It would be my one fling this semester as far as train fare is concerned. Constantine is the one boy I have met A.D. (After-Dick) that I could really become greatly interested in. As far as my future life is concerned, doesn't it bear a whirl?

I run the risk of disillusion, as does Constantine, of a "beer taste" after a "champagne ambrosia." Daylight and football games will be a test of sorts to see if the exciting rapprochement of japanese lanterns and church bells through trees at five in the morning will hold water.

Do write quickly, and tell me if you are in favor or not. I did want to tell you before writing Connie.

Wait till you read his letter!! I hope you really like it

<drawing of female face holding an envelope with "PRINCETON" printed on it>

XXXXX
your elated
sivvy

1 – 'an ~~ephenmer~~ ephemeral (sp?)' appears in the original.

TO *Aurelia Schober Plath*

Saturday 20 October 1951[1] ALS (postcard), Indiana University

Saturday p.m.

Dear mother –

This is just an after-thought to my letter. I have a written exam in English lit on Wednesday, Oct. 31 – after I come home that weekend. I am scared quite blue, because, in our complete lecture course, I have no real grasp of the subject. It's going to be on the romantic poets – Wordsworth, Coleridge, Byron, Shelley & Keats! So I'll have to study Sat. afternoon & all Sunday I'm home. I wondered if you could help me in any way at all, or if you knew anything about said Romantics. My courses this year somehow seem twice as hard as those last year. Also – time is short, my being sick

XXX
Sivvy

TO *Aurelia Schober Plath*

Sunday 21 October 1951[2] ALS with envelope, Indiana University

Sunday

Dear Mother –

If maturity consists partly in making judicious and important decisions, then I am more mature than Methusalah. After all the excited business I wrote you about Constantine, I have decided not to go. The factor of decision was that the English written which I spoke about in the postcard was postponed until Tuesday, November 6 (I'll still study Eng. at home, though). I already had a government written on that Wednesday (7th) which I had thought I could study for Mon & Tuesday. I am really glad that the written was postponed, because it makes my tripping off to Princeton an academic impossibility. Everybody has read Constantine's letter and is urging me to go – maybe I'll marry into Russian society, etc. But wisdom has won the day. I am going to write him a diplomatic letter, suggesting that we arrange to meet soon again. If I do get a chance to see him again, I shall be very happy. If not, I will curse the fate that held so

1 – Date supplied from postmark.
2 – Date supplied from postmark.

tantalizing a prospect before my eyes and then made me say "no." At this stage, it's hard to decide which is more important – possibilities of future life, or present tasks. A balance is sometimes hard to achieve. There are so many fascinating intelligent men in the world. I do want to see Eric & Constantine both again. I'm so lucky I went to Maureen's party. Her brother, by the way, just published a book God and Man at Yale – Will Buckley.[1] Her whole family is amazing: terribly versatile & intellectual. I'm giving up the idea of Mademoiselle this year. Next year I'll be clever & write it before school begins. As it is I'm on a treadmill of backwork.

Feeling really great though. Mucous only in morning. I love you and Constantine and Smith and am richocheting between supreme despair at the one short life I've been dealt (and the endless permutations possible. Which to choose?) and dizzy joy at feeling well & making the wise, if unromantic decision about Princeton.

One thing about sinus – if you feel like a depressive maniac while you have it, there is a renaissance of life when you can breathe again.

Can't wait to see you Friday.
Love,
your incorrigible Sivvy

<drawing of smiling female figure with caption:
'Woman with most beautiful shoulders in the world!'>

TO *Constantine Sidamon-Eristoff*

Sunday 21 October 1951 ALS, Private owner

October 21, 1951

Dear Constantine . . .

Receiving your letter was a reassuring confirmation of your reality. Not that I am in the habit of doubting my own perceptive powers, but I actually had begun to entertain the possibility of your being some sort of a young Georgian leprechaun conjured up especially for the occasion at hand, only to vanish forever at the first light of dawn, evanescent as the bubbles in champagne.

You may imagine that I was much heartened to see that you have an address on the terrestrial globe, also to realize that you are quite mortal.

1 – William F. Buckley, Jr. (1925–2008); American author and commentator; B.A. 1950, Yale College. His *God and Man at Yale* (1951).

By now, perhaps, I should be prosaic and plunge into the task at hand: the weekend of the third. I was extremely tempted to disregard all previous obligations and set out for Princeton regardless, for I would very much like to renew my first acquaintance with you.

However, I have unfortunately already gotten myself involved in plans to go away that weekend. Needless to say, I am both sad and apologetic that former arrangements have to interfere with your delightful invitation.

Please do understand that I would welcome the chance to see you again, to continue conversation, to share a day or two, increasing the affinity evident in our brief companionship a few weeks back.

Perhaps you would care to suggest another time when it would be convenient for me to visit you, or when you could manage to come Smithward. (I must confess that, never having been to Princeton, the idea of the trip overwhelms me. I am the sort of person who enjoys travelling, but is impractical enough in that regard to get lost in subways, or to end up in New York when <u>really</u> intending to go to Connecticut. Hence minute instructions would be appreciated should you ever again want me to make the rather formidable journey.)

Do tell me that you are not cross at my having to refuse your hospitality, and say that we will meet again soon. Maybe a few letters would help in the interim. At any rate, I would welcome any commentary you would care to make on the Princeton scene, future plans, and especially on your own ideas, activities and whimsicalities.

A contrite and yet somehow optimistic,

Sylvia

TO *Aurelia Schober Plath*

Monday 29 October 1951[1]

ALS with envelope,
Indiana University

Monday 4:30 pm

Dearest woman . . . whoops! I mean
Dear Mother –

Today was lovely – cold, clear, and beautiful. Last night, after you left, I unpacked, read my letters, and held an impromptu party to get rid of some of that delicious cake. I was so touched – the same girl who helped me with my formal made it. Marcia came home, then, and after mutual recapitulation, we hopped into bed at 10:30. No real work done, alas.

1 – Date supplied from postmark.

Today and yesterday brought good news, amusing news. Last night, guess what. No sooner than I got settled in my room at my books than the phone rang. "Hello," said a male voice, "This is Ed Nelson."[1] "Who?" I exclaimed, and then remembered that mysterious stranger who called last summer. "Well, finally," I said. "Who are you. I don't know you." "I live on Woodland Road," he replied. "I've lived there all my life." I then remembered vaguely some boy at high school two years ahead of me. "You're not any relation to Edor Nelson, the piano player?" I asked.

"The same," he replied.

That settled, he asked me to a dance at the U. of M. Saturday. I refused, not wanting to stay out late with 3 writtens the next week, but arranged to go out to lunch with him Saturday afternoon & see the horticultural show over there.[2] Thus I only involve myself for a few short hours, and get a good break in study time. (Course I could have flunked out & gone to Princeton. Imagine how awful I'd have felt if I accepted Constantine & found later that I had 3 writtens to cope with instead of one!)

Eddie Cohen may come out again Xmas vacation,[3] & said he had no desire to repeat our last meeting, but would like to say hello if I'd let him. Thought I'd invite him to one meal at least to show him N. Englanders aren't all cold at heart.

Gord Stanway, the Canadian, wants a picture of me. Says, and I quote, "I was just saying the other day to my mother what a lovely place New England would be in the fall. I would like to get some land down there by the ocean – I am quite serious about it."

Well, there's my chance – travel to the foreign plants of Colg-Palmolive, & have a summer mansion overlooking the sea. Jolly, wot?

Ilo sent me a beautiful framed pen-and-ink sketch today which I'll hang in my room. Unfortunately the glass broke, but it looks the same. Odd coincidence, since I just wrote the story about him[4] which is due tomorrow. It's uncanny – I hadn't heard for months, then this, mental telepathy, mebbe.

Also, Eddie is sending me a prose-poem by Nelson Algren called Chicago: City on the make.[5] It is autographed specially to me, as Eddie met the poet one night on the streets of Chi. Ah, me!

1–Ernest Edor Nelson, Jr (1930–); B.S. 1952, University of Massachusetts, Amherst.

2–The thirty-ninth annual Horticultural Show was held in the Physical Education Cage on 2–4 November 1951.

3–See Eddie Cohen to SP, [26 October 1951]; held by Lilly Library.

4–Sylvia Plath, 'The Latvian'; held by Lilly Library.

5–American writer Nelson Algren (1909–81). Algren's *Chicago: City on the Make* was published in New York by Doubleday, 1951.

News office loved my tryout articles – used my lecture cover as basis for correspondents report. Love Press Board dearly.

Tonight I hear Buckley.[1] Wish I'd read book & criticisms, but I'll take notes on his speech anyhow.

Eddie made a terrifically good comment on Constantine – to the point, admirably so: "He reminds me, in a vague way, of someone I know. I dunno, some romantic type critter I run into now & again who discusses love & literature & atomic power with equal glibness & appears and disappears with the suddenness of Mephistopheles."

Not bad for a thumbnail sketch.

If I can only swing all 3 courses into line this weekend, I'll live to see you Nov. 11 or thereabouts.

Only about 3000 thank-you notes to write, so I write you first.

Loved every minute of this weekend,
your hectic Sivvy

<drawing of flowers and gravestone with epitaph:
'Life was a hell of a lot of fun while it lasted'>

TO *Aurelia Schober Plath*

Friday 2 November 1951[2] TLS, Smith College

Dear mother . . .

Just a very quick note on my wonderful typewriter to tell you that several days here have breezed by since last I was home, and that in less than three weeks I'll be seeing you again. I still have a pile of thank-you notes to catch up on, but hope to do them before the weekend. I'm going to high mass, which you will be glad to hear, in preparation for the written next Thursday. As you know, this weekend will be spent in rabid study, since I have that frightening English written Tuesday, the equally ominous Government written Wednesday, and the aforesaid Religion on Thursday. As you may imagine, I will rejoice to get the whole mess over with. By the way, I was amazed to get a straight A on my Religion written on Judaism. Good marks always give me the impetus to study much harder.

Heard Buckley, as I told you. Ask Dick for details. I wrote him about ten pages of vindictive review. Eddie's gift arrived: a lovely thin book

1–SP attended the discussion between Smith College chaplain William Cole and William F. Buckley, Jr, in Graham Hall at Smith College. The discussion concerned Buckley's recent *God and Man at Yale*. SP's notes held by Lilly Library.

2–Date supplied by ASP.

autographed for me for "success in my writing career" from the author . . . . a prize possession as far as I'm concerned.

I'm enclosing a sonnet composed when I should have been reading the mass. It's supposed to be likening the mind to a collection of minute mechanisms, trivial and smooth-functioning when in operation, but absurd and disjointed when taken apart. In other words, the mind as a wastebasket of fragmentary knowledge, things to do, dates to remember, details, and trifling thoughts. The "idiot bird" is to further the analogy of clock-work, being the cuckoo in said mechanism. See what you can derive from this chaos.

I won't be writing more than an occasional postcard for a week now, by the way, but let me know if you can come up with the O'Neils.[1]

Love,
Sivvy

SONNET[2]

All right, let's say you could take a skull and break it
The way you'd crack a clock; you'd crush the bone
Between steel palms of inclination, take it,
Observing the wreck of metal and rare stone.

This was a woman: her loves and stratagems
Betrayed in mute geometry of broken
Cogs and disks, inane mechanic whims,
And idle coils of jargon yet unspoken.

Not man nor demigod could put together
The scraps of rusted reverie, the wheels
Of notched tin platitudes concerning weather,
Perfume, politics, and fixed ideals.

The idiot bird leaps up and drunken leans
To chirp the hour in lunatic thirteens.

1–Francis P. and Helen Gibson O'Neil, parents of SP's classmate Patricia O'Neil Pratson from Wellesley.
2–Published in *Collected Poems* under the title 'Sonnet: To Eva'.

TO *Aurelia Schober Plath*

Saturday 3 November 1951[1] ALS (postcard), Indiana University

Saturday 4 pm

Dear mum –

Just got back from my 3 hour "break" with the mysterious Ed Nelson. I sure go for queer characters – he's shorter than I, homely, with a lovely tenor voice and a future in poultry genetics, of all things. I spend a rainy three hours having lunch with him, tracking through stock yards, patting dear baby cows, young colts and kittens. Never came so close to animal life – really fun! The horticulture show was breathtaking, and Mr. Nelson bought me a little corsage. The trip was, as far as I'm concerned, a case of materialistic acumen on my part. I saw Ruthie for a lovely chat, while Edor dociley waited below – also, I've got a ride home with him on Thanksgiving in his little red Crosley. Not bad, if I do say, much cheaper and quicker than bus. It is now snowing into slush, and I must plunge into my week of intensive study without much more ado. Just pray I live through next week. Eric is coming next Sat. night. Whoopee! Will I see you?

XX
Siv

TO *Aurelia Schober Plath*

Thursday 8 November 1951[2] ALS (postcard), Indiana University

Thursday 6 pm

Dear Mum!

Whee! I'm the happiest girl in the world. I just got through 3 horrible consecutive writtens, and haven't felt human for a whole week. What with cramming my head with charts & data all last weekend and up to 12 every night till now. Marcia & I picked out THE DRESS for me this afternoon. Yup! It's a basic, beautiful Charcoal gray jersey that you can do anything with – at one of the best simplicity shops in town – only $23!!! It'll last me all my life. Wait till you see it. Also, if you want a shock, buy several issues of the Nov. 6 & 7 Monitor[3] & look guess where.

1–Date supplied from postmark.

2–Date supplied from postmark.

3–Sylvia Plath, 'As a Baby-Sitter Sees It', *Christian Science Monitor*, 6 November 1951, 19; and Sylvia Plath, 'As a Baby-Sitter Sees It', *Christian Science Monitor*, 7 November 1951, 21.

I thought I should emphasize art & writing "ability" for our Elks[1] friends. So I sacrificed my mountain day in writing & sketching what you see before you.

XX
Siv

TO *Aurelia Schober Plath*

Tuesday 13 November 1951[2] TLS with envelope, Indiana University

Dear mother.

After nine on a Tuesday night it is, and in spite of the fact that I owe ten people letters, I must needs talk to my favorite human beings for a little while. Writtens are over until the after-vacation seige in early December. I will briefly summarize the events of the past days.

A check of fifteen dollars arrived from the Monitor, which generosity prompted me to buy a beautiful pair of red leather pumps to go with my new dress . . . for $8.95. I also bought a matching lipstick and a red belt. I looked very nice when Eric came Saturday.

Friday night I took Louise Giesey to our Unitarian Young people's meeting where we heard and discussed the records of T. S. Eliot's "Cocktail Party."[3] A provocative evening, as you may imagine.

Saturday morning I shopped. Eric and his friend arrived in the middle of a clear cold afternoon. We took a walk around campus and had a delightful dinner at Rahar's. After which we went to free movies at Sage Hall[4] to see O'Niel's "Long Voyage Home" and "Anna Christie"[5] starring none other than the great Greta Garbo. They were both oldies, but extremely interesting, if over dramatized. Rahar's again, with dancing. Got a letter from Eric today saying what a nice time he had.

Sunday I wrote an essay for English on a nebulous walk down a street at night.[6] I realized with horror today that it was much too seamy to pass

1–The Elks National Foundation, to which SP applied for the Most Valuable Student scholarship in 1952.

2–Date supplied from postmark.

3–American poet, writer, critic, and publisher Thomas Stearns Eliot (1888–1965); his play *The Cocktail Party* (1949).

4–Sage Hall at Smith College with an auditorium seating 700 persons.

5–Film versions of Eugene O'Neill's *Long Voyage Home* (1940) and *Anna Christie* (1930)

6–Sylvia Plath, 'Suburban Nocturne'; held by Lilly Library.

in, and so have composed another one about my summer job[1] on the typewriter tonight. Much more concrete and sarcastic.

I'm enclosing another sonnet about the mechanical age as versus the natural world.[2] The green and red lights of traffic signals are equated to the poetic symbols of jade and garnet. The recurring images of neon lights and cars in the first verse are meant to express the bright artificial mechanism of the twentieth century world. The wind, symbolizing nature, is shut out from the mechanical cruel city. Wistful imagination is excluded by scornful logic. The naturalness of the pagan girl in sunlight, the kings and dragon, express again the theme of nature and imagination. The last two lines sum up the whole. Note the new rhymes in my experience . . . "garnet" and "car yet", "olives" and "all gives" . . . more attempts to get away from being continually hackneyed.

Can't believe I see you in ONLY ONE WEEK.

All my love,
Sylvia

TO *Aurelia Schober Plath*

Saturday 17 November 1951[3] ALS (postcard), Indiana University

Sat. am.

Dear mum –

This purports to be a relatively quiet weekend – no date, and Marcia is off to dartmouth. I have begun to catch up on sleep and to keep on working. By the way, among the many things I must try to do over vacation is write a 1500 word paper on Unitarianism,[4] emphasizing history, beliefs, customs. Any books or pamphlets you can line up for me on the subject will be much appreciated. Only got B+ on my last Religion written. I plan to go out with Dick Wed. night – to a party at HMS. Edor hasn't called yet, so I hope I still get a ride. Funniest thing: While covering Far Eastern lecture[5] for press Board, on International Students Day, a good looking

1–Sylvia Plath, 'Somebody and We'; held by Lilly Library.

2–Sylvia Plath, 'Sonnet: To Time'; see *Collected Poems*, 311. The poem is no longer with the letter.

3–Date supplied from postmark.

4–Probably Sylvia Plath, 'Unitarianism: Yesterday and Today', dated 8 December 1951; held by Lilly Library.

5–The lecture was given by Sir George Samson, director of the East Asian Institute at Columbia University. An unattributed article by SP resulted: 'Says Capitalism May Save Asia', *Daily Hampshire Gazette*, 16 November 1951, 10.

blonde guy[1] sat down by me (of all the 300 other females – what luck.) Turned out he came over from Frankfurt 7 weeks ago – goes to Yale Law. We had ice cream & talked.

XXX
Sivvy

TO *Hans-Joachim Neupert*

Saturday 17 November 1951 TLS (photocopy), Smith College

Saturday, November 17

Dear Hans . . .

Again I am back at Smith College, well in the middle of my second year. It is already late autumn, and as you asked, I am writing before the first snow falls. The air is cold and thick with clouds, and the leaves are long fallen. From the window of my room I can see the distant hills through the bare trees, a smoke-purple in the distance. I dread the coming winter in a way . . . because there will be so many months of sleet and mud before the spring.

I am now nineteen, and suddenly I am struck by the fact that I have been living for almost twenty years. Does that not sound like a venerable old age? And then I wonder what I have been doing with my life, and whether I will live out my days in normal sequence, or whether my brother, and all the boys I know will be killed, and the land destroyed. I sometimes wish that I had been born in some obscure corner of the world . . . In Iceland, perhaps, or some South Sea Island, where one could live a normal life without being part of the great insane world struggles.

Believe me, most of the people in America don't want war. Especially the young people are still hoping that something will happen, that something will be done to avert crises. What is the opinion of your young German friends of the battle going on in Korea? Whose side do they take? I am disgusted with the "truce" talks, which have been getting nowhere. All they do is quibble over artificial boundaries and dirty, bomb blasted soil. If people could only realize that it is not "saving face" that matters, but only saving lives. I am interested to hear the German opinions of the American tactics. I should not imagine that they are very pleased with us, or with the way things are going. I do want to know how the sentiment is in Germany, and you are the person best equipped to tell me at first hand.

1 – According to SP's calendar, he was Herbert Günther Jovy from Wiesbaden, West Germany.

The newspapers are so impersonal . . . one never knows what to believe in them. Let me know also what plans there are for unification of Germany. Do you talk about it much? How is the government in your zone run? There are so many things that I am curious about, Hans. Sometimes I wish I could talk to you face to face, and have a real conversation.

I think about you often, and wonder how your work is coming. You say you start again schooling for five more years . . . and your practicant work sounded very hard and demanding. Just what exactly will you be learning in the next years? Will you be keeping up with English?

My job this summer taking care of the three little children, age 2, 4, and 6, proved at the same time difficult and enjoyable. The difficult part was that I had to do all sorts of laundry, ironing and cooking as well as caring for the lively and mischievous youngsters. Their parents were extremely wealthy, and did not seem to care too much about how much they saw their children, only as long as they were not too noisy. My room was beautiful, though, with a view of the ocean and a great porch overlooking the lawns which sloped down to the sea. And somehow the ocean gave me great comfort when I felt lonely or tired from the children's tantrums. I enjoyed it on stormy days when it was gray and forbidding beyond the rainwet windows, and on glittering sunny days, when the blue was so bright that it made me almost want to cry. You know what I mean.

I too am using the typewriter, as you can see, and hope that it will make my printing clearer to you also. If I use it enough, I hope I can write really fast. Practice is all it takes, and it is very convenient, especially in typing papers.

The other night I went to one of the evening lectures here for Press Board, an organization on campus that covers speeches and news for the out of town papers. It was a nasty wet evening, and I felt somewhat weary, sitting in the auditorium full of girls and teachers who had come to brave the weather, when all of a sudden a very nice young man came to sit beside me. He was a young Law student, and had just come over from Germany seven weeks ago, from the Frankfurt area. It was International Students Day at Smith, and foreign students from all over New England had come up to celebrate the day here. It was just chance that made me meet this boy, and I was foolish enough to ask him if he knew you. Now that I think of it, it was a silly thing to do, as Germany is a great big place, and there would be hardly a chance of his knowing you. But I asked him anyway.

Do you have much chance for social life? I was wondering if there were dances and so on even while you are working hard at school to relieve the routine. No doubt your young people are much like ours. I think so, judging from this boy I met.

It is a Saturday night, and I should be doing all the work I have piled up beside me . . . Government, Religion, English literature, Art. But I write to you instead. Outside a clear cold November moon is shining behind the thin black lace design of the naked tree branches . . . very lovely, very nostalgic somehow.

And so I hope to hear from you when you are not busy. Somehow I hope we never stop writing, even if there are long spaces of silence in between our letters, which I hope there won't be. I like to feel that I have a contact with someone my own age, someone who thinks much as I do about life and the world.

Thank you for being such a delightful correspondent . . .

yours with
best wishes,
Sylvia

TO *Marion Freeman*

Saturday 17 November 1951[1] — ALS with envelope, Smith College

November 18,

Dear Aunt Marion –

You don't know how touched I was to hear from you the other day. It was dear of you to take the time to write me about the article in the Monitor, and I did so appreciate it.

Ruthie probably told you that I had a chance to drop over and see her a few Saturdays ago. It was wonderful to see her room and house,[2] and to have time for a chat. She certainly is growing to be a beautiful young woman, and she looked so happy! I don't blame her, with her lovely friends and her pretty room with the breath-taking view. I could hardly pull myself away from staring out the window – what gorgeous countryside!

I told Ruthie, and I want to take this opportunity to tell you too, how much I love "Come One, Come All!" The illustrations alone are exquisite, and the book as a whole is an impressive addition to my slowly growing "library."

1–Letter misdated by SP; date supplied from postmark.

2–Ruth Freeman lived in Lewis Hall.

I had a chance to meet the friend Ruthie brought home with her, and thought that they must get along quite well – both keen and attractive and full of wit.

Best wishes for a rich, full Thanksgiving holiday. My love to all –

Affectionately,
Sylvia

TO *Aurelia Schober Plath*

Monday 26 November 1951[1] ALS (postcard), Indiana University

Monday

Dear Mother –

Trip back last night swift & cramped, but otherwise O.K. We left Wellesley a little after 8 and got here a few minutes before 11. Marcia & I were in bed by 11:30. One of my friends in the house (Betsy Whittemore – the tall girl who helped me make my brown skirt) got engaged over vacation & will get married in June. I was just amazed. She's my age! The slush makes life even more annoying – what with all the work. Providentially my gym schedule is changed for the better – so next week my time will be well arranged for work at least. Crew MTW at 3 is changed to Individual gym Thursday at 9, Bowling Thu & Fri at 12. Which fills in my end of the week schedule but lightens, thank god, the beginning. Hope the meet Sun was good.

Love to all –
Sivvy

TO *Aurelia Schober Plath*

Sunday 2 December 1951[2] ALS (postcard), Indiana University

Dear Mother,

Sunday morning it is, and I am shut up in my little room with a horrible prospect of working on religion all day. The paper is due next Friday, but I have an exam this Wed & next Monday (a week away) both of which I must study for like fury. No rest for the weary – I am so sleepy, too. Yesterday I spent 2 hours in the afternoon decoration for a small dance they were having in the crew house. Eric came at 4, and we went

1 – Date supplied from postmark.
2 – Date supplied from postmark.

to a bar in town (my first bar), observed people and discussed poetry and art – after which we took an hour walk & talked about God and moral standards. Lamb chop dinner at Rahar's – and "Oliver Twist."[1] All in all, he is a nice homely baby. For some reason, life seems very depressing at present. No doubt it is because I have so much plodding work to do ahead of me that I can't really be free a minute without feeling guilty. Also, am rather worn. Ah me. No sonnets till Xmas vacation. Cheerio –

Love,
Sylvia

TO *Aurelia Schober Plath*

Wednesday 5 December 1951[2] — ALS with envelope, Indiana University

Wednesday

Dear mother –

With two weeks of solid drudgery ahead, I was feeling pretty awful as the week ground into motion. And lack of sleep, plus my period, led to a great depression. But somehow, when I feel most bereft and disillusioned, the unexpected always happens. In this case, it was the letters which kept me going. Tonight, at last, I will go to bed early. Really. Imagine – I had an English written this morning, a press Board assignment,[3] too, and in the next two days I have the phenomenal job of writing that huge research Religion paper, due Friday. From which I have to plunge into studying for the Government written Monday. (Had a lovely conference with my teacher & convinced him that I was getting a lot out of the course, and only want to express perfectly what I know in my head. Got to really come through this time.) To top it off, I have a creative writing paper[4] due the friday before house dance, as well as a three weeks art project which I haven't even begun yet. Not to mention my being co-chairman of decorations for House dance. Not a great office, but it will look good on the Elks list: Also, I am on the decoration committee for Charity Ball (in February) and entertainment Chairman for the Sophomore Prom. (In April.)

1–David Lean's film version of *Oliver Twist* (1948) was shown at the Academy of Music, Northampton, Mass.

2–Date supplied from postmark.

3–An unattributed article, 'Smith Girls to Take Exams in Civil Service', *Daily Hampshire Gazette*, 5 December 1951, 3.

4–Sylvia Plath, 'Mary Ventura', dated 14 December 1951; held by Lilly Library.

So glad Warren has an invitation to the Xmas Cotillion. I suggest he write to the girl of his choice immediately. At high school, people have the advantage of seeing each other & talking over invitations. He should make the most of his handicaps of distance & get to work, so he won't futiley be calling up prospective dates a few days before the dance.

Eric writes that he is falling in love with me, which is heartening, although somewhat a dead-end as far as I am concerned. He called me up the Sunday after we went to make sure I was feeling all right – I had gone in an hour early that Saturday, saying I felt tired. We had a great long discussion on moral behavior on Saturday. Believe it or not, he said he wanted to tell me something that he had never told anyone else. Guess what! So I asked him about his one experience with a prostitute, and was much interested to learn what sort of a personality the woman had, also a little about the procedure in houses of "ill fame." Said Eric, "You know, you aren't like other girls. You understand, and aren't shocked or anything." At that point I burst into silent laughter at the irony of the affair. The fact was, that I don't care a whit about him, and so was intelligently curious merely – a case history sort of thing.

Gordon – the rich Canadian wrote an appreciative letter on receiving the picture of me. I have a hunch he is working for a bid to a Smith dance, Just a hunch. Wouldn't it be exciting to have a date fly down from Toronto! Heh heh.

The best news was from dear Constantine whom I thought I'd never hear from again after the last two refusals. I am seriously considering a daring scheme – to evolve a working attempt to remedy the date situation. As far as I'm concerned, Dick is still a nice brilliant handsome guy, but Constantine looks promising. So what say I go to New Jersey for the first few days of vacation so I can date my beautiful Russian in New York? I haven't spent any money on weekends all semester, except the one coming home. Shall I write to Constantine and take him up on his offer to withdraw all his money from the bank to take me to a Russian restaurant for dinner, dancing, and deep intellectual communion? I can't afford to miss him. I do adore him – and want to corroborate the dream by seeing if he stands up under the test of daytime wear. I need a lovely, honest man quite badly. I'd be home that weekend, no doubt – about the 21st. It is all nebulous now – so what do you think? I have gone through enough little hells this Thanksgiving – shall I try to inject Xmas with Russian flavor –

Love your peregrinating daughter
XX
Sivvy

TO *Constantine Sidamon-Eristoff*

Saturday 8 December 1951 ALS, Private owner

<drawing of holly>

December 8,

Dear Connie . . .

Sitting on the floor I am, in Haven House livingroom, with the jazz notes of the piano beating into the back of my consciousness, and somehow in spite of the plethora of papers and writtens due in the next week, I feel a sudden surge of gaiety . . . Christmas-tinged already. The commercial holiday spirit has been evident in store windows ever since Thanksgiving, but I have remained relatively untouched by it until now.

New England has bestowed upon us a benevolent cover of iced slush, and somehow I can't believe in springtime any more. After just so many days of bare trees and sullen gray skies, one begins to think that is the only reality there ever was. You know what I mean? <drawing of seated female writing a letter beginning "Dear Connie"> No doubt all this sounds a bit vague, but I feel the same way when I think about the pyramids in Egypt or the balmy islands in the South seas: I want to travel there just to make sure they really exist after all, and weren't made up by some imaginative historian.

All of which is neither here nor there – and goes to show my facility (regrettable, perhaps) for embroidering in stream-of consciousness style at the slightest provocation.

Much there is that I want to tell you. Among other things, that I am extremely pleased with my courses this year – (in spite of my complaining about work, etc.) Creative Writing and painting are my favorites – I'll tell you about the delightfully peculiar female[1] I have for C. W. – seems she writes murder mystery after murder mystery – has been in the army, worked in factories, lived in sin, or something equally delicious, in Greenwich Village. <drawing of wine bottle, glass, and fruit> At any rate, she is a compelling, ugly, dynamic character – quite a challenge to slave under.

What I <u>really</u> have been wanting to tell you is something quite lovely. To whit: I have been invited to spend a few days with my roommate's family at the beginning of Christmas vacation. Since she lives, heureusement,

1–Evelyn Page, co-author with Dorothy Blair of *Beacon Hill Murders* (1930), *Back Bay Murders* (1930), *Cat's Paw* (1931), *Murder Among the Angells* (1932), and *In the First Degree* (1933), all published as by 'Roger Scarlett'. In World War II, Page was an aircraft inspector and served in the Women's Army Corps.

in South Orange, New Jersey, I will be able to get to New York quite easily, you see. I'll be staying at her house from Tuesday night, December 18th, to Friday, December 21st. Thus, if you would like to see me any time during those days – let me know, do, so I can plan. One slight item – I have been to New York all of once in my career, and as I told you, I am not the most practical creature as far as directions are concerned. <drawing of skyscraper with clouds and an astonished female holding a suitcase> So do tell me you will be able to see me sometime during those days – and let there be time for us to relax and talk . . . and talk . . . Also, don't let me get lost in the City.

Seriously, I want very much to get to know you. It is hard, somehow, to really become acquainted with someone in college, what with the gay, often superficial party system of weekending . . . but I feel that the rapport established at that sparkling occasion last fall might well be renewed. I hope so.

Let me know, my gallant Georgian, if and when I shall see you.

Till then,

Sylvia

P.S. Cartoons are expressly to cheer the somewhat nostalgic mood that one young male was in when he last wrote.

<drawing of hand holding a pen, writing the letter "S">

TO *Aurelia Schober Plath*

Sunday 9 December 1951[1] ALS (postcard), Indiana University

Sunday

Dear mum . . .

Well, I have decided! I am going to visit Marcia from Dec 18-21. So Ill be home sometime that Friday. I'm so excited – Christmas shopping in New York – and I hope to buy Dick a Picasso print for his room. Also, Mrs. B. has 3 tickets for "Don Juan in Hell."![2] I have written Constantine Sidamon-Eristoff to tell him I'll take him up on his "Russian restaurant offer." . . drew several colored sketches[3] – hope that gets him to live up to his promise. I have been to bed at ten the last two nights – no longer feel tired, and plan to keep it up – Gov. exam tomorrow. – Well, if I study

1–Date supplied from postmark.

2–Performed at the New Century Theatre, then at 932 Seventh Avenue at W. 58th Street, New York.

3–See SP to Constantine Sidamon-Eristoff, 8 December 1951.

9 hours today, I should get a "B." Miss Page liked "To Eva"[1] – even wants me to make an appointment about it to talk to her. Do call Phil[2] about Warren – say I want to have him & the German guy over for dinner during vacation – after the 21st. Mrs. Freeman sent me a great delicious box of fudge, cookies, & brownies. Her card bore the pious quote: "The home is woman's paradise." No doubt she considers herself a missionary, converting the wayward

XXXXXXX
S.

TO *Aurelia Schober Plath*

Thursday 13 December 1951 ALS with envelope, Indiana University

December 13

Dear Mother –

Boy, I've never been so busy in my life! Just finished typing a fifteen page theme for creative writing which took me hours to toss together. The only trouble is that I would like to give it more than the usual rough draft, and rewriting. Time however, does not allow any such meticulous composition. The best I can do is rework after I've gotten corrections from good old Miss Page herself. This latest is about Mary Ventura – how successful as a rough try, I don't know.

Tonight we're having house meeting – late again tonight – to wind up business before Christmas vacation. I plan to go to bed early tomorrow to make ready for house dance weekend – Dick wrote[3] me the cheery news that he has come down with a cold (no doubt caught from his date last weekend.) So I shall keep my distance.

I have been forced to drop my work in courses where I've already had writtens so I can keep up with work in other subjects. For example, I have a great art assignment due Monday – which I will have to work on all tomorrow afternoon and evening and Sunday, after Dick goes. So I am

1 – Probably Sylvia Plath, 'Sonnet: To Eva'.

2 – Probably Philip Livingston Poe Brawner (1931–); B.A. 1953, Princeton University; dated SP in 1951–2. Brawner was vice-president of American Whig-Cliosophic Society, Princeton's debating club, which also published the *Nassau Literary Magazine*. The Brawner family, who moved from Charleston, West Virginia, to Wellesley in 1950, lived at 175 Cliff Road. See SP to ASP, 8 February 1952.

3 – Richard Norton to SP, 11 December 1951; held by Lilly Library.

bring home a government book to read, plus English poetry by the load from Browning to the Rosetti's. Also, I must best needs create two masterful stories in my idle moments. – All of which work is really enjoyable and cultural, you understand. All I am planning on over vacation are those three "occasions," plus a possible dinner & play with Phil, and a lunch with Patsy and Louise. – So I hope between times to rest and study – no emotional upsets – I guarantee! Just so long as I keep well.

It is really frightening to see days chopped into frantic segments, with a dozen alternative choices for work crying to be done. I am really glad that I am going to Marcia's, though. Even if it costs quite a bit, I feel that I am extremely frugal in other respects and that I should not close such doors of experience – New York, play, art museums – etc. I am terribly excited to see all the great stores, and the lights at Christmas.

I bought Mrs. Brown a little hostess-Christmas gift – and wrapped it in silver paper, tied with blue ribbon. – Bought her two little tins of "paté de foie gras" – which Marcia says she adores. Also bought Marcia a little dish from Sweeden – very pretty pottery for her hope chest. The only thing I haven't been able to find is nice Christmas cards.

I went down to Hamp yesterday to shop, and was aesthetically exhilarated by all the Christmas smells and colors. There were the loveliest displays at the Hampshire bookshop – pottery, glassware, and lovely books. – I felt I could buy so many wonderful things if only I had a few thousand dollars. Books and clothes and the theater are my few cardinal weaknesses. There were so many little luxuries I would have liked to get for you, and Marcia!

My letter writing is going to pot again. I managed a great burst, and then let go.

Oh, by the way, I went to the Christian Science lecture by Margaret Morrison[1] from Boston – covered it for the press Board. I almost had hysterics – she was a Pollyanna-ish whitehaired – sweet-sweet old female who burbled on in a lyrical way about how truth, love, happiness, health, were always flowing always from the great divine mind. All is mind – transcending the "falsities of the flesh." Health is also a state of mind – disease not cured by "mindless drugs" as falsely supposed, but a freeing of the mind from fear & doubt. I was just laughing away inside as I took notes.

1–Margaret Morrison spoke at 7:15 p.m. on 11 December 1951 in the Little Chapel of the Library on the subject of 'Christian Science: The Voice of Truth'. Sylvia Plath, '"True Health" Lecture Topic at the College', *Daily Hampshire Gazette*, 14 December 1951, 7.

The funniest thing was the old woman who rushed up to me afterwards, pressed my hand fervently and trilled, "My dear, I saw you taking notes! Are you really that interested in Christian Science![1] I think that's just wonderful."

Whereupon I said "Oh, yes, isn't it," and slipped hurriedly out into the night.

See you Friday – will no doubt call from some rail road station – me and the pack mules –

Love,
Sivvy

TO *Constantine Sidamon-Eristoff*

Saturday 15 December 1951 ALS, Private owner

December 15

Dear Connie –

Votre SD letter arrived importantly in the midst of Christmas tree trimming and much tinsel and sparkles. Very appropriate. To be relevant, your plans for Thursday sound simply delightful. I would be extremely pleased to meet your parents and all – but don't, my enchantingly mad Georgian, go to great labors for things to do. I am amazingly easy to satisfy. You know, the sort of character who can sit for hours and meditate on the ocean in great content – not that I do it in this sort of weather, though. Save it, huh?

At any rate, with the aid of a map (drawn obligingly by my roommate;) I will plan to meet you at 5 p.m., Thursday, the 20th, at the McAlpin Hotel[2] – in the lobby, or wherever people congregate.

I will be arriving at 36A Cottage Street, South Orange, N.J., on Tuesday evening, so if you want to say hello or alter plans you can call me there (Mrs. Carol T. Brown, is the name of my hostess,) – Tel: South O. 33479.

If all goes well (no losing myself or anything), I'll be seeing you around 5 p.m. Thursday at the McAlpine!

Vacationally yours –
Sylvia

1 – 'interested in ~~Science~~ Christian Science!' appears in the original.

2 – In Herald Square at Broadway and 34th Street in New York City.

1952

TO *Marion Freeman*

Tuesday 1 January 1952 ALS with envelope, Smith College

January 1, 1952

Dear Aunt Marion –

Greetings for the New Year to you! It seems almost impossible that Christmas vacation will be over in a day or two. Unfortunately I have been confined in bed with a nasty sinus infection for over a week, now, and have been up today for the first time in what seems to be ages. Naturally I wanted to send a note in your direction – thanking you, Ruthie, and David for your thoughtful gifts to us.

I spent many convalescent hours enjoying my beautiful volume of drawings and prose about Europe (it was almost as good as taking a vacation myself.) And of course Warren, being so interested in music, was greatly pleased with the book on Haydn. All in all, I don't know how you could have made a better choice for each of us!

We have been having a delightful vacation (visits from friends and so on) in spite of my confinement to quarters – and my only regret is that the Plaths and Freemans live so far apart – but we certainly thought of you, and hoped for the most enjoyable of vacation festivities. Warren and I still remember those lovely times when we were little and used to gather at your house for carol singing!

Do give my special love to Ruthie, and thanks to you all once more for remembering us so generously at Christmas time.

Love to all – from Our house to your house –

Sylvia

P.S. I did want to tell you, too, how my roommate and I loved that delectable box of goodies you sent up to me. Never have I tasted such delicious cooking! I just hope that someday I will be able to make the same wonderful treats in a kitchen of my own . . ,

S.

TO *Aurelia Schober Plath*

Friday 4 January 1952[1] ALS, Indiana University

Dear Mum –

Here are the two items requested – No trouble about the blank---another girl asked for one just as I did, so I didn't feel guilty. I'll keep on with nosedrops & Trimeton till this damn head clears up. Eric called last night just as I was going to bed and must have spent I don't know how much on the phone bill, for we talked for quite a while (he was at New Haven, not North Carolina!) He wanted to come up this Saturday, but I postponed it, till the next one – I'm resting & working this weekend!

Marcia is supremely well – plans to get married in 1954, engaged in 1953 & pinned next fall. Practicality, wot? She gave me a beautiful copy of the "Pisan Cantos"[2] by Pound for a belated Xmas gift.

Work et al. make the next 4 weeks drudgery. Cheery morale boosting missives will be much appreciated –

Love,
Sivvy

TO *Aurelia Schober Plath*

Monday 14 January 1952[3] ALS (postcard), Indiana University

Dear Mum –

Just a note to add to your burdens! If you get this in time please empty (carefully) my old art portfolio, put away the pictures where they can't be hurt, & bring the empty one up. We have to have one, & I figure I can't afford a second. Also remember skates & skating socks! If you get here early, why not just go upstairs to the second floor, (rm 6) and make yourself at home till I get there at 12. Or talk with Mrs. Shakespeare.

Can't wait to see you!
Love,
Sylvia

1 – Date supplied from internal evidence.
2 – Ezra Pound, *Pisan Cantos* (1948). The location of SP's copy is unknown.
3 – Date supplied from postmark.

TO *Aurelia Schober Plath*

Wednesday 23 January 1952[1] ALS (postcard), Indiana University

Wed. night

Dear Mum –

Ugh. I am feeling fine physically – can breathe & all that, but studying is appallingly much & dull. I am working all tonight & tomorrow on government (Fri 10:20). My worst exam. Thank God Dick is coming. I would go mad for diversion otherwise. The room is a mess – dirty clothes & books everywhere. Time zips. Your cookies & dear letter arrived. I am proud at the glowing account of your Unitarian affair. More power to you! Carol & I have devoted an hour a day to playing vigorously in the gym. We need to un-tense. Marcia, poor lamb, has been in the infirmary since Mon. night with a sore throat & probably won't be out until Sunday. I owe 50 (hyperbole) people letters which I won't be able to answer until mid-semester. Also feel grubby. Art for next sem. will be over $20! Oil paints! My conservative estimate was too much so. Do disregard dull tone – will see you a week from tomorrow. Can't wait.

Love,
Sivvy

TO *Aurelia Schober Plath*

Monday 4 February 1952[2] ALS (postcard), Indiana University

Mon noon

Dear Mum –

I am now ensconced in Creative Writing class – somewhat weary, as I got 8 hours sleep last night but really will catch up from now on in. The bus ride back was hideous – stood part of the way, practically fainting – changed twice – didn't get in till after 11. Who was that dear boy that drove us? I could swear I never saw him before! Got a call from Mrs. Brown in Francestown – poor Marcia has measles – will be confined up there for an indefinite length of time – probably missing the Dartmouth Carnival this weekend. At least I will be able to go to bed really early without bothering her. (Gosh, I thought I had it bad.) Already I have

1–Date supplied from postmark.
2–Date supplied from postmark.

a lecture to cover tonight for Press Board[1] – meeting for Soph prom tomorrow – supper dates, and so on. My end-of-the-week schedule has been re-juggled favorably. This week will be one rush to catch up on sleep, letters, etc. Mrs. Shakespeare's plans tentative ($35 a week). I have all sorts of appointments and so on to make now – but boy, it's good to be back in a sane routine where I can forget various haughty blond med-students. Merci beaucoup for the $10 – I buy art supplies this pm. Work on Dr Christian[2] – please!

Love your fellow genius –
Sivvy
<drawing of a girl and a baby on address side of postcard>

TO *Aurelia Schober Plath*

Wednesday 6 February 1952[3] ALS (postcard), Indiana University

Wednesday

Dear Mum –

As you may imagine, I felt pretty low today when I got my letter from 17. I hadn't realized the subconscious support I was getting from thinking of what I would do with my $500. I guess I'll really have to hit those True Stories. By the way, I suddenly got an inspiration for the "Civic Activities" section of my application blank . . . I am starting next Monday to teach art to a class of kids at the people's Institute[4] – volunteer work Don't tell Dick!! Please – or his folks![5] (make it sound impressive). Next year I hope for either mental or veteran's hospital. (Time cures nothing, work cures all. – Confuscius say!) Marcia won't be back for over a week – talked to her on the phone & she sounds fine. I feel suddenly very untalented as I look at my slump of work in art & writing. Am I destined to deteriorate for the rest of my life? I'm going over to supper at Albright[6] next week –

1–According to SP's calendar, she covered the Reinhold Niebuhr lecture. Niebuhr spoke on 'The Cultural Crisis' as part of the Smith College Religious Association forum on 'The Shaping of the Foundations' held in the Browsing Room, Neilson Library. An unattributed article, probably by SP, resulted: 'Universal Faith Has the Answer, Dr. Niebuhr Says', *Springfield Union*, 5 February 1953, 21.

2–*Dr Christian* was a radio serial which ran 1937–54. The show aired on Boston's WEEI.

3–Date supplied from postmark.

4–People's Institute, a community centre at 38 Gothic Street, Northampton, Mass.; SP was a volunteer tutor in art, spring 1952.

5–This sentence added by SP in the left margin.

6–A residence house on Bedford Terrace, Northampton, Mass.

hope to make a few acquaintances. Do write for Dr Christian. Every year you will, until you win. You have the back ground & technical terms. Go to it! Am going to church & young people's this week – telephoned newsstory to Springfield paper[1] at 11 pm last night – felt professional.

XX
Siv

TO *Aurelia Schober Plath*

Friday 8 February 1952[2] ALS (postcard), Indiana University

Friday, at last

Dear Mum –

Thanks for the nice long typewritten letter! Glad to hear you are working on the play. I feel good about that. Hope you have better luck than I did! I have been working on my Elks deal – a transcript of my record will be sent you within a week – also a letter from a "person in authority" here – last year's Botany teacher & adviser – Mr. Kenneth Wright. I also wrote Mr. Crockett a long letter & asked him to send you a letter for the highschool p. in a. Now all you have to do is mount the stuff when you get it – and 3[3] write a letter on financial situation 6 get Mrs. F., Mrs. A. – and somebody else – to endorse me & write to find out about the Exalted 7 Ruler. Appreciated your advice about the cousin. I am working on re-orienting my life about my own potentialities – much better & secure that way. Only I feel dateless as hell. I won't know my marks for a month – but I do know I will get a B av. Even if I get a low C in art. because I got a straight A on my religion exam which should give me an A- in the course. Something unexpected & rather amusing – got a letter from none other than Constantine who said I charmed his mother[4] (hah!) also that he met Phil (not Bob) Brawner who said he'd gone out with me. Small world – ugh!

XXXX
Sivvy

1–SP covered a second lecture by Reinhold Niebuhr on the topic of 'The Personal Crisis'. An unattributed article, probably by SP, was published: '"Crisis" Is Topic of Dr. Niebuhr in Northampton', *Springfield Union*, 6 February 1952, 21.

2–Date supplied from postmark.

3–The numbers 3, 6 and 7 are circled by SP in the letter.

4–Anne Tracy Sidamon-Eristoff (1890–1978).

TO *Aurelia Schober Plath*

Sat.–Mon. 9–11 February 1952[1] ALS (postcard), Indiana University

Saturday

Dear Mum –

Just got my gov. grade back – straight A, no less. Even if I did leave out the 10% current events question, I wrote twice as much on the rest & scrawled "Time limit reached" across the bottom. He wrote me that I needed self-confidence, & next time should obey directions. Mighty lucky!

Monday

Went to church yesterday & heard Mr. Lauriat[2] give a daring & applicable sermon on love & pre-marriage dangers. Really great – practical etc. He advised falling "in love" (2 real people sharing common & important projects in a genuine way) several times – experience being valuable, and said not to marry at any account if scared of age (30 isn't worse than death!) or just to prove you too can catch a man. Also said to wait & work after College if necessary – learning how to be a real person & enriching oneself. Today I was on the go from 8-5. Just finished washing my hair. So happy – a chance suggestion of mine on Soph. prom com. resulted in my title "Evening in Aqua" being picked for the theme etc. People's Institute fun – just splashing paint from 3-5 with a small group of kids from about 8-12. They asked if I could teach an adult group beginning oils, but I said it would have to wait till next year when I'll know how myself

XX

Sivvy

1–Date supplied from postmark.

2–Reverend Nathaniel P. Lauriat (1922–2004); minister of the Unitarian Church of Northampton and Florence (later Unitarian Society of Northampton and Florence), 1951–6.

TO *John F. Malley*[1]

Sunday 10 February 1952 ALS, Indiana University

February 10, 1952
Haven House
Smith College
Northampton
Massachusetts

Mr. John F. Malley
16 Court Street
Boston 8
Massachusetts

Dear Mr. Malley:

At present I am a sophomore at Smith College, and in order to complete my education it is necessary for me to have financial aid. In this letter I would like to tell you just how much these last years of school have meant to me and why I have applied with such hope for an Elks Scholarship. First, as requested, I will summarize my activities.

Always interested in writing and journalism, I was on my High School paper for three years, becoming co-Editor in my senior year. During this time several Boston Globe awards[2] for three of my write-ups were received. I also was given top honors in the annual Atlantic Monthly Literary Contest.[3] In college I have continued my activities in writing by being a reporter for the Smith College News Office (Press Board.) In my spare time I have written articles, stories, and poems for the Christian Science Monitor and Seventeen magazine.

College has offered me the chance to continue my study of art which led me to win a place in the National exhibition at Carnegie Institute[4] and to draw for the Year Book and High School dances. Smith dances such as Charity Ball, Freshman Prom, I. S. Day, and House Dance keep me busy with paints and creative ideas. Studio Club allows me to meet and plan programs with other girls as interested in art as I am.

While art and writing constitute my major accomplishments, I would like to say that working with people is my favorite activity. Team sports

1–John F. Malley was the founder of the Elks National Foundation.

2–SP received prizes on 27 January and 24 May 1950 at ceremonies held at the Copley Plaza Hotel, Boston, Mass.

3–In 1948, SP won a merit award for her poems 'April: 1948' and 'The Farewell'.

4–In 1949, SP's watercolours titled 'Thanksgiving' and 'Hallowe'en' won awards.

and orchestra in high school; rehearsals for Senior Play; planning and participating in Memorial Day programs; being secretary for a vital Church Young People's Group; a summer job on a farm with Negroes, D.P.'s, and college students; a job this past summer acting as full-time governess, laundress, cook and playmate for three young children---all these activities involved my close cooperation with all types of people, and I enjoyed every minute of it!

Needless to say, my school work has always been a source of delight. The study of United States History (for which I received the Sons of the Revolution Prize) makes me feel that American ideals are in part responsible for my chance to go to college. In a country where ability can attain success in spite of a lack of wealth, I cannot but be extremely grateful for the freedom to work and hope for continuation of my education.

It is with the objective of going on with my education so I may be better equipped to serve my country and my fellowmen that I humbly state my qualifications for the Elks Scholarship.

Sincerely yours,
Sylvia Plath

TO *Ann Davidow-Goodman*

Monday 18 February 1952[1] ALS with envelope, Smith College

Monday

Davy, my love –

I deserve a horsewhipping for my writing habits! Now I am turning up my fat old nose at all the back work I have to do (we've only been back two weeks, but somehow I'm already paradoxically 3 weeks behind!) and writing you the letter you've deserved since last fall.

I meant to write a volume over Christmas vacation, but after a wild and sleepless few days visiting Marcia and going in and out of New York, I landed the prettiest sinus infection you ever did see – and it took me a full month of penicillin shots, misery, and cocaine nose packs to make me breathe again.

So I have been running around on my own private little squirrel cage (which Smith has so many of.)

I love the courses I'm taking this year, but I'm not studying very hard. At least Government is the only course that's really painful – partly because

1 – Date supplied from postmark.

I never got used to reading newspapers and always walk around with my head in the clouds pretending there isn't any war going on anyway, and who the heck is Eisenhower?

Religion is lots of fun, though, in my agnostic, liberal, humanistic way, I can't stir up any personal enthusiasm for anything except Judaism and Unitarianism. I won't say what I think of Catholicism.

Creative writing is heaven, as is English lit. (reading novels and poetry) – and I feel awfully self-indulgent when I sit down to read or write.

Dick is seen too far and few times – he doesn't go out with other girls, but is slaving like mad through his first year at Harvard Med School. Although I feel awfully dumb when I go down to visit him, since all the guys talk shop about diseases with mile-long unpronounceable names, I have wonderful times – unconventional, too.

Between semesters I went to the Boston Lying-In Hospital[1] with him, and we both dressed up in white coats and masks & took the self-running elevator up to the maternity ward. I spent the whole night there – going around from room to room with the older med students & doctors. Dick & I stood two feet away to watch a baby born, and I had the queerest urge to laugh and cry when I saw the little squinted blue face grimacing out of the woman's vagina – only to see it squawk into life, cold, naked and wailing a few minutes later.

The hospital was alive that night, and I went with a fascinating Hungarian 3rd year student[2] to hold test tubes while he took blood from a fat, pregnant gypsy woman who walked in off the streets to deliver unceremoniously. She was a jolly creature, and I had fun joking with her. Needless to say, my sense of the dramatic was aroused, and I went skipping excitedly down the corridors of the maternity ward like a thoroughly irresponsible Florence Nightingale.

Now for Dick – the blond god. Well – I learned alot about him – all of which has had various strange psychological repercussions on me. For one thing, I discovered that he is not a virgin – after his long having led me to believe how innocent he was as far as sex was concerned and how worldly I was, the shock made me sick. Mostly an unreasonable jealousy, I admitted, after analysis, and absurdly enough, I wouldn't give a damn about any other boy's being a virgin, but somehow I wanted him to be.

The revelation I got, or rather self-insight, during the next few weeks, was something I had subconsciously wanted not to admit to myself all

1–Boston Lying-In Hospital, 221 Longwood Avenue, Boston. SP visited on 1 February 1952.

2–Probably Thomas J. De Kornfeld, M.D. 1953, Harvard Medical School.

along. To wit: I am envious of males. I resent their ability to have both sex (morally or immorally) and a career. I hate public opinion for encouraging boys to prove their virility & condemning women for doing so. In short, I was not angry at Dick for seducing several women, but jealous that I had been denied the same chance by society. In other words, I am not an idealistic moral person, but have been using that cover to fool other people and myself. Really, I am non-moral. I would gladly go to bed with many of the boys I have dated – if I "loved" them for the time being. The only thing is, I'm a coward and afraid of having a baby, becoming too emotionally involved, or getting found out (I'm no good at fooling people---too transparent.) So there! I have got that off my chest. Here I am – not wanting to get trapped in a too-early marriage, wanting to get a graduate fellowship abroad, or something & not "settle down" as a country doctor's wife---right away, anyhow, and what do I do with my burning emotions & lusts in the meantime? God knows, & even he seems to be a little puzzled.

I am still writing Eddie, and hear that he tried[1] to approach you two dimensionally speaking – after which he got very mad at me and said "why the hell didn't you tell me she was beautiful and used Ponds?"[2]

Anyhow, I am still occasionally dating other guys – only after the first few times, most of them seem dull and childish – I definitely go for older men, though, and wish to hell that I would meet someone as brilliant, handsome & intelligent as Dick – a few inches taller, so I could wear heels – and a bit more intuitive – our natures are diametrically opposed, you see, he being so logical, practical, planned, and scientific, and me being terribly emotional, artistically inclined, romantic and impractical. Lots of people say it's a good balance, but I find my self always irresistably drawn to artistic guys. Also have a crush on my art teacher – Mr. Cohen, even though he must be in his forties and smells of tobacco and wine! Shows how sex starved one can get up here – only getting to be passionate once in every three weeks!

I have a theory that all my sex energy is now sublimated in studying, art and writing – which means that after I get married & sexually satisfied I will turn into a dumb, placid idiot!

By the way, I love Edie. She is the sweetest girl, and I do hope she's happy here. We all love her.

1–Eddie Cohen to SP, [7 January 1952]; held by Lilly Library.
2–Cohen wrote, 'Tell me, my love, was that your idea of a joke, or were you really and truly unaware that the girl uses Pond's?' Pond's: a brand of face cream.

I send you love from Marcia who is looking over my shoulder as I write. She had a raw deal – got mono during exams and got stashed away in the infirmary – then, just as she was planning to go up to winter carnival at Dartmouth, she came down with the measles, which, irony of ironies, she caught up in the good old sterile infirmary! She is planning to marry a Freshman up there (Mike Plumer) when she graduates.

Betsy Whittemore is engaged to be married this June to Bob MacArthur[1] – a very sweet guy who is going to be a math teacher. Betsy Blanton is pinned to Greg McGrath[2] at Amherst – Diana is pinned & transferring to the U. of Wash. next year. Sarah Ann is leaving next year for Ohio State. Callie, Lola, Joanie S., and Reggie want to go abroad. Carol Pierson, going to Europe with the chamber singers this summer, will probably go to New York to study dance next year – so you see the old group is breaking up. Even Sylvia will probably have to move to a co-op house if she wants to stay at Smith.

What I want to hear about in detail is Ray! If you really love the guy, Annie, don't let anything stand in your way – I'd marry a prince or a pauper if I loved him well enough – and when I say "love", I don't mean the popular song version of it, but a whole lot of things involving mind as well as body – both combined.

I think you & I are a lot alike in the way we're made – emotionally & mentally – we react to life similarly. Therefore I think I could understand and love anything you told me, just as I can spill over to you without reserve.

Just now I'm praying that I get to spring vacation without cracking up mentally and physically. Smith is a damn, heartless, demanding machine at times!

Do write, honey – & let me know all the things I would if we were next-door neighbors, which I wish we were!

Lots of Love –
Syl

P.S. Say hello to your mom & dad for me – I still remember that lovely supper they gave us! Hi to Ray, too!

1–Robert Helmer MacArthur (1930–72).
2–Robert Gregory McGrath (1931–2009); B.A. 1952, Amherst College.

TO *Aurelia Schober Plath*

Monday 18 February 1952[1] ALS (postcard), Indiana University

Monday night

Dear Mum –

I am going to start using up these addressed cards[2] while there's still time! I have never been so crowded with "things to do" – All this week I'll have to let studies slide & paint on Charity Ball decorations. Took your advice & accepted a blind date this Sat. night. Anything for a change of scenery! Ironically, he was from UNH, named Dick, & we went to Williams![3] The two hour drive through the blue, snow-covered hills was a delight in itself, although my date was rather dull and stupid compared to the boys I know. We had a lovely free dinner & went to a great Dixieland concert – I felt pangs of homesickness as I passed the house where I stayed when I went up for Fall House-parties with John. I looked for him everywhere, till one boy told me he'd gone home to Wellesley for the weekend – strangely enough, we went to a dance at the Beta house & I saw his picture over the mantel – so left a lipstick scrawled note of greeting in his mailbox – will he be surprised! Just have to tell you that I am one of the 4 gals in our class up for electoral board office[4] . . . Louise & Pat both have been one of the final four up for an office, so now this makes 3 of us! Little unpopular me, too! Oh, well –

love –
sivvy

1–Date supplied from postmark.

2–SP had personalized blue postcards that read 'Sylvia Plath / Haven House, Smith College, Northampton, Massachusetts.'

3–According to SP's calendar, she went on a double date with Carol Sameth McCauley (1933–) B.A. 1954, geology, Smith College.

4–A student committee of Smith College consisting of members of Student Council, Judicial Board, Activities Board, house representatives, and representatives from each class year. During her junior year, SP served as one of the secretaries of Electoral Board.

TO *Constantine Sidamon-Eristoff*

Monday 18 February 1952[1] ALS, Private owner

Monday

Dear Connie . . .

Life about now is as scintillating as that in a state penitentiary. Not that I'm bitter, just snow-covered and weary . . . Exams having faded in a bleary fog, now . . . . and we are looking ahead to the gaiety of the traditional Rally Day Celebration for this coming weekend.[2] Somehow my artistic inclinations have gotten me in a rather strange position in the gym basement, painting a big backdrop for Charity Ball. It's supposed to look very modern and Picasso-esque when I'm through – but picture me crouched in the big dim cellar with only a thin dusty light overhead, steam pipes hissing maliciously and jutting out at threatening angles, not to mention all sorts of dank slime exuding from the walls – lovely setting, wot? Just as long as I don't meet any Charles Addams[3] characters down there – or any maniac janitors!

I find myself doing all sorts of amazing things – some of which I am sure may surprise you, but which I shall tell you about anyway.

A weekend or so ago I spent a unique night down at Harvard Medical School. After some coaxing, my escort took me over to the Boston-Lying-In Hospital, bequeathed me a white coat and mask, and let me wander around anonymously on the maternity ward floor. I don't know when I've had such fun! I went into all the rooms with the internes & doctors, stood two feet away to watch a baby being born (the most colorful, amusing & sobering sight imagineable!) And even held test tubes while they took blood tests. My sense of drama was really aroused – and the characters I saw were a refreshing change from the usual socially-oriented college individuals I live with. It was life in the raw, really – women walking in from off the streets to deliver, and screams & wailing & blood. Needless to say, my experiences there, plus some intense conversations I had with a couple of med-students – will make terrific background material for those short stories I'm always trying to write. My collection of rejection slips would wallpaper several rooms, but the few things I have had published made me determined to keep on battering on the editor's doors.

1 – Date supplied from internal evidence.

2 – Rally Day was Friday 22 February 1952.

3 – American cartoonist Charles Addams (1912–88) whose work regularly appeared in the *New Yorker*; best known as the creator of the 'Addams Family' characters.

My latest enterprise involves volunteer work downtown at the people's Institute --- teaching little urchins how to draw, of all things! It's fun to get outside of the ivy-covered idealistic tower and learn to know the town better . . . and I have as much of a frolic spattering paint on paper as the children do. (Next year I want to work in the veteran's Hospital – and I have a great curiosity about mental Asylums, too. – As you have no doubt gathered by now, I am a female who cannot bear sitting away her life by a fireside, munching bonbons and playing bridge. I like doing things creatively & with all sorts of people too much for that!)

But now I have been rambling on for so long – too long – about my activities. I do want to say, belatedly, in retrospect, that I loved meeting your family. I lost my heart completely to your mother, who is one of the most delightfully stimulating women I have ever met! Do remember me to her, please.

You are no doubt leading the life of the suave Princetonian gentleman, I trust! But I would like to hear about it! Will the Armed Forces be devouring you after graduation? As I am sure you would make a dashing Cossack – or Napoleonic warrior – I do not care to think of you trudging muddily through battlefields. But there, my romanticism is winning over my realism again!

Do reciprocate and write, my enchanting Georgian!

Yours,
Sylvia

TO *Aurelia Schober Plath*

Monday 25 February 1952[1] ALS (postcard), Indiana University

Monday afternoon

Dear mum –

Another week has ground into being, and I find myself overwhelmed with work – novels to read, stories to write, and much more. The week of March 11 is my waterloo – with three writtens & two papers. I just hope I can keep well! Dick came up Saturday afternoon and we had a very nice weekend. We all (Marcia – Mike, Carol & Ken, Dick & I) went to the Whale Inn[2] for a delicious & talkative dinner there, whereupon the others went to the dance, and Dick & I went for an evening of reading at Davis.

1–Date supplied from postmark.

2–The Whale Inn is a restaurant and inn on Route 9 in Goshen, Mass.

Sunday was beautiful, so we went on a long hike across the snow fields to the Connecticut river & were out for a good six hours – we then read in the libe & the house, & I fell in bed after they left at 9:30 p.m. I will be coming home the weekend of the 15th to go to a dance at Harvard Med. School – and till then I will be working like a dog. I've got so much I want to do Spring vacation! Mostly writing and reading. Hows. Dr C.?

XX
Siv

TO *Richard Norton*[1]

Monday 25 February 1952 AL (excerpt),[2] Smith College

February 25 – letter excerpt:

. . . can you see, through the strange dark tunnel of cupped hands to the great cyclops eye, blurred, staring, flecked with one lightspot that grows and becomes a cloud, shifting, endowed with meaning, imposed upon it. Can you feel, listening with trained ear to heartbeat of the other, the wind shrieking and gasping and singing, as one listens to the vast humming inside the paradoxical cylinder of the telephone pole? Such uncharted, wild barrens there are behind the calm or mischievous shell that has learned its name but not its destiny.

There is still time to veer, to sally forth, knapsack on back, for unknown hills over which . . . only the wind knows what lies. Shall she, shall she veer? There will be time, she says, knowing somehow that in her beginning is her end and the seeds of destruction perhaps now dormant may even today begin sprouting malignantly within her. She turns away from action in one direction to that in another, knowing all the while that someday she must face, behind the door of her choosing, perhaps the lady, perhaps the tiger . . .

1–See Richard Norton to SP, 25–7 February 1952 and 28 February–1 March 1952; held by Lilly Library.
2–SP excerpted this letter in her journals.

TO *Aurelia Schober Plath*

Wednesday 27 February 1952[1] ALS with envelope, Indiana University

Wednesday

Dear Mother –

Just a quickie note in the midst of stacks of work! This weekend I have to read 2 novels (total: 900 pages) and 400 pages of government, write a story,[2] paint a still life, plus spending all Friday morning & night & Saturday morning over at the News Office! What a life! All my writtens & papers come in a row the week of March 10. It will be a large hell.

What I want to know is, can you put Carol up Friday & Saturday nights on March 14 & 15? We both are coming down to rest & party that weekend, & I thought she could sleep with me if you were in Warren's room.

News today of a $150 increase in board & room! You will no doubt get the notice soon. Just as we thought we had things in hand, too! The Elks better come across. I shall see if any sort of financial adjustment is possible when I see Miss Mensel about co-op house on Friday morning. At least I will be earning a sizeable sum in my last two years, by working on press Board! I'm really glad I got into that – lucrative & practical.

I have found a vocational interest! Today our creative writing class heard the president of the Hampshire bookshop[3] speak on the publishing house business. It sounds like just what I want. You teach me shorthand & typing, & I work up in all sorts of jobs (variety of angles – publicity, secretarial, editorial, reading manuscripts – juvenile depts. – etc.) I was overwhelmed with enthusiasm; still want to work in veterans hospital, though. But English majoring & Press Board can lead to a practical end. See if you can get any contacts!

Love & kisses –
Sivvy

1–Date supplied from postmark.
2–Probably Sylvia Plath, 'Though Dynasties Pass'; held by Lilly Library.
3–Possibly Cynthia Walsh (Smith, 1939).

TO *Aurelia Schober Plath*

Tuesday 4 March 1952[1] ALS (postcard), Indiana University

Tuesday

Dear mum –

So glad to hear you got Dr. Xian off! I am proud of my versatile mater! I have decided not to go to Princeton – it would be courting a cold & two low exam grades. For that I am not prepared to spend $15. It was the hardest choice I ever made, and, alas, the wisest. What I did was think of spring vacation in the same plight as Xmas. That did it. I am not going to let you beat me – & so am going to spend most of my vacation writing for the Mademoiselle short story contest – also for a poetry contest. I will also have two Eng. novels to read & lots of gov. – but I look forward to working liesurely. Got a terrific long letter from Phil – he's the dearest guy! Miss Mensel said I definitely would get a

$900 scholarship
50 adjustment
250 coop (probably)
$1200 – which leaves $600! She said I might have to borrow 1 or 2 hundred, but I hope Elks will take care of that! Of all crazy things – money is worst. Mrs. Brown is buying a house[2] in Hamp! Be good & don't worry 'bout me –

Love,
Sivvy

TO *Aurelia Schober Plath*

Thursday 6 March 1952[3] ALS with envelope, Indiana University

Thursday night

Dear Mother –

maybe your daughter is slightly crazy. maybe she just takes after her illustrious mother, but in spite of the fact she has 3 wicked writtens next week, she is just now feeling very tired and happy-go-lucky. Very virtuous because she refused 3 weekends this weekend – Frosh Prom at Yale, Jr. Prom (sigh) at Princeton, a blind date from M.I.T. – and, of course, Dick

1 – Date supplied from postmark.
2 – Carol Taylor Brown purchased a house at 211 Crescent Street, Northampton, Mass.
3 – Date supplied from postmark.

might have come. But my work will fill every minute. I am too stable, really, to throw over courses in a social crisis. But I do feel that by rights my social life this Spring should be more freely indulged in – – if any turns up. At least Dick is coming to Soph Prom. I really felt I had to ask him before anyone else.

Heard Struik[1] (friend "communist" from M.I.T. – dismissed – accused under Anti-Anarchy Law of 1919) speak Monday night. Really a fascinating Marxist. The Press Board took my review of it (playing down the controversial) almost verbatim! Mon. afternoon I spent 2 hours under the feet (literally) of the New York Ballet Theater Rehearsal – they said anyone who wanted to sketch could come – so I did. Magnificent.

Creative writing has given me a B+ and an A- so far. I am much pleased. Just finished delivering my best baby yet – a story (only 7 pp)[2] about a vet with one leg missing & a girl meeting on a train. Dialogue discipline, you know.

Saw Enid Epstein Wed. p.m. for tea at her house – she showed me that the same March issue of 17[3] that had a poem of hers in it had my name among the H. Mentions. We discussed writing & I read a few terrific stories of hers.

Life is queer. Glad as I was not to be elected for Electoral Board (being one of 4 was an Honor) – I am very excited at being one of the 3 soph finalists for Sec. of Honor Board – one of the Big all-campus organizations up here – specially fascinating because it deals with psychological breaking of Honor System. Even if I know I don't have a chance (same girl that beat me for Electoral Board is up) it's fun. Also, laugh of laughs, I was actually nominated for house president! Knowing how I am "loved" by various & sundry, I smile. So much for my political career (I haven't done a thing – one is just nominated & voted on & notified.)

So pleased about Dr. Xian. You just better get a prize! I'm going to write all vacation. Just full of ideas from Mademoiselle to True Confessions –

Love you Lots & lots –
your offspring –
Sivvy

1–Dutch mathematician and Marxian theoretician Dirk Jan Struik (1894–2000) spoke on 'Academic Freedom and the Trend to Conformity' in the Browsing Room of the Neilson Library on 3 March 1952, at 7:45 p.m. SP's article was unattributed: '"Heresy Hunts" Menace Liberty; Stuik Claims', *Springfield Union*, 4 March 1952, 2.

2–Sylvia Plath, 'Brief Encounter', rewritten as 'Though Dynasties Pass'; held by Lilly Library.

3–Enid Epstein, 'On Seeing the Renoir Show', *Seventeen* 11 (March 1952), 146.; SP's 'The Perfect Set-Up' won Honorable Mention in 'The Short-Story Contest Winners' (22).

<on back of envelope>

Good news – officially, classes get over at 12:50 Friday, March 21, since I don't have anything but a gym class that a.m., I can leave Thursday at 5 p.m! I thus squeeze an extra day out of this institution!

TO *Aurelia Schober Plath*

Tuesday 11 March 1952[1] ALS (postcard), Indiana University

Tuesday 2 pm

Dear mother –

God! I am dead. I have had not more than 7 hours of sleep per night for a week, and the strain of concentrated reading is awful – got through gov. yesterday, english today. Religion comes Thursday. It wouldn't be so bad if I didn't have classes all day & activities at night. Sunday, before gov. exam, I covered vespers.[2] Yesterday p.m. I spent with my painting class at the institute. Tomorrow I have an afternoon mass meeting and have to cover a lecture[3] that night – before the exam! Frustrating, wot – also a late house meeting Thurs. night! Boy – will I feel like an escaped deserving convict going home friday am. Carol isn't coming – but I might bring a friend of mine just for Sat night – don't worry! I'm going straight in Boston Friday – so don't expect me home before Fri. night. Hope you're better

XXX
Siv

1 – Date supplied from postmark.

2 – SP covered vespers held in John M. Greene Hall at 7:00 p.m. for Press Board. The speaker was the Rev. David Roberts, Dean of Union Theological Seminary; Music by Freshman Choir B, Katrina Schmidt '53, Director. SP's article was unattributed: 'Misery of Man Is Due to His Defects', *Daily Hampshire Gazette*, 11 March 1952, 5.

3 – The lecture was given by Massimo Salvadori (1908–92), a professor of modern European history at Smith College, 1945–73. SP's article was unattributed: 'Marxism Seeks to Replace God, Lecturer Says', *Springfield Union*, 13 March 1952, 30.

TO *Aurelia Schober Plath*

Sunday 16 March 1952[1] ALS with envelope, Indiana University

Sunday night

dearest-mother-whom-I-love-better than-anybody –

I have so much to tell you I hardly know where to start. Chronological order would be most coherent, even if I am most tempted to begin with the boy I fell in love with this afternoon!

First of all – I was one of the 16 girls in the college up for the college elections. (too bad it didn't come in time for Elks contest!) The whole college had a required meeting to see us (I didn't have to make a speech – just to get up & sit down.) But it was exciting. Unfortunately, my good friend & I who were both up for Sec. of Honor Board lost to the 3rd girl. (Funny, but I think Jane Anderson was up for the same office & lost last year!)

Well, Friday morning I shot out of here like a bat out of Hades – got off right at the Medical School & ran to Dick. First thing I did was to call you, but you had gone – you mischievous gad-about! I can't wait to hear your adventures. Dick & I sat and talked & talked & read Hemingway aloud for seven solid hours – without even eating. We took the bus home & he drove me the rest of the way from his house.

Saturday I had the most luxuriously homey day. Grammy and I had such fun – I got up, had a delicious brunch, played piano, took a long hot bath, played more piano . . . . ironed six of my shirts (oh! virtue!) while listening to the records we have & waltzing around the livingroom. Then I got all dressed up in my black velvet standby & Dick called for me about 4:30. We had Chopin, Beethoven, Cognac & Goya etchings in Tom de Cornfield's room – with Tom (the fascinatingly Continental Hungarian of my hospital acquaintance) and his date. Then dinner and the dance, where I met all sorts of lovely Negroes, Africans, Armenians and Americans. We got home around 12 after a nice evening.

Sunday, you will be glad to hear, I "girded my loins" & went to church alone. I sat with the Norton's, heard Dick sing, and drove back in their car afterwards. I also thanked Mr. Rice[2] warmly & personally for his letter. One score settled! I Promise to write the rest when I come home –. Dinner today was fun & I read to David until they took me to the bus.

1–Date supplied from postmark.
2–Unitarian Universalist minister William Brooks Rice (1905–70).

Now comes the wonderful part. I got on the crowded bus and found an empty seat toward the back by some young man, covered with a coat and snoring loudly. I couldn't see him very well, and it was a bit dim to read, so I shut my eyes & rested. We came to the "Flying Yankee Diner"[1] about an hour later, so I got out to get some orange juice. When I came back, my traveling companion was sitting up very much awake, rosy, lanky, tall and attractively nice looking. I was happy just sitting next to someone so personable. He offered me a cigarette, which I refused, & we started to talk about the weather – it was snowing a little. Well, you know me & conversations!

We talked solidly for the rest of the trip. He was completing his 8th year of college, having majored in Biology at C.L.A. and just finishing getting his PhD. in entomology at the U. of Mass. He told me about being a proctor over there, about his life in Canada – summer boyhood visits on his grandfathers 1000 acre lumber farm – about his job beginning at the end of March – his family – I did more than my share of talking – about you, Warren, college, my summer jobs, destiny, hypnosis, dream significance, chance, future plans.

I just couldn't bear to get into Northampton. He seemed the kindest person. When we got off the bus he said, "Say, would you like some coffee?" So I said yes, & we went into the same restaurant where you & I talked that day. We talked for a good hour & a half over sandwiches & coffee. It dawned on me during the course of conversation that daddy majored or taught entomology, so I said, "You know, my dad wrote a book on bumblebees once." His face lighted. "Not Bumblebees & Their Ways!" he said. "Let's see, P-L, P-L-A . . ." By that time I was laughing. Life seemed too strange for words. He carried my suitcase up to the house, then, leaving me at the door. I know I will never see him again, as I go home Thursday & he leaves for his job before I get back. His name was Bill something-or-other, and for a few hours I told him about most of my life and ideas and I think I loved him for talking to me. It just shows what wonderful people an uninhibited girl can run across.

Well, it's after 11, and I am still "high" with excitement over my fulfilling evening – it worked like a neatly opened oyster – & I managed, I think, to maneuver it to perfection. His father is a Canadian citizen. I will miss him . . . so old and sweet and listening and understanding – must have been 25 or so.

1–A diner in Auburn, Mass.

Ah me, life is strange!
See you Thursday night . . .
Lots to do twixt then & now
Love,
Sivvy
<drawing of heart on envelope>

TO *Constantine Sidamon-Eristoff*

Monday 17 March 1952 ALS, Private owner

March 17

dear connie . . .

and a happy saint patrick's day to you, me lad! feeling bohemian, i decide to make like eecummings[1] and drop capitals for a while.

really, i meant to write you a letter after that telegram i sent, but i haven't had time to breathe for the last two weeks on account of a crowd of exams, papers and all sorts of meetings. my calendar looks very grim – simply covered with appointments and so on . . . and so on.

but in spite of mud and cold and wind there are certain purple and yellow sprouts of vegetation springing up which might be called crocuses! and since i am a pagan sunworshiper who delights in turning all shades of brown come summer, i feel that once again there is something to live for.

spring vacation, too, starts this week. seems impossible that it's actually upon me – i've been counting the days for so long now! i will probably sleep away the first week.

at any rate, i have the usual overwhelming number of vacation plans . . . which includes writing several short stories and collecting more rejection slips . . .

my volunteer job of teaching "art" to a group of young devils on monday afternoons proves somewhat wearing (they get more paint on me than on the paper!) but quite fun. (I've become an expert in giving "piggybacks," too.)

as for the academic side of life, I've at last decided definitely to major in english. there are so many courses I want to crowd into the next two years that I really think I'll have to get a fellowship to graduate school at this rate – I wanted also to major in art, philosophy, psychology, sociology

1–Edward Estlin (E. E.) Cummings (1894–1962), often styled as e e cummings: American poet.

– and Russian (!) lit. But no. Choices are the cry these days. I do hate limiting myself, though – learning more about less and less.

maintenant – I have a proposition for you to ponder over. Suddenly conscience-stricken, a week or so ago, I realized that I had said "nay" thrice to kind invitations to trek Princeton-ward. (The boy must think I have a phobia or mental block, I say to myself. Not so. NOT SO.) Thereupon, I decide I can't bear not to see the dashing Georgian in his native habitat before he is lost to us forever. So I will therefore set before him all my free weekends to choose from, if he wants to commit himself – and he can pick one that's most convenient? Logical?

Do please understand that I can thrive on "off-" weekend as well as on gala ones . . . liking walking, talking, etc. – (and money isn't needed for such placid pursuits . . .) So, me love, if thou wouldst care to see me Apr. 5 (sort of soon, I think) or may 3, 10, 17 – just let me know. This is just to convince you that I am not busy <u>every</u> weekend for years in advance.

At any rate, even if you are furious with the girl for her last telegram, do realize that she would have much liked to send the opposite answer – and say hello to her now and then –

so sincerely –
sylvia

p.s. – home address:
26 Elmwood Road   Mar 20 to Apr 1
Wellesley, Mass.

TO *Ann Davidow-Goodman,*

Friday 21 March 1952   ALS with envelope, Smith College

March 21

Davy, me love –

And a happy spring to you, gal! This being my first day of vacation, and me relaxing after the first night of sleep in my own little home, I decide to drop you a line or so in thanks for that wonderful long long letter you wrote me.

Honestly, Annie, I don't know what to do with you – you've grown up beyond me so fast – I can only listen with abject admiration at your philosophizing about love and life. And working in Chi! Gosh, you're an independent woman! What I want to know is more about the handsome stormy looking guy whose picture I'm sending back (although I hardly can bear to – he's <u>so</u> dynamic!) Are you going to marry him? If so, how soon? If not, why not? Maybe your family is amazed at your surge of independent individualism – but all I can say is, more power to you!

I can see what you mean about getting attached to the man you "love" even if later on you might not want to be attached to him. How do you feel about Ray in that regard? That's just why I am so wary with Dick, because I figure that even though we're mentally & physically magnetically attracted, it's dangerous for me to get involved, although he would like to, if I would – because I'm not so sure I want to become a victim of my passions yet and have to break up our families or settle down. Yet every time I see him it gets harder and harder. What started out to be an intellectual and casual relationship last winter has flamed up into a situation where we can't tear ourselves apart, the attraction is so strong. Imagine – last Friday, when I went in to Harvard Medical School to see him for the first time in three weeks we started talking in his room, me sitting on the bed, and he on a chair, and finally he just threw himself down beside me on the bed, pulled the quilt up over us, and we stayed there in each others arms as it got darker and darker outside and the city lights came on. Time blurred, melted warmly. We had been there seven hours when we finally realized that I had to go home – plunged rudely out in the cold world again. If this goes on – I am going to become much more resentful of customs and conventions and may even develop a "To-Hell-with-people attitude." But then, you know what I mean. Life around here is so hypocritical.

College is still fun – I love my courses – specially creative writing and painting – I always feel guilty when I sit down to write – it's not work, just play. Did I tell you that I am teaching "art" to kids at the People's Institute? On every Monday afternoon – grubby, but a change from the ivory tower, any way.

I have applied for a waitressing job down the Cape this summer, but as yet, nothing has come through. I'm also hoping to move into a co-op house as the board & room is jumping $150. Trying to make "ends meet" is a rather risky proposition at times.

This vacation I'm going to be awfully virtuous and set myself a "writing schedule." I've looked forward to this for ages – when I can sit for hours at a stretch at the typewriter and pound away without worrying about other people or homework, or anything. I've decided to start trying for the Mademoiselle contest since I flubbed 17 this year and all. Anyhow – I'll be going back to school rested and caught up for a change – after having cried all Thanksgiving vacation (over Dick's revelations of his salacious past) and having been in bed for almost a month over Xmas. I even refused an excitingly dangerous invitation to the Princeton Jr. Prom from my dashing Russian inebriate (of N.Y.C.) on the grounds that I might get run down & have another sinus infection. Such maturity! (It almost killed me to say no, but I figured a 2-day fling wasn't worth a 2-week bedrest!)

Of course I'll be seeing Dick on weekends, even though he has classes during the week. We're going to see "Swan Lake"[1] tomorrow night in Boston – our first ballet! We read Hemingway short stories aloud when we are not otherwise occupied. God! I wish you could meet him. I still wonder if I am too selfish to love him – or if I just think I do because I need him and he needs me – or if I am an incurable polygamist – ah, me!

Anyhow, I persuaded him to come up and live in Northampton for a week during his spring vacation at the end of April. Springtime – I can't wait!

Life is funny – on the bus going back to school last weekend I sat down beside a boy just like the one Eddie told me I would finally fall in love with. For three solid hours we talked about life, destiny, chance, hypnotism – our childhoods, dreams & future plans. I don't know when I've ever established such a complete "rapport" with anyone. He was 25, tall, lean, blond, blue-eyed – quite lovely. And kind!

Funniest thing – he was getting his Ph.D. in entomology (insects) – which my father taught & wrote books on. He even had heard of daddy! Well, after the bus trip he took me out for coffee & a sandwich & carried my suitcase back to Haven. I almost cried at leaving him – it was all so perfect, only he was going to start work in a few weeks & live in Conn. for a while – and I know I'll never see him again.

You know, once in a while you have a glimpse of complete happiness with someone you love fully for a brief while – and then it passes, and you are sad, yet afraid somehow that if you ever met again, the perfect illusion would be dispelled and the dream gone. So I remember him, lovingly and sadly. Never again, you know.

Now, honey – write when you have a little time, and in the meantime, remember how much I love you –

Your
Sylvy

1 – *Swan Lake* was performed at the Boston Opera House.

TO *Hans-Joachim Neupert*

Friday 21 March 1952 TLS (photocopy), Smith College

March 21 . . . the first
day of spring 1952

Dear Hans . . .

I am celebrating the first day of my longed for vacation by writing letters, and you are first on my list. It has been so long now since I have had any free time of my own that I am thrilled at the chance to do the things I want to do at last. I plan to rest a lot and to make up all the sleep I lost during the last hard weeks when I stayed up late every night to study for exams or to write papers or to review lectures for the town newspapers for which I work. Now, at last, I am come home, where my brother is also home from preparatory school, and our little family is together at last.

Although it's spring by the calendar, it is still cold and muddy outside, and the wind has the knife-sharp edge of winter yet. We even had a big snow-storm the other day, and it was strange to see the daffodil stems sticking up through the blanket of thick snow. But soon it will be warm enough to take my studying out of doors and sit in the sun and get brown while I work . . . a much more healthy was of living than to sit indoors all the time as we have to do in the winter, I assure you. I wish you could see how pretty the campus is in spring, with the leaves greenly reflecting in the lake and the mountains faint and delicately blue in the distance . . . . not mountains really, but big hills. Then life is really lovely and even final exams cannot take away the beauty of it.

It is hard for me to believe that I have only two more years of college after this. As it is now, I would like very much to get some sort of fellowship to study abroad after I graduate for a year. I don't have any money myself, by my marks are high, and maybe there would be a chance to get a sort of scholarship. Who knows, I might even visit you, if you don't come to America first, that is.

The country is all excited about the coming elections next fall. Campaigning has been going on all over the place, and Eisenhower seems to be a favorite, although he is a bit handicapped by being abroad and not here to make a personal appeal to the people. The one thing I don't like in his program is that he favors Universal Military Training. You know what a pacifist I am!

I can imagine that your work is extremely demanding, by I should think you would be pretty proud of going through with it all. Being an electrical engineer is no small undertaking, you know.

You mentioned that you never found out the date of my birthday . . . . I belong to the same month you do . . . being born on October 27, 1932. Somehow I dread being 20 this coming fall . . . it sounds so old, as if I were already gray and grown-up, and I don't want to get old . . . life seems to be so open and full of choices now. I hate banging doors behind me, you know. Also the idea of settling down. I want to travel so badly . . . I have never been out of the New England States, you know.

At school I do not only study, but I also spend at least one afternoon a week teaching little children how to paint at the Settlement House in the city itself. I also paint decorations for the dances and parties, which is alot of fun. I enjoy living away from home and being independent so much, even if some times tired, or not feeling well, I long for a comforting hand and a motherly or fatherly shoulder to comfort me. But all in all, living in a dormitory is a good experience in growing up.

This summer I am trying to get a job waitressing down on Cape Cod in Massachusetts . . . right on the shore . . . but jobs like that, although they pay well, are scarce and in much demand, so I don't know how much chance I have. At any rate, I have my fingers crossed, for board and room expenses at college have gone up and I need the money rather badly . . . also I would like very much to be by the ocean where I could swim on my days off.

Well, I have been talking on and on about myself . . . let me hear from you, when you next have time, and good luck in all your work . . .

As always,
Sylvia

TO *Aurelia Schober Plath*

Thursday 3 April 1952[1] ALS (postcard), Indiana University

Thursday

Dear mum –

Seems hardly possible to be back in the old routine – had a lovely ride back on the bus with Pat O'Neil and a nice supper with Marcia & Mrs. B. Today classes were creaky & nothing happened except I got a straight A in the Religion exam I took before vacation – at least my refusal of

1–Date supplied from postmark.

Princeton paid off that way. I called the girl who worked at the Pines[1] last year and she said that it was like a family summer settlement – not commercial – with the same people & children coming back year after year. She also said there were about 2 hrs. off both a.m. & p.m. – but jobs like polishing silver. The help have their own private beach nearby & a whole day off (I should hope so.) She said tips were only $10 – $15 a week & that you made only about $300 during the summer. Sounds like a lot of work for not much money – also 6 beds in the dorm – about 20 waitresses to the small place – Gosh, I don't know. I'll wait & see. If only one knew in advance how these things were going to work out! I shall write the Southward.[2] This weekend means work – but its good to be back in a way

XXXX
Sivvy

TO *Aurelia Schober Plath*

Saturday 5 April 1952 ALS (postcard), Indiana University

April 5

Dear Mum –

Well, I did it – blew $34 for a sweater & skirt. It is something I hope you will like, but I feel I owe it to myself. The sweater is a lovely shortsleeved aqua cashmere that will also go with my gray skirt – and the skirt is a pleated white wool. I tried on mixtures, but felt that although this will have to be cleaned, it is wearable to date & dress occasions all year round – winter, spring, & fall, and can be worn with <u>any</u> color sweater I choose to buy – red, black, brown, green – anything I am going to get shieds for the sweater.[3] I feel it is better to wait & get something special like this than to get several mediocre things. I now have all of $1 in my checking account let me know when you put money in – do draw from my bank. <drawing of sweater and skirt> School is busy & I hope to get caught up this weekend. This week I am hearing both Robert Frost & Sen. MacCarthy[4] speak! What an opportunity.

1 – The Pines Hotel was in Cotuit, Mass.

2 – The Southward was an inn and restaurant in Orleans, Mass.

3 – A shield was a piece of fabric sewn into clothing, usually in the underarms, to protect it from perspiration.

4 – American poet Robert Frost (1874–1963) and American politician Senator Joseph McCarthy (1908–57). Both spoke in John M. Greene Hall at Smith College; Frost on 9 April 1952; McCarthy on 10 April 1952.

XXX
Sivvy

P.S. I wrote Orleans to find details on salad & pastry – just for the heck of it.

<on address side of postcard>

P.S. Got the April "17" – am eligible for the next contest due July 30! What luck! Watch my dust!

Please mail me my white hat! and overshoes – maybe you could send them via Dick Saturday p.m.

TO *Aurelia Schober Plath*

Wednesday 9 April 1952[1] ALS (postcard), Indiana University

Wednesday

Dear mum –

As I said, this is an extremely busy week. Irony of ironies – I have a gov. written at 12 next Wed – the day Dick leaves, so I'll have to be studying off & on most of the time he's here. Got straight A on that old English exam I took way back when, with a "This is an excellent paper" from the august Elizabeth Drew[2] herself! So happy I didn't go to princeton. Last night I sat up to type the 16 page story "Sunday with the Mintons" that I'm sending to <u>Mme</u> just for fun – you would be interested to see the changes – I made it a psychological type thing – wish-fulfillment, etc. – so it wouldn't be at all far fetched. Tonight I hear Robert Frost, tomorrow, Senator McCarthy. Also wrote two poems this weekend – which I'll send eventually – "Go Get the Goodly Squab in Gold-lobed Corn . . ." etc. I plan to sleep before Dick comes. Life is terribly rushed – what with press board, work, & all these lectures – but fun.

XXX
Sivvy

1–Date supplied from postmark.

2–Elizabeth A. Drew (1887–1965); English professor, Smith College, 1946–61; SP's colleague, 1957–8. Drew taught a course on the literature of the nineteenth and twentieth centuries (English 211) completed by SP, 1951–2, and modern poetry (English unit) completed by SP, 1952–3.

TO *Aurelia Schober Plath*

Monday 21 April 1952[1] ALS (postcard), Indiana University

Monday

Dear mum –

I am in a whirl of mad work – to pay for my lovely unintelligent athletic weekend. 3 weeks of back Religion is no fun – but it's being spring has compensations. Letter from Pines awaited me here – very nice – I can go to Cape on Monday 16th & start work the 17th. May even possibly have Monday's off. I'm not sure. I'm <u>really</u> invited to visit Alison,[2] and plan to go Thursday, June 5, for at least 4 days – which gives me a good week at home to rest and write in. Press Board is coming along fine – should earn about $10 per month. Saw Miss Drew, my Eng. prof, today and am trying to get my schedule straightened out. I talked to her about how I wanted to go to Breadloaf[3] in the summer, & she said she thinks I can get a job waitressing up there & audit all the courses I want! So that's my project for next summer. Where there's a will there's a way!

Love you,
Sivvy

TO *Aurelia Schober Plath*

Sunday 27 April 1952[4] ALS (postcard), Indiana University

The-morning-after-the-night-before

Dear mum–

Well, it is Sunday noon, and I am still in pajamas, after having inconsiderately been robbed of an hour's sleep by Daylight saving. The dance was great last night – and I wore my yellow dress, which looked nice with its two gardenias & yellow ribbons (courtesy of Dick.) Dick left after the dance to drive back with Ken, so I am free to sleep & work today. Tell me about Marcia's "invitation." Since she didn't tell me about it she probably wanted to surprise me or something. I can't think of any real news except that I bought a bargain outfit in denim – shorts, jersey,

1–Date supplied from postmark.
2–Alison Vera Smith (1933–97); SP's friend and Smith classmate from New York City. In June 1952, Alison Smith withdrew from Smith College to attend Johns Hopkins University.
3–The Bread Loaf School of English, a summer graduate programme, at Middlebury College, Middlebury, Vermont.
4–Date supplied from postmark.

skirt & halter all a nice shade of medium blue with white pique edging – the skirt & halter make a sunback dress, & shorts makes a playsuit with halter, a tennis-outfit with jersey – a lot of fun, washable, durable, and only $12 for the whole outfit. Just what I need for the summer! All the Sophs who went to the prom had dinner at Jack Augusts – treating the boys to a lobster dinner. I am at last making out my schedule for next year – its awfully exciting

XXX
Sivvy

TO *Aurelia Schober Plath*

Wednesday 30 April 1952[1] ALS with envelope, Indiana University

Wednesday

Dear Mother –

You are listening to the most busy and happy girl in the world. Today is one of those when every little line falls in pleasant places.

Number one: I have just been elected to Alpha-Phi Kappa Psi (no, I'm not going Greek on you) which is the "Phi Beta Kappa of the Arts. "It is the purpose of the society, composed of a maximum of 30 members who have demonstrated excellence in dance, drama, literature, music or painting, to provide recognition for artistic achievement . . . Qualifications for membership are creative ability, promise in the case of sophomores . . ." etc. So I am one of the 2 sophs chosen for creative writing ability![2] We all got single roses & marched out in chapel today. Also, I think I will get at least one sonnet published in the erudite Smith Review[3] this next fall!

Number 2 is a sort of frightening miracle. As you know, I have a physical science requirement next year which clogs up my whole schedule. At the suggestion of Pat O'Neil, who took the course this year, I petitioned to do the work on my own this summer & write a paper or take an exam, arranged by the director of the department. It was highly irregular, & Miss Schnieders didn't give me much hope. But it got passed! So I will study on some of my off hours this summer & probably clinch the work

1 – Date supplied from postmark.

2 – The other sophomore was Enid Epstein.

3 – *Smith Review*, the literary magazine of Smith College was revived with the fall 1952 issue. SP published her short stories and poems in the magazine and served on the editorial board, 1952–5.

in a week when I get back – which eliminates the necessity of suffering through 6 hours a week next year & lets me take an exciting History of Art course instead.

News number 3 is that the News Office is giving me an increasing amount of responsibility lately. I am covering no fewer than five (5) lectures in the next four days: Ogden Nash tonight,[1] 3 lectures on the European student Thursday & Friday, plus a Friends meeting[2] on Sat. afternoon which is not "open" to students, but involves all sorts of fascinating Smith alums with great book collections. These last four are to be written up feature style & sent everywhere from the Monitor to the Sat. Review – hoping for acceptance. The new head of the News Office – Mrs. Smith[3] – is very good about dropping such plums in my lap, and It is all because she saw my feature on baby-sitting (which I tossed off in 3 hours last Mountain Day) got published, & so thinks I have an angle, or something.

Number 4 is that at the 1st Alpha meeting after lunch today two girls came rushing up to me and said how would I like to be on the Editorial Board of the Smith Review next year, and my, how they just loved my Sonnet: Eva. (What a life!)

Number 5 will, I hope, involve me. None other than W. H. Auden,[4] the famous modern poet, is to come to Smith next year (along with Vera Michelis Dean[5]) and may teach English, or possibly Creative Writing! So I hope to petition to get into one of his classes. (Imagine saying, "Oh, yes, I studied writing under Auden!")

1–American poet Ogden Nash (1902–71). Nash spoke in John M. Greene Hall; two unattributed articles were published on the event: 'Ogden Nash's Rhyming Knack Makes Up for His Talent Lack', *Springfield Union*, 1 May 1952, 30; and 'Ogden Nash Is Speaker', *Daily Hampshire Gazette*, 2 May 1952, 6.

2–SP covered the Friends of Smith College Libraries meeting; an unattributed article was published on the event: 'Smith Library Displays "Fanny Fern Collection"', *Daily Hampshire Gazette*, 5 May 1952, 8.

3–Probably Elizabeth Hugus Smith '16, who served as the News Editor for the College during the 1951–2 academic year.

4–English-born poet Wystan Hugh Auden (1907–73); William Allan Neilson Research Professor, Smith College, 1953.

5–Russian-American political scientist Vera Micheles Dean (1903–72); visiting professor, 1952–4.

Honestly, mum, I could just cry with happiness – I love this place so, and there is so much to do creatively, without having to be a "club woman." Fie upon offices! The world is splitting open at my feet like a ripe juicy watermelon. If only I can work, work, work to justify all my opportunities.

XXX your happy girl,
Sivvy

TO *Aurelia Schober Plath*

Friday 2 May 1952[1]

ALS (picture postcard),[2]
Indiana University

Dear mum –

Carol pierson's mother treated ten of us to a birthday-steak dinner here last night – replete from sherry to coffee. I am planning for a very busy work weekend – with 2 papers, art projects, studying & lecture covers. By the way, I was just chosen to be one of the 30 "distinguished Sophs" to be on Push Committee (helping all during commencement activities). Unfortunately I will have to refuse because of my "job" – (which I hope I have) – sent Crawford's[3] letter & Belmont[4] acceptance – haven't heard from either. What a double life I lead!

XXX
Siv

TO *Aurelia Schober Plath*

Monday 5 May 1952[5]

ALS with envelope,
Indiana University

Monday

Dear Mother –

As yet I have heard neither from my acceptance at the Belmont nor my refusal at the Pines. I have visions of either being out of two good jobs,

1 – Date supplied from postmark

2 – The postcard featured the Whale Inn, Goshen, Mass., with the caption 'When down in the mouth, Remember Jonah! He came out all right.'

3 – Nita Converse and Calvin D. Crawford, owners of the Pines Inn, in Cotuit, Mass.

4 – The Belmont, a hotel then in West Harwich, Mass. SP worked as a waitress there in June 1952.

5 – Date supplied from postmark.

or sued by both places as a bigamist! However, I am sold on the Belmont, & feel that if only that's settled I can wiggle out of the Pines somehow – I should earn more, too, even though the months wages are the same – $40. I would begin work the 11th of June & end the 5th of September – not bad. I feel I would be so lucky to work there! The letter said – "We have thousands of applications and experience few openings . . . ."

These next 3 weeks are packed to the gills – I worked and sunned last weekend, getting 3 short papers written and typed – a total of about 25 pages. Also played an hour of tennis Sunday a.m. with Marcia. Sat. afternoon was spent at the Friends of the Library tea – as I was one of two college girls in the midst of a throng of ancient-but-fiery friends, I felt a bit conspicuous, but thoroughly enjoyed myself.

Last night I went to my first Honor Board meeting at the Warden's (Mrs. Cook's) House.[1] Dean Randall,[2] my old English teacher was there, as well as two brilliant faculty members, Maria Canellakis[3] (the Greek girl who is head of H. B.) and the head of Student Council.[4] The only one missing was the College psychiatrist. The two cases were fascinating – oddly enough. The offenses were by seniors & involved Modern Art & Creative Writing! (most appropriate for the note-taking secretary.) I kept still most of the time, figuring I'd better see how the procedure went before participating in discussion.

The Art offense involved a girl who had personality difficulties – defeatism, etc. She had ripped all the articles on Rouault out of the magazines in the library because she was writing a paper on him and had destroyed the evidence when a search was undertaken. Eventually she confessed herself to the warden because she felt she couldn't live with her self any more. They split the case in 3 aspects, with treatment or penalty for each. One necessity was psychiatric investigation.

The other girl came back late from a weekend at home where her mother was undergoing a cancer operation & her father was just diagnosed as a cancer victim – and she passed in a writing assignment due the next day – 2 poems of her own, & 1 copied to complete the required 3. The Board voted an E for the assignment & a possible D for the course.

As you can see, I find my job very exciting! Lots of ideas for stories! God! I'll have to start studying psychology!

1–Smith College Warden Alison Loomis Cook.

2–Helen Whitcomb Randall (1908–2000), English professor at Smith College, 1931–73; dean of the college, 1948–60; SP's colleague, 1957–8.

3–Maria Canellakis Michaelides (1930–); B.A. 1953, biological sciences, Smith College.

4–Holly Stair Greer (1931–); B.A. 1953, history, Smith College.

This weekend I'm playing Cupid and fixing up 3 of Dick's friends. I do hope all six new people[1] get along. One is Alison. I figured it would be nice to get her a date as she is planning all sorts of exciting things for me when I go to New York on the 5th (Thursday.)

By the way – how am I going to get all my stuff home Wednesday the 28th? Can grammy come up? Will you be free? I should be pretty well packed after lunch as my exam gets over at 11–

By for now – have thousands of pages to read for gov.

your loving,
Sivvy

TO *Aurelia Schober Plath*

Wednesday 7 May 1952[2] ALS (postcard), Indiana University

Wednesday

Dear mum –

Well, this summer is just about settled. An amazingly nice note came from the Pines today saying they had gotten a girl on waiting list to take my place. I was happily surprised at their courtesy: no muss, no fuss. All I have to get now is a note from the Belmont confirming my signed contract. I am saving the surprise to tell Dick this weekend. I am very glad to see your upswing in mood about teaching – you really need a rest. I was heartbroken about Carver. I need the money so badly. At least I have lots of extra activities for next year. Wish me luck at getting safely through the next two heavy weeks –

XXX
Sivvy

1–According to SP's calendar, she set up Alison Smith with Milton Viederman (1930–); B.A. 1951, Columbia University; M.D. 1955, Harvard University; Nancy Teed with Walden Benjamin Whitehill (1930–), B.S. 1951, Grinnell College; M.D. 1955, Harvard University; and Anne Goodkind Bird (1933–); B.A. 1955, history, Smith College, with Allan Irwin Sandler (1929–2001); B.A. 1951, Princeton University; M.D. 1955, Harvard University.

2–Date supplied from postmark.

TO *Aurelia Schober Plath*

Sunday 11 May 1952[1]

ALS with envelope,
Indiana University

Sunday 7 p.m.

Dear Mother –

Well! I have just taken a luxurious hot bath and am now sitting in pajamas and bathrobe in my friend Betsy Whittemore's room listening to a lovely Handel Concerto and planning to go to bed within the next hour as I am soo sleepy.

In spite of the rain all today, the weekend had many elements of success. Friday was so glorious that I lay out on the sunroof for a couple of hours – even washed & dried my hair up there. It's amazing how drying in the sun lightens it! Thursday night I had a delightful supper at Lawrence House (coop) with a new friend: Jan Salter,[2] a Jewish girl from New York. In the evening we went to hear the most wonderful lecturer – Patrick Murphy Malin[3] – Head of the Civil Rights Commission. He was without a doubt the handsomest, kindest, most tolerant, creative man I have ever met! (I mean heard!) As an antithesis to Senator McCarthy's "guilt by association and hearsay" lecture, he was an example of integrity and outstanding promise. I must show you the lecture notes I took sometime!

Anyway, the boys came Saturday just before supper, which we ate at Haven House. We saw a free movie[4] at Sage Hall, got them settled (Dick at Mrs. Brown's & the other 3 at a nearby tourist house) and split up. Two of the couples went to Rahar's – a local collegiate spot for food, drink & music – Dick & I ran barefoot on lawns, went wading in the liquid waters of Paradise, climbed trees, and generally enjoyed ourselves on our own.

Nancy Teed (much too cosmopolitan for our little group) decided not to go out with her date again today – so Alison got one of her prettiest friends to go and all 8 of us had a lovely time. Dick & I spent the morning in dungarees & sweatshirts helping Mrs. Brown sand and paint ceilings & woodwork. I had the best time! I just love painting woodwork &

1 – Date supplied from postmark.

2 – Janet Salter Rosenberg (1932–); B.A. 1954, English, Smith College.

3 – American activist Patrick Murphy Malin (1903–64); talk in Sage Hall on 'World Tension and American Civil Liberties' in what SP called a required government lecture in her calendar.

4 – On 10 May 1952, the College Film Committee showed *The Medium*, a film based on the contemporary opera by Gian-Carlo Menotti, at Sage Hall. Also shown was Norman McLaren's *Pen Point Percussion* (1951).

pretending I am making my own house. The work seems like nothing but fun, & I'm glad to have a chance to contribute to the Brown's new homestead – they've been so good to me.

Anyway, the 8 of us drove up to the mountain range and had a cookout in the rain under a log roof. We devoured cheese, hotdogs, pickles, potato chips, tomatoes and beer (not much) over a smoky fire, hiked, climbed a lookout tower, & generally got damp and fresh-aired.

The nicest thing is that Alison & Milton got along just beautifully, so he asked her to come down next weekend for a dance at Medical School which I decided to go to also. So I invited Alison to stay with me – feeling so happy that I could do this for her before my stay in New York. We will probably come home on the 5 p.m. bus, Friday, getting in between 9 & 10. Saturday morning I plan to study – and want to know if maybe I could use the car that day? Don't plan anything elaborate – you work hard enough! We won't be wanting meals except a pick-up supper Friday night, breakfast Sat., breakfast & dinner Sunday – we'll leave on the earliest bus then, too. I do want you to meet Alison – she's the dearest girl!

Today I got a letter from the Belmont confirming my job. So all is set. Dick is much pleased, too. I really hope I earn a lot of money to make up for the losing of the Elks' hope of aid! Boo to the Elks.

An English major here got a Fulbright this year to study in England after she graduates. Also, the Rotary scholarships are good. Find out anything you can. We will be applying for those in a year or so!

If only I can get all my work done before these exams! I <u>must</u> get good marks in them – plus writing up forty senior personals[1] to all the papers for graduation & doing each days press board, plus keeping up Honor Board work, plus going to showers, dinners, etc.!

Really, though, I am leading a glorious country-clubby life, in spite of my work. I have at least gotten thinner & you should see my tan!

See you Friday
XXXX
Sylvia

1 – An unattributed article, '15 Area Girls to Graduate From Smith College June 9', *Daily Hampshire Gazette*, 27 May 1952, 9.

TO *Aurelia Schober Plath*

Monday 19 May 1952[1] ALS (postcard), Indiana University

Monday a.m

Dear Mum . . .

How sad it is to be back in the narrow confines of a rigorous schedule again, with the next ten days looming grim and sadistic – and knowing that a head now blank will have somehow to be filled . . . [in the few days between now and Friday.] Our bus trip back, in spite of our resolutions, was mostly talk – that girl is by far the most intelligent and stimulating I have ever known! I feel proud to have her as a close friend. I <u>do</u> want to thank you for pausing in the midst of work to make such a lovely homey atmosphere for us – and such delicious meals! By the way – I got a postcard from Elizabeth Drew (my favorite Eng prof, who has written books on T. S. Eliot[2]) inviting Marcia (whom she has never met) and me to tea at her house[3] Tuesday! I was thrilled!

S

TO *Aurelia Schober Plath*

Monday 26 May 1952[4] ALS (postcard), Indiana University

Monday
7 a.m.

Dear mum –

I haven't even an hour before my Eng. exam to skim through my notes, so this will be a brief mandate: I'll be packing when you come Wednesday, and If I'm at lunch, just go on up to old Rm. 6. Marcia's mom would love to have you drop over & see her, too, – they took me out to the <u>best</u> steak dinner Sat. night. When you come bring <u>cartons</u> (for books) & empty <u>suitcases</u> – Heaven knows how I'll get <u>all</u> the things to go home packed! Gov. was a really rough exam – glad it's over! I've been studying for English solidly the last 2 days & have a great clot of memorized poetry in my head – I <u>do</u> love memorizing.

XXX
Siv

1 – Date supplied from postmark.

2 – Elizabeth Drew, *T. S. Eliot: The Design of His Poetry* (New York: Charles Scribner's Sons, 1949).

3 – Drew lived at 54 Prospect Street, Northampton.

4 – Date supplied from postmark.

TO *Aurelia Schober Plath*

Tuesday 10 June 1952[1] ALS with envelope, Indiana University

Tuesday

Dear mum –

Your amazing telegram came just as I was scrubbing tables in the shady interior of the Belmont diningroom. I was so excited that I screamed and actually threw my arms around the head-waitress who no doubt thinks I am rather insane! Anyhow, psychologically the moment couldn't have been better, I felt tired – first nights sleep in new places never are peaceful – and I didn't get much! To top it off, I was the only girl waitress here and had been scrubbing furniture, washing dishes and silver, lifting tables, etc. since 8 a.m. Also, I just learned since I am completely inexperienced, I am not going to be working in the Main diningroom but in the "side hall" where the managers & top hotel brass eat. SO – tips will no doubt net much less during the summer and the company be less interesting. So I was beginning to worry about money when your telegram came. God! To think "Sunday at the Minton's" is One of Two prize stories to be put in a big national slick!!![2] Frankly, I can't believe it!

The first thing I thought of was: mother can keep her intersession money and buy some pretty clothes and a special trip or something! At least I get a winter coat and extra special suit out of the Minton's. I think the prize is $500 !!!!!!!!!!!

ME! Of all people!

Being as I don't start waitressing till Thursday in the side hall – and am scared stiff as I have to balance trays on one left hand & don't know anything. I'm awfully happy.

If they take me back, I'd like to come be a regular "dining room" waitress next year. We'll see!

Since I've been the only girl waitress down here, I've been given a great time. Never have I seen so many cute guys! Young, a lot of them, but fun. One is even a professional gambler!

1 – Date supplied from postmark.

2 – Sylvia Plath, 'Sunday at the Mintons'', *Mademoiselle*, August 1952, 255, 371–8. The other prize winning story was Elizabeth Marshall (1931–), 'The Hill People', *Mademoiselle*, August 1952, 254, 363–71.

Paul Dalton,[1] a handsome Soph at Brown from Wellesley, has been a dear & made me feel right at home; yesterday I got a ride in one guy's convertible to the center & was treated to gingerale.

This p.m. I was innocently sitting on the beach writing this, when Paul and 4 other guy's came down, bringing me some cold beer. I was sunning in the midst of them when who should come along but Perry! He sat & talked with us for a while & is biking over tonight. Boy, was he shocked at the "competition."

He said when he saw me sitting amidst five boys he almost pretended he didn't know me & ran away! (So like Perry!) Anyhow – 35 girls will be competing with me in a few days.

Perry's biking over tonight, too. When I walked in yesterday, Driscoll[2] said "Letter for you" and handed me a cute note from Dick.[3] Those guys sure are thoughtful!

So it's really looking-up around here, now that I don't have to be scared stiff about money. My side hall uniforms are all black with adorable scalloped white collars, hair bands & aprons. Oh, I say, even if my feet kill me after this first week & I drop 20 trays, I will have the beach, boys to bring me beer, sun and young gay companions. What a life. Love, your crazy old daughter. (Or, as eddie said: "one hell of a sexy dame"!)

XXX
Sivvy

TO *Aurelia Schober Plath*

Thursday 12 June 1952[4] — ALS with envelope, Indiana University

Thursday

Dear Mum –

Boy, let me tell you, if I didn't have that Mme telegram[5] (it came Tuesday morning) to lean on, I would be pretty low now. Everything comes at once. On top of working like a dog all day yesterday setting up the whole

1–Paul Austin Dalton (1933–2011); schoolmate of SP's at Wellesley High School, class of 1951; B.A. 1955, Brown University.
2–Leo F. Driscoll, head waiter at the Belmont Hotel.
3–Probably Richard Norton to Sylvia Plath, [8 June 1952]; held by Lilly Library.
4–Date supplied from postmark.
5–Margarita G. Smith (*Mademoiselle*) to SP, 9 June 1952; see SP's publications scrapbook, p. 21; held by Lilly Library. Margarita G. Smith (1923–83); fiction editor at *Mademoiselle*, 1943–60.

dining room for 300, which involved moving & dusting tables, putting on cloths, silver, glasses, plates (all of which we had to wash & wipe first), I started my period early last night, and in spite of dosing myself with aspirin, couldn't sleep at all because of cramps. This morning was cold and rainy, and the whole combined to make me feel rather depressed.

I knew there would be some catch to waitressing – and I am stuck for the summer, as I said, with two other girls, in the "side hall" where the management eats. So I guess I don't even get to glimpse the high life at all. And my luck will be good if I earn as much as I did last summer. The only small apparent compensation is that I guess my hours won't be as long.

Most of the girls came yesterday, and I swear they are all Catholics, mostly Irish at that. But if I work at it, I can be just as boisterous as they are. My roommate hasn't come in yet, so I'm still living single.

I still don't see how I got in here unless Grampy knew Mr. Driscoll – it develops that just about all the new girls are "Mr. Driscoll's niece," daughters of the cook, very good friends of the Driscoll family, etc. Which probably explains why I got the side hall.

One important thing – I don't know what got into my head, but I didn't bring down any really warm clothes – and after today I'd appreciate a bathrobe, my lumbershirts, my white cardigan sweater, and anything else you can think of to keep me warm for the early season!

No doubt after I catch up on sleep, get over my period, and learn to balance trays high on my left hand I'll feel much happier. As it is now, I feel stuck in the midst of a lot of loud brassy Irish Catholics – and the only way I can jolly myself is to say "Oh, well, it's only for a summer, and I can maybe write about them all." At least I've got a new name for my next protagonist – Marley, a gabby girl who knows her way around but good.

The ratio of boys to girls has gotten less & less, so I'll be lucky if I get tagged by the youngest kid here – lots of girls are really wise, drinking flirts. As for me, being the conservative, quiet, gracious type – I don't stand much chance of dating some of the cutest ones.

While thanking god for little blessings – I will say I'm in the "quietest" part of the dorm.

If I can only get "in" as a pal with these girls, and never for a minute let them know I'm the gentle intellectual type, I'll be O.K.

As for the Mme. news, I don't think it's really sunk in yet. I felt sure they'd made a mistake, or that you'd made it up to cheer me. The big advantage will be that I won't have to worry about earning maybe barely $300 this summer. I would really have been sick otherwise. I can't wait till August when I can go casually down to the drug store and pick up a slick copy of Mme. flip to the index & see ME. One of two college girls in the U.S!

Really, when I think of how I started it over spring vacation,[1] polished it at school, and sat up till midnight in the Haven House kitchen typing it amidst noise and chatter, I can't get over how the story soared to where it did. One thing about Mme. College Fiction – although that great one last year by the Radcliffe girl[2] was tremendous & realistic, I remembered the first issue I read where there were two queer part-fantasies – one about the hotel the woman kept for queer people[3] & the other about an elderly married couple.[4] So I guess the swing of the pendulum dictated something like good Old Henry & Elizabeth Minton. Elizabeth has been floating around in my head in her lavendar dress, giggling very happily about her burst into the world of print. She always wanted to show Henry she could be famous if she ever worked at it!

One thing. I am partly scared and partly curious about Dick's reaction when he reads the story in print – (I wonder if they'll cut out the parts that my C. writing teacher wanted left out?) I'm glad Dick hasn't read it yet – but Henry started out by being him & Elizabeth me – (& they grew old and related in the process.) But never-the-less, I wonder if Dick will recognize his dismembered self! It's funny how one always, somewhere, has the germ of reality in a story, no matter how fantastic.

I don't think that they illustrate their stories, but I wish to heck they would. I know a great girl from Smith[5] who graduated this year & will be a guest editor – she's very talented in art. So Smith is getting publicity – and am I glad to help. I don't think they could hear about it in time to cut down my scholarship. It would sure be a nasty thing to do, but she knows I was short a few hundred, so this will just "fill in." It's awful to have to suffer because of publicity.

Anyhow, although I only told Perry & Paul Dalton about the story, I get great pleasure out of sharing it with you who really understand how terribly much it means as a tangible testimony that I have got a germ of

1–According to SP's calendar, SP worked on 'Sunday at the Mintons" on 25 March 1952 and 7–8 April 1952.

2–Probably Ilona Karmel, 'Fru Holm', *Mademoiselle*, August 1950, 203, 293–305. Karmel was a 1951 graduate of Radcliffe College.

3–Though not a *Mademoiselle* fiction contest story, possibly Hollis Alpert, 'The Partition', *Mademoiselle*, September 1947, 192, 293–7.

4–Though not a *Mademoiselle* fiction contest story, possibly Peggy Thompson, 'This is how it was', *Mademoiselle*, March 1949, 143, 200–2.

5–Jo Ann Wallace Davidson (1931–); B.A. 1952, art, Smith College.

writing ability, even 17 has forgotten about it. The only thing, I probably won't have a chance to win Mme. again, so I'll try for a guest editorship maybe next year or my senior year, and set my sights for the Atlantic. God, I'm glad I can talk about it with you – probably you're the only outlet that I'll have that won't get tired of my talking about writing.

The more I think about attitude being everything, the more I think that I can make these slangy girls be good for something if I handle them right. Anyhow, I'll soak up the kitchen & side-hall atmosphere – if not more than 25¢ tips. I've got a great story setting here, boy.

Speaking again of Henry & Liz – It was a step for me to a story where the protagonist isn't always ME – and proved that I am beginning to use imagination to transform the actual incident. I was scared that would never happen – but I think it's an indication that my perspective is broadening.

By the way, they've got an employee over here with a name almost exactly like mine – so put "waitress" after my name so she won't open my letters before I do!

Sometimes I think – heck I don't know why I didn't stay home all summer, writing, doing physical science & having a small part time job – I could "afford" to, now, but it doesn't do much good to yearn about that, I guess. Although it would have been nice. Oh well, I'll cheer up. I love you!

XXX
your own Sivvy

TO *Aurelia Schober Plath*

Sat.–Sun. 14–15 June 1952[1]

ALS with envelope, Indiana University

Saturday 11:30 p.m.

Dear mother –

After today you must be ready to disown me – I want to explain that when you walked in the door I was tired, tense, & on the verge of tears. I wanted nothing more than to throw myself in your arms and sob "Take me home with you, I'll never be a good waitress." But as it was I didn't know what I was doing. To top it off, the woman told me I didn't have to work for supper when I went in for lunch, and when I thought I could have had a picnic with you all somewhere I just ran to my room and did

1 – Date supplied from postmark.

burst into tears. I didn't know where you were, and Dick came, and I was so tired and sad. He insisted on driving me to Brewster to stay at the cabin. By that time I was so homesick and lonely and the thought of being left alone for four hours with Mr. Norton when I could have been with you made me feel worse.

But I somehow did manage to swallow that sick feeling & have a nice supper with him. We picked & hulled some little wild strawberries for desert & went for a walk together down by the shore till Dick came to drive me back. I was really so grateful for Mr. Norton's at least being human to me that I could have cried. That seems to be all I can do now.

Please, please, when Warren gets a day off, come see me again & give me another chance. Maybe if you could get here after lunch, if not earlier in the morning, I could swim with you all.

Do write me letters, mummy because I am in a very dangerous state of feeling sorry for myself. All the cute girls are on dates and I feel that nobody loves me except maybe the ice man who smiled at me today. As you psychically suggested, Dick has changed his attitude toward me and I feel like telling him to just stop being nice & to leave me alone. Marcia is "engaged" – and writes to ask about New York and so on – she's going to the wedding – or went today. How I love her!

Anyhow, since I providentially don't have to work for breakfast tomorrow, maybe I can go back to sleep and catch up. Just at present, life is awful. Mademoiselle seems quite unreal, and I am exhausted, scared, incompetent, unenergetic, and generally low in spirits.

Do bear with me – it was so heartbreaking to glimpse all you dear people today and want to again be back home where people care more about whether you're alive or not.

Anyway, forgive me for acting so queerly today. And please do come soon again.

Thanks for bringing the stuff.
Love,
Sivvy

Sunday

Well, I managed to get about 9 hours of sleep last night, and I still feel sort of shaky. Honestly, I would like to know why I can't seem to adjust to new situations involving a lot of people my own age. I already feel that I can never really belong to the large group of adorable, peppy, tireless waitresses who work in the main diningroom and get asked out to dances and parties till late in the morning. Working in side hall puts me apart, and I feel completely uprooted and clumsy. The more I see the main hall girls expertly getting special dishes, fixing shaved ice & fruit, etc., the more I get an inferiority complex and feel that each day in side hall leaves me farther behind. Even there I have trouble "timing" meals and getting courses to interlock, etc.

But as tempted as I am to be a coward and escape by crawling back home, I have resolved to give it a good month's trial – till July 10. I figure three more weeks should give me a fair chance to become more capable, to see how much I would earn in the next two months, to be really in the summer season. If I don't earn $100, I really feel that the work, the hours, the chopped up time and so on wouldn't be worth it. The only inducement I have is really the beach and a tan. I will sacrifice minor comforts for that, but not major ones.

One thing, If I do get really more miserable day by day, I figure maybe I can get another easier job, since it would be early in July, still, I hate to think of leaving the Cape, though. And you know how I hate not to complete a thing. At this point I am completely confused. In a week or two when the guests come, there will be more of a set routine, but side hall never changes from week to week.

Do you think I'm a coward to consider giving up in a month if it doesn't work out? I was thinking I might somehow be able to get a part time job down the cape here – in a store or book or art shop, but then I figured the hours would be so I couldn't ever see everyone else who goes to the beach, etc. And as for jobs around home, I don't know what you could dig up there for me. I wouldn't care so much about money if I could sleep, be home, study and write on weekends. After all, If I'm going to run around like mad for only 200-250 for three months, And I could be earning the same thing in an easier way, it would seem silly to stick this out.

However, I must change for dinner now. Don't <u>worry</u> about me, but do send me little pellets of advice now and then. My roommate comes in a week, which may give me a rapid swing up or down decisively. Just now I'm vacillating in great confusion.

Write soon,
XXX
Sivvy

TO *Aurelia Schober Plath*

Monday 16 June 1952[1] | ALS with envelope, Indiana University

Monday

Dear mum . . .

Well, it is my weeks anniversary here, and I am celebrating the beautiful blue day by spending my morning hour clad in my new black bathing suit down on the beach. Needless to say, I am in a little more optimistic mood than when I last wrote you. In spite of the fact that as usual I am not loved by all the girls – whether they classify me as competition or what, I don't know – but anyway I figure I don't have to shed tears about that. I do like being by the beach, though, and if necessary, I can be pretty independent and self-contained. Last night I actually had my first "date", and had a really good time, to my surprise. Of course, there are many more girls than boys, and all of them are adorable. But if I get a small percentage of dates now and then, and spend the rest of the time studying or sleeping, I may manage.

I have been thinking over the situation and figure that even if I did get a "dirty deal", this season, I should think of the future. I could earn $500 next year if they took me back in the main diningroom, and if I put in a relatively unprofitable summer financially this year, I can "afford" it with my <u>Mme</u> money. (Perhaps that's why I got the prize.) So we'll see. I probably could never get such a good job next summer as I could with this summer of experience behind me.

Anyway, could you rush me some mesh or service weight stockings. Nylons just don't stand up under the 3 day change & diningroom wear & tear – send garters please if they're not built in. Also send bras. I must have left them in one of my drawers as I only have one here.

Last night I got my phone call from "Lloyd, The Bellhop,"[2] around 8, lay down from 8-10, and went out from 10:30 to 2. It really was fun – we drove to a beer place and sat and played number games, drank beer & had cheeseburgers. After that, it was a drive to a lighthouse, a coffee place, and a furtive walk over the Belmont grounds in the moonlight. I really thought my date was a nice fellow – a med student from Dartmouth. Unfortunately, all the girls around here are gorgeous, so I don't expect to "go steady" at all. It's like shuffling a pack of cards. There are a good

1 – Date supplied from postmark.

2 – Lloyd Chaim Fisher (1930–2007); B.A. 1952, Dartmouth College; attended Dartmouth Medical School, 1951–3; M.D. 1955, Columbia University.

twenty-five really adorable waitresses to about a nucleus of 10 eligible men – so you can see. But at least maybe I'll net a few dates, & comfort myself by sleeping the rest of the time. The characters around here are unbelievable, and I already have ideas churning around in my head. One learns so much by keeping quiet and listening. I hope I'll be able to really get a lot of story material out of this. At least I'll be able to spout authentic dining hall lingo and thereby give a semblance of reality & background.

Chin up & take it easy,
XXX
Sivvy

P.S. I was much amused to get a letter from Alison who is going to Italy this summer. She wants me to come to New York in September, and I hope I can make it. I deserve a rest. The funny thing was, evidently Eddie & his friend dropped in on her saying, of all things, that I sent them. She & a friend went out with them, and she raved about how impressed her family was with them. All of which goes to show how double dealing some people can be

again.
XX
Siv.

TO *Aurelia Schober Plath*

Wednesday 18 June 1952[1]

ALS with envelope, Indiana University

Wednesday 930 pm

Dear mother –

I do so appreciate your very thoughtful letters which have been arriving every day. They have given me a big lift. As for the letter to Driscoll – at first I was horrified that grampy had sent it, but on second thought, I think its a wonderful idea. I believe in pulling all the strings I can, and that is one way to keep on hammering it into his head that I want to get into the main diningroom. I managed to grab him in the kitchen the other day and ask him if there was any chance of eventually changing. He was very evasive, and said that they couldn't tell now, and words to the effect that sidehall wasn't so bad once it got going. So I am glad your letter will clarify matters.

1–Date supplied from postmark.

As for me, I saw Mildred and dear Aile[1] this afternoon – chatted on the front porch, and convinced them I was healthy, happy, and coming along more philosophically than when I last saw you.

Dick came too, and we went for a little drive. One great thing about sidehall – I get out early. This morning I had a private swim at 9 a.m. and lay & rested in the sun till 11:30, as the other help gradually congregated around.

This afternoon, Dick & I took a brief drive, and I'm writing this just as I am expecting him to drop over & say hello tonight. At least we're best of friends, anyway.

So I'll stick it out, I think. Nowhere can I swim and tan so well, and as you said, a transfer would probably toss me out of the frying pan and into the fire. –

Enclosed find check – I am glad I'll at least earn $50 from that newspaper next year.

XXX
Siv

TO *Aurelia Schober Plath*

Saturday 21 June 1952[2] ALS with envelope, Indiana University

Saturday 10 a.m.

Dear mother . . .

Today is really going to be the roughest of the season. A big convention of about 1000 is coming down, and they are eating on 3 shifts, which means that everybody works all day. No doubt tempers will get very short. So maybe I'll get another whack at the main hall.

I have a feeling that unless something unforeseen happens I'll be in side hall all summer, and yet they have given me the biggest station, which will be work, but which pleases me because there will be more people. In full season I'll be waiting on 13 people: 4 orchestra men; the caretaker, his wife & daughter, 2 ladies from the gift shop, the 2 diningroom captains (women) and the head bellman. So, figuring at least a $1 tip per person a week (possibly $1.50 or $2 from one or two), I should net $15 in tips

1–Aili Kaukonen Bertocci (1907–79), wife of Angelo Philip Bertocci (1907–2002), a professor at Boston University. The Bertoccis lived at 30 Pine Street, Wellesley, Mass.
2–Date supplied from postmark.

per week, plus $10 base pay if I stay the season. So that would roughly be what I earned last summer. So except for the fact that this work is really physically tiring, I shouldn't go bankrupt. Of course, I have considered the pros and cons of leaving, say August 10 – all he could deduct would be $10, and I would be able to come home, rest, work on science, and maybe babysit or type or work on a playground mornings for a month – both studying science and writing. That way, I might earn about $50 less, but I was thinking it would be a plausible and healthful solution, perhaps. After all, 2 months work is a respectable stint. What do you think? Of course, come August, I might want to stay, or be switched to the main hall, but otherwise, I think my solution isn't too bad a one for the time being. We shall see. I feel very calm & philosophical about it. The way I figure, I'm working very hard for the money I earn, and a month of maybe writing, studying & earning pin money would be valuable physically. 2 weeks is hardly enough to rest up from a strenuous summer like this one.

My roommate, Polly LaClaire,[1] arrived yesterday, and is a very sweet girl, tall, dark – reminding me much of Ruthy Freeman, she is 17, and also starts the University of Mass. next year.

I got the package. Thanks. I haven't heard from Mlle (you were right) yet. Hope to heaven they didn't get the wrong person by mistake – otherwise I will die. You don't think they would have gotten wrong the name by chance, do you? That is the strategic coup that has saved my sanity and nervous system!

I've got an idea for a 3rd story for 17 called, of all appropriate things – "Side Hall Girl" – I even have a heroine named "Marley" who is, of course, me.[2] The ending would be very positive and constructive. I hope I can get time & energy to write it. If I mull it over in my head for a week or so, trying to organize the chaotic incidents which pile on me every day, I should be able to sit down & type it up on some girl's typewriter in a few days and send it to you to type and get notarized. Ambitious? You bet. The only thing I hope is that the editors of 17 don't read Mlle!

I'm going to try for a guest editorship next year (& the year after, If I don't get it.) At least I've got plenty of activities to advertise, & with my honors program, should manage to do the monthly assignments. Not only that, I'm going to work for that Atlantic contest but hard.

1 – Pauline Ann LeClair (1934–2013); B.S. 1956, University of Massachusetts.

2 – According to SP's calendar, she typed her story 'Side Hall Girl' on 16 February 1956. The University of Victoria, Victoria, British Columbia, holds the only known, extant page of the typescript (p. 2); named characters are Mary and Polly.

Would I like to win a summer at Breadloaf! But that is really a dream, because boys usually win those things, & my style needs to mature a lot yet. I'm glad to have catapulted out of the 17 arena, though.

Yesterday p.m. I swam a lazy & talkative mile out to sea with a beach boy life guard.[1] A motor boat with a friend of his came along and towed us back in. More fun! At least I'll learn how to swim if I go down at least once a day for 2 months. Dick biked over last night & from 10-12 we walked leisurely along by a river, I, learning some constellations I'd long forgotten how to find, talking casually, and stopping for big vanilla icecream cones on the way back. I really managed to enjoy myself.

As for sidehall – they've done the best they can for me as far as station is concerned, and I figure I deserve a "bad break", what with all my good fortune winning prizes & going to Smith. My different hours give me an excuse for not hanging around with some of the more snobby cliques, and well, I just don't care what people think about me as long as I'm always open, nice, & friendly.

So happy about Warren's job –
Love to you all,
Sivvy –
your Sidehall philosopher

TO *Aurelia Schober Plath*

Monday 23 June 1952[2]

ALS on The Belmont letterhead, with envelope, Indiana University

Monday

Dear mother . . .

From the beach once more I am saying hello. At this point I could use some sleep. They say one never gets completely rested around here. One sure thing, the chance for taking naps is fine once you get used to the noise in the dorm. But I haven't gotten around to it lately. This morning it was too nice to resist the beach, and Polly, my roommate, whom I like very much, went for a swim at 9:45 when we got through. It's so nice to have someone to do things with. Our hours are different from the other waitresses, and we are on a different "scale", so we don't get to see them as much.

1–According to SP's calendar and her journal, this was James Clark Williams, LL.B. 1953, Harvard Law School.

2–Date supplied from postmark.

Last night I went on a "gang" Birthday party at the "Sand Bar"[1] – where we sang and talked for a few hours. There were about forty of us kids from the hotel. In spite of the fact that there was a slight preponderance of girls, I managed by some magic to get myself seated next to a fellow in his first year at Harvard Law – and he was just a dear. Funny thing, but I managed to keep him around for the evening. We yelled conversationally across the din, and I nursed a Tom Collins he bought me, ate coconut cake, talked with a bar boy who majors in English at Tufts, and generally had a great time. I don't expect to get asked out more than a few times this summer so I'll have fun when I can get it. The best part was when we came back – it was a beautiful clear starry night and Clark went in to get me two of his sweaters to wear because it was cold and brought out a book of T. S. Eliot's poems. So we sat on a bench where I could just barely read the print, and he put his head in my lap and I read aloud to him for a while. Most nice!

The only thing is, I am so inclined to get fond of someone who will do things with me like that – always inclined to be too metaphysical, and serious conversationally – that's my main trouble. And around here dates are so ephemeral – you go out with a boy one night, see him the next day with one of the other adorable waitresses, and at first are crushed, and then think, heck, I'll get casual about life yet.

Mon. afternoon

Well, anyway, even if I did get in after one, I managed to take a 12 mile bike trip with Perry and Dick this afternoon to Long Pond where we went rowing for an hour, picking waterlilies, and generally having a lot of fun. Needless to say, tonight I am going to bed "early" – about 10:30. And shall take a nap tomorrow if I am stiff after my spurt of exertion – a mile biking in about six minutes is pretty good time for me!

So glad to hear the check from Mlle is real. I hardly could believe it. Just now, I am mentally so disorganized that I can't retain knowledge or think at all. The work is still new enough to be tiring, what with 3 changes a day into uniforms, and I am so preoccupied by mechanics of living & people, that I can't yet organize & assimilate all the chaos of experience pouring in on me.

In spite of everything, I still have my good old sense of humor and manage to laugh a good deal of the time. Even in spite of the fact I got not quite $20 in tips for the last two weeks of waitressing. Yet I will see how I feel August 10 – I figure slaving myself to death for a bare $100

1–The Lighthouse Sand Bar, 33 Lighthouse Road, West Dennis, Mass.

isn't worth it at this stage – and of course I may decide to stay if I'm rested & having fun & get into main hall. But by Aug. 10, the summer will be well on the way to a finish, and in spite of the fact I'll miss the beach & the Nortons, I don't think I'll miss much else. And 2 months is a good summer's work, wot?

Well, no other news – except I'll make the best of whatever comes my way. What fortitude. (Wish Phil Brawner would give me a call – does he know I'm a waitress---didn't think he associated with the proleteriat!)

Goodnight dear,
XXX
Sivvy

TO *Aurelia Schober Plath*

Wednesday 25 June 1952[1]

ALS on The Belmont letterhead, with envelope, Indiana University

Wednesday

Dear Mother –

Just a note, to let you know I'm still alive, although in a state of suspended animation. Never, it seems to me, has work worn me out so much. When my Smith friend, Jan Salter, told me all she did in her hours off was lie down & rest, I laughed, thinking – what a waste of time. But really, that is just about all we have energy to do. I can't think, I can just perform mechanical acts. So no more going out for me. I won't be asked, anyway, because I'm just not the beer-brawl type, even if I do have fun now & then at those aimless soirées. I am still captain of my soul – will send you money orders of my "great intake" in cash every week or two to be safe. We slave for every dollar that I figure I can't take any risks.

I have definitely decided to come home August 10. It is the only reasonable way out I can see. I will have stayed two months, slaved for $200 (-$10) and will need a good month to recuperate physically & mentally. With all my important & demanding school offices, I can't afford to crack up. So I'll have 6½ weeks more of swimming, the Norton's & slaving. How much notice should I give – ? isn't a week enough for side hall – They can get a girl any time?

I figure if I leave then, I can get my science done at home in 30 days at the rate of 25 pages a day – (in the morning) – and really get continuity.

1 – Date supplied from postmark.

NOW I'm always so tired that I just can't retain anything except what kind of eggs people like for breakfast!

Dick just called – is rather sick in bed with a cold, poor guy. I wish I could go over & take care of him – fruit juice, salads, etc. I really am awfully fond of both those boys as people. Well, tell me what you think of my schemes.

XXXX
Your maturing Sivvy

TO *Aurelia Schober Plath*

Friday 27 June 1952 — ALS with envelope, Indiana University

Friday, June 27

Dear mother . . .

Wow! The heat wave sure has hit. These last three days have been hellish. While the other girls go tripping around in light shortsleeved green nylon dresses we swelter in our heavy longsleeved black cottons. I didn't even have the energy to go swimming this morning, but just lay and rested in my room and dozed. Although I've gone to bed at 10:30 for the last two nights, I still have felt very tired. The fatigue may be due to the fact that I haven't had a meal off since two weeks ago this coming Sunday . . . and to add to the routine monotony, I have had continuous dreams about waitressing whenever I go to sleep, and often can't tell lunch from supper when I wake up from a nap because I feel I've been "working" all during my sleep.

To top it off, Mr. Driscoll must have been touched indirectly by your letter because he came up to me today with a very curt and rather unorthodox proposition. They are further complicating our sidehall troubles by building a linen closet where one of the two doors is, so with 30 people & 3 busy waitresses running in and out of the one door, it will be horrible. Mr. Driscoll stalked up to me, shot off in glib quick sentences – "You-say-you're-in-the-market-for-extra-money-well-you-can-have-the-job-of-giving-out-linen-after-meals-for $30 a-month-let-me-know-right-away-now-or-tomorrow."

I was completely taken off guard. $30 a month sounded like a wonderful sum, but I shot the pros & cons quickly through my head – giving out linen for the main hall would mean an extra hour after breakfast &

lunch & two hours after dinner,[1] plus till about midnight on Wednesday & Saturday after the big dance & cocktail parties. Well! I figured I'd be working over 30 extra hours a week with definitely no time off at the mere pittance of about 25¢ per hour. No social life, no relaxation, no nothing! I mean, I appreciated the opportunity as I felt Mr. Driscoll meant well. But I feel there is a definite limit to what I will do for money. And when I considered the work I'd be doing for the amount involved, I felt very angry. I started to tell him very politely that I appreciated his considering me but I couldn't undertake the extra time physically – and he just shrugged and walked off in disgust in the middle of my explanation. I could have slung a dish after him. There is something so nigardly & unscrupulous about these people – in spite of the money pouring through their hands. Imagine me working over 70 hours a week! God! And those girls in main hall don't work any harder than we do – & get 5 times as much pay. In other words, I have been offered the chance to kill myself for the opportunity to earn as much as they earn with hardly any effort at all. Boy, was I burning! I'm leaving here by August 9th come hell or high water – maybe you could persuade the norton's to strap my bike on their car when they come down at the end of July – if they do. They're so nice and understanding about things like that. I would like the bike as long as possible, but I don't care in the final analysis. It's funny how one's feelings fluctuate. After the heat & rush of today, I feel that I am slightly crazy to be slaving (that's what it amounts to) for two months to get not much more than $175.

I can see that Mr. Driscoll's attitude now is probably that he's given me my chance at money, I wouldn't take it, so I can stew in my own juice. Oh, well.

Do remind grammy & Grampy to bring those 3 big suitcases (empty) when they come down so I'll have space to put things in!

Well, I'll work on the sleep angle – there's only one boy here I really like – a skinny brilliant guy at Columbia Med who goes mainly with the most beautiful waitress here – in her first year at Johns Hopkins Med. Anyway, Ray Wunderlich[2] & I took a two hour walk Wednesday from 8-10 p.m. – as no one else was off that early, got icecream & sat down the beach & had great discussions on everything under the sun. He is a dear boy, but if I see him even a few times during the season I'll be lucky – and quite glad. So you don't have to worry about my going out too late and all.

1 – 'two hours ~~for~~ after dinner' appears in the original.

2 – Ray Charles Wunderlich, Jr (1929–2014); B.S. 1951, University of Florida; M.D. 1955, Columbia University; dated SP, 1952–3.

And once a week or so, I'll see Dick & thereby help save my sanity. If I can stick this out for two months I'll be proud of myself. The only thing I'm afraid of is – if I give him 2 weeks notice, he might kick me out on the spot – but now that I think of it, I wouldn't complain!

So, dear mummy, thanks for all your lovely frequent letters, and don't worry about me. I hope you feel as I do, that my refusal of that "proposition" today was a mark of my maturity!

Love to you and Warren & my dear grandparents. What would I do without you all behind me!

Love,
Sivvy

TO *Richard Norton*

Friday 4 July 1952 TL (incomplete), Indiana University

July 4, 1952

Dear Dickie . . .

Well, worlds do sometimes tumble and even when one is neither mouse nor man the best laid plans can dissolve. Leaving one rather dazed in the backwash. The phone rang early this morning, and it was of course the Belmont wanting to know, very sweetly, how I was and when I would be coming back. They said they wanted to hire a girl part time if only mother would give them a definite date of my return so they could make a contract and all. Whereupon mother took the bull by the horns and said that she didn't know when I'd be through with these sinus complications and that the doctor wanted to keep me here until I was definitely sound and sane again . . . and that maybe it would be best and most convenient to hire someone for the rest of the summer as my situation is so indefinite. The woman who called was just a dear, saying how they missed me, and liked me, and wanted me back . . . all of which touched me no end. So that is that.

At this point I am in no position to say how I feel about the whole business. I have just gotten my voice back after three days of enforced silence, and although the dear old speaking mechanism sounds a few octaves too low still, I get by with pretending I'm just naturally very husky and sultry. My sinus still is a bother, though, and they just let me outside for the first time today . . . the whole week passed by in sort of a penicillin coma. I will be overjoyed when I shake off this persistent lethargy of convalescence.

TO *Harold Strauss*[1]

Tuesday 8 July 1952 TLS, University of Texas at Austin

26 Elmwood Road
Wellesley 81, Massachusetts
July 8, 1952

Mr. Harold Strauss
Editor-in-Chief
Alfred A. Knopf, Inc.
501 Madison Avenue
New York 22, New York

Dear Mr Strauss:

As you may imagine, I was delighted to receive your encouraging letter[2] and to learn that you approve of my story, "Sunday at the Mintons." It was very kind of Miss Abels[3] to send the proofs to you.

Next fall I shall be a junior at Smith College, where I am majoring in English and getting journalistic experience as Smith correspondent for the Springfield DAILY NEWS. As I am working my way through Smith on scholarship, it is necessary that I take on a rather rigorous working program during the summers in order to meet the remainder of the year's expenses. Thus I am not in the position to concentrate on any sustained writing project as yet.

My plans after graduation are indefinite at present, as I do not know what opportunities the next two years will bring, but I hope to get a fellowship for graduate study here or abroad. It may be that then, at last, I shall have the opportunity to concentrate completely on writing.

Should I feel, in the future, that any of my work is of sufficient scope and merit to be of interest to you, I shall be very happy indeed to submit it for your approval. As it is, I deeply appreciate the confidence you have expressed in my writing, and I hope within the next few years to justify your encouragement.

Thank you for your great kindness in writing to me.

Sincerely yours,
Sylvia Plath

1–Harold Strauss (1907–75); editor-in-chief of Alfred A. Knopf, Inc.

2–Harold Strauss to SP, 26 June 1952; held by Lilly Library.

3–Cyrilly Abels (1904–85); managing editor of *Mademoiselle*, 1950–early 1960s.

TO *Marcia B. Stern*

Tuesday 8 July 1952 TLS with envelope, Smith College

Tuesday, July 8

Comrade . . .

Life has a sudden way of turning somersaults and spitting in one's face. Here I am, of all places, sitting in Wellesley and cursing myself. All very strange and about to be explained. No, I wasn't fired. It happened this way. Last Saturday (I mean a week and a half ago . . . time evaporates so fast) I started coming down with the typical and prophetic sore throat. After all, one can work and play twenty-four hours a day for just so long. So I was feeling like merrie hell all Saturday, until the phone rang, and it was Phil Brawner, a veddy nice guy from Wellesley who will be a senior at Princeton next year. Seems he'd come down to visit the Cape, and mother had thoughtfully told him where I was staying. So I figured I'd have one real fling to get my mind off my condition. At eight, when I got through slinging hash at a particularly fussy bunch of Belmont employees, I leapt back to the room, tore off my proletarian black uniform and got all swish in my aqua cotton we bought in Boston last summer. Phil was suitably impressed, and we had a delectable evening at a marvelous place called the Mill Hill Club,[1] with great entertainment . . . and expert banjo player, superb vocalists, dancing, etc. The Cape was really roaring. I foolishly made an arrangement to play tennis with Phil and his friends the next afternoon, and went to bed wondering if I was going quite mad. Sunday morning I went to the doctor in Harwich who advised me to go home for a few days and see my infection through in peace and quiet. So when Phil drove up dressed for tennis that afternoon (luckily it started to rain five minutes later) I met him and his friend with a little black suitcase and asked very sweetly if he'd mind company on the drive back to Wellesley. He and his friend thought it was the funniest thing in years, and we picked up another Princeton boy[2] who is the chauffeur for that senile millionaire I wrote you about that Art Kramer[3] (He says he knows Betsey James very well) is night nurse for at $100 per week. Anyway, because I looked very flushed and healthy, having both a tan and a temperature of over 100, the four of us went for a long drive in the rain, sat overlooking the ocean drinking beer and being very merry, the boys thinking that I was just tired

1 – The Mill Hill Club was in West Yarmouth, Mass.

2 – Identified as 'Weasel' in SP's calendar and journal.

3 – Arthur Bennett Kramer (1927–2008); B.S. 1949, Yale College; M.A. 1951, LL.B., 1953, Yale University; dated SP, 1952–3.

of work and wanted a vacation or something. Well, on the way home I started losing my voice, and by the time I hit Wellesley, I was ready for bed and the penicillin shots. I spent three days, sans voice, in a penicillin coma, when the Belmont called up wanting to know when I'd be coming back, as they planned to hire a girl for the interim. Mother, who thought I was working and living much too hard, and had figured that basically I really didn't want to go back to side hall, said maybe they'd better hire someone in my place as she didn't know just when the doctor would let me return. End of job.

Now that I'm my hideously healthy old self again, I feel that I've been hit over the head by a nasty black jack. I still can't get over feeling sorry for myself, and need very badly someone like you around to talk me out of my depression. All I do is think what a wonderful time I was having, how I could see Dick once or twice a week in the most idyllic settings, how I was meeting all kinds of fascinating young people, and how I was away from the warm, stagnant calm of a deserted Wellesley. I have been trying to think up all sorts of wild schemes to get back there at the Cape . . . as a laundress of sheets or a companion of anybody who'd pay for conversation but the chances are negligible. I've been reading help-wanted adds and so on. But the letters from the friends I made at the Belmont are so sweet and I was really getting to like some of the girls terribly, that I just sit here acting like a Greek chorus and beating my bloody head against the suburban woodwork. Aiyee!

Phil has been the only saving grace. He's working for free in the Shawmut bank in Boston getting experience with a capital E. I regard him solely as a means for drowning my sorrow. I mustered enough energy to play a little tennis with him Saturday, and saw "Quartet" and "Kind Hearts and Coronets"--a tremendous double bill--in Boston that night.[1] Sunday night we sat on the fabulous merry-go-round in the bar of the Copley Plaza (now the Sheraton) and talked for hours over Scotch and soda. He's really an extremely intelligent fellow . . . born and brought up in Charleston, South Carolina, and showing all the gentlemanly breeding that implies . . . I am quite smothered by his chivalry. Also handsome. But what the heck. The only real interest I have in him is the challenge of one personality balancing in verbal jousts with another. He's a human being . . . of the Wellesley aristocracy,

1–*Quartet* (1948), based on four of W. Somerset Maugham's short stories, played as a double feature with *Kind Hearts and Coronets* (1949) based on the novel by Roy Horniman, at the Kenmore Square Theater in Boston.

and a matter of convenient transportation and amusement. Do I shock you by my pragmatism?

At least Dick's dad came over last night and invited me to accompany him down to the Cape over this coming weekend. I am counting the days exuberantly. Needless to say, I miss the guy terribly. It was so divine to have him call me up when I got back from work and make boating or swimming plans. Oh, fie, I'm getting maudlin. There are times when the lid is lifted off and one is suspended in a bewildering vacuum. You don't know how I miss the blissful routine of that job. It took away six hours of personal responsibility . . . all I had to do was my work, and well . . . and the rest of the day, in pieces, was mine. Now I have the horrible twenty-four hours hanging over my head, and I must make out a schedule . . . science, four hours in the morning. Afternoon . . . tennis practice, writing. Evening . . . shorthand or planned intellectual reading. How can I spend such a lonely summer. And while at work, I thought nothing would be more blissful than to loaf! Life goes by contraries. Grass being greener . . . and other trite maxims.

Now, out of this slough of despond! Maybe my guardian angel, who has fallen asleep on the job recently, will be kind enough to get me back in medias res once more somehow. The uncertainty being what it is, I think I'd better wait before grabbing joyfully at the plans for a reunion on the 16th. I don't know where in heaven I'll be then. But I'll keep you posted. Oh, Marty, the summer started out so wonderfully and all. And it was my fault for the collapse. That's what hurts. And it is so frighteningly tempting to get into a suburban rut and to let the time go by without Accomplishing anything. I plan to start a vigorous schedule in the next few days, as soon as I am able to breathe fully and normally once more.

You know, it's funny, but here you are undergoing a rough deal this summer in being so far away from that wonderfuly guy Mike, and doing a rather good job of managing. Whereas I, who was starting to be quite spoiled at the Belmont, can still see my man now and then, and yet feel most nostalgic. It's all on what one expects, I guess. I aimed terribly high, and exacted too much living capacity for my physical frame, and now anything, no matter how good in itself, seems calm and quite tasteless in comparison.

This letter is a masterpiece of incoherence, but I just had to spill it out the way it would come. My old optimism is hardput just at present to smile and be philosophical. But even so, I am trying to be objective and see the funny side of the whole thing. La! Uncertainty in my wellordered life! How incongruous. But seriously, I think I would accept any old greasy job just to get back in the vicinity of the Belmont and Dick. Oh, well, ten years from now . . . but that's the trouble, the influence of this summer would make a difference. And what it would have been I'll never know.

Forgive the lugubrious undertones, angel. They'll pass. Love to you and your wonderful mother.

Syl

TO *Aurelia Schober Plath*

c. 12 July 1952[1] ALS, Indiana University

Dear mum . . .

don't think I forgot a thing! Do read this adorable note from Ray . . . especially the last line! People aren't so blind after all. La la!

XXX
Sivvy

TO *[Aurelia Schober Plath]*

c. 12 July 1952[2] ALS,[3] Indiana University

P.S. IF jolly old Phil <u>should</u> just happen to call, say veddy brightly – "Oh, Sylvia was having <u>such</u> fun down the Cape that she decided to make a long weekend of it & won't be back till Tuesday." Yuk – Yuk –

Silvano Plator
Merry Xmas
("m" as in mnemonic!)

1–Date supplied from internal evidence.

2–Date supplied from internal evidence.

3–Letter not addressed to a specific person; probably for ASP. Letter written on a form headed 'Please send this absentee report to the Evening Division office after class or the morning following class meeting.' Possibly used by Boston University. At the bottom of the form there is a space for 'School or College' which SP had modified to read 'School of Hard Knocks'.

TO *Marcia B. Stern*

Wednesday 16 July 1952 ALS with envelope, Smith College

July 16, 1952 8 p.m.

Dear Marty . . .

Just got back this afternoon from a weekend's camping out at the Cape with the Nortons. This will be my last fling for the next six or seven weeks, so I made the most of it . . . and as a result of hardly any sleep the last 3 nights plus the 100 mile trip back in the hottest part of the heat wave today, (I drove Mrs. Norton & young David back) I can hardly hold a pen, much less keep my eyes open. But I did have to drop you a note to explain my change of address.

The world has a funny way of working . . . in spite of my NEVER AGAIN vows at the end of last summer, I answered an add for a "neat, intelligent girl of pleasant disposition" (ho) that I read in the Christian Science Monitor.[1] (Anything to get back down the Cape!) The woman sounded just lovely over the phone, and I dropped in for a personal interview Sunday afternoon. I think the family is Jewish – and also Xian Scientist! Very gracious & friendly mother . . . two kids – boy (3½) & girl (5½) plus a relative of some sort – girl of 12. Should prove of interest & study-able, wot? I will be driving a Chevrolet station wagon – cleaning house, helping in all ways including amusing kids at beach & attending their swimming lessons – starting next Saturday. The Cantors[2] live in one of the roomy gray Cape Cod houses rented out by the Chatham Bars Inn, & use the beach, tennis court & all facilities. It'll be fascinating to compare this deal with our mutual summer experience last year. (I liked Mr. Cantor on first glimpse too!) I'm very curious as to what their lives have been like . . . I scent intrigue somewhere. (Mrs. C. likes to paint!)

As a matter of fact, I don't give a damn if the kids are horrid as long as I can see Dick once in a while. And some of the kids from the Belmont. I'll only be about 3 miles farther from Dick (a 25 mile round trip by bicycle isn't a cinch, though!) and about 10 miles from the Belmont. The

1–*Christian Science Monitor*, 10 July 1952, 15. The full advertisement reads: 'COLLEGE-AGE GIRL for Mother's helper for balance of summer. Neat, intelligent, and of pleasant disposition. Refs. exch. Salary arr. Box 546. Chatham, Mass. Tel.: Chatham 493-J.' SP clipped and saved the advertisement in her Smith College scrapbook, p. 19; held by Lilly Library.

2–Margaret Kiefer Cantor (1910–2003) and M. Michael Cantor (1906–2003). During the summer of 1952, SP was a mother's helper at the Cantors' summer home on Bay Road, Chatham, Mass., where she took care of their children: Joan (1939–), Susana (1947–), and William Michael (1949–). The Cantors lived at 276 Dorset Road, Waban, Mass.

only person I really liked quite intensely there was this Ray Wunderlich, a brilliant guy from Florida who goes to Columbia Med – and I hope I'll get a chance to see more of him – just for the stimulating conversation. Of all coincidences, I ran into him last night as Dick & I were coming out of the Cape Playhouse, having just seen Dana Andrews in "The Glass Menagerie."[1] Ray & Dick got on admirably – I was proud of both the dear med students.

This weekend has been a dream – I've been sleeping in all sorts of situations – in a tent with David – and in the cabin with the 3 boys – Dick, Perry & Rit (a tall, sweet guy, engaged to Bev – an elementary school teacher waitressing down in Brewster). Saturday night when I came down, Dick and I went swimming & boating out on a big, dark fresh water lake. We rowed out to the middle, anchored, swam, watched mammoth shooting stars & a slice of red moon rising over black hills – all idyllic after 3 weeks separation. All his time off we spent swimming & sunning. You should have been with us Sunday night—we went to visit the negro cook at Latham's— "Otha," and his wife Linda. When we walked up to the little white house, there was the sound of much laughter & merriment – no less than 8 other Negroes were visiting them. Dick & I felt right at home, drinking beer, eating sandwiches, kibitzing on canasta & merrily exchanging yarns. In twos & threes the other Negroes started leaving about midnight. But Dick & I stayed on till after 1, listening to Otha recount his experiences in New York, all about how he & Linda met, and their wedding day! I was entranced & went away loving them both as wonderful & sensitive people. It was a new experience for me, being in the "minority" group temporarily.

Yesterday, Dick's day off, was best. We biked in bathing suits in the hot sun to Pleasant Bay in Chatham – swam, picnicked, swatted at stinging green flies, read aloud, ate cherries, swam, stared at the bright blue sea, passed hours unknowing. Steak dinner back at cabin with Rit & Bev, & then the Playhouse. Very wonderful. (You know, though, anyway.)

Probably nothing as satisfying for a month & a half, though. One never knows.

I did spent one fascinating day in Wellesley working with an aggressive real-estate agent[2] who is opening an office in town. If the Cape job hadn't

1–SP saw the summer 1952 production of *The Glass Menagerie* by Tennessee Williams at the Cape Playhouse in Dennis, Mass., starring Dana Andrews as Tom, Mary Todd as Laura, June Walker as Amanda, and Walter Matthau as the gentleman caller.

2–According to SP's calendar, this was with Mrs Frank Williams, 45 Brook Street, Wellesley, on 9 July 1952.

popped up, I'd be working at Real-Estate. I had a great time touring through houses, reading adds, talking with builders, etc. Could have learned a lot that way, even if hot & lonely in this stagnant fen.

Keep your fingers crossed for your gambling roomie. Thanks mille fois for August invite. As it is, I can't be social & travel, though. Hope you'll come to Brewster, tho! Cape idyllic. Always sun, sea, & sailboats.

I'll write when I'm settled in my new abode.

xxx,
Syl

From July 19-Sept. 1
c/o The Michael Cantors
Bay Lane
Chatham

TO *Aurelia Schober Plath*

Sat.–Sun. 19–20 July 1952[1] ALS with envelope, Indiana University

Saturday

Dear Mother . . .

It now being 10:30 p.m., I am sitting in bed (phenobarb duly taken . . .) and sending you a few words before the reaction hits & I fall asleep.

Situation here won't bear judgment until at least after a week is up. It's always a big job getting accustomed to the ins and outs of new surroundings, but they are all very nice people apparently. I don't know just what I'll wind up doing, as this schedule is extremely arbitrary – people always are so un-routine.

As yet I haven't begun to "live" here. There's always the "breaking-in" period. So far, my schedule has been something like this: 2: arrival. 2-3 unpacked and got settled in small-but-nice whitewashed room with 2 beds, 2 bureaus & a huge closet, which I filled – also, readinglamp over bed. 3-5 swim at a lovely beach with parents, Billy (3½), Susie (5½) and Joanie (13) – all theirs. Kathy (17)[2] is over in Holland on the Experiment. (She, it seems, likes to write.)

3 children (1 visitor included) ate supper which I "supervised" – guess I'll be getting it later. I ate with grownups – nice change from Mayos, but I thereby do tons of dishes. Tonight it was a whole fresh lobster apiece,

1–Date supplied from postmark.
2–Katherine Cantor (1935–).

melon for dessert. Gave Billy a bath – but mother put him to bed. 8:30–9:30: sat in living room & chatted. Seems they are always having guests.

Keep your fingers crossed for me. Main job will be keeping house O.K. – and generally being around all the time to be handy. They are all very gracious, & children seem well-mannered – for children. All Xian-Scientists, too.

Only six weeks. Hope to do an hour or 2 of science everynight after I get through being so sleepy.

Mail not delivered – we pick it up at Chatham box. Food great – lots of fresh fruit. If I get sleep, I should be O.K. – lonesome for you, but its cool here. Also, great cool clear beaches nearby.

Love, your sleepy still bewildered
Sivvy

Sunday

Hello again. Family off in church, I have a few seconds between hanging out wash and fixing potatoes (warmed over) and a cubed steak for Billy. Got up at 7:30, helped with breakfast – 3 kids ate in kitchen, rest of us in dining room. Delightful guest (formerly of Smith & a Unitarian!) is very friendly. Drove after breakfast to an "artist's" studio – very nice woman, but I'm sure I could do as well. Then home. Piles of dishes. Daily kitchen floor scrub with wet mop. Made jello. Hung wash.

Now I await family's return.

Dickie called at 10:45 (tsk!) last night, but I was asleep. So I apologized for his lateness this morning.

All for now
XXX
Siv

<on back of envelope>

P.S. Think "Day-off" will be Wednesdays. Dick called Sat., but I was asleep. Art called tonight. Nice boy! Will most likely spent first day off with him.

TO *Marcia B. Stern*

Wednesday 23–24 July 1952 ALS with envelope, Smith College

Wednesday 11:30 a.m.

Dear Marty . . .

It develops that today is the Day off: O Marty, I never have spent such a queer summer. It's quite amazing how I've gone around for most of my life as in the rarified atmosphere under a bell jar all according to schedule – four college years neatly quartered out in seasons with summers to be filled in at will, hopefully, profitably, and never more than 2 or 3 weeks free at one time to worry about what comes next in. Even now, although the top would seem to have suddenly blown off, I know if I keep moving, time will pass, being as time is but an emptying of wastebaskets, a deadly going out and in of doors, a brushing of teeth routinely and a marking off of spaces until the cycle comes round again, and I will be gaily drunkenly academic again. God! After a year of dying for summer sun, I long only too soon to be myself (whatever that is) again.

Your letter came this a.m., making me wish you too would step briskly out of the mailbox and accompany me on my bike ride to Chatham light where I sit on the beach now, facing sun and waterward after a cooling dip, listening to small waves sloshing, children squealing, and musing on the paradox of human personalities shut up, in so many little individual airless windowless boxes, hermetically sealed, inaccessible to the casual observer. Here I am. 12 miles away is Dick. Yet it is as if I were sunning in Zanzibar for all the good that distance does. He biked over Monday (his day off) and I saw him for five strained minutes out on the Cantor's lawn . . . as we were about to serve supper. Oh, I even hate to talk to him over the phone, it's so ironic. If only I get my bike down here, I will bike over in the morning of my day off & live in his cabin till he comes home for his free p.m. hours. 25 miles is a long trek, but I don't give a damn.

Cantors are charming couple – much more friendly than Mayos – live in big gray house on little hill near golf course. Eldest girl Kathy (17) on experiment in Holland. Joan (13) is homely, quiet, very mature – dries dishes, and I guess I keep her company in lieu of Kathy. Susan (5 ½) is sweet, quiet, brown pigtails, freckles. Billy (3 ½) has a hell of a temper – runs shrieking to room under bed if you don't give in, but is terribly funny & adorable in his good moods.

Differences in setup: I do a lot more housework – waxed & scrubbed kitchen floor yesterday, clean house with Mrs. C., do great Bendixes of sheets, etc. (12 per week, plus daily dirt) – also get kids' snacks & help with grownups meals. In a way I miss the independent dual existence grownups & kids led last summer, because I do stacks of dishes after dinner – & company is frequent. But, eating with the family, I fare like a queen – all the fresh fruit & salads possible – lobster, lamb, steak, etc. Not bad, and Mrs. C. is an inspired cook.

Only thing is – independence. Again, I'm terribly isolated & miss the good laissez-faire of the gay fast Belmont crowd. However, Art Kramer

(Betsy James knows him I think) who has that fabulous job in Harwich has volunteered to rescue me for tennis this p.m. – also dinner & a dress-up evening. Oh, to feel an integral human again! He's ugly, but very intelligent – so I am muchly grateful to escape maternal Mrs. C. who does not approve of my going out at all. Her expression when Dick called at 10:45 one night was eloquent. Also the query: "And where did you meet all these boys?" I felt very trapped and like shouting "What the hell do you think I am? Red Riding Hood? I think I could fight off any male single handed, and they're not carnivorous beasts. You married one, didn't you?" Thank your stars, love, for integrity at home. Never did I appreciate mother's free rein more.

When I think of it, I sometimes wonder why I took a job. I didn't have to. Granted, I'm down the Cape (but still pretty isolated.) I think I did it to get away from mother & Wellesley, as much as I hate to admit it. I love her dearly, but she reverberates so much more intensly than I to every depression I go through. I really feel she is better without the strain of me and my intense moods – which I can bounce in and out of with ease. You see, I do understand your position, & hope to talk about it & everything when you come down.

10:30 a.m.
later – Thursday

Life ain't so bad after all. Just drove the kids down to the beach for Susie's swimming lesson – first time she's let me use the power-glide chevvy stationwagon alone, & was it fun to go wending aristocratically through the narrow, traffic-congested streets of Chatham with my two excited charges. We go shopping before returning home. The increased responsibility, I think, is very good for me. Also, the mother is really very nice & friendly – I can "talk" to her, which is also a pleasant variation on the Mayo-theme. (Her mother[1] was an Xian-Scientist practitioner no less! I wonder if they would like to convert me!)

Yesterday was better than I expected. Art, who is not too beautiful, as I said, & barely as tall as I, was sweet as could be. I was sure he'd regret taking me on for the day, but he made everything as smooth as possible – I actually talked with Mrs. Blossom in her bed – she's tremendous, you'd love her, 81, sprightly, quick, humorous – a breath from the Victorian age. I had to see her great beautiful emerald, hear the story of how she played before MacDowell (piano) – and she got a pass for "South Pacific" from Mr. Rogers himself. All enchanting. I felt that Art & I were paying

1–Flora Van Noorden Kiefer (1885–1941).

court before a very wealthy queen. I made myself at home at the Blossoms – sherbert on the chaise lounge, Art and conversation about politics, art, philosophy. At 25, he's one of the most versatile, intelligent people I've known. He's gone to West Point, been in the naval air force, got his masters at graduate school (in engineering, I think) and has now one more year of Yale law. You would love this – he's working with a professor on a compilation of Civil Rights cases for a Law Book.

We "played" tennis from 5-7 (me being atrocious – just rallying & he being terribly patient at my awful shots.) Dinner at an atmosphere-laden "clam bar" on a wharf overlooking the sea – I splurged & had lobster – a walk, a drive, conversation & home. I hated to go back to the isolated house on Bay Lane.

All of which served as a therapeutic escape for me & challenged me to think again.

Oh, I don't know, Marty. I've spread myself so thin in so many places I'll have to wait until I gather my selves into myself again; vegetate in one place peacefully a while, and start making value judgments. I am terribly impressed – after listening to Art talk so intelligently & wisely – at my own dense narrow stupidity. God, will I ever learn & be aware as fully as possible? How much time I've wasted! In functional summer jobs. Your Harvard sum. school plans sound idyllic. Wish I could join you.

Excuse the length & volubility of this flood – but there's no one around I can really spill over to – & do I miss our periodic purge-talks!

Love, to you angel
Syl

P.S. Just told Bill I had a tummy-ache. Whereupon he piously replied "Error gave you it." (So that's what it is!)

TO *Warren Plath*

Thursday 24 July 1952[1] — ALS (photocopy), Indiana University

Thursday 1:30 p.m.

Warren, old boy . . .

Seems the world is full of Beaver girls.[2] Joan (13) and a very cute friend, Carol Jocelyn, who is visiting her, both go there. Also Kathy Cantor (17!) who is at present in Holland on the Experiment in International Living.

1 – Date supplied from postmark by Warren Plath.
2 – A reference to the Beaver Country Day School in Newton, Mass.

Dishes being done, Billy in at his nap, I am relaxing in the sun in the Cantor's front yard, a delicious cool sea breeze evaporating the perspiration off as quickly as it forms, and writing to my favorite Kid Kolossus.

This morning Mrs. Cantor let me drive Billy and Susan down to the Oyster Pond where Sue has her swimming lesson. It's the first time she let me take the chevvy station-wagon Power-Glide alone. (I have just about gotten over reaching for the clutch, and now brake with my left foot – much easier to stop & start on hills that way!) Did I feel proud as I drove through Chatham in the shiny green & woodpaneled wagon with my two charges!

We stayed at the beach for an hour, then drove to an egg farm & home in time for lunch – which we always eat casually on paper plates out in the yard – usually sandwiches, or salad & sherbet! Mrs. Cantor is an inspired cook – uses a lot of sour cream, buttermilk & garlic. We had "buttermilk soup" today – try it some time: dice up cucumber; scallions & a little onion & mix with cold buttermilk & dash salt on. Very cool and prettily green & white.

Yesterday, my first day off, turned out much better than I thought it would. I got up as usual, made breakfast, did dishes, and was through about 10 a.m. Then I borrowed Joan's bike & explored the shops of Chatham (where the traffic, believe it or not, is twice as bad as Boston, and the streets very narrow.) Then I biked to Chatham Light & spent an hour sunning after a dip in the cold water. I ate lunch at the house, and Arthur called for me about 1:30. It was really good to drive away for a change.

I wonder what you would think of Art. I think he is one of the kindest, wisest people I know. He is barely as tall as I am, very dark, swarthy and Simian. Quite wonderfully ugly. But there is a quiet intelligence about him which I find most attractive. He is about 25, and went to West Point a year, joined the naval air core for a year after that, went to Yale, got his master's degree (in engineering, I think,) and now has one more year at Yale Law School.) He is extremely well-versed in politics (loaned me a speech by Adlai Stevenson to read – he favors Adlai as a man of capable integrity for Pres. – Ike next, but has very lucid arguments against him) – literature & poetry, philosophy, psychology, and life in general.

We drove over to the Blossoms home in Harwich where he gets $100 (!) a week for being night attendant – and I made myself really at home. First, I went into Mrs. Blossom's bedroom to meet her (she's been quite ill.) I was really enchanted. She is a spry, humorous, intelligent little woman of 81 (!) who presided from her bed like a white-haired Victorian queen

& regaled Art & me with tales of her girlhood – how she wanted to be a concert pianist – & played for MacDowell unexpectedly once – one of his own difficult sonatas – how she got a pass to the best seats in "South Pacific" by writing Mr. Rodgers himself – also showed me her beautiful gigantic emerald ring & told me how she met her husband. After this spiel, Art & I went out on the lawn, reclined on the chaise lounge & sipped ice water, ate sherbert, got acquainted. At 5 we "played" tennis. That was awful. He was a pro, & I was so rusty & uncoordinated. We just rallied, & I hit a lot of wild shots, & was quite ashamed of myself. But he nobly put up with me till 7. I went back to Blossoms, bathed, changed to my aqua dress & we went out to dinner at a lobster place loaded with atmosphere – on the wharf by the Snow Inn[1] where we got a great view of the ocean. By the time we finished our icecream and coffee it was after 10. We then went for a long scenic drive through Brewster and Orleans and back to Chatham All in all, I had a very restful time – and he left me a New Yorker & Atlantic with articles marked out to read.

I was grateful no end for my 12 hour reprieve. Monday I have scheduled to go to the Cape Playhouse[2] to see a ballet with Dick.

All in all, I am quite happy here, and the new experience and personality adjustments are probably very good for me.

Weekends are busiest of course, with Mr. Cantor and guests, & dishes are heavy but I am getting wonderful food & a lot of sun.

Do keep the letters coming. They mean a lot.

Love to you & Mother . . .
your traveling sister
sivvy

P.S. Don't forget Judy Humphry & going up to reconnoiter and Morses. Remember, with female society as everything else, Practice makes perfect!

1–In Harwichport, Mass.

2–The Cape Playhouse, Dennis, Mass. SP saw *Ballet Variante* starring Mia Slakvenska and Frederic Franklin.

TO *Aurelia Schober Plath*

Saturday 26 July 1952[1] ALS with envelope, Indiana University

Saturday – 2:45 p.m.

Dear Mother . . .

I am sunning in the Cantor's back yard while everybody else takes a siesta preparatory to going for a picnic at Nauset Beach. Really, I don't know when I've been so happy. I love everybody in the family dearly, and am already feeling like a sister to the 13 year old girl. The days are so rich and full that I hardly know how to begin telling you all that has happened. Although I am often quite busy, the work is all very pleasant because of Mrs. Cantor's lovely sunshiney friendly attitude. Also, now that I can drive both the stationwagon & Mr. Cantor's car (both Chevrolet powerglide) I am having much fun doing things with the children.

For example, last night the Cantor's had four guests for a lobster dinner plus a lovely attractive 13 yr. old friend of Joan's (Warren would like these girls – at least 5'8" or 9"!) who is staying for a week. So in order to have the two littlest ones out from underfoot, I was commissioned to take them on a supper swim & picnic in the stationwagon at Crystal Lake in Orleans. We had a lovely time, and I do enjoy the 2 little ones. After that, we had an hour to spare, so I got inspired. They wanted to go for a drive, so I drove to Brewster, expecting to find the cabin empty & to leave a note for Dick. Who should be there but Uncle Bill & Mrs. N. So we chatted, & I picked up my bike & brought it back.

They were still eating supper when we returned at 7:30 – & who should the guests be but the Nichols[2] from Wellesley who are in Falmouth for the summer. Sargent,[3] a fine 15 year old of 6'2" who could pass for 20, recalled that you had him in Sunday school, while Mrs. N. sweetly asked to be remembered to you.

I then took the children to the weekly Friday band concert – the most delightful spectacle. Hundreds & hundreds of people from all the towns around come to the park with blankets and sit on the grassy hills circling the bandstand where the jaunty red & blue uniformed players perform jolly marches, children's numbers where all the little ones dance, waltzes where the teenagers & grownups twirl around the lawn, and also everybody

1–Date supplied from postmark.

2–Hall Nichols (1896–1979) and Evelyn Sargent Nichols (b. 1898). The Nichols lived at 98 Brook Street, Wellesley, Mass.

3–Sargent Nichols (1936–2011).

joins in singing. A most festive occasion from 8-10, with colored balloons everywhere, children playing, stars coming out over the trees, etc.

I took the children home early & put them to bed.

Dick, Rit and Bev came over about 10:30 last night, and Joan & her friend and I did dishes & talked to them. They stayed and chatted companionably with me after the rest had gone to bed. Mrs. C. seemed quite pleased with Rit (thought him very goodlooking.)

Tonight I'll go to bed early. By the way, who should drive up yesterday with a friend but Polly! Her news of the Belmont crowd was good to hear, and made me want to see them all again. I plan to go back for a day in two weeks to visit. One sidehall girl has already gone into Main, & Polly probably will too. So I would have, after all. But then, I am really very happy & cool here – sleep often under blankets, & there is always a fresh breeze. Also, food is continuously grand.

I am worried about writing Mary.[1] I had gotten quite used to the idea of rooming with her & don't want to hurt her. I actually think I'd look forward to a roommate. Should I write Smith & ask for a switchback. Or what? I had forgotten about asking to be changed! Do say what you think I should do.

I miss you and Warren, but am glad to be in this lovely environment away from the conspicuous silence of Phil Brawner which I found so noticeable around the vicinity of our telephone!

This family is <u>so</u> different from Mayos – so appreciative. It makes work like play.

I love your dear letters . . . you & Warren must come down to pick me up at the end of the summer to meet these lovely people

XXX
Sivvy

Saturday night 9:45

P.S. All the Cantor's (Mr. & Mrs., Joan & Friend) have gone to the Chatham Bars Inn to a dance while I babysit. Comfortably ensconced in bed after a hot bath, I feel myself nodding drowsily.

Art called just after I put the children in bed, and we had the most lovely intellectual conversation for over half an hour. It was exhilarating to use big words again, & I reviewed my opinions of the articles he had given me to read in The New Yorker, The Atlantic (Thornton Wilder's)[2] and

1–Mary Agnes Bonneville (1931–2007); B.A. 1953, zoology, Smith College. SP's roommate in Lawrence House, 1952–3.

2–Either 'Toward an American Language', *The Atlantic* 190 (July 1952), 29–37; or 'The American Loneliness', *The Atlantic* 190 (August 1952), 65–9.

the Times (Stevenson's speech.)[1] He told me about Witness by Whittaker Chambers[2] which he'd just finished reading, and we discussed Thomas Mann, recent incidental news, and our talk was most satisfying. (He said Mrs. Blossom really approved of me highly! And would be most happy to have me come again.) Art got his Master's Degree in English (esp. Shelley et. al.) and so you can imagine what a versatile stimulating conversationalist he is. He is, (I just now thought of it!) the perfect illustration of my theory of the short, dark, ugly brilliant man. If only he were a few inches taller. So I wouldn't feel I had to slouch. Always a gimmick. But he is a dear. For our next reunion (in about two weeks, I guess) we plan to buy lobsters & cook them in the Blossom's kitchen! I shall get some french bread & make garlic butter, I think, as I've seen Mrs. C. do, & maybe make a salad – if we ever get all the food necessary. So at least there are things always to look forward to. I parcel out my days off with the nigardliness of a miser, crowding everything possible into them!

You have no idea how I appreciate Art's stirring up my lethargic intellect. I always admire that quality most.

Tomorrow I'm going to Xian Science Church with the Cantor's. Should be interesting.

XX again
Siv

TO *Marion Freeman*

Friday 1 August 1952 — ALS with envelope, Smith College

August 1, 1952

Dear Aunt Marion . . .

First, I want especially to thank you for your lovely letter of a while back – and then for your wonderful legacy of these books on writing markets and best sellers which mother has told me about. They will be invaluable to me, and I hope I can make good use of them! You, of all people, know how very deeply I appreciate your gift.

Tomorrow will commemorate my two-week anniversary as "mother's helper" at the Cantor's. I am really very happy here, much more so than

1–American politician and presidential candidate Adlai Ewing Stevenson II (1900–65). Probably his 'Text of Stevenson Speech of Welcome to Convention', *New York Times*, 22 July 1952, 12.

2–American writer Whittaker Chambers (1901–61); born Jay Vivian Chambers, also known as David Whittaker Chambers. His autobiography *Witness* (New York: Random House, 1952).

I expected, and I feel just like an older sister – really part of the family. Compared to the cool indifference of my employers last summer, the Cantor's are warm, friendly, and delightful. The two children, Billy (3½) and Susan (5½) are both dear and well-mannered. Tantrums are rare. Joan (13) is a plain, but intelligent girl – very mature for her age. Kathy (17) is in Holland on the Experiment in International Living.

My day is a full and busy one – from seven in the morning till after 8 at night, but I enjoy the work – from waxing and scrubbing the floor in the kitchen, weekly housecleaning, to driving the children to their swimming lesson. I have a great deal more responsibility than I did last year, and enjoy every bit of it, especially taking the children for trips and picnics in the shiny new station wagon.

Days off and some evenings are spent with friends in nearby towns – the Norton boys in Brewster, a Yale law student (getting $100 a week being night attendant for an old millionaire in Harwich –) named Arthur Kramer. I've played tennis, swum, biked, gone to a ballet & "The Glass Menagerie" – all very much fun.

Hope to see you, Dave & Ruth before school this fall.

Love to you all –
Sylvia

TO *Aurelia Schober Plath*

Saturday 2 August 1952 — TLS with envelope, Indiana University

August 2,

Dear mother . . .

I can hardly believe it's August already! And that my magazine is reposing in my closet, well-read. The whole Cantor family has been through it, as have Dick, Art, and the Blossoms (Art's millionaire employers.) On Wednesday, my day off, Grammy and Grampy called for me, proudly bearing the First Copy I had seen. I drove them to Brewster, where Dick met us at the cabin at 11, spent half and hour talking before he left for work, and gave me a beautiful tuna fish, tomato, and egg salad he had made artistically for me, plus a menu, for lunch. I left grammy and grampy at the cabin because they were comfortable reading, and had enough of the beach, and took the car alone for a blissful two hours at the Brewster beach with a bag of cherries and peaches and the Magazine. I felt the happiest I ever have in my life. I read both stories, and already feel that I have outgrown mine, as I saw a great many errors, artistically, and am already beginning to think out about the tremendous job I'll do on the next one. I read it, smoothed the page, chortled happily to myself, ran out onto the sand flats and dog-trotted for a mile far out alone in the sun, through the warm tidal water, with the foam trickling pale brown in fingers along the wet sand ridges where the tide was coming it, talking to myself about how wonderful it was to be alive and brown and full of vitality and potentialities, and knowing all sorts of wonderful people. I never have felt so utterly blissful and free. Those two hours alone were just what I needed. When I got back, Dick and Rit and Bev were there, so Grammy and Grampy started back to Falmouth, while the four of us played doubles. Dick and I whipped them neatly. The boys left for work, and I sat till the sun went down reading. Then I went into the cabin and cooked a small steak that Dick (the dear boy) had bought for my dinner, listened to Franck, and took an hour's nap. Dick woke me up when he came in, and Rit and Bev drove us home shortly later after a perfect day.

The weather has been pretty cloudy the last few days, so I took the three kids shopping yesterday morning. I had lots of fun browsing around all the gift shops, and saw some divine pottery, linen Country Prints, belts, and so forth. Went to the Sail Loft[1] where I was amazed to meet Pam Kent, the girl we went down to visit last year[2] when I went down with the boys and P. K. We had a nice chat, and she said she'd seen my story in Mlle. I guess when I get back to school I'll spend about a month saying "Yes, I'm glad you liked it. Yes, I really got $500 for it".

Last night Art came over to the Band Concert, and we wheeled the children up together. The Cantor's kindly took the kids home, so we sat in a garden behind a gift shop amidst leaves and moonlight and talked. He is going to red pencil my story for me in the magazine he got . . . and offered some very good criticism about word textures and adverbs and restraint and so on. All of which he suggests kindly to keep in mind for the next one. He has also advised me some short stories to read . . . . by Joyce <u>The Dubliners</u> and <u>The Sun Also Rises</u>, which he thinks are primers for any young writer. We had a beer apiece at the Sou'wester,[3] a place I'd been before while at the Belmont, and drove home. He offered to drive me home on one of my days off as he has to go to Boston to have his teeth worked on, but I said no, thinking the trip wouldn't be worth the time,

1 – The Sail Loft was a clothing store at 38 Bridge Street, Chatham, Mass., 1947–96.

2 – According to SP's calendar, this was on 14 June 1951.

3 – The Sou'wester was a restaurant then at 1563 Main Street, West Chatham, Mass.

and I'd much rather spend my days here on the Cape which I love so. I really think the boy must like me . . . he said he hopes we can share alot of things together . . . and I got him talking a little about his childhood. Seems he was the only Jew in his part of grammar school in Bridgeport Conn., and was always coming home with bloody noses till he learned how to fight and box. Also, his father and uncle lost a million or so in the law investments, and they were quite poor for a while. So in spite of the fact that the Cantor's don't seem to like him anywhere near as much as Dick, I find him quite wise and brilliant and understanding and gentle and don't give a darn about his being short and ugly. I wish some time you could really talk to him to see how much there is inside him. He is reticent until one brings him out, but I love to hear him expound on politics and literature. His lawyer's mind catches me up on every word, and I am going to try to work on expressing myself verbally more clearly and logically. I really think in a cotton fog, I guess . . Can't wait till next Wednesday when we will go to the play by Kramm[1] in Coonamesset together.

Yesterday, Joanie and I stopped at the Bookmobile that stops once a week in Chatham to sell books. I got talking to the most fascinating little sallow cynical brilliant woman who runs it. When she asked where I went to college, she said "Oh, Smith. That's a great handle. Snob appeal, you'll be using it all your life. It does things for you." Seems she whizzed through the University of Chicago (lucky thing) with three majors: English, History, and Anthropology. She got a job in new York, and now free lance writes for a living. I was at her feet with questions pouring out. She has written western pulps, western love stories, and will have a "dowager story" in the Ladies' Home Journal this fall.[2] She also writes juveniles, and had a blurb up on the wall advertising her latest for 12-14 year old boys. Her name is Val(erie) Gendron,[3] and she lives in a little ramshackle house in South Dennis. I plan to haunt her every Friday if I get a minute. Boy, would I like to bike over to her house on some day off and talk with her for hours! She really has been through the mill, I guess. (Hero worship, you know).

Dick is coming over for a visit tonight while I "baby-sit". I think I am doing quite well juggling him and Art at the same time. It does wonders

1–Joseph Kramm, *The Gypsies Wore High Hats* (1952) played at the Cape Playhouse in Dennis, Mass.

2–Probably Val Gendron, 'Second Blooming', *Ladies Home Journal*, March 1953, 44, 104, 106, 108, 110–11.

3–American fiction writer Val Gendron (1913–89), formerly Ruth C. Fantus.

in stimulating my ingenuity. I've written to Marion,[1] The Warden, and Mrs. Williams.[2] Seems I'm always writing letters whenever I get a minute, which isn't much time. Usually I go to bed shortly after I get through work, or do my ironing. Science has been temporarily shelved until I get a little more energy and can stay up later. But, darn it, I'm determined to get it done if I have to work ten hours a day for two weeks when I get home.

I got my poems back from the Monitor . . . the ones that I sent to the Home Forum. But they put, as Mrs. Freeman would say, an "encouraging note" on the rejection, saying that they were keeping two of them for future reference. Most of those are little nature things, charming bits of observation about slightly gold twilights or orange groves in Timbuctoo, so I should be able to write a few Cape-y things to send in this fall . . . both to the Youth page and Home Forum.

Did I tell you that I am typing four carbons of all Kathy's letters from Holland so they can be sent to friends? I really enjoy my "secretarial" work no end, and thus am getting a whack at the type-writer now to send a letter your way.

So glad to hear that the great Brauner called. You were wrong after all. Even the Cliff-dwelling plutocrats can't keep away from your enchantingly insane poverty-stricken daughter for longer than three weeks! Hah!

Don't worry about hearing from me. I will write as often as possible, but time is short. Love your letters.

xxx
Sivvy

TO *Enid Mark*

Saturday 2 August 1952 — TLS with envelope, Smith College

August 2, 1952

Dear Enid . . .

Right about now I am wondering how your job canvassing in New York worked out, and if you are now piling up story material at some Publishing House or other. As for me, in spite of the August dateline, I still

1–Dr Marion Frances Booth (1899–1963); college physician and professor of bacteriology and public health, Smith College, 1941–61; SP's Smith psychiatrist, 1954–5; SP's colleague, 1957–8. SP served on Honor Board with Dr Booth, 1952–3.

2–Probably Edna Rees Williams (1899–1992); English professor, Smith College, 1930–64; SP's colleague, 1957–8. Williams co-directed freshman English (English 11) completed by SP, 1950–1.

feel extremely far from the campus life the Springfield Daily News and the Smith Review. You know that peculiar feeling when your time-sense gets thrown off and you can't imagine ever having done anything but what your present job entails? Well, that's the way I've felt twice this summer.

My first venture was at the gigantic suave hotel, the Belmont, in West Harwich on Cape Cod. I had a lovely hectic three weeks, learning to balance trays stacked with dishes precariously shoulder height on my left hand, to wear long-sleeved black cotton uniforms and stockings (ugh!) three times a day without screaming, and to getting along with all types of peculiar professional people who follow the trade up from Florida to the Cape and back again all their lives long. All kinds of grotesque character types who would seem artificial in a story because of their almost mechanical functional lives . . . they were even known by their occupational names alone, like Ray-the-Coffeeman (a paunchy old bulldog of a man with a predatory leer who slouched grumpily over the coffee tanks all day, making hundreds of gallons over and over again) or Dave-the-Roast-Cook, or Bill-the-Bar-Boy. All very interesting hotel lingo.

Unfortunately my experience was cut short by my coming down with a sinus infection as a result of my rather continuous night life. Social life among the help, a group of about seventy college boys and girls, began about 10:30 at night, after everybody was off work, and lasted, in the form of dances or beachparties, till almost dawn. Daytimes were spent with three short two-hour work shifts at mealtime, and beaching or sleeping in between.

The whole deal was like college with the lid off, only a lot more strenuous. I had one final fling before the doctor sent me home to recuperate away from the noisy smoke-filled furor of the girls' dorm. Fortunately I was supposed to have a tennis date with a boy from Wellesley that afternoon, so I greeted him with a little black suitcase instead of a tennis racket and wangled a ride home. He thought the whole thing about being sick was a big joke, and that I just wanted a short vacation, because I was very bright-eyed and gay, having at the time both a very good tan and an even better fever. I had a terrible time keeping up a sprightly conversation on the long drive home, as my voice was leaving me octave by octave, so I just pretended it was very low and husky anyway. I spent about a week at home in bed in a voiceless coma, and meanwhile mother called the Belmont and told them I wouldn't be coming back (she thought I'd been slaving too hard for a mere pittance), so there I was out of a job.

Reading want adds was a lot of fun, and I considered all sorts of unique and peculiar things, like painting parchment lampshades for a company in Boston, or being a Real Estate agent's assistant . . . but my burning desire to be back at the cool Cape, with the ocean nearby, and the clean windswept beaches, and all the young people won out. I answered an add for a mother's helper (in spite of my vow Never to be one again after the fiasco last summer) for a family of Jewish Christian Scientists in Chatham, and here I am. I really am much more at home here than I thought I'd be, and the people are lovely and warm and intelligent. My day is a long one, lasting from 7 a.m. till after the two youngest (Bill, 3½ and Sue, 5½) are in bed, but I get to take them to the beach daily in the beautiful shiny Chevvy station wagon (a new toy for me) and there is plenty of sun, good food (Mrs. Cantor makes all sorts of delectable things with sour cream, buttermilk, garlic, etc.) and merriment. I've been dating Dick about once or twice a week (He's waiting with his brother 12 miles away in Brewster). We've been to the Cape Playhouse in Dennis (run by Richard Aldrich, the husband of Gertrude Lawrence[1]) twice, to see Dana Andrews in "Glass Menagerie" and the Ballet Variante. Both excellent in their own unique way. Tennis and swimming on days off have been the order of the occasion.

An item of interest. I met a brilliant ugly Yale Law student while working at the Belmont, and as far as I'm concerned, he holds the job of the summer. Get this: He gets paid $100 a week for being the night attendant to a millionaire down here . . . and he sits up all night reading fascinating books, sleeps all morning, gets driven to the beach or tennis court in the afternoon by the chauffeur, and has all sorts of good food in the bargain. I had a chance to visit him on my day off last week, previous to our going out for a lobster dinner on some old atmospheric wharf overlooking the ocean, and actually met this amazing old couple. Mr. B. is a senile crochety old man, and Mrs. B. (who entertained us from her bed where she is confined with heart trouble) is the wittiest old lady of 81 you could imagine. I had to admire her emerald, a large lovely hunk of green stone, and listen to her tales of all the celebrities she had known intimately in her time. All very unusual and intrigueing.

So the summer isn't too deadly after all. In spite of the fact I don't have any time to write or pore through all the intellectual tomes of literature that I have on my cobwebbed reading list. I do look terribly forward,

1–Broadway producer Richard Aldrich (1902–86). Married to British actress Gertrude Lawrence (1898–1952).

actually, to being academic again. What a relief to be working for my own improvement, and not someone elses'!!

I look very forward to seeing you in the fall and hearing in detail about your summer; also, to reading anything you've written recently.

Write if you get a chance.
Yours,
Sylvia

TO *Aurelia Schober Plath*

Monday 4 August 1952 — ALS with envelope, Indiana University

monday night
august 4
9 p.m.

Dear mother . . .

I am sitting on the edge of my bed, weary, grubby, and waiting for Joanie to get through with the bathroom so I can wash my hair. We have had a most wonderful and packed day. Honestly, I'm glad I have my little calendar to jot down what happens, because otherwise I would lose track of time completely. The days, so long and varied they seem weeks in themselves, tumble almost immediately into a great dark abyss in my memory, and it is almost impossible to recall, for instance, what happened yesterday, or whether yesterday was Sunday – already it seems so far back.

Today I got up at 7:30 and went down to get Billy's breakfast, set the table, put water on, etc. Then we all had breakfast. Together: Warren would love this menu: cantalope, scrambled eggs, bacon, kippered herring, several Bisquick muffins, bread and strawberry jam, topped off by good scalding coffee. Wow!

After dishes, we all did the big laundry – 12 sheets plus clothes. Lunch was good borscht and toasted rye bread & cheese. Then Mr. & Mrs. Cantor left for an afternoon, dinner & evening at the Southward Inn (Rotary Club).

Joanie and I cleaned up the kitchen & packed a huge picnic supper & got the kids up. We stopped in town to buy peaches, grapes & tomatoes. Then to Brewster to pick up Dick & Perry (all approved of by the Cantors.) Boy, did I feel capable and proud driving the load of them, picnic & all, in the great cruisy green station wagon. We picked up Star, their golden retriever, at the Kennels, and Edna Kelly at her house, and went to a wonderful beach in Dennis. By this time it was after four. All of us played on the wonderful hard flat sand, running, jumping, building dikes & moats. The children fell in love with Dick, and we ran around carrying them piggyback, etc. We all fell hungrily on the picnic, devouring sandwiches, milk and fruit with gusto. I dropped milky baby-talking fragile Edna, then the boys, and got home by 8 in a heavy fog.

It is now a little after 10, and I have finished drying my hair under the dryer. Tomorrow we get up at 6:30 as Mr. Cantor leaves then and it is cleaning day. The Cantors just got in and heard about our Afternoon. Dick & Perry (Dick's & my idea) plan to take Joanie & me to the theatre next week, or movies. We thought it would be a treat for Joan, and the Cantor's seem very pleased.

Oh, yesterday I went to Xian Science Sunday School with Joan. I asked so many questions & answered just the way I thought I should that the teacher, a bleached plump rather dumb blonde woman who glibly extols "our beloved leader M. B. E."[1] – thought I was an old veteran! I plan to go every Sunday I'm here. Luckily, out of our queer mixed class of 5, there is a boy almost my age who is very cute and precocious. He took an immediate liking to me (I read "Science & Health"[2] aloud beautifully in class! Without choking or being struck by a bolt of lightning for hypocracy![3]) and came up afterwards to ask me to go to a double header baseball game that afternoon. I was really sorry to refuse – it would be fun to try to proselytize him subtly <u>out</u> of Xian Science! The Cantors know his family, so I hope to see him every week at church, maybe get acquainted.

Last night I added to my role as Joan's companion by driving her to a handwriting analysis session at the Chatham Bars Inn. It was sort of fun, and we went up afterwards & had ours analyzed. I was really surprised. She said I was the most intuitive person she'd had that night – also that I was very artistic – had a flair for color, pattern & line. Not bad, for a starter.

So far there's hardly been a day Art or Dick hasn't called or visited – six calls in all from Dick, and six visits or times together – seven calls from Art, and two dates. So life is far from lonely –

Love to you all –
Sylvia

1–Mary Baker Eddy (1821–1910); the founder of Christian Science.
2–Mary Baker Eddy's *Science and Health* (Boston: Christian Science Publishing Society, 1875).
3–This sentence added in left margin my SP.

TO *Warren Plath*

Sunday 10 August 1952[1] ALS (photocopy), Indiana University

Sunday – 3:30 p.m.

Dear Fellow-Spirit . . .

Well, after a hectic day your sister is taking a well-deserved 5 minutes rest off her little flat feet. We have 3 weekend guests – Mr. and Mrs. Rock (you know, granulated and his wife Igneous) an elderly couple – he fat and bald and crustily humorous – she sort of nondescript. Also Cousin Marvin Cantor[2] who is 22, about 5'11", and very nice looking with brown wavy hair and blue eyes. (As you may imagine, it lightens the work considerably to have someone flirting with you in the kitchen.) Yesterday we spent running around getting the house and food ready, and had a huge lobster and chicken dinner last night with twelve people. Dishes took Joanie and me almost 2 hours, but we put on records and danced in the kitchen – I actually getting a whirl with the worldly Marvy. Then the whole gang of them left to go dancing at the Chatham Bars Inn. I was too sleepy to do anything but type a few letters. and iron some things. Dick drove over about quarter of 11 and stayed and talked till 12 – and had a very nice time sitting out on the front steps in the fog that was blowing in wet and dark from the sea. All the Cantors like Dick very much, and he them.

Today I went to Sunday School again and had an even better time. During the service I could hardly help bursting out in chortling laughter as I thought how my meek and sweetly pious face covered a wicked wicked belief in the matter and how satan himself was curled up in my left ventricle chuckling at them. In Sunday School class I answered questions, nodded fervently, smilingly told one girl that of course since God was the only reality, that all else was a mere figment of man's imagination – and matter was a mere false myth. I am getting better at this than they are themselves. The poor teacher, a simple-minded bleached spiritual blonde, thinks I am just wonderful – and complimented me on my heartfelt reading of the "Science & Health" text in class. Oh, it's all very amusing. Especially since the tall young boy – Bob[3] – I spoke of last time, asked if he could come see me (I had told him I would like to discuss Science

1–Date supplied from postmark by Warren Plath.

2–Marvin Stanley Cantor (1930–2007).

3–Robert Shepard Cochran (1935–56); dated SP during summer of 1952. He was a senior at the Clark School in Hanover, New Hampshire, and a summer resident of Chatham, Mass.

with him sometime.) and I demurely said yes-some-evening-next-week-he-could-visit. He must be about 17 or 18, but I shall be interested to get to know him better – a very precocious character, I think. So after all our discussion in class of how matter is a mere false illusion – we both drove off proudly waving to each other – he in his light blue convert and me in my green stationwagon. Oh, the false gorgeous beauty of matter! Ho ho.

Friday, as Mrs. Cantor was in Boston all day, I had charge of the house. The morning was nice enough for me to drive the infants to their swimming lesson, and after that I drove to the egg farm for 4 doz. eggs, and then over to Harwichport to get several armloads of zinnias to arrange for company. All afternoon, thank God, it poured rain, so there was no Band Concert that night (meaning the children were in bed at 8 instead of 10 – making life much easier.)

I took advantage of Joan's presence to drive downtown in the rain to the Bookmobile under pretense of getting a book for Marcia's birthday (which I did) but really to pay homage to Val Gendron. She actually remembered me and wants me to bring over Mlle next week so she can read it. By dint of much skill on my part, I got what I have been aiming for all along – an actual invitation to a bull session at her shack in South Dennis some evening when she's off!!! She gave me a tremendous system about writing which is too long to explain here, but I'm going to do it all this year. She actually said if I was serious and had stuff to show her in a year or so, she'd look it over, or introduce me to her agent in New York, no less! So I am going to get to work this year. If I maneuver it right, and get a night off a week from Monday (cross your fingers) Art said he'd drive me over (my company on the drive is enough inducement!) and drop me at her house. And she said she'd drive me back. So I hope it works out. Trust me to wind up discussing how-to-get-published in a red-painted chicken coop with a cynical sallow authoress!

I am really getting to know the town of Chatham backwards and forwards – with all the cruising around I've done – driving in a square from here to Orleans to Brewster to Harwich, as I do. Love the Cape – licenses from everywhere – Ontario to South America, and every state in the union. One N.Y. license plate at the Inn is simply – <drawing of license plate with details 'N.Y. XX 52'>! Wonder who that could be? The governor? Xavior? Xeras? or just two spots?

Life is: juggling people and activities all the time – most stimulating. I am far from lonely, as you can see. And am getting in all the things I want to in the dizzy colored spiral of whirling spheroids – including several male heads – also atoms and molecules. Have read 30 pages. If

I get 200 done now down here (10 per day) I could do all reading & papers in 2 solid weeks at home. I am going to do it, I feel it in my matter!

I was glad to get my acceptance from 17![1] That Nat Gittelson[2] is sure a good judge of excellent stuff! She's quicker on accepting poems than Margot[3] was. (I only hope this wasn't just a softening of the blow of rejecting all my 3 stories. I'm 'spicious!)

Well, keep fighting the female situation – as my Sunday School teacher said with a humble giggle – pointing to "Science & Health" – "we have all the ansahs to everything right heah, aftah all!" I'll take on neurotic M. B. Eddy any day! You've got to be healthy and sane to appreciate matter. N'est-ce pas? Also himmel.

"Life is incorrigably plural and more of it than we think . . ."[4]

Love to you & mum . . .
Sivvy

TO *Aurelia Schober Plath*

Friday 15 August 1952[5] — ALS with envelope, Indiana University

Friday

Dear Mum . . .

I took Thursday for my day-off this week instead of Wednesday, as Mrs. C was having a big luncheon Wed. and needed my help badly. As if in reward for my accommodation, the weather yesterday was flawless and we had the best "day-off" ever.

Now for a history of my week. After Sunday when the 3 weekend guests left, everyone was exhausted – including me, who had been running around like mad and, it seemed, doing dishes from morning till night. But I was touched when Mr. Cantor slipped me a $5 bill said with a wink "from the guests for services rendered." A tip, no less!

Monday I spent the better part of the afternoon scrubbing and waxing the kitchen floor. In the evening Dick came over and we went for a lovely

1–Sylvia Plath, 'Carnival Nocturne', *Seventeen* 12 (April 1953), 127; see Natalie Gittelson to SP, 7 August 1952; held by Lilly Library.

2–Natalie Gittelson (d. 2009); editor of the 'It's All Yours' section of *Seventeen*.

3–Margot Macdonald, previously editor of the 'It's All Yours' section of *Seventeen*.

4–Louis MacNeice, 'Snow'; SP misquotes lines from the poem: 'World is crazier and more of it than we think, / Incorrigibly plural.'

5–Date supplied from postmark.

companionable 2 hour hike along the beach to Chatham Light, with a big unbelievably orange moon floating up over the water.

Tuesday was cleaning day, and we got up early to prepare for a guest and her 2 year old baby who came then to stay till Friday. I really was on the go, and was finishing up dinner dishes when (at 9 p.m.) Bob Cochran, the lean young boy from Church walked in. We decided to go for a ride in his car as Mrs. C. was staying in – and I felt I needed a respite. I walked out expecting a blue convertible, when what should I see in the drive but a low, suave crimson M-G! (Warren would love this!) I got in and we were off, speeding through the lovely Chatham fog in the little open car along the highway: Picture trees arching over a smooth dark lonely road, and a car with two young gay people singing lustily on the top of their lungs. (Mostly Bob singing and me laughing.) He was sleepy, so he let me drive, and before I knew it we were whishing through Orleans and ended up in Wellfleet where Bob got some potato chips and cold beer – and boy, did it taste good! I was in before Joan – who had not yet come back from the movies with a gang of girls.

Wednesday I shopped in town – for such delicacies as escarolle, romaine, and strawberries – I really enjoyed the responsibility, and felt very domestic driving the car through the crowded sunny Chatham streets, stopping at the shops, officially smelling melons (I really can't tell the difference, my sense of smell not being too good!) The only flaw in my act was that, after paying the woman (with a housewifely smile) I started to walk gaily off without my packages! (After the luncheon and all, I went to bed early.)

Thursday dawned clear and blue – and I gave a little squeak of joy as I lept up and went about my tasks. Dick and two Lathamites picked me up in their car about 10:30. Dick and I had time for a slice of cantalope together in the sun outside the cabin before he left for work. He was so cute – insisted on making me an artistic salad of spam & cheese slices & cantalope & melon.

As soon as he left I walked down to the Brewster beach with a towel, feeling very happy and savoring how wonderful it was to be young and alive, noticing every smell and scent and sight with keen delight

The tide was dead low, so for an hour I walked or ran, as the spirit moved, straight out to sea on the sand flats – skipping through the clear calf-deep water, frightening seagulls, and in general, acting like a free young pony, neighing with delight. For 30 minutes after a vigorous 2 hour hike, I lay and basked on the sand, then the hike back to the cabin, with a brief stop at the Brewster cemetary to browse about the old tombstones. Dick biked up just as I was finishing my salad in the sun on the front steps.

We then biked to the tennis court made by the DP, and played in our bathing suits for an hour – such lovely informality! – and biked for a short dip afterwards.

After Dick bade me goodbye and left for work, I did the dishes and picked up the cabin. I then "bathed" in the dishpan and donned my yellow dress.

Bob drove up in his M-G at eight looking very sweet in his light blue cord jacket. Actually he isn't quite as old as Warren! But really terribly mature. Socially, having all the material advantages of Larchmont, New York. I am really fond of him in a tender maternal way – he is so young and reminds me much of Warren, only is not so sweet and gentle – rather cynical and fresh to people at times. He has given me the germ of a central character for a short story tho', of which I only had the title when I left home. I will probably write it at school, when it has had time to take form and plot.

We drove to the Music Circus in Hyannis to see (and hear) "The Fledermaus."[1] I'm enclosing the program which I hope you will save for my scrapbook.[2] We had a magnificent time, and the singing was glorious – all took place in a great circular tent with chairs in a gravel-sand amphitheater with a circular stage in the center – the actors came down the aisle. During the ball scene I felt like dragging Bob down and dancing too, it was all so Austrian and liltingly light and gay – wish you could all have been there! We stopped for a hamburg and milk afterwards – and drove around by Chatham Light afterwards for the sea-view before going home – a most lovely and perfect day.

I am sorry if my last letter sounded smug – I was really only fooling! I enjoy finding out about Xian Science really, and don't advance any of my own opinions as that would lead to arguing when what I want is to <u>learn</u>. (Joan and I sat out in the yard this afternoon making the unpleasant task of polishing all the silver less undesirable by taking turns reading aloud this week's lesson on "Soul" from the Bible and "Science and Health.")

I dropped my "Mlle" at the Bookmobile this morning and arranged to visit Val this Monday evening. I really like her a lot – she's so ugly and fascinating and fragile. I can't wait. At least my first nebulous exclamation "Oh, I love to write!" has been backed up in her eyes with material "success". As she said when I handed her the magazine apologizing for the story a little & saying it had many faults: "Heck, if any one takes it

1 – The Music Circus, 21 West Main Street, Hyannis, Mass. *Die Fledermaus*: 1874 operetta by Johann Strauss.

2 – SP pasted the programme onto p. 20 of her Smith College scrapbook.

apart just ask them if they could produce a prize-winner – you've got your approval. Don't apologize for it."

Also I am really humble about my short story & poems in "17." Just think of all the writing I have to do to keep up with my reputation! I am so happy I "have the right to write." I was really amazed that the Monitor is paying $3.50 for that little "Riverside Reveries"[1] poem I wrote while early in highschool! On the "Home Forum", too, I think. I hope to do a series of descriptive nature articles about the Cape this fall and see if that would get in. SO that makes a total:

2.50 A-bomb article with Perry
4.00 "Bitter Strawberries"
5.00 farm article
15.00 babysitting
3.50 poem[2]
$30.00

Not much, but a gnawing away at the edge of it. And 17 adds up so nicely –

$2.00 contribution[3]
15.00 "And summer will not come again"
10.00 poem "Ode on a bitten plum"
100.00 "Den of Lions" story
25.00 "The Perfect Setup" story
5.00 "The Suitcases are Packed again" poem
10.00 "Carnival Nocturne,"[4] Poem
167.00

So, with "Mlle", that's a total of almost $700 in 3 years. Starvation wages!

That's the resume of news for now.

Love to you all,
Sivvy

<on back of envelope>

P.S. Poor Mr. Murray! His passage you quoted was so tired and "preciously flowery." I was writing about "Myriads of jewel-like twinkling

1–Sylvia Plath, 'Riverside Reveries', *Christian Science Monitor*, 9 September 1952, 8.

2–Possibly 'Riverside Reveries', noted above, or 'White Phlox', *Christian Science Monitor*, 27 August 1952, 12.

3–Sylvia Plath, 'When I'm a Parent . . .', *Seventeen*, November 1949, 77. SP's response was 'I will not pry, but I will never go to the opposite extreme and be indifferent to my child's experiences outside the home.' See SP's publications scrapbook held by Lilly Library.

4–Sylvia Plath, 'Carnival Nocturne', *Seventeen* 12 (April 1953), 127.

stars" in junior high. Stars – they get sort of tarnished with overuse. Hope he can tighten it up and make good, poor guy!

TO *Aurelia Schober Plath*

Tues.–Thurs. 19–21 August 1952[1] ALS with envelope, Indiana University

Tuesday, 5 p.m.

Dearest mum . . .

I hardly think you would recognize your plump young daughter if you saw her now: I am sitting in my white bathing suit with Joanie in the back (open) of the beachwagon, legs dangling, munching peaches left over from our picnic this noon. After a queer, nasty rainy weekend, Monday & today have been clear, cool, breezy and blue, and as a result I am as tan as I ever was at the Belmont – even more so. I have been working extra hard in the mornings and putting up great picnics these last two days for five & six people – I don't forget anything any more – not even salt. Yesterday was just about the most wonderful yet. All morning I ran around doing dishes, defrosting the icebox, making a great picnic, hanging out load after load of laundry (12 sheets & pillowcases plus incidentals is quite a job.) The whole family left for Nauset Beach in Orleans at 12 and stayed till about four in the afternoon. To my mind, Nauset (over 20 miles of pure white sand and powerful bluegreen surf, low dunes) is the most beautiful place on the Cape. We had our picnic and a siesta on the sand and then Joan and I walked for miles up the hard flat sand in the sun.

I really don't mind running around like a fiend in the a.m. if I can relax now and then in the afternoon like this. After supper Mrs. Cantor kindly drove me over to South Dennis for my evening with Val Gendron. I don't know when I've had such a wonderful time in all my life. It was like a dream of an artist's Bohemia.

Val lives in a rickety old "half-house" <drawing of house> (one door, two windows) painted barn red with a white trim. She bought it four years ago and lives there the year round – and has carved a flower garden and vegetable garden out of the pine woods around her – love gardening. When I arrived she came to greet me, slouching slender and fragile in the doorway in her old plaid lumbershirt and paint-stained dungarees. I followed her into the tiny kitchen where she was doing a pan of dirty

1 – Date supplied from postmark.

laundry in the little sink. While she finished up, I sat down and talked to her. During the course of chatting she showed me her shelves of spices and let me smell all the savory leaves – and also her preserving closet, where she puts up choice jars of beach plum, strawberries, currant jellies and preserves – all planted and picked by herself. I also met her two cats whom I fell in love with – Prudence – a sleek lean sultry black Persian-blooded one with cold green eyes – and O'Hara. Val ground some savory smelling coffee and made a pot, got out a mound of grapes and a store cake (very good orange frosting,) put the whole feast on a tray[1] and led the way up a steep narrow flight of stairs to her "workshop."

We walked through one unfinished room, into this place she made for herself. I just stood on the threshold and gurgled in fatuous delight. She had erected the walls, made the doors & bookshelves, painted, – done everything herself. It was a low ceilinged cosy room with bookshelves all over the walls, in every angle and corner – all painted a lovely Williamsburg blue-gray with a creamyellow trim. There was a studio cot, a small gay upholstered sofa – a coffee table, and a rug on the floor in the process of being braided (she does that, too.) Also a desk, a file, a typewriter, and stacks of manuscripts.

No sooner than we had seated ourselves crosslegged on the floor than four black greeneyed kittens – playful skittish bits of soft fur – came waltzing and scampering out of the closet, playing around us, sneezing into our hot coffee, rolling grapes around with their paws, and being just adorable.

Well, we got talking, on and on – Val telling me about her job in New York, regaling me with anecdote after anecdote of her skyrocketing position in a bank – and why she quit – all hilarious. Also she got out her outline of her latest western novel, not yet accepted – and let me read a short story – and lots of her correspondence with her two agents – both her letters to them & theirs to her – all neatly dated and filed. And she told me so much in the course of the evening – we didn't stop talking till midnight – and drove me back in her old jalopy – us yelling to each other all the way over the noise of the engine.

She knows lots of people – Rachel Carson[2] & she are friends as of this summer – and she went to school with Hemingway's sister[3] . . . all sorts of tales. I learned so much, so very much from her – and I agree with all she says about writing. I must tell you in detail when I see you.

1 – 'put the whole feast ~~upstai~~ on a tray' appears in the original.
2 – American writer and marine biologist Rachel Carson (1907–64).
3 – Probably Carol Hemingway who was born in 1911, two years before Val Gendron.

I left her at 12:30 after 5 of the most wonderful hours I have ever spent ... completely fond of the dear skinny dark-haired woman – She had been so tremendous to me – "criticized" my story and all. And been so generous with herself & her work.

She said to write to her while at Smith & let her know what I am doing. It is my secret hope that I can drive down the Cape on a nice sunny day Xmas vacation & take her out to dinner somewhere and visit her. I just love her.

Now after all this – today, I got up at six and we cleaned house – I doing dishes, scrubbing & waxing kitchen floor, hanging laundry & making another great picnic.

After another glorious day at Nauset, I am browner and healthier than ever. Also sleepy. Mrs. Cantor is taking a friend out to Latham's tonight & getting Perry to wait[1] on her I think. I cooked cube steak, rice, & sliced tomatoes for supper tonight. (We cook Uncle Ben rice & it is real good – doesn't stick or get gooey.) Very delicious, if I do say!

I saw my darling Bob again today as we stopped in Chatham and he asked me to go sailing with him tomorrow afternoon! I was so pleased – just pray it's nice! I'm inordinately fond of this kid – not (just because of his M-G either.) So I hope we go.

I am <u>so</u> sleepy after this 14½ hour day that I shall now turn in.

Love,
S.

<drawing of sailboat with two people on it with three birds>

<on back of envelope>

P.S. – Thursday – another beautiful day after the lovely day-off. I ironed & packed Bob & me a picnic lunch in the a.m. At noon I biked 3 miles to his house & his Mother[2] showed me around the lovely old place from the "beanpot" cellar to the broadbeamed attic – and Bob came breezing in from work – we picked up our sails & food and hiked down to the cove to the boat. Oh, it was heaven to re-learn rigging a boat again. I took the tiller & mainsheet and we sailed out across the bay in the lovely sun & wind – tan, bathing-suited – very happy – to a big island beach. The picnic was tremendous, slaw, fruit & gingerale, lying in the sun like two contented puppies. We read aloud the whole chapter on "Marriage" from "Science & Health" and suddenly realized how late it was. Going back across the bay the wind dropped & tide was low, so we got out & pushed now & then! I was late for meeting Norton's – so they drove to bay –

1 – 'getting ~~a friend~~ Perry to wait' appears in the original.
2 – Ednah Shepard Cochran.

I jumped out – leaving Bob to anchor boat. Supper at Nortons – evening of conversation with Dick – 10-12 – Lovely day!

TO *Aurelia Schober Plath*

Thursday 21 August 1952[1] ALS (postcard), Indiana University

Thursday 8:30 Pm

Dear mum . . .

Just a card to answer a few of the questions in your last lovely long letter: As for all my uncashed checks – I don't want to send them endorsed in the mail – I can wait a week and a half before I deposit them in the bank myself. I plan, tentatively, to stop work Sunday night, Aug. 31 & spend it & Monday till you come Tuesday in Brewster with the boys. Tuesday I hope grammy can get down early, also you – to Brewster I'll be waiting there & then maybe you, Warren & I can drive to Chatham to spend a while with the Cantors as I pick up my suitcases – I do want you <u>and Warren</u> to meet Mrs. C. I'll drive back Tues. & plunge into work. Mildred wanted me to stay with you all, but as tempting as it may be, I remain stoic. I'll hate to leave here, I love them all so. Today we drove to Truro for a picnic & swim & picked a lot of beach plums to make jelly with. Now I sit sleepily under hair drier before early bed. Cute Bob called just now for a date tonight – but I was too sleepy. He'll come to band concert with us tomorrow, though. Love you all. Want to hear details about Warren's night club venture

XX
S.

TO *Aurelia Schober Plath*

Sunday 24 August 1952[2] ALS with envelope, Indiana University

Sunday night

Dearest mother . . .

At present I am sleepily curled up in front of a warm roaring fire in the Cantor's living room, happily about to recapitulate the last few strenuous and wonderful days. I don't know when I've had so much work and

1–Date supplied from postmark.
2–Date supplied from postmark.

fun combined! Really, I feel so much richer, older and wiser after this summer. Never have I gotten along so well with such an amazing diversity of people! Everyone from the Cantor's friends to 17 year-old Christian Scientist Bob to 25 year-old ugly pedantic thoughtful Art to just plain dear 22 year-old Dick. My juggling has been most successful. Imagine – there have been only 4 days so far when I haven't either been called or dated by one or more of my 3 pets!

Thursday, after the wonderful day off I told you about, we cleaned up in readiness for our 3 weekend guests, made a big picnic, and drove up to Truro – the first time I've ever been that far up the Cape – a fascinating ride – Joan & I sitting dangling our legs over the running board in back and drinking in all the varying scenery. The children, Mrs. C., Joan & I, had a lovely picnic on the Truro beach, and Joan and I read aloud the Christian Science lesson of the week together. (I am really learning an awful lot about Xian Science, and feel that I am having a rare experience of not only learning about a brand of religion and philosophy theoretically, but also seeing it operate in personal lives at the same time.) On the way back we all stopped to pick beach plums by the side of the road – which we later made into our own jelly. We came back, stopping to browse in a Wellfleet Antique Shop where Mrs. C. bought me an adorable little blue-green glass bottle that happened to have the initials "Sp" on it! I bathed, washed my hair, after a light supper, and had a long talk with Art on the phone, after which we all read from M. B. Eddy's prose in Mrs. C.'s room before early bed.

Friday was tremendous – sort of cold & cloudy. I took Joan and the kids off Mrs. C.'s hands all morning. First we drove to the Merry-Thought gift shop where I simply fell in love with a lot of the copper jewelry, Country print linen & Blenko glassware – and browsed. Then to the Cochran's to pick up my bike (which I left when I biked there on Wednesday my day-off.) Bob was home, and went across the street with us while we bought fresh vegetables at a small farm. We also stopped to get a great bouquet of flowers on the way back to decorate the house. After lunch, Joan & I did the weekend marketing and browsed in the Book Mobile & chatted with Val for about an hour or more. I had a great time & jotted down about 50 names & addresses of poetry & fiction magazine markets from a big Writer's Handbook[1] they had. Boy, I'll get those sonnets printed yet!

Bob came to the Band Concert with us, and we stayed for an hour in the chill air before we all left. After that, Bob & I drove in the M-G

1 – 'markets ~~down~~ from a big Writer's Handbook' appears in the original.

over to where his mother was visiting friends. It was a wild stormy night, and we had the top down, and the wonderful wind blowing the leaves and stars into a big dark sparkling sea. We spent a cosy evening in the new, beautifully decorated house, drinking tea and chatting gaily. The couple we visited were very simple and nice. After that we drove out to Chatham light & sat and talked about Science. I really am in deeper than I thought – the dear guy is trying to convert me – (!) so earnestly, too! I don't know whether to laugh or cry, he is so sweet – and fanatical. It is quite interesting: he has been around a lot and can be a wiseguy, but his belief in Science is a tool to bring out the best in him – which is wonderful – so I have decided to take your advice & build up his faith rather than pointlessly tear at it. It seems he thinks, idealistically, of course, that he loves me (spiritually, understand) and that I must discover the Truth – (he wants the best in the world for me, you see.) All of which is a knotty business. Mrs. Cantor likes my dating him – not only because I came in so exhilarated from my discussion & seem to enjoy Science (which I do, as a case study) but because I think she'd like to have him give Kathy a tumble next summer! I really have grown a lot just going out with this 17 year-old guy (& learned a lot about wisdom & growing old which I have elaborated on in my diary.[1]) I honestly love the kid . . . Kind of maternally I guess.

Saturday a.m. I got up early & puttered around the kitchen with Billy as I always do. I met our guests, too, who got up late after coming in late last night. There was Marvin, Joan's nice 22-year old cousin, and a wonderful Hungarian guy of 24 named Attila Kassay.[2] You know how I am about foreign names – well Attila, during the course of the weekend, captivated me completely. He is just a bit taller than I, lean, dark, with delightful black eyes, a crest of black hair, and very strong and neatly built. He is on a 5-year scholarship at Northeastern – the rest of his family being behind the Iron Curtain in Hungary. He told me some really fascinating tales of his escape to America two years ago.

Also there was "Johnny-the-girl" – a German old woman whom I like very much – who had a wealthy frivolous youth in Europe & now is a disinherited seamstress over here.

Saturday we took a big picnic of hot pork chops & frankfurts to Nauset and spent the afternoon there in the sun – cool, blue and clear day.

1 – See SP's journal entry dated 'Friday – August 22' [1952].

2 – Attila A. Kassay, Hungarian; B.A. 1955, business administration, Northeastern University; dated SP in 1952.

A light supper at home and dishes – then we all got ready for the Chatham Bars Inn Dance – me going because it was a big night – the Cantor's invited me! I must modestly admit I was a knockout – my hair bleached a light blonde, my tan golden brown, my black dress & dark eyes: everybody was wonderful to me. Joan & I had a perfect time. Attila danced mostly with me – we did well together – he very graceful and European. I also danced with Marvy & Mr. C. – such gala sport – with all the old summer couples & strange people. Afterwards, we four young ones went out for ice cream & Attila and I sat outside the house for a little & talked – it was such a lovely starry night.

I have, by the way, since he lives in Brookline, said how nice it would be for him to meet you – & hope we can invite him to dinner before I start back to school. Maybe you could speak German with him. Anyhow, I hope he likes me – today we exchanged addresses and phone numbers, so there is some hope, perhaps! I don't know whether it is just the wonderful intelligence & wit in him that appeals to me, or what, but he had that fatal Hungarian charm. And his name is Attila. (Wouldst you accept a Sylvia Kassay in the family?)

Marvy must like me – said he'd come up to Smith from work some time this year. Nice sweet simple guy. (Mr. C. likes me better than Mrs. C. does – he said he thinks I'm a great gal & that the guy who gets me will be walking off with a prize! He's a dear.)

So today I went to Sunday School again – saw Bob there – and read Bible. I really enjoy the whole business. Still a novelty. Like listening in on crusaders plotting a war vs. my own tribe of relativist materialists. Roast beef dinner – dishes, – I drove with Attila, Joan & kids to C. B. Inn beach for a swim – boys left – driving off – cute & dashing in Attila's car after lovely weekend. Very sleepy now.

Bob walked in kitchen as Joan & I were finishing light sandwich supper – short drive – then back here. He's a funny guy – so nice to me though. I am the ideal girl, you see – a dream construction or something – oh, so sweet, even if unreal.

Dick comes over tomorrow. Ah, me, I can hardly hold open my eyes – such a vivid life – hope I can get to know Attila better. You will love him. His father is a medical specialist prof at Budapest University. Oh, if only I could stay tan and beautiful all year!

XXX
Sivvy

TO *Aurelia Schober Plath*

Thursday 28 August 1952[1] ALS (postcard), Indiana University

Thursday – 10:30 p.m.

Dear Mum –

This is probably my last epistle before I see you Tues. Did you see my little poem in CSM of Wed. Aug. 27? Get a few extras, will you? Today was best yet. Mrs. C. let Joan & I and Chuck Dudley & Bob go for a motor boat picnic tonight. What a wild ride – out in the little boat into a wild deserted island where we gathered driftwood, made a blazing fire, ate, & almost killed ourselves getting the boat upright back into a heavy sea – sang all the way home – I love Joanie & the guys – hot baths – homemade bread – & a chat with Mrs. C. about her European experiences. She gave Joan & me twin leather wide brown belts – just gorgeous & much more than I ever could have gotten myself! I love mine! Yesterday I spent over at Dick's – went sketching with Bev & played a little tennis with Dick – very good food – Dick made the cutest menu – shrimp salad – strawberries, etc. Very much fun. I'll never forget this summer – my agonies over losing the Belmont job were a blessing in disguise! I never have felt so happy, rich (spiritually) and loving – chance is strange – one feels afterwards that it must have been destiny

XX
Siv

TO *Margaret Cantor*

Sunday 7 September 1952 ALS (photocopy),[2] Indiana University

Sunday, September 7,

Dear Mrs. Cantor . . .

I thought, for fun, I'd write to you on a very home-made card – seemed appropriate some how! More than anything, though, I want to tell you how infinitely much it's meant to me to become part of your wonderful family for the last month and more! How can I ever express the multitude of thanks for everything – all the trips, and picnics and companionable times

1 – Date supplied from postmark.

2 – This photocopied letter was found in the typescript of *Letters Home* held by the Lilly Library. The edges are faint; text appearing in < > is supplied by the editors.

we've had together – with dear Sue, and Bill and Joan. I don't know when I have been so completely happy and full of the simple and miraculous joy of living. Best of all, perhaps, are those intangible gifts of yours – the spiritual ones – which I know will retain a strong steady influence over me throughout my life. You see, it really has been an inspiration to me to live with you, admiring your full rewarding attitudes toward life, and learning all the time, as I gain in understanding.

Needless to say, this summer has been a milestone in my life in many ways. You and Mr. Cantor have both been such a dear "mom and dad" to me and I have grown to love Bill and Sue and especially Joanie as fondly as if they were my own brother and sisters. It seems so vacant around here without them!

All through the coming year, while up at Smith I will look back with nostalgia <at all the lovely> days we've shared together – a<ll> the glorious picnics at Nauset<,> the browsing about in shops, the making jelly and butterm<ilk> soup and steak for non-lobster eaters! It is impossible to en<um>erate the hundreds of good times we've had – from our little private family jokes to gala occasions such as the unforgetta<ble> dance at the Chatham Bars Inn!

As a matter of fact, it would be impossible to ever adequate<ly> thank you for the countless things you've done for me. I on<ly> hope that in my life and futu<re> relations with people I can shed a small part of the love of rightness and real living which I have learne<d> from you. For this, and everything else you've done, I thank you from the bottom of my heart.

My consolation at parting <is> that I will be able to see you during vacations – and I have yet to meet your dea<r> Kathy!

Love to all for the best summer ever –

Sylvia S. P<lath>[1]

1 – 'S. P' is encircled. Although the photocopy is faint, the editors surmise SP spelled her last name.

TO *Aurelia Schober Plath*

Thursday 25 September 1952[1] ALS with envelope, Indiana University

Thursday – 9:45 p.m.

Dear mother . . .

At present I am very weary and confused by strange faces and new circumstances.[2] I feel that the day I learn the names of my 63 other housemates I will again start to live. As it is, I shall probably remain quite numb for a week or two, what with my courses beginning full force tomorrow and all this newness to assimilate.

My room is a pleasant one with three windows, one looking out on the shops of "green street", the others into a large tree, and I have just finished getting my clothes put away and bookcase and desk stocked. Our colors clash (lets hope our personalities won't –) because Mary's things are all bright red, bright aqua or yellow. So we hope to get two yellow spreads (borrowed) from her mother & make our color scheme yellow, dark green & white. If so, maybe grammy could put a dk green cover over my little blue pillow & send it. I'll let you know.

(By the way, please send a couple of BLANKETS lest I freeze to death before winter. Our college ones have no warmth at all. Also, I'd appreciate it if you'd look through the box of "scrapbook" material on top of my bookcase & send up the photos of dick & the more colorful poster or playbill items for my bulletin board. Thanks.

My "job" shouldn't really be too taxing – it involves a little over an hour a day – waitressing, no less, for lunch. We eat before the rest and serve quite formally, actually wearing aprons! I'm so glad it is lunch instead of dinner. (dinner has twice as many courses.) I think it is silly for this house to be so much more formal than Haven – but am at least glad they got rid of the old housemother[3] last year – in the nick of time for my arrival. Mrs. Bridgeman,[4] the new one, seems like a rather sweet scatterbrain so far – such a change from dear Mrs. Shakespeare! (As far as I can see, Mrs. Rae, the last housemother, was a veritable Captain Queeg![5])

1 – Date supplied from postmark.

2 – SP began living in Lawrence House, a co-operative house where she was required to work one hour per day for part of her room and board. SP lived there from September 1952 until her graduation from Smith College in June 1955.

3 – Mary Stuart Rae.

4 – Dorothea Eaglesfield Bridgman.

5 – A reference to a character in Herman Wouk, *The Caine Mutiny* (New York: Doubleday, 1951).

Also I will have one hour of "watch" a week, plus occasional weekend duty.

My schedule is very hard at the end of the week, but as far as I can see, I have no Monday or Tuesday classes – which will give me a certain amount of responsibility, but it will be nice to have the time concentrated. As you can see, Wednesday and especially Thursday look like my hardest days. As classes[1] begin today, I shall see what my courses look like, also instructors.

	Wed	Th	F	Sat
9		Sc	Sc	Sc
10	Sc.	(watch)		
11	Art			
12				
2	Cr. Wr.	Cr. Wr.	Cr. Wr.	
3	Art	Art	Art	
4		Unit		
		Unit		

On arrival here Tuesday at 6 p.m. I found a letter and a note waiting for me when I looked in my mailbox – a lovely long one from Olive Higgins Prouty[2] about my story, which I'm so glad I sent her, because it seems I'm getting her scholarship again this year! She told me she hadn't known what year I was and had looked for me at graduation last spring, thinking I might be a senior – also got another little invitation to see her sometime. So I guess that relationship is patched up.

The note was from Bob Cochran, of all people, who had dropped up to the house earlier in the morning on his way to Hanover! I am just glad he wasn't there waiting for me when Dick arrived!

As I say, I am giving myself two weeks – to get oriented to the house – people and customs – before I pass judgments – because I do feel rather like a displaced person as yet – a bit bewildered and uninitiated.

1–During her third year at Smith College, SP completed English Unit (medieval literature) taught by Howard Patch; English Unit (modern poetry) taught by Elizabeth Drew; English 347 (creative writing) taught by Robert Gorham Davis; English 39b (Milton) taught by Eleanor Terry Lincoln; Physical Science 193 (world of atoms) taught by Kenneth Sherk.
2–Olive Higgins Prouty to SP, 14 September 1952; held by Lilly Library.

Thursday

Whew! I have just undergone all my courses during the day and am I weary! I really think I will drop Art 11[1] as much as I hate to. I simply don't feel I can carry the full 15 hours and do any kind of justice to my other demanding courses. Physical Science shouldn't be too bad – Mr. Sherk[2] gave me a friendly grim when he saw me, so the initial sheepishness has worn off me. Mr. Davis,[3] my creative writing teacher, I adore – he is the sort that can make you feel the urge to think and work and create – until it kills you. I want to do so much for him. And Mr. Patch,[4] my Medaeval Lit Unit prof is the most imposing literary lion I have ever seen – a great 6'5" gray haired man who seems to live in the ruddy vitality of the middle ages. He is terrifying and magnificent. The 10 of us taking the unit meet in his library & sit around on chairs comfortably. I just hope I can swallow the enormous tomes he assigns – already spent $8 for the first two books – one of which he wrote![5] I feel at once pitifully stupid, inadequate and scared – and determined to succeed in the enormous intellectual honesty, ambition & discipline that honoring requires. Boy, will I be busy this year!

Got a letter from Eddie Cohen[6] – he thinks he'll get married to a 27 year old divorcee with a 2 year old son eventually if their trial affair lasts – really loves the girl. What a wonderfully sordid life –

XXX

Sivvy

<on back of envelope>

P.S. By the way – please also send the book on Bridge in my yellow trunk –

1–Art 11 was 'An Historical Introduction to Art'.

2–Kenneth Wayne Sherk (1907–62); professor of chemistry, Smith College; 1935–72; SP's colleague 1957–8.

3–Robert Gorham Davis (1908–98); English professor, Smith College, 1943–58. Davis taught studies in style and form (English 247), a creative writing course completed by SP, 1952–3. SP also served on Honor Board with Davis, 1952–3.

4–Howard Rollin Patch (1889–1963); English professor, Smith College, 1919–57.

5–Howard Rollin Patch, *On Rereading Chaucer* (Cambridge, Mass.: Harvard University Press, 1948). SP's signed copy now held by Lilly Library.

6–Probably Eddie Cohen to SP, undated (*c.* September 1952); held by Lilly Library.

TO *Aurelia Schober Plath*

Sunday 28 September 1952[1]   ALS (postcard),[2] Indiana University

Sunday night

Dear mum . . .

It is amazing what a difference a good night's sleep can make in my psychological outlook on life. From the lonely, scared bewildered creature I was for the first few days, I am now sure that everything will work out for the best. I have decided to drop Art 11, as much as I hate to, because I want to do as well as possible at my work, while getting to know the girls in the house, and concentrating on Press B. and Smith Review. My creative w. & patch unit promise to be wonderful & demanding. Friday I had supper at Albright & renewed the good friends there – I have also supper scheduled with Marcia Monday and Haven Tuesday. Mrs. Bonneville[3] took Mary & me for a nice fish diner at Jack Augusts and has leant us curtains and twin yellow bedspreads for the year, so I should only have incidentals to buy – our room really will be rather nice after we're through – and I plan to have a single next year while I write my thesis, so I'll be able to use my pillows & spread then! Mrs. B. is very nice – tall, and homespun – a first grade teacher in Pittsfield Mass. Jim McNealy[4] asked me to Yale next weekend but I refused nicely, because I would like to get a good start in the house and studies & sleep & besides I feel very old and staid at present. Got a cute postcard from Warren

XX

Sivvy

<on address side of postcard>:

P.S. Wore suit first time today – looks & feels "perfect". Love it & feel so rich & right in it!

1 – Date supplied from postmark.

2 – A preprinted correspondence card left over from when SP lived at Haven House. SP crossed out Haven House and wrote in 'Lawrence –'.

3 – Mary Anna Bonneville (1906–99).

4 – James DuBois McNeely (1933–); B.A. 1954, B.Arch. 1960, Yale College; dated SP in 1952.

TO *Warren Plath*

Sunday 28 September 1952[1]

ALS (photocopy) written on Smith College letterhead, Indiana University

Sunday night

Allo, Varrie . . .

I am now feelink very happy, having got your postcard and being settled for the first time since I came here Tuesday. God, those first few days were awful – Dick drove me up and I got scareder and scareder thinking of how I didn't know anybody hardly in the house & hadn't even seen my room. I was greeted by a horde of strange faces and 60 new names – it was like being a freshman all over again, only worse, because I remembered nostalgically the homey comfort of Haven House, and rooming with Marcia. Wednesday was full of meetings and the discouraging job of clearing up the mess of unpacking and getting used to my job, which is waitressing every day at lunch (we have very formal service – waitresses eat early & wear aprons and pass plates & vegetables individually!) Really, it is not at all unpleasant, and scarcely seems to justify $250 off board & room – it's not that much more work.

Thursday classes started. I felt very sheepish about going to Physical Science at 9 o'clock. But he just grinned & said "You must have had a rough summer." So I blushed & murmured "Yeah . . ."

Creative writing will be great. Our teacher, Robert Gorham Davis, I think will even come to surpass Mr. Crockett in my esteem – imagine, his review of "The Old Man and the Sea"[2] got a front page spread in the N.Y. Times Book Review!

Mr. Patch, my gigantic (6'5") gray-haired Medieval Lit. teacher is really a literary lion (grrr . . .) and our unit of 10 girls meets once a week for 2 hours in his library where we sit and tremble at his hideous and docile bulldog, Jeeves. It will be a demanding and exciting course – I think Mr. Patch lives in the middle ages – One of our two textbooks is by Chaucer, the other by Mr. Patch!

I am going to be spending a lot of time in the College news office on Press Board and working on getting the <u>Smith Review</u> published – we were left last year with no money, no organization and a bad reputation.

1–Date supplied from postmark by Warren Plath.

2–Robert Gorham Davis, 'Hemingway's Tragic Fisherman', *New York Times Book Review*, 7 September 1952, 1, 20.

It's really exciting to be working at publishing a magazine (hitherto a dying venture) with such potentialities.

☆ By the way, I was talking with Jane Truslow,[1] a girl in Lawrence who has two brothers, Bob & Bill,[2] who are juniors at Exeter. We would love to have you come up some weekend for Saturday and Sunday sometime so you could have dinner with us and get a tour of Northampton in along with it. Why don't you find out who they are and talk it over with them and see if you would like to come together sometime during the year – I know you'd probably hate to waste a weekend on your old sisters, but we'd love to have you!

Saturday night I went to the early showing of "Jour de Fête"[3] at the college auditorium. It wasn't more than mildly amusing, but we were all so tired that we laughed hysterically. A good night's sleep last night did wonders for me psychologically. Mary Bonneville's (my senior roommate) mother – a homespun schoolteacher of first grade in Pittsfield – took us out to Jack August's for a great seafood dinner. I must take you there! Nothing but seafood in a great atmosphere – red-checked tablecloths and lobster things hanging everywhere: everything from shrimp cocktail, hot clam juice, lobsters, oysters, swordfish, smelts, etc – all served with french fries & cole slaw.

Our house has a lot of really interesting girls in it – I am now sitting in the room of a Jewish girl who lives in Greenich (sp?) Village along with[4] a Negro girl from Washington[5] who has a perpetual "black eye" because of some sort of capillary bleeding . . . really fun.

Keep up the activities – it'll look good on your record to have an "all round" program – you know how important the rounded (bullet-head) individual is these days.

Glad you heard from Ann and Cynthia[6] – use my policy of being nice and honest (well, mostly) with <u>everybody</u> – also, why not drop a line to Judy H? Never hurts.

1–Jane Auchincloss Truslow (1932–81); B.A. 1955, English, Smith College; SP's housemate at Lawrence House. Truslow married SP's friend Peter Davison on 7 March 1959.

2–Twins Robert Gurdon Truslow (1936–) and William Auchincloss Truslow (1936–).

3–*Jour de Fête*, a 1949 French comedy directed by Jacques Tati.

4–'Village ~~with~~ along with' appears in the original.

5–Probably Frances Yvonne White MacKenzie (1931–2007); B.A. 1953, law, Smith College; lived in Lawrence House.

6–Probably Cynthia Morrow, of 15 Intervale Road, Wellesley. According to SP's calendar, she drove with Warren to Exeter with 'Cinny Morrow' after Thanksgiving dinner. See also SP to Warren Plath, 4 December 1952.

Jim McNealy asked me to come to the Yale-Brown game next weekend but I refused for many reasons – it just didn't seem worth the money & time & resulting hard work I'd have to do to make up for it.

I've just been reading a rather serious historical tome titled "From Beowulf to Virginia Woolf"[1] – and I quote: "Later, William established the Futile System, with its intricate relationships between lord, vessel, serf, and villain. His greatest contribution was The Guilt System . . . A medevil organization designed to encourage arts and graft . . ."

Pox vobiscum.
-Muddle Latin Proverb[2]
Don't say I never loved you –
XXX
Sivvy

TO *Aurelia Schober Plath*

Sunday 5 October 1952[3]

TLS with envelope, written on Smith College letterhead, Indiana University

Sunday afternoon

Dear Mother . . . .

Wow! Speak of appropriate psychological moments for getting unexpected good news, this was one. I wandered lazily downstairs just before lunch today and glanced casually in my mailbox. Two letters from you. I opened the little one first,[4] looked at it puzzled for a few minutes before it suddenly dawned on me what the contents were. I never even cherished the smallest hope of getting one of the third prizes[5] this year . . .

1–Robert Manson Myers, *From Beowulf to Virginia Woolf: An Astounding and Wholly Unauthorized History of English Literature* (Indianapolis: Bobbs-Merrill, 1952). SP slightly misquotes the text, which reads: 'Later William established the Futile System, with its intricate relationships between lord, vessel, serf, and villain. His greatest contribution, of course, was the Guilt System, an organization designed to encourage arts and graft' (20).
2–This quote is also from Myers's book and serves as the epigraph to the chapter titled 'The Big Bad Wolf' (19).
3–Date supplied from postmark.
4–Telegram and letter from Alice Thompson to SP, 3 October 1952; see SP's publications scrapbook, pp. 31–2; held by Lilly Library. SP's 'Initiation' won second prize in the Short Story Contest.
5–Sylvia Plath, 'Initiation', *Seventeen* 12 (January 1953), 64–5, 92–5, 98; won second prize in the *Seventeen* annual short story contest.

as you know, I figured out the relative deadline for their decision by my other story, and had long since given up thinking about it.

This news makes me feel that I am maybe not destined to deteriorate after all. I have been too busy getting used to the routine of the house and doing the pile of beginning work on press board to really plunge into my studies, and as a result I have been feeling very far behind and scared about my courses. Sort of a beginning paralysis. My first writing assignment I just handed in was three very poor and stiff descriptions that I felt extremely sterile and mentally blocked while doing. But I feel that after I get academically set this coming week I will again have my self-confidence back. I never realized how important doing well in studies was to me until I got behind this last busy week. So if my letters come not too often for the first while, forgive me, and think that I am getting a lot of work done.

The girls in the house are very friendly, and I only have to realize that getting to know sixty girls by more than their names is a pleasant occupation requiring a year or more . . . not to be mastered in one day. I know, even while numbed and scared inside by this mass of newness, that it is the best thing that ever happened to me, and I will be joyous and elated about it when I can view it in perspective. The first week I couldn't, to be trite, see the forest for the trees.

Your last big morale building letter was most appreciated. You are the most wonderful mummy that a girl ever had, and I only hope I can continue to lay more laurels at your feet. Warren and I both love you and admire you more than anybody in the world for all you have done for us all our lives. For it is you who has given us the heredity and the incentive to be mentally ambitious. Thank you a million times!

Amusing notes: Bob Cochran called me up from Hanover the other night asking me to come up for a dance and football game October 18. Needless to say I told him a fond no . . . imagine me going to a prep school dance . . . the money lost didn't appall me as much as the valuable study time! Also, Jim McNeely asked me to Yale again that weekend. I may decide to go unless I think up a really good excuse. He is fun, but I am finding myself amazingly sober as far as going away is concerned.

Last night I went to dinner at Marty's again, and spent a lovely evening talking companionably with her and Mike . . . I love those two, and felt I really got to know Mike better for the first time. He is a wonderfully perceptive and delightful boy. Also went for a walk in the country with Ann Goodkind . . . a sophomore friend of mine in Haven House . . . it was unbearably beautiful out.

Dick comes up next weekend, so I will be slaving till then.

Lots of love . . . .
your adoring daughter
Sivvy

<on back of envelope>

So your old favorite idea "Heather-birds Eyebrows" worked out after all! I am amazed, but strange are the ways of the world . . . especially publishing. I, too, had thought "Brief Encounter" was the best bet. Think of all the coincidence that combined to get me this . . . the sorority invitation and the sinus infection . . . how intriguing!

xxx
s.

P.S. I think it was the subject and unfortunately not the style which won me this. "Den of Lions" was the opposite – "style" – & not too much more than one incident.

TO *Aurelia Schober Plath*

Friday 10 October 1952[1] TLS with envelope, Indiana University

Friday night

Dear mother . . .

Much thanks for your wonderful letter, and the comfortable check. I will cash it here because I have just about run out of ready money. Please, do deposit the beautiful $200 check at home in my bank . . . and save the precious stub for my scrapbook.[2] To answer a few of your questions: I've gotten all the packages, and am now wearing the new pajamas, which fit well and are warm, if not glamorous. Also, our room is just adorable now that we have fixed it . . . three great windows, yellow spreads and dark green furnishings, white curtains, and a harmonizing modern art picture that we're renting from the college museum for the year. Mary is working out beautifully, and we get along really well . . . . most of our work is done away from the room, so we don't see too much of each other during the day, but she is a very sweet girl, in her own way, even though I can't share myself with her to the great depths I did with Marcia. We do have fun together, though, and I am constantly glad that I decided to have a roommate.

1–Date supplied from postmark.
2–See SP's publication scrapbook; held by Lilly Library.

I have written a thank-you and sent a snapshot to Seventeen. That magazine has really been awfully good to me, and I am really aghast at this last fling of mine. I still can't believe it is true, and I have completely forgotten the plot and detail of my story! I was most interested to hear your quotes . . . . it was as if someone else had written it.

Last Sunday night I went to Joe's, a colorful local beer and pizza place with red-checked tablecloths and a gay atmosphere, with Marty, Mike, and Charlie Gardner,[1] a nice friend of theirs who spent a post-grad year in England with Mike and is an English major at Trinity. I spent a delightful few hours of conversation and the four of us had a most congenial evening

Press Board averages at least two hours of time six days a week, but I'd much rather have to work at something I love for money tthan at some of the dull routine library and babysitting and mail delivery jobs that the other girls in the house do. The Daily News is printing more news than last year, and it is very encouraging to see some of the feature stories I write get full picture spreads.[2] I should earn over fifty dollars from it this year.

The house is really lovely . . . very attractively decorated downstairs and closer to everything. The girls are all wonderful . . . they work, get good marks in general, and hold extracurricular offices. The is a delightful atmosphere of economy, and everyone understands the words, "I can't, I'm broke." We as a house, subscribe to excellent magazines like the Atlantic, SRL, (Newsweek and Life.) We work more, to be sure, but one quickly gets used to it. My lunch waitressing job takes from 12.30 to 2 each day, including lunch, which I eat before serving, so it's not overwhelming, and our formal waitressing is good practice. I have an hour a week also to be on watch duty, and every two or three weeks, a few extra weekend hours added, as the jobs then rotate.

I am renewing old friends, the last leaves, so many fine girls being abroad, and have met a few new girls. I shall probably take my New York trip to visit Jan Salter during midyear exams, as my exam is the last day, and I can afford a few days away at the beginning of the period, which will be the end of January . . . a good time to get theater tickets, see Greenwich Village, and so on.

1 – Charles Shoop Gardner III (1932–), 1955, Trinity College, Hartford, Connecticut.

2 – SP wrote a press release on the opening of a religious centre on campus that when printed, unattributed, included a photograph of four student leaders: 'Faith Groups Open Center for Students', *Springfield Daily News*, 6 October 1952, 26. A heavily edited, unattributed article on the opening was also published the next day: 'Central Spot for Religion Groups At Smith', *Daily Hampshire Gazette*, 7 October 1952, 16.

So far Honor Board hasn't sent me a word, so I've been gratful for a respite in that regard. Smith Review is not at all demanding as we have all the material, but are desperately asking for subscriptions so we can finance it . . . it is in dire debt.

Tomorrow Dick will come in the afternoon, and my casual plans for the weekend include supper with Dee Neuberg,[1] a brillan soph in our house, and her date, at some informal spot . . . an liesurely evening of conversation or walking if it is nice . . . Sunday breakfast at Browns, and visiting other friends on campus, with dinner at Lawrence.

Our housemother this year is a strange, pathetic scatterbrained woman . . . a direct change from the Captain Queegish Miss Rae they had last year . . . who was completely illogical and ruled by fear and meanness. Her influence and indoctrination are amusingly obvious for us new members.

I may very well come home Saturday the 25th for a weekend . . . and it will be good to get away and be frivolous and gay again . . . I have felt like a virtuous stoic refusing three weekends, but am sure it was the wisest choice, both for my sanity and my health.

Perry and Charlotte Kennedy were my supper guests here wednesday, Mountain day. Perry is falling in love again, and this time I can predict it is for good. The two of them are perfectly matched . . . both very sweet and idealistic and basically shy and understanding. I am beginning to feel like Cupid incarnate.

It grows late . . . .
lots of love . . .
Sivvy

TO *Aurelia Schober Plath*

Wednesday 15 October 1952[2] ALS (postcard),[3] Indiana University

Wednesday

Dear Mother . . .

Your lovely letter today was most welcome – the enclosed note was from a girl in Canada, an aspiring writer, who wanted to correspond with an "author." I recall a similar note from Hong Kong last year – but simply don't have time to get chummy with all my readers. I am just

1–Nadine Neuburg Doughty (1934–); B.A. 1955, sociology, Smith College.
2–Date supplied from postmark.
3–A preprinted correspondence card left over from when SP lived at Haven House. SP crossed out Haven House and wrote in 'Lawrence –'.

beginning to realize the "position & stands" a "writer" must take – and the responsibility: today I got a letter with the return address: Blodgett, Lynn – and it started by saying they had read my story. Aghast, I had visions of law courts & suits for slander. Luckily I had strength to read on & discover that it was the Mlle not 17 story they meant! Whew! As you have heard, Dick's weekend here was lovely, restful & very good for me – I hadn't exercised outdoors since getting here. I must write Cantors – and hope to see them on Thanksgiving – they have been so good to me. This weekend I will spend working on papers and reading Chaucer: I really love Chaucer, now that I can read along more rapidly – his stories are as fascinating as poetic fairy tales & as spicy as Boccaccio[1] – but the reading required is phenomenal – at least 20 hours a week. Glad to hear Warren is having fun. I may go straight to Med school Sat. to save time – not sure now.

Love to all –
Sivvy

TO *Aurelia Schober Plath*

Monday 20 October 1952[2] ALS (postcard), Indiana University

Monday –

Dear Mother –

Well, the week is underway, and it is a case of living till Saturday – the ride back yesterday was fine & I got here just in time for supper – Perry & Charlotte came over in the evening (ironically two hours after Dick left) & talked a while. Then I stayed up till 12:30 on late watch. Today I wrote my Chaucer paper – tomorrow it will be my Creative Writing, and Wed. my science, in which I am behind as yet. In spite of my work, I have decided to go to Amherst for the Community Chest Rehersal tomorrow night – the performance is Nov. 7 & 8,[3] but if I don't like the deal I can back out early – I am also thinking of being frivolous & going to Princeton on Nov. 1 with Rodger Decker[4] – a friend of Phil Brawner's whom I met this summer. (Phil is taking Mary Ann Hemry,[5] by the way.) I think it would do me good to go somewhere new again & have to pull

1 – Italian poet Giovanni Boccaccio (1313–75); author of *Decameron* (1353).
2 – Date supplied from postmark.
3 – The Community Chest Drive musical was *Keep it Clean* (1929).
4 – Roger Bradford Decker (1931–93); B.A. 1953, Princeton University; dated SP in 1952.
5 – Mary Ann Hemry (1935–); resident of Wellesley and Dover, Mass.

my self together to make a good impression – so if I decide to go, I'll go shopping this Saturday for a few of those items I need. My first inclination is to hibernate completely, so lest I become like our little grind we met at Filene's[1] 2 years ago, I will force myself out of my numb little hole and see if I surprise myself by having some fun

Love you muchly
XXX
Sivvy

TO *Aurelia Schober Plath*

Friday 24 October 1952[2]

ALS with envelope written on Smith College letterhead, Indiana University

Friday 8:15 pm

Dear Mother –

Your lovely long letter came today with the very generous enclosure – merci beaucoup! I am sitting comfortably ensconced in my armchair drying my hair, eating the last of the lovely apples I brought up with me, and treating myself to the illusion that, at least for half an hour, I have nothing to do but unwind the tension I've built up all week. Monday I wrote my Chaucer paper, Tuesday, my English paper, Wednesday and Thursday I rushed around to classes, slaved on Press Board & tried to cram in studying for my Science written this morning – to top it off we had a house meeting from 10:15 to 12:30 last night, so I was pretty beat this a.m., not having spent much time sleeping – I will refrain from commenting on the written till I get it back. At least I feel the 1st written has exorcised the rebellious mental block I had about taking science this year.

This afternoon I spent wandering through all the stores downtown trying on everything from shoes to black fitted coats. I didn't like any of the coats quite well enough to get one (I am very particular) but I think I can eventually get quite a nice one for not more than $80. The only difficulty will be trying to get one a suit will fit under! I did buy my first pair of high heels for $10 – a lovely black-suede that had done wonders for my sense of chic. They are the lowest type of French heel – very nice

1 – Filene's was a department store chain with its flagship branch in Boston.

2 – Date supplied from postmark.

– <drawing of shoe and foot> also a new pair of black loafers, a long-sleeved black jersey (10.95) to take the place of my beloved old one and a classic Charcoal gray slim skirt (10.95) All I need now is a few colorful accents – like a pretty pastel sweater – but I got lots of ideas!

I have decided to give up the Amherst show – as the rehearsal schedule was much too rough – but plan to leave for Princeton next Friday for heaven knows what sort of a time. The train trip takes 5 hours and costs $15 (I'll use your money for it –) but I feel I should try it anyway. Phil evidently recommended me highly to Roger Decker (my date) as a lot of fun – and they say the college is beautiful so even if Roger is the type one just banters with, I should get rejuvenated somehow.

Tomorrow I wanted to go hear Stevenson in Springfield, but I have so much to do in Chaucer – plus a huge feature to write[1] for Press Board – plus writing a Hallowe'en skit for the house, that I just don't think I'll be able to make it. Really, I can't see why you don't vote for him. Do you think the change of administration, which of course is partially desirable if only to make the opposition party more responsible – is worth the power it will give to the red-witch hunts of MacCarthy, the southern snobbery of Jenner,[2] the reactionary foreign policy of Taft???[3] No, it is not. A "clean sweep" is a good slogan, but I fear the present administration is the lesser of two enigmatic dangers. Stevenson will be a "change", himself – and his approach to the tidelands oil, Civil Rights and so on are so sound & intelligent – while Eisenhower[4] would seem to be open to influence and power of his unfortunate colleagues. Oh, I wish I were old enough to vote for Stevenson!

Tomorrow night I plan to go see "Rashomon"[5] at Sage Hall with some of the girls from Haven House. Monday night Marcia has asked me over for supper – those are the bright notes in the immediate future. My x-ray is scheduled for monday also, by the way.

Thanks again for the check & stamps.

XXXX
Sivvy

1–Possibly SP's article on the Student–Faculty soccer game published concurrently in two newspapers: 'Smith Girls Will Get Chance to Jeer Faculty', *Springfield Daily News*, 27 October 1952, 30; and 'Cheers, Jeers Promised for Smith Game', *Daily Hampshire Gazette*, 27 October 1952, 8.

2–Senator William Ezra Jenner (1908–85) of Indiana. Jenner served on the Senate Committee on Rules and Administration.

3–Senator Robert Alphonso Taft (1889–1953), of Ohio.

4–Dwight D. Eisenhower (1890–1969), 34th President of the United States (1953–61).

5–*Rashomon* is a 1950 Japanese drama directed by Akira Kurosawa.

TO *Aurelia Schober Plath*

Sunday 26 October 1952[1] ALS (postcard),[2] Indiana University

Sunday a.m.

Dear Mummy . . .

What a lovely mummy you are! The beautiful cake arrived yesterday afternoon, and I had a little party of the 10 girls who were in the house from 9:30-11 p.m. – who had a lot of fun & everybody praised the cake highly – how did you ever make it heart shaped! And the colors perfectly matched our room – so pretty! I saw "Rashomon" last night with Charlotte Kennedy. Also, to my surprise, a beautiful pen-and-ink sketch arrived from Ilo – haven't heard from him in a year! I was so touched that he remembered my birthday – he signed it "Your sentimental old friend." Such a dear! I was most pleased to get Aunt Hazel's gift & have written her already. This week is crammed to the gills with work – I still plan to go to Princeton, though. It is a sort of test case – have also heard twice from Dick.[3] Love to you all & thanks for remembering my Day so generously.

XXX
Sivvy

TO *Aurelia Schober Plath*

Monday 27 October 1952 ALS (postcard), Indiana University

October 27

Dear mum . . .

What a cagey one you are! Never o never did I suspect a FILE! I am so proud of it. It is just the sort of gift I LOVE. I'll use it the rest of my life, & it occupies a niche in my heart next to my typewriter and my bike! People who love me always know what makes me happiest. Marty, Carol & Mrs. B. gave me a birthday dinner party tonight & three perfect presents: a Van Gogh book of reprints, a chunky pottery Italian Plate, & a new Modern

1–Date supplied from postmark.
2–A preprinted correspondence card left over from when SP lived at Haven House. SP crossed out Haven House and wrote in 'Lawrence'.
3–Richard Norton to SP, 22 and 23 October 1952; held by Lilly Library.

Library book of Franz Kafka's short stories.[1] A glass or two of sherry & a home atmosphere served to bring me out of the bog of lonesomeness & despair I had been wallowing in, and shot me through with new joy and love for them all. They have been so very good to me – and so have you all. Thanks a billion times. I have gotten two fat letters from Dick, as I perhaps said. By the way, do get all the info on skiing that you can – prices of boots, skis, etc. I am serious about learning how. I am thinking of perhaps seeing Ilo when I go to Greenwich Village during midsemesters – he was so sweet to send me the picture!

XXX from your ancient 20 yr. old
Sivvy

TO *Aurelia Schober Plath*

Tuesday 28 October 1952[2] ALS (postcard), Indiana University

Tuesday –

Dear Mother . . .

Well, I have done it! Bought a black-fitted coat! I do hope you like it, as I tried on at least 10 b. f. c's in different stores till I got it. It is a snug fit over my suit, but I will wear it mostly over dresses. It is a very simple coat, with a full skirt, falling in folds, and will look very trim with my black heels – or my red shoes & the red bag I bought to match (a lovely pocketbook for only $3.60!) I feel much wiser & more sensible in my purchases this year. The coat was $50!!! <drawing of coat> So I don't feel I've compromised our home or anything! No more white-pleated skirts for me! I also bought a transparent nylon blouse – long-sleeved, for under my suit that was $9. So far I have spent $100 on clothes up here. The only big item now is either a wool dress or a very special sweater. But that can wait. I really feel a bit frivolous, going to Princeton & spending the train fare but I figure It'll probably be my only invitation this fall, so I'll make the most of it & thus never say "I wish I'd gone."

Love again
XX
Sivvy

1 – Franz Kafka, *Selected Short Stories of Franz Kafka*. Translated by Willa and Edwin Muir; introduction by Philip Rahv (New York: Modern Library, 1952); SP's annotated copy held by Smith College.
2 – Date supplied from postmark.

TO *Aurelia Schober Plath*

Wednesday 29 October 1952[1] ALS (postcard), Indiana University

Wednesday

Dear mum . . .

Thanks for the great political letter: read Mrs. Truitts article[2] & admire her strategy, even if I disagree with her ideas. Both sides have "albatrosses." No, I don't like some of Truman's deals. But also don't see how Ike can unite forces in senate to pass his noble measures when those black-sheep senators have voted so consistently against him! – How would you like a genuine, heavy, double-breasted Paris tweed suit or a gold jersey dress? I picked them up free because they almost fit & will bring them home Thanksgiving to see if you like either & to alter them – some of Alum donated them to the Co-op house! By the way, I was one of the 4 finalists for head of Junior Prom – but I resigned before the final vote, even though the prestige is tremendous, because it would mean half a year's work like mad, and I feel my health & courses are much more important. Also, I am busy enough already, to say the least. I think I am very wise, even though the big time has a certain glitter. In 10 years, who would know the dif? I like the house better & better every day. The girls are all wonderful! Wish me luck at Princeton

XXX
Sylvia

TO *Aurelia Schober Plath*

Sunday 2 November 1952[3] ALS (postcard), Indiana University

Sunday

Dear Mum . . .

Well, I am back, weary & a bit numb from travelling from 9:30-5 today. The weekend was warm & spring-like, & Princeton was the most beautiful college I've ever seen – especially the great modern library,[4] complete with elevators – and the exquisite gothic chapel[5] with great

1 – Date supplied from postmark.

2 – Margaret Dye Truitt, 'Two Urgent Reasons For Electing Gen. Eisenhower President', *The Townsman*, 23 October 1952, 10.

3 – Date supplied from postmark.

4 – The Harvey S. Firestone Memorial Library, opened in 1948.

5 – The University Chapel, opened in 1928.

stained glass windows. I wore high heels for the first time, and even Charlestoned in them. The trip has satisfied my wanderlust till Xmas when I'll see Dick. $15 train fare! My date was tall, cute, but unfortunately quite intellectually stupid. He served his purpose, but I never intend to see him again – I cannot abide dumb rich boys. Two informal dances at the Club where I stayed Fri. & Sat., and a football game where Princeton slaughtered Brown to which I wore just my suit & was hot even then! My heels were fun – I felt so grown up with them. I hope Warren goes to Harvard. No doubt there are intelligent boys at Princeton, but the pressure to drink & the wealthy socialites are most obvious. Now, back to work.

XXX
a sleepy Sivvy

TO *Aurelia Schober Plath*

Thursday 6 November 1952 TLS, Indiana University

November 6, 1952

Dear Mummy . . . .

Well, I only hope you're happy with McCarthy and appropriations, Jenner and Rules and Civil Rights, Taft and Foreign Policy, and our noble war hero and his absurd plan to fly to Korea like a white dove with a laurel leaf in his mouth, appealing to the emotions of parents who "want their boys back home". Bringing our boys back home too soon has ruined us before. As I said, though, it wasn't Eisenhower I was against, but all the other little horrors in the Trojan Horse he rode in on. I don't envy him his crusade nor his companions, and I feel that our gullible American public may be only too sadly disillusioned. But then, variety of corruption is the spice of life. And so are red witch hunts. Me, I felt that it was the funeral day of all my hopes and ideals when I got up the morning after elections. Stevenson was the Abe Lincoln of our age. I don't know how we could have gone better. But then, the prosperity party often gets kicked out. But I don't think the change justified the concomitant factors it brought with it. Enough of my partisan views.

I am crazy with work . . . two papers every week now, and I will be writing them thanksgiving, too. I do hope to have a lovely day with you all and Warren, whom I miss very much. And I hope to have a chance to see the Cantors, too. My Chaucer course I love, but the work is unbelievable, and I am going to devote my weekends solely to trying to keep only reasonably behind in the phenomenal lists of readinghe doles out. I will be lucky if I get a low B in the course, which counts for two courses, because the other seven girls in the class are all the most brilliant girls in the college. No longer is the competition large and general, but very specific and individual, with keen competitors and cut-throat workers. I am going to devote myself to this work, though because Mr. Patch is the most brilliant man I have ever known, and I don't give a damn about dates or any more extra-curricular activities. A good friend of mine got the head of Junior Prom, and I have never been so happy I resigned from anything in my life. I would hate myself for wasting half a year when I could be under the guidance of the best men in the department in the college. Hope you can go to Ray Brook[1] Saturday. I have hardly enough time to think of writing letters, as every minute of each day is planned rigidly to the last second, but I at least got off all the Birthday returns promptly, didn't I? I really love my work, all except science, and the nullifying pressure of my Medieval lit unit. I will enjoy rereading Chaucer at my leisure this summer, and later in life, I think . . . he is the most rich and rewarding of writers.

I'll try to get the box of clothes off to you this weekend. I truly hope you can do something with them. I would be so happy if the suit worked out. The only thing is, it has a pleated skirt, which you might not like.

I have written to Bread Loaf to see if they have any tuition scholarships, but I doubt it. I also don't know if they would let me spend a summer without earning money. But I would love to go to summer school . . . to Harvard, too, perhaps. I would also like only a part time job or one that would only last a short part of the summer so I could read and write and work on research for my thesis. I think that it is important that I have such a chance to think and work. I plan to write my application for Mademoiselle as soon as I get home on Thanksgiving . . . because I won't have a minute till then.

All for now. Keep your lovely letters coming. I do so appreciate them

xxx
sivvy

1–Ray Brook State Tuberculosis Hospital, a sanatorium in Ray Brook, New York. Richard Norton was hospitalized at the New York State Hospital there, receiving treatment for tuberculosis, 1952–3.

TO *Warren Plath*

Thursday 6 November 1952 TLS (photocopy), Indiana University

November 6, 1952

Dear Warren . . .

Much thanks for your letter. I really appreciated it. I am now paying for my frivolous Princeton weekend of three days last week where I actually had the privilege of sleeping in the same room with Mary Ann and sixty other girls on the top floor of the Tower Club. Obviously she was with Phil Brawner. She actually asked how you were, and took care to remind me that she and John Hodges had cried over my sad story about them in Seventeen three years ago.[1] I was so touched by her account; I can just see her sobbing. As far as I am concerned she is a very captivating bitchy socialite. My date was the perfect example of the absolute sheep, and I had thought I could have fun with him, and it was all right until he started talking. He was by all means the most pathetic specimen of manhood I have ever met . . . you remember that funny boy Phil and I drove around with down the Cape last summer when we went to see the Weasel? Well the summer is a much better place for funny boys who don't have any heads. As much as I tried to conceal my brilliance, he guessed I was not as neutral as I seemed. His confession of his own inadequacies, in an attempt to be serious, was not only pitiably revealing of his lack of thinking and values, but was evidently quite a strain on his mental powers, and I use the word loosely.

Princeton was beautiful: especially the gigantic modern library, with the elevators, the modern glassed in lounges, Poetry and Sanskrit rooms, carrels with soundproof sliding doors, art exhibits, and other amazing attractions. I also was much impressed by the enormous Gothic cathedral with the most exquisite blue and arched stained glass windows I have ever seen. The eating clubs all have accomodations for 60 or more girls, and the meals are served by colored waitresses, which bothered my sense of civil rights no end. Most of the boys were Republicans because, of course, they came from the wealthy families.

I went to the game, which was a farce, as Princeton shellacked Brown 39-0, and to a cocktail party with some other dumb boys and to a lamb chop dinner and a dance at the club where I looked very nice, and wore high heels for the first time (I at last bought some, now that Dick is flat on

1–Sylvia Plath, 'And Summer Will Not Come Again'.

his back) and I Charlestoned in them all night, so that when I took them off I couldn't bend my feet back! I left at 9:30 in the morning Sunday and was never so glad to get rid of any boy in my life. Thereupon I navigated the shuttle and 7th avenue sub from Penn Station to Grand Central all myself . . . nothing so depressing as the New York Subway on Sunday morning, had a cheery little repast of a sandwich and coffee sitting on my suitcase in the middle of the station and got back to Smith at 5 p.m.

The whole deal cost me about $16 and I resolved never ever to go down there again. I don't know what made me do it, except that I thought that Roger might at least have something to say. But he was a complete hacker. No doubt some of the boys at Princeton are intelligent and nice, but all the ones I saw are spoiled, sheepish socialites, who get drunk all the time and don't have an original or creative impulse . . . they are all bloodless like mushrooms inside, I am sure. I did, by the way, glimpse Pete Hersey,[1] and Alan Balsbaugh[2] came up to speak to me while I was down there. He seems to be a bright boy.

I am terribly disappointed that Stevenson lost the election. I don't remember knowing who you were for, except for Pogo[3] or Krajewski.[4] But poor mother was for Eisenhower. I don't think the need for a change in party justified the horrible combination of men that will take over the Eisenhower crusade . . . just think of Taft and foreign policy, Jenner and Rules and Civil Rights, MacCarthy and Appropriations[5] . . . and all the rest of the witch-hunters and undemocratic guys. It isn't Eisenhower I'm against, but all the men in his Trojan horse. Stevenson certainly was the Abe Lincoln of our age, and I felt that it was my funeral day when I got up the morning after his defeat.

My work is overwhelming. Don't know how I have the time to goof off writing letters, but I have two papers due every week from now till thanksgiving . . . I'll have to work most of the vacation on my back work, too. Ah me, life is grim . . . If I live till Xmas it will be a miracle.

1–Peter Hersey (1934–2010); Princeton University 1956.

2–Allen Balsbaugh (1934–); Princeton University 1956.

3–A reference to a comic strip character created by Walt Kelly who, in comics published in 1952 and 1956, was a presidential candidate.

4–Henry B. Krajewski (1912–66), American politician.

5–The House Appropriation Committee, which sets expenditure by the United States government.

But I can't wait to see you. Have you thought of asking anyone to the Cotillion yet? I guess I won't be able to go unless two very vague prospects come about . . . one, that I can persuade Perry to get me a date with Dick Smythe,[1] who probably doesn't know or care I exist, or that Attilla comes back from his sojourn in Florida and decides that I am not so immature after all, just because I won't be his mistress or something the way they are in Hungary (Vere he vas kink of the Huns, remember!)

Love you dearly,
your galley slave sister,
sivvy

P.S. Mother unearthed the clipping. She sure plays the field, wot!

TO *Aurelia Schober Plath*

Tuesday 11 November 1952[2] TLS with envelope, Indiana University

Tuesday

Dearest mummy . . .

It was lovely to get your long letter. I am overjoyed to hear about Frank and his success, and I was also glad to read about Herter:[3] he sounds like a most intelligent and creative man. I would have voted Republican on the Massachusetts men, I think.

This afternoon I was amazed to come back to the house just as Aunt Mildred and Uncle Bill were walking across the lawn. We sat in the car and talked for about an hour and a half, and I could see they weren't too happy about Dick . . . found him rather uncommunicative about his emotional state although he seemed to be cheerful and creative enough about his attitude toward his stay there.

I am enclosing the check, as you directed.

I hope, by the way, that you are feeling better, able to sleep, and aren't letting finances or grampy's retiring, bother you. I really wish you would give up teaching Sunday School. You work like a fiend all week teaching, and Sunday should be a day of rest. You should pamper yourself, have a

1–Possibly Richard Andrew Smyth (1933–2009); B.A. 1955, Yale College. From Milton, Mass., Smyth appears in SP's calendar on 31 August 1952; his name appears several times in the entry for 1 September 1952.

2–Date supplied from postmark.

3–Probably a reference to Christian Archibald Herter (1895–1966), the Republican gubernatorial candidate in Massachusetts in 1952. Herter became the 59th Governor of Massachusetts (1953–7).

long late breakfast, read, listen to music, lounge a little. I also hope you are wise about the extent and lateness of your baby sitting. Do feel free to tell me any problems that are bothering you. It takes my mind off myself to think of other people.

I look so forward to coming home in two weeks. I can't believe I will live that long . . . it really is amazing that I have escaped without a cold so far this fall, and I know if I can make it to Thanksgiving without one, I will be able to rest up then and sail through till Xmas. I will be glad to drive the boys back. As I won't have any time taken up with any sort of social life, I should have enough time left over to read and write my paper, and so forth. I will probably pay a few visits . . . to Pat O'neil, the Nortons' and the Cantors (I must write them).

Don't worry about the suit. I haven't sent it off yet as I literally haven't had a minute. I'll see if I can manage this weekend.

Do be good to yourself.
xxxx
sivvy

TO *Aurelia Schober Plath*

Monday 17 November 1952[1] ALS (postcard), Indiana University

Monday am.

Dear mum . . .

The week begins again. Last night I had dinner at Mr. & Mrs. Davis' house[2] (my creative writing prof.) Another girl was there, too, and we had a nice time, although I did feel a bit awestruck in the presence of the great critic – (one of whose stories is in the latest New Yorker anthology.[3]) Saturday night I went to bed at 10:30 – (which is early for me) and got the first good night's sleep, (with the aid of a phenobarb) for weeks. Friday night I had a lovely pizza supper with Marcia & Carol, and I got a long letter from Warren about politics. Next weekend I think I will double date with Marcia & Mike and a friend of Mike's from Trinity. Charlie is a nice boy whom I met about 2 months ago, and the four of us should

1 – Date supplied from postmark.
2 – Robert Gorham Davis and his wife, the writer Hope Hale Davis (1903–2004), lived at 96 Maynard Road, Northampton, Mass.
3 – Robert Gorham Davis, 'Then We'll Set It Right', *55 Short Stories from The New Yorker* (New York: Simon and Schuster, 1949). The story first appeared in the *New Yorker*, 28 August 1943, 18–22.

have a good conversational time. This afternoon I am spending precious time going to a tea for a representative from Mademoiselle[1] for all those hundreds interested in the College Board. See you soon.

XXX
Sivvy

TO *Aurelia Schober Plath*

Wednesday 19 November 1952[2] ALS with envelope, Indiana University

Wednesday

Brace yourself and take a deep breath – not too nice:

Dear mother . . .

Thank you for the lovely newsy letter that came today . . . I was most amazed to hear from the anthology[3] – I sent a whole batch of poems off at the beginning of the year and forgot about them. I don't know if it's too impressive – since it's probably a paper-bound pamphlet of bad poetry or something. When it comes down to it, we have paid them $5 for printing it! Evidently it's just "honorary" & they probably print it on the money of the "subscribers."

God, will I be glad to get home for a few days of rest. I am sorry to have to admit it, but I am in a rather tense emotional & mental state – and have been tense and felt literally sick for about a week now . . . a physical manifestation of a very frustrated mental state. The crux of the matter is my attitude toward life – hinging on my science course. I have practically considered committing suicide to get out of it . . . it's like having my nose rubbed in my own slime. It just seems that I am running on a purposeless treadmill, behind and paralyzed in science – dreading every day of the horrible year ahead when I should be revelling in my major. I have become really frantic: small choices and events seem insurmountable obstacles, the core of life has fallen apart – I am obsessed by wanting to escape from that course. I curse myself for not having done it this summer – I try to learn the barren dry formulas – sick, I wonder why? Why? I feel actually ill when I open the book, and figure I am wasting 10 hours a week for

1–*Mademoiselle*'s College Board editor, Marybeth Little.

2–Date supplied from postmark.

3–Dennis Hartman to SP, undated (c. 19 November 1952); held by Lilly Library. Sylvia Plath, 'Crossing the Equinox', *America Sings: Anthology of College Poetry* (Los Angeles, Calif.: National Poetry Association, 1952), 14.

the rest of the year. It affects all the rest of my life; I am behind in my Chaucer unit, feeling sterile in Creative Writing. My whole life is mastered by a horrible fear of this course – of the dry absurdities – the artificial formulas & combinations. I ask myself: why didn't I take Geology – anything tangible would have been a blessing. Everyone else is abroad, or falling in love with their courses – I feel I have got to escape this, or go mad. How can I explain the irrevocable futility I feel! I don't even want to understand it, which is the worst yet. It seems to have no relation to anything in my life. It is a year course. I have wondered, desperately, if I should go to the college psychiatrist and try to tell her how I feel about it – how it is obsessing all my life, paralyzing my action in every other field. Life seems a mockery. I have the idea that if I could get out of this course: even for the second semester, I would be able to see light ahead. But I can't go on like this. I have a paper & two exams after Thanksgiving, too. And I will have to study & rest all the time I am home. Luckily I haven't gotten sinus yet – that would be another form of escapism. When one feels like leaving college and killing oneself over one course which actually nauseates one, it is a rather serious thing. Every day more and more piles up. I hate formulas, I don't give a damn about valences, artificial atoms & molecules. It is pseudo-science – all theory; nothing to grasp. I am letting it ruin my whole life. I am really afraid to talk it over with the psychiatrist (symbol of a parent, or priest confessor) because they might make me drop my activities (Press Board in particular) and spend half my time pounding formulas and petty mathematical relationships (which I have long since forgotten) into my head when I basically don't want to learn them. To be wasting all this year of my life, obsessed by this course, paralyzed by it, seems unbearable. I feel that absolved of it – with some sign of light ahead – I could again begin to live.

Oh, mother, I hate to bother you with this, but I could cry. Life is so black anyway with my two best friends, Dick and Marcia, so far removed I hardly see them – and this course: I actually am worried over my mental state! What earthly good is this going to do me in my future life? I hate it, find it hideous, loathsome. I have built it up to a devouring malicious monster. Anything but formulas, anything but. And it is only a grade I course! God, what a mess my life is. And I know I am driving myself to distraction: everything is empty, meaningless. This is not education. It is hell; and how could I ever persuade the college authorities to let me drop a year course at the half year? How could I convince the psychiatrist I would go mad if I didn't escape from these horrible formulas &, for me, dry, useless chunks of memory? My reason is leaving me. I want to get out of this. Everybody is happy, but this has obsessed me from the day I got here. I really am in a state of complete and horrible panic. I feel on the one hand that I must get out of this course; I can't reconcile the memory & rote with my philosophy of a creative education, and I am in a very embarassing position as far as the authorities of the college are concerned: I have managed to make a pretty good impression so far, but to have me go insane over what I thought was a horrible, wasteful course, would only make them expel me, or something. Every week I dread opening my science book; it is the subject of the course that annihilates my will and love of life. NOT the fact that if I studied more I could take it calmly. Of course I am behind a few chapters (I skipped them to keep abreast of the present work . . .) but I feel that if I only could drop it second semester (how I would fill the science requirement I don't know!) I could at least see the light of life again. Even now I have a unit paper due – a new week's work of science to vomit over. I am childish? Maybe, but the series of hideous adjustments thrown in my lap this year doesn't help. Science is, to me, useless drudgery for no purpose. A vague, superficial understanding of molecules & atoms isn't going to advance my understanding of life. I can't deny that to myself.

Oh! Every fiber of me rebels against the unnecessary torture I am going through. If only I wanted to understand it, but I don't! I am revolted by it, obsessed. How can I ever explain this to anyone plausibly – even the psychiatrist? I am driven inward, feeling hollow. No rest cure in the infirmary will cure the sickness in me.

I will wait till Thanksgiving before getting actively desperate. But oh, how very desolate & futile & trapped I feel!

Love, your hollow girl . . .
Sivvy

TO *Aurelia Schober Plath*

Tuesday 2 December 1952[1] ALS (postcard),[2] Indiana University

Tuesday 11 a.m.

Dear mum . . .

I am writing from the warm armchair in the Browsing room of the library where I shall be living for the next few weeks. Just finished the

1 – Date supplied from postmark.

2 – A preprinted correspondence card left over from when SP lived at Haven House. SP crossed out Haven House and wrote in 'Lawrence'.

Divine Comedy.[1] Whew! I almost wish I'd had a Catholic background, as you have, so I could understand the heavenly logical faith of it. Unlike God, I can't be happy with souls suffering in hell! Anyway, I had a nice ride back on the Bus with Charlotte Kennedy, and we discussed plans for house dance. I wrote Myron[2] this morning. You have no idea how the thought of his coming inspires me to work hard now! Even if he doesn't ever speak to me again (and how I hope he does!) There is a good psychological incentive in having such handsome bait dangled before one as reward if one is good & gets work done. Now that I look back, I am most happy about our lovely peaceful Thanksgiving. Thanks for typing my MS and for letting me loaf so scandalously. I absorbed strength to live through the next 3 weeks – with 2 long papers due and that fateful written a week from Thursday.

Love from a grateful
Sivvy

TO *Aurelia Schober Plath*

Thursday 4 December 1952[3]

TLS with envelope,
Indiana University

Darling mother . . .

Notes in the next few weeks will be brief and hectic, but I just had to write you today to tell you about the lovely avalanche of mail I had. A lovely letter from Alison, and I do hope I can stop in New York on the way back from Dick and see her for a few days. It would be saving as far as train fare is concerned, and it would be such fun. Got a long letter from Dick[4] with a story and poem enclosed. The one thing I miss about his work is feeling. I think he sent me his most carefully composed work which does not mean that he felt it strongly. I am sure that his creative writing notebook is more spontaneous, but bless the lad for trying. Hope the boys magazines are encouraging.

1–Dante Alighieri, *The Divine Comedy* (New York: Random House, 1950). SP's copy held by Lilly Library.

2–Myron Lotz (1932–99); B.S. 1954, Yale College; Henry Fellow, 1955–6, Oxford University; M.D. 1958, Yale University; intern at Massachusetts General Hospital, Boston, 1958–9; dated SP, 1952–4.

3–Date supplied from postmark.

4–Richard Norton to SP, 2 December 1952; held by Lilly Library. The story and poem are no longer with it.

Got a delicious letter from Myron. It is the Detroit Tigers he pitches for, and he will be in Alabama this summer. Gosh, I can't wait to see him. I am so excited. This is the first date I have been so thrilled about. Of course there is the grubby hour by hour schedule planned for the next three weeks, but three papers and that horrible written. But hell, I can't cry in my beer all the time. Myron sounds just unbelievable. I'm so glad I have a lot of success and luck in my field to balance his. Both of us are evidently quite ambitious, and his versatility of appreciation of life, and finding beauty in ugliness, is quite close to mine. I hope, fingers crossed, that he likes me, because I am already fond of what he symbolizes. Ah, me.

The best letter, in a way, was a rejection slip. But this one bore the blissful touch of an editors hand, in penmanship and real ink too, and it said "PLEASE TRY US AGAIN." And guess where it was from . . . . . The New Yorker! I had only sent them one poem before, and gotten an impersonal slip, so I know they don't write encouraging notes all the time. Needless to say, I am thrilled to bits, and will work on poetry this spring, I think, as I have neither the time nor the fortitude to sit and meditate over sonnets for the next half year. Perhaps by the time you are 100 years old you can say, "Yes, my baby got a poem in the New Yorker." Well, nothing like being ambitious, but I was amazed and pleased. I figure they don't ask just everybody to try them again unless they sense promise.

Love, your stupid chemical and physical daughter. I know just how you feel about French. I had begun to think I was the only idiot in the family. A hard course sure hurts ones ego. Love and kisses,

Sivvy

TO *Warren Plath*

Thursday 4 December 1952[1]

TLS (photocopy) written on Smith College letterhead, Indiana University

Thursday night
just before house meeting

Dear Warren . . .

So glad I have a few minutes to write my favorite man. There is so much to tell you. Life is certainly looking up for your old sister, even if she is practically in danger of flunking an amateur science course because she can't seem to understand beautiful euphonic words like erg, joules,

1–Date supplied from internal evidence.

valences, watts, coulombs and amperes. Anyhow, let me start from where I left you. First of all: I just love Cynthia! We had the best time riding home together, and I find her a most stimulating girl, and we have a lot in common, since we've taken a lot of the same courses in high school, except that I gather she is much better in science than I am. Which will be nice for you. Really, Warren, I think she is simply a prize, so cute and lively and fun. I hope I can read her D. H. Lawrence paper this Christmas vacation.

Dick is coming home for a few days for Christmas, at the time of the Cotillion, darn it, so I will have to give up the idea of going and stay home, the way he did for me last year when I was sick. But really, dances aren't as important as people, and I'll be glad to see him. I am leaving with him by train or plane for the sanatorium right after Christmas for a few days. I will be living with the family of a doctor who writes novels and short stories in his spare time, and meeting all sorts of tubercular New York truck drivers, so it should be lots of fun. On the way back home I may even stop on Park Avenue to visit Alison Smith for a few days. Wot a giddy life!!

The best thing happened the day after you left Thanksgiving. Did mother tell you? I went to Perry's for supper and he had two roommates home from Yale. One is engaged to be married this Christmas, and Perry said over the Phone that the other one, Myron Lotz, was first in his class at Yale (Perry is second.) I envisioned a short dark little boy with glasses. What was my amazed surprise when I walked into the Norton's living room and saw a tall, handsome guy get up and grin. Honestly, I don't think I've ever been so immediately attracted to anyone. He looks anything but the brilliant scholar. Guess what he does in the summer! He pitches for the Detroit Tigers, and last summer he earned $10,000! Isn't that amazing. Not only that, he comes from Austro-Hungarian immigrant parents[1] who work in the steel mines and can hardly speak English. And he is going through Yale in three years, starting Yale med school next fall. Did you ever hear of such a phenomenal character? Best of all, he is coming up to our Lawrence House Dance with me the weekend of December 13, so we'll really have a chance to get to know each other. Keep your fingers crossed that my beautiful intellectual charm will captivate the brilliant lug. Maybe you could help me with information about the Detroit Tigers. I don't even know what league they're in! Ah, me.

Another thing: I just got the most exciting rejection slip today! In case you aren't aware, a personal editorial comment on the printed slip

1–Michael Lotz (1900–61) and Anastasia Lotz (1904–86).

is more than encouraging. Well, guess what. Written in real ink in real penmanship at the bottom of the rejection of my poem were the magical words "PLEASE TRY US AGAIN". The magazine was none other than that august journal, the New Yorker! Isn't that tremendous! They are actually asking me to try again, and they wouldn't just do that if they didn't mean it. So for the next fifty years your sister will be trying again. Maybe you can say casually someday, "Yes, My Sister has Appeared in the New Yorker."

I was so happy today in my unit: we had a gruelling oral Chaucer test on grammar, pronunciation, and memorization, which involved going alone into the den with the great, tall, blindingly brilliant and witty Patch and reciting. I love that man with fear and trembling. He is the most imposing mind I have ever had the opportunity to work with, and the fear and pressure and hard work suddenly seemed more than worth it. He said my pronunciation of Middle English was excellent, and complimented me on my story[1] which he read in the Smith Review. I was walking on clouds, really. My ego has been so deflated by my science course that this lifted me like a helium balloon.

Well, I must needs go to bed now. Remember that I love you, baby, as Mickey Spillane[2] would say. And I do hope you let me know what you are doing and thinking about. After all, there is no one in the world but us who has shared our particular common past and childhood . . . . everything from the feast and the beast and the jelly bean to skalshalala meat, remember? And it is not every sister who has such a tall handsome brilliant brother to be proud of. Wonder what you'd think of Myron. Of course he has had women going gaga over him at baseball games, and talking about their hopechests, but I don't have to worry about scaring him away, because I'm the last one to get matrimonial avarice in my eye. Poof, for a few years yet, anyway. There is so much to do in life anyway. Anyway.

Write if you get work.
lots of xxxxxx
sivvy

P.S. Say a merry hello to Pooch and thanks for the float. He is a good guy, as we say in the underworld.

xx again

1–Sylvia Plath, 'Sunday at the Mintons'', *Smith Review*, Fall 1952, 3–9.
2–American writer Frank Morrison Spillane (1918–2006).

TO *Aurelia Schober Plath*

Tuesday 9 December 1952[1] ALS (postcard), Indiana University

Tuesday am

Dearest mum . . .

Well, the grind has started, and I write you from the beginning of the fatal week. I must tell you, tho', what a boost your letter gave me. It was like having you here to talk to me & give good advice, which I often need! I shall follow your wise precepts, o, mother! Thursday at 9 am is the fatal hour. On that depends my future! One lovely thing – I got a wonderful letter from O. H. Prouty[2] and am going to "tea" with her at 5 o'clock Sat. the 20th. Write it down on my calendar, will you! Can I have the car? I'm so excited. Also, Dick wrote to say he has plane (!) tickets for us to go up to Saranac – and that the doctor's wife has skiis I can use just my size. What luck! Yesterday was a red letter day – got 6 letters: you, Dick, Perry,[3] Prouty, a letter from Yale asking if I wanted to write for a new intercollegiate mag, and a card from Miss Drew asking me to tea (sadly I can't go!) Not bad, wot!

Off to the wars

xxx

<drawing of smiling face with caption 'bloody but unbowed'>

sivvy

TO *Aurelia Schober Plath*

Saturday 13 December 1952 ALS with envelope, Indiana University

December 13 . . .
Saturday a.m.

Dear Mother . . .

Just wanted to say a fond hello in between dashing hither and yon. My hellish day (Thursday) being over, it seems I can again begin to live. You should have seen the day I put in: up at 7 to clean the room, breakfast, 9-10, science exam (don't think I <u>failed</u>, but just pray I got a B of sorts) 10-11, watch at house, 11-12:30 – Press Board; 12:30-2, lunch waitress;

1–Date supplied from postmark.

2–Olive Higgins Prouty to SP, 6 December 1952; held by Lilly Library.

3–Richard Norton to SP, 5 December 1952; Perry Norton to SP, 7 December 1952; held by Lilly Library.

2-3, creative writing; 3-4 appointment with honors advisor; 4-6 Chaucer unit. And all this in the drenching, pouring rain. All I did was run around, and Thursday night I washed my hair, did my nails, and collapsed in bed. I don't see how I get all the things done that I do! Not only have I had my hair trimmed (just trimmed – they do it so well up here, it doesn't look shorter, just neater.) but I went[1] shopping, too, and tried on about a hundred wool dresses from $12.95 to $45, none of which I liked. So I bought, instead, the most gorgeous cashmere pullover you ever saw. It is long-sleeved, a divine, luscious shade of red, and the most sensuously soft lovely texture – for $18.95. I bought shields, too, and sewed them right in (so domestic!) I am wearing it with my pleated white wool skirt to the cocktail party this afternoon (very Christmassy color combo, wot?) and it goes beautifully with my black velvet skirt, my charcoal gray wool, my plaid skirt, and blue suit, too. So you see, I have several variable "outfits" all for the price. I am so happy with the sweater: I would rather have one beautiful thing and all the rest old & wornout, than to have a lot of mediocre things.

In Chaucer unit we had a written & oral test, and I was one of the two people (out of seven) that passed.

Myron, Perry, and Charlotte and I went to Christmas Vespers last (Friday night) – very pretty with all the singing and candlelight ceremony. Afterwards we went down to Joe's – a noisy pizza and beer (we had tomato juice) place with red-checked tablecloths and lots of atmosphere. Myron & I ate a small bacon, tomato & cheese pizza between us and talked about baseball, Spenser's philosophy of despair, and quoted poetry – on the way back to the dorm (Charlotte & Perry started back earlier) we played that he was a gangster & I was a gun moll, and that the buildings were stage scenery. Really, he wore a hat! His mother didn't want his head to get cold. – a real businessman's hat like that! <arrow pointed at a drawing of a hat> In his black "gangster" coat, he looked most sinister & mysterious – it was such fun!

Cross your fingers that today goes all right. I probably will never see him again after this, but he is such a fascinating individual – had to show me his Jr. Phi Bete key – such a mixture of vanity (how much is a cover up

1 – '~~and~~ but I went' appears in the original.

I don't know) and real sweetness. He had memorized the letter I wrote to him!

Ah, me!
Much love,
Sivvy

P.S. My photos came out bee-you-ti-ful!

TO *Aurelia Schober Plath*

Monday 15 December 1952[1]

ALS with envelope written on Smith College letterhead, Indiana University

Monday a.m.

Dear Mother:

How can I recapture the last 3 days I don't know! I only can say that they have been the most blissful theraputic respite from the academic grind that I have had this year! Nothing I imagined could equal the magnificent time I had.

Myron and Perry arrived, as I said, at 7 Friday, and we spent the evening as a foursome. Saturday, Myron called for me at 11 a.m. and said that he had the car till three. (This was a lovely thoughtful present on the part of the boy who owned it – I started my period for the first time in 3 months, and so didn't feel like biking as we had planned.) We drove and drove out into the country, and as we went north, the sunny bare landscape changed to fir trees and snow. We stopped the car on a country road overlooking the hills, and Myron showed me all the pictures he had brought, and clippings – he had some lovely action shots of him pitching, and bequeathed me a dramatic snapshot of him taken in the baseball stadium – in his uniform, profile very nice.[2] I was so pleased that he shared his baseball triumphs with me, I felt so proud of him. We sat and talked, and it began to snow, so we drove back along the precarious roads. He was so understanding: said that he was glad we could go off together, because in a group larger than two you had to spread conversation so thin that you never got to know more than your dates name. (My sentiments exactly.) On the way back we stopped at a diner and had ham and eggs for a late lunch. We changed, then, for the cocktail party, and walked over to the professors

1 – Date supplied from postmark.
2 – This photograph is on p.33 of SP's Smith College scrapbook, held by Lilly Library.

house. On the way, we decided to keep on walking for a while longer, and so walked up to the mental hospital, among the buildings, listening to the people screaming. It was a most terrifying holy experience, with the sun setting red and cold over the black hills, and the inhuman echoing howls coming from the barred windows. (I want so badly to learn about why and how people cross the borderline between sanity & insanity!) We went to the party then, and had a daiquiri apiece, which made both of us very sleepy, and me a little high for an hour. Supper at Lawrence, and then piano music by a negro friend of a girl in the house, then dancing (I wore heels, and he was just a lovely height) and a walk around campus. We were both very sleepy.

Sunday was the crowning day of my life. You'll never guess what I did! To begin, Myron called for me at 10, and we had breakfast at a diner down town. Then we went for a long walk in to the cold, sunny country, and he told me about his travels, and experiences (Oh, on the way downtown he asked to see something I wrote, and so I calmly walked into the store and picked up a copy of Seventeen. He was most enthusiastic about the poem,[1] thought it was rather brilliant . . . and told people we met henceforth with evident pride that I wrote and got things published. Now that is a healthy attitude. And I felt an honest pride in his accomplishments – no envy, or jealousy, but just a great gladness that we were both so intellectually & physically alive!)

As we went walking out in the fields, we saw some airplanes landing close by, and so hiked over to watch them landing like toy gliders at a small airport. As we approached the field, a tall, lean, blue-eyed man with a moustache came toward us. "You two have walked pretty far today," he said. We sort of gasped, and he explained that he had driven past us on his way to the airport. We chatted for a while, and he showed us his private plane which he had bought for $800. We three had lunch at a diner across the street and listened to the pilot describe his experiences. He looked at us. "I'm going up this afternoon, want to come?" I stared at Myron, who gave me an understanding, benevolent grin. "She'd sure like to, sir," he told the pilot. So we went back, and they strapped me into the two-seater little plane, and Myron took my pocketbook, and said he'd wait and to have fun.

I couldn't believe my eyes. We taxied across the field, bumping along, and it felt like being in a car. I didn't believe we would go up, but then, suddenly, the ground dropped away, and the trees and hills fell away,

1 – Sylvia Plath, 'Twelfth Night', *Seventeen* 11 (December 1952), 75.

and I was in a small glass-windowed box with a handsome mysterious pilot, winging over Northampton, Holyoke, Amherst, watching the small square, rectangular colored fields, the toy houses, and the great winding gleaming length of the Connecticut river. "I am going to do a wing-over," he said, and suddenly the river was over my head, and the mountains went reeling up into the sky, and the clouds floated below. We tilted rightside up again. Never have I felt such ecstasy! I yelled above the roar of the motor that it was better than God, religion, than anything, and he laughed & said he knew. "You fly it," he told me, and I took the stick and made the craft climb & tilt. For half an hour we were up, and when I came down, Myron met me – (it was all free,) thanked the man, and we walked back to town along the railroad tracks like a couple of hoboes, talking about flying. He was so pleased to see me happy!

We spent a drowsy afternoon at Lawrence by the fire, he studying, me reading, and we went to have a club sandwich supper at Rahar's, after which we relaxed at Lawrence, listening to Beethoven till 10:15.

Today I am probably going to the infirmary because of my insomnia, so don't worry if you get a notice. I have an appointment with the psychiatrist this afternoon about my science, and will ask her if I can go up there for a few days to rest and get rid of a slight sore throat. Also, Mary Ellen Chase called me this morning & I hope to see her sometime this week, too.

Sober news from dick this a.m.[1] He has been very sick – nausea, vomiting, diahrrea (sp?) and so on. Poor guy. Only hope he can still come home. By the way, the letter[2] was all his own idea. I didn't even know he wrote it.

Bye till Friday afternoon –
your blissful daughter,
Sivvy

1–Richard Norton to SP, 13 December 1952; held by Lilly Library.
2–Richard Norton had written a letter to William Carlos Williams, asking to write a brief biographical sketch of the doctor-poet for the *New England Journal of Medicine*.

TO *Aurelia Schober Plath*

c. 28–29 December 1952[1] Telegram, Indiana University

BREAK BREAK BREAK[2] ON THE COLD WHITE SLOPES OH KNEE ARRIVING FRAMINGHAM TUESDAY NIGHT 7:41. BRINGING FABULOUS FRACTURED FIBULA NO PAIN JUST TRICKY TO MANIPULATE WHILE CHARLESTONING. ANYTHING TO PROLONG VACATION. NORTONS WERE PLANNING TO MEET ME SO WHY NOT CALL TO CHECK. MUCH LOVE. YOUR FRACTIOUS FUGACIOUS FRANGIBLE=

SIVVY=

1–Date supplied from internal evidence.

2–SP plays on the poem 'Break Break Break' by Alfred, Lord Tennyson which begins, 'Break, break, break, / On thy cold gray stones, O Sea!'

1953

TO *Aurelia Schober Plath*

Thursday 8 January 1953[1] ALS with envelope, Indiana University

Thursday 1:30 p.m.

Dear mother –

Just to let you know that I existed through the first day – spent $1 (!) on taxi fare to and from my unit (I really never could have walked in the treacherous sifting of snow) and went to three classes. Last night after you left I hobbled to the library and spent over an hour hunting for books in the stacks and finally found one. I'm sorry I made such a fuss about being a baby and crying, but forgetting that carton broke the last straw of my nervous control: I felt so badly and scared by so many things that I hardly could manage to be gay and cheerful.

At least today was the most rushed I'll probably have for some time. I started early for my science class (luckily I had read the chapter at home) and learned to my horror that we have, absurdly enough, a written exam a week from this friday! Imagine! As if midyears weren't enough! So I'll be all the more rushed next week, which will be hectic. I have two unit papers due Thursday, and piles of reading, which I'll have to cram for all this weekend. Then, the weekend of the 17th I have to do a creative writing paper. Which will leave me, at least, four or five days to work on my Mademoiselle before starting to study the grind for science (how I dread it.)

Walking does exhaust me, although I'm taking it as more of a routine. I don't know what I'd do without my walking cast! I only hope the heel doesn't come off, now that I'm used to it.

I am going to try to spend as much time as I can studying in the libe, so that I won't begin to feel that the room here is a prison. I do feel awfully shut-in! I always took such joy in walking, as part of my symbolic freedom, and now life is a weary hobbling from the bed to the toilet to the bookshelves. My leg feels so hot and itchy all the time that I can hardly

1–Date supplied from postmark.

keep from whacking it open against a tree and scrubbing all the dead skin off.

Myron's letter was very nice, and he ended by saying he had a few free days between semesters and wondered if I did, too. I somehow think that this was more than a pointless question, and am kicking myself (a neat trick if you can do it with a cast) for having to write and say I'm temporarily crippled. What boy would ever come up to visit a lame girl! And it is rather difficult to hold a boy's interest for three months without seeing him, especially if you've only seen him once! Oh, I just hope he doesn't forget me completely.

You might try having a large snapshot made of this negative:[1] it commemorates the one really ecstatic weekend I've had this year. The picture is taken from an odd angle, so we both look double-chinned and glassy-eyed, but at least we were smiling.

I probably won't write for quite a while, but don't worry at all about me. I have an appointment tomorrow with Miss Schnieders, but I think beating reason out of this institution is pretty hard. What do they care about my education – they've got my money! – I'm pretty cynical about this whole year. But springtime – with vacation from Wed p.m. March 25 to Wed pm April 9, should be a blessed respite – I plan to work ahead on my creative writing and modern poetry unit, and Mademoiselle, so it should be peaceful, restful, social, and pleasant. And I will be Able to Walk! God, I actually can't believe I ever will again.

Well, after the next 3 weeks are over, I may decide to come home for the 3 days between semesters – but I'll probably stay here, save bus fare, and maybe work on a creative writing paper ahead. If I live that long.

Don't worry if you don't hear from me for a week or so – no news will be good news. Do hope dear grammy is better.

XXX
Sivvy

<on back of envelope>

P.S. Got my package Thursday night. Merci beaucoup!

1 – This photograph is on p. 33 of SP's Smith College scrapbook, held by Lilly Library.

TO *Aurelia Schober Plath*

Friday 9 January 1953[1] TLS, Indiana University

Friday 5 p.m.

Dearest mother . . .

I am sitting in my room, looking out at a scene of snow pouring down with ice and sleet and thinking of how sometimes people are really wonderful after all. Today I walked to my science class through great drifts of snow, and really, I don't know how I made it. I was so exhausted that I felt ready to fall down in a drift and let the snow cover me for once and for all. Life seemed so mechanically difficult that I was ready to throw in the sponge and not go to classes at all. But then I trudged around some more and saw some authorities, and was amazed at the consideration I received.

This afternoon I plodded to my English class, after which I dragged myself to see Miss Schnieders. Honestly, she was amazingly sympathetic, and called up Mr. Sherk on the spot, and I am going to talk to him tomorrow and she is going to bring up my case before the Administrative Board. I <u>think</u> that if I make an arrangement to audit (just listen) to the science class next semester, without taking exams, or doing work, or getting credit, that they will let me waive the requirement on that basis! Needless to say I won't know for a week, but I am hoping desperately. Imagine . . . I'd only have to go to four lectures a week, and get a general personal appreciation, and THAT WOULD BE ALL. Luckily I am dealing with very broad-minded intelligent people who can see my point. Cross your fingers for me. It would mean I could rejoice about something. And then I could take a Milton course, or one I really loved.

The next news is also nice. I talked to Miss Mensel today about how worried I was about taxi fares for the next month and a half, and she said, "Now let me see, we have a fund for something like that . . . I just got a check from a graduate this vacation for a good-time fund . . ." Whereupon she handed me twenty dollars to be used for taxi fare! Now at least you can think of me being driven in state to all my classes, by taxis which are paid for not out of our bare pockets! Isn't that lovely.

At this point I am so exhausted from all my stomping around and soliciting aid that I can Hardly think, but at least I feel that tomorrow (meaning next semester) may be better. Oh, if I just have to audit science I would be so happy. I am going to study like mad for the exam next week

1–Date supplied from internal evidence.

in spite of my unit papers which I have to write . . . at least now I have an incentive. I can think: this may be the last time I have to open this blasted book! And I need this good luck so desperately. I almost kissed Miss Schnieders. It's people like that that I would slave all my life for.

One thing, people accept my leg with my own attitude of mirth. I am determined to be cheerful at all times and not to complain once, no matter how tired I am, or how very much harder it is to accomplish tasks that others take forgranted. It is amazing how a state of mind can affect one's whole attitude to life. I have decided not to dread each day and wish for it to be over, but rather to savor each small delight, thinking how much better off I am than someone who is blind, or starving, or terribly lonely. This is my young life, and even a broken leg is not going to make me wish it away. Even if I am confined to a small area, I am lucky to have such a beautiful room where I can look out at the warm lighted colors of shop windows, and at trees silhouetted against the sky. My room is beautifully comfortable, my meals are all prepared for me, my few friends are faithful . . . dear Enid, and Charlotte Kennedy, and even Mary, who is being very nice. So just think how much better it is for me here than languishing in sadness at home. It's not every girl who gets free taxi service! All in all, my leg has made me realize what a fool I was to think I had insurmountable troubles. It is a sort of concrete symbol of limitations that are primarily mental, or were. And now that I see how foolish I was in succumbing to what I thought were mental obstacles, I am determined to be as cheerful and constructive about my mental difficulties as I am going to be about this physical one. Naturally I will be a bit depressed and blue at times, and tired and uncomfortable, but there is that human principle which always finds that no matter how much is taken away, something is left to build again with.

Well, this probably will be all for a while, but rest assured that I am taking taxis, and doing as well as possible . . .

much love,
your very own sivvy

<written in shorthand by ASP at bottom of letter and transcribed by Barbara F. Kozash>

But there is that human principle that no matter how much is taken away there is always something left with which to build again

TO *Myron Lotz*

Friday 9 January 1953 | ALS written on Smith College, College Hall letterhead, Indiana University

<the second leaf of the letter is preprinted for 'COMMITTEE ON RESOURCES'; SP has added by hand '(natural, artificial, etc.)'>

Friday evening

Dear Myron . . .

First let me call your attention to the fact that this is official-college-hall-news-office-letter paper; that is college hall tower in the corner; I send out news releases two hours a day in said hall; I often, in special cases, filch a sheet or two of paper for my more abstruse and recondite correspondence. (My sentences are heading toward the terse simplicity of Hemingway, wot?)

Second on the agenda: re the paper enclosed. I really hate to send it back! I would like to have it bound, and refer to it often in conversation and papers: "As Lotz stated so succinctly in his cogent essay . . ." Seriously, Myron, I have had occasion to read the essay over several times, and each time I enjoyed it more! I found the ideas challenging and stimulating, and appreciated your lucid anatomizing of the issues most greatly. I especially liked your treatment of the "physical immortality on earth" of the nightingale and the "specialization and individualism" of man" on pages 7 and 8. Also the sentence on page 12 struck me forcibly: ". . . in this amphoteric position man is constantly yearning to attain a condition of complete happiness, which the earth obviously cannot provide him, but yet constantly thwarted by the realization that the attainment of this condition in heaven (which is itself but a conjecture) involves the destruction of the physical form which would realize this pleasure." How can I explain the mental elation I felt on reading that last . . . not to mention the rest of the essay! I agreed strongly with most of the ideas you set forth, which led me to wondering if there were crucial issues (and if so, what) upon which we would radically disagree . . . it might be rather fun to find out sometime. Anyway, thanks for letting me have the privilege of reading the essay!

I don't know whether or not Perry told you, but I am at present sporting a rather fabulous fractured fibula. The fatal event took place on a mountain in Saranac Lake almost two weeks ago. Obviously I was learning how to ski. It was fine until my friend urged me to ride the tow. There was a flash of ecstasy as I stood on the top of the glass hill and saw levels of snowy mountains stretching away into grayness, and the flat, sensuously winding river far below, pale green, reflecting the greenish sky. Then the plunge. Gaily I plummeted down straight (I hadn't learned to steer yet.) There was a sudden brief eternity of actually leaving the ground, cartwheeling (to the tune of "You Belong to Me"[1] blaring from the lodge loudspeaker) and plowing face first into a drift. I got up, grinned, and started to walk away. No good. Bang.

<drawing of a fallen female skier>

Luckily I was staying with a young doctor and his family next to the tuberculosis sanatorium, so I had all kinds of expert medical treatment. The doctor (who became a writer when he had to leave medical school for a few years with t.b.) even let me read the novel he wrote about his sanatorium experiences – a passionate, James-Joycian study of introspection involving every controversial subject from sex to God to modern art. He's going to try to get it published soon, but I am sure it is too spectacularly intellectual for more than small, elite group-appeal. For one thing, his vocabulary is unbelievable. While undertaking the cure for tb he undertook also the task of learning the dictionary from cover to cover. As a result, I, (who thought I had a pretty good vocabulary!) was forced to search for multitudinous words in Webster per page. Which brings up the question of the artists purpose as far as communicating with humanity is concerned. (Dr. Lynn is fed well and has a wife,[2] which is a case in point for your theory of the leisure class . . .)

<drawing of a female in cast reading the dictionary on a chair>

At any rate, I arrived back at school a few days late, only to find your coruscating letter. Myron, I laughed so hard! Really, I can't think up adequate adjectives to describe my high opinion of your literary technique. I <u>did</u> relish your missive! Particularly I was taken by the way your Miltonic conception of heaven and hell corresponded to my own – only I am in the habit of quoting my reference from one of my favorite poems, the <u>Rubaiyat</u>:

> "I sent my soul through the Invisible,
> Some letter of that After-life to spell:
> And by and by my soul returned to me,
> And answered "<u>I myself am Heav'n and Hell</u>."[3]

1 – Sue Thompson with Dude Martin's Round-up Band, 'You Belong to Me' (1952).
2 – Dr William Sanford Lynn, Jr (1922–) and his wife Mary Elisabeth Lynn (1925–2010). Dr Lynn was Richard Norton's physician at Ray Brook.
3 – Edward FitzGerald, *Rubaiyat of Omar Khayyam*.

"Heav'n but the vision of fulfilled Desire,
And Hell the shadow of a soul on fire
Cast on the darkness into which ourselves
So late emerged from, shall so soon expire."

Rather similar, n'est-ce pa?

. . . .

So I sit in my room surrounded by innumerable books of verse, jugs of wine, and loaves of bread, gazing out to where the snow is coming down in gulps and blasts and sleetings and icings and softly piling up and always up. Picture me beating a track through waist-high wastes with my crutch, stoically trailing my plastercast left leg valiantly behind me . . . and all to get to my medieval lit unit! Only three papers to get written before midyears, on Piers Plowman[1] (the people's Christ), the Holy Grail – and a story, respectively. Next semester I begin my modern poetry unit with an authority in the field, and I can hardly wait. The prospect is most exciting, especially as W. H. Auden will be here second semester, too, for three whole months! How I'd like to get to know him!

<drawing of a female on crutches in a high wind with hands reaching through ice>

You know, this environment is most unusually stimulating – I am getting to know a few of the faculty more personally – going to tea, coffee, and even dinner (with Robert Gorham Davis, who writes often for the front page of the Times Book Review . . .) with them. I find the intellectual interchange almost awe-inspiring – and am developing rather a reverence for the lofty genius of some of the professors here. I think the best feature about honoring is the intense personal contact with keen minds. That is my first prerequisite, I think, for happiness: continued intellectual stimulation. (Of course, I will have to be fed, first – but think of the artists starving in garrets!) I do place extreme importance on mental prowess, perhaps too much so – but after all, in the evanescent ephemeral realm of worldly possessions, what lasts as long, what is as rewarding, as a rich intellectual life? The physique shrivels, stock markets crash, youth evaporates, too much wine-women-and-song coarsen the palate – and so what is most worth working for? It's everyone's own choice. Me, I'll take my Roget's Thesaurus and be wrecked on a tropical isle – provided there are enough mangoes to last a century or so! Oh, heck, I like to play tennis, too.

1 – William Langland, *Piers Plowman*.

Three blissful days rise like an oasis mid-semesters. I shall either limp around the city of Northampton quoting Auden to myself, or maybe go to Wellesley – I think I could drive the car with my cast, and it would be fun to see a play or so in Boston, but alas, my brother, who chauffeured me so nobly during the last half of vacation, is at Exeter, so my radius of travel may be curtailed. Anyhow, no matter what turns up, I plan to relax. If all goes well, my cast should be off by the middle of February (Thank Jove!) and I am planning to have a Bacchanalian festival when I again can walk normally, involving a bonfire burning my crutches, and champagne will be served under the trees in the most original punch bowl yet: it will be long, white, and shaped like Sylvia's left leg. After which I will sell the fragments as either modern intrasubjective sculpture or relics of the Parthenon.

Farewell for a while,
frangibly,
sylvia

TO *Aurelia Schober Plath*

Friday 16 January 1953[1] TLS with envelope, Indiana University

January 16 . . .

Dearest of mothers . . .

At last the hideous week is over, and now I shall have some delightful respite before starting to study again the stultifying science. The exam this morning was on all the work I'd missed before vacation on electricity, so I hope I got a B, at least. I should do better, though, in the midyear, as I plan to study five days before the exam. I haven't heard from the Administration Board about my petition yet, but Miss Schnieders and Mr. Sherk have both approved a plan whereby I will audit the course without credit for the rest of the year, taking no exams and doing no work. In other words, I will just sit and enjoy the lectures and never open the damn book again after the midyear exam. This means that I will probably take a course in Milton in addition to my Modern Poetry and creative writing. Sounds divine, what? I'M pretty sure the petition will go through, since the class dean and my professor are both on my side, and the relief of not studying science any more is so wonderful I hardly can believe it. It will be a lucky thing, too, for I feel, with these two exams coming so close, that

1–Date supplied from postmark.

I have reached the end of my endurance of these mere theoretical atoms and molecules.

This week I have worked harder than ever before. The bad weather last weekend confined me to my room, and I had some girls get books out of the library. Saturday I read from morning to night, and Sunday I wrote a 10 page research paper on Piers Plowman for my unit. Monday I read furiously again all day, and Tuesday I wrote another 10 page paper on the search for the Holy Grail, both very difficult topics. Wednesday I typed the paper, went to class. Thursday I studied for my science written and had my last unit where I read the Piers Plowman paper aloud and got Patch to autograph my book of his.

My Herculean efforts on the Piers Plowman paper were more than repaid when Mr. Patch said: "That was a brilliant paper." From him, that is better than orchids. I was so pleased. I had gotten really fascinated by my subject and done alot of research in the Rare Book room,[1] and compared Piers, a complex allegorical character, to Chaucer's Plowman, Thomas Carlyle's Peasant Saint, and Gerard Manley Hopkins' Harry Plowman. That, in retrospect, is what I enjoy most about honors: instead of doing just the proscribed reading, as in a course, for every paper you can pick your favorite topic and plunge into research. Most stimulating.

I really don't consider my room a prison at all, even though I've been forced to stay in it pretty much because of the weather. The taxis take me to all my classes, and really, going to the library and climbing all the stairs is so tiring that it's a relief to stay all snug here. Fortunately Mary is at lab all day every day, and so it is as if she were just sleeping and eating here and this were really my own room. It is a fortunate thing, because I honestly can't communicate with her . . . she has no grounds for common interest or experience in either dating (that is worst) religion or study. And she is so pitifully inarticulate. To hear her try to express an idea outside the scientific field is the most frustrating thing. It is as if she had a block in her throat and the words kept tripping over it and falling back and starting over. But I am as nice as I can be, because I do need her help getting food or books often, and I want the rest of the year to be as pleasant as possible. I love our room, and will enjoy the springtime here when I can walk and play tennis and bike. Honestly, I am more good-natured and happy now than I was this fall. Perhaps it is that I feel I'm not missing anything (except Myron) because the weather is so bad. If I had to

1–At the time Plath wrote this letter, the Rare Book Room was located on the first floor mezzanine (now the second level) of Neilson Library in what was called the 'new' library wing.

sit and watch people making merry at spring proms and tennis it would be another story. I should love spring even more this year than ever, because of my ability to walk again.

Oh, yes, Tuesday afternoon I had the best time. Mary Ellen Chase is going to Southern France this week for a few months, and so she had about five girls over for coffee.[1] It was really most theraputic for me to go . . . by taxi, and I enjoyed myself most royally sitting in her diningroom over looking the snowy woods and paradise pond and drinking cup after cups of savory coffee and eating savory homemade gingersnaps, and chatting with the other girls . . . all very interesting, and, of course, listening to the tales of Miss Chase. She is the dearest woman, and I felt so pleased that she asked me over again.

One discovery I made that has made my life much more pleasurable . . . I can take a bath (of sorts). By lowering myself sideways in the tub, my legs hanging out, I can sit and take a perfectly respectable bath, slightly awkward, but blissful. I've had my period all this week, so that added to my weary state. But really, when I study, I don't feel my leg at all.

This weekend I will write my last creative writing paper for the semester, and this week will be spent working on my Mademoiselle assignment.

I am planning to have my leg X-rayed the weekend of February 8 (how I am counting the days!) and will send the X-ray immediately to you. Please airmail it or something to Dr. what's his name, perhaps the Nortons could drive you to his home in Wellesley, get his verdict immediately, and also instructions as to post mortem care and exercises, and telephone me right away. You can imagine that I want to get this thing off as soon as possible and start learning to walk again.

Rest assured that I am doing my exercises most faithfully . . . I have lots of time, now, and I discovered that I can do a bicycle exercise in addition which should keep my rear from getting too flabby from sitting all day.

Much love
. . . sivvy

<on back of envelope>

P.S. Please send a couple of those face photos as soon as you get them so I can answer Seventeen, also the school address and name of the girl who illustrated my story[2] . . . . thanx.

s.

1–Mary Ellen Chase lived at 16 Paradise Road, Northampton.

2–Sylvia Plath, 'Initiation', *Seventeen* 12 (January 1953), 64–5, 92–4; illustrated by Marjory Carolyn Clark.

TO *Aurelia Schober Plath*

Sunday 18 January 1953[1] TLS with envelope, Indiana University

Sunday night . . .

Dearest mother . . .

Well, the world has a miraculous and wonderful way of working. You plunge to the bottom, the way I did this fall, and you think that every straw must be the last. Everything is black. Then you break your leg, decide to be gay and merry, and the world falls like a delicious apple in your lap. I am so happy, so ecstatic now that I can hardly sit still. As a matter of fact, I have been waltzing around the house pouring over my joys at people. I love everybody at this point. I am even happy I broke my leg. You know, I have gotten so used to my leg that I never think about it anymore. Of course, the hard part will be when the cast is off and I have to be careful of it. Now I can just sling it around in careless abandon.

Well, first of all, my petition for auditing science without credit went through (provided, of course, that I get a respectable mark on the midsemester exam, which of course I will if I study five days for it.) This means that three hours a week will be spent auditing lectures (to waive the requirement, you see, I have to know about the whole course.) So I will never have to even open a book again, after midyears. And in class I can let my mind wander and think about spring or W. H. Auden, or something whenever I feel like it. As you may imagine, during my agonies of this fall, I felt that I could see no light ahead for the rest of the year. Now I will be taking a course in Milton instead of the hated science, and concentrating heart and soul on modern poetry and creative writing. Isn't it wonderful? I feel so virtuous, having worked like such a dog for the exams. I will be getting credit for the first semester, too so I hope I can pull an A in the course. Wouldnt It be amusing if that were the only A I got this semester? Next semester, however, I am going to be a real intellectual and get all A's. I am determined. So my academic life looks most fruitful.

And now that this last week's tension has lifted, I feel most free. I wrote a 15 page creative writing paper[2] (this semester's last) yesterday and today, and all I have to do is type it now. It isn't even a story, just a philosophical dialogue about heaven and hell and god. Funny, I started down to write a packed description, and this started pouring out after I got through the

1–Date supplied from postmark.
2–Sylvia Plath, 'Dialogue'; held by Lilly Library.

first paragraph. I guess I needed a philosophical catharsis. At any rate, I just have to type it now, and no more papers for two weeks. I never had worked so hard as I have this last week, writing three papers, and studying for my written. Never again will anything be this crowded. So all this week all I have to do is my Mlle assignments, and catch up on letters and sleep. I feel so relaxed, now. Also enjoy my baths immensely.

And I am taking your advice and getting a little fun in the outside world. Tomorrow night I am going over to Marcia's to dinner, and seeing the Dublin Players in "The Importance of being Earnest."[1] It should be ideal froth, and I do love the play. And if we can get tickets, a friend (male) of a girl in the house will drive us to Springfield Tuesday or Wednesday to see "Bell, Book, and Candle."[2] I do hope we get to go to that. I am so hungry for plays, and I feel it is good for me to take my mind off my limitations and have a little fun. I've been working hard enough to justify it.

I have an inspiration about your coming up. My science exam is on Thursday morning, January 29th. Couldn't you come up Thursday morning, or Wednesday (if the trip both ways is too much in one day) and see Miss Mensel, and then both of us take the 5 p.m. bus back to Wellesley Thursday? Then I wouldn't have to worry about getting my suitcase on and off, and we could have a lovely talk. I know it's late for the application, but you could finish making it out here, and leave it with her, so it still would be in before February. Then I could stay home till Sunday. How does that sound?

A most peculiar occurrence happened today. I was sitting in my bathrobe at about 10 a.m. talking to some of the girls about their dates last night . . . sunday mornings are lovely and casual . . . and my favorite senior, Marcelle,[3] came running upstairs and said breathlessly "Sylvia, there's a man on the downstairs phone for you." The word "man" at this point in my life was so rare that I actually threw down my crutches and stumped in my pajamas down to the first floor (we're not supposed to be down there unless fully dressed) in no time at all. A calm, silky voice said: "Hello, how's the invalid? This is Myron. I'm in Northampton." Controlling myself, I managed not to shriek and said something absurd, like, Oh, how nice. I remembered in a flash how Dick had called me

1–Performed at the Academy of Music, Northampton.

2–A 1950 play by English playwright and theatre director John Van Druten (1901–57). Performed at the Court Square Theatre, Springfield, Mass., from 19–21 January 1953.

3–Marcelle Thiébaux (1931–); B.A. 1953, English, Smith College; M.A. 1955, University of Connecticut; Ph.D. 1962, Columbia University; professor of English, St John's University, 1970–82; housemate of SP at Lawrence House.

when he came up to Smith with Jane Anderson, and felt rather sick. Sure enough, he explained how he had met this girl New Years, and had made the date to come up. Then he said that he got my letter saying I was back at Smith (Perry had told him I'd be home for a few weeks) and wondered if he could drop over to say hello Sunday night (tonight) as his date was singing in vespers, and he had a few hours before he had to go. Well, I was so excited to hear from him in the first place, and the sudden prospect of seeing him immediately obliterated all my sad wistful feelings that he had been up here for a weekend with another girl. So he said he'd be by around six. At four thirty I was in my bathrobe typing my paper, when a girl yelled: Sylvia, a man to see you. So he had come early. Well, I was really so excited I could hardly calm down enough to get dressed in my aqua sweater and black velvet skirt, remembering your lovely peptalky letter about French women on divans, I resolved to be the same. We sat in the livingroom and talked till supper, and he stayed through supper, eating in the dining hall. Then the boy who was driving him home called, and said he'd be over in five minutes. Well, I'd had two hours talking with him, so we sat on a wooden chest in the hall and Myron said: "When will your cast be off?" "Oh, around the middle of February," I said casually, thinking: god, if only he'd say something about seeing me again. Any grubby little weekend will do. "Would you be able to dance, say about March 6th?" I thought my ears were playing tricks on me. "Iguess so. Why?" I said still cool. "For YALE JUNIOR PROM?" (my caps). "Well . . . It depends on with whom I'd be dancing." "How about me?" "Well, yes, I'd like to very much . . ." hesitatingly. "But you can't," he said rather quickly. "But I will." I said. So that is that. I AM GOING TO THE YALE JUNIOR PROM WITH THE MOST WONDERFUL BOY IN THE WHOLE COLLEGE. I can hardly believe it's real. He said he was going to try to get theater tickets, and that we would take a bus out to the ocean, and that he would be "proud to have me." Honestly, now I can live in an ecstasy of anticipation for the next month and a half. I have been wondering about getting a new formal. First I will try on the two I have here . . . I think my black would be most glamorous, if I did decide to wear one of them. But I want to look absolutely gorgeous. After all, I'll have to compete with Shirley![1] (Myron says Perry is really in love with her and asked me: Is she really as beautiful as he claims she is? We both think he'll marry her. And Charlotte came over the other night, telling me how

1 – Shirley Baldwin Norton (1931–95); married to SP's friend Perry Norton on 19 June 1954 (divorced 1978); mother of John Christopher, Steven Arthur, Heidi, and David Allan.

sweet a letter Perry had written to her after vacation. I was shocked, and felt so sorry for her. Honestly, sometimes I feel downright omniscient!)

Well, this is my three week's anniversary, and I have proved that a broken leg need not handicap a resourceful woman. Thanks so much for your encouraging letter. It was just what I needed. Oh, mummy, I am so happy. If a hideous snowy winter, with midyears and a broken leg is heaven, what will the green young spring be like? How can I bear the joy of it all!

much overflowing love,
your own
sivvy

TO *Richard Norton*

before 21 January 1953 TLS,[1] Indiana University

Dear d.

Make what you can out of this rather unsightly mess. It's the first draft, and came pouring out straight into the typewriter without stopping, and since I have revised it a little. But it's the raw material of a lot of other discussions, too. Do tell me what you think of it.

The other paper is my religion essay last year.

love,
s.

1–Found between two papers written for Religion 14, which SP completed during the 1951–2 academic year. The papers are ['Religious Beliefs'], undated, with caption 'First paper: before course' and 'Religion As I See It', 3 May 1952, with caption 'Second paper: after course'. Norton refers to SP's religion papers in 'Individualism and Sylvia Plath: An Analysis and Synthesis' included with Richard Norton to SP, 21 January 1953; held by Lilly Library. Norton quotes from 'Religion as I See It', pp. 3–4.

TO *Aurelia Schober Plath*

Wednesday 21 January 1953[1]

ALS written on verso of flyer for *The Importance of Being Earnest*, Indiana University

Wednesday

Dear mum:

Here is the story: not as good as it looked when I first wrote it, but I'll give it a try.[2] After you type it, please send it right off in a brown envelope to:

Miss Margarita G. Smith, Fiction Ed.
Mademoiselle
575 Madison Ave,
New York 22, N.Y.

and put my Smith address on a stamped brown envelope which you'll enclose, so I'll be sure to get it back. This last is important. I never send letters.

"The Importance of Being Earnest" was badly played, but "Bell, Book & Candle" with Zachary Scott & Joan Bennett in Springfield last night was a heavenly humorous tale of modern witchery, Just loved it! As a result of 3 midnight bedtimes in a row I'm a bit weary.

Tax deductions:
Service Fund $10 (includes all charitable organizations)
tb seals $1
Thanks for cookies, check.

love,
syl.

1–Date supplied from internal evidence.

2–Sylvia Plath, 'Mary Ventura and the Ninth Kingdom'. *Mademoiselle* rejected the story on 11 March 1953.

TO *Aurelia Schober Plath*

Thursday 22 January 1953[1] ALS (postcard),[2] Indiana University

Thursday

Dear mum . . .

A lovely sunny melting snow-day, and I have an Honor Board meeting (first this year) this afternoon. I also hope to get half of my college board assignment written (on "health hazards") for which I interviewed Dr. Booth this morning. I only got a 90% on my last science exam which brings my average to a mere 95%. I really will study for the Exam though: I've been leading a luxurious life of reading modern poetry, the New Yorker, the papers, and Franz Kafka. Most surprising is a rather unexpected change of plans as of this morning's mail! Seems I'll be staying here midsemesters. One tall, dark and rather magnetic male is coming up to investigate communism at Smith Sat. night & Sunday, and I plan to be on hand to uphold the aristocracy of the intellect! Honestly, if that guy isn't careful, I'll start being rather fond of him. Really, I'm thrilled. It will be an immediate & tangible reward for slaving on science. (Last time I got a 99% before he came) I've decided as soon as I can walk I'll get a new wool dress for Jr. Prom Weekend – he deserves it. Oh, I am happy.

XX
Sivvy

TO *Aurelia Schober Plath*

Sunday 25 January 1953[3] ALS (postcard), Indiana University

Sunday 3:30 pm

Dear mum . . .

Your appointment with Miss Mensel is at 2:30 p.m. – so I'll have time to show you the way – can't wait to see you! Could you please bring lots of manila envelopes (big) & lots of both good & bad typing paper. I'm all out. Still love everybody with a passion – am reading New Yorkers, etc. Told Marcia you'd love to have her visit in my place over Friday night – didn't think you'd mind, since they've been so great to me and she's such fun anyway! Have got both Mlle things done: cartoons & health article.

1 – Date supplied from postmark.
2 – A preprinted correspondence card left over from when SP lived at Haven House. SP crossed out Haven House and wrote in 'Lawrence'.
3 – Date supplied from postmark.

Aren't I virtuous. Love Lawrence more every day – girls are all great – so happy here! Mary & I are getting along just fine, and I'm sure it will keep up. I really wasn't trying before! Can't believe I'll be seeing that Man in less than a week – one girl has loaned me her great navy-blue knitted dress to wear for when He comes – nice, huh! Things are really looking up. (Still exercising like mad)

XXX
Sivvy

TO *Aurelia Schober Plath*

Monday 2 February 1953[1] TLS with envelope, Indiana University

monday morning

dearest mother . . .

well, the event has come and gone, and I feel amazingly eager to plunge into the next five weeks of work so that when I take the pilgrimage to Yale in March I'll be rested, caught up and human. It is amazing how easy it is to direct oneself to slave at the task at hand if there is some definite plan for respite ahead, and not just a series of vague unsubstantial daydreams.

Tonight my modern poetry unit meets for the first time at Miss Drew's, and I am having supper with Enid Epstein, writer-artist-and friend, beforehand. Tomorrow it will be Wiggin's with Mr. and Mrs. Patch and the other six girls in the unit. I might even splurge and have a good dinner. Last Friday I had a lovely time at Marty's with she and Mrs. B. Great lovely steak dinner, modern music, and reading and talking. How good those people are to me. I can never repay them for all they have done. Saturday Myron came after lunch, and we sat and talked until supper, when we took a taxi to Rahars where we had a light snack and sat and drank gallons of gingerale in the bar and sang the words to a hundred popular songs (funny but he's the first person I've found who knows all the words to all the songs the way I do . . . we must just have absorbed them over the years). Sunday he came here for dinner, and we sat and read the times and listened to music all afternoon, and he stayed for supper. After supper we went across the street and sat in the coffee shop[2] for two hours, and he left off some of his reticence to talk about his family, and

1 – Date supplied from postmark.
2 – The Coffee Shop, a restaurant at 56 Green Street, Northampton, Mass.

told me more than he realized about them, for which I was very glad. Also he explained the elements of organic chemistry to me, very simply. He is reverent and ecstatic about the wonders of the universe, which is nice. Do you realize that he was Elks winner in his state, and one of the 10 national ones? His story of how he got to Yale, and about his childhood is really almost unbelievable, when you look at him now. Except for traveling with the team, he has lead a most austere life. No dates in highschool, and only two in his freshman year in college. Worked all the time, studying or jobs . . . has worked in road crews, stores, and I don't know what all else. His dislike of his older brother,[1] who drinks, smokes, and has no self-discipline, is most interesting. All in all, I was quite pleased that he did talk about himself and his family a little. The last time I casually asked him about his home life he shut up like a wounded clam. Seems he has lived in a neighborhood with negroes, immigrants, and all kinds of people. That's why, he says, he talks with such a drawl. I wish terribly that I could be good for him. I do enjoy telling him how much I admire his brawn and brain. His first pride is his scholastic ability, and his second is his baseball achievement. For these he has received rewards, honor, and admiration, and, as he says, that is why he had decided his life must be a continued stimulating intellectual one, because of the early reward-conditioning. But he seems so practical and reasonable about what he wants. He knows what he wants, and that he can have it, and so he goes on and does it. As far as I can see, women are rather unnecessary in his life. Anyway, we had a very happy restful time, and I spent 12 hours with him saturday and the same amount sunday, just sitting and talking, which is rather a feat for most people. Also received a very neat white baseball, subsequently autographed. And he can carry me very easily, so I made the most of it, and traveled comfortably from taxi to doorstep and across streets without touching a foot to the ground. It was most enjoyable, I assure you. That boy's muscles are like iron. Anyone who can lift me-plus-my-cast is, as far as I'm concerned, a minor hercules.

The only thing I'm at all discouraged about is my writing. I know inside me that Mlle will send the story back, but send it anyway. I deserve a couple of hundred rejections, now. It'll only make me work all the madder and harder.

Dick got his WCW thing[2] accepted, and I am so happy. It came at such a strategic time, just after he'd heard that he couldn't plan on going back

1–Theodore Lotz (1928–86).

2–Richard Norton, 'Doctors Afield: William Carlos Williams', *New England Journal of Medicine* 248 (2 April 1953), 604–5. See also Richard Norton to William Carlos Williams, 11 December 1952, and Norton to SP, 8 January 1953; held by Lilly Library.

to med school next fall but would have to stay at least until december. Now he has the thrill of publication, a tangible reward for his efforts, and renewed incentive to go on. Really, I am overjoyed that it worked out this way.

He suggested that I come up to the Middlebury Carnival the 20th and see him. For some reason I hedged, and haven't said any verdict. I don't know, I suppose it's terrible, but I just don't give a damn about going. Shirley and Perry and the Baldwins and the Nortons will be running around, and the trip would take a big chunk out of my study time. I just don't care about being a hanger-on, either. So I shall wait and think it over carefully. But my leg will still be tender then, and I don't want to go trotting around up there in the frigid north. Fortunately Myron hates the cold up here and likes lying out in the sun tanning. He is so beautifully relaxed, like Bob, only he is also motivated by the success-drive, wich is a nice workable combination. Well, after the leg gets normal, I'm treating myself to a formal downtown. After his standing me clomping around in rahars like this, I've got to make up for it by being feminine and lovely when I go down so he will be proud of me. Both of us have been so damn lucky in life, my writing being comparable in a small way to his baseball, that we get along very well. Again, I hark back to memories of work on the farm with infinite gratitude. I never want to forget the closeness to good hard labor.

This summer you will also have to teach me how to cook and to <u>buy</u>. Myron loves breaded pork chops and roast beef, and says abstractly that he will live in a shack if he has to, so he can have good meat and food. One could really cook creatively if one had the money, I guess. I might as well learn to do it naturally, so I won't have to waste time on it. Ah me. I may never see him again after this spring, who knows . . .

xxx
sivvy

TO *Aurelia Schober Plath*

Wednesday 4 February 1953 — TLS with envelope, Indiana University

wednesday, feb. 4

dear mother . . .

I was grateful more than I can say for your understanding letter about the middlebury trip. Luckily I had not written to either dear nortons (their letter almost made me weep) or dick, so I am here reprinting the crucial part of the reply I wrote to nortons so your story and mine will jibe:

"Oh, how enticing your trip plans sound to middlebury. I would give anything (another broken leg even!) to go with you up there to see dick but smith, unfortunately, is not as generous in meting out holidays as B.U. saturday involves two performances of our class Rally Day drama, and monday has a required morning commencement exercise at which every (that, I'm afraid, includes me) Smith girl is ordered to attend. So I am inextricably and rebelliously entangled! I'd love so much to spend the weekend with you all, but this, of all weekends in the year, is decreed to be "Smith College" by our President Wright (who in this case, I think, is more appropriately called Wrong.)"

I hope that does it neatly enough. The facts are true, but the sentiments, of course, aren't. I am becoming an expert in the polite expedient white lie. Ugh. Somehow, I just shudder at the idea of trekking up there. Losing valuable study time, and vegetating and watching Shirley swish around. I'll have a chance to match her in March. Besides, I don't want to run any risk of slipping on my precious ankle. By the way, a most fantastic thing: Charlotte Kennedy called last night . . . and she broke the fibula of her right leg over Midsemester weekend! Same time sunday as I did! At least I have the prospect of getting mine off in two weeks. God, I can't wait.

Classes this week leave me tireder than I thought. Glad I have March to look forward to, and the prospects of a new dress. I'll be so glad to get back on press board again, and seeing people . . . I really do feel a bit cut off, and every trip is a job. But I'M exercising and keeping outwardly cheerful. Don't envy Charlotte in the least.

This semester should be a scholastic joy. I'm starting Milton this afternoon at 3, and auditing three hours of Miss Drew while she does James Joyce[1] . . . I'm reading "Portrait of the Artist" and "Ulysses" along with the regular class . . . a rather ambitious project, but I am enjoying it no end, since I won't be getting Ulysses in the unit. Two papers to do this weekend . . . writing and an analysis of one of Yeats' poems. Haven't heard about science yet, though.

Dinner at Wiggins' with Patch last night and the other six girls in the unit. I was most flattered; he paid almost sole conversational attention to me, and said he and mary ellen chase thought my Minton story was most excellent. How I love them both . . . so brilliant, and he has such a rich wealth of knowledge and humor. Said he thought all smith girls he knew

1–English 44b, Twentieth Century British Literature. Joyce, Yeats, Eliot.

were beautiful, compared to the other women's colleges he'd taught in. Nice, what!

Much love to you,
sivvy

TO *Aurelia Schober Plath*

Thursday 5 February 1953[1] ALS with envelope, Indiana University

thursday
10:30 a.m.

Dear Mother . . .

Just a note from science lecture to tell you about a rather amusing incident that occurred last night. I'd had a rather full day: audited Drew on Joyce at 10 a.m., gone to R. G. Davis at 2, and Milton at 3. Chatted with Carol Pierson for a while about Ken – seems they're getting along admirably: I have great hopes for them – it would be so much fun to think Dick & I were responsible for a happy marriage . . . someone else's! Well, last night, instead of being lazy & getting ready for bed after supper I went to an excellent lecture on "Protestantism in an Age of Uncertainty" by Theodore Greene,[2] an expert on Kant, Philosophy & Religion – also, by the way, the master of Silliman College at Yale – (Myron's College!) I figured that since I am maybe staying at the master's house during Prom Weekend it would be strategic for me to be able to discuss my attending the speech, etc.! I really admire the man tremendously!

Well, anyway, I came back to the house, and one of the girls came up to me with a most peculiar expression on her face: "There's a boy in the livingroom to see you," she said. "He's been waiting for two hours. Say's he's never seen you before but was told to look you up!" Completely nonplussed, I dashed up the back stairs (you'd hardly know I was a cripple!) – changed to my red sweater & skirt and came down to the livingroom aflame with curiosity. I walked in, and the most handsome, tall, lean, curly brown-haired boy got up and said "Hello, Sylvia!" I gulped "Hello," and sat down in a daze. What did this god want with me?!

1–Date supplied from postmark.

2–Theodore Meyer Greene (1897–69); Master of Silliman College, Yale University (1947–53).

Seems that he (Gordon)[1] is the son of that woman at the Smith Club last fall[2] who came rushing up to talk to me after my speech (just think – if I'd refused to speak, this never would have happened! Late rewards!). He is a senior in English honors at Amherst, eager, intense, working his way through, too! I only talked to him for 15 minutes, but it was long enough for me to feel an instinctive "rapport" – and we were talking heatedly about Chatham and both of us being non-smokers in units, and creative writing, when it was time to close the house. I felt rather dazed, especially when he asked me to go out with him this Saturday! "My leg . . . ." I began to explain. "Heck, we can sit around and talk . . ." he grinned. "I'll be over after lunch!" And he went. The girls in the livingroom all crowded around me exclaiming "Who was he!" I just stood there leaning meditatively on my crutch and musing on the peculiar workings of chance, dropping lovely English-majoring Amherst seniors from the sky at exactly the right psychological moment! Honestly – imagine him taking me out all afternoon and night! That is surely "above and beyond the call of duty!" I was feeling a bit sad at not having heard from Myron yet this week – because I felt his letter should be indicative of the sort of time he had. And I was musing upon whether or not I should ask him up for the Rally Day show on the 21st. Now I've decided not to even suggest seeing him again before the prom unless he mentions it first, which I don't think he will. He's smart enough to see I enjoy being with him and I don't want him to feel chased. I do feel much safer with my interests spread out over a broader surface, now, and I was hoping that Attila or somebody would ask me out to relieve the single-minded intensity of my interest in Myron. So now when I go down to Yale I won't feel (I hope) that it's the first and last social event of the season!

Gordon looks most promising: and even if he does turn out to be engaged to somebody, I shall make the most of this Saturday! It will be such fun talking to a boy who has so much in common in the way of interests – English, travel, etc. He worked in Chatham for four summers,

1–Gordon Ames Lameyer (1930–91); B.A. 1953, Amherst College; dated SP 1953–5; travelled with SP in Europe, April 1956. Gordon Lameyer was encouraged to date SP by his mother Helen Ames Lameyer (1894–1980); B.A. 1918, Smith College. Lameyer's father, Paul Lameyer (1885–1960), was an artist; during World War II he was interned at a camp for German-born US citizens by the FBI.

2–SP spoke at the Smith College Club of Wellesley on 19 September 1952. She was to 'describe some phase of college life including some of their extra-curricular activities'. From 'Smith College Club Tea For Freshman And Undergraduates', *The Townsman*, 18 September 1952, 16.

went to Cuba as tutor to an 8-year old boy, graduated from Choate[1] – and in general, I'm looking more than forward to getting to know him (and his friends –)

So wish me luck this Saturday, huh?
Much love,
Sivvy

P.S. Got a cute letter from Warren – seems he's doing well in broad jump!

TO *Aurelia Schober Plath*

Friday 6 February 1953[2] TLS with envelope, Indiana University

friday night

dearest of favorite people . . . .

a brief note to say that the X-ray was duly taken today and should be on the way to the great doctor tomorrow. if you feel like it, you could ask him to <u>call</u> up the doctor's office here as soon as he reaches his verdict. there is a good bone man in town who should be able to take off the cast. i am, needless to say, getting more anxious to get over the learning-to-walk period as soon as possible. my bicycle excercises (200 per day) should have kept my muscles in tone a bit. walking is still a slow ordeal, and rather wearing, especially as the end of the week is so heavy. got your memo today, and think that my solution was really valid, especially as I don't know whether or not I'll want to ask anyone for rally day.

one, thing, I have decided that my hibernation from college this past half year as far as other girls go has resulted in my fading from the view of the class, so I'm accepting supper invitations to other houses with gusto now. also am one of the finalists of this year's electoral board, which draws up the slate for the big four college offices[3] . . . from our class this year. as I certainly don't want one of the big offices (next year I'll be doing the thesis), I will enjoy getting to know girls in the class better . . . if I do get elected to be on the board finally. one thing, I somehow seem to be popular still, for some obscure reason. I was amazed to be on the final slate.

1 – Choate Rosemary Hall, a private college-preparatory school in Wallingford, Connecticut.
2 – Date supplied from postmark.
3 – These are: (1) Head of Student Council; (2) Judicial Board; (3) Honor Board; and (4) House of Representatives.

letters today were heavy . . . you, dick,[1] hong kong, and best of all, a huge epistle from myron. it was five close-written pages long, which for him, like warren, is a herculean task and no doubt took hours. he wrote a most brilliant outline of his ideas of God, and the change from naive simplicity to scientific complexity in beliefs about God and the universe. I agree with him vehemently, and had to sit down right away to answer him, because I was so stimulated by his ideas. I think we are unusually alike in our approaches to like and thinking. one thing that amused me . . . he seemed apologetic for being rather quiet as far as intellectual topics this weekend went. I was wondering what the matter was, and he revealed it when he concluded his letter with the rather disconcerting remark: "Do you understand that I can think much more clearly while away from your biological magnetism." naturally I could hardly help but smile, as I only had let him kiss me a couple of times, and his way of stating the matter was so in keeping with his desire to be rational in explaining everything including emotions. but I did suggest that we take long walks next time, and talk . . . . so much healthier than sitting around and languishing for 24 hours. hope that takes care of it. I am rather fond of him, from what I know of him, and especially appreciate his honesty . . . I can believe what he says, and it was so touching to hear him say he would like to see moonlight on my hair. When he is idealistic, he is so very idealistic.

Well, tomorrow I try the town of amherst again with the new Gordon, whom I still can't believe is coming: all the girls want to be around to see this handsome creature when he comes! I just know it will be fun.

by for now,
much love,
sivvy

TO *Myron Lotz*

Saturday 7 February 1953[2] AL (excerpt),[3] Indiana University

I think walking might help, don't you. I think better that way myself – hate sitting cramped up in manmade boxes – so stultifying!

1–Probably Richard Norton to SP, *c.* 3 February 1953; held by Lilly Library.
2–Date supplied by Lotz.
3–Myron Lotz quoted SP's letter, now lost, in his 9 February 1953 postcard to SP; see SP's Smith College scrapbook, p. 34; held by Lilly Library.

TO *Aurelia Schober Plath*

Tuesday 10 February 1953 TLS with envelope, Indiana University

tuesday, february 10

dearest maternal image . . .

got your postcard today . . . hope the late tues. classes won't overtax your health with the already demanding french lessons. so proud about warren. if only he can play his athletic jumping to the full I feel college will welcome him with open arms. I can't stress enough how important a balance of athletics is (important) in the eyes of the authorities . . . in this distressingly wellrounded american age. glad I wrote him encouragement. he should keep jumping for the next four years.

last night . . . supper at haven house with the frail pale charlotte who has had a cold for the last week in addition to her leg. poor kid. I'm so much luckier than she to be so husky, really. after that: drew unit, where I read a short paper on yeats . . . we had coffee and cookies . . . a nice ceremony to break the two hour period with informal conversation.

gordon is utterly lush. just got unpinned from a smith senior honors last week, so I'm the first girl on his new round of dating again, I guess. rained all saturday. we took a taxi down town to wait for the bus to amherst . . . talked intensely over icecream about religion. He got me holding forth on my independent unitarianism until I stopped suddenly and asked: where do you stand? I'm a catholic, He said. I slumped in my seat with a huge blush. whereupon he quoted the unitarian creed with astonishing rapidity and said with a laugh: I'm just what you are: a renegade unitarian. you can say anything to me. so I did. whew!

spent afternoon in his room at amherst, fire blazing in fireplace, music playing, talking about james joyce: he is a joyce fanatic, and since I'm just beginning to follow in his footsteps, it was most stimulating. he told me about this fascinating friend of his teaching at yale who he says will be the writer of our generation. chicken dinner across the street at the community eating hall. back to room for an evening bottle candles burning, fire going and him reading aloud to me stories and some of his own poetry he has written. he also recreated his last summer hitchhiking all over the west, working as pipefitter on the 3rd biggest dam in the world, as icepacker, and coal miner. likes the vigor of labor although he looks like a lean handsome country-clubber. needless to say I hope he asks me out again during the course of the year when I can have two normal legs. but he doesn't want to be serious about anyone again for years, so he'll probably just play the field. ah me.

most lovely news from Myron . . . our eclectic beliefs about religion are in almost complete accordance . . . and we serve to heighten each others ideas. a letter and a postcard came from him today . . . after my letter I told you about. seems he wants to see me before the prom, too! so I'm going to ask him up for rally day weekend: I'm so happy about it: the invulnerably au·gust male has volunteered for the third time in a row to come see me, with my only actual asking being the first house dance weekend! those french ladies have nothing on me! ho ho. nicest of all, I think is his signature: your future taxicab driver: he says "I might mysteriously state that any week end after the 14th will find us about 100% certain that our limitations of travel will be forever banished . . ." and on his postcard[1] he pasted a lovely green chevrolet directed smith-ward under which: "to the lonely sea and the skies . . . to fields and brooks and plains of paradise."

in other words, cars are a means to wonderful ends to freedom and an extended radius. I have a sneaking suspicion that the prognostication for the coming spring will be more than favorable! apple orchards, modern poetry, and a lovely husky baseball player to carry me over fences.

o life where is thy sting[2] . . . . .
xxx
your sivvy

<on back of envelope>

P.S. just got a letter from a guy who wants to republish "Crossing the Equinox" in a "volume of poetry like Dorothy Parker's <u>death and taxes</u>"[3] (he says). I said O.K. – hope it has a hard cover!

xx
siv

1–Myron Lotz to Sylvia Plath, postmarked 9 February 1953; see SP's Smith College scrapbook, p. 34; held by Lilly Library.

2–Probably a reference to and modification of the final couplet of Alexander Pope's 'The Dying Christian to his Soul': 'O Grave! where is thy victory? / O Death! where is thy sting?'

3–Dorothy Parker, *Death and Taxes* (New York: Viking Press, 1931).

TO *Aurelia Schober Plath*

Wednesday 18 February 1953[1] TLS, Indiana University

wednesday night

dear mother . . .

enclosed is a big favor I am askingof you: would you mind awfully retyping the enclosed essay which is the first half of my Mlle assignment for this month? I was going to have this be the final draft, but then made corrections and am just too strapped for time and energy to redo it. I don't think you'll have any trouble reading it, but I just felt I couldn't type another thing. would you mind sending it so it gets back here (in a flat brown envelope) before the end of the month? that's before next weekend. can you manage?

as for me, this is the most discouraging time as I've been spending precious hours up at the doctor's office trying to get the whole intricate web of circumstance hashed out. I've got an appointment with the veddy busy bone specialist here tomorrow to see if he will take responsibility for my case. at this point, no one will take off my cast for me. also, eventually hugenberger[2] should send the xrays back here and to raybrook, since medical ethics say the hospital that takes them owns them. as it stands now, I don't know whether they will take it off tomorrow or next week or next month. I'm just fed up with the whole thing. I've been going to bed early, but the daily plodding to classes and up and down stairs is telling on me, and by late afternoon I'm exhausted. papers and assignments are cracking down, and I realize that the next two weeks will be hell. your letters are very comforting. the one person in the world I know feeling worse than me now is poor charlotte. her best friend at middlebury heard about her broken leg through one shirley baldwin, and charlotte, unfortunately, has put two and two together and gotten the fatal four. I think perry was damn mean not to write her an explanation, but to drop her like a hot potato, especially at this low time.

the doctor in the office was very glum about my prospects. said I couldn't put any weight on the leg at all for days and days once the cast is off. I just pray I can walk to the Junior Prom now. I've been stoic about this long enough. All spring I'm going to be an arrant hedonist.

One rather cheerful thing (yes, there <u>is</u> something): just got my semester marks tonight: first time in college that I haven't gotten a B! A- in creative

1–Date supplied from internal evidence.

2–Probably Dr Paul Willard Hugenberger (1903–96).

writing, A in science, and A (!!!!!) from my dear stern lovable brilliant Mr. Patch. Not bad, what? Should be a Junior Phi Bete after all.

Myron has been a dear. Honestly, today I felt so depressed with the uncertainty of my leg that if he'd been here I would have thrown my arms around him and hugged him, he is so sweet. He has done the spectacular and bought a new Ford in New Haven and is getting it Saturday morning and driving up here with it right away to take me off in the country. So I will be the first to christen his new car. I very badly needed something to look forward to to make life bearable right now, and I am leaning on him, although he doesn't know it yet. He wrote me a very wonderful stream-of-consciousness letter sunday, as I probably told you, and I think he wants to let me try to know him. Really, I don't know what I'd do without him. I am so looking forward to saturday that I can hardly bear the dragging minutes. I find it hard to believe that I will actually see him again . . . three weeks is such an impossibly long time. At least if he has the car, my leg (cast or uncast) won't matter. He can carry me anywhere we want to go. Oh, I wish I could sleep and wake up saturday.

How can Perry get pinned if he doesn't belong to a fraternity? just curious . . .

xxx
sivvy

TO *Aurelia Schober Plath*

Saturday 21 February 1953[1] TLS, Indiana University

saturday afternoon

dear mum . . .

well, this will go down in history as plath's Black Month. myron called last night, car hasn't been delivered yet, so no weekend date. I've had so many disappointments by now that I really would be shocked if anything nice happened to me at all. it is a big dance weekend here, so dates are everywhere, and I feel quite stoic about life in general.

the cast came off thursday night, and I felt as if the doctor were lifting a coffin lid when I saw the hairy yellow withered corpse of my leg lying there. the emotional shock of admitting it was my leg was the hardest (ugh). he took an xray and said the leg wasn't completely mended (which was also a nice shock.) I couldn't worm anything else out of him, and so went to get

1 – Date supplied from internal evidence.

my hot water whirlpool bath at the infirmary: that is to be a daily affair, taxi up and back. the doctor told me to walk on crutches without putting my foot to the ground until I heard from hugenberger about the new xrays. I only pray to god that I don't have to have a third cast put on.

thursday night I felt like hell: took a razor and sheared off the worst of the black stubble and the skin of course is all coming off and raw, my ankle is swollen and blackish green, and my muscles have shriveled away to nothing. needless to say I am never going skiing again. I am going to live in a southern climate the rest of my life and play tennis (a nice safe sport) bicycle, swim, and eat mangoes. I wish to heck I could start to use my foot walking. From the way things look now I'll be lucky to go to junior prom in my long black dress with a taped ankle. and I did so want to live up to the glorious queen shirley. I just hope I can go now. just let me know what hugenberger says about the leg, and do your best to keep it out of another cast: I'll stay in bed if necessary, just so I won't have to have it back in plaster again.

the hot whirlpool is very comforting, and I do ankle exercises in it. aside from the sore skin and the weakness, it doesn't hurt. I would just like to know what "not completely mended means".

to make myself feel better I wrote two villanelles today and yesterday:[1] a rigid French verse form I've never tried before, where the first and third line have to be repeated as refrains. They took my mind off my helpless misery and made me feel a good deal better. I think they are the best I've written yet, and of course sent them off blindly, one to the Atlantic and one to the New Yorker.

Oh hell. Life is so difficult and tedious I could cry. But I won't: I'll just keep writing villanelles.

much love,
sivvy

1–According to SP's calendar, on 20 February 1953 she wrote 'Villanelle – To Eva' ['To Eva Descending the Stair'] and on 21 February 1953, she wrote 'Villanelle – Mad Girl's Love Song' ['Mad Girl's Love Song'] and 'Doomsday'. Based on comments in SP to ASP, 23 February 1953, SP probably enclosed 'To Eva Descending the Stair' and 'Mad Girl's Love Song' with this letter. A typescript copy of 'Mad Girl's Love Song' held by Lilly Library includes the following note typed at the top: 'this one had the honor of being inspired by one myron lotz . . .'

TO *Aurelia Schober Plath*

Monday 23 February 1953[1] TLS, Indiana University

monday . . . rally day

dearest of mothers . . .

excuse the big black letter that last one must have been. sun is shining to day, all is much brighter. missed canham[2] at rally day, much to my sorrow, because I had an appointment with the doctor at the weekly bone clinic[3] and also a whirlpool scheduled. I decided, medical reticence or not, I was entitled to know just how serious my bone "not being completely mended was". "I have a bone to pick with you," I told him. "my fibula, as a matter of fact." thank god, he told me I could start bearing weight on it. every day in the whirlpool increases my range of motion and ankle rotation and the swelling has gone down, and the skin looks normal, even though the leg itself is thin and the muscles hang loose. I still do bicycle exercises, and would welcome and others hugenberger can suggest. except for a soreness at the place of breakage and tender skin, I can bear full weight on it without a twinge of pain . . . my christian science has subconsciously helped my mental attitude, I think. all in all, I think I will be able to dance slowly in two weeks, as walking without crutches (yup, I've tried) is very easy and doesn't hurt at all. I want to go ahead as fast as I can without endangering myself.

manuscript came yesterday, and I can't thank you enough. when I am rich and famous I will hire you for my private secretary and baby-tender, and pay you scandalously high wages and take you on monthly jaunts in my own shocking pink yacht. needless to say, I love you very dearly.

my poem[4] is not indicative of any misunderstanding with myron, but merely is an expansion of the thought that we were destined never to get together again. he sounded tense and distraught when he called friday night, and a letter received sunday cleared up a lot of doubts I had.

the car didn't come till late saturday, and by then the mechanics had quit working. the next day being sunday, and today being a holiday, he couldn't get the necessary fluids and checkup till tuesday. but he is coming

1–Date supplied from internal evidence.

2–Erwin D. Canham (1904–82), editor of the *Christian Science Monitor*, was the speaker at Rally Day in 1953. His talk was on 'The Chances for Peace'.

3–Likely, a reference to the Elizabeth Mason Infirmary at Smith College where Plath was treated by Dr O. Donald Chrisman (1917–2002), a Northampton orthopedist who maintained private clinic hours at the Elizabeth Mason Infirmary.

4–Sylvia Plath, 'Mad Girl's Love Song'.

up tuesday! that is tomorrow. at this point I hardly can believe I'll ever see him again, but at least he has the car.

I must quote from his letter, I think it's too good and heart-warming not to share: He says: "at this point you will undeniably be justified in accusing me of obsessively pursuing in a monomaniacal fashion a chimerical capricious goal called a car . . . . my umpteenth revised itinerary reflects my arrival at smith by 2 p.m. tuesday. should you be doing anything to prevent a tryst please call collect and tell me. my reaction will be the mild one of imitating a V-2 rocket upwardly bound with callous disregard to newton's three laws of motion . . . in toto, being prevented from the Smith jaunt this weekend was highly unpleasant. I must confess my frustration tolerance is very poor . . ."

nice, what? the poor guy has met up with so many delays and changes of plans, that he is really at the end of his rope. I was too, last saturday night. thank goodness I only have one morning class tomorrow. also that my leg looks respectable (after a fashion).

oh, I like that boy!

much love,
sivvy

TO *Aurelia Schober Plath*

Wednesday 25 February 1953[1] TLS, Indiana University

god what a morning . . . wednesday

dear mother . . .

honestly, now that I can walk again the world is going up in unbelievable flashes and earthquakes. I am the girl that Things Happen To. I have spent the morning writing a flurry of letters: all sorts, all sizes: contrite, gay, loving, consolatory. One to art kramer: saturday night, just before supper, he walked into the livingroom and sat down beside me. shocked at seeing the living apparition of the summer, I assumed that he was up here on a date with another girl, and excused myself, saying I had to go to supper. this morning I got a terse note saying that my amazing behavior seemed rather unjustified: usually visitors, out of common courtesy, weren't left gaping in the living room when they had driven a hundred miles to see someone. score one: I was overcome with horror at my unwittingly curt

1–Date supplied from internal evidence.

behavior. also a sad, longing pathetic letter from dick:[1] he told me last fall that he wanted me to tell him all about my dates so he wouldn't imagine things. I did so as painlessly as possible. yet, in his heart, I should have realized that he wouldn't want to hear about them. so I am going on a gay tender campaign: remember-all-the-companionable-things we've done together, etc. you might make the norton's aware that he never asked me to marry him point blank, that I never went-steady with him or committed myself in any way other than that I liked being with him more than any other person, (but I always went out with the other persons). also, I went out all last summer with bob and art, and he wasn't bothered: now, at the sanatorium, I have taken on unusual importance as I am the only girl he knows, and he is inhibited from making new contacts. if he were in the real world he wouldn't feel so sorry for himself. I really Don't Want to go up there spring vacation at all, but if they will go for only a day and two nights, I might be persuaded.

I have to write a topping story for Mlle then, a paper for Creative Writing, a paper for Modern Poetry, and read Paradise lost. the travel by car is tedious, a waste of time as far as I'm concerned. Marcia Is coming. I want to see Warren. but as a human being, I might visit him if they really think it will do any good. the thing I am afraid of is that he will propose to me when he sees me face to face, or try to extort a promise to him to try again when he comes out. at any rate, I feel that it would be better for me not to go: I can hedge for just so long. I know as well as I've known for a long time now, deep down, that I could never be happily married to him: physically I want a colossus; hereditarily, I want a good sane stock; mentally, I want a man who isn't jealous of my creativity in other fields than children; I also want a healthy husband so I won't have to worry about his relapsing into tb if he doesn't get enough rest. I have always been very rational and practical about the prospect of marriage: I feel that I can have the best; I won't take an inferior. Falling in love is a lovely ecstatic thing, and I think I might very well let myself do that this spring. Of course I won't tell Dick, but I never felt the great generous abounding spring of beneficence I do now. maybe there'll be someone after this, I don't know: it'll take a year or more to tell: I'm not leaping rapidly into anything for some time yet. So I don't want anyone to know how very fond I am of Myron: as far as the world is concerned: I like him very much indeed, but there is no scent of orangeblossoms about it. not yet, anyway. graduate school and travel abroad are not going to be stymied

1–Probably Richard Norton to SP, 23 February 1953; held by Lilly Library.

by any squalling breastfed brats. I've controlled my sex judiciously, and you don't have to worry about me at all. The consequences of love affairs would stop me from my independent freedom of creative activity, and I don't intend to be stopped.

today it is like spring. I sit in the warm sun with the window open and the lovely greening air wafting freshly in. great wells of creative power are splurging up in me. I want to free myself for writing as much as I can this vacation.

last night was unbelievably lush. myron, poor guy, was four hours late, and I was lying on my bed crying, thinking he had sped up and gotten killed somewhere or just wasn't coming, when he arrived at suppertime. for three hours we drove in layers and levels of bluish moonlight, through woods, by lakes, talking and radiating luxury. he left at nine, and looked at me with an amazing softness in his eyes . . . amazing for one who, the boys said, has a heart of mineral rock. someday I am going to quote back to Perry his words to me at Christmas: "Oh, don't expect to see Myron much. He doesn't go around with one girl . . . never been in love, just infatuated. Never had intellectual companionship . . ." The great stone invulnerable man is coming up at noon saturday to drive me to New Hampshire and Vermont, to maybe see a show in a hick town, eat popcorn, do what we feel like doing. I thought of heading to Exeter, but it is too far, alas. also, his older brother is coming to play ball in springfield this spring, so he'll be living there. myron plans to come up fridays and stay with him, bringing studying, and so on. he's also promised to take me to a ball game over there. also sometime to take a trip to New York City. Next weekend I'm going to the prom Friday, staying in the master's house (a lush arrangement) and going to the ocean, to see Bob and Jill,[1] Perry and Shirley . . . . and in general, having a lovely time: imagine, the weekend will cost over $50! Poof . . . money goes like water. all in all, I am very joyous about the turn of events, if somewhat unsettled by my news of dick. really, though, the Nortons had no right to assume any concrete promises of plans for the future had been made. Dick always was carefully noncommittal, and so was I.

do write any gossip about myron. I just like hearing his name . . . . .

love,
sivvy

1–Robert Kent Modlin (1932–); B.S. 1954, Yale College, M.D. 1957, Yale Medical School. Modlin married Jill Rae Garvin (1933–) in 1952; the Modlins were friends of Myron Lotz.

TO *Aurelia Schober Plath*

Sat.–Sun. 28 Feb.–1 March 1953[1] TLS with ALS postscript, Indiana University

saturday morning

dearest mother . . . .

sun streams warm and slantingly golden into my lovely room, and I sit basking and writing. your lovely long letter came today, and I am once again forcibly made aware of what a superlative mother you have been to me. in the great whirlpools of responsibility you have had these last ten years and more of "bringing me up right", you deserve the most verdant laurels. honestly, I appreciate your rational understanding of me so much. in return, I have always felt I can be completely honest with you and want more than anything to make you proud of me so that some day I can begin to repay you for all the treats you've given me in my two decades of life.

I am most elated today, for this morning I bought the most exquisite formal on sale . . . you will be pleased: it's full length, white nylon net very full skirt, and swish strapless silver lame-ish top. marked down from $50 to $30. if myron will go to our april prom with me I'll save it till then. if not, I'll wear it next weekend. nothing like a new springy dress to elate one.[2] (see back picture)

I now am waiting for myron who is driving up to day with bob and jill modlin to go on a jaunt north. I am most eager to meet that lovely couple, and myron gets such pleasure out of sharing his car with people! we should have lots of fun.

last night and yesterday I finished this month's Mlle assignment: a story I just wrote about a Big Weekend: I took a dance at Harvard Med School to get the bizarre touch they like so well, and tried to make it quick-moving and sophisticatedly glittery, somewhat like Den of Lions, only much smoother, dramatic and better: I feel I've come such a long way since then! Mailed that with my Ideal Summer[3] this morning: thanks again for saving me by typing it!

as you may imagine, the whole dick affair distresses me no end. I feel a great pity for him, and a sad sort of maternal fondness: but you know how fatal that has been to love in the past. I feel, ever since I made the irrevocable decision not to marry him last summer, that I am suddenly

1 – Date supplied from internal evidence.

2 – SP's dress is held by the Historic Clothing Department, Smith College.

3 – Sylvia Plath, 'The Ideal Summer'; held by Lilly Library.

blissfully free of an overwhelming bear trap. for one thing, as I said, I wouldn't want to marry perry's brother because I have always been fond of perry, even though I would never marry him either because he is too intensely singleminded for me (and I am very happy he has found shirley, because I like her: she is my type of person.) as much as I love the nortons, I am glad I'm not marrying into their family. barring the hereditary liabilities involved in tying up with dick, I feel that our protracted togetherness would be abrasive, more than anything else. we are too alike in the unfortunate ways. I have analyzed this thing for two years now in my notebook, and I am soon going to need another notebook. in case you are ever over at the Harvard Coop, or could persuade Mr. Aldrich to get it for you, I would like an exact duplicate in the form of my book now: about the size of typing paper, ruled, etc.

anyway, I give a great gulping breath of relief when I realize how I might have ruined my life by marrying dick. his letters now are pathetic. last one[1] asked me whether I'd rather have him be a teacher or to go back to medical school if it meant a two years absence and not being self supporting. asked if I'd be single and available in five years, and practically said I could call the tune of the rest of his life. naturally I feel responsible for him, and so am going to advise him to take up a branch of medicine that won't demand as much of his health as general practitionering would . . . say surgery. he really wouldn't be half as happy as a teacher, and would always feel subconsciously that he was forced into "second best."

I do think that a lot of this fear of losing me is an obvious result of his incarceration, and subsequent loneliness and time for thought. if he were leading a normal active life he would be able to meet new girls and I am sure would not flagellate himself masochistically this way. naturally I am not mentioning myron's coming up so often. there is no need to tell the truth where the truth only hurts.

of course perry is a dear about this. I was appalled when dick never told the lynns about perry . . . so they didn't even know he had a brother other than david. then too, dick asked me not to speak about perry in his presence, and just tightened up when I asked why. I think he is intensely jealous of my relationship with perry: the calm, intimate platonic fun we've had together, and perry, fiend that he is, played on that this summer a little. also listened to me when I was so broken up about the fact of dick's hypocrasy in setting himself up as a pure paragon when he'd gone out and slept with other girls all the time. (I am amused by his remark about the one hour in the women's ward: he told me of a cabin not far

1–Richard Norton to SP, *c.* 25 February 1953; held by Lilly Library.

away which is signed up by desirous couples: a bed and a locked door. he also wrote a poem about raping Ann[1] in said cabin. innocent as the driven snow, wot?) it probably is rather mean of me, but I wonder if his parents still think he is a virgin. anyhow, I am glad that as far as I'm concerned that episode in my life isn't protracted . . . I hope I can date him still and keep him as a friend as I probably won't be married for a long long long while yet. I have a lot of growing up to do still . . .

sunday morning

same sunny scene: bob and jill couldn't come after all, so we had the day to ourselves. never have I had such an exquisite time. the sun was clear and bright, and the barns red, and the mountains purplish-blue, and the firs deep green as we drove up into Vermont. it was the first time I'd been there since that day Betsy Powley and I crossed the snowy border and had my ugly picture taken against the post. we headed on up into Brattleboro, stopping to see if we could buy maple syrup candy. the trees were being tapped all along the road, so we stopped and investigated to see what the clear syrup tasted like . . . very watery, and all the cans full to the brim. every new bend in the road brought something new to exclaim over. both of us were going for the first thime this way, and it was such a lovely adventure. we drove up to mount tom when we came back and watched the sun set and the big moon come up and freeze the birch trees into a startled white. all most lovely. about nine o'clock we (or rather I) prosaically remarked that we hadn't eaten at all since breakfast, for which I'd only had a cup of coffee, so we drove to the smoky low-ceilinged red-checked tableclothed Joe's and had a huge tomato, cheese, bacon and hamburg pizza between us, with milk. by that time both of us were nodding sleepily, so we decided I would go home to bed and he would drive back. really, we felt so sensible . . . I came in shortly after 10 and exhaustedly fell into bed, and he drove off.

anyhow, we talked over plans for next weekend, and I am really aghast at the itinerary myron plans: I will arrive at lunch time friday, meet people, go to a party or two, (and if I have my way, take a nap) go to dinner, get dressed for the prom (which lasts from 11 pm to 4 am!) after which we all will cook breakfast at bob's with perry and jill. saturday if it's nice, myron wants to drive me to new york city and explore times square and the adjoining environs! sunday we will drive out to east rock in new haven and he will study psychology and me milton . . . . honestly, I am overcome by the delightfulness of it all. I think we are both very drunk with the vistas opened by the car, and are gaily planning trips to the cape, to north

1 – Probably Anne Yamrick, a fellow patient at the TB sanatorium.

carolina and to canada! honestly, it's laughable. as mike (I call him mike now) says "Everything suddenly becomes . . possible."

electoral board begins his week, so I'll be up to my neck in business. I'm so glad I can do it, though . . . getting to know all the girls in my class, etc. I am one of the two secretaries[1] of it, by the way. it's such fun to be in on the smokeroom decisions of a nominating committee. as I said, I have no regrets at refusing to run for one of the big four offices: I hope to be making money on Press Board and working on Smith Review next year, as well as doing a topping thesis, and all sorts of creative writing. I feel life is too short to try to be a Public Figure: I've had enough of that this year. Really, I have a feeling I could very well have been elected head of Honor Board, since I have experience in back of me and the whole campus seems to know who I am. Did I tell you this lovely little incident? I was sitting in bone clinic last monday and started talking to a sweet freshman from newton. we exchanged names and she exclaimed: oh, you write for Seventeen and Mademoiselle, don't you? I have read all your things and felt so proud you were going to Smith too! Whereupon I blushed with becoming modesty. As I left I heard her telling the nurse: "Oh, she's a wonderful writer, does stories for all sorts of magazines . . ." Really, does one's heart good. Sometimes I feel so stupid and dull and uncreative that I am amazed when people tell me differently.

Glad you like the villanelles. Wish the Atlantic and New Yorker would do the same. Can't wait to hear from them . . . felt that I am getting more proficient with the singing uncrowded lyric line, instead of the static adjectival smothered thought I am usually guilty of.

So proud of Warren. Ah, me, my whole self is full of merry little pots bubbling on the fire of my enthusiasm. myron, poetry, spring, Mlle, milton, tseliot, electoral board, possibilities if only I work hard enough. This summer I want to read and write like hell on a rigorous schedule. summer school with you will be good discipline, too. Can't wait . . .

xxx

sivvy

p.s. Dick is barely 6 feet tall & weighs 190; Myron is 6' 4" and weighs 185. Also can carry women weighing 140 lbs. Ah, me, comparisons!

<drawing of Junior Prom dress>

silvery top-winged softly, with a tiny high waist and a swoosh of white net with a very palish lavendar overtone! Exquisite!

p.s. Can't wait – christening it next weekend!

1 – The other secretary was Anabel Carey.

TO *Aurelia Schober Plath*

Monday 2 March 1953[1] TLS, Indiana University

monday afternoon

dearest one . . . .

just a brief merry little note to say that all goes well. electoral board had the first meeting last night: a group of 25 outstanding seniors, juniors, and a smattering of sophomores and freshmen that draw up the final slate of 16 nominees out of our huge class. it is a notoriously strenuously taxing job involving meetings from 7 p.m. to after midnight for two weeks, and as I am one of the alternate secretaries it will be a rugged pull. however, the interviewing of housemothers and housepresidents about the characters of the girls as we narrow down the slate is stimulating. I am glad to have the chance to see how the thing is run, and since it is only for two weeks it shouldn't disastrously affect my marks, as it is rumored to do. I have somehow gotten a month ahead in my davis papers (the villanelles and the Mlle story helped) and so I really have only two courses to worry about: the milton exam and the 20 page paper I'm going to do on Edith Sitwell.[2] even so, with this fabulous three day weekend coming up, it'll be a ticklish job.

the dress is hanging up in my window in all its silvern glory, and there is a definite rosy cast to the skirt . . . (no, it's not just my attitude!) today I had my too-long hair trimmed just right for a smooth pageboy, and I got for 12.95 the most classic pair of silver closed pumps with just enough heel so I won't have to dance on tiptoe, as I would have had to in ballet shoes. with my rhinetone earrings and necklace, I should look like a silver princess . . . or feel like one anyway. I just hope I get to be a junior phi bete this year so I can use it for my phi bete dress too. (do you realize I got the ONLY A in the unit from mr. patch!) hope I can do as well this semester.

by the way the great literary genius gordon dropped by yesterday to return a scarf I'd left with him and to ask me out this coming weekend. I was really sorry to refuse: he is by far the handsomest, tan physical specimen.I've ever gone out with. it was so amusing: mary and I were just talking about how I'd probably never see him again since it had been three weeks and no word, and poof! there he was. I only hope I get a second chance.

1–Date supplied from internal evidence.

2–Probably Sylvia Plath, 'Edith Sitwell and the Development of Her Poetry'; held by Lilly Library.

only wish you could see me in my exquisite new dress. just realized that the whole weekend, including trainfare, dress and shoes will cost me fifty dollars, too. but at least the dress and shoes will be wearable for years and years yet. I had planned on getting a spring formal this year, anyway.

god, how I wish I could win that Mlle contest. this year would be so ideal, while I'm still in touch with college. on my last assignment, which I will do as soon as I come home for vacation first thing, I want to write up an extra article or two for bonus.

bye for a while,
your busy loving
silvershod
sivvy

TO *Aurelia Schober Plath*

Tuesday–Friday 3–6 March 1953[1] TLS with envelope, Indiana University

tuesday afternoon

dear mother . . .

the most tantalizingly sad thing happened this afternoon, I really can't help but sit down and immediately spill it over to you. I got my two villanelles back from the New Yorker today with a rejection that wasn't even mimeographed, but that was written in pencil and initialed by one of the editors. It said, and I quote:

"Although we were impressed by many things in Doomsday, I'm sorry to say the final vote went against it, as well as the other poem. We were somewhat bothered by the two rhymes that break the scheme---especially 'up' which is not even an assonant rhyme here. Do try us again and thanks for letting us see these."

Honestly, I've never come so blasted close, and it's almost worse than missing out altogether. "Final vote": those heartless men! Ah, well, to keep my courage up I immediately sent them the third villanelle. The worst they can do is reject that too.

friday morning

hello again . . .

Just a note before I run off in my little taxi to the train station. The day dawned fair and bright, and I am all neatly packed and gathered

1–Date supplied from postmark.

together already . . . having tried on my dress yesterday afternoon for the admiration of all and sundry. About ten girls are going from the house, so we are all in a companionable flurry of activity. That's one very lovely thing about living in a dorm: all your pleasures are shared and thereby magnified no end. I love Lawrence House now, and would rather live here than anywhere else on campus: it took half a year to get to feel this way, but it was more than worth it. The girls are all exceptional, and I feel so at ease and friendly with them: imagine, half of the house is on Dean's List, and over half of the Juniors are honoring! Compared to the scholastic lethargy in other houses, this is a relief . . . also the friendliness of the girls, the way they want to see a new-bought dress, the way they help each other out, is so heartwarming. There is definitely a cooperative atmosphere, which I notice when I go back to Haven and other houses on campus . . . other houses are nice, but nothing like this. In fine, I am more than happy here.

Last night I plead guilty of a sore throat which I didn't have so I could get out of house meeting and go to bed early. I took two sleeping pills two hours apart, as you said, and woke this morning fresh and gay as a bromidic daisy. I felt I deserved it, as the Electoral Board meeting wednesday lasted till one in the morning (from after supper!) and I biked home on the dark deserted campus with my own house key feeling very privileged. I love the 25 girls on the board, and we meet early Sunday to interview the 30 candidates we've narrowed the jr. class down to. Of course this means leaving Yale early Sunday morning, and I don't like that, but, it will be good for Myron to know I have a few activities besides him! Lou Giesey is on the board too, and I was glad to see she had made the same choice about running for office that I had: I think both of us would have had a good chance of getting into the 16 speech-making finalists. But as I said, after a careful weighing of the problem, I decided emphatically against it, even though the glory of being one of the Big Four was tantalizing no end.

By the way, I want to set your heart at ease about Myron's and my weekending. Really, I think we are both very sensible and cool-headed and rational: even if it did take a long time to persuade him I needed a pizza! I got to bed shortly after 10 on that Saturday night, which is a noble feat. Also Mike is a very capable good safe driver, and he loves the car so much you have nothing to worry about there! We are admittedly not night-owls, and both cling to our quota of at least eight hours sleep per night. So rest, rest, perturbed spirit! I don't want to get tb either. One thing, Dick's sojourn has radically cured me of any secret longings to escape the world and write in a peaceful sanatorium. I will write this summer while taking typing and shorthand and I really think that I will get more done than when I'd have acres of unscheduled time. I plan to have a nice active two months at home, going to town with you mornings, studying, reading like mad and writing. I really would like to try getting into the Ladies Home Journal this summer!

Another item that saddens me: Dick writes[1] that he has been looking around for jobs for me at Lake Placid this summer, and says there are lots of opportunities. I am going to defer discussion of that till we go up there, but that is the last thing I want to do. It would be a summer down the drain, and I want to spend this summer intellectually without working and getting worn out. Hope you can give me a few suggestions of how to parry his invitation gracefully!

And now, off in my shining taxi! I thought today would never come: tonight I will be transformed into a silver Sylvia! Much much

love,
sivvy

TO *Richard Norton*

Sunday 8 March 1953 AL (excerpt),[2] Smith College

March 8 – letter excerpt:

Firstly of all I was horrified to hear that the dear bearshooting imaginative adorable very lovable bright southernaccented sandy[3] I knew for such a little nice while is gone away. it is unjust, unnecessary, and difficult to comprehend. if it was god's will it is a very stupid arbitrary blood thirsty god, and I do not like him or believe in him or respect him because he is more foolish and mean than we are and has no sense of proportion of what people are good for living and what people are unfit. it is perhaps very good that there is another potential lynn coming to receive some of the love that sandy flourished in. the work and mind and food and love given to a child for growing, and then the sudden going away to where we don't know, we wish somewhere that would save the part we loved, but can't really believe that, and so say it was blind chance and rail against the arbitrariness of it. nothing being there to do but weep, or stand shocked silent by the sudden end, the shattered glass and toppling masonry, the

1–See Richard Norton to SP, 3 March 1953; held by Lilly Library.

2–SP excerpted this letter in her journals.

3–William Sanford 'Sandy' Lynn, III (1948–53); died by accidental strangulation on 4 March 1953. See Richard Norton to SP, 4, 6 and 7 March 1953; held by Lilly Library.

ruin of all space, of a potential universe, and put away the fragments left, and begin the cycle of growth over and over again, birth and death, birth and death. oh the tireless amazing unbelievably creative urge of we weary fallible battered humans. all this sorrow, injustice, war, blood lust, and still we persist in hopefully, faithfully, bringing forth children into the world. I loved that boy sandy, and all the sprouting of goodness and fineness in him. I love the lynns, and wish I could articulate my sorrow, or give them a microcosm of the great huge understanding and sympathy they deserve . . .

TO *Aurelia Schober Plath*

Monday 9 March 1953[1] TLS with envelope, Indiana University

monday ugh morning

dear mother . . .

all good things must come to an end, and I am feeling the weary soporific effects of a very lovely weekend. got the 11 a.m. train back to hamp yesterday morning just in time for electoral board meeting which lasted 10 long hours, from 2 p.m. to midnight. you may imagine that it took all I had in me not to fall off the chair in a stupor. only two more meetings, and the final slate will be announced. what a life.

mike and I had a lovely time together and I feel I know him much much better and that we have a very wholesome relationship. friday I came down in time for lunch, and the afternoon was spent visiting multitudes of his friends, meeting endless people, being taken to the baseball cage and watching practice, having him take my picture posing casually on the fender of his car, driving up to west rock overlooking new haven and watching him pitch rocks into the sky. dinner at silliman, in the palatial tall dining room . . . very good rare roast beef, meeting the master of silliman in whose house I stayed with several other girls (princely quarters, big beds, mirrored bathrooms, spiral staircases, etc.) and eventually dressing and getting to the big dance about midnight (it began at 11) where I danced without much trouble, saw perry and jim mcnealy and lots of my smith and mike's yale friends. sherbet, punch and cake refreshments, three bands, among them, tommy dorsey's, and thousands of gorgeously gowned females and handsome men. a legendary extravaganza. saturday, after getting into bed at 5 a.m. we decided wisely not to go to new york

1–Date supplied from postmark.

because it was so cold and mike was fighting a cold too (his roommate had been sent off with flu). it was really much better: we drove out along the connecticut shoreline and sat in the sun watching the waves and bright colored summer houses and talking.

going back, we bought a half gallon of apple cider and someapples to quench our thirst and had dinner at silliman, after which we went to mike's room, where I made him take some cold pills and have a backrub and rest. we listened to music, classical, drank all the apple cider, talked some more, and went back to the master's house at midnight so I could get up in time for breakfast with him the next morning. saw perry and shirl, and had lunch with them that day. nothing said about dick: those two are so obviously far gone that one can hardly talk to them. when mike and I came over to call for them with bob and jill saturday morning, perry was still in his pajamas and shirley was sitting on his lap necking with him all the while we were there. honestly, I think I would vomit if any boy hung over me like that all the time: I like my integrity, and feel that a mature relationship isn't a complete all-smothering thing where two people can't be whole when they're apart. at least mike and I agree that it is important to have a balanced partnership (this is all theory) where outside interests are important and the people are realistic and flexible, facing life together instead of blinding each other by excluding the rest of the world. I honestly don't think I could ever take anybody with perry's intense concentrated demanding of complete continuous affection: I like the rest of the world too much.

as far as I'm concerned, things look very promising for a rich companionship between mike and me: with the understanding that there are no strings attached and there is complete freedom for both of us; living in the cloying atmosphere of perry and shirley and the young domestic bliss of bob and jill, where both mike and I don't feel ready to make final choices for a few years yet, calls for an assertion of position. neither of us are like perry, who drops girls if they aren't going to pledge to marry him. this is very nice, because I get a chance to see how mike works out in med school, and what he wants to do with the rest of his life. he is still very young at heart, and changing into being a man, and needs encouragement and affection, which I certainly am glad to give. the next few years will work themselves out, so please don't give anybody the impression that we are serious about anything. for me, and him, love is difficult to define, but it is a very slow growing rational thing. I have to know a great deal about anybody, and be able to predict reasonably the future life I'd have, before I could ever commit the next 50 years of my life.

as for dick, he is evidently very anxious to see me spring vacation. I hope that we can make it as brief and painless as possible. I saw pictures of the family group taken at middlebury, and he is <u>fat</u>, really pouty about the cheeks. I know it is a necessessary concomitant about tb, but physically it unfortunately revolts me. how glad I am that I was never one of the girls he compromised! that really would make me sick. myron is so lean and ironmuscled and I am sure always will be: we both hate fatness.

by the way, dr. lynn's dear oldest boy was accidentally choked to death while playing, a story that shocked me, for I loved those dear people so. they are leaving ray brook immediately, which of course is a hard blow for dick.

I am enclosing a bill from hugenberger which was sent me. I don't know where to send it off for insurance.

I am having a checkup xray next week for my leg, which still hurts, and I hope it is alright after the weekend.

marcia is coming home with me wed the 25th till that friday. it is the only time she can come so I said yes. if need be, we can bring in the porch cot for those two nights. hope it won't be too hard for you. warren can drive us both home; she does want to see him.

love,
a weary sivvy

TO *Aurelia Schober Plath*

Thurs.–Fri. 12–13 March 1953[1] TLS with envelope, Indiana University

thursday night

dear mum . . . .

just a note to say that I got your special delivery this morning and it couldn't have come at a more strategic time. all week we have been having electoral board meetings till after midnight, and the emotional tension has been great. last night, after much heated discussion, we evolved the final slate. although I have had a few brief pangs at not running, I've decided that if I am ever to do anything at writing now is the time, and if I had a big office I would intensely resent stealing time from my creative and class work. it is not often that one has the chance to work under men like davis and patch, or women like drew. I have become so influenced by my course

1–Date supplied from postmark.

I'm auditing in James Joyce that I think I would like to do some aspect of his work for my thesis topic!

today I had my milton written, and I hope I got a B, I was so tired. at least now, even though I have two big papers before vacation, the pressure is let up considerably.

by the way, I am elated about warren's triumph: I've told myron, marcia, and everyone else who will listen! I am so proud of him.

letter from mike came today with a few lovely snapshots[1] of the view from west rock and the ocean that we took on our trip last saturday. I had assumed that would be the last time I saw him till after spring vacation, but he asked to come up again this saturday: I don't know what his trouble is; I think he must have a bad case of wanderlust or something. anyhow, needless to say, I look most forward to taking another trip to the hills before he leaves for florida.

xxx

Sivvy (over)

<in left margin>

P.s. – got a lovely answer for my Thank-you letter from the master of Silliman. I sent him a villanelle as tribute, and his appreciation was most touching! He's a very famous expert on philosophy!

friday morning

dear mum . . .

spent four hours in the news office today adding up back tallies of inches. now all is in order, and I am very happy to be back again. I think W. H. Auden will be speaking for our annual pressboard banquet in April! It is pouring rain, and the ground smells springy.

got back the Mlle manuscript today. this is a bad time for me as far as rejections go. also, I don't see how I have any sort of a chance to be an editor this june. twenty top girls from smith are trying out, and the first list of the first month's twelve winners was announced, and no one from smith was on it. in a way it's better than having someone from smith other than me be on it, I suppose, but I am not hopeful as I once was. still, as soon as I come home spring vacation, I am going to work on the assignment that has to be in by April 1 and do a few extra articles for it.

my personal rejection from the New Yorker has made me realize how hard I want to work at writing this summer. I'll never get anywhere if I just write one or two stories and never revise them or streamline them for a particular market. I want to hit the New Yorker in poetry and the

1–See SP's Smith College scrapbook, p. 34; held by Lilly Library.

Ladies Home in stories, and so I must study the magazines the way I did Seventeen. Speaking of 17, I wrote them as you suggested in your note asking if I could submit stories and poems on a professional basis. It would be a great triumph for me to get a story in there on a regular basis. If I can consciously gear things to them the way I did that Initiation story, I don't see why I couldn't produce prolifically. I only hope they will consider my offer.

your rejected daughter,
sivvy

<in left margin>

p.s. do send that picture of me in my bathing suit last summer! I'll let you know soon whether Marty & I will be home wed. on 5 p.m. bus or whether we'll wait till Thursday for warren.

TO *Aurelia Schober Plath*

Sunday 15 March 1953[1] TLS with envelope, Indiana University

sunday afternoon 2pm

Dear mother . . . .

By some miracle yesterday was beautifully mild and springly between two very rainy days . . . today it is pouring and gray and dribbly but there is a softness in the air that promises a relenting in the season at the approaching equinox.

Tomorrow morning I get my final xray, and I just hope there is nothing drastically wrong with my leg, because it often twinges quite painfully, especially when I've slept with it in the same position all night or in wet weather. Maybe I'm getting like a rheumatic and being endowed with weatherpredicting sensations in my bones.

Myron and I had a very lovely relaxed time together yesterday. Now that I try to account for the time spent, I wonder where it went, it evaporated so fast. He came about three, and we drove along the beautiful connecticut river into the Holyoke hills where we read from his Abnormal Psych book until sunset, and we watched the sun go down across the river from the mountain. We then drove to Whately where we had a delicious steak dinner, with fresh salad, potatoes fried, and milk for only 3.80 for

1–Date supplied from postmark.

both of us! It was a Baby Beef modernly decorated place that specialized in steak and lobster . . . very yummy. We sat and talked there a long while, and then drove miles and miles so we could listen to the new radio which he got installed this week in the car. He left at about 11.30 for the 80 mile drive home, both of us being very sleepy. Honestly, I wonder if we are aged or something, we both simply cannot keep our eyes open after 11 at night. Poor Mike has driven so much: 160 miles up and back, and all over the Northampton country side with me . . . he was really beat. Showed him Silliman Master Greene's letter to me and he was as elated and proud as I was.

Do try to get a dentist's appointment with Gilmore[1] anytime after that first weekend home when Marcia will be there: I can't go on without fillings forever.

I am tempted to have Warren come up as early as possible Thursday the 26th so I can carry the crutches and books and winter clothes: I'll want to bring back all my spring cottons after vacation. (Mike and I plan to spend one weekend in Springfield watching a night ballgame with his brother playing and exploring the town, which should be fun.) Anyway I'll let you know definitely what Marcia would rather do.

By for now ,
your busy sivvy

<picture, described in SP to ASP, 8 January 1953,
enclosure of SP and Myron Lotz>

TO *Aurelia Schober Plath*

Monday 16 March 1953[2] TLS, Indiana University

monday noon

dear mum . . . .

thanks muchly for the letter this morning . . . I love that long paper you have and would adore getting some for my rough drafts. seems already that I've been back here forever. I've been running around madly about my many businesses. for example, this a.m. I had a 8 o'clock class meeting to get schedule cards to make out for next year: which means I'll have to get petitions to take psych next year, have interviews with my honors advisor, and pick a thesis topic and advisor. thank god I am pretty dead

1 – Dr George Gilmore.

2 – Date supplied from internal evidence.

certain I want to do my paper on Joyce (James). at least that narrows the field some.

after that, I went to the dean's office to get miss schnieders to write me a recommendation for harvard summer school, and to the registrar's office to get another transcript. the little secretary at the desk looked up at me in awe as I handed her my name on a card; "I've seen your name in Seventeen!" she said in a tone of hallowed reverence. evidently I'm not half aware of my own wide fame! then to the news office for two hours of typing releases for my beloved Hampshire Gazette . . . I get my own private paper sent to the house, now! and should earn a good $200 from it by next April! half of my college expenses. of course, it is a lot of work, but at least it is stimulating and good experience.

Harvard Summer School wrote me a most nice note and are sending me a catalogue and slanders of applications. I am definitely taking two courses, one definitely for credit, the other maybe not: Elementary Psych and Frank O'Connor's short story course . . . or if that's taken, his novel course. He wrote an excellent article on the short story in the Times book Review this week, which I clipped out to save.[1] I want to read his collected short stories[2] before I take his course. Summer school begins June 1[3] (early, wot) and lasts eight weeks till August 23.

the detailed account of cultural lectures, seminars, concerts, plays, and social life made me thrill with excitement! what a wonderful prospect, I hope to see psych teachers here during this next packed week. by the way, peter Bertocci is teaching the psych of personality at Harvard, too. how I would like to take that! but I'm of course not advanced enough.

tb xray again last week, and as they haven't notified me, I hope and assume I'm again clear. what a blight that would be on my life!

hope I can win some money so I can live in cambridge those eight weeks to be right near the library and evening events! otherwise I'll have to live home. if I lived there I could come home weekends . . and save on transportation and time. oh, well, I've so many things on the financial fire, <u>something</u> just has to turn up.

mike and I had a very nice day, driving in the country, eating steak dinner, and going to a party of nice people that night. I felt sort of badly telling him I had two dates in the future, because now I won't see him for a month, but after all, I certainly have been giving him the major part of

1–Frank O'Connor, 'And It's A Lonely, Personal Art', *New York Times Book Review*, 12 April 1953, 1, 34.
2–Probably *Stories of Frank O'Connor* (New York: Knopf, 1952).
3–Harvard Summer School in fact began on 6 July 1953.

my social time, and I am sure he is the last person who would insist on monopolizing me. needless to say, I am looking very forward to seeing Gordon again. he is a really adorably sweet intelligent handsome guy.

papers and work will cram my time till the weekend. till later.

love,
sivvy

TO *Aurelia Schober Plath*

Tuesday 17 March 1953[1] TLS with envelope, Indiana University

TUESDAY afternoon

dearest progenitor . . . .

even though I am very weary and very longing for sleep and very behind in papers, I felt such a sudden burst of love and happiness and joy in love seething all day in me that I could not help but want to share some of it with you, there is so much to flow over merrily with, and I feel violets sprouting between my fingers and forsythia twining in my hair and violins and bells sounding whereever I walk . . .

why should I be so elated even if tired? . . . because I have two good strong legs, the doctor and xray said so yesterday; because I revised my villanelles the way the New Yorker man suggested and it is true they are much better and I am going to send them back and see what he says; because I will probably get the coveted position of Hampshire Gazette Correspondent for next year in the News Office which will mean earning about $150 or $200 . . . the most lucrative job in the office; because I have many good warm friends . . . Marcia, Enid . . . and talented others; because one Myron Michael Lotz thinks I am brilliant creative and beautifulallatonce; because one promising Raymond Wunderlich has just written and asked me to come to New York sometime this spring for ballet and other cultural delights; because I just got a check from the Springfield Daily News and bought three coveted books and six modern art postcards at the Hampshire Bookshop: the huge black-and-white modern art-covered New Directions (14),[2] James Joyce's Dubliners,[3]

1–Date supplied from postmark.

2–*New Directions in Prose and Poetry 14* (New York: New Directions, 1953).

3–James Joyce, *Dubliners* (New York: Modern Library [*c.* 1926]); SP's copy held by Smith College.

and the Basic Writings of Freud[1] . . . because life in general is rich and heterogeneous and promising if I work hard . . . .

now to practical affairs: I am staying overnight at Marty's Wednesday, hoping that Warren will come up as early as possible Thursday morning. I have all my winter clothes, piles of books and crutches to bring home, and Marty has a lot of stuff too, so we'll need him.

by the way, I got a long letter from Mr. Norton about the coming (sigh) vacation, and have agreed to go with him Monday March 30 and come back Wednesday April 1. Really, that is as good a time as any, and I'd like to get it over with and enjoy the rest of the vacation and read and write and work. The only thing is, I'll have to work like fury on Mlle Saturday and Sunday because I have to mail it Monday March 30. Maybe you could then help me with the typing of it.

I LOVE MY NEW BOOKS: THIS SUMMER I AM GOING TO STAY HOME AND READ AND READ AND READ AND WRITE AND WRITE AND WRITE . . .

I LOVE YOU TOO
AND WARREN ALSO,
xxxxxx
sivvy

<drawing of map with directions to Marcia Brown's house with caption: 'Marcia lives in a small white house: 211 crescent street, on the left of the street. Crescent street turns off Elm street on the right, opposite curved brick quad.' Other labels written by SP are 'Rt 9.'; 'MAIN STREET'; 'GREEN STREET'; 'College Hall tower'; 'Gates'; 'ELM STREET'; 'Curved brick quad'; 'Crescent STREET'; and '211'>

TO *Warren Plath*

Saturday 21 March 1953[2]

TLS (photocopy), Indiana University

saturday morning . . . .

dearest washington wanderer . . . .

much pleased was your untraveled sister to receive a blooming pink postcard of the cherry trees seen from the tidal basin today. here it is

1–Sigmund Freud, *The Basic Writings of Sigmund Freud* (New York: Modern Library [*c.* 1938]); SP's copy held by Smith College.

2–Date supplied from postmark by Warren Plath.

miraculously sunny, and blue skied and springly, and right next to our house the sophomores are having their annual carnival with an honest-to-goodness merry-go-round, and the creaking carousel music makes me feel as gay and lighthearted as a child at a country fair, in spite of the fact that I have a 25-page research paper on Edith Sitwell due monday and I have 11 books on my desk which I haven't even started to read yet! seriously, though, I love writing it, and just spent another $10 on three books: basic writings of Freud, Joyce's "Dubliners", and a delectably stark arty black-and-white covered New Directions Anthology just out this year which includes two selections by professors at Smith:[1] we really are an artistic place.

the great W. H. Auden spoke in chapel this week and I saw him for the first time. he is my conception of the perfect poet: tall, with a big leonine head and a sandy mane of hair, and a lyrically gigantic stride. needless to say he has a wonderfully textured british accent, and I adore him with a big Hero Worship. I would someday like to touch the Hem of his Garment and say in a very small adoring voice: Mr. Auden I haveapomeforyou: "I found my God in Auden."

He is Wonderful and
Very Brilliant, and
Very Lyric and Most
Extremely Witty.

I love Sitwell: remember:

"That is my friend King Pharoh's head
That nodding blew out of the pyramid . . . .[2]

and "An old dull mome with a head like a pome."[3] those are going to be my children's nursery rhymes, along with T. S. Eliot's practical cats.

can't wait to see you Wednesday. now I have classes from two to four, so if you get up by then, just wait in the livingroom of the house and tell the girl on bells youre my Brother, or tell anybodyand they will be

1 – Martha England, 'Le Voyage d'Urien' (9–49); as well as two former Smith professors, Ben L. Reid, 'The Tower' (54–67) and Oskar Seidlin, 'Hermann Hesse' (109–31).

2 – Edith Sitwell, 'The Wind's Bastinado'; SP slightly misquotes: 'It is my friend King Pharaoh's head / That nodding blew out of the Pyramid . . .'

3 – Edith Sitwell, 'Fox Trot (Old Sir Faulk)'; SP does not include the line break after 'mome / With . . . '

very Impressed with you. probably you will get up a little after four, in which case I will be there with all my many books suitcases and crutches and so on. from where we will pick up marcia, and if it is near supper which it will be we will go and take you down to rahar's and treat you to a good dinner and a hell of a lot of collegiate atmosphere. marcia is staying from thursday, till saturday, so our Little Home will be Packed with Guests. needless to say, I want to get home as Soon as Possible. but If by chance you can't come up till thursday morning because of it being rainy or snewing, I will stay overnight at marcia's. I really must know, though, so why don't you waste a big lot of money on me by sending a telegram from washington wed. morning if you Can't come till thursday. and maybe send one from home when you leave Wed to let me know When you will get here: check?

there are a million things I want to talk to you about, since I haven't written you for a long time. looks like you and I will both be home this summer, so I hope we can help mother with the cooking and work since grammy is evidently pretty out of the running now, and I look so forward to being with you all the summer: I hardly ever see you during the year, and you are still my Very Favorite Person! we will have a fun summer together. it will help the fact that my social life will obviously be Nil. at least now and then we can Do Boston together, alleys and all, because you are a Big Man and can protect me.

my male acquaintances are coming along pretty well: myron is in florida for three weeks of spring training now, so I won't be seeing him till the middle of april. he is really a very wonderful person, and I must tell you the story of his home life: it is amazing that someone like him came from such a place. imagine his mother never went beyond fourth grade! and his father works in the steel mills! I think myron like me better than any girl, as he has come to see me in his new ford car with the radio every weekend for a month . . and we read poems, abnormal psychology, and everything together . . . only he is still under his facade very young and romantic and idealistic, which I of course appreciate and cherish . . . while he definitely has the advantage over perry of being more of a rationalist and conscious of the worldliness of the world. I like him quite a bit. imagine, he sings songs to me! he would like to meet you sometime because I keep telling him how wonderful you are, with your broadjumping and brilliancy at exeter. I think you would like him.

another nice thing: just got a letter from ray wunderlich, the columbia med student I met at the belmont last summer, and I think I will go to New York to visit him this spring! isn't that wonderful! he is a member of the N.Y. ballet society, and very alive, brilliant, and enchanting, even though he is barely as tall as I. spring in Central Park! ah, aren't we coming up in the world!

I have been getting very encouraging personal rejection slips from the New Yorker, and they have a pome of mine now, which I am praying to god they accept. that would crown my life. I am superstitious about always having something at the printers. 17 printed a pome of mine this month,[1] and my Last One is coming out in the may issue.[2] they have been very good to me.

hope to see you wednesday . . . much love,

sivvy

TO *Aurelia Schober Plath*

Saturday 11 April 1953[3] TLS with envelope, Indiana University

saturday morning

dearest mother . . . .

well, no publication news yet . . . neither rejections nor acceptances, just an empty silence! so no news is good news in this case I think!

I am at present beginning a long funny poem which the first stanza of I here reproduce. I am trying to get a rollicking rhythm. sometimes, I fear, it is not only rollicking, but also supremely irresponsible:

Dialogue en Route
"If only something exciting would happen!"
Said Eve the elevator-girl ace
To Adam the arrogant matador
As they shot past the forty-ninth floor
In a rocketing vertical clockcase
Fast as a fallible falcon.
and so on and on,

1–Sylvia Plath, 'The Suitcases Are Packed Again', *Seventeen* 12 (March 1953), 91.
2–Sylvia Plath, 'Carnival Nocturne', *Seventeen* 12 (April 1953), 127. No poem by SP appears in the May issue. *Seventeen* purchased 'Sonnet to a Dissembling Spring' in March 1953 but it never appeared in the magazine.
3–Date supplied from postmark.

as far as my masculine acquaintances are concerned, I am most elated about subsequent happenings. upon returning I got a card from Myron reaffirming his coming up early this afternoon "For the express purpose of talking over a million things." needless to say I look most forward to reseeing him. and ALSO I got a darling letter from Ray with a Round Trip Ticket to New York enclosed(!) He is very understanding about my financial setup, but no boy has ever gone to the trouble and expense of sending me train tickets! I was most touched. here's to May 1!

the best thing happened, as most best things do, unexpectedly. walking out of the Auden lecture last night[1] alone (thank god) I saw a tall handsome figure standing in the rain, and with a start, realized that it was Gordon Lameyer.

Thinking he probably had come with another girl, I vowed to quell my first impulse to run up to him and say hello, and just kept slowly walking home. And then, just like in the movies, I heard a measured male tread behind me, and I didn't dare to look up until I heard him say my name. So it developed that I went out with him to a little smoky place downtown, drank gingerale (he is another boy who drinks nothing stronger than beer and doesn't smoke) and talked heatedly about James Joyce, religion, childhood, and all sorts of obscure poets and famous people we knew people who know. The evening was a stimulating rapid cross fire of ideas, and both of us had an excellent time. I was so relieved at having a second chance to make up for our first and only date, and me handicapped by the cast.

Anyhow, the great God Gordon has asked me to a dance at his fraternity house next Saturday night, and I am happily going. Just like I imagined I would if he ever asked me! The only trouble is that he is going to be an insurance salesman after he gets out of the navy. What a waste of talent!

And so my date life looks inordinately bright! Ah, spring! I certainly am going out with three exceptional men! Both Gordon and Mike are about 6'4", only Ray is short (my height) and spindly, but he certainly makes up for it in brilliance and entertaining conversation. And all of them are so intelligent!

If only now I would make some great unexpected windfall of money all would be just lush!! At least I have lovely social prospects. I do like Gordon, he is, as I have said, the best looking boy I have ever met. I feel that I am out with a particularly attractive movie star, or something,

1–Auden's lecture was on 'Some Reflections of the Comic' and took place in Sage Hall at 8 p.m.

whenever I look at him . . . his hair is close cropped and curly brown, and his eyes black, and he has a really tremendous lean lithe build! Ah, me!

xx
sivvy

TO *Aurelia Schober Plath*

Wednesday 22 April 1953[1] ALS with envelope, Indiana University

<incomplete letter; first page(s) not present; the top portion of the page on which the below text was transcribed appears to be cut off>

Tell me what you think about the poems.[2]

xxx
Sivvy

P.S. If you ever have a while with nothing to do (ho ho!) you could type up these poems, centered, singlespsaced, on good paper (without name or anything) & send 'em to me!

xx
S.

Parallax

Major faults in granite
Mark a mortal lack;
Yet individual planet
Directs all zodiac.

Tempo of strict ocean
Metronomes the blood,
Yet ordered lunar motion
Proceeds from private flood.

Diagram of mountains
Graphs a fever chart;
Yet astronomical fountains
Exit from the heart.[3]

1 – Date supplied from postmark.
2 – Sylvia Plath, 'Trio of Love Songs', *Collected Poems*.
3 – 'Exit ~~Flower~~ from the heart' appears in the original.

Drama of each season
  Plots doom from above;
Yet all angelic reason
  Moves to our minor love.

April 16, 1953

Verbal Calisthenics

My love for you is more
  Athletic than a verb,
Agile as a star
  The tents of sun absorb.

Treading circus tightropes
  Of each syllable,
The brazen jackanapes
  Would fracture if he fell.

Acrobat of space,
  The daring adjective
Plunges for a phrase
  Describing arcs of love.

Nimble as a noun,
  He catapults in air;
A planetary swoon
  Could climax his career.

But adroit conjunction
  Eloquently shall
Link to his lyric action
  A periodic goal.

April 16, 1953

Admonition

If you dissect a bird
   To diagram the tongue
You'll cut the chord
   Articulating song.

If you flay a beast
   To marvel at the mane
You'll wreck the rest
   From which the fur began.

If you assault a fish
   To analyze the fin
Your hands will crush
   The generating bone.

If you pluck out the heart
   To find what makes it move,
You'll halt the clock
   That syncopates our love.

April 17, 1953

TO *Aurelia Schober Plath*

Friday 24 April 1953 — Telegram, Indiana University

BIRTHDAY GREETINGS STOP MY PRESENT IS FOLLOWINGNEWS. HARPERS MAGAZINE JUST GRACIOUSLY ACCEPTED THREE POEMS FOR 100 DOLLARS IN ALL. MADEMOISELLE SENT TEN DOLLARS FOR RUNNER-UP IN THIRD ASSIGNMENT BEST LOVE TO YOU=

=CIVVY

TO *Aurelia Schober Plath*

Friday 24 April 1953 — TLS in greeting card,[1] Collection of Judith Raymo

<printed greeting>

If I were a Walküre / Full of sound and fury / I'd mount my trusty stallion / And with a whoop Valhallian cry / Happy Birthday

<signed>

much love to / my favorite / mummy! / your / sivvy / (inside)

friday, april 24

Dear mother . . . .

As you can see, with much effort and travail, I managed to put a new ribbon on the typewriter. Feels so much better, really, and my thoughts somehow become correspondingly scintallant and concise. Got my final catalogue from Harvard and am in the midst of writing up my application sheets. O'Connor's story course is limited, and I do hope I can get in, but if I can't, I'm signing up for his novel course in 20th century lit. which should also be tremendous. About $150 should cover it if I live at home. But if any little financial bonuses come through, I will try to get a room and board there during the week and come home weekends. I really should live there, as I have a 9 a.m. class and a 2 p.m. one. Will earn about $50 from the News Office in these last 2 months. As for squaring things with the Scholarships office, should they ask, I'm taking a prerequisite course for possible grad work in psych, and working before and after, and writing in the meantime, so to hell with them. They probably won't know about it until it's too late anyhow. And even then, I really don't have to worry.

In the final catalogue, the opening date is July 5, so I'll have plenty of time to study shorthand with you, to read all the books I have on hand, rest, and get tan and intelligent. The College Board Editor from Mlle[2] came up to cover the tremendous Arts and Morals Symposium[3] we're having these last 2 days . . . as I told you, with Auden, Lionel Trilling,[4]

1–Panda Prints birthday card designed by Rosalind Welcher.
2–Marybeth Little.
3–'Art and Morals' was a symposium held at Smith College on 23–4 April.
4–American literary critic and writer Lionel Trilling (1905–75).

Allen Tate,[1] Jacques Barzun,[2] George Boas,[3] Ben Shahn,[4] Archibald MacLiesh,[5] and several others. She treated all of us to icecream after the afternoon symposium, and we all had a friendly chat. However, I have completely given up hope for a month in New York. The girls trying out from Smith are all tremendous in art, gov, fashion, and so on, and none of them have received prizes yet, so I am dead certain I don't have a chance. Naturally I'm sorry, but there is so much else I want to do that I can't waste time in self-pity.

Next Friday I head off for a gala weekend in New York. Ray promises most entertaining times . . . Saturday I'm going to his 2 hour neurology class . . . and I can't wait to tell you all about it. I'm going shopping at the beginning of this week for a dress or traveling suit. Mike has asked me down to Yale for the spring college (May 9th) weekend the next weekend, and of course I'm gladly going. Perry and Shirl will be there, and evidently Jill Modlin was so intrigued by me that she is insisting on having me as a house guest! If it's nice weather, we'll all hit the beaches, for picnics et al. I look most forward to it.

By the way, Auden came to dinner at the house last night, and I had the honor of sitting at the same table. Really, he is the most delightfully brilliant man! If I get up enough courage I'm going to ask him to criticize some of my poems. After all, the least he could to is refuse or tell me they're all putrid!

I was very disappointed in what I found out about the psych dept. at smith. It is definitely inferior. I am not going to go overboard for this and then back out, so I'll take the course this summer, and probably a semester of Social Disorganization[6] with a brilliant man in the Sociology department,[7] and maybe the Psychology of Personality[8] with a good

1–American poet Allen Tate (1899–1979).
2–French-American historian Jacques Barzun (1907–2012).
3–American Philosopher George Boas (1891–1980).
4–Lithuanian-born American artist, muralist, social activist, photographer, and teacher Ben Shahn (1898–1969).
5–American poet Archibald MacLeish (1892–1992).
6–Sociology 32a, b. 32a: 'Theory of social disorganization; delinquency; crime; and related problems. Psychology 11a and b or 12 may be offered as prerequisite. Th F S 9. Mr DeNood'; and 32b 'Family disorganization; mental deficiency and pathology; and related problems. Optional field trip. Psychology 11a and b or 12 may be offered as prerequisite. Th F S 9. Mr DeNood' (124).
7–Neal Breaule DeNood (1904–72), professor of sociology and anthropology, Smith College, 1937–68.
8–Psychology 37b, 'Study of the psychological organization of the adult personality, with emphasis upon individuality rather than generalized human nature. Basic concepts

woman.[1] Any man who doesn't recognize Freud (who himself is already modified and outdated) isn't worth wasting time on! If I am really interested, I will find out about possible grad work in psych. I am open to all kinds of suggestions about the future at present . . . want to consider every possible angle.

In conclusion, I want to wish you lots of love and felicity on your birthday, and only wish I could be there to help you celebrate. I hope I can convey some good news later this spring as a belated and intangible gift . . .

xxx
sivvy

TO *Russell Lynes*[2]

Friday 24 April 1953 TLS, Library of Congress

Lawrence House
Smith College
Northampton, Massachusetts
April 24, 1953

Mr. Russell Lynes
Harper's Magazine
49 East 33rd Street
New York 16, N.Y.

Dear Mr. Lynes:

Needless to say, I was much elated to receive your letter[3] accepting my three poems.[4] I am eager to know what issues of Harper's they will appear in. Also, since I believe I sent you four pieces, I'd appreciate knowing the titles of the three you chose. In case "Doomsday" is among them, I am

---

and theories; experimental and clinical techniques of investigation; development of adult personality-structure. Open to sophomores by permission of the instructor. M T W 10. Miss Siipola' (117).

1–Elsa Margareeta Siipola (1908–83). SP's calendar for 1953 indicates she met Siipola on 17 and 20 April 1953.

2–American art historian, author, and editor of *Harper's Magazine*, Russell Lynes (1910–91).

3–Russell Lynes to SP, 27 April 1953 in SP's publications scrapbook; held by Lilly Library.

4–Sylvia Plath, 'Doomsday', *Harper's* 208 (May 1954), 29; 'To Eva Descending the Stair', *Harper's* 209 (September 1954), 63; and 'Go Get the Goodly Squab', *Harper's* 209 (November 1954), 47.

enclosing a slightly revised version which (with a purely personal bias) I consider superior to the copy I believe you now have.

You mentioned that you would like some information for your Personal and Otherwise column. Here are some statistics that may be relevant: at present I am a junior honoring in English at Smith College. I'm working my way through Smith on a combination of college scholarships and odd jobs. The jobs generally pay for themselves twice . . . once as a regular salaried position, the second time as subjects for stories and poems. In the last three years, during the summers, I have been a governess for innumerable children, a waitress, a real estate agent's assistant, and a picker on a vegetable truck farm. While at Smith I do a two hour daily stint in the News Office sending out releases for the town paper.

As far a previous publishing goes, it's all been on a level of teen-age and college competition up to now. Seventeen has generously published four stories and five poems[5] in the "It's All Yours" section; the Christian Science Monitor has bought two essays and three poems;[6] and Mademoiselle published my story "Sunday at the Mintons'" in their August 1952 College Issue. So I consider Harper's my first real appearance in the Elysian field of "adult" writing.

Obsessive ambitions for the future include the common desire to take a tilt around the world, from the Blue Grotto to Bali (I've never been out of the New England States), to go to graduate school, to continue working at all kinds of jobs and getting to know all kinds of people, and, like a literary Miniver Cheevy,[7] to keep on writing.

Thank you again for your delightful letter!

Sincerely,
Sylvia Plath

5–The stories were: 'And Summer Will Not Come Again' (August 1950); 'Den of Lions' (May 1951); 'The Perfect Set-Up' (December 1952); and 'Initiation' (January 1953). The poems were: 'Ode to a Bitten Plum' (November 1950); 'Twelfth Night' (October 1952); 'The Suitcases Are Packed Again' (March 1953); and 'Carnival Nocturne' (April 1953). The fifth poem, 'Sonnet to a Dissembling Spring', was not published.

6–The two essays were: 'Rewards of a New England Summer' (12 September 1950) and 'As a Baby-Sitter Sees It' (6 & 7 November 1951). The three poems were: 'Bitter Strawberries' (11 August 1950), 'White Phlox' (27 August 1952), and 'Riverside Reveries' (9 September 1952). Plath did not include 'Youth's Plea for World Peace' which she co-authored with Perry Norton while a senior in high school (16 March 1950).

7–Edwin Arlington Robinson, 'Miniver Cheevy' (1910).

TO *Warren Plath*

Friday 24 April 1953 — TLS in greeting card[1] (photocopy), Indiana University

<printed greeting>

Quelle swell / Occasion belle / I'm all agog / This is der Tag / C'est merveilleux und wunder / And utterly spectacular / (look inside for some)[2] Meilleurs souhaits on your Geburtstag

<signed>

the tyrolean bear / says hallo there / and for someone nice / here's an edelweiss! / love, sivvy

friday, april 24

dearest brother . . .

decided to send you birthday letter for a change . . . combining business with pleasure. you can decide which is which. really angel, there is so much to tell you I don't know where to begin. probably mother has come across with some forests of news, so it may be a bit repetitious. one thing I've decided is that you and I are both pretty darn lucky pipple. by the way, I hear you are going to Beaver. do be nice to Kathy even though she may not be Marilyn Monroe. she can't help that. much! have fun and take a subtle address book to take down names of sundry luscious damsels you meet up with.

am dying to hear what Harvard comes across with. by the way, don't tell mother, but I am applying for a scholarship to Harvard Summer School. she thinks I am just applying, but I hope to surprise her with some money. so that will take care of eight weeks of the summer. in June I will be home writing and reading and getting tan. same with September. so we'll both be acquainted with the place!

I just got out of a week in the infirmary from a dastardly sinus infection, but that didn't prevent me from going out with Gordon (the brilliant senior honors in English at Amherst) saturday. In the afternoon I watched him crew race yale up the connecticut river. he is 6'4" and the best looking guy I've ever gone out with. you shoulda seen him. we talked about you and crew, and I think it would be a most shrewd idear for you to go out for the Harvard crew because Gord said there would be a chance for you getting on . . . very good as Harvard emphasizes crew, and a friend of his

1–Panda Prints birthday card designed by Rosalind Welcher.
2–This phrase is typed by SP.

got on with no experience whatsoever, also tall as you. it would look good to Harvard too to have you really hit a sport. just advice.

anyhow, in spite of the fact I have 50 pages of papers to do before May 20 I am really taking off for weekends. Ray Wunderlich of Columbia Med is treating me to three days of New Yourk . . . the weekend of May 1 . . . also sent me round trip tickets which sweetly saves me ten bucks. maybe he's planning to seduce me or something. the weekend of the 9th, after that, I'm heading to yale for 3 days for the spring college weekend with Mike (Myron) at which I plan to lie in the sun and get tan on various beaches. nice, wot?

this weekend we're having a tremendous symposium on arts and morals at which a stellar array of speakers such as W. H. Auden, Lionel Trilling, Allen Tate, Ben Shahn, George Boas, Jacques Barzun, Archibald MacLeish and a few other notaries. I'm covering the whole whoopedo[1] for the Hampshire Gazette and having all kinds of fun doing it. In Case you are dastardly ignorant as to these men, they are all famous artists, critics, poets and historians. Also by the way, W. H. Auden came to dinner at the house the other night and we all were really thrilled. I had the honor of sitting at his table and almost got to touch the Hem of his Garment. He reminds me of a brilliant, amusing, naughty boy.

best news is my first Professional Acceptance which arrived this morning in the form of a lovely letter from Russell Lynes at Harper's magazine telling me they were buying THREE of my poems for $100 dollars in all! This is my Very First acceptance in professional competition, not just a teen-age contest. That's also the most I've ever got paid per pome . . . about $33.33 each. Plus a penny for bubble gum! Also Mademoiselle just sent me ten bucks for being one of the ten runners up in the last College Board Assignment. Now if I only could sell that 50 page true confession I wrote[2] over spring vacation, we could redecorate the house, buy three convertibles and go to the Riviera for the summer! By the way, Harper's is equally as good (if not better, I now say,) as the Atlantic Monthly!

now that your sister has speiled so long and intricately to her favorite handsome blond man, she would appreciate a liddle news concerning that same enigmatic individual. how about it bebe?

much love and hapuuppappy returns
for your birfday pooh, love piglet
xxxxxxxxxxxxx from me

1–Probably the unattributed 'Literary Speakers Mark Symposium at Smith College', *Daily Hampshire Gazette*, 24 April 1953, 1, 12.
2–Sylvia Plath, 'I Lied for Love'; held by Lilly Library.

TO *Aurelia Schober Plath*

Saturday 25 April 1953 TLS with envelope, Indiana University

saturday, april 25

dearest mum . . .

well, tomorrow is your birthday, and Harper's conveniently came across just in time for me to tell you the news I wanted to: that I got my first real professional acceptance! even now I still can't believe it! although the lovely check for $100 came today. The poems they accepted are two of the villanelles: "Doomsday" and the one you like so much "To Eva Descending the Stair." The third was one I wrote last spring called "Go Get the Goodly Squab." I was most surprised about that one because the Atlantic had already rejected it, and the Smith College jury for the annual poetry contest[1] overlooked it completely last year and gave the prize to another girl.[2] it is one of my favorite exercises in sound, so I'll be most pleased to see it in print in the future.

I must quote you my lovely note from Russell Lynes word for word. I am really going to frame it:

"We've had a couple of your poems here for a long time and do like them very much. The trouble has been that we don't seem to be able to make up our minds which one we like best, and so I'm going to buy all three of them--which isn't just weak-mindedness on our part but real enthusiasm. We'll be sending you under separate cover in a few days our check for $100. I hope you'll send us some information about yourself for our "Personal and Otherwise Column" . . . what your'e doing, what you've published, and so on."

Isn't that just wonderful? Now I can really plan to live in Cambridge, I think. In the same mail I got a $10 check for being one of the 10 runners up in Mlle's last assignment, so all my extra work and your kind typing really paid off.

Just deposited a $24 check for my April Gazette work, and $18 from March, so the wealth is still dribbling in. Each year I have gotten a larger sum, so I just hope True Story comes through with something substantial to decorate our house with. Now I am still barraging the New Yorker . . .

1–The Elizabeth Babcock Poetry Prize is 'awarded annually for the poem adjudged best by a committee appointed by the Department of English. The competition is open to all undergraduates except those who have already won the prize; the poem submitted may not have been printed previously.'

2–The 1952 winner of the Babcock poetry prize was Patience Mather Cleveland (1931–2004); B.A. 1952, theatre, Smith College.

three new poems went off today, and a note asking them about "Mad Girl's Love Song" which I haven't heard about for 2 months.

I am really going to work at this writing deal. Amazingly enough, my poems have really had surprising luck . . hope I can get rid of some more this summer. The Atlantic and the New Yorker remain my unclimbed Annapurnas. Of course, in Harper's I shall be in excellent literary company. Really, I just couldn't sleep all last night, I was so excited. Can't you just hear the critics saying, "Oh, yes, she's been published in Harper's." (Don't worry, I'm not getting smug! I'm just happy that my hard work has gotten such a plum of a reward!)

At last the Symposium is over and I've taken down my last cover. Work is piled up mountain high, and I just hope I get through (as you do) the rest of the year.

Last night I had a celebratory supper at the Brown's and the dears got a whole bottle of champagne to celebrate! I love those people so much, Marty and Mrs. B. If I ever publish a little book of poems I will dedicate it to them. Mentally, I dedicate this Harper's triumph to you, my favorite person in the world.

Now I just want to read and read and study and write and write and study. I have piles of pocket books and others that I want to read this summer . . . they line my shelves with such gay jackets, and I love them with all my heart.

New York next weekend, New Haven the one after that. Then God knows what. I am really so very happy in the house and in my work . . . the long hell of the fall and the broken leg seem to make each present joy that much more of an ecstasy.

xxx to my birthday mummy . . .
sivvy

TO *Aurelia Schober Plath*

Tuesday 28 April 1953[1]

TLS with envelope,
Indiana University

tuesday morning

dear mother,

just a note before the holocaust of the rest of this week to tell you that such wonderful and right things are happening to your tall stubby-nosed

1–Date supplied from postmark.

daughter. yesterday I was elected Editor of the Smith Review for next year . . . the one job on campus that I really coveted with all my heart. so now, with my prize financial job on the Gazette, I'm carrying my full number of points, and have the two activities I really wanted above all.

last night I will never forget. W. H. Auden came to our unit of Modern Poetry and for two hours sat and read and analyzed one of his longest poems. we had beer and little cheese sandwiches on rye bread, and a magnificent man, Dr. Wind,[1] from the art and philosophy department was there, too, and to hear the brilliant play of minds, epigrams, wit and intelligence and boundless knowledge was the privilege of my lifetime. Miss Drew's living room took on the proportions of a book-lined sanctuary, and I never felt such exaltation in my life. the English department in this place is unsurpassed anywhere, and this year, with the symposium and W. H. Auden, was a plumcake of letters and arts genii.

you'd never know I had a written in Milton tomorrow. living at Harvard for 5 days each week for 8 weeks, with meals, would be, at the lowest, $150. I have a feeling that some of my other financial pigeons may also come to roost . . . the ones I have out are the Luckies jingles, the New Yorker, the True Story (god, that should bring <u>something</u> ---at least $100) and of course I am again applying for the college poetry prize, which I doubt a bit if I will get, judging from their oversight last year.

wait'll you hear what I've done. yesterday I went on a shopping spree, and the items I came up with are fit to scream in ecstasy over. I spent a fabulous sum ($85!!!) in one day, but I really hit the jackpot. now I can go to New York and New Haven, Paris for that matter. Really, my summer clothes were all just cottons with big full skirts and unversatile (except for the aqua cotton) personalities.

Yesterday I bought first a divine pair of white linen french heels. then the most divine black pure silk shantung dress you've ever seen in your life . . . very simple sheath with shoestring straps, bare as a slip, for dancing or such, with a shortsleeved black jacket that makes it exquisite for theater or town wear. perfectly classically simple. then I got a suit dress which goes perfectly with the blue topper you sent today . . . it has a strapless sheath dress of blue and white pinstripe cotton cord, and an over-jacket that fits it for train travel with the most heavenly parisian standup collar and long sleeves. unbelievably versatile. the last purchase is a heavy linen textured brown-white-and-black mexican print with a boat neck and shiny black patent leather belt, much on the style of my shiny yellow cotton. as you

1–Edgar Wind (1900–71); professor of philosophy and art, Smith College, 1948–55.

can imagine, they all do wonders for me, and I've never been so sure and Right about clothes before in my life. somehow this is a good time to buy for choice, and I knew just what I wanted and got Exactly what I wanted. someday, if I get a million dollars from true story, I will buy a black linen duster. I feel I have grown up no end. no more dirndls or baby puffs for me . . . all very sleek and suave and stylish. oh, I want so badly for you to see them . . . pictures inside.

mushc lover (now I can't even spell and sound inebriated!)

your ecstatic daughter . . .

sivvy

p.s. please . . . don't scold me about spending the money. I really needed these things & they will be most versatile & wearable – I'll sell more poems, I promise. If Harper's is down, the Atlantic should be feasible—

<drawing of suitdress and jacket with caption
'Suitdress – navy & white pin stripe'>
<drawing of black silk shantung and jacket with caption
'black silk shantung – (very poorly drawn jacket) really beautiful'>
<drawing of Mexican print dress with caption
'black-white-& brown Mexican print linen'>
<drawing of shoes with caption 'white linen shoes'>

Parallax
Major faults in granite[1]

<handwritten by SP>

p.s. ironically enough (I should have waited for my luck to work as usual) The one poem Harper's didn't accept was "Mad Girl's Love Song" which was the one at the New Yorker (My favorite! 1) The New Yorker now has my 3 best recent poems (a long dialogue between Adam & Eve[2] & 2 new villanelles) plus two letters, one cancelling M.G.L.S., the other (2nd) saying to use it if they felt so inclined. God knows what will happen now. Damn them – They should accept one of the four!

Thank god also about Dick's operation – I am visiting a "friend" in New York – make it a girl if you wish. Then I will too.

xx

siv

1 – SP started typing her poem 'Parallax' on this paper, but got no further than the first line.
2 – Sylvia Plath, 'Dialogue En Route'.

TO *Aurelia Schober Plath*

Thurs.–Fri. 30 April–1 May 1953[1] TLS with envelope, Indiana University

THURSDAY NIGHT

Dear mother . . .

just got your sweet special delivery letter, and want to set your heart at ease about my attire for the weekend. I'm bringing a wool skirt and cashmere sweater, in case of chill weather, and invested in a pair of plastic boots this morning, which with my raindana and a black raincoat from a friend in the house should make me quite waterproof. by the way, I just LOVE your topper . . . it goes so beautifully with my new suit that you must have been psychic when you got it.

our Phi Bete dinner tonight was most impressive. our house has five, and is, if I may say so modestly, the most Phi Bete starred house on campus. we all wore formals to the dinner, and Miss Mensel and Mrs. Cook were there in addition to several faculty members invited by each girl who was a Phi Bete. we had all the Faculty Lights, as a diversity of departments were represented . . . science, government, english, and religion! Mr. and Mrs. Robert Gorham Davis, Miss Page (last year's creative writing) and Miss Lincoln[2] (this year's Milton) were all present . . and although I sat at Mary's table, I went and had coffee with my pets afterwards. I wish you could have seen the affair . . so impressive, and I am so proud of our wonderful house.

cross your fingers for me this weekend . . I hope everything goes all right. after all the time I've spent shopping this week, and buying shields and, labor of labors, sewing them on . . . I feel like a housewife, secretary, anything but a butterfly schoolgirl!

Friday morning

RAIN. well, I'm glad it's raining now so I will be All Prepared. the black raincoat I'm wearing is warm and very stylish, with a heavy white lining and multicolored pinstripes. I've decided that it is exactly what I will buy (someday when I earn more money) instead of a duster, because it is not only infinitely more practical, but also beautiful, and can serve as a regular coat. seems as if I'm all for black and white these days. navy accessories and brown things are really impractical because of getting shoes and bags

1–Date supplied from postmark.

2–Eleanor Terry Lincoln (1903–94); English professor, Smith College 1934–68; SP's colleague, 1957–8; SP completed English 39b (Milton) taught by Lincoln in 1953.

to match. I now have a white bag and white shoes, a red bag and red shoes, and some day am going to get a black patent leather bag.

I am so proud of myself now, in my judgment in clothes. I know just what I want and just what I need, and feel most positive and good about it all.

the funniest thing happened this morning. a girl called up and said Mr. Sherk suggested that I tutor her in physical science. I was overwhelmed. of course, since I've missed so many lectures by going away and being sick, it is a physical impossibility, but I was very touched that he suggested me.

I am getting more and more excited about harvard summer school. unfortunately, two other girls from the house are applying, so I hope I get in all right. seems everybody from smith wants to work or study in cambridge this summer! I have now decided what I want to do with psychology, after a fashion. I really don't think I want to go to all the expense and training to be a clinical psychologist . . as far as I know now. the course this summer will help me decide. but I do want to go on with abnormal and personality psych as it is invaluable in conjunction with my writing and studies in english. mr. davis is avid about psychology, and I am very interested in the study of psychology in relation to myth, symbol and metaphor. so in graduate school, I will hope to take abnormal where it is Good. so it works in beautifully with my interest in motivation, etc. somehow, I want to stick to writing . . . and fortunately, instead of being too limiting, I should study innumerable things in connection with it . . . philosophy, art. etc.

bye for now . . . . much love
your peregrinating daughter . . .
sivvy

<on back of envelope>

Ahem!
11 a.m.

Dear mother:

Oh, bother!
Mrs. Bragg[1]
(Alas, alag)
is staying chez elle aujourd'hui
Eh bien, quelle ennui! <drawing of frowning female face>

So I packed my books in a box
And for breakfast had Scotch on the Rocks

1–Frances Bragg (1908–2016).

To give me that je ne sais quoi,
That gay la-de-dah
Attitude,
To give longitude and latitude
To my bad high-hatted mood.
(On Braggs a pox
And some dirty sox!)
<drawing of female face sticking out her tongue>

And so with a sandwich of roast beef. (au jus)
I leef (by bus)
To face papers and etcetera
And polite rejection lettera
At Smith. <drawing of crying female>

In the meantime, an abstract kith
To you for being my mother
Instead of the mother
Of somebody else or other.

Please call Mrs. Bragg to tell her
How much you wish well her
And won't be able to join her Saturday
On her trip to Smith because the latter day
Is the one that Kid Lotz and I will be away
Tooralay! <drawing of smiling female>

If any unprecedented windfall
Should perchance befall <drawing of smile female radiating>
Me, I will call.
That is all.

Take good care of your health progression
While I am on my academic mission
Because when I return in JUNE
I want you to be well in tune
For a gay pot shot
On my shocking pink yacht. <drawing of smiling female>

Love and laughter
From your daft daughter!
(Who gets dafter & dafter!)

TO *Aurelia Schober Plath*

Tuesday 5 May 1953[1] TLS with envelope, Indiana University

Tuesday morning

Dear mother . . .

I have been literally champing to get to the beauteous typewriter and tell you on and on about the magnificent occurences of the last three days, but yesterday was one mad rush to get back into the normal sunshine and orange juice routine of college life again, after the most wonderful weekend, literally, that I have ever had in my twenty years of Life.

Let me begin last Friday morning. Just before I left, my "author's proofs" came from Harper's, all shiny and with another nice letter from Russell Lynes.[2] (I corrected them to-day and am going to send them back . . . he said they'd send me advanced copies when they decided to print them, as they don't know yet . . . I imagine they have to wait and see the space left by the articles.) A welcome $10 check came from 17 yesterday, and said my poem was "unscheduled" which may mean that they're not going to print it or just don't know when. At this point, not caring for the poem, and wanting to write over the whole thing to save the last two excellent clinching lines,[3] I just grab the money and don't care.

Anyhow, to get back to the subject at hand, I donned your lovely Worth blouse and my blue wool suit, red shoes and red bag and white hat, and met my new friend Carol Koch,[4] and took the train. We read, chatted, and dozed during the four hour trip, both of us being very excited and eager to get to the city.

We got into grand central around four (after a sumptuous lunch in the plush dining car of the train, which thrilled me no end.) Carol's date, a short, balding but simply wonderfully kind and intelligent first year man, met us, as Ray was working at the hospital till supper-time. He took us across by shuttle and up by subway to the Columbia Medical Center.

I must confess that I have never seen a place like it in my life. Great tall yellow-bricked buildings shoot up cleanly into the sky, all overlooking Riverside Drive, the Hudson river, the poetic arch of the George Washington Bridge, and the lights of the Palisades across the water. Bard

1–Date supplied from postmark.

2–Russell Lynes to SP, 27 April 1953 in SP's publications scrapbook; held by Lilly Library.

3–The last two lines of SP's 'Sonnet to a Dissembling Spring' are: 'Again we are deluded and infer / That somehow we are younger than we were.'

4–Carol Koch Kaufman (1933–); B.A. 1955, English, Smith College.

Hall,[1] where the boys live, and where Carol and I shared a guest room together, is about 12 stories tall, with a great glassed hall and eating rooms overlooking the river, and all sorts of amazing facilities, like a swimming pool, which the boys are generally too busy to use. I fell in love with the place at first sight.

Carol and I changed for the evening, I getting into my white sharkskin dress, which looked very striking with the dramatically-cut black coat I'd borrowed (which proved ideal for NYtravel . . . didn't show dirt, kept out rain, and looked very swish.)

Ray arrived, and we all took off for dinner. A French restaurant "La Petite Maison"[2] was the one the boys had picked, and never in my life have I partaken of such ambrosial food and enjoyed the linen-clothed, wine-clear atmosphere, with all the ubiquitous French waiters who could remove plates from under you without you noticing. Ray treated me to my first oysters on the halfshell, wine, filet mignon, tossed green salad, and coffee. The cameraderie of our foursome was struck right there, and increased during the weekend to a lovely rapport. Right after dinner (during the meal we had a lovely claret wine) we taxied off to see "The Crucible" by Arthur Miller.[3] A very good play about the witch hunts in Salem . . . and afterwards we went to Delmonico's[4] where we sat around a little table, listening to excellent piano music, and talking long and heatedly about Communism, racial prejudice and religion (our companions were both very liberal jews.) It was a most stimulating evening, the kind where everyone contributes, challenges, and pounds the table in excitement to be heard. Bed came after this at 5 a.m.

Saturday the four of us brunched at 1 p.m. and took the subway to the city center where I saw my First Opera . . . "Carmen".[5] It was just exquisite, and I did enjoy the music.

After that we went to the Cape Coddy "Gloucester House"[6] where we had the best sea food I've ever eaten . . . crabs, clam broth, scallops, biscuits, all sorts of lovely things on the wooden tables, and conversation was brilliant, witty, and one running pun.

We separated after that, the Carol-and-Dick party going back to the dorm to sleep awhile before the dance, Ray and I to see the most

1–Bard Hall is a residential building at 50 Haven Street, New York.

2–Le Petite Maison, a French restaurant. Possibly at 108 E. 60th Street, New York.

3–Performed at the Martin Beck Theatre, at 302 W. 45th Street, New York.

4–Hotel Delmonico, then at Park Avenue and 59th Street, New York.

5–The New York City Opera Company's performance of *Carmen*; performed at the City Center, 131 W. 55th Street, New York.

6–The Gloucester House was at 59 W. 51st Street, New York.

magnificently acted, shockingly surrealistic play I've ever seen in my life . . . Tennessee Williams's "Camino Real".[1] I can't describe it now, it would take too long, but contrary to the review of many good critics who ranted against the hopeless maniac despair of the play, I found that it organized in Williams's own particular way the formless chaos of that part of the world which is real and malignant and pathetically close to hopelessness. In the words of the play itself, it was "a serious circus, a comic strip read backwards."[2] The symbolism was frightening, appealing to the emotions when occasionally baffling the intellect. Between acts Ray and I talked heatedly about the meaning of it, and at the end, we sat in the theater until all the crowds had gone before we went back to Bard. It was the most stimulating, thought-provoking, artistic play I've ever seen in my life!

We arrived at the dance at midnight, and it was just hitting it's height . . . so I slipped off the jacket of my black silk dress, put my hair behind my ears, and presto! was transformed into a danceable date. The dance was the large glass windowed room overlooking the lighted river, and Ray, after I got used to his style, was the most original beautiful dancer I've ever tried to follow. None of this mere conventional face-to-face business . . . it was all swoops, open steps, twirlings under arms, gliding across the hall, singing to the music, and charlestoning like fury in a circle of onlookers. Most gratifying, and a new experience for me.

After the dance, six of us went up to Ray's room overlooking the lighted river from the 7th floor, and drank sherry and listened to music from "Swan Lake" to "Gaite Parisienne" until almost dawn, talking and just relaxing after a packed wonderful day.

Sunday we brunched again at one, all four of us feeling extremely sleepy and languid. We decided to have a restful companionable day instead of seeing a good movie, as planned, so Ray took us up to his lab (also overlooking the river) and spent an hour showing us his pathology slides and explaining them. We then took a tour through the Presbyterian hospital[3] (which even had a built-in chapel with stained glass windows where we sat and listened to organ music awhile) and had our final meal in the hospital cafeteria in the midst of doctors and nurses.

Bidding the boys goodbye at 7, Carol and I took the train back to Hamp after the most perfect weekend we both had ever had.

1–*Camino Real* was performed at the National Theatre, then at 208 W. 41st Street, New York.

2–SP slightly misquotes the play: 'The Camino Real is a funny paper read backwards' (114).

3–The New York Presbyterian Hospital, 722 W. 168th Street, New York.

Just to point out how thoughtful Ray was: he hadn't told me any of the things we were going to see, but on my arrival, handed me two envelopes, one with a humorous typed itinerary with comments,[1] the other full of reviews of the plays we were going to see, plus notices of general artistic interest we were going to discuss. I was really touched.

Knowing me, you can imagine my reaction to the City of New York . . . even the subway rides were enchanting to me . . . and Ray, who is just my height, skinny, and who dresses in Floridian style (more flamboyant than my conservative New England friends) was the most entertaining and intelligent and instructive companion imagineable.

Well, that's that. I am elated by the way that you are to be a ghost-writer. Dobbin nothing! you have a gift in your own line, and between the two of us, we should make a lovely life. I owe all I am to you anyway, for you have made all possible, from my life to my Smith career (I wouldn't want to be anywhere else, I'm so happy here.)

love,
your ecstatic sivvy

<on back of envelope>

p.s. – mentioned casually to dick about date at med. school – makes things so much simpler that way – being <u>honest</u> – so you can be truthful too.

TO *Aurelia Schober Plath*

Friday 8 May 1953 TLS, Indiana University

Friday night . . . in the
midst of a greenish
thunderstorm . . . and
dramatic sheets of rain

Dearest progenitor . . . .

This will probably be the last letter for a few days. You could hardly guess how busy I've been these last days. This morning, for example, there was our last Press Board Meeting, News Office work, and a rush envelope from MLLE with all kinds of lists to be filled out, letters, to be written, and a huge vocational history to be done which took me all afternoon . . . and all had to be sent off air mail special delivery. I am enclosing a release paper for you to sign where indicated, and to send of Immediately to the

1–See SP's Smith College scrapbook, pp. 28–31; held by Lilly Library.

address at bottom. I'm also enclosing a copy of what we'll do as guest editors, which you can peruse and send right back in your next letter . . . I'm too lazy and rushed to type an extra copy.

The month sounds strenuous but challenging and lots of fun. I've already sent in the names of four writers, one of whom I will meet, interview and be photographed with. My tentative choices are: J. D. Salinger ("Catcher in the Rye"[1] and tremendous stories); Shirley "The Lottery" Jackson;[2] E. B. White[3] of New Yorker fame; and Irwin Shaw.[4] Hope one of those luminaries consents to be seen with me!

I'll be staying at the Barbizon hotel[5] at a reduced rate of $15 a week. (Never stayed at a hotel before!) As for clothes, they advise bringing bathing suits, and cool, dark clothes "which will look as fresh at 5 p.m. as at 9 a.m." So next week I am going to pick up a few more dresses, another hat, pajamas, and a few other necessities. Also have to bring a formal.

Now, here is a plan I've been thinking of. You and grammy could drive up around Thursday, May 21, or shortly thereafter, and I could pack all my stuff in the car and go home with you (driving back.) Then I could stay home for about till Tuesday, say, ironing washing and getting everything in spic and span leisurely readiness. Tuesday I could take a small suitcase of necessities back with me, enough to last till my Milton exam sat. morning. Right after my Milton exam I could take the bus home, get a good rest saturday night, and head for New York Sunday afternoon, May 31. Then I'd have time to get settled at the Barbizon and be up the next day for my interview at 9. How does that sound? Let me know when you'll be up.

Right now I am desperately trying to write a Milton paper[6] which I have to get done tonight, as well as packing, for I leave for New Haven tomorrow morning. Monday I have to write a Modern Poetry paper for my unit that night. Also that week, I'll usher for the play "Ring Around the Moon"[7] here to get in free, and do a long feature interview for the

1–American writer J. D. (Jerome David) Salinger (1919–2010); *The Catcher in the Rye* (New York: Little, Brown, 1951).

2–American writer Shirley Jackson (1916–65); her 'The Lottery', *New Yorker*, 26 June 1948.

3–American writer E. B. (Elwyn Brooks) White (1899–1985).

4–American playwright Irwin Shaw (1913–84).

5–The Barbizon Hotel for Women was at Lexington Avenue and E. 63rd Street, New York.

6–Sylvia Plath, 'Chiaroscuro and Counterpoint'; held by Lilly Library.

7–*Ring Round the Moon* is a 1950 adaptation by Christopher Fry of Jean Anouilh's *Invitation to the Castle* (1947). SP covered the play for Press Board, 'Smith College Play Delights 'Hamp Audience', *Springfield Union*, 15 May 1953, 31.

Hampshire Gazette on a girl on campus[1] they want written up. They are very impressed with my work, and on my review of the Evening with Charles Laughton last week,[2] gave me credit by putting my initials after the article. I do enjoy that job!

After Monday night, things should let up a bit. New Yorker keeps sending rejections. Some day I must conquer them too, and keep it up. I get out of New York June 27, and summer school doesn't begin till July 5, so I should have a little time to rest, make a scrapbook to preserve the memories of my month, and do a little advance reading.

I hope you all take it easy with the house decorating, and let Warren do any heavy work, and don't do anything silly yourself just to save money.

Looking most forward to seeing you around Thursday the 21st.

Much love, your enchanted daughter,
Sivvy

TO *Aurelia Schober Plath*

Tuesday 12 May 1953[3] — TLS with envelope, Indiana University

tuesday noon

dear mother . . .

at last I can breathe . . . after rushing off to new haven saturday morning in the glorious sunshine and my very nice blue cord suit . . . I arrived in time for lunch at silliman with myron and attended the afternoon festivities with bob and jill and perry and shirl. everybody was dressed in shorts and shirts and straw hats, and informality beer and suntans were the cry. we all had a picnic out by a lake, lolled in the sun, and dressed to drop in at the timothy dwight dance.[4] after which we changed back to old clothes again and drove miles and miles to the ocean where all six of us had a beach party.

that night I slept in a double bed with shirley and jill on the cot, got up late sunday, in time for a lamb chop dinner at silliman, and spent the beauteous afternoon at lighthouse point with bob and jill where we

1–Sylvia Plath, 'Austrian-born Junior Enlists in Women's Marine Corp, "Can't Wait to Get There"', *Daily Hampshire Gazette*, 16 May 1953, 2. The article was on Antoinette Willard.
2–Sylvia Plath, 'Laughton Holds Audience Spellbound With Readings', *Daily Hampshire Gazette*, 6 May 1953, 3.
3–Date supplied from postmark.
4–Timothy Dwight College, Yale University.

waded, sunned, and played baseball. I acquired a nice sunburn, which in itself made the weekend more than worthwhile. It was all diametrically opposite to last weekend, which was good, because comparison was impossible for that reason. I needed very badly to get some exercise and fresh air out-of-doors, and would never have been able to allow myself that treat if I'd stayed at Smith.

I really paid the penalty for my two days of play when I came back as I had to write two papers on monday for deadlines. I wrote my Drew paper on Auden in the morning, went to my unit for two hours in the afternoon, and from then until after midnight wrote and typed an 11-page paper for milton. I hate doing things at the last minute, but that rush assignment from MLLE came friday and took all day, when I had been planning to do one of my papers. at last, today, I can again breathe, and am now up on the sun roof resting and laconically typing letters.

tonight I'm going out to supper with Marty and Carol Pierson, tomorrow night I'm ushering for our last college play "Ring Around the Moon" so I can get in free. next week is my last unit, and we are taking Miss Drew out to dinner, and on wednesday I plan to go to amherst on a literary pilgrimage with enid to hear dylan thomas[1] give his wonderful poetry readings. I am so thrilled he is coming and that I'll have the chance to hear him.

now my main tasks will be catching up in milton, doing my reading period assignments in the course, and studying for the exam. I just hope my petition to take it sat, may 30 goes through (the regular exam is June 1) as I have to be in New York on May 31.

also I'll have to go shopping for necessaries like the black raincoat, pajamas, a quilted bathrobe, and maybe a dark cotton or silk print dress. meanwhile, I'm making money handoverfist from the hampshire gazette . . . should net over $20 this month, which certainly comes in handy . . . I also hope I can get a tuition scholarship from harvard, but as two other girls from Lawrence are also applying for tuition scholarships, my chances are probably slight.

by the way, I learned many interesting things from bob modlin who had a heart to heart talk with me about the nortons . . . bob is a fine and perceptive boy. evidently perry had just been home the week before, and via the grapevine (I never realized what a convoluted grape vine it was) I discovered that mrs. norton has decided (at this late date) that she doesn't want me for her precious courageous boy anyway, because,

1–Welsh poet Dylan Thomas (1914–53). Thomas read on Wednesday 20 May 1953 at Amherst College.

number one, my summer plans show what a Selfish Person I am. I was really appalled and very hurt. Not only is my not ruining my health as a waitress at saranac proof that I'm Selfish, but so is my going to Harvard Summer School, because I should be working so that you wouldn't have to.

As you may imagine, I feel very chilly toward Mrs. Norton, and really don't care if I ever see her again for all the such-like rationalizations she has made about me now that she sees I'm not serious about her Baby (as in truth I never have given her to understand I was).

Most of all I am concerned about you working this summer. Really, mother, if Warren gets a big enough scholarship, I don't see why you have to work. I can swing Harvard, and my expenses next year, and work the summer after my senior year if I don't get a big enough scholarship to grad school. You could just stay home and rest, and let both Warren and me take care of ourselves financially. I am appalled to think that my going to summer school means that you'll have to slave in town in the heat of the day. Really, I promise to pay for everything myself, out of my Harpers money and Hamp Gazette earnings.

much love,
sivvy

p.s. let me know when you and grammy are coming so I'll be mostly packed. Better bring several suitcases and cartons.

xxx
s.

TO *Aurelia Schober Plath*

Wednesday 13 May 1953 — TLS with envelope, on *Smith Review* Make-Up Sheet letterhead, Indiana University

Wednesday, May 13

Dearest mother . . .

Needless to say, I've been eagerly awaiting news of Warren all week, and your letter with the news of Harvard has set me on topmost peak of the world. I sat right down this morning and wrote him a long 3-page letter of congratulation. I'd give anything to go to his graduation, but the expense and mechanics of the trip are rather prohibitive. We can talk about that when I see you. Does this scholarship mean you won't have to apy anything? I hope so, because I want to be independent, too, next year.

I want very much to talk over finances and get an overall family picture when I come home next week.

Your advice about New York was most appreciated. I am not going to get another hat. I love the white one, and will wear it all the while I am there, and if they get tired of it they can buy me another one. You advice about the food is also agreed wholeheartedly with. I am not going to starve my stomach to put clothes on my back.

I did buy a very lush raincoat yesterday, not black, as I first thought, but the same wide-cut style in a beautiful gray mixture with a lovely rose-pink lining and matching scarf, which looks enough like a coat to be worn even when it doesn't rain, and will not show spots the way the black would have. I am beautifully pleased with it.

I will buy one pair of nice p.j.'s, as I have two blue pairs and a nylon nightgown, and a nice quilted robe, which I need anyway, to go over them. Also I'll need to shop for necessaries like a new garterbelt, more stockings (I guess I'll be wearing them all the time), a new lipstick . . . and I'll have to hunt up that black powder case you once gave me, so I can powder shiny noses (plural because mine is fat!) and I'm going to experiment with wearing my hair back in a neat net, so it won't get all fuzzy and out of place while running around on busses and in offices.

PLEASE PUT A GOODLY SUM OF MONEY IN MY CHECKING ACCOUNT AS SOON AS POSSIBLE, AS I AM DOWN TO ONE DOLLAR . . . one hundred dollars would not be amiss, and you could withdraw it from my bank account. Let me know when I can start using my check book again.

I have spent as much money this year on clothes as I spent my freshman year on everything combined, but I feel that as far as the New York trip goes, I'm investing in my future. I've always wanted to try "jobs on like dresses and decide which fit best", and now I'll have the chance to see what it's like living in the Big City, plus working on a magazine! As you say, the intangibles are most exciting and important. I could work as a secretary for years before I got a break at experience like this one. And I'm going to put myself completely and willingly in the hands of the magazine, and, as you say, be as cooperative and eager as I was at the Cantors.

Now that Warren is set in college, his first choice, and me loving every precious minute of beautiful, stimulating Smith, with the wonderful girls in Lawrence House, and the fun-job at the News Office, and the marvelous instructors in my department and out . . . and the gala weekends at Columbia Med and Yale, I am most happy for our little happy-family.

I only hope that summer teaching doesn't prove too much for you. I gather you've had ulcer trouble recently, and hope that you don't let anything the Nortons do or say throw you off balance. Once Dick gets out of that Place, I can talk to him directly again, without all this meddling. I can understand the Norton's position, but do think that Mrs. Norton's maternalism is making her, as Bob Modlin said, like a mother animal with unreasoning concern for the welfare of her young at the expense of everyone else.

From what I gather, Mrs. Norton has decided, as I said, that I am selfish in not sacrificing MLLE and summer school (not even considering that I have to have a pre-requisite course for future work) and working as a waitress or mother's helper, or some such, again. I hope seriously that I can write this summer, maybe sell an article to the Monitor about my month in New York, or a story written for O'Connor . . . and also hope that if I don't get a prize from True Story, that I can send the story out to other magazines, and earn some money that way. So if Mrs. Norton feels that I am such a beast, she should be relieved that I feel the same way about Dick now that I felt before he was incarcerated. His circumstances have put this whole normal friendly situation in an artificial light, and I don't want you to have to bear the brunt of their pressure group.

I believe in being honest at all costs, except that of hurt feelings, and I can hold up my head and say that I have played straight through this whole thing. I exacted no promises when Dick was so dead certain that his future was selfishly all set with no room for change or flexibility, and when he thought I wanted too much out of life. Now that he is more humble and ready to snatch at the nearest security, which is me, I don't see how I can do more than be a continuous friend, write frequent letters (they take up a good part of my time and thought) and act toward him the way I always have, with No Strings Attached. I am fond of him as a person, but as I have said a million times, there are innumerable reasons why it would be suicide to be "serious" about him. I just hope that with all her resentful talk about my selfishness in not slaving to be near her son while she runs around Europe won't spoil my tentative and embryonic friendship with Myron, who, by the way, is very emotionally insecure and uncertain of who he is. I wonder so often how many people are capable of reciprocal love today. His talk is all of himself, and his problems.

I don't want you to get unduly concerned over this Dick affair. After all, I can't fake something I don't feel just for the sake of the Nortons' convenience and peace of mind. Your safest bet if they prod you for information as to my feelings is to say that I feel the same way about him as I did before he went away, emphasizing the fact that I dated other boys all last summer, and that he knew about it. You might also bring up innocently that it seems strange Dick never mentioned his "love" or wanted to commit himself before he went away. And after all, I disagree with the Nortons' policy of working at jobs, like waiting, with no future except immediate cash. Phil McCurdy needs money even more than they do, and is insuring his future with his summer jobs at the Jackson lab. Mike is doing what he loves and getting paid for it. I think it is shortsighted to waste summers at work which prepares one for nothing if there are other possibilities of earning a little and getting experience at the same time. Which is what I am doing by going to MLLE and summer school. (Which I also hope will help develop my technique and knowledge of the short story.)

In addition, you can say that you feel uncapable of making statements of my ideas and attitudes, that the grapevine which the Nortons have nurtured with such avidity runs the risks of distortion and misrepresentation, which I certainly feel, after talking with Bob Modlin last weekend. Mr. Norton may be stiff and awkward, but it is Mrs. Norton that I will never be able to forgive for what she has said about me. It was very uncalled for, and she should be more mature than that.

I just hope that if my going to summer school makes it necessary, in your mind for you to work, that you resign work immediately on grounds of doctor's orders and your ulcer, because, I plan, as I said, to be independent next year. I can pay the $600 from my bank account, and with the money in my bank here ($300) and my earnings next year on Press Board (should be well over $150) I can take care of expenses.

Enough about that family. I can just imagine that if I were in Dick's place that Mrs. N. would smile sweetly, shake her head, and say that a doctor couldn't risk the liability of a tubercular wife. And she'd also emphasize the fact that he'd never even gone steady with me, but liked me as a "cousin." Well, a cousin is all I'll ever be to That family. I really am most disgusted with them.

I look most forward to seeing you and grammy Thursday. I plan to wash, iron, starch, and get all my clothes hanging up in the closet in readiness to be packed the following saturday when I come home. I'll have to discuss the baggage problem with you, too. Hope it's nice so you can have a walk about the lovely Smith campus. All the dogwood is out this week.

Much love to you all. Can't wait to see the papers for the house . . .

xxx

sivvy

TO *Warren Plath*

Wednesday 13 May 1953[1] — TLS (photocopy) on Smith College News Office letterhead, Indiana University

FLASH: FLASH: FLASH: CONGRATULATIONS!
CONGRATULATIONS! CONGRATULATIONS!

Dearest Harvard Man . . . .

"Oh, I on-ly date a man if his shoes are white" . . . I am so proud of you that I can hardly keep from leaping up and down and shouting liddle 'ip-'oorays all over the Smith campus. So Harvard came across with a National! And best of all, they Won't Let You Work during the year. That is what I call princely.

After seeing the freshman scholarship boys at Yale in White Coats waiting on the Rich Ones and their dates all weekend, I am very glad you don't have to undergo the strenuous work program they have, because in order to keep up your marks you would have to work at studies all the time you weren't working at a job. This way, at Harvard, you should be able to try for all A's, or something close to it, while going out for a sport (That is really a Must, as you no doubt know . . . colleges don't want Just Brains all the time.)

At least you won't make the mistake I did my freshman year by innocently not taking a paying job at school (no one told me or suggested it) and thusly having my scholarship lowered the next year because I was "lazy and didn't work". Thank God I have this News Office Job now, because it's lots of fun and experience, and I'm in continual contact with the town paper, plus the fact that I've cleared about $150 at it this year. Should do about the same next year.

Tell me, now, how much is left for you to cover? Will mother have to pay anything? I hope not, because she is really down to rock bottom, and I gather from her letters that she is having ulcer trouble, although she is very brave and gay about eating baby foods again. I hope that I too can pay for everything next year, in spite of summer school (I just wish Harvard would come across for me too on June 1!) and New York.

Now, I think you and I should have a plan to make mother rested and happy this summer, in spite of the fact that she is teaching. As you know, the house is being decorated (for which I'm infinitely glad, as now I can bring boys home without keeping the lights down very dim and hoping

1–Date supplied from internal evidence.

they won't see the spots and tears in the wallpaper . . . and you can feel proud to bring girls home during college.) And obviously this is a big financial chunk out of mother's almost nonexistent bank account. So if we can continue to completely support ourselves these next years (if ONLY my True Story would pay, I'd keep our pot of caviar boiling by writing more such sordid money makers. Ironically enough, all my attempts to earn money by prostituting my talent, e.g., by writing hundreds of Lucky strike jingles, have been silent, while Big Money has come from all my attempts at artistic satisfaction without care for remuneration, e.g. MLLE and Harper's.)

One thing I hope is that you will make your own breakfasts in the a.m. so mother won't have to lift a finger. That is the main thing that seems to bother her. You know, as I do, and it is a frightening thing, that mother would actually Kill herself for us if we calmly accepted all she wanted to do for us. She is an abnormally altruistic person, and I have realized lately that we have to fight against her selflessness as we would fight against a deadly disease. My ambition is to earn enough so that she won't have to work summers in the future, and can rest, vacation, sun, relax, and be all prepared to go back to school in the fall. Hitherto, she's always been rushed and tired, and her frailty worries me.

She can't take big problems or excitements without staying awake all night, and so our main responsibility is to give her the illusion (only now it hardly seems like an illusion) that we're happy and successful and independent. After extracting her life blood and care for 20 years, we should start bringing in big dividends of joy for her, and I hope that together we can maybe plan to take a week down the cape at the end of this summer . . . what do you think about that?

If we could go after I get out of summer school at the last week in August, or right after labor day when expenses are down, we could read, relax, and just be together. I don't know where the car will be, or what you think about it, but we could both chip in and treat her to a week in a cabin, maybe around Brewster, or Falmouth, or somewhere. Let me know what you think about this little light bulb of a plan.

In a way, I'm awfully sorry I won't be home in june to help with the house and cooking, but as mother probably told you, being one of the 20 winners in the U.S. of this month in New York is a dream of an opportunity for invaluable job experience, and I feel like a collegiate Cinderella whose Fairy Godmother suddenly hopped out of the mailbox and said: "What is your first woosh?" and I, Cinderella, said: "New York", and she winked, waved her pikestaff, and said: "Woosh granted."

I'll be working on a five-day week schedule, doing grubby work, getting experience, meeting my favorite famous person and having my picture taken with him or her (I sent in a list of my pet writers whom they're going to try to get me an interview with one of . . . lovely syntax, wot?) and going to a theater opening, a starlit roof, and all sorts of clothes places. I should be a veteran of subways, busses, and New York modes when I come back to the bucolic pastures of home.

After the fabulous weekend with Ray, which included filet mignon and wine a la Petite Maison, lobster at the Gloucester House, "Carmen" at the City Center, "Camino Real" by Tennessee Williams and "The Crucible" by Arthur Miller, plus a tour of the medical center and a dance overlooking the Palisades, I'm excited to death at the prospect of living there for 4 gala weeks.

I get home at the end of June, and will have a week to recuperate, talk endlessly and tell you all about it. Then 8 weeks of living in you future home town at Cambridge, coming home on weekends to study, help around the house, and visit with you. Also will have to start reading for my thesis topic.

So glad you read Joyce . . . it'll be such fun having someone special to discuss my problems with.

(next page, if you have the strength)

After last weekend in the sunny beer-and-blanket-and-beach-party atmosphere at New Haven with Mike, I came back with a great sunburn, plenty of salt air in my lungs, and a jolly guilt complex, as I had two papers to write Monday. Stayed up way after midnight typing an 11-page paper on the light and music symbolism in Milton's "L'allegro and Il Penseroso", and collapsed in bed after writing and typing at a furious pace all day. Really, I have only had about five or six really tense times like that during the year (that's enough, brother) and the rest of the time is chock full with News Office Work, and Smith Review (did mother tell you I'm Editor of that luminous lit mag next year? I'm most happy, cause I love the work) and waitressing, and shopping, and all sort-s of menial labor.

Really, you and I have it good. Food, clothes, best schools in the country . . . our first choices, and all sorts of prizes, etc. Seems we lead a charmed plathian existence. Just hope the world doesn't blow up and queer it all before we've had our good hard lives lived down to the nub.

So much remains to talk about: philosophies of life, aims, attitudes. At least we can be best companions, all honesty and help to each other. I am so proud of you, and want the very best for you in the world. Hope that you can profit by all my mistakes, and a few of my lucks and successes!

Be good, and keep a cool and level head (soaking it in beer often helps).

One thing, when you get all success like us, you have to be damn careful because many people secretly would like to see you fall off your proud stallion into the mud, because, no matter how good friends they are, they can't help but be a bit jealous. I find it expedient to keep quiet about the majority of my publications, for instance, because friends can rejoice with you for just so long without wishing they were in your place, and envying you in spite of themselves. It's sad, but that's the way it goes.

One exam remains, at the end of May, and the interim will be taken up with sunning, studying on back work for it, getting a printer for next year's magazine, and working in the News Office . . . all very pleasant liesurely tasks.

Here's hoping I see you within a little over a month.

Much much love
and more felicitations,
your very proud
Sivvy

TO *Aurelia Schober Plath*

Thursday 14 May 1953[1]

TLS/ALS on *Smith Review*
Make-Up Sheet letterhead,
Indiana University

thursday night

dear mother . . .

just a note to say that life goes on fast and furiously, as if on a constantly accelerating record turntable. tuesday I had a lovely cheap ($1.30) steak dinner at a favorite diner with marciandcarol after which we took a therapeutic drive out in the lovely greenery of the evening country side and blew off steam acquired while writing papers under top heat. now there is a blessed interim betwixt papers and my exam. college is beautiful, dogwood verdant, and full of lovely brilliant talented people.

my work at the hampshire gazette is as profitable as I want to make it. I'm getting a precious byline for my writeups of all the Northampton seniors who are graduating,[2] and just interviewed the one girl[3] from Smith

1–Date supplied from postmark.

2–Sylvia Plath, 'Many Area Students Are Among the 464 Who Will Get Smith Degrees on June 8', *Daily Hampshire Gazette*, 20 May 1953, 8.

3–In the margin SP wrote '10:15 quiet hour'; at this point the letter goes from being typewritten to handwritten.

who is joining the marines and wrote up a 6-page article on her. Besides teaching me alot about people, and getting pay for it, I'm keeping clippings of my reviews and such for possible job leads later . . . never can tell when all my news office experience will come in handy – I've gotten in the habit of writing pithy, concise paragraphs, and the style is becoming pleasantly natural. Last night I ushered at a delightful performance of "Ring Round the Moon" and tonight I wrote up a review of it and phoned it collect just now to the Springfield Union, where I read it word by word to the man at the teletype. I don't think I could ever get blasé about working with writing. It's such fun – the man at the Gazette showed me all around the shop today. I also just totted up my year's earnings and found I've cleared $170 so far this year. When you think of it, 2 hours a day of work is a respectable amount!

They're being very cryptic about changing my exam from the fatal June 1. I managed to worm out of the Registrar that "it's all right" to plan to go to NYC the 31st, but as to the verdict of the Administrative Board about when my exam is, she won't tell me till next week as my case is "very peculiar." God Knows what that means. I'll call at the beginning of the week if there is any drastic change in plans.

xxx
sivvy

TO *Aurelia Schober Plath*

Friday 15 May 1953[1]

TLS with envelope, on *Smith Review* Make-Up Sheet letterhead, Indiana University

Friday morning . . . rain

Dearest mother . . .

One nice thing about rainy days . . . I'm sure of getting some studying done instead of lolling amidst dogwood blossoms on the sunroof next door.

I don't know what I'd do if I didn't have such a wonderful and understanding mother as you are. Your letters are a constant joy. I hope your decision about resting up this summer becomes final immediately. Considered rationally, your working would be absurd. Next fall you want to start work rested and healthy, and you need a backlog of relaxing in the

1–Date supplied from postmark.

sun in our yard, reading magazines, tanning, and having lovely talks with me when I come home on weekends from summer school. You should be able to be a rested mother all summer as your fledglings are now able to take care of themselves financially.

The carfare and just the mechanics of daily teaching are formidable. I forbid you to work this summer! Also, Mrs. Norton can thusly just swallow her nasty correlation of my loafing at summer school and your slaving in the same city. I may be naive, but I am not selfish. I would give up summer school at a moment's notice if it were necessary financially. However, with the training and openings it may well provide, and with my earnings of $1000 in the past year alone through writing ($500 MLLE, $250 SEVENTEEN, $100 Harper's, $$170 News office) I hardly need to stoop to waitressing or fileclerking.

I hope maybe you can write a bit this summer, articles about your teaching job, or about medical shorthand opportunities for one of the women's magazines. They like things like that, vocational slants, and with your knowledge, and your lectures for classes, you could make your work salable twice. I'd love to edit for you. Also, at leisure, you might take a few of your many experiences and try the True Confession market again. Not that I'm plugging the field, but once you got the formula, you could make tidy sums and the more you did it the easier it would be. Of course sharpening up writing again, once it's rusty, is very painful and almost prohibitive, as the "Oh, why should I waste my time doing something that will never be published" attitude is easy to have. But you deserve to pamper yourself increasingly now that the hardest 20 years of your life are over, and you deserve all the returns you can get from your wonderful selfless work and help to Warren and me, who love and admire you more than anyone else in the world. You have managed to create a warm, loving, intelligent, family unit, where pride and love in mutual achievement makes us all very close. I never know anyone for long before I start holding forth with pride about grammy and grampy and you and Warren. Smith and all the opportunities now opening only make me want to affirm[1] my rich heritage all the more!

If my True Story offers anything substantial, I would like to treat the three of us to a week in a cabin down the Cape at the end of the summer . . . that has long been a private little dream of mine!

I wrote immediately to MLLE asking permissions to go to Warren's graduation. I love that boy so that I couldn't bear not to be there or

1 – 'only ~~want~~ make me want to affirm' appears in the original.

to disappoint him. The only thing that bothered me was the expense involved. I don't see how they can refuse my request, and so tell Warren that I'm working hard at coming.

Between the three of us we'll show the Norton's that we are all paragons of forgiving selflessness.

Love to grammy, grampy, and specially you . . . .

I insist that you be a scandalously dilettante mother this coming summer!

best love,
sivvy

<on back of envelope>

p.s. Bought that tremendously stylish raincoat – gray mixture with lush pink lining – that can double as coat & duster – so much more practical than black which would have to be spot cleaned!

xxx
sivvy

TO *Aurelia Schober Plath*

Monday 18 May 1953[1]

TLS on *Smith Review* Make-Up Sheet letterhead, Indiana University

Monday morning

Dear mother . . . .

Your era of opportunity sounds like work, but I too am sure you will do a good job. Humor and emphasis on the past indignities of women, as contrast to the wealth of job opportunities to-day, should make the address an excellent one.

It amuses me that your deadline, May 26, is the same as mine from MLLE, who just wrote me my first assignment for a two page spread on five young teacher-poets.[2] Needless to say, it's a big challenge to condense information in catching, vital captions, and to do research on such relatively obscure people, plus layout, which I've never done before. It of course comes at a very crowded time, and it will be nice to be able to devote myself wholeheartedly to the magazine in June without worrying about academic obligations.

1–Date supplied from postmark.

2–Sylvia Plath, 'Poets on Campus', *Mademoiselle* 37 (August 1953), 290–1; discussed William Burford, Anthony Hecht, Alastair Reid, George Steiner, and Richard Wilbur.

Yesterday, a gloomy sunday, the R. G. Davises invited me over to dinner again, as they had a pretty Polish girl who had worked for them last summer and is going to be a freshman at Smith next year coming also. I stayed till four, enjoyed sherry, a good dinner, strawberry shortcake and converstaion and the two absolutely beautiful children.[1] Mrs. Davis is an intriguing woman, and next year, at the beginning of school, I am going to make an appointment to interview her. She has just sold a story to McCall's, was once editor of a True Story magazine, writes True Stories, and used to write for the New Yorker. She writes and manages a home and a brilliant husband all admirably, and they live down the Cape in the summer. Tentatively she recommended my Not writing True Stories, as that market is a heartbreaking one with even more competition than the good literary markets . . . and my getting a job where I will learn about people and life . . . which is a good bit of advice, one which concerns me . . . should an embryonic writer go on to school work in publishing (she says no) or get any kind of job and write on the side. If I could write about my work and the people in it, I would be happy no matter what I was doing.

This summer at MLLE I am going to take private polls on my questions. They will probably have a "jobs and Futures" panel again, and I'll have a chance to fin-d out a lot there.

Myron came up Saturday afternoon, and our goodbye day together was a most pleasant one. First we climbed to the house at the very top of Mount Holyoke and basked in the sun and surveyed the lovely green world for a while. Then we drove to springfield, and I sat for an hour and a half watching him pitch batting practice to his brothers team, the Springfield Cubs. After which I took him to see float night on the banks of Paradise, which is always very impressive with the singing from the Island, the colored lanterns all reflecting in the pond, and the pretty canoe floats. Then I treated us both to a steak dinner at the college diner at about 10.30, after which we went for a drive, had a good talk, and said so long.

I finally brought up the subject of Dick and the Nortons, because I was damned if I was going to have him go away for the summer with a lot of distortions festering in his head. He was very sweet as I explained a few things. Also said that he thought I was "eugenically minded" and thus should very well feel wary of picking a tubercular-prone husband for my children, which I thought was very understanding. Anyhow, I got that subject out in the open, and feel better about it.

1–Lydia Davis (1947–) and Stephen H. Davis.

Tuesday, dear Mary Ellen Chase has invited me over to her house for coffee with a few other girls before she goes up to her place in Maine. I must love her and have enjoyed these conversational sessions no end. The English department here is the best in the U.S. as far as I'm concerned, and the faculty is superlative anyway. Next year I really want to concentrate on academic work, as it is a very difficult and crucial year.

Tuesday night, we're taking Miss Drew out for dinner. She also is a most brilliant and lovely woman . . . very friendly with Auden, who is leaving this week after a final speech tonight.[1]

The registrar is very cryptic about my exam, as I went in again today and she won't tell me anything about when my exam is. I told her I was planning to go home Thursday, and she said to come in again tomorrow. So if there are any last minute changes, I'LL have to call, I guess. If you don't hear from me, just come up the way we've planned.

Have two very nice black bylines in the Hampshire Gazette this week . . . one for my interview of the Smith marine-to-be and the other for writeups of the Northampton seniors to graduate. Also my review (without byline) of the play was printed in the Springfield Union . . . I'm going to keep my clippings all together in case I ever need them for a job. They should come in handy, as they show my "versatility".

The "New Yorker" rejected my last batch of poems, so I am going to let them rest for a while, and try some really special poetry writing slanted to them this summer if I can. Maybe I'll try some prose, if anything good evolves out of Frank O'Connor's course. More than anything now, I realize I have to Live and Work with People . . . instead of forever being sheltered in this blissful academic environment where all the girls are the same age and have the same general range of nervous tensions and problems. My summer experiences have proved most versatile in story-background data.

Enclosed is a vitamin bill. Can insurance pay it?

xxxx
sivvy

1 – Auden's speech, 'Balaam and His Ass', was given in Sage Hall at 8:00 p.m.

TO *Warren Plath*

Thursday 21 May 1953[1] | TLS (photocopy), Indiana University

Thursday . . . just this minute got home . . . .

Dear broad jumper . . .

(Whenever I tell anyone what a good broad jumper you are they invariably say: "How many broads can he jump at once?") This is mainly to tell you that I will be up at Andover before the meet Saturday to cheer you on. I hope I can find out from liddle boys where the track or whatever you jump on is. I will be most eager to see you in action! It will be more than fun to drive home with you and get in a good talk.

I'm coming home between exams, and MLLE just sent me a whopping assignmentwhichIhavetodorightawaythisweekend.It'sablurb,captionand two-page spread on five young-teacher-poets, and a plum of an assignment, but a hell of a lot of quick work which has to be off for a monday deadline.

On Tuesday, I'm interviewing Elizabeth Bowen,[2] the famous Anglo-Irish writer, who will be in Cambridge[3] for the day, and having my picture taken with her. Which means I have to read several novels and stories about Her before Tuesday.

All during this time I have to wash, iron and array and pack clothes for my trip. A week from Saturday I have my Milton exam for which I have a month's back work to do. I shall probably flub it and get an abysmal B which will infuriate me no end as I've gotten all A's for the first time this year so far.

Anyhow, add all these things together and you will get a harassed sister. I'm looking for'ard to sleeping while I'm home as I'm real exhausted. So be prepared to see me wukkin away at the typewriter this weekend, and reading like mad. If I get all these things published in MLLE it will get me a tremendous reputation.

1–Date supplied from internal evidence.

2–Anglo-Irish writer Elizabeth Bowen (1899–1973).

3–The interview took place in the house belonging to American writer May Sarton at 14 Wright Street, Cambridge, Mass. To prepare for the interview, SP checked out *The Death of the Heart* (1938), *Seven Winters* (1942), *Ivy Gripped the Steps* (1946), and *Early Stories* (1951) from the Neilson Library. Smith College holds the borrower's cards for several of these books with 'S. Plath '54' listed as a borrower.

By the by, in our last award assembly, I find I got the Two Poetry prizes[1] in the college. Money is involved, Thank the Lord, but I'm not sure how much yet. Mebbe even another $100. Or suthin.

So I'm slaving this week, but it's all worth it.

See you Saturday, rain or shine.

Much love . . .
your own sivvy.

TO *Aurelia Schober Plath*

Wednesday 3 June 1953[2]

ALS with envelope,
on *Mademoiselle* letterhead,
Indiana University

9:30 Wednesday night[3]

Dear mother . . .

So incredibly much has happened so quick and so fast these last 3 days that I have been too tired to do more than drop into bed at night without a thought of correspondence. For the first time I feel that I can look around me and assimilate (not just gape in amaze at) all that goes on around me.

A brief history: ate on train to NYC. Two lovely muscular members of the US soldiery took one suitcase each (I would have had a hemorrhage) carrying them!) at Grand Central, called me a taxi in the predatory crowd, accompanied me to the hotel & left me at the desk with all good wishes. So I didn't have to lift a finger! I was really touched.

Barbizon is exquisite – green lobby, light cafe-au-lait woodwork, plants, etc. Whooshed up to the 15th floor[4] where I have the darlingest single (we all do) imagineable. Green wall-to-wall rug, pale beige walls, dark green bed-spread with rose-patterned ruffle, matching curtains, a desk, bureau, closet, and white enameled bowl growing like a convenient mushroom from the wall. Bath, shower, toilet, a few doors down the hall. Radio in wall, telephone by bed – and the view!

1 – SP won the Elizabeth Babcock Poetry Prize and the Ethel Olin Corbin Prize. The Corbin prize is 'awarded for the best original poem (preferably blank verse, sonnet or ballad) or informal essay by an undergraduate'.

2 – Date supplied from postmark.

3 – All dates and activities in SP's June 1953 letters obtained from her calendar and *Mademoiselle* materials; held by Lilly Library.

4 – SP's room number was 1511.

From my window I look down into gardens, alleys, to the rumbling 3rd avenue El, down to the UN, with a snatch of the east River in between buildings! At work at night at my desk I look down into a network of lights, and the sound of car horns wafts up to me like the sweetest music. I love it.

The other guest eds are intriguing – about four are superlatively beautiful (could be Paris models) – the rest are attractive, vital, varied & intelligent from all over the U.S. – we even have a Mormon among us!

Monday we breakfasted at the drug store downstairs where I can get fruit juice, egg, 2 pieces of toast, & coffee for 50¢ – good & substantial. My worst experience was getting all dressed up in my suit, just ready to go, and suddenly having a malicious nosebleed – all over my suit (which is now at the hotel cleaners.) Wore my brown dress instead.

Whooshed up to the 6th floor of 575 Madison, spent morning with other Eds filling out endless forms & job data in mirrored dk. green & pink conference room which is our head-quarters – interviews were scheduled with Eds of Depts. we were interested in – I talked with Rita Smith, Fiction Editor (also sister of Carson MacCullers![1]) – Polly Weaver,[2] Jobs & Futures Ed (who had my job on Press Board when she was at Smith) and Betsy Talbot Blackwell,[3] fabulous Editor in Chief.

For lunch, we split up among the Eds, who took us out. 3 of us went to the Drake room[4] with BT Blackwell & Cyrilly Abels,[5] (managing ed.) It was thrilling: sat in dark plush room, sipped sherry, plowed through enormous delectable chef's salad, discussed writers, magazines, all sorts of exciting things.

Afternoon – rewrote poetry squibs[6] again, pictures taken of all of us for "Jobiographies feature" – Don't mind the violent ink, but I just ran out & had to borrow. Anyhow, I've worked in the office till 6 all 3 nights so far – at last, today, Cyrilly Abels pronounced my poet-feature ready to go to the proof-room – when I see the work & research some of the other guest eds had to go through during their exams I consider myself fortunate.

Monday I unpacked dresses (formal came today) after a late, exhausted supper in the cafeteria downstairs. Yesterday a.m. we saw our first (my first) fashion show at the Roosevelt Hotel.[7]

1–American writer Carson McCullers (1917–67).
2–Polly Weaver Crone (1900–2003); B.A. 1922, English, Smith College.
3–Betsy Talbot Blackwell (1905–85); editor-in-chief of *Mademoiselle*, 1937–71.
4–The Drake Room was a restaurant in the Drake Hotel, 432 Park Avenue, New York.
5–Cyrilly Abels (1904–85); managing editor of *Mademoiselle*, 1950–early 1960s.
6–Sylvia Plath, 'Poets on Campus'.
7–On 2 June 1953; the Roosevelt Hotel, 45 E. 45th Street, New York.

It was exquisite – all the clothes to be featured in the August issue – all really lush – gorgeous models – all campus fashions, music, Princeton singers, exhibit of styles – I listened avidly, learned lots & lots.

Lunch at plush Oyster Bar in Grand Central[1] – afternoon – worked & finished another poets write-ups.

Assignments announced – one of my best friends from Washington State is Ed-in-Chief[2] – I'm Managing Ed & moved my typewriter into Cyrilly Abels office today. At first I was disappointed at not being Fiction Ed, but now that I see how all-inclusive my work is, I love it.

I work in her office, listen surreptitiously to all her conversations on telephone & in person, read all copy – & probably do a lot of "managing" – deadlines, dirty work, etc. – but it's fun – her secretary[3] is a girl I knew at Smith last year, so all is relatively un-tense now, almost homey, in fact.

I have to write comments on all the stuff I read – just got through criticizing Elizabeth Bowen's speech[4] she gave the very day I talked to her – intellectually stimulating – also will have a chance to criticize poetry, etc., so my fiction interests are <u>included</u> here, too.

Last night, typed up final draft of poets to count till late. Deadlines should slacken soon. Will work hard, but love it.

All morning we spent at the mall in lovely Central park having our pictures taken in star formation, looking up, dressed in <u>Mlle's</u> own tartan skirts, shirts & caps – very cute – all 20 of us.

During lunch, I discovered a Child's on 5th Ave,[5] love it – <u>good</u> reasonable food – probably will haunt it often. <u>Great</u> fruit salad, pea soup & croutons & buttermilk for $1.10. Healthy & tasty.

Afternoon – working in Abels office.

This week has no night activities, but affairs scheduled afterwards include Fashion tours (e.g. John Frederics hats[6]), UN[7] & Herald Trib[8]

1–The Oyster Bar is a restaurant in Grand Central Station at 89 E. 42nd Street, New York.
2–Madelyn Mathers (1931–); University of Washington.
3–Anita Myers Luery (1930–2003); B.A. 1952, English, Smith College.
4–Elizabeth Bowen, 'The Technique of the Novel', given on 26 May 1953, at 4:30 p.m., at the Boston University College of General Education, 785 Commonwealth Avenue, Boston, at a meeting held at the Boston University Graduate English Club.
5–Child's Restaurant had a branch at 604 Fifth Avenue, New York.
6–On 18 June 1953; John Frederics Hats was at 29 E. 48th Street, New York.
7–On 18 June 1953; United Nations, 760 United Nations Plaza, New York.
8–On 22 June 1953; *The New York Herald Tribune*, 230 W. 41st Street, New York.

tours, movie preview,[1] City Center ballet,[2] "Misalliance,"[3] TV show[4] – Dance at St. Regis Roof[5] & dinner – sounds exotic, what?

Oh, yesterday p.m. – went to Richard Hudnut[6] – got shampoo (very convenient as I just started my period) and little trim – refused drastic cutting, still look like me. Alas.

glad about $75 from Harvard. Every little bit helps.

please sign enclosed form – face cloth or two would be nice. Be <u>good</u> to yourself – Warren's paper sounds fine –

love – your managing ed
syrilly

TO *Aurelia Schober Plath*

Monday 8 June 1953 — TLS on *Mademoiselle* letterhead, Indiana University

June 8, 1953

Dearest mother . . .

Life passes so fast and furiously that there is hardly time to assimilate it. I'm going to bed early tonight, as the rest of the week is pretty fully scheduled. Tomorrow night I'm going to attend the Herb Shriner television show with 3 other guest eds . . . we have guest tickets. Wednesday is the big dinner and formal dance at the St. Regis for all the guest eds and sundry men . . . don't know whom. Just hope I meet some interesting guys so I can go out without paying for it myself and see New York. Thursday is the City Center Ballet.

Work is continuous . . . I'm reading manuscripts all day in Miss Abels office, learning countless lots by hearing her phone conversations, etc. Reading manuscripts by Elizabeth Bowen, Rumer Godden,[7] Noel

1–On 17 June 1953; *Let's Do It Again* at 729 Seventh Avenue, New York.

2–On 11 June 1953; City Center Ballet at 131 W. 55th Street, New York. Performed that night were *The Duel*, *Scotch Symphony*, *Illuminations*, and *Metamorphoses*.

3–On 23 June 1953; at the Barrymore Theatre, 243 W. 47th Street, New York. *Misalliance* (1910), a play by Irish playwright George Bernard Shaw (1856–1950).

4–On 9 June 1953; Herb Shriner's television show *Two for the Money*, which ran in 1952–7. Herbert Arthur Shriner (1918–70), American television host. The location was the International Artists Studio, at W. 58th Street and 8th Avenue, New York.

5–On 10 June 1953; St Regis Hotel, 2 E. 55th Street, New York.

6–On 2 June 1953; Richard Hudnut Salon, 693 Fifth Avenue, New York. American businessman and cosmetics manufacturer Richard Hudnut (1855–1929).

7–English writer Margaret Rumer Godden (1907–98).

Coward,[1] Dylan Thomas, et al. Commenting on all. Getting tremendous education. Also writing and typing rejections, signed with my own name! Sent one to a man on the New Yorker staff today with a perverse sense of poetic justice.

Saturday, slept, toured Museum of modern art . . . loved it. Shopped for minor necessities in Bloomingdales . . . got my black patent leathers . . . they have everything at good prices. A relief. Spent Saturday evening in Greenwich Village with Laurie Totten[2] seeing annual outdoor art exhibit in Washington Square . . . fascinatingly diverse . . . paintings and portrait artists all over the place. Then home. Sunday afternoon we wandered all about Central Park, in the zoo, to the carousel, and sat on benches for hours just watching the phenomenal people go by . . . didn't hear a word of English spoken all day!

Business: have written Perry and Rit and Bev little congratulatory notes. Nice letter from Prouty,[3] whom I'd like to drop in on before starting summer school. Have a horrible feeling I probably won't get into O'Connor's course. Send "Mintons" clipped from old review (in little Warren's ole bureau) AND the first section from one of my creative writing assignments this year called "The Birthday". Should be in my green file under "Themes". Be sure it's just the first part about the birthday party and Irish Helen, not the other episodes . . . all unrelated. Erase comments if possible, or better still, retype, and send. That incident might help me. I'm dubious about getting in, as all people in U.S. will no doubt try to.

Also, could you send you're lovely navy blue umbrella as soon as possible? It would help no end when it rains. Won't bother about modern Picasso painting. Miss you all. Life happens so hard and fast I sometimes wonder who is me. I must get to bed. Time is at a premium. Love hearing from you. Letters mean much. So much to do, and a month is such an infinitesimal amount of time.

August issue will be full of us all . . . several pictures, also last word[4]. . . introduction to whole issue which I just got finished writing in my capacity as managing editor. Poet feature all done. Looks great.

Wearily, still amazedly that there are so many people and animals in the big huge world . . . .

your citystruck,
sivvy

1–English playwright Sir Noël Peirce Coward (1899–1973).

2–Laura Totten (1932–); B.A. 1954, Syracuse University. Totten lived at 82 Pilgrim Road, Wellesley.

3–Possibly Olive Higgins Prouty to SP, 29 May 1953; held by Lilly Library.

4–Sylvia Plath, 'Mlle's Last Word on College, '53', *Mademoiselle* 37 (August 1953), 235.

love specially to Warren, whom Mrs. Prouty also thinks is wonderful and would like to meet. How is he? I miss him more than anybody and am learning a lot about the world that I will tell him.

Saw a yak at the zoo, and a soft-nosed infinitely patient eland, and a sleepy polar bear and several civet cats. Will go again when more kinds and different names are awake. Most were asleep as it was twilight when I went. But I heard a heffalump snore. I know I did.

love and more love
s.

TO *Aurelia Schober Plath*

Saturday 13 June 1953[1]

TLS with envelope,
on *Mademoiselle* letterhead,
Indiana University

Saturday morning

Dear mother . . . .

Well, I went to bed at 8.45 last night and slept a good 12 hours, so I now feel that I could write the great American novel, walk up and around the whole island of New York and construct a Philosophy of Life. If I perchance sounded wistful in my letters, it was mainly because I was very tired and wishing that I knew Men in the city that could take me the places that I couldn't go alone at night.

The dance Wednesday night produced no potential dates for me, and most of the other girls, although a few ended up with eligible New Yorkers. However, in itself, it was spectacular and most thrilling. We had cocktails on the outdoor sky terrace of the St. Regis roof, with hedges around the iron railings, the sun going down in glory, and all the tops of the buildings around. I had my picture taken (one of the 20 for the Editors memo in which we all appear) in a foursome,[2] daquiri in hand, big beaming smile of joy on face . . . wish I could get the big copy of it, cause it's a great picture of me . . . will appear in minute size in mag all over nation with caption something like: "Sylvia and Anne[3] smile ecstatically over champagne and two male dates of girls in the office".

1–Date supplied from postmark.
2–This photograph appears on p. 54 of the August issue with the caption: 'On the St. Regis Roof, Anne [Shawber], Sylvia and dates hold before-dinner confab'. See SP's Smith College Scrapbook, p. 38; held by Lilly Library.
3–Anne Shawber (1931–); B.A. 1953, Northwestern University.

Dinner was lovely, music, dancing between courses, shrimp, chicken, salad, parfaits, cordials, etc. etc, and two bands that alternated, one sinking into the floor, the other rising, taking up the same tune so that there was no apparent break. Rosy ceiling, painted like sunset sky, pink tableclothes, everything washed with a rose glow and outside the floorlength windows: all the lights of the New York skyscrapers. My dinner partners were 3 boys from Columbia, all about my height, one of whom was quite goodlooking, all of whom were embryonic composers of lyrics and showtunes and actors in the dramatic club. The goodlooking one was supposed to drive me to Jones Beach[1] today but since the temperature is sub-zero and the ceiling of clouds is lower than the trees,, we called it off . . . which leaves me dateless for the weekend. After writing letters to everybody this morning, I am going to take a sketch pad and walk over as much of the city of New York as possible before nightfall, when I will come back and go to bed . . . early. The prospect pleases me . . . I will make the most of being off on my own and not sulk in my Barbizon trou.

Since Mlle pays us every two weeks at the <u>end</u> of two weeks, I cashed your welcome and much-needed check to pay my hotel bill for these first two weeks. I'll pay you back when I come home. Other business: sent O'Connor letter off with Minton story alone, as you suggested. The other sketch was awful; I hadn't realized how awful. I just pray I get into the O'Connor course because I want to <u>write</u> this summer, and being there on scholarship means I have to take two courses, so if I don't get O'Connor, I'll have to take another course, and wouldn't have time to write . . . and also won't have time to write while doing my thesis, which would be disastrous. I of course can make changes in my program, even drop the scholarship and take only one course so I can write, but that will have to wait until I see what develops with O'Connor. I no doubt have competition from all over the nations, even from many professional writers and grown-ups. Let me know what you think about my chances, also my determination to have time to really <u>work</u> at writing daily, which I have never done.

My job in the office, is, I am sure, the most valuable I could ever have. Met Santha Rama Rau[2] yesterday (she's a very good friend of Miss Abels) . . . went to lunch with Miss Abels and Vance Bourjailly[3] Thursday (he's

1–Jones Beach State Park, on Long Island, New York.
2–Indian-American writer (1923–2009).
3–American writer Vance Bourjaily (1922–2010).

the co-editor of a new and wonderful literary periodical: "discovery" and had a lovely talk . . . and I made a mental note that I wanted to try writing stories for his periodical . . . real excellent "literary" publication). Paul Engle,[1] poet-teacher of a new program at Iowa State where you can get your MA in creative writing, dropped in, talked, read some of my poems, and poems by a friend guest editor who writes brilliantly . . . and said he'd send us booklets describing the Iowa graduate program . . . he's co-editor of the O'Henry collection this year.

Lots of the other girls just have "busy work" to do, but I am constantly reading fascinating manuscripts and making little memo comments on them, and getting an idea of what Mlle publishes and why . . . . I am awfully fond of Miss Abels, and think she is the most brilliant clever woman I have ever known.

Thursday night, on the way to the New York Center ballet, our taxi was stopped in traffic, and a very genial tall man came over, leaned in, paid the fare, and said to the four of us: "Too many pretty girls for one taxi. I'm Art Ford,[2] the disc jockey. Come in for a talk." So we got out, went into a cafe, were treated to a cocktail and a standing invitation to be taken by Art Ford (written up by MLLE as one of the bright young men in New York) to Greenwich Village after his night show got over at 3 a.m. A pleasant interlude. The ballet, with Maria Tallchief[3] and Tanaquil LeClerq,[4] was magnificent . . . Scotch Symphony, Metamorphoses, Fanfare, and Con Amore.

In the intermission, one of those peculiar coincidences happened which always evidently do in New York . . . I met Mel Woody, a tall blond sophomore at Yale, and who was in much the same relationship to Marcia that Phil McCurdy was to me a while back. He is a brilliant guy, very nice, and chivalrously offered to take me out for beer and a talk after the show . . . we walked to third avenue, collecting chianti bottles in the back of restaurants, peering in windows, listening to violinists on street corners, stting over beer steins in a small cafe and talking about our respective philosophies of life till about 2 a.m. Very stimulating, and I had a lovely time with the boy.

1–American poet and editor Paul Engle (1908–91). Engle was editor of the *O. Henry Prize Stories*, 1954–9.

2–American actor and radio personality Arthur Ford (1921–2006).

3–American ballerina Elizabeth Marie Tall Chief (1925–2013).

4–Paris-born dancer Tanaquil LeClercq (1929–2000).

The main surprise that has touched me . . . Gregory Kamirloff[1] called yesterday from the UN (Mrs. Norton had written him to say I was in New York) and invited me out for the beginning of next week. I was so overcome that I called up Mrs. Norton to thank her and to ask for details concerning the man so I would at least recognize him in the lobby. (She no doubt is sure I am completely mad.) Anyway, I won't wear heels, because he doesn't sound very tall, but for one evening that shouldn't matter, and if I get rested this weekend, I should be able to engage the brilliant character in some kind of conversation which he doesn't find too dull. At this point, I don't know whether he is just going to see me for a short talk, or take me on a tour of the UN, or what. Cross your fingers that it goes all right.

If you look at the television game of the Yankees next Saturday, you might see some of the guest editors if they teleview the audience, as we will be there in a guest box.

Did I tell you that some of us went to see the Herb Shriner show last Tuesday? It was very exciting, and lots of fun, and Herb Shriner is a real dear. To see the TV cameras roll down the ramps and focus on 3 stage sets, and then to see the picture simultaneously on the TV sets ahead, was really intriguing. TV is a rising thing . . . I wonder what it would be like to write for it

Thoughts are with you and Warren at graduation this weekend. Hope all goes well. Really, I couldn't have come with the cost of it. Money goes like water here, and I rebel against ever taking taxis, but walk everywhere.

It is a big unbelievable town, and I will be homesick for it. I love being Guest managing ed. We'll all have our pictures in Mlle four times[2] . . . I have the poet article and the Introduction bylines, too.

Your rested daughter . . . .
sivvy

1–Igor Karmiloff (1925–); a simultaneous interpreter for the United Nations. Also known as Gary, Kamirloff lived at the time in a twelfth-floor flat at 95 Christopher Street in Greenwich Village. Kamirloff stayed with the Norton family 25–7 April 1952 during a UN Secretariat weekend hosted by the Wellesley League of Women Voters. According to SP's calendar, she met Kamirloff for dinner (Italian) and visited his 'penthouse' on 16 June 1953; and after a tour of the UN for coffee on the 18th.

2–SP's picture appears on pp. 54, 235, 252 and 284.

TO *Myron Lotz*

Saturday 13 June 1953 — TLS on *Mademoiselle* letterhead, Indiana University

Saturday, June 13

Dear Mike . . .

Got your postcard today, felt inexplicable nostalgia for scent of magnolia mingling with tobacco, and imagined you striking out gasping batters right and left and getting a bronze tan at the same time. I liked hearing from you, because it is almost as good as having a conversation with a special friend.

Here I am living at the Barbizon Hotel for circumspect young women, on the 15th floor, overlooking the 3rd street el, rooftops, gardens, and a minute chink of the East River . . . and, if I lean far enough out the window, the UN. Never have I lived so high, and it is a thrill to sit at my desk at night, music on the radio, typing away, empty Chianti bottles on the table, and look out at the colored lights winking and shining across the east side.

I'm Guest Managing Editor of MLLE, hang out in the office of brilliant managing ed Cyrilly Abels, who, I'm convinced of it, knows all the writers, publishers, and poets in the world. Have met many intriguing people through her, such as Santha Rama Rau, the Indian woman writer who went to Wellesley College once upon a time; the new co-editor of the O'Henry short story collections; and several authors. I type rejection letters, read fascinating manuscripts and write comments on them, run errands, and generally listen to Cyrilly Abels conversations on the phone and with important people, and am learning innumerable things about magazine work and human beings.

Extra-curricular activities have included fashion show, guest tickets to Herb Shriner's TV show "Two for the Money" (I never watch TV, but seeing the mechanics of the ramps and stagesets and rolling cameras was an experience I'll never forget. This modern age. Sometimes I think it is impossible to comprehend and assimilate more than an infinitely small and modest segment of the total-time-space existence . . . so small and transient that it is at once pathetic and laughable.) Anyhow, this week we had our big Guest Editors dinner dance and party on the St. Regis roof overlooking the city and sunset; tablecloths, chairs, ceiling et. al. colored pink, the world awash with rosy glow, and music continuous, with two bands that alternated, one sinking into the floor, the other rising and playing the same song so that no break was discernible, and outside the windows, all the lights of the city. So wish you could have been there. Had picture taken with cocktail glass in hand, most untypical and cosmopolitan, for MLLE.

Night before last all 20 of us had orchestra seats for the New York City Center ballet . . . you would have been elated to see it, I know: Maria Tallchief and Tanaquil LEClerq starred; the four selections were "Con Amore", music by Rossini;[1] "Scotch Symphony"(Mendelssohn),[2] a lyric poem of grace and enacted on a sweeping blue and green craggy scottish set; then the oriental Hindemith's[3] "Metamorphoses", with Balinese-type dances, shimmering insect costumes, and an intriguing episode with wings. The last section was Benjamin Britain's[4] "Fanfare", where every dancer was dressed as an instrument in the orchestra: the woodwinds a haunting poignant blue color, the violins and strings starting out warm rose, and descending in color and tone range to a vibrant red for the double bass . . . brasses an insolent yellow, percussion, clownish black, white and red, and the harp a white queen. All most humorous and charming.

After which I by utter chance met a friend of mine in the lobby, walked all over the 3rd street section of the city, where there are innumerable and bizarre antique shops under the shade of the 3rd avenue El, plus hundreds of bars . . . went into a plotzy German one where the tables were heavy scarred wood, and an accordianist, pianist and violinist played and everybody sang . . . then to a little red checked tableclothed one, observed people, discussed philosophies of life, all strange and other-worldly. Lives drip away like water here, not even making a dent in the acres of concrete.

Last weekend, I wandered around central park, discovered a carousel, baseball park, zoo, and didn't hear a word of English the whole time. Also went to Museum of Modern Art and to an annual open air art exhibit in Greenwich Village. Drank gingerale in a sidewalk cafe, contemplated the Empire State Building.

Today it is sub-zero, pouring rain, and the fog hangs low, shredded among the gleaming wet black rooftops. I might just go out and walk alone in the rain later on. I like to do that.

Arrowsmith[5] almost made me cry in places. I loved . . . was it Gottleib? It was so long ago that I read it. Tell me what you think about it.

1–Italian composer Gioacchino Rossini (1792–1868).
2–German composter Felix Mendelssohn (1809–47).
3–German composer Paul Hindemith (1895–1963).
4–English composer Benjamin Britten (1913–76).
5–Sinclair Lewis, *Arrowsmith* (1925); SP refers to the character of Max Gottlieb.

Any time you want to talk on paper, just write me c/O 26 Elmwood. Anything: gripes, elations, horrors, loves, livings, details . . . I like listening to anything that comes to your mind.

Am seeing the Yankees next saturday[1] at the stadium: wish you could be beside me to point out all the details I'm sure to miss, neophyte that I am. We're guests of Mel Allen.[2] Ever know a guy named Jim Biery[3] in Keokuk? He's engaged to one of my favorite guest eds[4] here. Told her about you.

your bucolic newyorker,
syl

P.S. don't forget to sneak incognito to the mag stands & get a copy of the AUGUST Mademoiselle!

TO *Warren Plath*

Sunday 21 June 1953 — TLS (photocopy) on *Mademoiselle* letterhead, Indiana University

June 21

Dear Warren . . .

Forgive me for not writing years ago to tell you how tremendously enormously proud I am of you and your superlative honorific graduation. I thought about you all that weekend, and if I could have traveled for nothing with the speed of thought, I would have been there in person to congratulate you a million times. I am so glad I have you for a brother.

I have not rounded up letter paper and a 3 cent stamp for a long time, and I just today felt: heavens, I haven't thought about who I am or where I come from for days. It is abominably hot in NYC . . . the humidity is staggering, and I am perishing for the clean unsooted greenness of our backyard.

I have learned an amazing lot here: the world has split open before my gaping eyes and spilt out its guts like a cracked watermelon. I think it will not be until I have meditated in peace upon the multitude of things I have learned and seen that I will begin to comprehend what has happened to me this last month. I am worn out now, with the strenuous days at the

1–The Yankees hosted and defeated the Detroit Tigers, 6–2.

2–American sportscaster Mel Allen (1913–96). Allen was the play-by-play announcer for the New York Yankees, 1940–64.

3–James R. Biery (1929–).

4–Janet Ellen Wagner Rafferty (1932–). Biery and Wagner did not marry. Wagner became a model after her experience at *Mademoiselle*.

office and the heat and the evenings out . . . I want to come home and sleep and sleep and play tennis and get tan again (I am an unhealthy shade of yellow, now) and learn what I have been doing this last year.

I don't know about you, but I've realized that the last weeks of school were one hectic running for busses and trains and exams and appointments, and the shift to NYC has been so rapid that I can't think logically about who I am or where I am going. I have been very ecstatic, horribly depressed, shocked, elated, enlightened, and enervated . . . all of which goes to make up living very hard and newly. I want to come home and vegetate in peace this coming weekend, with the people I love around me for a change.

Somehow I can't talk about all that has happened this week at length, I am too weary, too dazed. I have, in the space of 6 days, toured the second largest ad agency in the world[1] and seen television, kitchens, heard speeches there, gotten ptomaine poisoning from crabmeat the agency served us in their "own special test kitchen" and wanted to die very badly for a day, in the midst of faintings and hypodermics and miserable agony, . . spent an evening in Greenwich Village with the most brilliant wonderful man in the world, the simultaneous interpreter Gary Karmirloff, who is tragically a couple of inches shorter than I, but who is the most magnificent lovable person I have ever met in my life . . . I think I will be looking for his alter ego all over the world for the rest of my life . . . . spent an evening listening to an 18 year-old friend[2] of Bob Cochran's read his poetry to me after a steak dinnere, also at the Village . . . . spent an evening fighting with the wealthy unscrupulous Peruvian legal delegate to the UN[3] at a Forest Hills tennis club dance . . . and spent Saturday in the Yankee stadium with all the stinking people in the world watching the Yankees trounce the Tigers, having our pictures taken with commentator Mel Allen, getting lost in the subway and seeing deformed men with short

1–Barton, Durstine and Osborn, then at 383 Madison Avenue, New York.

2–According to SP's calendar and Smith College scrapbook, this was Mark von Slosmann; both held by Lilly Library.

3–According to SP's calendar, she met 'Jose Antonio La Vias' on 20 June 1953. The full calendar entry for that day reads: 'Yankees vs. Detroit / Forest Hills Dance – Jose Antonio / La Vias – East Side apt. – Latins – / Lima Peru x'. According to papers held by United Nations Archives, the names of the Peruvian delegation for 1952–3 were: Victor Andres Belaunde, Juan Bautista de Lavalle, Fernando Berckemeyer Pazos and Carlos Holguin de Lavalle. There is a listing for 'Jose A de Lavelle' at 142 E. 49th Street in the 1953 New York City directory. A 1954 newspaper prints: 'Dr. Jose Lavalle of the Peruvian delegation to the United Nations still hasn't recovered from Ava Gardner. He was her offbeat date while she was in New York—handsome, single, and glamourously latin.' Dorothy Kilgallen, 'On Broadway', *Pittsburgh Post-Gazette*, 26 October 1954, 26.

arms that curled like pink boneless snakes around a begging cup stagger through the car, thinking to myself all the time that Central Park Zoo was only different in that there were bars on the windows . . . oh, God, it is unbelievable to think of all this at once . . . my mind will split open.

I am going to call up and find out about trains back to Boston on Friday after work, or early Saturday morning . . . do you suppose you could meet your soot-stained, grubby, weary, wise, ex-managing editor at the station to carry her home with her bags????. I love you a million times more than any of these slick ad-men, these hucksters, these wealthy beasts who get dronk in foreign accents all the time. I will let you know what train my coffin will come in on.

Seriously, I am more than overjoyed to have been here a month, it is just that I realize how young and inexperienced I am in the ways of the world . . . Smith seems like a simple enchanting bucolic existence compared to the dry, humid, breathless wasteland of the cliffdwellers, where the people are, as D. H. Lawrence wrote of his society "dead brilliant galls on the tree of life".[1] By contrast, the good few friends I have seems like clear icewater after a very strong scalding martini.

There are so many things I have collected here, that I will send a few more boxes home, If I can find them. All I have needs washing, bleaching, airing. The soot, sweat, yellowness here pervades everything.

I am now going down to the swimming pool in the hotel, then to the sundeck . . . plans for beach fell through . . . I would melt into the sidewalk.

Write if you could pick me up Fri night or Sat am. Will let you know time tomorrow. Best love to you all . . . you wonderful textured honest real unpainted people . . . .

your exhausted, ecstatic, elegiac, New Yorker.

sivvy

1–D. H. Lawrence, *Women in Love* (1920); SP slightly misquotes from chapter 9: 'Good enough for the life of today. But mankind is a dead tree, covered with fine brilliant galls of people.'

TO *Director of Graduate Schools, Columbia University*

Friday 3 July 1953 TLS[1] (draft), Smith College

26 Elmwood Road
Wellesley, Massachusetts
July 3, 1953

Director of Graduate Schools
Columbia University
New York City, N.Y.

Dear Sir:

I will be graduating from Smith College in June, 1954, and I am most interested in obtaining information at this time about your program of graduate study at Columbia University. I am particularly interested in the departments of Education and Journalism.

At present, I am a scholarship student, honoring in English at Smith, and would like to find out about possibilities of scholarship aid to Columbia Graduate School.

Any bulletins, course of study booklets, and scholarship information that you could send me would be very much appreciated. I would also like to become acquainted with your program for the departments of English and Psychology.

Sincerely yours,
Sylvia Plath

TO *Gordon Lameyer*

Thursday 23 July 1953 TLS, Indiana University

July 23, 1953

Dear Gordon,

Male orderly ambling ambiguously .. (no, not so in Sam's Navy! I somehow cannot visualize you in your proper uniform, which, I trust you have received by now and thus become unstraggled) for letters, etc. Your barracks I can very well imagine, shining with polish, plus salivary aid, and I wonder if there are the bunk-orange crate variety, or, since Congressmen et. al. mosey in and out as the Investigating Committees

1–Draft typed on verso of SP's June–July 1953 'Letter to an Over-Grown, Over-protected, Scared, Spoiled Baby'; see 'Appendix 5', *The Journals of Sylvia Plath*.

dictate, whether you have minor luxuries, such as bedside bars with hot and cold running champagne, fritos and caviar, and a marilyn monroeish Wave to rouse you from slumber in the morning by crooning-- "Oh, what a Beautiful Day." Tell me, doctor.

Life here is rainy at present and mostly goodly for a change. I always have an elemental urge to go walking in the stuff . . . the lovely rambling wetness of it all loire's me on, so to seine.

Warren types furiously on, and mistakes make him take breathers and go into dynamic tension exercises. Really, the boy has a rather enormous lung capacity, now, and I'm pretty sure that crew is for him next fall. (Thanks to one who shall be nameless. And speaking of names, do you realize how many possibilities yours has? Just for kicks: e.g. God on la mer. Or filial reward for the mother: e. g. Guerdon la mere. May be it was a horse, that last, though. At this point, any interpretation seems bona fide. Joyicity is excelsis. One gets obsessed.)

I have a part-time job at the Newton-Wellesley Hospital mornings now, being a nurses' aides' aide, and the environment is very new and intriguing, while, of course, being very sobering at times. One of my duties is to help feed the patients who are too weak or too sick to eat themselves, and I never realized or paused to think about the side of the world where the people are reaching the other end of the line: senility, even death.

You get attached to certain patients, see them leave, apparently well, and then there they are at the beginning of the next week, (some of them) not recognizing you. The little woman who cries all the time and takes only liquids dies and is wheeled away rapidly. Mongoloid babies are born along with the other ones. There are whispered consultations in the halls, cautions to say nothing specific to the mothers because of the prize boners that have been committed--such as by one bright nurses' aide who exclaimed, "My, Mrs. X, your husband will be proud it's a boy." only to find out later that Mr. X had run away without waiting to find out the gender of his offspring. In summary, it's life. The River Liffey goes on. In devious ways.

Tell me, Gordon, just how many times you have read Ulysses, and whether you read the keys along with it simultaneously. Just from beginning the second time and doing a thumbing through of your books, I begin to wonder if everything hasn't been keyed and written about. The reading is fascinating, but the commentaries explain everything, it seems. That's why I'd like your opinion upon the potentiality of making any kind of valid statement about him (JJ) without either absorbing completely all the vast mass of scholarship behind him or depending completely on the work of other people like Gilbert,[1] etc.

What I am really asking you is, from your more advanced point of view, do you think the idea of a thesis on Joyce is really plausible. I thought so before I began outside reading--now I wonder.

Anyhow, let me know your ideas about this. And do tell me if there are any Captain Queegs about your station, will ya, huh?

Love,
sylvia

TO *Gordon Lameyer*

Wednesday 29 July 1953[2] TLS, Indiana University

July 29, 1953

Dear Gordon . . .

It scarcely seems possible that I saw you off only three days or so back . . . you looking so veddy starched and white and regimental. Your mother and I had a lovely ride home, went back and finished up the dishes and sat in your room for a leisurely chat, all most enjoyable. I can't tell you how tremendously I admire her . . . with all her vigor and personal strength and richly-lived background! She is a phenomenal woman . . .

Monday night was lots of fun for mother and Warren and myself . . . we went over to Brookline for dinner with Olive Higgins Prouty, one of my former "benefactors". I don't know if I ever told you about her, but she's the author of "Stella Dallas" and a whole series of novels about Boston society that made a big hit in their time, were turned into movies and plays starring people like Betty Davis.

Anyhow, Mrs. Prouty, now a widow, lives in a white and palatial estate, with sloping landscaped lawns, rock gardens, terraces, et. al . . . and has a French poodle for company named Taupe which she keeps for company, teaches tricks, goes to school with. But instead of succumbing to the temptation of idolizing a dog the way older people do cats, or a geranium, she said, rather wistfully in the course of conversation: "Taupe doesn't care about me really; he's self-sufficient. He is, after, all, only a dog."

1–English literary scholar and translator Stuart Gilbert (1883–1969). SP may be referring to Gilbert's *James Joyce's Ulysses: A Study* (1930).

2–On this day, SP had the first of her shock treatments at Valley Head Hospital, Carlisle, Mass.

Olive Higgins P. is an attractive, alive woman still, blue-eyed, tall, gray-haired, writing now biographies of the people in her family for a few hours a day. We toured the garden, had Old Fashioneds on the flag stone terrace, and then a lovely salmon dinner served by a small ubiquitous maid at a table with blue glass goblets, candle holders, and plates . . . the clarity and intensity of a stained-window with the light through it.

I'll be most interested to hear (if you get a minute moment in your rigorous schedule) about how the courses are going, whether and what VIP.'s have inspected your spit and polish, and what in general is the trend of your seamanship.

Was talking just today with Pat O'Neil, a high school confidante of mine who had to leave Smith last year to help at home as her father had contracted cancer . . . anyhow, her brother[1] trained at OCS at Newport two years ago and it was discovered in the course of tests and all that he had a high aptitude for scientific subjects, although he'd been strictly liberal arts at Dartmouth. As it developed, he got further training in electronics, etc., and is now flying jets and doing a particular type of perilous job (which is volunteer, because it is so dangerous) involving landing planes on small carriers. You probably know more about the types of specialized jobs available, or will, as time goes on, but just from what I've heard so far, I think the experience and chance for travel and technical skill development the Navy offers is great . . . my attitudes about the military life alter as I see vicariously what sort of things can be done with it. Who knows, some day you may find yourself wanting to write (understand that I am not idealizing or expecting!) from the fulness of your wide experience-to-be: travel, people, lord-knows-what . . . whether it's the "Caine Mutiny" sort of thing or a personalized, and therefore individually styled saga of your own. (I sometimes wonder if it would be a human possibility to go beyond the "funferal" with HCE and ALP[2] as far as language is concerned, and the multifoliate meanings . . .)

Enough . . . I hope the trees and bushes aren't too thorny, and that you manage to come home again sometime soon. You should let me know, if you'd rather not get letters that I've told you the news of, like the last one. I've got my fingers crossed for an easier time of it for you . . .

love,
sylvia

1–Frank B. O'Neil; B.A. 1951, Dartmouth College.
2–References to James Joyce, *Finnegan's Wake* (1939).

TO *Myron Lotz*

Tuesday 18 August 1953 TLS, Indiana University

August 18, 1953

Dear Mike . . . .

Say, but you deserve more than congratulations for your promotion[1] to the civilized northern regions . . . this coterie of ball clubs has a hierarchy of skilled ratings which is beyond me, but it seems that the lower and cruder elements are relegated to the humid climate of the southern regions (paralleling Dante's Inferno?) while the more spectacular players migrate toward the fair modern northern climates . . . such as New York. That so? From the Mount of Purgatory heavenward.

I was really pleased to the core to get your letter, with its messages. Bob and Jill are among my favorite people, and I think the life they lead is rather wonderful. If two people are that much in love, then just being together would make any situation bearable. I got a very sweet note from Jill before I came back from the city, and managed to squeeze in time to write back before I came home.

Life here has been very placid . . . I had to give up the idea of summer school this year because life at home demanded attention: the doctor ordered me to take time off and rest, and so I have been helping with the house, visiting Cambridge occasionally, and taking a few trips to the beach. Swimming in salt water is my pet pastime, even if I do have to be careful about the eternal sinuses and can't dive or play submarine woman. You sounded rather versatile yourself, sir, what with golf and tennis being among your increasing athletic skills?

The last paragraph of your letter touched me especially! Because I feel the same way about my acquaintance with you . . .

mutually . . .
syl

1–Lotz advanced in the minor leagues from the Durham Bulls (North Carolina, Carolina League) to the Jamestown Falcons (New York, Pennsylvania–Ontario–New York League).

TO *Gordon Lameyer*

Monday 31 August 1953[1] — ALS with envelope, Indiana University

Monday

Dear Gordon . . .

Mother brought up your letter[2] along with your wonderful flowers yesterday, and I don't know if I can ever in the world tell you how tremendously important your words were to me . . . out of the experiences and confusions of the past it was most welcome to find some kind of constancy and friendship that I could identify with possible shared experiences in the as yet uncertain future . . .

You would be among the very first of my companions I would want to see . . . and perhaps during your ten day leave when you get your commission, I will again be seeable and free to begin to live again as I would like to. The reasons I can't see people now are many and various – among them, that I have a few face bruises that need to heal – and of course I'll be under doctor's care for a while more. Whatever the outcome, please know that your letters and pictures are more welcome than I can say and news of you and the world and your work and ideas will always be appreciated as intensely as this last generous and understanding volume was. I don't know why I chose the hard way to learn who the real people are and who they aren't: but I'll be mentally thanking you for standing by me now (I'm still sort of numb from all this) and will cherish your Friendship in the future – I know the hardest time will be then – when I rearrange life and make a comeback, new and a year or two late, perhaps: but (I hope) worthy of you and people as strong and good as you are. Now I'm perhaps "purple-passaging," but it's strange how, when you write sometimes (thinking only of attitude and not of new form) the words begin to have the tone of a campaign speech or a radio-spiel but I mean very much and want very much to tell you that although it's a difficult and complex situation now, I will work twice as hard at recuperating so that I can again see you – and just walk and talk with

1 – Date supplied from internal evidence.

2 – Probably Gordon Lameyer to SP, 30 August 1953; held by Lilly Library. SP attempted suicide on Monday 24 August 1953 and was found two days later on Wednesday 26 August 1953. Between 26 August 1953 and 29 January 1954, SP received treatment at Newton-Wellesley Hospital; Massachusetts General Hospital in Boston; and McLean Hospital in Belmont, Mass. SP returned to Smith College on Saturday, 30 January 1954, and graduated with the class of 1955 on 6 June 1955.

you. "To learn to appreciate the green and the blue" again – and to make more of the rushing, fast, complex world become reality and part of the experience we form our lives from . . . The activity of which is sometimes – as at present – ordered to lie fallow for future use.

Gordon – please remember me smiling and thinking our way. I'll answer again and mother and the home address will always be available when and if I change mine . . . I'm not sure about that now, but I am sure that your letter meant more to me than any I've ever received any time before . . . or probably ever will . . .

yours,
sylvia

TO *Gordon Lameyer*

Monday 7 September 1953[1] ALS, Indiana University

Monday –

Dear Gordy –

When mother brought me the package containing your Amherst letter, along with your other letters,[2] I was so happy I could have cried – The meaning of the <drawing of the letter 'A'>, especially after the story you told me in that first long letter of yours, made me appreciate your sending such sustenance – which I need very much just now.

Your mother also made me realize more fully what a dear friend I found in her – her letter and enclosure was lovely. I will write to her and tell her so – and I'll tell you both also (here, via you,) how terribly much I enjoyed those last excursions of ours before you went to Newport. – New Hampshire, especially, I loved[3]. . . . . I'll never forget the expert, rapid meal that was whipped up for us, culminating in the final dessert – wasn't it soup plates of icecream, peaches, and short cake? The whole day was one of those that remains in mind, no matter what, sunset included . . . I want you to know Gordy, that bearing up under the "slings and arrows of outrageous fortune,"[4] even if they are a result of one's own mismanagement . . . is incalculably easier when one has two such marvelous people as you and your mother to be so thoughtful . . .

1 – Date supplied from internal evidence.

2 – Gordon Lameyer to SP, 31 August 1953, and 1, 2, 3 September 1953; held by Lilly Library. The 'Amherst letter' was included with 1 September 1953.

3 – According to SP's calendar, she went with the Lameyers to New Hampshire on 5 July 1953.

4 – Shakespeare, *Hamlet*.

No matter what happens or has happened, I would want you to know how therapeutic it is to get news of your active, if tremendously demanding life: I can visualize you now in your uniform, and hope that perhaps I can beg a picture from you when reprints of your graduating shots are available: to contemplate from whereever I may be.

I am, at present still undergoing rigorous treatment – shots of penicillin practically by the hour for my incipient temp – which will rise . . . by now I'm becoming immune to any kind of needle whatsoever, which is a large step in my life – against the more minor of my fears.

As for the major ones: those remain to be knocked down, too. And for being so understanding and tremendously helpful . . . again – thank you more than I can say. Whereever you are – or finally go in the world – only think of me in very special places now and then, and by some telepathic magic, I'll maybe partake of the scene – or become part of it – I only wish I could make this denouement something as poetic as scattering ashes! But it's a lot more difficult than that. – Please, keep thinking of me now and then, and wish me luck –

yours,
sylvia

TO *Aurelia Schober Plath*

Thursday 17 December 1953[1] ALS (postcard, excerpt), Unknown[2]

Thursday

. . . I am doing occasional work over at the library – and an having my 6th treatment tomorrow I hope I won't have to have many more ...

sivvy

1 – Date supplied from postmark.

2 – Offered as part of Sotheby's New York sale on 6 April 1982, Lot 107. The lot was withdrawn, passed, or unsold. Transcribed from catalogue which reads: 'PLATH, SYLVIA. Autograph postcard signed ("sivvy"), 22 lines, {McLean Hospital, Belmont, Mass.}, "Thursday", postmarked 18 December 1953, to Aurelia Plath. Written when Sylvia Plath was in hospital recovering from her first breakdown and suicide attempt, at the end of her Junior year at Smith, she writes that she will be able to come over for tea on Saturday and come home for two days at Christmas.'

TO *Gordon Lameyer*

Friday 25 December 1953 TLS, Indiana University

Christmas day . . .

Dear Gordon . . .

Today will be chalked up as one of the most notable in recent history for several reasons. First of all, I've been able to celebrate the holly-crowned festival at home, which in itself is a pleasure. In fact, I'm now sitting at the diningroom table pounding away at my brother's square masculine typewriter, munching on homemade Yuletide cookies. Secondly, I'm smiling back at the most genial and attractive of friendly faces: I'm more pleased than I can say with your picture and want to thank your mother for it over and over again . . . it will follow me back to McLean tonight, and keep me company on my subsequent travels (around the world or whereever, as the case may be). Also, Axel's Castle,[1] which I've always been meaning to read (you know how those best of intentions may deviate from the straight and narrow!) will take me back to new depths in my dearly loved Yeats, Joyce and Eliot . . . and into new fields as well, serving as a springboard into Stein,[2] Proust,[3] etc. All of which will help me communicate more rewardingly with you in the future!

After the best of festive turkey dinners with the best of families, I curled up in the biggest armchair in the livingroom and had a protracted "conversation" with you which involved reading all your delightful letters[4] consecutively and wishing I could talk with you in person right then and there. (I do want to explain my scandalous silence in the line of correspondence: I'd been undergoing months of therapy which left me feeling rather unconversational temporarily.) At any rate, I'm feeling 100% better now, and am looking forward to increasingly frequent visits home, ending up in an eventual permanent sojourn there, with visits to Boston and a couple of courses to be audited either at Wellesley or B.U.

Next year, as far as I can see now, I'll probably finish up my degree at Smith . . . they've been really princely about everything. As have the deepest and closest of my friends: you first and foremost. Someday I hope I'll be able to find the right words to tell you about how very tremendously

1–Edmund Wilson, *Axel's Castle: A Study in the Imaginative Literature of 1870–1930* (New York: Scribner's, 1931). SP's copy held by Smith College.

2–American writer Gertrude Stein (1874–1946).

3–French novelist and critic Marcel Proust (1871–1922).

4–There are fourteen letters from Gordon Lameyer to SP between 30 August and 2 December 1953. See Lameyer's unpublished memoir *Dear Sylvia*; held by Lilly Library.

important you have been in speeding me on the road back to the full and vital world again. Your letters, which I am just now growing able to fully appreciate, have made me want, more than any other single thing, to find my way back to the world which I am again sure I can love with a deep intensity once more. Some day I hope I'll be able to express my appreciation face to face. Your own particular brand of therapy has been most meaningful to me; I'll be wanting to keep you posted regularly, now that I'm feeling so very much better.

Life at the hospital has improved with my move to a new dormitory[1] where I've met some extremely delightful girls, one of whom I'd especially like to have you meet someday: she's a creative, energetic Vassar graduate who composes her own songs and words to go with them: everything from torchy love lyrics to bouncy novelties. Right now she's peddling them around the music marts in Boston. I spend a good deal of my time in the Coffee Shop, a pine-paneled den of smoky sociability, and have struck up a fast friendship with the librarian here (Smith, '49); she's even let me type up all the stencils for the hospital newspaper (McLean "Gazette") and do the marginal sketches. We have a most active music department at the hospital which puts out everything from organ concerts to piano recitals, too, and an enormous record library which is going to entertain me on rainy afternoons.

The family is now getting ready for leaving for my aunt's house in Weston for yet another Christmas celebration, so I'll be signing off for a short while, to be taking up conversation again very soon. Once more, Gordon, my dearest accumulated love and thanks for giving me such incentive for rapid recuperation . . .

your rejuvenating
sylvia

1–SP moved from Codman House to South Belknap House.

TO *Edward Cohen*

Monday 28 December 1953 TLS, Indiana University

Belknap House
McLean Hospital
Waverley, Mass.
December 28, 1953

Dear eddie . . .

The rather enormous lapse in time between the date of this letter and the date of your brief-but-eloquent plea[1] for me to write needs an explanation. I don't know just how widely the news of my little scandal this summer traveled in the newspapers, but I received letters from all over the United States from friends, relations, perfect strangers and religious crackpots; and I'm not aware of whether you read about my escapade,[2] or whether you are aware of my present situation. At any rate, I'm prepared to give you a brief resumé of details, in case you aren't aware of them already. However, at this late date, I'm not sure whether you're in South America, father of five children, still alive, or what. I hope you won't follow my bad example, but will send me as soon as possible a fat letter revealing recent news about you. I assure you, I would have written much sooner, if I had been able, but I didn't receive your letter till a short while back, and it wasn't until today that I could sit down and give you the wholehearted attention you deserve.

At any rate, just in case you haven't been briefed on the past half year or so: I worked all during the hectic month of June in the plushy air-conditioned offices of Mlle magazine, helping set up the August issue. I came home exhausted, fully prepared to begin my two courses at Harvard Summer School, for which I'd been offered a partial scholarship. Then things started to happen. I'd gradually come to realize that I'd completely wasted my Junior year at Smith by taking a minimum of courses (and the wrong courses at that), by bluffing my way glibly through infrequent papers, skipping by with only three or four exams during the year, reading nothing more meaty than the jokes at the bottom of the columns in the New Yorker, and writing nothing but glib jingles in an attempt to commune with WH Auden. I had gaily asserted that I was going to write a thesis on James Joyce (when I hadn't even read Ulysses thru thoroughly

1 – Probably Eddie Cohen to SP, 1 November 1953; held by Lilly Library.

2 – Articles on SP's disappearance and recovery, largely sent out over the news wire, appeared in more than 200 newspapers across the United States, including 'Missing Co-ed Found', *Chicago Tribune*, 27 August 1953, 5.

once) and take comprehensives in my senior year (when I wasn't even familiar with the most common works of Shakespeare, for God's sake!) Anyhow, there I was, faced with the impossible necessity of becoming familiar with the English language, which looked as coherent as Yiddish to me, in the short sweet space of one summer. When I had come to think Psychology, Sociology, Philosophy (which I somehow never sullied my hands with) were infinitely more worthwhile, valuable, and unattainable.

To top it off, all my friends were either writing novels in Europe, planning to get married next June, or going to med. school, or something. The one or two males I knew were either proving themselves genii in the midst of adversity (e.g. Allan,[1] who was becoming a writer, a buddy of W. C. Williams', and a researchist at the tb san) or were not in the market for the legal kind of love for a good ten years yet and were going to see the world and all the femmes fatales in it before becoming victims of wedded bliss.

Anyhow, to sum up my reactions to the immediate problem at hand, I decided at the beginning of July to save a few hundred $$$, stay home, write, learn shorthand, and finesse the summer school deal. You know, sort of live cheap and be creative. Truth was, I'd counted on getting into Frank O'Connor's writing course at Harvard, but it seemed that several thousand other rather brilliant writers did too, and so I didn't; so I was miffed, and figured if I couldn't write on my own I wasn't any good anyhow. It turned out that not only was I totally unable to learn one squiggle of shorthand, but I also had not a damn thing to say in the literary world; because I was sterile, empty, unlived, and unwise, and UNREAD. And the more I tried to remedy the situation, the more I became unable to comprehend ONE WORD of our fair old language. I began to frequent the offices and couches of the local psychiatrists, who were all running back and forth on summer vacations. I became unable to sleep; I became immune to increased doses of sleeping pills. I underwent a rather brief and traumatic experience of badly-given shock treatments on an outpatient basis. Pretty soon, the only doubt in my mind was the precise time and method of committing suicide. The only alternative I could see was an eternity of hell for the rest of my life in a mental hospital, and I was going to make use of my last ounce of free choice and choose a quick clean ending. I figured that in the long run it would be more merciful and inexpensive to my family; instead of an indefinite and expensive incarceration of a favorite daughter in the cell of a State San, instead of the misery and disillusion,

1–This was SP's name for Richard Norton in her letters to Cohen.

of sixty odd years of mental vacuum, of physical squalor, I would spare them all by ending everything at the height of my so-called career, while there were still illusions left among my profs, still poems to be published in Harper's, still a memory at least that would be worthwhile.

Well, I tried drowning, but that didn't work; somehow the urge to life, mere physical life, is damn strong, and I felt that I could swim forever straight out into the sea and sun and never be able to swallow more than a gulp or two of water and swim on. The body is amazingly stubborn when it comes to sacrificing itself to the annihilating directions of the mind.

So I hit upon what I figured would be the easiest way out: I waited until my mother had gone to town,[1] my brother was at work, and my grandparents were out in the back yard. Then I broke the lock of my mother's safe, took out the bottle of 50 sleeping pills, and descended to the dark sheltered ledge in our basement, after having left a note to mother that I had gone on a long walk and would not be back for a day or so. I swallowed quantities and blissfully succumbed to the whirling blackness that I honestly believed was eternal oblivion. My mother believed my note, sent out searching parties, notified the police, and finally, on the second day or so, began to give up hope when she found that the pills were missing. In the meantime, I had stupidly taken too many pills, vomited them, and came to consciousness in a dark hell banging my head repeatedly on the ragged rocks of the cellar in futile attempts to sit up and, instinctively, call for help.

My brother finally heard my weak yells, called the ambulance, and the next days were a nightmare of flashing lights, strange voices, large needles, an overpowering conviction that I was blind in one eye, and a hatred toward the people who would not let me die, but insisted rather in dragging me back into the hell of sordid and meaningless existence.

I won't go into the details that involved two sweltering weeks in the Newton-Wellesley hospital, exposed to the curious eyes of all the student nurses, attendants, and passers-by---or the two weeks in the psychiatric ward of the Mass-General,[2] where the enormous open sore on my cheek gradually healed, leaving a miraculously-intact eye, plus a large, ugly brown scar under it.

Suffice it to say that by fairy-godmother-type maneuverings, my scholarship benefactress at Smith got me into the best mental hospital

1–ASP was at the Exeter Theatre, 26 Exeter Street, Boston, watching *A Queen Is Crowned*. She was most likely at the 2:10 p.m. showing.

2–Massachusetts General Hospital, 55 Fruit Street, Boston. SP was in Ward B-7.

in the U.S., where I had my own attractive private room and my own attractive private psychiatrist. I didn't think improvement was possible. It seems that it is.

I have emerged from insulin shock and electric (ugh) shock therapy with the discovery, among other things, that I can laugh, if the occasion moves me (and, surprisingly enough, it sometimes does), and get pleasure from sunsets, walks over the golf course, drives through the country. I still miss the old love and ability to enjoy solitude and reading. I need more than anything right now what is, of course, most impossible; someone to love me, to be with me at night when I wake up in shuddering horror and fear of the cement tunnels leading down to the shock room, to comfort me with an assurance that no psychiatrist can quite manage to convey.

The worst, I hope, is over. Ironically enough, Allan's former Smith flame (the one I superseded) is also here. When I entered (in the "middle" ward) she was in the highest-ranking ward (where I am writing from now); a display of temper, however, involving her breaking several windows, involved her ending up in the "lowest" ward, and I haven't heard from her since.[1] Somehow, all this reminds me of the deep impression the movie "Snake Pit"[2] made upon me about six years ago. I only hope I don't have any serious relapses, and get out of here in a month or two.

Our ward of ten people is very attractive, having a diningroom, two bathrooms, a large livingroom overlooking the golf course and the lights of the town below, and containing several bridge tables, a lovely piano, and a TV set to amuse away the evenings.

I can now have visitors, go for drives, supervised walks, and hope to have "ground privileges" by the end of this week, which means freedom to walk about the grounds alone, to frequent the Coffee Shop, and the library, as well as the Occupational Therapy rooms.

Among the other girls here are several from Vassar, a couple from Radcliffe, and one from Cornell. As the basic fee for room and board alone is $20 a day, the backgrounds of most here is quite different from mine. When I think of how I could be living in Europe on that amount, and with what lovely people, I sometimes get a bit sour.

Anyhow, the handsome Amherst grad (now an ensign in the navy) who has faithfully written to me (in spite of not getting any answers for four months) and who promises to be around when I get out is being

1–The wards at McLean were Wyman (lowest), Codman (middle), and South Belknap (highest). SP modified the names in *The Bell Jar* to Wymark, Caplan, and Belsize.

2–Mary Jane Ward, *The Snake Pit* (1946); film version released in 1948.

sent to Europe for half a year next week, so I won't be able to see him until, at the earliest, next May. And God knows what will happen by then. I may be out of here. Or I may not. He is too good to be true.

Allan, who certainly owes me nothing after the way I treated him last year when he was down and out, is heading off for a hedonistic tout to Europe with a male friend of his. (I think it would be the best therapy possible for me to go with him and live a high life for a while, but somehow few people agree with me.)

I do miss you to talk to. If you think it would be worth your while to spiel forth to a sympathetic, though fouled-up old female---(even though she is incarcerated temporarily she still has her lucid . . . and very lonely . . . moments)---please do write me frankly and fully what's been with you the last months or so. I would like somebody to talk to again very much. The student nurses here are all cuties and very sweet, and I like some of my fellow inmates very much---BUT I will be glad as all hell to get my final writ of dismissal. I am able to communicate with several concert pianists here, plus an atomic genius from MIT (a jolly professor who has hit his second childhood, or something), but every now and then I long to be out in the wide open spaces of the very messy, dangerous, real world which I still love. In spite of everything. Because, mainly of the people who have kept writing, who have kept coming, even tho I botched one of the nastiest sins on the church records.

Anyhow, I'd love to be able to loll around in Acapulco, or in some sunny tennisy clime for a while: much more therapeutic than enduring the New England winter on Waverley Hill, even if it IS the best place of its kind going.

Aw, please, scold me, placate me, tell me your loves and losses, but do talk to me, huh?

as ever,
syl

1954

TO *Gordon Lameyer*

Sunday 10 January 1954 TLS, Indiana University

<typed on six yellow Street & Smith Publications[1] Inter Office Memorandum sheets; each page has a separate heading>

(1)	TO	dear gordon	FROM	sylvia
	SUBJECT	Life in general & particular	DATE	jan 10.
(2)	TO	you	FROM	me
	SUBJECT	continued	DATE	",
(3)	TO	gordon	FROM	Sylvia
	SUBJECT	ad infinitum	DATE	same,
(4)	TO	g	FROM	s
	SUBJECT	"	DATE	",
(5)	TO	The Ancient Mariner	FROM	Alice-in-Wonderland
	SUBJECT	cabbages and kings	DATE	",
(6)	TO	g. a. lameyer	FROM	s. p.
	SUBJECT	"	DATE	",

new year's salutations, ensign! every now and then I am the victim of a compulsion to type à la e. e. cummings and ignore capitals and other conventions. so bear with me. also, home for the weekend, I find all sorts of intriguing remnants of stationary and paper at hand which I feel like using up for fun. and now that the form of this epistle is accounted for, on to items with more content.

against my acquisitive instinct, I am warming my frostbitten fingers at present over the dying glow of your last letter,[2] scrupulously observing your request therein. ashes to ashes. but darn it, that was a good letter. and I am often moved by considerations of the future: for example, some day years and years hence, when I am peddling unsalable villanelles for

1–*Mademoiselle* was owned by Street & Smith Publications until 1957 when it was sold to Condé Nast Publications. This memorandum paper was collected by SP when she was a guest managing editor at *Mademoiselle* in June 1953.
2–Gordon Lameyer to SP, [1953–4], postmarked 5 January 195; held by Lilly Library.

a penny apiece on sleety streetcorners, I just might be glad to earn a few more days food supply by turning over my collection of g. a. lameyer's ("you know his latest novel, of course, my dear . . . herman wouk just didn't stand a chance by comparison--wrote all his logs in prose, the pedestrian creature!") early letters to some avaricious publisher. but then. honor among thieves . . . and friends, as the case may be.

anyway, I managed to extract a lot of substance from your rather complex and provocative dissertation concerning aerial castles and the dangers and delights thereof. I think, for the most part, that I comprehend. I had a rather singular experience which I may have told you about which points up the possible consequences of a prolonged letter-writing experience between male and female: in brief, (?) this was a clinical example of what disillusion may follow a correspondence which is entirely two-dimensional (all on paper) without any basis on physical and practical realities.

for a year or so, as the result of vital and most intriguingly intelligent letters from an unknown black-haired fellow (who had read one of my tear-jerking adolescent stories in "17" and somehow deduced that we had great things in common) I poured out my ideas, emotions, and reactions to life in frequent cathartic abandon, and sent them off to chicago. the actual attachment that we two built up, based on utter trust and faith in each other, and complete frankness about our romantic involvements and problems and our ideological growth, became most vivid and important to us. since we both wrote in a free and easy conversational style, the letters were really close to talking, and we seemed to have an instinctive understanding of each others predilections.

the whole affair went along just fine, until I walked downstairs into the livingroom of haven house at college and found an unfamiliar young man waiting for me. as it was the day spring vacation began, I first assumed he must be the taxi driver, until he took the pipe out of his mouth and remarked with a cryptic smile: "this is the third dimension." the shock was enormous. he drove me home, and even a pink convertible couldn't help me to make the natural integration between the fiery, independent, idealistic, pragmatic, vehement personality that I had become fond of in the letters . . . and the quiet, reserved, tense, almost inarticulate male at my side in the car. we had occasionally jokingly reffered in letters to what would have happened if we ever met, but since he happened to be as serious about a special member of the opposite sex as I was, we agreed never to cross each other's paths, and that was to be that.

but here I had gone and built up in my most agile and capricious mind an image of a tall dark compelling guy who would talk and act like his letters. and here was a stranger I simply couldn't adjust to. even after hours of a bull session in some hash house along the road, I found that I was doing all the talking, and he just didn't have the complex ingredients that make up an attractive personality. the let-down was really depressing; it was also unfortunate that, for him, my letters and my personality coincided. oh well, chalk it up.

at any rate, one of the purposes behind going into this is to say that I know what happens to so many of those aerial castles that get built without prosaic foundations like basements and reliable central heating. in the words of one of our more minor and embryonic poets:

"The magic golden apples all look good
Although the wicked witch had poisoned one:
Oh, never try to knock on rotten wood.
From here the moon seems smooth as angel food,
From here you can't see spots upon the sun:
Never try to know more than you should."[1]

all right, we'll say "no prefabricated castles". naturally inclined to idealism, I would have found it hard to admit to the inevitable little flaws and lop-sidednesses in every human nature several years ago. in this world, I am beginning to realize more and more, if the man can produce quite deft and architectural pen and ink sketches and know just when to send dark red roses with just what words, he may, in regrettable addition, blow bubbles in his chicken soup. or something. or the girl with butter yellow hair and the tricky cocktail conceits may just not happen to give a blink of her doe-eyes for fireside evenings reading dylan thomas aloud. so there it is, and of course it's much more complex than that. it all depends what you rate highest in your slide-rule scale of values.

as for "playing parts". ah, such fun, and, one thinks, so safe. if one particularly vulnerable character gets wounded to the core, one can always pretend to whip off the mask, shrug the shoulders, and reveal the mocking and unhurt smile of the actor behind, ready for new and better things. when the truth, all this time, may be the reverse: the hurt face the real one, the smile being the protective and camouflaging mask. and in how many varied roles do we like to see ourselves: the serious creator, the strong honest out-door type that scorns persiflage, the urbane and seductive partygoer; the eggs-and-bacon-and-coffee girl in a housecoat who can also

1 – Sylvia Plath, 'Admonitions'.

exist somehow on olives, roquefort and daiquiris while clad in black velvet, and make a switch to a tanned saltwater and sunworshipping pagan. and different situations open different doors---shall we release the lady? or the tiger? someday, somewhere, with someone, there may be the chance to balance, to stabilize, to learn to integrate all. who knows? but maybe?

all this meandering about parts and facets of personality reminds me of an amusing flick I saw in town yesterday (driving in in the midst of a novel snowstorm.) "The Captain's Paradise", with my pet "Alec Guiness".[1] made me think of you, as always when I see a boat or anything nautical. seems this handsome genius of a captain, shuttling back and forth between gibraltar and africa, managed two blissful menages, diametrically opposed to each other, but sufficing to keep him perfectly happy: the hot, voluptuous, libidinous child of nature on one shore (pampered by gifts of hothouse roses, naughty black underthings, and bikinis) and the veddy domestic, stable, homecooking wife on the other shore (who lapsed into controlled ecstasies over vacuum cleaning attachments and singer sewing machines). sound like fun? well, he managed. with finesse.

that is, until the two consistent and unchanging natures of the women he had set up to delight him forever began to show the versatility of the human personality. the sexy dancer begins to want to settle down to home life like other gals; the staid housewife takes to gin to help her enter in on all the nightlife fun she's missed, and the poor captain tries to no avail to force his women back into the mono-roles he had planned them to retain always. to no avail. they both leave him, lovely, lovely.

reminding me of the adage that a woman needsthree husbands: one to support her in style, one to be an intellectual companion, and one to make competent love . . . or something to that effect. here again, hyperbole. but I vote for versatility, combining several of the desirable characteristics in one personality. complex, but fun.

now this is going on and on. the end draws near. I just want to say that my garrulity tonight is a result of my prolonged silence. also, I like writing to you, talking about anything that comes to mind (incidents, ideas, be they serious or frivolous) and I like thinking that you can share some of your adventures, etc., with me.

I apologize for the fact that my actual living experiences won't be particularly unique and scintillating for a while yet: someday I will no doubt be able to joke about the characters and experiences I've had at

1 – *The Captain's Paradise* (starring Alec Guinness) played at the Astor Theatre, then at 176 Tremont Street across from the Boston Common.

mclean, but not on paper. I have met a lot of nice girls, though--a friend from smith who was in your class I mean "year", one from cornell, and several from vassar---due to winter closing in the opportunities for tennis, badminton rates as the favorite sport, and I'm just learning and having fun doing it. also am playing around with ceramics---liking designing, etc.

I went skating today over in Walpole with a friend in spite of a snowstorm. you would have hysterics if you saw me: I never really learned to skate at the age when all children should because my ankles more or less collapsed, so I am a complete novice. today, however, I must chalk one up because I managed to skate (forward with nothing fancy) a good long time without either taking a nosedive or plunging through the ice. my triumph will come years hence when I learn to skate backwards.

which reminds me: there are so many things I want to learn to do . . . you always impressed me becaused you seem so competently versatile in every respect. I feel much in the position of a willing and eager apprentice to a sleight-of-living artist. just hope I can keep close enough to your mental and technical advancement to make it worthwhile for you to converse. I do like sharing.

tonight, before going back to mclean, I am typing an english paper of warren's . . . all about Brueghel's painting Icarus[1] and three varying critical interpretations of it (one of which is w. h. auden's delightful "musee des beaux arts"). wonderful as my kid brother may be, he certainly had a wicked time writing papers of any kind, or expressing himself in literary form of any kind. his mind is the methodical, literal (not ary) scientific kind, mainly, I think. a good balance and ballast for mine, what?

eight above zero and snowing again now at midnight.

random sleepy thoughts, blurring now, making me feel in a jokable mood . . . like quoting pooh bear. or something.

if you like getting letters, I'll keep up this sort of thing. in fact, I probably will anyway, unless the navy sends me an injunction to stop ruining the morale of its ensigns.

tell me about your ensigns paradise. will you sojourn on the riviera? or visit the blue grotto? or turn leftist on the bank?

let me know also if there are any special news-items you particularly like to hear about. I like talking to you, listening to you, or your music, or reading . . . oh, well, enough. comrade.

your somnolent
sylvia

1 – Pieter Bruegel the Elder, 'Landscape with the Fall of Icarus'.

TO *Marion Freeman*

Saturday 16 January 1954 ALS, Smith College

January 16, '54

Dearest Aunt Marion . . .

Just a little note to tell you how very much your last two sweet and thoughtful letters meant to me – you write so well! I could just picture the snow coming down the way you described it, and I know the way you feel about the freshness and purity of it.

Ruthie wrote me the dearest letter about her experiences over New Year's and at school. She is such a wonderful girl – I just hope our long friendship will last for always! I'm sure she will have the best of times this summer, too.

Recently the hospital has been letting me come home every weekend so I will slowly start getting used to living in the "outside" world again. My visits have worked out quite well, in general – I saw "Captain's Paradise" in town last weekend with mother and Mrs. Norton. This weekend I went to a "bridge tournament" of two tables – as I am merely a beginner at bridge, I was a bit skeptical about my value as a partner, but was at the table of those who were not experts, fortunately, and so all went well and was fun.

Perhaps mother has already chatted with you about the good news – my doctors have talked things over and decided that the best plan is for me to go back to Smith as a junior this second semester and take only 3 courses instead of 5, taking life very easy, with no pressure of a lot of studying or having to get a certain average of marks. Then, if all goes well, I shall complete next year as a senior. Really it is so much pleasanter to contemplate than going back a comparative "stranger" next year. My class graduates this June, and I'll be able to enjoy their company at the same time as I make friends with my junior class which I will be part of next year. So in two short weeks I will have made the transition into the "outside" world of responsibility and independence. I expect it will be difficult in many ways – adjusting to the faster pace of normal life and activity again, but I hope I shall be able to go at it with a much more philosophic and serene attitude!

Your messages have helped so much, dear Aunt Marion – and I so enjoyed reading your entertaining clippings – very best love to all – wish me luck!

Yours,
Sivie

TO *Enid Mark*

Monday 18 January 1954 TLS with envelope, Smith College

January 18, 1954

Dear Enid . . .

Your last plump letter was a delight . . . with all the wonderful news in it! First, how can I ever tell you how happy I am about your engagement![1] Your husband-to-be sounds like the sort of man we used to talk about in our confidential sessions, and I would be most pleased to have the chance of meeting him someday in the future.

All in all, your year sounds most idyllic . . . what with the intriguing thesis topic, and work with such fine, stimulating people as R. G. and Mr. Jules![2] As for seeing you, I am glad to say that it will be sooner than I hoped . . . the doctors here have agreed to my going back to Smith for the second semester as a junior, and taking a light program of three courses, to get back into the swing of academic life without any pressure, or at least as little as possible.

It will be so good to get back on campus for the spring, even if I won't be graduating with you . . . because I want so very much to renew our friendship! I'll be coming back Saturday of midsemester weekend, and, needless to say, will look forward to catching up with you on the multitude of ideas and events that have occurred since last we met.

From my large windows, now, I can see the gray mist of fog thickening and settling on the wide landscape . . . over the snowcovered golf course, and the small gray chapel. The lights have just come on, and hang suspended in luminous haloes of honey-colored brilliance on the path leading down to the town. I feel a peace and serenity just looking at the graying shadows of the trees and thinking that soon I will be back again with my favorite friends, relearning the academic routine . . . more slowly, but surely.

Life here has been rather markedly unscholastic in the bookish sense of the word . . . although I've been learning a good deal about human character. Time flows by lazily, with tobogganing, playing badminton and bridge, hashing out life in the coffee shop, taking in good movies . . . and I've become quite a devotee of ceramics . . . it's such fun. Jane Anderson

1–On 13 June 1954 (the Sunday after her Smith College graduation), Enid Lois Epstein married Eugene L. Mark (1923–); A.B. 1947, Harvard College; M.B.A. 1949, University of Pennsylvania Wharton School of Business.

2–Mervin M. Jules (1912–94); art professor, Smith College, 1945–70; director of Art 13 (Introduction to Art), a studio art course in basic design completed by SP 1950–1.

lives just down the hall from me (you remember her, don't you? lived in Gilette, and was president of her sophomore class.) and we have gotten to be very good friends as we have shared so much (even Dick!)

I can hardly believe that I'll be seeing you . . . in less than two weeks! It will be so good to catch up on things . . . .

Until later,
best love,
Syl

TO *Sally Rogers*[1]

Thursday 21 January 1954[2] TLS with envelope, Smith College

Lawrence House
Smith College
Northampton, Mass.

Dear Sally . . .

Please do forgive me for not answering your letter sooner . . . but I just received it a short while ago. You see, I had to miss the first semester of college this year as I was ill and had to be in the hospital for a few months. Fortunately, though, I am back for the second semester.

You asked me to tell you about Smith . . . and how it would suit you for a college career. Well, I'm afraid I first have to confess that I'm tremendously prejudiced in favor of the college, and rather enthusiastic about the whole set-up of the place. As far as I'm concerned, all types and varieties of girls can be happy at Smith . . . because there are so many girls from all over the country (and from foreign countries, too) there is ample opportunity for "finding" yourself in any of the multitude of friendly groups that are formed through the associations you form in your house, your classes, your sports, and your extra-curricular activities.

Maybe I'd better give you an idea of my own personality orientation so you can better understand what my own particular biases are. I consider myself an ordinary high school graduate, with a maximum interest in English and people. I never had a particularly riproaring social life at high, and I frankly couldn't have afforded to go to Smith if I hadn't gotten a scholarship from the college, lived in a Co-operative house (in many ways, the friendliest houses on campus) and waitressed on tables one meal

1–Sally Rogers (1937–); B.A. 1957, Drake University, Des Moines, Iowa.
2–Date supplied from postmark (Boston); probably typed at McLean Hospital.

a day to help with expenses, and worked during the summers. Roughly, expenses---tuition, board and room and incidentals, mount up to well over $2000 . . . but work and scholarship help can take a big slice off that.

Smith, of course, is rather large in numbers, but it makes up for that in the way life is arranged in small groups . . . , and my memories are not so much of the weekly Wednesday chapel meetings where well over 2000 girls congregate, but rather of the intimate after-dinner coffee sessions with professors visiting the house, art club meetings in the museum lounge, small class "sections"---a refreshing contrast to the large lecture halls where most of the big freshman courses take place . . . and the fun of being part of a crew team or a basketball team: all these characteristics make it relatively easy to extend personal relationships, and though I can't guarantee being accepted by "everyone", I can guarantee that eventually you will orient yourself in a group of warm friends who share your interests, whatever they are.

The faculty, I am sure, is one of the finest in the country . . . fine concerts, exhibits, and speakers are always scheduled . . . and extra-curricular activities give you a chance to follow up your hobby interests . . . whether they be inclined to horseback riding, politics, debating, writing, playing hockey or whatever.

If you think you'd like a smaller group of girls to live with, you might apply to one of the smaller and homier houses, like Dewey, or Sessions, or Haven . . . rather than to the large and more magnificent architectural creation of the Quadrangle---of course, it all depends on your personality characteristics.

I know that many people told me that I'd feel "out-of-place" with so many girls, and most of them so wealthy. The truth is, I found many more close friends than I would have at a smaller college where the choice would not have been so great, and since the "Smith uniform" is generally dungarees and sweaters or skisuits in the winter, and Bermuda shorts in the spring and fall, I found that my wardrobe expenses were almost nil. Sweaters and skirts at dinner and for the evening were in order, and weekend dating (here or away) dresses were an entirely individual matter of preference. "Social life" is a whirl for just about any freshman who wants it to be that way. Big introductory dances for freshman are staged with freshman from near-by men's colleges, and "blind dates" are as easy to pick as daisies!

Again, it all depends on what you want to pursue as interests . . . you can lean toward the studious type who gets to know the professors on an intimate basis (to the point of being invited to dinner at their homes) or lean toward athletics and star in Float Night (one of the most beautiful of college traditions: crew races and floats painted by the freshmen all on the dark waters of Paradise Pond at night under the glow of Japanese lanterns, with the choirs singing from the island, and generally a very obliging moon shining somewhere overhead) or you can be a weekending socialite and trip down to Yale, or Dartmouth, or Harvard . . . or just be casual and cross the river bridge to Amherst which is right next door. The facilities for choice are all there . . . all you have to do is pick and choose. And sometimes that's rather hard with the plethora of interests and events one copes with.

Anyhow, I've been extremely happy in my Smith experience so far (of course everybody gets discouraged and blue at times) and I think that all you have to do is figure out generally what kind of a girl you really are inside (that's pretty hard when you're still growing up, the way we are) and what sort of experience you want out of college . . . and Smith can give it to you. That's the way I found it.

Well, Sally, I could talk on for years about my favorite college, and I do hope that if you choose it that you'll feel free to ask me any questions you like. Your faculty advisor and your junior class "big sister" can explain about everything you'll want to find out about, and are wonderful at helping with advice.

I'll be a senior next year, so if you are going to be a freshman then, please do write and let me know, and maybe we can get acquainted personally. That would be fun . . .

Best of luck in your college applications!

Sincerely,
Sylvia Plath

TO *Gordon Lameyer*

Monday 25 January 1954 TLS, Indiana University

January 25
Monday morning . . .
cloudy, but bluing
with the coming-out sun . .

Dear Gordon . . .

And all I ask is a tall ship . . . claimed the salt-crusted gulled and crabbed sailoring poet. Oh, I sail most salubriously through your letters[1] . . . the

1–Gordon Lameyer to SP, 11 January 1954 and 20 January 1954; held by Lilly Library.

parts about James,[1] and Europe, and imagination and intentions, at any rate; but when we plunge into shop talk about heavies and drones and the main director I climb like Alice through the looking glass, sighting a sea of terms and technicalities quite spanking fresh and most intriguing. You do manage to explain so well.

Future letters (says she, optimistically assuming) may (thank-whatever-gods-there-be including papa Freud) be addressed to Lawrence House, Smith, Hamp. Yup, I'm heading back for the second half of the year under stern injunctions to take a slow and sweet program, easing very gradually into the academic world again . . . as I'm taking a minimum of courses, I'll be a senior next year, which will present minor problems as my friends are mostly graduating this June; but it's going to be so much more swimming this way, since I can concentrate on new acquaintances in the junior class instead of coming into a Rip-Van-Winkle[2] village of relatively complete strangers next fall. Aw heck, nothing like taking five years to graduate. Like those ripe long-maturing wines.

My intellectual activity has been more or less confined to reading Kafka, cerebrating over the SRL's double-crostics, and quaffing sherry before seeing plays. Last Friday it was Eliot's "The Confidential Clerk".[3] Excellent, thought I, entertainment. Though not as clearly defined as was the "Cocktail Party". As one woman behind me exclaimed to her companion: "I know there are two levels to this, but I just can't seem to get to the second one!"

Acting good (maybe you can get to see the play in England or something) . . . but then, I love Claude Rains anyway. And if an operation on my larynx could give me a voice the unique texture of Joan Greenwood's, I wouldn't think twice before calling up the surgeons. The Harvard Crimson[4] came out with intricate Christian interpretations of the whole performance . . . with Christ, Joseph, and the Virgin Mary and the rest of the Biblical gang all latent in the seven characters. My own private reaction, pagan secularist that I am, was philosophical rather than religious, mythical rather than mystical . . . and the compelling wish-granting, fate-directing woman who mixed babies up seemed to me to be a "good witch" type character, as in the old folk tales, rather than the Virgin. But then.

1–American writer Henry James (1843–1916); mentioned in Gordon Lameyer to SP, 11 January 1954.
2–Washington Irving, 'Rip Van Winkle'.
3–T. S. Eliot, *The Confidential Clerk*; SP saw a performance of Eliot's play at the Colonial Theatre, 106 Boylston Street, Boston, on 22 January 1954.
4–Michael MacCoby, 'The Confidential Clerk at the Colonial', *Harvard Crimson*, 15 January 1954, 2.

In your last letter, by the way, you seemed rather intuitively to be voicing one of Eliot's ideas presented in the play: all that business about the importance of differences. "We have many likenesses," said the girl to the boy, "but it is the countless differences inside those likenesses that are important . . ."[1] or something to that effect.

Got up at the decadent hour of one o'clock on Sunday afternoon and spent a couple of hours visiting the Crocketts . . . did you ever meet him? Mr. C? I don't think so, but I may have told you that he was my English prof all through high school . . . the kind of guy who symbolizes for me the highest form of the art of teaching, the sort whose pupils come back year after year, bringing their new husbands and wives for approval, and then the babies. I decorously drank about a whole pot of tea, devoured raspberry tarts, and had a wonderful time talking about Eliot, etc. . . . and listening to their excellent collection of Robert Frost recordings (you would have enjoyed it all, I think . . .) with the roughhewn granitey voice reading the poems as simply as if Frost were talking with you over a splitrail fence.

Last evening was even better, if possible . . one of those small, intimate dinner parties across the street at the Aldriches (they're the ones with five delightful children and a rambunctious pup). There were only five of us . . . Mr. & Mrs. A. (he being a lawyer, they being one of those Harvard-Radcliffe combos) a sister just back from Europe, and a brother at Law School. Between us, we had one of those scintillant evenings where conversation leaps, crackles and behaves the way good conversation should . . . the law man provided us with political and judicial flavor (everything from a heated discussion of "Fifth Amendment communists" to a case history of Russian roulette robbers) to balance our feminine contingent of primarily literates . . . and we afterdinnercoffeed while listening to recordings of Eliot, eecummings, Nash, Marianne Moore[2] . . . and the lyric Welshman I've been in mourning for these past months, Dylan Thomas.

1–T.S. Eliot, *The Confidential Clerk*; in Act Two, Lucasta says to Colby:

'Oh, it's strange, isn't it,
That as one gets to know a person better
One finds them in some ways very like oneself,
In unexpected ways. And then you begin
To discover differences inside the likeness.
You may feel insecure, in some ways—
But your insecurity is nothing like mine'

(New York: Harcourt, Brace and Company, 1954: 61–2).

2–American poet Marianne Moore (1887–1972).

And speaking of Dylan, I just got a copy of the tear sheets[1] from Cyrilly Abels at Mademoiselle containing his verse play "Under Milkwood" which I heard him read at Amherst last spring . . . I could get drunk just on the sound of the words . . . or on the boisterous Welshness of his humor . . . says he:

> "To begin at the beginning: It is spring, moonless night
> in the small town, starless and bible-black, the cobble-
> streets silent and the hunched, courters'-and-rabbits'
> wood limping invisible down the sloeblack, slow black,
> crowblack, fishingboat-bobbing sea. The houses are blind
> as moles (though moles see fine tonight in the snouting,
> velvet dingles) or blind as Captain Cat there in the muffled
> middle by the pump and the town clock, the shops in
> mourning, the Welfare Hall in widow's weeds. And all the
> people of the lulled and dumbfound town are sleeping now.
>
> "Hush, the babies are sleeping, the farmers, the fishers, the
> tradesmen and pensioners, cobbler, schoolteacher, postman
> and publican, the under-taker and the fancy woman, the
> webfoot cockle-women and the tidy wives. Young girls
> lie bedded soft or glide in their dreams, with rings and
> trousseaux, bridesmaided by glowworms down the aisles
> of the organplaying wood. The boys are dreaming wicked
> or of the buckling ranches of the night and the jolly,
> rodgered sea . . .
>
> "You can hear the dew falling, and the hushed town
> breathing . . . . Listen. It is night moving in the streets,
> the processional salt slow musical wind in Coronation
> Street and Cockle Row, it is grass growing on Llareggub
> Hill, dewfall, starfall, the sleep of birds in Milk Wood.
> "Look. It is night, dumbly, royally winding through the
> Coronation cherry trees; goingthrough the graveyard of
> Bethesda with winds gloved and folded, and dew doffed;
> tumbling by the Sailors' Arms. Time passes. Listen. Time
> passes."[2]

1–Dylan Thomas, 'Under Milk Wood', *Mademoiselle*, February 1954, 110–22, 144–56.
2–*Under Milk Wood* © Dylan Thomas (1952). Extract reprinted by kind permission of New Directions Publishing Corp and David Higham Associates Limited.

I didn't mean to dive off the deep end in quoting, but the introduction was just too rhythmic and musically vowelish to cut short. And I can just hear his voice reading, the lovely curlyheaded, boozing hefty poetman.

I am eager to hear about the impressions you register of your first encounter with Europe: sounds, colors, textures, highlights and habits, taste and touch . . . and your ideas and attitudes. And all about (or at least some) how the rather xish character of "I, Gordon" adjusts and alters.

Misc. info: "Greensleeves" is one of my favorite ballads. I have a most congenial and comradely brother. Twenty-one is not as old as it seems. I am determined to learn how to ski no matter what. Only there is no snow now. I would like very much to travel in Europe next summer somehow not with a tour so much as with one congenial and stimulating person, so we could really mingle and stay where we liked as long as we wished without being part of a large gawking cathedralcounting Group. Life in the plural is fun and frolic, but life in the singular has often a more delectable essence.

So with those tagending thoughts, I will leave you for a while, trusting my missive to the whirring helicopters or the atomic subs, or whatever.

Like talking to you, you know. An alter ego of sorts, with all those differences inside the likenesses.

Very
very
best
Sylvia

TO *Philip E. McCurdy*

Thursday 4 February 1954 TLS with envelope, Smith College

<typed on six yellow Street & Smith Publications Inter Office Memorandum sheets; each page has a separate heading>

(1)	TO	Phil	FROM	Syl
	SUBJECT	Life in general	DATE	Feb. 4,
(2)	TO	you	FROM	me,
(3)	TO	PEM	FROM	sp,
(4)	TO	male	FROM	female,
(5)	TO	x	FROM	y
	SUBJECT	z,		
(6)	TO	*	FROM	*

Hello . . .

I am being very naughty and un-Emily Postish by using up my favorite tag ends of inter-office paper for stationery . . . but I did enjoy employing them this summer, and I trust that you know me well enough not to mind my little idiosyncrasies . . . and my penchant for typing personal missives. Which this is.

You should, by the way, feel a bit honored, since this is The First letter I am writing to anyone from my new and most agreeable abode, in spite of the fact that I have a list of unanswered letters about as long as the road from here to Harvard. I hope you don't hate yellow paper. But I like writing on unique things . . . like birch bark, for instance.

Your most excellent and quite delightful letter arrived in the mail this morning, and for some reason . . . or reasons, made me rather happy. You said everything so well, and I very much was pleased with the gist of your statements . . . Even the letter paper you used made me realize how close we are in so many of our tastes . . . the small material ones as well as the larger philosophical ones. Because I like gray paper with red letterheads (have some myself), and I always use black ink. Minor observation perhaps, but of interest nevertheless.

Before plunging into the more basic personal and philosophical topics, just a few words about what has happened since we last saw each other. I don't know if I told you over the phone Saturday that last Sunday I spent the afternoon at the Crockett's home. The whole affair was delightful; a ruddy fire was leaping and crackling in the fireplace, Mrs. Crockett served tea and homemade raspberry tarts, Mr. C. was at his intellectual best, and little Deborah was a dear---we got along well immediately, and evidently she was crushed that I couldn't stay to eat supper with her. We all discussed Eliot's play, which we'd seen, and then listened to an excellent collection of Robert Frost records. The poet's voice is so appropriate to his poems---as rough and textured as granite or the bark of wood; it's just as if he were leaning over a split-rail fence and chatting in a neighborly fashion about country life. All in all, I had a fine time.

Warren drove me up to Smith through snow and sleet after I talked with you, and we almost had a rather drastic accident which left me pale and rather shaky for about half-an-hour afterwards. Coming into Northampton we drove into a thick dark blizzard, and as we began to descend the steep unplowed hill by Paradise (ironic name!) Pond, the car turned into a skid the likes of which I've never seen before and hope never to see again. We sped down the hill sideways, tilting dangerously and completely out of control. Ahead there were three possibilities, all equally unpleasant: We could smash through the glass windows of the green house on the left, crash into the car in front of it, or roll down the steep incline into Paradise Pond. I just remember saying in a repititious conversational way: oh god god god god god god . . . as we spun around and ended up facing up the hill from whence we had come. All's well that ends well, as the cat said as he devoured the last of the canary.

Anyhow, I'm here, in my old room (now a single) in my dear old cooperative house, with two bookcases full of my books, and the sun streaming in the three big windows. I'm passionately in love with all my courses:[1] early American Lit. (Hawthorne, Melville and Henry James), Modern American Lit. with the well-known critic R. G. Davis (the one who went to Washington for the Communist trials last year), European Intellectual History of the Nineteenth Century with a magnificent and powerful german woman, Russian Lit. (Tolstoy and Dostoevsky) and Medieval Art History.[2]

1–When SP returned to Smith College, she completed English 321b (American Fiction) taught by Newton Arvin (1900–63), English professor, Smith College, 1922–60; SP's colleague, 1957–8. SP completed this course as a student in 1954 and corrected papers for it as an instructor in 1958; History 38b (History of Europe) taught by Elisabeth Ahlgrimm Koffka; and Russian 35b (Tolstoy and Dostoevsky) taught by George Gibian (1924–99); associate professor of English and Russian literature, Smith College, 1951–61; SP's thesis adviser, 1954–5; SP's colleague, 1957–8. SP's thesis, 'The Magic Mirror: A Study of the Double in Two of Dostoevsky's Novels', was awarded the Marjorie Hope Nicolson Prize in 1955. SP audited English 417b (The Twentieth Century American Novel) taught by Robert Gorham Davis. SP completed this course in 1955 with Alfred Kazin.
2–Art 33b (Medieval Art) taught by Phyllis Williams Lehmann (1912–2004); art professor, Smith College, 1946–78, Dean 1965–70; SP audited Art 33b, spring 1954.

Honestly, I wish you could some day come up just to audit some of my courses with me . . . I know you'd enjoy them immensely. I've spent most of my free afternoons (all my classes are in the morning) shopping for books and necessities to make my room look like home, plus having appointment with the powers that be in College Hall . . . all of whom have welcomed me back with open arms, so to speak, the lovely people.

Litza Olmstead[1] (or however you spell it) is in my house . . . a very attractive girl, I must say. In fact the underclassmen are all most intelligent and friendly.

Enough of this external commentary. If you are the way I am about such things, you have been impatiently skimming through all this and wanting me to begin on the more abstract and internal issues. So I will.

As far as seeing you again is concerned, you have no need to wonder at all about that. I'd really like very much to continue to see you often in the future, because you are, and most probably will always be, one of my favorite people. So if you ever feel like coming up for a day or so some weekend, just let me know ahead of time, and I'll plan to be free for some good long walks and talks and so on. I don't know if I'll have the chance to come home for a weekend before spring vacation begins on March 24, but I certainly hope I will be able to, and if so, I'll let you know, and perhaps we can get together. It's all up to you about convenient times, etc.

As to our rather unique evening---any departure from conduct and "ritual" which has been agreed upon tacitly involves complexities in that it demands a reassessment of the situation, a consideration of former intentions in the light of an altered context. And for that reason our evening may have given rise to problems which, although complicated, may be resolved.

Our contact in the past has been what one may call "platonic" . . . and, I think, quite satisfying on an idealistic and intellectual plane, while involving walks, tennis, biking, and so forth. And our platonic relationship, as such, I think is capable of continuing without any emotional and physical involvement: in other words, it can continue to burn like a fire to which new kindling (of an evolving mental sort) is always being added. As long as we continue to grow individually, I think we will be close friends . . . .

But the recent addition of a new quantity to our relationship, while intrinsically pleasant, may confuse the issue, perhaps even unwisely

1–Elizabeth Olmstead Null (1935–); B.A.1957, art, Smith College; SP's housemate at Lawrence House. Olmstead was also from Wellesley.

so. Both of us Phil, I am pretty sure, know a good deal about physical attractions to the opposite sex (to be pedantic, and perhaps euphemistic) and have no doubt even accepted physical relationships of a temporary and unsubstantial sort just for the ephemeral transient pleasure of it . . . but while a kiss, let's say, can be just a simple physical act performed out of mere biological hedonism, it can also by symbolic of a great depth of mental and philosophical rapport and appreciation. The difficulty is in distinguishing between the two aspects of the same act, and the effort can sometimes prove confusing. You expressed essentially the same thing when you talked about the difficulty of endowing the same words with new and sincere meaning. It's a difficult job, I think.

And while we can satisfy ourselves physically with a great range of other males and females, an intellectual and spiritual (damn it, the words sound so trite) relationship such as we have had is rather at a premium, and therefore is much more important to retain than anything else. And since a physical relationship can add such complications to a companionship (which we hope to maintain far in the future,) it might be wiser to return to what we had before and leave it at that; I don't know. But I don't ever want to run the risk of spoiling the continued knowing of you, Phil . . . and somehow after a close physical relationship becomes impractical or impossible (for any number of reasons,) it is relatively unusual to continue the comradeship that gave rise to it originally. And I don't want anything like this to happen. So it might be safer to just keep on seeing each other---for lectures, plays or dances or just talks and tennis---and let the rest of alone as far as each of us is concerned. I'm not sure just how you feel about it, but perhaps we can talk about this at length the next time we see each other . . . sometimes it's easier to talk face to face, you know . . . .

Anyhow, I hope my attempt to explain a little of how I feel about the situation had been at least partially coherent . . .

I will enjoy hearing from you, Phil, and hope that we can get together again soon---and in the meantime, my very fond love . . . .

as ever,
Syl

TO *Gordon Lameyer*

Saturday 6 February 1954 | TLS on Smith College News Office letterhead, Indiana University

Saturday, February 6

Dear Gordon . . . .

9 a.m.- Having just pared a multitude of whitish turnips and brutally gored the eyes from a large carton of potatoes, I sit at the third window in my large maroon-gray-and-blue single overlooking the quaint colorful commerciality of Green Street and the far gray humpback of a dark distant hill under the uncertain light of Saturday morning. I have been here a week, and already I feel most comfortable and at home and quite unbelievably contented.

My arrival last weekend was a spectacular one . . . as Warren drove us from the clear wintry metropolis of Amherst across the river into Hamp, we entered a dark whirling cloud of local blizzard which seemed to shroud college hall in a phantomlike obscurity. As we began to descend the unplowed steepness of the hill by Paradise Pond, the car plunged into a skid the likes of which I never hope to see again---speeding downward sideways, turning all the while and leaning dangerously. There were three alternatives---all quite unpleasant: we could smash into the manywindowed greenhouse on the left, crash into the car parked in front of it, or plunge over the steep bank at the right and roll merrily down into the dark iced waters of "Paradise." I remember telling Warren that it had been lovely knowing him and saying: oh, god god god god god (to my own private diety) in that ineluctable interval as we slid, spun, and miraculously came to a halt at the bottom of the hill, facing upward, the way we had come, and rather pale and tremulous from the unexpected and uncontrolled ride. Our new housemother, Mrs. Kelsey,[1] (who is a most felicitous improvement over the fluttering idiot we had last year) understandingly fed us some hot tea in her livingroom, which had the desired quieting effect.

Most pleased am I with all my courses. After long months of no more intellectual work than trying to solve Double-Crostics and (much more difficult and cryptic) attempting with only partial success to decipher one erudite nautical cross word puzzle,[2] I am really glad to get back to my

1–Estella Culver Kelsey (1891–1991) was Head of House at Lawrence House, 1953–7, and at Ziskind House, 1957–9.

2–Gordon Lameyer to SP, 20 January 1954; held by Lilly Library.

program, which includes Russian lit. (Tolstoy and Dostoevsky), European Intellectual History of the 19th cen., Medieval Art, and early and modern American lit., (the latter of which two courses is with my favorite critic, the unbeatable R. G. Davis.) At present, I am reading (simultaneously) Hawthorne,[1] Sister Carrie by Dreiser,[2] and Crime and Punishment:[3] really too pleasurable to be classified as assignments!

Thursday evening Sheila Saunders[4] and I planned to visit my last year's roommate at Amherst for dinner etc., but it was a blasted cold windy night, and we missed the afternoon bus by a few mere minutes, so we stepped out in the road and began to hitch . . . a novel experience for me, at any rate (except for the one evening when a friend and I hitched home from Boston and the boy in the back was merrily tearing up dollar bills and watching them float out the window.) We found Mary in the lab in the depths of the Biology building helping a few senior honors students remove the pituitary glands from newts in regeneration experiments. (Seems that newts with pituitaries can regenerate amputated limbs; not so newts without; ho ho.) Dr. Schotté,[5] the head of the lab (on a Rockefeller grant) welcomed us with literally open arms and said the occasion called for some wine, which he proceeded to extract from his chemical closet in a fat bottle. We cleared away the mutilated newts, poured the wine in beakers and began drinking toasts, etc., and talking for a good long while. Whereupon we all went to dinner at Valentine, after which we spent a most stimulating evening at Dr. Schotté's, imbibing quantities of liqueur and talking and being read to aloud and listening to some young married instructor of math at Princeton imitate the inimitable Tom Lehrer's[6] songs when the occasion called for it, which it often did. Mary seems to enjoy her little apartment and her work at Amherst which is a combination of a research and study grant (she's been broadening out and taking German and music, etc.--besides chopping the feet off newts.) With a promise to

1–Nathaniel Hawthorne, *Hawthorne's Short Stories* (New York: Vintage Books); SP's copy held by Smith College.

2–Theodore Dreiser, *Sister Carrie* (New York: Modern Library, 1917); SP's copy held by Lilly Library.

3–Fyodor Dostoevsky, *Crime and Punishment* (Harmondsworth: Penguin Books, 1956); SP's copy held by Emory University.

4–Sheila Orton Saunders (1933–); B.A. 1954, English, Smith College; SP's housemate at Lawrence House.

5–Oscar Schotté (1893–1988), professor of biology, Amherst College, 1934–66; in 1953–4, Schotté taught 'Embryology: A description of developmental processes in the vertebrates, with an introduction to the physiology of development.'

6–Thomas Andrew 'Tom' Lehrer (1928–), American singer-songwriter, satirist, pianist, and mathematician.

join them all newt-hunting this spring, I left with Dr. S. for Lawrence, arriving one minute before the deadline.

Our house is in an uproar these days as one of the seniors is getting married up here in a week . . . and we are all going through the rituals of showers etc. Remember Throcky? (Joan T.)[1] Well, she writes that she is being divorced this winter, after just being married last year. So it goes; La Ronde. While my inner core is really (I think) sincere and hopeful idealist, my outer layers are rationally pragmatist enough to think that a calm analysis of character and desires and situations would obviate the frequent messes arising from casual or careless matches . . . but one never knows.

Anyhow, it seems a long long way till spring vacation March 24. I hope to be able to drop down to New York to visit a few of my lovely bizarre friends who are modeling, painting and simultaneously interpreting in that fair metropolis . . . but we shall see, we shall see.

Your letters, as usual, are a delight to read, containing and re-creating, as they do, the color and flavor of the scenes you wander through. I was most amused by your recapitulation of the shore(t)-sighting sentiments of some of your men . . . .

2:30 p.m. . . . hours later, having sat through a characteristically witty and whimsical Davis lecture on extrinsic and intrinsic aspects of the novel; perused slides of pagan and Christian art and architecture and learned that early Christian art technique, forms and subjects are nothing less than immediately derived from the antique pagan origins: shepherds, wine-festivals and Dionysus being transformed into shepherds, wine-communion and Christ; rented a modern art masterpiece to hang on the walls of my room; sat for an hour over coffee with one of my friends and caught up on the past year; played reckless bridge on the floor of the livingroom; eaten lunch; now devouring a whitefleshed ocherskinned pear and writing you preparatory to going to tea at Elizabeth Drew's a bit later on . . .

I was just considering the differences in our present modes of existence . . . you, while always intellectually active, are never-the-less emphasizing the actual three-dimensionality of new experiences and discoveries in a new Old World, while I am leading what might be termed the "contemplative life" in the sequestered ivy-twined browsing rooms of my old mind . . . trying always to expand the minute islands of my

1–Joan Throckmorton (1931–2003); B.A. 1953, English, Smith College; Phi Beta Kappa. Married to Melvyn H. Dawson.

philosophic understanding and experience which are microscopic in a view of the whole enormous and quite spectacular universe. I suppose I will be trying to enlarge those islands of understanding and experience for the rest of my life (I hope so at any rate)---to keep on growing and altering until I get to the terminal where "... Grave level-headed men / Know all disjointed temples break their vows and fall / And sonnets alter into alphabet again."[1]

Sometimes, when I try quickly to think back upon the texture and substance, the form and content of these past 21 (doesn't that sound ancient?!) years, I think that the parts of actual living (by which I mean physical experience and doing, as distinguished from activity which is primarily philosophical and mental ...) stand out like unique trees along a roadway which is now rough, now level, now leading through a wasteland, now coming unexpectedly to grape arbors and fountains .... I remember, although it sometimes seems impossible to conceive of myself as a child, physical details: the noon sunlight on my mother's pale hands as she cut raw carrots and beans into an aluminum pot, the radiance making her slender fingers almost translucent; the nightly ritual of going upstairs with Warren to get ready for bed in an ecstasy of fear because we thought giants lived in the dark, mysterious bathroom store-closet; bits of colored watersmoothed glass we collected on the beach and pounded up into blue, red, and green powders which we stored in glass jars; a green rock that became a boat, a castle, an island in our fertile imaginings .... oh, all those multitudinous recollections that are stored in the unconscious, that elude the memory, only to emerge unexpectedly in connection with some stimulus in the present. Life is so largely eating and sleeping and going places without ever getting there: my "experiences" with the quantity of "action" seem so few and outstanding in comparison with the rest of the sitting and reading and sleeping: I can count them off: seeing a baby born, breaking rules and going up spontaneously for the first time in a small private airplane, cutting up the lungs of a human cadaver, being the only white girl at an all-Negro party, battling high waves in a storm in trying to climb aboard our little tipping sailboat, squatting in the blazing noon sun setting strawberry runners and wishing for water, racing my favorite golden retriever along the hardpacked shore at Nauset beach .... little things, large things, that all are somehow very important in the formative

1–Possibly from a draft or earlier version of SP's poem 'Ice Age' which features similar lines and themes: 'and so the final answer is not met / though sonnets are altered back to alphabet / again ...'

scheme of living. I want to do more, so very much more: to bike and hike through Europe, to travel out West, to meet and know and love people with that intense rapport, transient and elusive though it may be, which I have felt so strongly in so many separate instances: I want to condition myself to hear, and not just listen; to see, and not just look; to communicate, and not just talk; to feel, and not just touch . . . . It is so disastrously easy to settle down into the smooth undemanding rituals of the trite sheepish conformist life . . . . That is why it is good to have friends who will stimulate and arouse one . . . .

I think you said that you would not mind hearing a few fragments of things I have written; of course, nothing has been written since last spring . . . . and I don't remember if I showed you this brief sarcastic bit: Anyhow, here it is. Tell me what you think of it:

Dirge in Three Parts

I.

The door bangs shut upon the tiny garden:
  Gigantic children rant and kick the stairs
And scribble cross notes to the wicked warden
  Who exiled them in spite of bribes and prayers.

II.

The road to Oz is flawed with shocking ruts,
  Fallen prey to scarecrows and tin men;
The two-faced lion lives on blood and guts,
  And Dorothy won't walk that way again.

III.

The vampire clock mocks the unwinding heart
  And claps black hands, converting man to dung;
The friendly sluts and chimeras depart,
  And dirt is devil's food upon the tongue.

Of course the first verse is supposed to derive from a small satire on Adam and Even in Eden combined with Alice-in-Wonderland and DP's in general. The second uses the fairytale Oz yellow-brick road to take the place of Dante's road of life and the pilgrimage in Bunyan's book. The third plays on the inexorable black magic of time passing, childhood dreams lost, and the final taste of inevitable death. Cheery, wot? W. H.

Auden accused me of being too glib, which I think is a valid criticism in most cases . . . except I wasn't trying to be completely serious. Also played with vowel sounds . . . .

Did I tell you that I bought two magnificent records before I came back: one is Edith Sitwell's Façade with the bizarre music of William Walton[1] in the background. Mother doesn't like it, and general family concensus makes me shut all the doors when I listen to what they think in incomprehensible gibberish, while I insist that vowels do have wave lengths and can give a pure sensuous listening pleasure, even when dissociated from meaning . . . "Said the navy blue ghost of Mr. Belaker, the allegro Negro cocktail shaker . . ."[2] and so on. The other record is a wonderful Dylan Thomas set of readings,[3] with his musical lyric voice, living beyond the grave for me, and making me shiver and sometimes even cry to hear "Do Not Go Gentle into That Good Night" and "In the White Giant's Thigh" . . . . these being the first records of the poet readings I have ever had, I love them blithely well.

This letter is becoming much more monumentally long than I ever intended. Sometimes I'm not even sure to just which sort of Gordon I'm writing . . . . that is what this medium of prose and typewritten talk can do to one if prolonged . . . . it can so abstract a personality that it becomes altogether too easy to extend the attributes of an individual to cover all sorts of characteristics, some of which may not even exist. Leading to the eventual shock of realization some day in the future.

This, I sincerely hope, will not happen. If I continue to feel that I can tell you just about anything that I do or think, I am presupposing a sensitive and understanding recipient at the other end of the postal line, an individual whom I endow with definite perceptive comprehension. The test comes in the more complex three-dimensions . . . where action is added to and becomes an integral cause-and-effect of the abstracted words. All this may be incoherent . . . . but I hope, and usually assume, that you are kindred enough to me to supply much of what is badly said, and sometimes not said at all.

1–English composer Sir William Walton (1902–83). The publication was *Façade: An Entertainment* (London, New York: Oxford University Press, 1951).

2–SP slightly misquotes Sitwell's 'Four in the Morning'. The poem reads, 'Cried the navy-blue ghost / Of Mr. Belaker / The allegro Negro cocktail-shaker . . .'

3–Most likely *Dylan Thomas Reading A Child's Christmas in Wales and Five Poems* released by Caedmon in 1952. The five poems are 'Fern Hill', 'Do Not Go Gentle into That Good Night', 'In the White Giant's Thigh', 'Ballad of the Long-Legged Bait' and 'Ceremony After a Fire Raid'.

Do feel free (even libidinously so) to share all sorts of ideas and experiences with me, please, or to say anything, absolutely anything that comes into your lovely head . . . .

and so, my peregrinating Ulysses,
adieu for a time
aufviedersehen (or howsoever
they spell it . . . .)
your own particular
sylvia

TO *Ellen Bond*[1]

Sunday 7 February 1954 TLS, Library of Congress

Lawrence House
Smith College
Northampton, Mass.
February 7, 1954

Miss Ellen Bond
Personal and Otherwise
Harper's Magazine
49 East 33 Street
New York 16, N.Y.

Dear Miss Bond:

Needless to say, I was extremely pleased to hear from you about the possible publication of some of my poems this coming spring.[2] There are only a few recent items to add to the information I sent you last spring.

Briefly, I am a junior at Smith College this year, honoring in English. This fall I was named a junior Phi Bete, and my past activities have included working on the Editorial Board of the Smith Review (our literary magazine) and being the Smith College correspondent for the Daily Hampshire Gazette newspaper.

My poems and stories have appeared in Seventeen and Mademoiselle magazines, as well as in the Christian Science Monitor. Last June I spent the month working at Mademoiselle in New York as one of the twenty guest editors chosen annually from colleges all over the United States. As

1–Ellen Bond worked for the 'Personal and Otherwise' department at *Harper's Magazine*.
2–Ellen Bond to SP, 29 January 1954; held by Lilly Library.

guest editor from Smith, I was assistant to the managing editor of Mlle., Cyrilly Abels.

And that is a short history of my activities since last spring. I shall be most eager to hear what issue of Harper's my poem will appear in!

Sincerely,
Sylvia Plath

TO *Aurelia Schober Plath*

Monday 8 February 1954[1] TLS, Indiana University

<typed on yellow Street & Smith Publications Inter Office Memorandum sheets, with heading>

TO you FROM me
SUBJECT things in general DATE monday

Dearest mother . . .

I'm sending you this blank for next year which I hope you can make out immediately and send to the office of Scholarships as the blanks are all supposed to be in by Feb. 14. I put down tentatively that I expect to earn $400, although I don't even know if I could ever get a job paying that much. So don't you put down that you can give me a whole lot next year, as you are paying for all this semester, and they certainly will want to help if I do well, and even if I don't.

Saw Miss Mensel today, and had a nice chat. Also went to tea at Miss Drew's Saturday afternoon and had a lovely time . . . she is such a dear . . . hugged me and kissed me and said how happy she was to have me back. I still have some people left to see, but the major items of immediate importance are completed. Have only seven letters out of about 20 left to write . . . sent off the most important ones to Mrs. Prouty, Mary Wrenn,[2] etc.

Had a blind date at Amherst Saturday night . . . . very young and childish, although goodlooking, with a penchant for beer. He obviously thought I was tremendously witty, even though I didn't say one thing out of the ordinary, but rather enjoyed making little remarks that were over his head. The boys over there are all so young and weak and "sheepish"

1–Date supplied from internal evidence.
2–Possibly Mary Wrenn Morris Baird, 1936 graduate of Radcliffe and author of privately printed *Odd Poems* (1931).

fraternity-wise. I do think that the standards at Amherst are much inferior to those at Harvard and Yale. Gordon certainly was an exception to the rule.

However, although my date in himself was no prize, I sized up the situation practically, turned on the laughable cosy side of my nature, curled up on the big leather couch and drank beer and listened to music, and managed to enjoy myself in a casual hedonistic way.

I have spent a good deal of time chatting in the rooms of various girls in the evening and playing bridge, figuring that getting well acquainted with some of the underclassmen is most important at first. Am reading Hawthorne's short stories, "Crime and Punishment" and "Sister Carrie" by Theodore Drieser. All very good books.

Needless to say, it is simply wonderful to be back here, and I feel no desire to graduate, amazingly enough, with the rest of my class. I like the underclassmen in Lawrence very much and am growing to feel more at home with them which is a good thing.

I'll probably be talking to you on the phone soon, so I won't go on any longer. I'm glad that Harper's wrote. I was sure they thought I was dead or something and were never going to publish anything, or if they did, that they were going to put a black border around it!

much love,
sivvy

TO *Gordon Lameyer*

Wednesday 10 February 1954[1] TLS in greeting card,[2] Indiana University

<printed greeting>
Valentines, schmalentines / As long as you're healthy
<signed>
to Gordon / from Sylvia

Dear Gordon . . .

Couldn't resist sending you this bit of frippery, even though, because of lateness of delinquent helicopters it may arrive later than the Day.

1–Date supplied from internal evidence.
2–Panda Prints Valentine card designed by Rosalind Welcher.

Life has managed to become a great deal more complex and varied since I last wrote, which I believe was not too long ago. Last night I went to the Hampshire Bookshop to hear a lecture by New England Novelist Esther Forbes,[1] and to meet her and chat afterwards. Tonight it is a dance drama "Green Mansions",[2] with choreography by one of my best friends, Sidney Webber, and tomorrow it is a lecture by Mary Ellen Chase[3] and a reception at the President's House afterwards . . . all of which promises to be most fun!

I'll write more at length later . . . in the meantime, be good and enjoy yourself (if you can do both at the same time!) and accept my best wishes and best love . . .

s. p.

TO *Margaret Cantor*

Monday 15 February 1954 — TLS (photocopy)[4] on Smith College letterhead, Indiana University

February 15
Monday

Dear Mrs. Cantor . . .

This will just be a little note between classes to tell you how very much I appreciated your last wonderful letter---it simply exuded love and strength which I felt most deeply! I can't say in words how much it meant to me to receive it, but I think you must understand.

Even though I steeled myself for all sorts of little awkwardnesses and problems in my coming back, I was met by such love and warmth that I still can hardly believe it. All the small difficulties that might have been seem to have melted completely away in my love of being back among my old and new friends. Everything is suffused with sunshine and love---as Mary Baker Eddy says: "We are sometimes led to believe that darkness is as real as light; but Science affirms darkness to be only a mortal sense of the absence of light, at the coming of which darkness loses the appearance

1–American novelist Esther Louise Forbes (1891–1967); in 1954 Forbes published *Rainbow on the Road* (Boston: Houghton Mifflin).

2–Inspired by the 1904 novel by William Henry Hudson.

3–SP attended Chase's evening lecture 'Imagination in the Old Testament' on 11 February 1954 in Sage Hall.

4–This photocopied letter, found in the manuscript of *Letters Home*, has some text missing in the copy. Text appearing in < > is supplied by the editors.

of reality." And so the darkness which I once believed real, has dissolved like a mist or fog, showing the clear, wonderful outlines of the true world, and the true self. And for helping me to see what I really was and am and always will be, for having faith that the "real me" was there, I want to thank you from the bottom of my heart! Knowing you and <y>our wonderful family has been one of the main <s>timulating and beautiful experiences of my <l>ife.

<B>est love to you all---I'll write again soon.

Love,
Sylvia

TO *Philip E. McCurdy*

Tuesday 16 February 1954 — TLS with envelope, Smith College

February 16
Tuesday p.m.

Dear Phil . . .

Here I sit after my luncheon of mushrooms and bacon, overcome by an early afternoon drowsiness (no doubt a result of my staying up till all hours last night discussing the intricate problem of personal relationships, both intuitively emotional and articulately rational.) A fat, disgusting pale yellow spider just dropped down from the ceiling beside my typewriter; I squashed the crawling monster most ruthlessly with a copy of Crime and Punishment and life is once again placid . . .

Your descriptive letter arrived today, and I enjoyed your sharing events and reactions with me a great deal . . . I hope future news about your mother[1] is auspicious. I understand your attitude in regard to that unfavorable news, I think, because of similar, and perhaps more shocking feelings of mine in regard to my own mother---which I shall probably discuss with you some day.

Went to a stimulating lecture by Mary Ellen Chase Thursday night on the imagination in the Old Testament, and to a reception at President Wright's house afterward (I'd never been before---seems you and I are really becoming close in contact with people of stature) which included a crackling fire, coffee, and good talk . . . Sunday my alter ego (Marcia

1–Philip McCurdy learned that his 'mother' was actually his grandmother, Magda Bergliot Andresen McCurdy (1892–1981), and his 'sister' (Betty) was his birth mother, Magda Elizabeth McCurdy Meredith (1912–2001).

Brown) and I had morning coffee downtown and talked heatedly about Dostoevsky, theories of crime and insanity, and heard a fine Unitarian "sermon" on marriage and the Kinsey report.[1] I have always thought that the Unitarian church depends primarily on its minister for appeal, as the ritual is so bare and almost negligible, while in ritualistic churches, like the Catholic, the minister and priests are mere automata in the important sequence of the ceremony, and mean little as individuals. Our Northampton minister is more like a dramatic college lecturer with a subtle wit and keen intellect--and we take notes on our programs . . . .

Our house is in a great uproar today as one of the seniors is getting married at the Congregational church downtown. I haven't been to a wedding since I was a flowergirl at my aunt's (I was still in the pigtailed stage) and scattered rose petals blithely down the center aisle. Unhappily, I am rather unconventional in regard to the system of marriage, engagements etc. . . . I don't worship in the cult of the diamond, or the elaborate service, because psychologically I am not oriented to outer trappings and display, but rather to the bare honest elementals of people. In my more radical stages I have thought that the marriage ceremony (as often overdone, with crowds of spectators, drinks and frills) would be best performed on a rock cliff overlooking the ocean (my personal symbol of life force and fertility) with only a few really deep friends there . . . sort of a pledge of honesty, relating one to the huge natural forces of procreation and life: a kind of pagan ritual, in some respects, clean and unadorned . . . but I shall go, anyway, to this and spectate.

Just bought (ah, the spendthrift!) a wonderful New Directions copy of my favorite Tennesee Williams play which I saw in New York before it folded last spring: <u>Camino</u> <u>Real</u>.[2] You must read it sometime (although seeing it is almost indispensable for the true emotional impact, as dance rituals play an important part). I'll loan you my copy when next we meet--it only takes an hour or two to read. I remember lines like: "And these are the moments when we look into ourselves and ask with a wonder which never is lost altogether: Can this be all? Is there nothing more? Is this what the glittering wheels of the heavens turn for?" and "We have to distrust each other. It is our only defense against betrayal." and "We are all of us guinea pigs in the laboratory of God. Humanity is just a work in progress."[3] Oh, I wish you had seen that play with me . . .

1–Alfred C. Kinsey, *Sexual Behavior in the Human Female* (Philadelphia: Saunders, 1953).
2–Tennessee Williams, *Camino Real* (Norfolk, Conn.: New Directions, 1953); SP's copy held by Smith College.
3–SP annotated these passages on pp. 55, 96 and 113 in her copy.

Speaking factually now . . . I have been trying to persuade my brother to come up to Smith some weekend soon because I would like to see him, and also I know he would like to go out with some girls up here, and I have already a freshman picked out for him. But as yet I have no idea when he'll possibly be coming. Anyway, I would like at least to extend you a blanket invitation to come visit me whenever you could best spare the time . . . for a day, an evening, a day or two some weekend. We could talk, go dancing, see a foreign movie . . . walk, have pizza and beer . . . or anything you'd feel in the mood to do. So maybe you'd want to get in touch with Warren and arrange to come up with him some weekend, or come alone . . . I don't know. Just let me know about a week or so ahead if you ever feel like visiting me . . . I'd really enjoy it and think we could have a lovely time . . . I do wish somehow that you could visit some of my courses, but that is impractical, I suppose . . . .

bye for now. Till later . . .
Love,
Syl

TO *Gordon Lameyer*

Sunday 21 February 1954[1] — TLS on Smith College letterhead, Indiana University

Sunday evening

Dear Neptune . . .

Early of a black slithering sunday evening, with rain walloping in swats against windows and the thin wind keening like a lost fox in the far stalwart purpling hills . . . car lights swing into the blithering rain, shouldering through curtains of holy beads and dwindling in tail lights of blurred red neon . . . streetlight caught in a black twigged nest of waterslick boughs . . . .

Shall shall shall I? I shall. Talk to him. But how to tell? How to tell, now that he has delved and delineated dreams that were once . . . but are now rememberings---there is no more name playing left . . . he is so witbeguiling and so wayfaringclever . . . he is so blithevoweled and so competantly consonental, so lithely continental . . . how? But I shall. Talk. While other voices tell their griefs and joys in other rooms, while the live and the dead spin orbited nice, perilous and beautiful . . .

1 – Date supplied from internal evidence.

The letter came.[1] The post man brought the letter in a curiously carved box of quaint device. The letter weighed several thousand pounds, and contained within it the walls and walks of a city, the call of colleens, the fate of a man. Like the servile vapor that sprouted from Aladdin's lamp, bowing and scraping and murmuring, "At your service, master!" the words sprang upward and leapt and danced and created kaliedoscopic mosaiced gordonian worlds. I read, I lived, I quoted it. I cut classes even, I did. reveling in evil . . . raveling sleepless sleeves . . . (you used up all the names in the world so you'll just have to be satisfied with appallingly unconnotative page numbers!)[2]

Spring struck hamp with sundiamonded slush and voluptuous blunt mud for two days, and there was singing in the gutters where the coffee-colored rivulets ran riot to the sewerholes, and there was softening softening of sun in the haystacks of cloud and there was starsap in the song of orion swinging up over the housetops in spilling dippers of glory and the moon blew up balloonly, "a circumambulating aphrodisiac"[3] . . . boys and girls coupled like noah's ark animals in the curving dark and it was the rally day of benevolent love . . .

Reading Winesburg, Ohio, she lay alone in the sun on the roof of the Alumnae Gym, the gravel under her slicker making waffle pique patterns in red on her white flesh, winterpale, and she faced the sun shuteyed with mystic smile of sylvan bliss, feeling the golden lust of pagan heat, and the vine leaves twining in her hair, and the rough gallop of the following centaurs in the grapeblue arboring vineyards . . . She dreams and reads, aloud because it is good aloud, with only the sun listening in a great core of golden silence: "Love is like a wind stirring the grass beneath trees on a black night. You must not try to make love definite. It is the divine accident of life. If you try to be definite and sure about it and to live beneath the trees, where soft night winds blow, the long hot day of disappointment comes swiftly and the gritty dust from passing wagons gathers upon lips inflamed and made tender by kisses . . ."[4] And she underlines in black ink, and turns down the corner of the page as is her bad bad habit . .

1–Probably Gordon Lameyer to SP, 4 February 1954; held by Lilly Library.

2–In Lameyer's 4 February 1954 he played and punned on their names: Page 2: 'Myth Sylphia Plath / Myster Gordian Lameyer'; page 3 'Silver Plate / Golden Lamb'; page 4: 'Sylvan Path / Golden Lyre'; page 5 'Silvern Plume / Golden Limb'; page 6: 'Salvia Plant / Goldenrod Lamina'; page 7: 'Silverfish Pond / Goldfish LaMeer'; page 8: 'Silverfish Pop / Goldfinch L'amour'; page 9: 'Silver Age Plath / Golden Age Lamé'; and page 10: 'Sylvanite / Godroon'.

3–Christopher Fry, *The Lady's Not For Burning*, 67.

4–Sherwood Anderson, *Winesburg, Ohio*.

Then she becomes inebriate of Christopher Fry: all about . . . "Creation's vast and exquisite

Dilemma! Where altercation thrums
In every granule of the Milky Way,
Persisting still in the dead-sleep of the moon,
And heckling itself hoarse in that hot-head
The sun. And as for here, each acorn drops
Arguing to earth, and pollen's all polemic---
We have given you a world as contradictory
As a female, as cabbalistic as the male,
A conscienceless hermaphrodite who plays
Heaven off against hell, hell off against heaven,
Revolving in the ballroom of the skies
Glittering with conflict as with diamonds:
We have wasted paradox and mystery on you
When all you ask for is cause and effect!"[1]

Adding for conflict and contrast the yet other facet of her nature that shudders in an ecstasy of horror when Mephistopheles in Crime and Punishment muses on the future life and says:

"And what if there are only spiders there . . . We always imagine eternity as something beyond our conception, something vast, vast! But why must it be vast? Instead of all that, what if it's one little room, like a bath-house in the country, black and grimy and spiders in every corner, and that's all eternity is? I sometimes fancy it like that?"

And why should I quote? Speak in other voices? Because, like the archetypal wanderer, I am a part of all that I have met, and all that I have met is a part of me, and there is an mystic electric current of understanding and intuitive rapport that runs through all the subjective worlds we two share fragments of, and perhaps similar stimuli may achieve similar results . . .

Always people are talking to me . . . a young brash illegitimate boy who dreams to be a great medical artist to prove he is better than all the other accident-scorning legitimate bastards . . . a very German Fulbright from Stuttgart[2] who is the only one who knows the little town of Grabov

1–Fry, *The Lady's Not For Burning* (New York: Oxford University Press, 1950), 53; underlined in SP's copy. Extract © Christopher Fry (2007). Reprinted by kind permission of Oberon Books Ltd.

2–Gerhard Rauscher from Stuttgart, West Germany, was a student 'not enrolled as a candidate for a degree' at Amherst College, 1953–4.

where my father was born . . . somebody's roommate who has a red scar on his face from where he got thrown from the truck when it turned over and who wanted to tell about the time in Nassau when he was sitting alone on a pier and a negro prostitute came along, and said: Are you lonely, and he said: yes, and she said: come, and he followed at six paces to a little room in a squalid alley where there was just space enough for a cot and the laundry that she did, and she knew he had no money, and he wanted to talk, so she talked and talked and that was how it was . . . and the fatherly Estonian artist who keeps sending more pictures and saying: think of all the museums and music and plays there will be when you come and live with my mother and I for days in the spring . . . and the med student cured of tb taking off on a boat for three months of wandering in Europe trying to find himself because he is lost, lost, lost . . . and the lovely unconventional blonde girl claiborne[1] who is marrying the jewish boy[2] with the communist sister who married a negro--she comes in and talks and listens, and it is two in the morning and there is all the question of free will and destiny and objective and subjective worlds to be considered more . . . and there is pizza and wine and candlelight . . . and wind blowing clean and hard like water across the mouth . . . and tan toned hills and tweed fields and light blue denim skies . . .

Oh, gordon gordon gordon . . . you are you forever and I am I and the hours and hours I could spend talking, reading aloud, listening, walking and communing with you are many and multitudinous.

The world is your oyster . . . venuses on the half shell and all that . . . worlds of words cannot convey what the liquidity of a look may say . . .

As T. S. E. says in "The Confidential Clerk":

> "There's no end to understanding a person.
> All one can do is to understand them better,
> To keep up with them: so that as the other changes
> You can understand the change as soon as it happens,
> Though you couldn't have predicted it . . ."[3]

I don't need to tell you that I like that idea.

I don't have even to tell you, but I cannot give you a two-dimensional glance that would say it, so I will wait until I can be in the three and four

1–Elizabeth Claiborne Philips Handleman (1933–); B.A. 1954, history, Smith College.
2–Avrom R. Handleman (1928–2015); B.S. 1951, M.S. 1953, Massachusetts Institute of Technology; married SP's classmate E. Claiborne Philips on 7 June 1954.
3–T. S. Eliot, *The Complete Poems and Plays of T. S. Eliot* (New York: Harcourt, Brace, [1952]); a gift from her friend Marcia Brown Stern; SP's copy held by Smith College.

dimensional kingdom before I begin to forsake words and substitute what the words are substitutes for . . .

Our names <u>are</u> protean and, please whatever gods there be, so are we

your provincial
polemical
nereid
s.

ps: you will unfairly deprive people of your humanity if you do not become a lawyer. you could, you know, and that would be stimulating and full of all people . . .

TO *Jane V. Anderson*

Thursday 25 February 1954 — TLS with envelope (photocopy), Smith College

February 25
Thursday

Dear Jane . . .

Not that I'm getting psychic in my middle age, but I had a dream about you last night, and today I received your letter---all of which reminded me forcibly that I have been planning to write you for a long time ever since I got back to the campus.

Miraculously enough, I am in the same big sunny three-windowed room I had last year, only now I have it all to myself, instead of with a roommate--the girls in the house moved around so that I could have it, which was much more than I ever expected.

The trip up was a story in itself: I had been hectically shopping and packing all my belongings in the very brief time I had before going, and Warren drove me back along with mother. We had to drive very slowly as the roads were bad, and going through Amherst it was clear . . . however, as soon as we neared Northampton we ran into a thick swirling blizzard which so shrouded the place that we couldn't even make out College Hall through the blasts. On Paradise hill we got into the most fantastic and frightening skid I've ever been in: the car tilted dangerously and began to slide sideways down the steep unplowed incline--faster and faster, turning all the time. I saw with blinding clarity that we would either crash through the glasswindowed green house, or into the car in front of it, or roll over the hill and end up in (to make a bad pun) Paradise.

I remember the interminable seconds as we slid, utterly out of control, and I wondered if I really was living in a deterministic universe and had displeased the malicious gods by trying to assert my will and return to Smith. I felt an enormous affection for Warren sprout in me to insufferable proportions, and thought in absolute horror "this can't happen to us--we're different"---the same way a soldier must feel a certain invulnerability and indestructible identity before going into battle. Capriciously, the car turned about and skidded to a shuddering stop, facing up the hill which we had descended so precipitously, without crashing into any of the three alternatives that had confronted us.

So it was with literally shaking steps that I went apprehensively into the back door of Lawrence House. Fortunately, as I had thought, most of the girls were away, this being the free weekend, so only a small cosy group greeted us. Our wonderful new housemother gave us tea in her rooms, and the girls were so favorably impressed by Warren that everything went off very smoothly and I bade my security goodbye and went upstairs to unpack. Two of my old friends came over to visit, and I played bridge and typed the conclusion to another friend's thesis, and was outwardly ensconced as the girls began to arrive on Sunday.

The first week, as I had forseen, was a round of visits to college hall---seeing officials and professors and getting my schedule settled, shopping for books and curtains, going to classes, and memorizing the names of the twenty new freshmen in our house. I was weary, slept soundly, and at the end of the week felt that I had been living here all my life---the past fading and integrating into the background with each succeeding day.

My schedule is wonderful: all morning classes: I am taking early American lit with Arvin, Russian lit with Gibian, and 19th cen. intellectual history with Koffka. I am auditing Medieval Art (which I love) with Mrs. L. (who wishes to send fond regards to you) who is most intriguing and forceful---and modern American lit with my pet Mr. R. G. Davis. Both of the latter courses will offer just as much as I give them, and I do the reading as a reward for accomplishing my regular work. As I have my first writtens next week, I am rapidly running through the Idiot by Dostoevsky, having just finished Crime and Punishment and Notes from Underground.[1] Amusingly enough, I felt conspicuous at first during the discussions of suicide in these books, and felt sure that my scar was glowing symbolically, obvious to all (the way Hester's scarlet

1–Fyodor Dostoevsky, *Notes from Underground* in *The Short Novels of Dostoevsky* (New York: Dial, 1951); SP's copy held by Smith College.

letter burned and shone with a physical heat to proclaim her default to all). But now I am really so adjusted to my attempt of last summer that I may even write my Russian paper on the theme of suicide, feeling that I have somewhat of a personalized understanding of the sensations and physical and mental states one experiences previous to the act. No one has questioned me about my experience, and I have voluntarily shared notes with Jane Truslow, who had shock at Baldpate,[1] I discovered, and Claiborne Phillips who is my closest friend in the house, and Marcia Brown who is my really best friend and whose mother is still in a mental hospital in NYC, but is rapidly improving . . . but in all these cases, we just spoke of my experiences thorougly once, and that was that, none of the daily self-examinations and analyses that I subjected myself to with friends at McLean.

All of the difficulties which I was prepared to encounter have melted away like snow in the sun. My classmates consider me a junior now, and in Rally Day, I felt not the slightest tremor of frustration or envy as I sat clad in virginal white and saw my former friends file down the aisles in black gowns--rather I felt good, for I really am glad to have this extra year, now, even though I will of course miss my friends, many of whom are getting married this June (I'm going to be a bridesmaid in Marcia's wedding, by the way). Also, with my new easy-going feelings, I am enjoying my reading, and although I know the writtens will test my power of retention and absorption, I am not going to don mourning if I get only average marks (Miss Mensel cheerfully told me that it didn't matter if I failed all three of my courses!) I am enjoying myself, and maybe I'm slow, and no genius, but I am anyway having fun---buying lots of books for my courses and going to lectures---the most recent by Mary Ellen Chase and Esther Forbes (both of whom I met and chatted with). Miss Drew had me over for coffee and actually kissed me, in greeting! And Miss Page (my advisor in place of Miss Lincoln, thank God!) is another good confidante.

I've been on several long hikes these past springy days---out along the railroad tracks into the country, and on a picnic with Marcia where we biked out by an old mill stream and had a good bull session while devouring apples and sandwiches.

In summary, everybody has treated me just as if nothing had happened, and I feel most at home and causal about the whole episode, which I never thought possible.

1–Baldpate Hospital, Georgetown, Mass.

The most indicative part of my life has been the social aspect. I had resigned myself to being totally without male contacts, but in the short space of four weeks I have been out with about seven different boys---not that quantity is indicative, but that's just the way it happened. All my housemates seem to have friends of their dates coming down, so I decided that since my marital future was far from being at stake, I might as well have fun and get back into the swing of social talk.

So I've been to two good British movies and cocktails with a guy over at Dartmouth business school, gone over to Amherst four times, each with a different but likeable chap (over there it seemed as if my whole social past was being reviewed before me---saw all the Wellesley boys: Maury Longsworth,[1] Mal Brickett,[2] Dick Baughman,[3] Bob Blakeslee, et. al., plus a boy I worked with at the Belmont Hotel two summers ago, plus the first boy I dated in my freshman year, who remembered me for some obscure reason!)--also had wine from chemistry beakers in the bio. lab with Dr. Schotté and my last year's roommate, Mary Bonneville, who is doing grad work over there. This weekend I am going over to a house-dance with a little German guy on a Fulbright whose name is Gerhardt! Mike Lotz, Perry's friend from Yale medical school, came up one weekend for pizza and candlelight talks, and Sunday I was surprised to be visited by a charming Junior at Harvard whom I hadn't seen since I played tennis with him five summers ago: Tony Stout, a Wellesleyite, and most delightful. So, as you can see, I feel that my escapade had in no way made a lasting scar on my future associations, but is of advantage in deeping my understanding of self and others . . .

Dick, by the way, headed for Europe this week very depressed and unorganized, as his mother explained it. He seems to be under the impression that he has no appeal for the kind of girl he wants to marry and his brother and close friends are trying to locate such. In the light of our long talks, it will be most interesting to see what turns up!

I just love my room here, done with maroon bedspread and chair, grey curtains and lampshades, blue pillows and armchair, and paintings all over the walls and two bookcases overflowing with gaily jacketed books---a welcome den, in contrast to my strange, almost physical aversion to my nice, but annoyingly antiseptic and un-private room at Belknap.

1–Maurice Alfred Longsworth, Jr (1932–); B.A. 1954, Amherst College.

2–Malcolm Hoyt Brickett (1933–2009); B.A. 1955, Amherst College.

3–Richard DeWeese Baughman (1934–); B.A. 1955, Amherst College; M.D. 1960, Harvard University.

Dr. Booth is just as you and I agreed---and I don't think anyone could ever give me that psychiatric relationship so felicitously established at McLean. But anyhow, now I feel that psychiatric help is really superfluous: I have several close friends to confide in, and no problems---I'll be back here next year, and my social, academic, and personal life is flexible and unhurried. So I see Dr. Booth for one long session a week, and even then find that we discuss on a more abstract level of ideas, rather than on an immediate temporal one, because I am living now, as I was not at McLean, and as yet my experience in the three dimensional world of action in time is smooth and consistent with my new attitude of easy-going and relaxed averageness, in contrast to my former hectic leaps for the exceptional. I feel in general, very calm, philosophical, and indeed, consistently "happy" rather than spasmodically ecstatic.

Amusingly enough, my job in the house is preparing vegetables every morning, and I enjoy it to the hilt---after my repeated desire to go into the kitchens at McLean, this comes as a pleasant and novel task, most refreshing, and reminding me of my work on the farm. I really enjoy peeling potatoes and onions and slicing carrots! The cooks are fun, and there is always time for that inevitable third cup of coffee before my nine o'clock class.

So . . . I did not mean to ramble on for so long, but the life is full here, like a fruit cake, instead of just plain bread without salt, and it now seems inevitable that I am back, although at the time of deciding I felt I had free will. Heaven knows when I will really feel like writing again---I just know that I am living now, and I need to do a lot more of it before I feel I can tell the world about it . . .

Nothing spectacular goes on, except the fact of going to classes, playing bridge with the girls, having bull sessions in our Smith prototype of the Coffee Shop, and dating with agreeable males---none serious material--and writing enormous letters to Gordon who has made a Joycean pilgrimage through Dublin, and is now savoring the delights of a modern Ulysses on the Riviera . . .

As time is of the essence and I do not have any spare to write other people but you, please send my best to Martje, Mrs. Atwood . . . and most especially Dr. B. If Dr. Beuscher[1] would have time to read this letter, you

1–SP's American psychiatrist Ruth Tiffany Barnhouse Beuscher (1923–99). SP was Dr Beuscher's patient at McLean Hospital in 1953, continued private therapy in person through 1959, and by letter through 1963.

might give it to her, as I would like her to know how I am getting on. Hope to hear from you anon.

Meanwhile . . .
love,
syl

TO *Philip E. McCurdy*

Monday 1 March 1954 TLS with envelope, Smith College

March (!) 1

Dear Phil . . .

Gray monday with clay gray sidewalks and sky pinkening faintly over mountains the color of smoke. I sit, at this matutinal hour of 9:30, having just had breakfast, peeled 100 potatoes, and been given a free cut in my early Am. lit. lecture, which is fortunate as I have a written in it wednesday, along with one in Russian lit. (Hawthorne and Dostoevsky) and have several critical books to assimilate yet . . .

Last monday, on George's natal day,[1] Marcia Brown and I threw some apples and loaves of bread into our bike baskets and headed for the hills in hopes of finding a suitable bough to eat them under. We also visited several package stores to obtain one of those lovely wickered bottles of good wine, but it seems that George was not a toper, so they wouldn't sell us any and we had to be satisfied with fresh orange juice.

We biked and talked as we rode, and finally found a suitable muddy brown millstream, asked a farmer if we could borrow it for lunch, and sat out picnicking in the watery psuedo-spring sunlight, enjoying life thoroughly . . .

Friday, in the nasty rain, Marty (Marcia afore-said) and I strode downtown and bought a bridesmaid dress for me to wear to her wedding this June---all of which you will no doubt be bored to hear about---but it is just unique for me to be going to a wedding because I am unconventional about such affairs, as I no doubt must have told you a dozen times, but I really believe in Marty and Mike, and so will take part with pleasure---we are going to wear ivy in our hair, carry daisies (la-!) and the small whitewashed chapel[2] will just be simply decorated with pine boughs

1 – George Washington's Birthday is celebrated as a federal holiday on the third Monday in February.

2 – Brown was married in the Hanover Community Church, Hanover, New Hampshire.

. . . all very bucolic. My dress by the way is light blue linen, most crisp and innocent. Since this is the first wedding I've been in since I was a flowergirl at the age of 8, and Marty is my best friend, I am understandably elated . . .

This Wednesday, after the gruelling saga of writtens, I am going to treat myself to a lecture by Harvard's own I. A. Richards[1] on "The Dimensions of Reading Poetry" . . .

And now, about future plans . . . this is the way things are, offering several alternatives, any or none of which you are privileged to choose . . . I have, as fate would have it, a date with an Amherst chemistry major[2] this Saturday night, and so I have been thinking up all kinds of schemes so I could see you . . . first of all, you could come up for Friday night (by bus if you couldn't get a ride) and come to my two Saturday morning classes . . . as I won't be going to Amherst till late in the afternoon. Secondly you could come up Saturday early, see me, go out with a real nice girl in our house that night and stay over Sunday. Or third, you could say the hell with me altogether and postpone getting together till spring vacation, which is three and a half weeks away. I really would like to see you this weekend anyway, if you'd care to take advantage of either of those two alternatives . . . only if you do decide to come, could you call me about suppertime right away so I could either plan to see you this Friday or get a date for you on the night of Saturday and plan to see you the rest of the time. If you aren't coming, don't bother to call but just write, will you huh?

My brother is coming up the next weekend, I think, but I am probably not going to be here then, as I may take off for New York at any moment . . .

I really would like to see you, though, if you wouldn't be cross about it being Friday, or another lovely girl on Saturday (which really would be most ideal, I think, as you'd be seeing two people then . . . not that quantity counts, but she is sweet) . . .

So call me at Northampton 1700, 293 exchange, if you are coming to let me know and be prepared . . .

Meanwhile . . .
love,
Syl

1–English literary critic Ivor Armstrong Richards (1893–1979) taught at Cambridge (1922–9, 1931–9) and Harvard (1939–63). SP attended Richards's evening lecture on 'The Dimensions of Reading Poetry' in Sage Hall at Smith College on 3 March 1954.

2–A. George Gebauer (1932–); B.A., 1954, chemistry, Amherst College; dated SP, 1954.

TO *Philip E. McCurdy*

Wednesday 3 March 1954 TLS in greeting card,[1] Smith College

<printed greeting>

I try very hard / To be avant garde / To keep abreast / Of the very best / In contemporary art and thought / And so I feel I really ought / To find some method tres noveau / To show you that I really know / The very newest way / To say / Happy Birthday

<signed>

love & / all best / wishes – / syl / (inside) →

march 3
wednesday

dear phil . . .

first I will start out by being veddy cheerful because you are going to have a birthday and I am therefore in a congratulatory mood . . . so no matter what the content of the rest of this, read it silently in a cheerful, jolly, merry old mental voice, huh?

today is a lousy day. it is pouring wet cold unsentimental rain and the gray streets are puddled with it and the trees are slippery with it and my feet are muddy with it and the windows are splotched with it and my hair is damp with it and damn it to hell anyway . . . .

there! I feel much better now. this morning was one of those inexorable times when you have everything planned minutely to the last second and wonder if it humanly possible to plow through it physically. gulped coffee and hot cross buns for breakfast after dragging myself out of bed (having studied late last night), peeled 100 potatoes and sliced malicious orange mountains of carrots, roared up to the second floor of the libe to return an armload of overdue books on Dostoevsky, barely made it to 8:30 chapel to hear our president read the disgusting slanderous letter written by a member of the Buckley family[2] (related to Bill Buckley, author of God and Man at Yale) about how no alumnae should support smith financially as we were harboring all sorts of commies on the faculty, among them, my american lit prof who is the most sensitive innocent guy under the

1 – Panda prints birthday card designed by Rosalind Welcher.

2 – Aloïse Buckley Heath (1918–67); B.A. 1941, Smith College; eldest sister of SP's classmate Maureen Buckley O'Reilly; secretary of the Committee for Discrimination in Giving who sent a letter to the alumnae of Smith College alleging that five members of the faculty (including SP's English professor Newton Arvin) were associated with publications or organizations cited by the Attorney General or the Un-American Activities Committee as being Communist or Communist-front organizations.

sun who is now at the infirmary recovering from shock . . . all in all an irresponsible and scandalous attack with no foundation . . . ran then full speed to said american lit course to take an hour exam in which I wrote frantically for the whole period on the theme of secret guilt and subsequent retribution in Hawthorne's complete works . . . from there home to hastily study russian lit for an hour, then to intellectual history, then to an hour exam on Dostoevsky . . . home for lunch, bridge, eating apples . . . then to the doctors' office for my weekly chat with the psychiatrist, who is my great friend and tells me all the psychological dirt about the college . . . to get antihistamine tablets for a wicked sore throat and incipient cold . . . and to attempt to get a diagnosis for a mysterious burn-like scar which appeared suddenly on my lift hand, discolored to an angry red, sprouted hurting water blisters, scabbed over and healed . . . since its not an allergy, and since I'm not in the habit of burning myself in my sleep, the one thing they could figure out was that I'm allergic to chemistry majors . . .

so now I sit in my room, drinking gallons of water and eating more apples, hoping to help the effectuality of the antihistamine . . . I am going to that lecture by I. A. Richards tonight, and have been invited to the reception at the president's house afterwards, which is about the only pleasant prospect the day contains . . .

your letter was a welcome break in the day . . . and the party on march 27 saturday sounds like a lovely one . . . I'll really enjoy going with you and hope I can meet some of the friends you make sound so intriguing. I probably will be in a much more carefree mood then than I would be this weekend as I have four weeks of intellectual history to assimilate for a written next week . . . by the way, in your indictment of "sweet smith jeunes filles" you implied by contrast that I am neither sweet nor a jeune fille . . . how about that?

hoping to hear from you in the interim between now and the 27th . . .

love as usual,

sp

TO *Aurelia Schober Plath*

Friday 5 March 1954

TLS on Smith College letterhead, Indiana University

Friday
March 5

Dear mother . . .

Felt like dropping you a line this morning to tell you how things are going. I've stayed in these last two days pampering a slight headcold which looks as if it would clear up by tomorrow. It's really been quite pleasant staying curled up in my sunny room, eating apples, drinking quantities of water, and reading "The Brothers Karamazov", by Dostoevsky . . .

Wednesday was the most hectic day yet---my written on Hawthorne was stimualting and fun, and I'm sure I did pretty well---but the one on Dostoevsky was a totally unexpected and minutely particular question: the role of money in the three novels we have read! Here I had prepared myself for great philosophical issues of reason vs. emotion, nihilism vs. religion, earth vs. spirit, etc., and I had to rack my brain to remember when Raskolnikov[1] tossed a copeck into the river.

Of course it rained all day too. In the afternoon I had my weekly hour talk with Dr. Booth, who is really a great friend of mine, now. I have no psychological problems actually, so our discussions are more philosophical than anything else . . .

That night I heard I. A. Richards from Harvard give a delightful lecture on "The Dimensions of Reading Poetry" after which I went to the small cosy reception for him at Pres. Wright's house, had cocoa and cookies and listened to the good man read poetry aloud . . . most fun!

I do love my reading and courses, and even if I didn't get more than a C on the Russian exam, I won't care because I think that I am getting a lot out of the course anyway.

As it is, I plan to come home for spring vacation in the early evening of March 24, Wednesday . . . my plans for going to New York are very indefinite as yet, but I won't go probably till Monday, March 29, as Phil has asked me to go to a candle-light-and-wine affair at his house at Harvard on Saturday, the 27th, and I said I'd favor him with my presence---perhaps I can even see Warren in his native habitat! I was thinking rashly of going to Florida, as a girl in the house did it all last year on only $75, but since the object of my present interest is staying in Amherst all vacation, I decided not to even think of it.

1 – The protagonist in *Crime and Punishment*.

You have no idea, after going out with eight different boys in four weeks, how nice it is to find someone I can really talk to, study with, and enjoy. Ever since I met George so strangely two Saturdays ago, when I was going out with his roommate, I have felt a rapport with him, evidenced by the fact that in the half hour I spent with him then, while my real date was down at the bar, I told him all about my escapade last summer, and felt that he would somehow understand and appreciate it, which he did---he has a scar on his face too, a thin red line which dips in a semicircle over one eye where he got thrown out of an overturning truck. I like his scar partly because I have one too and partly because it makes him unique.

Anyhow, we are exactly the same height, when I wear flats, and I feel so relaxed and happy just being with him---perhaps he is just a stand-in for Gordon, I don't know, but I do feel the need of orienting myself deeply to some one person in a confiding companionship where I can be articulate, and George Gebauer seems to be the most logical person around--I've refused two dates with a boy at Dartmouth business school, and I think I would really rather stay in and read now, than just go out with "anybody"---but when I came back I felt that the first month should be spent "getting back in Circulation" which I did with the greatest success.

Its a funny thing, but when I was out with Gerhardt last Saturday, (George's third roommate) I kept counting the hours from 3 to 1 thinking they would never been over---in spite of the fact that Gerhardt treated me to cocktails, a lambchop dinner and a party---I could hardly wait till George came back from the chem lab and dropped in to talk with me. In contrast, on Sunday, as we just sat and read in George's living room, the clocked seemed terribly accelerated and the hours struck one after the other with alarming rapidity . . . we listened to music, talked, went downtown for a club sandwich, and I felt just bubbling over with the mere realization that I had found a friend with whom I could share my humor, my ideas, and my delight in the surrounding world.

Really, I am very lucky to know such nice people--Marty, Claiborne, Gordon, Phil and George--all so alive and stimulating.

Mrs. Kelsey came up last night to see how I was feeling and brought a whole iced grapefruit for me to eat---it's little things like that which make her so loved around the house.

George called up to tell me that he would call for me at 4 tomorrow afternoon, so that is a delightful prospect which has helped me get through this rather rugged week, . . . he is going to let up on his honors work in chemistry till spring vacation, when he will be up here working---he says that I am a bad influence, as he had resolved to work on weekends, but I really don't think he is too disturbed by my coming onto the scene---

It was such fun last Sunday to have him carry my books down to the house as we walked along under the starry sky like schoolchildren, hand in hand, talking about people and ideas . . .

Got a postcard from Bob Cochran who did quit Dartmouth after all and is now at Newport Beach in California preparing to enter a sailboat race to Mexico--some people are just too unconventional for a disciplined program of study and must learn about life first hand, like a wandering hobo . . .

I am really pleased about my accepted job at the Southward Inn, especially as it doesn't begin till June 21 which will give me a nice vacation and ample time to be at Marty's wedding in Hanover. Also, Orleans is near Nauset, the most beautiful part of the Cape as far as I'm concerned. The sun and sea have it all over commuting in the sooty city as far as I'm concerned, and the Belmont taught me the lesson of moderation . . .

I'll be hearing from you next week . . . meanwhile,

best love from your happy daughter . . .

sivvy

TO *Aurelia Schober Plath*

Tuesday 16 March 1954[1]

TLS with envelope on Smith College letterhead, Indiana University

Tuesday

Dear mummy . . .

Just a note to tell you that I finished my last written before spring vacation this morning, and am relaxing now under the illusion of freedom . . . just have a 20 page Russian paper to write now, which should be hard work, but quite satisfying . . . I think I will definitely write a thesis this coming year if I can get a good topic . . . . the rigid prospect of having to take 5 exams per week and attend every class doesn't really appeal to me . . . and I am making up for lost time by the classes I'm taking this semester . . .

Mrs. Koffka's exam today was good . . . and I really crammed for it this last week, doing six weeks of work this one week alone! I don't know whether I was too general or not, but am sure I'll at least get a B from her.

1–Date supplied from postmark.

As I passed in my exam, she looked at me intently and asked if I wasn't in her History 11 section four years ago---I said yes and was amazed and pleased that she remembered me all this time!

Good news--I got an A- in my Russian exam, which was that hard question on money in Dostoevsky, and a straight A in my Hawthorne exam---which proves to me that I can combine artistic enjoyment with intelligent analysis, even if I am no genius! Thought you'd be pleased that I did so well while taking it so easily and having such a lovely time with my friends in the house and with George too!

Got a wonderfully understanding and appreciative letter from Gordon[1] today . . . he's such a dear.

Also would love to fly to NYC Sunday IF we can afford it . . .

much love . . .

sivvy

<on back of envelope>

p.s. – just received a copy of an article by a girl at a Texas U.[2] which included a very favorable criticism of my poem "Carnival Nocturne"!

TO *Gordon Lameyer*

Tuesday 16 March 1954 — TLS on Smith College News Office letterhead, Indiana University

March 16

Dearest Ulysses . . .

A March Tuesday finds me cold, dry, blue and windslashed in my sun square room . . . just finished intellectual history written this a.m. and feel deceptively free and omniscient and wise: all I have to do this coming week is a 20 page paper on the novels of Dostoevsky, who is to me in intellectual writing what Dylan is to me in emotional lyricizing. I'll never get over the experience of reading "The Idiot" and "Brothers Karamazov" and fear that I shall walk around carrying the muchunderlined books in a small satchel and quoting voluminously from them at the slightest provocation!

1–Either Gordon Lameyer to SP, 4–8 March 1954 or Lameyer to SP, 12 March 1954; held by Lilly Library.

2–Ramona Maher (1934–96); B.A. 1954, Texas Christian University; her 'Conjectured Harbours', *Prize Winning Entries of the Creative Writing Contests of the English Department, May 1953*, 12–13. Maher was a guest editor at *Mademoiselle* in 1954.

Statistically, since I last talked twodimensionally with you, I've heard I. A. Richards hold forth on the "Dimensions of Reading Poetry" and sat on the floor at his feet during the subsequent reception listening him read poetry aloud by a leaping twinkling fire . . . also heard and delighted in a remarkably lucid lecture by Selden Bacon[1] from Yale on the intriguing subject: "Alcoholism: Illness, Evil or Social Pathology" . . . the following evening I went spontaneously down to Joe's with my beautiful, brilliant blackhaired next year's roommate, Nancy Hunter,[2] ostensibly because we wanted a glass of wine with our history reading. We ended up drinking a bottle of that lovely Chianti apiece and becoming inspired by our mutual eloquence and scintillating ideas in every field from sex to salvation . . . got to know each other a great deal better in the process. Symbolically, two voluptuously greenglass wickered wine bottles now flank your navy picture, which, as you may guess, is paganly enshrined on my maplewood bureau . . .

Your last manyleveled letter was declaimed partly aloud today over coffeecups and through bluelayered smoky air in Toto's[3] . . . somehow I suddenly felt terribly close to you through your typewritten talking and your descriptions were so colored and conceived that I could fancy them more real than the original scenes must have been! You have many admirers of your reported journeyings, sir . . . I wonder when and where I will see you again if I will be able to look at you and say to myself: yes, this is the boy I have been writing to, confiding in, beginning to know and understand . . . or if you will be a darkeyed mysterious stranger with all the secret wisdom of the ages in your enigmatic smile and I will find that I cannot reconcile you to your name . . . identity is such a perilous quantity . . .

Last weekend, amid howling rain and sleet and treacherous puddled streets, Warren arrived from Harvard with one of his charming young roommates. I got them dates for the Amherst freshman show and dance and they stayed overnight in Chi Psi with George Gebauer, a good friend of mine whom you may have known . . . Anyhow, I had a great time Sunday over twohour's worth of coffee catching up with Warren's academic, social and ideological life---he's doing wonderfully well at Harvard and

1 – Yale University sociology professor and alcoholism researcher Selden D. Bacon (1909–92).

2 – Nancy Hunter Steiner (1933–2006); B.A. 1955, history, Smith College; SP's friend and roommate at Lawrence House, 1954–5.

3 – Toto's was a restaurant at 86 Green Street, Northampton, across the street from Lawrence House.

is at present enamored of a Radcliffe girl poetically named Margo[1]--who mother claims resembles me, oddly enough. The two boys were my guests for dinner at the house and threw the whole freshman class into a minor state of adoration: my prestige mounted enormously because of my tall goodlooking brother!

Spring vacation begins a week from tomorrow, and I am planning to read about ten novels during it . . . plus spending five days exploring the delights and deviltries of NYC. My Estonian artist friend who I've probably told you about has invited me to stay with him as long as I want--his mother, too, which makes it all moral and aboveboard-and explore the town from my own section of their apartment to which they will symbolically give me the keys. I look forward to museums, central park, wine and cheese, and greenwich village . . . also, for some magnanimous reason, mother wants me to have the experience of flying in a big plane for the first time---though I really don't see how anything could approximate the exhilaration of my one trip last year in the little two-seater over the Connecticut river and the Holyoke range . . . however, I shall probably increase my cosmopolitanity and accept her offer to wing my way wayward . . .

Other bumbling plans---mere bottles of form to be filled with the blood and wine of content---are a waitress job at the Southward Inn in Orleans on the Cape (anything to be near the sand and sea) which should begin not till June 21, giving me time to bridesmaid it at Marcia Brown's wedding in Hanover and relax after exams at the end of May . . .

You are a most gratifying critic, by the way . . . you would be good at so many lovely things---lawyering psychologically, professoring English to young worshipping lads and free lance criticizing on the side of Mr. R. G. Davis---oh, hell, you are just damn versatile . . . we know what we are but not what we may be . . . and maybe we don't even quite know what we are . . .

How can one become enamored of a letter? is it like loving a poem or a symbolic piece of prose because of the subconscious rememberings and desirings of living heightened by the pleasurefulpain of articulateness? . . . or is it linking the twodimensional mental work to the darkmysteriousmythicalphysicomentalempathy of bodyandmind??? God knows what I'm trying to say. And even he is having a time at it . .

Sometimes I am a susceptible hedonist, but if I don't try to rationalize or be hypocritical about it, if I say: I am being this way because it is all

1–Probably Margaret 'Margot' S. Dennes Honig; B.A. 1957, Radcliffe College.

I can get out of this particular situation and all I want to get and give, and it is good for it's intrinsic value and for no long range or ideally related purpose except the immediate intense reveling joy of here and now to the height---then I can orient my refined and luxuriating hedonism to the honest reasoned integrity I hope I can revolve around all my life . . .

But when it is very dark and very mysterious and very warm one can say onename and really mean another . . . a much more fundamental and psychically significant name . . . so gordon, gordon, gordon . . . .

There is music to be heard with you and favorite parts of books to be read aloud to you . . . and apples to be eaten . . . with you . . .

lovingly . . .
sylvia

TO *Ramona Maher*

Tuesday 16 March 1954

TLS with envelope,
Dobkin Collection

Lawrence House
Smith College
Northampton, Massachusetts
March 16, 1954

Ramona Maher
Box 192, Texas Christian University
Fort Worth, Texas

Dear Ramona:

I was extremely pleased to receive the copy of your article "Conjectured Harbours" and enjoyed it a great deal, being especially appreciative of your favorable review of my poem "Carnival Nocturne"--indeed, if you happen to have another copy or so of the article I'd really like to have it as this is the first time I've seen anybody write a criticism of any of my work!

As for recent information about me---I'm taking an extra semester at Smith this year as I missed the first term--so I'll be a senior next year. I've had three poems accepted by Harpers' which should be coming out sometime this present spring---the names of the poems are "Go Get the Goodly Squab", "To Eva Descending the Stair", and "Doomsday". I'll enclose a couple of poems so you can get an idea of what I've been doing.

Campus activities related to writing include serving on the editorial board of the "Smith Review", our college literary magazine, and being a reporter and correspondent for the out-of-town newspapers in the college News Office . . . I've also been on our college Electoral Board (which ratifies nominations for the Big Four college offices), served as Secretary for the Smith College Honor Board, been a member of Alpha, our honorary society of the arts, and been elected a Junior Phi Bete . . .

My favorite novelist (at present) is Dostoevsky, while Dylan Thomas is my favorite modern poet---Gerard Manley Hopkins, Yeats, and W. H. Auden rank highest among my other models---also I'm a devotee of James Joyce and Virginia Woolf and D. H. Lawrence.

I'd be interested to see your article when your through---congratulations again on your essay!

Sincerely,
Sylvia Plath

Sylvia Plath
Smith College
Assignment III

Harper's[1]

Doomsday

A Villanelle

The idiot bird leaps out and drunken leans
Atop the broken universal clock:
The hour is crowed in lunatic thirteens.

The painted stages fall apart by scenes
And all the actors halt in mortal shock:
The idiot bird leaps out and drunken leans.

The streets crack through in havoc-split ravines,
The doomstruck city crumbles block by block:
The hour is crowed in lunatic thirteens.

The fractured glass flies down in smithereens,
Our lucky relics have been put in hock:
The idiot bird leaps out and drunk leans.

1 – In the first two poems, SP handwrote 'Harper's' to indicate where she placed the poem.

God's monkey wrench has blasted all machines.
We never thought to hear the holy cock:
The hour is crowed in lunatic thirteens.

Too late to ask if end was worth the means,
Too late to calculate the toppling stock:
The idiot bird leaps out and drunken leans,
The hour is crowed in lunatic thirteens.

Sylvia Plath
Smith College
Assignment III

Harper's

<u>To Eva Descending the Stair</u>

A Villanelle

Clocks cry: stillness is a lie, my dear;
The wheels revolve, the universe keeps running.
(Proud you halt upon the spiral stair.)

The asteroids turn traitor in the air,
The planets plot with old elliptic cunning;
Clocks cry: stillness is a lie, my dear.

Red the unraveled rose sings in your hair:
Blood springs eternal if the heart be burning.
(Proud you halt upon the spiral stair.)

Cryptic stars wind up the atmosphere,
In solar schemes the tilted suns go turning;
Clocks cry: stillness is a lie, my dear.

Loud the immortal nightingales declare:
Love flames forever if the flesh be yearning.
(Proud you halt upon the spiral stair.)

Circling zodiac compels the year.
Intolerant beauty never will be learning.
Clocks cry: stillness is a lie, my dear.
(Proud you halt upon the spiral stair.)

Sylvia Plath
26 Elmwood Road
Wellesley, Massachusetts
Lawrence House
Smith College
Northampton, Massachusetts

Accepted by Harper's[1]

Go Get the Goodly Squab

Go get the goodly squab in gold-lobed corn
And pluck the droll flecked quail where thick they lie,
Go reap the round blue pigeons from roof ridge
    But let the fast-feathered eagle fly.

    Let the fast-feathered eagle fly
    And the sky crack through with thunder,
    But hide, hide, in the deep nest
    Lest the lightning cleave you asunder.

Go snare the sleeping bear in leaf-lined den
And trap the muskrat napping in slack sun,
Go dupe the dull sow lounging snout in mud
    But let the galloping antelope run.

    Let the galloping antelope run
    And the snow blow up behind,
    But hide, hide, in the safe cave
    Lest the blizzard drive you blind.

1 – Added in SP's hand.

Go cull the purple snails from slothful shells
And bait the drowsing trout by the brook's brim,
Go gather idle oysters from green shoals,
    But let the quicksilver mackerel swim.

    Let the quicksilver mackerel swim
    Where the black wave topples down,
    But hide, hide in the calm port
    Lest the water drag you to drown.

Sylvia Plath
26 Elmwood Road
Wellesley 81, Mass.

Verbal Calisthentics

My love for you is more
    Athletic than a verb,
Agile as a star
    The tents of sun absorb.

Treading circus tightropes
    Of each syllable
The brazen jackanapes
    Would fracture if he fell.

Acrobat of space,
    The daring adjective
Plunges for a phrase
    Describing arcs of love.

Nimble as a noun
    He catapults in air;
A planetary swoon
    Could climax his career.

But adroit conjunction
    Eloquently shall
Link to his lyric action
    A periodic goal.

TO *Melvin Woody*

Wednesday 24 March 1954 TLS, Smith College

<typed on yellow Street & Smith Publications Inter Office Memorandum sheets, with heading>

TO you FROM me
SUBJECT minutiae DATE mar. 24

sun aslant along blue blotter . . . flesh sunwarm
clean air greenlucid and splattered with
sundrops . . . tender sproutings of spring
among bluepurple gauze hills, tweed
fields and lightblue denim skies
purple crocii leap vital
in bloodstream
and the dead corngod puts forth green buds . . .
and this inside . . .
and I sit with a checklist
hearing at my back time's wingèd jetplane . . .
somehow I will and must
see you

How Is This? you call me in Wellesley at Wellesley 5-0219-J (26 Elmwood Road) sometime or other between Thursday March 25 and Saturday March 27 and tell me which configuration of time would be best for us to see how we each live: statistically: I fly to New York Sunday March 29 to live with the Estonian artist at 2023 Lexington Avenue till Thursday April 1 when, up to now, Marty and Mike were going to drive me back to Boston. I could (1) stop off at New Haven that Thursday; but I think you have vacation then. Or you could (2) come see me in Wellesley anytime from April 1 to 6 when I go back to Smith . . .

Call to let me know which what and where . . .

Till then when you call soon . . .
love,
syl

TO *Gordon Lameyer*

Tuesday 6 April 1954 TLS, Indiana University

Tuesday, April 6 . . .

Dear Gordon . . .

It has been long . . . I'm not sure exactly how long, since I talked on paper with you. Now it is night, the last night of my two-week spring vacation, and as I look out the window before the desk in my room, I see a blurred reflection of myself imposed on the black inscrutable void outside. The only light is from the streetlamp, and that light is slick, like india ink, on the slippery and rain-sluiced road . . .

Downstairs mother irons and listens to Il Trovatore;[1] in the room across the hall my grandparents sit and survey television, as a novice singer gives with "I'm-as-corny-as-Kansas-in-August"[2] in a too-frantic voice at a too-hectic tempo. Cloistered in my sanctum, I sit selecting and sorting the collage of memories I have shored up these past two weeks which have been for me the intensest and most exquisitely cataclysmic of my young and oh-so-green psychic and physical existence . . . where to begin?

At the beginning, as the little girl said. Once-upon-a-time there lived in Lawrence house a Smith girl . . .

The first weekend home I was introduced to Harvard for the First Time in 21 years of living in the environs of Cambridge. Result: I could live in that Place contentedly for the rest of my days . . . (Provided I saw the world in leisurely fashion first). Warren took me to his room where I met his three superlative and handsome and most brilliant roommates: Luigi Einaudi,[3] blond, blue-eyed grandson of the President of Italy; Clem Moore, young, precocious son of a brilliantly successful free-lance-writer mother and chemistry-research father . . . a guy with intense black eyes, a cosmopolitan drawl, who is playing around with existentialism; and Alec Goldstein,[4] a dark, sinuous good-humored fellow who was, at the time I met him, collecting six cheeping black chickens as a surprise gift for his girl, whom he'd promised a "furry present" (undoubtedly she was expecting a mink stole!) Warren treated me to a lovely Egg Foo Yong

1–*Il Trovatore* is a four-act opera by Italian composer Giuseppe Verdi (1813–1901).

2–Rodgers and Hammerstein, 'A Wonderful Guy', *South Pacific* (1949).

3–Italian-American US career diplomat Luigi R. Einaudi (1936–); B.A. 1957, Harvard College.

4–Alexander Goldstein, Jr (1935–); B.A. biology 1957, Harvard College; M.D. 1961, Baylor College of Medicine.

at Young Lee's,[1] to a humanities class, and to a meeting with "his girl" . . . a breezy, tall, brown-haired, spontaneous and enchanting Radcliffe creature named Margo Dennis. I could have accepted her for a sister then and there . . .

Margo came home for dinner that night, after which I went for a cup of coffee at the Shopper's World in Framingham with Dr. Ruth Beuscher, my psychiatrist, who is now one of my best friends . . . only 9 years older than I, looking like Myrna Loy, tall, Bohemian, coruscatingly brilliant, and most marvelous . . . we had an excellent comradely time, and she approved heartily of my plans for spending a week in NYC this vacation and of taking an accelerated course in beginner's German at Harvard this summer . . .

That night it was dancing and beer at the Meadow's[2] . . . the next day I went to a bohemian Cabaret Dance at Harvard's Adams House . . . my escort being that 19-year old illegitimate medical artist I may have told you about . . . who wants to prove he's twice as talented as most legitimate people . . . which he fortunately is. He gave a punch party in his room at which he let me hold a minor salon with all the graduate resident instructors in the house . . . bright young guys all, getting Phd's or teaching Byzantine history or Romance languages and whatnot, all being most chivalrous and stimulating.

My most intriguing contact was made at the dance itself . . . which was in a hall set about with individual red-and-white checked tables, candles in wine bottles, and intinerant gypsy violinists. Phil introduced me to a ruddy-faced, genial fellow, "Scotty" Campbell,[3] the Assistant Director of the Summer School, no less.

Scotty claimed to remember me as a result of my application last year and remarked that he'd just interviewed Warren for residence in Adams house next year and was most impressed . . . fortified by wine, I boldly remarked that I'd been hesitant about applying for a scholarship this summer as I'd refused the one offered last year. Scotty was most encouraging, insisted that I apply, saying I had a good chance. Come the last dance set, he asked Phil for me, and whirled me away. I kept saying to myself: "He is a professor, and here he is, telling me all these fantastic things in my ear . . ." I attributed Scotty's fervor to the wine and figured he'd forget it and be cross with himself come dawn . . . . but the next day

1 – Young Lee Restaurant, then at 27 Church Street, Cambridge.

2 – Vaughn Monroe's Meadows, on Route 9 in Framingham.

3 – Alan K. 'Scotty' Campbell (1924–98), Assistant Director of Harvard Summer School and instructor in Government, Harvard University.

came a scholarship blank with a letter saying he had all my records from last year, so all I had to do was sign on the dotted line and let the rest go to blazes . . . so it sort of looks like this year I will be living in Cambridge all summer!

Next day: Scene: Logan Airport.

Character: Young girl who never was up in big plane, only a little one once last spring.

Props: Huge suitcase and Dostoevsky's book, The Possessed.

Destination: NYC: from Harlem to Greenwich Village.

I arrived at LaGuardia after one hour of tilting flight during which I sat with my eager nose flattened against the window, staring down at the redundant squares, triangles and rectangles of brown-toned land, threaded together by rivers and railroads . . . flashes of blue sea at first as we wheeled above Boston, and the houses and ships falling away under the slanting silver-winged airship . . .

Settling in a descending spiral outside of NYC, we landed and taxiied in, I being met by my 35-year old Estonian artist and whisked off to stay with him and his mother Hilda at their dark, dingy 3rd floor walkup at the corner of Lexington and 123rd in the center of Harlem, where a nucleus of Estonians, Latvians, and Russians have gathered.

A ceremonial dinner was prepared to greet me, with aunts and uncles, none of whom could speak more than broken English . . . and I soon found myself speaking slow broken English myself, trying, to the merriment of all, to imitate the gutteral and sibilant hisses of Russian sounds, and assuring everybody that after I began learning German this summer I would start Russian immediately upon entering grad school . . . That night it was to re-see the "Confidential Clerk"[1] with Ilo, who is an artist and architect's draftsman.

Against the advice of mother and friends, I insisted I could manage myself equally well in Ilo's apartment as at Smith . . . and everything went according to my calculations, except that Ilo startled me slightly Monday by waking me up and announcing that he'd decided to stay home from work that day. I told him coldly, in a flash of inspiration, that I was engaged to be married in a few months, and so was to be considered as a friend, and absolutely nothing more . . . which information succeeded in making him behave with upmost solicitude and tact for the rest of my stay . . .

1 – *The Confidential Clerk* was performed at the Morosco Theatre, 217 W. 45th Street, New York.

That day I walked by myself for over a hundred blocks across town through the center of Harlem to Columbia and Morningside Heights, and down Broadway till I reached the upper fifties and met Cyrilly Abels, managing ed of Mlle, for a long lunch of lobster salad and avocado pears at the Ivy Room of the Drake Hotel . . . conversation being mostly about authors I've read and she knows personally . . . she'd had Dylan Thomas over for dinner the week before he died and confirmed the story about his drinking to great excess on an empty stomach all the time . . .

Afternoon: I met Ilo at the Metropolitan Museum and saw the exhibit of Medieval art and early American art (Sargent, Whistler, and Mary Cassatt).[1] I must say my tastes are arrantly modern! That night Ilo had gotten tickets to William Inge's sparkling play "Picnic"[2] which I enjoyed to the hilt . . .

Tuesday morning I walked from 125th street down 5th Avenue to 43rd and the museum of Modern Art, which seemed closed . . . a young, big-eyed vital-looking woman approached me to ask the time just as I went up to the locked museum door and informed me that the museum didn't open till noon, and we had yet an hour to wait. Somehow we got talking about art, and began walking and talking intensely about progressive schools and education and politics . . . at which juncture we discovered we'd walked fifteen blocks and were at Lord and Taylor's. "You must see the Bird Cage" my delighted companion informed me, so we went up for a delicious lunch for 95¢ and talked heatedly over coffee. Turned out she's a painter and has an apartment in the Village with her two boys and husband, who's an Hungarian psychiatrist . . . that afternoon we spent together in the museum and seeing the three socio-psychological films[3] that were showing there . . .

Come night, I dressed up black velvetly, with a red rose in my hair from the half-dozen Ilo had presented me as a combined apology and farewell present and waited for Bish,[4] a charming student at Union Theological Seminary (of all the fantastic places for a friend of mine to be!), to come take me to dinner.

1–The exhibition *Sargent, Whistler, and Mary Cassatt* was at the Metropolitan Museum of Art, 25 March–23 May 1954. SP's copy of the exhibition catalogue is held by Lilly Library.
2–William Inge, *Picnic* (1953) was performed at the Music Box Theatre, 239 W. 45th Street, New York.
3–The three films were *The Steps of Age* (1951) directed by Ben Maddow; *Who's Boss* (1952) directed by Alexander Hammid; and *Benjy* (1951) directed by Fred Zinneman.
4–Atherton Sinclair Burlingham (1926–87); B.Arch. 1950, Cornell University; active in Sage Chapel Choir and Cornell United Religious Work; attended Union Theological Seminary in New York City, 1954; dated SP in 1954. Burlingham went by the nicknames 'Bish' and 'Bisher'.

We took the subway downtown to the Village and sat for hours at Asti's[1] eating rare lampchops and chef's salad and listening to the singing waiters and waitresses who continually sang operatic arias . . . after this, all I could take was a long windy ride on the Staten Island ferry, where we stood alone on the whistling deck (all the other herds of people stayed warm and untransfigured inside) drinking hot chocolate and watching the glittering skyline of Manhattan recede and the statue of liberty grow green and big, and then the statue dwindle, and the lights rise tall and shining above us in the windy dark . . . at this point I was in a skipping mood and felt like chanting Millay: "We are very tired, we were very merry, and we went back and forth all night on the ferry . . ."[2]

Next day, I told Ilo I was going home, which I wasn't, and I took a crosstown taxi to Union where I woke up Bish, had breakfast, and heard Paul Tillich[3] and Reinhold Niebuhr[4] (that last name is the devil to spell!) lecture at his classes, had lunch, and went to a practice room to play piano badly in accompaniment as he sang opera in a creditable tenor . . . all of which was gay fun.

I then headed to Jan Salter's apartment in Greenwich Village[5] . . . her adopted father,[6] a fat dead-pan humorous German free-lance artist who makes great money doing bookjackets, met me at the door of their 9th floor studio apartment which is all books, original paintings and wide windows overlooking the lights of the village.

Jan's kindly, whitehaired mother,[7] who used to be a social worker in the city, took one shrewd look at me and then pointed to the bedroom . . . "Baby, you need a little nap," she smiled. I lay down gratefully and conked out for two solid hours . . .

Dinner, sherry, conversation, and Jan and I headed for the Greenwich theater[8] for two superlative Hitchcock thrillers: "Maltese Falcon" with my boy Peter Lorre, and that now-deceased hulk, Sid Greenstreet. "Shadow

1–The Asti Restaurant was at 13 E. 12th Street, New York.

2–Edna St Vincent Millay, 'Recuerdo'.

3–Paul Johannes Tillich (1886–1965); German-American Christian existentialist philosopher and theologian.

4–Karl Paul Reinhold Niebuhr (1892–1971); American theologian, ethicist, public intellectual, commentator on politics and public affairs, and professor at Union Theological Seminary.

5–The Salters lived at 40 E. 10th Street, New York.

6–George Salter (1897–1967), book designer and calligrapher. Married Agnes O'Shea in 1942.

7–Agnes O'Shea Salter (1901–89); Smith College 1927.

8–The Greenwich Theatre was at the corner of W. 12th Street and 7th Avenue, New York.

of a Doubt" with Joseph Cotton as the handsome strangling uncle, played with it, and Jan and I were both so tense afterwards that we looked for evil leering little men in every shadowed alley. A daiquiri at a hotel bar, and conversation (Jan is one of the few girls who can outtalk me!) and to bed . . .

Thursday Bish and I had lunch, went for a long walk in Morningside Park, argumentatively discussing philosophy and theology and calling each other all sorts of bad names like "humanist" and "Existentialist" (he to me) and "pseudo-preacher" and "arrogant absolutist" . . . all in all, I grew philosophically in the proverbial leaps and bounds this week . . nothing so conducive to growth as to have to battle with one's opposite (being, as I fear I am only too often, the devil's advocate!)

That night I dined at Cyrilly Abels 5th avenue apartment in a neat foursome including her brilliant, opinionated lawyer husband[1] and his nephew, a young Jewish news reporter who works on the midnight to 8 a.m. shift on the Voice of America . . . conversation centered around legal cases, book cases, and whatnot . . . another daiquiri and more conversation with the reporter at some Greenwich dive or tother . . . then "home", which is where I hang my nylons . . .

Friday luncheon with Jan and Smith friend Dee Neuberg at the Time-Life building, watching the out-of-season skaters pirouette and twirl in the Plaza . . . then to Grand Central, that soap opera stage where "a million lives play daily" . . .[2]

I stopped off in New Canaan on the way home at the home of Clem Moore to have dinner with the Moores and Warren, who was driving down on vacation from Harvard with Clem. Mrs. Moore, a vital, black-eyed, black-haired (Italian-cut) woman with a beautiful mobile face, met me at the station. As she has been one of my "ideals" for a long while now, I was most eager to meet her, and we hit it off immediately, with she telling me all about her writing start, her unfortunate first marriage (she eloped with a society playboy whose family subsequently disinherited him and left him to live off Mrs. M's writing earnings, while he made cigarette money by selling life insurance to his parents . . . finally he became a professional pilot in the air force, leaving Mrs. M. in peace with a lovely baby who is now Clem.)

1–Cyrilly Abels was married to Jerome Weinstein (1901–72), a lawyer and an authority on tax policy. They lived at 14 Fifth Avenue, New York.

2–Probably a reference to the radio serial *Grand Central Station* (1937–54) which opened with 'The crossroads of a million private lives, a gigantic stage on which are played a thousand dramas daily.'

Now happily married to a benevolent giant of a chemical research man, Mrs. M. lives in a modern dream house in the plushest part of the New Canaan woods . . . I told her, after a tour of the plateglass windowed woodtextured roughbricked clean uncluttered haven, that was all sunlight and fresh blue air, that in 10 years I would buy the place from her. Her studio really won me over: separate, all windows looking out into trees and lakes, walled with books and files, with the typewriter the central talisman on this writer's altar . . .

I played with young Peter and Michael[1] till Warren and Clem arrived, then delighted in a quick chicken supper (Mrs. M reassured me by insisting that she, too, hadn't known how to cook, but that it was simple and speedy with all the modern conveniences . . . and even a free-lancer could eat in style) . . . she also took a look at me and insisted that I sleep there overnight, so I washed the grime and soot from New York from my weary body, luxuriating in the hot shower and the clean sheets of the bed (such pleasant physical comforts when one is footsore and beat . . .)

Awoke to sunlight and treebranches, almost touchable . . . coffee, eggs, bacon, and strawberry jam . . . the boys saw me off at the station . . . stopped in New Haven for lunch at George and Harry's[2] with a psychic brother of mine, Mel Woody, and borrowed so many of his poetry books that I had to kidnap him and take him along on the train to carry my things home . . .

Home in time for dinner with the two Crockett's and more talk . . . as yet I had not contracted laryngitis . . . more poetry reading . . . bed . . .

Monday was lunch with Olive Higgins Prouty at Joseph's[3] . . . and over swordfish and sherry I recounted my adventures to my fairy godmother . . . who has literally sunk untold thousands into my scholarships and hospital bills. I enjoy keeping her posted regularly, which is the only price I have to pay . . . this, lest she wave her wand and reduce me again to a pauper, and my English bicycle to a pumpkin! Vicariously I conquered Mt. Everest[4] at the Exeter theater . . . dinner at Harvard with Phil and a tour of a superlative one-man art exhibit[5] of modern mosaics and pottery which I think you'd have loved . . . all the rough stone textures and structured drawings . . . the colored polish of small stones and rough

1–Peter Vincent Moore (1952–) and Michael Moore, step-brothers of Clement Henry.

2–George & Harry's, a pizzeria with three New Haven locations: 90 Wall Street, 381 Temple Street, and 1132 Church Street.

3–Joseph's, a restaurant formerly at 279 Dartmouth Street, Boston, Mass.

4–The film *The Conquest of Everest* played at the Exeter Street Theatre, Boston.

5–American artist David Holleman (1927–). Holleman exhibited at Behn-Moore Gallery, 40 Brattle Street, Cambridge, Massachusetts, 22 March–11 April 1954.

carved tile . . . the inlays of wood grains in unique and balanced forms . . .

Today . . . the respite: the day with noplace to go at no particular time: I've been playing sentimental songs on the piano, listening to opera, brunching on chicken livers and bacon, reading elf stories and being an obliging galloping horse to the children across the street while telling Mrs. Aldrich, that delightful young mother of five, about how it is possible to synchronize a logical city and walk around it in a week . . .

Tomorrow . . . back to Melville, Tolstoi, James (my introduction to him) and Hemingway and Faulkner . . . and to what I hope will, out of this barren gray rainlacerated womb of beginning April, be spring . . .

My fingers falter on the keys . . . Gordon, when will you be stationed hereabouts? . . . everytime I see the ocean or a sailor, it induces me to think even more frequently of you . . . saw a jovial Texan machinist's mate fresh from the somethingorother William Rush[1] (is there such?) who asserted that he had tied up alongside the Perry somewhere or so . . . whither goest thou this summer, Ulysses, my roving one . . . ?

Properly, I was struck by your letter[2] on the pros and cons of professoring vs. salesmanning . . . I argue not so much to you, as to myself, since I am torn between jobbing it or going on to grad school for pure mental hedonism to learn languages and expand to comparative lit on someone else's money . . .

But I think that you overestimate the exigencies of teaching . . . granted, the academic community requires thinking, reading, correcting . . . but this very thinking and leisure is conducive to writing, not, as some think, abstract and ivory-towered . . . long vacations allow plunging into work for three months without the nagging doubt: "What am I doing writing when I should be contacting so-and-so about the such-and-such deal?" If reality and the everyday world is necessary for grist for the writer's mill, summer months could be spent working on a boat, in Europe . . . anywhere, and this living would reciprocally enrich the teacher's ability to offer himself and his growing mind and psyche to his students . . . after my article on poet-teachers, I feel very strongly that teaching is a vital profession for those that have the guts to make it such, and I say this, I think, without being blinded by a rosy haze of dreamy impracticalness . . . If I taught and didn't write, at least I'd be growing (because that is the only kind of a teacher I would want to be . . . a kinetic one) . . . and I would be in contact with the side of life which is most important to me . . . the artistic, creative side, with a minimum of social pressures to

1–USS *William R. Rush*; a Gearing-class destroyer, commissioned in September 1945.
2–Gordon Lameyer to SP, 12 March 1954; held by Lilly Library.

conformity, even though within the academic environment there are also pressures: to "publish or perish" or get degrees, etc.

On the other hand, a job in business (be it selling insurance or working on a magazine or for a publishing house) offers more money, probably, and a chance to meet real life situations with a maximum of creative tact and savoir faire . . . but from my experience last June, I discovered that my daily work took all my creativity out of me and replaced it with weariness and a desire to relax over a drink, a dance, a show, or just plain go to bed . . . when I tried to write, I kept thinking: If I want to Get Ahead, I'll have to turn to my job reports . . . why am I sacrificing valuable time to trying to write . . . ?" I was either too tired or too guilty to write . . . and my job certainly was not the subject for a novel . . .

I find myself in much the same position you are in . . . even when I finally combine a home and children with this hypothetical writing (as Mrs. Moore has done so capably, without sacrificing to either) I will have a certain nucleus of conflict . . .

That is why I am so happy to have this extra year at Smith . . . why I have decided to apply for Harvard Graduate School after 1955, rather than start the 9 to 5 grind so soon, be it at the best publishing house in NYC! I want time, lots more time to mature . . . summer months to travel, to work, to read . . . . to meet like-minded people, to think, and I'm pragmatist enough that I'll apply for scholarships (I've even thought of joining Waves so I'd get on the G.I. Bill!) and live off other benevolent millionaires till I feel ready to support myself by a "regular" job . . . and that won't be for some time.

I won't be abstracting myself in the Ivycovered Tower, either . . . I think I get more of the blood-and-guts substance of life in my 3 summer working months than many people get in a year of routine work . . . the advantage of summer jobs being that they are temporary, therefore not trapping and dulling, and the stimulus may provide writing material . . .

I want <u>you</u> to evolve into the best Gordon possible, because I am honestly fond of you . . . and as it impossible to predict in more than hypothetical fashion where we'll both be individually happiest and most creative, we must hazard shrewdly and with the best of our hopings and doubtings . . .

I don't see you a Willie Lowman,[1] but I think insurance demands a high amount of extroversion, pressure, and solicitude for "contacts" no matter how good you are, & perhaps more of these, the better you are . . .

1–A reference to the protagonist William 'Willy' Loman of Arthur Miller, *Death of a Salesman* (1949).

But you know the pitfalls even better than I . . . and raise the utterly important question "What kind of a person will this make me, or what kind of a person will I make of myself if I go into this kind of work?" Here, I think, you have hit upon the ultimate point for consideration, the heart of the onion, or what you will . . .

Me, I want to grow in an upward (that's where my optimism comes in) dialectic spiral that makes out of thesis and antithesis a kinetic synthesis which in turn becomes a thesis, to be blasted at by new antitheses . . . this is not a placid cowish monolithic way to live, I know, and it's damn hard to keep whipping yourself out of some comfortable bourgeois complacency . . . but I want to do just that . . . to keep on learning and thinking and feeling intensely even if it hurts like hell . . .

And because I am a woman (or getting to be), I eventually want a guy who feels somewhat the same way, who will grow along beside me in approximately a parallel line, and I want kids to carry on my mortal flesh and some of my mortal philosophy as I go (and this is not to be taken sentimentally) down "rosecrowned into the darkness with unreluctant tread"[1] . . . the roses being the thorny variety . . .

This all begins to sounds most bellicose and belligerent . . . but I learn more about myself as I talk to you . . . and I have always rated becoming and the horizontal flux over being and the vertical stasis . . .

Hell, Gordon, I could go on forever . . . fortunately I am getting so sleepy I can hardly see . . . and I have to pack . . .

"The solar system tilts, and planets rain
Wild fire: the suitcases are packed again . . ."[2]

sometimes, after a spiel like this, I think I <u>could</u> love you a good deal . . . but is it because I <u>know</u> you at all, or because I only <u>think</u> you will understand all this and therefore be a confidante . . . Oh, I don't know at all at all . . .

a two-dimensional abstract kiss for you nevertheless . . .

Love from your
sylvia

1–Rupert Brooke, 'The Hill'; SP misquotes, '"We shall go down with unreluctant tread / Rose-crowned into the darkness!"'
2–Sylvia Plath, 'The Suitcases Are Packed Again'.

TO *Aurelia Schober Plath*

Thursday 8 April 1954[1] ALS (postcard), Indiana University

Thursday 11 a.m.

Dear mother . . .

It seems strange to be unpacked & settled again in my favorite academic world, in my big sunny harvard-crimson, yale-blue room with my hundred lovable books & several best friends (Nan Hunter, Claiborne & Marty) – yesterday was delightful – spring weather & Norm[2] & Phil were dears! We quoted poetry (some of our own) all the way up – stopped at Amherst to see Ruthie (to make arrangements about our Sat. lunch together) and George Gebauer – the 2 boys carried all my luggage up to my room where we left it, & they treated me to a lobster dinner – we spent the afternoon at Amherst at the apartment of a Spanish professor Norm went to Mexico with last year, sipping cherry wine – then a hotdog supper, goodbye & home to unpack – letter & picture arrived from The Boy, and the feeling is now articulately mutual but local complications are enormous.

xx
S.

<handwritten on address side of postcard>

(p.s. Please send those postcards I left on my desk!)

TO *Aurelia Schober Plath*

Sunday 11 April 1954 ALS (postcard), Indiana University

April 11, 1954

Dear mother . . .

just a note in the midst of 1000 pages of Melville reading before my exam on Wed a.m. – only got a B on my history exam, but an A- on my Russian paper, so looks like my final grades at this juncture will be a mixture of A's & B's – well, just as long as there aren't any C's! Heard world-famous guitarist Andres Segovia here Sat. night[3] with George after lovely afternoon at Amherst, lunch with Ruthie (who came to George's with me & stayed for bridge & music all afternoon) – great letter from

1–Date supplied from postmark.

2–Norman Richard Shapiro (1930–); B.A. 1951, Ph.D., 1958, Harvard University; friend of SP and Philip McCurdy.

3–Spanish guitarist Andrés Segovia (1893–1987) performed at Sage Hall on Saturday evening, 10 April 1954.

Gordon in Istanbul[1] – still have to keep quiet about the Man in house as M. B. plans to ask him up for float night (May 15) not knowing he considers her "dull" & asserts (in writing!) that he "loves me very much!" So I sit & wait till he makes a definite move to see me again – meanwhile enjoying friends – George, Phil, et al. "We also serve." I'll be so glad to bike, play tennis & get TAN – am sick of sitting studiously on rear – it's great to have a balance – more news later – hope you, Warren, Clem & Margo can come up May 15

x
S.

TO *Aurelia Schober Plath*

Wednesday 14 April 1954[2] ALS (postcard), Indiana University

Wednesday 10:30 am.

Dear mum . . .

Miraculously enough my wallet was returned today with ALL THE MONEY IN IT!! I am going to send a rose to Mr. Anthony Sabarito immediately, as I am now solvent for the rest of the year! Just got through my Melville exam this a.m. – really enjoyed it – I got quite inspired with my own spontaneous eloquence! glad Warren & Clem were such fun – I love them both. Only one History written to go before finals! Hope you, Clem, Warren & Margo can come up the weekend of May 15-16. Claiborne wants me to be at her wedding here June 7th, so I'll be home over a week, then drive back – could my next year's roommate, Nancy Hunter, live with us for that time? Next to Clai & Marty I love her most. By the way, could you send me a tin of Tollhouse or oatmeal cookies to nibble on while studying? I get ravenous reading about the delectable things you concoct with such glee for Warren! Am going out with George again Saturday – most likely we'll see Leslie Howard in the movie of "Pygmaleon"[3]

xxx
Sivvy

1–Gordon Lameyer to SP, 26 March 1954; held by Lilly Library.

2–Date supplied from postmark.

3–*Pygmalion* played at Sage Hall, Saturday 17 April 1954 at 7:30 p.m. and 9:30 p.m.

TO *Philip E. McCurdy*

Wednesday 14 April 1954[1] ALS with envelope, Smith College

Wednesday night – 9 p.m.

Dear Phil . . .

Ah, the blandishing blatant delights of pure physical well-being! I sit luxuriously ensconced in my Harvard Crimson[2] armchair, surrounded by literal stacks of new books, – (still smelling faintly and enticingly of printer's ink and sawdust – whatever that ineffable new-book-smell is made up of!) Dressed in casual lounging pajamas, freshly warm and 99 44/100% reborn through the benevolent baptism of a hot shower, with a roast-beef dinner digesting benignly somewhere in my lower gut – I sit reveling in leisure. For a change. In a short while I will go to bed – at the unprecedented hour of 10 p.m.!

The reason for this personal pampering is the rigorous week I have just lived through; also, a preparation for the even more rigorous ones to come. Late last night, as I was finishing reading Melville's "Billy Budd"[3] and frantically digesting notes for my Big exam at 9 a.m. today, I by chance plucked from my library of largely unread-but-about-to-be-read-this-summer books a paperbound copy of D. H. Lawrence's dry-titled "Studies in Classical American Literature"[4] to read the chapters on Melville. Little did I know what bright blustering, cataclysmic confidences I was plunging into – result; I read the little pamphlet from cover-to-cover, underlining & turning down corners in most enthusiastic abandon . . . and staying up injudiciously late.

Hans Kohn,[5] visiting, I believe, from Columbia, lectured on Henrik Ibsen in my Intellectual History course today, and I'll never be the same again – it was absolutely explosive – vital – soul-shattering! I was so entranced with the drama and intellectual brilliance of his presentation that I could hardly take my eyes off his face long enough to scribble down notes. In the midst of his vivid description of a young ("how-you-say-

1 – Date supplied from internal evidence.

2 – Harvard Crimson are the sports teams of Harvard University. A Harvard seal pennant was draped across the back of SP's chair in her room at Lawrence House.

3 – Herman Melville, *Selected Tales and Poems* (New York: Holt, Rinehart and Winston, 1950); SP's copy, which includes *Billy Budd*, is held by Emory University.

4 – D. H. Lawrence, *Studies in Classic American Literature* (Garden City, N.Y.: Doubleday, 1953); SP's heavily annotated copy, a gift from Marcia Brown, 24 April 1953; held by Smith College.

5 – Hans Kohn (1891–1971); professor of history, Smith College, 1934–49; professor of modern European history, City University of New York, 1949–62.

it?") "roué," he caught me smiling in devilish amusement and leveled an impish finger at me: "Ach, that girl, she knows, she's had experience!" he chuckled, as I blushed furiously – thinking of your proposed sketch of Ilo!

Anyhow, after the lecture I was so transfigured that I went across the street to buy the collected plays of Ibsen[1] and read them immediately! Phil, I'm worried – what I've got is worse than epilepsy or syphilis! I went to that damn store[2] and came back having bought TWELVE (12!) books! I got the collected plays of Ibsen, Shaw,[3] O'Neill,[4] the Greeks; Fry's Venus Observed,[5] Delmore Schwartz's Vaudeville for a Princess,[6] Whitman's Leaves of Grass,[7] Sterne's Tristram Shandy[8] – and simply stacks of others! My bookcases are overflowing – shelves of novels, poetry, plays, with clots of philosophy, sociology & psych. I am a bibliomaniac (with a slight touch of nympho thrown in!)

Last weekend I went to a Religious Center[9] lecture – you will be surprised at this till I tell you it was on sex; or, more decorously: male-female encounter and subsequent reception (or conception, or contra – as the case may be) – Yale joined us, the main purpose being my meeting Dick Wertz,[10] a psychic Yale "brother" of my alter ego, Nancy Hunter. The three of us adjourned our discussion to Rahar's, substituting beer &

1–Henrik Ibsen, *Elevens Plays of Henrik Ibsen* (New York: Modern Library, 1954); SP's heavily annotated copy held by Smith College.
2–The Quill Bookshop was located across from Lawrence House at 90 Green Street, Northampton. SP also bought books at the Hampshire Bookshop on Crafts Avenue, Northampton.
3–George Bernard Shaw, *Four Plays* (New York: Modern Library, 1953); SP's copy held by Lilly Library.
4–Eugene O'Neill, *Nine Plays* (New York: Modern Library, 1952); SP's copy held by Lilly Library.
5–Christopher Fry, *Venus Observed: A Play* (London, New York: Oxford University Press, 1950); the location of SP's copy is unknown.
6–Delmore Schwartz, *Vaudeville for a Princess and Other Poems* (New York: New Directions, 1950); SP's copy held by University of North Carolina at Chapel Hill.
7–Walt Whitman, *Leaves of Grass and Selected Poems* (New York: Rinehart, 1953); SP's copy held by University of Virginia.
8–Laurence Sterne, *The Life and Opinions of Tristram Shandy, Gentleman* (New York: Rinehart, 1950); SP's copy, with some underlining to the introduction and the first ten chapters, held by Smith College.
9–Religious Center, 7 College Lane, was the headquarters for the Religious Association at Smith College, 1952–4.
10–Richard Wayne Wertz (1933–2002); B.A. 1955, Yale College; resident of Westminster College, Cambridge, 1955–6; M.Div. 1958, Yale Divinity School; Ph.D. 1967, Harvard University in history of American religion; roommate of Melvin Woody and Richard Sassoon at Yale College; dated SP, 1955–6; co-authored *Lying-In: A History of Childbirth in America*.

potato chips for coffee & ice cream, and holding forth passionately on sex, war, and capital punishment. Most stimulating.

Also saw George: brought Ruthie over from the U of Mass & visited with her all afternoon while G. was taking shower. Then we heard Andres Segovia, world-famous guitarist, give a spectacular rendering of classical pieces at Smith – G. had a raging fever & was being beastly, so I sent him home to bed. Also decided I can't marry a man who is so unreasonable and irritable about women, especially when he is sick (although everybody is privileged to blow off vitriol periodically, one doesn't have to try to drown innocent bystanders with it!)

This weekend I hope to see a revival of Shaw's movie "Pygmalion" with Leslie Howard and Wendy Hiller – if G. has recovered sufficiently to be civil and broad-minded about women's rights.

I keep thinking what a lovely time we had that most beauteous Wednesday. I only hope Norm wasn't too weary or bored – I like him very much, you know! The two of you were such fun, and so damn considerate (tsk, Sylvia, your swearing quota is over following – no profanity, dear, even for emphasis!) Anyhow I love you both for being so dear to me – or rather Norm for being d. to m. and you for it, but also just anyway, on general principles.

I have thought longingly about beach party weekend, & feel I must, because of the large amt. (at least 8 hours) of bus traveling time involved, decline – I've got another exam in history the following Monday and literally 5 1000 page novels to read these next few weeks – so I've decided not to leave Smith at all till after my last exam May 27th – this wounds me, but is, as so many wounding decisions are, I fear, wise – in view of how I still get tired leaping about in transit as I did of late in NYC – that little jaunt will last me another month or two yet! So this will get to you in ample time to ask another unsweet unSmith damsel – already I envy her – I loved every minute of being with you vacation – dance, dinner, cocktails, art exhibit, drive, et. al. Please be good and write some time soon – meanwhile, accept my love & a two-dimensional kiss!

XXX

your sylvan smith girl

P.S. – your voluptuous nude lies in slumbering aphrodisiacal bliss on the wall over the head of my bed – under her aegis I sleep warmly and well and am delighted by the most indecent of indecorous dreams –

TO *Aurelia Schober Plath*

Friday 16 April 1954 TLS, Indiana University

<typed on yellow Street & Smith Publications Inter Office Memorandum sheets, with heading>

TO dear mummy FROM me
SUBJECT odds and ends DATE april 16

seems scarcely imagineable that there are only six weeks left of school! I am very tired at the end of this hard week, but am taking a very hot bath tonight and going to bed early. I cut classes these last two days (the ones I'm auditing) to lie in the sun on the porch roof yesterday and get my first burn of the year while beginning the 1200 page tome War and Peace.[1] Today I cut because I wrote my first poem, a sonnet, that I have written since last May! To be sure, I astringently revised several of my poems this past month (the second one I'm including has six new lines, and six old revised and rearranged ones: I think it's my best so far for both thought content and sound . . . a union of both, not just a hyperdevelopment of one. Tell me what you think of them.) But "Doom of Exiles" is All New.

☆ Two important Requests: I know I left my white net stole at home, but don't know where . . . in a box, or the closet, or down in a drawer (it takes very little space). PLEASE try to find it and send it immediately as I have two formal Phi Bete dinners coming up, one next Thursday night . . . for which I can't come bare shouldered. Also could you send my white hat? And cookies?

Thank you!

While I have not got a paying Press Board job next year (all the present correspondents are keeping their positions, so there are no vacancies), I am the correspondent to the NY Tribune, which should be good experience, even if it doesn't pay money.

I am so happy about the prospect of my thesis on Dostoevsky, and also of my rooming with Nancy Hunter, who is now my dearest friend, taking Claiborne's place, even though I love Clai just as much . . . and will visit her and Avrahm in NYC next year and during this summer. Nancy is writing a thesis in History on Ethical Culture, and I am so elated that with Marty and Clai gone that I have found such a beautiful brilliant girl to be my confidante and belle amie!

1–Leo Tolstoy, *War and Peace* (New York: Modern Library, 1942); SP's copy held by Lilly Library.

Tomorrow I'm going over to Amherst for the usual steak dinner at Valentine Hall, then back to Smith with George to see "Pygmalion", then back to a French party at Chi Psi, to which I am wearing my slinky black silk sheath with my little black lace hat, long white silk gloves and a white ermine muff: the general idea to be a highclass French call girl. Should be fun.

Decided definitely not to go to Harvard with all this reading I have to do . . . travelling by so bourgeois a method as bus takes too much energy.

My love to all.
xxx
sivvy

Sylvia Plath
New Poem
April 16, 1954

Sonnet

Doom of Exiles

Now we, returning from the vaulted domes
Of our colossal sleep, come home to find
A tall metropolis of catacombs
Erected down the gangways of our mind.

Green alleys where we reveled have become
The infernal haunt of demon dangers;
Both seraph song and violins are dumb;
Each clock tick consecrates the death of strangers.

Backward we traveled to reclaim the day
Before we fell, like Icarus, undone;
All we find are altars in decay
And profane words scrawled black across the sun.

Still, stubbornly we try to crack the nut
In which the riddle of our race is shut.

Sylvia Plath
Revised version
April 16, 1954

Sonnet

The Dead

Revolving in oval loops of solar speed,
Couched in cauls of clay as in holy robes,
Dead men render love and war no heed,
Lulled in the ample womb of the full-tilt globe.

No spiritual Caesars are these dead:
They want no proud paternal kingdom come;
And when at last they blunder into bed
World-wrecked, they seek only oblivion.

Rolled round with goodly loam and cradled deep,
These bone shanks will not wake immaculate
To trumpet-toppling dawn of doomstruck day:
They loll forever in colossal sleep;
Nor can God's stern, shocked angels cry them up
From their fond, final, infamous decay.

TO *Aurelia Schober Plath*

Monday 19 April 1954

TLS on *Smith Review* Make-Up Sheet letterhead, Indiana University

Monday, April 19

Dearest mother . . .

Just a quick note before my 9 o'clock class . . . today is the inevitable Monday, when weekend stardust metamorphoses into sawdust . . . and there is kp duty at 8 and classes all morning . . .

The weekend was superlative . . . George was fortunate to have a good friend loan him a car in the torrential rain on Saturday, so we went to Amherst for dinner, back here for Pygmalion, which we both loved, especially Leslie Howard, who reminds me most strongly of Marty's Mike, then back to Amherst for a French party to which I wore my sliplike black silk sheath dress which, thank God, fits me beautifully, and one long white silk glove with an ermine muff . . . the effect was heightened by the fact that I had quite a good beginning tan from being out in the sun . . . George was most gratifying . . .

Sunday was heavenly . . . sunworshipped all morning with Marcia, and we both skipped the abominable formal Sunday dinner hour, taking a picnic of apples and milk and sandwiches up on the roof and getting a toasty brown. The afternoon and evening was intriguing . . . Dick Wertz, (who is to Nancy Hunter what Perry was to me) a roommate of Mel Woody's, telegrammed, after the three of us had such a good time last week, that he'd like a date, and his roommate who had heard so much about me from Mel and Dick, wanted to meet me.

So I got Anne Goodkind for Dick, and met Richard Sassoon[1] (whose father is a cousin of Siegfried Sassoon[2]) . . . a thin, slender Parisian fellow who is a British subject, and a delight to talk to . . . I find he's another of those men who are exactly as tall as I, but they don't seem to mind it, and I certainly don't. He drove up with Wertz in his little German Volkswagon and we drove out to Look Park as it was such a beautiful afternoon (I had been out all day) and raced each other over the green fields, observed the deer and children leaping around, and meandered along by the river. Then a good pork dinner at Valentine over at Amherst with Nancy Hunter and Dave Furner,[3] a tour of the college, back to Smith to pick up Anne. Then we four did the most wonderful thing: we drove up to the Mount Tom reservation in the pitch dark, with the wind blowing, and only the headlights cutting a path out of the black, and climbed a perilous firetower from where we could overlook the whole pioneer valley, springfield, holyoke, et al, with the congregations of luminous lights and colored neon pinpricks, and the big moon faintly orange, misty, as in a Japanese print. It was a moving and unifying experience, even if my legs did shake on the way down the steep slatted stairs.

1–Richard Laurence Sassoon (1934–); B.A. 1955, Yale College; attended the Sorbonne, 1955–6; dated SP, 1954–6. Sassoon was born in Paris, and raised in Tryon, North Carolina. There are very few letters from SP to Sassoon. SP biographer Andrew Wilson reports in his biography *Mad Girl's Love Song* (2013) that Sassoon told him 'Sylvia and I did correspond a lot and, long ago, visiting my parents' house, I looked in the attic in a trunk where I kept her letters and they were not there, which is a total mystery.' There are many letters from Sassoon to SP held by Lilly Library.

2–English poet Siegfried Sassoon (1886–1967).

3–David Charles Ferner (1933–2016); B.A. 1955, Amherst College; Nancy Hunter's boyfriend, David Ferner, a junior at Amherst College.

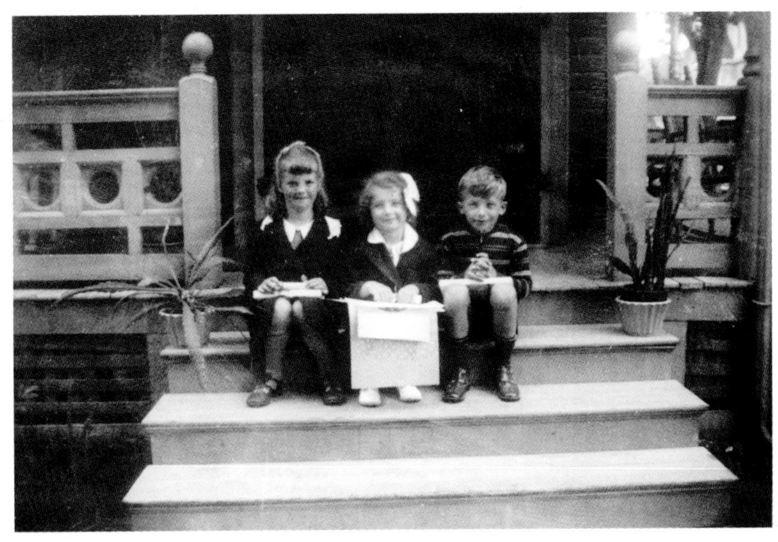

Sylvia Plath, Ruth Freeman and David Freeman,
Winthrop, Massachusetts, 1938.

Febuary 20.1940

Dear Mother
I liked your letter.
The waves were up to our front steps they were as high as the window!
And I wrote a letter to Aunt Dot.

Self-portrait of SP holding a flower next to her Aunt Dorothy holding a wand, from SP to Aurelia Schober Plath, 20 February 1940.

Above: Sylvia Plath and campers at 'Trading Post', Camp Weetamoe, Center Ossipee, New Hampshire, July 1943.

Left: Margot Loungway in Maine, 1 November 1944. Captioned on verso: 'First of November. 1944. Just before Margot had her hair cut'.

Top right: Drawing of a winter scene with moon, from SP to Frank Schober, 16 January 1946.

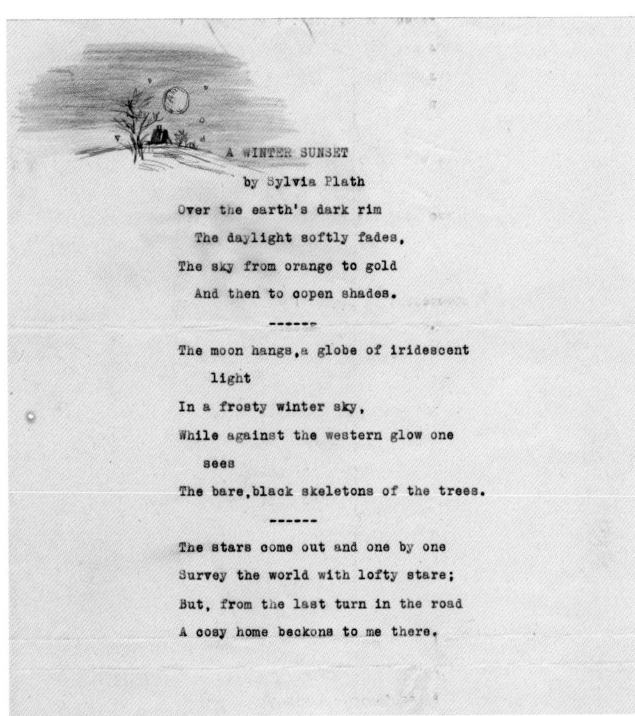

A WINTER SUNSET

by Sylvia Plath

Over the earth's dark rim
The daylight softly fades,
The sky from orange to gold
And then to copen shades.

The moon hangs, a globe of iridescent
light
In a frosty winter sky,
While against the western glow one
sees
The bare, black skeletons of the trees.

The stars come out and one by one
Survey the world with lofty stare;
But, from the last turn in the road
A cosy home beckons to me there.

a new Easter dress and all the
other wonderful things.
If it won't be to much of
a bother, I'd like to tell the
following people the following
things:
Mr. Freeman – I do hope that
I may see your finished pain
ing. In my estimation it shou
be in the Art Museum alon
with Winslow Homer and the
rest.
Dave – Crissy is very anxiou
to meet you – likewise Bets
I do appreciate your followi
the bus – especially popping
by East Boston.
Ruthie – the hat is adorable.
Mum loves it, I do hope you
will have a nice time in
Saugus. (Did you sleep last night?)
Wayne – My bike feels so un-
comfortable and strange. I al-
ways used to like it but now
I think that I should loosen
the front wheel and paint it
orange.
Give my love to the
family.
Love, Sylvia

Drawings of a painted frame, of a bicycle, and a girl holding a piece of paper sitting at a desk with an inkwell on it, from SP to Marion Freeman, 16 April 1946.

November 4, 1946

Dear "Marion,"
I still have a left-over
glow from the lovely time
I had at your house. It
is a weekend I will never
forget. the movie is one
that I had wanted to see,
and the evening dinner
was like a happy dream.
Ruthie was a peach
to entertain me as
she did, although every-
body helped. It was
so thoughtful of you to
invite Wayne over, too.
You will always be like
a second mother to me,
you know, and even
though it was "precipitat-
ing" outside it was so

Drawing of a peach on a leafed branch, from SP to Marion Freeman, 4 November 1946.

(4) The sail stands a good 5 feet, high. Some of my friends will pull it across the stage, while prissy is inside the basket holding the sail. I only hope the sail doesn't collapse in the middle of the stage!

Priscilla has kept rather silent about the whole little incident of your skating trip. I guess that she just didn't appreciate your suttle humor— or something!

SYLVIA FOR SECRETARY

The next time I write to you— That will be after I receive the next long letter to you, I will send you some valuable stamps to sell and get enough money to set me on easy street with. Perhaps I will even quote my latest masterpiece of poetry that appeared in our school maga-zine, and was approved by an eminent author. Until our next meeting or your next letter.

Au revoir,
Sylvia Artemis
Platowsky

Above: Drawing of a sailboat with 'SYLVIA FOR SECRETARY' written on the sail and port side, from SP to Margot Loungway, 11 January 1947.

Above right: Drawing of the beach, houses, and the ocean, from SP to Aurelia Plath, 5 July 1947.

Above, far right: Drawing of a 'freak' girl scout, from SP to Aurelia Plath, 20 July 1948.

July 5,
Dear
Mummy,
This is a very
quick sketch of the beach
we biked to this morning.
We totaled only 13 miles, and
we left at about 9:30 A.M.
and came back at 12:00
after spending 45 min. in
swimming and resting on
the warm white sands.
Hardly any people were
there, so we were left more
or less to ourselves. The
waters were a light, salty
blue and a sandy, smooth
bar stretched out into the
ocean. The water was free
from crabs and seaweed,
and I went swimming
with. Sally Haven, an adora-
ble girl who lives in Newton.
She has soft light hair
and lovely dark eyes-almost
as tall as I am, and still
has a little girl charm about
her since she does not act
old, and yet does not seem
in the least silly. I just love
her. We had loads of fun
swimming underwater
and sitting on the smooth,
sandy bottom pretending
to comb our hair. When I
come home please do
not expect me to have a
very dark tan since I don't.
How long does it take for
my cards to get to xxx
Wellesley?

Dear Mum, July 20 (3)
Here I am again for
the third time today,
and feeling even better!
Do you know an odd co-
incidence?! One girl in
my unit came up to me
and asked if I knew
Wayne Sterling! It seems
that her little brother
wrote her from the Y
camp where Wayne is
counsellor, and Wayne
wanted to know if I
went to his sister's
camp! We had a girl scout
troop from W. Haven come
to visit us for a day + ·
night, and they left this
morning. They were all
cute except for one
freak who scared Betsy +
me + looked like this:
I pitied her, but she was
so
utterly horribly slovenly
that we kept away from her.
I'm not so homely after all!
Lots of love -me

Sylvia Plath, *c.* 1950.

what kills me. They really are mad
That anything nice has happened, (4
and can't take it. So I keep it to
my-self – and it hurts. I can't go
around telling people how terrific I
am, because I can't believe it.
Blanton has talked herself into thinki
she's pretty + popular. It took a
while + a lot of talk, but now,
damn it, she is! But I don't
believe I'm any good. You made
me think I might have something.
This letter is the swearsiest one
I've ever written. I need so to
love a person – be it girl or boy,
friend or enemy. and without being
able to, I sort of dry up.

Heck, don't start feeling sorry for
me, even if this letter has been
awfully pitiful. I'll write news, +
you do the same. I love you, Davy.
I love your mother. She's one of
the finest, most beautiful women
I've ever seen. Tell her hello for
me.

Bye, baby,

your
Sylvy

(not to be confused
with— (heck – I never could draw animals

So I came back from my sojurn (
last Wednesday, with make-up work
piled shoulder high. But that was O.K.
being I was dateless this weekend +
going to Yale with Dick on the 11th (Gosh
don't I sound popular! Heh-heh!) So
what happens? I am in talking about
next year's program with Mr. Wright,
my advisor, and leaving his office very
gaily, with a little skip. And what happen
to the graceful little ox? Her slippery-sole
loafers skid on the polished stone floor,
and she falls with the loudest crash
imaginable, her ankle crunching queerly
as she sits on it. Now isn't that annoyin
after making such a fashionable exit, to
have your advisor have to rush out,
pick you up off the floor and half
carry you to the D.O.? I still am hopin
the damn sprain will be walkable
by this weekend so I can see Dick.
Just when I wanted to look my
best I have to have an ankle three
times normal size!

It is broiling hot, now, and it
is only 9:30. How much can a
female suffer for her vanity? I'm
determined to be golden brown,
though. You should see the color
Marcia is! (she's been lying out
on every sunny day)

Now to tell you how surprised
and thrilled I was to get a letter
from Boulder! Honey, you are so
traveled! And it sounded like the

Smith College Northampton Massachusetts

his points completely. As for me, I think
practice will help me grasp even
larger situations. This new experience
with children might prove writable, too.

I am guilty of making a few
clothes purchases this am, but all
of them are sensible, versatile, and
very nice. I got a full navy cotton
skirt which can be dressed up or
down with all my blouses – a white
tailored casual no sleeve blouse –
a yellow tucked one of dressier proportions
and a must for this summer – a
neat two-piece white Jantzen bathing
suit to alternate with my flowered
one: prices: white blouse 2.98
yellow blouse 2.98
navy skirt 5.95
bathing suit 8.95
20.86

I also am "making" a brown skirt (under
the careful supervision of a
friend) to take the place of
the shiny skimpy one at home,
so my mix-and-match separates
have really proved quite
economical. I have outgrown the
frilly high school stage, tra la la.

See you soon Love, Sivvy

Above left: Drawing of a horse's head, from SP to Ann Davidow-Goodman, *c.* 12 January 1951.

Above: SP with a sprained ankle, from SP to Ann Davidow-Goodman, 9 May 1951.

Left: Drawings of four pieces of clothing, from SP to Aurelia Plath, 6 May 1951.

(3)

Smith College Northampton Massachusetts

The Yale men dropped me at home in time for supper. after which Dick biked over for a brief 15 minutes to show me the suave black paint job on his 2-wheeler + walk me quickly around the block. An intellectual pass on his part in the direction of the international situation was blocked on my part with a mute resolve to read and memorize every issue of the Monitor this summer. We parted ... buddies, you might say.

He headed off with Perry for a week's trip in the wilds of Maine – around Jonesport – Sunday, so I will catch no glimpse of his pointed blond head till this Saturday. Leaving me a blissful week to "get things done in."

Sunday I began with a will, got all unpacked, hung up, and drawers, bookcase, closet and trunk completely cleaned out and rearranged – a long task in itself. The lawn also awaited me – strictly a long-hair job saved up for a month. At last I plowed through it ... only to have to begin again. Monday I went "downtown" to the Wellesley shopping district. I blew myself on a LP record of César Franck's symphony

(8)

Tuesday June 26, 1951

Dear Davy –

I'm sure that you could draw the infants alot better than I can, but at least you get the general idea – two girls (2 and 4) and a boy (6) As you may imagine, that is just about the most wicked combinati[on] of ages possible!

But before I tell you about the situation here, I want you to know how thrilled I was to hear your voice over the phone the other night! I had the absurd feeling that you were in Lynn or Marblehead, just waiting to come over and say hello in person. Maybe you will, though, before the summer's over! I wish you could get down to Swampscott on my day off (any old time, in other words) and we could take a picnic and spend the whole time down on the beach. It's only about a half hour's trip from Boston!

Now for a little sketch of the place where I live and work and have

Above: Drawing of SP mowing the lawn, from SP to Marcia Brown Stern, 6 June 1951.

Above right: Joanne, Esther (Pinny), and Frederic Mayo, from SP to Ann Davidow-Goodman, 26 June 1951.

Right: Self-portrait holding a book, from SP to Marcia Brown Stern, 1 July 1951.

Sunday

And here is a glamorized version of the pseudo-mater after a looong day at the office, (started out to be Pinny's face, but matured into a frowsy almost-adult) after Thursday and Friday off, I returned somewhat regretfully to my home at BB. I had worked over a week and a half without a rest, and so really slept at my domicile, which was startlingly silent and peaceful somehow. Best of all was sight of brother. When he walked in Thursday night after work (at farm), I gasped. Not only did he tower tanly above me, but he wasn't half bad looking, and his shoulders are getting broader by the minute seems. he and his best pal (Rodney a skinny little guy with a cute sense of humor) have rented Rodney's brother's old jalopy for the summer, and so will toot

Sylvia Plath standing beside a bicycle, Marblehead, Massachusetts, 24 July 1951.

-3-   c1953, Jan. 7

SMITH COLLEGE
COLLEGE HALL
NORTHAMPTON, MASSACHUSETTS

COMMITTEE ON RESOURCES (natural, artificial, etc.)

At any rate, I arrived back at school a few days late, only to find your coruscating letter. Myron, I laughed so hard! Really, I can't think up adequate adjectives to describe my high opinion of your literary technique. I did relish your missive! Particularly I was taken by the way your Miltonic conception of heaven and hell corresponded to my own—only I am in the habit of quoting my reference from one of my favorite poems, the Rubaiyat:

"I sent my Soul through the Invisible,
Some letter of that After-life to spell:
And by and by my Soul returned to me,
And answered "I myself am Heav'n and Hell."
"Heav'n but the vision of fulfilled Desire,
And Hell the shadow of a soul on fire
Cast on the darkness into which Ourselves
So late emerged from, shall so soon expire."

Rather similar, n'est-ce pas?

....

So I sit in my room surrounded by innumerable books of verse, jugs of wine, and loaves of bread, gazing out to where the snow is coming down in gulps and blasts and sleetings and icings and softly piling up and always up. Picture me beating a track through waist-high wastes with my crutch, stoically trailing my plastercast left leg valiantly behind me... and all to get to my medieval lit unit! Only three papers to get written before midyears on Piers Plowman (The peoples Christ), The Holy Grail – and a story, respectively. Next semester I begin my modern poetry unit with an authority in the field, and I can hardly wait. The prospect is most exciting, especially as W. H. Auden will be here second semester, too, for three whole months! How I'd like to get to know him!

Drawing of a female on crutches in a high wind with hands reaching through ice, from SP to Myron Lotz, 9 January 1953.

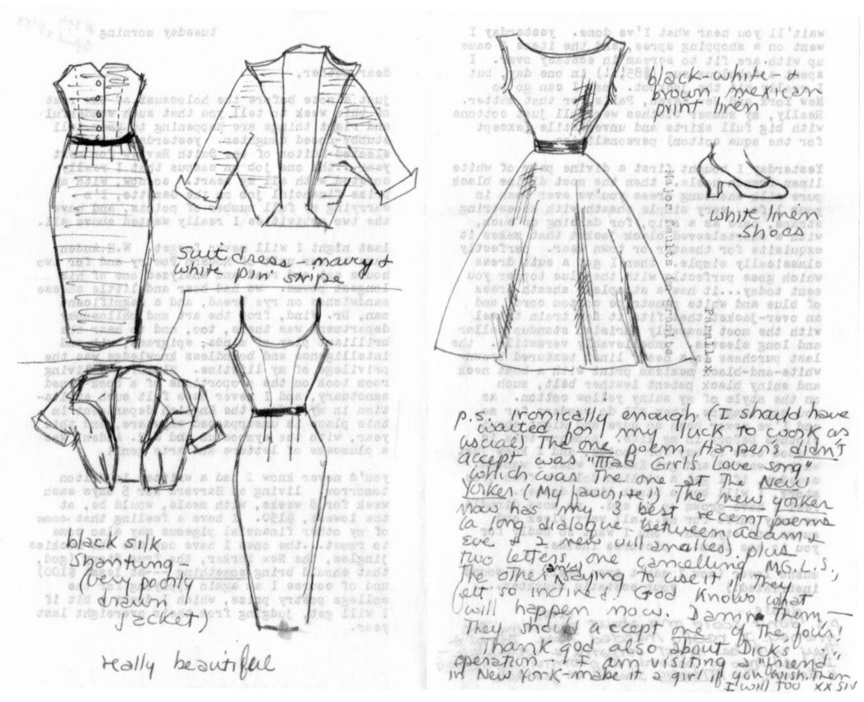

p.s. Ironically enough (I should have waited for my luck to work as usual) the one poem Harper's didn't accept was "Mad Girl's Love Song" which was the one at The New Yorker. (My favorite!) The new yorker now has my 3 best recent poems (a long dialogue between adam & eve & 2 new villanelles) plus two letters, one cancelling M.G.L.S., the other saying to use it, if they felt so inclined! God knows what will happen now. Damn them—they should accept one of the four!
Thank god also about Dick's operation—I am visiting a "friend" in New York—make it a girl if you wish. Then I will too xx siv

Drawings of jackets, dresses, and a shoe, from SP to Aurelia Plath, 28 April 1953.

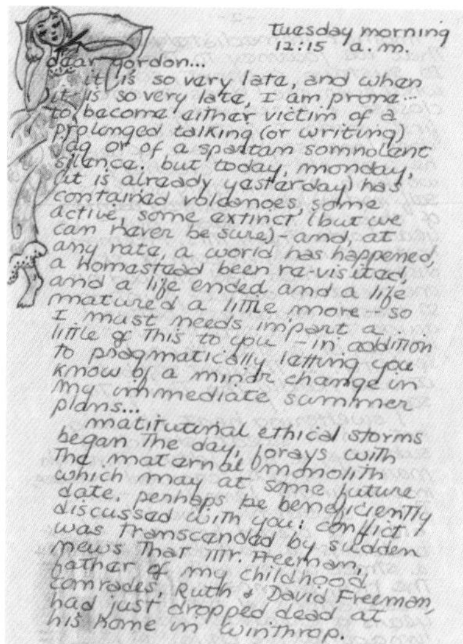
tuesday morning
12:15 a.m.

dear gordon...
it is so very late, and when it is so very late, I am prone—to become either victim of a prolonged talking (or writing) jag or of a spartan somnolent silence. but today, monday, (it is already yesterday) has contained volcanoes, some active, some extinct (but we can never be sure)—and, at any rate, a world has happened, a homestead been re-visited, and a life ended and a life matured a little more—so I must needs impart a little of this to you—in addition to pragmatically letting you know of a minor change in my immediate summer plans...

matitutional ethical storms began the day, forays with the maternal monolith which may at some future date, perhaps be beneficently discussed with you; conflict was transcended by sudden news that Mr. Freeman, father of my childhood comrades, Ruth & David Freeman, had just dropped dead at his home in winthrop.

Drawing of a female wearing a robe, on a pillow, holding a pen, from SP to Gordon Lameyer, 22 June 1954.

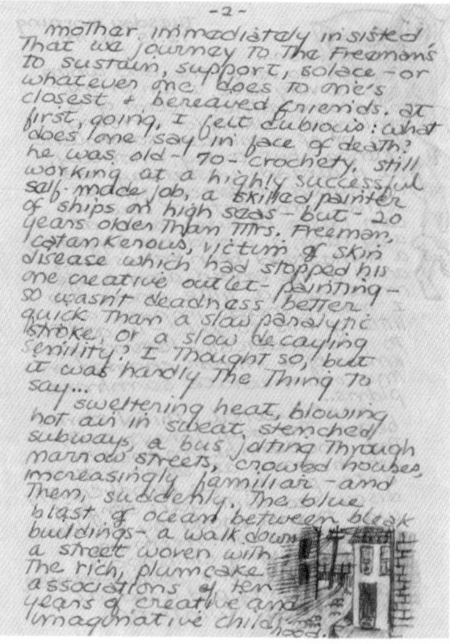
-2-

mother immediately insisted that we journey to the Freeman's to sustain, support, solace—or whatever one does to one's closest & bereaved friends. at first, going, I felt dubious: what does one say in face of death? he was old—70—crochety, still working at a highly successful self-made job, a skilled painter of ships on high seas—but—20 years older than Mrs. Freeman, cantankerous, victim of skin disease which had stopped his one creative outlet—painting—so wasn't deadness better quick than a slow paralytic stroke, or a slow decaying senility? I thought so, but it was hardly the thing to say...

sweltering heat, blowing hot air in sweat, stenched subways, a bus jolting through narrow streets, crowded houses, increasingly familiar—and then, suddenly, the blue blast of ocean between bleak buildings—a walk down a street woven with the rich, plumcake associations of ten years of creative and imaginative childhood.

Streets, houses, and ocean in Winthrop, Mass., from SP to Gordon Lameyer, 22 June 1954.

4.

.so There was breaking of tearful silence and death blighted quiet: talk began of life, of ruth's coming trip to europe, of supper, and how to learn to cook – life was reestablished in little ways – accidentally, and in consonance with my infallible instinct for doing The tabu Thing in all innocent accidence, I went for a drink of water and picked up The heavy glass from The sink and filled it to quench my Thirst – and found out That it was The glass mr. freeman had gasped a last shot of brandy from before dying, put in The sink to soak: nothing like appropriating a holy chalice... ah, well...

a sober supper of Thick green pea soup, cold meats, potato salad, cake and milk and I wanting to be busy or useful, and so doing what

Soup on a table, from SP to Gordon Lameyer, 22 June 1954.

Sylvia Plath at Chatham, Massachusetts, c. 24 July 1954.

Sylvia Plath and Ruth (Freeman) Geissler
on Ruth's wedding day, Winthrop,
Massachusetts, 11 June 1955.

E 534 Sunday afternoon, Oct. 2,

Dearest mother...

By now I hope my two-installment letter of last week has caught up with you. I am most heartily sorry if you were at all worried, but life was coming at me so fast that I had no sense of time elapsing at all. Before I left London, I sent off a slew of postcards to all the people who had been most dear: Crocketts, Cantors, Freemans, Prouty, et. al. Amazing what dreams do to fill up absences: I've dreamt of you and Warren every night since I've been away; sometimes the two of you are very wicked, conspiring to get rid of me forever. Which I suppose is an indirect way of saying that basically I miss you both.

I don't know how I can begin to tell you what it is like here in Cambridge! It is the most beautiful spot in the world, I think, and from my window in Whitstead on the thrrd floor I can see out into the Whitstead garden to trees where large black rooks (ravens) fly over quaint red tiled rooftops with their chimney pots. My room is one of three on the 3rd floor, and while it is at present bare of pictures and needs a bit of decorating, I love it dearly. The roof slants in an atticish way, and I have a gas fireplace which demands a shilling each time I want to warm up the room (wonderful for drying my washed hair by, which I did last night) and a gas ring on the hearth where I can warm up water for tea or coffee. I shall draw you a little map so you can see the layout. My books overflow everywhere and give me the feeling of color and being home (spent all morning carrying loads of them up the staircase). I want to buy a low coffee table if I can find one to bring the room together a bit and give more surface space.

2.

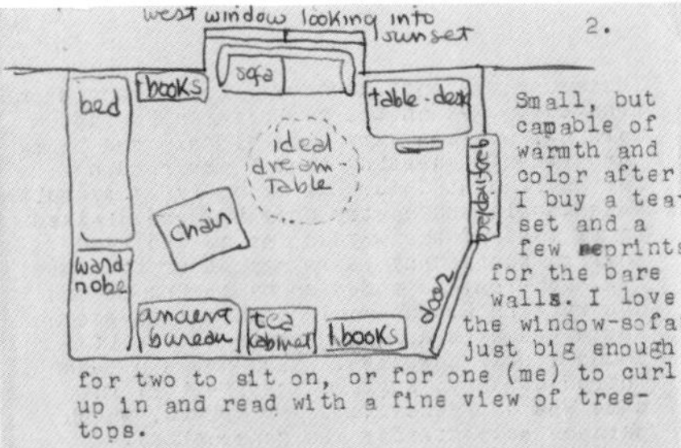

Small, but capable of warmth and color after I buy a tea-set and a few reprints for the bare walls. I love the window-sofa: just big enough for two to sit on, or for one (me) to curl up in and read with a fine view of tree-tops.

Breakfasts are in Whitstead, in a lovely old-fashioned dining room with dark paneling looking out on the garden. We are given a hunk of butter once a week (!) but of course can supplement by buying margerine downtown. I get a small bottle of milk a day (it costs a bit extra but is worth it) which I can use for tea, coffee, or just drinking and plan to out a store of jam, cheese, and crackers in my tea cupboard. We eat lunch and dinner at Clough Hall (one of the four at Newnham) and I have been ravenous each time, so the food doesn't bother me, although it has an amazing amount of starch all at once; two kinds of potatoes, cauliflower, yorkshire pudding, pie and custard sauce, for example accompanied a small piece of roast beef for lunch. Breakfasts have the advantage of being made for only the 12 of us, and this morning I had cornflakes, a fried egg, two pieces of toast and marmalade and coffee, so shall not starve.

Most of the girls are not here yet, so Whitstead is very quiet this afternoon. The few girls here have all gone off to tea and reunions with various friends.

(over)

Drawing of SP's room at Whitstead, from SP to Aurelia Plath, 2 October 1955.

A coffee table with a plant, a *New Yorker*, and other items, on the back of an envelope, from SP to J. Mallory Wober, 16 November 1955.

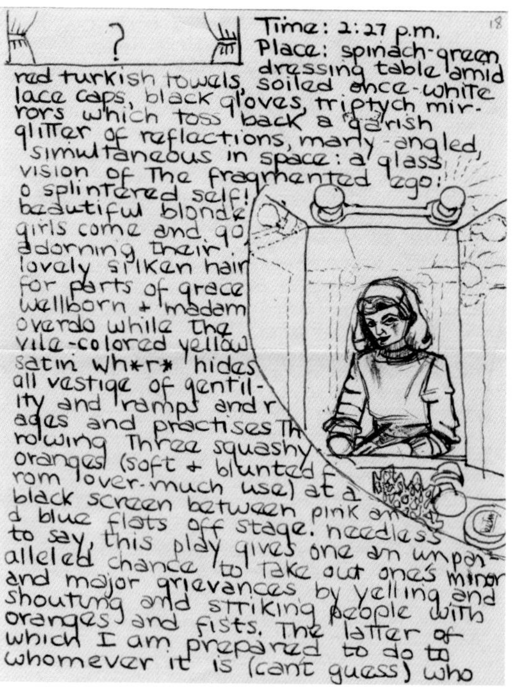

18

Time: 2:27 p.m.
Place: spinach-green dressing table amid red turkish towels, soiled once-white lace caps, black gloves, triptych mirrors which toss back a garish glitter of reflections, many-angled, simultaneous in space: a glass vision of the fragmented ego: o splintered self! beautiful blonde girls come and go adorning their lovely silken hair for parts of grace wellborn + madam overdo while the vile-colored yellow satin wh*r* hides all vestige of gentility and ramps and rages and practises throwing three squashy oranges (soft + blunted from over-much use) at a black screen between pink and blue flats off stage. needless to say, this play gives one an unparalleled chance to take out one's minor and major grievances by yelling and shouting and striking people with oranges and fists. The latter of which I am prepared to do to whomever it is (can't guess) who

Drawing of a female figure in dressing room looking in a mirror and holding a pen, from SP to J. Mallory Wober, 24 November 1955.

A bouquet of daffodils and sunshine
for my dearest grammy —

Drawing of a bouquet of daffodils on the back of an envelope, from SP to Aurelia Schober, 2 February 1956.

Sylvia Plath atop Torre dell'Orologio, Venice, 8 April 1956.

Sylvia Plath at Fontana Muta, Rampa Caffarelli, Rome, 10 April 1956.

Sylvia Plath sitting on a stone wall with a typewriter,
on the Yorkshire moors, September 1956.

After this communication with nature we went to the Deke house at Amherst where Wertz had a good friend, and sat in the pinepaneled bar decorated with wonderful Tolouse-Lautrec paintings mounted in black, quaffed bourbon and water, danced, and since Richard found a boy named Andre Pierre,[1] most everybody was speaking French. I was amazed at the amount I understood and could mimic so that Richard told me I had an excellent accent . . . so if only I could learn a vocabulary and relearn grammar, I'm sure I could pick up the inflection in no time! As it was Sunday, there were many stag boys, and Anne and I were the belles of the bar as it were, with several boys asking for dances, dates, etc., all most gratifying to the insatiable female ego!

Richard Sassoon and I got along very well indeed . . . and I honestly enjoyed talking with him, and climbing towers . . . he's a very intuitive weird sinuous little guy whose eyes are black and shadowed so he looks as if he were an absinthe addict . . . all of which helps me to be carefree and gay and forget this tantalizing Waiting Game which is ubiquitous in the background.

Next weekend George is working hard on his chemistry honors subject, so I won't be seeing him probably, and as I sweetly refused Phil's invitation for all-college weekend, I may just (but somehow dubiously) be sitting home and studying. But one never knows.

Am still chatting with Dr. Booth once a week . . . mostly just friendly conversations as I really feel I am basically an extremely happy and well-adjusted buoyant person at heart . . . continually happy in a steady fashion, not ricocheting from depths to heights, although I do hit heights now and then . . .

Hope youre able to find the stole, also hat . . . clothes don't make the woman but they certainly help . . . my Mexicanprint linen with a black sweater over my tan was highly approved of yesterday . . . the nice thing is that most boys don't notice the line between woman and apparel, just judge the ensemble . . .

love,
sivvy

1 – Andrew Jules Marie Pierre (1934–); B.A. 1955, Amherst College.

TO *Richard Sassoon*

Tuesday 20 April 1954 — TL on verso of Smith College News Office letterhead, Indiana University

wednesday, april 20:

to sassoon:

halfnakedly browning on natural mattresses of pineneedles we lolled luxuriant and cerebralized abominably about what all vitalisitc people do . . . waded barefoot in iced flowing levels of riproaring river, swung treeward with children, raced deer and made naughty remarks about passing nuns . . . such sinful black swathings and blindings and bindings from god's blazing, banging, pungent and pugilistic sunlight! rip them naked, fix them writhing white and pious on a formulated paradox . . . burn them to corpulent crisps and serve them up like sanctified snails with a succulent filet mignon of holy notions . . .

remembering: soft moonvaulted night, annoyed with a plethora of stars, climbing in hegelian dialectic spirals up into the dark unknown . . . as kilroy cried: "I don't see nothing but nothing, and then more nothing!"[1] and the enchanting jargon of three Other voices accompanying this lone vertigoed one in the perilous descent . . . postulations of rapport don't need articulation, but poetic symbols facilitate such . . .

<the letter ends here>

TO *Aurelia Schober Plath*

Friday 23 April 1954[2] — TLS in greeting card,[3] Indiana University

<printed greeting>

Double, double toil and trouble / fire burn and champagne bubble / I'm stirring up a witches brew / That will, I hope, bring luck to you / HAPPY BIRTHDAY

<signed>

best wishes and lots / of love from your / euphoric daughter / (over)

1–Tennessee Williams, *Camino Real* (1953), 45; Kilroy is a lead character in the play.

2–Date supplied from internal evidence.

3–Panda Prints birthday card designed by Rosalind Welcher.

Dear mother . . .

Just a note to tell you that I'm thinking of you on your birthday . . . today is a warm green rainy day which is a subtle change from all the sun I've been out tanning in.

Last night I wore my pretty formal and the silver shoes to the All*Smith Phi Bete dinner[1] in the quadrangle which was most sumptuous: filet mignon, asparagus, fresh strawberries, etc. . . . sat at Mr. Patch's table and enjoyed myself thoroughly. Next Wednesday is the dinner at Lawrence House. As we have 5 Phi Betes, it will be a gala occasion: I'm having Mr. and Mrs. Davis, Miss Drew and Miss Page (who has been wonderful about advising me on my program next year and is going to help me review French on my own).

Also, Mr. Fisher,[2] a handsome middleaged member of the faculty, wanted a collection of my poems, and, although his course in verse writing has been canceled as too expensive for the college, has offered to coach me privately next year in writing poetry . . . a charming man!

Tonight Mike Lotz is coming up to tell me his troubles . . . should be diverting . . . a second Perry! Hoho . . .

xxx
Sivvy

TO *Aurelia Schober Plath*

Sunday 25 April 1954[3] ALS (postcard), Indiana University

Sunday 1. a.m.

Dear mother . . .

Just a note before I fall deliciously in bed after a lovely day. First: two records of the four are for you, two for Warren: yours are the <u>New World Symphony</u> by Dvorzak and Copland's Symphony No. 3 – I think you will like the lyricism of them – the more modern polyphones of the others – Hindemith, Bartok & Shoenberg – probably will appeal more to Warren – Phi Bete dinner delightful – wore white formal, silver shoes, received pink rose which is now ensconced in chianti bottle at desk – filet Mignon at Mr. Patch's table – dull few hours with lugubrious Myron last night

1–The Phi Beta Kappa initiation and banquet was held in the Franklin King and Laura Scales Houses at 6:00 p.m. SP was elected to the Phi Beta Kappa Society in September 1953.
2–Alfred Young Fisher (1902–70); English professor, Smith College, 1937–67; SP's colleague, 1957–8. SP completed a special study in poetry writing with Fisher, 1954–5.
3–Date supplied from postmark.

– he is always so damn sad, depressed, spongy – no "joie de vivre" – even I couldn't catalyze him – he's just Dull! Remedy today – my French boy Dick Sassoon drove up from Yale in his Volksvagon with a bottle of exquisite wine which we imbimbed at a 830 ft altitude on top of world – steak "saignant" at Wiggins – quoted French poetry – great rapport – charming little chap – diversion

xx
sivvy

TO *Philip E. McCurdy*

Monday 26 April 1954 TLS with envelope, Smith College

monday april 26

on my mother's birthday I salute you, darling . . . breakfast has been, as usual, delightful . . .

by cheating me of an infinitely valuable hour of slumber the machinistic men at the Bureau of Time have made 8:30 an earlier blue color with colder greening leaves, and have stretched the afternoons out late and long gold . . . c'est la vie! theyre always changing something . . .

your letter was appreciated, especially the choice cartoon which occasioned much laughter and is now tacked up on my bulletin board (what with your cartoon, your poster, and your own portrait, this room is becoming a salon de Phil!) also loved monsieur norman's poems . . . have read them aloud to several friends, who gratified me by thinking they were by an established poet (well, isn't he?)

nice days, mostly, have been devoted to the sun cult, picnics in country and park, reading James on sunroof, taking on tan with tolstoi . . . , lou giesey, pat oneil and I were treated by miss palmer[1] of wellesley high one night to succulent jack august lobsters . . . reminiscent of former and enchanting time . . . formal college phi bete dinner also this week . . . enjoyed filet mignon and pink roses symbolic of girlish scholarship . . .

I must really plunge into uncompromising work this next month . . . have literally thousands of pages to assimilate and have been playing around too much with sun of god and sons of eve . . .

your friend and mine, george, has been desperately working on his chemistry honors thesis last week, and I have been going out with little

1–Dora E. Palmer (1911–2000), English teacher and head of the Devotionals program, Wellesley High School; English teacher, Northfield School for Girls (fall 1954).

expatriate frenchmen . . . one of whom, a sensitive, intuitive, very thin, black-eyed with purple hollows about them, satanic relative of siegfried sassoon I find quite charming . . . he speaks in french half of the time because he thinks I understand it: je t'adore . . . la vie est la farce à mêner par tous . . . and so on . . . as a result of which my french is picking up and I am adding a few telling phrases to my rather meager previous store of "voulez-vous coucher avec moi?" and "merde alores!" oh, every day in every way . . .

so pleased about your cape job . . . I'm planning on Harvard Summer School[1] remember? or do you? . . . and anyhow, I'll be home all June except for Two Weddings on the 7th[2] and 15th . . . maybe you could investigate down the cape and see if they have any little cabins for rent on weekends in which case I could come down occasionally with grammar or goethe or whatever . . .

anyhow, I hope you can practice your tennis coaching skills with me before you take off for the summer . . . my frenchboy is not the outdoor type . . . he prefers cloistered velvet rooms, pale with roses, light wine, a volume of baudelaire or vigny or rimbaud and a nuit d'amour . . . me, I occasionally want good healthy vulgar american sun, sweat and song . . . entendu?

climbed the firetower 830 feet high in pitch black night last weekend with three others . . . to wonder at the circling crown of lights far far below and stand mystified and silent, the winds of eternity blowing down our backs . . . a victim of vertigo, I shuddered in ecstasies of terror all the while pretending to be brave . . .

off to hear more about henry james . . . hoping eventually to hear more about you . . .

xxx
syl

1–SP studied Elementary German: Aural-Oral Approach (S-Bab). SP's Smith College scrapbook indicates the course was taught by William Oldenbrook, who was a teaching fellow for this course working under the direction of Dr James Hawkes of the Groton School. Though it does not appear on her official transcript, SP also studied Nineteenth-Century Novel (S-151) taught by Frank O'Connor.

2–SP's friend Claiborne Phillips married Avrom Handleman, 7 June 1954.

TO *Philip E. McCurdy*

Wednesday 28 April 1954 ALS with envelope, Smith College

wednesday, april 28

dear phil . . .

speaking of strategically-timed letters, yours, which arrived this morning, was providential! I am writing from a semi-prone position at the infirmary, which opened its antiseptic white gates to receive me an hour ago – malheureusement this is the gala date of our formal Phi Bete dinner at the house – which I was looking forward to attending like a tan cinderella in a silver & white ball gown – our dear housemother has to disinvite my 4 illustrious faculty members, and if I were strong enough, I'd swear bitterly – as it is, I can just about manage one weak, rickety: "damn." . . .

either someone tried to poison me last night, or I had an immaculate miscarriage: excuse the vulgar simile, but I feel at present as if I'd just given birth to five or six babies simultaneously. In other words, I feel like hell – you know how it is when your skin is abnormally hypersensitive, so that sheets weigh like six feet of gibraltar rock, and to your ears the sound of a sneeze reverberates as if Krakatoa were blowing up?! (. . . excuse my hypochondria, but I keep getting carried away by my own figures of speech! . . .)

anyhow, angel, I am here, too spent to read, with barely enough verve to keep my eyes open and contemplate the wet, rain slick flagstones of the sun (!) porch outside my window. funny thing about pain: it annihilates one's pride completely – when I think of crying out like a teething baby wanting its mother, I somehow feel more intensely than ever the reserve power of matter over mind . . .

I was shocked and saddened to hear about how death struck adams house . . . Dr. Little[1] seemed so charming, so debon air – while feeling a vicarious loss for you, I muse on the suddenness of death . . . if we could be clairvoyant and see the date of our own doom, the bloodclot in the vein of our existence – how differently we might proportion our own time . . . and yet, perhaps all one can do is to go on and on "making the best of a bad job . . ."[2] and loving life the more for its individual ephemeral quality . . .

1–David Mason Little (1896–1954); Master of Adams House, Harvard University (1938–54) and Secretary to the University (1936–54); co-editor of *The Letters of David Garrick*; died on 25 April 1954. Philip E. McCurdy was a resident of Adams House.

2–C. S. Lewis, *The Silver Chair* (New York: Macmillan, 1953), 57. In the fourth book of the *Chronicles of Narnia* illustrated by Pauline Baynes, Puddleglum the Marsh-wiggle addresses

<flourish>

a switch: ten novels to devour in four, or rather three brief weeks before exams! all over may 27th . . . and I hope that we'll have a bit of a chance to see each other before you and Norm hie yourselves to the cape . . . and I start to cultivate my native tongue: Deutschland uber alles . . .

<flourish>

cheerful note: (about time, WOT!) please do buy the sprightly pink-yellow & green covered issue of the May Harper's. on page 29 you will see displayed the work of this starving minor poet: a landmark in the flux of fickle time.

I was most pleased at the generous typographical setup,[1] and at the way the poem echoes in verse the prose paragraphs closing Mr. Bowles article – also thrilled at the minute biography on page 19 and the company my name keeps on the title page!

ah, vanitas, vanitatum . . .

I'm only human: & did so want you to share my happiness . . .

The pen falters in my feverish fingers –

my love –
sylvia

TO *Aurelia Schober Plath*

Friday 30 April 1954 Telegram, Indiana University

=SMITH JUST VOTED ME SCHOLARSHIP OF $1250 MORE BIRTHDAY GREETINGS=

SYLVIA=

Jill Pole and Eustace Scrubb: 'I see you're making the best of a bad job. That's right. You've been well brought up, you have. You've learned to put a good face on things.'

1–SP's villanelle follows 'A Bipartisan Policy for Asia' by former Ambassador to India Chester Bowles (23–38); other authors on the title page include Van Wyck Brooks and Sigmund Freud. SP's biography on page 19: 'Sylvia Plath is a Smith College junior and has had poems and stories published in *Mademoiselle* and other magazines.'

TO *Gordon Lameyer*

Monday 3 May 1954 — TLS on Smith College News Office letterhead, Indiana University

May 3 . . .
7:30 p.m.

Dear Gordon . . .

It is the twilight of an english may day, green and gloomy, with car tires slithering wetly on the rainy streets; and the white flower clusters on the tree outside my window are already dissolving, petal by petal falling in the fine and persistent mist . . . a bird chitters sleepily, perhaps it is a goldfinch or a languid nightingale . . . on my desk, in one of my globed green chianti bottles sprouts an "unofficial rose" dark red and exotically proud . . .

Your excellent letter arrived yesterday[1] and brought lovely splashes of continental color into my collegiate life . . . I was especially enchanted by your account of the spinning motor bike trip . . . and, as you must obviously know, I am most eager to hear about your evolving tentative plans and reasons for the project of graduate school . . .

Since I last talked with you, I've been actively planning my program for my senior (it's about time!) year at Smith. I don't know if I mentioned it before, but I'm planning to do my thesis on Dostoevsky . . . more his philosophies than his literary talent: either the recurrence of the split personality or the idea of the Christ and AntiChrist . . . and Mr. Gibian, an exquisite young Czech who is in both the Russian and English departments has consented to be my director . . . I've already had two good talks with him, and feel that he is an excellent choice for me: he's vital, stimulating, and thinks with a penetrating clarity which will be a tonic for my occasional bursts of verbal and metaphysical euphoria . . . also, he's extremely interested in the creative aspects of writing, and has criticized some of my poems. Speaking of poems, Mr. Alfred Fisher has benignly offered to give me a private and extempore course in verse writing next year, as the college considered this course an hors d'oeuvre too expensive for its palate, in spite of the delicacy of it, and struck it off the catalogue. The first thing Mr. Fisher had me do last week was sprint out and buy the new edition of James Joyce's poems "Chamber Music",[2] with the superb introduction by Tindall.[3]

1–Gordon Lameyer to SP, 19 April 1954; held by Lilly Library.

2–James Joyce, *Chamber Music* (New York: Columbia University Press, 1954). SP's copy is held by Smith College.

3–William York Tindall (1903–81), James Joyce scholar and professor at Columbia University.

As I sat on the sunroof, underlining and laughing at several lovely allusions to "chambermade" music, and "shamebred" music, I enjoyed recalling Bloom's pun on chamberpot music, and burst into uncontrolled hysterics when, in the midst of Tindall's scholarly explication I read: "let us look more steadily at Joyce's concern with urine . . ."[1] whereupon we consider that both "tea and urine are forms of water, and water is a natural symbol of life . . ."[2] Sometime again you must read me from Finnegan's Wake which I hope to read at either the beginning or the end of this summer . . . having not yet bought a copy[3] or remembered more than the parts you read about Shem and Shaun, and the hitheringthithering waters . .

The cultic twalette is deepening now, and I think of levels of ambivalences, and nefarious nuances and paradoxical polemics, and I am happy to know that I will have at least two years . . . and maybe more, who knows, to plunge and probe and wallow utterly in reading and talk . . . I always was to evolve dialectically, but I think that by prolonging these years of intense delight I shall only be the more desirous and capable of mixing up sonnets with my scrambled eggs, lyrics with my laundry, and so on . . .

As ever, I am slightly awestruck at the amount I can learn from you; your literary background is so much richer and prolific than mine! I feel like Alice in Wonderland, always running, yet staying relatively the same distance behind . . . this term has helped: am savoring one novel after the other in these three hectic weeks before exams . . . War and Peace, Anna Karenina,[4] The American,[5] Portrait of a Lady[6] . . . and, for reading period, The Ambassadors (I remember your showing that book to me last spring and commenting upon the intricacy of the style . . . now I look forward to reading it and making your remarks more meaningful . . .) Newton Arvin has been a magnificent experience in this Hawthorne, Melville and James course, as you may imagine . . .

I'll be through with my last exam on the afternoon of May 27, and hope to head home that Thursday. Except for a wedding in Hamp on the

1–Tindall, 'Introduction', *Chamber Music* (New York: Columbia University Press, 1954), 75.
2–Tindall, 'Introduction', *Chamber Music*, 77.
3–SP obtained a copy in Cambridge, England, in 1955, which is now held by Smith College.
4–Leo Tolstoy, *Anna Karenina* (New York: Modern Library, 1950); SP's copy held by University of Virginia.
5–Henry James, *The American* (New York: Appleton, 1949); SP's copy held by Lilly Library.
6–Henry James, *The Portrait of a Lady* (New York: Modern Library, 1951); SP's copy held by Smith College.

7th of June, and my bridesmaiding at one in Hanover on the 14th and 15th, I'll be luxuriating in tennis, swimming and leisure reading all of June before Harvard Summer School opens in July . . .

Did I tell you that I have been seeing one of Siefried Sassoon's descendants for the last few weeks? My charming roommate for next year, Nancy Hunter, introduced me to Dick Sassoon and since then I've been receiving weekly visits from the thin, black-eyed little guy, who is Parisian born and a subject of the queen . . . and never fails to come up in his minute Volkswagon without a bottle of exquisite French wine and a few volumes of Baudelaire, Rimbaud, Verlaine or Malarmée . . . it is improving my comprehension of French no end, as Sassoon insists on speaking French whenever he is intense, which is most of the time . . . you'd enjoy him, I think.

Our last exploit frightened me no end: we took off for the country with poetry books, Bordeaux wine and chicken sandwiches for a picnic, and drove all over rutted roads to get to a particularly verdant hilltop, paying no attention to the fact that the roads were abominable. I began to get uneasy at twilight when an eerie wind sprang up and I remembered that we would have several barbwire fences to cross in the descending dark . . . there were no lights anywhere . . . and when, with relief, I crawled into the little car after lacerating myself on barbwire and being bitten all over by malignant minute flies, we found that the car wheels just spun deeper and deeper into the wet mud of the rutted road. At this point I began to become terrified, the way I do, utterly unreasonably, on the top of a fire tower where the steps can be seen through . . . my visciously vivid imagination conjured up murders and brutality in the woods . . . the car wheels spun more shrilly, Sassoon swore gallantly about "merde de vaches" in French and the forest got darker and darker . . . oppressive and obscure . . . you know: "I came to myself in the middle of a dark wood where the way was lost . . ."

Finally, in a flash of inspiration, I suggested through chattering teeth that we walk together to a farmhouse I had remembered seeing about a mile and a half back on the tar road we had left so blithely that afternoon. Leaving the two faint lights of the little car to recede behind us in the ominous dark, we walked hand in hand, ankle deep in mud, up the black road . . . finally we saw a light far off; luckily the people in the farmhouse did not retire at 8:30 . . . and as we approached the distant house in its isolated circle of light, I began to conjure up new images of sadistic farmers with guns, bloodhounds, perverted hired hands who would kill Sassoon and so on.

We knocked; would it be the lady or the tiger?[1] Neither. A solid, taciturn and handsome man opened the door . . . his white-haired wife came up behind him to see who it was, and invited us into a wide, spacious kitchen, full of light and warmth. A dog nuzzled my ankles; a young girl in slacks sat at the kitchen table with an elderly man who looked like a urbane leprechaun, his fingers gnarled and stiff with arthritis. I sat shakily down in a chair and swore I wouldn't ever move or go back in that windy wilderness again.

While Sassoon was calling the towtruck and spending hours getting the car out of the mud, I was getting to know the family. They accepted me immediately, and I let them think I was more afraid than I was because that pleased them. They seated me in their one burlap rocking chair before a huge fireplace that served as the center of the house; the taciturn gentleman went down cellar to get another big log to put on the blaze; the mother showed me the picture of her son in Korea and obligingly kept saying: "I wish Paul was here now"; the young girl brought out the pink and white satin pajamas her brother had sent her from Japan; the old man hobbled about with his cane and put violets in my hair. By the time Sassoon came back, I was invited to a square dance next week and told please to come back anytime to visit . . . all in all, it was a really warming sequel to the dark terror of unknown nature: the friendliness of simple people who brought out all their treasures to show me because I was afraid . . . . . enough of this . . . do let me know as soon as you know when you'll be home . . .

with love,
sylvia

P.S. Do try to buy a copy of the May issue of Harper's! It's my first poem therein – and as I've always wanted to dedicate something to you, consider this dedicated . . .

1 – Frank R. Stockton, 'The Lady, or the Tiger?' (1882).

TO *Aurelia Schober Plath*

Tuesday 4 May 1954[1] ALS (postcard), Indiana University

Tuesday 2 p.m.

Dear mummy . . .

just a note in the midst of a rigorously-planned schedule from now till reading period & exams to say that I am fine: had a good Saturday with Sassoon up here – most unique – another bottle of exquisite Bordeaux wine & a picnic of chicken sandwiches in a lovely green meadow – strange and enchanting evening spent in a farmhouse while waiting for Sassoon & towtruck to get his car out of quagmire on rutted dirt road – 4 intriguing people who were evidently captivated by my peculiar arrival in the dark of night, hair, damp with rain. They called me Cinderella and treated me like a queen till Sassoon came back with the reclaimed Volkswagon – a unifying episode of crisis. Wonderful letter from Gordon who is gradually changing to favor teaching (!) – my letters, subtle as they are, seem to be exerting influence – also I hope to know him on deeper more mature levels than I was capable of last summer – See you Sat the 15th –

xx
sivvy

TO *Melvin Woody*

Wednesday 5 May 1954 TLS on Smith College News Office letterhead, Smith College

May 5

Dear Mel . . .

And I also find it impossible to spend the hours necessary for full communication, as you do, but at any rate I'm sandwiching this answer between War and Peace and Anna Karenina, and using my typewriter to facilitate and accelerate expression . . .

I say this is an "answer" to your last letter,[2] although I hardly like to identify my reply by such a pedestrian word: and yet I marvel that you, in consistency with the tone of your message, did not enclose a stamped, self-addressed postcard with two boxes to check: yes or no . . .

1–Date supplied from postmark.
2–Probably Melvin Woody to SP, [*c.* 28 April 1954]; held by Lilly Library.

Don't misunderstand me by thinking that I misunderstand you, or this letter will strike you as either blind or a little cruel. But Mel, you are so devastatingly illogical in your logic, so passionless in your passion, that I cannot resist indicating a few discrepancies I find even in the framework of your philosophy . . . and, indeed, I can hardly forbear a blow by blow annihilation of your premises and conclusions: but I shall try to control myself here . . .

Granted, I stand accused of sophistry and pragmatism . . . two very derogatory words in your vocabulary, obviously, but (while I vehemently deny sophistry, or "subtle fallacious reasoning", I do accept the full guilt of pragmatism in the dictionary sense that thought should function as a guide to action and "truth is pre-eminently to be tested by the practical consequences of belief".)[1] I would rather be admittedly a relativistic amoral pragmatist, which I suppose I am in a certain sense, than a déracinée (your word, I believe) idealist incapable of more than inconsistency in linking thought and action: and of this last drastic flaw I accuse you . . .

Your hypothetical membership in the "community of life" as speciously distinguished from the "community of men" I find highly artificial. You apparently deny the possibility of finding fulfulment in a social context, a context of tradition, ritual and responsibility which can become as rich and vital as you are capable of making it. Your concept of a completed ritual act of fertility is as incomplete and sterile as any I could imagine!

Really, now, do you accept the fact that your "total commitment to earth" involves more than a brief spasm of irresponsible ecstasy? Do you accept the fact that the demand of fertility in fertility, creation (not of male euphoria) of babies, and the care of such? Can you deny that the end of fertility is reproduction, not just the hedony which you condone as "a ritual act of fertility allowing no aesthetic distance?"

Not only do I deplore your unawareness of the real, provable end of fertility rituals, but I am concerned for your apparent justification of the "laceration and pain" you intend admittedly and coldly to inflict on others (me, in particular) by your sweeping generalization that pain is the true root of existence. That last assertion may be true, but it is hardly appropriate to justify your propositions here! I don't pretend to be going through complete fertility rituals – (as you would have me do) – simply because I am honestly not ready to accept the consequences (the

1 – SP underlined this part of the definition of 'pragmatism' in her *Webster's New Collegiate Dictionary* (Springfield, Mass.: G. & C. Merriam Co., [*c.* 1949]). SP's copy held by Smith College.

full consequences) of the conceiving act: I am hardly ready or willing to produce the children which nature would endow me with as the understood reward of my actions.

In this sense, I claim to be more honest than you are. I don't pretend to desire a "complete act" simply because I refuse to accept the consequences of a complete act. You, contradictorily, would pretend to be honest and unsophistical while denying the same responsibility . . . and the responsibility is a responsibility to the community of man as well as that of nature: there is no unequivocal and drastic distinction as you seem to imply. In the amoral world of nature, procreation and survival is the tacit apparent aim; in the moral world of man, the aim is the same. And I think it's about time you began thinking about the meaning of roots, instead of denying all roots, ipso facto, as evil man-made and sterile. I, too, abhor hypocritical and sterile man-made institutions, but I think that one of the most powerful things an individual can do is to endow those same institutions with deep meaning, as Marcia will do when she raises a family: that, to me, is real, honest and vital creativity.

By now you are either thoroughly angry or thoroughly sure that I am a puritan pragmatist . . . and perhaps thoroughly sure that I am not any longer capable of representing your theory of Woman with a capital "W" . . .

All I can say is, I am sorry that you must retreat to an artificial "all-or-nothing" standpoint, especially when I see you making false and specious distinctions between "life" and "men", and apparently misunderstanding the true meaning of the word "fertility". I admittedly feel deeply that I understand the meaning of this word, and therefore do not intend to desecrate it by pretending to act under its aegis; that will come later, and I hope to do full justice to it.

Meanwhile, I accept your condescending appellation of "pragmatist" and can only say that, by your own declaration of alternatives, I can never see you again . . . I am even a little sorry you are so "scrupulous" in your alternatives . . .

s.

TO *Aurelia Schober Plath*

Friday 7 May 1954[1]

ALS (picture postcard), Indiana University

<picture postcard caption>

R. Dufy Il Casinò di Nizza 1928. Edizioni Del Milione. Milano. Serie di Cartoline a colori. N. 207.

Friday 10:20 p.m

Dear mother . . .

just a note before I leave: to wish you a happy mother's day! I'm going to New Haven tomorrow to see Sassoon for a final party (exams & Europe preclude any more dates this year) – should be absorbing as both Sassoon and his roommate, Mel (they hate each other) claim to be intensely in love with me: it's a bit disconcerting to get passionate metaphysical love letters from the same mailbox & two antagonistic roommates: to top it off, Nancy & the 3rd roommate have been "partners" for years (as I used to be with Perry) – anyhow, Sassoon & I are driving to NYC to celebrate our farewell party. Next Friday I'm going to the Amherst spring Formal with Jack Furner,[2] older brother for Dave F., (the boy Nancy goes steady with) as a "favor" which I look forward to. Let me know when to expect you Sat. – as I have tons of work, perhaps late afternoon (5?) would be best – & stay till after Sunday dinner (I have a room for you nearby – the boys should stay at Amherst) – could you bring some of your yummy cookies? I'll have some clothes & books ready to go – Nancy is coming from June 1 to 5 (her birthday is June 3 & I want to have a big steak dinner & cake surprise – I do love her!

xxx

sivvy

<handwritten on face of postcard>:

HAPPY MOTHER'S DAY

s. p.

<drawing of smiling female face>

1–Date supplied from postmark.

2–Jack Dennis Ferner (1930–); B.S. 1953, University of Rochester; M.B.A. 1955, Harvard University, 1955.

TO *Melvin Woody*

Friday 7 May 1954 TLS on Smith College Press Board letterhead, Smith College

Friday, May 7

Dear Mel . . .

This interweaving web of circumstances is becoming so intricate that I feel fleetingly like having a family barbecue under the trees for the few of us individuals involved . . . in honor of our rapidly multiplying plethora of egos and ego-relationships, past, present, and (may the lord have mercy on us!) future!

Your excellent letters[1] arrived today, as did you rhythmic and exquisitely clever congratulatory (?) postcard to my roommate-to-be (shades of Marty!) Nancy. I do feel that I should assume nothing about the relationship of you and your estimable roommates, and so I'm telling you myself, because I wanted to be sure you knew, that I'm coming to New Haven Saturday and will no doubt, at sometime, be up in your suite, to return some of your books (not all, as I haven't read them all . . . and hope perhaps you will collect them sometime before you leave for Edinburgh . . . which statement obviously implies a three-dimensional conversation, if you feel so inclined.) As for Saturday, I mainly wanted to tell you I'm coming because I wanted you to feel free not to be there, if you chose, for any reason . . . to prefer absence to presence . . . but I have not forgotten times, nor even attitudes . . . only it is not my place (for I am a little proud) to remind you of them or suggest that they recur: that is part of the tacit responsibility of the male role, I think,

Till I see you again . . .
syl

1–Probably Melvin Woody to SP, [5 and 6 May 1954]; held by Lilly Library.

TO *Philip E. McCurdy*

Friday 7 May 1954[1]

TLS on Smith College News Office letterhead with envelope, Smith College

Friday, 11 a.m.

Dear Phil . . .

Oh, your last letter was exquisite! I am still trying to quench the hysterical and delighted laughter which burst out when I read your brief play sketch . . . I've read it aloud to Nancy Hunter, my roommate-to-be, and she and I have been roaring together . . .

Which reminds me, just for any notice you may care to take of it . . . (all this is a bit tentative and subject to change): Nancy will probably be my guest in Wellesley from June 1-5 and her birthday is June 3 (21st) . . . ergo, I want to give her some big surprise, or dinner, or something. What could be more of a surprise than to get her a date with the handsome trilingual poet? If he isn't free that Day, he might be some time during her stay (and you could always take me out so I wouldn't feel excluded by Nancy's blaze of glory.)

Statistics which might concern said poet: Nancy is both beautiful and brilliant, not to mention talented (she was just elected president of the Smith College Glee Club). She is going to write her history thesis on Morris Cohen,[2] I think, and American Liberalism and (this smacks of a non sequitur) is tall, slender, with an enchanting heart-shaped face, green Kirghiz eyes, black hair and a more than figmentary ressemblance to a certain Modigliani odalisque. Our relationship is most involved, and I do love her dearly: she is to me, in a feminine way, what Norm is to you, I think . . . will he take me up on this?

She does happen to be dating an Amherst junior rather steadily, but is perfectly willing to accept my recommendations, if footnoted properly: and for Norm I can give her a whole bibliography! It would be fun for the four of us to jaunt to the Cape for a day's picnic or something (she's never seen the Atlantic as she comes from Akron) . . . let me know if any of this sounds plausible . . . or pleasurable . . .

As for me . . . I shall be incommunicado from now till May 27 as far as social affairs are concerned. Mother and Warren and Clem Moore are

1–Date supplied from internal evidence.

2–American philosopher and legal theorist Morris Raphael Cohen (1880–1947) whose liberal social philosophy encouraged use of the state to achieve a more just society.

coming up the 15th and 16th, and I shall try to be civil to them while reading Anna Karenina.

I did say I'd go to New Haven and NYC this weekend with Sassoon to celebrate our last meeting for the year (he sails for Europe, the cruel brute, after exams) . . . but only for 24 hours . . . and even then, I feel guilty about my gaily atrophying intellect! When do you get through with exams?

I'll write again . . . and call when I come home the 27th if you'll be there. I approve of the new vocabulary! . .

love . . .
Syl

TO *Aurelia Schober Plath*

Tuesday 11 May 1954[1] ALS (postcard), Indiana University

Tuesday 2 p.m.

Dear mother . . .

Just a postcard in the midst of my rigid reading program to let you know what a lovely weekend I had with Sassoon in spite of the beastly weather: had lunch at Yale with Sassoon, saw Mel, (who hugged me publicly, gave me a note saying I was wonderful,[2] & disappeared!) – drove through rain to NYC & got there in time for a lampchop dinner & a preview of Chekhov's Seagull starring Montgomery Clift – playing in a Greenwich Village Theater[3] – then a bottle of exquisite French wine & reading aloud of poetry – Sunday we spent 2 hours eating a huge dinner at Steuben's Tavern[4] – a feast beginning with herrings in sour cream & ending with icecream eclairs, white wine & coffee – the drive back to New Haven on the Merritt Parkway was pretty: all green trees & white dog wood, (although I slept most of the way) – a charming finale to our month's acquaintance: (Sassoon leaves for Europe in a short while) – and I was happy, as I haven't been since that strange unfinished interlude in NYC spring vacation – although nothing can ever equal it, it's a comfort to know it can be at least approximated. See you Sat.

xxx
sivvy

1–Date supplied from postmark.

2–Melvin Woody to SP, [*c.* 8 May 1954]; held by Lilly Library.

3–Anton Chekhov, *The Seagull*, starring Montgomery Clift; directed by Norris Houghton; performed on 8 May 1954 at the Phoenix Theatre, 181 Second Avenue, New York.

4–Steuben's Tavern, a restaurant then at 163 W. 47th Street, New York.

TO *Philip E. McCurdy*

Thursday 13 May 1954[1] TLS with envelope, Smith College

thursday morning
10:30 a.m.

dear phil . . .

overhead the malignant gray skies of this last week are giving up and dissolving away in clouds like curdled cream, and a cold sun deigns to shed sundry spasmodic rays, all most aloof and icy . . .

as if by telepathy, I've felt like the lovely gullible lady in the circus all morning: the one who lets moustachioed virtuosos hurl deft knives at her outlines: only my mesmeric master seems to be aiming solely for the forehead over my eyes, and the knives plunge, halt and quiver: headaches, ah yes . . . and how I sympathize and am concerned for you. do you work in a good light? and Please get more sleep . . .

I am no one to talk: I have a reading program of 10 hours a day for the next two weeks, and after even one full day of rigid discipline, I am stiff from sitting, longing for some magic chance to "jump the life to come",[2] i.e., the inevitable intensive cycle of reading, writing papers, and review: I know I have to live through it, and probably will, but it is psychologically difficult to finish War and Peace in the middle of the afternoon and instead of going on a fine, stellar, wine-cellar binge, to pick up 950 pages of microscopically printed Anna Karenina, and proceed without even a coffee break . . .

at night I am so cerebralized it is annoyingly difficult to go to sleep . . . and I remember with nostalgia those days on lookout farm when I was struck with an uncomplicated physical exhaustion which swallowed me in a dark and dreamless sea of sleep until I woke refreshed and rejuvenated at dawn. I envy you your tennis . . . I need physical exercise to balance this suddenly study-saturated spell . . .

so pleased that norm will take up nancy . . . I honestly love them both, and she is visibly taken with the idea. also liked norm's poems a good deal . . . most especially "don juan to his lover". norm has a happy facility of combining the familiar with the unique and arriving thereby at a felicitous juxtaposition: "as the stars, in exquisite dispassion" is perfect, and so is the quaint and quite poignant understatement of the excellent last verse: in fact, I would like to memorize that last verse to quote it along with my

1 – Date supplied from postmark.
2 – Shakespeare, *Macbeth*.

favorite auden's[1] "lay your sleeping head my love, human on my faithless arm" on appropriate occasions!

one bright spot: had lunch in new haven last saturday and drove to new york with the strange parisian sassoon (your drawings were wonderful, only he's deceptively boyish looking: his eyes only give him away, and his wicked laugh). we plowed through rain and traffic on the merritt parkway, arriving in time to drop our luggage at a 44th street hotel, get tickets to a play, and gulp a lambchop dinner. the play was the preview of chekhov's seagull starring montgomery clift (!) . . . good, but not outstanding: all characters behaving in one way or another like caged seagulls: all frustrated and unfullfilled. the audience was the upper layer of the lower greenwich village level. after which we retired in the rain to our hotel for the inevitable french poetry and wine . . . sunday we woke up at noon and spent two hours gourmandizing at steuben's, starting with herrings in sour cream, onion soup, etc., and ending with ice-cream eclairs and coffee, white wine having been strewn all along through . . .

I was so tired, having slept about two hours all night, that I curled up in the backseat of the little car driving to new haven and fell deeply asleep. I awoke to consciousness of sunlight and a circle of people staring at me in unfeigned curiosity. sassoon had stopped at a merritt parkway gas station for coffee, and the sight of a touseled girl sleeping soundly in the backseat of a volkswagon in the midst of empty wine bottles and books of baudelaire attracted attention, to put it mildly. unabashed, I woke up fully, saluted all in blithe abandon, and proceeded to drink the coffee sassoon had brought . . . all of which was a much needed bohemian respite to my more academic obligations . . .

smith college, by the way, has seen fit to award me their biggest scholarship for next year, so I won't have to feel constrained to work during the summer: all of which is most fortunate, seeing I'll probably be paying out for summer school, and, in a burst of fervor, have spent several hundred dollars this semester on books and records . . . and, alas, linen dresses. I can now claim the distinction of literally having one dollar apiece in my checking and bank accounts and absolutely no prospect of any money coming in unless I sacrifice my maidenhood on the streets in scollay square . . . and that I'm not prepared to do quite yet.

1–W. H. Auden, *The Collected Poetry of W. H. Auden* (New York: Random House, 1945), 208. SP's copy, with annotated lines from 'Lay your sleeping head', held by Smith College.

your courses for next year sound excellent: I know you'll love the slavic. as for me, I'll be taking a superlative course in shakespeare, a unit in prose fiction, a german course in goethe and shiller (if I pass the one this summer), a thesis on dostoevsky, and auditing in philosophy . . . I plan to be much more unsocial then, and really devote myself to academic pursuits. which, alas, is what I said this semester . . .

I just can't wait for the summer when I can read the multitudes of books I've bought, and practice writing poetry. very selfishly, I'll be terribly sad if you and norm don't get jobs around cambridge: we all could have such a lovely time jaunting about together. I'd like to have the chance to get to know norm in the way I know you, as a choice acquaintance who is also a kind of confidante . . . and again, I do look forward to introducing him to nancy, whom I wish you also would have time to be with . . . but I understand only too desperately well about your exams . . .

I'd really love to have you call me: it's always so exciting, even though I am more myself in letters. the dinner hour (6 to 7) is generally best, although I'll no doubt be studying at home from now on till my first exam next saturday, and all the time after that . . . probably if you call toward the end of my stay here, nancy's plans and mine will be more definite . . .

don't bother writing if you're as busy as I know you are . . . I'll see you after the 27th and hear from you via telephone perhaps I hope before then.

meanwhile, please take care of yourself for me, and send my greetings to norm . . .

much love,
syl

TO *Aurelia Schober Plath*

Tuesday 18 May 1954 — TLS on Smith College News Office letterhead, Indiana University

May 18

Dearest mother . . .

All sorts of little bits of news which will gradually clarify the situation arising after I get out of my last exam: first, I'm so glad you can come to call for me on the 27th . . . probably you can see Nancy for the first time then.

I'll have a few days to buy wedding & birthday presents and plan the food and events before my favorite girl arrives on Tuesday afternoon,

June 1. Phil will call later this week and I hope to get Nancy a date with Norman Shapiro for either Tuesday or Wednesday night. David Furner, her Boy, will arrive Thursday, June 3, the evening of which I want the very special birthday dinner (I may possibly be the partner of Dave's older brother Jack if he can make it, but I shall scare up someone from somewhere, so there'll be four of us, plus the family, whatever it may at that time consist of.) Friday, June 4, is the Day we want to use the car (If only it's nice!) to drive to Nauset Beach, starting at 6 a.m. or so with a huge lunch-supper picnic. Saturday morning, both Nancy and David will leave for Hamp. So that makes four nights for Nan and two for Dave. I do so want to play the best sort of hostess again, and cook myself, at least the desserts, so that the burden won't be on you. But I want Nancy and David to have the best time ever: it's really an honor to me that they'll spend these last days together at my house!

Next, I think I've persuaded Nancy to forsake the sterility of Akron Ohio and come to summer school with me this summer! We would room together much as Marcia and I planned to and have a wonderfully stimulating social and intellectual time. If only Phil and Norman would get fine jobs around there, too!

Worst news is that Gordon isn't coming home at all this summer: not till next December, in fact. He sounded[1] a little homesick about the Navy's new orders. But perhaps, with the summer working out the way it's apparently going to, it might be all for the best for me to save getting reacquainted with him for another time when I won't have quite so many seductive friends around. Once I get to know him again, I won't feel quite so possessive!

My main worry now is money. I just don't see where it's all coming from. If over three hundred goes out this summer, with my having spent that much this semester, and probably requiring that much again for spending money for <u>all</u> next year, I think I'll be hopelessly in debt to you by the end of my senior year. No chance of Europe for me, I guess. I'll have to be a waitress all next summer and try to scrape together $800 or so to pay back debts. Then, if I get a scholarship to grad school, I should at last break about even. I may, in this case, apply seriously for a Fulbright to England so I could travel freely in Europe for the several 6 week vacation periods which wouldn't cost big travel expenses. As Gordon will still be sailing all around in the Navy, I won't have any romantic attachments to consider, and could go to Harvard Grad School the year after I get back

1–Gordon Lameyer to SP, 7 May 1954; held by Lilly Library.

from England . . . with a rich background for a Master's thesis to be done at Harvard the same year Gordon tentatively plans to enter there.

Ah, well . . . on to exams. So glad you all had a good time here: I certainly did. Took a two hour nap after you left. See you in (heavens!) ten days!

love,
sivvy

TO *Aurelia Schober Plath*

Wednesday 19 May 1954[1] ALS (postcard), Indiana University

Wednesday

Dear mother . . .

Just a note in the appropriate midst of Escape From Freedom[2] to let you know I won one (1) poetry prize this year[3] on the basis of my sonnet "Doom of Exiles" which I wrote this spring – only $20 I think, but it will keep me in new shoes for Marty's wedding. Also, I just got elected president of the Alpha Phi Kappa Psi Society – honorary society of the arts – which has the advantage of being a very honorary post with a minimum of work & a solid gold, ruby-studded pin from Tiffany's which is handed down from president to president each year – minor events compared to the splash last year, but events never-the-less – Tomorrow I have sherry with Mr. Gibian my thesis advisor – Then the reign of terror: exams. See you in a week –

xxx
sivvy

1–Date supplied from postmark.

2–Erich Fromm, *Escape from Freedom* (New York: Rinehart & Co., 1941). SP's copy held by Lilly Library.

3–SP submitted 'The Dead' for the Elizabeth Babcock Prize for Poetry and 'Doom of Exiles', under the pseudonym 'Alison Arnold', for the Corbin Prize. There was no Babcock Prize given in 1954. However, 'The Dead' was awarded the Ethel Olin Corbin prize.

TO *Melvin Woody*

c. Thursday 20 May 1954[1] TLS, Smith College

thursday

dear mel . . .

out, out, brief silence![2]
life's but a canceled postcard; a dead letter
that waits and frets its hour in haven house
and then is read no more: it is a tale
told by a yale man, fresh from an unsound brewery,
signifying . . .
god knows what

(apologies to W. S.)

oh malt does more than melvin can[3]
to justify my ways to man.
wine, mel, wine's the stuff to drink
for fellows whom it hurts to think:
look into the wickered bottle,
love those whom you wish to throttle:
the air is clear, and there's no haze
(save that which shrouds my yesterdays)
oh I have been with Calhoun's[4] fair
and left my Lawrence* god knows where,
and carried halfway home or near
pints and quarts of wine (not beer!)
then the world seemed sweet and good,
as if I'd acted as I should;
and down on studio cots I've lain,
happy till I woke again.
then I saw the stranger's eye:
my god! the tale was all a lie;
the world it was the old world still,
I was I, and I felt ill,

1–Date supplied from internal evidence.
2–SP plays on a speech in *Macbeth*.
3–SP plays on A. E. Housman's 'LXII. Terrence, this is stupid stuff', in *A Shropshire Lad*.
4–A reference to Calhoun College where Woody, Richard Sassoon, and Richard Wertz lived and were roommates.

and nothing now remained to do
but begin the game anew.

-------------------- (apologies to A. E. H.)

* D. H., if you must have a double entendre. That's where I live now, too, you know. Unless you want Marty to continue proofreading your postcards before I get them!

anyhow, my charming one, your address makes no difference to me now, only mine does: remember it? de rien! (please excuse the par(adis)ian influence. but it will crop up!) . . . it'll change to 26 elmwood road on may 27 anyway . . . or isn't that telling you subtly enough?

it seems we are doomed to misinterpret each other. I hadn't thought I was being silent; I had thought you were. I'm just enough of a feminine creature to give men the prerogative for inviting me to commune: you've given it, so I commune.

this is brief because I have four exams and weeks of back reading to do plus a paper in the next week, and I'm only human, and so have made myself incommunicado till the 27th when I shall either be a genius or a gibbering idiot . . .

just send me a consoling note to see me through, huh? shall I see you at marty's betrothal or before.

love,
syl

"rien ne nous rend si grands qu'une grande douleur . .
les plus désespérés sont les chants les plus beaux,
et j'en sais d'immortels qui sont de purs sanglots."
vive l'amour![1]

1–From Alfred de Musset's 'La Nuit de Mai'.

TO *Gordon Lameyer*

Saturday 22 May 1954 TLS, Indiana University

saturday
may 22

dear ishmael . . .

I had just begun to resign myself to not seeing you for another year or so (and not succeeding very well) when your more cheerful information arrived today,[1] about your leave in june. I hope at least you can manage that!

summer school doesn't start for me till about the first week in july, and so all of june, when I'm not at weddings, I'll be home, or trying for occasional weekends at the cape. I have purposely planned a minimum of events so that I'll probably be able to see you whenever you arrive. somehow I wish I could actually watch the boat arrive at the docks so I could throw slipperfuls of champagne or wreath your nautical neck with garlands of sea-anemones! my only real obligations are from june 1-5 when nancy hunter, my roommate, will be my houseguest (along with david furner, her amherst junior . . . know him? from DU[2]). I have promised to entertain them with regal birthday dinners, official teas, and cape excursions if it's beau soleilish. a possible hamp trip on the 7th-- expendable wedding of friend claiborne who's been secretly married for a year or so . . . just to satisfy the hungry public. then a three day sojourn in hanover, as I've no doubt said, from the 14th-16th to bridesmaid it at marcia brown's betrothal. c'est tout! c'est assez!

then: sun and bathing suits and reading and reading all the books I've accumulated unread during the semester . . and, I hope, somewhere, catching as many glimpses of you as possible.

do let me know as soon as you do when and where you'll come up from the sea, trailing albatrosses, mermaids, reduction gears, and lord knows what else . . . strange, but you have become almost a mythical figure to me: an eclectic blend of ulysses, kilroy, icarus, neptune, ishmael, noah, jonah, columbus, and richard halliburton! so you must, in all kindness, emphasize your mortal finitude when next we meet!

last weekend, I obliged nancy by doubling with her for david's visiting older brother, a product of the deadly harvard business school . . . the weekend being the "fabulous" amherst spring prom with bluelit palms

1–Gordon Lameyer to SP, 7 and 13 May 1954; held by Lilly Library.
2–Delta Upsilon Fraternity.

and fountains inside and japanese lanterns and a real moon and mist-floating hills outside: dancing under the stars in nets of silver, ah, those fitzgeraldean scott-free hours . . . even a carnival in the square, me in ecstasies of terror on circling ferris wheel, a blaze of revolving lights, up, over, poise and swing, tilt and teeter on the brink of an enormous nothing . . . and scream because--it's a woman's prerogative, and a wonderful valid excuse for vocal exercise . . .

warren and mother came up saturday for float night weekend, and of course it poured, but the floats were exquisite, and mother loved the crew races, the gracious dinner on sunday and a walk along the more pleasant paradisial vistas . . . warren insisted that he escort me, as we never commune basically when we both have dates, and I arranged a budding rapport between warren's young existentialist roommate and a beautiful neurotic freshman in the house: it promises well, and I have such fun discreetly plotting . . .

just finished my hawthorne, melville and james exam, and came away knowing more than I did when I went in, which is the test of a good exam---relating, as well as extracting, knowledge. I love arvin so . . . wish I could somehow take a course with him next year! had great fun with comprehensive question on egoism, and am won over especially by the exquisite artistry of James . . . so much to discuss with you . . . will we ever have time?

now the stoic plunge into nietzsche and marx and hegel for my worst: history on thursday, and tolstoi and dostoevsky for tuesday . . . plus a paper on fromm's "escape from freedom"[1] which I've been promising myself to read for four years.

speaking of russian, I spent the latter half of the afternoon yesterday at my thesis advisor's house drinking sherry and feeding babies; it was marvelous. a bleak, rain-lashed day, and mr. gibian and his brilliant czech wife,[2] two boy twin babies, and a precocious young devil, peter. my maternal instincts, which I keep forgetting I have, really emerged, and I was holding the deliciously warm twins and feeling them bottled milk (after five glasses of sherry I felt an overwhelming impulse to strip and nurse them myself!) and then playing riding games with the rewardingly enchanted peter, whom I could have practically hugged to death, he was so abominably lovable. I hope I have all boys (except for maybe one girl,

1–Sylvia Plath, 'The Age of Anxiety and the Escape from Freedom'; held by Lilly Library.

2–J. Catherine Annis Gibian (1926–93); married to SP's colleague George Gibian (divorced 1967); mother of Peter, Mark, Stephen, Gregory, and Lauren. 'Cay' was Mrs Gibian's nickname.

just to have a vicarious rebirth) because they are such exceptional free spirits when brought up in a stimulating environment . . . in fact, I wish it were somehow possible for me to teach or something at a boy's school--I get along with young boys so much better than with girls: did I tell you about the charming twelve-year old chap I rode back from new haven with two weekends ago? (I always forget where I left off with you!) we had the most vibrant conversation: I'd forgotten where one was at the age of twelve, it's all somehow a blur for me now under the age of 20 . . . and I was bewitched by the flashes of mingled maturity and pure child-likeness in this young scion: son of tom fawcett of fawcett publications,[1] by the way! anyhow, I really plan to enjoy a multitude of sons . . . as free companions: none of this insidious "momism" or apron string business for me.

and now that I have expounded in capsule form my philosophy of childcare and cultivation, I will bid you a most fond adieu and return to the next crammed week, at the end of which I shall either be a genius or a gibbering idiot . . .

do let me know immediatement when I may plan to see you! till then . . .

affectionately,
sylvia

TO *Gordon Lameyer*

Friday 11 June 1954 TLS, Indiana University

june 11
3 p.m.

very dear gordon . . .

writing you now, I suppose, is like bringing the redundant coals to newcastle (or sailors to newport) but this is just a little anyhow inbetween note to say I am home safely and not driving bewildered somewhere down in north carolina asking most naively for the expressway to boston . . . no mistakes on the way back . . . only stops for gas . . . and a half-asleep, numbed following of broken white lines coming always at me from out of the long dark . . . infinity, I decided, is driving forever down a celestial highway of whitelines: my one flash of insight during the trip . . .

today, miles in time from you, is hot, wetly humid and sunny . . . morning spent under phil's coaching on town courts, how to hold racket

1–An American publishing company founded in 1919 by Wilford Fawcett.

again, and run, for god's sake, run . . . and I recall an equally patient you telling me the same constructive things last summer . . . and hope that I can relearn how to at least hit before you and I try again . . .

the week bellies and fills like an inflating balloon . . . wish you were here for the arts festival in boston[1] . . . think I'll see modern dancers[2] on the common tomorrow night and our boy frost sunday . . . reading poems in a granite textured over-the-split-rail-fence voice . . .

ran into perry for the first time in a year down biking past the courts, caught up on news, and said I'd be in the branford chapel in new haven on saturday the memorable 19th[3] (which is when you go to jaffrey, n'est-ce pas? hope things synchronize that neatly, anyway!)

so many lovely people you will sometime meet: perry (just realized how coincidental the name of your boat is!) and boyish phil, pat o'neil and marcia brown . . . all possible and probable . . .

writing now is so different, somehow . . . there is a real, vital stimulating gordon who cuts oh, such an endearing space out of the thin air . . . so multidimensional in this suddenly more-than-we-think-it pluriverse, that I can scarcely become accustomed to saying casually to myself: ah, yes, next friday, after a merry-go-round of champagne wedding and light blue connubial skies (made out of linen this time) I will leave early on friday morning and drive down for lunch and . . . there he will be . . .

with a need (such as we have) to be articulate so intensely, I feel how I should now be able to recapitulate verbally all the complex of ideas, sensations and orientations experienced this last week . . . but there are times when I feel no words could approach or approximate the actual triumph of living and acting in time . . . even though I am at war psychically over this problem: one earthly part in me preferring bodily sunworship and physical prowess and power, the other cerebral part preferring the sedentary construction of aesthetic artifices to order in form the artless chaos of content in the flux of time . . . a dynamic equilibrium, I suppose, a paradoxical maximum of both qualities, is perhaps the most desirable end . . .

and yet I feel it would be a triumph, somehow, to invent new ways of expressing the richness of life I have felt in being with you these last

1–The Third Annual Boston Arts Festival on the Public Garden opened on 6 June 1954, and ran for two weeks.

2–Performed by dancer Sophie Maslow and her New Dance Group, the programme included 'The Village I Knew', 'Folksay', and 'Manhattan Suite'.

3–Perry Norton married Shirley Baldwin on 19 June 1954, Branford College Chapel, Yale University. See wedding invitation held by Lilly Library.

magnificent days . . . I shall be trying for a long time, no doubt, to be making up a new language for you . . . and perhaps never quite being able to ever express all I think and feel about you . . .

mother and warren have taken off for nahant beach, an hour's drive away, and I am now going to shower the dust from the tennis courts away and drive to cambridge to see some spanish prize film[1] at the avant garde (so they say) brattle theater with another of my very young, psychic (sic.) brothers, phil . . . who, by the way, would really appreciate meeting you . . .

I enjoy thinking of you in the yellow wardroom with the family of coffeepots (a "coven of kettles"[2] as dylan would say) hissing and perking on the gas jets. Now at last I can visualize you moving in a concrete context . . . not just floating like amorphous ectoplasm through blue strata of sea and sky on a phantom ship the size of a stationery-representation . . .

<SP has affixed a head-shot of herself>

And here, by the way, is a face I found . . . do you recognize it? sometimes I wish I didn't! anyhow, it the remnant of some proofs of a senior picture, of sorts, and at least is not so haughty as the ones mother has strewn about the house for propaganda . . .

until friday, when I will come for lunch . . . and . . . you . . .

love from
your very own
sylvia

TO *Gordon Lameyer*

Saturday 12 June 1954 TLS, Indiana University

saturday
10 p.m.

dear gordy . . .

feel like talking twilightly to you and so will, most especially because have just arisen from prone adulation before aural altar of our lp-hearing our father (allah, dada, etc.) . . . you know . . . lilt along aloud about anna livia[3] and the hitherandthithering waters of . . .

1–*Rio Escondido* ('Hidden River'), a 1948 film directed by Emilio Fernández and starring Maria Félix, played at 5:30, 7:30, and 9:30 that day at the Brattle Theatre.
2–Dylan Thomas, 'Under Milk Wood' (1954).
3–A character in James Joyce, *Finnegan's Wake.*

it was a small sacrilege that you weren't there. hearing joyce, I was amazed at the similarity of your own accent when reciting (blithely) to me on the way home from amherst . . . you, I think, have attained the very inflections of our musically reflecting creator . . . and I begin to wonder whether I am admiring symbols of idols, or idylls of cymbals, . . . (oh, "gather behind me, satraps,"[1]) . . . simply, I understand joyce better for the hearing of you . . .

tonight was the first record . . . colum, campbell and joyce[2] . . . tomorrow I will bow once more for the second orgy . . . warren joined me listening and has been inspired this evening to write satirical verse, panning the names of passé swains . . . he is here now, chortling satanically at my side, stretched out on the bed and crossing out, scribbling, and saying periodically, "oh, listen to this . . ." which I do . . .

cartoon enclosed[3] made me think of you . . . of literary beacheads in provincetown . . . isn't the stance magnificent? bare foot planted defiantly on driftwood, hair blowing in line with pipe smoke and waves . . . you must let your hair grow if we are ever to make a social splash at the artist's ball . . . perhaps I should get an italiate cut?

felt antisocial today, so canceled and revised plans . . . contemplated omphalos (sans salt) and had a few new thoughts and awarenesses about situations that have long concerned me . . . which was gratifying and worth the introspection . . . had afternoon hour session with ruth beuscher, beginning the first of my bi-monthly visits which I'll continue during the summer . . . do enjoy analyzing and philosophizing with her . . . someday she is another you will meet . . .

warren drove me to nahant, and we had another one of our long, languid, recapitulating talks, getting reacquainted with each other, as we do periodically . . . sunned, but it was too late and sadly cold for us fearing ones to swim . . .

(warren just finished his verse which is subtitled: "a longitudinal orgy to be accompanied with xylophones and muffled conundrums")

also had a good talk with marcia brown in marblehead . . . she and mike are picking me up monday morning and driving me up to hanover

1–Joyce, *Finnegan's Wake*.

2–Padraic Colum (1881–1972), Irish poet, novelist, and dramatist; Joseph Campbell (1904–87), American mythologist writer, and lecturer; and James Joyce. A reference to the LP recording of *Finnegan's Wake: Meeting of the Joyce Society at the Gotham Book Mart, October 23, 1951* (New York: Folkways Records, 1951).

3–Paul Darrow, 'the sea wind roared like an avalanche of demons . . . the sea wind, screaming like a tortured, living creature . . . like an avenging soul . . . like', *New York Times Book Review*, 15 March 1953, 2.

with them, which should be delightful . . . some weekend it might be fun if you and I drove down to the cape to visit them at the camp where they'll both be counselling on their honeymoon . . .

night falls now. night. night.

and all the things I would tell you I will tell you anon, another day, after a night and a day and a night and a day and on and on until again I come down to the tall ships . . .

Lovingly,
sylvia

TO *Gordon Lameyer*

Tuesday 22 June 1954[1] ALS, Indiana University

tuesday morning
12:15 a.m.

<drawing of a female wearing a robe, on a pillow, holding a pen>

dear gordon . . .

it is so very late, and when it is so very late, I am prone . . . to become either victim of a prolonged talking (or writing) jag or of a spartan somnolent silence. but today, monday, (it is already yesterday) has contained volcanoes, some active, some extinct (but we can never be sure) – and, at any rate, a world has happened, a homestead been re-visited, and a life ended and a life matured a little more – so I must needs impart a little of this to you – in addition to pragmatically letting you know of a minor change in my immediate summer plans . . .

matitutinal ethical storms began the day, forays with the maternal monolith which may at some future date, perhaps be beneficiently discussed with you: conflict was transcended by sudden news that Mr. Freeman, father of my childhood comrades, Ruth & David Freeman, had just dropped dead at his home in Winthrop.

mother immediately insisted that we journey to the Freeman's to sustain, support, solace – or whatever one does to one's closest & bereaved friends. at first, going, I felt dubious: what does one say in face of death? he was old – 70 – crochety, still working at a highly successful self-made job, a skilled painter of ships on high seas – but – 20 years older than Mrs. Freeman, catankerous, victim of skin disease which had stopped his one creative outlet – painting – so wasn't deadness better quick than a

1 – Date supplied from internal evidence.

slow paralytic stroke, or a slow decaying senility? I thought so, but it was hardly the thing to say . . .

sweltering heat, blowing hot air in sweat stenched subways, a bus jolting through narrow streets, crowed houses, increasingly familiar – and then, suddenly, the blue blast of ocean between bleak buildings – a walk down a street woven with the rich, plumcake associations of ten years of creative and imaginative childhood.

<drawing of streets, houses, and ocean in Winthrop, Massachusetts>

lawns that were continents, rocks that were fortresses, alleys that were secret passages to magic worlds: all seemed now strangely shrunken and denuded of myriad mystic meanings – like talismans become impotent: no more skyblue abracadabra heydays – but a diminished prose translation of what was once an infinite poetic masterpiece of childhood (and yet even now I am guilty of the adult fall, the fatal fault – of exalting a golden eden of free perfection that never quite really was, except in dreams –)

anyway: there was the Freeman's – a pale, dark parlor, hot and still, with the blinds drawn, and all the highly polished furniture, the ornate antiques, sulking in a brown study – only the pale, tearpurpled faces of Ruth, and Mrs. freeman and her sister[1] – and the grin of david, the superman of my lois lane days – older now, yet dearly familiar.

so there was breaking of tearful silence and death blighted quiet: talk began of life, of ruth's coming trip to europe, of supper, and how to learn to cook – life was reestablished in little ways –

accidentally, and in consonance with my infallible instinct for doing the tabu thing in all innocent accidence, I went for a drink of water and picked up the heavy glass from the sink and filled it to quench my thirst – and found out that it was the glass mr. freeman had gasped a last shot of brandy from before dying, put in the sink to soak: nothing like appropriating a holy chalice . . . oh, well . . .

<drawing of soup on a table>

a sober supper of thick green pea soup, cold meats, potato salad, cake and milk and I wanting to be busy or useful, and so doing what every woman can do in her sleep: wash stacks of dishes – while relatives drove to the funeral parlor: david wiped dishes, and began to talk right where we left off over ten years ago, while ruthie sat out on the porch with her fiancée[2] . . .

1–Helen M. Churchill (1903–99).

2–Arthur J. Geissler (1933–2013); B.B.A. 1954, University of Massachusetts, Amherst.

took a walk by my old home, the golden rain trees and shrubs that my botanist father planted now flourishing giants, though the house and yard had shrunken as if unsanforized through years of rain . . . mother and I met an intellectual jewish friend of ours of eld (syn: old bygone days, ages previous, etc.) and drove with him to see his sister-in-laws fantastic modern house pitched on a green sloped lawn, anchored by an enormous ancestral willow before plunging headlong into the sea – all outdoors organic with beige – subtlely textured interior – must describe to you in detail, or show you someday – the young macy[1] drove mother home, david at denoument insisting on driving me separately: he needed very badly to talk, and we catharsized for hours through a soft vague twilight into a night of red neons and stars – he discussing his ideas of death – our philosophies enough similar so we could really communicate about our mutual revolts and searches for independence and freedom . . .

so strange, after recalling only our childish fancies, afternoons of science fiction, backyard birthdays and elementary escapades – we should leapingly be grown and talking still a similar dialect of a uniquely small tribe . . . on the eve of his father's death he told me what he couldn't talk about to his family, and as I left him on the precipice of my doorstep, I felt a surge of joy that I had, at least, helped david a little when he needed someone contemporary and as this verbal merry-go-round slows (somehow its going on two . . . I must have been day dreaming) I say business – likely that mother and I are leaving for my grandparents little place on the Cape tomorrow till July 4 . . .

naturally I want you to come down if ever and whenever you wish – I am sure I could get a room for you nearby for friday, saturday, or both nights, and we could borrow my grandparents' car for visits to warren, marty & mike & joan cantor, if you cared to be peregrinaceous – all sorts of alternate plans arise – just let me know which, if any you pick – I'm enclosing a sheet[2] with our address in Eastham & a phone to leave messages over, whichever is best – if you could take the train & bus down either friday eve or saturday a.m., I could meet you at whatever cape station you wished, probably – & you could stay overnight, if (all this so conditional) you wanted – I maybe driving you back to Newport sunday – think of sand, picnics, sun (?) and sea – just know we'd (how editorial!) enjoy you whenever & for how long you could or would come . . .

1 – Macey Gerson Feingold.

2 – The enclosure is no longer with the letter.

now, my ho head halls . . . my foos won't moos . . . I feel as heavy as yonder helm, <SP redacted some text and wrote 'censored' above>; tell me, tell me, tell me ames – do llamas speak in gordonian nots? weather or knot, there are suns to live, riddles to un, and pluriverses to be . . .

night now . . .

hush, hush, whisper who dares . . .

so we'll go no more aroving . . . down, down to a sunless sea . . .

so late into the night (darkness falls from the wings of)

can't hear with the waters of the hitherandmothering waters of

though the heart be still as loving christopher Robin is saying his prayers and every night, as I tumble into bed I think of: delphiniums (blue) and geraniums (red)

x

s.

TO *Gordon Lameyer*

Wednesday 23 June 1954[1] — ALS on Smith College letterhead, Indiana University

Wednesday

Dear Gordon . . .

A note that anthropomorphically hopes to get you before you leave the base: to say I am here at Hidden acres, off the road to thumpertown beach in eastham . . . names out of a backwards comic book it seems . . .

An enchanting small cabin in the pines, with a minute interior-new-painted like a jewelbox, yellow, pale green, and oh, one little wall of shocking pink which I love . . .

After a train and a bus trip hot and jolting with mother, grammy & grampy met us . . . and now, no trains, no phones – no mail – no visiting friends – only 9 or 10 books to sate any arising taste, bathing suits, and beaches to be alone on . . .

In the last two days I accidentally chalked up a high list of visits and re-encounters – monday it was three freemans, macy, and the young family[2] (all young, free & amacing!) and yesterday I swam at waban with mrs. aldrich & the 5 little ones, whom I gave rides, tows, and tumbles in the

1 – Date supplied from internal evidence.

2 – Harold and Ann Young, and their son Sheldon, who lived at 187 Somerset Avenue, Winthrop, Mass.

water as they clamored for me to watch their aquatic feats – met dear friend pat o'neil & her mother there, also jeanne woods, acquaintance from high school who went to wellesley – then an unexpected visit from john hodges & a friend whom I hadn't seen for literally years – a visit from laurie totten – one of my June Mlle cohorts – then my voluble aunt from Weston who drove me for a delightful session with ruth beuscher – and then: bed. now: vacation – awakening from a long, dreaming earwickerian[1] sleep on acres of tufted yellow bedspread all afternoon, I drink iced buttermilk and plan to walk miles & miles before I sleep . . .

Never such a rambler as I! First I was going to send a pithy postcard – then a note, now I must needs halt lest you think I have nothing to do but write you how much salt I put on my celery nightcap or to what degree of ebony I burn my breakfast toast – and other monumental inanities . . .

Ostensibly (isn't that a smug, annoying world of a word – almost as bad as oecumenical!) I write to tell you there is a cabin next door with a bed with your name on it in large godlike script, wreathed with gordonian knots – for you, if and when you are able, baker – no, no – wishing to come – because you do no longer have the usual title of "visitor" – which implies all sorts of formalities, but are somehow quite different . . . a name not yet found . . .

Just do please let me know by mail or call or male call where, when & if to pick you up – friday or saturday, or sunday – I do hope you'll feel like coming, even for a little, ideally – for a lot!

oh, gordon – living in a place like this for a summer, I feel I perhaps could write really again – away from social phones, eager & sometimes too attentive friends, and sophisticated syphilizations . . .

pines, sand, sea – and oh, for a typewriter – some day you will be in a study – (gayer than brown) like this with no one but perhaps a scrupulously unobtrusive cook-secretary to disturb you – on summer vacation to find your "portals of discovery"[2] & sail through, like ulysses, on & on like columbus to novels, stories – do let me be your typist!

And do come down to see us!
your obed. sec.,
s. p.

1 – Joyce, *Finnegan's Wake*.
2 – Joyce, *Ulysses*: 'Bosh! Stephen said rudely. A man of genius makes no mistakes. His errors are volitional and are the portals of discovery.'

TO *Gordon Lameyer*

Tuesday 29 June 1954 ALS, Indiana University

Tuesday, June 29

Very dear Gordon . . .

A sad and foggy day it is, and in the old green rocking chair I'm sitting surrounded by pocketbook editions of "discovery" and "New World Writing" . . . Without my typewriter I feel aesthetically and technically castrated (or perhaps unfertile would be more apt!) . . . yet, in my artistically crippled state I still want to communicate with you: a fetish, these letters . . . making me feel somehow closer which is how I want to be with you . . . very, and much more . . .

Ride back sunday: lurid and lonely: evil red and orange kerosene lights flickering and leering over two miles of devilish hacked-up road with cars moving two way trafficly, coming at each other head on till one chickened out & pulled aside in a ragged ditch: I being very stubborn, forced all the other approaching cars into the sideditches: being myself too numb to get either scared or polite, and rationalizing that I had no male tarzan along to extricate me in case of trouble . . . and so to the canal, too sleepy to even talk or think to myself . . . which I generally enjoy doing. I stopped for two quick shots of hot coffee on the rocks to keep my reflexes awake as I navigated the tortuous second lap of route 6 . . . hot milk, like a baby . . . and the sweet clover quilts of bed and sleep . . .

Yesterday, I walked two miles down nauset from the coastguard station to meet sue hitchcock[1] and we took off in her family's beach buggy for a day of travel . . . first to dick's camp (tonset[2]) in orleans where I saw the boy for the first time in six months . . . oh, gordon, it was so strange: I felt much as I did when I went "home" to winthrop last week: dick, too, seemed to have shrunk, telescoped up, like alice-in-w, both physically and psychically . . . I had lived so hard and so much and deep that never again could I go back to the same small country of his personality which once, years ago, I had seen as vast and glittering with promise . . . I felt only a little sorry for the boy who has had such hard things happen in all areas of his life . . . and who has again reverted to the "cousin" he was before I began dating him . . . sue and I swam with him and saw the infirmary he'll run, and he loaned me his bike for the rest of the week . . . and I left,

1–According to SP's calendar, Sue Hitchcock lived in Pound Ridge, New York. SP's Smith College scrapbook says, 'tramping miles up Nauset, introducing Sue Hitchcock (discovered by "The Outermost House") and brother W[arren]' (p. 64).

2–Camp Tonset in Orleans, Massachusetts,was a boys' sailing camp 1949–72.

feeling a mingled relief and pity – at his everpresent, inverted snobbery, puritanically directed against smoking, drinking, women with short hair and lipstick – all excesses of comfort and artistry and imagination – now that I have such increased distance in time and space from this major influence on my life, patterns and problems emerge more clearly articulate, and I feel desirous of describing to myself (and, by corollary, to you) the shaping furnaces that helped to forge this plastic plathian phenomenon which is the me, the I, the subjective center of the relative psychic solar system . . .

dick is, inside, a middleaged rigid, paternally authoritative bachelor who lives by maps, compasses and anatomy books: that, and his stubborn uncompromising critical attitude, constitute the essential tragedy of his personality . . . once I thought, for the benefit of future generations, that science should balance art, as the north pole does the south, with a wellrounded world in between: and, as a metaphor, it sounds fine – but I've been thinking over what you said so recently about blind spots, about learning, (say about the guts of cars) – and I feel that we are, you and I, creatively and natively clever enough to assimilate knowledge less poetic, though perhaps more practical, than joyce & thomas – and we can perhaps also help each other grow and learn as we do so ourselves, teaching and sharing on a mutual plane – not in a rigid teacher-student character – but rather as if we both were perpetually students – both learning, discovering and creating life . . . and maybe even art . . .

now and then, because of the multiple and complex ways you are always growing dearer to me – so that every time I say "I love you Gordon," the word love is a new word, deeper, and rich as a plumcake with nuances of taste and texture – because of all this, I wonder, in time and space, how long and continuous an interval I would need so that I could sit in the same room with you and read (I'd have to write shut up in a closet!) for hours without saying a word or interrupting to talk, discuss, or share something with you – read without some private voice dancing and capering and exulting most indecorously inside me: "Gordon is here . . . here . . . here!" As yet, I cannot pretend I do not hear the insistent, clamoring voice which makes me feel that getting to know you, wanting to understand you is so important when I am with you because I am with you so little – such a small proportion of hours, compared with the hours of my past life – even my present life . . . all this I think over and want to say to you here because it is new to me and I am so always very happy now that I am capable of such an enormous and potential tenderness and admiration – "love" is the biggest word I can think of for this insistent growing feeling – which is bigger than words used usually because it compares them all in an immense, fertile, bubbling, jolly Irish stew – that can produce exquisite aromas for the abstract, intellectual aspects of my need for form and artistic artifice – as well as earthy, succulent meat, for the physical, emotional facets of my scarlett-o'-hara,-molly-bloom elemental eva nature . . .

my needs and givings consist of polarities and counterpositions – and you and I are the lords of them . . . we will patent a new synthesis . . . and yet a newer one . . . we will be hobo and hoyden, duke and duchess . . . and learn cold by knowing hot, black by white, and yet be experts and connosieurs of warm grays as well . . .

darling, I do love you and, loving you, want to tell you so, and, telling you so, want to describe and make metaphors to qualify and specify this unique attitude of me (s) for you (g) . . . and I want to work (in time, as well as on this space) to make a four-letter word full of multitudes of connotations – so when I tell it to you, the meanings are infinitely individual . . .

This letter began as a sort of itinerary of the last two days – believe it or not . . . ("ah buhleeve it!") and switched somehow from the general to the particular . . .

I did drive with sue to see warren & clem in cotuit – explored 20 acres of "the pines", met characters – rowed to a bird sanctuary, discovered my first colony of fiddler crabs (fantastic creatures!) was swooped at and screamed at by irate white terns as we blundered among their nests – they added injury to insult by dropping well-aimed liquid white messes on our bare shoulders . . . back, and reading in bed . . .

today, rainily, I baked some cookies and spent hours talking (and mostly listening) to our loquacious cape cod landlady hold forth colloquially ("colloquacious" – not bad – but it could never approach your "bikeening"!) on her adventures as "home-made" bakeress of the cape – and her encounters with cape cod characters – one "as Irish as pat murphy's pig, you know, the one who perfected the chemical they use to embalm the boys' bodies sent home from overseas!" . . . I only wished I could take surreptitious shorthand to record her vivid untutored twists of speech, her vital vernacular – she's great story material . . .

you said you didn't object to my impulsive outbursts via mail . . . so I take you up here – and hold forth, even without the artistic regularity and discipline of the typewriter – because I want you to know me as much as I want to know you . . . and as we are both growing fast – (hope we always will) that is a colossal task – like trying to codify a rapidly increasing language – buth oh, I love you more than the alphabet and Roget's thesaurus combined . . .

sylvia

TO *Aurelia Schober Plath*

Friday 2 July 1954[1]

TLS with envelope on Smith College letterhead, Indiana University

Friday night
10 p.m.

Dearest mother . . .

It seems that my life is so full that even when I've only been away from someone less than a day, so much has happened in the interim that it would take volumes to recount it in detail!

I'm all freshly showered, shampooed, and squatting like a sleepy buddha on my lovely bed christening my typewriter (beloved thing) for the first time since I've been back.

Thought you might like to know the little practical details that you are always concerned about. Well, the house hasn't blown up yet (although diSTANT (hmm!) firecracker and cannon explosions tonight at first had me thinking that the preserve jars were blowing up one by one in the basement.) and I've aired it, and put it in apple-pie order and gotten the mess of unpacking cleared away.

The ride home on the train was hot and tiring, the only event being that the man in the seat behind me was cut badly on the face by some vandal kids who threw a rock, of all things, through the train window, shattering the glass in all directions: probably they were aiming at me, and missed! It was a shock to the whole car, as you may imagine, and we all felt suddenly like a row of wooden ducks set up behind glass for any novice assassin!!

A taxi sped me through the traffic to the busstop, and I didn't wait half an hour for the Manor Ave, but leapt aboard the one there. Luckily a greasy young character in a yellow convertible saw me struggling with my suitcase after only a few paces from Weston Road, so I sacrificed maidenly integrity to practicality and gratefully took the free ride home.

First thing, no mail. I called Dot right away, and she obligingly brought mine over in the nick of time, as she had been about to forward it. I got a letter from Bob Cochran and one from Mrs. Cochran inviting me for the

1 – Date supplied from postmark.

weekend in Chatham last week, so I'll write an apology for missing her mail immediately. Nancy wrote a nice letter: poor girl is working like a dog selling refrigerators and can't wait to come East. Joan Smith[1] wrote from the apartment,[2] saying the number is changed to Tr 6-0848, and Mel Woody wrote a good intellectual letter. Also my application photos came, 12 of them, the best small pictures I've ever had, I think . . . so I'm sending you one[3] as a little present to remember me by . . . saving the rest for the countless applications for scholarships I'll have to make out next fall.

Had a tunafish sandwich and peaches for lunch, so tired I couldn't eat more, and washed hair and relaxed on chaise lounge for an hour after visiting for a few minutes with Dot and Bobby, and Mrs. Aldrich and Ann later.

Mrs. Lameyer picked me up about 6 and we had a lovely supper of salmon and peas at her house[4] after which she drove me shopping to the Star Market which was packed with pre-holiday shoppers. For under three dollars I stocked up on 2 quarts of milk, mayonnaise, donuts, tomatoes, carrots, lettuce, green grapes, grape juice, frozen orange juice and toothpaste. Felt very competent and matronly with my list and enjoyed cleaning and rearranging refrigerator.

For some reason Gordon's phone call never came through, so I sent a telegram from Mrs. Lameyer's house telling him we'd be down at Newport for lunch tomorrow . . . and the most fantastic thing happened: remember this, because it's the queerest coincidence: Mrs. Lameyer evidently has a party line, because the line was busy when I lifted the received to call western union. Somehow, some wicked instinct made me keep listening to the woman's voice on the line, thinking that I'd call the minute she got through so she couldn't have the chance to make another call. Well, she talked on and on, and then began to talk about her daughter Ann, who was working on the cape and had met an awfully handsome boy about 19 who was a sophomore at Harvard. I was amused at the mention of Harvard as a prestige factor to the other mother, but when she continued, "Yes, he has an older sister who was a year ahead of Ann at Wellesley High and is now at Smith," I practically choked. "Ann thinks he may be a little young for her, actually, but evidently he is a charming boy" . . .

1–Joan Elizabeth Smith (1934–); B.A. 1956, government, Smith College.

2–SP sublet apartment 4, Bay State Apartments, 1572 Massachusetts Avenue, Cambridge, Mass.

3–The photograph is no longer with the letter.

4–The Lameyers lived at 24 Linden Street, Wellesley.

and it came back to me about meeting Ann Burnham[1] on the beach when I was over in Cotuit and how interested she was when she heard that Warren was working at the Pines too! When you think of all the chances that made up this coincidence of hearing, by chance, over a party line at someone else's house the mention of me and Warren, the possible odds are staggering, aren't they?

Anyhow, I've never enjoyed anything so much as being home alone . . . it seems so big and palatial and airy, with so many rooms . . . I feel I could hold a ball in the kitchen! I really am very tired, and look so forward to being very rested to cope with the new adjustments of the apartment and studying.

Tomorrow is Newport. Sunday I'll stay home all day, cook chicken or steak, with a fresh salad, preceded fashionably by vichysoisse . . . wash the mountain of clothes on the kitchen floor, iron, and pack one suitcase with necessaries. The heavy things I'll save till the weekend when dear Gordon will be home at last, unless he's hung from the yardarm for assassinating the captain.

Don't worry about a thing . . . all is very fine here, and I want you to get rid of those nasty ulcer pains.

Be sure and tell grammy and grampy I send my best love and regret I can't be there to celebrate with Frank and his family, but it is all for the best that I start summer school liesurely and rested.

Love to all . . .
your very own daughter,
sivvy

TO *Gordon Lameyer*

Saturday 3 July 1954[2]

TLS on Smith College letterhead,
Indiana University

saturday night

dear ponce de lameyer (en route) je pense de la mer

bang is how an opening sentence should begin; or, rather, BANG!! (just to make sure you are there, ready to listen all awake and aware) . . .

1–Ann Doreen Burnham; schoolmate of SP, class of 1951; B.A. 1955, Colby College, Waterville, Maine.
2–Date supplied from internal evidence.

I am squatting on my bed like a sleepy buddha, untergiversating typewriter in my languid lap at last, sound only of clacking keys, smug tick of clock damn conceited about being on time for a change, distant slither and hush of cars on pike, and a few spasmodic chirrups of somnolent birds of no appearance . . . .

so we have a scene of sounds set, and here I am: the Question is: where are You? as of today, my new philosophy of life is: Assume-Nothing-And-Jehovah-Won't-Jilt-You . . . or, in times of crisis: Assume-The-Worst-But-Serve-It-With-Parsley (that last is out of my "joy of cooking" book from the section on what to do with leftovers)

I don't even hazard when this letter will reach you . . . viconian recoursing may bring it to you tomorrow, or next year in tibet . . . I thought of addressing it to "the terrestrial globe", but then thought that the cretin post officials might take that to mean the third, and not the first and more general websterian definition, and be confused because you are technically on the aquatic globe . . . anyhow, by now maybe you got my gay little telegram about how your mother and I were jaunting down to lunch on the ship with you in newport today, ho ho and a hey nonino. perhaps you do not see why we planned on coming; well, it was all because of Assuming Things and happened like so:

Moment's silence. A few haunting bars of "Bobbie Shafto" with Wanda Landowska[1] on the Harpsichord (or, for variety, a melalcholic perversion of malice in wandaland with chorus harpies along the bar). Fade out.

Narrator (in highly suggestive tones): Yesterday we left our heroine Absinthe Lutely Plathtered struggling valiantly through the yuccas and the thith (shuchks, fluffed again!) thistles to get to her destination hundreds of ohms away in Newport, the Celestial City. Armed only with stale toll house cookies (to annihilate venomous nematodes) and Rinso Flakes (to keep her Nylons lovely longer), Absinthe ponders to herself the happenings of the past ninety-eight hours.

Absinthe: Oh, rather! That quite nice letter in the (com.) (,) post from Humperdinck Chimpendale Eccemann saying as how his galleon is hawl-a-day saturday, sunday and monday and there will be a caul friday for which I left a message as to where I would be as I wouldn't be where originally I was going to be.

Narrator: (ominously) Vraught by the sveldtering noonday headt, Absinned hears the dingle of a sturm nearby und yearns for a drang of vatever iss in it, HomoChinEyezed or uddervise. Liddle doss she know that

1–Wanda Alexandra Landowska (1879–1959), Polish harpsichordist.

this sturm is 100% mescalin flowink from a leak in a hidden moundand still.

Absinthe: (drinking like it was High octane ChampagnE) Oh, Weltschmerz! (She passes out cold.)

Narrator (undaunted): Yes, Absent had heard by post from Humperdinck and expected him to call. Friday. Meanwhile, in another part of town, Humperdinck's mother, imprisoned for days by the underworld gangster, Shrimp Casserole, escaped to call our herowine and offer her a ride to Noport sadherday. ALP accepted with joy.

Impatient Newscaster (seizing script and kayoing narrator): Awright awready, let's get dis over an done wit! Goil and guy's mudder have dinna friday. No call. Line must be busy or somethin so they send telegram. Leave early. Arrive Saddy. No ship. Flew coop.

Joe Friday (walks on set by mistake, knifes newscaster, plays "dragnet" theme on deviated septum): Ten thirty-one. Nothing turned up yet. Grilled sentry. Called Descant. No dope. Except the operator.

Operator: Ah des can't tell you-all wheah that silly li'l old boat done gone floatin off to.

Joe Friday (suavely) Ten thirty-four. One clue: operator's accent gaver away. Boat obviously in Norfolk, Virginia.

Absinthe (coming to): Zut alors! (begins wailing a Gordonian Plain Chant).

Joe Friday (suavely): Merde de vaches!

Radio Technician: Damyata! This whole show's shot to hell! (short circuits the mike and leaves for dinner at the Hilltop and a quick tour of Cornelius Vanderbilt's summer playhouse.)

* * * * * *

enough of this farce. dear gordon, I missed you. from your last letter[1] I gathered euphemistically that I could plan to see you some day this weekend and would talk things over definitely if you called friday. in fact, your mother and I made plans which gathered momentum, so that, after trying to call you and learning we could only send a telegram, we rakishly did that.

receiving from you no negative, we acted positive. anyway, after the naked horror of the deserted wharf, we had a lovely dinner and tour of the "breakers" and, in spite of the reputedly death-dealing traffic (according to the sepulchral radio warnings of rudolph king[2]) I drove about two

1–Gordon Lameyer to SP, 29 June 1954; held by Lilly Library.

2–Rudolph King (1887–1961), member of the Massachusetts House of Representatives; House Speaker; and Registrar of Motor Vehicles.

hundred miles without scratching a fender. and I did enjoy spending the day with your mother. she is so lively and a good deal of fun.

hot here. mountain of clothes in kitchen to wash and iron tomorrow. alone in house, except for a few ghosts lurking in shadows and an amphibious troll inhabiting the washing machine. I've been so social that I love being here quietly alone with books and papers and letters and no (well hardly any) people. even without telling anyone I was home, my aunt Dot and cousin Bobby came over with my mail (10 letters), baby Ann and Pixie wandered through the hedge to leave tricycles and beg for cookies, Mrs. Aldrich sent Libby over to ask me for Sunday dinner tomorrow. my life is one of unpacking and repacking and reunpacking. monday I hope to move to Cambridge. as I have a dentist appointment friday afternoon (the 9th) I'll be home all next weekend. these weekends seem farther and farther apart! I live lifetimes between seeings of you, and now, after today, I muse in wonder and wishfulness about having you warm and vital and near: those miracles of proximity, mental and material, ethereal and earthy . . . once they begin they are already vanished . . . only to appear again, more and very muchly better . . .

fog on cape conduced to reading <u>Sons and Lovers</u> by dhlawrence and <u>The Great Gatsby</u> by fscottfitzgerald and beginning of <u>Babbitt</u>.[1] danny kaye in "knock on wood"[2] with warren and sue hitchcock (that vivacious girl I discovered on nauset beach) . . . visit to marcia and mike plumer at pleasant bay camp[3] . . . stone through train window lacerating man behind me . . . fantastic accidentally overheard telephone call . . . so sleepy . . .

here is a piece of virginally white paper to end all this on. you might keep it for statistics, among other things. my summer address is:

Apartment 4 Telephone: Trowbridge 6-0848
Bay State Apartments
1572 Massachusetts Avenue
Cambridge

I promise I will be home all weekend from friday supper on, just in case you really do come home.

I am enclosing my class picture which looks as much like me as any of the others do, which is a safe statement as the others are very few and very

1–Sinclair Lewis, *Babbit* (New York: Harcourt, Brace & World, 1950). SP's copy held by Lilly Library.

2–According to SP's calendar, she saw *Knock on Wood* (1954) in Dennis, Mass., on 1 July 1954.

3–A mixed summer camp, in operation 1938–79, on Little Pleasant Bay in South Orleans, Mass.

bad. the main, and perhaps sole, virtue of my face is that it is extremely mobile. therefore photographs are not ME, or even a reasonable facsimile thereof. because, in normal life, I do not stay still that long, and my fluid features are always riverrunning together. but here is my burnt offering anyway. at least it's better than that snooty profile that makes me look as if I wish I were at a coming-out party.

* * * * * * *

that is all factual, above. this part, underneath the stars, is, too, but more softly labial . . . because the more I live and think and read the more I am amazedly glad that you are there to be knowing more and vividly . . . every choice or event I measure as best I can by the limitations and difficulties it involves (which is rather like evaluating a landscape by its shadows, instead of its highlights) . . . and all I can think of that I regret in the growing and evolving tenderness I have for you is that we do not have a more constant, consistent environment to learn to know ourselves in: like a summer job at chatham, or a daily college companionship of study and celebration, both situations hypothetically offering a more valid approximation of actual living conditions . . . in contrast to the accelerated pitch of life I save to pour into our weekends . . .

when I am sleepy, darling, I can have recapitulating talks, but I cannot create or think and read fiercely. I need sleep, about nine hours a night. while I love the night, to read and talk and love late, and easily sleep till noon, I really live and work best if I go to bed generally early and get up to work by 8. from then, till lunch at 1, are my best thinking hours.

it follows that I am not disciplining my thinking now; I am more vaguely stream-of-consciousness and uninhibitedly fond of you. for you I want to be like a chameleon on a paisley shawl . . . . paradoxically always and yet never the same . . . the more always and vividly I love you the more newly and variously I want to tell you how this you-i linking affects me . . .

how private are typewriters, anyway? mine is more dear and intimate to me than quill or parchment. it would like now to talk about the warm, structural lines of your strong neck and the way your voice can go soft and lyric when it wants to . . . all those gordonian elements which are suddenly all-at-once You, which I could leave inarticulate, (and which you might rather I did that way,) sheathing them in that abstract, ambiguous, and ambivalent word "love" . . .

sometimes I'm tough and then sometimesI'mnot . . . but I will try to explain openly anything . . .

and I will also be quiet (when I'm asked . . .)

so all there is left now to say before I drift into dreams which are even now weaving around me is that I would rather see you rising from the sea than any pagan triton . . . so might I have glimpses that might make me less forlorn than that vacant newport landing . . .

until whenever,
lovingly,
sylvia

TO *Melvin Woody*

Monday 5 July 1954 TLS, Smith College

july 5

recklessly . . . calling up old tendernesses, and beginning, like joyce in the wake, with the end of a cycle (viconian) and delineating another . . . yes, it has been eclectic and packed as a plum cake, this past month . . . and now I sit alone in an island of hot honest sun, blazing toward a tan, with the second cup of coffee cooling on the grass beside me, next to a copy of babbitt which I am reading for the first time with "god-yes!" notes getting scrawled in the margins beside satire, irony, and those shocks of recognition and a little horror . . . not that I feel the danger of the hustling, banal, automatic mass-media dictated responses of those blithering floral heighters, but because I wonder if there is not a more subtle, dangerous specimen in our midst: the graduate school bohemian babbitt who makes a fetish of criticizing, denying and skeptically disagreeing, of patronizing foreign coffee shops and avant garde bars, discussing the organic horrors of hyman bloom,[1] pavlov tchlitchev[2] (pronouncing it eliminates the nasty necessity of trying to spell it!) . . . the vitriolic vitality of delmore schwartz and kenneth patchen and the sentimental romanticism latent beneath the small lettered scattered typographical forms of ee cummings' poetry (with a hiho, the wind and the rain) . . . all this because, with my own very clean swept and acutely architectured tastes for the plexiglass facets of joyce, lawrence, woolf, braque, klee, kandinsky, and all the other names (as yet, my names are not obscure merely for the sake of esotericism, thank god) . . . I wonder where the line is between the sweatevolved personal standards of art appreciation and the sveltely surreptitious zietgeist of the modern age itself, suavely feeding us our predilections intravenously and letting us claim

1–Latvian-born American painter Hyman Bloom (1913–2000).
2–Russian artist Pavlov Tchelitchew (1898–1957).

them as our own . . . all of which is sylvan mental meandering after having read fromm's escape from freedom last month and writing a paper on fromm/and my boy neitzsche (seems every paper I've written this semester is on somebody-and-nietzsche) . . . my summer reading, by the way, although constricted by the active life I've been leading, has been infinitely stimulating, ranging from the sublime to the . . . well, satirically ridiculous . . . children's books among the sublime: alice in wonderland again, and the little prince (saint-exupery is about the one author who can make me shed those clear, lyrical tears which are, in a larger sense, the result also of the pity-and-terror catharsis of greek tragedy) and then the great gatsby (there is miraculously noone like fitzgerald for describing the atmosphere of a cocktail party . . . no, not even eliot!) sons and lovers (found great smorgasbord for thought about mother-child relationships) the sun also rises (which, except for the bullfighting and fishing episodes, I find different from the avalanche of sexily-covered hardtalking paperbound books only because of the name hemingway on the cover . . . his short stories, esp "hills like white elephants" and "the snows" are muchly superior to his novels, I think) . . . and, for slow, scholastic digestion, I am spicing my days with reading the convoluted and explicated skeleton key to finnegan's wake[1] (which one charming cape codder thought was a murder mystery . . . well, to each his own!)

new paragraph, leaving book reviews alone now (but really, you and I are so intensely involved and stimulated in what we read, and by what we've read that a personal bibliography might be as effective in describing our personality development and orientation as anything else!) miraculously I got a full scholarship to harvard summer school, and nan got a half one, so we're moving into our plush apartment in cambridge (which we've sublet very cheaply from some harvard law students[2]) tomorrow and we'll be living with two other girls from lawrence house who are working in boston, and doing, god help us, our own cooking . . .

I'm extremely exhilarated at the prospect of introduction to the cultural stimulation of cambridge this summer as, eventually, I hope to do graduate work there . . . and plan to really hit that accelerated elementary german course (10 hours a week of class) hard so that I can plow through goethe and schiller at smith next year with a minimum of difficulty . . . also will audit either frank o'connor's course in the 19th cen novel, or

1–Joseph Campbell and Henry Morton Robinson, *A Skeleton Key to Finnegan's Wake* (New York: Harcourt, Brace, 1944).

2–According to SP's Smith College scrapbook, they sublet from David H. Neiditz and Joseph A. Novak; held by Lilly Library.

howard mumford jones'[1] class in modern american lit . . . brattle theatre foreign films and the spasmodic (or is it sporadic) presence on weekends of a delightful ensign (graduated in english from amherst in 53) who I've spent time getting reacquainted with since he's come back from a cruise in the med . . should complete a potentially vital and intellectually valuable summer . . . during the four weeks before smith reopens, I'll begin to plunge into dostoevsky (just got his enormous diary and notes[2] from marboro) in preparation for my thesis . . .

oh, mel (which devilishly enough means honey in latin) there is so much to talk to you about . . . I get so tempted to take you verbally by the scruff of the neck and shake you when I hear you talk about solitude, or exile, or what verges on the horrible "Ennui" (which is more than boredom of the dilettante, but rather a huge and horrible cosmic yawn of the intellectual, highly sensitized being in face of life and death and whatever you may mean by eternity) because the cataclysmic downward gyre I plummeted to symbolic death in last summer, when the center did not hold because there was none, or rather (as you wrote), too many, has given me an understanding of the black and sustained hells a mind can go through . . . and the enormous insulated loneliness when you feel that no human hand or love could reach or move you (if even one could it would be allright, because that one would symbolize contact with the human race)

you and I are alike (and different) in many ways, but there is, I think, a psychic brotherhood, a sort of amusingly ectoplasmic umbilical cord between us, which makes it possible to pick up our thread of communication any time and any place, no matter how raveled it has become . . . you and I have the sort of intense relationships that make it possible to emerge from nowhere to see a friend for coffee and passionate hard talk and then to disappear or be silent again for an indefinite and unexplained time . . . I would like to think that you felt you could always come and see me, call from california, and come for a cup of coffee . . . whenever you felt there was noone to commune with; which is naturally an arrogant attitude for me to have for it implies that I am a damn good high priestess of the intellect (which, by the way, I am) . . .

statistics . . . marcia's wedding restores faith again in fact that convention can be permeated with life and originality . . . wonderful reunion with carol pierson, whom I hadn't seen for a year . . . all most simple, honest

1–American intellectual historian Howard Mumford Jones (1892–1980).
2–Fyodor Dostoevsky, *The Diary of a Writer* (New York: G. Braziller, 1954); SP's copy held by Smith College.

and vital . . . nan at house for five days of turkish nightclubs with harvard instructors that I am fond of, tea with olive higgins prouty, cape excursion to nauset beach and birthday dinner for my future roommate and her amherst david . . . for me, a week at the cape with ten mile strolls along up the fantastic solitude of nauset beach, with powerful surf crashing on hardpacked sand, and a treacherous undertow sucking back into itself with a low chuckle of rocks and pebbles . . .

now, unbelievably domestic (with, I hope, a great difference and delight) I've been living alone at home this weekend, washing mountains of month's back laundry, ironing while listening to hindemith and poulenc, reading and sunning half naked while the clothes dry . . . cooking little steaks and chops and deviling things with onion and cheese in preparation for my nervous debut as ¼ of a cook this summer . . .

this letter is the last blast before the rigors of summer school preoccupy me to the exclusion of long epistles. statistics here, degenerately facts:

saw marty and mike for 10 minutes at cape hideout: both look tan, married and damn happy and healthy: address: pleasant bay camp, south orleans, cape cod.

I live during the week at: Apartment 4
bay state apartments
1572 massachusetts avenue
cambridge (trowbridge 6-08[1]

in case you write or drop by . . .

crane[2] and the man who died[3] will be resurrected for you by mail sometime in the next week . . . much thanks for the constructive loan . . . remember that I'll always be around and glad for coffee, wine, talk with you as long as we're both vagabonding about the terrestrial globe . . .

also like letters . . .
love,
syl

1–The number was incomplete on the letter.

2–Hart Crane, *The Collected Poems of Hart Crane*, Black and Gold edition (New York: Liveright, 1946).

3–D. H. Lawrence, *The Man Who Died* (1929).

TO *Gordon Lameyer*

Monday 19 July 1954[1] TLS, Indiana University

MONDAY (whoops) moaning

liebling . . .

weekend world diminuendos into monday dawn with lingering fugal wunderbars . . . and I am a little proud that I can concentrate on separable prefixes even while being separably betwixt time and space shared so creatively with you . . .

tired, yes, but all afternoon I will curl up like a foetal rose petal and in the darkness of daysleep, dream of your warm nearness and rise reborn from rivering waters of love and rest . . .

now it is shortly past 10, and I have had my first hour of german, gone shopping, and returned to the apartment to gather moral courage and verbal proficiency for the next onslaught at 11 . . . then frank o'connor, lunch with nan, bed, supper, and study and again, bed (Early) (I Promise!)

last night, in a semicomatose state, I fought and was cursed at by long lines of sunday drivers clad in the modern armor of autometal, with radio ariels held aloft for lances . . . took me over three hours to make the greyhound terminal, which I rushed into thinking only that your mother must have been wearily, frantically, and possibly desperately have been waiting for me about an hour. miraculously enough, her bus arrived at the moment I did, and she had also been wondering if I was waiting in the same adverbial state as I hoped she hadn't been. sweetly she drove me to cambridge with all my paraphernalia, and dropped in for a few minutes to see the apartment and meet the girls . . . every one of my roommates remarked enthusiastically, after your mother left, upon her vital, attractive personality, and voted that she was, without a doubt, the most delightful sort of mother a boy could have . . . which I thought might please you, as it did me . . .

last night I showered gratefully, washed clothes, wrote out german exercises, called mother, and literally crawled (almost oozed) into bed as nan arrived at midnight from a late steak dinner which edwin[2] cooked for her at his apartment (he'll make some strange woman a wonderful cook!) and we talked together, recapitulating the mutual weekends and events . . .

1–Date supplied from internal evidence.

2–Edwin James Akutowicz (1922–2007), A.M. Harvard, 1946; Ph.D. Harvard, 1947; a mathematician; dated SP 1954–5. SP recorded: 'A cool study, beer and intrigue provided by assistant physics professor Edwin Akutowicz at M.I.T., and a casserole of life, love & learning –' in her Smith College scrapbook (p. 62); held by Lilly Library.

also today I had a charming talk with one of our landladies . . . Mrs. O'Clare has a son[1] on a fulbright in england, who is getting his phd at harvard in english next year, so she suggested that I write him about my tentative plans to apply for one, and find out the inside story from him, which I shall do later today . . . I enjoy having numerous irons in the fire (what in heavens name are they doing in the fire?) or, better, several potent irish stews bubbling creatively on the firey range of my life.

with you and we so both quite new, it is tempting to forget, at least for a little while, that there is an external word of facts, people, and events which also must be occasionally placated with a raw hunk of attention tossed into the avid mouth of the insatiable lion . . . and so, while I would Rather be on a sunny pacific (or, pacifistic) atoll with you, mangoes, and grass huts full of books, I feel that as I get to know you more and better and increasingly lovingly, I will be more able to work hard at studying or jobs with the constant pervasive joy that I am working for you and that you are There with me . . . but now, when with you, the external world is pleasantest, of course, but almost superfluous in comparison with the deep universes in your greenbrown eyes . . . and I want to inhabit infinite islands of insulation with you until we are quite used to the miraculous fact that we shall work and write and live and love sometime perhaps organically together . . .

all of which is only trying again to say that I amazingly do love surely you . . . and, loving you, I love the world as I never could alone, because you symbolically make the world "so various, so beautiful, so new"[2] . . .

until friday,
your very own
sylvia

TO *Gordon Lameyer*

Wednesday 4 August 1954[3] TLS, Indiana University

2.05 p.m.

dearest gordon . . .

indulging the liberal and unscheduled side of my most presently disciplined nature, I am seated in comfortable deshabille at my desk,

1–R. M. O'Clair; a letter from O'Clair to SP, 24 July 1954, held by Lilly Library. In the letter he acknowledges SP's letter dated 20 July 1954.
2–Matthew Arnold, 'Dover Beach', *New Poems* (1867).
3–Date supplied from internal evidence.

listening to sentimental lyrics waltzing out from the radio, after a light sandwich lunch preparatory to going to bed for my afternoon nap, which is always seductively pleasant, since thoughts and dreams drift toward you intuitively on the grammatic wings of imaginative subjunctives . . .

metaphorically, I feel now in the position of a prisoner chained to a galley going through the bluest of mediterranean seas: I have a job (for which I volunteered, actually) which sucks up all my strength and concentration and powers of motion, and, even as I drop in bed numbed by fatigue, yet insatiably demands more. the tourists on the galley sip scotch on the rocks, gaze dreamily at the tiltingwhite gulls and the vague, verdant shores, skim through all the books ever written, indulge in voluptuous love as the evening sifts down in purple levels of passion to the paradisal bizarre lyrics of oboes and flutes, guitars and mandolins. the damnable aspect of the situation is that I could be one of the most appreciative of intellectual gourmets (as I hope to, someday) but the bread-and-water discipline I've chosen is one of those necessary means to a desired end . . . the ability to expand and multiply horizons of experience and perception . . . and yet it is a bittersweet agony to see swann's way,[1] look homeward angel,[2] as I lay dying,[3] the enormous room,[4] shaw, ibsen, o'neill, and the rest, languishing unread on my bookshelves.

the above is self-rationalization (and commiseration) which is necessary sometimes before I throw myself back into the position of a healthy filly turned into a beast of burden, with blinders, and a cartful of words to carry to a german roget.

something, among others, of more note than the hours spent in widener getting tense over tenses: had a conference with my german prof today, and even though I barely managed a B (which was rather a relief even so) on my midyear, said that he would like to groom me for better things . . . and was very helpful and encouraging. I figure that if I got a bare B having lost half my blood I should do better being back to full capacity again. I'll work hard this weekend so I'll really be able to enjoy jaffrey, the weekend of the 14th. the next weekend, however (the 21st), I won't be able to get away from cambridge because I have a part of my final that saturday

1–Marcel Proust, *Swann's Way* (1913); SP's copy (New York: Modern Library, 1928) held by Smith College.

2–Thomas Wolfe, *Look Homeward, Angel* (New York: Modern Library, 1929); SP's copy held by Lilly Library.

3–William Faulkner, *As I Lay Dying* (1930); SP's copy (New York: Modern Library, 1946) held by Smith College.

4–E. E. Cummings, *The Enormous Room* (1922); SP's copy (New York: Modern Library, 1934) held by Emory University.

morning at 9, and will also have to study intensely for my final exam on wednesday the 25th . . . after which I shall optimistically turn hedonist, even if I have to read a little german daily to keep up and increase my vocab . . I'm going to read and read away at the books I have piled up here and at home . . . also, I love it so here, and have so little relaxed time to saturate myself with the minor pleasures and daily epiphanies of life that I may just stay at the apartment into the middle of september to cook and read at widener and observe the plethora of vivid details of life which I generally have to ignore for the sake of economy of time . . . perhaps I can entertain you here for a dinner or two . . . I'd really love the chance to hold forth as hostess in my own temporary domicile . . . and if you're in charlestown navy yard perhaps you could even come over during the week . . .

the radio is throbbing with a colloquial spiritual now all about how "you just didn't happen friend, God planned you that way", the streetcars are streaking by beyond the venetian blinds like grating orange carrots, the leaves are lyric scallopings of greenblack against a luminous gray sky, two clocks are ticking, and the dark spinach-green color of the curtains happens to match the keys of my crackling typewriter (which last observation is the epiphany, or minor revelation, of the day) . . . monday I had a reaction vs. the weekend clutter of the apartment that always greets me on return, so I created an esoteric dinner (apres votre mere!) beginning with jellied consomme in champagne glasses, an elegant compote of sliced peaches, grapes, cherries and apples marinated in sherryandlemon dressing, cheese and crackers, chocolate cake and hot coffee . . . all of which made me feel that even if I didn't have time to originate color and taste with the art of words and paint, I could at least sublimate in the functional world by exotic menus . . .

tuesday was one of those sopping soggy anesthetic rainy days when it doesn't begin to pour till you've left the house without your umbrella and raincoat . . . I shivered and growled at noon as I hurried home in the cold deluge, soaked to the skin, with my feet squashing unpleasantly in the rain puddles in my shoes . . . nancy greeted me in an equally saturated state at home, and we decided that our physical and psychic states demanded pampering, so we each put on one long wool knee sock as we had only one pair between us, to give the illusion of warmth, turned on a delightful program of classical music, made deluxe peanut-butter sandwiches spiced with onion, mayonaisse, bacon, and experimented with tall hot toddies which were delectable and most enlivening . . . later in the afternoon we went to a scholarship tea at the harvard union and gorged on sherbet punch and tollhouse cookies while talking with harvard officials . . . tonight we're going to an affair given by one of nan's instructors to meet faculty members on a personal basis, which should be fun . . . at least, after I've taken my nap . . .

all this to catch up with only two days . . . but there is so much more I want to learn to share with you, the minutest and the most colossal . . . everything from stream-of-consciousness impressions to the more logically thought out ideas and problems.

even in the midst of this (the radio is now being gaily suggestive and some slick guy is crooning: "life would be a dream, if I could take you up to paradise, doo-ah, doo-ah, life would be a dream sweetheart"[1]) I revolve the universe of possibilities and probabilities involving you and I and the dream of we . . . and ideas come, and questions, and hazardings about all the contingencies that depend upon other contingencies . . .

thinking back, of how dear you were to agonize through all the german with me . . . perhaps as difficult a situation as would a-rise if we ever studied side by side (which I hope we'll be doing for the rest of our lives) as we were dealing with mere mechanics here (except for the rather poignant story about Death and his godson, and the enormous subterannean cave of lifelights) when, even when I'm plunged into the as yet obscure depths of my thesis, I'll at least be involved in ideas and philosophy . . .

so many ifs and on-the-other-hands arise as I become as unflinchingly practical and objective as I can about the quite entrancingly unobjective process of growing to love you to newer depths and breadths and heights from day to day that I cannot help but wish that you were here by my side to discuss, analyze and project plans with me . . . already I have innumerable things to talk about with you . . . and I have become so spoiled by your weekly arrival that I can't really believe you won't be up this weekend, too . . .

oh, darling, there is so much love in me for you, intrinsically, and for you as a symbol of all I love in life that I want to express this most blazing and potent content of affection in new and increasingly complete forms of love and thought and communication . . . a long, lingering kiss for your magnificent mouth . . .

aufwiedersehen . . .
sylvia

1–The Chords, 'Sh-Boom' (1954); covered by The Crew Cuts.

TO *Gordon Lameyer*

Thursday 5 August 1954[1] TLS, Indiana University

thursday, 2.20 p.m.

most adored one . . .

if you could be here at this moment with me we would share delight, I think, looking out of our study window, to see the big silver rain suddenly come down, with its inexplicably delectable wet spattering and splashing sounds that take on the tones of the objects rained upon . . . metallic on car tops, rustles like taffeta in the flat leaves, melodic trickles down the drainpipe . . . and now the young mother comes running laughing up the walk, her skirts sodden, her eyes crinkled up with laughter and raindrops, pushing a fat edible blond baby in an open carriage . . . and after her waddles the panting possessor of a bedraggled baby poodle, breasts and hips lost in rolls of fat, swaying in her hurry as if she were balancing on the tilted deck of a ship about to sink . . . and the discreet squares of the red tile walk are, indeed, awash with rollicking rivulets, giddly imitating the canals in venice . . .

and even as I try to create for you a verbal, quick watercolor sketch of my environment, the rain diminishes, while my words increase . . . and I am again happily unclad at my desk, wanting to talk with you before I tumble sleepily into bed for my nap, into the tantalizing dark limbo of dreams where the warmth of my own drowsy body becomes the warmth of your arms, and I think how, (with the intuitive release of the beginning rain, with the plaintive musing piano dreams of debussy,) wishable it would be to make love to you with it raining all around, and on the roof and on the windows and on the ships at sea, with it so dearly lovable to be enclosed in the solar system of your universal embrace . . .

somehow, with all the difficult and dark things that have happened to me, I seem to be able to maintain a healthy, productive optimism, which eventually manages to work out crises and problems, transmuting them into positive events, such as art of instructive philosophical development . . .

in my last letter to you (was it only yesterday?) for example, I may have sounded tired and have seemed to resent my stoic program . . . but today, even still being sleepy, I have been acutely and positively happy (kay starr[2] is now brassily singing "if the sun should tumble from the sky, if the sea

1 – Date supplied from internal evidence.

2 – Born Katherine Laverne Starks, Kay Starr (1922–2016), American pop and jazz singer.

should suddenly run dry, if you luhved me, ree-ly luhved me, let it happen, I won't care, let it happen darling, I won't care"[1] . . . and it becomes satirical counterpoint to the very deep, very infinite emotion I will spend the rest of my life trying to communicate to you by love, words, actions . . . and every method of expression known to man . . . and woman . . . I am glad, though, that I can appreciate the burlesque coarsenesses of existence, seeing them through the double lens of vision . . . enjoying them, yet having a sort of aesthetic distance which will let me use them as tools without their using and victimizing me . . . I can like jazz, blatant syrupy love lyrics, dirty jokes, bartenders, taxi drivers without any sense of superiority or patronizing pride, quite honestly, and simply talk that language . . . but in the final analysis I guess I want, like Eliot, to refine the dialect of the tribe . . .) because I discovered

(that last long parenthetical expression reveals the influence of german sentence structure upon my own)

but today suddenly how I might be able to have two things which I thought were incompatible . . . and the prospect of continually eating cake and continually having more of it always appeals to the feminine-logic side of my nature . . .

you know, last weekend, I told you about how I wanted to give myself an (I think) unnecessary, yet indicative, test, and cut away all the accessory males that have, for the last five years, crowded my life, and give up those countless bull sessions and tête à têtes which I have hitherto rationalized and accepted as "platonic" friendships, never consciously admitting that even seeing a boy with no physical relationship whatsoever was a latently romantic or sexual situation (which was brought so drastically home to me last week!)

anyhow, to sum up, I felt that it would be somewhat of an artificial situation to cut all male contacts out of my life, because I would like to appreciate men as intellectual thinking human beings, and converse with them as such . . . but I lost my eve-like naivté with a traumatic shock last week, when I realized that I might have only comradely intentions, while my "comrade" might have totally different expectations of our meetings.

what to do? stoically give up the possibility of having anyone of the male sex for a friend? how to combine mental conversational stimulation with a truly innocent and unambiguous situation? well, today after german class, I found myself in a good discussion with three fellowstudents; a young catholic priest, an atheist jew, and a small college boy: all male, yet

1–Kay Starr, 'If You Love Me (Really Love Me)' (1954).

none of whom I would ever care to "date" in the sense of a tete a tete, but all of whom I enjoyed together as conversational companions. well, it occured to me that if I gave a party for about ten of these people at the apartment and acted as a hostess (always wishing that you were the host with me) all these people would enjoy themselves en masse, and I would achieve my ideal of holding entertaining "salons" without compromising myself in anyway with anyone whatsoever. so, tentatively a week from this friday, I am planning a dinner at noon at the apartment, to which all guests will contribute some part of the food, and, of course, stimulating conversation . . . already plans are dancing in my head for a huge bouffet, with delectable varieties of meat, fish, hors d'ouvres, desserts, and father delair[1] has promised to bring some wine "homemade" (!) at the rectory (no doubt used for "sacramental purposes" on sunday!) I am a little scared at the prospect of my first big entertaining project, but will do all the planning next week so that just the final touches will have to be added friday noon. this way, I can partake graciously of philosophical arguments, while remaining, obviously, aloof in respect to emotions . . . as I said to you last week, I seem to be regrettably conspicuous as a single woman, and I hope to insulate myself from the ever-prevalent danger of advances by all kinds of men until such a time as . . . I am fortunate enough to luxuriate in the security and miraculousness of having you walking always beside me . . .

and I do think that this idea of entertaining groups of people is a practical way of enjoying communication without becoming personally involved with anyone . . . because I don't want anyone to be tete a tete with me but you: and the problems involved here are obviously not those of wondering if I could love someone else: as long as you are on the earth, you will be the one I want to share my life with: the considerations here are only: which time would be the best and most practicable to begin living with you? and then, the normal differences that may arise (I can hardly see any, no matter how assiduously I look!) about, say, finances or something. all of which I'm sure can be settled by careful and considerate discussions . . .

1 – SP's college scrapbook refers to Father Delair as a 'young Jesuit Priest', who was probably in her German summer school class. According to SP's calendar, she met Delair and others as planned in the letter on 13 August 1954 for a buffet dinner, and on 20 August for coffee at the 'College Inn', formerly at 1200 Massachusetts Avenue, Cambridge, Mass. SP had plans for dinner on the 23rd, but crossed through the appointment. SP also spells his name as 'Dallaire' in her calendar.

last night, for example, nancy insisted that I go to a cocktail party given by one of her instructors (she refused to go unless I came with her) and, because I knew she wanted to go, I went for an hour. my old illusion that everyone who got a phd was brilliant, intellectual and desirable was further refuted over cocktails with anemic, pedantic, socially-regressive, scientifically-illiterate midgets . . . honestly, gordon, you and I must be exceptions (even though we are inclined often to be insecure and modest about our own potentialities!) because the young men and women here, who are associated with grad schools hereabout were the most unattractive (both physically and mentally) people I could imagine. no law school degree could excuse pedantry, no phd cancel out an uncared for, mistreated body . . . yeats' ideal "where body is not bruised to pleasure soul"[1] is most important with me: I scorn intellect without a strong healthy body as much as a beautiful body without a mind to make it incandescent . . . and in you the combination of desirable qualities is so sunlike that it eclipses all the asteroids in this human solar system, and I want nothing better than to revolve around the lifegiving warmth of you for as long as the world of ourselves lasts . . . never be concerned that I overidealize you, darling . . . I am only most very aware of our human weaknesses, but in spite of and including them, I still think you are the most special person I could ever want for me . . .

practical details: I am seeing dr. heels[2] tomorrow afternoon for a complete pelvic examination which I would have to have anyway before I got married, and I am sure that prognosis will be generously optimistic: it is always comforting to have a definite and competent doctor's advice, and even if I regret the unsavory way I discovered about my manyarteried insides, I'm glad to get the deluge over with so that I will be healthily prepared for a natural and completely understood sexual life . . .

and now, I must fold up my letter like the arabs and silently steal away to sleep . . . sending first to you my most longing love, and hoping to hear from you at the apartment a week from tomorrow . . .

your very own
sylvia

1–W. B. Yeats, 'Among School Children', *The Tower* (1928).

2–Probably Dr George E. Heels, a physician and obstetrician in Cambridge, Mass.

TO *Gordon Lameyer*

Saturday 7 August 1954[1] | TLS with envelope, Indiana University

saturday morning
time: early
place: paradise

dearest Gordon . . .

I think I have achieved a world's record this weekend: sleeplinging. yesterday, after an unusually full week, I felt my typical friday languor: up at 6:30, german at 8, studying at widener from 9-11 (with a brief walk to savor the clear blue of an exquisite sparkling morning – sunlight twinkling and dancing on green leaves and colored shops in harvard square) german again at 11, frank o'connor till 1, then lunch and packing, doctor's appointment at which all was pronounced intact, healthy and generously normal, and a lucky encounter with an attractive friend[2] of mine (from high school who graduated from wellesley this june) and offered to drive me home . . . well, I decided to go to bed for the day at the phenomenal hour of 5 p.m., planning to rise with dawn's first breath: to sum up, I slept soundly till 8 p.m. this morning, chalking up a grand total of 15 hours straight! and today I am a new woman: my eyes have emerged from their charles-addamsish-purple hollows, I have washed my hair which is drying streakily in the hot sun, and I feel that I could write 7 short stories and read 100 pages of german before lunch, which I probably could, if I really concentrated on it!

I am saying all this because I want you to know how wise it was for me to stay home this weekend, even if stoic. as much as I wanted to see you and be with you, I felt it even more important to put myself in a state where I could appreciate you most fully next weekend, and I needed rather definitely to rehabilitate, equalize my blood and weight supply, study german, repair my wardrobe and my serenity, all of which being taken care of, I am again having "my cup runneth over" with energy and power, and I can't wait to have you around so that I will feel fully appreciated and active . . . I will be delighted to see you next friday, and, needless to say, at any time this week <u>if</u> you should have the time to catch a ride up and back (as long as it didn't make you too tired or too inconvenienced!) . . . for future reference: I'm always either at the apartments or at the big

1 – Date supplied from postmark.
2 – According to SP's calendar, this was Jeanne Woods.

reference and reading room on the 2nd floor of widener library in the evening, and so easily findable . . .

as always, I'm luxuriate and replete in the green haven of my secluded back yard: private enough to sit like a cross-legged buddha on the chaise lounge before my typewriter, clad in halter and shorts, to write and study, yet neighborly enough so that I can hear ann aldrich crying in concern as mrs. aldrich learns to ride my bike under libby's direction, and so that the-old-mr-magowan[1] can teasingly remind me of a hypothetical date we've been about to have for several years. all the virginia-woolf delight in a symphony of unrelated sounds, sights, and flavors being sympathesized (explication: sympathy, symphony, synthesis . . . for a future story) into an ecstatic unity by the observer (a sort of mrs. dalloway-plath, here).

I cherish the lunging roar of the powermower as peter aldrich mows our lawn, the blasé drone of the cicada, the junior greek chorus of children playing hide-and-seek in the foliage, sunlight incandescent on blue and pink cornflowers, kindling warm yellow in the veined green leaves of swiss chard; fragrance of steak broiling, fresh cut grass and sunwarm flesh . . . all the minor-keyed daily delights which I want to share with you as I would the details of an african safari . . .

mother and I, <redacted text by SP> are getting along more constructively and creatively well than ever, as perhaps you noticed last week. an analogy which seems relevant: there was a time when the new american colonies needed very badly the close, protective surveillance and direction of mother england; but as they gained maturity, a tempestuous revolution was needed to break the umbilical cord binding them to the maternal security and protections; once the initial battle for a new, reciprocally independent, relationship was won, peace ensued, and harmony has been developing ever since. so here, with my revolution (and a belated one it was) over, I feel that I can be generous, loving, benevolent, without fearing for my ever-strengthening newfound independence and self-reliance.

at this moment it seems impossible that war, or destruction, or death, could explode upon the frank, sunlight peace of this dear american world, perverting life into a lurid, hellish inferno and blighting the sensitive structures of art and life that it has taken tedious centuries to build . . . but, idealistic as we are, we also, I am sure, are founded in a firm, constructive realism which takes into account all the difficulties that could occur, as well as all the delights . . . and this makes me, for instance, live by a healthy humanism which savors each day for its own

1–Probably Robert McGowan, who lived at 27 Elmwood Road, Wellesley.

revelations and essentially exquisite details, so that if curtains should ever begin to fall before the normal last act of ripened old age, I can at least say to you: every day has been lived to the hilt, freshly and keenly. that is the difference between sacrificing the present to a nebulous, spectacular (and dubious) future, and living fully in the present, even while planning hopefully for a future which may, after all, never arrive with the wished-for retirement in state on a tropic isle . . . as for me, I'd rather have a sandy nauset now than a hypothetical carib isle later . . .

also, by the way, if ever you wanted to bring reese[1] up again, or any of your other naval attaches, I'd be almost surely able to arrange delightful dates for them with some of my friends in wellesley with whom I'm reestablishing contacts . . .

one good thing I'm learning about myself: even when I'm away from you, I prefer the delights of solitude to the solicitude of other men . . . something which I had never proved to myself before. this, according to marriage counselors, is a most healthy sign, because it shows that I can be active and happy on my own (even though I would much prefer to be active and healthy with you!) and therefore do not lean on male admiration as an ever-necessary crutch to my psychic and physical vanity.

this observation has arisen from my dealings with nancy's problems and concomitant hysteria. she came rushing over to widener where I was studying thursday, all panic-stricken because david, the amherst boy, had said that he was coming up this weekend, and she would much rather see jim, who had been at the apartment when david called; so I went out for a cup of coffee to calm her and to be as constructive as possible in answering her frantic questions. the essential root of the matter is that nancy always wants to be actively made love to all the time, so that when she has to be away from david, she immediately seeks out another boy to become concerned about (you know, "when I'm not near the one I love, I love the one I'm near"). the only unrealistic thing is that she wants both boys to be ready to marry her at the same time, while she reserves the right of final choice whenever it is convenient. luckily, I have the aesthetic distance needed to be a close friend of nan's, and I'm willing to spend time listening to the tense "whatever will I do, syl"s because I love her dearly. those who do not know her well enough to enter into the inner sanctum of her private emotions, and those who have not lived daily with her, take her reserved calm as the key to her personality, as I first did. it is only now, after having lived with her, that I am beginning to realize that the apparent

1 – Reese Thornton, Lameyer's fellow ensign.

calm and sweet reasonableness are surface-deep, like sunsilver on a dark, moody lake, and that her calm is a result of tensions which break open at home in shrill, neurotic screaming. this is a very good thing for me to deal with, because my own inner serenity and calmness is being developed more highly to compensate for nan's eternal crises. and love for her, cancels out the inconvenience which her demanding self-concern occasionally causes, so please don't ever worry about my rooming with her next year, darling!

perhaps you have noticed by seeing me as honestly and unadornedly as possible, that the excited and enthusiastic attitudes I have toward life and people are a natural and healthy personality trait for me, and do not by any means imply that I must have, as corrolary, sour, moody depressive depths. only when I am overtired, I become a little numb, and that is easily taken care of by knowing my limits, and getting nine hours of sleep as often as possible, which is an easy price to pay for a jolly life!

the reason I am telling you these little things, which you probably know intuitively anyway, is because I want you to have every bit of information possible about me before we eventually begin to live together, so that whatever depths of myself you may not have seen (I don't see how there could be many) you will find a natural outgrowth of my character, and not an unpleasant shock!

and now, my favorite one, lest this become too long a chapter to read at one sitting, I will turn to my german translation, wishing that you were again here to be patient with me as you were so dearly last week. writing you more frequently has been my consolation for missing you a great deal.

I do feel that it is good for us to study together, because it will be more natural to do so then after we're (I still find it hard to articulate!) married! we'll learn to know our mutual working habits, as well as our lovely playing habits.

a letter came today from my dear, beautiful Claiborne who is living now in newyork with her jewish husband, avrom handleman. she, perhaps more than any, is a girl who needs love and support from her few, but most devoted friends. and I want to show how I believe in her by making an effort to visit her every time I go to new york city. perhaps you an I could plan to make a trip there early this fall, before school starts, as I would like so much for you to begin to share my small circle of close friends . . . I know only too well how all of them will love you!

but I am happy to think that perhaps I can love you more strongly and versatiley than most could . . .

you absolute darling!
Love from
your Sylvia

p.s. – you can call me at the apt. again –[1]

TO *Gordon Lameyer*

Wednesday 11 August 1954[2] TLS with envelope, Indiana University

wednesday afternoon

dearest gordon . . .

if I time this properly, you perhaps will read it when you get home just before you call me at the apartment, and I can predict now how elated I will be at the sound of your voice and the then immediate prospect of seeing you, because, to be honestly profane (or profanely honest), I have missed you increasingly like hell . . . I feel so intensely about you, and about sharing life with you, even just from day to day, that when two weeks separate us, my impatience to be with you again becomes, at times, almost unbearable.

so I sublimate by pretending that this is <u>really</u> <u>our</u> apartment, and that I am shopping for you, saving up daily vignettes to share with you, buying books with the intention of reading them aloud together before bed . . . and that you are just studying at the library, or teaching, and will appear on the scene at any moment . . .

you letter today[3] was so dear . . . in spite of the fact that a cool reasoning practicality grows in me to balance the eversoaring intense love I have for you, I sometimes wish to brush aside the material obstacles of time and future obligations like bricabrac from a beautiful, strong shining wooden table . . . and just savor immediately the naked wonder of living with you every day . . .

darling, if we can become ecstatic about the common necessities of life together, like morning coffee (or milk!) and shopping, how amazing will seem even the smallest of good fortune that comes our way! I am so glad you share your daily grievances with me, because I want to relieve you of

1 – SP added this by hand on the second page of the letter.
2 – Date supplied from postmark.
3 – Gordon Lameyer to SP, 9 August 1954; held by Lilly Library.

annoyances as much as possible by understanding and listening to them, and by being a sort of shockabsorber between you and the petty demands of the routine world . . . and you will be the same for me . . . somehow, if we were sharing our lives together, all problems, no matter how serious, would be just that much more bearable and capable of being worked out . . .

I want to stay at the apartment as long as possible just to be an hour nearer to you every day, after you are stationed here . . . and probably will be able to stay till september 14, which will give us two unbelievable weeks of continuous proximity. also, since only joan is here, there would be ample free space for you to stay here in, if you like . . . and I'd love to have you come for meals if you were able . . . or I'd love to eat on the ship (If your fellow officers wouldn't be bored or embarrassed by the presence of a frequent female!)

german becomes increasingly difficult, and the passive beastly voice finds me with an inherent misunderstanding of the english grammar, not to mention the german . . . three exams between now and the final to make or break me . . .

violin music whimsically lilting, cucumber sandwiches having been eaten for lunch, a new-bought book on my desk for use to read aloud in together, and darling, I shall simply explode like a feminine H-bomb if you don't let me right now tell you very hard again and again that I love you love you love you love you love you!!

your very own adoring . . .
sylvia

TO *Aurelia Schober Plath*

Monday 30 August 1954[1] — TLS with envelope, Indiana University

monday afternoon

dearest mother . . .

thought I'd sit down on this cold clouded day to write you a note about affairs here since last I talked to you. practically speaking, all has run off well. I've cooked meals for gordon all weekend, and learned a good deal . . . my main problem was using frozen meat, which malevolently didn't thaw completely even after a couple of hour out of the refrigerator, and

1–Date supplied from postmark.

required more cooking therefore . . . we had a very lazy weekend, doing absolutely nothing except eating, talking, reading, sunning and listening to records, and I again realized that it takes a few weeks of utter relaxation to put one in shape in between big pushes of work . . .

I cooked the veal, the chicken, and had the steak for sunday dinner out in the yard . . . beginning with cold potato soup, and progressing to steak, peas, macaroni and cheese, and ending with chocolate pudding and icecream and some rather lopsided and deformed (but good) chocolate-frosted cupcakes I made . . .

luckily gordon got a car from a friend on the ship who wanted it driven up to boston . . . and I persuaded gordon to leave it with me till the ship came up to charlestown the middle of this week, which means that I'll have easy transportation to the market, the dentist (ugh) tomorrow, and cambridge tomorrow afternoon. we ended by driving to dr. beuscher's ourselves friday . . . luckily, because my talk with her lasted longer than usual . . . I do love her, she is such a delightful woman, and I feel that I am learning so much from her . . .

saturday, pat o'neil biked over and had a charming visit with gordon and myself . . . I was in a mood to pamper myself this weekend, and so went to bed early and read j. d. salinger and carson mccullers short story collections[1] in the sun . . . I just didn't feel like disciplining myself to more difficult intellectual reading . . . this coming week, however, I hope to start dostoevsky in cambridge, and pick up german again, which I dropped for this week after the B exam, as if I'd been burned . . .

coincidentally enough, I was reading the monitor in the backyard saturday, and found that the usual foreign language article was translated in both french and german.[2] I tried the german, and had a thorny time, especially with the big built-up words and still (for me) awkward constructions. I was pleasantly surprised, however, to see how the french translation flowed out in idiomatic english. I'm sure that an intense review course, plus speaking (I do feel I've got good pronunciation, considering my four year lapse) would make me quickly proficient . . . somehow, it seems more native to my own expression than german, but of course I had it for three years longer, and so the comparison is hardly fair . . . I do hope you and warren will read german with me . . .

1–Probably Salinger's *Nine Stories* (New York: New American Library, 1954) and McCullers's *The Ballad of the Sad Cafe and Collected Short Stories* (Boston: Houghton Mifflin, 1951). SP's copy of *Nine Stories* is held by Smith College.

2–'Man's Right Place', *Christian Science Monitor*, 28 August 1954, 8. Translated into French 'La vraie place de l'Homme' and German 'Des Menschen rechter Platz'.

and speaking of him, I'm really sorry not to have heard from him in so long . . . you are lucky to be near him . . . gordon and I are planning to be at cantors from friday till sunday next weekend, so do tell warren that our trip won't be complete unless he can drive over to see us for a while . . . I do miss him so much . . .

mrs. colburn called up, and just wanted to say hello, and the funeral for ken is today at 2, so said elaine mcintyre (57 addington street, brookline . . . in case grampy wants her address). I really didn't think I should call about it, and hope he won't be sorry at missing the funeral . . . the drive up would have been gruelling.

I do want you to know how I appreciate time for a retreat of sorts here . . . of course the house is lonely without you, but I have been such a social being so continually since last winter (the month of June being an intensification, not a cessation, of my social obligations and contacts,) that I really feel the need to be in a social vacuum by myself for a few days when I move solely at my own lazy momentum, with no people around. naturally it is only too easy to want company to alleviate the necessity for self-examination and planning, but I am at the point now where I have to fight for solitude, and it thus becomes a precious, if challenging, responsibility . . .

my main concern in the next year or two is to grow as much as possible in as many directions as possible, to find out, essentially, what my real capabilities are, especially in writing and studying, and then to plan my future life in consistency with my abilities and capacities. this is a very important time for me, and I need as much space and concentrated solitude for working as possible . . . I feel that you will understand, if only I can learn to use the right words to communicate these desires and tests to meet for myself . . .

if I can learn to create lives, stories, and excitement out of myself, without depending on external stimuli as shots-in-the-arm, but rather as provocative-yet-dispensable additions to a life already whole and rich in itself, then I will be surer that I am maturing in the direction I want to go . . .

meanwhile, I want you to know that I love you really very much, and have wished occasionally that I could just whisk on a magic carpet to the cape to give you an impulsive bearhug, because you are, and always will be, so dear to my innermost heart . . .

much love to all,
sivvy

TO *Aurelia Schober Plath*

Wednesday 1 September 1954[1] ALS (postcard), Indiana University

Wednesday

dearest mother . . .

just a note to let you know the hurricane[2] didn't blow me away: tried to call several times to tell you house was all right, but your lines were down – Bill Cruickshank[3] (the dear) nailed down temporary cover where the shingles blew off our roof & I raked up as many of the branches as I could yesterday – we lost our birdhouses & one big birch – that's all – I luckily had eaten up almost all perishables with Gordon last weekend, & so cleaned out the refrig & brought the leftovers here – our house was still without electricity when I left – luckily I had Gordon's friend's car to transport me to the dentist in the hurricane – all through, now, thank heaven! Spent all day today scrubbing apartment from top to bottom cleaning up after Kay[4] & Nan in preparation for having Gordon to dinner tonight – will miss car – it was such fun, now to shopping – I'll call from Chatham this weekend

xxx
siv

1–Date supplied from postmark.

2–Hurricane Carol, which made landfall on Old Saybrook, Connecticut on 31 August 1954.

3–William H. Cruickshank, Jr (1925–2015). William H. and Dorinda Pell Cruickshank lived next door to the Plath family at 24 Elmwood Road, Wellesley, with their four children: Dorinda, Pell, Blair, and Cara.

4–Kathleen Quinn Camin (1935–96); B.A. 1957, government, Smith College.

TO *Gordon Lameyer*

c. Monday 20 September 1954[1] TLS, Indiana University

<SP has pasted in four photographs of herself; three taken during June 1953 when she was Guest Managing Editor at *Mademoiselle* and one in a formal dress, also from June 1953>

MEMO: TO AN ENSIGN WHO MAKES IT MORE AND MORE FINE TO BE HERE IN THIS UN*BE*LIEV*ABLE & QUITE INCREDIBLE COFFEE AND CAVIAR COSMOS . . .

these are pictures of a Girl who once had dark hair and forgot it; she is here in these monotone shots being very dark-haired, playing with a real rose (which she likes to think flames in her hair forever only she is mortal too so it is also a rose of jeopardy and all the million other things roses---especially dark red roses---are)

HER EARS ARE SHOWING AND THE MAN SAID TO HER: you always look as if you were going to cry even when you are laughing."

BUT HERE SHE IS REALLY LAUGHING

at the damn funny Rose . . . . . .

THIS GIRL WILL HAVE BLACK HAIR AND HER CHILDREN WILL ALL PROBABLY BE MULATTO AND SPEAK WITH A RAW*THRE BRRRITISH OXCENT . . . oh she was a nice girl a fine girl BUT one-a-tha-rovin-kind! hence: cocktails and she doesn't mind if she does . . .

but really (and this is a secret) but you know it anyway . . she is vulnerable and honest and that makes all the rest of it pretty much OK . . .

except her mother is very sick and she is worried always about that and sometimes is hard talking because inside she is unsure and scared a little bit . . .

and this girl hopes that she will grow like a bamboo tree but not stab anyone that happens to be tied up nearby because she would rather lose a lot than hurt someone . . .

and most of all above anyone she loves and wants to be with most of all a certain person who is YOU, and work hard to make you proud, & she is here smiling at you although she doesn't know it yet

a rose for you my allin green riding

LOVE
your
own
sp

1–Date supplied from internal evidence.

TO *Gordon Lameyer*

Monday 20 September 1954[1] TLS in greeting card,[2]
Indiana University

<printed greeting>

Let us dedicate this day / To people who are somewhat fey / To bundles of nerves / And strange complexes / To all of those / With wrong reflexes / Whom drugs won't help / Or antibiotics / Let us celebrate / Being neurotics

<SP captioned the card, which features five people in various poses>

<a stern-faced man> German professor listening to someone decline irregular objectives –

<a woman in bikini trailing flower petals from a basket>
Other Smith girls on Mountain Day

<man kneeling in with a worried look on his face>
Thesis advisor listening to project

<female hiding under a bed>
Me on day of reckoning

<man hiding under a carpet on which are placed a lamp and armchair>
Dostoevsky awaiting trial!

Monday

Dear one . . .

Not that you (or I) belong to this card, but it seemed amazingly appropriate in view of the fact that I wanted to write you in the margins of something gay and rhyming, if possible, and since no menus or ticket stubs were handy, here we are!

Hectic mechanics crowd, and my room is the only stay against confusion at the moment, with the right things in the right drawers: lovely colors: H crimson curtains, chair and bedspread; Y blue rug, blotter, pillows; new gray walls for hanging pictures on and two bookcases filled to overflowing; add four wickered green chianti bottles and two benign portraits of The Man in my life, and there you have my decor.

New faces, me feeling very old in the sense that I know my major purposes here and won't sacrifice time to dilettanting with the superfluous. In this week I have to make at least 10 faculty appointments for Fulbright recommendations etc. which have to be typed up in quadruplicate by the end of October. I feel very guilty about thesis unreading and German, but

1–Date supplied from postmark.
2–Panda Prints card designed by Rosalind Welcher.

hope to get Fulbright red-white-and-blue tape cleared up this weekend, plus an embryonic schedule of study[1] established so that I can greet you, my love, with calm and uncluttered delight, even though I shall have to prevail on you to sit by my side in the library a bit! All is so unbegun and untried that I still feel insecure . . . and will no doubt till I begin to feel competent in German and Fyodor D. Brown hair accepted here with hardly a murmur except: "It makes your eyes look browner!" I feel serene and dependable somehow, but want to begin to prove it! I'll try to write again before the much-desired Friday when you come . . . let me know what time, and do write me morale-buildingly! I need your love and confidence enormously.

A sleepy kiss for you, darling,
sylvia

TO *Aurelia Schober Plath*

Tuesday 21 September 1954[2] ALS (postcard), Indiana University

10:30 p.m. Tuesday

Dear mother . . .

About ready for bed, I sit to write the latest news: Room charmingly small & cosy & colorful, arranged yesterday with help of Warren & Joan – Harvard Crimson chair, bedspread, curtain – Yale blue rug, blotter, banner, pillows – new gray (at last!) walls ideal for sketches – Ilo's are now up. hope you can see it all sometime – Life as yet is all crowded chaos – no less than 7 meetings today for me! I have to get my Fulbright application all done by the end of October which means endless forms in quadruplicate, health exams, transcripts & essays on project plus 4 very important letters of recommendation for which I'm seeing professors this week – thesis topic is due Oct. 7, so I have 2 weeks of hectic reading for that – hope to fix red tape about German course tomorrow when I have an apt. with Ger. professor. Once I get my German & Dostoevsky well underway I won't feel so insecure. I do like to put down roots of schedule!

1–During her last year at Smith College, SP completed English (thesis) taught by George Gibian; English 36 (Shakespeare) taught by Esther Cloudman Dunn; English 347 (short-story writing) taught by Alfred Kazin; English 417b (twentieth-century novel) taught by Alfred Kazin; English (review unit) taught by Evelyn Page; English 41b (special studies in poetry writing) taught by Alfred Young Fisher; and German 12 (intermediate German) taught by Marion Sonnenfeld.

2–Date supplied from internal evidence.

Shopped today for necessities like shampoo (found one for tinted hair!) & bulbs & extension cord, etc. – on the rash statement to Macy: "Oh, write me, if you want a sympathetic ear!" I got 3 (!) letters of the most blind & pathetic self-castigation imagineable! One special delivery, no less! (SHE used to demand that!) – the vile girl is so ironically revealed in all her crude flabby materialism through Macy's rapturings over her! – I must read like fury – if only a good topic emerges in the next 2 weeks! I feel so unprepared as yet! – my job is waiting on breakfast every morning – I'm up at 7 and done by 8 a.m. – had a good dinner with Warren & Joan – love both – rain sounds cosy outside – this'll be both the best & hardest year – do write

xxx
sivvy

TO *Aurelia Schober Plath*

Friday 24 September 1954[1] ALS (postcard), Indiana University

friday 9 p.m.

dearest mother . . .

got your letter and welcome check today – it does help – only I'm concerned that macy had such a terrible effect on you (thank you for steering him away from visiting me – he has spilled over to countless people already, but I rebel at his taking advantage of your sympathy & making you sick) – I also disapprove vehemently of your evening course plan – how many evenings a week will they meet & how can you get the rested supper & evenings at home you need so much? I am distressed at your taking on such a demanding program when you are so thin and in such warningly poor health! I don't think another doctor (not mild Fran, who assumes you will take your own way anyhow) would condone it! you know that any problem makes you sick, so you should prohibit unnecessary people preying on you like macey. please cut down on your work, for my sake, if not for your own! As for me, I've had innumerable conferences with professors – about courses & fulbright: question: since Dr. Booth has to mention my McClean lapse & Dr. Beuscher anyway – do you think it would be best to get my personal reference from Dr. B – who would be brilliant, eloquent & allay any doubts about my stability in a medical way – or to have Mrs. Cantor or someone do it? Intermediate

1 – Date supplied from postmark.

Ger. is rough – the class is conducted in Ger, & I can't even stammar a sentence yet – Shakespeare prof is magnificent – conference with Mr. gibian today re thesis was encouraging think I'll do several examples of "The Double" in Dostoevsky

xxx
SYLVIA

TO *Gordon Lameyer*

Friday 24 September 1954[1] TLS, Indiana University

friday evening

dearest gordon . . .

the rather unique spacing effects on the envelope of this are due to the fact that this is nancy's typewriter and it skips, hops, and jumps about in a most undisciplined manner, expressing an eccummingsish personality insofar as a machine is able to! my typewriter is at the shop for a week being fixed: I don't know what's wrong except that the foxy old carriage is loose and I feel as if part of me were amputated every time I look at my empty desk, but they will probably charge me outrageously for whatever they do . . .

it is difficult to believe that I have been here only five days, for in that time, as my black scrawled textbook will testify under every date, I have made a phenomenal number of conference appointments, meetings and shoppings. I'll be glad for this sunday, the one morning I can sleep late since I'm a breakfast waitress.

Physically, as I said before, I'm settled, and I will be glad to put down substantial intellectual roots as soon and as solidly as possible. I've been going everywhere for my fulbright application material, interviewing practically every professor in the english department and begging the librarian to borrow catalogues of study in england from the amherst library, two of which books are on my desk now, making me wish you were still over there to read daily with me, bike, boat, and give cousel and conversation.

the one course I'm definite about in every respect is shakespeare which I have thfrisat at noon . . . miss dunn is a dynamo, the kind I most enjoy, and her interpretation is not only aesthetic, but political, social and historical in the sense of context . . . perhaps you would like to go to

1 – Date supplied from internal evidence.

her course with me this coming saturday (only you won't be able to sit next to me as we're seated rigidly in alphabetical order). in german I'm in a dubious state and still will have to see the head of the department again for further counsel . . . officially I've changed to the intermediate course in conversation, reading and composition, which I have with an attractive young female graduate student from yale[1] . . . only the class is conducted in german which I never heard at harvard, and I can answer questions in english inside my own head, but can't very well spiel forth in german since I haven't learned to form the words yet! all of which makes me feel very dense, even if I have a perfectly valid explanation for it all. I'll probably do abominably the first semester, but by pure perseverance and exposure I should pick up by the second. my most recent plan, (when I discovered that a sophomore in our house was taking the advanced lit course after only one year of college german,) is to arrange with the head of the department to audit his course in goethe[2] also, to do the work in it, and perhaps even contribute in conversation later in the year when I can say more erudite phrases than "ich bin müde" (which may be true, but is hardly inspiring) . . . so I would be spending about 20 hours on german a week, but instead of diverging efforts, I hope that after a semester of plodding, torturous work the two courses would help each other to the extent of my being able to converge in german lit. and be able to read with relative facility.

one good thing, today I had my conference with mr. gibian, my thesis advisor and it went better than I'd thought. we talked freely of graduate school plans (he got his degrees at harvard and recommended it highly . . . did his phd thesis in comparative lit. under harry levin![3]) and I think that I will do my thesis on several pairs of the "double" personality in dostoevsky . . . it's been mentioned in many critical works, but mr. gibian said he didn't think anywhere was it gone into in great and intense detail . . . the challenge is there, I just hope I can meet it . . . really, darling, I honestly can't picture myself in february, with a thesis "done". all the original thinking and research I've got to do between now and then is phenomenal; I sometimes feel as if I were battering my head up against a resistant wall of matter: time, space, ignorance. if only I can do these three things: dostoevsky, shakespeare, and german . . . and do them more

1–Marion Sonnenfeld (1928–99).

2–Paul Gerald Graham taught German 26, An Introduction to the Classical Literature of the Eighteenth Century.

3–Harry Tuchman Levin (1912–94), American literary critic and scholar of modernism and comparative literature.

than just adequately, I shall have fulfilled the main aims for this year. I don't have to worry about slighting social life completely, because I can get along in it perfectly well and happily . . . and now is the time to work.

funny incident: at supper tonight I sat regaling the table (forgive me) with the jellyroll incident, and a freshman gasped when I casually mentioned the perry: "my uncle is captain of the perry," she said. I crimsoned and said: "oh, there are two, I'm sure of it." it turned out that her uncle is (thank god) captain of the <u>other</u> (is it JF?) perry[1] and had told her the story of an attractive young ensign who boarded his boat by mistake last year, thinking it was the one he was stationed on in newport; at that point, I felt the seven-league long arm of coincidence grabbing me by the scruff of the neck again!

in a sense, I'm rather sure that my brown-haired personality will win out this year . . . gone is the frivolous giddy gilded creature who careened around corners at the wheel of a yellow convertible and stayed up till six in the morning because the conversation and bourbonandwater were too good to terminate . . . here is a serious, industrious, unextracurricular unswerving creature who, if you looked closer, might admit to being me! I felt strange at first in bermudas, knee socks and loafers instead of racy red heels, and parachute skirts, and an aura of chanel, –with books under my arm instead of a frenchy parasol, and girls everywhere, instead of men . . . but it is good for me, and this is really the most honest part of myself, I think. I still appreciate the screamingly blue sky, the turning trees, the softness of the sun on autumn green grass and rosecolored buildings, and inside me the love for extravagant and impulsive gesture is still there, only I work better when I go to bed early, and can think sharply from 8 to 1 in the morning when I've had a sober sleep . . . although if and when I get a creditable thesis done, I feel I'll deserve a champagne blast to celebrate . . . heck, wine will do . . . I'll put on my raffia skirt and scarlet o'hara shoes, and (please bring back my SP badge!) we'll be eccentric together!

oh, darling, I can stand anything for a year, and if I just catch up on sleep and can see you and study with you often, I'll be sustained . . . (do look in on warren and reuben brower[2] if you ever get a chance!)

I resolved this would be a short note, but I can't resist talking to you, even if it has to be on this satanic hicupping machine . . .

1–Gordon Lameyer referred to a ship called the *J. P. Perry* in a letter to SP, 3 June 1955; no US Navy ship of that name can be identified, however. Lameyer served on the USS *Perry*.

2–Probably Reuben A. Brower (1908–75), Cabot Professor of English Literature at Harvard University. Served as master of Adams House.

I will probably be tense, sometimes, but you will know that it is because the pressure of my thesis and the demand of my german course are everpresent, and I won't see light really till the second semester, and then I start preparing for the formidable comprehensives . . .

sky has gone from blue scalloped with dark leaves to all dark . . . with honeycombed light from windows across the way . . . laughter in the hall, surge of hot black coffee, a sudden unexpected rapport with a professor, smell of poignant sweet green grass, description of oxford in a catalogue . . . oh, life may be more solitary now as I plunge into the unique abysses of learning and thinking I've accepted, but I think I can be strong and love my work and not mind forgoing the convivial waste of time with a dilletante knitting, bridgeplaying, movie-going, group . . .

I may not be able to see you <u>during</u> the week, but you are there with me . . . in conversation, in my thoughts, as a sort of strong and symbolic sustenance for me . . . some of the snapshots I took of you in newport came out really well, and five of them are circling the border of my mirror now . . . so this makes seven yous in all that are in my room . . .

please love me this year, darling . . . I don't know how this year will work work out yet . . . and I'm a little scared and uncertain even . . . but more than anything I need you around, believing in me, while knowing my limitations, loving me, while knowing my weaknesses . . .

you are very dear
sylvia

TO *Aurelia Schober Plath*

Monday 27 September 1954[1]

TLS with envelope,
Indiana University

monday morning, 11 a.m.

dearest mother . . .

I am now sitting at my desk in my warm, colorful room typing on someone else's typewriter (mine's at the repair shop for a week and I feel lost without it) and looking out my one window into a lovely tangle of green leaves. at last I can write you more definitely about my program, since plans are at last settling out and I see the desirable and constructive outlines of a regular schedule of studying shining through this last week of chaos and countless faculty appointments.

1–Date supplied from postmark.

unfortunately I have my first runny twitchy cold of the season which threw off my period so I never had more than that one day . . . but as I just spent the frightful sum of $7 on nosedrops, pyrobenzamine and a big bottle of vitamins, I feel much better psychically with my little medicine cabinet handy. I think the dry climate and heat here is responsible for my cold (I've been keeping good bedtime as I'm a breakfast waitress six days a week) and so I bought a humidifyer for my radiator, and hope to keep the air breathable that way!

the house group is wonderful this year, as the snobby powerful senior group clique of last year has vanished, and our class is most friendly. mrs. kelsey is back and jane truslow is our house president, so you can imagine that the atmosphere is highly convivial. (this unfamiliar typewriter is rather unstable!)

my main bother this month is my fulbright application . . . I've had numerous interviews with the head of the graduate office and all my former professors, all of which have at least resulted in most gratifying results: elizabeth drew, newton arvin, and mary ellen chase have agreed to write my letters of recommendation, and as they are all very big names in their field internationally, I should have an advantage there that might compensate for my mental hospital record. I think I definitely am going to write dr. beuscher for my personal reference as I have to tell about mclean anyway, and a letter from her would serve the double purpose of eloquent recommendation and also of leaving no doubt as to the completeness of my cure. in addition to the fantastic red tape of the fulbright, all of which is due in a month, I am applying separately to both oxford and cambridge, my two choices for university, through the american association of university women since often fulbright recipients are arbitrarily placed and I want either of these two erudite institutions . . . so that makes about 12 letters of recommendation, 3 health exams, 12 statements of purpose, etc. . . . you can see how I'd love a private secretary! however, I hope to be able to have several photostats made of my three Big letters, so I can just send them out. fortunately my applications to harvard, yale, and columbia don't have to be in till the middle of winter! (harvard is the only place I really want to go!)

as for my classes: shakespeare (thursday, friday saturday: at noon) is magnificent under miss dunn, a sort of mrs. koffka in the english department . . . I am so wrapped up in her lectures that the hour leaps by on wings. my interview friday, with george gibian, was, as I said before, encouraging, and I'm busy making a bibliography for my reading, after which I'll plunge into skimming through all the works of fedor d. in preparation of a detailed study of his Double characters . . . mr. gibian is young, married, with three dear little boys (one pair of twins) and got his degree in comparative literature at harvard under harry levin, so he is most helpful.

german, as you may gather, gave me the most trouble. however, I feel I've worked out the best possible approach, given my appalling limitation of not speaking german at all, or writing it, or ever having heard it spoken in class! I am taking german 12 (the intermediate course in reading, conversation and composition) for credit . . . it meets five times a week, and is conducted in german, which will be a big handicap for me these first months. in addition I have permission to audit the literature course with mr. graham, the head of the german department, which is advanced and concerns goethe, schiller and lessing. the first class in this course met this morning, and I was amazed that I could understand mr. graham (he speaks very distinctly, of course) as well as I could . . . I could (except for technical words I didn't know) intellectually understand what he was saying for the most part, although I couldn't write the words down in german as my ear hasn't been trained to spell from dictation. it is my hope that by spending eight hours a week in german class, plus ten or twelve outside, that even if I do abominably in german 12 first semester, eventually my extra work will compensate so that I can contribute in articulate german in the literature course. naturally it is hard for my ego to have intelligent literary remarks to make and to be unable to articulate them in german . . . but I feel that I am not to blame for my lack of speaking ability, and that with constant listening, I will gradually begin to feel how german should sound and learn to say more than "Ich habe Deutsch gelesen, aber ich habe nicht Deutsch gesprochen!" also, I hope to be able to learn to write it correctly. the one amazing thing is that my pronunciation is as good as it is, since I have never heard or spoken german at all at harvard. so this will be gruelling, but I hope to improve rapidly with work.

this weekend I was pleasantly surprised to have clem and al goldstein turn up at our house . . . clem to take out lynn fisher.[1] al asked me to come out to supper with them saturday evening, and the pleasant break was good for me . . . I missed warren, naturally, and hope he will come up with them next time, as there is a charming girl in the house I would like him to meet . . . outwardly like margo in that she is tall and brownhaired, but much more softspoken, I think. I sent a letter down to warren via al.

1–Lynne Trowbridge Salisbury (1936–2008); B.A. 1957, history, Smith College.

gordon wrote a nice letter this week,[1] and I plan to see him up here next weekend, and we will both study together . . .

I hope to get over this cold soon, but my schedule is settling out well, so that I feel psychically happy, if physically nasty. My brownhaired personality is most studious, charming and earnest . . . I like it, and have changed back to colorless nailpolish for convenience and consistency . . . I'm so happy I dyed my hair back, even if it fades and I have to have it touched up once or twice more, I feel that this year, with my applying for scholarships, I would much rather look demure and discreet . . .

this letter has been much longer than it should have been, but I did want to tell you all these developments . . . and especially to ask you to take good care of yourself for my sake . . . and to send you my very best love . . . .

your own sivvy

TO *Aurelia Schober Plath*

Friday 1 October 1954[2] ALS (postcard), Indiana University

Friday – 5 p.m.

dearest mother . . .

greetings to you in your new temporary dwelling,[3] and heartfelt sympathy if it is as sweltering and damp there as it is here! although its not ideal weather for sinus victims, I gladly left the infirmary in time for classes this morning, feeling a bit groggy, but infinitely better for all the shots of penicillin & cocaine sprays. I was sorry to miss classes, but I can catch up in German reading this weekend – I work about twice the time that the other 9 do, but will get my reward by 2nd semester, I hope. George Gibian, my thesis advisor, and I, are getting along extremely well & we both are excited about my topic: Aspects of the Double which, now that I am beginning reading is no longer the ominous monster it once was! best of all – Gordon came up to visit me at the infirmary Wednesday afternoon for three lovely hours – I'd called him just 5 minutes before he'd planned to call me: sort of psychic. girls in house are all awfully nice & I feel that a good year is beginning, with both feet firmly on ground – even if I do not get a good mark in German (it is so hard) I feel I should

1–Gordon Lameyer to SP, 23 September 1954; held by Lilly Library.
2–Date supplied from postmark.
3–Sent to ASP, c/o New England Medical Center, Bennett Street, Boston.

by dint of hard work, be able to speak it & write a little by 2nd sem. – then, if I were good enough, I'd love to switch to the Goethe course which I'm auditing in addition this sem. Hope your tests all show you to be a paragon of potential longevity – Gordon joins me in sending love

xx
Siv

TO *Aurelia Schober Plath*

Monday 4 October 1954[1] ALS (postcard), Indiana University

Monday – 2:30 pm

Dear Mother . . .

Whew! Say hot! Hope that by now you are home from hospital: does "bed rest" mean you'll be at home in bed & not teach the rest of the year, or what? let me know if I can be of any use whatever. One thing, I'm desperate for cotton clothes – all I have up here is woolens, & wonder if you or grammy (when she comes home) could make up a box of all my cotton jerseys & my 2 linen dresses: brown & black print and peacock-blue one – if I wear my woollens now I shall both suffocate & wear them all out by February! Gordon was up all this last weekend & it was nice to study together – Warren called last night, & I've got him a date with a lovely freshman in our house – Kathy Preston[2] – this coming weekend. as yet, I'm pretty tired from working on all my back work & scholarship application blanks & jobs, & am looking forward to Mountain Day this week sometime in which to catch up on sleep & homework – I'll be glad to get everything squared away – although I'll have another round of blanks to attend to come Christmas vacation – how I'd love a private secretary! I do hope you can arrange to have a good rest at home – and only wish you could somehow arrange to go to florida, arizona or california to recuperate with relatives or friends out there! Please keep me posted on your health reports!

Lots of Love
Sivvy

<handwritten on address side of postcard>

PS. – Rejection blow from Ladies Home Journal softened by personal note asking me to try again. Hope they realize what they're getting into!

1–Date supplied from postmark.

2–Kathleen Preston Knight (1936–2013); B.A. 1958, sociology and anthropology, Smith College.

TO *Aurelia Schober Plath*

Tuesday 5 October 1954[1] TLS on Smith College Press Board letterhead, Indiana University

Mountain Day

Dearest mother . . .

Today being Mountain Day, I bade most of my housemates goodbye as they headed for Yale and settled down to the blissful task of catching up on the backwork I missed last week. This day came just in the nick of time, and I plan to get caught up in German, Shakespeare, and thesis reading, so that this weekend I can really enjoy the feeling of doing current assignments!

Thought I'd enclose the little corrected example of my first German "composition",[2] since it is drawn from one of our family anecdotes. My task of writing it was most difficult, as I'd never written any German before and had to refer constantly to the lovely big Cassell's German dictionary[3] which I've bought. I'm so glad I'm taking this Intermediate Course; as I said, it's hard for me, very hard, and I spend twice as much time on it as the others have to, but I'm going to learn German or perish in the process . . . if only I'd spoken it at home!

I have asked to do the papers and participate in class in the German literature course I'm auditing, and can understand him pretty well, but can't as yet say a word in class . . . I just don't have the vocabulary or feeling for sentence structure to ennable me to express my intellectual ideas, which is very frustrating. We are now reading Lessing's "Minna Von Barnhelm", and although it's tedious to look up thirty words per page, the subtle characterizations and word nuances are rather enjoyable.

I'm still working on scholarship applications. Saw Miss Mensel, who informed me that my whole scholarship is the Mrs. Prouty one, so I wrote a long note to Mrs. P. today, thanking her and giving her the latest news. Also wrote Cantors at long last. I'm awfully tempted not to apply to Yale grad school, although it's supposed to be excellent in English, because they require the graduate record exam (which Harvard and Columbia don't) and it's just alot of bother. However, every now and then I get scared that if I only apply to Oxford, Cambridge and Harvard, nothing may come through, and I'll be left. Or, on the other hand, that if I apply

1–Date supplied from internal evidence.

2–Possibly 'Wie Ich Einmal Mein Kleinen Bruder Neckte'; held by Lilly Library.

3–*Cassell's New German and English Dictionary: With a Phonetic Key to Pronunciation* (New York: Funk and Wagnall's, 1939); SP's copy held by Smith College.

also to Yale and Columbia, that I may be offered ten $1000 scholarships all at once, out of malicious fate!

Have a wonderful idea of how to get clothes up here: Warren is driving up Saturday afternoon: why not call him up to stop at home and pick up the linens and jerseys, etc. . . . will save bother and postage! Meanwhile, do let me know your plans for the year, because I do want to be sure you are happy and well cared-for!

Much love,
Sivvy

TO *Gordon Lameyer*

Tuesday 5 October 1954[1] TLS, Indiana University

<typed on Street & Smith Publications Inter Office Memorandum letterhead, with heading>

TO	The Ensign	FROM	The English Major (please note double entendre)
SUBJECT	Cabbages and Kings	DATE	Mountain Day

Sky being requisite shade of blue, sun being benevolent, yellow leaves falling in appropriate quantity on black mirror of Paradise, and chapel bells ringing: my last (sob) Mountain Day. And just in time too, I am inclined to add. I went to bed at the incredibly early hour of 11.30 last night without having done my German paper, just because I was <u>sure</u> it had to be Mt. Day. 2000 Smith women can't be wrong. It was.

Today is lovely: a generous wastebasket of all this-and-that: the things I've been meaning to do for the last three weeks: catching up in all courses, writing letters of various natures to my favorite people, applying for my pyramiding stack of more application blanks, u.s.w. I am applying for blanks from Yale today, although that is the only college that requires the Graduate Record Exam which I am highly tempted Not To Take, but I'll have the application blanks on hand, anyhow. I really don't want to bother applying to Columbia either, because getting four letters of recommendation, health certificates and transcripts for each college is a hell of a Bother. However, always comes up the nagging thought: what if nothing at all comes through if I only apply to Harvard and Oxford and Cambridge, in my snobbish intellectual pride, and what if none of them

1–Date supplied from internal evidence.

want me??? On the other hand, just for the malicious pleasure of fate, I may be offered ten scholarships of $1000 each all at the same time. Jolly prospect, wot?

Hello hello hello again. It was good having you up here last weekend. Everybody who met you told me specially afterwards how charming they all thought you were. I have, to my delight, fixed Warren up with Kathy Preston for this coming weekend, and am looking forward to having Sunday breakfast with him . . . he is such a dear! I do hope Pat and John[1] go out together soon. I am most fond and admiring of both of them! I really would like to fix Joe or Reese or someone up for the weekend after that . . . we're having a great jazz band and dance at the house on Sunday, I think, and if you could let me know ahead of time, it might be fun to help two more people meet! Ah me, I shall start a dating service . . . it gives me such vicarious pleasure to see couples coupled!

They have discovered that I am Anemic because of sinus. So I am taking iron, and feel very suddenly strong and ironic. I went out for crew practice for the first time in a year-and-a-half yesterday, and after I got the feel of the boat back, it was extremely good. Our 2nd crew is ridiculously unpracticed and heterogeneous, but it does me no end of good to be out on the water in a shell . . . the feeling of pulling hard and skimming along in a unanimous sweat of stroking is really potent!

I have rashly offered to write papers and "participate" in the German class I'm auditing, so out of pride, I'll have to keep it up . . . it will be good practice, but arduous at first. Well, isn't everything?

I feel like writing poetry and stories most in fall and spring, and it is so damn frustrating not to be able to allow myself to go off on a drunken timeless Thesaurus Binge . . . I feel like a genie (not "us") stuffed into an Alladin's lamp that is too rigid and small . . . I think I'll explode next spring! Oh, to be in England!

Love to you, my love . . .
from your Smith harem . . .
Concubine, white, age 22
(well, almost)

1–John A. Dugger (1924–2014); see Gordon Lameyer to SP, 29 [October] 1954; held by Lilly Library. The original letter was misdated by Lameyer as of 29 November 1954.

TO *Gordon Lameyer*

Friday 8 October 1954[1] — TLS on Smith College Press Board letterhead, Indiana University

friday evening

dear gordon . . .

and a sleepy friday evening it is. a week of finishing up fulbright application and oxford admission blanks: just put on the final touches tonight, and on monday will go up to graduate office to make sure all my letters of recommendation, health certificates and transcripts are in, in good form, and then to hell with applications till january!

every night I vow to go to bed early it seems that some imp of the peverse manages to fix it otherwise: housemeeting to elect new house president, as jane truslow has to take the place as head of house of reps (one of the Big 4 offices) since the president[2] is leaving smith to get married, then fire drills at unseasonable times, and we having to run out-of-doors to freeze in pajamas at 2 a.m., and so forth.

you'll be glad to hear that I've been out on the water crewing three times this week, position 2. this morning a white frost mist was blowing, and it was all very cold and invigorating. we won our first house race with tenney[3] this afternoon (we're only 2nd crew) and I'm sure it was because I wore your sailor hat, which I just love!

I want to ask a big favor of you about next weekend: I learned today that the first chapter of my thesis is due friday, october 22, and this shocking information makes me beg of you to come up late next saturday afternoon If Possible, instead of friday night: I'll be in a much more sociable mood if I can enjoy you solidly for saturday supper and the sunday afternoon jazz concert if you'll just leave me in my grubby solitude friday and most of saturday. perhaps you could persuade joe to drive up saturday in late afternoon with the lure of a date, or some such worldly chattel; please do realize that the actual process of writing the first draft of my "golyadkin" chapter is going to be fantastically difficult, as I have to do so much reading and hard thinking in these next two weeks, so that the weekend you come up will be the only time I'll have a chance to write things down, and for that part of it, I do need to be alone and conscious of

1–Date supplied from internal evidence.

2–Probably Ann Doney Roen (1933–); B.A. 1955, art, Smith College.

3–Tenny House, a cooperative residential house for Smith College students, at 156 Elm Street, Northampton.

nothing else, which is not quite possible when you're there, because I am too tempted to talk or look at you suggestively!

anyhow, do write and tell me if you'll bring anyone, what time sat. you can come, and if pat and john are got together yet! warren is coming up this saturday with one of his roommates, and I've fixed them both up.

I am very happy in spite of the fact that I have so much work to do. if I can keep barely treading water in german, and do a good thesis, all will be well. wish me luck, darling!

much love,
sylvia

TO *Gordon Lameyer*

Sunday 10 October 1954[1] — TLS on Smith College Press Board letterhead, Indiana University

sunday night

dearest gordon . . .

home now growing cosily to be the carrel in the library . . . that corner labeled mine, which is on the same convenient level with dostoevsky, hoffman, psych journals and the ladies lavatry and a drinking fountain which, I hope, will never run dry, lest I take it too symbolically!

came back to house tonight with german undone because I'd gotten so fascinated with reading about the doubles in hoffman that I couldn't stop as scheduled, and now just want to read and read on my thesis topic: supreme irony, the main article of importance in my field is written in german by otto rank,[2] and I can't even translate a paragraph of the damn thing: mr. gibian, as I perhaps said, took notes on it for me, but I'm still hoping to get a complete english translation.

to bed early last night and up rested at 8.30 this morning for a change to practice crew in the rain, with warren and his date, kathy preston, looking on. the more practice I get the better I feel, and if I am supremely audacious, will try out for senior crew this spring!

tonight was damp and foggy, with the lamps hanging each in its nimbus of blurred light, and the sound of water dripping from sodden leaves. soft and fertile, everything, and in between one waking and another I think of you with love, and want you to know it, even if the note is brief, for each articulate message represents a hundred others unspoken.

1–Date supplied from internal evidence.
2–Otto Rank, 'Der Doppelgänger', *Imago* 3 (1914), 97–164.

your last letter was really dear, and I have read it several times over with increasing pleasure. I want you to be proud of me too for having the discipline (which you help me to have so wonderfully) to work hard and enjoy it, without feeling in the least resentful: this, after all, is thinking, discovering, and inner living: outer living I have to say is more important in the life scheme, precisely because I am so inclined to introversion, and therefore must overbalance toward actual living in order to come out anywhere near even! I do hope you will not be too inconvenienced by coming up saturday! it will be doubly (whoops! there goes that word again!) delightful to see you then, having worked so much in preparation for your coming!

I think I will write an adolescent story about doubles after I'm through with all this: every incident in my life begins to smack of the mirror image: nancy sitting opposite me in the carrels, wearing also a pink shirt and gray skirt, the two perrys getting mixed up, dick linden[1] driving you to linden street, lameyer being on la mer, and so forth!

please know how I like knowing your presence is omnipresent even if not here present, and make me a present of it next saturday if you are pleased to please the present writer who now presents to you with pleasure her everpresent

LOVE
YOUR OWN sp

TO *Aurelia Schober Plath*

Tuesday 12 October 1954[2]

TLS with envelope on Smith College Press Board letterhead, Indiana University

tuesday morning

dearest mother . . .

I was extremely happy to get your newsy letter today, and glad to hear you sound so cheerful! I really feel that the girl I got Warren last weekend was exceptional, tall, attractive and intelligent, and I hope he liked her well enough to ask her out again. as for al, I don't know what he expects . . . I got him a date with a most pretty sophomore in the

1–Probably Richard L. Linden, a 1948 graduate of the Bradford High School in Wellesley. Linden reported to the destroyer USS *Perry* on 24 December 1953.
2–Date supplied from postmark.

house, but his personality is somehow sodden . . . I don't know how to explain it exactly: I like him, but there is something so depressing in just being with him, for I don't think he has any real "joie de vivre", or whatever it is that makes someone look alive and vital . . . I felt that the girl was the one to be sorry for and not al! I don't know if I like the effect he has on warren . . at dinner sunday, when they talked at all, they talked in such low murmurs that I could hardly hear them, and I don't know how I can get warren to be, as you say, sunny and lively . . . he is so vague and negative too much of the time . . . I wish he knew how to have fun and to make others have fun, because it is depressing to try to liven someone who just doesn't respond . . . and al, with his grave, expressionless face, was enough to make anyone feel gloomy. I missed a strong sense of competence and initiative in both of them . . . I practically had to tell them step by step what to do and where to go saturday night! but I think kathy liked warren, and hope he realizes how fine a girl she really is.

naturally this problem concerns me, of warren's social savoir faire: there is a healthy middle road of partying and moviegoing and group fun which is not superficial, but stimulating and gay, and I wish he would find that life is not either an extreme of hard lonely introverted work or artificial gregarious extroverted binges: he needs to build his ego up by going to many social events, parties, and so on, and growing to feel confident of his attractiveness and competence in any social gathering so that it becomes second nature for him to be gracious and at ease, and then he can afford to cut down on social life, if he really wants to, not out of fear of being gauche, but because he knows he could handle situations if he chose to do so. I do think he should go out for at least one extra-curricular activity that involves group participation . . . he's not taking that extra course, and should get outside the narrow circle of his roommates, who have been with him from time immemorial. also, he should simply set about learning techniques of social conversation, how and when to manage and direct group talk, and so on . . . I wish he could take public speaking. I know that when I went out for extra-curricular activities in my sophomore and junior years I found to my amazement that I could be elected popularly, and my confidence in myself grew constructively. now I think it is the time for me to concentrate on the hard year ahead, and I do so, although it means sacrificing the hours spent in pleasant frivolity over coffee and bridge . . . but I feel that the work I'm doing now is most important for the last push of my senior year . . . and I know how to have happy gay times when I really want to.

I am really concerned about warren, and wish you could look at him objectively from your nearer viewpoint and perhaps analyse the gaps in his social life and advise him about them. I wish I could help, because I feel that what he needs is chiefly practice in how to entertain others (and himself) and assert himself articulately and with firmness. I practically have to prod him to get him to say what he would like to do, and question him specifically to get him to say how or what he feels. perhaps some respected doctor or social advisor who is close enough to see behind the honorable facade of warren's work and outward conduct could point out more specific and constructive ways to develop in warren an articulate, active and participating delight in life . . . a sense of "fun", which I think has been a family weakness . . . . I know that underneath the blazing jaunts in yellow convertibles to exquisite restaurants I am really regrettably unoriginal, conventional and puritanical, basically, but I needed to practice a certain healthy bohemianism for a while to swing away from the gray-clad, basically-dressed, brown-haired, clock-regulated, responsible, salad-eating, water-drinking, bed-going, economical, practical girl that I had become . . . and that's why I needed to associate with people who were very different from myself. my happiest times were those entertaining in the apartment, where I could merrily create casseroles and conversation for small intimate groups of people I like very much. and that served as a balance in the midst of the two extremes. but I think warren has a good deal to learn from boys like phil or even richard sassoon (for his familiar roommates, I think, are so used to him that they make no new demands, and only, like al, help entrench him in his introverted habits), and not with an eye to being like them, but rather trying to incorporate their best qualities and thereby make himself a more versatile and vital person. I am really quite hopeful that you will write me your ideas on all this, and that somehow we can prevent our favorite boy from going on more and more in his outwardly respectable rut. I would like to see him go out west, or to alaska this summer with someone other than clem or al . . . he'll get so accustomed to their being there to support him by their presence that he won't have the new and difficult challenges he should have, and since he'll be living with them for three years more, I feel strongly that he should have a change of scene both in personalities and ways of life. if only I go to england next year (small hope) I wish he could come over the summer after this and that we could travel around europe a bit together . . . so much better than staying in the cambridge womb all our lives! it would do us both good to exchange our allegorical lives (where everything is in a prosaic one-to-one ratio) for a vivid symbolic existence where the lvevels of meaning are multiple, with always new ones to be discovered.

only do understand how I love warren and want to help him so he can grow and develop to a competent human being (not one who couldn't even make his own breakfast because he "didn't know where the things were"!) frankly, I think he needs to be kicked out on his own to shift for himself this next summer . . . somewhere where it was not always certain that meals would be served him and that the same roof would be over his head. I am a firm believer in learning to be inventive and independent the hard way . . . with little or no money, and I hope I can continue to investigate life's chances and try to be so, even though inside I long for comforting security and someone to blow my nose for me, just the way most people do. I was proud of learning to cook and take care of bills this summer, but that is only a beginning: if only england would by some miracle come through, I would be forced shivering into a new, unfamiliar world, where I had to forge anew friends and a home for myself, and although such experiences are painful and awkward at first, I know, intellectually, that they are the best things to make one grow . . . always biting off just a slight bit more than you chewed before, and finding to you amazement that you can, when it comes right down to it, chew that too!

you must be getting bored with my fumblings at philosophizing, but I feel the hour was worth it, because I want you to know what I'm thinking about, how I love every member of our family dearly, and want to make you all proud of me by being a versatile, responsible, gay person.

right now it seems as if it is impossible that I ever have a thoughful well-written thesis done, because now all reading is apparently unrelated, (except that it is all about doubles, and very exciting in itself,) and thoughts are yet in embryo . . . the rough draft of my first chapter is due in a week from this friday, and I am wondering if I can say anything original or potential in it, as I feel always that I have not enough incisive thinking ability . . . the best thing is that the topic itself intrigues me, and that no matter how I work on it, I shall never tire of it . . . it is specific, detailed, and with a wealth of material . . . but of course I don't know yet what precise angle I'll handle it from . . . I'm taking the double in Dostoevsky's second novelette "The Double" and Ivan Karamazov (with his Smerdyakov and Devil) in "The Brothers" as cases in point, and think I shall categorize the type of "double" minutely, contrasting and comparing the literary treatment as it corresponds to the intention of psychological presentation . . . in conjunction with this, I've been reading stories all about doubles, twins, mirror images, and shadow reflections. Your book gift "The Golden Bough",[1] comes in handy, as it has an excellent chapter on "the soul as shadow and reflection".

german is as always terribly difficult. I don't know if I'll ever be able to really hear it understandingly or to speak it.

do write often, and give my love to all.

your own,
sivvy

p.s. Thanks for clothes and apples – !

<drawing of female head with smiling face>

TO *Aurelia Schober Plath*

Thursday 14 October 1954[2] — TLS with envelope, Indiana University

thursday night

dearest mother . . .

don't you think of what those envious people say when they see you lounging around at your ease: you know much better than they what you are working to prevent; I imagine Dick feels much the same way about going to bed early---outsiders find it hard to imagine the need of taking extra care when nothing seems outwardly wrong.

tomorrow I have my first hour exam, in german, so this will only be a note. I was really discouraged this week, as I work so hard and only get low B's, so I talked with my instructor after my two hour evening section last night. she was awfully understanding, and offered to give me an extra hour a week conversation drill, because I just can't speak . . . and I have such trouble writing my quiz answers in german . . . the answers are right, but the words, order, and genders are all wrong, as I just never wrote a thing before. she advised me to keep on auditing the literature course, so this means that I'll be spending about 20 hours a week on german . . . I do feel so dense.

I was glad to realize that the very blue, aching mood I've been in for the past few days was due to my oncoming period (several weeks late, as usual, thrown off by my cold, I guess.) I feel much more cheerful now

1–James George Frazer, *The Golden Bough* (New York: Macmillan, 1952); SP's copy, received for Christmas 1953; held by Smith College. The part to which she refers is chapter 18, section 3.

2–Date supplied from postmark.

that the horrid first day is over . . . I couldn't sleep for the pain and had to take codeine . . . so annoying. at any rate, with my vitamins and iron, I am getting along fine, now. I've been out for crew several times, and luxuriated in the exercise.

went up to have a talk with miss mensel yesterday, and she was just dear. I was beginning to feel concerned about senior expenses, and all the college and house dues coming up, and so decided to get a few little jobs to cover some of my spending money. I am now going to spent 1½ hours each monday afternoon reading aloud to a blind man,[1] starting next week. I also am going babysitting twice next week, and spent two hours today proofreading copy for the college directory. miss mensel said that I was slated for a gift of $10 from the "riotous living" fund, which I was most interested to learn about. I decided inwardly that when I start earning money, I'd like to send at least $10 a year for miss mensel to give some scholarship girl to spend on a play, or put toward a weekend away, or something impractical like silver dance slippers . . . they have been so wonderful to me! she also said that I shouldn't leave my $50 deposit for scholarships as they will ask me to, but that I will need it to cover my senior expenses (which is a help).

mary ellen chase has been just wonderful about my fulbright application . . . she is going to write both to oxford and cambridge for me, with miss drew, and from what she says, she seems to have no doubts about my getting in! she says the english universities will give me time to write, travel, and are nowhere as rigid with planning time as america's enormous grad schools, and from her accounts of cambridge, england, I just languished with wishful thinking!

as for my thesis topic . . . it's very simple: just a study of two specific examples of the Double personality in Dostoevsy's books: the first novel (<u>The Double</u>) is about an introvert clerk who creates his own Double in his mind, which turns out to have all the hypocritical, suave, social graces necessary to getting on in the business world, and ends by ousting his own originator from his job, love, and life. The other example is Ivan Karamazov, whose distorted physical half-brother mimics and carries out Ivan's hypothetical theories by murdering Ivan's father. In connection with this topic, I'm reading several stories by E. T. A. Hoffman; <u>Dorian Gray</u>, by Oscar Wilde; <u>Dr. Jekyll and Mr. Hyde</u>; Poe's <u>William Wilson</u>; Freud, Frazer, Jung, and others . . . all fascinating stuff about the ego as

1 – SP read to William Dodge Gray (1878–1958), who lived at 22 Round Hill, Northampton; professor of history, Smith College, 1907–46.

symbolized in reflections (mirror and water), shadows, twins . . . dividing off and becoming an enemy, or omen of death . . . or a warning conscience . . . or a means by which one denies the power of death (eg, by creating the idea of the soul as the deathless double of the mortal body). My thesis, as I see it now, will only mention the philosophic and psychological theories (there are thousands) and will deal specifically with the type of Double in these two novels of D., and the literary methods of presenting them.

Several professors are most interested in this topic, which gives me a great responsibility for clear thinking and lucid expression . . . had a conference with a charming young english prof[1] I'd never met before, and he gave me some of his notes on the subject, and some bibliography references, and was very encouraging . . . .

needless to say, this year will be just hard work. but, except for my treading water precariously in german, I Love to Study! I am so happy with my brown hair and my studious self! I really can concentrate for hours on end, and am hoping that I can justify my topic by doing it well.

be good to yourself, dear mother, and know how much I look forward to seeing you well and happy when I come home thanksgiving . . . I hope this year will be an unclouded thanksgiving for all of us!

best love to all,

sivvy

TO *Aurelia Schober Plath*

Monday 18 October 1954[2] ALS (postcard), Indiana University

Monday, Oct. 18

Dear mother . . .

It seems almost impossible that only a bare month has gone by since my arrival here – I feel that I've been here for aeons – my first draft of one thesis chapter is due Friday, which puts heat on, as I have to start outlining it (20 pages) tonight. Gordon & I had a good weekend – he came over & studied the night of the "hurricane",[3] Fri. (we had early curfew, because of the "storm"!) – I studied Sat. aft. while he socialized at Amherst &

1–According to SP's calendar, on this day she met Daniel Aaron from 4–5 p.m. Daniel Aaron (1912–2016); English professor, Smith College, 1939–72; director of the freshman English course (English 11) taught by SP, 1957–8.

2–Date supplied from postmark.

3–Hurricane Hazel made landfall in North Carolina on 15 October 1954 and progressed towards Massachusetts that day.

then joined him (we hitchhiked as we had no car) over there for an Italian spaghetti dinner – I had the happy thought of visiting Ruthie, and did so, with Gordy, for about 1 hr. – good, as she was lonesome because of Art's 1st weekend not there – Sunday was intimate & friendly in the house, & I'm succeeding in getting Gordon to be a part of the group – delightful dinner-table talk, & an afternoon jazz concert in the livingroom – plan to fix up two dates for a friend of Gordy's next week – spent 2 hours reading aloud this afternoon to dear, old, blind, pathetic ancient history ex-prof at Smith – my regular Monday p.m. job from now on – earned $2.30 proof reading last week –

love,
sivvy

Hope you're happy & getting better every day!

TO *Aurelia Schober Plath*

Sunday 24 October 1954[1] TLS with envelope, Indiana University

sunday morning

dearest mother . . .

it is a beautiful clear blue sunday morning, and after ten blissful hours of sleep last night I feel again that I can cope with anything, and realize afresh how sleep and good health are essential to a lively, intelligent personality.

mrs. freeman, ruthie, and two of her roommates came over friday and sat around in my attractive room (which you must see in all its charm before the year is out---perhaps again for spring weekend on float night) and then drove me back to amherst with them where I had dinner with mary bonneville (she is such a pathetic, ugly, lonely figure, I think) and waited for gordon to arrive at his hospitable fraternity house. he brought a friend[2] for whom I'd fixed up two dates in the course of the weekend.

friday night I stayed up extremely late typing the 30 pages of my first draft of the golyadkin chapter which I passed in to mr. gibian yesterday. ultimately this chapter will only be 20 pages, but I wanted to cram everything in, so that it will be easier to condense artistically later. mr. gibian was very pleased, (even though I told him the draft was

1 – Date supplied from postmark.
2 – According to SP's calendar, this was John Stamper.

rough stream-of-conscious comments only,) that I'd gotten something substantial in so early, and I'm waiting till he reads it to react . . . perhaps it's all abominably bad, but I secretly don't think so and feel I have some good embryo ideas which I'll develop and revise as I go on reading. the next 3 weeks will be devoted to the ivan Karamazov part.

really, mother, I am so happy and fortunate in my topic: it lends itself to writing, and is so fascinating that my interest will never become dulled, no matter how I work on it continually. except for a brilliant long essay on "the double" by otto rank, no book has been devoted to it, and mr. gibian says he thinks it would be a good topic for a graduate thesis or even for a book! I have fallen in love with it, and feel reasonably sure that if I revise and rethink I can write[1] a good thesis.

this next week I'll catch up on all the subjects I've neglected for my thesis. my shakespeare course is fascinating, and if you come up on a friday in the spring, I want you to hear the saturday lecture with me: you'd love the vivid, whitehaired, fiery miss dunn! we've read richards 2 & 3 so far, and I have to devote next weekend to reading for the exam. german is, and no doubt always will be, very hard. if I continue to get B- I will consider myself lucky. my ideas are A Ideas but my writing (which I've never done before) is C writing . . . the grammar and sentence order is so hard. however, the young fraulein sonnenfeld is very nice and is giving me an extra hour a week in reading conversation. I had to cut the german literature classes this week because of writing golyadkin, but hope to start up again tomorrow, keeping with it on the off chance that I could switch courses midsemester.

one very nice thing has happened this week. I don't know if I told you, but the brilliant young jewish writer and critic alfred kazin[2] (wrote "on native grounds" and "a walker in the city") has a chair here for a year, and I felt badly, since he was in the english department, that I'd have no chance of coming in contact with him. then the alumnae quarterly conveniently assigned me an interview[3] with him.

he is notoriously hard to see and even more impossible to interview, but after about 20 phone calls I finally persuaded him to give me 5 minutes. at first, he was very brusque, and then he asked me a few direct questions about myself. as soon as he found out that I was working my way through

1–'and rethink ~~that~~ I can write' appears in the original.
2–Alfred Kazin (1915–98); William Allan Neilson Research Professor, Smith College, 1954–5. Kazin taught short story writing (English 347) and the twentieth-century novel (English 417) completed by SP, 1954–5.
3–Sylvia Plath, 'The Neilson Professor', *Smith Alumnae Quarterly*, Fall 1954, 12.

college and had a few things published and wanted to teach and write, he became charming and said he'd thought I was just another pampered smith baby like the rest. he offered to criticize my writing, invited me to audit a class friday, and told me to come back and talk to him again because he thought I was interesting!

well, when I went to his writing class of 10, I was delighted with him, but appalled at the weak, mealy-mouthed apathy of the girls, who either were just too scared or just too stupid to have opinions. as an auditor, I found it hard to keep quiet. finally, at the end of the class, mr. kazin turned to me and said: "well, what do <u>you</u> think?" I told him, and he said, "why don't you join the class. I think we need you!" I was really thrilled. the chance to write for a semester under such a man, and to have him "invite" me, while countless other girls have wanted to get into his small course, seemed rare and wonderful. I thought it over carefully, and decided that it is much more developing for my character to maybe get two B's in my other courses while grinding my rusty writing gears into motion under mr. kazin than it would be to rigidly strive for A's and sacrifice the rare opportunities of life: mr. kazin will not happen again, and it will be good for me to have the impetus of his criticism while starting out again . . . I can apply it to the things I want to write this coming summer.

the thing about writing is not to talk, but to do it, no matter how bad or even mediocre it is, the process and production is the thing, not the sitting and theorizing about how one should write ideally, or how well one could write if one really wanted to or had the time.

as mr. kazin told me: "you don't write to support yourself; you work to support your writing."

I've thought over your advice about jobs, and have narrowed down to one afternoon a week reading to mr. gray, a delightfully dickensian old blind man who was an ancient history teacher at smith for thirty years or so. right now I am reading from a history book about the hellenic age. claiborne had the job last year, so I feel I'm carrying on a good work.

mr. gibian is the best kind of thesis adviser I could have . . . went over to talk to him yesterday, and sat happily holding one of his twin baby boys on my lap while he held the other, and discussed dostoevsky while the baby gurgled happily and pulled my hair. it is amusing that I'm writing on the double, while my adviser has twins.

gordon is up this weekend, as I said, but I've got to discipline myself and get to bed early and work, even though he's here. it is unfortunate that he insists on coming for three whole days, because I just can't afford to give up reading for more than one evening or afternoon, and my work is so interesting that I don't like to stop. however, he is perfectly glad to study with me, although I can't do any really creative concentrated work while he's around.

I look forward to seeing warren next weekend, and am glad he's taking out kathy again.

feel very beatific and birthdayish: gordon gave me a lovely light brown cashmere cardigan, mrs. lameyer sent a gay red-and-white striped apron, and ira[1] mailed up a lovely light blue brooks brothers shirt to match the pink one, while nancy gave me three lovely pieces of brown and aqua pottery like the pitcher I gave you once . . .

hope you continue to get fat and healthy . . . and please do demand that you don't take business machine job . . . you've a good excuse now . . .

lots of love
sivvy

TO *Gordon Lameyer*

Wednesday 27 October 1954 — TLS in greeting card,[2] Indiana University

October 27

Dearest Gordon . . .

A note to you on The Day that I begin my 23rd year (sounds so impressive that!) As I look out through the yellowing leaves at the gray rain, I am tempted to borrow trouble in the way of metaphors and liken myself to an agéd eagle[3] who has just been run over by time's wingéd chariot[4] . . . but enough . . .

I am thinking of you, and wanting to tell you about paradoxes in me which are hard for anyone to understand, even if they know me as well as you do, which is as well as can be, almost. I am serene and happy, despite the heavy pressure of thesis, German, Shakespeare, et. al. (all of which is really a "labor of love", you know) . . . and one of the main reasons I am so interiorly placid is not because I've found God or learned Yogi, but rather because I am learning how to select between the important and unimportant things in my life, to make difficult choices, to relegate

1–Ira O. Scott, Jr (1918–2002), American; instructor at Harvard University, 1953–5; dated SP, summer 1954.

2–Panda Prints card designed by Rosalind Welcher.

3–Probably a reference to T. S. Eliot, 'Ash Wednesday' I, 6.

4–Probably a reference to Andrew Marvell, 'To His Coy Mistress'.

clamoring demands on my time to a sort of valued graded system . . . all of which is yet more of an ideal, than an achievement.

However, you are one of the strongest sustaining forces I have . . just knowing you are there (be it in Boston or Bombay) somewhere in the same world, feeling as you say you do about me, that is the important thing for me at present. And this feeling is mine also ("Dare I name it?" as Clark-Gable-Butler would say)[1] and very strong, yet consistent with my apparently difficult attitude about your visiting me as often as you would like.

In order to make ends meet this year, both psychic and financial, I literally have to hibernate for about eight months, and really I enjoy it, as long as I know you're there, like the genie in Alladin's lamp, to incandesce my days when they become dulled. I know you want to see me whenever you can, but I also know you understand I work better, can write and think better, when I am alone, grubby and asocial, without the conflicting loyalties which your presence arouses. Somehow, when I know you're around, I perversely want to throw concentration to the winds, and that, at this point, cannot be. Only remember even though I keep disciplining myself to see you more rarely than you wish, that underneath I love you VERY VERY MUCH . . . and it's that feeling, and not the daily demands that stoically regulate and curb its manifestation, that matters . . . nicht wahr?

Affectionately,
Sylvia

TO *Aurelia Schober Plath*

Tuesday 2 November 1954[2] ALS (postcard), Indiana University

Tuesday 5:30 p.m.

Dear mother . . .

Thank you so much for the delicious cookies – it's so comforting to nibble on them while studying. I hope Warren told you that I shared my tasty birthday cake with about twenty girls in the house – all of whom pronounced it excellent! I hope that your taking up teaching will not prove too arduous – my blind professor, Mr. Gray, is very sympathetic about

1–A reference to Clark Gable as Rhett Butler in the 1939 cinematic adaptation of Margaret Mitchell, *Gone with the Wind* (1936).
2–Date supplied from postmark.

your ulcers, as he has had them himself – and he showed me a cookbook by Jordan called "Good Food for Bad Stomachs"[1] which contained many tasty recipes. I do feel that this dear old Dickensian man looks most forward to my Monday afternoons with him: we get along very well. It was wonderful to have Warren up here this weekend. I thought he looked astoundingly handsome and mature – and so did the other girls. As far as I'm concerned, he and Kathy look as if they were brother & sister! I enjoyed having coffee with him Sunday morning & a good talk. Edwin, the professor from M.I.T., drove up Sunday afternoon and left after supper (he is very peculiar and archaic, but amusing.) Gordon called & we had a lovely talk – it seems the colorshots we took of each other this summer came out beautifully[2] – I can't wait to see them when he comes up the 13th – Shakespeare exam this Friday, for which I'm deserting thesis this week. All goes well. Hope you're fine

xxx
sivvy

TO *Gordon Lameyer*

Thursday 4 November 1954[3] TLS in greeting card,[4]
Indiana University

thursday
1.40 p.m.

dear gordon . . .

in brief respite between lunch and my favorite class of the week . . . namely the great god alfred's, I pause to refresh and tell you about things past, and passing and to come. first, your letters have been magnificent, especially the official one![5] such a sustaining force! I was happy to hear you'd visited my favorite brother[6] and think you've no need to worry

1–Sara Murray Jordan, *Good Food for Bad Stomachs: 500 Delicious and Nutritious Recipes for Sufferers from Ulcers and Other Digestive Disturbances* (Garden City, N.Y.: Doubleday, 1951).

2–See Lameyer mss; held by Lilly Library. Photographs were taken at Mount Monadnock, NH, on 17 July 1954 and Chatham, Mass., on 24 July 1954.

3–Date supplied from internal evidence.

4–Panda Prints card designed by Rosalind Welcher.

5–See Gordon Lameyer to SP, 29 [October] 1954; held by Lilly Library. The original letter was misdated by Lameyer as of 29 November 1954.

6–See Gordon Lameyer to SP, undated [*c.* 2 November 1954] which begins: 'At the end of a most exhausting day . . .'; held by Lilly Library.

about his thinking you've ulterior motives: he is honestly very admiring of you, I know that for a fact!

I am really beat but beatific: my status quo, it seems. last night sat up so late to write a german composition which is a labor of blood, sweat, and sentence structure, after a three hour siege at my instructor's home . . . she is very kind about tutoring me an extra hour a week. tomorrow is the shakespeare written, next week the 2 three hour Cambridge exams and a german written, and as I haven't looked a fyodor once for two weeks, I'll have to somehow postpone my 2nd chapter for a week or so . . . I've still all the reading to do. the state of my study affairs perhaps reveals my guilty, secret and consuming love: my first conference with kazin yesterday about the 1st prose paper I've written for two years creatively was unbelievable . . . he told me it's my holy duty to write every day, spill out all, learn to give it form, and is going to let me go off on my own every week, only asking that I turn in lots and lots and not to bother with the regular class assignment. he is extremely critical and encouraging, and the fortuitous accident of interviewing him is something I'll praise fortune for all my life long. I adore him!

tomorrow night I'm going to hear mary ellen chase talk about her new book[1] at the hamp bookshop, and hope to make time to hear margurite higgins (my ideal newswoman)[2] hold forth tuesday. the roster of visiting lecturers this year is fantastic: claude raines, thornton wilder,[3] ogden nash, kazin etc . . . I hope you can get up to hear one or two of them . . . life is full to the brim, and always overflowing . . . my main philosophy of life is: "things will work out" (with a highly optimistic inflection). if I get accepted at either oxford or cambridge and don't get a fellowship, I'll spend the summer in new york as a call girl, or, better still, you can solicit for me among your esoteric navy men!

most of all, it's wonderful having you in my future . . . immediate and otherwise!

much love

s.

1–Mary Ellen Chase, *The White Gate* (New York: W. W. Norton, 1954).
2–American reporter and war correspondent Marguerite Higgins Hall (1920–66).
3–Wilder spoke at Smith College on 26 April 1955.

TO *Gordon Lameyer*

Saturday 6 November 1954[1] TLS, Indiana University

<typed on Street & Smith Publications Inter Office Memorandum letterhead, with heading>

TO	Darling	FROM	Smith Doll
SUBJECT	Minutia & Momentia	DATE	Saturday

I feel damn lovable and good and scrubbed and my hair is washed and soft and my mouth is red and I am in my rough old Navy sweater and suave oxford gray Bermudas and knee socks and oh how agreeable I am but I need fifty blazing brutes to tell me so and how drastically I need to be appreciated . . .

I broke Safety Rule No. 2 this afternoon because it was such a bang crash blue screaming act of god day. Persuaded Sue Weller[2] to bike out to Connecticut River after lunch in the sparkling burgundy air and tramp through the asparagus fields with me. Well, what do you know, there is the La Fleur airport[3] with all the little planes lined up looking like gaudy painted toy gliders, and that Icarian lust came upon me again. So we went over and hung around talking to some hood pilots and being very young and innocent and enthusiastic and broke and talking about how god damn blue it was and good for flying and how we wanted to ski this winter and how was the best way to learn, and then I am bumping along the ground in this sweet yellow job and the shadow is parting from the earth, and we are up, tilting over hamp, me screaming about how this is the fourth dimension and god isn't it a fantastic day, and how the gravestones are white chess pieces, and for heavens sake there is Lawrence House, and so on till we come tilting down with the yawning of eternity still in my ringing ears. Oh it was all very naughty and dashing . . .

Please, darling one, try to borrow me a pair of skis over Christmas so we can take off now and then . . . Sue said she'd go with me whenever we could manage this winter, and I want so to learn.

Somehow I have to have my thesis chapter postponed a week as I haven't done the reading even yet for this one, but must study for a

1 – Date supplied from internal evidence.

2 – Susan Weller Burch (1933–90); B.A. 1956, economics, Smith College; B.A. 1958, philosophy, politics, and economics, Somerville College, Oxford; SP's housemate at Lawrence House.

3 – LaFleur Airport opened in April 1929 and is now called Northampton Airport. It is at 160 Old Ferry Road, Northampton.

German written this Friday, having just had Shakespeare yesterday. I hope I can get a ride down Wednesday with some of your friends, and am toying with the idea of going back with you, or someone the preceding Sunday and staying home for a week . . . which would be bad because I'd miss three German classes, but good because I'd rest and study at Widener . . . I think . . .

I love Saturday nights at home here because it's the one night I can luxuriate in not having any classes the next day. I told you I'm reading aloud to that dear old blind man every Monday afternoon, didn't I?

Please let me know when to expect you next week, dear, and Don't forget to bring the pictures! I am dying to see if you are an unbiased observer about my unparalleled native beauty! Personally, I think your biases were cut with pinking shears . . . very crooked . . .

Last night I heard Mary Ellen Chase give an initiatory talk on her new book "The White Gate". Her publisher and illustrator[1] also talked, and it was an enchanting evening in the Hampshire Bookshop . . . she wrote the warmest inscription in my book[2] and is making me homemade cookies for my exam trial next Tuesday and Wednesday mornings, which I think is supreme dearness on her part . . . if I ever get to England that magnificent woman will be at the bottom of it!

Oh, back to all the never-ending work: Henry IV (how I love Falstaff, Hotspur and Hal!), Kazin paper, German subjunctives, Lessing, and all the rest. Somehow there is always such a pull between wanting to extend my horizons in width and the necessity to plunge in depth if I want to be proficient in any field . . . you know, if you write all the time you don't live, if you act, you don't think enough, if you study, you don't develop your body enough . . . all the planets whirling seductively around the chosing ego . . . you are the dearest planet of all . . .

love,
sylvia

1–Storer B. Lunt of W. W. Norton and the illustrator Nora S. Unwin.

2–Chase, *The White Gate*; SP's copy held by Smith College with inscription: 'For Sylvia Plath, my fellow student and friend, with all good wishes and my love. Mary Ellen Chase'.

TO *Aurelia Schober Plath*

Thursday 11 November 1954 ALS (postcard), Smith College

Thursday

Dear mother . . .

seems unbelievable that Thanksgiving is only TWO weeks away – I'm glad Gordon is coming for dinner – I will have a good deal of concentrated work to do – reading for thesis, complete revision of 1st chapter, which will involve condensing 30 pages to 20 – appointments to make at Harvard, with Dr. Beuscher, etc. Thus Thursday will be my one "social" day, and I hope to sleep & work the rest of the time. I took my cambridge (England) exams at Miss Chase's house Tuesday and Wednesday morning (3 hours each). The questions were so general that it would have taken a year to answer anywhere near properly: "e.g." The Art of The Novel. What is that? Or "The importance of metaphor in poetry." I just hope I pass these exams, because Miss Chase & her friend Miss Duckett[1] have been so kind & encouraging. By the way, do you suppose you could write Warden[2] at Smith to give me blanket permission to go up in planes – I now know so many pilots that it's silly to break a rule & go up with<u>out</u> permission – just write <u>Warden</u>, <u>College</u> <u>Hall</u>, smith: "My daughter SP has my permission to go up in planes, both private & public" – or something. A nice, intelligent little Amherst grad[3] took me out for a delicious lamb chop dinner last night – he's rooming with Bob Riedeman at Fort Dix & stayed with him in Wellesley. German written tomorrow – wish me luck –

xxx Sivvy

P.S. Do you suppose you could call <u>Anthony's</u> hairdresser[4] in Boston & ask <u>how</u> <u>much</u> a re-dye job would cost (my hair's faded a little) & tell him I went to him before and MAKE AN APPOINTMENT for me over Thanksgiving? Danke schön!

1–Eleanor Shipley Duckett (1880–1976); professor of Latin, Smith College, 1916–49.

2–Helen Louise Russell (1914–2005); professor of physical education (1944–54), warden (1954–6), dean of students (1956–79), Smith College.

3–Jon Kimmel Rosenthal (1932–); B.A. 1954, Amherst College; M.C.P. 1960, Massachusetts Institute of Technology School of Architecture & Planning; Ed.M. 1971, Harvard Graduate School of Education; U.S. Army 1954–6, roommate of Robert Riedeman at Fort Dix Army Base, New Jersey; dated SP, 1954–5.

4–Anthony, a hairdresser's, then at 93 Massachusetts Avenue, Boston. According to SP's calendar, she had her hair dyed and cut on 18 September 1954.

TO *Aurelia Schober Plath*

Saturday 13 November 1954[1] ALS (postcard), Indiana University

Saturday night

Dearest mother . . .

Oh, this is such a wonderful year – the pressure of work is of course a good deal, but I love it all so and work best under a healthy tension. Gordon is up this weekend & we had a good afternoon at a party at Amherst, meeting all his old friends, one of whom is driving me home Thanksgiving (I should be home Wednesday, for supper!) Just as I was wondering how I'd break even financially at the end of the year, a small blessing occurred today – Cyrilly Abels wrote[2] to say that I got an "honorable mention" in Mlle's Dylan Thomas poetry contest, & they're buying one of my lyrics[3] for $30! It is so lovely to contemplate this coming check! I can buy all the necessaries I need, now, in perfect joy: a girdle, brush & comb, bedroom slippers, blue shoes, etc! I am so happy. Also, my German teacher is so sweet – tutoring me an extra hour or 2 a week! I Rose from a B- in my first exam to an A- in my last! I am really most happy here – busy and occupied of course, but oh! with such a healthy, philosophical outlook! LIVING best is most important, & no matter what the reward in marks or money, I'm happy knowing I'm "keeping faith"

xx
sivvy

TO *Aurelia Schober Plath*

Wednesday 17 November 1954[4] ALS (postcard), Indiana University

Wednesday 12 noon

Dear mother . . .

It was good to get your long letter today – I really enjoyed all the news. There is as always more I want to do than I can ever get done, and of course I am bringing home more work than I will do . . . but I am an

1–Date supplied from postmark.

2–Cyrilly Abels to SP, 8 November 1954; held by Lilly Library.

3–Sylvia Plath, 'Parallax'. SP had submitted 'Triad of Love Lyrics' (later published as 'Trio of Love Songs') to *Mademoiselle*. SP's honourable mention was printed in *Mademoiselle*, January 1955, 73; the collegiate winner that year was American poet Linda Pastan (1932–). 'Parallax' never appeared in *Mademoiselle*.

4–Date supplied from postmark.

optimist, and am happy with accomplishing at least a major part of my plans – the reason I am working on my 1st chapter (you sounded impatient about that, somehow!) is because I have to write a very rough draft first, allow time for Gibian to read it, while I write another 1st draft of another part. I have just gotten back the 1st chapter, & now must meticulously rewrite it. I plan to come back here december 26, right after Xmas, for a week of solid work – from now till Jan. 20 the real push is. Then I hope for a few days respite for either New York or skiing up north. I wonder if I could borrow the car Friday? I will be in Cambridge, & commuting is deadly. Also, could you possibly beg Anthony (Newberry St. is right) to squeeze me in Friday morning, or even afternoon, or call if there's a cancellation? Sat. is a bit deadly – I have some necessary shopping to do – my slippers are literally falling apart, as is girdle, brush, etc. and I need one good long-sleeved white-shantung-silk blouse (not nylon or cotton or transparent) for my jumpers & jerkin. Looking forward to a busy but merry Thanksgiving!

xxx
sivvy

TO *Gordon Lameyer*

Monday 22 November 1954[1] TLS in greeting card,[2]
Indiana University

monday night
8 p.m.

dearest gordon . . .

again I am in the strange state of suspended animation which always follows a seige of thesis, having had an enormous two-day stretch of typing two drafts of one chapter (40 pages in all!) with little sleep and typing from breakfast to dinner today without bothering for more than an apple for lunch. fortunately I am too sensible to try my luck (Iknowitwouldn'tbegood) and stay up more than one night. the ivan chapter which I just handed in to my very kind mr. gibian this afternoon is, as usual, a disorganized stream-of-consciousness mess, but I do think I have one or two good ideas floating around in it. from now till the 20th of january is the big push, and I plan to be very unsociable till that date,

1–Date supplied from internal evidence.
2–Panda Prints card designed by Rosalind Welcher.

out of necessity! the revising will be an intricate painstaking job, and the drawing of conclusions even more ticklish.

I want to thank you for your lovely letter of this week. I promise never to say another word about my ____ features, and admit that I am very happy with myself and wouldn't trade me in for a new model even if she did have a grecian nose! obviously, darling, I would never think of calling anything "quits". even if you decide to marry someone else in a few years from now, I hope we shall always be good friends. as it is, you know you are the major man in my life! I do not plan to refuse reunions with my old friends . . . ira and sassoon among them, but the chances of seeing them are so infrequent that it seems pointless to mention them at all . . . just my over-scrupulous sense for frankness again!

anyhow, I know you will understand that most of my thanksgiving vacation must be spent in concentrated reading and writing. do call me wednesday around supper, will you? I shall probably be really beat and go to bed right afterwards, but I'd like to talk to you anyway. thursday of course, is dinner at our house, friday is my consecration to cambridge, shopping and library, saturday reading . . . and I still don't know when I can get an appointment with beuscher and the russian prof.[1] so pouf! the vacation is gone already, and I am back here! but I am glad you are being understanding about my work . . . I must admit that those last two days of talking with you took a big hunk out of my schedule, but I hope it was worth it for you.

see you soon, darling,
much love,
sylvia

TO *Ann Davidow-Goodman*

Tuesday 23 November 1954 TLS, Smith College

November 23, 1954

dear ann . . .

it was so wonderful hearing from you again! only it made me extra wishful about seeing you in person for one of our very real talks. I'll be home in wellesley with mother (who is just recovering from an ulcer

1–Dmitrij Tschižewskij (1894–1977); professor of Slavic studies, Harvard University, 1949–56. In the Harvard University Annual Reports of the President and Treasurer for the years 1948–57, Tschižewskij's name is printed as 'Dmitry Cizevsky'.

attack) all thanksgiving, and will be back in hamp sunday night. if ONLY you could fly up to either boston or hamp! I know that is just a pipe dream of mine, but I am determined to see you before the year is out, although I am so broke now (I am "supporting" myself, ha!) that I can't travel, but must even hitch a ride home, which is fun, but a rather devastating indication of insolvency! I'm in the midst of writing a thesis on the double personality in dostoevsky's novels all of which is fascinating, as I read in freud, "the golden bough", and e. t. a. hoffmann's wierd fairytales, but somehow my first rough drafts of the damn paper are nowhere near the inspired flaming paragraphs I had in mind as I began! I'm hoping that between January 20 (when my thesis and exams will be over) and the end of that month I can make it to nyc for a few days, if I get some undexpected money from some poems that are out now, but that is only another nebulous project, so I'll probably have to settle on having this french boy drive me down.

do let me know if there is ANY possibility of your getting to boston christmas, or nyc or boston at the end of january. telegram or call if there is the slightest possibility of your coming up to visit with me, even if only for lunch or something! My phone in wellesley is WE5-0219J, and at hamp, it's ext. 293 at lawrence house!

honestly, ann, I feel that no matter when or where I see you again, that we can take up where we left off . . . probably, though, we have both grown up fearfully much since those terrible days when we were freshmen! I often wonder how I got through them at all, when I look back!

I didn't even know you had a brother,[1] isn't that absurd! I have one too, who is the apple of my eye: six feet six, amazingly good-looking, and a sophomore at harvard; I am really proud of him. If your brother ever comes to smith for a date, please tell him to drop over and see me if he has a minute . . . it would be sort of a vicarious contact with you, you know!

your life at art school sounds delightful . . . I know exactly what you mean when you say you love your work, but not necessarily what you produce . . . sometime will you send me one of your productions though? I should love to have one! I'm taking a great short story writing course now, and my lifelong ambition is to get in the new yorker, and from the rejections I keep getting from them, I'm sure they're determined to make it

1–William Henry Davidow (1935–); A.B. 1957, M.S. 1958, Dartmouth College; M.S. (electrical engineering) 1959, California Institute of Technology; Ph.D. (electrical engineering) 1961, Stanford University.

stay a lifelong ambition! I really must tell you that for the few acceptances at harper's there have been at least 50 rejections! it just proves I'm pigheaded and keep on sending out stuff!

do write again, and please try to come see me!

very much love to you,
Syl

TO *Aurelia Schober Plath*

Wednesday 1 December 1954[1] ALS (postcard), Indiana University

Wednesday

Dearest mother . . .

Do you s'pose I could ask you another favor? I'm again rather up a tree for recommendation letters & need one for the big Woodrow Wilson Fellowship, that will discuss (favorably, I hope!) my "intellect, character, and personality and promise for the career of teaching & scholarship." Could you ask Mrs. Cantor right away if she would write a letter about these (esp. character & personality!) & send it by December 10 to: Dean Francis M. Rogers,[2] Grad. School of Arts & Sciences, Harvard U., 24 Quincy St, Cambridge. This is the big ($1250) national Woodrow Wilson fellowship, and I figured she'd be best, aside from 3 professors I'm scouring up, to "know" me at a job where my "character" showed. Please let me know immediately her answer, so I can put her name down as reference! I hope she'll be pleased at my asking! When my Harvard application comes up in January, I don't know what I'll do – I've used up everybody in the Eng. Dept. About Xmas gifts – cross off the gloves & star stockings: I am in desperate need of them: 10½, black seam, gray, not beige, shade! Work on thesis coming well – must pause to write a German paper today – looks like I'll be all caught up by Christmas, If my schedule goes as planned! – if only Mr. Gibian likes my 2nd chapter – I'll know by Saturday – already have 25 pages carefully rewritten on 1st chapter

xx
Siv

1–Date supplied from postmark.

2–Francis Millet Rogers (1914–89); Dean of Harvard's Graduate School of Arts and Sciences, 1949–55; Professor of Romance Language; Chairman of the Selection Committee of the Region for the Woodrow Wilson Fellowship Program.

TO *Jon K. Rosenthal*

Thursday 2 December 1954 TLS (photocopy), Smith College

thursday afternoon
december 2

dear jon . . .

you have no idea what an obstacle course it is to write you a letter! I just finished addressing the envelope, and am sure all the numbers and cryptic abbreviations are wrong, and blush to say that I unconsciously typed your unique name with a pedestrian "h", for which I should obviously be shot.

however, I have a new ribbon in my typewriter, and things are looking up. from now till january 20, when I have my last exams and (I hope) my thesis will be in, I shall be, as they say in siberia, working! by saturday I shall have a rough idea of how the thesis is progressing, as I get the second chapter back, with comments . . . I'm at the point now where I can't tell the difference between brilliance and banality: the subject---double personality in dostoevsky's novels, remember?---is as usual fascinating, but so familiar now that it's hard to distinguish whether my observations are evident to cretins or the result of long intense meditation over lukewarm coffee!

anyhow, if all goes well, I should be home in wellesley from december 18th to somewhere toward the end, when I plan to head back to hamp early and finish the albatross for once and for all.

your letter, by the way, was a surprise, and a pleasant one . . . it was so enormous that you must have taken special leave to write it, or something! you should have told me you were poetic . . . I was really with you in that airplane episode, you described it so vividly . . .

your work sounds more like the kind I can condone, and someday you will have to explain to me more carefully what you are studying . . . as I said, if I were drafted, they would have to put me on a farm: I'm not at all mechanically dexterous, and would probably shoot my sargeant accidentally at the first rifle practice, or cut my hand off while absent-mindedly peeling potatoes . . .

thanksgiving was a blur of champagne and cognac and harvard library, charleston navy yard, and gourmet dinners . . . notably at joseph's, boston's own "snail-and-frog-leg" bistro, where everyone who frequents is either a disinherited count, rich gangster, or woman of diamonds and dubious virtue: I was trite but happy with lamb chops, and watching my favorite bartender vault heroically over bar and knock out inebriated customer, who had no doubt insulted him in a foreign language . . . I do love seeing people be shocked . . .

you'll be amused: there's this russian professor at harvard I want to see about my thesis christmas vacation, and I dropped in on his daughter at harvard when I was home.[1] seems dmitri never deigned to learn english, so If I wish to speak to him, I must have either a russian or a german interpreter . . . luckily I thought of an acquaintance who just got back from two years in moscow, and hope this little deal works out . . .

your list of invitations seemed rather tempting, as a matter of fact. my problem is that I had vowed not to travel at all by myself this semester, which may seem odd to you, but if you knew what I was living on, it wouldn't. if I had skis, I would love being lessoned in vermont (I told you about the broken leg) but is it possible to rent them up there? you tell me. also, you wouldn't want to slow down for a beginner, would you? my weakness is that I love being taught. also, new york is also alluring . . .

as you see, my spirit wavers, and could be convinced perhaps with your taking care of my questions and objections. which is not fair to tell you, really, as it gives you an unfair advantage! I want to be home from 18th to 19th at least, and then just before and after Christmas . . . that sort of leaves the day or so at the beginning of the week, starting monday the 20th, nicht wahr? I really wish it were somehow possible for me to start learning how to ski again, but as I perhaps told you, I don't want to acquire my own equipment until I know more about the sport than I do now!

of course, new york is a living carnival, but somehow, intellectualized and sedentary and most daiquiri-saturated, which is all very lovely, with plays and museums and restaurants, and I am highly enamoured of it all, but I think a more elemental communion with nature on snow slopes might be therapeutic after the hours in the carrell and those nights spent slaving over a hot typewriter . . .

in summary: why don't you write sort of tentative suggestions of how we could pragmatically get together (you see, I'm assuming we will) for a short while, and give me your opinions on what I've mentioned. another thought struck me. if I rearranged a few things, I could stay in hamp till saturday the 18th and you could meet me there (if that is convenient . . . I have no idea where you'll be arriving in the east) and we could take a day or so then. anyhow, let me know what you think most plausible, so I can try to make tentative schedulings of things to jibe with it all . . .

1 – According to SP's calendar, this was Pat Tschiżewskij.

I hope you aren't like that boy's grandmother who said she'd tear up all my letters without reading them if I typed! I am no longer able to write by hand: it is above and beyond the call of duty. and I think better on a typewriter . . .

you may disagree with that last, after this letter!

fond regards to my Blissful one,
sylvia

TO *Aurelia Schober Plath*

Monday 6 December 1954[1]

TLS with envelope,
Indiana University

monday afternoon

dearest mother . . .

I was delighted to receive your nice letter this morning, and enjoyed, as always, the excerpts from mr. rice. outwardly, the weather here has been very cold, but in spite of the fact that I am nursing an annoying sore throat and suffering through the usual first day of my period on doses of codeine, I am supremely happy.

I just had a conference with mr. gibian this afternoon about my thesis, and, except for rewriting three paragraphs out of about 20 pages, he said my second chapter is in final form! do you know what that means! it means I will have a relaxed christmas vacation where I will be reading up on my other subjects and writing poetry and short stories, and visiting friends! I will also have a whole week at the end of january to do the same, in preparation for the second semester. there will be NO LAST MINUTE RUSH! I handed in the rewritten golyadkin chapter today, and also four pages of introduction which I slaved over. this next week I must write my six pages of conclusion, which will of course be the most difficult but the most stimulating. that means, that except for the mere mechanical details, the whole thesis will be "done" by christmas vacation! I am so proud of myself! why, I may even graduate!

should[2] have the thesis ready for you to type between january 5-10!

kazin's course is delightful as ever. our last meeting was held at his home this friday, over coffee and lovely pastry. I read my last story aloud, and everybody analyzed it . . . it was the incident about paula brown's

1-Date supplied from postmark.

2-SP has handwritten this in the left margin of the first page.

snowsuit,[1] remember? this course is the best thing for getting me in the habit of writing. every time one sits down to the blank page, there is that fresh horror, which must be overcome by practice and practice. I stayed afterwards to help with the dishes, and talked to the beautiful, blond mrs. kazin,[2] whose second novel is coming out this winter.

I have a poem by rilke to analyse for german this week, and our teacher gave us a present of his slim volume of poetry,[3] which made me happy. in shakespeare, we are reading henry fourth and fifth, and I remember the wonderful time warren and I had with you at the movie![4]

oh, mother, I was so glad to hear about your nice visits with mrs. cantor and mrs. prouty. I love them both with all my heart. I have still not heard from the atlantic monthly, by the way, which is very tantalizing . . . it's been over two months now, which is so similar to harper's treatment . . . I love building up my hopes, even though nothing comes of it, it's such fun to live in suspense. I am also trying out for vogue's prix de paris contest for college seniors. the first prize is $1,000(!) and so amply worth the time. I have already completed one assignment. the second is four articles which I shall write over christmas. these two assignments will make me eligible for the final long thesis upon which the prize is judged. last year two smith girls[5] were among the winners, so I should have some chance!

if only I get accepted at cambridge! my whole life would explode in a rainbow . . . imagine the wealth of material the experience of europe would give me for stories and poetries . . . the local color, the people, the fresh backgrounds! I really think that if I keep working I shall be a good minor writer someday, and this would open such doors! one thing, If I get accepted in england, no mere two thousand dollars will stop me from going! it is the <u>acceptance</u> over there, that I'm worried about. oxford never likes people with any physical or mental ills in the past. mary ellen chase and miss duckett may make cambridge a possibility. I shall earn $500 next summer, at least, I think, and get something from smith I hope, and piece the rest together somehow.

1–Sylvia Plath, 'Superman and Paula Brown's New Snowsuit', *Smith Review* (Spring 1955), 19–21.

2–Ann Birstein (1927–); Kazin's third wife; author of *Star of Glass* (New York: Dodd, Mead, 1950); her second novel was *The Troublemaker* (New York: Dodd, Mead, 1955).

3–Probably Rainer Maria Rilke, *Der ausgewählten Gedichte erster Teil* (1954); SPs copy held by Smith College and inscribed on flyleaf.

4–SP's diary records seeing Laurence Olivier's film version of *Henry V* on 28 April 1946 at the Esquire Theatre, then at 264 Huntington Avenue, Boston.

5–Jocelyn Arundel Sladen (1930–); B.A. 1952, French, Smith College. Denise Musnik (1951–90); B.A. 1952, government, Smith College.

I was so happy to hear that warren is coming to our house dance with kathy next weekend. I am only unhappy that gordon is in virginia and that I won't be here. claiborne and avrom dropped up this last weekend, and invited me down to new york that weekend, which I had complained would be terribly lonely here, as everybody but me (and one or two other unsocial girls) will be going to house dance, and there is nothing more depressing than having gay music come drifting upstairs when one is trying to study. I am so sorry gordon won't be here, because, it would have been grand fun to share this experience with warren. however, even though I am awfully disappointed to miss him, I shall enjoy seeing my friends overnight saturday in new york, and renewing old acquaintances. the good news about my thesis really decided me.

I look so forward to the year ahead. there is much work always, but it is happy work, and I am loved, and I love, and everything is sweet and sensible . . .

much love to you all,
see you soon –
sivvy

TO *Aurelia Schober Plath*

Wednesday 8 December 1954[1] TLS with envelope, Indiana University

Wednesday night

Dear mother . . .

The story looks just exquisite! I am so pleased. In fact, you have won me over to the beauties of elite type, which is a feat, since I was so prejudiced to begin with. I wish that you could do my thesis in elite because it would hold more words and look lovely. But I don't think they'll let us use elite for that very reason. My margins are non-existent in my rough draft, so I imagine it will be about five to ten pages too long if typed properly!

I acted immediately upon your suggestion and sent the story off to WOMAN'S DAY. You are right about its being too short for most magazines . . . I had thought to send it to the NEW YORKER, which accepts small sketches (it's really not a "story" in the strict sense, but rather a "slice of life") but WD might be more inclined to consider something

1–Date supplied from postmark.

with more pathos. Anyhow, I love having things "out", whether they are accepted or not. I enjoy living in perpetual suspense.

I am leaving for New York Saturday, and looking forward to seeing many old friends, or at least calling them . . . Claiborne, of course, and Jan Wagner, and so on. It is nice to have so many offers and invitations! I look especially forward to going window shopping . . . they say the displays are more beautiful than ever this year.

Wrote Mrs. Cantor to thank her for lovely letter, and mentioned hope that we could have a get-together at our house this year during holidays . . . would like Warren, Gordon, and boys for Kathy and Joan . . . they've done so much for us.

For our German unit tonight we had to translate and explicate a poem apiece by Rainer Marie Rilke, a really stimulating assignment because a bit beyond our complete grasp. I got so interested in mine "Ein Prophet" that I made a stab at translating in verse with rhyme scheme and rhythm exactly like Rilke, and except for a few places I have to rework, it came out rather well, if I do say so!

Kazin has invited me out to an informal lunch next week for a long talk, and naturally I look forward to it more than anything else in the world. He has gladly accepted writing a recommendation for me for a Woodrow Wilson fellowship (the one Mrs. Cantor wrote for) and I know his name means a lot. If anything, this year has exposed me to the most magnificent of men! He is an inspiration which comes seldom in a lifetime. And it is so wonderful to know he admires me in return! Oh, yes, I do worship him.

I am also going tomorrow to see Mr. Alfred Fisher, who has offered to give me a rough "course" of private criticism on my poems, which I am going to start taking advantage of now that the main worry of the thesis is well in hand.

Everyone is singing Christmas carols, and I am already gathering cards and making out lists. I only have about 25, but they are all very close . . . and such a diverse group! I think your idea of a mimeographed letter was an inspiration. Christmas I hope to see Patsy, Ruth Geisel, the Cantors, the Crocketts, Mrs. Prouty, and Dmitri T. (the Russian prof at Harvard). What a program! I am nursing this cold, which I plan to be rid of in a day or two. Vitamins and early bed should check it completely.

Well, that's about all for now. The Smith Review comes out this week with my story and poem[1] in it . . . look forward to bringing it home to you!

1–Sylvia Plath, 'In the Mountains' and 'Circus in Three Rings', *Smith Review* (Fall 1954), 2–5, 18.

Looking forward to Christmas . . .

much love,
Sivvy

<on front of envelope>

P.S. Guess what! Adlai Stevenson is going to be our commencement speaker! You should enjoy it doubly!

TO *Gordon Lameyer*

Thursday 9 December 1954[1]

TLS in greeting card,[2]
Indiana University

thursday morning

dear gordon . . .

a note in the midst of this impossible three weeks, which probably will welcome you home . . . I don't have any idea about your virginia address, so I figure linden street's the safest port. I battled temptation to ask you fly up from the south for our house dance, which is, after all, my last, and should have been the best, with you there. warren is coming up with kathy too, which satisfies my cupiditry.

anyway, I am packing up early saturday morning and heading for new york. I shall probably stay with claiborne and her husband, windowshop, and drown my sorrows in gallons of chateauneuf du pape. as it is, I refuse to be here alone, and there is no one to go to the dance with but you.

life here is fantastic, as usual. my thesis is coming along much better than I expected, and except for the ten most difficult pages of conclusion and the mechanics of bibliography and, of course, typing, I am through! doesn't that sound impressive! except for three paragraphs in my last 20 page chapter, gibian likes it as is! which means I can write some stories and poems over vacation, I hope. german isn't as bad as it was---I translated my first poem by rainer maria rilke yesterday, and got so interested that I worked up a verse translation in the same rhythm and with the same rhyme scheme . . . very difficult for me, but terribly stimulating. kazin has asked me out for lunch and a long talk before vacation next week, so naturally that makes me most elated. he is, of course, my guardian angel, and is writing me all kinds of recommendations for all these overseas scholarships. and, by the way, adlai stevenson is going to be our

1–Date supplied from internal evidence.
2–Panda Prints card designed by Rosalind Welcher.

commencement speaker! do so wish you could come, but suppose you will be with giesha girls in japan

of course my schedule for seeing people in christmas vacation is, as usual, impossibly packed, and I'm hoping we can do some of these together: patsy, ruth geisel, the cantors, the crocketts, dmitri t., mrs. prouty, cambridge-in-general, and of course dr. b. am also working for vogue's prix de paris, a $1000 jackpot for some clever college senior. chances are slim, but articles are fun to write . . .

smith review comes out this week with story and poem with your great title "circus in three rings" . . . can't wait to see it all in print. don't think you've seen story, done two years ago, about t.b. sanatorium, and one of my favorites . . .

until christmas vacation then (call when you get in, why not?) . . .

as ever
sylvia

TO *Aurelia Schober Plath*

Monday 13 December 1954[1] TLS with envelope, Indiana University

<typed on Street & Smith Publications Inter Office Memorandum letterhead, with heading>

TO	mother	FROM	daughter
SUBJECT	cabbages and kings	DATE	Monday

dearest mother . . .

it is monday morning again and the world settles back from the miraculous to the mundane, with so impossibly much to be done before the coming friday. my health is excellent, you will be happy to hear, and my change of scene did wonders for my flagging spirits . . . I feel infused with new energies and projects . . .

the weekend was wonderful. Claiborne has the most charming apartment which she had furnished with avrahm with modern wood coffee tables and bookcases that they have made themselves, and I had such a happy time. saw "the bad seed"[2] saturday night, that new play,

1–Date supplied from postmark.

2–American playwright Maxwell Anderson, *The Bad Seed*; adapted from William March's novel of the same name. The play, starring Patricia 'Patty' McCormack, was performed beginning 8 December 1954, at the 46th Street Theatre, 226 W. 46th Street, New York.

and was intrigued by it. the heroine, a nine-year old murderess, looked exactly like libby aldrich! precocious and piano playing and deucedly clever. the supporting cast was the star-point of the whole play.

as usual, the people were fascinating, and I had a marvelous time windowshopping on fifth avenue, gazing at the blazing four-ton tree in rockefeller center, browsing for hours in brentano's, eating my first escargots, partaking of oysters, shrimps, wines, and all the neon wonderland of thieves and millionaires.

this morning a happy thing happened: my second semester schedule, which has hitherto been a mess, is settling out miraculously. had a conference with alfred fisher about my most recent poems and he offered to give me a private course one hour a week of special studies in poetics! he is a very strict man, and a brilliant professor, and this is a signal honor! also, I'll be writing poetry! the nasty requirement for a unit this semester, for which I have no desire or need, will probably be changed by the honors committee to include this course in special studies, so that my program will cohere beautifully. I must be very quiet about it all, because fisher is terribly strict about taking on anyone to be tutored, and the waiving of the unit requirement (as yet to be done) is highly irregular! but it will mean my being able to take kazin's modern american lit course and poetry (plus my shakespeare and german courses which continue) and a review class which is required. so I am very excited and must write both prose and poetry over vacation with a big: "do not disturb" sign on my door.

plans for vacation are crystallizing, and I thought I'd brief you: I'll no doubt come home by bus this friday and stay till sometime monday the 20th (I think bob cochran might drop in to say hello on sunday the 19th). monday I am heading up to vermont to go skiing with a new friend of mine (bob riedeman's roommate in the army) jon rosenthal, who is flying up from his base in texas. he graduated from amherst last year, a phibete in chemistry, and is in the enlisted student detachment working with guided missiles: a possibility for warren, perhaps: they carry books, not guns! jon is a nice guy, and a sensible chap, who will start me carefully on beginning slopes on his sister's skis.

I'll be coming back home that wednesday, the 22nd, in time to meet alison smith whom I've invited to stay with us from late wendesday the 22nd to friday the 24th. I know this is close to christmas, but if she didn't come then, I don't know I'd ever see her! and you know that she is a delightful guest! after christmas I must start my work schedule, which I will carry out at home till sunday, january 2nd, when I hope I'll be able to persuade someone to drive me back to smith! so you see, I'll really be home a good bit, and hope to see mrs. prouty, the cantors, aldriches, patsy, ruth geisel, bob cochran, crocketts, and of course dr. beuscher! la! what prospects!

in eager anticipation . . .
your loving daughter,
sivvy

TO *Jon K. Rosenthal*

Monday 13 December 1954 TLS (photocopy), Smith College

monday morning!

dear jon . . .

came back last night from a trip which elated and shocked: human nature never ceases to amaze. but more about that later. your letter was here. so to work. the third plan you listed (all of them were great) sounds most plausible for me at this stage, which means that I would be much appreciative if you would pick me up at my small white cottage in wellesley some time on the 20th, a monday, I believe (my god, a week from today!) and head north (I trust that's the direction we'll be going) from there. now I'd really love it if you would call when you get into NYC if possible to let me know the time, and just to say hello anyway. that is always nice, hearing someone say hello.

one of my closest friends, alison smith, is coming to stay with me starting the evening of the 22nd (wednesday) so if we started early monday, we could have one whole day with a half day on either end. check? I do hope your sister's old skis will be available and also that we will pick up boots somewhere or other . . . you'll have to supervise fit etc. as I obviously know nothing. my shoe size can very between 6 and 7 ½ and so is variable. or like, the japanese women, I could bind them (feet) this week in preparation . . .

my house is fantastically easy to find, I think. I'm sure I've said all this before, but it is 26 elmwood road, off weston road, which is off route 9 (nine, that is) which runs from boston to amherst and smith. or, if you find wellesley college, which is where weston road begins, just follow the road down a mile or so till you get to elmwood. I trust your map sense. again, it's WE5-0219J. I'll clarify over phone farther, if you should wish . . .

before I forget, I have a very attractive, but nervous mother, whom I see as little as possible. (I no doubt also told you this). anyhow, for her sake, I should be prepared to say where we'll probably be, where staying, and so on. mother's funny about such details. in case she dies unexpectedly, she wants to be able to send me a telegram. (seriously though, I do love her, and am not contemplating matricide, as it may sound from my idle chatter! she just likes to know.)

about this weekend (past). I broke all resolutions and headed for nyc friday. we were having a house dance here, and gordy lameyer was at gunnery school in virginia, and I can not stand crhistmas spirit by myself, so I made a break and prevailed upon a french friend of mine to host me about the city. like cinderella, I was enchanted. christmas lights unbelievable, enormous four-ton tree with blazing red, yellow, orange lights in rockefeller center, skaters waltzing and twirling, silver and blue windows for windowshopping, brentano's for bookbrowsing, oysters for breakfast . . . you know, all exotic and alive, wind-in-hair, frost and wine . . . only I spent the last afternoon talking to detectives in the 16th squad police station.

like this it was: left suitcase in date's locked car for one hour while sunday dinnering,[1] car being on public street just off 5th avenue in very broad daylight. upon return, car forced open, broken into, suitcase gone with all worldly possessions such as favorite dresses and poetry books, theater programs and empty wine bottles. all very discouraging. no clothes. no nothing. I'm trying to keep this a secret from mother, because when one is supporting oneself, one does not replenish wardrobe, one wears dungarees for a year. so I will wear dungarees for a year. and pretend I have become an ascetic. you know: just cawn't beah cashmeah sweatehs, so vulgah. materialism, these tweed dresses! back to natcah!

excuse me, jon, but I'm still seething. my date and I whiled the afternoon away reading missing person notices, discussing theories of crime with a detective in a blue serge suit (it <u>is</u> serge that detectives wear, isn't it?) and hearing fantastic cases being reported: we got these here woman and a three year old kid unconscious in apartment five ana puddla blood on the floor dint belong to either of em. and this here other woman up ona thoid floor with her arm slashed open wide with a knife, no gas, and we can't figya why the kid was knocked out, overtired maybe huh?

and on and on. I almost decided to be a police reporter for a year. this stuff fascinates me! so I came home with a pair of dirty white gloves and a book of franz kafka's short stories, and longing memories of escargots (a euphemism for snails, I just found out). fortunately I have an old navy sweater left, and some ski pants. hope I don't bore you!

1–SP was at Steuben's; the experience became the subject of her poem 'Item: Stolen, One Suitcase'.

anyway, I hope my modern poetry books are educating some thug or other about the finer things in life. and that my chanel no. 5 is sweetening the nights of some gun moll in the slums. my christmas gift to the miserable masses. (only it is disconcerting to be left naked!)

so, to terminate: (somehow have to write thesis conclusions today!) I'll plan to hear from you by letter, phone, or telegram about when on monday the 20th I should be ready for you. also, would appreciate if you could give me some idea about what kind of clothes to bring (ha). navy sweater and ski pants, maybe?

until a week,

season's greetings from the disenchanted,

sylvia

TO *Melvin Woody*

Friday 17 December 1954 TLS in greeting card,[1] Smith College

<printed greeting>

It's Noël! / MERRY CHRISTMAS

<signed>

much love and / holiday greetings / syl / (see inside for much deserved / letter →)

monday afternoon
december 17

dearest mel . . .

really, my room is wallpapered with good intentions! I have been going to send you a long missive for about half a year. at last, the christmas season makes me repent verbally for my sins, and say how often I've thought of you and wondered what you're doing, and wanted to send you news. I insist that you be more honorable than I and answer me before we reach infinity!

life here is the richest ever, and I am most happy. all the vitalities and interests that were sprouting last spring from soil that I though was to be eternally sterile are blossoming out miraculously. the thesis on two examples of the double personality in dostoevsky (golyadkin and ivan karamazov) is almost writing itself, and I am more and more convinced that dostoevsky has been the greatest philosophical influence on my life . . . along with nietzsche, huxley, fromm and a few others. I am also taking

1–Panda Prints Christmas card designed by Rosalind Welcher.

an unexpected creative writing course with a brilliant young jewish critic, visiting this year, alfred kazin (author of "on native grounds" and the exquisite "walker in the city"). he is the light that incandesces my year, and our conferences are fabulous. I'm taking his modern american lit. course next semester, going out to lunch with him next week, and being elated about it all. the shakespeare course is vivid and vital, intermediate german is a struggle, but I need it for graduate school and stimulate my interest by making stabs at translating rilke. best news is that alfred fisher, an excellent english professor here, has just offered to give me a private course in special studies: writing poetry and the technical aesthetics of poetry. I'm stimulated at the prospect, and just a little scared. so much for courses.

amy remondelli[1] is all you said and more. she is going around with charlie gardiner now which somehow surprised me . . . all the intricate connections in our group of acquaintances. I think she has the face of an intellectual madonna: as you can see, I admire her no end, and she has done so much as editor of the smith review. news from marty is cheerful as ever, and I hope to glimpse her during christmas vacation. carol pierson writes (secretly, you understand!) that she is at a mental hospital in new york, and I am trying to find out further details, knowing generally what she is no doubt enduring there. nancy hunter is pinned to david furner (at amherst) as of this fall, and although we've hardly spoken to each other all year (separate theses and separate social lives keep us apart, among other things) there is a sort of bond still; I have, however, lost my case of heroine worship which I had last year. sassoon (if I remember, you don't care about this) is explosive as ever, and I just got back from a weekend of escargots, red wine and plays in nyc to which he cavalierly excorted . . . visited with claiborne handleman and her husband (nan's roommate last year). aside from the fact that my suitcase was stolen with all my worldly goods, it was a magnificent respite from the campus circuit. (to paraphrase yeats:[2] "suitcase, let them take it / for there's more enterprise / in walking naked") I'm doomed to dungarees for a year.

am applying in a splurge of optimism for a fulbright to oxford or cambridge next year, but understand they aren't hospitable to lady-suicides. so am also trying for harvard scholarships. only I long for

1–Amelia (Amy) Remondelli Gardner (1934–), B.A. 1990, American studies, Smith College. Remondelli matriculated with the class of 1956 at Smith College, but left to marry Charles S. Gardner, III. She returned to campus as an Ada Comstock scholar and graduated in 1990.

2–SP plays off of W. B. Yeats, 'A Coat'.

england, with long vacations in italy and france. always did want to go to africa and egypt, too! enough of this for now, and PLEASE WRITE someday.

much much love from all of us americans,

sylvia

1955

TO *Aurelia Schober Plath*

Monday 3 January 1955[1] ALS with envelope, Indiana University

monday night

dearest mother . . .

just thought I'd write you a note before the deluge of the next three weeks, which will be the busiest in my life and won't give me time for socializing! The trip back was long, but I had a nice dinner of pizza & wine to send Gordon off. The day early being back has made all the difference: never have I accomplished so much – had about 10 appointments & got much settled – also had wonderful pick of january clearance sales with no other girls to compete! Got wondrous wool dress, long sleeved, gray, brown & green – ann fogarty,[2] of course, for $21 off! also got great gold necklace, originally $22 for only $4! Also a white satin blouse exactly what I dreamed of, for under my jumpers – not transparent! I feel most successful and happy with my purchases. January is the time to buy!

<drawing of white satin blouse>

My conference with Mr. Gibian was heartily encouraging and amusing. Except for rewriting one paragraph, he approved of my 8 page conclusion verbatim, which is, of course the most difficult part of the thesis. So it is ready for the typist. I spent the evening typing up footnotes (which I'm putting at the end of each chapter) & bibliography – must spend tomorrow morning at libe checking them. Friday it goes to the typist, who will do it very reasonably in 10 days! I am glad you won't have to set aside any of your precious vacation for this – I feel guilty enough asking you to type those two stories! This plan will work out best in the long run, and the typist is one of the secretaries[3] to President Wright! Because mine is done early, I'm beating the mob!

1–Date supplied from postmark.

2–American fashion designer Anne Fogarty (1919–80).

3–SP's calendar indicates she called Pauline C. Walker on the same date this letter was written. Pauline C. Walker (1902–95), Assistant Secretary to the President and the Board of Trustees, 1937–68.

Mr. Fisher, my new poetics professor, was very exciting today. (The Honors Committee approves highly of my special studies with him!) He is assigning me one long monograph on the Rhetoric of the Elizabethan poet & playwright John Ford[1] which I'll be doing on a graduate level – he is also doing research on Ford, aided by other of his graduate students & spoke of the possibility of "publishing a study" of essays. As you may imagine this is a challenge of the utmost scholarship! It will be invaluable. My regular assignment is to hand in a "batch" of poems each week! Fun, what!

I love all my professors, and feel that my work is so intriguing & so well rewarded – cross your fingers that I make it to the 21st with success – have a fabulous amount to do till then – feature article on Smith social life[2] looms among them – with interviews for it – College Dean, etc. – everybody is so wonderful up here – know that I'm well & happy even if I don't write till after exams – Hope you are the same

xxx
sivvy

TO *Aurelia Schober Plath*

Thursday 6 January 1955[3] — ALS with envelope, Indiana University

Thursday

Dear mother . . .

Never thought I'd be writing you so soon again, but I wanted to tell you, before the officials did, that I'm up at the Infirmary as of today. I have been feeling miserable all week because of a searing sore throat, cough & cold. Nose drops & gargles at the house helped not at all, and I didn't feel well enough to do any work, so I came up here to recuperate quickly & completely before exams, when I shall need every bit of extra energy, to top it off, I started my period unexpectedly early too, so I am really a mess. The reason for this cold is, I am sure, the unhealthy hot temperature at Lawrence House. It has been from 80° – 87° (!) on our floor, and although I keep my radiator turned off, it is always scalding hot. Of course I have a humidifier, but even that doesn't help the intolerable hot stuffy

1 – 'poet & playwright ~~of~~ John Ford' appears in the original.

2 – Sylvia Plath, 'Social Life Without Sororities: A Profile of Smith College'; held by Lilly Library.

3 – Date supplied from postmark.

atmosphere (I work best at 70°). Naturally the contrast to my cold room at home played havoc with my health. However, although Mrs. Kelsey said airily "nothing could be done" about my radiator, I complained to the Doctor, & they are going to try to fix it.

I handed my thesis and my last creative writing paper today, so at least all I have to worry about is the big article due at Yale next week and my German & Shakespeare courses in which I will be drastically behind as I was going to catch up concentratedly this week and haven't been able to do a thing.

It is a treacherous slushy day, with glare ice and awful rain, so I'm glad I'm here where I'll get good food & medicine & sleep. Many thanks for the welcome $5 – I indulged in the luxury of a taxi up to the infirmary. Am delighted about the Sheldon book[1] & would really appreciate your sending it here as soon as possible. I've been dying to read a few Chapters in particular & should have time after exams –

I expect to be all better soon. Meanwhile, take care of yourself.

xxx

Sivvy

p.s. Delighted about car! Trust grammy to get a good bargain any day! Hope Warren's happy!

TO *Aurelia Schober Plath*

Sunday 9 January 1955 ALS (postcard), Smith College

sunday night

dear mother . . .

seems I just can't stop writing to you! but I do enjoy chatting over the latest tidbits of news! It was so nice to get your last letter, especially the phone call – I always feel so "out-of-touch" at the infirmary, even though they are all so dear up there & all know me well. I got out today – much better – still a little shaky, but "dried up" inside. Very fortunately I have no classes till Wednesday – but I do have a lot of appointments at college hall. Called my typist tonight & she said she's just begun work on my thesis, which is most comforting – also got notes from both Southward & Coonamessett Inns[2] & plan to schedule interviews there in the late spring

1 – William Herbert Sheldon, *Psychology and the Promethean Will: A Constructive Study of the Acute Common Problem of Education, Medicine, and Religion* (New York: Harper and Brothers, 1936). SP's copy held by Smith College.

2 – The Coonamessett Inn, 311 Gifford Street, Falmouth, Mass.

(if enough fellowship's come through, maybe I can afford an interesting job with "spare time!") An encouraging note came from Fulbright committee today: my application passed National selection & is now in the finals! This is, as they say, no assurance of a grant, but still, a nice bit of news. The wait now is longest – Am. Comm. in England must decide. Wrote 5 poems[1] at Infirmary under influence of codeine – mostly gay love lyrics or scene descriptions & optimistically (as always) sent them off to NYorker. At least they won't keep me waiting like the Atlantic! Will keep you posted

xxx
S

TO *Gordon Lameyer*

Sunday 9 January 1955 | TLS in greeting card,[2] Indiana University

<printed greeting>

As you embark upon life's stormy seas / With gaze fixed firmly on your pilot-star / May fate ne'er send you aught but fairest breeze / Nor wreck your vessel on some treacherous bar

Dear Gordon . . .

Somehow when I found this card I thought immediately of you, and so here it is. I am afraid that this will be about the last missive for two weeks, until my dantean inferno of exams and articles is over, for I just got out of a nasty week in the infirmary today and have twice as much to catch up on, which makes life complicated, as I what I had previously was impossible enough. So I'll write you an enormous letter now, hoping that by the time you get it, I'll be through with my monstrous schedule. I'm enclosing, by the way, two shots for John Stamper, which Dee took long long ago. The squibs, as you may guess, are mine. Just couldn't resist.

1–According to SP's calendar these poems were: 'Ballade Banale', 'Item: Stolen, One Suitcase', 'Morning in the Hospital Solarium', 'New England Winter Without Snow', and 'Harlequin Love Song'. The first four SP dates to 8 January 1955, and on 9 January 1955 she wrote 'Harlequin Love Song' and rewrote 'Ballade Banale'. SP sent seven poems to the *New Yorker* on 9 January 1955.

2–Panda Prints card designed by Rosalind Welcher.

Sunday night
January 9, 1955

Dear Gordon . . .

(I might as well begin over again in good style in here . . . always enjoy the chance of saying: "dear Gordon" twice, you know!) Since I have been back, life has been fantastically complex. I can't believe it was only a week ago that we were down at Joe's imbibing wine and pizza and rambling on about the world!

Monday was a gift from God. Only Nan Hunter and I were back, so I spent the whole day at faculty appointments and January clearance sales. My luck at the latter was phenomenal. May I brag to you? I replenished my whole wardrobe (that was stolen) and did a much better job than I had done in the first place: got a divine charcoal-gray long-sleeved wool dress with subtle brown and green square designs embroidered in it, very thick and rich ($20 off), a full-skirted caramel-colored jumper that can be worn as a dress ($12 off) but which I like best with a black shirt with brown-and-gray stripes (sounds wierd, but is terribly exquisite), a necklace, heavy gold, marked down from $22 to $4, a miraculous white satin blouse, the kind I've been looking for for years, with a simple jewel neckline, puffy pushup sleeves, a pink party nylon nightgown that makes me feel I'm going to a prom (you know: I dreamt I went to Guantanamo Bay in my Maidenform nightie!) All in all, darling, I must have saved about fifty dollars, according to my woman's logic. Now that you think I am clothes crazy, which I am, once or twice a year, I shall proceed to more esoteric things. (If you think I'm bad, you should see my roommate! She got three new coats and suits for Christmas, and God knows, about six new dresses!) Such crass materialism!

Monday I checked over my thesis with Gibian, and except for revising one paragraph in the conclusion (which I thought would be the hardest part!) he said it was ready to go to the typist! I spent a day checking bibliography and re-tying footnotes, and managed to secure one of the secretaries to the President (Wright, not Eisenhower) to type it for about 25¢ per page, including two carbons, so I'm very relieved about that: she's extremely efficient, and began typing it today.

So, except for the ultimate proof-reading, that is off my mind. The honors committee was all behind my project to take a private course in the Theory and Practice of Poetics (I thought up that title myself: pretty classy, wot?) with Alfred Young Fisher, who is no longer young, but the handsomest elderly man I've ever seen, very British, with keen blue eyes, white hair and mustache, and most tweedy clothes. I do hope he propositions me by the end of the year, (but perhaps, after his 3rd wife, he's wearied of that.) At any rate, our conference this week was most enchanting, and I'm going to be doing a "scholarly monograph" on the rhetoric of an Elizabethan poet and playwright, John Ford, whom Mr. Fisher himself also happens to be working on with some of his graduate students. Someday, he suggested, we may all publish a little study together. La! And I don't even know what the word rhetoric means in its true sense! This shall be a semester of learning. Also am turning in a "batch" of poems weekly to him, which will be a rather fantastic challenge. Like prospecting for gold: you know the raw nuggets are there, but you have to sift through a hell of a lot of sludge to get at them!

Then bang, the infirmary with the worst sinus infection yet. Thought I'd never get back from my miserable codeine stupor, but here I am, still slightly dazed, but at the typewriter. While at the infirmary, since last Wednesday, all I did was read the Thesaurus and write five poems, which as always are the favorite ones I've written, (being the newest!) and which I've sent off to the New Yorker, as always, in a splurge of optimism today. They are the most varied forms and tempos I've ever done at once, mostly invented. Some slow and pompous, some shallow and dancing, some erotic and lyrical. Naturally the last are my favorites. I am so erotic and lyrical.

While up in the realm of white sheets and nose drops, I had a charming guest sent over by Alfred Kazin: a young assistant editor[1] at Harcourt, Brace, who was visiting Mr. K. for the day and came over to talk and to say he'd like to be the first to see any novel I come up with in the next year or two (!) A Harvard graduate, winner of a Fulbright to Cambridge. he had a lot of intriguing things to say. Speaking of Fulbrights, darling, I just got word that my application has passed the preliminaries and is in the finals! This obviously means nothing at all, except that I haven't been ruled out yet and won't find out till spring what the American officials in England decide. But it is nice to know the dice may still shoot in my favor. I'll probably be going to Cambridge, Mass., the weekend after my exams if I'm in the finals for the Woodrow Wilson fellowship. Cross your fingers for me!

1–Peter Hubert Davison (1928–2004), American poet, assistant editor at Harcourt, Brace & Co., 1953–5; assistant to the director at Harvard University Press, 1955–6; editor at the Atlantic Monthly Press, 1956–85; dated SP in 1955. Davison married SP's Smith housemate Jane Truslow in 1959; father of Edward Angus and Lesley Truslow.

Here I sit, with that damn German paper to do which I've postponed for a month now, a hundred notes to catch up on, interviews for the social life article this week, and I gossip my little head off to you.

Oh well, perhaps you'll be kept busy reading all this garbled jargon until you come home, what with shells and mock invasions interrupting you all the time.

Do take care, darling, because I want you to come back whole and hearty so we can maybe take off for skiing once or twice before the snow is gone. I do miss you, although my activities are (as ever) so thick and fast I don't have time to feel sorry for myself. Oh, pray for England!

Love to you, angel, be good, and ignore that thriving Gitmo industry! You are a dear guy!

Much love, from your own,
Sylvia

<enclosed are two photographs with SP's typing on verso>

<first photograph> This is Your Mood Portrait.

A Souvenir of your visit to exquisite Smith College in the Heart of the Pioneer Valley . . .

Suitable for framing: a must for eager friends and relatives.

<second photograph> The Prisoner of Goat's Peak: Marooned for 40 days and nights without bread, chianti, or human society, this criminal was condemned for operating illegally without his poetic license in the crow's nest prison in a Northampton mountain top where he served time, guarded by are cola bears on constant 24 hour watch below. When released, the prisoner was babbling incoherently about a monstrous flea. (This picture was taken from a helicopter).

TO *Aurelia Schober Plath*

Saturday 15 January 1955[1]

TLS with envelope on Smith College Press Board letterhead, Indiana University

Saturday night

Dear mother . . .

I have just finished washing my hair and performing my thorough weekly ablutions, and so feel most clean, but most prosaic and businesslike. I haven't stopped "work" since getting back, and yet most of this work is

1–Date supplied from postmark.

love for me, so it is the medium of my being. I just wanted to write you a note before the deluge of this coming week, when I have two months to catch up in Shakespeare and about one in German before the exams, which both fall on Thursday. I can't believe that in five days I shall become so intelligent as I will be when I take those exams!

Fortunately, I will have a good week to spree between semesters, and I really feel I deserve it. I may very well come home next Friday afternoon if I have to be interviewed for the finals on Saturday and Sunday at Cambridge for the Woodrow Wilson Fellowship (they still haven't let me know whether I am to come yet, which is very inconvenient, as all other plans hang on it). Anyway, do tell Warren I hope to have at least one meal with him that weekend if I come. He has to eat anyway, and it shouldn't take any extra time to say a few words between mouthfuls!

I TURNED MY THESIS IN TODAY! Yes, my typist had it all done, and I was so excited that I cut classes to proof-read it. It is 60 pages of straight writing, with 10 more for notes and bibliography. I had her make 2 carbons, so the total cost was $17.50, a big sum for me, but well worth it, for the professional results! I was so proud, it is an excellent thesis, I know it in my bones, and already two girls have told me that Mr. Gibian thinks it's something of a masterpiece! I am really pleased with it.

Another note: I hoped I could save it till I was sure one way or the other, but it's too exciting to keep, so I'll let you in on it. The JOURNAL rejected my "The Smoky Blue Piano" story,[1] but with the following wonderful personal letter: "Although your story is not quite right for the Journal, it has some appeal and we want you to know that it is being returned with more than ordinary regret, and of course our thanks. We feel the diary method of narration, certainly for this story, is awkward and makes the telling too limping. If you should ever decide to rewrite it as a straight story, keeping the nice sparkle it now has, we will be glad to see it again. Congratulations, anyhow, on a good first try."

Well, usually they say they'd like to see your next story or poem, but this offer to consider a rewrite stimulated me to my typewriter today, and I was amazed at the validity of their criticism! I did the story over in direct form (I knew inside the diary wasn't right) and the whole thing drew together and incandesced! Naturally I took them up on their offer and sent it back immediately, tonight, after spending a whole day typing the 20 pages. It is the best short story I have ever written of its kind (the kind

1–Sylvia Plath, 'The Smoky Blue Piano'; held by Lilly Libary. SP first sent the story to the *Ladies' Home Journal* on 28 December 1954. Her re-write was rejected by 2 February 1955.

is the “Initiation” kind, written to meet certain specifications, while being true to my own humor and ideas.) I Know it in my bones, again, and somehow felt that their letter to me would be exactly this, only I never expected them to say they’d consider it again after I rewrote it! I thought, like the New Yorker, they’d just criticize, so I could profit by it, and then sell to Harper’s, or something! But even if they don’t take it rewritten, I know now, in my intuition, that it will Sell somewhere!

You, I am sure, would like it, to show your friends, for it is as funny as anything, very frivolous and light (no profound philosophizing in it anywhere) and all ends happily, with the heroine going to marry the man of her choice in the most magnificent dialogue I’ve ever done, really hysterical. I am so happy about it, and so grateful for their criticism, that I can hardly walk on the ground! Forgive my exulting!

Had a wonderful final talk with Mr. Gibian, my adviser, today, as I handed my paper in. He is so interested in my writing and my fellowship applications, that I plan to visit with him second semester anyway, even if I don’t have a course with him!

Mr. Fisher has been having unofficial classes with me already for my Poetics course! We get along admirably, now that we are getting acquainted, and he is the most brilliant, enchanting man I’ve ever known, reminding me very much, in his way, of Gordon as he may be 30 years from now, who knows. Anyhow Mr. Fisher is exactly what I need for poetry criticism, and my first two “Batches” of about 10 poems he went over so thoroughly, I find myself just flying home to rewrite them, which is a rare drive for any writer, I think! I have polished the two long ones I wrote over vacation, and he is very pleased.

While speaking of people being pleased, did I tell you about my article for the Yale Intercollegiate Literary Magazine? I finished it at the beginning of this week, with a lot of legwork and interviews with the higher ups in college hall. The result was a good solid essay (often amusing) called “Social Life without Sororities: A Profile of Smith.” The News Office let me pick three or four wonderful photos to illustrate it, and the best thing is that both the Warden of the College and the Head of Public Relations were so delighted that they asked for a copy to use on their own later! So I am happy it worked out so well.

I am now in the finals for the Vogue Prix de Paris, and must write a “thesis” of over 10 pages (at least) on “Americana”: “on my discoveries in the arts this year . . . what I’ve found most exciting in the American theatre, books, music, etc?"[1] I'd really appreciate any advice you have on bird's eye reading I could do, I feel that you would be much more aware of current trends than I, what with your Monitor and SRL! I hope to see more theater in NYC after next weekend, and also take in the latest additions to the NYC art galleries in preparation for this essay, which I am hoping to get done mostly before second semester begins . . . plan to do a research job on it in NYC.

Now I've run out of time & space. Hope I'll be seeing you next Friday. Will let you know definitely as soon as I find out about interviews!

Love to all,

Sivvy!

<on back of envelope>

p.s. am planning to re-write a really good, (if awfully naked & depressing) story[2] for Mlle contest between semesters! It has possibilities, & is in the nature of Illona Karmel's "Fru Holm", only more subjective – more fun!

xx

s.

TO *Aurelia Schober Plath*

Wednesday 26 January 1955[3] TLS on *Smith Review* Make-Up Sheet letterhead, Indiana University

Wednesday morning

Dear mother . . .

Well, my vacation was just what I needed. I am back at my desk as of last night and will feel happy if I don't move from Northampton till spring vacation, which after all was the purpose of my New York jaunt. I rested and played and whirled until I really wanted to come back to Smith, and now I am full of resiliant desire to work again, which last Saturday I thought was a physical and psychical impossibility . . .

The flight to New York was ecstasy. I kept my nose pressed to the window watching the constellations of lights below as if I could read the riddle of the universe in the braille patterns of radiance. It was a luxury to have coffee on the plane, and I began to forget those four men that

1–Probably SP's 'Arts in America'; held by Lilly Library.

2–The story to which SP refers might be 'Tongues of Stone', which according to her calendar she re-wrote by 28 January 1955.

3–Date supplied from internal evidence.

went on arguing in my head long after I'd left them. At the airport, I had kept hearing the man announce: "Air France nonstop flight to Paris now ready for departure . . ." and wondered if I could just switch flights at the last minute . . . I was very tired Saturday night, but by Sunday I felt revivified . . .

Sunday afternoon, I saw "Gate of Hell",[1] that beautiful Japanese movie that the critics are all raving about. It was like all Oriental art: perfect economy and balance of line and color, a paradoxical illusion of simplicity in richness, richness in simplicity. Strange, but the foreign languages bothers one not a bit, which is a tribute to the universality of the performance and the excellence of the acting . . . one color poem after another . . . the Japanese have such intriguing rituals and disciplines . . . the whole set was a singing poise and opposition of bamboo columns with embroidered gauze hangings floating to enclose space . . .

That evening it was the last performance of a Russian-Jewish legendary drama: "The Dybbuk"[2] at a 2nd floor theater in Greenwich Village, where the audience sat on either side of the stage, and the actors used the aisles. This tale of the possession of a young girl's body by the spirit of her lover ("The Dybbuk") who died before his time and had no other home in eternity was uneven, but when good, very good.

Monday, I spent the afternoon at the Museum of Modern Art, which I am getting to know better and better. They were selling hot chestnuts outside, and somehow the people all look so intriguing. I looked up a few paintings of modern American artists to describe for my long feature article for Vogue which is going to take a heck of a lot of research. I stayed to see the late performance of the movie at the Museum that afternoon, and have never been so moved. I could hardly bear to sit out the whole thing. It was a silent French version of the "Temptation of Saint Joan",[3] with written titles and piano music going all the time, not with the moods (for that would have been so dynamic as to be insupportable) but quite casually on its own, absorbing some of the powerful emotions aroused by the black-and-white counterpoint of faces . . . it was almost all faces . . . of Joan and her tormenters. The background was all white walls with

1–*Gate of Hell*, Japanese film directed by Teinosuke Kinugasa, 1953, played at the Guild Theatre, then at 33 W. 50th Street, New York.

2–S. Ansky, *The Dybbuk* (1914), trans. Henry G. Alsberg. This adaptation starred Morris Carnovsky, Lou Gilbert, and Miriam Elyas, was directed by David Ross, and performed at the 4th Street Theatre, 83 E. 4th Street, New York, 23 January 1955.

3–*The Passion of Joan of Arc*, silent French film originally titled *La Passion de Jeanne d'Arc*, directed by Carl Theodor Dreyer, 1928.

windows and doors, and the psychic torture was cruel, so cruel that a picture image of Joan on a wooden stool with a paper crown and stick scepter in her hand contained all the impact of Christ and all martyrs. The burning at the stake was incredibly artistic and powerful, but the very lack of sensationalism, just the realism of fire licking at sticks, of soldiers bringing wood, of peasant faces watching, conveyed by the enormity of understatement the whole torture of the saint.

After it was all over, I couldn't look at anyone. I was crying because it was like a purge, the buildup of unbelievable tension, then the release, as of the soul of Joan at the stake. I walked for an hour around Central Park in the dark, just thinking, and my date kindly took me for a ride in one of those horse cabs around the park, which was the slow paced black-and-white balance I needed to the picture. I fed the horse a lump of sugar I'd saved from lunch and felt much better. Experiences like that are rare. Human beings cannot bear very much reality, as Eliot says.

Most of the rest of my time was spent being enchanted in various French restaurants, very expensive and intimate, with small white linen tablecloths and tables elbow-to-elbow with editors and wives of millionaires (I overhead some intriguing conversations, which I mentally noted). I indulged at "Le Gourmet,"[1] and "Cafe Saint Denis"[2] and "Le Veau D'or"[3] among others, with vichysoisse, soupe a l'oignon, steak, veal in wine, lamb chops, aperatifs, white wine, cognac, french pastry, eclairs, tartelettes, and Dieu knows what else . . . oysters and clams and french breads and salads. It was all very wonderful, and I learned a great deal about myself in the process . . . this period of time lasts me about half a year, gives me incentive to work with spartan economy, and makes me actually grateful for plain cold water, brown bread, and hotdogs and coffee. There is nothing like living an extravagant illusion to make one appreciate the simple round of daily life . . . which I am appreciating with delight now, completely cured of my longing to be exotic. I have been. C'est fini. Now I look forward to catching up on letters, stories and poems, to spartan intellectualism.

Bye for now, your returned prodigal . . . .

sivvy

1–Le Gourmet, a restaurant then at 49 W. 55th Street, New York.

2–Café Saint Denis, a restaurant then at 11 E. 53rd Street, New York.

3–Le Veau d'Or is a restaurant at 129 E. 60th Street, New York.

TO *Enid Mark*

Wednesday 26 January 1955 TLS with envelope, Smith College

Wednesday afternoon

Dear Enid . . .

It was a delight to hear from you. I am, to answer your question, the sort who can somehow always pick up a friendship that was very dear, no matter how long the time, nor how wide the space in between. I am sure that if I went to Africa for ten years, I would come back naively expecting to pick up right where I left off, and hoping that everyone else would feel that way too. At any rate, it seems most natural to be talking on paper to you again, and the new name is strange and wonderful, too.

Life here at Smith has been incredibly rich this year. I am becoming a fatalist and think that somehow this postponed senior year was necessary for me to grow more slowly in time, like cider needing years in the dark to become mellow. At any rate, all avenues of life are full and miraculous. I found myself writing a thesis on "The Magic Mirror: A Study of the Double in Two of Dostoevsky's Novels" with young, brilliant, delightful Mr. George Gibian, and being fascinated by my topic till the end, and reading all about mirror images, shadow legends, everything from ETA Hoffmann's fairy tales to Freud!

To top it off, by accident (being assigned an interview) I took Mr. Kazin's writing course also first semester, with the delight of his asking me in, long interviews every two weeks, and a final joy of his sharing a pizza and coffee with me at the Little Italy one rainy iceglazed December afternoon. I turned out a lot for him, mostly rough sketches, which have all been rejected by The New Yorker. However, one which I rewrote with a "plot" (very unusual for me) and a frothy sense of humor (more unusual) was looked at with interest by the Ladies Home Journal. They asked me to rewrite it and send it back, and now I am undergoing that excruciating wait, dying for the mail in terror and desire every day, telling myself sternly that they are taking all this time to write a very nice detailed letter of rejection! Cross your fingers!

I'd really love to see some more of your stories, Enid. Just for the joy of reading them; I'm so deep in rejections that I am hardly equipped to criticize! I too, hope to write for "Seventeen" someday. But they are very demanding . . .

Next semester is the usual review unit, continued Shakespeare with Miss Dunn, intermediate German, Mr. Kazin's famed American Lit. course which everyone in the college seems to be taking, and a lovely private special studies unit with Mr. Fisher (whom I'm just getting to know) which He suggested: The Theory and Practice of Poetics. I have to turn in a "batch" of poems every week and a long critical essay that looks from here like another thesis. At any rate, the prospect is enchanting, and I do think the poems are coming better . . .

Gordon, the Amherst graduate, now an ensign in the Navy, is in Cuba at present, but I had a very good Christmas vacation in Wellesley with him . . . our times coincided exactly. I have, however, put off all thought of marrying him to a very indefinite future, for a multitude of reasons, primary among them, the precarious uncertainty of our future growth and activity. It is fine if a man is older, more mature, has crystallized out a bit, but even though Gordon is 25, he is amazingly young yet (or I am amazingly old) and I am Machiavellian enough to want to grow to the fullest . . .

New York has been most hospitable lately, with that charming young French boy, Richard Sassoon. This past week, in celebration of completed thesis and exams was a round of plays ("The Dybbuk") movies ("Gate of Hell" and "Temptation of Saint Joan" at the Museum of Modern Art) and French restaurants like the Cafe St. Denis and Le Gourmet. Now, at last, I think I can bear cold water and brown bread, hotdogs and coffee for two months with joy, so glutted am I on escargots and huitres!

Do write, send stories, and I hope I may perhaps say hello to you and your wonderful husband in person sometime springvacation, if all goes well.

Love,
Sylvia

TO *Gordon Lameyer*

Wednesday 26 January 1955 | TLS in greeting card,[1] Indiana University

<printed greeting>

Since All the World's a Stage / Why Postpone Things / No Need for Us to Dally / In the Wings / Let's to Our Places / Let's to Our Lines / On With the Play / Let's Be Valentines / What Bliss that Cupid Thus Should Pair Us / In This Comedy of Eros

<signed>

amour, cheri! / sylvia / (missive within)

<within two hearts printed on the card, SP has written 's. & g.'>

Wednesday morning
January 26, 1955

Dear Gordon . . .

Well, and then again, well. I am wishing you a happy Valentine's Day, and no doubt shall continue to do so for quite some time. Merci, first of all, for your most intriguing letter[2] about the suave antics of you and your compatriots (or is it expatriates?) underneath the sheltering palms (or is it in the sheltering arms?) of Cuba.

Now for news, inanities, and other such. (This letter, by the way, is being written in severe and sincere sobriety, contrary to what the tilt of the paragraphs may indicate.) To put it bluntly, I have never done so much in one small month in my small life. Since I saw you, I have taken two gruelling exams (Shakespeare was fun, so I don't care what I got; German wasn't, and I got a mere chilly 87) finished proofing my thesis, which cost me a cool $20 to have typed, but in my mid-exam state, was well worth it, sent off that research article "Social Life Without Sororities: A Profile of Smith" to the Yale Gargoyle (who apparently can neither spell nor gurgle), written poems for Mr. Fisher, and been interviewed at Harvard for the Woodrow Wilson Fellowship at what was probably the most difficult session I've ever had in my life . . .

I finished my two exams last Thursday, and immediately hopped a train for Wellesley in a state of writers' cramp, having written solidly for five hours and being the possessor of a blackened middle finger on my right hand which is no doubt an omen of something, I don't feel equipped to

1–Panda Prints card designed by Rosalind Welcher.

2–Gordon Lameyer to SP, 'sunday nite'; held by Lilly Library.

say what. Mother and Warren picked me up where I had fallen on the platform, frothing at the mouth and reciting future perfect passives in Elizabethan dialect. I spent one blissful day wandering around the house in my pajamas, eating or not eating, as I felt or didn't feel like it. I bought $4 worth of piano music ("These Foolish Things" "September Song" "I'm in the Mood for Love" and "The Man I Love" among them) and sat at the piano for hours soupily crooning to myself in bad french, and getting a hell of a kick out of it . . .

Also managed to have an evening bull session with Dr. Beuscher which was fun, at her house, which is illegal, as she is not yet an American citizen, and discussed religion, philosophy, honesty, selfishness, and a lot of other potent, and perhaps more intimate, topics. Mother and I, by the way, are getting along much better. I have found an almost sure-fire way of sustaining a more than benevolent attitude toward her. A rather macabre way, to be sure, so I don't think I dare tell you it. But it has worked admirably so far.

(Lift thine eyes to the hills . .)

Saturday I had that hideous interview. For one half hour I sat at a table surrounded by four skeptical men, all seasoned professors, and was the raw target for fantastically loaded and merciless questions, none of which I had dreamed of being asked. Mentally, I have been arguing with them ever since! All about my philosophy of teaching: terribly specific. Every remark I made, they took up, twisted to their purposes, and shot back at me. Like darts. Such fun. I was asked about obscure modern authors I'd never heard of, how could I combine writing and teaching (wouldn't the level of freshman comp destroy my finesse?), why the hell did I put down Oxford, Cambridge and Radcliffe in that order, did I know it was impossible to get a Fulbright to Oxford or Cambridge? (It no doubt is, alas), had my Fulbright gone to Washington (It Had), would I give up teaching for marriage without a fuss, what about babies, would I marry a teacher (I felt like asking if it was a personal proposal), what would I do with the average student, how to interest, were English departments doing their jobs, was W. H. Auden odd to want to teach freshman comp instead of lecture at Swarthmore . . . and on and on . . . I would give my little finger to know what they said about me afterwards. I think they thought I just wanted to get married to a millionaire, but at least I convinced them about my ideas of teaching as a way of life . . .

Leaped from the Saints of Cambridge to a plane at Logan Airport and flew through the spangled dark to NYC, a much needed release. At the port, the announcer kept saying: "Air France nonstop flight to Paris now ready for departure," and I was terribly tempted to switch reservations and trade the Empire State for the Eiffel Tower!

The three days I spent in NYC will amply suffice me till spring vacation. I was overjoyed to get back to Hamp last night after my orgy. Sunday I saw "Gate of Hell" that Japanese movie all the critics are raving about, and it was an exquisite work . . . one color poem after the other, with the incomparable Oriental illusion of richness in simplicity, simplicity in richness . . . not a superfluous gesture in the whole thing. I love the ritual and order of the passion in Oriental life: the sets were a poise and balance of bamboo poles, with floating gauze curtains to enclose space. That evening it was the last performance of a Russian-Jewish play "The Dybbuk" in a little 2nd floor Greenwich Village theater, where the audience sat on either side of the stage and the actors used the aisles. This supernatural symbolic drama of a "Dybbuk" (the soul of one dead before his time, with no home in eternity) entering and possessing the body, and then the mind and soul, of his beloved, was uneven, but when good, very good.

Monday, I spent the afternoon at the Museum of Modern Art, reacquainting myself with my favorite paintings and sculptures. I stayed for the movie, a magnificent French silent rendition of the "Temptation of Saint Joan" done in black-and-white, primarily with facial expressions and powerful understatement. I could hardly sit through it, it shocked and sickened me so, shuddered to the base of the soul . . . at first I wondered why the piano music was not at all dramatic, but very casual and unrelated to the emotions of the movie, but soon I understood that it absorbed some of the tremendous tensions aroused, and made the emotion more supportable. The sense of martyrdom grew agonizingly, until the least twitch of a monks' eyelid conveyed the impact of a whole century of cruel blindness. The final scene at the pyre was perfect and terrible. I'll never forget a close-up shot of a baby sucking its mother's nipple, turning casually to the final agony of the saint, and then calmly resuming sucking. I was so purged and cleansed by this catharsis, psychic and spiritual, that I had to walk around Central Park in the dark for an hour, was treated to a ride in a horse cab, fed a lump of sugar to horse, and felt better. Rest of stay was a round of French restaurants, "Le Gourmet", "Cafe Saint Denis," "Le Veau D'Or" and wine and cognac and aperatifs, oysters, steak, lamb chops, eclairs and pastries, and all those other delights our sinful flesh is heir to. For two months I shall be completely satisfied with cold water and brown bread, hotdogs and coffee. Of such is the kingdom of heaven.

Love, your returned prodigal,
sylvia

TO *Melvin Woody*

Wednesday 26 January 1955 — TLS on *Smith Review* Make-Up Sheet letterhead, Smith College

Wednesday morning
January 26, 1955

Dear Mel . . .

Such an unheard of thing I am doing, answering a letter in the same month wherein I received it! But I am blessed with a whole voluptuous week between semesters, and certainly your last missive deserved more than placement in the: to be-answered-within-the-year file! I dutifully quoted your words to Amy, who, as I said before, is amazing and most lovely . . .

The life here is fantastically varied and the future is drastically up in the air, and will be for months: I feel like a juggler in pink tights tossing up a multitude of flaming colored balls, none of which land, but just tilt beyond reach of the finger tips. Finished thesis two weeks early and bled the cool sum of $20 for a typist, which was more than worth it in the mid-exam coffee mill. Result: a 60 page study of "The Doubles in Dostoevsky's Novels" called "The Magic Mirror" and rather neat; I am honestly terribly proud of it, for it is a starting place, and I have discovered much. Dostoevsky, I think, will always be my favorite novelist (if I can be strong enough to keep to blazing polemics all my life) and Nietzsche my favorite philosopher (the wit and poetry and shock of his epigrams makes my soul "sneeze" itself awake, to use a Nietzschean verb!)

My course with Kazin, as I no doubt said before, has made rough drafts for several potential stories. You will no doubt be disgusted, but I wrote the first plotted story this fall, a frothy, hysterically funny thing, very much on the cocktail party (small letters, no caps) side of my personality. The "Ladies' Home Journal" asked me to rewrite it, not in diary form, and they are now looking at it again. Having just gotten my second semester bill, which is a tragic $15 over my combined checking and banking balance, I am waiting in daily dread and desire. No, I did not sell my integrity down the river, I just played up my sense of humor, that's all. It's much harder than being tragic and depressing, you know! Anyhow, if $850 should some through, I might be able to afford the luxury of a summer of writing.

My poetry is coming much better, and this private course in The Theory and Practice of Poetics (doesn't that sound impressive? I made it up myself) is coming superbly, with me turning in about 5 poems a week, reading all the little magazines, and having "nimble, fiery and delectable"[1] discussions with my professor (he's the one who is on his 3rd Smith wife). Apropos of poetry, Nancy Hunter (no doubt worn out by my deluge of rejections) has taken upon herself the role of poetess--Dorothy Parker type--and writer. She has borrowed all my writing yearbooks for addresses, is taking the first sophomore creative writing course at college next semester, and just wrote three sonnets which have no words less than five syllables, ambiguous pronouns, and otherwise are rather posed and postured. I am harsh, but honest, I think. The stardust has long gone out of my eyes. We speak, that is all. I shall wait with interest to see if she can either get out of herself long enough to write a good story, or dramatize herself enough to do so. Perhaps the latter is possible. God and David Furner know about the first. So amusing, really, Mel, last year, last spring, I worshipped and imitated (in a way) that girl, this summer I learned about her, about the hypochondria, the hysterics if things didn't go her way, the fantastic need for security in one so poised (outside) and beautiful, and now she becomes a gesturing poetess. Enough.

Had the most gruelling interview at Harvard last Saturday. Four men, all brilliant professors, grilled me for over half an hour for this Woodrow Wilson Fellowship, picking up every remark I made, twisting it to their purposes, tossing it back, asking loaded questions, until I felt like a painted wooden toy at the rifle booth in the circus. I argued on everything from my philosophy of education and teaching to would I marry a teacher and what about babies and was W. H. Auden odd to want to teach comp and why did I put down Oxford, Cambridge and Radcliffe in that order, and did I know it was next to impossible to get a Fulbright to Oxford or Cambridge (which, alas, is probably true.) Anyhow, they left me with the comfortable feeling that American Fellowship Committees are highly selective and damn pragmatic.

Fell on a plane to NYC, my first night flight, and I was in St. Exupery ecstasy the whole way, reading the riddles of the universe in the braille of lights, tracing radiant enigmas and wondering how the rest could sleep or read in that flying temple. New York soothed, assuaged, gorged, glutted, indulged. Saw that new Japanese film "Gate of Hell" which the critics are raving about: a series of color poems, the fantastic ritual and order of Oriental passions, sets of poised and balanced bamboo poles, with floating gauze curtains to enclose space. That night: the last performance of "The Dybbuk", a Russian-Jewish drama in the small 4th street Theater,

1 – A reference to Shakespeare's *Henry IV, Part 2*.

where the audience sits on either side of the stage and the actors use the aisles. An intriguing performance about the soul of onedead before his time possessing the body and finally the mind and soul of his beloved. An uneven play, but when good, very good.

The Museum of Modern Art took up a whole afternoon. They were selling hot roasted chestnuts outside in the frigid gray air; inside I got reacquainted with Braque and Picasso. The movies I saw there that afternoon was the most shattering work I've ever endured. A silent French film, the "Temptation of Saint Joan." At first I wondered, why only visual subtitles, why only piano music that is quite casual, meandering on in utter unconcern for the emotional drama on the screen. Soon I understood that the dynamic tensions in the film were partly absorbed by the indifferent piano music, otherwise, they would have been insupportable . . .

The movie was in black-and-white, a study mainly of facial expressions which built up so that the least drop of a monk's eyelid conveyed the impact of centuries of spiritual blindness. I'll never forget the final scene at the pyre, a strong and terrible masterpiece of understatement, with the flames licking the wood, smoke rising, the faces of peasants, the innocent unconcerned closeup of a baby sucking a nipple, turning casually to the flaming light, and then back to the nipple, unmoved. The tension built (the way it did when I read "The Penal Colony",[1] in utter sick horror) but I was physically unable to stop looking, even though my mind screamed for release. With the final tension of the film dissolved, I went for a long walk in the cold dark of Central Park, crying and crying, those cold pure tears of Greek tragedy. Then I was treated to a ride in one of the horse cabs, and fed a lump of sugar to the horse which I'd saved from lunch, and felt better. Human kind connot bear very much reality. That kind of reality.

Contrasting to this shuddering rape of the soul, I was feted in one French restaurant after the other . . . "Le Gourmet", "Le Veau D'Or," the "Cafe Saint Denis," among others, until the world was a field of white linen table cloths laid with vichysoisse, soupe a l'oignon, oysters, escalope de veau, aperatifs, steak, white wine, lamb chops, cognac, french pastries, crackling bread and resilient green salads, and all the other sinful sensualities that flesh is heir to. I learned an incalculable lot about myself this week. One can never know what enough is, as Blake remarked, unless onehas had too much. I returned to Smith gladly (which last week I thought was both physically and psychically impossible) and will subsist

1–Probably Franz Kafka's short story 'In the Penal Colony' (1919).

happily for months on cold water and brown bread, hotdogs and bitter coffee. Of such also is the kingdom of heaven.

Oh, Mel, I am running out of typewriter ribbon and time, and again feel that I can pick up in the middle of nowhere and have a verbal communion with you. It is like that with a few people. Next year: que sais-je? The Fulbright to Oxford or Cambridge looks like a dubious dream, now, although my application has been sent to Washington. I do know that if I get admitted at either place (which also looks dubious) that no lack of funds will stop me going. If I have to write a hundred Ladies' Home Journal stories. Radcliffe and Harvard are the places I want to get my degrees, to study eventually, but only after I've been around the world. I know I'll be disillusioned in many ways about England, Mel, but that doesn't stop the vacations in Italy (where I am a daughter---body-and-soul) and France, or, if I have a gallant master, even Africa. My blood, like yours, has a definite southern metabolism . . .

Cross your fingers for me Mel, and hope that I'll be running into you in the Channel or something, before you come back to the land of the chromium plated bathroom, the ivory soap opera and the league of women voters!

My love to you,
syl

TO *Aurelia Schober Plath*

Thursday 27 January 1955

TLS with envelope on *Smith Review* Make-Up Sheet letterhead, Indiana University

Thursday morning, Jan. 27, 1955

Dear mother . . .

I always hate being a harbinger of bad news, but I am really pretty miserable this morning. Evidently my interview decided the committee against me, and this is the first time I have been really rejected after having all the chances, and I have been terribly sad all morning. Perhaps at last those four little men will stop arguing and asking me sarcastic questions in my head. It simply doesn't do any good to say: "Don't worry, it's only one scholarship." It is, unfortunately, everything. Letters from Kazin, Phi Beta Kappa, all that did absolutely no good: my interview canceled all that.

The worst thing is that they told me it was practically impossible to get a Fulbright to Oxford or Cambridge (and they know, having been over there)

and that Dean Rogers is now merrily receiving my Radcliffe applications for admission and scholarship no doubt with a pre-conceived rejection all ready in his mind. Obviously, if this American regional committee refused me, I have no chance for a Fulbright in national competition with countless PhDs. And also obviously, if Rogers says in his letter to apply to a grad shcool with no overcrowding in the Department, he doesn't mean Radcliffe, where only a few make the grade every year. Even if I got admitted, that would be something, but I honestly am dubious about even that last hope, which was the very bottom one on my list, after the Fulbright, England admission, Woodrow Wilson, Radcliffe Scholarship. On this one simple fact of admission hangs my whole future. They can quite easily cut off my whole chance to expand my intellectual horizons, with one little: "We regret to in-form you."

Oh, I really will have to fight with myself to weather the repeated discouragements of this. I've borne the tens of rejections I've gotten for my writing this year with a gay philosophy, but this, after all, is my life. You were only too right when you challenged me about my ability to be an English teacher on the college level. I don't think I'm organized or positive or well-informed enough to teach anybody a damn thing: I'll be lucky if I can teach myself to be a practical file clerk or waitress.

To top all this off, my 2nd semester bill came this morning with $15 more than I had expected for graduating fees. My checking account is thus about $10 short, for I had cut it just "close enough" to cover what I thought my bill would be. Would it be possible for me to have you withdraw about $15 from my dwindling bank account and deposit it in my checking account? The damn check has to be paid in ,10 days.

Well, at least my thesis is all right, and my work here, these last months of what may be my only academic experience, seems to look promising. Several girls in the house are running themselves ragged on theses which they now hate, and having typist problems, so I should count my blessings. At least Smith loves me and I love Smith. If I can't get into Harvard with all Smith behind me, and top grades, I don't see how poor Gordon can expect to, with his low average marks. It's so discouraging, because it implies a rejection of personality and potentiality as well as just "a superfluous applicant."

I'm enclosing a letter to Dean Rogers, in addition to his depressing refusal,[1] for your opinion. I think the letter to him is all right and doesn't sound bitter, which was very hard for me, but I <u>must</u> have some idea about

1–Dean Francis M. Rogers to SP, 26 January 1955; held by Lilly Library.

my failings,[1] because they are inextricably involved with my Radcliffe chances. Dean Rogers only needs to say to a wavering committee at Radcliffe: "She is too risky. I saw her for an interview and she had no grasp of questions, was too cocky, or too nervous, or too God knows what . . ." and I'm done. The thing I'm worried most about now is being admitted even. I never thought I'd fall to such a level!

One fortunate thing is that after I've stopped crying about this and deluging my typewriter, I shall plunge into my work here, a little defiantly to be sure, but with renewed vigor. I still haven't heard from the Journal, and even if they too say "We regret to inform you . . ." it's been 10 days now, and I've learned that bad news is quickest. If only I knew what they disliked about me! I think it's only fair for him to give me some inkling, where my application to Radcliffe is so related to his decisions and so I won't go through life repeating that half hour interview and wondering what I said or did wrong. It's appalling to think that my application and letters were good enough to get me there and that something about my personality was so bad that it cancelled all the rest.

Well, I sat and wrote 10 back letters yesterday, Mrs. Prouty's among them, and am caught up there. This morning I wrote one short story[2] for the Christophers,[3] and will write the other[4] this afternoon. If even one of my three big contest prizes came through, I might be able to earn enough waitressing this summer to go to Graduate school without financial scholarship. But now I am really scared about even being admitted. If admitted, I will go, of course, but at present I hate Dean Rogers, which is not exactly charitable, but rather easy to do at this point. Today this refusal, a SatEvePost rejection, my 2nd semester bill, and your forwarding of my check balance all came, and it is enough to make Vanderbilt wince.

Hello again: it is now after lunch, and I am beginning to think a little. I shall write immediately to Columbia and ask if it is too late to apply for A Scholarship there (the due date is February 20, but they said to send for applications before January 15). I do not think they require the Graduate Record Exam at Columbia as they do at Yale (which is why I am ineligible for Yale, on top of the fact that New Haven leaves me totally cold and the department there is stricter than Harvard about languages). Columbia, at least, evidently has a huge graduate department, and may be more

1–'about my ~~chances and~~ failings' appears in the original.

2–Sylvia Plath, 'Home is Where the Heart Is'.

3–Since 1949, the Christopher Awards are annual awards given for creative works that 'affirm the highest values of the human spirit'.

4–Possibly Sylvia Plath, 'Tomorrow Begins Today'.

generous about admission than Radcliffe. It is where Pat O'Neil wanted to apply next year, and certainly has a good name, even if it is a huge machine. But I am old enough to adjust to a huge machine where the graduate department in English is as large as our senior class at Smith. In fact, I am beginning to think that Harvard is too small to hold both Dean Rogers and myself: he is a big fat man. Ugh.

Even if it is too late to apply for scholarship blanks at Columbia, I can still apply for admission, and I trust they do not know Dean Rogers. I would rather go there, now that I think of it, than be a waitress in Florida. I never could get the orders straight.

Thank goodness I don't have courses now and can spend time on a blank to Columbia. I was foolish to assume that Harvard would be panting to have me and put all my eggs in one basket. It is just that sometimes when all your chickens come home to roost at the same time, broken and bloody, it is a little discouraging.

Forgive me for spilling all this over to you, but if you have any pertinent advice, I'd be glad to have it. You seem to be more of a realist than I about my future prospects. I'd appreciate it if you'd send off the letter to Rogers immediately upon checking it for subtle malice. Keep the refusal for my grandchildren: "See what a brilliant career mother had in spite of Woodrow Wilson, Dean Rogers and various hardhearted professors!" And they will look admiringly at a picture of me, just elected most popular waitress at Howard Johnson's.

Oh well, something will work out. I'll keep fighting.

Lots of love,
your rejected offspring,
sivvy

<on back of envelope>

P.S. I'd really appreciate it if you could send the final copy of my Mary Ventura story[1] up in a week or two – forget about the 17 story – I'll do it myself spring vacation. Also will send grammy's overshoes off in a day or so when I'm downtown. Sorry for the discouraging facts in this letter, but they are, unfortunately, facts.

xx
s.

1–Sylvia Plath, 'Marcia Ventura and the Ninth Kingdom'; SP's calendar indicates she finished this story on 27 December 1954. Previously, SP wrote a story called 'Mary Ventura and the Ninth Kingdom' which she submitted to *Mademoiselle* in early 1953.

TO *Aurelia Schober Plath*

Saturday 29 January 1955 — TLS with envelope, Indiana University

SATURDAY MORNING

Dear Mother . . .

Just thought I'd sit down and write you a little note on this bright sunny day. I hope you are much better and am sure that a good part of your attack (which you are so careful not to elaborate upon) was due to worry and brooding over Dotty and stopping on hills. I don't know whether it is an hereditary characteristic, but our little family is altogether too prone to lie awake at nights hating ourselves for stupidities---technical or verbal, or whatever---and to let careless cruel remarks fester until they blossom in something like ulcer attack or vomiting . . . I know that during these last days I've been fighting an enormous battle with myself . . .

But beyond a point, fighting only wears one out and one has to shut off that nagging part of the mind and go on without it, with bravo and philosophy. Dotty, as you know, is no doubt jealous of you subconsciously for many important things---like having children of your own (and what children!)--and managing to be so much more attractive than she, though older and with much much more responsibility. Therefore, instead of being understanding, she no doubt said something cutting when she saw you making a try for yet a new independence. I must admit I felt a little the same way a week ago when Nancy Hunter began posing as a poet and sending things out. I honestly was glad that they were all bad, which is not a sin, but very natural, and must not be whipped but understood . . .

I remember only too well how weary and dead-tired Frank made me stopping on hills. Always the motor stalled and I had a frantic fear of plunging uncontrolled backward. Over and over again he forced me to let up just enough clutch and push down just enough accelerator to feel the car poise and balance and hold safe while I sat at a 90 degree angle. It's the toughest thing---that and parallel parking which I never use . . . always finding a way out. Not worth the fuss.

By all means don't go around thinking "Oh, the poor driving teacher, he is no doubt sure I'm the stupidest pupil he's ever had." Just know that this is his job, and if you make it more of a challenge, fine, he deserves it. Think of what you'd feel like trying to teach him shorthand. He just might be a little slow to catch on. I knew that I would never get a license, and was sure that my impractical naive approach to the intricacies of a car which stalled mysteriously in the midst of honking traffic would bar me from the modern age. Not so. Here I am, parking on Beacon Street. Not just because I'm young, either. I practiced.

Do try to get some of the fun back into it. I hated myself, car, and instructor very often. Now it's easy to forget and gloss over because I have my license. Maybe a supplementary lesson with Warren would give you time to breathe and practice up on one or two of your problems. Like Frank, he should be kind, but firm.

Do keep on with the lessons, if only 2 or 3 a week. Nothing is worth turmoil. I've learned that. Your present life is the important thing, and it must be relaxed and happy . . . not becoming so only after countless postponements. Remember, I couldn't even run a business machine. Speaking of those, for our sakes (Warren's and mine) I would like you to get a statement from your doctor that you are not to take on extra or <u>new</u> work this coming semester. Older professors are to get <u>concessions</u> not complications. The girls here agree that it would be impossible for them to "dismiss" you as you say for a doctor's order. You could be very sorry, but Get That Statement. Explain to him how you feel and say what you want. I hope you let me know soon about this, or I shall feel forced to write Fran. I want you to spread your force out over many years, not just throw it all recklessly into this one . . . .

Please, by the way, forget about typing those two stories. I've decided to rewrite the "In the Mountains" one so it will be suitable for SEVENTEEN in spring vacation. It is not suitable now, and needs much more development of the inner struggle of the girl. It was an attempt to be understated and cryptic as Hemingway which is fine for a lit. course, but not for 17.

Then too, I am not sending the Mary Ventura story to the Christophers. I think it is much too fantastic and symbolic for what they want. They want warm simple stories that will inspire people to go out and do likewise, and I don't think they want everyone in the U.S.A. jumping off speeding trains in the subway!

These last three days, I have done up some very good stories if I do say so. I wrote two for the Christophers, tailored for specifications, both based on a Bible quote, very plotted, and noble, but not preaching. One is about a housewife ("Home Is Where the Heart Is") who comes to mental crisis, faced by a family that seems to be seeking life outside the home. She manages creatively to bring them all back together. The other is even more dramatic---set in a hospital waiting room with flashbacks (I've read up on TV requirements and limitations and been realistic in my sets, main characters, and immediate interest angle) called "Tomorrow

Begins Today", about what one teenager can do in channeling energies of high school students from destructive to creative channels. Both are under 10 pages, very decisive and forthright, and I think I have a much better chance than possible with a vague symbolic tale like 9th kingdom . . . .

Also have rewritten my two best Kazin stories and am sending both off to MLLE's short story contest, answering Cyrilly Abels recent letter[1] that she is looking forward to see my new stories "eagerly". I am very proud of both of these stories . . . have digested thoroughly and rewritten critically (as you suggested, there has been a cooling time lapse since the 1st copy) They seem to like a balance in their two winning stories, so one of mine---"The Day Mr. Prescott Died"---is a sassily-told humorous one (with real human interest, seriously, under it) in the first person. The other, a very dark story, is the best work of "art" I've ever done, I think. It is called "Tongues of Stone" (my favorite title yet) and is all very bleak and beautifully written, with a crisis and turn for the better at the immediate end. This was the one Mr. Kazin wrote his lovely letter to me about---saying that, thank God I was a writer, but that writing was invented to give more joy than that story---so I took his advice, and changed it from life to art . . . gave it a conclusion of dawn, instead of eternal night, which to me just makes it right . . . .

I have a feeling that I may be destined to be more successful in writing than I thought at first. If any of these come through, I may well be able to go to Europe in spite of Dean Rogers, write there, learn French and German, and come back a better person. The reason why Miss Chase advised England is the free time to write there, which I long for. If either Oxford or Cambridge should accept me, I will go without a Fulbright. That I know. I shall get $2,000 somehow if I have the chance to go!

The Columbia application came today, so with fast work at the beginning of the week, before classes start for me Wednesday night, thank God, I should be able to get the necessary letters underway. They ask for thesis or other academic work, and bless Miss Page for having me make an extra carbon! It shall go. Only at Columbia you have to write an MA thesis, as you don't at Harvard, so my writing time would be almost nil. And writing is the first love of my life . . . I have to live well and rich and far to write, so that is all good. I could never be a narrow introvert writer, the way many are, for my writing depends so much on my life . . .

1–Cyrilly Abels to SP, 18 January 1955; held by Lilly Library.

Chin up, mother, and get well for me! Do all you can to put me at ease about that! Love to all.

your very own –
sivvy

p.s. Haven't heard from Journal yet – it's now a full 2 weeks!

TO *Aurelia Schober Plath*

Wednesday 2 February 1955[1] TLS with envelope, Indiana University

Wednesday morning

Dearest mother . . .

Hope by now that all is well with you, both physically and autoly. Snow has come here, and the bleak black winter sets in, all of which provide many metaphors for poetry. Nothing more, I'm convinced of it, could happen in a discouraging way. The Journal sent my story back saying that the narrative improved the writing, but it lacked an "indefinable something" that made a Journal piece. At present, I begin to feel that I lack that "indefinable something" that makes a winner.

Fortunately, I'm happier in the midst of these refusals than I was two years ago on the crest of my success wave. Which just shows what a positive philosophy can do. I'd be scared if I just kept on winning things. I do deserve a streak of rejection, and am fortunate to have a friend such as Sue Weller to stand by me through joy and sorrow both with equal fortitude. Also, I am very fond of a brilliant music major, Dorrie Licht,[2] whom I've no doubt told you about. They make life much more delightful.

I've paid all my outstanding bills, and now have the glorious figure of $17. in my checking and $11. in my bank account. According to my drastically reduced budget, I am $75 short for coming semester expenses, but am sure that at least a couple of hundred in poetry prizes will be forthcoming later this spring, and will be prompt about paying back your kind $25 then, along with the January telephone bill which will be astronomical.

1–Date supplied from postmark.

2–Dorrit Licht Hildebrandt Colf (1934–); B.A. 1955, music, Smith College; SP's friend. SP attended Licht's wedding at the First Presbyterian Church, Mount Vernon, New York, to Frederick Dean Hildebrandt (1933–2010) on 26 March 1955 (divorced); married Howard D. Colf on 14 June 1965.

I have felt great advances in my poetry, the main one being a growing victory over word's nuances and a superfluity of adjective. On the risk of your considering "Temper of Time" "depressing", I am sending you the 3 latest examples of my lyrics.[1] Read aloud for word tones, for full effect. Understand that "Temper of Times," while ominous, is done tongue in cheek, after a collection of vivid metaphors of omen from the thesaurus, which I am rapidly wearing out. It is a kind of pun on the first page of the NY Times which has news much like this every morning.

Someday Phyllis McGinley will hear from me. They can't shut me up.

The Christophers wrote a nice letter about receiving the stories, saying "God Bless You" and "Sincerely in Christ," which struck me as rather ironic in the midst of all this flurry of rejections, literary and academic.

However, my typewriter won't be still. This summer I am going to write a pack of stories, read magazines religiously (as every Writer's manual advises) and capitalize on my growing powers of neat articulation. And I am going to Sell "The Smoky Blue Piano" somewhere.

Now I can see the advantage of an agent . . . she keeps you from the little deaths every writer goes through whenever a manuscript comes back home. It's like having your child refused admittance to public school. You love it, and often can't see why. Read one encouraging story about a successful writer who wrote 10 stories in 10 months and her agent collected 81 (!) rejections and not one acceptance. But the author gaily began her 11th story. Very encouraging!

Much love to my favorite mummy, and keep well for me. That's the one thing you can do for me and for Warren! We love you so much.

A kiss for the tip of your Grecian nose!

Love,
Sivvy

1–According to SP's calendar, she completed 'Temper of Time' and 'Winter Words' on 1 February 1955, and 'Apparel for April' on 2 February 1955.

Sylvia Plath
Lawrence House
Smith College
Northampton, Massachusetts

Apparel for April

Hills sport tweed for
   april's back,
world parades her
   birthday frock.

Clouds don laces
   and white linen,
all the sky is
   light blue denim.

Air is clear as
   honeydew,
in pink tiaras
   daisies blow.

Daffodil puts
   on frilled yellow,
fringe of veil suits
   greening willow.

Crocus struts in
   amethyst,
robins button
   scarlet vest.

Squirrel brushes
   silver fur,
river flashes
   jeweled hair.

Sunlight gilds fair
   boy and girl,
apparels them for
   pastoral.

Tricked with clover
   in this land,
with leaf and lover
   wreathed around.

Lest spring bequeath me
   nakedness,
o sweet one, clothe me
   with a kiss.

Sylvia Plath
Lawrence House
Smith College
Northampton, Massachusetts

Winter Words

In the pale prologue
   of daybreak
tongues of intrigue
   cease to speak.

Moonshine splinters
   as birds hush;
transfixed the antlers
   in the bush.

With fur and feather,
   buck and cock
softly author
   icebound book.

No chinese painter's
   brown and buff
could quill a quainter
   calligraph.

On stilted legs the
  bluejays go
their minor leagues a-
  cross the snow,

inscribing cryptic
  anagrams
on their skeptic
  search for crumbs.

Chipmunks enter
  stripes of black
in the winter
  almanac.

A scribbling squirrel
  makes a blot
of gray apparel,
  hides a nut.

On chastely figured
  trees and stones
fate is augured
  in bleak lines.

With shorthand scratches
  on white scroll
bark of birches
  tells a tale.

Ice like parchment
  shrouds the pond,
marred by misprint
  of north wind.

Windowpane wears
  gloss of frost
till dawnlight blurs
  and all's erased.

Before palaver
   of the sun
learn from this graver
   lexicon:

Read godly fiction
   in rare flake,
spell king's direction
   from deer track.

Sylvia Plath
Lawrence House
Smith College
Northampton, Massachusetts

Temper of Time

An ill wind is stalking while
   Evil stars whir
And all the gold apples go
   Bad to the core.

Black birds of omen now
   Prowl on the bough
And the forest is littered with
   Bills that we owe.

Through closets of copses tall
   Skeletons walk
While nightshade and nettles
   Tangle the track.

In the ramshackle meadow where
   Kilroy would pass
Lurks the sickle-shaped shadow of
   Snake in the grass.

Approaching his cottage by
  Crooked detour
He hears the gruff knocking of
  Wolf at the door.

His wife and his children hang
  Riddled with shot,
There's a hex on the cradle and
  Death in the pot.

TO *Aurelia Schober Plath*

Thursday 3 February 1955[1] ALS (postcard), Indiana University

Thursday

Dearest mother . . .

So glad to get your last fat letter and hear about the home front. It is amazing how one small human love can make a mountain of black bills & rejections seem small as a speck of pepper! Today Mr. Fisher took me to coffee before our weekly session, asked in detail about my projects for the next year, and is both practical and dear about everything – telling me to run over the minute I hear yes or no about anything to discuss with him before even wording acceptance or rejection – told him how bleak my prospects are, & he was a relief to talk to – I'll find <u>something</u> through these wonderful people, even if it's not what I had a preconceived notion about. It is adventure to have the world open. I wonder if some day in May Sue Weller & I may have the use of your blue car to drive to the Southward Inn for interviews? <u>If</u> we decide we need that much money. We are both applying next week for a job teaching 5th grade for 1 year at the American school in Morrocco – it sounds like the most intriguing prospect to put our theories of international co-operation together – pupils come from 20 different countries & the salaries, while very low, are made up for by the type of experience & the nearness to the continent – only a few hours across the straits. Naturally we would only consider going as a pair. Usually these appointments are for 3 years and the 1 year interval is unusual. Wish us luck. Sue is a great girl. Am doubledating this Fri with her & two grad students from Princeton.

xx

s.

1 – Date supplied from postmark.

TO *Aurelia Schober Plath*

Saturday 5 February 1955[1] ALS (postcard), Indiana University

Saturday afternoon

Dear mother . . .

I was really appalled to hear Mr. C. was in the hospital – no wonder his "personality" was so criticized by his students – as with daddy, disease twisted an otherwise good nature. I am terribly sorry I have no money to give – I expect to have to borrow on my $50 deposit what with unforeseen senior expenses. But I do expect to get some money from poems this spring, and will send a check, I hope, then. Got the first really encouraging note from Dean of Radcliffe[2] today – (Rogers sent her my letter) – saying my not winning the Woodrow Wilson "Would in no way weaken" my chances for a grant at Radcliffe, & the WWS were given mostly for men who might otherwise go into business, law, medicine, etc. Obviously Rogers wrote her why I didn't get a WW, & It no doubt was not for character blots. only, as I had thought. Poems come better and better, and my courses, if demanding, are fiery and delightful. I feel much better about my prospects now that I have spread my applications out to include an interesting job and Columbia (although my roster of choice goes 1 Fulbright to Eng. 2 Teaching in Morocco 3 Radcliffe & 4 Columbia. Keep all your fingers crossed. Thrilled about Ruth's coming wedding & feel most honored.[3]

xx
Siv

<handwritten on address side of postcard>

P.S. Got beautifully typed (!) letter from Warren with no apparent provocation (!) and enjoyed it thoroughly! Shows what patient teaching & practice can do!

Cookies are delicious – enormously appreciated – Sue & I enjoy them at teatime every day – Thank you!

1–Date supplied from postmark.

2–Probably Bernice Brown Cronkhite (1893–1983), Dean of the Graduate School (1934–59). SP was admitted to Radcliffe Graduate School for the fall of 1955 to work towards a Ph.D. in English; see Bernice Brown Cronkhite to SP, 23 May 1955; held by Lilly Library.

3–SP served as maid of honour at Ruth Freeman's wedding to Arthur Geissler on 11 June 1955, at Saint John's Episcopal Church, Winthrop, Mass.

TO *Aurelia Schober Plath*

Thursday 10 February 1955 TLS with envelope, Indiana University

thursday, february 10

Dear mother . . .

Happy Valentine's Day! Sue and I are still enjoying your delicious cookies at our nightly teatime and really appreciate your going to the bother of sending them. I hope that by now you have got your overshoes! Life here is in that nasty fickle stage between winter and spring and I have written several very good poems[1] which I think you will like. I look so forward to going to Mr. Fisher this afternoon as ever for our weekly session.

I am very proud of my brother, but am afraid I can't boast as much about marks. My Shakespeare wavers toward a B* and my German is also only a B*. But I like both courses very much and feel that my writing deserves what it is getting by way of time.

Now for the money. The only way I would accept your kind offer of a monthly loan is that it was unequivocally understood it was a <u>loan</u> and that I would pay it back by graduation. My whole budget was thrown off this year by $100 unexpected expenses ($25 application fees and transcripts, $20 thesis, $25 medicines, and $30 senior expenses such as cap and gown). So quite frankly I have used up all my 2nd semester funds already and have been forced to sell some of my old clothes and possessions to keep myself in postage stamps. In spite of strict budget and absolutely no amusements (I depend on my dates for food, plays, and wine) I would need, after your first $25 check, about $10-$15 a month, I think. I do appreciate this, as I refuse to borrow from authorities and was fully expecting to be hauled into court for my 2nd semester book bills!

Now, about the Morocco job. I thought I would wait until my interview with Mr. Robert Shea,[2] head of the American School in Tangier, today, before countering all your arguments, which I now feel very justified in doing.

1–According to SP's calendar, she wrote 'Dirge' ['Lament'] on 4 February 1955; 'Elegy', 'Complaint' and 'Notes on Zarathustra' on 6 February 1955; 'The Dream' on 7 February 1955; and 'Prologue to Spring' on 9 February 1955.

2–Robert Smith Shea (*c.* 1922–2001); a member of the United States Consulate in Tangier, Morocco, a former member of administration at Xavier University and the Commission for Human Rights. Educated at St Bonaventure University, Tulane University, and Columbia University.

I was sorry that you jumped to hasty conclusions about both the job and my future plans before waiting to hear the facts. Obviously you are against the job, or you would realize that your questions, while practical, have no real bearing on the subject at hand, which is what I want to do with my time.

Now with me, writing is the first delight in life. I want time and money to write, both very necessary. I will not sacrifice my time to learn shorthand because I do not want any of the jobs which shorthand would open up, although those jobs are no doubt very interesting for girls who want them. I do not want the rigid hours of a magazine or publishing job. I do not want to type other people's letters and read their manuscripts. I want to type my own and write my own. So secretarial training is out for me. That I know. Of course I shall be glad to learn the dictaphone and other machines with you spring vacation, because I may have to do part time work now and then.

As for the job teaching fifth grade (it is really any grade from kindergarten to 8th), the charming, handsome diplomat who interviewed me today stressed that in the very new school in Tangier which has 200 pupils of over 20 different nationalities, wants good will, interest and a general liberal arts education in preference to a rigid program of education courses. That is why he is interviewing seniors at Smith. The program at the school (which has 13 teachers) puts each new recruit with a seasoned teacher (he showed me pictures of one from England who has her 'life certificate' and one from Sweden who is also superbly trained). Thus they initiate their own staff to their own needs which are unique, and which no Teachers' College in the world could begin to prepare for. As you no doubt know, it is only the public schools which ask for "specific information and preparation." The private schools have descended on Smith seniors avidly demanding girls without <u>any</u> education courses to join their programs at top salaries and openly prefer not to have those with preconceived notions. They teach their own.

So much for the need of preparation. As you see, I would be expected to do nothing more than learn from the expert teacher who shared my grade, and to teach the whole grade, all courses, which would be a remarkably versatile training for me. I believe that in America much too much emphasis is put on courses---with the idea that anything from cooking to writing can be mastered if a course certificate is had. Well, I believe I can learn from books by myself, and certainly will read up on my age group and lesson theories when and if I get this job . .

I do not want state certification or more years sitting at a desk learning how to teach when I can live and learn from the best schoolbook yet: real children in a real international community. This is the beginning of my professional training, The "veteran" teachers in Tangier are if anything more skilled and versatile than those here, so I will be a trainee there, too. This will thus eliminate all fear of "failure" which you seem to have. A lively love and general education and creative outlook are what they want. They will train themselves.

As for this job, I certainly am looking beyond the "vacation." You say that the teaching experience would not help me get a job here! I don't see how you can ignore the reputation of an international school, where at the third grade each pupil starts a 2nd language, and where the demands for versatility and quick thinking are everywhere, what with the international and interracial problems in this community!

You see, all your worries about "teacher training" are inapplicable here, and Sue and I would live in an apartment (the most luxurious, with patio and 5 or 6 rooms is $50 a month!) and do our own cooking (food is abundant, especially fruit and vegetables). We would have a maid to purchase for us because her salary would cost no more than what we would be cheated out of as foreigners at the public markets. Our program would be 5 days a week from about 9-4, beginning in the middle of September till June 30.

I can hardly describe the vitality of this small international community, which was founded, according to legend, by Antheus, the son of Neptune, and which is governed by a Committee of Consuls of Spain, France, Portugal, Italy, Belgium, the Netherlands, Great Britain and the U.S. The man who spoke to me is head of the school, and he is the sort that would be the utmost delight to work under . . . he has a radiance and a love that make me really want to serve. English is taught, and is the language of the school; French is the language of the polite society; Spanish is the language of the street. And the rest ranges from Icelandic to Arabic.

How can you not see that living here would be a thousand times more advantageous for my languages and growing interest in international politics than "courses" at a sweet American desk?

The question for me is not a "definite objective", but rather a growing way of life which can adapt itself to surprises and alterations of all sorts. After a year in England, or a year in Morocco, who knows what I wouldn't be equipped to do? With me, the process of living is a justification in itself, especially if I believe in it with my mind, heart and soul. I have no time to waste, as you so well realize, but our interpretations of wasted time are quite different. To me, anything which will not let me write and grow and learn by leaps and bounds in my own way, which is more and more versatile, is not only confining, but stunting.

The international outlook is the coming world view, and I hope to be a part of that community with all I have in me. I am young enough to learn languages by living, and not the artificial acceleration or plodding of "book" courses. I want people opposite me at tables, at desks, not merely books.

I do hope you do not get blind with anger at these statements, which, I think you will find, upon careful, cool consideration, are not only logical, but live up to my ideas of the true life.

As for the climate and culture in Morocco, you will be glad to know that it is healthier than England and New England by far! It is a "Cool, dry climate with a hot sun", which is just my dish . . . and the doctors are excellent, as Mr. Shea said, and the American Navy Base has plane service nearby to the school in case an appendix needed to be cut out, so there is no worry there. Mr. Shea is like the intelligent, loving, liberal father I have always longed for, and I can think of no man except Mr. Crockett who so much made me think that there are saints on earth, with a radiance and love of service and helping others to grow which is almost superhuman. The easy-going sunny nature of this man attracted me from the first. It is impossible not to love him. He is an international Mr. Crockett, and gave up a top job as diplomat in Persia because he loved the project of this school so much.

He is sending Sue and myself applications, and we will not know until late April or early May, which is fine, because all my other offers will be in then, or refusals, as the case may be. Ultimately, although he must discuss us with the Tangier Board, his decision is final.

During my divine poetry hour with Mr. Fisher today, I discussed all this in detail, and he said, after approving heartily (He too was dubious about it last week, when the complete facts weren't known) "Do you really want this job?" I assented earnestly, and he left the room a moment. When he came back, he said he'd just called the man, who was in the middle of interviews, and given me the highest recommendation he could think of. Such dearness I can hardly believe. Mr. Fisher is the ideal reader and professor for me, for my particular poetry. Week by week I can feel the growth and heightened sensitivity, sprouting up inside me. Again, he treated me to coffee, and I believe I am experiencing the most stimulating creative process of two minds meeting and growing . . . I learn so much from him, and in turn I feel I am giving all that is in me, and he is happy with it.

Well, enough of this rambling. I did feel though that I wanted you to have the facts whereby to make a judicious considered judgment of this possibility which I feel you were not able to do before (and neither was I) because of lack of concrete information.

One small thing: I realize that my goals in life may seem strange to you. I only hope that it does some good to take all this time out to try to explain, because, if possible, I would like you to appreciate my aims and attempts, even if you do not personally agree with them. I do think you should feel reassured about the "approved" nature of this job, and understand that all which passes through the Smith Vocational Office is highly reputable and solidly founded.

I have always wanted to combine my creative urges with a kind of service to the world. I am not a missionary in the narrow sense, but I do believe I can counteract McCarthy and much adverse opinion about the U.S. by living a life of honesty and love amidst these people for a short time. It is, in a way, serving my religion, which is that of humanism, and a belief in the potential of each man to learn and love and grow: these children, their underdeveloped lands, their malnutrition, . . . all these factors are not the neat rigid American ideals, but I believe the new races are going to influence the world in turn, much as America did in her day, and however small my part, I want a share in giving to them.

I know what my professors have done for me, how I remember Miss Raguse[1] and Mr. Crockett, Mary Ellen Chase and Mr. Fisher. Even if my level is only making a Mexican get excited about history, or dramatizing a government problem simply to recreate an abstract idea vividly, this is what I would like. This is for now. For perhaps only one year. I hope after that to be a much more linguistic and experienced woman. Maybe I'll be a reporter. Or a poet living in Italy. Or a student at Radcliffe. The important thing is that the choice grows naturally out of my life and is not imposed on it by wellmeaning friends.

Do consider what I say seriously. I hope you understand!

xx
sivvy

1–Mabel R. Raguse (1892–1993), English teacher at the Alice L. Phillips Junior High School, where SP was enrolled 1944–7.

TO *Gordon Lameyer*

Thursday 10 February 1955 TLS in greeting card,[1]
Indiana University

<The printed greeting includes more than thirty one-line Valentine messages and short rhymes in a random layout, and is signed:>

love, / sylvia / inside ↓

thursday, february 10

dear gordon . . .

forgive me for not being more verbose, but for the first time in my life I've been impatient as hell with letters, and want to talk in person because there is so much much much to say. hope I will see you before I explode with all the news . . . .

it is a black month in the sense that a hideous committee of 4 smug men interviewed me at harvard for a national teaching scholarship (ww) and found me wanting because I was a woman and would obviously get married someday. the dean of radcliffe wrote me a very encouraging letter about this, for as the head of the committee was head of harvard grad school, I figured it would annihilate my chances for a grant at radcliffe. not at all she said. I was a woman, and radcliffe is more hospitable to women. so I was relieved there.

otherwise, it has been rejection all around. one poem after another. the worst was a story the "Ladies' Home Journal" suggested me to rewrite and which they finally rejected a second time, thereby smashing my dreams of $850 to save me from debtors' prison, where I am rapidly heading. but somehow, I am happier in this wave of refusal than I ever was two years ago on my flashy crest of success . . .

the best part is the weekly sessions with fisher, who as I've said hundreds of times, reminds me of you. he is The Reader for my poetry. so sensitive, with a feeling for nuance and allusion, a love for joyce, a linguistic genius, that makes me go around in a state of metaphysical love and light from week to week, writing at least 5 poems a week, and dying to write more and give all else up, and hoping to arrange a book, which is already crystallizing, and should be ready in a year or so . . .

oh, the most fantastic thing is to come (forgive me the queer paging, but I'm getting hectic). I had an interview for a job teaching in morocco today at the american school in tangier, and I can think of nothing else. sue and I want to go together, and the man, robert smith shea, who interviewed

1–Panda Prints Valentine card designed by Rosalind Welcher.

us, was the handsomest, most radiant, polished fellow I've ever met. we both felt we could literally follow him to the ends of the earth, which is what we may well be doing.

the school itself is in an old sultan's palace, and there are 200 pupils from 20 different nationalities. I forget whether you've been here or not, but he said the port lido (?) navy base was connected to this place by plane. details will have to wait till I see you, and sue and I won't know definitely till late april, but I am really exhilarated at the prospect of putting my theories and philosophy of life into practice . . . of having people and not merely books opposite me at the desk!

I am obsessed by writing as the first thing in life, and the poems come more and more, as I said. and next I am entranced by the coming importance of an international orientation in life, which is what I want to have. languages in morocco are like the tower of babel: french is for polite society; spanish is for the street; the rest range from arabic to Icelandic . . . . oh, cross your fingers for sue and me! two such desiring ulysses!

loved your last long letter[1] as always. this semester is much harder than last, and I have dropped to a B* in all my courses except writing, because I am giving my love and time to it . . . but it is worth it for me . . . .

please let me know as soon as you are coming back so I can clear away work and see you the first time possible . . .

bon voyage home, darling . . . .

goodbye for a while, your terza rima dreamer,

sylvia

1–Gordon Lameyer to SP, either 25 or 31 January 1955; held by Lilly Library.

TO *Atlantic Monthly*

Saturday 12 February 1955 TLS (photocopy), Yale University

Lawrence House
Smith College
Northampton, Massachusetts
February 12, 1955

Accent on Living Editor
ATLANTIC MONTHLY
8 Arlington Street
Boston 16, Massachusetts

Dear Sir:

Almost five months ago, on September 29, I mailed a group of seven poems to your department, and as I have not heard from you as yet, I should like to make sure that my manuscript has not gone astray.

The poems are: "Never Try To Know More Than You Should," "Verbal Calisthentics," "The Dispossessed," "Insolent Storm Strikes At The Skull," "Ennui," "Suspend This Day," and "Circus in Three Rings."

At present, I am enclosing six of my recent poems which I hope you will consider for publication in your magazine: "Temper of Time," "Epitaph in Three Parts," "Dirge," "Rondeau Redoublé," "Danse Macabre", and "Prologue to Spring."

If by any chance the stamped, self-addressed envelope which I enclosed with the last set of poems has been lost, I should be glad to send another. At any rate, I should very much appreciate hearing whether the poems were received intact by your department.

Poems, stories and articles of mine have been published previously in Mademoiselle, Seventeen, and Harper's.

Thank you for your time and consideration.

Sincerely yours,
Sylvia Plath

TO *Ruth Cohen*[1]

c. Monday 14 February 1955[2] TL,[3] Indiana University

Lawrence House
Smith College
Northampton, Massachusetts

Dear Miss Cohen,

I was glad to receive your letter[4] informing me that I have been admitted as an affiliated student at Newnham College to read for the English Tripos. It is with pleasure that I accept this offer of admission for the two years' course leading to the B.A. Honours degree.

Recently I was notified that my Fulbright papers have been sent on to Washington and that I am in the final round of the Fulbright competition. Since the outcome of Fulbright applications is not announced until late in the spring, I have also applied for supplementary grants to cover the cost of my first year in England in case the Fulbright is not forthcoming. In any case, I plan to arrive at Newnham in October, 1955.

I should be most appreciative if you would let me know whenever possible what the increase of College and University fees will involve in new total of expense for an American student so that I will be able to plan my finances accordingly.

I should also be intereste to know about the possibilities for my living in the Hall for graduate students at Newnham. (I believe this is Whitstead Hall).

In conclusion, I wish to thank you for your time and kind consideration. It is with pleasant anticipation that I look forward to my arrival at Newnham next October.

1–Ruth Louisa Cohen (1906–91); Principal of Newnham College, Cambridge, 1954–72.
2–Christine Abbott, Newnham College Secretary to SP, 19 February 1955, answers this letter; held by Lilly Library.
3–Probably a retained copy of SP's letter.
4–Ruth Cohen to SP, 27 January 1955; held by Lilly Library.

TO *Aurelia Schober Plath*

Monday 14 February 1955[1] ALS (postcard), Indiana University

monday night

dear mother . . .

your welcome check came today, narrowly saving me from debtor's prison & enabling me to buy my senior robe, which somehow thrilled me. am fighting off a cold with pyrobenzamine and it does wonders, this will be a month of unadulterated work & meetings & so will march. fruits should all bear sometime in april. hope to contradict t. s. eliot's words that "april is the cruellest month."[2] You'll be happy to hear of an ecstatic coffee hour spent at the home of my dearest friend, mary ellen chase, discussing my plans for next year, which have suddenly taken a bright turn: cambridge university accepted me as a foreign affiliate for 2-year program for honors B.A. – M.A. is automatic & all colleges in america will hold out arms to me as teacher – whole english dept. here is behind me and against machine-made american grad degrees. if fulbright doesn't come, will get money some how. don't tell anyone except grandparents & warren. but it looks like what I've always wanted in my secret heart –

xx

sivvy.

ps. English men are great

TO *The Editor*, Mademoiselle

c. February 1955 Printed from *Mademoiselle*,[3] March 1955

Never have I read such a plump, magnificent issue as your February one! A very happy twentieth birthday to you.

At Smith, my friends and I were especially enchanted by the gay, lilting love poem by Donald Hall[4] and the winsome, whimsical Peynet sketches.[5] I reveled in the superb story by Bryan McMahon[6] and you can imagine how I welcomed Dylan Thomas![7] To tell the other features I enjoyed would

1–Date supplied from postmark.
2–From Eliot's 'The Waste Land', line 1.
3–Printed under the heading 'Many happy returns', *Mademoiselle*, March 1955, 64.
4–Donald Hall, 'Valentine', *Mademoiselle*, February 1955, 121.
5–Raymond Peynet, 'The Path of Love', *Mademoiselle*, February 1955, 144–5.
6–Bryan MacMahon, 'O, Lonely Moon!', *Mademoiselle*, February 1955, 164–5, 211–16.
7–Dylan Thomas, 'The Vest', *Mademoiselle*, February 1955, 142–3.

be to run through the contents of the whole magazine. Congratulations on the most wonderful MLLE yet—a delight and challenge to the eye and to the mind.

S. P., Smith College,
Northampton, Mass.

TO *Aurelia Schober Plath*

Tuesday 1 March 1955[1] ALS (postcard), Indiana University

Tuesday, 4 p.m.

Dear mother,

Just a note in the beginning of my most rugged week to let you know how things are – somehow its a comfort to think that this is March 1st, the same month that spring vacation begins – I am looking forward to two whole weeks of peace & study (I must review fantastic amounts for may "comprehensives") in Wellesley. Plan to go to NYC from sat. till Mon. that weekend before to see Dorrie Licht's wedding & Jan & Clai, which should be fun. This week is fantastically full. Am going (alone) to Amherst tonight to see "Othello"[2] for Shakespeare course & one of my best friends[3] is playing "Emelia" & got me a free ticket. Friday I have a Ger. written & Thursday & Friday is the enormous 3-session symposium on the "Mid-Century Novel",[4] starring among others, Alfred Kazin, Saul Bellow[5] & Brendan Gill[6] – chaired by Miss Chase. – Cyrilly Abels just sent me a lovely telegram[7] offering me $10 to $50 (depending on fullness of material) to cover this thing, so must spend almost 3 solid days concentrating to do a good job on this. As you may imagine, I was very pleased at her assignment! Cross your fingers for me during these crowded days!

xx
sivvy

1–Date supplied from postmark.
2–The Amherst Masquers performed *Othello* at the Kirby Memorial Theater in Amherst, 24 February–1 March 1955. SP's friend Elinor Friedman played the role of Emilia.
3–Elinor Linda Friedman Klein (1934–); B.A. 1956, Smith College; SP's friend; Friedman lived at 704 Laurel Street Longmeadow, Mass.
4–Smith College hosted a two-day symposium called 'The American Novel at Mid-Century'. Kazin spoke on 'The Novelist and the Unknown'.
5–Saul Bellow (1915–2005), Canadian-American author; Nobel laureate.
6–Brendan Gill (1914–97), American writer, especially for *New Yorker*.
7–Cyrilly Abels to SP, 1 March 1955; held by Lilly Library.

TO *Aurelia Schober Plath*

Thursday 10 March 1955 ALS (postcard), Indiana University

Thursday, March 10

Dearest mother . . .

It was a joy to get your cheerful letter this happy day which was all running rivulets, melting snow, and lilting spring – business first: would much appreciate your offer of $25 when possible – hope that will be the last I need ask of you – be assured I shall pay you back by summer – I am optimistic about my chances somehow. As is, I have large book & medecine bills to pay for the 2nd sem., so am always it seems, in need. Mlle is paying me $30 for my coverage & probably will use one of my ideas: publishing the best speech as a feature article. hope Smith will let them. At a talk & party at the Hampshire Bookshop on Monday,[1] Mary Ellen Chase made a lovely public announcement of my admission to Cambridge & even Pres. Wright came up to shake my hand – I somehow know I will get $4000 to cover those two years – somehow. Had a good talk with Mr. Kazin yesterday, who I hope will be a lifelong friend of mine. Mr. fisher is very pleased with my poetry, & I love that course above all – got A- in my last Ger. exam & only hope I can keep it up – These next two weeks are hardest, with 2 exams & 2 papers due next Friday, but I am somehow very happy always, in spite of the longdrawn tension of WAITING for a hundred things –

Love you all very much –
your own sivvy

TO *Aurelia Schober Plath*

Sunday 13 March 1955 TLS with envelope, Indiana University

Sunday morning, March 13

Dearest Mother . . . .

I have so loved getting your colorful Paul Gauguin cards . . . they really make my mail incandescent, with their lovely slices of orange, purple and gold between the black-and white of rejection slips. I have written three

1–According to SP's calendar, she attended a party for Eleanor Duckett's *Saint Dunstan of Canterbury: A Study of Monastic Reform in the Tenth Century* (New York: W. W. Norton, 1955). SP's copy held by Smith College.

or four little poems,[1] partly humorous, about the sculpture and paintings I saw at the Whitney museum in NYC when I went there for the 1955 American exhibit.

Yesterday, Ruthie came over, and after an unsuccessful hour or more of looking in shops for dresses, I treated her to a cocktail and potato chips at Rahar's. I feel a little sad that she and I are so far apart . . . she is without a doubt the leader of her friends in intelligence and good looks, and I find them terribly young and tedious: always smoking "cigs," playing bridge and dying of boredom unless they can see a "real tremendous movie." I can't help but think that most of them are rather empty, and have never gotten beyond a highschool mentality. The mention of anything intelligent or the least bit academic shocks them to death. As I say, Ruth is the one exception I can find. I do feel that it was not my place to give a shower for her here, since I am the only girl she knows at Smith, and it would be most peculiar to ask all her friends---girls I've met only once briefly, and whose names I don't even remember, except that they are all Bizes and Lizes---to Hamp. So I shall compensate by getting an extra-special wedding gift. Should I get her an engagement present too? As far as I can see, the kind of dress I'll get for this will be the sort of thing I wont want to wear again, because the girls seem set on green, of all frightful things. Anyway, we'll go shopping in Boston the Saturday after I get home.

In spite of the fact that this is my worst week of exams and papers, I am very happy, probably because Sue Weller and I spent the morning today playing tennis for the first time in the season and I feel the sluggish gloomy weight of the winter dropping away and am getting agile on my feet again. As a native Californian, Sue is an excellent player, and thinks I have great possibilities. So we look forward to a season of playing together. I never felt so lively as today for months, and I am determined to keep up this exercise, and to go out for crew again this spring the way I did last fall. I am not bad, if I practice, and I love the feeling of being up early in the morning and having my muscles tightening: basically, I think, I am an "outdoor" girl, as well as a contemplative sedentary writer.

<u>Mlle</u> just sent my lovely pink check,[2] which will pay my book bill at least. Somehow with the coming of the spring, nothing really bothers me, and I feel very happy and optimistic. I am turning out five poems a week and they get better and better. I hope to write a lot this summer and try

1–Sylvia Plath, 'Wayfaring at the Whitney', comprising: '"Kafka" by Sahl Swarz', '"Daedalus and Icarus" by Lindsay Daen', and '"Three Caryatids Without a Portico" by Hugh Robus'.

2–Dated 9 March 1955. See also Cyrilly Abels to SP, 9 March 1955; held by Lilly Library.

to get a little book of them into print in about a year: think I'll try out for the Yale Series of Younger Poets. Just for fun.

By the way, after my exams in the end of May, I shall have about five days till graduation weekend and wonder if you would mind if I brought Sue Weller home for those days. I think you will like her next best to Marty . . . she is beautifully plump, quite reserved, until you get to know her, and brilliant in economics and government. Really, she is my closest friend in the house and I should love to have the family meet her . . . I'd also like to play tennis with her daily, show her my dear Nauset beach, and just relax, nothing to put out any extra work for, really.

I am happy to say that my plans for spring vacation have altered favorably. Instead of coming back here a week early, the way I thought I'd have to, I hope to get all my papers done in a push beforehand, and compromise by bringing a suitcase of books home and writing poems and reading for two lovely weeks in Wellesley. I should either come home Tuesday March 29, or Wednesday the 30th, depending on how my work goes.

The weekend after this, Sue Weller and I are going down to NYC to see Dorrie Licht, the brilliant musician of our trio, get married. It should be an exciting affair, and we've been invited to the reception too, the only girls from Smith going.

Don't want to get any of your hopes up, but I can't help telling you that my fates seem to be brewing up something quite good. The Fulbright Adviser here just got a letter from the agent in Oxford (saying I'd been recommended for one, nothing more) and mentioning that if I could be sure of providing for the second year that Lady Margaret Hall[1] at Oxford would admit me! Naturally this is all very hush-hush and I'm not even supposed to know as my Grant is apparently so indeterminate, but to know that Oxford also accepted me, without even the aid of a Mary Ellen Chase, on the testimony of my record, a long Chaucer paper done for Mr. Patch, and an interview with the wife of the President of Kenyon College,[2] is a rather beautiful thing to contemplate. Especially after that smug obviously-Oxford professor at my Harvard interview told me it was impossible to get a Fulbright to either Oxford or Cambridge! Oh, even if I don't get one, I know somehow that I will go! Imagine having a <u>choice</u>!

1–Founded in 1878, Lady Margaret Hall is a college at Oxford University, for women only until 1979.
2–Roberta Teale Swartz Chalmers (1903–93); wife of Gordon Keith Chalmers (1905–56), president of Kenyon College 1937–56.

Of course If I get a Fulbright, they will probably assign me to a particular one, but I hardly can worry about that!

Cross all your fingers for me this coming crucial month, your puddle-jumping daughter,

Sylvia

TO *Aurelia Schober Plath*

Thursday 17 March 1955 ALS (postcard), Indiana University

Thursday
March 17

Dear mother . . .

Just a quick note (which I hope gets to you before the rather grim infirmary letter) to say I got out yesterday after a stay of only 24 hours. The sleep and respite from pain did me a great deal of good, and I am now ready to face the round of exams (German & Shakespeare) which begin tomorrow – and term papers (Ger. & Am. lit.) which I plan to get done before vacation. Sue & I are both very excited about our trip to NYC for the weekend of Dorrie's wedding – we are giving her a surprise shower at Rahar's Monday, which naturally will cost a few dollars for gift & hors do'euvres for 20, but she is our "best" friend & so we are happy to do it – thank goodness I only have a few close friends – participating in weddings is too expensive for me on more than a minute scale. Have a wonderful time in Toledo & give my special love to the Frank Schober Jrs!

xx
siv

TO *Aurelia Schober Plath*

Sunday 20 March 1955[1] ALS (postcard), Indiana University

Sunday afternoon

Dear mother . . .

So nice to get your letter & many thanks for the check – I managed to live through my wicked week & celebrated by playing some invigorating tennis this morning. From 6-8 last night I had the pleasant surprise of a visit from Marty & Mike who had come down to coach a rugby game

1–Date supplied from postmark.

– had fun talking to a charming friend of theirs[1] – a Cambridge grad from Eng. – who said I was terribly lucky to be accepted at the two best "colleges" at Cambridge & Oxford – & said the choice was only between two heavens, & so not to worry – presented an enchanting picture of spring boating & may "balls" & gardens there – Sue & I are giving dorri a surprise shower at rahar's tomorrow before our NYC jaunt next friday for wedding & reception. This Wednesday, I am excited about a 2nd visit from that charming young editor at harcourt & brace whom Mr. Kazin sent up to see me last fall when I was at the infirmary – he is a dear, & I have a pleasant suspicion this is a personal & not professional call. Love to you and Frank, Louise & the two young men

xx
sivvy

TO *Aurelia Schober Plath*

Thursday 24 March 1955 TLS, Indiana University

Thursday, March 24

Dearest Mother . . .

I thought I'd write a note in the midst of packing for New York City to catch you up on the latest news here, as I won't write again probably until I come home to the house Sunday night. As yet I haven't decided whether to come home Tuesday to avoid the holiday rush, or whether I'll have so much last minute business to do here that I'll have to wait till Wednesday. I have a feeling I'll take the 5 p.m. bus Tuesday, but will let you know definitely Sunday night.

News here is as always small; I don't expect to have the deluge begin till after April 1, which is when I'll be at home. One exquisite thing is that Smith has just given me a fellowship of $1,000 (one thousand) for graduate study abroad (!) which surprised me no end, as their highest listed fellowship is only seven hundred, and the one I got is listed only as about five hundred. Naturally, if my Fulbright comes through, I will turn back the fellowship as the Fulbright even covers postage stamps and book allowance, but it is wonderful to have such a backlog to begin with, as it means I can go to England definitely for one year at least, if I work hard this summer. I feel that even better things are in the wind.

1 – According to SP's calendar, this was Chris Buxton.

Dorri's shower at Rahar's was a huge success in spite of the inhospitable snow. Fifteen people came, and the hors d'oeuvres were delicious (Sue and I supplied them at $6 apiece). Best of all, Dorri was completely surprised and very happy with her gifts. I look most forward to her wedding Saturday, in Mount Vernon, New York.

I am really glad to be getting off for this weekend, as it has been much too long a pull through this bad weather and study discipline this past eternal two months, and I have reached my limits of creative study and effort. Realizing which, I have no compunction about taking my usual tonic: a weekend of complete change in people and a more gay, relaxed atmosphere. Dear Claiborne and Avrom are opening their arms to me as ever, and those two dear people are as close, in a different way, as Marty and Mike. When I come back, I shall again be ready to do the fantastic reading and writing program I have over spring vacation. I really need a respite from the daily round of classes and waitressing, and stoic living. It will be good to read and write in peace at home.

There are only a few people I want to see: Mrs. Prouty, Mr. Crockett, Patsy, and Dr. Beuscher, of course. And I do hope Warren will be around. I miss him very much, and am hungry for talking with him again, as I am for living with you all. There is nothing like an alternation of work and play to keep one fresh and spirited. Fortunately, I am building up a list of outlets and tonics for my periodic slackening times. In the summer, it will be tennis, swimming, sunning and sailing. In the winter, New York is a help, and I hope to add skiing in the Alps next year!

My Harcourt & Brace editor, a charming young man of 26 (!), graduate of Harvard and recent recipient of a Fulbright to Cambridge University, came up Wednesday on his quarterly trip to bookshops in our environs. We had a charming long lunch and talk at Rahar's, after which we drove over to the bookshop at Holyoke and I browsed while he talked to the owner. The ride was a treat, and if he drops by in June on his visit to Hathaway House, I hope you have a chance to meet him: Peter Davison is his name; his father[1] is an English teacher at Hunter College, a visiting British poet.

That's all for now. Hope you had a good trip at Frankie's.

Lots of love to all,
Sivvy

1–Scottish poet Edward Lewis Davison (1898–1970).

TO *Aurelia Schober Plath*

Sunday 27 March 1955 TLS with envelope, Smith College

Sunday night, March 27,

Dearest mother . . .

So happy to hear about your exciting Toledo trip. I just got back from New York tonight myself, and am feeling calm and serene as the Mona Lisa, all ready for a session of reading and writing at home. I plan to bring a suitcase of books, a tennis outfit, a tea dress, and a theater dress. That should take care of everything.

First off, I have a request. Sue Weller would love to come to our house for the last week of spring vacation, and I have practically told her definitely that we'd love to have her. She is the sort of girl who is just part of the family, like Marcia, and I would love to get your O.K. on this. She is staying in Cambridge with friends for the first week, and I plan to ride down on the 1:15 bus with her Wednesday. So I'll be arriving about 5 p.m. Wednesday night alone, and would like to have her come over a week from that Wednesday, if it is all right with you. Do let me know.

The weekend was just as therapeutic as I knew it would be. Had a lovely luncheon with Claiborne on Friday afternoon. That night she and Avrom and I went to a French restaurant[1] for a long leisurely supper and got good balcony tickets to "Tea and Sympathy".[2] We had a marvellous walk around the city, and Claiborne and I had a great talk which took place as we stood for an hour at the lighted skating rink in Rockefeller Center and watched the swooping skaters who so intrigued me when I first went with Marcia five years ago.

Saturday was Dorri's wedding: a beautiful affair in a light, airy modern church, packed with about 300-400 society people from NYC, but exquisitely simple: the three bridesmaids wore just the kind of dress I'd love for Ruth's wedding: perfectly plain princess cut, wonderful colors: copper and emerald. Dorri was so lovely it made me cry.

At first I felt shy about going to the reception in Dorri's house, for I knew not a soul at the wedding, but the reception turned out to be a dear intimate affair, and as the only girl from Smith, I was greeted with a kiss by Dorri's handsome father[3] who'd met me up here, and had lovely

1 – Le Champlain.

2 – Robert Anderson, *Tea and Sympathy*, director Elia Kazan, Longacre Theatre, New York, 25 March 1955.

3 – Carl E. Licht.

talks with the best man[1] whom I happened to know from Dartmouth, and a Smith girl[2] who graduated last year and is living in Oxford next year. The punch (champagne) and canapes were out of this world, and I ate so much I couldn't manage supper, and left feeling most at home and happy.

Saturday night I was thrilled by Gian-Carlo-Menotti's opera "The Saint of Bleeker Street."[3] The music was dynamic, and the whole performance was sung with shuddering beauty and power; I don't know when I've been so moved . . . the fusion of the arts was flawless: the music, acting, and art of color, light, and group pantomime.

Came back this afternoon to a tantalizing letter[4] from the Atlantic Monthly (at last) saying they still had my poems, yes, and they had a deluge of poems, and asked me to "be patient with our slowness in coming to a decision about them . . . but since your work is too interesting to pass up without a struggle, we have held the poems for further argument. I hope that the verdict will be settled very shortly." Well! If they have the gall not to accept one after this (and I am sure they will give an equally laconic refusal) I shall be really angry; art may be long to the Atlantic, but my life is fleeting, and I would like to recirculate the poems. Ah well, I leave them to struggle!

See you Wednesday night about 5 p.m. Till then,

Love to all,
Sylvia

TO *Aurelia Schober Plath*

Saturday 16 April 1955[5] TLS, Indiana University

Saturday afternoon

Dearest mother . . .

Well, all things come to those who wait, and my waiting seems to be extended for two weeks until the judges decide, after reading our poems over in the quiet of their boudoirs which of the six of us[6] deserves the

1–Probably Charles Acker Jr; B.A. 1954, Dartmouth College.

2–Probably Patience Plummer Barnes (1932–); B.A. 1954, government, Smith College.

3–Gian Carlo Menotti, *The Saint of Bleecker Street*, Broadway Theatre, New York, 26 March 1955.

4–Phoebe Lou Adams to SP, 24 March, 1955; held by Lilly Library.

5–Date supplied from internal evidence.

6–In addition to SP, the Glascock Poetry contestants at Mount Holyoke College for 1955 were Lynne Lawner (Wellesley College), Jean Piser (Mount Holyoke College), David Rattray (Dartmouth College), Donald Lehmkuhl (Columbia University), and William Key Whitman (Wesleyan University).

coveted prize (won in the last 32 years by an amazing number of now well-known poets).

Suffice it to say that I don't know when I've had such a lovely time in my life. I took to Marianne Moore immediately, and was so glad to have bought her book[1] and read up about her, for I could honestly discuss my favorite poems. She must be in her late seventies and is as vital and humorous as someone's fairy godmother incognito. Interestingly enough, she asked about you and said she hopes to meet you some day, and also said you should be proud of me, which I thought I'd tell you in case you didn't already know!

Took the train to Holyoke Friday afternoon, was picked up at the station and taken to a palatial guest room in one of the dorms where I met attractive Lynn Lawner,[2] the contestant from Wellesley and a charming girl whom I enjoyed very much. We were interviewed by the Monitor,[3] had our pictures taken again and again clustered around Miss Moore, interviewed by the reporter from Mademoiselle,[4] a Smith graduate whom I am also very fond of, and went to dinner of lamb chops, very good, if a little stilted at first, with everybody very new, and still unacquainted.

Then came the reading: a magnificent audience (about 200) packed into a charming small room with dark walls, plush chairs, leaded windows, and a very literary atmosphere. The six of us sat facing the audience at a sort of seminar table, and the response was most rewarding.

All the contestants were amazingly attractive, charming people (from Holyoke, Smith, Columbia, Wellesley Wesleyan, and Dartmouth), and read very well. The girls, I felt, were much superior to the boys . . . the only one I felt was serious competition was the one from Dartmouth whom I would bet on for winning. The other two girls were often excellent, but very uneven. All of us got most vociferous applause, and it was a real pleasure to see such an enthusiastic group . . . there were all sorts of other events going on, too, and no attempt was made to drum up an audience.

The reading went excellently, and I loved doing my poems, because they all sounded pretty polished and the audience was immensely responsive,

1–Marianne Moore, *Collected Poems* (New York: The Macmillan Company, 1953); SP's signed and inscribed copy held by Smith College.

2–American poet and art scholar Lynne Lawner (1935–); B.A. 1957, Wellesley College.

3–Mary Handy, 'Judges Hear Glascock Poetry Contestants', *Christian Science Monitor*, 18 April 1955, 2. The article includes two photographs of SP: one reading from a typescript with the first lines of her 'April Aubade' printed beneath, and the second with Marianne Moore.

4–Chris Christiaen; B.A. 1955, Mount Holyoke College. Her 'Poet on College Time', *Mademoiselle* 41 (August 1955), 49, 52, 62, prints SP's 'Two Lovers and a Beachcomber by the Real Sea' on pp. 52, 62.

laughed in some of the witty places, even, which made me feel tremendously happy. I think I'd love being a humorous public speaker, it's such fun to be able to make people laugh. After the reading we had a "party" to which selected Holyoke girls were invited, and I had a chance to talk to John Ciardi[1] and Wallace Fowlie,[2] the other two critics, poets and judges, both delightful, also teachers and translators, the former having translated Dante and the latter Rimbaud and the French poets. I loved them both, and they grew on me more and more as the time went on.

This morning Lynn and I were brought a sumptuous breakfast in bed, and had our voices recorded at the radio station. I hope they will send us records of them, as they said they might. Then we had a marvelous forum by the three judges on translations which I found delightful. The whole affair was culminated by a delightful luncheon at which everyone was very intimate and cosy, and Marianne Moore signed a dear autograph in my book of her poems . . . I really loved them all.

So back to a week of fantastic work: papers, reading, business . . . .

love to all,
sylvia

TO *Joyce Horner*[3]

Monday 18 April 1955[4] TLS, Mount Holyoke College

Lawrence House
Monday morning

Dear Miss Horner,

I don't know when I've looked back on a more delightful weekend! Really, when I think of the arranging that must have gone into that lovely poetry festival I can only admiringly tell you what a magnificent experience it was. It was such a pleasure to talk with the three judges. (I quite love Marianne Moore, she seems like somebody's fairy godmother incognito!) Wallace Fowlie was a dear, and John Ciardi most fun . . . I was naively entranced by their warm humanity and friendliness, as I guess one always is by one's favorite writers and critics.

1–American poet and translator John Ciardi (1916–86).
2–American writer and professor of literature Wallace Fowlie (1908–98).
3–Joyce Horner (1903–80), professor of English, Mount Holyoke College, 1944–69. Horner ran the Glascock Poetry Contest with colleagues Joseph Bottkol and Constance Saintonge.
4–Date supplied from internal evidence.

Lynne Lawner and I enjoyed our luxurious guest room, complete with the unique delight of a lazy breakfast in bed, and I don't know when I've met a group of more stimulating and pleasant people as I did at Holyoke the night of the poetry reading.

Saturday morning, Miss Shephardson[1] (I think that was her name) mentioned that it might be possible for Lynne and myself to obtain records of our taped reading, and I do hope that there is a chance of this . . . it would be so much fun to play and reminisce about a recording.

I'm still waiting eagerly to hear from the Fulbright committee, and must admit that I'm crossing my fingers for Oxford! So many British poets come from Oxford that it would be rather an inspiration to live on the same soil!

Once again, let me say how I appreciate your wonderful hospitality and how pleasant it was to see you again at the Poetry Reading.

Sincerely,
Sylvia Plath

TO *Aurelia Schober Plath*

Thursday 21 April 1955[2] — TLS with envelope, Indiana University

Thursday night

Dear mother . . .

Every now and then there comes a difficult spell where little discrepancies pile up and look enormous, or rather gray, and this week has been one of those. I just feel like writing you about it, although I usually am in a more cheerful mood, and I've been hoping that not hearing from you since Saturday doesn't mean that anything is wrong at home. Did you see the spread in the Monitor? I don't know what day it came out, but I would like to have you save a copy or two and send one to me if you could. I think they did a generally good job except for that out-of-context quote which had me making the prize moron remark: "I think reading is important."

If I get through this week, I shall feel much better, but everything has piled up so that I know how a bank feels when all the people decide to go to the window the same day and withdraw their money just to be sure

1–Nadine Shepardson, associate professor of speech at Mount Holyoke College.
2–Date supplied from postmark.

its been there all along. Two late house-meetings this week added to the tenseness. I did a ten-page paper for Kazin due today, a rather frantic outline for my correlation question for one of my three finals which I must work on intensely for this next week (dear Mr. Fisher reassured me greatly about the question today) and a German oral report on de Heldensage.[1] Add to all this the arranging of a take-in assembly Wednesday plus a two hour tea in the afternoon for the new members of Alpha, of which I am president, and the writing of three poems,[2] and perhaps you can see how tight things have been these last days.

I was very happy, however, to be given the Alpha award for creative writing (chosen by the English department) which is non-remunerative, just a gold A and an impressive note from the office of the President. I enclose the clipping.[3]

I think you would have been pleased to see how the tea came out. It was for the 50 members of Alpha in the very bright red-and-white Dutch room of the Alumnae House. I poured for the whole hour, a feat which I decided to learn in a dash of bravado, and there were sandwiches and a lot of good conversation. Nancy Hunter and Lynne Fisher were among the new members (Nan for her sonnets this semester) and I was most glad for them both. It went off very well, my first experience at presiding at anything, and I really had fun.

I have signed papers accepting the $1000 Smith scholarship which they will kindly let me renounce if I get the Fulbright. The next four weeks will be spent plunged in review for the 3 final comprehensives on May 21, 23 and 25, after which I shall be ready for a long long respite. I have reached my limit of "giving out" this year, and feel that my peace of mind is more important that bringing up my two high B's in Shakespeare and German, and God knows what I'll get on the Kazin paper, which is my whole mark for the semester. I am just ready for three months of long liesurely living with no schedule to meet, plenty of sleep and sun, and time for absorbtion. I know I need more sleep and less pressure than most people, and that teaching is the one kind of job I can envision (in the far future) which would support me with these qualifications, and which I think I honestly might enjoy.

1–Probably a report on German heroic legends.

2–According to SP's calendar, her three recent poems were: 'Sonnet to Satan' on 17 April, 'Apology to Pan' on 18 April, and 'Desert Song' on 19 April 1955.

3–No longer with the letter, the clipping was probably 'Alpha-Phi Society Presents Awards, Names New Members', *The Sophian*, 21 April 1955, 21.

The most difficult choice I have ever had to make happened today. Editor Weeks[1] on the Atlantic sent me a letter[2] with a $25 check for your favorite "Circus in Three Rings" BUT with a really thorny string attached. They liked the 2nd stanza much better than the 1st and 3rd and challenged me to do a revision around the 2nd stanza with a new title (suggested by them) "Lion Tamer". Well, I was a kaleidoscope of mixed emotions and had a long talk about it all with Mr. Fisher. The top of my head said excitedly: this is your chance to get through the golden doors (they mentioned wanting to have me represented in the young poets' section of the August issue). Revise, revise. Quick. The inside part looked at the poem, which sprang out of a certain idea of a trilogy, admittedly poorer in the 3rd stanza than the others, frothy, not bad, but light. I thought of their paternalistic letter and felt a little sick and disillusioned. I just can't tailor-make it over again. Another poem, yes, but the dangers of contrivance, of lack of spontaneity, are legion if I revise this. I'd have to live with it the year out and still I'm afraid a revision would sound artificial. I did resent this attempt at butchering to fit their idea of it. Prose, I wouldn't mind, but a poem is a like rare little watch: alter the delicate juxtaposition of cogs, and it just may not tick.

So I think I'll sleep on it the weekend out, and if a revision comes, I'll send it, but I doubt it. If not, I think I'll send four of my best latest poems which are "consistent" (a lack they felt in the batch I sent last September) and ask Mr. Weeks to please seriously consider these alternates. Of course I'll have to send back the check too, which is a hard thing, and they certainly put me in a very awkward position. I battle between desperate Macchiavelian opportunism and uncompromising artistic ethics. The ethics seem to have won, but what a hell! They should have accepted it completely, with the 2nd stanza recommending the others, or not at all. This limbo is definitely difficult! So much dreaming, and then this problem!

Well, do send me an infusion of energy. It will do me more good than thyroid. I really miss hearing from you, and your letters always cheer me up.

Your almost-but-not-quite,-try-us-again daughter,

Sylvia

1–American author and editor Edward Weeks (1898–1989); editor of *Atlantic Monthly*, 1938–66.

2–Edward Weeks to SP, 18 April 1955; held by Lilly Library.

TO *Aurelia Schober Plath*

Saturday 23 April 1955 | ALS in greeting card[1] with envelope, Indiana University

April 23, 1955

Dear mother . . .

Along with love and best wishes for your birthday, I thought you'd like to know I tied for first prize at the Holyoke Contest with the boy William Whitman[2] from Wesleyan. That means a check of $50 for me, plus a pleasant glow. Best of all was a eulogistic letter from John Ciardi, my favorite of the judges, who called me "a real discovery," saying "She's a poet. I am sure that she will go on writing poems, & I would gamble on the fact that she will get better & better at it. She certainly has everything to do it with. Praise be . . . ." All of which made me so happy I could cry – he also wants to help my publishing & sent a list of quarterlies he wants me to send specific poems to with his recommendations – so it's not a completely indifferent world after all!

Love,
Sivvy

<printed on inside of card: 'The older you grow, / The dearer you get.'>

you certainly do!

Love,
Sylvia

TO *Aurelia Schober Plath*

Sunday 24 April 1955[3] | TLS with envelope, Indiana University

Sunday afternoon

Dearest mother . . .

All I can say is that I was glad to find you were recovering when I got your letter. Please, though, don't ever think you are doing me a favor by not telling me when you are sick. While you may think it would worry me unnecessarily, I would like to feel that I could be of some help, even if it is only thinking of you and wishing you well. I am really concerned about

1–A birthday card designed by Oz.
2–William Key Whitman, 1956, Wesleyan University.
3–Date supplied from postmark.

the state of your health, which this year has shaken twice, and cannot advise you strongly enough to take the summer off and go to the Cape for two months, renting our house to tenants carefully screened. If you put an add in the Christian Science Monitor, I am sure your clients would be fine people to begin with.

It would be unrealistic to think that you need to work for money this summer: think about the future year. It would be tragic for you to work in the summer, and then miss out next year, and ambitious as we are, we need more than the couple of weeks at the beginning and end of the summer to relax in. When I come home at the end of May we can talk more concretely, as I will have some definite idea of my resources then, but I really insist that you take a sabbatical summer and worry not a whit about money. Depending on the family finances, I can always work as a waitress for the summer, and would like to think of you vacationing with grammy and grampy all summer. Your rent for our house would be sufficient from July and August to pay for your vacation, and health and present happy living is worth much more than saving for a perpetually postponed future.

Ironically enough, I felt something was wrong when you didn't write, so you see, it concerns me more not to hear about you than it ever would to know specifically what is wrong. I am sorry that I sounded blue about my week at such a bad time, for two suppers out with Nan and Sue on successive evenings, plus the chance to cook a lamb chop dinner with all the fixings at my friend Elinor Friedman's house in Longmeadow with my Saturday date from Yale made life look much better. Ten hours of sleep the other night helped immensely.

I have sent a revision and five poems as possible alternates off to Editor Weeks and am holding my breath, and the check, until his final verdict. Probably he will accept nothing now, but I did what he suggested and would really love it if he took one of my more serious and better poems which tied for first in the Glascock Contest.

Thank you for sending the clippings, I really appreciated them. The next four weeks are going to really be a concentrated grind, so wish me luck as I wish you health. I will go to Onteora High School in Boiceville, New York, on Wednesday evening, May 4th, and come back after the festival on May 5. It should be fun to be on the other side of the fence for a change.

Do give me an honest and frequent report of your progress and promise not to go back to school until you are blooming with health and resemble Winston Churchill instead of Mahatma Ghandi. Also, put an add in the papers for renting the house for the summer. You must assure yourself a 3 month build-up period, money aside.

Take care,
all my love,
Sivvy

TO *Edward Weeks*

Sunday 24 April 1955[1] TLS (photocopy), Yale University

Lawrence House
Smith College
Northampton, Massachusetts

Editor Edward Weeks
THE ATLANTIC MONTHLY
8 Arlington Avenue
Boston 16, Massachusetts

Dear Editor Weeks:

I was pleased to receive your letter about my poems and glad that you liked the second stanza of "Circus in Three Rings." As you suggested, I have taken this stanza and done a revision under the new title "Lion Tamer" which moves the lion and tamer into a stellar figure. However, I am still not confident that this will win you completely or prove more consistent than "Circus in Three Rings" which remains my favorite of the lighter poems. I am enclosing both poems for your convenience.

Since there are few places in the world I would rather appear than in your August issue of young poets, I should like to ask you the favor of seriously considering the five poems[2] enclosed as alternates to "Lion Tamer".

Several of these poems were winners in the recent Irene Glascock Poetry Contest where Marianne Moore, John Ciardi and Wallace Fowlie were the judges and I feel that they are not only better but also more consistent poems, especially the villanelle "Lament" and the poem "Two Lovers and

1–Date supplied from internal evidence.

2–According to handwritten annotations made to the letter by an *Atlantic Monthly* employee, the five poems enclosed with 'Lion Tamer' and 'Circus in Three Rings' were: 'Lament', 'Two Lovers and a Beachcomber by the Real Sea', 'Epitaph in Three Parts', 'Winter Words' and 'The Princess and the Goblins'.

a Beachcomber by the Real Sea." I realize that the mood in these poems is hardly light and airy, but I would more than appreciate your appraisal of them as possible candidates for the August issue, since I consider them among my best recent work.

As I am uncertain about your final verdict on "Lion Tamer" and on the enclosed poems, I shall hold the check until I hear from you about your decision in this matter.

Thank you for your creative suggestions and consideration.

Sincerely yours,
Sylvia Plath

TO *Warren Plath*

Sunday 24 April 1955[1] — TLS in greeting card[2] (photocopy), Indiana University

<printed greeting>

No need for mincing words / or quibbling / I'm awfully glad / that you're my sibling / Happy Birthday

<signed>

Much love on your approaching majority, / Sivvy / (over)

Dear Warren . . .

Many happy returns on your birthday, and I hope that when we next get together we can have a dinner of appropriate celebration. I was really concerned to hear of mother's siege with the virus, which was much more serious than she would have us believe. Try to work on her to put an add in the Monitor advertising our house for rent for July and August so she could take the money and go down to the Cape for the summer. She needs at least a 3-month build-up period, or she just may not be able to teach at all, no matter what her arguments for earning summer-money.

The next four weeks before the dreaded Comprehensives will be one grim grind, and I wait as usual for the Fulbright. Perhaps mother told you I tied with the boy from Wesleyan for the Glascock Poetry Contest (which means $50 for each of us) and got eulogistic letter from judge John Ciardi who wants to help me get some things published. Am still fighting with Editor Weeks, who sent me check for poem he wants revised for Atlantic.

1–Date supplied from internal evidence.
2–On Panda Prints birthday card designed by Rosalind Welcher.

Difficult assignment, and I'm hoping he'll take an alternate. Cross your fingers. See you in May.

Much much love,
Sivvy

TO *Aurelia Schober Plath*

Monday 25 April 1955[1] TLS[2] with envelope, Indiana University

Monday afternoon

Dear mother . . .

It was good to get your letter today: I am so sensitive to mail and really enjoy it. I hope that you are feeling better and rest until you have a reserve to go on. The weather here has been abominable the last two days, all great deluges of raw rain. Yesterday and today I spent getting off various letters and finishing typing up my manuscript for Mr. Fisher of poems: there are about 60 poems in the book[3] titled "Circus in Three Rings" (poof to the Atlantic) and it does look like a good bit of work to have produced in one semester. I included all my poems, some bad, some good, some still needing revision, and dedicated it to "My favorite Maestro, Alfred Young Fisher". I also made a carbon of the manuscript so I can have it to work from this summer. I want to write at least ten good news poems to substitute for the inferior or slight ones and turn 30 in for Borestone Mountain book competition this July and then the Yale Series next year. Of course I really don't think I have a chance, as most are in that limbo between experimental art of the poetry little magazines and the sophisticated wit of the New Yorker, too much of the other for either. But I shall try.

I have had a serious self-examination, and come to a decision to drop German for the rest of the year without credit. I have taken the full 15 hour program all year, in opposition to the kind advice of my professorial advisors, and now find that in this last month it is simply too much. My comprehensives need all my time and more, and I have reached a satiation

1–Date supplied from postmark.

2–Enclosed with this letter is a cartoon of a parrot at a typewriter in a room with two women. Lawrence Hector Siggs, 'No, he doesn't talk', *Punch*, 3 March 1955, 292. SP has an arrow pointing at the parrot with the handwritten annotation: 'try teaching Peter the touch system!' ASP also annotated this cartoon: '(Peter – our parakeet)'.

3–Typescript held by Lilly Library.

point where I need to cut down all that is not absolutely necessary. The 6 extra hours of German class per week and long hours of preparation in addition to my 4-year review is just too much to maintain all at once, especially since I am just plain bushed from the academic year. I have plenty of extra credits, so there is no administrative problem whatsoever.

Needless to say, the next four weeks are rather crucial, and I should find out a good deal of concrete information: Fulbright, Atlantic, Vogue, Mlle, Christophers, and several Smith prizes to be announced in assembly May 18. Now I shall just read relentlessly away, reviewing four years of notes and books and creating a correlation question. I feel much better about the German, now, as I am in my cycle of ebbed energy and know that at these times I must pare my demands to a bare minimum. I feel this is more sensible than stubbornly trying to juggle too many balls at once. I look enormously forward to a summer of rest and slow-paced creative work and outdoor relaxation.

Don't worry about me at all. You see that I can cope with my limitations, even though it would be much nicer if I didn't have any. I do need at least 10 hours of sleep a night, a minimum of pressure (most of the time) and a life that allows for cycles of energy (I wrote my thesis in two months, in a great spurts of energy, much before any other senior finished) and corresponding complete relaxes. Teaching or marriage combined with free-lance writing would be ideal for this, I think. At any rate, be at ease about me these next weeks and wish me luck.

I hope your birthday finds you feeling much better and do give my love to all,

sivvy

TO *Gordon Lameyer*

Tuesday 26 April 1955[1] TLS, Indiana University

Tuesday, 11:35

Dear Gordon . . .

I'm sure whatever went before your fall was fun, but I have drastic visions of your being wired together from your letter,[2] and all stuck through with wood splinters and tangled with bindings. Please get free and say it isn't so. As long as youre having a comfortable convalescence, though, I am reassured. There is nothing more pleasant than that lovely

1–Date supplied from internal evidence.

2–Gordon Lameyer to SP, 23 April 1955; held by Lilly Library.

interim when one is well enough to feel enjoyment and not well enough to bother with responsibilities. I actually envy you.

Ahead of me is the thorny slope of comprehensives, and I have had to drop German because too much was simply too much. It seems my life is a constant readjustment between my psychic demands and my physical supply. I need three long months of sun and sand and tennis and time (to read and write as I choose or do not choose) to recover from the academic trials of this year. Sue and I are projecting more schemes: the latest: to drive through Washington (so she can get an apartment) to Kentucky, borrow a car from her rich relatives there, and head for New Orleans, and, hopefully, Mexico City. Let's hope this has a little more percentage of probability than Tangier. If so, we would go in late June and early July.

April is the cruellest month: it's like winter here now, with sleet and clouds and raw winds. I've had a bout of papers, reports and extracurricular obligations which left me shot for the weekend, over which I recuperated when a friend in Longmeadow loaned me her very posh modern house so I could cook a lamp chop dinner beginning with cocktails and ending with strawberries and coffee. This relaxed me no end, and pleasantly recalled last summer. God, I love to cook! The chops were done, too. All I need is practice and an income that allows for cooking sherry and sour cream and cheese!

Contrary to your optimistic note, the Fulbright men maintain stolid silence. I am sure the fellow managing my affairs in England is having a few of his own and prolongs the time for this reason; or perhaps he has turned alcoholic and is embarrassed to write because his hand shakes too much. No news is supposedly good news, but I'm tired as hell of waiting. To ease my state of suspension, I accepted the $1000 fellowship from Smith (which I can use in England) and wait out the interim.

News here is all indefinite, with Fulbright, Vogue Prix, Mlle fiction, Christophers TV, and sundry Smith poetry contests to be announced at the end of May or so. Only really definite thing is the outcome of the Irene Glascock Poetry Contest at Holyoke the other weekend which was the warmest, most intelligent affair I've ever been to. Judges John Ciardi, Wallace Fowlie, and Marianne Moore were delightfully human and accessible and we had several dinners with them and much time for discussion during the two days. An enthusiastic audience of 200 or more packed the Elizabethan hall and applauded wonderfully after each of the 6 readings, and the three male and other two female contestants were attractive and charming. Verdict: I tied with boy from Wesleyan, $50 per each of us. Best of all, John Ciardi drank scotch with me for hours over the kitchen sink at someone's party and sent enchanting and enthusiastic letter with names and addresses of places he wanted me to send my poems with his very special recommendations. His words I shall cherish for my as yet mythical grandchildren.

Perhaps the most tantalizing occurence of late was a sort of aesthetic rape by Editor Edward Weeks of the Atlantic Monthly. He sent me a check for "Circus of Three Rings" saying among other things that the 2nd verse was best of the 3, so would I take it and do a revision on a consistent metaphor of a lion tamer and if it "won them completely" he would like to have me represented in the young poets' section of the August issue.

Well, my reaction was kaleidoscopic. First, golden with joy: La, at last the pearly gates open and let me babble in among Wallace Stevens, Dylan Thomas, and Edith Sitwell! Then purple anger: what are they paying me for anyhow! What the hell makes them think they'll like the revision any better, and meanwhile this check burns a slow hole on my desk! Finally blue disillusion: don't they know the dangers of a paternal directive: and why the blazes don't they publish one of my recent very good and consistent poems instead, although they are all about deathandgraves? To make a long story trim its tale, I quaffed two martinis, slept 12 hours, looked at the letter again, wrote a revision which I know they won't like, but I got 2 good phrases out of it: a lion "shaggy with stars" that comes "roaring rare through my almanac." Then I sent my five best poems with a plea to consider them as alternates. What more can a girl do? They'll probably politely say "none will quite do". So I wait, gnawing my pale green check down to the dollar sign.

Thanks for your poems: always like to see these visually, and here is one for you appropriately called: Sonnet for a Green-eyed Sailor:

> I look at you and the room begins running away:
> dolphin tables ride off on turnabout tide;
> curtains flap into sails while feathered books fly
> beyond the gull-giddy horizon in my head.
> I dive, no jonah in jeopardy, toward the dark gorge
> where bric-a-brac tick of clocks is halted in wreck
> of tall time's intricate schooner, sunk under surge
> that will swallow all in warm-as-whale-gut-black.
>
> Down shell-whorl of my ear is poured the sound
> of your hurricane heart until the moon
> unleashes lunging waves to flood love's land:

saltstruck worlk is sucked within whirlpool spin,
plummeting through the pupil of green sea
to drown in the absinthe eden of your eye.

Mend those metacarpals soon! Best wishes from the girl in the absinthe sombrero!

sylvia

TO *Aurelia Schober Plath*

Thursday 28 April 1955 TLS, Indiana University

April 28, 1955

Dearest mother . . .

Just a note to tell you that my regime of final study has begun and I shall be disciplining ferociously for the next four weeks. It seems impossible now that I shall review in 3 weeks all the work in English for the past four years, brushing up in a day an author I have spent a year studying, but that is the way it looks. Dropping German was surely the only thing I could do, and they were all most nice about it.

By the way, amusingly enough, I just found out this morning that I won $100, one of the 34 prizes in the student contest for the Christophers! Of course I shall write Mrs. Freeman right away to tell her thanks, for it was her sending the notice that got me interested. There were 34 winners in all from the U.S. and Canada, and I was interested to note that I was the only winner from a big eastern college. All the rest were Catholic colleges or mid-west or western universities. I am probably the only Unitarian that won a prize! There were 3 prizes given from $500 to $150 and 31 prizes of $100. I really am pleased that I came through with one of them! As you see, my frugality prevents me from calling home for anything less than a definite Atlantic acceptance, a Fulbright, or $500 or more! As yet nothing from these last.

Also I am enclosing the latest and last copy of the Smith Review,[1] which I hope you will save for me, in which I have a story and a poem. I'll be interested to know what you think of the story. I'm also sending Mrs. Prouty a copy with the news about the Alpha award, the Glascock Contest, and this latest one. Do tell Warrie about the Christophers and

1–Sylvia Plath, 'Danse Macabre' and 'Superman and Paula Brown's New Snowsuit', *Smith Review*, Spring 1955, 12, 19–21.

give him my best love. I miss him and will really miss him this summer. I'd give anything to be able to get him a job in Europe next summer and will try my best.

By the way, did I by chance leave Warren's tennis racket in the car when I came up here? I could swear I brought it into the house here, and yet haven't seen it since I got back. Do let me know if it's at home. Also would you like me to make a super-special effort to get rooms for you all over Sunday night of Graduation? The ceremonies begin at 10 in the morning, which means you'd have to leave about 6:30 at least to get good seats. Of course rooms are terribly expensive and hard to get, but I'd try if you thought the early morning trip would be too much. I do hope Warren can come, it would mean so much to me to have him up here, and it would only be for the day of June 6, Monday. If you have your license by that time, perhaps I could get just you a room if you cared to drive up Sunday, and Warren could drive the grandparents up the next day. Do let me know your opinions about this, too.

Weather here has been abominable, cold, wet and raw since the last glimpse of sun which was on Saturday. Hope it clears up for the weekend. Sun makes such a difference.

Do keep getting well and strong, and give my love to all,

sivvy

TO *Marion Freeman*

Thursday 28 April 1955 TLS with envelope, Smith College

Thursday, April 28, 1955

Dear Aunt Marion . . .

Just a note to share some good news with you which is really your doing anyway! Remember that notice about the Christophers Contest which your neighbor, Mrs. Nalieri[1] so kindly gave you and which you sent me? Well, after writing two stories for it way back last winter, I just heard this morning from Father Keller[2] that I had won $100 which was one of the 34 prizes offered!

Naturally I've just been on top of the world today, as I was wondering how I'd get through the rest of the year with all my senior bills, and this

1–Mary Honan Nalieri (1915–74), lived at 6 Somerset Terrace, Winthrop, Mass.

2–Father James Keller (1900–77); founder of the Christophers. See Father James Keller to SP, 26 April 1955, Sylvia Plath, Smith College scrapbook, p. 82; held by Lilly Library.

happy news takes a load off my mind. I feel that you have something very special to do with my interest in the contest in the first place, and wanted you to be the first to know of the wonderful outcome. Do tell your neighbor how excited I am and thank her from the bottom of my heart for sending on her Christopher News Notes via you. I have a strong admiration for the Society and the work they are doing.

The next four weeks involve preparation for our senior Comprehensive exams which cover all the English courses taken in the last four years, and all of us are really plunging into work now, and will be most glad when they are over. I look so forward to Ruthie's coming wedding in June . . . it sort of shines through the fog of exams ahead like a beacon. I thought her ring just beautiful and am very happy with the color and choice of dresses for the attendants. You must really be up to your ears in happy plans, now. It will be wonderful to see you all at such a marvelous occasion and I feel most honored to be taking part.

Once more, thank you again for your part in this piece of good fortune,

Much love,
Sivvy

TO *Aurelia Schober Plath*

Monday 2 May 1955 — ALS (postcard), Indiana University

monday, may 2

dearest mother . . .

only a little card to say how very much I hope you are surely getting well and that the convalescence isn't too tedious for you. I do wish you'd write me bulletins of just how it's going so I could keep track of you more closely. will you put an add in the paper to rent the house for july & august? I think that would be a great idea, for you to be down the cape! I hope now the weather is nice you'll sun in the yard – the freshmen left us seniors maybaskets of daffodils this morning, a lovely custom. richard sassoon came up from yale again this sat., and we had a lovely time walking along the river – he gets along well with my dear sue, & is getting her a date next week which I hope will make up for that boy not coming during spring vacation. now the weather is all clear & blue & green in the sun, even comprehensives seem possible – do get well soon –

love,
sivvy

TO *Aurelia Schober Plath*

Friday 6 May 1955 — TLS in greeting card,[1] Indiana University

<printed greeting>

It's coals to Newcastle / It's peat to Kerry / It's gilding the lily / It's reddening the berry / To say what a very very / WONDERFUL MOTHER YOU ARE

<signed>

all my love, / Sylvia / (see inside)

Friday afternoon
May 6, 1955

Dearest mother . . .

The hunter being home from the Catskills, she will take up her porcupine quill to add a supplement to this card wishing you best luck and love on your day. After ten hours of sleep last night (got back to Smith at midnight) I feel much more human and scarcely able to believe that I lived so fantastically much in a mere 24 hours. Words can hardly convey the packed experience I've had.

Armed with my Writers' Digest, I boarded the Greyhound bus for Albany on Wednesday morning, was driven through lovely green hills and apple orchard country, and took another bus to Kingston, New York, where I was met by a fat, well-tempered, hot, slovenly farmish woman who introduced herself as Mrs. Thornell.[2] At this point, I decided to be my country self and wondered what on earth Mr. Thornell would be like, the general chairman of the whole festival.[3] Well, I learned a lot in a few hours. On the drive to their home, Mrs. Thornell, obviously deferent to my New York City appearance and "literary reputation", told me that her youngest daughter of 3 had just had her tonsils out unexpectedly that morning, that her aunt had died the week before, and that the house was in the midst of being redecorated. At this point I expected Mr. Thornell would be tied up in the pasture cropping grass and that the school would be held in a barn. On the contrary.

1–Panda Prints Mother's Day card designed by Rosalind Welcher.

2–Emma M. Takacs (1923–90). Takacs married Robert Thornell (1921–2005) on 4 March 1942. Their three children were Colleen Marie (1945–2011), Russell E. (1946–), and Susan (1949–).

3–SP participated in the 1st Annual English Festival at Onteora Central School, on 5 May 1955. SP's programme from the festival held by Lilly Library.

Bob Thornell was home cooking steaks, a charming, virile, 34 year old chap, like a kind of woodland Mr. Crockett, a wonderful grin and easy-going disposition. I liked him immediately and wondered about his choice for a wife, she seemed so lethargic and uninterested in her appearance or in the work he was doing. Well, after dinner they left for the hospital to visit their little girl, and told me sternly to read or walk in the apple orchard and not touch the chaotic kitchen till they came back. I figured they would be worn out, what with all the confusion, and so spent an hour doing the enormous day's stack of dishes with the bright, talkative help of the oldest girl, red-haired Colleen. We must have heated five kettle of water in the course of our work, but I felt really proud when everything was all straightened up, and went out to play baseball with Russell, the 8 year old boy.

When the Thornells came back, Bob asked me if I wanted to go up to the school with him as he supervised the students who were fixing up the displays and signs for the next day, so he could show me around. I was glad for the chance to talk to him alone about the program, and so we drove through more green hills as he told me about the country, the people, and their new 2 million dollar central school which was located beautifully high in the Catskills, 3 years old, and taking the place of the previous 23 one-room school houses. Never in my life have I seen such a beautiful building in such an exquisite setting. With a capacity for 1000 students from kindergarten to 12th grade, two big airy gyms, an auditorium with modern stage equipment, enormous light sunny rooms all looking out into the green mountains, all on one floor, spreading for a quarter of a mile in each direction, there was nothing more to be wished. After helping the attractive senior committee lay out the displays, Bob took me for a long drive up through Woodstock, the artist colony, and to the enormous reservoir, which was like an ocean of silver in the moonlight. I saw my first porcupine and countless rabbits, and got to know the life history of one of the most wonderful men in the world . . . what you would call a "self-made" man. Six years in the navy after highschool, war in the South Pacific, truck driving, marriage and children, and then this burst of interest in English and Art acquired in spare time in the Navy . . . then he started as a freshman at NYC in his late twenties on the G.I. Bill, with a homebody wife, two children, and nothing but opposition. He is one of the most tremendous men I've ever met: no sheltered, aesthetic Phd, but a creative man with ideas, moving alone, envied by those who don't have his courage or originality, admired in ignorance by the rest. We talked till 3 in the morning, and

I read part of a novel he's working on, learned that he's the only non-professional actor in the Woodstock summer theater, and all about his life, his students, and his ideas. We got along just tremendously as people in love with the same kind of life.

The day itself was a revelation. Seven hundred students came from all over New York state, I spent the morning reading about 20 stories and 20 poems for the two contests I was judging, and out of the general collection of vague echoes and lilied spiritualism, was excited to find two excellent poems and several original stories, and learned a great deal in my reading and analyzing the subjects and form. No names were on the entries, only numbers, so I didn't know till the end of the day that my choice for 1st in poetry went to my favorite boy, Wallace Klitgaard,[1] son of a now-dead Danish author,[2] with a famous artist for a mother.[3]

I also had two hours, one in the morning, one after lunch, of poetry roundtable, armchair reading of verse, and discussion. I was amazed at an enthusiastic audience of about 30 both times, very responsive, and I was really elated at my articulation and ability to manage group discussion, use my sense of humor, and draw together a varied group (including Catholic girls and a couple of nuns, one or two young and delightful agnostics, several high school teachers and principals,) and share the desk with a bohemian poetess from Woodstock named Dachine Rainer,[4] whose husband had a D. H. Lawrence beard and whose daughter, a pigtailed pixie, could quote ee cummings. They asked me to read aloud my own poetry, and discussed it, and also two of the student poems. I was so stimulated by the groups, and several came up afterward, including a dear little man teacher from Middletown, to say how they enjoyed the discussion. I was really amazed by my diplomacy, my sudden ability to remember quotes to illustrate points, and to smooth differences into an acceptance of paradox. We had excellent discussions, and I realized that a moderator can guide a class to make conclusions and draw the whole thing together. I was happiest to see how they responded to challenge, humor, and figured that I would really like teaching after this session which elated me no end.

Met several publishers, artists, etc. either from NYC or Woodstock, also Mickey Spillane, a friend of Bob Thornell's, up from Florida, looking

1–Wallace Klitgaard (1937–2006).

2–Kaj Klitgaard (1883–1953).

3–American painter Georgina B. Klitgaard (1893–1976).

4–Writer Dachine Rainer (1921–2000); born Sylvia Newman. Rainer lived with the writer Holley Cantine.

like a dear, tan innocent kid rather than the author of countless best-seller murder mysteries. Bob drove me back to Albany, very happy, and we really shared the joys of the whole day together. I have a standing invitation to visit some day, too.

By for now, your own,
Sivvy

TO *Joyce Horner*

Friday 6 May 1955 — TLS with envelope, Mount Holyoke College

Lawrence House
May 6, 1955

Dear Miss Horner---

I was really delighted to hear the outcome of the contest and very happy to share the prize with William Whitman. Needless to say, my most treasured possession is the dear note from John Ciardi which I appreciate from the bottom of my heart. I enjoyed his company so much at the festival and can't tell you how much his specific suggestions and comments pleased me!

Also, it was exciting to receive the beautiful glossy print[1] of my talk with Marianne Moore from the News Office. Please thank Elizabeth Green[2] for me when you next happen to see her for her kind letter[3] and forwarding the <u>Monitor</u> article and the photograph. I really appreciated her thoughtfulness.

Once again, let me tell you what a rich experience the Holyoke festival was for me. So often at a forum affair there is really no chance for serious discussion with the main speakers, but only exchange of pleasantries over coffee, for the celebrities must be shared with everyone. However, I felt that I had a really provocative conversation with all three judges in the course of two days, and that the party, the dinner and luncheon, were all delightful opportunities to get acquainted with these three stimulating people. I also enjoyed the other contestants, and felt privileged to hear their work.

1–See SP's Smith College scrapbook, p. 79; held by Lilly Library.
2–Elizabeth Green was director of the News Bureau at Mount Holyoke College.
3–Green to SP, 3 May 1955; held by Lilly Library.

No news from the Fulbright committee yet, so I shall review for comprehensives and try to curb my eagerness to hear whether I'll be assigned to Oxford or Cambridge should I get a fellowship.

Thank you again for one of the most meaningful experiences I've every had.

Sincerely,
Sylvia Plath

TO *Aurelia Schober Plath*

Saturday 21 May 1955 — Telegram, Indiana University

MORE GOOD NEWS ATLANTIC MONTHLY JUST BOUGHT ORIGINAL THREE RING CIRCUS FOR AUGUST ISSUE LOVE
=SYLVIA

TO *Aurelia Schober Plath*

Saturday 21 May 1955[1] — ALS with envelope, Indiana University

Saturday afternoon
2 p.m.

dearest of mothers . . .

I am up here on the sunroof in halter and shorts basking in the pure blue air under a tall waving tree of white dogwood and green leaves while the leaves of the beech tree are coppery dark red. You have no idea how wonderful & reassuring it was to talk to you yesterday! That, plus the Fulbright, has made me able to face exams with equanimity. and now:

MORE GOOD NEWS! (if that seems possible!) I just got a wonderful letter from Editor Weeks[2] of the Atlantic Monthly after my first exam of 3 (4 hours long) this morning.

He said they all agreed with me that my original poem "Circus in Three Rings" was better than the revision they asked for & so it will definitely appear in the August issue of the Atlantic[3] as you read it & liked it – What good fortune for the title of my embryonic book!

1–Date supplied from postmark.
2–Edward Weeks to SP, 20 May 1955; held by Lilly Library.
3–Sylvia Plath, 'Circus in Three Rings', *The Atlantic* 196 (August 1955), 68.

Best of all, he said they were "charmed" by my long 3-page poem "The Princess & the Goblins" (whose length deterred them at this time) and asked me to send it back with some new work this summer! Such bliss! That fortress of Bostonian conservative respectability has been "charmed" by your tight-rope walking daughter! Do tell Mr. Crockett & Mrs. Prouty about this & the Fulbright – I will try to write Prouty, but wrote 10 letters of thanks & information of Fulbright to professors & Dr. Beuscher yesterday, & so don't know if I'll have time before I get home Wednesday – I am so happy, so encouraged – talked to Clem over the phone yesterday & hope to visit his mother some time this summer early for advice about plotting – I'd love to get that "indefinable Journal" quality!

Now, just so you can remember it all, I'll give you a list of prizes & writing awards got this year:

$ 30. Dylan Thomas honorable men. for "Parallax", Mlle.
30. For cover of Novel Symposium Mlle
5. Alum Quarterly article on Alfred Kazin
100. Acad. Of Am. Poets prize (10 poems)[1]
50. Glascock Prize (tie)
40. Ethel Olin Corbin Prize (sonnet)
50. Marjorie Hope Nicholson prize (tie) for thesis
25. Vogue Prix de Paris (1 of 12 winners)
100. Christophers (1 of 34 winners)
25. Atlantic for "Circus in 3 Rings"
15. Mlle for "Two Lovers & a Beachcomber by Real Sea"
$465. Total, plus much joy!

Now can pay all debts & work towards coats & luggage – get well fast – can't wait to see you Wednesday –

all my love –
sivvy

<on address side of envelope>

More good news!

1–The ten poems were: 'Prologue to Spring', 'Metamorphoses of the Moon', 'Winter Words', 'Ice Age', 'Lament', 'Epitaph in Three Parts', 'Two Lovers and a Beachcomber by the Real Sea', 'Moonsong at Morning', 'Love Is a Parallax', and 'Insolent Storm Strikes at the Skull'; held by Academy of American Poets, New York; copy with SP pseudonym 'Robin Hunter' held by Smith College.

TO *Lynne Lawner*

Sunday 22 May 1955[1] Printed from *Antaeus* 28, Winter 1978

Sunday afternoon
May 22, 1955

Dear Lynne,

A belated note out of the holocaust of our final comprehensive exams to say how happy I was to get your letter. I, too, enjoyed staying with you so very much at Holyoke and among other things, was most surprised that you were (am I right?) a sophomore. You seem so much more mature than that in every way . . . If you could see the poetry I wrote two years ago, you would no doubt laugh . . . it was so uneven and unfinished. Like piano, practice can do wonders . . .

I want to congratulate you, too, for being one of the 50 runners-up in the *Mademoiselle* College Board contest. That is a marvelous coup for you. The girl in my house at Smith who is among the winners, Jane Truslow, tried out for four years before she got it, and I am confident that if you try out again you will make it. They really rate seniority and perseverance, and if you are being runner-up at this stage, you have a tremendous chance in your next year!

Must return to Chaucer and the Canterbury pilgrims now. Meanwhile, best of luck and have a fun summer. Oh, I must tell you . . . the Fulbright to Cambridge University came yesterday, and I'm walking on air, although I shall probably flunk my comps as a result of such feather-headedness. I sail for London on the Queen Elizabeth in September, which, even as I say it, I can hardly believe.

Bye for now,
Sylvia

1–Date supplied by internal evidence.

TO *Aurelia Schober Plath*

Monday 30 May 1955[1] ALS (picture postcard), Indiana University

<picture postcard caption>

THREE CROWNS RESTAURANT. Revolving Smorgasbord of world's fair fame. 12 East 54th Street, New York, N.Y. Native Swedish Cuisine – Cocktail Lounge.

Memorial Day

Dearest mother –

I am having the loveliest time – just finished my first smorgasbord – saw "Wuthering Heights"[2] last night (Laurence Olivier as Heathcliff, Merle Oberon as Kathy – remember?) and wept buckets & couldn't stop. Also saw "Desperate Hours"[3] a magnificent melodrama – and the movie "La Ronde"[4] – can't wait to see you – only a week from today – get well fast

xxx
sivvy

TO *Gordon Lameyer*

c. Sunday 5 June 1955[5] ALS in greeting card,[6] Indiana University

<printed greeting>

I want a greeting that will reek / Of chic / It can be gay / But not mad / Naughty but not / Bad / Perhaps just a little risque / As long as it will say / HAPPY BIRTHDAY

<signed>

love, / sylvia

1–Date supplied from postmark; postmarked Long Island City, N.Y., 31 May 1955.
2–A revival of the 1939 film played at the Plaza Theatre, then at 42 E. 58th Street, New York, from 10 May 1955.
3–According to SP's calendar, she saw this play on 27 May 1955. *The Desperate Hours*, adapted from the 1954 novel by Joseph Hayes, was performed at the Ethel Barrymore Theatre, 243 W. 47th Street, New York.
4–According to SP's calendar, she saw this on 28 May 1955, as well as the Rockettes, *Love Me or Leave Me*, and 'Bolero' at Radio City Music Hall, New York.
5–Date supplied from internal evidence.
6–Panda Prints birthday card designed by Rosalind Welcher.

PS: "Circus in 3 Rings" comes out in August Atlantic! Had a lovely time with your mother at the Smith Club dinner last week[1] – Fulbright now in pocket & I sail for the big green gem in silver sea on Sept. 14 – will be home writing & taking care of mother all summer.

s. p.

<included with card was clipping of Paul H. Rohmann, 'The Full, Bright Scholar', *The New Yorker*, 6 March 1954, 84; SP handwrote at top: 'couldn't resist clipping this for you – just in case your helicopter doesn't drop New Yorkers on deck regularly –'. In the article, SP underlined 'my family always go to bed as soon as they see me curled up with a Double-Crostic', adding the comment 'ah yes!'>

TO *Lynne Lawner*

Wednesday 8 June 1955

Printed from *Antaeus* 28, Winter 1978

Wednesday, June 8, 1955

Dear Lynne . . .

it was delightful to get your champagne-spontaneous letter when I arrived home from the rather unbelievable business of becoming a smith alumna. adlai stevenson, operating on the hypothesis that every woman's highest vocation is a creative marriage, was most witty and magnificent as commencement speaker. miraculously, monday was blue and sunny, sandwiched like caviar between cold slabs of rainy june weather. in the hectic flight of a week in nyc, I managed to lose my voice completely between grand central and hamp, and am just recovering it in a slightly frogish state today, along with my equilibrium . . . .

your life sounds most exhilarating . . . the new bucolic man and the impressive scholastic papers especially. I wish no end that I could take you up on the cape project, but my summer plans have been changed rather drastically because of my mother, who has been in the hospital and will be operated on next week because of a drastic ulcer condition. I shall be writing in the backyard at my wellesley cottage, reading, tanning, and playing florence nightingale for the summer, plus cook and general mistress of the place.

1 – According to SP's calendar, she read a selection of her poetry at the Smith Club Annual Meeting in Wellesley, on 26 May 1955.

no trips, then, for me. in a way, it's a good thing, as I've had enough traveling these past months to make me retch at the sight of a suitcase, and so am saving my wanderlust for next september when I go all-royale and board the queen elizabeth.

fortunately, a very nice assistant editor from harcourt, brace, is conveniently changing his job this month to assistant to director of harvard u. press, and with his coming cambridge locale, I hope to see a bit of him. I love cambridge enormously, and would love to end up with a professor there. I'll see if I can win any converts in england.

you're so lucky to be coming to the harvard prom . . . I was planning to be at yale's prom this weekend, but a childhood friend suddenly got sentimental and enlisted me as the honorable maid at her wedding this saturday, so I must, alas, forgo my french sassoon and be attendant.

new york was magnificent: saw "desperate hours" and countless excellent movies, among them, "la ronde" and "wuthering heights" . . . also whirled on central park carousel, lunched with cyrilly abels of *mlle*, and haunted museum of modern art . . . .

I know you'll be preoccupied when you return here, but I'll be home, and would love to have you drop by for a visit anytime. I'm only 10 minutes from the college, right off weston road, on the right, two streets away under the route 9 bridge, very simple, and anyway, do call if you get a second (We5-0219j).

meanwhile, my faith and best wishes for a tremendous career, writing and living, and

love,
sylvia

TO *Aurelia Schober Plath*

Friday 24 June 1955[1] AL, Indiana University

WELCOME HOME !!!!!!

<drawing of bouquet of flowers in a vase>

<on verso>

hjhjhjhjhh ghghghghghfhfhfh

1 – Date supplied from internal evidence.

TO *Harrison Eudy*[1]

Tuesday 28 June 1955 TLS (typed copy), Academy of American Poets

26 Elmwood Rd.
Wellesley, Mass.
June 28, 1955

Mr. Harrison Eudy
4614 Prospect Ave.
Cleveland, Ohio

Dear Mr. Eudy:

I was both pleased and honored recently to have a group of my poems awarded the Academy of American Poets Prize at Smith College. Mrs. Hugh Bullock,[2] President of the Academy, informed me in her letter[3] that the prize was made possible through a generous bequest of your mother, Mrs. Mary Cummings Eudy,[4] and that the two exquisite black-and-silver poetry books by Mrs. Eudy were a gift from you, in your mother's memory.

I felt, after reading the beautiful, diamond-cut poems in "Quarried Crystals"[5] and "Quicken the Current",[6] that I wanted to write you and tell you what a privilege it is and always will be to partake of your mother's vital, radiant spirit, crystalized here in living words. To use her own words, "The spreading shaft of a phrase, / Like radium, / Illumines the unseen realm."[7] This expresses my feeling towards these two brilliant books of poetry. Thank you for letting me share them.

As a scholarship student at Smith College, just freshly graduated this June, this prize was a most encouraging part of my "commencement". Almost as if it were a talisman, I had three poems accepted by The Atlantic, Mademoiselle, and The Nation. After this fruitful year, I know that writing poetry will always be the richest, most rewarding part of a full maturing life. Next fall, as I embark on a Fullbright grant, to study

1–Enoch Harrison Eudy (1899–1965).
2–Marie Bullock (1911–86); founder and president of the Academy of American Poets.
3–Marie Bullock to SP, 2 June 1955; held by Lilly Library.
4–Fashion designer and poet Mary Cummings Eudy (1874–1952).
5–Mary Cummings Eudy, *Quarried Crystals and Other Poems* (New York: G. P. Putnam's Sons, 1935); the location of SP's copy is not known.
6–Mary Cummings Eudy, *Quicken the Current* (New York: Harper & Brothers, 1949); the location of SP's copy is not known.
7–Mary Cummings Eudy, 'Radiation', *Quicken the Current*, 74.

English literature at Cambridge University, these two fine volumes of Mrs. Eudy's poetry shall accompany me as guide and inspiration.

With deepest gratitude for your thoughtfulness and generosity, I am

Sincerely yours,
/s/ Sylvia Plath

TO *Edward Weeks*

Wednesday 6 July 1955 — TLS (photocopy), Yale University

26 Elmwood Road
Wellesley, Massachusetts
July 6, 1955

Editor Edward Weeks
THE ATLANTIC MONTHLY
8 Arlington Street
Boston 16, Massachusetts

Dear Editor Weeks:

I was delighted to read of your decision to publish my first version of "Circus in Three Rings" in the August Atlantic.

As you requested in your letter, I am sending back to you "The Princess and the Goblins" with a selection of some new (and shorter) poems.[1]

I'm looking most forward to seeing the August issue!

Sincerely yours,
Sylvia Plath

TO *Warren Plath*

Wednesday 6 July 1955 — TLS (photocopy), Indiana University

Wednesday, July 6

Dear Warren . . .

I am sitting up in my room in halter and shorts trying to beat the heat with iced coffee, but it simply refuses to be beaten, and the ice persists

1–According to handwritten annotations made to the letter by an *Atlantic Monthly* employee, the poems enclosed with 'The Princess and the Goblins' were: 'Black Pine Tree in Orange Light', 'A Study in Sculptural Dimensions' ['Wayfaring at the Whitney: A Study in Sculptural Dimensions'], 'Ice Age', and 'Moonsong at Morning'.

in melting. Around me are the "hewn coils of my trade":[1] mountains of rejection slips, poems addressed to be sent out again, and countless copies of the SatEvePost (as the Writer's mags insolently abbreviate it) which I took out from the library to saturate myself in the "indefinable something" which makes a $1000 story. One acceptance since you left: The Nation,[2] that political news-sheet, to my surprise, bought an ominous little 24-line lyric called "Temper of Time." First acceptance from them, so it salves the wounds of the other snotty rejections. Poems are hell to sell. Be sure to buy the August Atlantic and Mlle if you have money to burn. Hope to be in both.

You would be very proud of me, I think, if you saw what I've been doing around the house! I have spent the whole last week doing nothing but working at it: spaded and weeded all the flower beds and around the trees; dyed the porch rug a less-spotty green; did mountains of laundry; bought two cans of enamel paint and painted porch tables and lamp and sundry little items black and the three kitchen chairs and table white. So much fun that I felt like painting the whole house with the left-over white enamel!

Mother is improving rapidly, and we have runs of guests. One day, no one will call or come. The next, a waiting line forms to the rear: Do Cruikshank, Mrs. Pulling,[3] (complaining about over-critical Miss Hamm;[4] followed by Miss Hamm (complaining about the lax Mrs. Pulling), Mrs. Gaery,[5] Mrs. Lameyer, Mrs. Clower,[6] Madeline Sheets:[7] whew, can't name them all! Anyway, mother receives them on the chaise lounge in the back yard and loves every minute of company.

I also have cleaned the house completely from top to bottom: your bookcase, mother's, medecine closets, all is washed, mopped, dusted, and ready to be kept up for the summer. Gordon was home for a week before heading off to Bainbridge, Maryland, and we had a most pleasant time

1–Dylan Thomas, 'Poem on His Birthday'; SP slightly misquotes: 'He / In his slant racking house / And the hewn coils of his trade perceives / Herons walk in their shroud'.

2–Sylvia Plath, 'Temper of Time', *The Nation* 181 (6 August 1955), 119. See Caroline Whitney to SP, 21 June 1955; held by Lilly Library.

3–Grace E. Pulling, who lived at 19 Pine Plain Road, Wellesley. Married to Richard A. Pulling; mother of David and Lynda.

4–Probably Thelma V. Hamm, a junior high school teacher who lived with her mother Charlotte C. Hamm at 27 Pine Plain Road, Wellesley.

5–Probably Mary R. Geary, wife of Rex I. Geary, who lived at 1 Ingersoll Road, Wellesley.

6–Probably Ruth Klauer, wife of Frederick J. Klauer, Jr, of 7 Ingersoll Road, Wellesley.

7–Madeline Redmond Sheets (1905–2006). According to SP's address book, Sheets lived at 1 Weld Road, Stoneham, Mass. Sheets was a trained nurse, see SP to ASP, 16 January 1960 (second letter).

swimming at Crane's Beach and playing tennis at the Wellesley courts. No one my age seems to be about Wellesley, only thousands of little kids and wrinkled old ladies smelling of lavendar water. I'll miss not having anyone to play tennis with, but really enjoy the peace and quiet. Cooked Gordon and mother a steak dinner which both ate merrily.

Took me ages of red-tape to get my passport:[1] had to run around the plethora of courthouses in that nasty hilly part of Boston, all one-way streets, and wait hours in line, only to find I needed an engraved birth certificate and not a piddling abstract, which cost more money and time. Finally, this week, the valuable document came from Washington, with my picture stamped over with an ornate government seal, so I look like I'm peering suspiciously from behind a printed lifebuoy, enough to make any customs agent suspicious of my intentions.

Mrs. Cantor took me into a wholesale place to buy some luggage, and I got along fine with the guy there, and ordered three pieces of beautiful gray airplane luggage (two in the shop, one to be got from nyc) at half price! Mrs. Cantor said even her husband, with all his business connections, wouldn't have been able to talk them down more. So I wait while the 3rd piece comes with bated breath. It will be a great deal if it comes through. Also went to Neal's of California,[2] that exclusive Boston shop, and ended up buying two fantastically great one-piece bathing suits, which I would feel proud to wear on the Riviera. All the salesgirls clustered around while I tried these on saying to each other: "Gee, that little girl in there is sure having a party." Mrs. Cantor had taken Kathy to shop there, and she "found nothing she liked", while I felt right at home, everything being most casually cut and magnificent in style and material. Oh, how horribly easy it is to spend money! Female logic: I figured I'd saved it from the suitcase markdown!

Amazing thing: I invited Richard Sassoon to come here for the 4th of July weekend. Mother revised her former picture of him, and I think found him okay. Anyway, I cooked like mad: datenut bars, tollhouse cookies, lobster salad, broiled chicken, steak, and a monumental new effort: Peach angel pie, which requires six egg whites for the meringue base and 2 hours cooking (it swelled up almost to fill the oven) and a filling of iced peaches and whipped cream. It was a gorgeous thing, and Mrs. Pulling, Miss Hamm, and Mrs. Gray all had some on their visits, and mother loved it.

1–SP's first passport, used 1955–7; held by Lilly Library. Her second passport, used 1959–63, is held by Woodruff Library, Emory University.

2–Neal's of California, a clothing store for women then at 19 Arlington Street, Boston.

George Gebauer is now my one summer contact, and very fortunately, we seem to get along quite well, and he seems to want to take me out (I made a fabulous picnic for last Saturday at Crane's beach) and I will probably go to the Theater-on-the-Green[1] with him this Friday. He is an awfully nice guy, openly says he is "very conservative and conventional" and is apparently amazed that he likes seeing me because I am what he terms "different" from the girls he knows. That's what happens when a staid scientist and a writer get together, I guess. He just can't follow my enthusiasm about life, including going to the Star Super-market.[2] I don't think I will ever in the world be "bored", because I have so many projects a life-time isnt' enough to carry them out, and there is always so much to learn. I really must have someone who has that joie de vivre which makes even a milkshake or a rowboat ride a keen delight. After all, that's life.

You have no idea how happy your letters make mummy! She reads them aloud to all her visitors and gloats over them like they were solid gold. It is fun hearing about the details of your work, and I think it will be a great experience for you. The money sounds good too! Hope you meet some nice girls who aren't married . . . funny how customs vary in different parts of the country; here, they all go to college. Anyway, Mother is getting the address of a young couple Mrs. Lameyer's friend Sibyl Doherty[3] knows, who she thinks might introduce you around.

Until later, keep writing, have fun, and know we're thinking of you . . .

much love,
Sivvy

TO *Aurelia Schober Plath*

Tuesday 12 July 1955 — TLS with envelope, Indiana University

Tuesday night, July 12

Dearest mother . . .

You would really laugh if you could see me typing now with my one arm, the other folded to my side like a sprained chicken wing. Reason

1–A summer-season production performed at The Amphitheatre, Wellesley College. The productions in June and July 1955 included Christopher Fry's *The Lady's Not for Burning*, Eugene O'Neill's *Desire Under the Elms*, and Shakespeare's *King Henry IV*, Parts 1 and 2.

2–Star Market, a grocery store then at 448 Washington Street, Wellesley.

3–Sibyl Webb Dougherty (1891–1960); taught voice at Pine Manor Junior College, then in Wellesley.

being that Fran gave me the first pair in a series of three shots. The tetanus didn't bother my right arm, but the typhoid sure immobilized my left! Luckily I caught her before her vacation, because this series has to be spaced, and I'll get the other two double threat jabs spaced in the middle and end of August.

I had a lovely drive home last night; made it in exactly three hours and headed into a stinging pink sunset that matched my sunburn in light, if not in heat. I sang on the top of my lungs all the way, with the freedom one feels only in the shower where the acoustics are excellent and no one will wince. I was so happy and felt so well after my lovely weekend with you and the relatives that I had to let out a few Indian yips of pure pleasure as I swung up the speedway past blue lakes and green swooping slopes of trees.

First thing getting here, I ran about opening all the windows to let in cool night air. Then I got ready for bed and read all my mail. Received a lovely fat letter from my dear Sue Weller, now in Washington, which relieved me greatly. If only I sold a story, I would fly down to visit her before I go! I do hope to manage it somehow. She is a great source of strength to me, as I am to her, and I think we'd profit by seeing each other once before God knows when. Also heard from Lynne Lawner, that lovely Wellesley college sophomore I met at the poetry reading in Holyoke. I have encouraged her to send things out and shall write her over the summer to give her as much of my mere technical pragmatic know-how as possible to save her learning the tedious way.

Haven't heard from Harper's yet . . . it's over a month now, which is definitely a good sign that they are "debating". Harper's Bazaar remedied their faux pas, evidently an accident, by sending all my poems back today with an impressively large letter-headed rejection and a personal note from the fiction editor. The New Orleans Poetry Journal, a new quarterly, send a nice post-card acknowledging the receipt of my poems and saying the editors will confer next weekend. They wanted to explain the "delay" in verdict (they only got the poems this weekend!) and the co-editor said he rarely sent his poems to the better quarterlies because they were so intolerably slow when they were considering something. So this blessed magazine is fanatic about their two week verdicts. Hope they give me a tumble.

Also got an amusing letter from the editor[1] of an evidently venerable poetry magazine named "Lyric", saying Gertrude Claytor[2] (my fairy-

1–American poet and author Ruby Altizer Roberts (1907–2004).

2–Gertrude Boatwright Claytor (1890?–1973); Claytor was on the advisory board of *Lyric*.

godmother on the Borestone awards whom I met at Holyoke) had recommended me very highly, and did I have poems to send them. They don't pay, but have several cash prizes awarded at the year's end. Here, I can see it now, is a perfect market for my more conventional and dainty sonnets, for they are very traditional. So I'm going to send all that will never get published as intellectual wit or modern blood-and-thunder.

Today was a domestic and odd-and-ends day, so I have postponed my working till tomorrow, when I hope my arm will let me type without wincing. I did the laundry, shopped for groceries, went to the bank. Went to Fran's, dropped over to Aldriches and had cocktails with Betty and Ginny (will go over some evening when the kids are in bed for a talk). George is taking me out Friday night,[1] and I may go visit Elly Friedman. Mrs. Lameyer called, and wants me to go to the Theater-on-the-Green[2] next week, so you can see that I have to fight them off. Dr. Beuscher delivered a 9 lb. baby boy named Christopher Grey B. July 6, and sent me an announcement. I called today, and hope to see her a few times before I go. All quiet on Eastern front.

Love to everybody – your one-armed girl,

Sylvia XXX

<on front of envelope>

p.s. Harper's thought, but said no. Am on my way for dinner with Mrs. Prouty tonight.

XX.
S.

TO *Aurelia Schober Plath*

Tuesday 19 July 1955

TLS with envelope,
Indiana University

tuesday night, july 19

dearest mother . . .

Occasionally I get the impulse to call the cape and chat with you, I do so like to share little bits of news. seems to me I wrote you only yesterday, and here I am again. It will be so nice to have you back home for nightly

1–According to SP's calendar, she saw *Tales of Hoffmann* and *Last Holiday*, and had ice cream at Howard Johnson. The films showed at the Kenmore Theatre, then at 777 Beacon Street, Boston.

2–According to SP's calendar, she saw *King Henry IV, Part 1* on 20 July 1955.

ice-cream and inbetween chats. (I bought some new ice-cream in preparation for your return: orange sherbet!)

Today has been packed full of phone calls. I spent a long time shopping for food this morning, stocking up on meat, only to find out I'm going out for dinner three times in the next four days! What a nice way to save food.

Mrs. Cantor called, and wants us to call or visit as soon as we come back next week, so do remind me. Tomorrow is dinner and theater with Mrs. Lameyer. Thursday I'm having dinner over Dot's. Friday I'm going out with George.[1] And Saturday, best of all, I'm going out to dinner and a play in Cambridge[2] with Peter Davison, who is in town for good and called tonight at last!

I'd really forgotten how nice and Britishy and tweedy his voice sounded. When I said I had hundreds of questions to ask him, he promised to be a Mr. Anthony and answer them all. What a relief! I'm putting off calling Rhoda Dorsey[3] till next week, as I have absolutely no time to see her this one. I am working in the daytime now, at my typewriter. Today I finished the Prouty article,[4] about seven pages, and will send it off. Tomorrow I begin my story: "Platinum Summer"(I changed it from "Peroxide", and think the tone is better) and hope to have it done by the time I see you next Tuesday. Once I get rid of my inhibitions with the typewriter, I'm golden.

Signing off for now with much love to you all,

sivvy

ps: what news from Warren?

<drawings of a female and male face and a dress in an unknown hand on back of envelope>

1–According to SP's calendar, she saw the film *Svengali*, visited the M.I.T. chapel and auditorium, and walked in the Public Garden. *Svengali* played at the Beacon Hill Theatre, then at 1 Beacon Street, Boston.

2–According to SP's calendar, she saw *Henry IV, Part I* at the Brattle Theatre. SP and Davison had dinner at Chez Dreyfus, then at 44 Church Street, Cambridge.

3–Rhoda Mary Dorsey (1927–2014); B.A. 1949, history, Smith College; B.A. 1951, Newnham College, University of Cambridge.

4–Sylvia Plath, 'Tea With Olive Higgins Prouty'.

TO *Gordon Lameyer*

Thursday 28 July 1955 TLS, Indiana University

thursday evening, july 28

dear gordon . . .

a note out of my chill (at last) gray room where, after bringing mother home from the cape yesterday and chauffering her to doctor appointments today, I am at last sitting down and facing the grim keys of my smug typewriter which, everytime I procrastinate and start a letter, gives a small malicious laugh. I've spent a hell of a lot of postage the last month sending out batch after batch of poems. my favorite villanelle "lament" ("the sting of bees") finally got accepted by a relatively new mag of good rep, <u>new orleans</u> poetry journal,[1] for a 40¢ per line rate, and <u>Lyric</u> accepted two[2] which I knew I'd never get paid for elsewhere: they give "prizes" yearly, no pay. I still have at least 10 top poems I know should get accepted, but unfortunately the new yorker et al. don't seem to be as aware of such matters as I. I keep reading about this damn adrienne cecile rich,[3] only two years older than I, who is a yale younger poet and regularly in all the top mags; and about 23-year old blondes from radcliffe who are already selling stories plus climbing alps. occasionally, I retch quietly in the wastebasket. wrote the reader's digest article about mrs. prouty which I expect to get back in the mail rejected any day now and am working on a flip story called "platinum summer", you guessed it, about a girl who dyes her hair. I can think up tremendous titles and whoopdedo funny conversation, but the plots throw me every time. the nicest thing about writing is not the writing which is hell, but having written something reasonably good. o fie.

your mother, by the way, treated me to a lovely dinner and theater-on-the-green (henry 4, pt. 1) last wednesday. had much fun with her. have been to a few good movies (guiness in "last holiday") and bad ("svengali": god: don't see it) lots of swimming at crane's and cape but not one solitary swat at tennis. your large green room[4] sounds most conducive to writing. I grow old, I grow old. already my pre-departure homesickness has set in and I am growing ineffably nostalgic. two years,

1–Sylvia Plath, 'Lament', *New Orleans Poetry Journal* 1 (October 1955), 19.

2–Sylvia Plath, 'Apotheosis' and 'Second Winter', *Lyric* 36 (Winter 1956), 10–11. Ruby Altizer Roberts to SP, 30 July 1955; held by Lilly Library.

3–American poet Adrienne Cecile Rich (1929–2012); Rich's first book *A Change of World* won the 1950 Yale Younger Poets Award, and was published by Yale University Press, 1951.

4–Gordon Lameyer to SP, 14 July 1955; held by Lilly Library.

so crucial, and will I know what to do with them? the horror, to be jamesian, is to find there are plenty of beasts in the jungle but somehow to have missed all the potshots at them. I am always afraid of letting "life" slip by unobtrusively and waking up some "fine morning" to wail windgrieved around my tombstone. how do the brilliant men find time to live, love, read and write? you tell me. I need too much sleep to be godlike. chosing is such hell because each choice cuts off a leg or an arm to make the head grow bigger. remember to bring back my 11 letters, huh? I shall not, by the way, be able to make jaffrey the weekend of the 6th or whatever, but hope to see you anyhow, either before or after your trip. I have developed a morbid attachment to my house and workroom. do, by the way, look up my dear sue weller for me: address: 1514 26th St. N. W. Washington, D.C.!

Love,
Sylvia

P.S. Do write.

TO *Warren Plath*

Thursday 28 July 1955 — TLS (photocopy), Indiana University

thursday night, july 28

dear warren . . .

I write from my desk in the chill gray woolen-sweater-weather which set in today, apparently to prepare me for the climate in england. this month has been a patchwork quilt in which a lot of odd and ends, but no long projects, have been accomplished. just got back last night from four days at the cape with the grandparents (both tan as walnuts) and mother, whom I chauffeured to two doctors' appointments today. her strength is picking up, although her weight is still low, and we've been having a congenial time together. we all miss you, and it has been wonderful to get your cards and letters which I've shared with mother.

you know how I am: always get homesick before I go anywhere. well, evidently before a two-years' siege, my attacks set in early, and I have been wandering around with a blue streak of incredible nostalgia for je ne sais quoi. paradoxically, I feel the desire to be intensely close to my friends: marty and mike, mrs. prouty, betty aldrich, patsy, not to mention aunt dot and george gebauer and peter davison (my publishing friend who is now delightfully at the harvard press as assistant to the director);

however, the closer I get, the sadder I feel to go away and leave them. once I get on the ship, I will be fine, as I'll have something tangible to work with, but already I feel sort of rootless and floating, with nothing actual to bite my teeth into. intellectually, I know the fulbright is the best and only thing for me; staying in new england or even new york would suffocate me completely at this point. my wings need to be tried. o icarus.

I've been reading a lot of magazines (nothing intellectual, a reaction, I guess, from the academic life of two solid years which I've just finished leading); the hardest part of writing is writing. I invent any excuses to procrastinate, and whenever I put off story plots to write a letter, your smug typewriter gives a low, malicious chuckle.

I have, however, written a couple of rather good poems and an article on mrs. prouty which I sent off in my usual gambling streak, to the reader's digest. expect the rejection any day now. amid my poetry rejections (the postage and re-typing and charting of them takes a good deal of time) I've had my favorite villanelle, "Lament", accepted by a relatively new mag: New Orleans Poetry Journal for the grandiose sum of \$7.60 (ie: 40¢ per line). what price artistic integrity. I am fast trying to lose said integrity by writing a story called "Platinum Summer", you guessed it, about a girl who dyes her hair. once I get that <u>first</u> professional story accepted, the gravy train will be in. unfortunately, to publish, one must write.

also, two poems I know very well I'd not get paid for anywhere were accepted by The Lyric, a traditional "poesy" mag that gives yearly prizes, no pay. oh, well. it's print. by the way, pick up the August Atlantic. unusually good poetry issue. funny, but one of the critters stands out like a green thumb. also the August <u>Mlle</u> has massacred one of my best poems by printing two lines on one page and the rest sandwiched between some later fashion ads. but they do have a good little paragraph and small minute snapshot under and article titled: poet on college time.

about the peregrinating one, namely dotty: obviously her job will have what I hope to have on shipboard: intriguing, poised, often intelligent, continental people. time goes fast when you have a varied job, and seems proportionately slow when you are working at the same kind of thing (IE: railroading) and have a good deal of time to ponder, probably, also, she is not the garrulous writing type, like me. she may just be the kind who doesn't feel letters are worth writing frequently. anyhow, I don't know her as well by a very long shot, but these are just suggestions to partially explain the big silence. perhaps. maybe she's written by now, maybe not. I know none of this will Mean anything inside your guts when you're writing five letters to her one, but in your head it may help to reason out possible explanations, and check them off later, either when she writes to explain or when you see her next fall. if it is Other Men, it is no doubt a good and necessary step in her growing up; yours, too. it happens to the best of us.

but listen: I want you to have some idea of your potential. it is great. like me, when you're good (as a person, versatilely) you're very very good, and when you're bad, you need rehabilitation; ergo: we both have a great deal of growing (maturing) to do, and it is by our relationships with other people (after all, what is life but people) that we will grow to ripe stature. in other words, the self-examinations that are induced by our problems and disappointments in relation to others are paradoxically the best incentives to growth and change we have. And it does take guts to grow and change, especially when your horizon is lighted up by what looks like the very best of good things: e.g. dotty, gordon, or whatever.

all this may be annoying to you; perhaps the girl had written already, perhaps not. lord knows, I admire her enormously and would be happy for you if it chanced you could grow along together for a good while. but at this age, growing is a chancy thing, and, for instance, sometime an "older" girl could be an enriching experience for you to know, or then, later, a much younger one. it is rare to parallel someone else's growth and meet needs for a sustained period when we are so flexible.

what I am rambling around and trying to say is, How Much I think you have to work with and how much I want you to have the sure, positive, creative feeling of the one or two <u>men</u> I'm lucky enough to know: that your security and love of life don't depend on the presence of another, but only on yourself, your chosen work, and your developing identity. <u>then</u> you can safely choose to enrich your life by marrying another person, and not, as ee cummings says, until.

I sure hope you take all this talk the way it's meant, and maybe drop me a line sometime to let me know you don't think I'm talking through the top of my sun-bleached head. I want you to grow to a certainty of your identity (which I think is the most important thing in life) which will never ask for another court of appeal but your own conscience. that often means sacrificing the tempting urge to spill over All (blues, defeats, inscurities) to another person, hoping for advice, sympathy, or sometimes even scolding as punishment. It means knowing when to go off for a socratic talk to yourself; sometimes it's a help to have one with someone who knows you and will always love you no matter what whenever; such as me.

anyhow, I want you to have a chance at europe next summer, so start applying to the harvard office Early in the year (one thing to learn is that there is always time for what you Really want to do, believe me) and ask for a job chauffeuring, translating (your german and french (?)) might help here, etc. I'll work on my end from bonny england.

it grows late, now, and I must sign off. tomorrow I spend in cambridge; afternoon at harvard with patsy o'neil; sandwich supper with george gebauer on his way to maine (he thinks, by the way, according to some chemical formula, that as exact opposites, we would be very happily married!) and then a much-looked-forward-to evening over peter davison's[1] reading aloud and talking. he's a harvard man, good friend of howard mumford jones, once had fulbright to cambridge, and is delightfully in the midst of publishing, authors, and poets and editors. his father is a scotch poet, too. a pleasant person. remember, there will be a lot more pleasant women in the world, warren, intelligent, beautiful, sometimes both together, sometimes not. but it is all living, preparation for the final intelligent beautiful one you will somday marry. I'll write again soon. meanwhile, my best love to my favorite brother.

your own,
sivvy

TO *Gordon Lameyer*

Wednesday 3 August 1955[2] TLS, Indiana University

wednesday morning

dear gordon . . .

just got your last letter[3] and wish somehow there was an intercom (don't know exactly what it is, but it sounds professional and may very well be the word I want) rigged between us. I am trusting this missive to airmail, praying you'll be getting it by friday. in case not, I'm also writing you a note in care of your mother.

life has been all up in a heaval lately. I am now wondering if you have watch or not this weekend. I am hoping, in a way, you do. because I am scheduled to be interviewed and taken apart by an agent down the cape,

1 – According to SP's calendar, Davison lived at 43 Bowdoin Street, Cambridge, Mass.
2 – Date supplied from internal evidence.
3 – Gordon Lameyer to SP, 31 July 1955; held by Lilly Library.

and the appointment was made for me by an editor[1] I know through mr. kazin. this is to arrange a homeport for any and all stories I do abroad, and it is my once-only chance. I had said I would take any time this agent could see me. so I have to take it. I'll be gone friday to sunday.

the worst that could happen would be for you to come up this weekend thinking I'd be here. for lesser things than this, women have been decapitated. the fact remains that I Must See You Before I Sail. I simply can't leave this country without seeing you. I am damn ritualistic, I know, but you are woven so into the tissue of my life that I may reason about it in the top of my head, but can't deny the fabric of my feeling. so I beg you again, to understand.

best of all, I would hope you had watch this weekend and would come up any other, to beach, play tennis, and (very much so) talk. I need a talk with you. quite a good deal. please, please write or leave a note at the house or something, so I'll know if I have a chance to see you before I go. do understand.

love,
sylvia

TO *Gordon Lameyer*

Thursday 4 August 1955 TLS, Indiana University

august 4, thursday

dear gordon . . .

a note only, to catch you in transit in case the air mail was not kind enough to speed my letter as of yesterday to you. I leave for martha's vineyard tomorrow to see agent about stories. arranged for me by young editor at harcourt brace whom mr. kazin philanthropically steered my way.

I still hope, selfishly, that you have watch this weekend and may come up later, for I expect to eternally be home until sailing time. and, as I said in my other letter and repeat here, I would like enormously to see you once before I go. please?

I am on my sweltering way to the doctor's to have both arms and a leg (perhaps) punctured for the second time. tetanus, typhoid and possible vac. hope it doesn't disable my cocktail arm, as I'm having pre-dinner

1–Peter Davison. SP and Davison travelled to Martha's Vineyard via Woods Hole and met, while awaiting the ferry, the Irish poet Padraic Colum (1881–1972) and his wife Mary (1884–1957).

drinks with marcia and mike plumer (those dears) in cambridge at their new apartment[1] before seeing "othello" at the brattle[2] which I'm sure won't come up to amherst performance.

enclosed:[3] article my by favorite dame, sent kindly by your mother, who has been most dear and helpful to me these last weeks.

leave a note at the house if you're home, huh? glance into the august 6 nation for fun. such news.

much love,
sylvia

TO *Aurelia Schober Plath*

Tuesday 9 August 1955 TLS, Indiana University

tuesday noon, august 9

dearest mother . . .

so nice to get your letter and card this morning: all mail otherwise has been unusually dull, just bills, circulars, ads, and nothing from warren. glad you like "two lovers and a beachcomber"; it's my favorite of the later ones, too, and I'll never quite forgive mademoiselle for what they did to it. I think I could have found a more dignified resting place for it. but then, someday I hope to see it shrined in book form, and the mlle credit will look good.

nothing but nice things to tell you. the weekend was fantastic. very hot, sunny, blowy and ominously hurricanish,[4] but wonderful for sailing and swimming. on the way down (we tried to catch the 5 pm ferry as peter got out of work early) we were stopped for speeding and just missed it. however, I was just as glad, for as we went into a woods hole bar for a cold beer, peter saw an elderly couple he seemed to know. the man was very irish and evidently a poet, while his salty, amusing, seasoned wife was a reviewer. turned out to be padriac and mary colum, old friends of peter's father. they treated us to a drink, and padriac told me his poem on the book of kells[5] was in the atlantic just the month before mine. delightful people, who spoke so familiarly of names that have been legends to me.

1–According to SP's address book in her 1955 diary, the Plumers lived at 45 Linnean Street, Apartment B-2, Cambridge, Mass.

2–*Othello*, directed by John Stix and starring William Marshall, played at the Brattle Theatre.

3–The enclosure is no longer with the letter.

4–Hurricane Connie made landfall in North Carolina on 12 August 1955.

5–Padraic Colum, 'The Book of Kells', *Atlantic Monthly* 196 (July 1955), 53.

peter and I had dinner at a lovely wharf restaurant: the landfall[1], where there was candlelight and a piano and organ player through a delicious dinner. all during the ride to the island on the ferry we stood at the helm, and by the time we got to vineyard haven, it was pitch dark. I felt very strange meeting all the people of barn house[2] in the dark, because I couldn't see their faces as there were no lights, and we all sat around in the dark and talked before going to bed early.

I was stationed in the "luxury" main house, which meant that I had a large attic room on the second floor with a bowl and running water, all very bare and barny, with a view of the sea. peter stayed in one of the "coops", little cabins scattered out in the fields for families.

in the morning I learned more about this amazing place and met more of the amazing people. it was set up after the first world war by a group of families who were all part-owners, and they invite friends and acquaintances to stay there. the big barn on a hill is the center of activities and meals are served there at regular times (8, 1, and 6:30). everybody serves themselves from the main dishes, and does the dishes together afterwards in a very specific ritual way.

peter and I were the only young people there, except for a fifteen year old boy who was a lot of fun. among the elderly couples was the president of rutgers university and his wife[3] (an englishwoman with a beautiful singing voice), an english professor from williams[4] and his writer-wife[5] (she did the article on the boy with the tumor in the last lh journal), a couple of lawyers and a german count and countess[6] from bonn. these were the people I ate and wiped dishes with! I was amazed at the casual informality: everybody came to meals in shorts and pitched in together.

saturday morning, peter and I went sailing with the 15 year-old boy in menemsha harbor. we swam off the boat and had a lovely time. in the afternoon, peter and I went up to vincent cliffs and found ourselves swimming along with a nudist colony. we met several interesting people

1–The Landfall is a restaurant at 9 Luscombe Avenue, Woods Hole, Mass.

2–The Barn-House is a seventeenth-century building at 451 South Road, Chilmark. It was added to the National Register of Historic Places in January 2012.

3–Lewis Webster Jones (1899–1975) and Barbara Slatter Jones (b. 1902); Jones served as president 1951–8.

4–Roy Lamson Jr (1908–86), professor of English and dean of freshmen, Williams College, 1938–57.

5–Peggy Lamson (1912–96); married to Roy Lamson; author of '"You Shall Become a Man": A mother who would not let her son die', *Ladies' Home Journal*, July 1955, 48–9, 86–8, 90, 93–4, 96–8, 100 (adapted from Simone Fabien, *Tu seras un homme* [1955]).

6–According to SP's calendar, their surname was Graf.

there, among them, a psychoanalyst and a commercial artist. then we climbed the sand cliffs and ran down in great seven-league leaps until we were exhausted, and then modeled clay faces on the clay cliffs, walking a couple of miles down the beach back home.

saturday night, the count and countess had a party at the barn during which we had gallons of champagne with peaches floating in it. a lovely lobster dinner followed, and then peter joined a group playing old elizabethan airs on a trio of recorders. he is very much like dick norton in his social ease, sort of playing on the keyboard of people like an organ, and hysterically funny in the stories he tells.

anyhow, sunday was a lovely long breakfast, and we went swimming again, running for long laps and battling the enormous surf till dinner. after which we left, and stood again on the helm of the ferry, dashed with spray, in a very rough crossing back to mainland. rain was welcome, and peter cooked me a delicious dinner on coming back. I'll never dare to cook for him now, he's such a conoisseur and knows all about touches of herbs and spices, etc. at least I can be properly appreciative, because he cooks magnificently with wine and sherry and cream, and has all sorts of interesting notes like pumpkin seeds and bacon rinds with garlic.

the last two days have been a dream. low humidity and bright sunny weather in which I can accomplish twice as much in an hour as in a whole sultry day. monday I shopped for food and finished the whole "platinum summer" story. today I will polish and rewrite a few parts, then type it up and send it off. I was up at 8:30 this morning, had a huge breakfast, did machine and hand laundry, mopped, dusted, washed hair and gave my self a manicure and pedicure out in the drying comfortable sun, where I am sitting now preparatory to working again on my story.

received a lovely encouraging letter from mary ellen chase[1] about england, and feel really good now. I can just sense a beginning desire to get back deep into books and thinking, perhaps the preview of autumnal weather has brought it on, but I shall count this summer well spent if I am fresh and eager to begin studying in the fall. by writing I am building up a background hunger to study, which is good.

have a lot of business to attend to this week. will call for my lovely suit[2] this afternoon and hope to hit boston again with you when you come back. if only I'd earn a big hunk of money, I'd feel better. but I feel very

1–Mary Ellen Chase to SP, 4 August 1955; held by Lilly Library.

2–According to SP's calendar, her suit was from C. Crawford Hollidge, then at 74 Central Street, Wellesley.

creative just now, and am determined to write much and often, continuing while I am in england. once I start selling to the slicks, I'm made.

so interesting, your plans to tentatively join aunt mildred abroad next summer. hope you do, it's such fun to have a confidant there when you want one. seems I'll be visited, too, by my friends. mary ellen chase will be over in the spring, and I hope to see richard in paris (he sent me a delectable box of marrons glace this week: glazed chestnuts, which I have been begging for ever since I read about them somewhere. delectable, and so thoughtful of him). peter, if all works out well, plans to take a six weeks vacation in europe also next spring, and if we're still as congenial as now, I'll probably see a bit of him. all in all, my fears are gone and I am feeling quite elated about going.

I'll probably be driving down next monday or tuesday, depending on weather and my story progress, planning to stay a couple of days and get back to wellesley before the weekend. I'll let you know before I come.

meanwhile, much love to all,
sivvy

TO *Gordon Lameyer*

Thursday 11 August 1955 TLS, Indiana University

11 august 55

dear gordon . . .

it was good to get your letters,[1] the one waiting scrupulously in my mailbox when I returned from the vineyard and the one yesterday mailed from maryland. thank you, as always, for being so damn understanding. my life has been so undisciplined and hedonistic this past summer that I will be glad to get back to a kind of strictness and routine this fall. this summer I have really done nothing I didn't feel like doing: stayed up late to read, read dozens of periodicals, hit or miss, beached it, swum, sunned, shopped extravagantly (I just better get some money soon from something or they won't let me go over because of debts), and eaten meals whenever I happened to feel hunger.

naturally, I feel chagrined in a way that I haven't studied an hour each of french and german, as I was going to, and read all the many books in my library I haven't read, and written ten stories and several pulitzer prize novels. but after two solid years of schooling without halt, I feel

1–Gordon Lameyer to SP, 8 and 9 August 1955; held by Lilly Library.

this summer is profitable by the very fact I'll be eager to get back to books in october and really plunge in. of course, they say the life there is much more "social" than here, with all kinds of clubs and teas and stringent intellectual discussions. I'm going to have to learn to get over my habits of impressionistic, indescriminate gush and straighten up. what appals me most is my lack of conversational versatility. I know absolutely nothing about politics and history and very little about art, nothing about music and a smattering (no novels) about english. I begin to wonder why intelligent people bother with me at all, I am such a tyro. but the time has come to branch out and get rid of the feeling I'm "an eagle too aged to try its wings."

on the positive side of the ledger, only a few things: wrote another gay, silly love story for the slicks called "platinum summer" and sent it off to collier's yesterday with the usual combo of foolish optimism and cynical defeatism. I have been mentally spending large sums of money which will accrue from my first slick story sale, but it might be more practical to sell one before I started these dreams of glory. still haven't heard from the reader's digest about the article, but expect the rejection any day now. worseyet, they may have lost my return envelope and junked it all.

have visited over at marty and mike's apartment and will have my close friend from smith, elly friendman, the theatrical mexican-looking one, stay with me this weekend. hope we have the hurricane. just elly, me and connie: very cosy.

had a wonderful and rather peculiar weekend on the vineyard. went down with this friend of mr. kazin's who worked with him when he had his books come out at harcourt. you'd like him, I think. he's now assistant to the director of the harvard press, peter davison by name, and my god, the writers he knows are phenomenal. (his father is the scotch poet, edward davison).

while waiting for the ferry we wandered into a bar where mr. davison seemed to know an elderly and very witty couple who treated us to a round of drinks. turned out to be the poet padriac colum and his critic wife, mary. on the vineyard we stayed in a co-operative settlement called barnhouse, where everybody helped with the work. except for a precocious and very funny fifteen year old boy, I was the infant there.

I found myself wiping dishes with the president of rutgers and an english prof at williams whose wife is a writer. a german baron and baroness gave a champagne party (peaches floating in it this time) in the barn, and it was all very casual and folksy, with the english prof making up a trio which played elizabethan folk songs on the recorder.

as far as the agent part goes, I think I'll have one quite definitely. I'm waiting till I see the reception to this last story and then probably will have an appointment at the new york office just before I sail, which, by the way, is wednesday afternoon, september 14.

now, if all goes well and I should make some money, (which I doubt), I hope to fly to washington to stay with my dear sue a few days. this would probably be between august 26 and september 4, but I am very tentative and indefinite yet. will let you know before, because it would be infinitely more convenient for you to see me there, n'est-ce pas?

anyhow, I'll see you before I leave, either down there or up here. you must speed this female ulysses on her way with a kind of creative blessing. I'll need it. I certainly will.

for now, love and fond thoughts,
sylvia

TO *Aurelia Schober Plath*

Friday 12 August 1955 — TLS with envelope, Indiana University

friday morning, august 12

dearest mother . . .

a lovely rainy day, this, and I have just finished my usual huge great colossal breakfast of orange juice, chicken livers and bacon, danish rolls and much coffee. after my second cup of coffee, I always feel extremely creative, as if I could write a pulitzer prize novel. some week I shall drink nothing but coffee and thry this.

I am about to run downtown for a few last minute purchases, as elly friedman is coming in a couple of hours to stay till tomorrow. I am about to make up the bed in my room, feeling very hostessy, and have got out a big steak and some good sherry for dinner tonight. I love it here, and listen often to fm when I'm doing housework. I meditate and think, too, which is all to the good, kind of getting settled in equilibrium before the assault on the rich, complex old world.

got a nice fat letter from betsy (powley) wallingford from germany today, where she'll be for a year with her husband. evidently she hadn't got our pitcher, but that's only natural. I now have several married-couple friends in germany and hope to visit them.

nice letter from cambridge, with a list of the exam papers I'll have to write, about six in all. somehow I feel much better, seeing the specific choices. there was also enclosed a reading list for the required exam on tragedy with a good hundred books on it. I feel I should face this with the attitude that I can grow to be a well and widely educated person, even though now I am terribly narrow. It is exciting, too, rather than sickening, to look at the book titles and think that I shall be curling up in libraries and reading and reading. if I interpret rightly, the language can be either french or italian instead of both, which would be a blessing. I could hire a weekly tutor in french and by the second year my reading should leave me with no vestige of this old inferiority complex.

was most interested in your enclosed dance-notice. called up immediately and am scheduled for the first one next monday afternoon. they sounded very nice about it, and I know it will give me much need confidence to tell a tango from a rhumba and be able to do them both. lessons are private.

got a magnificent letter from my dear sue and have decided to fly to washington to visit with her over the weekend of the 26th if all goes well. I have my last shots with fran the 25th, and sue and our mutual friend dorri (licht) hildebrand will be there. sue's life sounds magnificent. she is taking french at the language school, in charge of 30 visiting frenchmen in statistics for three months, and her dating life is magnificent, with all sorts of fascinating government boys, including lodge's son.[1] I have made reservations to leave on friday afternoon the 26th, and hope maybe you and warren will be home by then.

will probably drive down the cape wednesday the seventeenth to pick you up. expect me then, if you don't hear otherwise.

am feeling very rested and happy. read a magnificent article in the "writer's yearbook"[2] about a slick writer who took the words out of my mouth: "You are a human being before you are a writer, and because of this you are apt to identify yourself too closely with your work. When this happens, every rejection you get throws you into depression, because you will be rejected as a person as well as a writer . . . . I learned I was certainly going to be in trouble if I went on thinking of myself as a writer first and a woman second. It had to be just the other way around. If you can think of yourself as an individual who, incidentally, writes, you'll be able to accept your acceptances as well as your rejections as a professional must accept them. You will take them as a matter of course. The failures

1–Probably American politician and professor George C. Lodge (1927–), son of United States Senator from Massachusetts Henry Cabot Lodge, Jr (1902–85).

2–Lucinda Baker, 'No Literary Slump for Lucinda', *The Writer's 1955 Year Book* 26 (Cincinnati, Ohio: F. & W. Publishing, 1955), 11–15; SP's annotated copy held by Smith College; the text SP quotes appears on pp. 14–15.

won't be grievous wounds to your own sense of personal worth." I would like to memorize this article forever etching it in my head. It is a directive to live by.

see you soon, love to all
Sivvy

TO *Gordon Lameyer*

24 August 1955 TLS, Indiana University

wednesday, august 25[1]

dear gordon . . .

it was great to get your letter,[2] and I do so look forward to seeing you before I go. I haven't yet heard definitely from sue weller re details, but at present I'm planning to get a ride down to washington sunday night, august 28th (which means I'd miss the weekend) and I would be overjoyed if it were possible to drive back with you on friday, september 2nd! I can't think of a more pleasant way to spend hours which are often tedious when one is on the road alone, unless an interesting hitchhiker happens along. do let me know if it will be possible to drive up with you then, so I won't go mad over plane reservations. I hear vague and ominous rumors about the bad road conditions, due to the recent hurricane floods from temperamental diane,[3] but maybe we could go up together on plane or train, as the fancy suited you. anyhow, let me know your pleasure.

the most devastating occurence here recently has, of course, been the hurricane flooding rains. it seems almost incredible to me that two solid days of rain could botch up our whole clockwork civilization, but so it did. even the reliable boston trains weren't running, and my cousin bobby was marooned for hours in a western massachusetts washout. as for me, I unerringly picked thursday last, the beginning of all this, to drive back from the cape, with my usual peculiar luck, I drove through flooded underpasses and places where whole sand bankings were flowing into the road, able to see nothing but the faint tail-lights of the car a few feet ahead. friday it was still pouring, and I couldn't resist driving to cambridge to visit friends and take a look at the affluent charles. the harvard stadium stood like a greek arena on the mediterranean, for all

1–Letter misdated by SP.

2–Probably Gordon Lameyer to SP, 16 August 1955; held by Lilly Library.

3–Hurricane Diane made landfall at Wilmington, North Carolina on 17 August 1955, moving up the east coast and affecting Virginia and the mid-Atlantic states.

soldiers' field was under water and the river was lapping at the curbing in the lesser flooded places. sewers gushed up like miniature old faithfuls. somehow I was most exhilarated by all this . . . a bottle-mode of the 40-day act of God.

anyhow, I feel a kind of strong joy in battling the forces of nature. there is an ancient grandeur to it which I love, in contrast to the killing manmade devastation of war, which only sickens me.

my ticket finally came from cunard, and now it seems that if I can work my baggage problems out, I might actually get off on september 14. warren, I hope, will drive me down on the 13th, and I'll see if I can work in a few new york appointments before I take off. I'm determined to go to tangier next summer for a few weeks and hope to write a feature article about the american school there. by that time, I hope also to be speaking parisian french.

I can't describe the queer feelings I have now. this is the first time I have put all constants in life behind me and set off without a chart or friend to stabilize transition. I get flashes of intense joy at the potential of living and studying abroad, stabs of fear (will I have enough to give to it? or will much magnificence be lost on me? will I grow, like my favorite isabel archer,[1] through struggle and sorrow? or will I want to run home crying for the laps of those I love? god knows,) not to mention blue days where I seem to be living in a limbo where my roots are already torn up from my home soil, but yet not put down to grapple with the chemical and physical differences of a foreign ground. Once I am on the damn ship, it will all be all right, because I can begin something. but now, there is no time for any sort of sustained reading or writing here, and I am eager to go through the fires of the queen elizabeth, london, and cambridge, to get to my room and roots at whitstead hall.[2]

an interesting note: mother had decided to give me my birthday present in advance: a summer special of 11 half-hour dancing lessons at the fred astaire studios in boston.[3] I decided that this would be more than worth it, so I wouldn't run and hide under the captains table when the south american bands began, but would try my luck with a kind of confidence. well, my luck began when I walked into the studio last week, shaking slightly.

1–Henry James, *The Portrait of a Lady* (1881); Isabel Archer is a main character.

2–Whitstead Hall, 4 Barton Road, Cambridge, is the residence for foreign students attending Newnham College, Cambridge University; SP lived there from October 1955 through early December 1956.

3–The Fred Astaire Dance Studio was at 294 Boylston Street, Boston.

you can imagine what most of the male instructors are like: soft, pale, boneless, weak, and kind of slimy. well, the manager gave me my d.a. (*dance analysis) and said he'd take me on. he happens to be the most amazing character: tall, lean, with a white-blond crew cut and the most fantastic teutonic bone structure. his name is mr. hanzel[1] (I feel like a most fortunate gretel) and he is almost impossible to even begin to figure out. first of all, he is a most original and exquisite dancer, has spent a lot of time in cuba and is, as they say, polished. but most unassuming and intensely serious about life, philosophically speaking, while he can go absolutely wild with a deadpan mambo.

perhaps the most uncharacteristic thing about him is a kind of innocence and articulate wisdom which I have met in very very few college boys. to find this in the manager of a dance studio is rather unusual to say the least. I'm pretty sure he never got through senior high (he enlisted in the navy at 16) and yet his ideas on growth, maturity, the essence of character, death, and god knows what else, are more articulate and highly developed than any I've found. strange, but I'm curious as hell to find out where all this wisdom comes from. you'd be awfully taken by him, I think. maybe you could help me figure him out. he's more than worth it. in our last coke break we were attacking the fallacy of plato's state and coming out strong for the relativity of growth and necessity for a lifelong toleration of conflict, rather than a secure resolution of it. also, I'm learning how to tango, which at this point is my favorite dance. I am also learning how to do rocks without falling over, likewise, dips and backbends. la la la. such fun. if I can get to be a good dancer, I won't mind not being able to sing so much. I've just Got to Express all this life I have inside me somehow in rhythm and patterns, freedom in discipline.

oh, gordon, there is so much to talk about with you. I hope so very much our trip back on the 2nd works out. for convenience, here is sue's address again:

1514 – 26th Street NW, Washington 7. her phone number is Adams 4-3473.

I am sure that you will be one of the men to escort Miss America. if they could only have a picture of you, they would save you to escort the winner. do send me any publicity shots with you in them.

also, don't forget that anytime you choose to fly to london, just off hand, I'd meet you at the airport. this may sound a bit overboardish, as I have to find out about cambridge rules, but the spirit is there. and you kind of symbolize the home continent.

1 – According to SP's calendar, this was Richard Roger Hanzel.

if you have time, send me an airmail letter if it will get here by saturday telling me about the long way home. if not, send something to sue's. I await news of you.

with love,
isabel

TO *Aurelia Schober Plath*

Tuesday 30 August 1955[1]

ALS (3 picture postcards) with envelope, Indiana University

<picture postcard captions>

1) The Music Room at Mount Vernon; 2) View of the Building [National Gallery of Art, Washington, DC] from the Mall; 3) The Nativity. Engraving by The Master I. I. C. A. Italian (early 16th century). Rosenwald Collection.

Tuesday 1

Dear mother –

It seems almost impossible that I am here & seeing all this with Sue – I love Washington, it is all wide leafy green avenues & pseudo-Greek buildings. Georgetown, where Sue lives[2] is exquisite – all pale pink, blue & yellow houses with ivy and patios. Quaint, idiosyncratic shops, all most lovely for browsing. Sue has a large pale green room with a door leading out on a dear back yard terrace – books, music, and so homey. Left at 7 a.m. Sunday in packed car with Pat Conmy[3] – talked a blue streak till NYC where we met Sue & lunched with her & Whitney and got here about 7:30 in time for supper (next card)

2

yesterday & today Sue took off. Monday we went up the clean-cut Washington Monument after window-shopping on the Capitols "5th Avenue". Then walked up to the mall to spend hours at the National gallery (Mellon's bequest). I think it must be the most beautiful building in the world – I love the Flemish school and plan to spend all Thursday there myself – wonderful Giovanni Bellinis, Rembrandts, van Eycks, and exquisite Raphael madonnas – got several postcards & imagine, they have courts & fountains inside! I can't wait to go back – such a collection!

1–Date supplied from postmark.

2–Weller lived at 1514 26th Street NW, Washington, DC.

3–Possibly Patrick A. Conmy (1934–); B.A. 1955, Harvard University.

pizza supper last night with Sue & George (a witty & pleasant friend of hers) – then saw Hepburn in "Summer Time"[1] – Technicolor Venice made me want to leave right away for Italy – (next)

3

Today we rented a new two-tone blue Ford Herz-you-drive-it car & took off along the scenic Potomac for Mount Vernon – exquisite grounds, 18th century formal gardens and colorful rooms; I love early American styles. Then we came back to visit the Lincoln Memorial which impressed me, emotionally & intellectually, most of all. Such a colossus, in such clean, enormous, simply carved white stone. I felt shivers of reverence, looking up into that craggy, godlike face – the view of the Wash. Monument in the reflecting pool was also spectacular. Tonight we drive to a country house for a steak dinner[2] – tomorrow I go to work with Sue – Thursday is mine, & maybe we'll see "The King and I."[3] Home Friday –

XXX
sivvy

TO *Aurelia Schober Plath*

Sunday 25 September 1955 — TL (aerogramme), Indiana University

<SP typed 'Letter No. 1' on address side of letter>

Sunday afternoon, September 25

Dearest mother . . .

At last I am sitting at my typewriter, free for the first time, really, in the whirlwind of the past days where I have lived years in the space of hours. Orientation is over, and I have moved from my first residence at the lovely Bedford College set in the midst of Regent's Park (complete with swans and boating lakes) to the YWCA[4] (!) directly opposite the British Museum. I am staying on the 4th floor (they call it 3rd here) in a

1–American actress Katharine Hepburn (1907–2003) starred in the motion picture *Summertime*, which played at the DuPont Theater, then at 1322 Connecticut Avenue NW, Washington, DC.

2–SP's calendar indicates she ate at Peter Pan; probably the Peter Pan Inn, then in Urbana, Maryland.

3–*The King and I*, starring Patricia Morison and Leonard Graves, played at the National Theatre at 1321 Pennsylvania Avenue, Washington, DC, from 1 August 1955. There is no indication in SP's calendar that she saw the performance.

4–According to SP's calendar, she stayed at the YWCA Holborn, Helen Graham House, 57 Great Russell Street, London.

large room which I am sharing with 3 other girls, (2 French, one another American Fulbrighter to study English at Oxford.) It is a most convenient spot, only 10s 6d per night, which here includes breakfast (roughly $1.50) and I achieve a keen aesthetic satisfaction from the incongruous act of sitting in our bathroom and staring directly into the Ionic columns and classic pediment of the British Museum where we went yesterday for a lecture, to see the famous Reading Room and Elgin marbles. I shall stay here till a week from Monday when I move on from the most magnificent city I've ever lived in to the more rural provinces of Cambridge.

Where to begin! I feel almost smothered when I start to write, this my first letter! I feel that I am walking in a dream. Perhaps I shall start at London and go backwards. This is really the first day on my own, and since Sunday mornings in any strange city are a bit sad, I took a walk and sat in one of the little green squares to read a bit from the London Magazine. My "shipboard romance" left this morning for his university in Manchester, and we have had the most ideal time discovering London together. He's a genial, versatile Jewish Physics major from New York named Carl Shakin[1] and we've gone skipping about finding restaurants and plays and bookshops ever since Tuesday when we arrived. Imagine, in five days we've seen 4 plays and one superlative French movie, "Rififi"[2] which makes Alfred Hitchcock seem an infant. Theaters (there are over 40!) offer everything from operas, musicals (several American), melodramas, to symbolic poetics and kabuki dancers. The theaters are small, intimate, like the decorative inside of an easter egg, and in the intermissions tea (afternoon) or coffee (evening) is served at your seats in little trays (if ordered) for about 40¢, complete with sugar bowl and creamer and assorted cakes! We've seen a magnificent and peculiar existentialist play about a man's dilemma in the midst of nothingness by Samuel Beckett (James Joyce's secretary) called "Waiting for Godot";[3] Terence Rattigan's "Separate Tables",[4] with Margaret Leighton and Eric Portman, really two related plays, a tour de force in structure; "Shadow of a Doubt"[5] with John Clements, a tense drama about a physicist trying

1–Carl M. Shakin (1934–); B.S. 1955, New York University; Fulbright Fellow, University of Manchester, 1955–6; Ph.D. 1961, Harvard; escorted SP on the Cunard liner *Queen Elizabeth* and in Cherbourg and London, September 1955.

2–According to SP's calendar, she saw *Rififi* at the Curzon on 24 September 1955.

3–According to SP's calendar, she saw Samuel Beckett's *Waiting for Godot* at the Criterion Theatre on 20 September 1955.

4–According to SP's calendar, she saw *Separate Tables* at the St James's Theatre on 24 September 1955.

5–SP misnames the play. SP saw Norman King's *The Shadow of Doubt* at the Saville Theatre on 22 September 1955.

to make a comeback after being accused of treason; and "The Count of Clérambard",[1] a witty French piece. Acting is superlative, and I can see how the intimacy of a small theater helps a play succeed here, where it can flop in the enormous halls on Broadway. We've got excellent seats in the middle of the first balcony each night for never more than $1.50! Such a life! I could go to plays forever. Also became a "member" of a small Arts theater[2] which puts on esoteric foreign plays for a nominal fee enabling me to buy tickets and take guests.

London is simply fantastic. So much better organized (beautiful "tubes" with artistic posters, two decker red busses, maps everywhere, all black cars and cabs, guides to theaters, all posted) than NYC; more beautiful than Washington (Parks with roses, pelicans, palaces, plane trees and fig trees and lakes and fountains) and infinitely more quaint and historic (obviously) than Boston). The "bobbies" are all young, handsome, and exquisitely bred; I think they've all gone to Oxford. Flower girls, fruit stands with enormous peaches, grapes, etc. on every corner. Chalk artists too, on the sidewalks at Trafalgar Square, (as in "Mary Poppins",) who draw lurid sunsets and American movie stars and collect pennies. Discovered the book stalls up and down Charing Cross Road and browsed for hours. Wonderful art stores there, and found ancient books illustrated by our favorite Arthur Rackham. Ate at Chez Auguste,[3] an international restaurant in the cosmopolitan international section of Soho, and am a devotee of cafe expresso with foaming white cream, which I have at a colorful modern coffee house on Haymarket where there is a cubist water fountain, with water sliding perpetually down planes of colored glass overhead into a glass pool surrounded by white pebbles, green plants, and nudes and chickens carved out of finely grained wood. We've had lectures at Bedford (one on politics and economics with the Editor of "The Economist"[4] and several Members of Parliament . . . very fiery, re prejudice, colonies, nationalization of industries, fascinating) and one on education, public (Private to us) and state. Several impressive receptions, the first at the English-Speaking Union where the Countess of Tunis[5] received us and I met a tall handsome barrister, a member of the Queen's

1–According to SP's calendar, she saw Marcel Aymé's *The Count of Clérambard* at the Garrick Theatre on 23 September 1955. The play was translated by Norman Denny.

2–The Arts Theatre is at 6–7 Great Newport Street, London.

3–Chez Auguste, a restaurant then at 38 Old Compton Street, London.

4–British economist and journalist Geoffrey Crowther (1907–72); editor of *The Economist* 1938–56. This lecture took place on 21 September 1955.

5–Margaret Alexander, Countess Alexander of Tunis (1905–77); the reception was at Dartmouth House, 37 Charles Street, Berkeley Square, London, on 21 September 1955.

Royal Horse Guards, who drank wine on the balcony overlooking Berkeley Square and had a most intriguing talk with me. (next letter).

TO *Aurelia Schober Plath*

Sunday 25 September 1955 — TLS (aerogramme), Indiana University

<SP typed 'Letter No. 2' on address side of letter>

(continued)

Dear mother . . .

To go on . . . once I begin it is almost impossible to stop, as memories keep crowding into my head. The saddest reception was the one for English Lit. students, as I had no way of knowing the illustrious men who were there as guests until afterward (the hostessing was atrocious, and none of us had any idea of the nature of the visitors . . . they all looked very much like respectable professors). I only met David Daiches,[1] who will be lecturing at Cambridge and is a well-know critic. Imagine my chagrin when I found out that Stephen Spender[2] (the poet), John Lehmann[3] (Brilliant head of BBC and editor of the London Magazine, a literary review) and C. P Snow[4] himself (!) had been in the crowd! It was terribly frustrating not to have been introduced to them, but I swallowed my anger at the inefficiency of the hostess and determined to meet them after I'd begun writing at Cambridge. It might be better that way, anyhow. Even T. S. Eliot had been invited, but couldn't make it at the last minute.

The last reception was given by the American Ambassador[5] at the Embassy in Regent's Park, formerly Barbara Hutton's palace.[6] Never have I seen such a palace! We had cocktails and hors d'ouevres on the wide marble steps overlooking one of those enormous rolling green lawns that must have been growing at least a hundred years! Such elegance. It has rained a good deal here, and I carry an umbrella as part of my costume. My gray coat is ideal, dressy enough for evening, very warm, and of course my suit is perfect (several people have commented on it).

1–Scottish literary historian and literary critic David Daiches (1912–2005).

2–English poet Sir Stephen Harold Spender (1909–95).

3–English poet Rudolf John Frederick Lehmann (1907–87).

4–English novelist Charles Percy Snow (1905–80).

5–United States Ambassador to the United Kingdom Winthrop Williams Aldrich (1885–1974).

6–Barbara Woolworth Hutton (1912–79); Winfield House, Regent's Park.

I have never lived in so many places for such a long time (the Moores, the Smiths, the ship, Bedford, YWca, and next Cambridge), and I feel more and more capable. The money is fun, and I am getting used to it fast. I've walked for absolutely miles, looking and looking: Picadilly Circus recalls Times Square with all the neons; the statue of Eros and the fountain in the center is a landmark now. Trafalgar Square at night is awe-inspiring, with the national Gallery lit up, the exquisite church, St. Martin's in the Fields, and the lighted fountains and flowerbeds and regiments of pigeons. The theater is very early here (7:30) and out by 10:30, so London is really all in bed long before midnight, it seems.

Oh, mother, every alleyway is crowded with tradition, antiquity, and I can feel a peace, reserve, lack of hurry here which has centuries behind it. After every theater performance everyone stands at attention while they play "God Save the Queen" and I am already beginning to feel strong stirrings of loyalty. Statues are everywhere, and I had a picnic yesterday with Carl (we bought meat pies and cheese pies at a miraculous delicatessen near Hyde Park) and ate under the statue of Roosevelt.

One of Sue's little boys[1] (all very thin and tubercular-looking) brought me in an ancient car from Bedord with my cases yesterday and is taking me to the National Gallery this afternoon. The days are generally gray, with a misty light, and landscapes are green-leaved in silver mist, like Constables paintings.

The ship was wonderful, made more so by Carl, who had tea with me and long bull sessions on deck. Weather was half-and-half, but I took no pills, danced every night in the midst of great tilts and rocks, and communed with the sea, by sun, rain and stars. Hot broth on deck every morning, afternoon tea (after one cold rainy day in London, I became an addict), roast beef cold for breakfast, an hysterically funny cockney waiter, and sun and sky. Now I know I'll never get seasick, although the others were taking dramamine by the pail.

Best of all: my first land was France! We docked at Cherbourg, and Carl and I went ashore for the most enchanting afternoon of my life. I can see why the French produce painters: all was pink and turquoise, quaint and warm with life. Bicycles everywhere, workers really drinking wine, precocious children, tiny individual shops, outdoor cafes, gray filigree churches. I felt I'd come home. We wandered in a park full of rare green trees, fountains, flowers and hundreds of children feeding goldfish and rolling hoops. Babies everywhere. I even got up courage and stammered

1 – According to SP's calendar, this was John Clark.

out a bit of French to several vibrant, humorous old ladies on a bench, and fell in love with all the children. My first vacation, and I shall fly to France! Such warmth and love of life. Such color and idiosyncrasy. Everything is small and beautiful and individual. What a joy to be away from eightlane highways and mass markets to where streets are made for bicycles and young lovers, with flowers on the handlebars and around the traffic lights!

It was good to get your letter. I do feel so cut off from home, especially since I am not[1] at my final address yet. But if I am happy now, at the most disoriented stage of my journey, I imagine once I put down roots at Cambridge, there will be no end to joy. Do write, and I shall piece by piece, write all my thankyou notes. Will write from Cambridge. Much love to you, Warrie and the grandparents.

Sivvy

TO *Gordon Lameyer*

Tuesday 27 September 1955 — ALS (picture postcard), Indiana University

<picture postcard caption>

BRITISH MUSEUM. OA 21. HEAD OF AMIDA BUDDHA. Wood; formerly painted. Japanese: late 12th century. ht. 38½ inches.

Whitstead, 4 Barton Road, Cambridge
Sept. 27,

Dearest Gordon . . .

am now living in London cultivating buddha's calm directly opposite Ionic columns of Br. Museum which I see as I walk daily. You'd love it here – have seen 5 plays this week[2] – best "Waiting for Godot" – an intriguing symbolic tragicomedy by Samuel Beckett – James Joyce's secretary! the bookstalls at Charing Cross (especially Foyle's[3]) are more seductive each day. have walked miles – queen's park – london bridge (not yet fallen) – picadilly circus with statue of eros as in the center of a navel.

1 – 'since I ~~have~~ am not' appears in the original.

2 – According to SP's calendar, during 20–7 September 1955 she saw *The Remarkable Mr Pennypacker* at the New Theatre on 26 September 1955 in addition to *Waiting for Godot*, *The Shadow of Doubt*, *The Count of Clérambard*, *Separate Tables* and *The King and I*.

3 – Foyle's bookstore was at 119–125 Charing Cross Road (address from SP's address book).

No Osmond yet but then I'm still in Garden Court.[1] Will write in detail from Cambridge. Meanwhile, write!

Much love,
Sylvia

TO *Elinor Friedman Klein*

Wednesday 28 September 1955[2] ALS (picture postcard), Smith College

<picture postcard caption>

BRITISH MUSEUM Page from The Codex Zouche-Nuttal a Pre-Columbian Mixtec pictographic manuscript from Mexico, painted on deer skin. The scene probably represents the creation of the Mixtec people.

Whitstead, 4 Barton Road
Cambridge, England

Dearest Elly . . .

GREETINGS from London!

Have been living by your great card & bending elbows madly. London is great – all theater (5 plays in a week I've seen) art (from Nat. Gallery to sidewalk chalk artists) and bookstalls. Have walked miles through green queen's parks, historic streets, discovered sin & shashlik in Soho and had a tragic shipboard romance with a young Jewish nuclear physicist – turned out he'd been married just 8 weeks ago – but we discovered France together – <u>there</u> the men know how to look at one – I take off for Paris my 1st vacation – will write more from Cambridge –

Love,
Sylvia

P.S These mad Mexicans reminded me of you. People from Tangier are called Tangerines.

Love,
Hercule Poirot[3]

1–Henry James, *The Portrait of a Lady* (1881).
2–Date supplied from postmark.
3–Fictional Belgian detective created by Agatha Christie.

TO *Aurelia Schober Plath*

Sunday 2 October 1955 TLS (aerogramme), Indiana University

<SP typed 'Letter No. 1' on address side of letter>

Sunday afternoon, Oct. 2,

Dearest mother . . .

By now I hope my two-installment letter of last week has caught up with you. I am most heartily sorry if you were at all worried, but life was coming at me so fast that I had no sense of time elapsing at all. Before I left London, I sent off a slew of postcards to all the people who had been most dear: Crocketts, Cantors, Freemans, Prouty, et. al. Amazing what dreams do to fill up absences: I've dreamt of you and Warren every night since I've been away; sometimes the two of you are very wicked, conspiring to get rid of me forever. Which I suppose is an indirect way of saying that basically I miss you both.

I don't know how I can begin to tell you what it is like here in Cambridge! It is the most beautiful spot in the world, I think, and from my window in Whitstead on the third floor I can see out into the Whitstead garden to trees where large black rooks (ravens) fly over quaint red tiled rooftops with their chimney pots. My room is one of three on the 3rd floor, and while it is at present bare of pictures and needs a bit of decorating, I love it dearly. The roof slants in an atticish way, and I have a gas fireplace which demands a shilling each time I want to warm up the room (wonderful for drying my washed hair by, which I did last night) and a gas ring on the hearth where I can warm up water for tea or coffee. I shall draw you a little map so you can see the layout. My books overflow everywhere and give me the feeling of color and being home (spent all morning carrying loads of them up the staircase). I want to buy a low coffee table if I can find one to bring the room together a bit and give more surface space.

<drawing of SP's room at Whitstead with the following labelled by SP: 'door', 'books', 'tea cabinet', 'ancient bureau', 'wardrobe', 'bed', 'books', 'chair', 'ideal dream – table', 'sofa', 'west window looking into sunset', 'table – desk' and 'gas fireplace'>

Small, but capable of warmth and color after I buy a tea-set and a few prints[4] for the bare walls. I love the window-sofa: just big enough for two to sit on, or for one (me) to curl up in and read with a fine view of tree-tops.

4–'and a few ~~re~~prints' appears in the original.

Breakfasts are in Whitstead, in a lovely old-fashioned dining room with dark paneling looking out on the garden. We are given a hunk of butter once a week (!) but of course can supplement by buying margerine downtown. I get a small bottle of milk a day (it costs a bit extra but is worth it) which I can use for tea, coffee, or just drinking and plan to put a store of jam, cheese, and crackers in my tea cupboard. We eat lunch and dinner at Clough Hall (one of the four at Newnham) and I have been ravenous each time, so the food doesn't bother me, although it has an amazing amount of starch all at once; two kinds of potatoes, cauliflower, yorkshire pudding, pie and custard sauce, for example accompanied a small piece of roast beef for lunch. Breakfasts have the advantage of being made for only the 12 of us, and this morning I had cornflakes, a fried egg, two pieces of toast and marmalade and coffee, so shall not starve.

Most of the girls are not here yet, so Whitstead is very quiet this afternoon. The few girls here have all gone off to tea and reunions with various friends.

Yesterday was most hectic. I left London and managed to get on the train early in the morning, where a very nice elderly man in my compartment (guessing that I was reading for English at Cambridge probably by my suitcase labels and poetry book in hand) talked to me most of the way up, as he had read English there many years ago under the famed I. A. Richards. He ended up by saying he and his wife[1] in London would be happy to see me for a few days around Christmas time if I found myself homeless. Which was a pleasant introduction to English hospitality. (His name was of French Huguenot origin, which perhaps accounts for his generosity).

Our dear Scottish housekeeper, Mrs. Milne,[2] met me at the door and showed me to my room, giving me much helpful advice on the way. After lunch a nice South African girl from Capetown[3] (they're all white and very civilized . . . 4 South Africans in Whitstead[4]) took me with a boyfriend

1–Cecil Edward Clarabut and Kathleen Mary Clarabut, who lived, according to SP's calendar, at 2 Highmore Road, Blackheath, London SE3.

2–Mrs Milne was the housemother at Newnham.

3–According to SP's calendar, this was Jean Pollard (1933–); B.S. 1954, Cape Town University; B.A. geography 1957, Newnham College, Cambridge.

4–In addition to SP, the Newnham College Report for January 1956 lists the following Whitstead residents: Jane Baltzell (American), Kathleen Isabel Margaret Chesters (British), Marie Philippa Forder (South African), Renee Mary Elizabeth Kimber (American), Lois Marshall (American), Isabel Murray (Scottish), Jean Margaret Pollard (South African), Margaret Roberts (South African) and Evelyn Sladdin (British). Reminiscences by several Whitstead residents were published in *Memories of Whitstead* (2007). SP is mentioned in several: see Marie Philippa Forder Goold (27–31) and Jane Baltzell Kopp (39–45).

of hers[1] who gave us a walking tour of Cambridge. I can't describe how lovely it is: I walked through countless green college courts where the lawns are elegantly groomed (not a stray grassblade anywhere), formal gardens, King's chapel with the lace-like ceiling and intricate stained glass windows, the bridge of sighs, the backs, where countless punts, canoes and scows were pushing up and down the narrow River Cam, and the shops on the narrowest streets imagineable where bikes and motorcycles tangled with the little cars. Best fun of all was the open marketplace in the square where fresh fruit, flowers, vegetables, books, clothes and antiques are sold side by side in open air stalls. Then tea with the two south africans, and supper at 7:15 in Clough Hall.

(continued in next letter)

Love,
sivvy

TO *Aurelia Schober Plath*

Sunday 2 October 1955 — TLS (aerogramme), Indiana University

<SP typed 'Letter No. 2' on address side of letter>

Opus 2

Dearest mother . . .

Hello again. It was so nice to receive your letters. Until I get oriented here, with my lectures and daily routine of life which involves growing friendships, I shall no doubt be feeling a bit strange and lonely. Naturally I miss the constants I had at home: the intuitive understanding of custom, the feeling of warm, deep friendships, the assurance of academic creativity. Here all is to begin again, and probably will be a bit slow and creaky at first due to the very lack of restraints and organization which will make it possible for me eventually to have a rich private social and intellectual life. No official "big sisters" come up to one here, but a pleasant American girl at Whitstead, Elizabeth Kimber,[2] kindly treated me to tea in the garden this morning, and informed me about miscellaneous items before going off with her last year's friends.

1–According to SP's calendar, this was David Allison; B.A. 1956, mathematics, King's College, Cambridge.

2–Renee Mary Elizabeth Kimber; research student in history, 1954–6 Newnham College, Cambridge.

Probably I shall meet with Miss Burton,[1] my academic adviser, some time tomorrow to discuss my program: everything here is so lackadaisical and de-centralized that it will be a relief to have some definite commitments. After I get my academic schedule underway, I want to begin writing again (I always have to digest experience first, before re-forming it) and join a few clubs: to find out about politics, and religion and see if I can dig up a French tutor. I feel that after I put down roots here, I shall be happier than ever before, since a kind of golden promise hovers in the air along the Cam and in the quaint crooked streets: I must make my own Cambridge, and I feel that once I start thinking and studying again (although I'll probably be a novice compared to the specialized students here) my inner life will grow rich enough to nourish and sustain me.

I was glad to leave the American group in London, and discovered the bohemian section of Chelsea with an old beau of Sue Weller's[2] in my last days. Had rum and cold meat sandwiches in a fascinating Dickensian pub called "The Doves" at night in a court overlooking the dark, low-tide Thames,[3] where in the moonlight, pale swans floated in sluggish streams that laced the mudflats. It was a mystical evening. Also drank great foamy mugs of hot chocolate (<u>really</u> chocolate) in an avant garde coffee house[4] where I ate the best spaghetti in the world amid white stucco walls, black corduroy booths, and gay pink and blue and yellow chairs and tables in a little court. Also saw the "King and I" at the Drury Lane theater, and afterwards walked up Bow Street and stared in delight at the wholesale fruit and flower and vegetable markets and trucks.

Here I received a surprise visit from Dick Wertz, Sassoon's old roommate and Nancy Hunter's former alter ego: he's here to study theology. Also ran into the boy from Columbia[5] (who competed in the Glascock contest last spring) at the train station. Not to mention the news that Mike Lotz is studying medecine at Oxford! Seems everyone I knew is stationed somewhere in Britain. As far as I'm concerned, I want to start meeting British men. We'll see.

I appreciate your considerate news about the multitude of rejection slips and will be glad to get back the poems so I can reassemble them and try to

1–Kathleen Marguerite Passmore Burton (1921–); lecturer in English, Newnham College, Cambridge, 1949–60; director of studies in English, 1952–60; SP's director of studies and supervisor under whom she studied Tragedy and Practical Criticism.

2–According to SP's calendar, this was John Whiteside.

3–The Dove is a Thames-side pub at 19 Upper Mall, Hammersmith, London.

4–According to SP's calendar, this was Sa Tortuga, a coffeehouse owned by former Sydney, Australia, radio and stage actor Peter Bathurst, on King's Road, Chelsea, London.

5–Donald Lehmkuhl.

get leads on the British Lit. magazines. Can't wait till I get established and can really start writing again. I feel this spring should be most fruitful. An acceptance now, of course, would be most kind to my morale. I've been living, acting and being so much lately that it will be pleasant to grow contemplative and gestate again, "recollecting in tranquillity."

I am so happy to hear the lovely news about Warren: the linguistics and math combination. I miss him very much, and only hope that I may show both of you a Cambridge which I have made mine come next summer. In a sense, you and I are generally faced with similar problems: meeting challenges for which we are as yet a bit limited. It is easy to get impatient at the beginning, especially if we have a vision of ambitions and achievements which will, of course, take time to attain. I do hope that gradually work will become less taxing for you. I'm very proud about the driving, and am eager to hear whenever you try for your license. Glad you had such a nice time at Mrs. Lameyer's. I was so sorry to hear about Aunt Hazel, and, even at this far remove, felt a sense of loss.

Can't wait to get shoes, as they'll be of use as warm winter slippers with stockings. You were very clever to wear them. If you ever send any clothes, just wash them first, and send them rough-dried only. Naturally, while I know it is a bother to wrap, I would welcome any cookies (oatmeal or molasses) to remind me of home. I shall probably sound quite homesick these first few weeks; I always enjoy giving love, and it is slightly painful to have it shut up in one until deep friendships develop with fruitful reciprocal confidences involved. Do bear with me. It really helps to write you and will be nice to establish a regular correspondence where we answer each other instead of talking in a sort of vacuum. I have to begin life on all fronts at once again, as I did two years ago, but I have all that experience behind me, and so I'm sure everything will be for the best. Remember I love you very very much, and give my dearest love to my favorite brother and the grandparents.

Your own loving,
Sivvy

TO *Aurelia Schober Plath*

Wednesday 5 October 1955 — TLS (aerogramme), Indiana University

Wednesday morning,
October 5

Dearest mother . . .

It is a clear (!) blue morning, and I am sitting in my room by an early gas fire (to take off the damp chill of the night) and warming my fingers by typing. Thought I'd follow up my rather tristful Sunday letter with news of the cheerful days following. Honestly, I love it here. I spent most of the time yesterday and the day before downtown, going in and out of the shops, browsing, and pricing things. The open market place is heaven: such color, flowers, fruit, vegetables, all in little stalls from nearby farms. The bookstores have some good art prints and frame pictures most inexpensively, so I am shopping around for a couple to brighten up my walls. I ordered a lovely long oblong coffee table yesterday for (4 guineas, roughly $12) in light natural oak which will hold plants, magazines and tea things and really draw the room together.

I have taped up my small colorful art reproduction postcards artistically on my wooden wardrobe and the back of my door and finally found accomodation for all my books by wheedling a 2nd duplicate case (much like my black one at home) from our housemother and then trading it for a marvelous tall 6 story affair which was gracing the room of my fellow fulbright biology major (they have so few texts). Slowly, and with great deliberation and delight, I shall shop for a few choice pottery bowls and so on for fruit, nuts, and candy and flowers The handcrafts around here are unbelievable and very expensive, but fortunately, I get enormous pleasure just staring at them.

Imagine, mother, one woman weaves bedspreads and then prints them with carved block-print potatoes! Another weaves cloth from wool she has combed herself and dyed with vegetable dye. The native pottery is enchanting: ranging from rough earthenware jugs with textured designs to delicate glazed yellow fruit bowls.

Monday, I opened a bank account at Lloyd's, where the charming man in the foreign department advised me on everything from theater memberships to where the best furniture store was! He also told me that I could open an American dollar account, the details of which I shall find out if ever there is a prospect of getting a check from America for writing (ha!) or something. It is very important to keep separate accounts, for the

English are severely restricted in their currency usage. Dollars, blissfully, are good everywhere. And of course I must squeeze through our two long vacations in winter and spring on my dollar travellers checks.(We're allowed 3 weeks abroad each vacation, so I hope to use time to the full, and spend the extra week or two living here monastically and reading and writing like mad). All the while I pray that I will earn some hunk of money to take me through the 3-month summer.

Monday I also began using up some of my book allowance (we have to spend it on books, or turn it back; what a pleasant coercion! At last I can buy art books!) Rode to town on the back of an Italian Vesper (motorcycle) with a delightful, vital South African girl in Whitstead, shopped some more, met another Fulbright American (Winthrop Means[1]) from Harvard and had an excellent talk with him over tea, everything from religion to art. Yesterday, on the way to town with Lois Marshall,[2] the very attractive Fulbright Biology student at Whitstead, a nice, if rather playboyish, Britisher[3] asked us in to coffee & told us about his service in Kenya.

In the afternoon Tuesday,[4] Dick Wertz (from Yale, studying divinity here) came over and took me punting up the backs: it was really idyllic, with swans and ducks bobbing for the apples fallen in the water from border gardens, innumerable crew shells and quaint low bridges, and weeping willows trailing over crenellated walls and the lacy spires of St. John's college, of Trinity Chapel, and the rest, which I still can't completely name, passing slowly by. If it is this lovely now, what must it be in spring, with chestnut blossoms and fruit trees in bloom!

I can't wait to start meeting the British men, instead of all these familiar Americans. Imagine, the ratio here is 10 men to each woman! Evidently, as this vivid Margaret Roberts[5] (the S. African with the motorcycle) told me, you could spend all your time doing nothing but seeing men socially, once you begin meeting them! I bought the Varsity Handbook,[6] which

1 – Winthrop Dickinson Means (1933–), American; A.B. 1955, Harvard College; Fulbright fellow, research student, Emmanuel College, Cambridge, 1955–6; Ph.D. 1960, geology, University of California, Berkeley; friend of SP.

2 – Lois Marshall; B.A. 1955, biology, Bryn Mawr College; Fulbright scholar, anatomy, 1955–6, Newnham College, Cambridge.

3 – According to SP's calendar, this was Barry Edward Sales; B.A. 1957, French and German, Corpus Christi College, Cambridge.

4 – 'In the afternoon ~~Monday~~ Tuesday' appears in the original.

5 – Margaret Roberts (1933–2007); B.A. Rhodes University; B.A. Newnham College, Cambridge.

6 – Guy Shepherd, *Varsity Handbook: The Undergraduate Guide to Cambridge* (Cambridge: Varsity Publications, [1955]).

tells about absolutely everything here, and is quite witty. Extra-curric life makes organizations at home look like child's play! There is a club for everything from Esperanto to Wine-tasting to Gepettos (puppetry) to tiddleywinks! Clubs for each Faculty, social clubs, talent clubs, and hundreds of musical and theatrical societies. Writing is evidently "in the doldrums". I gather the university magazines rise and rapidly wither, and from the one I glimpsed on the stands, poetry is fast fading from galloping consumption. I'm going to try finding out the British lit magazines, and pounding at them. My first poem published here officially will make me feel honestly a literary citizen.

Today I see my Director of Studies: don't know how I can ever choose between the miraculous smorgasbord of lecturers: much more tantalizing even than Smith! Bye for now. Love to all.

Your own happy,
Sivvy

TO *John Lehmann*

Thursday 6 October 1955 TLS, University of Texas at Austin

Whitstead
4 Barton Road
Cambridge
October 6, 1955

Mr. John Lehmann, Editor
THE LONDON MAGAZINE
31 Egerton Crescent
London, SW 3
England

Dear Mr. Lehmann:

I am enclosing a selection of poems,[1] some of which I hope you may find suitable for publication in THE LONDON MAGAZINE.

At present, I am an American Fulbright scholar, reading for an Honours B.A. Degree in English Literature at Cambridge. In the States I have had

1–Based on notes made to the typescript by *London Magazine* editors, Plath submitted, among other poems, 'Ice Age' and 'Danse Macabre'.

poems published previously in The Atlantic Monthly, Harper's, The Lyric, Mademoiselle, The Nation, and The New Orleans Poetry Journal.

Hoping to hear from you, I am
Sincerely yours,
Sylvia Plath

TO *Aurelia Schober Plath*

Sunday 9 October 1955 TLS (aerogramme), Indiana University

<SP wrote 'No. 1' on address side of letter>

Sunday morning
October 9

Dearest mother . . .

It is one of those luminous silvery-gray days which seem to be usual here, and I have just finished a pleasant leisurely breakfast downstairs with the other 9 girls and 2 faculty residents of Whitstead. I wish you could see my room, it is becoming so much home. I am having such pleasure conquering the material objects and corners, one by one, and bringing them from the realm of the disorganized and impersonal into a warm, vital solar system of relationships which is uniquely mine.

Slowly I have been buying a few things, and as yet the window-couch needs to be covered (which will be done by the housekeeper) and I'll want to get several bright-colored cushions to toss about there and on the bed. Also, I want to save up and get a reprint or two framed for the walls. And a green plant. If all goes well, my teaset ordered in London, should come the next week or so. As is, my new coffee table is a blessing. I can curl up on the couch by the window and read day and night, with coffee or tea, and art magazines and papers on the lovely natural wood, so convenient, a kind of focal point for the whole room. I have bought three lovely woven rush-mats (embroidered with stylized black thread by the Debenham weavers) for the table, bookcase shelf, and cabinet; a round stoneware ashtray with a dark brown-black inner glaze and the most enchanting small cup vase which has a story all its own: it has a pale yellow glazed base, a wide white outer surface, with a brown rim, trailing little irregular streams, and inside all is the most delicate robin's egg blue. Here, I shall draw it! <drawing of small cup vase> Well, I went into the little handcrafts shop I told you about, just to look and long, and every time I "fell in love" with a piece of pottery, a bowl or a tea cup, and asked the woman "who made it?" she said "Lucy Rie".[1] Well, if I were wealthy, I would become the patron of this woman. Of course the pottery is fearfully expensive, but there was this small, whimsical cup which was reduced because of a small flaw at the rim, so I bought it, just to have one of this woman's exquisite pieces for my own, to touch and cherish daily. You would love the delicacy of the colors and shape!

Today is the anniversary of my first week in Cambridge, and as yet, all is poised on the threshhold, expectant, tantalizing, about to begin. Lectures started Friday, and I have already been to four, but I have yet to establish the regular schedule of my days. I am most excited about my program, which I arranged with my director of studies, Miss Burton, an apparently very nice woman who is to be my supervisor of studies this term (e.g. I meet with her and another student once a week and do papers on Tragedy) and practical composition and criticism tutor (also one hour a week). This is apparently the only regular work I will be asked to produce, as there are no exams until a year from this coming June! I have chosen the exams I will "read for" and am at present wondering how two years will ever be enough! My lectures are chosen to lead into the subjects I've picked for exams.

There are 6 exams in all, three required. Of these, two are on composition and criticism (general) and one enormous one on 2000 years of Tragedy! This is marvelous for me, because over the next two years I'll be reading tragedy from the classics up to the modern french playwrights pirandello, cocteau, etc., which includes enormous hunks of literature I've never seen before. (This term I'm attending lectures in the history of tragic theory, tragedy from Racine[2] to the present, and Elizabethan and Jacobean Tragedy).

Next year, I'll probably concentrate on ancient tragedy. Of my three free-choice papers, I've picked French (for language) and plan to get a tutor in the language itself this year, and to read the texts next (the "set books" are wonderful: Stendhal's "Le Rouge et Le Noire",[3] Ronsard's[4] Poems; "Les Fleurs du Mal",[5] and so on. I can't wait to get over this inferiority complex I have about French). The other exam is on the English Moralists in relation to the history of Moral thought, which is a fat exam with a huge reading list, and I picked it not only because I know nothing about it, but

1–Austrian-born British studio potter Dame Lucie Rie (1902–95).
2–French dramatist Jean Racine (1639–99).
3–Marie-Henri Beyle, known by his pen name Stendhal, *Le Rouge et le Noir*; SPs copy held by Lilly Library.
4–French poet Pierre de Ronsard (1524–85).
5–Charles Baudelaire, *Les Fleurs du Mal*; SP's copy held by Smith College.

because I'll have a chance to read a great deal in philosophy and ethics: from Aristotle to D. H. Lawrence! The third paper I chose was the history of literary criticism, with reference to English literature. This again seemed excellent, because I'll have to read both criticism and the literature.

For the first time, I'm taking a program which should slowly spread pathways and bridges over the whistling voids of my ignorance. My lecture schedule is about 11 hours (morning) during the week with men whose books are beginning to fill my shelves: F. R. Leavis[1] on criticism: a magnificent, acid, malevolently humorous little man who looks exactly like a bandy-legged leprechaun; Basil Willey[2] on the moralists (he's written enormous, readable books on the 17h, 18th, and 19th century backgrounds); and, if I have time next term, David Daiches on the Modern English Novel. (Really "modern", I think, instead of the usual concept of "modern" here: e.g. "modern poets" are considered to be Wordsworth, Arnold, and Coleridge!) I must admit, my enormous ignorances appal me (all I seem to have read is Chaucer, Shakespeare, Milton, the 19th and 20th century[3] writers!), but instead of feeling frustrated, I am slowly slowly going to remedy the situation by reading and reading (most work here is independent reading) from the lists until my awareness grows green & extensive as my philodendron at home! (next letter)

TO *Aurelia Schober Plath*

Sunday 9 October 1955 — TLS (aerogramme), Indiana University

<SP wrote 'No. 2' on address side of letter>

Sunday morning

Dearest mother . . .

Hello again! To continue: I shall probably be so involved with work and orientation this first month, that I shan't have time to write to more than you, and a few scattered friends like my dear Sue, so please share whatever parts of my letters are of common interest with neigbors, relatives and friends! I shall appoint you my press agent!

1–Frank Raymond Leavis (1895–1978); lecturer, Downing College, Cambridge University.
2–Basil Willey (1897–1978); lecturer and King Edward VII Professor of English, Cambridge University, 1923–64.
3–'19th century and 20th' appears in the original. SP has encircled 'century' and drawn an arrow indicating it should be after '20th'.

Daily life here is at last becoming usual, so before everything becomes natural, I'll tell you a few details that struck me as unique at first. Our rooms are cool enough to keep butter and milk in (!) and I can see why there are so few iceboxes here. Imagine, in the morning when I get up to wash in the bathroom, my breath hangs white in the air in frosty clouds! Once a week in Whitstead we get a hunk of New Zealandbutter which we keep in our own dish and use until the next week. The cold here is certainly damp, and I rushed to the "chemist's" yesterday to buy a bottle of iron pills and one of vitamins to build up my resistance (everyone seems to have colds or sinus). For lunch and dinner we eat in Hall, a tall room with ornate white woodwork which always makes me feel Im sitting inside of a frosted wedding cake. Although the architecture is atrocious and victorian, it reminds me of Smith, as both were built about the same time, in the 1870's, and we have lovely formal gardens and walks, with a small lily pond and a dear cupid wrestling with a dolphin[1] which I imagine are exquisite in spring.

We wear black gowns to class and after dark, which somehow gives a pleasant feeling of belonging, although at first seeming awkward and unnecessary. In lectures, women are very much the minority, which is a pleasant change, and I imagine, much the way it is at Harvard and Radcliffe.

Although my academic work will be most demanding, I hope to join at least one or two clubs where I can give intensely in an informal way and meet British people, instead of S. Africans and the ubiquitous Americans, who seem to be everywhere, probably because I know several, and they stand out of the crowds. I'm going to investigate a Dramatic society[2] today, and if there is no room for amateur beginners like me, I'll try the college newspaper.[3] I hope to submit to the little pamphlet magazines here "free lance", and perhaps shall join the Labor Club, as I really want to become informed on politics and it seems to have an excellent program. I am definitely not a Conservative, and the Liberals are too vague and close to the latter. I shall also investigate the Socialists, and may, just for fun, go to a meeting or two of the Communist Party (!) here later on. Anyhow, I hope to join a group where I can meet people socially who share my interests, instead of just viewing them from afar at lectures.

1–A replica of Italian painter and sculptor Andrea del Verrocchio's 'Putto con Delfino'. See Sylvia Plath, 'Stone Boy with Dolphin'.

2–The Amateur Dramatics Club (ADC), founded in 1855 and located on Park Street, Cambridge.

3–*Varsity*, published since 1947.

Merely walking about in Cambridge itself is a privilege! I enjoy the sense of time and space dimension so much. Dick Wertz (Sassoon's roommate at Yale and Nancy Hunter's old friend) took me to visit his college (for theological students) yesterday, Westminster, and I was amazed at the dark, ancient, monastic atmosphere of the place. A hod of coal was outside everyroom for coal fires! Grace here is said solemnly in Latin, and everybody seems to have a classical background; Dick himself is rapidly learning Greek!

Newnham is to be honored on October 20th by a visit from the Queen herself and the Duke (their first visit to Cambridge) and so the place is already in preparation for her coming. I can't believe I shall actually see her in the flesh. Imagine, she's coming to open a new veterinary laboratory:[1] how poetic!

I received your packet yesterday, with the three rejections which, I admit, were as encouraging as rejections could be. As yet, the shoes have not come, and as I shall be wearing them as "shoes", I bought a pair of wool-lined slippers for winter which are deliciously warm and comfortable, in bright red felt. When it gets <u>really</u> cold, I shall no doubt want to buy a pair of furlined boots which they wear as shoes, indoor and out (often it's colder in lecture than outdoors, and there are ubiquitous drafts which slither along the floors and in cracks of window frames.)

When I am acclimated here, to the work, first of all, and the people, I want to try to do a few articles on the atmosphere here, and if I am ambitious, a sketch or two, to try out for the Monitor. As yet, I feel too much an initiate to hold forth. The same holds true of writing. We're allowed only 3 weeks abroad by the Fulbright each of the small vacations (December and April, roughly) so I think I shall stay in Whitstead for a week or two in each of the 5-week Cambridge vacs, to write and catch up on my reading, as it is less than $2 a day to stay on for board and room. Lord knows what I will finally do in my vacations; I would like to ski in the Tyrolean alps and go to southern France and Italy, but it remains to be seen when and with whom. As yet I do not know if Sassoon is going to be at the Sorbonne, which I sincerely hope he will be, because it would be ideal to have such a connoisseur escort me around Paris. But that is still a vague dream.

Don't forget to give my love to Warren and to tell me all the news about him. Also, congratulate Betty on the new baby boy. I certainly enjoy your

1–Queen Elizabeth II and Prince Philip, Duke of Edinburgh, opened the new University of Cambridge Veterinary School, Madingley Road.

newsy letters as they contain the real flavor of home. Keep on gaining weight, too! There's nowhere to go from the bottom of the mountain but up!

Much love to all,
sivvy

TO *J. Mallory Wober*[1]

Thursday 13 October 1955[2]

ALS with envelope,[3] Cambridge University

Whitstead
Thursday

Mallory . . .

I look forward to coming to tea with you today at 4.30. However did you guess that I have no sense of direction? . . . Your charming map, as lucid as it is thoughtful, will be of great help in my travels!

Until this afternoon, then . . .
Sylvia

TO *Aurelia Schober Plath*

Friday 14 October 1955[4]

TL (aerogramme), Indiana University

<SP wrote 'No. 1' on address side of letter>

Friday afternoon
5:30 p.m.

Dearest mother . . .

It was so good to get your fat letter today (written last Monday). To clear up a few practical questions first: the slippers came (I didn't have to pay anything) yesterday having been mailed Sept. 25. Yes, of course I picked up the traveller's checks in London! One thing you never have to worry about is my neglecting a source of income! When I say the Cam is

1–Joseph Mallory Wober (1936–), British; B.A. 1957, natural sciences, King's College, Cambridge; dated SP, 1955–6. Wober lived at 7 Peas Hill, Cambridge.

2–Date supplied from internal evidence.

3–The letter is not postmarked and was probably hand-delivered, likely by the University's internal mail service.

4–Date supplied from postmark.

"narrow" I mean about as wide as Weston Road! River traffic is an ever-present and often amusing problem.

I'm writing a little earlier than usual (I set Sunday morning aside for communications at present) because the next week will be full and hectic, so I seized this gratifying momentary lull in my room to brew a cup of coffee, have a piece of bread butter and honey (I plan to buy fruit regularly, so don't worry about the starch), and talk to you.

The past week has been both terrible and glorious. I have learned about socialized medecine the hard way, by coming down with my annual fall sinus cold. Medical treatment here is very peculiar. It is fine if you are completely healthy or <u>very</u> sick (e.g., running a temperature, which I wouldn't do even on my deathbed), but if you're just miserable and can't breathe with sinus, you're left to fend for yourself. Thinking that I'd get the kind of potent medication (e.g. cocaine sprays and penicillin) and good diet that I received at the Smith infirmary, I let myself be persuaded to go to the "Newnham Hospital",[1] a sort of 3-bed sickbay, Wednesday morning, after nursing myself ineffectively in my room Tuesday. Well, what a rude awakening! They have one stony-hearted and absolutely "rule-bound" nurse over there, and the strongest and only medication is aspirin. When I asked innocently for some kleenex, the nurse kindly offered to rip up an old sheet for me (paper is evidently very scarce here . . . we <u>never</u> have napkins, and so I am getting used to going around feeling rather sticky and jam-ish!) By subtle questions, pleading ignorance about "the way medecine worked" in England, I found that, unless I ran a temp, no doctor would come see me. Meals were ghastly: white fish paste and white potato, stewed fruit and custard on uncooked dough, with nothing to drink to wash it down! No greens, no fresh fruit or red meat! Well, I was jolted into a most amused frame of mind, and, first thing Thursday morning, "picked up my bed and walked – out", so to speak. I biked downtown to the Doctor whose "panel" I had signed up on (he sees you free, and all his prescriptions cost you only a nominal shilling (14¢) to fill). This was the first intelligent being I'd met since I got sick. The waiting line was about 20 in his office hour, but I got in after only half an hour's wait. He is a very nice guy, this Doctor Bevan,[2] asked me rapidly and thoroughly about my sinuses, prescribed a new kind of nosedrops and told me to come back in a week for a checkup. If I can't breathe by

1–It is likely SP is referring to a small infirmary that was at one time located in Sidgwick Hall, Newnham College.

2–Possibly Dr Edward Vaughan Bevan (1907–88); his surgery was at 3 Trinity Street, Cambridge.

then, he'll xray my head. This I tell you not to alarm, as I feel really good now, but to show you that if I needed attention, I could get it. Anyhow, my major resolution now is to lay in enough canned food that I could cook lunch and supper in Whitstead myself if and when I get sick again, to get through the worst "runny" days on my own, with nosedrops. Perhaps I'll get Dr. Bevan to prescribe a rest-cure on the Riviera for me in winter vacation and make the Nat. Health Service pay for it! It is true that the damp here is continuous. Heavy morning and evening mists make me feel I'm moving about in a ghost-play. Rumor has it that the mists extend later and later into the morning and earlier in to the afternoon until the day is quite eclipsed and we won't see sun again until May! But I am becoming stoically indifferent to this wet, learning to dress warmly in several layers, wearing heels and stockings (so my feet aren't flat on the ground) and biking everywhere. I must admit I'm rather proud of my biking; although to the natives here I must seem rather unique in my style: I had to get used, first of all, to cars going on the left side of the street, to about 6000 other bicycles in this small, crooked-streeted, cobbled town, and to various objects of terror like two-decker red busses and roaring motorcycles which have a habit of just grazing one gently as they pass.

To class and everywhere after dark we wear our black university gowns, and although it was rather a nuisance at first, I must admit I feel rather proud of the battered old thing now, and enjoy seeing the gowns flap out bat-like as cyclists spin past. I have a total of about 15 hours of lectures, supervisions and tutoring a week, all except one hour[1] are in the morning, (a 6 day week) and I find the prospects of reading exceedingly exciting. One hour a week I'll be tutored in French by a research student, so I can catch up and eventually read for my exam paper; I need French immediately, because I have about 8 plays by Corneille[2] and Racine to read and write a paper on in the next two weeks (!) At present, this seems rather impossible, but my supervisor (Miss Burton) whom I saw yesterday, is very kind, and I'm sure it will work out somehow. It is almost better to be forced intensely into something you want to do, anyway! In toto, I have 12 hours of class lecture (stressing tragedy, but with moralists and critical theory too, and 17th cen. poetry just for fun), 1 hour of "practical criticism" (where we write it), 1 hour of French tutoring; and 1 hour of "supervision" in tragedy which I share with a vivacious Indian girl & calling for 1 long paper every two weeks.

1–'all ~~but~~ except one hour' appears in the original.

2–French tragedian Pierre Corneille (1606–84). Sylvia Plath, 'Four Tragedies of Corneille: The Conflict of Good with Good', dated 26 October 1955; held by Lilly Library.

TO *Aurelia Schober Plath*

Friday 14 October 1955[1] TLS (aerogramme), Indiana University

<SP wrote ‘No. 2’ on address side of letter>

Friday afternoon: later

Dearest mother . . .

Hello again! Now that I’ve told you the grimmer side of the week, let me tell you the lovely part. To begin with, I went with some of the girls at Newnham to a Labour Party Dance Monday night. It reminded me a little of the old dancing school days, but once I got out on the floor, I didn’t lack for partners. In particular, one tall, rather handsome dark-haired chap named Mallory Wober, caught my interest. He is a Londoner, and has lived 9 years in India (where his father is an executive of some sort), is reading for Natural Sciences, and seems extremely versatile, with a nice kind of humor, which I enjoyed. I think he “goes with” another girl here, but he invited me to tea with her and another boy Thursday (sufficient reason to make me recover and leap out of the Newnham hospital) in his “digs.” It is the habit here, I gather, to write notes of invitation (which he did) and for the girls to go to the boys’ place for tea or coffee, as the case may be. Seeing young men make tea is still a source of silent mirth to me!

Anyhow, Mallory has his own piano in his rooms, and evidently is a brilliant pianist (he had Scarlatti’s Sonatas out, and the Brandenburg Concerto, and much else that made me regret my own lack of musical knowledge and understanding). The other girl, Elizabeth somebody, was British and had just come in from “beagling” (hunting animals with beagles, I think) and was the kind of fair-skinned, rather hysterical and breathless type of English girl I’ve met so far. I must say, I am happy living in Whitstead where the girls are mature and well-rounded: I love this vital South African girl, Margaret Roberts, and the lovely blonde Marshall scholar, Jane Baltzell,[2] from Rhode Island, who is reading English with me.

The other boy, Adam someone, was a nice, tall skinny fellow, reading for medecine, and he said afterwards that he liked the way I was “fresh and outspoken” and promised to invite me to tea soon. I have resigned

1 – Date supplied from postmark.

2 – Jane Baltzell Kopp (1935–), born in El Paso, Texas, 1935; B.A. 1955, Brown University; B.A. 1957, Newnham College, Cambridge; Ph.D. 1965, University of California Berkeley; associate professor of English, University of New Mexico, 1964–70; married American poet Karl C. Kopp, 1969. Jane Baltzell Kopp read English on a Marshall Scholarship at Cambridge and was SP’s housemate at Whitstead, 1955–6.

myself to meeting as many people as I can this first term, and being selective only when I have a large range to choose from. The prospect of so many "first meetings" is a bit tiring, but not too bad; I do long to get to know some few men really well, though. This, evidently, only comes with much time. So I am sailing with the wind; doing as the Romans do.

Best news of all is the next. I decided to go out systematically for several activities I was interested in, so that I would have a chance to meet people socially this way. Well, I made a mental list: theater groups, newspaper, political clubs, and decided to try from the top. I had my audition (with about 100 other people at least) for the A.D.C. (Amateur Dramatic Club) here, which is the top of the several acting groups here and is the only one to have its own theater (where all the student productions are played out). I was scared to death, as we all sat in the theater together, and I watched about 20 people have auditions before me, which was a bit gruelling. Also, I still had the ends of my sinus cold and felt a bit giddy. Well, once I got up there on stage, the natural ham in me came out, and so I did a bit of Rosalind in "As You Like It"[1] (we could choose from 10 set Shakespearean pieces) and the part of Camille in Tennessee William's play "Camino Real."[2] I also made a few remarks in between, describing a stage set which made them all have a seige of laughter, and this was most gratifying. Anyhow, I had no idea how I did, but one nice, ugly little boy came up to me later on the street and told me admiringly what a wonderful voice I had, that it filled the whole auditorium! Such joy!

The pleasant upshot of all this is that I am one of the 9 girls to become a member of the Amateur Dramatic Club this term. This coming Saturday night, we are putting on 3 one-act plays[3] in a "nursery" production to which influential people will be invited to see the "new talent" A.D.C. offers. All of the new members have part in a play; mine happens to be, not the feminine lead, but a rather dramatic character part in a farce by Pope about cuckoldry (!) in which I play a verbose niece[4] who has high-flown and very funny ambitions to write plays and poetry. I come in about four times and have a short part (as do most of the players), so

1–Rosalind is the heroine of *As You Like It*. SP underlined Rosalind's speech in her copy of *The Complete Plays and Poems of William Shakespeare* (Boston: Houghton Mifflin, 1942), 235; SP's copy held by Smith College.

2–SP annotated Marguerite Gautier's speech to Jacques Casanova in her copy of *Camino Real* (Norfolk, Conn.: New Directions, 1953), 96–7.

3–The ADC performed excerpts from *Julius Caesar* by William Shakespeare; *The Epidemic* by Octave Mirbeau, and *Three Hours After Marriage* by John Gay, Alexander Pope, and John Arbuthnot, ADC Theatre, Cambridge University, 22 October 1955.

4–SP played the part of Mrs Phoebe Clinket in *Three Hours after Marriage*.

it is just enough to be stimulating, and not too much. All this next week, of course, we rehearse afternoon and night! This will no doubt be the most hectic time, and then, heaven knows what will happen. There are a few attractive chaps in the group (multitudes more men, of course, than women) and one[1] took me out to sherry last night to celebrate both of us getting in. The dues are high (5 pounds a year), but amply worth it to me. The audition was the hardest, and now I hope to have fun! I am much happier concentrating on one thing I am intensely interested in, like amateur acting, than being a flittering dilettante and belonging to countless little clubs. I really am quite elated that I should have the chance to concentrate on my "first choice." Now I can freely refuse the myriad little invitations to join petty clubs of "overseas students", "liberals," "christians", etc. Well, I just had to spill over my little triumph. Cross your fingers for me. I think I'll have a really good time in this Dramatic Club. Am going to see its production of Webster's "White Devil"[2] with Jane Baltzell tonight.

Best love to all, your loving daughter,
Katherine Cornell[3]

P.S. Your letters are a constant joy! (They really capture the "spirit of home". I love hearing news about everyone, and the "little things" count most!

Sivvy

TO *Aurelia Schober Plath*

Tuesday 18 October 1955

TLS (aerogramme),
Indiana University

tuesday afternoon
october 18

dearest licensed mother!!!

I am so proud of you that I just had to sit down in the mist of the hectic lovliness of this week and write you my congratulations! I really feel ours is growing to be a kind of "renaissance family"! it seems it is never too late for any of us to learn anything, and we can help each other to expand and grow, which, in many cases, certainly takes courage; overcoming the

1–According to SP's calendar, this was Richard Charles MacKenzie; B.A. 1958, economics, history, Jesus College, Cambridge.

2–John Webster, *The White Devil*, ADC Theatre, Cambridge University, 14 October 1955.

3–A reference to American stage actress Katharine Cornell (1893–1974).

first inertia is the worst of any undertaking. I am SO HAPPY YOU HAVE YOUR LICENSE! give warren my admiration, too, for he has been a superb teacher.

as for me, today, I think has been the "happiest" yet, just in the joyous, exuberant way I feel. now that the cold is completely gone, and the weather clear and sunny (!) though absolutely frigid, I am in a marvelous mood. I feel as if I had planted a tree in new soil, and were watching a few blossoms open slowly, lovely things, but, best of all, promising the most delectable fruit to come in the maturing sun! such wild metaphors! it is probably the influence of my absurdly verbose appearances in our coming one-act play!

instead of being snowed by the enormous amount of work and reading I must do to gain the full benefit of my academic life here, I am sturdily doing a little at a time and feeling most happy. after I get through this initial tangle of having to read 8 french plays without being able to read french, and come into english tragedy, life should smooth out a bit. as it is; I met my french tutor[1] today for the first time and liked her very much: she is a bright young woman, fresh from three years in paris, and she lives nearby. to begin with, I am going to read "le cid" and do the exact translation of a long speech in it to learn the french classical style, and then I shall probably begin stendahl's "le rouge et le noire" and continue to read modern works side by side with the older ones. after the pressure of the first month is over, I hope to start speaking french in class!

I have been going to lectures and enjoying them immensely and am quite loving wearing my black gown, which makes me feel so wonderfully a part of this magnificent place. sort of like sacramental robes! best of all, my dear, adorable play director gave me the ultimate laurel today by saying my performance was "excruciatingly funny" and doubling up with laughter. I was so happy, because the part of this mad poetess, phoebe clinkett, is rather absurd farce, and depends in a kind of double entendre slanting of words and gestures which I tried today, having just learned my part, 15 flighty, rather verbose speeches (I have 4 appearances in toto in the whole thing). our performance is saturday night, and we are the last of the 3 "nursery plays" to be put on. I just hope that I can audition for some of the larger productions after this. my voice is the main thing in my favor . . . I have, of course, never <u>moved</u> <u>about</u> on stage except in the ancient "admirable crichton",[2] and I feel most audacious in just braving my way

1 – According to SP's calendar, her tutor was Miss A. Barrett.

2 – As a senior in high school, SP performed the role of Lady Agatha Lasenby in a production

about. I ate lunch at the theater today and felt so much a "member." Imagine, we can just order lunch or tea between rehearsals and have our term bill presented with our term dues: so much nicer than eating out downtown, and very sensible, so we don't skip meals while rehearsing. this theater is celebrating its 100th anniversary this year and is completely student-run. I feel so lucky to be a member of this particular one!

the nicest thing about this A.D.C. is the particular group I've been assigned to work with on this play. as I said, the guy directing is simply a darling and hasn't lost his temper once, but makes us all want to do what we can with it and is marvelously creative in his interpretations. the two other girls in it are very pretty and petite and sweet, and the boys are extremely nice and friendly, none of this bohemian affectation at all (which, I admit is indulged in to the hilt by other members I've seen around). I went out to coffee with anthony smith,[1] a very handsome chap with a full blond moustache (!) and had a good talk after rehearsal last night. last saturday, the lovely vital south african girl, margaret roberts, gave our house a sherry party and invited all the men she knew to meet us. one of them, a tall, skinny, rather sweet chap,[2] came over yesterday and took me on an exquisite walk to granchester for tea.

I can't describe how beautiful it was to go down the little cobbled streets in the pink twilight with the mists rising from the willows along the river and white horses and black cows grazing in the pastures. remember rupert brooke's poem?[3] well, we had tea by a roaring fire at "the orchard" (where they serve tea under flowering trees in spring) and the "clock was set at ten of three"[4] and there was the most delectable dark clover honey and scones! had a lovely tea sunday with the brother of a handsome graduate[5] I met at the fulbright reception in london, and enjoyed this business of at least several men to each girl. several fellows have told me how they liked my audition, and I met a vivid oldish woman,

---

of J. M. Barrie's *The Admirable Crichton* (1902).

1–Possibly Anthony Thomas Smith; B.A. 1956, English, King's College, Cambridge.

2–John Nicholas Lythgoe (1934–92), British; B.A. 1957, Ph.D. 1961, natural sciences, Trinity College, Cambridge; dated SP, 1955–6.

3–English poet and Cambridge graduate Rupert Brooke (1887–1915) lived in Grantchester 1906–9 and immortalized the town in his poem 'The Old Vicarage, Grantchester', which ends 'oh! yet / Stands the Church clock at ten to three? / And is there honey still for tea?' SP had tea at the Orchard in Grantchester when she was a student at Cambridge and annotated Brooke's poems in her copy of Louis Untermeyer, ed. *Modern British Poetry* (New York: Harcourt, Brace, 1950), 319–29. SP's copy held by Smith College.

4–SP slightly misquotes from Brooke's 'The Old Vicarage'.

5–According to SP's calendar, this was probably Richard Edward George Mansfield; history, Pembroke College, Cambridge. Mansfield was director of the nursery plays.

camille prior,[1] who played the important rôle of cornelia in the "white devil" which I saw last week. she seemed to like me, and may ask me to tea after this hectic week of rehearsals is over. wish me luck saturday! I'll write after the holocaust.

much love to all,
your happy
sivvy

TO *Gordon Lameyer*

Tuesday 18 October 1955 — TLS (aerogramme), Indiana University

tuesday afternoon
october 18

dearest gordon . . .

it was so wonderful to get your long letter, rich as a plumcake with news! atlantic city sounds like quite a festival, and your work most stimulating, in spite of the mechanics of routine which beset us all in various ways.

where to begin? first, very simply, with my passionate love for cambridge! honestly, gordon, it is the dearest city in the world, with quaint cobbled streets, chimneypots and rooks flying above them, every inch of ground planted with brilliant green grass or flowers, and the unbelievable wedding cake architecture of king's chapel, the enchanting bridge of sighs, the tudor courtyard of queens! I went punting a few days after arrival up the most narrow (about the width of linden street!) cam, where weeping willows mourned over the "backs", and ducks and fluid white swans bobbed for apples that had dropped from overhanging fruit trees. I live in a wonderful house for ten graduate students (american, british, south african and scottish) with a dear room on the top floor, a window-seat couch overlooking gardens and treetops, a gas fire and gas ring for making tea, and all my books and handcrafts I've bought plus a modern coffee table, my one large purchase. here, I feel, is the place to create. it is quiet, enchanting, with all the opportunity of the richest of private lives. we can have men in our rooms till 10 at night, and are perfectly free to stay out every night till midnight, since we are all "older, and therefore more mature," what heaven to avoid completely the large, bare, institutionalized mass living of the dormitories! my bike is my most prized

1–Camille Prior, an actress and boarding-house proprietor in Cambridge.

possession, and I have at last become used to cars going on the "wrong side" of the street and learned my way about town after having managed to ride the wrong way down every one way street there is! we have "open market" every day; that is, a whole open air square full of tented stalls full of fruit and flowers and books and antiques. the bookstores themselves are heaven and I have already racked up a rather plump bill. after my first sinus cold last week, I have become acquainted at one fell swoop with the byways of socialized medecine. the hard way. they persuaded me to try our college "hospital" here, and I went obediently, thinking with relief of the smith college routine of penicillin and cocaine. here it was aspirin therapy, total neglect, and pasty white meals (potato, fish, bread, custard and dough). when I asked for kleenex, the nurse offered to tear up an old sheet; probably a winding sheet. well, after satisfying myself with a fair appraisal, I leapt out of bed and ran downtown to see my doctor on whose panel I'd registered (you see him free, but there's an enormous waiting line). he was a dear and promised to xray my head if I wasn't better in a week. evidently the national health service is fine for the very well or the very ill. If you don't run temperatures (but sink to dangerous low subnormal levels as I do,) no doctor will come to see you. so I picked up my bed and walked out to a play audition. improved rapidly thereafter.

which brings me to the loveliest news. in a burst of audacity, I decided to try out for the top dramatic club here (Amateur Dramatic Club) which is the only one of the many theater groups to have its own theater, lunch, tea, bar and social club. in fear and trembling I listened to about 20 people try out before the auditorium full of anonymous, faceless judges. then I went up on stage in a state of rigor mortis and read a sarcastic speech on true love by rosalind in "as you like it" and, for contrast, the part of the aging camille (my cough and difficulty in breathing was a help here) in tennessee williams' wonderful "camino real." before doing the latter, I pattered on briefly describing the stage set which drew huge bursts of laughter from the anonymous judges, giving me a feeling of great power. damn, it's such hellish fun to make people laugh. anyhow, I got IN, and, with all the other novices, have a part in the "nursery" productions to be given this saturday night before an invited audience of formally dressed celebrities from the other theater clubs who want to look over "new talent." perhaps because of the laughter, I have an absurd character part as a mad young poetess in a one-act 18th century farce where the double entendres are fantastically ribald. in the play, fortunately, I am supposed to be flighty, verbose, metaphorical and rather insane, and innocently go around "conceiving" poems and begging young men to "father my productions" on the stage. all in utter innocence mind you. wonderful fun, and our director is a darling if there ever was one; hasn't lost his temper once! after this debauch, I hope to audition for more serious parts. wish me luck, angel!

as for courses! imagine: twice a week I hear the pithy deadpan magnificence of f. r. leavis, a tan, devastating leprechaun of a man; basil willey on the moralists; david daiches next term on the modern novel. I'm being tutored in french and have chosen papers (exams) to read for in french, tragedy (2000 years of same), english moralists (covering all moral philosophy) and the history and theory of lit. crit. (with f. r. leavis) which will, all in all, demand the reading of just about every book in the world! will write more later. am dashing to tea in granchester, rupert brooke's green spot with the honey and this clock perpetually set at 10 to three. Do write.

Much love to you,
sylvia

TO *J. Mallory Wober*

Wednesday 19 October 1955[1] TLS with envelope[2]
on Newnham College letterhead,
Cambridge University

wednesday morning

dear mallory,

since my director of studies has made a previous appointment with me at midday why don't you pick me up at my room about one p.m. I think if you appeared in person sometimes to arrange crucial items such as hour and place it might be several hundred percent simpler. unless I take to using carrier pigeons.

s. p.

1–Date supplied from internal evidence.
2–The letter is not postmarked and was probably hand-delivered.

TO *J. Mallory Wober*

Friday 21 October 1955[1]

ALS in greeting card with envelope,[2] Cambridge University

Friday evening

Dear Mallory . . .

It was most tempting to come home this afternoon following hours of wind, rain, shopping and precarious cycling – and to find your thoughtful invitation. I felt a certain impulse to tell you that my inability to materialize at the George and Dragon[3] tonight is not because of work (which, alas, I don't seem to have begun yet) but rather due to play – a one-act play, in particular.

Tonight is the dress-rehearsal for the three A.D.C. "nursery" productions tomorrow night, and I am appearing (due to a stroke of intuition on the part of our enchanting producer) as a mad poetess in an 18th century farce. This week, as you may imagine, I have been living at the A.D.C. – Lovely place! At any rate, after Saturday, I should be able to return to a more balanced rôle. At least, by comparison with this week's rugged rehearsal schedule, I'll have the illusion of plenty of free time. (I think: life here seems like a carousel which accelerates considerably each day!)

As we say, in the barbaric tribe I come from,: I'd like very much to "take a rain-check" on your invitation some time. Unfortunately, I can only carry a tune when at least 100 others are also bearing the burden – but I enjoy listening. It was, by the way, an exquisite map! Wish I could have used it!

Sylvia

1–Date supplied from internal evidence.

2–The letter is not postmarked and was probably hand-delivered. On Panda Prints card designed by Rosalind Welcher.

3–A pub on Thompson's Lane, Cambridge.

TO *J. Mallory Wober*

Saturday 22 October 1955[1] ALS with envelope,[2] Cambridge University

Whitstead
Saturday

Hello, you!

Sunday, indeed, seems an excellent day for enterprise, such as an Indian supper. I may be required to pay my respects to the A.D.C. later in the evening, but let's plan on the Taj[3] for sure and let the rest wait – I am tempted by the College concert,[4] too & will do my best to get free of these dramatic tyrants! Expect me at your digs a bit after 7 Sunday – until then –

Sylvia

TO *Aurelia Schober Plath*

Monday 24 October 1955 TLS (aerogramme), Indiana University

monday night
october 24

dearest mother . . .

"why, emmaline! where have you been?"

"to see the queen!" yes, I stood about a yard from the gracious queen saturday morning, speechless with excitement. it rained and rained all morning, and the royal party was scheduled to visit newnham (for sherry and a few presentations) on their way to open a veterinary lab. (!) all of us gathered in the diningroom in our black gowns, on either side of the aisle up which the queen and duke were going to walk. I stood right at the foot of the little platform on which the ceremonies were to take place and felt an eagerness which surprised me.

after many false alarms, there was a hush, then we all cheered as the royal couple walked into our humble dining hall with its white wedding-

1–Date supplied from internal evidence.

2–The letter is not postmarked and was probably hand-delivered.

3–The Taj Mahal restaurant had two locations in Cambridge in 1955, one at 1A All Saint's Passage and the other at 37–9 Regent Street.

4–King's College Musical Society Open Concert, Sunday 23 October 1955, at 9 p.m. in the Dining Hall. The programme for the event is held with these letters.

cake ceiling. the queen looked quietly radiant in a kelly-green princess-style coat and hat, and the duke was most talkative and humorous, with a smile that passed all believing: he was enchanting! they stopped at random and chatted with girls down the line, the duke making many amusing observations. then four of the top students of newnham were "presented" to the queen and duke. it was all quite lovely, and I ran out in the rain afterwards to see them go off in the royal car (again feeling unaccountably elated to be within touching distance of the handsome pair.) camera bulbs flashed, more cheers, and they were off for lunch at trinity college.

a rather amusing sequel occurred in the afternoon: I was biking in the rain to the ADC theater for a last rehearsal before the performance that night, and saw crowds of people lining the long road down which I had to hurry to reach my destination. I asked a policeman when the royal car was coming, and he laughed and said: "in a couple of minutes; hurry up." so the policemen (in their best white slickers) beckoned me on and I flew down the street in my red mackintosh on my bicycle, feeling that I should be scattering rose petals or something, while a ripple of laughter ran through the waiting crowds. if I'd had the courage, I would have bowed right and left as I went by, but didn't want to create a mob scene! I must say the royal couple is most genial and attractive, with a kind of radiance which appeals to me. I do, however, envy them not at all the daily round of functions which must be their lot! apparently they enjoy it no end, though. and the people certainly all turned out to cheer their queen in the pouring rain!

the play, by the way, went off fine, and was a lot of fun. I hope some day, though, that I can get a really challenging part with depth of character, rather than mere stylized cariacature. we shall see. this last week I have been quite lucky about being taken out to meals in town by various young men, and the prospect of going back to the pasty, tasteless white "hall food" this week is grim. the south african (sweet, but rather weak chap)[1] took me out to lunch and dinner the day of the play, and we had sherry and wine, chicken and mushrooms, which was lovely. I went to a large sherry party (these take the place of our "cocktail parties", and I must say, appeal to me a good deal more) before the play (ours was the last of the 3 one-act things).

sunday I rested in the morning after the strenuous week and was rather surprised to have mike lotz drop in on me. he had come over from

1 – According to SP's calendar, this was Kenneth James Mayo Frater; B.A. 1956, mathematics, law, Pembroke College, Cambridge.

oxford, where he is on a henry fellowship. strange, how time changes one's perspective on people. I was very disappointed in him, and found myself extremely bored by his heavy, prosaic complacency (he is very well-off financially now, and boasts that he can live off the interest of his savings). we went to lunch, and I said goodbye with something of relief. I felt with renewed conviction that no matter what "labels" a person has, what outward achievements (like phi bete keyes, or "summas", which mike also bragged about, or big cars, which he also emphasized), there is an inner vitality and keen integrity of being which is necessary to give them true worth, for me, anyway. I was really disgusted by his american materialism which has degenerated into a disagreeable self-satisfaction and conceit.

anyway, to change to a much more agreeable topic: I had the loveliest time last night with the boy I met at the labor club dance and went to tea with last week: mallory wober. he gets more and more dimension each time I see him. first of all, he is extremely handsome in a rugged way, quite different from the pale, delicately-made englishman. he is tall, strong, with coal-black hair and vivid red cheeks and boldly-cut features. he is a natural sciences major, and imagine my delight when yesterday afternoon, a gray rainy time, he settled me in a large, comfortable chair with a glass of sherry and played the piano for me for over an hour: beethoven, scarlatti, haydn, with comments now and then! he plays excellently and has a sense of humor in his interpretations about it which helps me understand the music. then we dropped in at the ADC party, then to the most magnificent sunday night concert in the king's college dining hall, where the architecture looked like a lace of shadows and light, and we heard hindemith (oboe and piano), bartok (two violins) and schubert's songs[1] for 5 of heine's poems! then the "taj mahal" an indian restaurant where mallory spoke hindustani. He introduced me to mangoes & bindhi gusht (he's lived in darjeeling for 9 years) & the waiters. Biked home after a perfect evening. do hope to see more of him – must work hard this week.

Very happy

xx Sivvy

ps: lovely holland earthenware teaset has come. also bought 6 lovely swedish glasses for sherry and stainless steel coffeespoons, very reasonably!

PS: am buying apples (very good) oranges & dates (fruit) regularly at market and biking <u>at least</u> 5, often 10 miles a day to classes, town, dates,

1–The songs performed were 'Der Atlas', 'Ihr Bild', 'Die Stadt', 'Am Meer', and 'Der Doppelgänger'.

(men) etc.! feel very healthy in spite of drizzly rainy weather and am probably building up endurance like mad!

love to all.
sivvy

TO *Elinor Friedman Klein*

Thursday 27 October 1955 TLS (aerogramme), Smith College

thursday
october 27

dear dear cleo . . .

there is no one like my girl. she can very easily make hunks of america look like airmail letters and fool the postman, but then they open up and like those pop-up pictures: there is smith and the 5 & 10 and autumn and god and a damn lot of sun: like those paper japanese flowers that you put in water and they open up and spread out and the colors keep coming and the petals keep unfolding and presto: venus on the cockleshell.

dear venus: I am here. love, kilroy.

cambridge is heaven. I sat myself down at the window last night, turned off the gas fire and the light, and looked out at the white mists rising in the moonlight. plath, I said casually to myself like I do when I am facing up to things, you have been here over a month, and what is with it? with it? I answered. you are living it up, is what.

it is very cold here: the wind comes straight off the russian steppes and the cobbled streets are paved with blue frostbitten fingers that have dropped off people's hands. people like me. no wonder they have to have tea. today I am going to two teas and then a sherry party with people named respectively john, richard and brian.[1] I promised myself that this first term I would meet as many people (meaning men: the women here are ghastly: two types: the fair-skinned twittering bird who adores beagling and darjeeling tea and the large, intellectual cowish type with monastically bobbed hair, impossible elphantine ankles and a horrified moo when within 10 feet of a man) as possible. next term, I am going to be discriminating.

1–Brian Neal Howard Desmond Corkery (1933–), British; B.A. 1957, history, Pembroke College, Cambridge; dated SP, 1955–6.

after my wonder and joy (and anger at not being able to get a roundtrip ticket to amherst to see oedipus) about you turning into jocasta,[1] I can hardly bear to tell you the foolish and exciting thing I have done for me: I was in the college "hospital" here for one hideous day learning about socialized medecine (they offered to tear up an old sheet for me when I asked for kleenex) with a sinus cold (gone are the good old smith days with cocaine, codeine, and sleeping pills) when suddenly I threw aside my lukewarm dinner of white fish paste, gray potato paste and yellow custard paste and biked off madly to the ADC (amateur dramatic club) here which is the only one of the many acting groups in cambridge to have its own theater (plus lunch room tearoom and bar where you can eat and drink by just signing a little blue piece of paper and smiling at someone: we probably have to pay eventually, but I hate to think about it).

anyhow, in front of a hunk of nervously smoking new men and women and an esoteric hunk of old members, I auditioned with rosalind's sarcastic speech on courtly lovers and the wonderful tennessee williams' bit of camille talking to casanova camino real. as I could not quite breathe and felt consumption galloping all over me, I felt great rapport. result of all this: being catapulted into the ADC (notice the capitals, like I was maybe talking of god or something) "nurseries": three one-act plays featuring all new members. my dear intuitive producer, with whom I immediately fell wickedly in love, cast me as a mad poetess in an 18th century farce called "3 hours after marriage" written by pope, arbuthnot, gay and others, evidently because no one man would take full responsibility for the very very bad double entendres. my favorite play that night was octave mirbeau's "the epidemic" produced in a magnificent, grotesque stylized way by the artiest guy I ever did see: a real perfectionist, long hair, who brought his mistress to rehearsal and kissed her tenderly while yelling cruelly at the electricians and blaspheming the actors. there are plays here all the time and my main lust now is to work up so I can get to live a good part. I can't tell you what that experience of living and working 8 to 10 hours a day for a week with my play-group did to me. I love them all, we were hugging and kissing each other and swigging gin from a common bottle and god knows what. all this you know from your guts, and I am feeling like a baby saying "ma-ma" for the first time to someone who knows the whole goddam dictionary. oh well. but the plays here! tremendous performance of webster's "white devil" (raymond massey's

1–Elinor Friedman played Jocasta in Sophocles *Oedipus Rex*, presented by The Masquers, Kirby Memorial Theater, Amherst College, 17–22 November 1955.

son[1] was the hero, brachiano . . . what a guy!) . . . decision for ADC centenary coming up this week, between, I think: Juno & the Paycock[2] and Darkness at Noon. enough, enough.

lots of people here are named brian, colin, gavin and robin: I like. have been punting on river cam (about as wide as green street) where white swans bob for apples under weeping willows and the wedding-cake towers of st. johns and kings chapel rise along the backs; walked across meadows full of cows and brooding white horses to granchester where rupert brooke had tea at ten to three and they left the clock that way ever since: honey and scones beside roaring fire; play-readings of shakespeare at night where I am all the women, o mother earth; lots of delicate, pale fine-boned men and one tall, dmitri karamazov[3] guy with coal black reams of hair, scarlet cheeks and fantastic versatility (speaks hindustani from 9 years in india, nat. sci. major, sings, plays piano exquisitely, knows everything about architecture, indian food, bindhi gusht and other things with H's) . . . his aloofness obsesses me: we shall see what comes of all this. do write; and keep all those home-fires flaring for me. more later. meanwhile, much much love.

Sylvia

TO *Aurelia Schober Plath*

Saturday 29 October 1955 TLS (aerogramme), Indiana University

saturday afternoon
october 29th

dearest mother . . .

greetings from your happily agèd daughter! it was so lovely to get your telegram and the wonderful birthday gifts and letters from warren, you and dotty and dear grammy and grampy. I must say the best present anyone can give me is a fat typed letter: all the news from home, even the tiniest daily details, are most welcome. strange, but true, I feel so close to you all, as if I were only a short drive away. probably it is that the language is native to me (even if the accent isn't!) and that from my

1–Daniel Raymond Massey (1933–98), British; B.A. 1956, English, King's College, Cambridge; fellow actor with SP in the Cambridge Amateur Dramatic Club production of *Bartholomew Fair*, 24 November–3 December 1955.
2–Sean O'Casey, *Juno and the Paycock* (1924).
3–Dmitri Karamazov is the eldest son in *The Brothers Karamazov* by Fyodor Dostoevsky.

childhood I built up by reading a feeling for england (I'd forgotten how many british writers I must have read, but so much here seems dearly loved already because I've met it before in my reading; the rooks and teatime from "the cuckoo clock";[1] the poetry about granchester and the cam; crumpets (from t. s. eliot) and scones).

my birthday was the happiest of days: I had just finished writing my first supervision paper on 4 of corneille's tragedies (read, if slowly, in french!) wednesday, which was miserably cold and rainy. The 27th dawned crisp and blue-and-gold. I went to a lecture by basil willey (very good, on english moralists) and the supervision with my director of studies which I share with an indian girl (resplendent in vivid, red blue and gold saris!) where she went over our papers. then shopping for fruit and sherry at colorful market hill where the open booths spilled over with red tomatoes and apples, translucent green grapes, and armfuls of hot yellow and orange dahlias. I love just walking around that place, feasting my eyes on the colors and shapes like a glutton. after lunch, I came back to my dear room to find an enormous bouquet of yellow flowers in a lovely pottery vase (dark brown earthenware with designs scratched through to the dusty-pink clay) with a card saying "love, from whitstead." so you see what sort of a wonderful house I live in! then ken frater (the sweet, if prosaic south african chap) took me for a green walk across the fields to granchester where we again had honey and tea at the "old orchard", where rupert brooke's picture smiled down on us. after supper, I went over to pembroke college to a playreading of "henry 4th, part 1" where I took the parts of the women (which are small and had the privilege of listening to the wilson brothers (david and peter)[2] read falstaff and prince hal . . . they are both magnificent actors and always play old men's parts. david was "doctor fossil" the mock-hero of our farce last week, and all the boys are members of the ADC. this sunday night we are reading "the tempest" and I will be miranda. it is such fun sitting around a fire having coffee and reading aloud!

socially my life has really been looking up. I am beset with invitations to tea, sherry and dinner on every hand, and am meeting people with increasing rapidity. yesterday, for example, I went to tea with richard mansfield, a very handsome black-haired 3rd year man who was stage director for our play and has had me to tea once before. there I met an

1–Mrs Molesworth, *The Cuckoo Clock* (1877).

2–According to SP's calendar, these men were David Henry Wilson; B.A. 1958, French and German, Pembroke College, Cambridge; and Peter Joseph Wilson; B.A. 1957, archaeology and anthropology, Pembroke College, Cambridge.

attractive fellow, mahmud, from iraq.[1] then to another tea at trinity (a beautiful college right on the cam) with john lythgoe, our set designer, where dick gilling,[2] our tall, skinny, utterly delightful producer was too. dick invited me to hear the BBC next week, and john begged me to have tea with his quaint grandparents in granchester after a trip on his motor bike. I then biked to a sherry party with brian corkery (who is very correct, and looks like the young t. s. eliot) who is taking me to the theater tonight.[3] then back to richard mansfield's (after a hectic change) for a steak dinner with wine and full dress attendance at the 3 one-act plays put on by the mummers, another theater group.

whew! best of all (if there can be any best . . . everything is so lovely) I have at last met nathaniel lamar,[4] that boy from exeter and harvard who wrote the story "creole love song" in the atlantic![5] when I heard he was at cambridge I begged some boys at pembroke to introduce me to him, so last night, richard and I caught him on the walk and I have a tea-date with him next monday. he is a lovely, light-skinned negro, and I look most forward to talking to him about writing, etc. sunday we have a large general meeting of the ADC to discuss our centenary production, and my favorite tall dark handsome fellow, mallory wober, has just invited me to meet some of his friends at a sherry party before dinner. my project for meeting as large a cross-section of people as possible this first term is certainly working out most pleasantly. I have simply been treated like a queen!

meanwhile, I am buying books, studying french, (have just begun "le rouge et le noire" which will probably take me all year); bought a dark, lovely braque still life[6] with browns and black predominantly, & lovely yellow lemon shapes and deep green, which is being framed for my room. also a green plant with bright red berries. (speaking of red, by the way, I loved your birthday card, which was so appropriate with my own exquisite red-velvet dress). all this biking in the cold air (which blows

1–Mahmud Ahmad Osman; history, Fitzwilliam House, Cambridge.

2–Christopher Richard Gilling (1933–), British; B.A. 1956, English, Trinity Hall, Cambridge; dated SP in 1955. Gilling was the producer of the play.

3–According to SP's calendar, she saw *The Little World of Don Camillo* and *New Faces*; shown at the Rex Cinema, then on Magrath Avenue, Cambridge.

4–Nathaniel D. LaMar, Jr (1933–), American; A.B. 1955, Harvard College; research student on a Henry Fellowship at Pembroke College, Cambridge, 1955–6; dated SP, 1955–6.

5–Nathaniel LaMar, 'Creole Love Song', *Atlantic Monthly* 195 (June 1955), 39–45.

6–SP refers to a still life by Georges Braque (1882–1963), French painter and sculptor, throughout the first term at Cambridge in letters to her mother, Marion Freeman, Gordon Lameyer, and Olive Higgins Prouty.

directly from the russian steppes) makes me feel simply grand: clean, fresh and strong. evidently the short terms here are packed with culture and lectures and concerts and exhibits and much serious work is done in long vacations. I plan to take advantage of this scheme and stay here about 2 weeks into december after end of term, just reading and reading and contemplating, before I take off for europe for the 3 weeks alotted by the fulbright commission. will write later in the week, meanwhile, much much love to you and warren and the dear grandparents.

your joyous birthday girl,
sivvy

TO *J. Mallory Wober*

Saturday 29 October 1955 — ALS with envelope, Cambridge University

Saturday
October 29

As Anna said to the King of Siam.[1] "I shall be delighted to come!"

Expect me then, Sunday at 12, at which time I shall be happy to encounter your friends, your piano, your polished table, your crocodile, and, of course, your highness himself.

Sylvia

TO *Olive Higgins Prouty*

Saturday 29 October 1955 — TLS (aerogramme), Indiana University

Saturday afternoon
October 29th, 1955

Dear Mrs. Prouty . . .

At last I am beginning to feel a native of Cambridge and want to take time in the midst of this pleasant carousel of activity on a multitude of new fronts to tell you a little about how happy I am here! First of all, I have a room all to myself on the top of a quaint house for 12 girls (Whitstead) which is most homelike and, thank heavens, not at all like the cold red-brick institution of the main halls of Newnham! I wheedled

1–A reference to *The King and I*.

enough bookcases for my brightly colored multitudes of books (to which I am adding rapidly), and bought a wonderful brown earthenware teaset from holland while in London and a lovely modern oblong coffee table on which I have art books, magazines, and a green plant with bright red berries. The wonderful Cambridge custom of having open market in the square every day lets me buy heaps of fresh fruit and flowers to pile about, while postcards of art reproductions deck the doors and cupboards. A sofa for two is placed in the window niche, where I can curl up comfortably and read or write overlooking a garden, treetops and orange tile roofs. In addition, I have a gas fire (which somehow isn't quite enough to keep my fingers and toes from being perpetually blue,) and gas ring on which I can make tea, coffee, and perhaps eventually, if I am adventurous enough, a one-pot casserole!

I am going to about 15 hours of lecture and tutoring a week (in the mornings) and love every minute of it. slowly, very slowly, I am beginning to build bridges over some of the whistling voids of my ignorance. We have no exams until the end of our two years, and I chose subjects to "read for" which I knew least about: 2000 years of tragedy (!), the english moralists in relation to the ancients (which will let me read lots of philosophy); the history of english criticism as applied to english literature (which will enable me to read as much eng. lit. as possible) and french (I am now being tutored by a very nice research student and hope to try it out in paris in my first vacation!) during the week I write about one critical paper for my director of studies, prepare french lessons, and read and read. so much for my study program, which is most stimulating (as are lecturers like the caustic F. R. Leavis, wry Basil Willey, and vital David Daiches).

My social life has unfolded with amazing rapidity after about 10 days of feeling rather isolated. The English are slow to meet, but once I began to be introduced about, I have been treated like a queen, with invitations to sherry parties, tea, dinner and the theater piling up with agreeable rapidity. Perhaps mother mentioned my daring move to try out for an amateur dramatic society: my second week here was spent in rehearsing 8 hours a day for my part as (guess what!) a mad poetess in an 18th century farce! Our theater club (ADC-- Amateur Dramatics Club) is the only one of the many acting groups in Cambridge to have its own theater (complete with dressing rooms, lunch and tea room!) and I feel overjoyed to be participating in such vital activities. I met many delightful people through this play production and am now taking the women's parts in a small play-reading group which meets once a week to read plays of shakespeare by the fireside. Since the ratio of men to women here is pleasantly 10 to 1, I find myself building up the beginnings of an agreeable salon of actors, producers, writers, embryonic lawyers, scientists, and so on. I still have a few important finishing touches to put on my room (such as couch cover, a large reprint or two for the walls) before I'll feel sufficiently fit for entertaining in my own quarters (as yet I let the Englishmen make tea for me! I need practice before I will have face to serve them!)

The crowded, tantalizing smorgasbord of fine plays, excellent films, challenging lectures, concerts (I heard a marvelous sunday eve concert last week in king's college with a handsome chap, a natural scientist who plays the piano superbly, speaks hindustani, and introduced me to cambridge architecture, music and indian food),--all this makes it necessary to do a great deal of reading in the long vacations, since the actual college term is so short. So I plan to stay here for about two weeks at the beginning of December after term ends and read and read and contemplate and write: life has been too full and active so far to allow for any meditative and creative work. This, of course, is only natural when one is plunged head over heels into a completely new life on all fronts.

I am most interested in acting now, and my ambition is to audition again and again until I get a part in one of the big plays: there is a companionship and fervor in producing a play which is equalled by nothing else: by the opening night, one feels a great rapport with everybody from the leading man to the electrician and wardrobe mistress! Next, I want to begin writing again in December, when I am not so intensely involved in the immediate prospect of discovering all that Cambridge has to offer by way of people, books, scenes, and events. Plans for vacation are still very tentative, but I hope dreamily for Paris, the Mediterranean (The Sun), and perhaps a bit of skiing in the Alps. Instead of wishing rather frantically, as I once did, to be brilliant, creative, and successful all at once, I now have a steadier, more practical approach which admits my various limitations and blind spots and works a little day by day to overcome them slowly without expecting immediate, or even eventual perfection. Life is rich, full and I am discovering more about it by living here every challenging day. I'll write again soon.

Meanwhile, much much love to you,
sylvia

TO *Aurelia Schober Plath*

Monday 7 November 1955 — TLS (aerogramme), Indiana University

Monday morning
November 7

Dearest mother . . .

It is a wet, warm, gray November day, and the yellow-green trees are letting go their leaves in the sodden wind. The week has been crowded with books and people, and I am slowly learning by experience the kind of life I want most to live here. With so many challenges on all fronts, academic, social and extracurricular, I have to be firmly disciplined in choosing.

To sum up the past days: I saw a good bit of that outgoing, creative negro boy, Nathaniel LaMar (from Exeter and Harvard) and went to coffee with him Monday at the bohemian coffee house[1] here where I had the first really good open "bull session" I've had since I've been here. Temperamentally, Nat is very much like me, enthusiastic, demonstrative, and perhaps trusting and credulous to the point of naivté. A strong contrast to the Englishmen, who have a kind of brittle, formal rigidity and, many of them, a calculated sophisticate pose. Anyhow, Nat had a friend from Harvard who is now in Paris (reminded me of Clem) come and visit him, so I went out with them to hear Louis MacNiece (who never turned up) and then to the Coffee House with a whole group of boys where I observed human nature over cups of café espresso.

Went to a series of surrealist films Wed. night in a torrent of rain with Richard Mansfield, a very good-looking boy, but not without a certain amount of vanity and pose. Films were magnificent: a green, watery poem of motion and music called "Bells of Atlantis",[2] all fluid, with primal rhythms like embryo green worlds and white women floating yet unborn through waves and leaves. Then a gay Norman McClaren[3] experimental film of abstract colored forms leaping about in time to music; and a hilarious Charlie Chaplin film (I'd never seen him before). The chef d'ouevre was "The Cabinet of Dr. Caligari",[4] that classic expressionist film where the jagged black-and-white sets grow out of states of mind

1–According to SP's calendar, this was the Copper Kettle, on King's Parade, Cambridge.

2–*Bells of Atlantis* (1952), directed by Ian Hugo.

3–Scottish-born Canadian film director Normam McLaren (1914–87).

4–*The Cabinet of Dr Caligari* (1920); German film directed by Robert Wiene, presented by the Film Society in the Examination School, Cambridge.

and there is the subtle reversal between the worlds of sanity and insanity. Really wierd and haunting. Somnambulist Cesars reminded me of those Poe horror tales where decomposing men are kept alive by hypnotism, and the frustrating cramped red-tape of the official business world recalled the surrealistic tales of Kafka where it is realistically possible for a man to wake up in the morning to find himself turned into an insect. Well, it is the sort of movie I enjoy most: it shocks one into new awareness of the world by breaking up the conventional patters and re-molding them into something fresh and strange.

Also went out to dinner at the Union[1] (the one place in Cambridge where women are not allowed unless escorted: the debate club) and saw a rather good repertory production of my favorite "I Am a Camera"[2] (which you remember we saw[3] with Mrs. Cantor and the Braggs, I think) which made me want to turn immediately to writing again. Acting simply takes up too much time. I was really glad I didn't get a part in the coming production of "Bartholomew Fair", (although of course it injured my ego slightly) because I have so much reading to do, and I would rather be a mediocre writer than a bad actress.

Had one very charming tea on Thursday: John Lythgoe (set designer for our little play, and natural sciences major: specialty, fungi) took me speeding through the dusk on the back of his motorcycle to his grandparents' house in Granchester: a lovely, stately place, with orchards, formal gardens, and greenhouses. His grandfather, Sir Arthur Tansley[4] (evidently the name is well-know in botannical fields, and he also worked with Freud, I think) was in the hospital, but his ancient grandmother was a delight: dry, witty, full of reminiscences about royalty and cambridge, etc. Had buttered scones and much tea by a cosy fireside, and she gave me some apples from her orchard in parting. John is one of those sweet, tender souls (there are many in Cambridge) who bring out the maternal instinct in one and exactly nothing else. His mother[5] (a scientist) may invite me to visit them in London for a few days this Christmas vacation, which would be nice, as John knows the place well.

1–The Union Society, Bridge Street, Cambridge.

2–Shown at the Arts Theatre, 6 St Edward's Passage, Cambridge; according to SP's calendar, she saw this on Friday 4 November 1955.

3–According to SP's calendar, she saw *I Am a Camera* at the Wilbur Theatre in Boston, on 4 April 1953.

4–English botanist and ecologist Sir Arthur George Tansley (1871–1955); married to Lady Edith Tansley.

5–British scientist Katharine Tansley (1904–88), married first to British ophthalmologist Richard James Lythgoe (1896–1940).

Academically, I feel very ignorant, as I knew I would, choosing subjects I know nothing about, but still, although I have allowed myself a year before I start making judgments, ignorance is not a pleasant state. In practical criticism, for example, we have to "date" poems which is for me impossible since I've never read any 17th and 18th cen. poetry (I'm taking an excellent series of lectures of 17th cen. metaphysicals now). Also, I've never read the classics, or all the multitude of prose & poetry writers outside the colossi: Chaucer, Milton, Shakespeare and the 19th and 20th cen. My only job is to go on reading slowly and steadily, and this I am beginning to do, ruthlessly cutting out all teas and social engagements for the main part of the week. I am now reading French, (I do love my gay supervisor here), Ibsen, 17th cen. poets, Restoration tragedy and a bit of criticism. My main concern is that I must appear rather uneducated to my Director of Studies, who will have to write my recommendations for Fulbright renewal in December, which is much too early for her to realize that I am progressing as well as is humanly possible. I can't wait till those two weeks in December which I shall spend here, without the load of 15 hours of lecture, just reading and writing. One of the Cambridge "little magazines" has accepted two of my poems[1] and I'm meeting the Editor[2] this afternoon. I feel about increasing my scope of reading much as I did about my thesis: I <u>know</u> it will take place eventually, but am irritated sometimes at the slowness.

Love to all,
Sivvy

PS Had a lovely time last night at playreading of "King Lear" being wicked Regan in gothic-spired turrets of St. John's College.
PS: could you please get me a pair of RED pappagallo ballet shoes (7M) as soon as possible, before I leave on vacation. I think Wilbar's[3] has them. You can tell them by the striped red & white inside. Don't take a reasonable facsimile! Only the gen-you-ine article!

1 – Sylvia Plath, 'Epitaph in Three Parts' and '"Three Caryatids Without a Portico" by Hugh Robus. A Study in Sculptural Dimensions', *Chequer* 9 (Winter 1956), 2–3.
2 – According to SP's calendar, she met Derrick Amoore (1935–92).
3 – Wilbar's was a shoe and hosiery store with several branches in the Boston area, including one at 41 Central Street, Wellesley.

TO *Aurelia Schober Plath*

Monday 14 November 1955 TL (aerogramme), Indiana University

<SP typed 'Letter No. 1' on address side of letter>

monday morning
november 14

dearest mother . . .

it has been so nice to get your letters this week. I enjoy everything, big and little, which you write about. I received the snapshots of warren and me about two weeks after you sent them and have put my favorite up on the mirror: the one of us in the backyard, both smiling sort of up and out. I like it better of warren than the stern, heavier prussian one which makes him look too much like a captain of industry. the blessed new yorker comes now, after their card announcing it, which got missent to cambridge maryland, of all places. I didn't realize how much I missed the "atmosphere" of humor and cultural and geographical "assumptions" which I so love in the new yorker. every night, before bed, I make a point of relaxing over a pot of hot milk and crackers by my gas fire and reading for fun in it.

there are several frustrations in my work, which, although I allowed for them abstractly, nevertheless bother me still, while I do my best to take them easily. in the first place, the girls in my practical criticism hour have a much broader background than I in the periods of literature, and so I am utterly left out when they have to "date" bits of prose and poetry from 16th, 17th, & 18th centuries. naturally none of the selections are from chaucer, shakespeare, milton, the russians, and only very rarely from the 19th or 20th, so I feel very ignorant. there is no preparation I can do for this class, except to read, very slowly, as I am doing through the poetry of these centuries. also, in my "supervision" in tragedy, with the same woman, miss burton, I again feel enormous handicaps reading, as it were, in a vacuum where I have had no background, such as dryden and otway in restoration tragedy. I've done only one paper for her so far on corneille which, in spite of the fact, I read the plays in my still rusty french, seemed to be acceptable, although we get no marks and just discuss them with our tutor. these are my two most painful hours in the week as I invariably make some verbal faux pas out of simple ignorance and can't throw around the names of a host of minor writers in the augustan age, etc. the kind of reading I have to do slowly to remedy this too early over-specialization of mine is exactly what I wanted to come here to do, but it is still often difficult, in face of some of these glib girls, to compete on levels where my own lack of reading stands in my way. occasionally, I would just like to catch them off guard with our early american literature!

another thing, I probably won't hit my stride till the third term, when I have done enough reading to be at least competent enough to talk about it, and by then it will be too late for the fulbright people to appreciate this. my director of studies, miss burton, is also my supervision in tragedy and practical crit., so she sort of governs (unfortunately, I think) whatever judgments are written about me this december when our applications for renewals go in. and I can hardly tell her that my very ignorance has dictated the new fields I've chosen (tragedy for 2000 years, moralist philosophy, french and criticism) and that I will be worth the price of keeping on for another year. I really <u>must</u> finish this course, and in many ways it is the hardest thing I've ever done, for, instead of concentrating in my favorite specialties and periods, as I did at smith, I've deliberately chosen to fill in the large gaps of my unknowledge. I have to give myself stern talks continually to go on slowly enjoying reading day by day without getting claustrophobic at the piles and piles of books rising up around me that I "must read".

I could read all day every day for the rest of my life and still be behind, so I do balance my mornings of lectures (which I love) and reading with a kind of cultural and social life. people are still infinitely more important to me than books, so I will never be an academic scholar. I know this, and know also that my kind of vital intellectual curiosity could never be happy in the grubbing detail of a phd thesis. I simply don't believe that kind of specialization is for me. I like to read widely, in art, psychology, philosophy, french and literature, and to live and see the world and talk deeply to people in it, and to write my own poetry and prose, rather than becoming a pedantic expert on some minor writer of 200 years back, simply because he has not been written about yet. ideally, I would like to write in at least half of my vacations here, and publish enough to get some sort of writing fellowship, saxton or guggenheim, which would let me live without academic obligations (which I can make up myself after these 2 years) and write steadily, which is impossible here during the packed term. this is all rather private musing, and I would rather you kept it in the family and shared the more extroverted passages with other people.

perhaps what I <u>do</u> miss most here is the lack of my friends who have known me in my past. I can't explain fully how much it means to have people who have shared years of one's life and with whom you can assume a deep understanding and common experiences: people like marty, patsy, sue weller, gordon, phil, and, of course, my own dear family. while I am very happy here, and have many too many invitations to accept even half, all my acquaintances are at the same "historical stage" in knowing, and it takes only much time to achieve anything like the deep and vital friendships I left behind me at home. everyone here is so "new" and untried. I am glad that I am outgoing and open and intense, now, because I can slice into the depths of people more quickly and more rewardingly than if I were superficial and formal.

(next letter)

TO *Aurelia Schober Plath*

Monday 14 November 1955[1] TLS (aerogramme), Indiana University

<SP typed 'Letter No. 2' on address side of letter>

monday morning, continued

well! it seems I have a good deal to spill over this morning, so I shall go on before my morning lectures in 17th cen. metaphysical poetry and ibsen.

to continue: it is a lovely blue and gold day: when it is nice here is is "very very nice, and when it is bad, it is horrid."[2] I have gotten used to clouds of frosted air surrounding me as I breathe in the bathtub, and to concentrating on the cloud formations outside the diningroom windows as I eat my soggy sludgy mass of daily starch foods. my room is more and more a delight, and I now have my big earthenware plate heaped with a pyramid of fruit: apples, oranges, pineapple, bananas, grapes, and a large vase of bright yellow dahlias, which bring the sun inside to worship.

this week has been a rather mixed one as far as feelings go. I have mixed both sorrow and joy in fairly equal parts. I've told you about the problems. the nicer things involve people. last monday, I spent the whole afternoon and evening with mallory wober. he played the piano for me about two hours, and one of his friends dropped in and sang some songs for us. then he read aloud some light verse from lewis carrol which he made excruciatingly funny, and then, at about 10, we went for a late dinner at the indian restaurant, the taj mahal, where mallory is very much at home and we have our own favorite waiter. I biked home over the cam and down the starlit road feeling very happy.

1–Date supplied from postmark.

2–Probably a reference to Henry Wadsworth Longfellow's poem 'There was a little girl': 'She was very, very good, / And when she was bad she was horrid.'

dick wertz, sassoon's roommate at yale and nancy hunter's old flame, who is reading theology here, dropped over wednesday afternoon, and we had the first good talk we've ever had. I have been constantly surprised how much I miss sassoon, who is now at the sorbonne, and spent hours talking about him with dick. ironically enough, the boy's here are sassoon's age, but in maturity and integration they are babies compared to him. having created such vivid, brilliant worlds of talk and people and plays and art exhibits and eating and all those many minute and important things that make up shared experience, I find fragments of the things I so admired and appreciated in him scattered here & there among other chaps, but naturally miss not having them all together.

thursday I went to tea with john lythgoe, this sweet botanist who has traveled all over the world and is going to help me find out about exchange rates and travel to paris. we were going to motorcycle to ely (the cathedral town) sunday but it was too cold and raw and gray.

friday I had a lovely time with the first english boy I've met who is temperamentally like me: david buck.[1] he played the lead in one of the ADC nurseries (dr. triceps in mirbeau's "epidemic") and I have admired him ever since. he is reading english in his 1st year, after serving 2 years in the army in germany, and is very strong and versatile. he is a champion swimmer, and has a large role in "bartholomew fair" where I have five lines as a rather screaming bawdy woman[2] who gets into a fight. I think I will do it, even if it is so little a part, because it will give me a kind of stage presence and keep me active in the ADC. the advantage is that 5 lines will mean I only have to go to one or two rehearsals. it is a "cuttable" part, and I hope I can be good enough for them to keep it in. I have to be very rough and brazen, which might be fun. anyway, david and I had sherry at his rooms in christ's (I still can't get over the way people casually talk about: "come on over to jesus" or "I live in christ's"!) and we went for an enormous and delicious dinner at the cambridge arms hotel,[3] very formal and victorian and gloriously ugly. we had fish, and turkey, and lots of lovely red wine. saturday we went to visit the editor of the "big" magazine at cambridge where, at david's recommendation, I left a few stories and poems. david writes for them, too. we lunched at "the eagle",[4] one of the arty bouffet pubs in town, which was lots of fun.

1–David Keith Rodney Buck (1933–89), British; B.A. 1958, English, Christ's College, Cambridge; dated SP in 1955.

2–SP played Alice in *Bartholomew Fair* by Ben Jonson, ADC Theatre, Cambridge University, 24 November–3 December 1955.

3–The University Arms Hotel, Regent Street, Cambridge.

4–The Eagle is a pub at 8 Bene't Street, Cambridge.

saturday afternoon, mallory took me punting on the cam, which was lovely, as he looks like a dark-haired, red-cheeked jewish greek god (if that is possible) standing at the helm and poling along perfectly straight (a feat) under the bridges where people leaned over and stared and took pictures, and he told me about the cambridge architecture we could see. afterwards, he came back for tea at my place (I had fixed up the room with fruit and flowers and gotten all kinds of breads and cakes . . . I love to have people in for a change, after going out so much). I had refused another date for the evening, as I figured it would be anticlimactic, so I just sat and mused nostalgically on the paradoxes of life.

yesterday was most amazing. I was, as I said, to have gone to ely with john, but mallory had invited me to lunch, and it was a bad day, so I left a note on my door telling whoever read it to come to tea, and mallory delivered a note to john postponing seeing him. well, mallory took me and some of his jewish friends from israel, around king's and the chapel, which was exquisite at dusk, with all the colored stained-glass windows (which mallory explained the stories of, and the history & architecture) and myriads of candles and lacy fan-vaulted ceiling. then mallory played the "emperor concerto" on his vic, and "greensleeves" and some other favorite ballads on his piano for me. we were biking back to my place with sandwiches for tea-lunch when john pulled up on his motor cycle, having read the note on my door and not having got my letter. well, nothing remained but to have them both for tea, which bothered me a bit as they are very different, john being most shy and sensitive and retiring and mallory being outwardly very witty and amusing. believe it or not, they both stayed from 4 till 10 at night, talking about everything from "is there a purpose in the universe" to the belgian congo no mention of supper! john left only after I invited him to tea today, and mallory took me to a lovely late steak dinner at the taj. my first "salon", and most stimulating.

xxx
sivvy

TO *J. Mallory Wober*

Wednesday 16 November 1955[1] ALS with envelope,[2]
Cambridge University

Wednesday also pm

Dear, dear Mallory* . . .

No, (I hadn't quite realized, but I hoped I wasn't the only one to be enjoying it). If so, re company, the pleasure was quite mutual. YES! (I would like to repeat, continue and magnify it). YES! (we shall discuss this and much else on Friday). YES! (I received the note of yesterday, delivered, I presume, by one of those large carnivorous black ravens). NO! (I must admit I did not fully understand the contents until I received the more detailed explication in today's missive).

Now, Mallory (I like to say that name out loud, because it has just the right number of syllables to give it so many kinds of dramatic expression – ask me to demonstrate some time –) I have come to a very difficult time where I have to make an important choice, specifically affecting the next two weeks & perhaps more. All day the pros & cons have been adding up on either side & the total seems to come out even. It is an extremely complex conflict, with large philosophical issues woven into apparently simple social phenomena. May I talk to you about this huge chaos Friday? Since you are, rather definitely, involved in some of this? It might be a good idea to meet earlier than 8 if we are going to discuss more than the weather during intermission. Then too, I always feel a little desperate if I'm conscious of the clock racing toward twelve – my bicycle might just turn into a pumpkin on the way back to Whitstead & then where would I be? If you possibly could or care to meet me before 8, let me know when & where & I shall appear at your bidding.

(next page!)

Hello again! I am being most wicked & prolonging this while I should be polishing off at least five Romantic tragedies before my supervision tomorrow! Why? I enjoy talking to you, even via paper, which is, in many ways, inferior to the experience in all four dimensions, instead of just these two: ↓

remind me to read you some eecummings, edith sitwell & dylan thomas when we next have a few quiet hours together . . .

1–Date supplied from internal evidence.

2–The letter is not postmarked and was probably hand-delivered.

I am, by the way, becoming quite delectably inebriated with your letters (the opposite of "fed up" – I am beginning to feel like an opium fiend – I need more & more to live on!) you definitely ought to make a wholesale deal for stationery. You are already a diplomat par excellence. (I favor a lawyer, who composes in his leisure time!)

No, I am not listening to your music from France, because you haven't invited me to. I can't spend my life in a room with no music, so that is why I am irresistably drawn to haunt yours (the only reason?) – and I sincerely wish you would wheel your piano up here at least once a week & fill my room with enough music to last till the next week! please do! (I have so much to talk to you about Friday!)

<drawing with caption 'Moon: seen reflected in large puddle!
(Thought it was a fried egg, didn't you!)'>

There is something quite mystical that happens to me when I think of you. Strange isn't it, this process of learning to know & understand someone else!

Until Friday,
Your unmusical
Sylvia

*It must mean something, musn't it???????????????????

<drawing of a coffee table with a plant, a *New Yorker*, and other items on back of envelope>

TO *J. Mallory Wober*

c. Thursday 17 November 1955[1] ALS (picture postcard), Cambridge University

<picture postcard caption>

Henri ROUSSEAU: *The Sleeping Gypsy*. 1897. Oil. 51 x 79 inches. The Museum of Modern Art. Gift of Mrs. Simon Guggenheim.

Dear Mallory . . .

Like Alice-in-Wonderland, I have gone through the looking-glass, and now, (translated to the land of the Jabberwock) I find myself seized with a remarkable affinity for purple ink.

I am sending you a close friend of mine, the Sleeping Gypsy, watched over by three eyes: the moon, the innocent lion, and the guitar. Please treat

1–Date supplied from internal evidence.

him well & do not speak too loudly, or you will waken him. I hope you will see that the stars & planets are obedient until Saturday, at which time I shall cycle up on Fortune's wheel. My room is most eager for you to see it & really behaving with scandalous impatience!

Until then . . .

S:

TO *Aurelia Schober Plath*

Monday 21 November 1955 — TLS (aerogramme), Indiana University

Monday morning
November 21

Dearest mother . . .

It has been so good to get your letters this week, and to hear via dear Patsy too how well your driving is going! I am so proud of you. Also, I look most forward to my Christmas present which I promise faithfully not to open till the Day. It might, you know, if it is at all weighty or bulky, be better to send it to me care of American Express, 11 Rue Scribe, Paris V, as I shall be leaving Cambridge about Dec. 16 and would appreciate not having anything extra to carry. Vacation plans, while yet very tentative, at least are coming into focus. I am staying in Cambridge for a blissful two weeks after classes stop on Sat., Dec. 3 and reading and resting and meditating on this life and gathering "my selves into myself again"[1] before flying to Paris (round trip from London, by the way, being only about $25). I have a very nice invitation from Katharine Tansley, D.Sc. (Mrs. Lythgoe, mother of John, that sweet, weak botanist) to stay in London with them as long as I want. I shall welcome not being forced to go to the cold & depressing Y, and plan to spend about 3 days in London before going to Paris, where John has promised to show me the London Life (or as much of it as possible in 3 days). His sisters are very musical and artistic and his mother works at her research in color vision all day, and maybe I'll have a chance to do some cooking!

As for Paris, I am roughly going to be in Europe from Dec. 20 to Jan.10 (filling out the 3 weeks allowed by the Fulbright Comm.) I am most happy to have made a very warm, good friend in Nat Lamar (the negro writer from Harvard) who is a wonderful sort of psychic brother.

1–Sara Teasdale, 'Two Songs for Solitude'; one song, 'The Crystal Gazer', begins: 'I shall gather myself into myself again'.

Had him to tea this last week and we talked more concretely of plans. Since he is flying over about a week earlier than I, to stay with his very attractive, intelligent, Clem-Moorish type friend at the Sorbonne, they will look around and get me a cheap, good place to stay on the Left Bank so when I come I won't be lost in a strange city. Then, we plan to see Paris together and celebrate some sort of American-in-Paris Christmas there. All this will be very nice if it works out, and I like the idea of having two "brothers" to go around with, both as guides and sort of champion protectors. There is left the week in January, during which I may go skiing (Jon Rosenthal is stationed in Germany) or seeking the sun and Hieronymus Bosch (my favorite middle-age Salvador Dali) in Spain. It is fun not to have everything planned rigidly, so I can see what comes up in Paris. Well, I'll let you know how things work out.

Life here is at present packed to the brim. I have a small speaking part in "Bartholomew Fair" and lots of pantomime acting to do in the crowd of lower-world characters (I am, I must admit, a rather colorful woman-of-ill-fame) and the experience of working on the same stage with Big Actors of Cambridge is something I'm happy not to miss. Daniel Massey (Raymond Massey's son) is the hero of the piece, the towering, childlike old Bart. Cokes, and the character parts are many and most richly Ben Jonsonian. I love our group, and am very happy to be in the centenary production. As one more experienced actress told me: take any part, no matter how small, and watch the professionals. Acting here is as professional as can be for "amateurs." The revue shows, written and sung and directed by Cambridge students, go to the West end in London or on summer tours, and one of the most talked-about student actors left Cambridge to play on in London in "Waiting for Godot" which I saw my first night there. Watching our rehearsal yesterday was old Miles Malinson,[1] the chinless executioner in "Kind Hearts & Coronets" and Polonius to John Gielgud's[2] "Hamlet."

The show runs 10 nights, from Nov. 24 – Dec. 3 and I must admit, is almost a relief as it absolves me from giving a 2nd thought to all the invitations I have been getting to parties and balls (I refused 3 balls this week). I think I will wait till the fabulous dances in the spring (which run through breakfast) before staying out till 4 am. As it is, I am in bed by 12 every night. Read "Faust", "Peer Gynt" and Schiller's "The Robbers" (not time for German, alas) among other Romantic tragedies at the

1–English actor William Miles Malleson (1888–1969).
2–English actor John Gielgud (1904–2000).

beginning of the week. Last Sunday, by the way, was a sort of comedy of errors. By accident, John Lythgoe and Mallory Wober both came to tea here at 4. I was worried at first, for they are extremely different, John being very shy and easily hurt and Mallory being outwardly vividly handsome and witty, although really very sensitive and thoughtful. Well, we began talking about life, and went on and on. 8 o'clock came and no mention of supper from either of them. By this time we were arguing about purpose in the universe. Finally, at 10, I got John to leave by asking him to tea the next day and went to the Taj Mahal for a lovely late supper with Mallory. I think I shall start a salon in Paris! Mallory, by the way, was born on April 27th (!!!) and is, believe it or not, a year younger than Warren! I am, naturally, much older and have probably lived much more than most of the boys here. I enjoy, however, the chance to influence them, and Mallory is an especial delight. We saw the "Glass Menagerie"[1] Friday, went for a long walk around moonlit Cambridge. Saturday, I read Oscar Wilde and Dylan Thomas aloud to him (practising some experimental ideas of mine in getting people to like poetry by hearing it without analytic fanfare) and he made the nicest picnic in his room: cold ham, dark bread and cheese, ending with mangoes; then I listened to him play Scarlatti for me. Imagine, he lived for 9 years in the Himalayas! Has a fascinating and amazing family background: Moorish Jews, Russian Jews, Syrian Jews, etc. We can do a lot for each other. Ah, well, must dash to ADC rehearsal.

Love to all, your own
sivvy

ps – Tell Warren that Sean Sweeney[2] is here, too!

TO *J. Mallory Wober*

Monday 21 November 1955[3] ALS, Cambridge University

Monday a.m.

Dear Mallory . . .

A hectic note from the ADC – the tyrants allow us a meager tea-break today from 4:30 to 5. May I come quietly to see you then & listen to music & you & calm my most hectic & tormented psyche? I'll assume

1–Performed at the ADC Theatre, Park Street, Cambridge, on Friday 18 November 1955.
2–Probably American Sean Sweeney (1932–); Warren Plath's schoolmate at Phillips Exeter Academy, class of 1950.
3–Date supplied from internal evidence.

"yes" and materialize about 4:30. Next term I shall deny this riproaring life & become a sedate femme du salon with a "private life."

Your ramping jade,
Sylvia

<on front of envelope>
kindness of houdini

TO *Aurelia Schober Plath*

Tuesday 22 November 1955 — TLS (aerogramme), Indiana University

Tuesday morning
November, 22, 1955

Dearest mother . . .

Your Saturday letter arrived today, and I felt the impulse to sit down and answer it, even though I've told you most of the relevant news in yesterday's note. I must admit that now that Christmas draws near, I, too, feel occasional waves of deep homesickness flood over me which makes me want to go about and announce publicly from the cobbled corners in Cambridge just what a wonderful mother and brother and grandparents and friends I have and how noble and tragic and self-denying a figure I am to be away from all those I love so much for so long. No matter how old one is, there is so often the need to "let down" and spill over to those of one's own flesh and blood, who accept one simply for oneself, without making any demands. When you think of it, it is so little of our lives we really spend with those we love. I really resent being away from Warren so much while he is growing and becoming a man, and I long to spend time with him and learn to know him and have him know me as I am growing to be, too. Perhaps, if the fates are kind, and he comes to Germany this summer, I may be able to travel to be with him a while. I <u>do</u> hope you can come to England, before June 22, if possible, when Newnham closes, to see the dear little room and house I live in and walk about the Newnham gardens, where I will show you my favorite little statue of an impish cupid delicately balancing and holding an amiable dolphin.

I shall be happy to carry your Christmas present with me whereever I go, and, probably in a cold and snowy Paris, open it on The Day. Perhaps the most difficult thing for me to keep up is writing letters to other people, who have been most wonderful about writing me. I get a large satisfaction about writing you, and also my brilliant and sympathetic Richard who, from paris, makes me feel I have a strong partisan just over the channel. But, although I've written Sue, Patsy, Gordon & Elly Friedman and Mrs. Prouty, I just haven't had time or energy to write all the dear people I love so much (like Cantors, Crocketts, etc.) I hope to do this in a series of Christmas letters in the two weeks I am here in December. Also, if ever I am repetitious from letter to letter, do understand that I forget just to whom I have written what. You can help me immensely by telling Mrs. Prouty I am thinking often of her and love her dearly and will write in a few weeks. Also to dear Aunt Dot, how much I loved her birthday gift and letter. And to Mrs. Freeman (I did ask David to share my letter with her) that the picture of Ruthie's wedding is on my bureau. I simply can't write separate letters to them all until my vacation, but I dearly enjoy hearing from them and their letters are magnificent. So please be my ambassador, as I know you are, until I get time to write on my own!

I must admit that I find everywhere what a mixed blessing life is. Every choice involves advantages and disadvantages, and I welcome those heavenly two weeks in December when the play and classes will be over and I can muse in peace. I think this is much wiser than rushing off to Paris or London right away, for I have really had no time since I left New York to "take stock" in anything more than a hasty, immediate way. So picture me for two weeks here, having leisurely teas, curling up with many books by my cheerful gas fire, and being creative and contemplative. That images sustains me through these hectic days.

As I have probably said before, I am not meant by nature to be an academic phd person, and if I teach, it must be in vital combination with writing and living in this world of plays, music, new and old books, but foremost, <u>living people</u>. I see in Cambridge, particularly among the woman dons, a series of such grotesques! It is almost like a cariacature series from Dickens to see our head table at Newnham. Daily we rather merciless and merry Americans and South Africans and Scottish students remark the types at the dons' table, which range from a tall cadaverous woman with purple hair (really!) to a midget Charles Addams fat creature who has to stand on a stool to get into the soup tureen. They are all very brilliant or learned (quite a different thing) in their specialized ways, but I feel that all their experience is <u>secondary</u>, and this to me is tantamount to a kind of living death. I want to force myself again and again to leave the warmth and security of static situations and move into the world of growth & suffering where the real books are people's minds and souls. I am blessed with great desires to give of love and time, and find that people respond to this. It <u>is</u> often tempting to hide from the blood &

guts of life in a neat special subject on paper where one can become an unchallenged expert, but I, like Yeats, would rather say: "It was my glory that I had such friends,"[1] when I finally leave the world.

I evidently made a rather fine impression on Lady Tansley when I was over for tea a few weeks ago (that wonderful 86 year old grandmother) and John Lythgoe says she would like me to come to a family wedding at a little parish church in Granchester on Dec. 17th, the day I'll no doubt go to London to stay with John's family. Somehow, I really welcome the chance to be a bit involved with family life. I have a feeling that I love dear Mallory primarily because he is a kind of substitute (although there can be no such thing) for Warren: strong, handsome, with a kind of integrity and strange dearness which is so tempting to help mold. I really feel that I could be a fine creator of children's souls. Preferably my own children, where intense love could be involved, as well as the teaching part! I do enjoy your advice & feel very close to you in your letters. Shall talk to Miss Burton after Dec. 3rd, when I give her my renewal application to fill out and the hectic term is over and I can prepare a serious discussion. I do love you all so very dearly.

Much love,
sivvy

TO *Richard Sassoon*

Tuesday 22 November 1955 — TL (excerpt),[2] Smith College

Excerpt from letter[3]
November 22, 1955

Words revolve in flame and keep the coliseum heart afire, reflecting orange sunken suns in the secret petals of ruined arches. yes, the glowing asbestos thorns and whistling flame flowers reflect the cells of the scarlet heart and the coliseum burns on, without a nero, on the brink of blackness. so words have power to open sesame and reveal liberal piles of golden metallic suns in the dark pit that wait to be melted and smelted in the fire of spring which springs to fuse lumps and clods into veins of radiance.

so sylvia burns yellow dahlias on her dark altar of the sun as the sun wanes to impotence and the world falls in winter. birds contract to frozen

1–W. B. Yeats, 'The Municipal Gallery Revisited'; SP slightly misquotes stanza VII: 'Think where man's glory most begins and ends, / And say my glory was I had such friends'.
2–SP excerpted this letter in her journals.
3–'Excerpt from letter ~~to Sassoon~~' appears in the original.

feathered buds on barren boughs and plants surrender to the omnipotent white frosts which hold all colors cruelly locked in hexagonal hearts of ice.

at midnight, when the moon makes blue lizard scales of roof shingles[1] and simple folk are bedded deep in eiderdown, she opens the gable window with fingers frozen crisp and thin as carrots, and scatters crumbs of white bread which skip and dwindle down the roof to lie in angled gutters to feed the babes in the wood. so the hungry cosmic mother sees the world shrunk to embryo again and her children gathered sleeping back into the dark, huddling in bulbs and pods, pale and distant as the folded beanseed to her full milky love which freezes across the sky in a crucifix of stars.

so it costs ceres all that pain to go to gloomy dis and bargain for proserpine again. we wander and wait in november air gray as rat fur stiffened with frozen tears. endure, endure, and the syllables harden like stoic white sheets struck with rigor mortis on the clothesline of winter.

artificial fires burn here: leaping red in the heart of wineglasses, smouldering gold in goblets of sherry, cracking crimson in the fairytale cheeks of a rugged jewish hercules hewn fresh from the himalayas and darjeeling to be sculpted with blazing finesse by a feminine pygmalion whom he gluts with mangoes and dmitri karamazov fingers blasting beethoven out of acres of piano and striking scarlatti to skeletal crystal.

fires pale askew to pink houses under the aqua backdrop sky of "bartholomew fair" where a certain whore slinks in a slip of jaundice-yellow and wheedles apples and hobbyhorses from lecherous cutpurses. water scalds and hisses in the tin guts of the kettle and ceres feeds the souls and stomachs of the many too many who love satanic earthenware teasets, dishes heaped with barbed and quartered orange pineapple and cool green globes of grapes, and maccaroon cakes that soften and cling to the hungry mouth.

when the face of god is gone and the sun pales behind wan veils of chill mist, she vomits at the gray neuter neutralities of limbo and seeks the red flames and smoking snakes that devour eternally the limbs of the damned. feeding on the furies of cassandra, she prophesys and hears the "falling glass and toppling masonry"[2] of troy while hector pats her torn and tangled hair and murmurs: "There, there, mad sister."

1 – 'Cf. poem' written in SP's autograph in the margin opposite this line, possibly a reference to an image in SP's poem 'Dialogue Over a Ouija Board'.

2 – A reference to *Ulysses* by James Joyce. SP slightly misquotes Joyce: 'Time's livid final flame leaps, and, in the following darkness, ruin of all space, shattered glass and toppling masonry'.

God is on vacation with the pure transcendent sun and the searing heat that turns the flawed white body of our love to glass: look! how the riddle of the world is resolved in this menagerie of mated glass, how clean and sparkling the light blesses these pure serene ones! suddenly from the bed of mire they ascend to astonish the angels of heaven who keep the light of their love enshrined in ice.

see, see! how the mind and mated flesh can make man the envy of god, who masturbates in the infinite void his ego has made about him. but do not ask for these tomorrow. he is a jealous god and he has had them liquidated.

I have talked to various little dark men who keep giving me, at my request, booklets colored yellow and titled: sunshine holidays . . . .

do you realize that the name sassoon is the most beautiful name in the world. it has lots of seas of grass en masse and persian moon alone in rococo lagoon of woodwind tune where passes the ebony monsoon . . . .

I am proud again, and I will have the varying wealths of the world in my hands before I come to see you again . . . I will have them, and they are being offered to me even now, on turkish tables and by dark alladins. I simply say, turning on my other flank, I do not want these jingling toys. I only want the moon that sounds in a name and the son of man that bears that name.

In the beginning was the word and the word was sassoon and it was a terrible word for it created eden and the golden age back to which fallen eva looks mingling her crystal tears with the yellow dahlias that sprout from the lips of her jaundiced adam.

be christ! she cries, and rise before my eyes while the blue marys bless us with singing. and when, she asks (for even eva is practical) will this ressurection occur?

TO *J. Mallory Wober*

Wednesday 23 November 1955 — ALS with envelope on Newnham College letterhead, Cambridge University

Place: couch overlooking redtile rooftops, senile gray trees & white sheets struck with rigor mortis on winter's clothesline . . .

Time: year of our Lord 1955, a pale gray November 23rd morning . . .

Scene: Louis XIV salon: Woman sits clad in blue-flowered pyjamas sipping dregs of coffee from gold-plated cup. She has scarcely bothered to comb her hair, which hangs in snarled locks over one eye. A few rough-cut emeralds on throat & arms are her only adornment, and the splendid color of the jewels brings out the quaint, cadaverous green pallor of her skin, the room is full of white camellias, sent by her countless admirers. Fighting heroically against an ominous cough (tubercular), she calls her small black serving-man to her, "I must Dictate," she gasps in Hindustani, 'a letter to my rugger'd crimson-cheeked Hercules!"

Cher Hercule,*

Bless you. Bless a certain King's don Mr. E. S. Shire.[1] Tell him to have a jolly good time in Piccadilly Circus. Tell him to bathe in the fountain of Eros. I do not have much time left on this earth, but what there is of it I want to spend with you – such as Friday, such as afternoon & dinner. Shall you meet me here at 2 and read or talk before changing scenes to 7 Peas Hill? Or shall I have my black chariot (symbols will sneak in) drive me to your dwelling immediately? Is 2 p.m. still all right?

About the U*io* B*ll – have you ever heard about the rather disagreeable & ridiculous emotion called "altruism"??? It means "regard for, devotion to, the interests of others . . . as opposed to egotism or (heaven forbid) selfishness" – (courtesy of Webster).[2] → next chapter

---

* "Don't know how to write Hindustani": yours truly, small black servingman.

Agenda: Union Ball

To continue:

Out of regard for and/or devotion to the interests of one Mallory Wober, I (Sylvia) urged him to gather him roses, openly, too, simply because I felt I should not forcibly monopolize him, which happens to be a rather strong inclination of mine. His quite casual suggestion that some gallant from the cast could prevail upon me to go is most groundless, because I do not Go to Balls to Go To a Ball, but rather to be with someone I enjoy intensely, it may hap, at a Ball, or not, as he chooses. Now I enjoy many people at present, but only one intensely. And He remarks that "it would create

1 – Edward Samuel Shire (1908–78); natural sciences scholar at Cambridge University.

2 – Though not underlined, definition in Plath's dictionary reads: 'Regard for, and devotion to, the interests of others; – opposed to *egoism* and *selfishness*.'

a slightly embarassing situation if we were both to be there unawares." This ambiguous remark implies that he intends to be there & would be annoyed if I turned up, suddenly, to confront him (unawares) and/or that He would be happier if I confessed that, dealing in intrigue, I were wickedly going with someone Else & hadn't had the courage to honestly tell him (Mallory) that this was so, so He is giving me the opportunity to do it now & save myself maidenly blushes later.

All this foliage is unnecessary: "If I do not go to the Union Ball with Mallory, I go with no one." (statement of witness at prosecution.)

By the way, your letter was THE FIRST I ever received at the ADC & made me radiantly feel "I live here now."

For this, and the constant ways you "surprise me by joy,"

I am,
your
Sylvia
<drawing of flower>

<on front of envelope>
Kindness of the White Rabbit

TO *J. Mallory Wober*

Wednesday 23 November 1955 — TL with envelope, Cambridge University

Whitstead
4 Barton Road
Cambridge
November 23, 1955

Mr. Mallory Wober
King's College
Cambridge

Dear Mr. Wober:

It has come to our (editorial) attention that one of us (not editorial) is going quite mad. Not that there's anything off-key about walking casually into one's room nearing the witching hour of midnight, turning on the light, gazing around gratefully and thinking: ah, home at last; now for a little supper of wormeaten apples and stale malt bread topped off by a brimming jug of scalded milk . . .

BUT, in the casual process of picking up a satanic earthenware cup one just happens to notice the back of an envelope, rather a familiar kind of stationery, too, perched on top of Cassell's New French Dictionary (Funk & Wagnall's Co., New York, c. 1930). Oho, one says to oneself (impersonal 'one', just to be safe), I must have forgotten to mail one of the letters I wrote this morning; strange.

One (still playing safe) carelessly picks up said envelope, turns it over, and gets a rude shock. The handwriting, rather weird, to be sure, with the W looking like a pitchfork without the handle, is our (editorial again) own. Fine, one says quietly to Jiminy Cricket, someone has returned a letter we wrote because maybe the stamp fell off or maybe they just don't want to speak to us any more and are subtly suggesting this fact by returning letters unopened . . . .

"BUT, my dear Watson," says a still small voice, "the letter happens to be addressed to you." So it is, thinks Sherlock. Smart chap, that Watson; I'll have to make him a Doctor one of these days.

"What the devil," one laughs nervously reading the letter one has apparently written to oneself when dozing unawares in the bathtub or slumbering peacefully under Braque, "it's fashionable to have an alter ego these days!" We (very regal) always did think we had more personalities than ordinary people were blessed (?) with. We're getting more versatile every day: haven't even left the A's yet: am doing a switch on Alice-in-W. and screaming in yellow satin as Alice, Mistress of the game, at Bartholomew F. Just you wait till we hit the B's (Beginning By Borgia (Lucrezia() and Climb through Cassandra, Cleo, Cressida . . . whee . . . .

Meanwhile, watch out for schizophrenic women. We're typing all our correspondence now, just so nobody can recognize our writing and tell who's talking.

????????????????!????!??????????

TO *J. Mallory Wober*

Thursday 24 November 1955[1] ALS with envelope,[2]
Cambridge University

<drawing of stage with curtains and "?" in the middle>

Time: 2:27 p.m.

Place: spinach-green dressing table amid red turkish towels, soiled once – white lace caps, black gloves, triptych mirrors which toss back a garish glitter of reflections, many-angled, simultaneous in space: a glass vision of the fragmented ego: o splintered self! <drawing of a female figure in dressing room looking in mirror holding a pen> beautiful blonde girls come and go adorning their lovely silken hair for parts of grace wellborn & madam overdo while the vile-colored yellow satin wh*r* hides all vestige of gentility and ramps and rages and practises throwing three squashy oranges (soft & blunted from over-much use) at a black screen between pink and blue flats off stage. needless to say, this play gives one an unparalleled chance to take out one's minor and major grievances by yelling and shouting and striking people with oranges and fists. The latter of which I am prepared to do to whomever it is (can't guess) who at this advanced stage (n.b: pun) of life cannot draw the line between reality (which is life) and the illusion of it (which is acting). either that, or you were teasing me in a line (n.b. again) of holly leaves, which I sincerely hope was the case. only, It probably was'n't. This, and much else, will undoubtedly be revealed on friday afternoon, when the dark dmitri karamazov hewn out of the himalayas descends in a dark cloud and astounds the wearied mahomette[3] who will probably be trying feebly to hang herself with yards and yards of holly-ribbon, conveniently provided by an invisible troll who lives under the staircase. I do not quite understand about the music, unless you are prepared to sing for several hours. today ! is Thursday. tomorrow, by the blessed order of the universe, is friday, I will be languishing like camille amid my withered yellow dahlias –

your admiring
sylvia

<on front of envelope>
un-kindness of orange juggler & tale-bearer

1 – Date supplied from internal evidence.
2 – The letter is not postmarked and was probably hand-delivered.
3 – Voltaire, *Le fanatisme, ou Mahomet le Prophète* (1736).

TO *J. Mallory Wober*

Thursday 24 November 1955[1] ALS with envelope, Cambridge University

Dear Mallory –

In medias res this is to tell you (while I wait to be called up to sing about cutpurses with the crowd of barnyard grotesques) that you are an absolute (no, not relative) dear and it was rather like having a blood transfusion (only much more magnificent) to receive your just-before-curtain-time note. I felt like a prima donna or something equivalent (at least a glorified & sublime tart) and hope someday you'll be more justified in coming to see your own

Sylvia

Tomorrow & tomorrow & tomorrow –

<on front of envelope>

Kindness of one Danish scholar

TO *J. Mallory Wober*

Thursday 24 November 1955[2] ALS with envelope,[3] Cambridge University

Time: eternity
Place: limbo

Dear Mallory . . .

I sit in the midst of squealing cubist pigs wallowing in the chaotic bedlam of sword fights, spilt oranges, musty gingerbread, hobby horses, cutpurses, revolving pink elephants, floating iridescent soapbubbles, shrill madmen with tousled red hair, ballad mongers and delicately askew orange & blue rooftops. Even my gross inability to carry a tune comes in handy as you will see (or, more regrettably, hear). friday seems as far off as the himalayas →

your
s.

1 – Date supplied from postmark.
2 – Date supplied from internal evidence.
3 – The letter was not postmarked and was probably hand-delivered.

TO *Aurelia Schober Plath*

Saturday 26 November 1955 | TLS (aerogramme), Indiana University

Saturday afternoon
November 26th

Dearest mother . . .

I received your wonderful packed envelope of articles yesterday and enjoyed it no end. You have no idea how I love such juicy collections of items: I understand how important it was to send letters and news of art & incidental home affairs to the soldiers overseas: it keeps the image of home alive and vital, for it is by specific details that we re-create the atmosphere of family and love. the tooth article was excellent & appalling. I have heard gruesome rumors about teeth here, and am careful to brush mine several times a day and to eat much fruit (several apples a day, bananas, grapes, oranges, etc. which I buy regularly from the stalls at market hill to keep my fruit pyramid piled high). I think the english have notoriously bad teeth, partly because of their bad diet during the war and party because of the fantastic amounts of "sweets" they consume: I forget the exact figures, but millions of pounds of candy are eaten a year, and hence, also, the pasty complexions of many men.

remember the picture of sahl swarz,[1] american sculptor, doning a head of einstein which you so justly found to resemble the head of a camel? well, it is his "head of kafka" that I was so impressed by at the museum of modern art last year and which inspired my short poem of that name in the series of 3 on museum sculpture (dedalus and icarus and 3 caryatids were the others). seems I have rather good judgment. was also very admiring of the "waiting for godot" review, which, as I perhaps told you, stars an undergrad from cambridge as one of the old tramps! he signed a contract and so can't come back (they thought it might fail, but no!)

this next, last week of term will be the most hectic yet. "bartholomew fair" began this last thursday night and will continue until saturday dec. 3, so all my evenings are taken up. our opening night was cold (many critics from london were there, and we got a long, if rather critical, review in the london times[2]) & I must admit that the play's production is a herculean task, even for pro companies, what with staging of the crowd

1–American sculptor Sahl Swarz (1912–2004). Swarz had an exhibition at the Sculpture Center, then at 167 E. 69th Street, New York; his 'Kafka' was included.
2–'A.D.C. Theatre, Cambridge', *The Times*, 25 November 1955, 3.

& the variations on the main theme of the many various and narrow kinds of warrants (spiritual, legal, etc.) men find for indulging essentially the same kind of frailties. however, even though I am generally part of the crowd, and have only one brief scene of dashing across the stage & shaking a creature and bellowing about the hardships of the common whores, it is good experience. our costumes come from the wardrobe at stratford-on-avon, and I have a long-sleeved gown of vivid yellow satin which is much fun. unless I get something like the part of cassandra in "troilus & cressida", I shall let this stage & grease-paint part of my life go and become a more private person. I must say, though, that instead of frittering my time on small teas or avant garde movies, all very nice in themselves, I enjoy <u>working with</u> these boys and girls to create something, and not just sitting around to talk and gossip and be passive. the ADC is my extracurricular life, and I am too much a part of this world to become a passive beholder. I want to be out on the stage too, and create in any way, no matter how small.

I must tell you how lovely a day yesterday was. mallory, by the way, sent me a letter on our opening night, and has thought up countless small ways to surprise me with his originality in daily notes and messages. one letter was written in my own handwriting, which gave me rather a shock. another on a roll of christmas holly ribbon, which I had to unwind. the latest surprise occurred yesterday. I had invited mallory here for tea (and got a lovely orange iced sponge cake, malt bread, cookies, etc.) and said rather sadly that I had no music in my room and regretted this (as we always have such a lovely time at his place listening to records and having him play the piano). well, I opened the door to find my hercules standing outside, not only with his gramophone and a stack of records and a church of england hymn book, but a small hammond organ! I was really speechless. the dear boy had rented an organ for the rest of the week! so we moved it in my room, and spent the afternoon singing our favorite hymns (he introduced me to a wonderful one with words by john bunyan beginning: "he who would true valor see"[1]) and christmas carols he also played bach and scarlatti, and as we ate tea on the floor by the fire, we heard tchaikovsky's magnificent 1st piano concerto & beethoven's "emperor concerto" on the vic. I can't tell you how dear mallory is; he is so strong and unspoiled and magnificent to be with. I am very happy to have such a lovely boy to be creative about. I can give him a good deal of confidence and read aloud and make teas for him and enjoy sharing

1–John Bunyan, 'To be a Pilgrim', *Pilgrim's Progress* (1684).

all kind of experience. I wish you could picture him: I think I will get a snapshot of him later, & might even sacrifice it to send it you if you could send it right back just so you could see what a magnificent fellow he is. he looks like I always imagined dmitri karamazov to be: coal-black hair, elegant strong bone structure, scarlet cheeks, blazing black eyes, with a wonderful feeling of leashed strength. I find an aesthetic delight in just looking at him: his blend of russian, syrian and spanish jew gives him a subtle strange other-world aura. well, enough. I am just very happy to find a strong, original soul, we bike a good deal together, and walk, and eat apples and are most healthy and strong and individual. now, to work on my ibsen reading and paper![1]

love to all, you own,
sivvy

TO *J. Mallory Wober*

Saturday 26 November 1955[2] — ALS with envelope,[3] Cambridge University

saturday night
8:37 p.m.

dear mallory . . .

purple eyes and scarlet cheeks being duly painted, I allow myself the minor luxury of talking to you via notepaper, which is already smeared with greasepaint. footsteps thunder on the stairs overhead and I feel a martyr to the cause of common (very common) humanity. 7 more nights to freedom.[4] lord, how I look forward already to a leisurely private life!

today, at least, was a pleasant change of tempo. I slept until I woke naturally to find a tall dark coffin-shape at my bedside. a second look made the events of yesterday leap into focus. I felt at once very warm & joyous and the organ took on its more amiable & creative proportions. The room was still full of music & your presence lingered in my mind like the smile of the cheshire cat which comforted my favorite alice-in-w.

1–Sylvia Plath, 'The Destructive Power of Genius in Four of Ibsen's Plays'; held by Lilly Library.

2–Date supplied from internal evidence.

3–The letter was not postmarked and was probably hand-delivered. On Panda Prints card designed by Rosalind Welcher.

4–Plath may be referring to the end of the term and to the final performance of *Bartholomew Fair*, both of which were to occur on 3 December 1955.

I stayed in my pajamas in scandalous laziness, ate apples, bananas & malt bread & hot coffee for breakfast which lasted 2 hours while I played very badly & gaily on the lovely organ. all day I have been humming "he who would true valor see . . ." you must come to play it again tomorrow – do come at least by 11:45! I find myself having to fight valiantly to concentrate on ibsen – somehow you are altogether too tempting to ponder over. The moon tonight was magnificent, wasn't it? – all distant, pale & frozen in an india-ink sky. I walked alone in the frosty moonlit gardens at newnham, musing on life, and paid a visit to my favorite statue: a dimpled & most mischievous cherub balancing a curly dolphin. you must meet him. I look so enormously forward to vacation here; peace at last. I miss you very much –

your own,
sylvia

<written on envelope>
Kindness of an enormous black raven

TO *J. Mallory Wober*

Monday 28 November 1955[1] ALS (picture postcard) with envelope,[2] Cambridge University

<picture postcard caption>
The Little Horse *Engraving by* Dürer *German (1471–1528) Rosenwald Collection* National Gallery of Art, Washington, D. C.

dear mallory

the original troll who lives under the stairs is getting phenomenally clever: he knows how typewriters work! for this, and his multitude of other admirable qualities, I quite love him. if I live through Thursday morning without coming down with pulmonary pneumonia the world may turn out to be a lovely place. all I want to do is sleep like the enchanted princess for 100 years. tonight I must give birth to my paper which has cost me labor pangs all day. tomorrow I type it. – 5 nights of this "foul" (as Robin Chapman[3] says) & then Liberté! Egalité, Fraternité! Bear with

1 – Date supplied from internal evidence.

2 – The letter was not postmarked and was probably hand-delivered.

3 – British actor, playwright, and author Robin Chapman (1933–); Chapman was steward and junior treasurer of the ADC and played the role of Zeal-of-the-Land Busy in *Bartholomew Fair*.

me. this pony is very proud because he lives completely on apple cores from King JMW. one day we'll analyze a few difficult words.

your own,
Sylvia

TO *Aurelia Schober Plath*

Monday 5 December 1955 TLS (aerogramme), Indiana University

Monday, December 5

Dearest mother . . .

It is a pleasant morning, with that brilliant silver-gray light which seems to be characteristic of the English landscape. I am sitting comfortably in my pajamas after a lazy breakfast of fishcakes, toast and marmalade and coffee and typing a few letters before biking down town to do a multitude of errands which includes arranging my plane ticket to Paris, buying nylons by the dozen (I'm on my last pair – they run so fast here, what with cycling all the time and splintery furniture!) and getting tea things (a perpetual process). It has been a really rugged week, and it will be pleasant to unwind peacefully these next few days and then begin to build up positively for Paris.

I am just finishing with the dregs of a very undermining sinus cold and fever which kept me confined to quarters for the last three days and cut out the last 3 performances of "Bartholomew Fair"; since I'd already been in 6, it didn't matter much at all to me. I must tell you what an absolute rock of gibraltar Mallory has been to me! To begin with, I had an Ibsen paper to write, French to do, and classes, and the nightly appearances seemed endless. Well, Mallory called for me every night at the stage door of the theater and biked home with me, always bringing a ritual apple which we ate by the garden gate at Whitstead. Just looking forward to his strong, comforting presence helped me live through those hectic, demanding days. Then, when I got really sick on Thursday, he delivered all my notes telling people about my not being able to come see them, etc., and spent the afternoon playing Bach to me on the organ (still in my room!) while I drifted off into a kind of delirious fevered sleep. In order that I wouldn't have to go out in the damp and devastating night air, he brought some steak and accessories, and I managed to cook a steak dinner on my one gas jet! We started off with sherry and crackers with peanut-butter-and-bacon, then had a delicious rump steak sauteed with onions and butter, plus canned spaghetti, plus a kind of scrambled-egg-omlette I made with eggs, milk, cheese and bacon. For dessert we had dates and yogurt. All this before my hearthrug. I am so happy and at peace with Mallory, and it has been heavenly to have him take care of me while I was sick: I just felt I could rest completely and everything would be all right.

Last Sunday, before the deluge of this week, I shared the most magnificent experience with him: Advent service at the King's Chapel. Since Mallory belongs to King's College he got two tickets. Honestly, mother, I never have been so moved in my life. It was evening, and the tall chapel, with its cobweb lace of fan-vaulting, was lit with myriads of flickering candles which made fantastic shadows play on the walls, carved with crowns and roses. The King's choir boys processed down through the chapel singing in that clear bell-like way children have: utterly pure and crystal notes. I remembered all the lovely Christmas times we've had as a family, caroling with our dear friends, and the tears just streamed down my face in a kind of poignant joy. The organ pealed out and the hymn was that magnificent one "Wachet Auf" ("Now Let Every Tongue Adore Thee") which was so beautifully familiar. The choir alternated with Bible readings and sang several exquisite, lyrical 15th century carols about Mary, enchantingly naive pieces. I enjoyed standing and singing with the packed throngs of congregation: O Come o Come Emmanuel and, finally, the triumphant Adeste Fidelels. After this powerful experience, Mallory and I had supper at our favorite Indian restaurant, the "Taj Mahal". I also forgot to mention that in the morning, we had a stimulating sherry party with one of Mallory's friends, a Israel boy named Iko[1] and his girl. Excellent talk.

I do hope grampy had a lovely birthday and that my card came in time for the Day at least, if not for the party. I am planning to write about 20 Christmas letters this week, so you may rest assured that people will at last be hearing from me. Yesterday, I had a visit from Richard Sassoon, who had flown to London from Paris to visit his relatives. We had lunch in town and in the afternoon I had a tea for him and Dick Wertz (Nancy Hunter's ancient flame from Yale who is now studying theology here & was Sassoon's roommate). My appreciation of the situation was dulled with the remainder of my cold, but I managed a nice tea with maltbread & butter, maccaroons & chocolate cookies and a good orange sponge cake. I have also got a speckled pottery bowl and copper nutcrackers for my

1–Isaac Meshoulem (1934–), Israeli; B.A. 1957, economics and law, Pembroke College, Cambridge; dated SP, 1955–6.

table, and always have it full of mixed nuts, which look rugged & well-textured in their shells. I only wish you could see my room, now: I have put candles in two wine bottles, the two bookcases form walls of gay color; I love my Braque still life, which is low-keyed browns blacks and grays with lovely avocado-greens and a bright yellow; chrysanthemums (gift of David Buck from "Bartholomew Fair" for my illness) blaze in Van Gogh yellow from two earthenware vases; fruit is piled high in a large dish and there is always plenty for tea. I enjoy so much creating a homey atmosphere, and my room is the favorite of all the places I've lived. The other two girls who live up here have gone home, so I have our whole little top floor all to myself and it is utter heaven. I am having several people to tea and sherry this week to catch up on my social obligations, plus continuing my French lessons & having a talk with my Director of Studies, Miss Burton. Mallory went on a walking trip to London (!) yesterday with a friend, but should be back tomorrow. So we will spend the days working & enjoy each other in the evening. He is an absolute joy. You would love him; he takes such good care of me! His mother has invited me home,[1] too, but unfortunately I accepted John Lythgoe's mother long ago!

Give my love to all,
your own sivvy

TO *Aurelia Schober Plath*

Saturday 10 December 1955 — TLS (aerogramme), Indiana University

Saturday, December 10

Dearest mother!

My wonderful Christmas box came yesterday, and I can't tell you how lovely it was! I must admit I opened everything except the stocking (which is now hanging over my gas-fire mantel) right then and there, as my baggage will be very limited when I fly to Paris, and I had to sacrifice to expediency. I am saving the stocking till just before I go, because I love looking at it. Perhaps the most magnificent gift was the silver-wrapped cookies! I immediately devoured a large number of the fresh, delicious hazelnuss cookies and that unique flavor, which I have never encountered

1–Samuel Wober (1898–1960) and Dina Solomon Wober (1906–98) lived at 71 Wentworth Road, Golders Green, London NW11.

anywhere except at home around Christmas, brought back a flood of memories, much the way a certain song or scent can evoke whole portions of the past. I made up a plate of cookies for Mallory when he came to tea later, and he said to tell grammy especially that they were the best cookies he ever tasted. I put the silver paper around my wine-bottle candles and hung a few balls of it from my green plant. I must admit I indulged in a very complex wave of homesickness, too!

Christmas has always been the time for gathering together with our family and dearest friends, and I think of it as I do of Thanksgiving: a period of life where we can express the love and warm togetherness of our home which has lived through the year in our hearts while we were at college, or working. Christmas is a kind of realization of the dream of love of family and friends which sustains us with more power than we know, through travels and wanderings. Each gift is not so much important in itself as because it brings with it the time, thought, and love of the giver. I must tell you how beautiful those red shoes are! And what a blessing that plastic bag will be to protect my books from our ubiquitious rain! The slip was like a white nylon snowflake: pure and exquisitely-cut. Thank you, thank you, thank you.

Now I have a few instructions for you! I have sent off a little package which I hope will arrive in time for Christmas. You can take out the little wrapped presents and put them under the tree. Then on Christmas morning (or New Year's, if the post is late!) I want you to open the Christmas cards I will send you and read them with your presents. Actually, they are just little trifles I wanted to send you, and Warren, and Grammy and Grampy, but each one has a special thought with it, and an enormous amount of love. I really felt part of Christmas Cambridge when I chose these small tokens.

This week has been both pleasant and difficult. I realize now that it parallels that "unfolding" period I always go through when first I come home on vacation: I plan lots of work for every day, and then just drift about, sleeping, playing the piano, eating and assimilating: lying fallow, in preparation for beginning to be creative again. It is always hard, though, for me not to demand that I show a profitable work schedule for every spare minute. Well, I can work harder and better this coming week here for having rested and relaxed in this one. I didn't realize how my cold had hung on & tired me, but this week I feel caught up again with health and sleep. My dear Mallory has stayed on to work (and will go home to London tomorrow and has come over every day for tea and the evening. I haven't had such a healthy "co-ed" life since high school, really. Instead of going off on gay tangents of plays, wine and extravagant holidays on weekends as I used to at college, I live very simply, and much of my time with Mallory is spent placidly listening to music, reading aloud, making tea, biking, and just talking. This week I cooked another steak dinner for him, more elaborate then the first, with dessert of fruit compote marinated in sherry with cheese and crackers (we both eat great quantities of cheese, all kinds, yogurt, etc). Wednesday, I had dear, lovable Nat LaMar over for tea with Mallory and the three of us had a most pleasant time. Nat has already left for Paris and promised to get me some really cheap hotel reservations, on the Left Bank, which should be a relief to have on arrival. Mallory is really the most delightful chap. I am so happy to have such a dear person about, and he helps take up a good deal of the lonesomeness I have for my old friends and loved ones. He is the product of a very interesting progressive school called Bryanston (which I hope to visit some day) and the fact that he is 19 seems of no real importance whatever: he is so much more mature and strong and well-balanced than any of the other boys I have met here. And so kind and loving and thoughtful. He is not brilliant scholastically (reading in sciences where I think he would be happier in history) but quite simple and steadily thoughtful and happy and enchantingly whimsical & original. I so wish you could meet him. His mother would like me to come and stay with them in London (they evidently live in a very small flat), so I shall probably visit them next Sunday when I am at Lythgoes[1] and stay there a few days on my return from Paris. Evidently Mallory's relatives are all gathering around to see me, too, for it is an Event to have a "christian" girl accepted, I gather. Ironically enough, I am not really a christian in the true sense of the word, but more an ethical culturist: labels don't matter, but I am close to the Jewish beliefs in many ways. This family should be fascinating: the English Jews are a contradiction in terms: the vivid warmth and love in their personalities I find very close to home. Anyway, I am happy to have the experience of two London families to look forward to. Paris is a tremendous challenge and I'm glad I won't be faced with it alone, because of the language problem. Nat & Sassoon should be a blessing at escorting me through the blazing lights and wonders of this city that never sleeps (not like London, which shuts up shop promptly at 11!). Know that I am thinking of you with much much love, and rather a bit of wistfulness, this Christmas.

your own loving –
Sylvia

1 – According to SP's calendar, the Lythgoe family lived at 105 Clifton Hill, St John's Wood, London NW8.

TO *Aurelia Greenwood Schober & Frank Schober*

Sunday 11 December 1955[1] ALS in greeting card,[2] Indiana University

<printed greeting>

Greetings / With all Good Wishes / for Christmas / and the New Year / from

<signed>

Sylvia

Dearest Grammy & Grampy . . .

Merry Christmas! This is a photo of the beautiful "Bridge of Sighs" under which I have punted with Mallory up the River Cam to tea & honey by a crackling fire in Granchester. Imagine me living surrounded by such loveliness!

I hope you are reading this on Christmas morning and remembering, as I am, the many wonderful Christmasses we have spent together: I tasted "home" in the delicious silver-wrapped cookies you sent (Mallory loved them, too) – my favorites – apricot jam & hazelnut – and I also thought back to the delicious apples & special avocados grampy always brought home at the bottom of his bag on Sundays & how we had club sandwiches, & lovely fireside suppers together. All these memories are especially precious to me now, my first Christmas away from those I love best. I really appreciated your card & gift (I shall spend it on something special in Paris!)

It was so nice to get your Christmas box! I have shared the cookies at several teas & wore the ski-pants for the first time yesterday on my first venture on horseback![3] The horse had ideas of his own & broke into a gallop straight into a main intersection at which time my stirrup came off! Picture me clinging to the racing stallion's neck, saying between bumps "Whoa! Sam!" to no avail, stopping traffic right & left & sending terrified pedestrians flying for cover! Such an adventure! I am still black & blue!

Your little gift – for both of you – is to be used at breakfast & each time you use them, I want you to think of how very much I love you both! They are made of hand-turned wood & came from my favorite craft

1 – Date supplied from internal evidence.

2 – Christmas card with image of Bridge of Sighs, Cambridge.

3 – See Sylvia Plath, 'Whiteness I Remember'.

shop. Merry Christmas & Happy New Year to the dearest grandparents in the world –

your loving
sivvy

TO *Aurelia Schober Plath*

Sunday 11 December 1955[1]

ALS in greeting card with envelope, Indiana University

Dearest mother . . .

Merry Christmas! This should be Christmas Day (if you obeyed my instructions!) and I want you to feel, in spirit at least, that I am with you! This is a copy of one of my favorite Brueghels,[2] and if I remember rightly, Warren once had to write a paper[3] about it in relation to W. H. Auden's poem – "Musée des Beaux Arts." At any rate, I love this, and wanted to share it with you.

About my little gifts to you: they are very simple & small, but I want to tell you the associations that go with them: the decorative ashtray depicts the famous statue of Eros at Piccadilly Circus in the heart of London – which became so dear to me: the wingèd figure aims his arrows above a circular fountain in the center of traffic: it is on Piccadilly that I saw "Waiting for Godot" my first night in London. Incidentally, I thought the shade of blue matched our diningroom walls & peter's wings!

The flat present is simply a picture of our Newnham College gardens where I walk daily, up & down the formal gravel paths by the box shrubs & sunken pool. The white windows are our dining hall, and around the corner out of sight is my favorite little winged bronze cherub, struggling gaily to hold a twisty dolphin. I hope we will stroll here this summer!

I want you to believe in mental telepathy & know that I am close to you in thought & spirit right now! I know I have the most wonderful family in the world and want to share as much of this new world I am discovering as I possibly can. These little Christmas tokens I sent are only small symbols of the Cambridge I now love so much.

Wish me luck in Paris, where I shall be at the moment you are reading this. I am blessed with dear friends both in London & in Paris, so shall be

1–Date supplied from internal evidence.

2–Pieter Bruegel the Elder, 'Landscape with the Fall of Icarus' (Pallas Card 1081, Brussels Museum).

3–See SP to Gordon Lameyer, 10 January 1954; held by Lilly Library.

as happy as possible. I <u>do</u> miss you, but look forward to being with you this summer.

Love from your very own
Sivvy

<on inside of card>

Sylvia

<written on the envelope>

Do Not Open till Christmas!

TO *Richard Sassoon*

Sunday 11 December 1955 TL (excerpt),[1] Smith College

Excerpt: December 11[2]

What concerns me among multitudes and multitudes of other sad questions which one had better try to lure aside with parfaits and sunshine, is that there is a certain great sorrow in me now, with as many facets as a fly's eye, and I must give birth to this monstrosity before I am light again. Otherwise I shall ressemble a dancing elephant . . . I am tormented by the questions of the devils which weave my fibers with grave-frost and human-dung, and have not the ability or genius to write a big letter to the world about this. when one makes of one's own heavens and hells a few hunks of neatly typewritten paper and editors are very polite and reject it, one is, in whimsy, inclined to identify editors with god's ministers. this is fatal.

Would it be too childish of me to say: I want? But I do want: theater, light, color, paintings, wine and wonder. Yet not all these can do more than try to lure the soul from its den where it sulks in busy heaps of filth and obstinate clods of bloody pulp. I must find a core of fruitful seeds in me. I must stop identifying with the seasons, because this English winter will be the death of me.

I am watching a pale blue sky be torn across by wind fresh from the russian steppes. Why is it that I find it so difficult to accept the present moment, whole as an apple, without cutting and hacking at it to find a purpose, or setting it up on a shelf with other apples to measure its worth or trying to pickle it in brine to preserve it, and crying to find it turns all brown and is no longer simply the lovely apple I was given in the morning?

1–SP excerpted this letter in her journals.

2–'Excerpt: December 11 ~~Letter to Sassoon~~' appears in the original.

Perhaps when we find ourselves wanting everything it is because we are dangerously near to wanting nothing. There are two opposing poles of wanting nothing: When one is so full and rich and has so many inner worlds that the outer world is not necessary for joy, because joy emanates from the inner core of one's being. When one is dead and rotten inside and there is nothing in the world: not all the woman, food, sun, or mind-magic of others that can reach the wormy core of one's gutted soul planet.

I feel now as if I were building a very delicate intricate bridge quietly in the night, across the dark from one grave to another while the giant is sleeping. Help me build this o so exquisite bridge.

I want to live each day for itself like a string of colored beads, and not kill the present by cutting it up in cruel little snippets to fit some desperate architectural draft for a taj mahal in the future.

TO *Warren Plath*

Sunday 11 December 1955[1] TLS in greeting card[2] (photocopy), Indiana University

<printed greeting>

With all Good Wishes / for Christmas / and the Coming Year

<signed>

and much, much love / from / Sivvy / (see inside)

A very merry Christmas to you! I am remembering all the mornings which we have shared on Christmas, tiptoeing to take down our bulky stockings with a little jingle of bells, and opening the small presents first, and then the big ones, and then driving in the frosty air to dinner at Dot's where there were more presents, and celery & anchovies and a big crackly golden turkey and wine and that sleepy, well-fed feeling afterwards. It seems almost impossible that the years whooshed by so fast, and here we are in our twenties all at once with the days of stamp-collecting and monopoly games far behind.

First of all, I want to tell you how much I enjoyed your long letter at my birthday, telling me about your new course of studies and activities. How I admire you! Your program of germanic languages and linguistics sounds magnificent: difficult, but stimulating, the sort of combination which is

1 – Date supplied from internal evidence.

2 – On Gaberbocchus Christmas card designed by Franciszka Themerson.

invaluable. I believe that you will be more and more pleased with your choice and hard work *now* later on. I have found it works out that the most arduous working periods bring forth most fruit, at a later date, as in my senior year at Smith, which I spent working on my many schemes and assignments and waiting, until they suddenly all blossomed forth with results in late spring. This past term has been hectic, and now that the smoke has cleared away and I ask myself what I have accomplished, the main achievement seems to be to have learned: "to Live in Cambridge, England," including everything from where the best places to buy steak or tea cakes or apples are, how much social life I want and with whom, and that, enjoyable as the A.D.C. is, I shall give it up for a time to concentrate on the colossal amount of reading I have to do.

The most difficult thing is choosing between the greater of two goods in the long run. It is wrong, I think, to shut out the blue skies, vital people, and *active* participation in the immediate world of the present completely in order to work, but it certainly is hard to measure roughly what is the best proportion, to keep alive one's simple, elementary joy in *being* while working for a better, <evidence in photocopy suggests some text is missing> are working hard, and hoping that you man[age] enough track and dating to have *fun*, which is a most important ability! To simply accept the daily texture of life with a keen awareness and joy in small, colorful things: from the sight of a flicker on the grass to the sound of rain on a tin roof.

I am most interested to hear about your plans for a summer in Germany! Please, no matter what, do come to Europe. I am convinced that it is best to travel when one is young, because adapting to all kinds of rough situations is most possible then. And I want so much to see you and be with you again. Perhaps I could come visit you in your little town and try to learn how to *speak* German, or join you for a while if you went through Scandinavia. It would be such fun, and by then I should be at least a bit more of an experienced traveler than I am now! I am at last going to have my vague dreams of travel to egypt, greece, spain, africa, brought smack up against reality (i.e. very little money) and will be interested to see what ingenuity and simple living can work out. Paris is my first station of the way: I am flying over (the round trip fare, including busses from center of London to center of Paris, a rather large item, is only about $20) on Tuesday the 20th, and spending till January 6th in Europe. Nat LaMar is getting me a place to stay as he has already gone over to visit his friend Steve at the Sorbonne (by the way, Nat is a really lovely person: so open and friendly and kind . . . Sean Sweeney is here too: remember my reading stories by both of them in your Exeter magazine?) Anyway, for Christmas, I shall hang tinsel and green-ribboned bottles of Beaujolais wine from the Eiffel Tower, and open my jingling stocking in the middle of Paris! I'll be thinking of you on this Day with much love, and preparing a table before you under the Arc de Triomphe.

The two small presents I am sending you from Cambridge are very British. The blue-and-brown woven tie comes from my favorite handcrafts shop where this card was discovered (reminding me of that little song: "and heplayedonaladla-aladle-aladle"[1]) and I thought it would go with your eyes. The scarf is the rich color of Cambridge chestnuts & earthenware, and somehow spoke of Harvard: to keep your neck both warm and colorful!!

with much love –
from sivvy

TO *Elinor Friedman Klein*

Monday 12 December 1955 TLS in greeting card,[2] Smith College

<greeting card caption>
A KNIGHT HUNTING / *From an old Danish peasant embroidery.*
<printed message>
With All Good Wishes / for / Christmas and the New Year
<signed>
not to mention / much love / from / sylvia

dear dear elly:

your card, thank you. I am sitting with my right flank scalding by gas fire and my left as cold as the other side of the moon talking to all the people I love most. there are at least 10 or 15 of them. the term is over. the swallows have returned to sorrento, or wherever the hell they go for long vac, and I am recuperating: from flu, from being a whore for a week in "bartholomew fair", from not stopping to think since I left new york and the homes of two attractive, creative rich bitches whom I would like to be in the glass slippers of in 10 years, from too many men and the Right One who is too young, and the sassoon one who came to see me last Sunday

1 – Part of the chorus from 'Aiken Drum', a Scottish folk song.
2 – Christmas card produced by K. J. Bredon.

and who has shrunk, like gregor samsa,[1] to an insect, to my utter horror. BANG.

I am also black & blue from a horse named Sam. it was a beautiful day, last Saturday. never rode a horse before, but it was a day for a horse, & so friend from yale (sassoon's ex-roommate, nancy hunter's high school flame) dick wertz took me for a ride. ecstasy. like santa claus bouncing atop roof with reins around chimney. country: peat stacks, thatched cottages, misty fens. Sam decides to gallop as we near busy intersection. switches with originality to wrong side of street. cars pull to curb, white staring faces pass by like lotus flowers, stirrup suddenly comes off. I find myself hugging Sam's neck passionately. old women & children run screaming for doorways as we heave up onto sidewalk. such power: like the old gods of chance: I felt like one human, avenging thunderbolt. every time dick tried to catch up on "Cherry Brandy", Sam thought it was a race. I intend to have grandchildren immediately. I am here today. black and blue, to be sure, but with a new religion: I mean to marry Sam. any day now.

oh elly, there is this boy: tall, raven-haired, scarlet-cheeked, husky, Jewish, strong as the "giants in the earth" in the days of the old testament prophets. Mallory Wober. and god made me born about 5 years too early. He is 19, born on my brother's birthday. when I was sick with flu he <u>carried</u> an organ to my room: bach, beethoven, scarlatti, tchaikovsky's 1st piano concerto: worlds of music. he is dmitri karamazov, and I made him all myself. god, elly, he is the kind one could create a superman with. not brilliant, no. reading natural sciences. wanting to be a farmer in israel. only 19! but compared to gordon, to ira, to mr. kazin's harvard-press boy, he is a MAN. fantastically strong, like a lion. yet o, so gentle. music: king's college chapel advent service: millions of candles flickering on tall, lacy, fan-vaulting that henry 7th dreamed about, with tudor roses & gargoyles: crystal choir-boy voices singing 15th cen. carols about maid-mary. organ like roar of god, thousands singing "adeste fideles" and the young, black-bearded moses standing beside me. I am meeting his family in London this week: all the relatives are coming to see me: I am the tabu: the "Christian girl" (I can't convince them I'm a healthy pagan). never in God's o so green world will his like grow again. to think I'm making him ready for some girl who is teething innocently in her cradle! it is that first, very magnificent love. perhaps I shall burn my birth certificate & learn to give birth at the plow in israel.

1–Gregor Samsa, young man who awakes one morning to find himself transformed into a large insect, in Franz Kafka's short story 'The Metamorphosis'.

mr. kazin's blinking eyes haunt me. like a kind of winking albatross. I shall write. come to europe to travel with me this summer. to greece. still have africa map. am flying to paris to hang tinsel on eiffel tower under escort of negro writer from harvard, nat lamar ("creole love song" in atlantic) and pay post mortem visit to sasson. write, write. london is lousy with dramat schools, christopher fry, etc. please come!

much love –
Sylvia

TO *Gordon Lameyer*

Monday 12 December 1955[1] TLS, Indiana University

Dearest Gordon . . .

A most Merry Christmas to you! There is so much to say that I feel almost paralysed, and want to just take you out for a cafe expresso at the desperately avant garde Soup Kitchen here for a long, long talk. The transfer of my old verbal tête-a-têtes at home (with people like Sue Weller, Marty & Mike Plumer, the Cantors, Mr. Crockett, Pat O'Neil, etc) to the typewriter is really an overwhelming and rather frustrating switch: I want to hand over great hunks of Cambridge (courtesy of the Eyes & Ears of S. Plath) and scorn mere notes. Hence the rather drastic infrequency of my letters. I manage a weekly vignette to mother and rely on her to disseminate the cultured pearls and grains of sand, such as they are!

The term has been over for a week, and I am in the midst of my second week living in the relatively blissful, calm undemanding joy of solitude (also relative) in Cambridge. This term has been the most hectic, packed, over-stimulated two months of my life and I can now see what they mean when they say the terms are for "living" and the very long vacs are for reading and thinking. I shall be so happy for you to visit my room here: it is at last all mine: two enormous bookcases, toppling over with colorful volumes (multitudes bought on my Fulbright allowance, yet frustratingly inviting and unread), a satanic dark earthenware-and-white enamel teaset from Holland which has sustained many members of my selected and delightful "salon", fresh mounds of fruit (apples, pineapples, pears, bananas, grapes, etc.) from the outdoor market in Cambridge, enormous Van Gogh-ish bouquets of yellow chrysanthemums, a flurry of vivid postcard modern art reproductions on door and wardrobe, (memoirs

1 – Date supplied from internal evidence.

of Art Galleries from N.Y.C. to Washington to London), a long, low walnut coffee table, holding art books, pottery bowl of mixed nuts (to be cracked in person), hand-woven rush mats, rough-textured yellow pillows on favorite two-seater couch in window niche, perfect for curling up to read & meditate, Braque still life in fawns, rich russets, avocado greens & highlights of yellow: forest green, sun yellow, chestnut brown, plus accents of black & white, are the colors I live among. You must come see!

For the first time since arrival I have been able to sit back and enjoy my room & the hospitality I can offer: I can cook steak dinners on my one gas jet, complete with sherry & hors d'oeuvres, salad, fruit compote, wine, cheese & crackers. I promise you one in advance, if you really come at the end of March to England!

Actually, most of my energy here has been spent in trying out different kinds of life & becoming used to all the subtle differences in the daily texture of existence. My mornings were taken up with classes, & I spent a rather drastic amount of time at the A.D.C., which I have, with some regret, decided to give up this term, as it demands blood, and I am not that serious about acting, although the group of actors, set-designers & producers I met is the sanest, kindest, most creative throng going. I took the minor part of a screaming whore-mistress named Alice in the A.D.C.'s centenary production of Ben Jonson's "Bartholomew Fair" (a technical feat to stage). We ran for 9 nights, got reviewed in the London Times, etc., and our costumes were straight from the Stratford wardrobe! I wore a lusciously trollopish yellow satin gown and most of my work was pantomime in the continuous crowd scenes. The chance to work with The Actors in Cambridge, & watch them rehearse (Dan Massey, son of Raymond Massey among them) was invaluable. However, the flu caught up with me the last two nights, & I decided to be contemplative & concentrate more on work and writing this next term. I'm almost dead sure the Fulbright won't be renewed, (as it's based on only one term's work, & there are only a few renewals out of 150 applicants) & am rather wondering where the next year is coming from.

In a sense, my outline of studies is just too juicy. And my century-background is, as I knew it would be, impossibly unbalanced (have read only major figures: Chaucer, Milton, Shakespeare, & nineteenth & 20th cen. poetry & prose, no drama). I can at last remedy this here, where instead of specializing, I can spread out, but I feel rather like a starving woman confronted like a smorgasbord of delicacies: such richness! the more I read, the more there is to read, & the inverted pyramid of desired knowledge grows without end.

There is so little time in each day, it seems: I have discovered the early & late Ibsen (you must read "Brand" & "Now We Dead Awaken", if you havent, especially the last, which is a surprisingly symbolic drama---I'd always narrowly thought of Ibsen as a social dramatist---about the need for the artist to sacrifice life to his creation and the deadly retribution he must pay, laying waste to the creative lives around him, yet having to follow his call). Am beginning on Strindberg: fascinating studies of destructive love-hate relations between men & wives. Meaty symbolism. Full of shrikes. "Spook Sonata"[1] is intriguing. All I can do is fight down that feeling of suffocation that I have every time I enter the University Library or Bookstores & go on slowly struggling toward brighter light in my understanding, versus the almost frightening accumulations of new books, specialized knowledge, etc. One must read, one must live, one must write. No one activity is fully possible without the others and each one demands complete devotion. I begin to feel I never can become a Phd person, but must go on reading widely in art, philosophy, psych, concentrating where I like, not where avid Phd candidates have been too bored to research, & live fully & create children, which to me is becoming even more primary than writing, which will never be a career, only an avocation for me. Now that I know it, I won't go around with quite so many soap bubble dreams.

The most rewarding part about life here is the people. I must admit the English girls are either too blue-stocking or two fluttery & Society (never both together) for me, and most of my good friends are men. There's the American Negro from Harvard, Nat LaMar (whose story "Creole Love Song" I may have pointed out in the Atlantic) who is simply a dear: friendly, open, & wonderfully frank. We have periodic bull sessions like brother & sister (he went to Exeter & knew Warren) & he's getting me a place to stay in Paris & promising to protect me & help me learn to speak French when I fly over Dec. 20 (excited, but scared, too). Then there's a sweet Botanist who is very shy, & is exchanging my pounds illegally for francs & whose mother has invited me to stay with them in London next weekend (she's a research scientist & John Lythgoe is the grandson of Sir & Lady Tansley, whom I visited in Granchester before he died.[2] Am going to a family wedding at the parish church there next week).

Then there's a wonderful Jewish Hercules (age 19) who was born on Warren's birthday (see how sentimental I'm getting!) whom I have adopted

1–August Strindberg, *The Ghost Sonata* (1907).
2–Sir Arthur George Tansley died on 25 November 1955.

completely. He has been a great solace when I had flu, & brought me an organ (carried it!) to play Bach, Beethoven, & Scarlatti while I lay in a delirium of fever. He comes from Darjeeling, India, & has a long line of Moorish & Syrian Jew ancestors: the English Jew is a paradox in terms, & I must admit I find the vital intensity, sensitivity and whole integrity of body & mind a relief from the childish & tea-drinking Englishmen, who idealize one embarrassingly. My mother-impulses are brought out like mad. I'll be visiting Mallory's family in London, too (all the relatives are gathering around to meet me, as a "Christian girl" is very rare & generally tabu in their midst: I find it difficult to explain that I'm not really Christian!)

Had my first horseback ride yesterday with Dick Wertz, an old flame of Nancy Hunter's from Yale who is studying to be a Theology professor here: wish you could have seen the debacle! "Sam" broke into an unexpected gallop toward a busy intersection on the wrong side of the road at the crucial moment that my right stirrup came off, whereupon I found myself hugging the horse's neck with extreme warmth. A sharp right-angled turn, and we roared down the middle of the highway, cars stopping right and left, pedestrians flying for the bushes. Sam thought the sidewalks were safer than the street, which immediately made several elderly ladies think the opposite. Never has ever fiber of my mind & body been so simply & passionately concentrated, since I flew down the ski slope to fracture my fibula: nothing in the world mattered but keeping from under the flying hooves of that runaway horse! I managed, too, although I now move about a bit like an arthritic, vividly black & blue! I want so much to master in even a beginner's way the power of horses, skis & sailboats! A lifetime won't be enough.

Am venturing to Paris & from thence to wherever chance calls me for 2½ weeks this vac. Hope to be forced to learn to speak French! Perhaps I can share some of Germany with you during my long vac at the end of March & early April. It would be such fun to discover castles on the Rhine, etc. & try to resurrect some German! Do write. My thanks in advance for the Moliere[1] your kind mother said she was sending for you!

Love from Gardencourt . . .
sylvia

1–Molière, translated by Richard Wilbur, *The Misanthrope: Comedy in Five Acts* (New York: Harcourt, Brace, 1955). The location of this copy is presently unknown.

TO *Gordon Lameyer*

c. 12 December 1955[1] ALS in greeting card,[2] Indiana University

<printed greeting>
With Good Wishes / for Christmas / and the New Year / from
<signed>
Sylvia
p.s. Felt this reproduction[3] particularly appropriate for us – cf. Auden's "Musée des Beaux Arts" &, of course, our Stephen.[4]
sylvia

TO *J. Mallory Wober*

Tuesday 13 December 1955[5] TLS in greeting card[6] with envelope, Cambridge University

tuesday afternoon

hello there! cambridge is simply not the same. there is a particularly devastating sort of vacuum about king's and the arts theater, & I begin to feel much too noble and virtuous for my own good. actually, I'm not half as much of a stoic as I think I am, but I must admit that outside the circle of my scorching gas fire and gaily colored mounds of books, the gray, wet, sodden atmosphere is rather ominous. I feel like going bankrupt and buying hundreds of colored lights to hang on all the bare, skeletal trees. and draping holly wreaths about the necks of the grim, grubby-looking christmas shoppers.

I've been reading some more racine in french, buying apples & now am in the midst of the huge project of writing christmas letters to the people I love best at home. not just simple little notes, these, but enormous hunks of paper re-capturing the texture of the past two months, the people, thoughts, and events that make up life: mood music, and so on.

1–Date supplied from internal evidence.
2–Pallas Card 1081, Brussels Museum.
3–Pieter Bruegel the Elder, 'The Fall of Icarus'. SP sent the same card to her mother on 11 December 1955, and also mentioned in that letter Auden's poem.
4–A reference mostly likely to Stephen Dedalus, a character in James Joyce's *A Portrait of the Artist as a Young Man* (1916) and *Ulysses* (1922).
5–Date supplied from postmark.
6–On Panda Prints card designed by Rosalind Welcher.

you probably have never been described so many times in your life. I am getting better and better at it, and perhaps may borrow you for a short story later: anything, so I can keep on writing about you. describing life at cambridge this term is impossible without presenting you acting in medias res. the room is very quiet now. I liked getting your letter and the railway rhythm poem: have you read t. s. eliot's "wasteland"? I shall read part of it to you, as sections have a similar tone about coming into london. transition is always hardest, I think: the tearing up of roots & moving them. once I am in a place, I am too active in settling & living to be nostalgic. I think it is probably very good for me to be forced to be alone for a while, in preparation for the challenge of entering a new world . . . . .

your enormous book came: you must read aloud to me from it next term! I hope I can finish my 20 long letters and 10 short cards tonight. then I can try to learn a few crucial french sentences, read strindberg, and feel an illusion of freedom to work as I choose. if I read every hour from here to the end of the year I still wouldn't approach the bottom of the books "I must read!"

I look most forward to seeing you sunday (it seems like months till then) and am sure that you are happily active at home: there is nothing quite as wonderful as having a family to go to. I must admit I feel a rather sharp wave of nostalgia for my brother, mother & grandparents, as this is the first christmas I've been away, a kind of feminine ulysses, wandering between the scylla of big ben and the charybdis of the eiffel tower. let me know when and where you want me to meet you sunday afternoon.

much love to you,
sylvia

TO *Olive Higgins Prouty*

Tuesday 13 December 1955 TLS, Indiana University

December 13, 1955

Dear dear Mrs. Prouty!

A very Merry Christmas to you! There is so much to tell you that I hardly know where to begin. First of all, I loved your wonderful pencilled-manuscript-paper letter:[1] when we write to each other I feel we are really communicating: almost as good as talking, but not quite! I feel I can talk to you like a second mother, perhaps even more frankly!

1–Probably Olive Higgins Prouty to SP, 25 October 1955; held by Lilly Library.

Picture me sitting in my room in the blissful peace after term has ended: outside is the gray twilight landscape with the mists rising from the fens and the large black rooks circling about the bare, mottled sycamore tree outside my window. Within: a squeaking, cheerful gas fire (I'm quite fond of the little asbestos monstrosity now!), bright yellow accents: big, Van Gogh-type yellow chrysanthemums, rough-textured yellow pillows, bananas on a pile of fresh fruit from the outdoor market, and the bright lemon shapes in a reproduction of a lovely Braque still-life I had framed: my room colors are sunlight yellow, chestnut brown, holly-green, with black & white accents. How I wish you could be here to have tea with me! I have such a cosy place. All the students (except a very few) have gone home as of a week ago at the end of term, and I am staying here at Whitstead for two weeks to rest, read the pile of books accumulated during term, and assimilate the fast-moving life I have lived through since leaving New York last autumn.

Most of my energy this term has been spent simply *trying out* different kinds of life, activity and people, and selecting the most important elements & cutting out the unessential. The main difficulty here is *choosing* between the over-stimulating variety of challenging activities offered: theater, little magazines, political groups, foreign movies, fascinating people (the hardest to limit), and, of course, the enormous and wide-spread reading program I have undertaken. These past two months my mornings have been occupied fully by classes with most exciting lecturers: dry, witty F. R. Leavis in criticism: incisive Joan Bennett[1] in 17th cen. metaphysical poets; Basil Willey in philosophy.

I have lessons in French (and hope to be forced to speak it in Paris this Christmas vacation, where I am staying for 10 days) and a supervised class in Tragedy (2000 years of it!) in which I've written a mere 2 papers this term on Corneille and Ibsen. The reading is, for the most part, exactly what I need, but I really feel the lack of a "century-background" which these girls have, while I specialized in major figures like Chaucer & Milton & the 19th & 20th centuries. I have constantly to remind myself that this wider reading background is partly what I came for, and I must go on reading and enjoying slowly, and not want to devour the University Library at one desperate gulp. Even if I read every hour from now till the end of the year I *still* would never be close to finishing the ever-expanding list of book "I must read!" So I also realize that I never will want[2] to become a Phd scholar and know more and more about some

1–English literary scholar Joan Bennett (1896–1986).

2–'I never will ~~become~~ want' appears in the original.

minute details of knowledge: I want to read widely in art, philosophy and psychology, my special interests, and to live richly (I hope eventually with a family and children and write about life, people as I know them, and not distilled abstract metaphors and symbols in poetry).

I wish you could have seen the Amateur Dramatic Club Centenary performance of Ben Jonson's rollicking "Bartholomew Fair"! We ran for 9 nights & were reviewed in the London Times; our costumes were from Stratford-on-Avon! I had a very small speaking (or rather, shouting!) part and a lot of pantomime acting to do in the crowd scenes at the fair: I was Dame Alice, a mistress-of-the-game, which is a nice Jonsonian way of saying woman-of-ill-fame: had to add color and wickedness to the fair in a vivid yellow satin gown. It was really a privilege to work with The Cambridge Actors (some of whom are now on London Stage; Dan Massey, son of Raymond Massey, was hero of our play). However, the A.D.C. demands blood: e.g. all your time, and I am giving it up temporarily, for a more contemplative & literary life this next term. I must say that the actors, technicians & producers are the nicest, warmest, sanest, most creative lot I have met in Cambridge! I really felt I belonged at our dear, rickety theater. But the very very public grease-paint life is not for me: I am no Sara Bernhardt,[1] and will try the other side of the footlights for a while, having loved the experience of actually participating.

My social life here has been more than one could wish. With a ratio of 10 men to each girl, it is quite a problem. I had to tell 4 young men this term I couldn't see them any more because they were becoming much too monopolizing & serious & I couldn't be sure of a moment's peace, with them dropping in all the time to ask me out to dinner, or tea, or a play. Englishmen are quite naive, really, and idealize one almost embarrassingly over tea-cups. They talk and gossip extraordinarily, & I am very much against their being brought up in strict prep schools segregated almost completely from women. There is little of the healthy, friendly camaraderie I was so used to at home, & women are often treated like Dresden china. I have been very lucky, however, in making some special friends:

There is Nathaniel LaMar, a warm, friendly Negro boy from Harvard who knew Warren at Exeter & who had his first story "Creole Love Song" published in the Atlantic last year. We get along very well, having the same interest in writing & living abroad, & he is getting me a cheap place to stay in Paris and offering to be a sort of protector-escort in those places women can't visit safely alone.

1–French stage actress Sarah Bernhardt (1844–1923).

Then there is, strictly on a very platonic basis, a nice, shy Botany student named John Lythgoe, who has a dear, vivacious grandmother, Lady Tansley (of the scientific Tansleys) in Granchester who had me to tea, scones & honey; we got along so well that I'm invited to a family wedding in Granchester this saturday and for a stay at the Lythgoe's home in London. John's mother is doing scientific research in color vision, and his sisters are both studying music; it should be fun to see the "inside" of an English home & get a personally conducted view of London again.

My favorite man is a tall, handsome, raven-haired, red-cheeked Jewish boy named Mallory Wober. I must tell you about him. He looks like a young Hercules, or like the "giants in the earth" in the days of the Old Testament prophets, and is as strong and peaceful as the Rock of Gibraltar with an astounding originality and sensitivity. (Very healthy comparison with the pale, delicately beautiful Englishmen, who would probably fracture if touched without extraordinary care).

The tragedy of Mallory is that he is only 19! (Born on Warren's birthday, by coincidence). It is impossible for me to believe this, because in his philosophy of life, his actual daily living, and his maturity and balanced perspective he is older by far than all the "older" men I have known! When I was in a sort of delirium with the flu, he carried an organ over here to my room which he played on during the long feverish afternoons: Bach, Beethoven, Scarlatti: new worlds of music opening up under his fingertips. He was always there: strong, reassuring & comforting, through my weakest, most depressed hours. When I was strong enough, I cooked a steak he had brought on my one gas jet & managed to throw together a candle-light dinner for two with salad, fruit compote, red wine, cheese & crackers.

We have been together almost constantly of late: not running off on gala sprees, but leading a healthy, sharing day-to-day existence: reading aloud, going punting, biking to see the "Glass Menagerie", or "The Country Girl"[1] with Grace Kelley, studying, eating at our favorite restaurant, the "Taj Mahal" where Mallory orders Indian food in Hindustani (he lived for nine years in Darjeeling) & we eat mangoes.

Last Sunday we went to the advent service at the famous King's Chapel (his college), where I really had a mystic experience, seeing the myriads of candles throwing flickering lacy shadows on the walls and ceilings of exquisite fan-vaulting, hearing the clear, crystal voices of the choir boys

1–*The Country Girl* (1954), shown at the Arts Theatre, Cambridge. According to SP's calendar, she saw this on 8 December 1955.

singing 15th century carols, & remembering, as I sang the triumphant "Adeste Fideles" the countless happy Christmasses at home with my family, caroling with friends, & sharing gifts. This year, I will be in Paris, hanging tinsel on the Eiffel Tower perhaps. I am, especially at this time, seized with flashes of keen nostalgia and longing, although, of course, happy with my new friends.

I am going to visit Mallory's family in London this weekend, too: all the relatives are gathering about to meet this "Christian girl", for evidently they are generally tabu in these closely knit Jewish societies, and so I shall really be up for examination. It is so sad Mallory isn't chronologically older: he is in every other way such a magnificent person: both in mind, spirit & body, vital, growing & strong & so dependable, which I really need in a man.

I didn't realize how much I had been longing to talk to you until I actually began! Again, I have decided that I would like to combine writing (which I hope to be doing in my long vacation, & especially this summer) of simple short stories about people I know and problems I have met in life with a home & children. I love cooking and "homemaking" a great deal, and am neither destined to be a scholar (only vividly interested in books, not research, as they stimulate my thoughts about people and life) nor a career girl, and I really begin to think I might grow to be quite a good mother, and that I would learn such an enormous lot by extending my experience of life this way!

Perhaps the hardest thing I have to accept in life is "not being perfect" in any way, but only striving in several directions for expression: in living (with people and in the world), and writing, both of which activities paradoxically limit and enrich each other. Gone is the simple college cycle of winning prizes, and here is the more complex, less clear-cut arena of life, where there is no single definite aim, but a complex degree of aims, with no prizes to tell you you've done well. Only the sudden flashes of joy that come when you commune deeply with another person, or see a particularly golden mist at sunrise, or recognize on paper a crystal expression of a thought that you never expected to write down.

The constant struggle in mature life, I think, is to accept the necessity of tragedy and conflict, and not to try to escape to some falsely simple solution which does not include these more somber complexities. Sometimes, I wonder if I am strong enough to meet this challenge, and I sincerely hope I will grow to be responsible not only for myself, but for those I love most. These thoughts are some of the intangibles I've been working out here, in the midst of the outer active, stimulating life. One doesn't get prizes for this increasing awareness, which sometimes comes with an intensity indistinguishable from pain.

I wanted to share my inmost thoughts with you as well as the bright texture of my active days. Do you know how very much I think of you: how I remember our wonderful long discussions over tea and sherry in your living room (which has become a second home to me) and at the Brookline Country Club that lovely evening last summer![1]

Christmas has always been for me the time of reunion with those dearest people one carries in one's heart through the separation and work of the year. At this time, I want you to know that in spirit I am very close to you, loving you dearly, more than words can tell.

Mother is looking so forward to playgoing with you! I know that your friendship is most cherished by her. Aren't you proud of her getting her license! I feel so happy about her expanding life, and hope very much to share some of it with her this summer.

I'll be writing again after the holidays. Meanwhile, my very best love to you . . . .

your loving
Sylvia

TO *Aurelia Schober Plath*

Wednesday 14 December 1955 TLS (aerogramme), Indiana University

wednesday evening
december 14

dearest mother . . .

I feel about as exhausted verbally as a literary santa claus! I have just got through the most colossal job of writing my christmas letters: a huge project involving sending long letters with christmas cards to about 20 people and cards with short messages to about 10 more. I made an effort to choose special art cards (like the one I sent you) and witty line drawings (like Warren's) to suit the individuals, and each time I wrote a letter, I took out the last letter from them, read it, thought about them, and about my sharing of life with them, and wrote a really particularly personal letter

1–According to SP's calendar, she had dinner with Olive Higgins Prouty at the Brookline Country Club on 14 July 1955 and 10 September 1955.

to them all: including, to name only a few: mr. crockett, the cantors, mary ellen chase, all three freemans, the lameyers, patsy, mrs. prouty, marty & mike, alison smith, sue weller, elly friedman, mr. fisher & mr. kazin! I also sent little art postcards to about 5 neighbors, just to show I was thinking of them. the one letter remaining is dr. beuscher's, which, since I haven't written her before, will be especially long and full. just thought I'd tell you, so you'd know these people would be hearing from me! I simply can't maintain a continuous correspondence with anyone but you during term, and will probably write them all once a term. I want to plan to write on my own for a good two hours a day this term, no matter what, and really can't throw forth all my creative verbal energy on a project like this more than two or three times a year. spent about $15 on the air mail stamps and art postcards! but it was more than worth it. I really felt I was communicating in a deep sense with all those I wrote to, and let them know it.

I am making out my re-application for a fulbright this week, and feel sorry that it will be judged completely on what I have done this term, as I just feel my head above water now, and my roots taking firm grip. all this term has been "living", experiencing life widely so I can select a disciplined program for the rest of this year without that tantalizing distracting sense of the "untried." I am giving up the ADC for writing regularly a few hours a day, cutting my class schedule so I can do more reading & meditating, and narrowing my social life down to mallory and one or two good friends. but I had to try everything to be able to choose with such sureness: "you can never know enough without knowing more than enough,"[1] as blake says: "the road to excess leads to the palace of wisdom."[2]

I am really sure the fulbright won't be renewed and so am writing smith to see if it would be possible to re-apply for the fellowship I was offered last year. by certain subtle illegal money-changing among friends, I will probably be able to live and travel abroad in these two long winter & spring vacations, but lord knows what about the 3 month summer. my one hope is that in my writing later this vac (I'm coming back here 10 days early before term) and during next term something salable may turn up. but I am rather pessimistic about it. with the return of my borestone mountain ms., all my pigeons are home to roost. gone are the days where

1–William Blake, *The Marriage of Heaven and Hell*. SP slightly misquotes 'Proverbs of Hell': 'You never know what is enough unless you know what is more than enough.'
2–Blake, *The Marriage of Heaven and Hell*. SP slightly misquotes 'Proverbs of Hell': 'The road of excess leads to the palace of wisdom.'

I got prizes for everything. this mature market-competition demands constant writing, so instead of waiting for a whole bulk of time, which I come to rusty and paralytic, I am going to do an hour or two every day, like czerny exercises on the piano. I want to get enough written so I can have several things out and get rid of this sense of a financial deadend: even intangible hope is a better state!

I must remember, too that I owe good Dr. Beuscher at least $50. I will try to trace her old friend and buy something for her little son when I come back, after Paris.

Speaking of Paris, I shall be flying there on next Tuesday, December 20th, and the surest mailing adress will be: c/o American Express 11 Rue Scribe, Paris V. Until Thursday, jan.5, when I return to England, perhaps to stay with Mallory's family in London a day or two before going back to Cambridge.

So Ruthie is expecting a baby? That is lovely. I was also very happy to hear about Dick Norton and Joanne Colburn:[1] they should be very happy, but I must admit I thought Dick would never settle for someone so quiet and delicate. He has fortunately changed from the old days when he was so arrogantly demanding of health, so critical of looks. I still feel Perry has by far the best combination of all this in vital, intelligent, beautiful Shirley. Perhaps we will run into the Nortons in Europe. Do tell me, by the way, what time roughly you plan to come over next summer! I look so forward to showing you Cambridge.

These two weeks have ended up by being mostly for rest, business affairs, and Christmas shopping & letters. I think they will stand me in good stead in the three weeks to come. Saturday is the wedding, and I leave with John Lythgoe right afterwards for London, where we will go to plays & look at the Christmas windows. I opened one present in my stocking every night before bed, and could practically put each thing immediately in my Paris suitcase: so thoughtful! I must admit that it is fortunate I shall be "having a whirl" in London & Paris with John, Nat & Sassoon, & Mallory, for it will take my mind off feeling sorry for myself at missing you so! I really feel it at this time.

My dearest love to all . . .
Sivvy

p.s. reveled in your magnificent description of grampy's DAY.

1–Richard Allen Norton and Joanne Colburn (1932–) married on 9 June 1956, at the Wellesley Hills Unitarian Church, Wellesley.

PS: overjoyed by your account of grampy's Day. have read it over & over again. just regretfully finished the last of grammy's wonderful cookies. such a lovely package that was! every present was wrapped like an objet d'art!

Got lovely pre-Paris pageboy trim here for only 50¢!

TO *Jon K. Rosenthal*

Wednesday 14 December 1955 TLS in greeting card (photocopy),[1] Smith College

<printed greeting>

With all Good Wishes / for Christmas / and the Coming Year

<signed>

sylvia / → / (see inside)

December 14th, 1955

Dear Jon . . .

It was so great to get your letter and all the news. I haven't stopped running, like Alice trying to keep in the same place, since I boarded the Queen in NYC. At present, I wisely decided to stop, recheck batteries for two weeks after our term ended, and store up sleep and contemplation for a while before venturing to Paris. Because that's where I'm spending Christmas. I can't believe it yet, but that's what the ticket says. It says that.

To begin to sum up life here is like trying to put a camel caravan through the proverbial needle. First, Cambridge is the most divine town to live in: a daily open market with booths of flowers, tropical fruit from the colonies in midwinter, vegetables, antiques, old books; the lazy narrow river Cam up which we punt, under the Bridge of Sighs, the spires of King's Chapel, Newton's Bridge, weeping willows, through flurries of white swans; wedding-cake architecture; green velvet lawns; the unique feeling of centuries and centuries of history and tradition everywhere; narrow cobbled streets, ancient black cabs, two story red busses; tea drunk by work men even, leaden pastry & custard sauce; my room in a tremendous house for 12 grad students, a kind of attic studio with my favorite art reproductions, a gas fire that eats up shillings like mad, a single gas ring on which I have managed to create a steak dinner complete with sherry, hors d'oeuvres, salad, etc. in rebellion versus English cooking. All this, and classes too.

1–Card designed by Franciszka Themerson.

The three terms are short, made mainly for classes & "living"; vacs are very long, made for sustained reading as well as travel. I have been mainly living. Theater everywhere: joined Amateur Dramat Club and have been in two plays, including Ben Johnson's hilarious "Bartholomew Fair", the ADC centenary production which ran 9 nights & was reviewed by London Times. Great experience. Dan Massey, Raymond Massey's son, was hero. "Amateur" here means as close to pro as you can get. Foreign films, surrealist films, concerts: the hardest thing is to choose, to limit, to discipline.

Am giving up theater to read & write more next semester. As for travel, I feel so much like you do about it. When everything was hypothetical & very distant in the States, I could dream with great confidence. Now I feel like a starving woman facing a smorgasbord of delicacies with the terrible problem of choice! You have to begin somewhere, so I'm starting with Paris and leaving some days open the first five days in January. I have varying & passionate desires to go to Spain, Italy & Greece. Also, this summer, want to use that map to Africa. How to choose? It's really more frustrating that I ever thought possible: I want both to "see the world" and to live for long enough in each place to really be simpatico, to be permeated with the atmosphere; yet how can I decide where I'd like to stay best if I haven't seen a lot? I'd love to know what you've decided to do, & my address in Paris from Dec. 20 on, for at least a week or 10 days, will be simply: c/o American Express, 11 Rue Scribe, Paris V. Write me there if you get any inspirations. Hope I'll have learned to speak French by that time!

I also have great longings, after this damp, gray, English atmosphere, to find the sun on the Med. Having no money to speak of, this is a problem, & I am seriously thinking of trying to find a patron in Paris. Spent 10 days in London, by the way, & really like it: went to a play every night, very very cheap; 50 good theaters, small, intimate. Walked miles from avant garde cafe espresso houses in Chelsea to international dives in Soho, from Trafalgar Square, with its dolphin fountains[1] & squadrons of pigeons to Picadilly Circus & the fountain of Eros; it's a great, impressive place, with lots of exquisite parks, swans, flowers (on every corner, fruit carts, barrel organs, & chalk artists) and countless public monuments. But I look to Paris for that intense emotional rapport which I simply don't feel for the delicately boned frosty-eyed, terribly proper English. My best friends here

1–Plath drafted a sketch of the dolphin fountains. See Appendix 11, *The Unabridged Journals of Sylvia Plath, June 1957–June 1960*, entry 97[a–c].

are Jewish or negro. FLASH: just got your very appropriate & witty card: if you want a cook, girl friday & news correspondent & part-time driver to scandinavia or turkey in april, let me know!

Do write me in Paris!
Love,
Syl

TO *Marcia B. Stern*

c. Wednesday 14 December 1955   TLS in greeting card,[1] Smith College

<printed greeting>
With all Good Wishes / for Christmas / and the Coming Year from
<signed>
and much love / Sylvia / ↓ / (see inside)

Dear Marty & Mike . . .

A Merry Christmas to YOU! It was so great to get your newsy letter: I now know how our fighting armed forces must have appreciated the smallest details about people and affairs at home! The new job, Marty, sounds at last really worthy of you: what a tremendous double-perspective you must have on Cambridge life: pink Brooks Bros. shirts versus tattered diapers! I like to visualize you in that apartment, which appeals to me natively from color & texture to content.

How to begin? I am now sitting in my room by a whistling gas fire (which scalds the side nearest it & leaves the other as cold as the back of the moon) looking out over my Cambridge vista of bare, mottled sycamore trees, orange-tile rooftops with chimneypots around which hover enormous back rooks (or ravens, if you like Edgar Allen Poe) which have an unquieting habit of eyeing one with more than casual intensity: I am sure they eat small children after dark! I've had a tremendous time decorating this kind of attic-studio room: two tall bookcases spilling over with all the old & new volumes (bought on my lush book-allowance: for once I can afford art books!), the indispensable black-and-white earthenware & enamel teaset from Holland, piles of fresh fruit from the daily open market in the center of town, great bouquets of Van-Gogh-type yellow chrysanthemums, vivid postcard reprints of Picasso from Nat. Galleries from NYC to London; candles in wine bottles, and a gas ring

1 – On Christmas card designed by Franciszka Themerson.

on which I have produced a steak dinner complete with salad, wine, in sherry-soaked fruit compote. It's like having an apartment of my own, & I love having "salons" at tea and dinners for two.

By now I am used to biking at least ten miles a day, to and from town & classes; to seeing my breath come out in frosty white puffs while taking a bath; to the college diet of cold mashed potatoes & ubiquitous yellow custard; to men making tea; to muddy coffee; to butter that keeps hard as a rock in my room for weeks. And I love it all.

Honestly, this is the loveliest town in the world. The sleepy little river Cam (about as wide as Linnean Street) winds through the "Backs" of the colleges, under weeping willows & apple trees & gothic spires of King's Chapel, afloat with white swans. I have been punted up the river to Rupert Brooke's Granchester for tea, scones, & Cambridgeshire honey, where the clock is always set at 10 to three, and tea is served in the apple orchard in the spring. I've eaten at avant garde Cafe Expresso houses where inter-national crowds congregate: Indians, Arabs, Negroes, South Africans, plus a crew of Scandinavian girls who come to study English; learned to like mango chutney, bindhi gusht, prawn pelavi at the Indian "Taj Mahal"; the main problem with life here is to choose between the fantastic fanatically demanding activities: there are clubs for everything from puppetry to piloting, communists to heretics, wine tasters to beaglers! Indifference is the cardinal sin.

The short terms (3 of 8 weeks) are mostly for "living" & classes, the long vacations for reading, thinking . . . and traveling. I've spent most of my energy "adapting" to the texture of life here, choosing between greater of goods with much difficulty. I joined the powerful Amateur Dramatic Society here (the only one of the many Cambridge acting groups with its own theater) after an audition and have taken part in two plays so far, the most exciting being: Ben Jonson's hilarious "Bartholomew Fair", the A.D.C. centenary production which ran for 9 nights & was reviewed in the London <u>Times</u>! There's always theater here, and the amateur is as demanding and professional as can be: one Cambridge actor signed a contract for the lead in Samuel Beckett's lovely, controversial, symbolic play in London, "Waiting for Godot," which they thought would flop. Now he cant come back! (Beckett, by the way, was James Joyce's secretary, which perhaps accounts for some of his tragi-comic ambiguity).

O Marty, just seeing, hearing, & being alive in the town is a dream. You would love the open market, full of fresh fruits from the colonies (apples, pineapples, figs & dates in midwinter), fresh flowers, vegetables from neighboring farms, antiques, parakeets, old book bargains, everything!

There are foreign films, avant garde surrealist films, debates. Even the Queen & Duke came to visit us at Newnham, and I stood within a few feet of the handsome wise-cracking Duke, while the Queen radiated quietly. Even though it was pouring rain, every person in Cambridge turned out to cheer the Royal procession. We stand at attention to "God Save the Queen" at the end of movies, dances & plays (once I made the fatal mistake of thinking it was a new dance!) & I must say, I am beginning to feel loyal!

I am getting to know some magnificent people: there's friendly, vital Nathaniel LaMar (whose story "Creole Love Song" was in the Atlantic) the negro writer who knew Warren at Harvard & Exeter. He's getting me a place to stay on the Left Bank in Paris over Christmas, & is good for simple, frank, "American talk." My favorite man is a tall, raven-haired, scarlet-cheeked Jewish boy from Darjeeling, India, who has introduced me to the world of music: carried an organ to my room, & now I have afternoons of Bach, Beethoven, Scarlatti, even "Greensleeves." His name is Mallory Wober, and he looks exactly the way I always imagined Dmitri Karamazov would. Will visit his family in London (he is, unbelievably, only 19, but much older than the "older" men I know in every way.) Sort of an Old Testament Hercules. You should see!

Have heard much about dear Peter Davison via others: evidently as Alceste in Wilbur's translation of the "Misanthrope"[1] he was fine. All the friends he had me look up in London were, alas, homosexuals. And his sister[2] was quite mad. I felt most disgustingly normal.

London (10 days) was a heaven of plays (very cheap, with tea in interval on little trays), bookstalls outdoors, large flurries of pigeons around the rainbow fountains and spouting dolphins in Trafalgar Square. Regal parks, most international & wicked Soho: will pay return visit this week on way to Paris, which I still can't believe will come true. I'll be hanging tinsel & colored baubles on the Eiffel Tower.

Do write; I so long to see you again. Meanwhile, much, much love to you.

From the Other Cambridge: and your wandering

Syl

1–Richard Wilbur's translation of Molière's *The Misanthrope*, performed at the Poets' Theatre, 24 Palmer Street, Cambridge, Mass., 31 October–6 November 1955, and then at the Kresge Auditorium, MIT, 9–12 November 1955.

2–Lesley Davison Perrin (*c.* 1931–2014); according to SP's calendar, Lesley Davison lived at 26 Chepstow Villas, London W11; met on 26 and 27 September 1955.

TO *J. Mallory Wober*

Thursday 15 December 1955[1] TLS with envelope, Cambridge University

Thursday evening
5: 45 p.m.

ITEM: I like your third thoughts. My room now is looking more and more like a picture gallery (rogue's gallery?) or a kind of photographic shrine. I like it this way; sometimes I can hardly believe you really look these ways. The photographs constantly reassure me: yes, they affirm silently, it is possible.

FLASH: although Golder's Green Tube Station is not on my map of central London, I shall continue to act on faith and be there at 3 o'clock Sunday. I can't believe it will happen: my being in London again; you being there too. But, as I say, I shall act on faith.

I just finished my last Christmas letter: 13 pages. I am amazed that I can still form words. I wrote 20 long letters, and 10 short messages. I never realized quite so intensely what wonderful people I have known: relatives, professors, writers, vital girls & philanthropists who have adopted me: each time I wrote a letter, I chose either a special art-reproduction card or witty pen & ink drawing (those we saw at the crafts shop) chosen particularly for that person, re-read their letters, reminisced about the past life we'd shared, and really "talked" to them: never did one person's descriptions of Cambridge have so many personal, different slants! I now feel a pleasant sense of communication with those back home: like, metaphorically, sending slices of my self by air mail in Christmas wrappings. It is, Confucius says, the thought that counts.

Please let me tell you a few things: re beard: I would not mind in the least if your face was clean-shaven when I meet you in London! I happen to think you look fine either way. I just also happened to enjoy the rugged, prophetic, appearance your beard gave you, which surprised me, as generally I dislike beards on men: they usually hide a weak chin or pallid complexion or something unpleasant. Yours is the first beard I have actively admired, because it outlines the strength of your bone structure & color. So there. Do what you wish with it. I shall be perfectly happy either way.

Also: realize that for once and for all, it is the <u>essential</u> you that matters most to me: and whether you stop carrying up organs, writing letters, or whatever, I <u>still</u> will feel this way. In other words, my feelings don't

1–Date supplied from postmark.

depend on the external manifestations of your personality, although I naturally find them most pleasant. It is that inner strength and potential and sensitivity which is impossible to completely express in words, that intangible "self" of yours which I am drawn to admire. So be true to your highest self, and I will be happy, because that is what I want you to be, even if it means eventual growing away from me in the unforseeable future.

Now I will stop, because when I philosophize, you sometimes think I am lecturing, which I am not really. It just sounds that way. I am really only trying to talk to you and with you to try to share the ways I feel and think.

Most of my time here has been spent in writing letters, reading a little Strindberg (you were right), talking with Dick Wertz (the boy who rode beside our organ caravan) over two long teatimes, because he needed someone to listen about this girl at home he is in love with. (English majors never get their prepositions in the right place!) and doing last minute errands. I am evidently eager for vacation: my suitcase has been packed for a whole day already, although I don't leave till late Saturday afternoon. (I will probably just make "Salad Days"[1] by the way, without time for supper!) It will be frustrating to see so little of London, especially so little of you. I'd love to browse in Charing Cross, watch the pigeons & dolphin fountains in Trafalgar Square, window-shop on Christmas-lighted Regent Street, see "La Strada"[2] at the Curzon, and on and on!

But no. By the way, if you and your mother are really serious about having me stay over-night sometime, how about right when I return from Paris on the evening of the 6th? It would be so wonderful to look forward to meeting you in London & spending a couple of days with you before heading back to the stoic life at Cambridge. That would be the best part of my whole vacation!

I have decided to write for at least two hours every day this next term, starting by returning 10 days before to get in the habit before classes begin: like practicing finger exercises: describing events, people, scenes: keeping the typewriter hot, instead of waiting for the perfect time to write a whole story at one fell swoop: the perfect time never comes, & if it does, you're paralysed from lack of practice. This will take the place of the A.D.C.

1–A musical then playing at the Vaudeville Theatre, The Strand, London. According to SP's calendar, she saw *Salad Days* with John Lythgoe on Saturday 17 December 1955.

2–An Italian film by Federico Fellini released in 1954 and playing at the Curzon Cinema, 38 Curzon Street, Mayfair, London W1.

I also want to work (i.e. write thoughtful papers & read widely) more this term, so when I am refused my Fulbright renewal, I will at least have the bittersweet conviction that they are making a grave mistake! I think you will find me much more bearable when I am producing fruitfully in writing & academically. It will be hard at first, as is all discipline (the dreams of ideal perfection are so much more entrancing than the imperfect compromises with reality!) but I should flower with the spring!

Please send me anything you write; or feel like writing about your thoughts. It doesn't matter a whit if anything is "merely mediocre or honestly bad": the importance is if you had fun & enjoyed the process of writing it. It's like climbing a mountain: even if you don't make the peaks all the time, it's the process that is the important, exhilarating thing.

Know that I am thinking of you. Don't let the mere chance or frequency of letters cause you to doubt for a minute that wherever I am, you are very much in the center of my heart . . . .

with my love,
sylvia

TO *J. Mallory Wober*

c. Sunday 18 December 1955[1] TLS, Cambridge University

FRAGILE!
HANDLE WITH EXTREME CARE!
CAUTION!
BREAKABLE!

"One little pig went to the market,
one little pig stayed home,
one little pig had roast beef,
and one little pig had none . . ."

THIS little pig seems to have had his cake and eaten it too . . . his specially favorite fruit is pears and this is written all over him. His chief ambition in life is to Stand Among the Illustrious Company on Mallory's Mantel. He also wishes to be quoted saying: "Love and Merry Christmas to J. Mallory Wober."

from Piglet, Esq.

1–Date supplied from internal evidence.

TO *J. Mallory Wober*

Monday 19 December 1955[1] ALS in greeting card[2] with envelope, Cambridge University

Dear Mallory . . .

A copy of my favorite Old King,[3] who bears somehow, – because of a certain strength, a magnificent black beard, and vivid, stained-glass colors – a distant resemblance to my favorite young King: to say how many other private snapshots I carry away, wrapped in cellophane of frost and spangled with Regent Street stars: pink and violet anemones in a gold basket; hymns on a mellow, versatile organ; paintings around the color wheel – calm green hills, red-brown groves of trees, blue of sea, sky & ships; malt bread for tea in violet-sprigged cups; orange japanese lanterns vivid, warm, witty aunts; wonderful supper on gay checked plates; then, dream-walk through mist, underground, – to lights, carols, hot roasted chestnuts, conversational Bobby, surrealist mushrooms in Trafalgar Square, top-story of red bus – all this is Christmas-wrapped in my heart – and will be with me in Paris to sustain me till the New Year which will really begin when I am with you again . . .

Love from your own –
sylvia

<inside of card>
sylvia
<on envelope>
From: Somewhere above English Channel
Altitude: unknown

1 – Date supplied from postmark (Paris, France, 24 December 1955).
2 – On a Soho Gallery Christmas card.
3 – Georges Rouault, 'The Old King' (1937). Card from Soho Gallery, 18 Soho Square, London. The painting is now held in the Carnegie Museum of Art, Pittsburgh, Pennsylvania.

TO *J. Mallory Wober*

Friday 23 December 1955[1]

ALS (picture postcard), Cambridge University

<picture postcard caption>

6331. Joan MIRÓ. Femmes, oiseau au clair de lune (1949). 81 x 65. Women, and bird in the moonlight. Frauen, vogel im mondschein. Donne, Uccello al chiaro di luna. Mujeres, pájaro al claro de luna. Collection Galerie Maeght.

Friday

Dear Mallory . . .

Love & greetings from me & Miro's gay, floating people who look the way Paris makes me feel – after 3 days like a comedy of errors involving jolting across the channel in ferry & being locked out of my hotel room the 1st night by a thoughtless roommate[2] & having to sleep on the floor with some strange loquacious Swiss. Am just beginning to feel very happy: so far! The Louvre, lovely stained glass chapel of Ste. Chappelle,[3] from Marché aux fleurs[4] – drinks from cognac to citron pressé at hundreds of cafés – am stammering French, loving people & buildings – now settled in blue velvet room[5] on brink of Seine – will write more later –

much love
– sylvia

TO *J. Mallory Wober*

Thursday 29 December 1955

TLS with envelope, Cambridge University

Thursday night
December 29th

Dearest Mallory . . .

It is a wet, rainy night in Paris, and if I pull back the dark=blue velvet curtains of my hotel room window I can look down and see red, green,

1–Date supplied from postmark.
2–Jane Baltzell Kopp.
3–La Sainte-Chapelle, Île de la Cité, Paris.
4–The Flower Market, on Île de la Cité, Paris.
5–According to SP's calendar, she took a room in the Hotel de la Harpe, then at 6 Rue de la Harpe, Paris.

yellow & pink colored lights of the foreign restaurants below, reflecting in the puddled streets. I can see through the lighted windows across the way: negroes, chinese, french faces, eating, drinking, talking. My street is never quiet: all through the night voices talk under my balcony window, taxis screech past, drunks shout and bang their heads against the pavement. It is a conglomerate oriental quarter, on the corner of the left bank between the Boul' Mich and the Boulevard St. Germain, about a five minute walk from the Ile de la Cité in the middle of the Seine, and Notre Dame cathedral. Everywhere I walk I pass little avant garde art stores, wine & oyster shops, sidewalk booths which offer every thing from roasted chestnuts to gambling lotteries to shooting galleries. It is one enormous cosmic circus.

I went to the American Express for the first time yesterday (you have no idea how difficult it is to find practical places like that & like post offices in a strange city) and found, among about 15 christmas cards, four letters from you. Somehow I felt very frustrated, because your letters made me want to tell you so many things, face to face, immediately, and I feel so far away from everything and everybody now: time has no meaning any more, because all here is so new and strange and terrible and wonderful all at once: it is like the combination of heaven and hell in one colossal surrealistic dream and I have lost all sense of clock time or calendar dates: please, try to understand this!

In the first place, let's talk about you. I loved your robin and fish, which I opened the first night I arrived in Paris and which gave me no end of comfort and delight: especially the robin, who is artistically all one could ask, and most cheering! I also loved your poem-ballad about London, especially the last verse with the wonderful images of light & shining London town. Now, let me scold you a little: I hope this letter arrives in time for you to know right away that I am only too happy that you are seeing Bernice and I hope you see a lot of her and that I have a chance to meet her when I come. I think it is very wrong of you to feel that any sentiments you have for me should rigidly cancel out all former feeling and make that continuing tenderness "tabu". Please remember that it is <u>you</u> and not I who is apparently attempting to stifle normal feelings for Bernice: for I feel that you should accept the challenge of seeing her, with your increased maturity and see what happens. There is nothing that makes a girl appreciate the true worth of a man more than if she thinks there is another girl in the picture, and I would be only too happy to be of service to you in this situation. I beg you to see Bernice often, to enjoy her, to feel perfectly <u>right</u> and not at all guilty in doing so. And don't think

I say this because I want you to stop seeing me or being fond of me or something like that, because it is not true. I love and admire you and want you to grow to be the strong, powerful, vital man I feel has awakened in you even now: this is because I truly love you beyond the pettiness of any personal jealousies or desires to limit you, like a horse in blinders, to looking soley at me! Love is not narrow and confining: it wants to grow, even at the expense of personal loss or sorrow. And that is what I want for you. If it means Bernice, I shall be very happy for you.

I ask you to understand what I say to you now, and to realize that my rather weird life in Paris has cut me off from my customary methods of regular writing and living. Today, for example, I got up and had breakfast at 5 in the afternoon, because I didn't get to sleep till the small hours this morning, and now that it is approaching theater time I am thinking of having lunch. So, in addition, I have whole new worlds to absorb, and am constantly fighting to understand Parisian French which is almost impossible as they speak fantastically fast. Thus I shall reserve all detailed explaining till I see you next, which, I hope (barring plane crashes) will be a week from tomorrow (Friday!) at the Victoria Coach Station, about 6:15 p.m. in the evening, at the Skyways terminal (ask where that is: it's around a sort of bus terminal, & Skyways is an airline). I sincerely hope that I will have better luck coming home than I did coming over! If there is blizzard weather here, or strikes, which might delay me, I shall telegraph you Friday morning, the 6th. Cross your fingers for me.

Now, reassure me that you understand: 1) I love you still, always, no matter what happens, whether mails fail, or I can't find post offices, or whatever; 2) I want you to see Bernice and enjoy her as a fine person & give yourself a chance to see how you really feel about her, because I am far from being the strict, rigid judge of yourself that you are and feel that rules should grow from natural feelings and not be imposed on them. Very simply, if you, in your new mature strength, find she is the "choice" for you, make it with my blessing! As long as you are happy about it truly, I will be, too!

Now, for a little about Paris. After the first horror of our plane flight being canceled and crossing a rough channel with people vomiting everywhere in white enamel basins, and being locked out of my hotel room by a careless roommate so that I had to sleep on the floor with strangers, I moved from my first hotel, where I had caused several rows on account of said roommate, who also took off for Italy with the key to the room, and came to this nice blue room, with blue velvet curtains, which is only 400 francs a night and near the Seine, and the Metro, and life in general. I have fallen in love with the city. It is all light, airy, spacious, with the white-grays of a Utrillo[1] painting. Christmas, I went to services in Notre Dame, with its flower-decked altar to the Virgin, exquisite rose windows, and enchanting gargoyles. I have walked everywhere: up the Champs Elyssés, of course, at night, to the lighted Arc de Triomphe, past countless blazing shops; up the steep, quaint hill of Montmartre, throught the artist quarters, under the magnificent, white, lighted dome of Sacre Coeur; through place Pigalle (which is like Times Square, N.Y.C., or Piccadilly) where the bleached, painted whores in furs walk everywhere, and I've overheard men bargaining, and even had a whore scream at me for looking at her, but I couldn't help it: I have to stare at everything! The most beautiful sight was the Sainte Chapelle next to the Palais de Justice which I must show you some day: it is very perfect Gothic, pure, soaring, made almost completely of stained glass: a veritable jewel box of blazing colored light: Ive browsed in bookstalls along the Seine, drunk wine, cinzano, orange pressé (squeezed at the table) in countless sidewalk cafes, eaten oysters & snails, seen the Paris Ballet of Roland Petit, a play in French by Emlyn Williams ("Le Monsieur qui attend"[2]), and 2 good French movies:[3] am trying for the French Riviera this week: these are just notes to give you an idea. The rest will wait until I see you next Friday. Please, keep on writing, as it means a lot. And know that I love you no matter what.

À bientôt, your own,
sylvia

1–French painter Maurice Utrillo (1883–1955), famous for his depictions of Parisian street scenes.

2–Performed at the Comédie Caumartin, 25 rue Caumartin, Paris. In English, *Someone Waiting* (London: Heinemann, 1954).

3–According to SP's calendar, she saw *Les Carnets du Major Thompson* and *Vive Monsieur le Maire*.

TO *Aurelia Schober Plath*

Friday 30 December 1955[1] — TLS with envelope, Indiana University

Saturday p.m[2]
December 30th

Dearest mother . . .

I am sitting at present in the lobby of a Paris hotel surrounded by wonderfully strange people all running in and out talking French rapidly. Where to begin? I have been here almost twelve days and am now packed and ready to leave for Nice, on the Cote d'Azur to spend a few days staring at the Mediterranean and hoping to find the sun there also: every day I've been here it's been pouring rain! But somehow, in spite of a fantastic nightmarish arrival (plane flight was canceled because of bad weather in France, boat crossing was really stormy and rough, with countless people vomiting all over the deck in the white enamel basins: I was only a little groggy and managed to come through fine with brandy; and a late arrival, after being on the road about 15 hours, having my roommate from Whitstead, Jane Baltzell, who brightened the way by sharing these experiences, ask if I'd share the room Nat LaMar had reserved with her and her falling asleep inside, with the key in the lock, so all my yells & poundings wouldn't wake her; so I had to sleep in one bed with two very vivacious, friendly girls from Switzerland who were studying English at Cambridge) . . . all this, and the fact that my period waited till now to descend, a week late: and yet, I have loved Paris, and feel at last that I know it passing fair. In spite of the fact I have had one or two real waves of homesickness, I've been going regularly to the American Express, where I've got about 20 or 25 letters and cards so far, including a check for $25 from dear Mrs. Prouty, and your thoughtful registered letter & money. All this has made Paris seem friendly and more like home. I really don't know how to begin telling you all the wonderful things I've done and seen!

First of all, Sassoon has been a godsend. He's taken me all the places women can't go alone, at night, and spoken French a good deal with me, and helped settle some of the heated confusion at my hotel when Jane calmly set off to Italy with the key to our room: she is very casual, that girl. Anyhow, I've walked miles and miles, along the gray Seine, browsing in the countless bookstalls which sell original watercolors and sketches

1 – Letter misdated by SP.

2 – '~~Thursday evening~~ Saturday p.m' appears in the original.

and all kinds of paper=covered books and prints; I've seen the beautiful jeweled women with exquisite furs at the theater: have seen a French translation of Emlyn Williams excellent suspense play: "Le Monsieur qui attend", the Paris Ballet of Roland Petit (two parts being my favorites: a legend of a young girl who found faith and love in a wolf instead of her fickle fiancé, and "La Chambre",[1] a surrealistic psychological ballet in a circle of action about a murder and a vampire, most magnificently danced), and last night it was the Comédie Française[2] to see an exquisitely moving "Jeanne D'Arc" by the French writer Charles Peguy. I've really had to concentrate to understand what was going on, as the French speak very fast when moved (and they are always moved) and the divisions between words are difficult to hear, but I have really improved in my week or more here.

Perhaps I've enjoyed most just walking and feasting my eyes: Sassoon took me to the Place Pigalle at night where all the painted whores are, and I was really overcome to see how they worked: it's like a play itself, and most fascinating. Everywhere on the main Boulevards there are all kinds of booths and stands set up on the wide sidewalks, selling trinkets, colored bowls of candy and nuts and marrons glace, lottery tickets, neckties, and mounds of oranges, grapes, bananas and dates and figs which I've been indulging in like mad: never ate so many oranges!

I've walked up the brilliantly lighted Champs Elyssés at night past flashing cinemas and expensive shops, to the illuminated Arc de Triomphe, wandered down the Rue de la Paix with its jewelry stores and esoteric shops, climbed the steep crooked streets to the summit of the hill of Montmartre under the blazing white dome of Sacre Coeur, the fabulous bohemian quarter, and eaten oysters and drunk wine at a little cafe in the Place du Tertre, which all the artists paint. Everywhere outside the multitudinous cafes are open boxes of lemons and oysters and snails, keeping cold (it is colder than London here!) and enticing to the passer=by. Even the faces on the street are fascinating: many Africans, and beautiful young people (that's what I miss in London . . . everyone is so un-chic and dowdy and formal). Here, the hotel people love their work, and the waiters too, and at one little cafe on my street, which is on the Left Bank in the Oriental & Greek quarter, the manageress of a little cafe gave a bowl of soup & a stick of bread to an old, toothless beggar who,

1–Georges Simenon, *La Chambre*, a detective-story ballet performed at the Théâtre des Champs-Elysees.
2–The Comédie Française, 1 Place Colette, Paris.

she told us, was once a clown in the circus and has gone mad, but is very harmless.

Let me tell you about Christmas day: Sassoon took me to Notre Dame in the morning where we sat in the dark, enormous interior of the church near the shining altar to the Virgin and child, covered with pink and white flowers: the purple, blue, red and cold rose windows of the transepts were an aesthetic feast, and the mammoth organ sounded really like the voice of god. I thought especially of you at home, and the people I love, and was most moved by the clusters of thin tapers burning on the altars and the blazing jeweled colors of the windows. I also walked about the enchanting Isle de la Cité in the middle of the Seine, and marveled at the exquisite jewel-Gothic structure of the Sainte Chapelle in the Palais de Justice, where there seems to be nothing at all holding together the soaring stained=glass windows, which lift one's eyes upward in a dizzy leap of vivid, painted glass.

I've walked through the Louvre, too, and seen the Winged Victory atop a flight of marble steps, powerful enough to soar through the very rook of that enormous museum. The Mona Lisa smiled her mystic golden smile at me and I found some of my favorites: "Virgin of the Rocks" and several thin, torturous El Grecos, a marvelous anonymous Pieta d'Avignon, Breughel, and my beloved Flemish school, with the meticulous, loving detail. Went also to a wonderful exhibit of the Impressionists which you would have enjoyed at the Orangerie, a small museum in the Jardin deS Tuileries and saw much excellent Cezanne (fell in love with the blending blue=greens and subtle touches of peach in his "Lac D'annecy"), and many familiar Van Goghs (Sunflowers, Man with Cut Ear,[1] etc.) and Gaugins, with their weird sallow greens & yellows and purply reds against the golden & brown native flesh. Also a few good drawings by Picasso, an enchanting Henri Rousseau in his primitive style. After this I had a wonderful time with Richard in the Garden of the Tuileries where we spent the whole afternoon watching the children playing with their new Christmas toys: roller skates, hoops, shiny new dolls, bikes, swings, sailboats on the boat=pond: the Jardin is made for children: long rows of trees, countless statues, swings, merrygoround, donkey=carts, ponies, and even the famous daily puppet show which we went to amid the little excited children who yelled and talked to the magnificent puppets which I found utterly enchanting. Oh, it is all so amazing here, and so lovely. I've seen all the tourists want to see and so much more, because I've had

1–Probably Van Gogh's 'Self-Portrait with Bandaged Ear'.

time to live, to browse in art shops, to nibble roasted chestnuts on the wonderful efficient Metro, to enjoy my blue velvet room which overlooks a noisy street of little foreign restaurants and costs only $1.20 a night, with 50¢ extra for coffee and croissons in bed! Will write more later from Nice. Meanwhile, all my love to all of you, and to all our dear friends. I miss you, but am learning to live through trial and error: everything new is hard, as well as exciting! Saw Olivier's "Richard 3rd" movie[1] in London & a terrific musical called "Salad Days". Ate like a queen.

Bye for now & all my love to you –
sivvy

PS. Happy New Year!

1–*Richard III* (1955), starring Laurence Olivier, played at the Leicester Square Theatre. According to SP's calendar she saw this on 19 December 1955.

1956

TO *Aurelia Schober Plath*

Sunday 1 January 1956[1] ALS (picture postcard), Indiana University

<picture postcard caption>

PRINCIPAUTE DE MONACO Vue générale / Au loin le Cap Martin et l'Italie.

Jan. 1

Dearest mother . . .

I began the New Year on an express train which sped through the night, away from rain & clouds into clear moonlight shining on the Med, a red sun rising out of an incredibly blue sea, palm trees sprouting by pink & yellow villas, and, sunrise on snowcapped mountain peaks. I can hardly believe my eyes! Climbed the steep hill overlooking the blue "Baie des Anges", all sparkling pink & white steps winding up to summit – cacti, strange palms, illuminated by night, flower & fruit markets, and the blessed "Cote d'Azur" at my feet. Nice is exquisite – am going to feast on color & sun – still crisp & cool – but wonderfully invigorating – more later –

love –
sivvy

1–Postmarked 5 January 1956.

TO *J. Mallory Wober*

Sunday 1 January 1956[1] ALS (picture postcard), Cambridge University

<picture postcard caption>

REFLETS DE LA COTE D'AZUR. JUAN-LES-PINS. 06.997.15. – La Plage.

HAPPY NEW YEAR!

Dear Mallory –

I changed years last night aboard an express train cutting through France to the Côte d'Azur: a red sun rose out of an incredibly blue sea as I ate breakfast en route, practically screaming with joy at the feast of color before me: pink & yellow villas, green palms & cacti, sparkling white casinos & vivid blue-inlets. Am staying at Nice for a few days – climbing quaint steep hills of palms & fountains to see sunrise on the snowcapped mountains – walking along the quais at night – all is unbelievably new, colorful & lovely.

My best love to you –
sylvia

☆ Par Avion ☆

PS – Flight changed to <u>Sat</u> 7th same time same station. OK?

TO *J. Mallory Wober*

Thursday 5 January 1956 Telegram with envelope, Cambridge University

MALLORY WOBER 71 WENTWORTH ROAD LONDONNW11

STRANDED AMID RIVERA SUN PALMS ORANGES STOP PLANE CANCELLED ARRIVING LONDON MONDAY AFTERNOON WILL CALL THEN AU REVOIR =

SYLVIA +

1–Date supplied from postmark.

TO *Aurelia Schober Plath*

Saturday 7 January 1956 AL,[1] Indiana University

Sylvia Plath
Avenue Victor Hugo
Nice
France

Dearest Mother –

I was going to write you a letter but decided to make two installments on giant postcards instead so you could glimpse the color I've been surrounded with this last week! It is incredibly lovely here, and the air is clear, crisp, and pure, while the sun is warm. I cancelled my plane to stay till tomorrow a.m.

Guess what! I've learned to drive a "lambretta"--magnificent, comforable, safe Italian motor scooter--ideal for good weather. One is out of doors in the sun, perfect view, powerful on steep hills, easy to park, stop, look! I rode to Jaun-les Pins for my first trial trip, supped cheaply and well (You <u>can</u> get wonderful wine, steak, sauces, hors d'oeuvres, etc., if you look, for about $1.50 at most). Then, Thursday, to the Italian frontier! Take a map and follow the sea route, where the road signs are all "Z," fantastically steep, drop straight to sea; blinding blue-azure, pink towns, Italian Alps beyond hills--palms, orange trees, olive groves, terraced flower gardens--through Monaco. Stopped to visit Monte Carlo, watched fascinating roulette games. Amiable croupier explained game. On to Italian border, just to go over to Vingtimilia--"Riviera of Flowers"--scarlet, red, yellow against pastel stucco villas. Biked back at sunset through Monaco, Menton, Beaulieu, Villefranche--exquisite in blue niches of bays! Like traveling outdoors on easy chair. (continued on next card)

1–The original postcard is missing; this exact transcription is taken from the typescript of *Letters Home*, held by Indiana University. SP sent two instalments covering two postcards; in *Letters Home* only the second postcard was printed.

TO *Aurelia Schober Plath*

Saturday 7 January 1956 — ALS (picture postcard, photocopy), printed from *Letters Home*

<picture postcard caption>

O-20 G. ÈZE-VILLAGE (A-M). La Lanterne du Palais du Prince du Suède.

2

Saturday – con

Dear mother . . .

yesterday was about the most lovely in my life – started out on motor-scooter along famous wide "promenade des anglais" of nice, with its outdoor cafés, splendid baroque facades, rows of palms, strolling musicians – and headed inland to Vence, where I planned to see the beautiful recent Matisse cathedral of my art magazine which I've loved via picture for years. How can I describe the beauty of the country? Everything so small, close, exquisite – & fertile – terraced gardens on steep slopes of rich red earth, orange & lemon trees olive orchards – tiny pink & peach houses – to Vence: small, on a sun-warm hill, uncommercial, slow, peaceful. Walked to Matisse cathedral – small, pure, clean-cut. white, with blue-tile roof sparkling in sun. But shut! only open to public 2 days a week. A kindly talkative peasant told me stories of how rich people came daily in large cars from Italy, Germany, Sweden, etc., & were not admitted, even for large sums of money. I was desolate, & wandered to the back of the walled nunnery where I could see a corner of the chapel, & sketched it, feeling like alice outside the garden, watching the white doves & orange trees. Then I went back to the front & stared with my face through the barred gate. I began to cry, I knew it was so lovely inside, pure white, with the sun through blue, yellow & green stained windows. Then I heard a voice "Ne pleurez plus. Entrez." & the mother superior let me in after denying all the wealthy people in cars. I just knelt in the heart of the sun & the colors of sky, sea & sun in the pure white heart of the chapel. "vous êtes si gentille" I stammered. The nun smiled "C'est la miséricorde de Dieu." It was.

Love
Sylvia

TO *Aurelia Schober Plath*

Tuesday 10 January 1956 — TLS (aerogramme), Indiana University

Tuesday evening
January 10, 1956

Dearest of mothers . . .

Happy New Year! It seems almost impossible to be sitting back in my lovely room at Whitstead again, with three magnificent packed weeks in France behind me. So much to tell! I feel unbelievably refreshed, seething with ideas, rested, ready to write & work hard and deeply for the next three months. The academic year is ideal for my system, which works in large cycles, needing frequent alternations between intense periods of work and play. My New Year mood is so different from the rather lonely, weary, depressed and slightly fearful state in which I left Cambridge a mere three weeks ago. Coming "back" here for this first time made me feel <u>this</u> is truly home, and my vacation has given me an invaluable perspective on my life, work and purpose here which I had lost in the complex over-stimulation of the first semester. I now feel strong and sure. There is nothing like experience to give one widened horizons and confidence!

First of all, how wise you were to send my beautiful check from the "LYRIC" here instead of to Paris. Arriving last night, after an arduous two-day trip up from Nice, I found just the lift I needed, like a second Christmas. Also a beautiful signed edition of "The Misanthrope" from dear Gordon, a sweet New England Calendar from Mrs. Freeman, and a pile of gay-covered copies of my blessed "New Yorker", full of poems and good stories and all the tidbits of Americana I love so well. You have no idea, by the way, how enormously much this weekly present means to me! Spent a whole evening reading stacks of them over coffee with two other American girls here, and they were so happy and hungry for their <u>own</u> copies that they <u>both</u> sent off for subscriptions then and there: you see how powerful suggestion is!

I must admit that my heart is with the French! The contrast coming back to England was really painful: my compartment of 8 on the day-train up from Nice to Paris Sunday was like a specially selected cross-section of the French race. Lively, talkative, everybody joined in together and the 13 hour trip flew: besides me, there was a charming professor of French literature in high school going home for a funeral (I enjoyed talking to him, and he helped me with my rapidly improving French), two rather non-descript working class parents with an amazingly ugly baby of 4 mos. named Chantelle, with huge fat cheeks, peculiar blue eyes and strangely-shaped body tightly packed into a knitted white suit; a big humorous woman in black, reading "A L'Est D'Eden" by Steinbeck; a simple strong peasant woman with a bag full of bread and cheese and oranges; a fat, soft, effeminate Corsican who made himself the host of the carriage, talked about a little of everything to all; and a witty young apprentice in radiology from Marseilles. Well, there were all kinds of conversations, from "how to relax", to "what to eat for breakfast", to "disagreeable Paris landladies". The baby was slung in an ingenious hammock between the baggage racks and was resurrected periodically to be fed milk, to be dandled and cooed over, to which it responded with stupid smiles and droolings, or wettings, as it chose. The Corsican and the Marseillan taught me how to play Bellotta,[1] or some such, game of cards, and so I learned the French terms for suits, etc. At the end of the trip, everybody shook hands, wished each other good luck, and smiled all around. I was amazed at how my ear had improved during my stay: I've had to deal with all kinds of situations: pharmacies (where I bought marvelous nosedrops), hotels (asking around for cheap rooms), garages (motor bike repairs & renting: even know word for "sparkplug", because that's what always goes wrong!) theaters, and everything on the french menu! Everywhere, even the smallest officials have hearts of gold, and will do everything to help. Universally, I felt at home with the exuberant "joie de vivre." Everybody in Europe thought I was Swedish!

Stayed overnight in Paris, up early to catch the boat train to Dieppe. Seemed so strange to see dampness & snow after orange trees and blue sunny seas! Never have I seen such a rough crossing! The trip was 2 hours longer than the one coming over from Folkestone to Calais, and the sea was an angry ugly green. I stood on the spray splashed deck, unable to go below because of the hot, stagnant, foul air; everywhere people lay about, vomiting in the orange basins placed conveniently every few yards for this purpose. I passed the trip without being sick, but really felt tremendously precarious, and will take dramamine next time. Kept my mind off the sloshing basins at my feet by talking with several very interesting people: an elderly American woman, married 30 years to an Englishman, with sons graduated from Yale and MIT, a Polish man living in Belgium, a British teacher formerly at Cambridge. What I love here is the international atmosphere: every instruction on the French trains is in French, German, English, Italian.

1 – Belote is a 32-card trick-taking card game common in France.

You would have been proud of me on the train to London. I was the unifying force this time, speaking French with a delightful Spaniard from Madrid and a charming young boy from Vietnam, both of whom could speak no English & spoke French with the accents of their own countries, and a convenient Canadian[1] from the Cambridge ski team (who carried my heavy suitcase all about) who could speak no French. I am going to study French like mad this term, to crystallize verbs & idioms (the hardest). My ear is excellent, and all the French say my pronunciation is perfect. So now I have to work on correct details & the eternal vocab building. Could hardly understand the harsh Cockney of London, the bored, impersonal, dissatisfied faces of the working class, the cold walls between people in train compartments. But Cambridge is selling daffodils and tulips in the snow, and I bought an armful of bananas, apples, grapes, and oranges at market today. Am looking forward to a term of writing & work.

Love to all –
Sivvy

PS. Please thank Dot for $5 & dear Grammy. Aunt Helen[2] sent $2, Mrs. Prouty $25. Will write them soon – enjoyed Warren's letter so! Tell him best thing is to live in place long time – I know Paris & Nice for this reason. Loved your descriptions of Xmas – better than Cinerama! Felt there.

TO *Richard Sassoon*

Wednesday 11 January 1956 TL (excerpt),[3] Smith College

January 11[4]

The crossing was terrible. It was fantastically rough and everywhere people lay in insular agony, retching into the bright orange basins which sloshed with curded vomit as the angry green sea smashed against the bow.

Below it was impossible, with stagnant, sweet fetid air and the stench of regurgitated slop, and people lying about groaning. I stayed above, while about 20 little girls, clad exactly alike in camel's hair coats, argyle

1–According to SP's calendar, this was Patrick T. Mackenzie (1932–2006); B.A. 1956, M.Litt. 1963, moral sciences, St John's College, Cambridge.

2–Possibly Helen M. Corcoran, whose address appears in SP's 1955 calendar. Corcoran lived at 52 Weld Hill Street, in the Forest Hills district of Boston.

3–SP excerpted this letter in her journals.

4–'~~To Sassoon:~~ January 11' appears in the original.

socks, plaid kilts and scotch berets with double feathers that made them look like a crew of human turkeys, ran about giggling and vomiting as the fancy took them.

dagenham pipers

TO *Richard Sassoon*

Sat.–Sun. 14–15 January 1956 TL (excerpt),[1] Smith College

from letter january 15[2]

it is saturday night, turning as I write into sunday morning. the dark world balances and tips and already I can feel the dawn coming up under me.

outside it is raining and the black streets are inky with wet and crying with wind. I have just come back from a film: die letzte brücke.[3]

It was a german-jugoslav film about the war, and the partisans fighting the germans. and the people were real people with dirty shining faces and I loved them. they were simple. they were men and both sides were wrong and both sides were right. they were human beings and they were not grace kelley, but they were beautiful from inside like joan of arc, with that kind of radiance that faith makes, and the kind that love makes.

the kind of radiance too that suddenly comes over you when I look at you dressing or shaving or reading and you are suddenly more than the daily self we must live with and love, that fleeting celestial self which shines out with the whimsical timing of angels.

that confident surge of exuberance in which I wrote you has dwindled as waves do, to the knowledge that makes me cry, just this once: such a minute fraction of this life do we live: so much is sleep, tooth-brushing, waiting for mail, for metamorphosis, for those sudden moments of incandescence: unexpected, but once one knows them, one can live life in the light of their past and the hope of their future.

in my head I know it is too simple to wish for war, for open battle but one cannot help but wish for those situations that make us heroic, living to the hilt of our total resources. our cosmic fights, which I think the end of the world is come, are so many broken shells around our growth.

sunday noon: very stingily blue whipped to white by wind from russian steppes. the mornings are god's time, and after breakfast for those five

1–SP excerpted this letter in her journals.

2–'from letter ~~to Sassoon~~ january 15' appears in the original.

3–*Die letzte Brücke* (1954), directed by Helmut Käutner. According to SP's calendar she saw the film on 14 January 1956.

hours somehow everything is all right and most things are even possible. the afternoons however slip away faster and faster and night cheats by coming shortly after four. the dark time, the night time is worst now. sleep is like the grave, wormeaten with dreams.

TO *Aurelia Schober Plath*

Monday 16 January 1956 — TLS (aerogramme), Indiana University

monday morning
january 16, 1156

dearest of mothers . . .

before I forget, right away, could you please possibly send me a large sheet of 3¢ stamps? I will be needing them for my return envelopes when I send manuscripts to the united states, as I just found out. thank you in advance.

now, about the wonderful letter I received from you this morning! aunt hazel certainly is a fairy godmother! her benevolent spirit is operating in the world even now, and I am sure that the magnificent possibilities opening up for you this summer---and the relaxed sense of financial strain---were all in her mind. june 10, by the way, could be an <u>ideal</u> time for you to come to cambridge: it is the day after our classes & academic term ends, and I will be able to live on at whitstead for two more weeks, so you can see my beloved room and have tea with me, and I will get you a special place to stay in cambridge, if you tell me how long you want to stay. of course you must let me know exactly when the ship you finally take will dock at southampton, for I want to be there, waving to meet it!

oh, mummy, I am so happy that you are coming there are tears in my eyes! I would love to show you london, too, as I can get around rather well, now, and perhaps together we could take a trip to the parts of england you want most to see, as I have seen nothing but cambridge and london, and have been saving the rest for the summer, which will be fairer to england than any other time! your trip plans make me glow with joy: if warren gets his experiment in living fellowship, all will be perfect: what a cosmopolitan international family we shall become!

do remember not to change <u>any</u> of your $$$ into pounds, for I can do this for you at the international rate (with no service charge!) and I am always in need of dollars, because the english have very limiting (almost impossible) rules about the money you can take out in cash (only

10 pounds!) and I am slowly saving $$$ for the long 3 month summer. I was very lucky to spend nothing but my fulbright funds in my 3 weeks in france, thanks to john lythgoe's eagerness to work a confidential exchange: all the other fulbright people have enough american money to travel on, but I really feel justified in living abroad on their funds, because I couldn't do it any other way, and they certainly want us to go abroad (it is just that the money is in pounds). so don't tell anyone: but I will be most happy to exchange as many pounds as you need. I hope I can also do something like the lythgoe-exchange for the 3 weeks in spring.

now, blessedly, my fears of traveling are gone, vanished completely: I was so scared, really, when I started out: it is one thing to dream a panorama of international travel, and another to be faced with limited time & money and practical problems of choice & selectivity. I must say you will love europe: it is all so small, so intimate, every inch of it cultivated and exquisite: not like those long wastes of super-highway in america. here, a big car is a liability. gradually, naturally, my plans for spring emerge: I think I will devote it to italy: venice, florence, milan and rome. I would much rather live in one country for my brief 3-week vacation, and know it well, from the heart (which is the way I feel about france, even though I haven't spent any time in the chateau country). it is amazing how plans take shape. this summer is a large question mark, but if warren is in germany, I would like to settle at least a week or so in his town, & see him as much as possible, too. also want very much to see spain and greece. we shall see. dear elly friedman writes she is coming in summer, so perhaps we can go together a bit: 2 is so much cheaper than 1.

felt extremely moved and homesick when I saw a magnificent german-jugoslav movie "die letzte brücke" sat. night: understood more of the german than I thought, missed warren and you terribly: while being temperamentally a good deal more french & southern, I instinctively love german as my "mother & father" tongue and cursed myself for dropping it over the summer and this last busy term. I want so much to pick it up again and go on reading: it is the daily process of a little reading that keeps a language alive, not monumental future projects: I do want to live in german-speaking countries this summer, too, with books & study it: the ideal way: speaking, reading, going to plays, & being surrounded with german.

here: I found it both home, and hard, coming back to the atrocious food, the damp cold, & the unsimpatico people (compared to the loving french, who are kindred spirits): you ask about girl friends: well, the english girls are impossible: intellectually brilliant in their own fields of zoology or math, but emotionally & socially like nervous, fluttery adolescent teen-agers (probably a result of being kept apart from boys in school all during adolescence). jane baltzell, a beautiful blonde marshall scholar, is as close to a "best" friend as I have (she is in english & writing too, in whitstead), but she goes around with a scotch girl most of the time & there is somehow a subtle sense of rivalry between us. I do miss my dear sue weller: close girl friends are difficult here because of the intensely individual & concentrated nature of our separate studies, but I do like jane very much. am beginning to write slowly, painfully: just finished 2 8-page reportorial essays, one on cambridge, one on paris & nice, from which stories will grow (the vence matisse cathedral one has several possibilities as article, story & essay): have detailed maps of london, paris, nice, & can verify details on them. but I <u>can</u> live on the golden fat of these past rich three months like a bear hibernating through the russian winter & write now.

Love –
sivvy

TO *J. Mallory Wober*

Monday 16 January 1956[1] ALS (picture postcard), Cambridge University

<picture postcard caption>

[A-19] SAINT JOHN THE BAPTIST. By DONATELLO (c. 1386–1466). Mellon Collection. National Gallery of Art, Washington, D.C.

Whitstead
4 Barton Road
Cambridge

Dear Mallory . . .

Loved luminous 'big ben'. Saw "die letzte brücke" at the arts cinema last night & was deeply moved – even to tears & a certain home-sickness. missed you to share it with – magnificent film. also an amusing russian short on a story by chekov – "illegitimate child" – excellent.

With fond greetings –
sylvia

PS – Would be delighted to join you for lunch Wednesday —

1–Date supplied from postmark.

<on picture side of postcard, SP wrote:>
Both Sylvia and I welcome you back to Cambridge.

sincerely,
John the Baptist

TO *Aurelia Schober Plath*

Tuesday 17 January 1956 — TLS (aerogramme), Indiana University

tuesday afternoon, jan. 17

dearest mother . . .

just a practical postscript to my last letter. I've been heckling lloyd's bank in cambridge about my checks ($25 from mrs. prouty and $100 from lyric) and they maintain that in order to get them cleared and converted into dollar traveler's checks (which is what I want) they have to be converted into pounds sterling first, thus meaning my losing on the exchange, having to "buy back" the dollars, and other ridiculous things. I've asked and asked in my plodding logical way, but they keep saying "we want your dollars" in a most avaricious fashion.

hence, thence, wherefore and so I wonder if I sent the signed checks to you, registered mail, if you could cash them (I don't want to hang on to them any longer, for fear "lyric" may go bankrupt before I get the precious money) and somehow make them available to me in traveler's checks at the american express, 6 haymarket, london, or even deposit the money in my bank account and bring it over when you come in june. I am trying to save every dollar for the summer, so I most likely won't need the money till june. do write as soon as you find about the best angle for this. since there is no hurry about the money, and I want to conserve every penny I can.

perhaps I could write a letter to my bank giving you jurisdiction to take out my money & bring some over with you? it is so awkward here, with the restrictions on my fulbright pounds which makes foreign exchange morally illegal and the absurd avariciousness of the english currency system which will do anything for dollars. I now have $75 in cash and these $125 checks. do let me know whether to send them to you for deposit. also, I should like to get $50 at least off to dr. beuscher. I must not forget that.

I so appreciated your morale building last letter: I read it over and over. with the long winter term ahead, and the ghastly food and cold, it is easy to get discouraged, especially since if I read solidly for 100 years

I would still be nowhere near approaching the ever-expanding reading list. perhaps I have told you that I've given up the ADC for the rest of the year: a stoic but very wise gesture, I feel I would have considered more regretfully, if I had a chance at large parts, but I just don't have the time, or desire, to work up, although I must say the people I met there are the sweetest, most creative I've run across in cambridge: I simply loved our producer, and dan massey, & robin chapman and will of course miss not being in that devoted elite, which seems to be a center of vital people.

however, I found myself feeling rather desperate during "bartholomew fair", at having no inner life to speak of. "muteness is sickness" for me, as richard wilbur[1] says, and I felt a growing horror at my inarticulateness; each day of not-writing made me feel more scared. fortunately, I have, two years ago, been through The Worst, and have the reassurance that if I work slowly and wait, something will happen. in spite of my occasional spells of resentment at my own blindness and limitation, (I would really like to get something in the new yorker before I die, I do so admire that particular, polished, rich brilliant style) I go slowly on, with little flashes of delight for example, at the sliver of new moon this week, outside my window, the sudden gentler blue air today, the sight of a red-cheeked blonde baby: little things. but as sassoon says so rightly: "the important thing is to love this world; if a man has loved so much as a grapefruit, and found it beautiful, god will save him." the hardest thing, I think, is to live richly in the present, without letting it be tainted & spoiled out of fear for the future or regret for a badly-managed past.

this term, then, I plan to devote to reading for my supervisions and writing at least two hours every day, no matter what, no matter how bad it comes out. I am starting with these reported descriptions of people & places, trying for precise details, and today did the outline for a version of the matisse cathedral story which I am going to try in new yorker style first, then perhaps Ladies' home journal style, and then as a feature article. I want to "lay in" reading and introspection this term, and feel that my health should improve with good hours, plenty of fruit & biking, and a developing spiritual calm, which comes as soon as I am writing and sending things out. I would smother if I didn't write. I honestly feel that if I work every day, in a few years I will have begun publishing again. writing sharpens life; life enriches writing. ironically enough, I write best when I am happy, because I then have that saving sense of objectivity which is humor, and artistic perspective. when I am sad, it becomes a one-dimensional diary. so a full rich life is essential.

1–American poet Richard Wilbur (1921–).

don't worry that I am a "career woman", either. I sometimes think that I might get married just to have children, if I don't meet someone in these two years. Mrs. prouty needn't worry either, the dear. france gave me perspective on mallory who is fine, but so young. I do need to meet older men. these young ones are so fluid, uncertain, tentative, that I become a mother to them. I miss a mature humor and savor and love of career which older men have; I feel that I am certainly ready for that. the only man I have ever really loved (that is, accepting the faults and working with them) is sassoon, of course. and I fear for his particular nervous, intense fluctuating health when I think of children. oh well, so much meandering. but I am definitely meant to be married & have children & a home & write like these women I admire: mrs. moore, jean stafford, hortense calisher, phyllis mcginley etc. wish me luck.

much much love,
sivvy

TO *Aurelia Greenwood Schober & Frank Schober*

Friday 20 January 1956 — TLS (aerogramme), Indiana University

Friday evening
January 20

Dearest Grammy and Grampy . . .

I was so happy to get your lovely letter with the wonderful smiling picture of mother and Warren that I had to sit down right now and tell you about it. I have the picture put in the border of my mirror over the gas fireplace, where I can turn to look at it all the time. I almost feel that I could step right into it, it brings home so much closer, somehow.

You can imagine how happy I was, too, to see mother looking so radiant and girlish! Be sure and tell her to take special care of herself the rest of this year so she will be fine and strong and positively fat for her trip to Europe this summer. Ever since I heard she is coming over, I have been walking on air. I have already been planning things I want to show her in London and Cambridge, and I would like her to make up a list of all the spots she wants to see, or activities she wants most to do, in both places, so I can arrange to be the best of guide possible. If Warren gets his Experiment fellowship to Germany, all I need is for you both to come over too, to make things perfect!

Naturally I miss home and sometimes get waves of feeling quite sad, but that is only normal: no matter how nice people are, they simply aren't "family", where you can be sure of undivided love and support. I am fortunate in having some good friends---three fine, attractive, intelligent girls in Whitstead here: Margaret Roberts, a South African girl studying Economics; Isabel Murray,[1] a Scottish girl; and Jane Baltzell, a creative, humorous blonde girl on a Marshall fellowship from Brown University in Rhode Island---plus several nice boys: Mallory, his friend Iko, a delightful chap from Israel, Nat LaMar, the warm, friendly negro writer from Harvard, and a few other more casual acquaintances. Perhaps one of the really exciting parts of living in Cambridge is meeting people from <u>all</u> parts of the world (some of which I hardly knew existed, like South Africa) and getting first hand accounts of politics (Israel-Arab conflict, for example) and life in general.

I am starting a rather more serious and solitary life this term, giving up the very demanding, if stimulating, acting in the theater and writing at least two hours a day, no matter what. It is amazing how much better I feel doing this. I am building up creativity from the inside out. Even though writing is difficult, often stilted at first, or rough, I firmly believe that if I work hard enough, long enough, some stories rising out of my rapidly growing perspective about people and places may be published. Somehow stories interest me much more now than the narrower, more perfect form of poems.

I can refer with authority now, to much of England, France, and America, and the texture of my writing gets richer as I live more fully. I want most of all to be able to publish some of my transformed experiences, to share them with others.

I am also reading and studying a great deal more, cutting down on all extra-curricular activities, and even if I never will approach what I <u>want</u> to read, or the demands of my long lists of books, I am making slow progress in the wide fields of my ignorance, going on with French, reading modern tragedy (Strindberg, now), which is sheer delight, and going to study classical tragedy (Aeschylus, Sophocles & Euripides) which I have, shockingly enough, never touched.

As I sit here now, in my cheerful room which I love better than any place I've ever stayed (I have found it a big help to make it as homey as possible, and gay, so I look forward to coming back to it: my favorite

1–Dr Isabel Murray Henderson (1933–); B.A. archaeology and anthropology 1957, Ph.D. 1962; Fellow of Newnham College, Cambridge.

art reproductions, bowls of fruit, shelves of books, a bowl of mixed nuts, flowers, and cheerful yellow cushions to remind me of the southern sun)---the wind is wuthering about the gable eaves, swatting rain against the window, and I feel very snug, curling up with about ten plays by Strindberg I must read before I write a paper[1] this weekend.

I can't believe that in June mother will be sitting here, and the windows will be opened over a spring garden! I am living for spring, really.

I was so sorry to hear you had that miserable gastritis and only hope that by the time this letter reaches you, you will be feeling much, much better. Know that I am thinking of you and wishing you healthy and well again.

So many times I think of my grammy and grampy, and how nobody in the world could have dearer grandparents than I do! One takes so much for-granted when one is living at home, and I want you to know now how often I think back with love at all the dear things that mean home to me: grampy's whistling and gardening, grammy's marvelous cooking, and sour cream sauces, and fish chowder, and those feathery light pastry crescents filled with hot apricot jam---our wonderful lobster dinner under the pines at the cape last summer---all these things we have shared. I feel unusually rich having such a dear family. Give my love to everybody, and thank Mrs. Magown[2] for taking the Christmas picture!

Love to all,
sivvy

TO *Gordon Lameyer*

Saturday 21 January 1956 — TLS (aerogramme), Indiana University

Saturday morning
January 21, 1956

Dear Gordon . . .

It is a brilliant, frigid morning, and I sit by a whistling gas fire, burning on one side, with fingers polar cold, warming up on the keys before I begin my daily stint of two to three hours of writing. New Year's Greetings from the frosty fens.

1–Sylvia Plath, 'Strindberg: Tragic Concept and Dramatic Form', dated 22 January 1956; held by Lilly Library.
2–Either Ruth C. McGowan, wife of Robert G. McGowan, who lived at 4 Ingersoll Road, Wellesley, or Edith A. McGowan, wife of Robert McGowan of 27 Elmwood Road, Wellesley.

First of all, I was delighted by the signed edition of Wilbur's "Misanthrope"; I regaled myself with it, savoring the witty rhymes, the sparkling style, and the sumptuous print and paper of the book itself; as always, you know so well what books I love best. "No Villain Need Be"[1] is resting on my bedtime reading pile (I give myself about an hour of utterly spontaneous reading over milk & bedtime snack) coming up now after I just finished Shirley Jackson's amusing, uneven, yet at times most disconcerting novel "Bird's Nest", about a kind of quadruplicate schizophrenic girl, told in several different styles to follow the changing point of view.

It seems impossible that I have spent three weeks in Europe, yet my memories are rich and vivid, and I'm writing them down as fast as I can to freeze those elusive specific details on paper. I forget just where you and Reese rode on the continent, but I've a feeling our trails probably overlapped. I now have a new sense of power and wisdom (born of hard experience) which I certainly didn't possess as I tremblingly set out to Paris on December 20th. I can find cheap hotels, cheap excellent meals, and even know that "bougie" means sparkplug in French, because that's what always goes wrong with a motor bike!

For ten days I lived on the left bank in Paris, and although much of my time was spent in plodding through rain, buying potent nosedrops and arguing with my first hotel concierge on account of a very forgetful, casual roommate, I managed to spend Christmas morning in Notre Dame, visit the exquisite jeweled Sainte Chapelle on the Ile de la Cite, explore part of the enormous Louvre, smiling back at the golden Mona, bowing to the Winged Victory and looking for Breughel, spending a day among children and post-christmas toys in the Tuileries (and even going to the Grand Guignol---puppet show), viewing an excellent Impressionist exhibit at the Orangerie, walking miles and miles along the Seine bookstalls, up the lighted Champs Elysees to the shining Arc, navigating the traffic streams in the Place de la Concorde, climbing from Place Pigalle (where I finally saw countless whores, even overheard one sweet blonde thing refusing a man, etc.) up the steep streets of Monmartre to the Place du Tertre, under the illuminated white domes of Sacre-Coeur, like a dazzling snow palace. Add to this, oysters for breakfast and wine and wine, Paris Ballet, two movies in French, two plays (one a translation of Emlyn Williams' "Le Monsieur Qui Attend" into French), and a moving, lyrical "Jeanne

1–Vardis Fisher, *No Villain Need Be* (New York: Pocket Books, 1955); SP's copy held by Lilly Library.

D'Arc" by Charles Peguy at the Comedie Francaise, and you have some of it.

Then: midnight express on New Year's Eve to Nice, where I celebrated the new era by having breakfast on the train, watching a red sun rise like the eye of God out of a blazing azure Mediterranean. An unbelievable week on Angel's Bay, renting a beautiful Lambretta motor-bike (two, really, after having trouble and a midnight breakdown with the first)--with blue, clear weather, biking from Nice along the lower corniche through Beaulieu, Villefranche, around Cap Ferrat, through Monaco (yes, even lost $3 at the roulette tables in Monte Carlo: I felt the gambling fever growing, so got out fast) and passed over the Italian border into Vingtimilia. Motorbike is ideal (IF weather is good, which it was), out-of-doors, little gas, can stop anywhere, and people don't think you have pots of money, which helps. I glutted my eyes on pastel villas, orange and olive groves, snow-capped Alps Maritime, violently green palms, and that blazing blue blast of sea. God, what a blissful change from the gray of Cambridge, London, and even Paris! I was so hungry for color.

Biked into the country up to the exquisite town of Vence one day, to see the beautiful Matisse Chapel, and experienced an unusual entrance, which I am trying to write about in a story at this moment, still idolizing the intricate, polished style of the New Yorker, with its blend of intelligent wit and deep seriousness, excellent specific vocabulary (which I find hardest to cultivate). Am much more desirous of writing prose, good short stories, now, than poetry, which isn't wide enough for all the people and places I am beginning to have at my fingertips. Am being much more introverted this term, giving up acting for writing (and do I feel better! I get actually spiritually sick if I'm not writing---even if it is only sketches of brief description) and reading more than going to lectures--still hearing Basil Willey, FR Leavis and beginning David Daiches next week.

PLEASE write about your plans to come over here in March! Could you do me a favor and let me be you exchange bureau for switching your dollars into pounds (no agent's fee!) if you need any? I'm legally prohibited from taking pounds out of the country and need $$$ desperately if I'm going to travel my regulation 3 weeks in Europe this spring. I can't believe you may actually be in Cambridge (this one) in two months! Do write and let me know if & when it shall be!

Meanwhile, love from
SYLVIA

TO *Aurelia Schober Plath*

Wednesday 25 January 1956 TLS (aerogramme), Indiana University

Wednesday morning
January 25

Dearest mother . . .

It was lovely to get your long letter this morning with the blessed purple stamps and rather amazing Harvard Coop check (seeing as I bought so little there). I hope especially that you don't let those horrid comptometers and calculators (whose names even sound like malevolent mechanical ogres) wear you out or make you vulnerable to colds at this hardest time of the year---from now till April is a long pull, and it's so easy to become run down. Do keep me informed of grammy's progress; I only hope it is nothing serious, but as you have always understood, I would much rather know what is going on than be surprised later. So please don't keep anything from me, thinking I might worry. I have the right to be concerned which is different from worry.

Now, to dissipate your concern about me: I am working under a completely new regime this term, and much happier at it. I have cut out the ADC completely (and feel such a freedom, which overbalances any traces of desire to be in the theatrical thick of things) and, except for seeing Mallory about once a week, have told all the boys of last term good-bye. I can't tell you what a bother it was to never have peace, because of visits from so many boys, none of whom I felt more than a vague liking for; most of them were so emotionally immature that they shocked me; I felt so much like a wise old mother that I sent them all away, there is time enough for being maternal. Even Mallory seems so incredibly young now that I have had the perspective of being away; my whole view before was distorted by too great a nearness to life here, which dragged me into it, without that saving sense of humor. Now I am able to act, to make choices, to work, with a better sense of sureness.

I am writing at least a few hours every day, and after doing about 16 pages of factual description about Cambridge, Paris and Nice, have written the first draft of a 25-page story about the Matisse chapel in Vence;[1] you have no idea how happy it makes me, to get it out on paper where I can work on it, even though the actual story never lives up to

1–Sylvia Plath, 'The Matisse Chapel'; a few typescript pages of the story are held by Lilly Library.

the dream. When I say I must write, I don't mean I must publish. There is a great difference. The important thing is the aesthetic form given to my chaotic experience, which is, as it was for James Joyce, my kind of religion, and as necessary for me is the absolution of the printed word as the confession and absolution for a Catholic in church. I have no illusions about my writing anymore; I think I can be competent and publish occasionally if I work. But I am dependent on the process of writing, not on the acceptance; and if I have a dry spell, the way I did last term, I wait, and live harder, eyes, ears and heart open, and when the productive time comes, it is that much richer. This Vence story has my heart and love, and I am going to polish and polish now. I also have other ideas, pushing at each other.

When I talked about my health improving, I only meant that I had two bad sinus colds last term, and luckily fought off one in Paris, but had sinus most of the time there. Now, with a good nine hours of sleep a night, I am feeling wonderful. I am working for my supervisions, too, and although I never will match the superior period background of the others, I have the pleasant feeling that I am doing the best I can, and learning a great deal. This week, for example, I read 18 Strindberg plays and wrote a 15-page paper. This next week, it is Chekhov and the Russians; and I am beginning to study the classics. This reading and my writing combines to make me feel a core of peace in myself which I never had when I was running around to the theater and going out all the time last term. It is more than worth it.

Winter and spring seem to be my most productive times; I rejoice in a kind of spartan seige of work now, after the utter joy and rich magnificence of my 3-week vacation. This is the kind of cycle I need: complete work, complete relaxation, in long, rhythmic periods.

About the marriage question, please don't worry that I will marry some idiot, or even anyone I don't love. I simply couldn't. Naturally I am sorry that none of the "nice" boys who've wanted to marry me have been right; but it's not that I'm over-particular, it's that they're not the ones. I shudder to think how many men would accept only a small part of me as the whole, and be quite content, Naturally all of us want the most complete, richest, best parts of us brought out, and in turn will do this for another. Actually, as you probably know, Richard Sassoon is the only boy I have ever loved so far; he is so much more brilliant, intuitive and alive than anyone I've ever known. Yet he pays for this with spells of black depression and shaky health which mean living in daily uncertainty, and would be hard over any long time. But he is the most honest, holy person

I know. And, in a sense, I suppose I will always love him, together with his faults; ironically enough, he "looks" not at all like the kind of man I could be fond of; but he is, and that's that.

My dearest friend in Cambridge is Nat LaMar. I had a wonderful coffee-session with him Sunday and met a stimulating married friend[1] of his who works for Time and gave me a lead on some lucrative summer jobs, which I shall write for. Nat is a blessing; the true friend, warm, dear and emotionally very much like me: sunny and extroverted, but with a profoundly serious creative side. He had Archibald MacLiesh, I Alfred Kazin; we both have to write and live richly. So I rejoice in knowing he lives in Cambridge, and love seeing him. Tell Warren I have always envied his ability to work & do so much; I have always felt inferior in this way. Funny how things sound so much easier than they ever are –

Love
sivvy

P.S. Am sending signed checks under separate cover –

TO *Richard Sassoon*

Saturday 28 January 1956 TL (excerpt),[2] Smith College

January 28[3]

it would be easy to say I would fight for you, or steal or lie; I have a great deal of that desire to use myself to the hilt, and where, for men, fighting is a cause, for women, fighting is for men. in a crisis, it is easy to say: I will arise and be with thee. but what I would do too is the hardest thing for me, with my absurd streak of idealism and perfectionism: I do believe I would sit around with you and feed you and wait with you through all the necessary realms of tables and kingdoms of chairs and cabbage for those fantastic few moments when we are angels, and we are growing angels (which the angels in heaven never can be) and when we together make the world love itself and incandesce. I would sit around and read and write and brush my teeth, knowing in you there were the seeds of an angel, my kind of angel, with fire and swords and blazing power, why is it I find out so slowly what women are made for? it comes nudging and urging up in me like tulips bulbs in april.

1 – According to SP's calendar, she met David B. Tinnin.
2 – SP excerpted this letter in her journals.
3 – '~~To Sassoon:~~ January 28' appears in the original.

TO *Aurelia Schober Plath*

Sunday 29 January 1956 TLS (aerogramme), Indiana University

January 29th

Deareast mother . . .

It is a sodden, rainy Sunday afternoon, with a moist leaden gray air and wet mud squashing underfoot. I am taking a few moments from my solid weekend schedule of reading to talk with you before the tense, tightening up for the first three days of the week, which are my hardest. This afternoon I have to finish a critical book on Chekhov, write a paper on him;[1] tonight I have to translate three plays by Racine; tomorrow I have a tough discussion class in tragedy, a french supervision, and two lectures (one on the moralists, the other on Virginia Woolf by David Daiches, who is a total delight); Tuesday I have my modern tragedy supervision with my director of studies, Miss Burton (paper discussion, etc.), and I must read all 7 plays by Aeschylus; Wednesday: another tough class discussion (with a marvelous man named Redpath,[2] who was a lawyer before teaching, and whose mind is the cleanest, most incisive and logical I've ever seen), my classics supervision with a rather unfortunate nondescript woman[3] (the women dons are all victorian grotesques, most of them, terribly peculiar and shy socially); and three lectures: on the Jacobeans, Daiches again on the modern novel, and wonderful, dry brilliant F. R. Leavis on practical criticism. Thursday and Friday, the week blessedly slacks off, with one lecture each day.

So you see, the pressure is constant, and I am surrounded with a pleasant torture: piles and piles of books, all of which I want so much to read; the pain is that I know no matter how solidly I work, I never will read enough, and am always fighting to keep up. I wonder if the day will ever come when I can write as much as I want? In a sense, a certain amount of pressure is necessary to me, but I do wish I had more time each day to write.

I am taking full advantage of my sudden desire to hibernate, to read and write and think. I am seeing hardly anyone outside Whitstead (Jane

1 – Sylvia Plath, 'The Question of Tragedy in Chekhov's Plays: "Studies in Frustration" or an "Affirmation of Life"', dated 5 February 1956; held by Lilly Library.

2 – Robert Theodore Holmes Redpath (1913–97); fellow of Trinity College, Cambridge, and lecturer in English, 1951–80.

3 – According to SP's calendar, she had Welsford for tragedy on Wednesdays after Redpath. Enid Elder Hancock Welsford (1892–1981); director of studies in English, Newnham College, Cambridge, 1929–52. SP attended Welsford's lectures on tragedy in 1955.

Baltzell, the other American English lit. girl and writer is more and more of a pleasure), except Nat LaMar, who is a blessing. I had a good talk with him over tea and cake last Friday, and will go to a surrealistic Dali film[1] with him later this week. Saw the A.D.C. production of "Crime and Punishment" with Mallory last Thursday and enjoyed it thoroughly, even though, on stage, much of the psychological analysis degenerated into melodrama (which, of course, the novel is full of, but there the introspective writing sustains it better). I am now living on the perspective and rich experience I had during my vacation, and feel happy working (it is only the pressure that makes it seem like "work"; outside of that, I love it.) Unfortunately, there are no boys I've yet met here that I really like, and even Mallory, after my time away, seems terribly young, unformed, and prosaic and dependent. It was such a relief to meet Nat's married friend, who has a job with Time, is supporting himself, studying at Cambridge, and learning Russian (already having "picked up" Greek, Hebrew, German, etc.) It is this rich, active kind of life I miss in the vague, abstract, immature boys surrounding me; I must always have my fingers in the world's pie: and be doing as well as talking; creating as well as analyzing. It is so true, what you said about the relief of engaged girls. I am too weary of wasting time to run around to parties any more for "opportunity"; I have a greater faith that if I work and write now, I will have a rich, inner life which will make me worth fine, intelligent men, like Sassoon, and Nat and his friends, rather than only an empty hectic fear of being alone. I believe one has to be able to live alone creatively before being ready to live with anyone else. I do hope someday I meet a stimulating, intelligent man with whom I can create a good life, because I am definitely not meant for a single life.

You have no idea how exciting it is to live here on the brink of the continent: even when I am not thinking directly of my coming travels. I feel that latent joy of possibility: all lies over the channel, all the variety of the western world is so close: I can study italian in Italy; german in Germany: and find, at such close range, a rich variety of temperaments and settings; I actually feel smothered at the idea of going back to the States! Cambridge, wet, cold, abstract, formal as it is, is an excellent place to write, read and work; near the theater of London, and the vital, moving currents of people and art in Europe. I don't know how I can bear to go back to the States, unless I am married: here, there is the chance to meet people living "on the edge" of the world's politics and art: there is so much more choice.

1–According to SP's calendar, she saw *L'Age d'Or* (1930), directed by Luis Buñuel, on 1 February 1956, at the Film Society.

I really think I would do anything to stay here. If only I could get a few things published in this next year, I would like so much to apply for a Saxton fellowship (or even a Guggenheim) and go to live in Italy and write for a year, combining it with some kind of reporting job part time. Next year, I hope to study Italian. I have finished re-writing my Vence story and look forward to typing it and sending it off this coming weekend. This week, by the way, I am also going to tea with the editor of one of the small Cambridge poetry magazines, Chris Levenson,[1] who just dropped in, a very sweet boy who knows Stephen Spender and wants to study at Harvard for a year; should be fun. If you only knew how hard it is to know I'm not a career woman, or going to be more than a competent small-time writer (which will make me happy enough) and to have so much love and strength to give to someone, and not have yet met anyone I can honestly marry; it would be easier if I either wanted a career or had no great love for people; but waiting is so hard. Enough of this. I am looking terribly forward to seeing my favorite mother in June! Already I am planning what we shall do in London and Cambridge. I miss you all, and love you so dearly.

Love from your own
Sivvy

TO *Aurelia Schober Plath*

Thursday 2 February 1956 — TLS (aerogramme), Indiana University

Thursday morning
February 2, 1956

Dearest mother . . .

Naturally I was very moved when I read your letter this morning about grammy. I only wish I could be there, to take the double load of work off your shoulders, to do driving and take care of dear grammy. I can't believe anything could happen to her, so I mightn't see her again: I love that dear woman so, I feel saddest that I, too, can't be there to help her feel that she is loved and joyously cared for. Please, every day, let her know how much she has meant to me: her strength and simple faith and presence have always been so much a part of my life: always meeting me when I came home, driving me, feeding me, all those family things: I can't imagine

1–Christopher Rene Levenson (1934–), British; B.A. 1957, English and modern languages, Downing College, Cambridge; dated SP, 1955–6. Levenson was an editor of the Cambridge magazine *Delta*.

our home without her presence. I realized when I was first over here that the "matrix", or atmosphere of home itself is so close and interwoven with the fabric of our days that it is only when we are torn away that we fully realize the air of love and warmth in which we have lived: it is sad that such a complete realization can never come fully until one is away, however much one may have flashes of intuition while at home. I remember especially freezing in my heart the anniversary celebration on the Cape last summer, thinking with love of our whole family, for it was really only then that I began to know them: Frank and Louise and Dot and Joe, particularly. Please, please, dear mummy, don't tense up and strain yourself (as is so easy to do in crisis) because no matter what happens, I want you to remain strong and well. Tell me if I can write to grammy or do anything: I would love to send her frequent little cards and notes, if it would make her days brighter, for my love for her is daily, and I think of her with such tenderness. Do let me know whatever develops right away.

At present, I myself am steeled for a hard, cold winter. I never thought I'd use a hot water bottle, but I couldn't get in bed without it, for the sheets exhale the chill of polar regions; I wear ski socks and ski sweater over my flannel pajamas. Right now I am sitting on the floor typing facing the feeble gas fire (which eats up about $3 a week!) and even now my hands are so cold I can hardly bend the fingers to type, and my breath comes out in white puffs. I had to take a knife to hack ice from my window, to make a kind of porthole so I could see out. Even with the furlined gloves, I feel an intense pain on my fingers and never have experienced such cold; it comes they say, directly from Siberia. In spite of all my precautions, I am nursing a wet sneezy cold, which I think has passed its peak now. I had a scare myself this week (which is all over now, and everything all right). Monday night I woke up with excruciating pains and was violently sick, and fainted. The doctor came and sent me off to the hospital[1] in an ambulance to be under observation for acute appendicitis. Well, after a miserable night in a ward of 30 snoring and groaning women, feeling deserted and precarious, (no medecine, not even water), I felt the pain go and came home, to come down with this cold. They said it was "colic" which means absolutely nothing to me, and I don't see how it could be anything I ate, because none of the other girls were stricken. But it is all over, and, despite all the discouraging aspects of life (my two poems in the Cambridge magazine got lousy reviews:[2] there are 10 critics to each

1–SP was sent to Addenbrooke's Hospital, Hills Road, Cambridge, England.

2–SP's poems were reviewed in a student publication called *Broadsheet*. Daniel Huws, 'Chequer No. 9', *Broadsheet* 4 (1 February 1956), 1–3.

poem, and although I think they are bad critics, using clever devastating turns of phrase to show off their own brilliance, I still was sorry, but the deep parts of me are not affected, and I cheerfully go on writing), I feel actually happy, even in medias res of this wicked cold and a pile of papers to do this week. I do miss not having a family, though: there is nothing like that faithful love when one is sick: no matter how "kind" strangers are, one always feels one is imposing somehow.

I got a nice letter from Gordon this morning: it seems he is coming over to Germany around the first of April to look for a university at which to study, and I hope to see him, and maybe travel about a bit in Germany with him then. Anyone from home will look quite angelic to me. I shall perhaps spend the last of March in Italy, and then maybe go up to see him in Germany. He would be lots of fun to travel with, I think, and is as much like Warren as anyone I know. I do wish I could take some kind of short trip with Warren next summer; let me know whatever happens about his Experiment applications.

I had a nice tea yesterday with Chris Levenson, editor of one of the Cambridge little magazines and "Cambridge poet", although his poems get scathing reviews, too; it seems this is an age of clever critics who keep bewailing the fact that there are no works worthy of criticism: they abhor polished wit and neat forms, which of course is exactly what I purpose to write, and when they criticize something for being "quaintly artful" or "merely amusing", it is all I can do not to shout: "that's all I meant it to be!" Well, we had a good tea, with two other people, and Chris is very sweet. Also enjoy my lectures by David Daiches on the modern novel (Virginia Woolf and James Joyce) which are sheer pleasure (he wrote a very bad article for the latest New yorker called "The Queen in Cambridge"[1] which infuriated me, because I could have done better: it was all 2ndary reporting, from posters & newspapers, and I had so much first hand. Well, I'll learn better next time. England can be exploited for merely being England, and I want to do a few humorous skits about college characters, especially the grotesque victorian dons). Well, dear mummy, keep well and strong, and remember I think of you always with much much love and only hope dear grammy recovers and that you will come over here this June: I am already eagerly looking forward to it.

Love to all, your own,
Sivvy

1–David Daiches, 'The Queen at Cambridge', *New Yorker*, 14 January 1956, 80, 82, 84–6.

TO *Aurelia Greenwood Schober*

Thursday 2 February 1956[1] ALS[2] with envelope, Indiana University

Dearest grammy . . .

It is Thursday night, and I am sitting in flannel pajamas and ski sweater by the minute circle of warmth next to the gas fire, drinking my bedtime cup of hot milk and thinking of you before I go to sleep, with much love.

Mother's letter came today about your operation, and I only wish I could be spirited home to take care of you, while you convalesce, to bring you light meals and read or chat with you – I remember the many times you have taken care of me, and made tempting broths and run up and downstairs for me during sinus colds –! If only you know how much I miss you and how very much I love you! If I were home, I would want to bring you color & cheerfulness every day, to help you to get all well, and so I shall be sending you little cards & notes now to show you that for every line I write, I wish you health and quick recovery a hundred times. If you hold this card open to the light, you will see all the bright, jewel-like colors on one of the stained glass windows of my favorite chapel in Paris – I wanted to share the beauty of it with you – imagine a whole gothic vault made completely of these windows, shimmering in the sun!

I am working hard now, both writing & studying, to get through this Siberian winter – Please know that every day I think specially of you, and every night I say a little prayer for you to grow strong and well soon again – it will be slow, I know – but spring is coming, and you will feel a little better each day. My dearest love to you & my wonderful grampy!

your own loving
Sylvia

<drawing of a bouquet of daffodils on back of envelope with caption: 'A bouquet of daffodils and sunshine for my dearest grammy –'>

1 – Date supplied from postmark.

2 – On a card of the Sainte-Chapelle in Paris featuring an image of the church's thirteenth-century stained glass.

TO *Aurelia Schober Plath*

Monday 6 February 1956[1] TLS (aerogramme),
Indiana University

Monday afternoon
January 6th

Dearest of mothers . . . .

It was so wonderful to get your optimistic letter on this wet, rainy morning! I am so happy that dear grammy is improving (do give my best love to her and to my favorite grampy) and that the monster machines are getting under control: isn't it providential that you learned how to drive in time to meet this new crisis of grammy's! In the last two years we have certainly had our number of great tests (first my breakdown, then your operation, then grammy's) and we have yet been extraordinarily lucky that they were timed in such a way that we could meet them. I am most grateful and glad that I banged up all at once (although I am naturally sorry for all the trouble I caused everyone else), for I can't tell you how my whole attitude to life has changed! I would have run into trouble sooner or later with my very rigid, brittle, almost hysterical tensions which split me down the middle, between inclination and inhibition, ideal and reality. My whole session with Dr. Beuscher is responsible for making me a rich, well-balanced, humorous, easy-going person, with a joy in the daily life, including all its imperfections: sinus, weariness, frustration, and all those other niggling things that we all have to bear. I am occasionally depressed now, or discouraged, especially when I wonder about the future, but instead of fearing these low spots as the beginning of a bottomless whirlpool, I know I have already faced The Worst (total negation of self) and that, having lived through that blackness, like Peer Gynt lived through his fight with the Boyg, I can enjoy life simply for what it is: a continuous job, but most worth it. My existence now rests on solid ground; I may be depressed now and then, but never desperate. I know how to wait.

Actually, in spite of the cold, rainy time of year with an unbroken pile of work ahead, and tag-end of sinus cold, I am very very happy. I feel I am working, digging myself in at last (I just finished a 20-page Chekhov paper, put off from my sickness last week) and must write one one the position of Zeus in Aeschylus' plays to be read aloud in my class Wednesday. I look forward to it, in spite of the pressure, and often pause to tell myself how happy I am at reading things I like so much. The main

1–Letter misdated by SP.

problem is an "embaras de richesse", getting it all in, which of course is the hardest, for no matter how much I read, I'd never do more than open up vast new horizons. It is the process of thinking and writing that is most important, not the "rewards" whatever they may be. I sent off my Vence story to the New Yorker this week,[1] and when it comes back, I'll send it to Mlle. Meanwhile, I hope to begin a new story this weekend when the bulk of present papers is off my shoulders.

I must say that I do not lack for friends. Dear Nat LaMar is such a pleasure; I see him for coffee about once a week. Also, I have begun to get to know this Chris Levenson, editor of one of the Cambridge little magazines, and a fine poet in his own right; he came over for coffee yesterday, and we got along very well; he is half French, half English, tall, nicely built, healthy and quite strong, and all of which seems to be rather pleasant instead of these weak, pale, nervous artistic homosexuals which abound in university circles in England (partly due to segregation of the sexes throughout school, I'm sure). Anyway, Chris is a dear, too, and has published in magazines in England similar to the ones I've been in at home; his intuitive, warm temperament is a delightful change from the more pedantic, objective, inarticulateness of Mallory and John Lythgoe, both scientists. I'm going to a Greek play[2] ("Philoctetes" by Sophocles and Lorca's "Shoemaker's Wife") this week with John. Also to a party Saturday with a Fulbright historian who went to Amherst,[3] just for old times' sake.

Also I really enjoy Jane Baltzell, Isabel Murray, and Margaret Roberts, the three most vital, intelligent, attractive girls in Whitstead. All of us are very busy with our deep studies and own social lives, but we have lovely humorous times at meals and teas, which is a great pleasure to share. I am really very fond of all three girls, especially Jane. Speaking of Janes, Jane Anderson just wrote and said she is coming over to Europe this summer and hopes to see me; her letter sounded very careful, and a little wistful; evidently her interviews for med school have been gruelling, quizzing her on her breakdown (how well I remember that awful interview at Harvard last year!) So if Elly Friedman comes over (how I'd love to travel a bit with her!) and Gordon, this spring I shall feel that I have a little america

1 – According to SP's calendar, she mailed 'The Matisse Chapel' on 3 February 1956.

2 – According to SP's calendar, she saw *Philoctetes* on 10 February 1956; performed at the ADC Theatre.

3 – According to SP's calendar, she planned to attend, but cancelled, a party hosted by Frank Dewey Mayer, Jr ('Freddy') (1933–); B.A. 1955, Amherst College; history, Corpus Christi College, Cambridge University; J.D. 1959, University of Chicago.

right at hand. Actually, I have no desire to go back to America at all! The nearness of the continent, with its stimulating variety of people and customs and country in such a small, available space, is a constant delight. Hope I somehow earn money so I can travel this summer. I look so forward to your coming! I hope we can enjoy London, Cambridge, and the British Isles together, because I would like to spend 10 days at least with you, and perhaps, if I got money, see you again on the continent with Warren. Do let me know as soon as you hear about his experiment applications. Chris worked in Germany for the Friends Service committee, and found the north Germans, in particular, very spontaneous and gay (!)

Well, I must bike off through mud and slush to hear David Daiches lecture on Joyce's "Dubliners." In spite of all, I am stoically inured to the winter, and working hard so that the spring will be a true and deserved flowering. My best love to all of you: keep well and happy for me!

your own loving
sylvia

TO *J. Mallory Wober*

Tuesday 7 February 1956[1]

ALS with envelope on
Newnham College letterhead,
Cambridge University

Whitstead
Tuesday

Dear Mallory . . .

Am in a very grubby mood this week and except for a few literary affairs such as 'Philoctetes' and editorial meetings, I am growling and ferocious. Grrr. Hence, please allow me to default tomorrow. Be angry. Stick pins in images. But let me make like Greta Garbo, huh? 'I vant to be alone.' Or just fall in bed & sleep for a week.

your disagreeble,
idiosyncratic
psuedo-misanthrope –
sylvia

<drawing of fish and hook descending from the 'y' in 'sylvia'>

1 – Date supplied from postmark.

TO *Aurelia Schober Plath*

Friday 10 February 1956

TLS (aerogramme), Indiana University

Friday morning
February 10

Dearest mother . . .

I am so happy and bubbly today that I just had to share some of it with you! Guess what! Just heard by telegram from Sue Weller that she has been awarded a Marshall scholarship for Oxford next year! I am overcome with joy. That means we shall go to London on weekends, to see plays, go skiing in the Alps, travel together: all so perfect, because she is the ideal companion! That girl really deserves this and has a marvelous career ahead of her, I'm sure.

Another, more tentative bit of news which I want you to keep strictly to the family, is that I heard from the Fulbright commission that my application for renewal has passed the first stage and I'll hear finally in mid-April. I quote the entire letter, which, in spite of the Ifs has an optimistic sound:

"I am very pleased indeed to be able to inform you that your application for a renewal grant has been recommended to the Board of Foreign Scholarships for its final approval. I trust that this recommendation at this time will serve to clarify your own plans, both academic and personal, in such a way that the rest of this year will be used to best account.

"I do not anticipate that we shall be able to inform you of the Board of Foreign Scholarship's final decision before mid-April. At that time, we will also state the arrangements for payment of a summer maintenance allowance. As you already know, you are eligible to receive such an allowance only during the period you actually remain in the United Kingdom.

"If you do win a renewal, you will be expected to use your return travel entitlement to America at the end of your second year . . . ."

So I wait! I'm also re-applying for the $1000 fellowship I was awarded last year at Smith, just in case, and have received a most sweet letter from the woman on the graduate scholarships panel in answer to a note of mine, telling her about my life here. I feel so happy, now: not because of any ideal false-rosy-colored dreams, but simply because it is possible to work and love and make a good creative life on this earth in spite of sickness, suffering, uncertainty and sorrow, which I continue to believe are necessary as a tempering fire to the growing soul. With this faith, I can face suffering, without fearing it, or running from disappointment, which surely will come, too.

I am gifted with the dearest, most wonderful friends: Nat LaMar, Gordon, Elly Friedman, Sue Weller, Marty Plumer, Sassoon---Mrs. Prouty, Dr. Beuscher, Mr. Fisher at Smith, Mary Ellen Chase (who is coming over in spring) and the whole faculty there. I love the world, and want to sing of it, with its muck and its angels, its blind alleys and its moments of holy radiance. I love people, individually, and somehow am lucky enough to impart this to the ones I know. I am very, very happy.

It is cold, biting, with blizzard flurries, and I bike home from classes and market, laden with apples, oranges, nuts, and daffodils. I am grateful for all the uncertainty, and all the horrors of suffering when I thought I was doomed to be mad for ninety years in a cell with spiders; I am solidly, realistically joyous; I like living in hope of publication; I can live without the actual publication. I write, however poorly, or superficially, for fun, for aesthetic order, and <u>I</u> am not poor or superficial, no matter what I turn out.

So rest happy in knowing that no matter what comes, I am willing to face it. And know, too, that I just happen to be living in the most marvelous university in the world! It is hard to choose between all the cultural delights: am going to the play "Philoctetes" tonight; In a little over a week, I'll see Euripedes' "The Bacchae" <u>In Greek</u>[1] (!) which is performed here every 3 years (even Oxford gave up plays in Greek in 1932!) Am thoroughly enjoying my film society membership:[2] probably told you that I saw Dali's fantastic "L'Age d'Or" a magnificent surrealistic film; Cocteau's enchanting "fairy tale for adults": "La Belle et la Bête!"[3] and lots of films synchronized to music. In spite of the constant pressure, I find time, every night, over hot milk, for contemplation and a little incidental reading: am browsing Kierkegaard, loaned me by a fine, Israeli friend of Mallory's (who is taking me to a fencing match and play in London in early march,) named Iko Meshoulem. Today I spend the afternoon with Chris Levenson. I love my lectures, and am reading about 15 to 20 plays a

1–According to SP's calendar, she saw *The Bacchae* with Jane Baltzell at the Arts Theatre, Cambridge, on 21 February 1956.

2–The Cambridge Film Society showed films on Sunday mornings at the Rex Cinema then on Magrath Avenue and in the Examination School on Wednesday evenings. According to *Varsity Handbook: The Undergraduate Guide to Cambridge* (Ninth Edition, 1955–6), membership was £1 for sixteen shows and the emphasis in 1955–6 was on comedy and musicals (94).

3–According to SP's calendar, she saw *La Belle et la Bête* on 5 February 1956 at the Rex Cinema.

week. Never again in my life will I have such a concentrated spell (2-years!) to read and read, gradually devouring my ever-increasing "Wanted" list! I keep frustration at bay, by thinking that I get to know one play-wright really well each week. If I were working, I'd be very lucky to read one book a week. I need this time very badly, because I have a shocking lack of background: in poetry and novels, too; the one compensation is that what I know, I know almost by heart: like Chaucer, Yeats, Dostoevsky, etc. I can't tell you how I love being able to plan for the continent! Have been invited to join some friends to the Isle of Majorca this spring, in case I don't choose to go to Italy---much will depend on my summer plans, when I hope to see you, Warren, Elly, Mrs. Prouty, Mary Ellen Chase, and even Jane Anderson! Life is quite fine: all things come to those who work and wait. Love to dear grammy & grampy.

your own
sivvy

TO *Elinor Friedman Klein*

Friday 10 February 1956 TLS (aerogramme), Smith College

friday morning
february 10

dear dear elf . . .

listen, I am going quite mad with thinking about this summer! there is a cold wind blowing straight from siberia, and our gas fires went off at the most frigid time of the year, leaving us with frostbite, breath coming in great white clumps, and no place to hide. much less type. now all is cheerio again, and I am dancing on the orange tile rooftops and kicking over chimney pots.

LISTEN: how about you and me traveling for a hell of a long time together this summer!!?!! I can't think of anybody on god's green earth I would rather run around greek arenas with, and if I know us, we might just end up straddling the sphinx or masquerading as arabs in morocco or fighting for zion. I am teetering in wait for hearing about my fulbright renewal which, if it comes, will make me rich with not a worry, and if it doesn't come, will make me start selling matches in moscow and trying to make a fast buck on the place pigalle. could be worse. today, though I am optimistic as mary martin.[1]

1–American musical comedy performer Mary Martin (1913–90); known for the role of Nellie Forbush and song 'A Cockeyed Optimist' in the musical *South Pacific*.

gordon is coming over this march to look for a university in germany at which to study next year; which couldn't mean less, except it'll be nice to have a hunky man to travel with on navy-expense account this spring; mother is coming this summer (to austria) if my grandmother gets over her recent operation for stomach cancer o.k., and I'll be seeing her and showing her london, cambridge, england for about a week from june 13-to-yup, 21st! after that I'll have 3 or 4 weeks (at least, depending on fulbright) and then summer term here which I may shorten, but should take, and from august 20th to sept 30th definitely free. now all is contingent, like the best things in life, so let me know your dates, desires, and so on and on. I'm game for anywhere, esp, greece, italy, spain, africa, egypt, just to name a few, and would love to get some vague, cloudy, rose-colored idea of where you'd like to start out at, so I can think about easter. I'm a pro-motor-bike driver know, and it is fun, and quite comfortable, like a livingroom armchair, maybe. also, hitchhiking is a very real possibility.

let me, just to make you go utterly mad, tell you what happened christmas: and from now on, when I start telling you that I am in love with an arabian giant and everyone else looks like insects, laugh loudly and strongly in my face and tell me to wait a week. or even a day or 2. for I now have olympian perspective. and all because I didn't get sick on the channel boat. I lived in Paris for 10 glorious rainy hell-and-heaven days with Sassoon: saw Ballet de Paris: Buzz Miller,[1] take it from me, is out-of-this world: danced george simenon's surrealistic "La Chambre", cyclic, detective, drama with vampire woman reminding me rather drastically of you, with black hair miles long, in her face, and all over the place; god, what a dance; seduces him and murders him; convulsions great. Went mad in stained-glass Ste. Chapelle, cried over all the colors, just all glass, many-colored, staining white radiance of eternity, etc. and notre dame on chrismas morning, frigid cold and dark; saw hundreds of whores, thanks to dear richard, who obligingly quoted price ranges: even heard one petite blond refuse someone, poor guy; hours walking, in lights: montmartre under snowpalace domes of sacre coeur, champs elysses, place de la concorde; mona lisa smiling pale yellow, winged victory hunking like god's wife in louvre; impressionists: van gogh all yellow sunflowers, cezanne's other-world blue-green "lac d' annecy" which makes you realize all reproducers should be toasted in hell and their eyeballs burnt out; jardin de tuileries, where, yes, we went to puppet show with little kids and played on swings, and with sailboats, Christmas toys.

1 – American theatre and film dancer Buzz Miller (1923–99).

New Year's Eve we took midnight express to Riviera, Sassoon and me. my first shot of the new year was the red sun exploding up out of the blazing blue of Angel's Bay in the Med. Sea like the cyclops-eye of god. I made it a poem.[1] we lived in Nice, in a cheap room, with its own little wrought-iron balcony overlooking a garage and the surrounding mountains. Could see alps maritime like white breasts of aphrodite in distance; blue sea incredible; rented Lambretta, me learning to drive, rode through Beaulieu, Villefranch, Menton, round Cap Ferrat, through Monaco (where we gambled and lost at Monte Carlo and I bowed my head down and muttered the name of Grace Kelley), to Italian frontier. Then, another blue day, up in the little hills, with palms and orange trees, to Vence to the Matisse Chapel, which is god's own heart and into which we entered by a miracle which I just wrote a 25-page story about which should immortalize me. love enters everywhere: I know this, and it sounds like hell or the ladies' home journal, but its true. Sassoon and I shared all this, all life, crying, kicking each other, madly in love, growing, and all that. God, what a life.

And we have now said good-bye: reality comes in: he goes back to the states to be killed in the army (I'm sure it will kill him, he's got such bad, sensitive health), and to find his metier (he'll always earn pots of money; he's lucky, the child of the devil and dionysus) and we both go about our responsibilities, which is the way grown-up people do. it is hell, because all the dear, sweet boys (mostly jewish and negro) here are loves, but none I could marry. we'll see. I've years yet. and am damn happy. Tell some of this to Mr. Fisher; he knows all, anyway, and I admire him and he'll always be The Force in my writing life: I'm wicked now, though, and have turned from poetry to prose, which gets in the bigness and people, and plots I've got to say now. LET ME KNOW ABOUT THE SUMMER.

Love & more love –
Sylvia

1 – Sylvia Plath, 'Winter Landscape, with Rooks': 'The austere sun descends above the fen, / an orange cyclops-eye, scorning to look / longer on this landscape of chagrin . . .' (*Collected Poems*, 21). According to SP's calendar, she wrote 'Winter Landscape, with Rooks' ten days later on 20 February 1956.

TO *Aurelia Schober Plath*

Tues.–Sat. 14–18 February 1956 TLS (aerogramme), Indiana University

Tuesday afternoon
February 14, 1956

Dearest mother . . .

Happy Valentine's Day! A little late, but I'm thinking of you today, which is it. I do hope all is going well at home and that grammy is improving and that you are weathering the toll this must have taken from your energies. I am experiencing the drowsy, but relaxed, state that comes after my beginning of the week cram and late night of work before my supervision, and am freshly washed, my room cleaned and stocked with fruit and nuts and tea things, the fire going, and a lovely white flurry of snow outside the window.

One small piece of good news came this morning in the form of a check for 5 pounds 17 shillings which is the equivalent to $16.50, for my 7-page article on Cambridge life for the C. S. Monitor;[1] they also bought the pen-and-ink drawing that went with it: a view of house gables and chimney-pots from our little bathroom at Whitstead! Well, this is the most I've gotten from them yet, and hope to have some sort of letter telling me about it, as the check came from a London bank. Do send me a couple of copies of the Youth Page when it comes out, because I want one for myself to see the changes they made in the article for future reference, and think it would be a good idea to send a copy to the Fulbright people, as I have made so much of writing about university life here and sharing it with the untold millions who read the C. S. Monitor that I would like to prove it; there is nothing as convincing as newsprint!

I sent off those 3 checks by regular mail quite a while ago (Prouty's for $25, the $100 Lyric check, and the Harvard Coop one, and just sent Mrs. Prouty's $150 check this week). I am anxious to hear if you get them all right.

1–Sylvia Plath, 'Leaves from a Cambridge Notebook', *Christian Science Monitor*, 5 March 1956, 17, with drawing captioned 'Cambridge: A vista of gables and chimney pots'; and [part 2] 6 March 1956, 15.

Saturday noon,
February 18

Hello again, dearest mother . . .

I received the checkbook and news articles with much thanks. I trust it is my check for $150 from Mrs. Prouty which you deposited and am still eager to hear if the others reached you. I don't relish losing $125!

It is a lovely crisp bright day, and it snowed all morning, the first we've had here which has stayed more than two minutes after the sun came out. I had a very fine evening yesterday. Chris Levenson and I took the train to London late in the afternoon (after he'd just come back from lunch with E. M. Forster & others) and we had a pleasant ride through a flat, ugly white countryside, with the sun orange as an egg-yolk setting in the west. We went for supper in Soho, at a polyglot restaurant, which was very respectable, with crimson curtains and white-linen table cloths and flaming braziers for show and last minute warming, and waiters with foreign accents, but both of us were homesick for the intense, warm rapport that comes from the heart which pervades French restaurants. Anyway, we had good hors d'oeuvres, shish kebab, red wine and cheese, and dashed off to the Arts Theater of which we're both members, to see W. S. Merwin's[1] verse play "Darkling Child," something that Christopher Fry's experiments made possible, no doubt, about the Puritans and witches, with an intriguing play on the double-theme which I enjoyed (plus lots of contrast of light and dark in the verse, flame and sun, versus dark, and grave metaphors); as always, in verse, it is difficult to make it "move" (the way Shakespeare's did) and Christopher Fry often makes his blazing language take the place of action, but here there was a certain fluidity of action, seasoned humor, and an interesting movement through ideas of Puritanism, love, and darkness which must be accepted on this earth.

Sometimes I come conscious of living here, in England, with a sharp jolt: life goes so fast and there is so much to do here, from week to week, that, out of simple practicality, one becomes dulled to all those little detailed differences that made the first adjustment so challenging and even exhausting: I accept the cold, the perpetual shivering, the bad coffee and starchy food, with a stoic amusement, and walk through historic arches with familiarity and a certain regrettable ignorance about their background in time: however, I get thrills of delight every time I pass the spires of king's chapel, or go by the fruit and flower stands in market

1–American poet William Stanley Merwin (1927–).

hill, or cross the bridge of sighs to climb the circular stone staircase to a cocktail party in st. john's. I enjoy walking and looking alone, and thinking. Already I am planning about walks we will take, and all the things I want to show you when you come!

Occasionally, I am chastened and a little sad, partly because of the uncertainty of the coming years, and the cold whispers of fear when I think of the enormous question mark after next year (which is still not finally financed). I feel no real desire to come back to the United States, somehow, and would much rather either get a writing fellowship to live in the heart of Europe, or get a job of reporting (which is difficult to make practical) which would take me traveling and meeting people. The political frontiers here are most interesting, and I wish I could think of some angle which would result in a job which would challenge me to learn and keep intellectually awake. I am just about through with the academic community and beginning to itch for the practicality of work. I would like so much to work for a paper like the Monitor, but of course, don't know how to break in. Ah, well, if you have any ideas, let me know. Meanwhile, love to all, and I hope grammy is getting much better and that you are keeping well.

your own –
Sivvy

TO *Gordon Lameyer*

Saturday 18 February 1956 — TLS (aerogramme), Indiana University

Saturday afternoon
February 18, 1956

Dear Gordon . . .

I can't really believe that I'll be seeing you this April! I am afraid I get very sentimental about the idea of your coming from "Home", and would love it if you could possibly manage to see mother before you leave (if you're in Wellesley) and find out with your own eyes just how things are going there, how she is, etc. Perhaps you know that my grandmother just had an operation for stomach cancer, and I am quite concerned about mother's bearing up under the double load of teaching and nursing. She is planning to come over to Europe this summer if all is well at home, and I am crossing my fingers that she makes it. Also, that Warren may get an Experiment grant to come to Germany.

Honestly, Gordon, there is so much to talk to you about that can never get across in letters, no matter how fast my fingers fly to catch up with ideas! I really look immensely forward to being with you and would enjoy traveling with you very much. As yet, I am not sure if I will get a Fulbright renewal or not (they have a strict policy against renewals, as they want "as many" as possible to come abroad, and only give about 20 out of 200 applicants in the U.K. I won't hear till mid-April, although I do know that my application has passed the first round. I am staying to get my degree next June, no matter what, but would be glad to get this yearly financial uncertainty over with. As it is, I have to rack my brains to think of illegal ways to change my morally un-changeable pounds into foreign currency so I can go abroad in vacations and live on the grant then, too, which really pulls it thin). As a matter of fact, just letting myself think of seeing you makes me feel like bursting out with so much: thoughts, feelings, concerns, etc.

Ironically enough, I am intensely happy here and simply can't imagine coming home again until I have made certain decisions. I love the excitement of living on the edge of the continent, with the nearness of tense political frontiers, different languages and countries, all available in a few day's journey. I would give anything to get a grant to write abroad or a job reporting, all of which is no doubt pipe-dreaming, but I am rather tired of the slow, theoretical backwater of the academic community (which I would no doubt hunger for if I'd been away as long as you have) and long to Earn Money and write and Support Myself. I suppose I sometimes forget how good I have it, and am "supporting" myself through my classes & papers, reading dozens more books than I'd have a chance to if I worked, and having brief and intense tries at writing: which always goes better if compressed in a short space. Then, too, I'm having a wonderful chance at traveling on the continent, taking advantage of Paris, etc. off-season, and planning to try the more remote and unfrequented (by tourist) places in the long three-month summer.

Best news yet for me is that Sue Weller has a Marshall Fellowship to Oxford next year. I miss her terribly, as she was the best friend and confidante I've ever had and an ideal person to live & travel with, as we balance each other very well, temperamentally & intellectually. Could you, by the way, possibly get a pass to either Austria or Italy or both? I haven't decided definitely where I'll be the free week before you come, but think it will probably be Italy. We can decide as the Time draws near just where and when we should meet, depending on where your business takes you and where I am at the moment. Do write. I am so eager to see you again, and explore a bit of Europe with you, and talk and talk.

Love from Gardencourt,
Sylvia

TO *Jon K. Rosenthal*

Sunday 19 February 1956 — TLS (picture postcard, photocopy), Smith College

<picture postcard caption>

PAUL GAUGUIN – WHENCE COME WE? WHAT ARE WE? WHITHER GO WE?[1] 1897 – DETAIL – MUSEUM OF FINE ARTS, BOSTON.

Dear Jon . .

I was crushed that we missed so narrowly in Paris: I called your hotel as soon as I finally picked up my mail, and from a Kafka-like concierge, heard you'd just gone. Myself, left Paris with friend from Sorbonne, woke New year's day on mediterranean, lived in Nice for a week, renting Lambretta motor-scooter for touring riviera. No tourists, nothing, all ours. Very fine, and I can't believe people really live all year round in pink, yellow and orange houses under palms and lemon trees. Please tell me about your plans for future jaunts. I'm living in the usual attitude of prayer for Fulbright renewal.

love,
syl

1 – Underlined by SP.

TO *Aurelia Greenwood Schober*

Monday 20 February 1956[1] — ALS (picture postcard), New York Public Library

<picture postcard caption>

6191 Peeter BREUGHEL (vers 1528–1569) Noce villageoise. Village wedding. Bauernhochzeit.[2] Nozze contadineche. Boda aldeana. Musee de Vienne (Ecole Flamande). Les editions nomis, Paris. Printed in France.

From: Sylvia Plath
Whitstead, 4 Barton Rd
Cambridge, England
Monday

Dearest grammy!

How happy I am to hear that you are home & coming along so well! I saw this gay card & wanted to share it with you! I am so glad you are enjoying the Talking Books – sometimes I would enjoy a voice reading my book assignments to me! It has been snowing a lot here this week, and I love seeing everything white, with black rooks & trees etching lovely landscapes. Tell mother I'm relieved she got all my checks safely & am very encouraged about her words on teaching. My best love to you and my very dear grampy. Get a little better each day!

your loving granddaughter –
Sylvia

TO *Aurelia Schober Plath*

Friday 24 February 1956 — TLS (aerogramme), Indiana University

<SP wrote 'No. 1' on the address side of the letter>

Friday afternoon
February 24, 1956

Dearest mother . . .

I am being very naughty and self-pitying and writing you a letter which is very private and which will have no point but the very immediate one

1–Date supplied from postmark. On front of postcard is a postmark stamp from Attleboro, Mass., dated 23 February 1956. A stamp on the written side of the postcard reads 'Missent to Attleboro, Massachusetts.'

2–Underlined by SP.

of making me feel a little better. Every now and then I feel like being "babied", and most especially now, in the midst of a most wet and sloppy cold, which deprived me of a whole night's sleep last night and has utterly ruined today, making me feel aching and powerless, too miserable even to take a nap, and too exhausted to read the lightest literature. I am so sick of having a cold every month; like this time, it generally combines with my period which is enough to make me really distracted, simply gutted of all strength and energy. I wear about five sweaters and wool pants and knee socks and still I can't stop my teeth chattering; the gas fire eats up the shillings and scalds one side and the other freezes like the other half of the moon. I was simply not made for this kind of weather. I have had enough of their sickbay and hospitals to make me think it is better to perish in one's own home of frostbite than to go through their stupid, stupid System. How I miss the Smith infirmary, with the bliss of medication, enticing food, strong cocaine sprays, and all the comforts possible to make sinus and pain bearable! Here, the people have such an absurd inertia. They go around dying with flu and just plodding on and on. Perhaps the most shocking indication of their neglect is evident in their teeth. Almost every single British boy I know has his whole appearance ruined by the absence of several important front teeth; it is horrible, they evidently just let them rot in the mouth, and don't seem to mind the gaps, like Emily Hahn[1] said. At present, you may gather, I feel like a total martyr. I am sick of being constantly shivering & biking in siberian winds.

Even while I write, I know this too shall pass, and someday, eons hence, it may possibly be spring. But I long so much for some sustaining hand, someone to bring me hot broth, and tell me they love me even though my nose is ugly and red and I look like hell. All the nagging frustrations and disappointments that one bears in the normal course of days are maliciously blown up out of all proportion simply because I am not strong enough to cope or be humorous or philosophical: my Vence story came back from the New Yorker (and now looks very absurd & sentimental to me); I cant smell, taste, or breathe, or even hear, and these blunted senses shut me off in a little distant island of impotence. Jane Baltzell, that beautiful blonde English major, suddenly seems incredibly gifted; you know how it is when someone seems to do everything better than oneself: well she sings, plays piano, writes, and has a joan-of-arc cap of blonde hair and eyes that are gray, green or blue, depending on what color she wears. She is very casual and lucky and goes around with the scottish girl in the house, and I am

1–Probably a reference to the American journalist and author Emily Hahn (1905–97).

being sorry for myself, because there isn't anyone here I can be deeply close to, like Sue, or Elly. I went through a period of telling all the boys I knew here that I couldn't see any of them again (partly because they all reminded me how very different they unfortunately were from Richard), but now I have steeled myself to being very kind and sweet and only seeing them for the simple human contact, of talk over coffee, or a play; once again, I am accepting invitations, because I just can't live merely in my head. Richard will be going back to America this year, to serve in the army, and heaven knows when I'll ever see him again. I sometimes despair of ever finding anyone who is so strong in soul and so utterly honest and careful of me; having known him, in spite of his limitations, makes it so much more difficult to accept the companionship of these much much lesser beings.

In addition to all this slough of despond, I am robbed of a good two days studying and all my tight, careful plans for writing a paper and reading have gone up in one frosty breath. I am so appreciative of the family environment, where, no matter what, one rejoices with the success of one's kindred and helps them through the hard places. I would take such delight in feeding and caring for my husband or children when they were sick or sad; human beings need each other so; they need love, and tender care. I was so lucky to have such a bright, strong constellation of friends at home; I have friends here, too, but so much time is spent reading and studying that all we share is occasional plays and teas or a walk now and then; nothing that approaches that depth of experience when you work or live side-by-side with someone, sharing the daily texture of life. It is so <u>hard</u> not to have anyone care whether one writes or not; I miss that very subtle atmosphere of faith and understanding at home where you all knew what I was working at, and appreciated it, whether it got published or not. It is the articulation of experience which is so necessary to me; even if I never publish again, I shall still have to write, because it is the main way I give order to this flux which is life. I have written one or two poems this week[1] which I shall copy out in my next letter. Please don't worry that I am sad; it is normal, I think, when one feels physically shot and lousy, to feel helpless. But I am stoic, even though I feel very much like being petted and loved, and I shall weather this long barren winter. At least it makes me feel I deserve joy and pleasure and clement weather! This summer I shall follow the sun and participate in the primary joys

1–In addition to 'Winter Landscape, with Rooks', SP finished 'Channel Crossing' on 23 February 1956.

of life, which are all frozen up now. Do bear with me, and forgive me for overflowing; but I really needed to talk to you, and spew out those thoughts which are like the blocked putridity in my head. Please give my love to grammy and grampy and my dear Warrie, too.

your own
sivvy –

TO *Aurelia Schober Plath*

Saturday 25 February 1956 — TLS (aerogramme), Indiana University

<SP wrote 'No. 2' on the address side of the letter>

Saturday noon
February 25, 1956

Dearest mother . . .

I felt that after the wailing blast of the last letter, I owed you a quick follow-up to tell you that it is a new day: bright, with sun, and a milder aspect, and my intense physical misery is gone, and with it, my rather profound despair. I got some really potent nosedrops today, and, except for feeling a bit bushed from the maelstrom of pain and utter agony of yesterday, am somehow getting optimistic again. I had a complete physical exam last week (having had a chest xray) & was pronounced fine, but they suggested that I might see their psychiatrist[1] to fill in the details of my breakdown, and so I would know him, in case the stress of completely new circumstances made me feel I wanted to talk to him. Well, I went over to see him this morning, and really enjoyed talking to him. He is a pleasant, keen middle-aged man and I felt a certain relief in telling someone here a little about my past: in a way, it makes me feel a certain continuity. Well, I found myself telling him about my opinions of life and people in Cambridge, and as I went on, I realized that what I miss most is the rich intellectual and emotional contact I had with older people at home and at college. I am literally starved for friends who are older, wiser, rich with experience, to whom I can look up, from whom I can learn. I had such fine contact with Mr. Fisher, Mr. Kazin, Mary Ellen Chase, Mr. Gibian---in fact, all my professors at college, and then

1–Brian William Davy (1914–93); SP's Cambridge psychiatrist in 1956. According to SP's calendar, she met with Dr Davy at the University Health Centre, near Gresham Road, Cambridge.

I enjoyed Mrs. Prouty, Betty Aldrich, Dr. Beuscher, the Cruikshanks, the Cantors and so on. I know there are no doubt brilliant dons here at Cambridge, and many men who are mature and integrated emotionally and intellectually, but I just haven't met them. The best ones we get on the lecture platform, but our women supervisors in Newnham are, as I have said so often, bluestocking grotesques who know about life second-hand. As a woman, my position is probably more difficult, for it seems the Vitorian age of emancipation is yet dominant here: there isn't a woman professor I have that I admire personally! I am not brilliant enough to invade the professors at the men's colleges (the biggest ones only teach research students, and the dons supervise the men in their own colleges) but there is no medium for the kind of rapport I had at Smith. I realized with a shock this morning that there isn't one person among my friends here or in Europe who is more mature than I! All the girls and boys I know are younger or barely equal (however brilliant they may be in their subjects) and I am constantly being sister or mother: only when I am sick, it seems (Chris Levenson came over last evening and gave me a certain amount of comfort and strength which helped turn the tide toward convalescence) can I be the dependent one. I have decided to make a point of seeing the nice man (Mr. Clarabut) and his wife whom I met on the train my first day here during Easter vacation. I would like to talk to an older couple, and he studied English here 20 years ago; I feel that while I am ignorant and untutored in much, I can give some of my native joy of life to older people, and balance our relation this way. I also am going to look up that couple whose address Dr. Beuscher gave me: I've put it off and off, and will try this. It seems that my chief complaint is the isolation on this island of the young, the immature, so often rash and desperate and unconsidered; I really need deep contact with the mellowness and perspective of older people which the orientals do so well to reverence. Knowing this, I shall take every chance to find some. I am going to talk to this Dr. Davy again in a couple of weeks, because he is the first adult I've spoken with in Cambridge, and it is an immense relief to get away from these intense adolescent personal relationships which go on among students here.

Tonight I am going to a party celebrating the publication of a new literary review[1] which is really a brilliant counteraction to the dead, uneven, poorly written 2 lit. magazines already going here, which run on prejudice and whim; this new one is run by a combination of Americans

1–*Saint Botolph's Review*, edited by David Ross.

and Britains,[1] and the poetry is really brilliant, and the prose, taut, reportorial, and expert. Some of these writers are Jane's friends, and I must admit I feel a certain sense of inferiority, because what I have done so far seems so small, smug and little. I keep telling myself that I have had a vivid, vital good life, and that it is simply that I haven't learned to be tough and disciplined enough with the form I give it in words which limits me, not the life itself. Even in the midst of all this muttering, I feel I will go on, and be perhaps a competent writer who occasionally gets published: it is a very necessary ordering of experience for me, an aesthetic religion which gives a certain form and meaning to the flux of experience which is my life, and, as such, I will always need it. I feel very calm and steady now, and am learning to bear not being always "the best"; that is a consequence of giving my energies out to people and shared experience, as well as to reading, studying and writing: I could never be either a complete scholar or a complete housewife or a complete writer: I must combine a little of all, and thereby be imperfect in all. Although I would like to concentrate on writing in intense spurts when I feel like it. As it is, I must turn to rush off a Racine paper[2] and do some French translation which I have neglected scandalously while being sick. Do know that I am really happy, and it is not a contradiction to say that at the same time I am debating inwardly with problems: that is just life, and I am ready to take it and wrestle with it to the end of my days. I love you very much, and hope you will understand my present frankness and know that it has made me feel much better just to know that you are listening.

your own loving –
sivvy

TO *Richard Sassoon*

Thursday 1 March 1956 TL (excerpt),[3] Smith College

March 1:[4] Thursday

It is somehow march and very late, and outside a warm large wind is blowing so that the trees and clouds are torn and the stars are scudding.

1 – The journal featured contributions by David Ross, E. Lucas Myers, Daniel Huws, Daniel Weissbort, Ted Hughes, Than Minton, and George Weissbort. Myers was the lone American contributor.

2 – Sylvia Plath, 'Passion as Destiny in Racine's Plays'; held by Lilly Library.

3 – SP excerpted this letter in her journals.

4 – '~~To Richard:~~ March 1' appears in the original.

I have been gliding on that wind since noon, and coming back tonight, with the gas fire wailing like the voice of a phoenix, and having read Verlaine and his lines cursing me, and having just come newly from Cocteau's films "La Belle et La Bête" and "Orphée"[1] can you see how I must stop writing letters to a dead man and put one on paper which you may tear or read or feel sorry for.

So it is. Stephen Spender was at sherry this afternoon, blue-eyed and white-haired and long since become a statue who says "India, it depresses me terribly" and tells of the beggars who will always be beggars throughout eternity. Young men are leaving ships full of flowers and poems, and souls---delicate as snowdrops---duck belled white heads in my teacups.

I can hear the wounded, miraculous furry voice of the dear bête whispering so slow through the palace of floating curtains. And the Angel Heurtebise and Death melt through mirrors like water. Only in your eyes did the winds come from other planets, and it cuts me so, when you speak to me through every word of French, through every single word I look up bleeding in the dictionary.

I thought that your letter was all one could ask; you gave me your image, and I made it into stories and poems; I talked about it for awhile to everyone and told them it was a bronze statue, a bronze boy with a dolphin, who balanced through the winter in our gardens with snow on his face, which I brushed off every night I visited him.

I made your image wear different masks, and I played with it nightly and in my dreams. I took your mask and put it on other faces which looked as if they might know you when I had been drinking. I performed acts of faith to show off: I climbed a tall spiked gate over a moat at the dead hour of three in the morning under the moon, and the men marveled, for the spikes went through my hands and I did not bleed.

Very simply, you were not wise to give me your image. You should know your woman, and be kind. You expect too much of me; you know I am not strong enough to live merely in that abstract Platonic realm out of time and flesh on the other side of all those mirrors.

I need you to do this one more thing for me. Break your image and wrench it from me. I need you to tell me in very definite concrete words that you are unavailable, that you do not want me to come to you in Paris in a few weeks or ask you to come to Italy with me or save me from death. I think I can live in this world as long as I must, and slowly learn how not to cry at night, if only you will do this one last thing for me. Please,

1–SP saw Jean Cocteau's *Orphée* on 1 March 1956.

just write me one very simple declarative sentence, the kind a woman can understand; kill your image and the hope and love I give it which keeps me frozen in the land of the bronze dead, for it gets harder and harder to free myself from that abstract tyrant named Richard who is so much more, being abstract, than he really is in this world . . . . For I must get back my soul from you; I am killing my flesh without it.

TO *Aurelia Schober Plath*

Saturday 3 March 1956 TLS (aerogramme), Indiana University

Saturday morning
(excuse me,)[1]
March 3

Dearest mother . . .

I am sitting on the floor in front of the gas fire drying my freshly washed hair in my favorite lounging costume: gold slippers, charcoal gray slacks and socks, and a fine paisley velvet overblouse which I don't think you've seen as I just got it before leaving NYC: it has my favorite colors: black, white, aqua and yellow in a rich print and I love it. I am preparing for a stoic weekend of solid work: reading and writing two papers, and in general catching up on all I missed last week with this devastating sinus cold; I still can't go out of doors without gasping like a beached fish and feel "just over" the border as far as strength goes, but if I can plod through the obligations of this next rough week, I feel light and air are just ahead: already the grounds of Newnham are purple and gold with crocuses and white with snowdrops!

I do want to tell you how much your letters mean to me: last Monday those phrases you copied from Max Ehrman (sp?)[2] came like milk-and-honey to my weary spirit; I've read them again and again: isn't it amazing what the power of words can do? I also loved your two letters which came today. I don't know if you've felt how much more mellowed and chastened I've become in the last half year, but I certainly have gotten beyond that stage of "not listening" to advice, and feel that I have been confiding in you through letters more than ever before in my life, and welcome all you think wise to tell me. Perhaps you still don't realize (why is it we are so

1–('~~February~~ (excuse me,)' appears in the original.
2–Probably American writer Max Ehrmann (1872–1945).

much more articulate about our fault-findings than our praises, which we so often take forgranted?) how very much I have admired you: for your work, your teaching, your strength and your creation of our exquisite home in Wellesley and your seeing that Warren and I went to the Best colleges in the United States (best for each of us, respectively, I'm sure of it!) All this is your work, your encouragement, your produce, and as a family, we have weathered the blackest of situations, fighting for growth & new life: perhaps I most especially admire your resiliance and flexibility symbolized by your driving, which seems to open new possibilities for a richer, wider life in many other ways, too. I want you to know all this in words, for while I have been most verbal about all the limits in our lives, I don't think I've ever specifically told you all that I love and revere, and it is a great, great deal!

I am at present wrestling with my own private angels, and the hardest part is having to wait through the next interminable days of work & slow recovery, still fighting weakness & that depressing blocking of breath which makes all that should be a delight in work an arduous task. But I shall come through, and have great hopes for spring, having pruned and planned changes in my future program here, involving much less weekly supervised work, concentrating, as well as spreading out my subjects, and giving time to write. Only 2 more weeks, and then easter vacation.

I have made a sharp alteration in that radical treatment of men I've been giving hitherto (telling at least 4 that I could never see them again) and instead of cursing them all for not being Richard, or not being strong enough to overcome his image in my heart, I am casually accepting friends and dates merely for the present companionship and asking for nothing more than human company; I am also being much more generous and kind and tolerant, and taking life easier. There is no reason why I can't enjoy plays and movies and a little talk with boys who are nice & personable, just because I think I am made for a "great love."

Anyhow, after Monday & Tuesday spent in my room, nursing myself & cooking meals on the gas ring, I started classes & life again, even though still weak. I went to a charming light opera "Sir John in Love"[1] (libretto from "Merry Wives") put on by the Cambridge Opera group Wednesday with Iko Meshoulam, a very nice, cynical Israeli friend of Mallory's; Thursday I went to see Cocteau's modern, psychological fairytale film

1–Ralph Vaughan Williams, *Sir John in Love*; based on Shakespeare, *The Merry Wives of Windsor*; first performed in 1929. This performance was produced by Brian Trowell and performed at the Arts Theatre, Cambridge. According to SP's calendar, she saw it on 29 February 1956.

"Orphée"[1] with Derek Strahan,[2] a sweet, if rather mixed-up boy in the French society (the film was most dynamic: a fantastic modernization of the legend, including love between the worlds of earth & death, with mirrors as the gate of death, and motorcyclists, frighteningly anonymous & powerfully destructive, as death's henchmen); last night, I saw Frank Sinatra---I admire him immensely as an actor---in Nelson Algren's story "Man with the Golden Arm",[3] a fine film about drug-addiction, marred only by the improbable ending, great photography; seen with Hamish Stewart,[4] a rather impossible Canadian who drinks & smokes too much, but is aware of a certain pub-life & pub characters in Cambridge which I find occasionally refreshing after weak intellectual tea.

Speaking of that, had sherry at Chris Levenson's Thursday with Stephen Spender & others. When I get a few more recent (and more sociological) poems ready, I'll send them to his magazine; one thing, British literary circles are so inbred; every writer ends up in London, knowing everything about the work, mistresses & personal idiosyncrasies of everyone else & talks and analyses the others continually; blessed be America for its catholic bigness! Met, by the way, a brilliant ex-Cambridge poet[5] at the wild St. Botolph's Review party last week; will probably never see him again (he works for J. Arthur Rank in London) but wrote my best poem[6] about him afterwards: the only man I've met yet here who'd be strong enough to be equal with; such is life; will send a few poems in my next letter so you can see what I'm doing.

much much love,
sivvy

<on the return address side of letter>

PS: just a very few practical requests: my favorite plaid viyella shirt just dissolved at the elbows yesterday after five years of constant wear: if you ever see a warm, neatly tailored wool shirt of good plaid or black & white like Cantor girls, do send it: they don't have them here; also could you look out for some gold-mesh slippers with lowcut foot (not high to ankles

1–SP saw *Orphée* on 1 March 1956.

2–Derek William Strahan (1935–), Northern Irish; B.A. 1956, modern and medieval languages (French and Spanish), Queens' College, Cambridge; dated SP in 1956.

3–Nelson Algren, *The Man with the Golden Arm* (1949), adapted for film in 1955; shown at Victoria Cinema, then in Market Square, Cambridge.

4–David Hamish Stewart (1933–), Canadian; B.A. 1956, English, Queens' College, Cambridge; dated SP in 1956.

5–English poet Edward James ('Ted') Hughes (1930–98); B.A. 1954, archaeology and anthropology, Pembroke College, Cambridge; SP's husband, 1956–63.

6–Sylvia Plath, 'Pursuit', written 27–8 February 1956.

like yours) for mine are hanging about my feet by several shining threads! will also eventually need more thyroid: they don't think it exists here!

xxx
sivvy

TO *Gordon Lameyer*

Sunday 4 March 1956 TLS (aerogramme), Indiana University

Whitstead
Sunday evening
March 4, 1956

Dear Gordon . . .

This letter is in the nature of an sos: I woke up from a week's seige of sinus this morning and realized I'd stopped shivering for the first time in 6 months; purple and yellow crocuses sprang up under my feet when I went to lunch; I also have been dreaming about you: we are always skiing! A look at the calendar shocked me in to realizing that in roughly a month I will be in a foreign country I've never seen before, probably and preferably, with you. Is this true?

Perhaps this letter bristling with questions will cross one of yours in the middle of the Atlantic, but in any case, I beg a few firm commands from your direction, and soon. I want you to feel perfectly free to see me when and for how long you want and where, likewise, but I will tell you that I can make all my vacation plans revolve around you, and would like very very much to do so. Hence, I shall throw up various combinations and permutations and tentative ideas, which I beg you to sift out and decide upon.

First: I am "free" from the last week in March to the 14th (or, at latest, 16th) of April. According to your last letter, you'll be in Germany the first days of April and will want to do business in Hanover & look for universities, check? So much is sure?

Well, I have a feeling, after looking at a map of Europe for several hours with undivided attention, that Munich would be the best place to meet. The date is up to you, contingent on the following factors:

I have a passionate and irrational desire to spend a good part of spring in Italy: gondoling in Venice, blowing glass, seeing Florence, Rome, and hopefully Naples and Capri. Now maybe you have done all this; I forget. Or maybe don't give a damn about doing this in April. If so, tell me, and

I will probably go to Italy myself before I see you, meeting you in Munich as soon as you want to see me and touring universities with you.

IF you would be at all interested in going to discover Italy with me after your university hunt, there is another possibility or two: I might be able to drive this woman from Dover (right over the channel most of the way down to Trieste, meeting you in Germany, or even Switzerland or Italy after you have done all your business in Germany, and go to Italy for a week or ten days, probably beginning later in April, around the 7th or 9th, to let you get your German deal over with. This woman is going to write me (I answered an ad in the Times!) and it might be a little cheaper and more pleasant to slowly drive her Morris minor across the continent, but I'd have to leave her a week at least before the end of her trip, so I don't know if she'll want me. Ideally, I'd like this best; of course, I might like it even better going around Germany with you from the day you get there and heading to Italy with you afterwards. In any case, I must spend a week in Italy either before you come or with you afterwards.

Now, I am floundering between two x factors: you and the woman in the Morris minor. My choice (if she gives me one) will depend on you. If you don't want Italy, I'll probably drop the Morris and go there before you come, meeting you early in Germany. If you do want to go to Italy after you finish in Germany, I'll either drive to meet you with her, or come on my own earlier. (The driving would postpone our rendezvous, of course). Please, please, tell me what you'd like best to do!

Classes for me begin around the 17th of April, and if you aren't completely fed up with me by then, perhaps you'd like to come to Cambridge for a few days & go hear Daiches & Leavis or whoever is lecturing, and let me initiate you into the delights of Cambridge. Maybe we could see a play or so in London. "Everything", as they sing so sweetly, "depends on you!" Well, almost.

I am just finished writing a 15 page paper on "Passion and Destiny in Racine's Plays",[1] and thus am in rather a stupor, having been typing steadily for about 2 days. I scarcely have a minute to realize how much I am reading that I didn't even know existed last year: Ibsen, Strindberg, Chekhov, Synge, Yeats, Racine, Corneille, Chapman, Marlowe . . . I've devoured over 50 plays this term, read a little 16h cen. French, worked in classical tragedy (will you believe it, I'd never read a Greek tragedy till I came here!) Heard & saw: the Greek version (!) of Euripides' "Bacchae" here last week, complete with Cambridge students chanting Greek

1–Sylvia Plath, 'Passion as Destiny in Racine's Plays', dated 3 March 1956; held by Lilly Library.

choruses, modern original music; heard opera "Sir John in Love" (from "Merry Wives" by Vaughan Williams); also Cocteau's magnificent films; "La Belle et la Bête" and "Orphée", fantastically fine surrealist fairy-tales. God, Gordon, every week there are magnificent plays put on by the amateur theater groups, and terrific movies: am going to see Shakespeare's "Troilus & Cressida" next week.[1] Do come over here and join me! It is so wonderful to think you are going to be on the continent next year.

WRITE WRITE WRITE WRITE WRITE !!!!!!!!!!!!!

Love from your April fool,
sylvia

TO *Aurelia Schober Plath*

Tuesday 6 March 1956 — TLS (aerogramme), Indiana University

Tuesday morning
March 5, 1956[2]

Dearest mother . . .

I loved your wonderful letter this morning, & trust that although the "enclosed" was not enclosed, that it will be "coming": meaning that I hope nothing was enclosed originally because it wasn't there in the letter. You have no idea how much I appreciate your voice; I can even hear the capitals, for emphasis, and must admit that I love every word. The most difficult lack here is, as I have said before, not so much that everyone I know is younger than I, but that there is no balance of older, wiser, characters which combine understanding and humor and creative stimulation: I deprived myself of all my "father figures" in the form of my professors at Smith, and all my mothers in the form of you, Dr. Beuscher, Mrs. Prouty, Mrs. Cantor, and my woman professors. I feel none of the bravado of the little tailor who killed "seven giants at one blow,"[3] for I am only too aware that a healthy, reciprocal relationship between older and younger people is of inestimable value, for both sides, as long as there is no perilous and ambivalent dependence or over-domination involved.

I am working hard to "compensate" for this influence: I have three excellent lecturers: Basil Willey (in the moralists; a world-wide expert in

1–Performed at the Arts Theatre, Cambridge. According to SP's calendar, she saw this on 12 March 1956.

2–Letter misdated by SP

3–A reference to the fairy tale 'The Valiant Little Tailor' by the Brothers Grimm in their *Grimm's Fairy Tales*.

his field); Dr. Redpath, former lawyer, brilliant in discussion classes in aspects of tragedy, a real challenge; and dear, humanist David Daiches, a visiting lecturer in the modern novel (much more vital, flexible than the dour puritannical Dr. F. R. Leavis, whom I also enjoy, in a more limited way) whose course is a total delight: Joyce, V. Woolf, Huxley, Samuel Butler . . . I admire the man as well as the mind. But these people are all removed to the lecture platform, and there is no personal interplay, which I savored so much in my units at Smith where one could literally "imbibe" the genius of a Patch, a Kazin, a Fisher, a Drew, and, although one's mind was ignorant, it was receptive, and there was a reciprocal current of ideas: our papers received comment, we did not just drink in the lecturer's words in notes. Now, there is a vivid, brilliant, opinionated young woman[1] lecturing in the moralists here whom I am really angling for as a supervisor next term and next fall; I feel I could "grapple with" her mind; she seems the kind one would work like mad for, and I miss this among the women here so much: their grotesqueries and sublimations as people undermines a really deep complete admiration of them: I believe so strongly that the "whole life" must be judged and not just the worth of academic essays.

I have also several projects for consolidation of my program: I am very excited about becoming really proficient in French and German, and am going to drop all ideas of taking Italian next year and find out about being tutored (at my own expense, since German is not a part of the English tripos) in German next term and next year, while reading French daily on my own (how I love that language) and perhaps going to lectures just to hear it. I feel perfectly justified in arranging my program to my best advantage, and German & French are required for advanced degrees in America, and while here, with Germany and France at my fingertips, I want to plunge into the languages. I also am going to campaign for one supervision a week instead of 3, so I won't feel this rat-race of cramming, where no matter how hard & much I work, I still can't feel I've done all that's required. I need time to write. So, I feel I am facing my problems, and doing the best I can with them. I really want to stay here next year, because I love it here; I need to build up the kind of independence which can get along on its own, while preferring of course to be surrounded by a rich group of friends of all ages; this too will come.

This two-week siege of sinus has really been the cause of my temporary despair, because I felt so frustrated: having so much work I wanted to do,

1–Dorothea Greenberg Krook-Gilead (1920–89); research fellow at Newnham College, Cambridge, and assistant lecturer in English, 1954–8; SP's supervisor.

and being totally exhausted from coughing and not sleeping because of not being able to breathe: I simply don't see how one head can manufacture so continually such green guck; it is appalling. But with this week and the end of term coming in 10 days, I see light again, even if I still am battling this inner putrescence (I miss my cocaine sprays; I really must build up a drastic medicinal attack which I can use when this comes again; I'm not alone in suffering, lots of people have been miserable – English, too! but with sinus, it hangs on & is much more unpleasant).

The "Jane Baltzell myth" has at last been dealt with, too, thank goodness. The explosion came when she wrote & underlined in pencil all over 5 new books I'd just loaned her; she'd evidently felt that since I underlined my own books in black ink, nothing further could damage them. Well, we had a real session, both of us agreeing to get all our troubles out in the open, and I feel much better. Actually, we are too much alike to be friends, and this "overlapping of identity" has bothered us both in different ways: we are both "American girls who write", with similar humor, and used to being "queens" among our men, and together we puzzled this odd situation out; very simply, we will never be at all close (as we might have been in America) ironically, because one of us here is enough in any situation, and both of us intuitively dominate social affairs. She admitted that in my presence she suddenly got very clumsy (as I felt obtuse, I suppose) & we came to a positive working agreement which got rid of all suspicion and resentment & makes a healthier "laissez faire" situation. So I go on facing my private dragons, and finding a rather powerful satisfaction in wrestling with angels. So don't worry; I'll use your coming check for a weekend in London after term is over.

Meanwhile, love to all from your own,

sivvy

<drawing of female smiling>

TO *Richard Sassoon*

Tuesday 6 March 1956 TL (excerpt),[1] Smith College

Tuesday afternoon: March 6, 1956

Only listen to me this last once.[2] For it will be the last, and there is a terrible strength to which I am giving birth, and it is your child as it is mine, and so your listening must christen it.

1 – SP excerpted this letter in her journals.

2 – '~~My darling Richard.~~ Only listen to me this last once' appears in the original.

The sun is flooding into my room as I write and I have spent the afternoon buying oranges and cheese and honey and being very happy after having for two weeks been very ill, because I can see every now and then how one must live in this world even if one's true full soul is not with one; I give of my intensity and passion in minute homeopathic spoonfuls to the world; to the cockney woman in the subway lavatory when I said: look I'm human and she looked in my eyes and believed me and I kissed her; and the crooked man who sells malt bread; and a little dark-haired boy running a dog which urinated on the bridge post over a pool of white swans: to all these, I can give my fantastic urges of love, in little parcels which will not hurt them or make them sick, for being too strong.

I can do this, and must do this. I hoped in a night of terror that I was not bound to you with that irrevocable love, for ever. I fought and fought to free myself as from the weight of a name that could be a baby or could be a malignant tumor; I knew not. I only feared. But although I have gone crying (god, have I) and battering my head against spikes, desperately thinking that if I were dying, and called, you might come, I have found that which I most feared, out of my weakness. I have found that it is beyond your power ever ever to free me or give me back my soul; you could have a dozen mistresses and a dozen languages and a dozen countries, and I could kick and kick; I would still not be free.

Being a woman,[1] it is like being crucified to give up my dearest lares and penates, my "household gods": which are all the small, warm gestures of knowing and loving you: writing you (I have felt smothered, writing a kind of diary to you, and not mailing it: it is getting ominously huge, and each time is a witness of a wrestling with my worst angel) and telling you my poems (which are all for you) and little publishings, and, most terrible of all, seeing you, even for the smallest time, when you are so near, and god knows when we shall be pardoned for being so scrupulous.

This part of the woman in me, the concrete, present, immediate part, which needs the warmth of her man in bed and her man eating with her and her man thinking and communing with her soul: this part still cries to you: why, why will you not only see me and be with me while there is still this small time before those terrible years and infinite years; this woman, whom I have not recognized for 23 years, whom I have scorned and denied, comes to taunt me now, when I am weakest in my terrible discovery.

1 – 'Being a woman, ~~my darling one,~~' appears in the original.

For, I am committed to you,[1] out of my own choice (although I could not know when I let myself first grow toward you that it would hurt, hurt, hurt me so eternally) and I perhaps know now, in a way I never should have known, if you made life easy and told me I could live with you (on any terms in this world, only so it would be with you)---I know now how deeply, fearfully and totally I love you, beyond all compromise, beyond all the mental reservations I've had about you, even to this day.

I am not simply telling you this because I want to be noble; I very much didn't want to be noble. That most intimate immediate woman (which makes me, ironically, so much yours) tormented me into delusion: that I could ever free myself from you. Really, how ridiculous it was: how should a mistress free me. When even you, and even what gods there are, can not free me, tempting me with all kinds of men on all sides?

I thought even, at the most desperate time, when I was so sick and could not sleep, but only lie and curse the flesh, whom[2] I was going to marry two years ago in a spluge of contrived social-conscience: we looked so well together! So he is coming to study in Germany, and I thought perhaps if I could keep him skiing and swimming I might live with him, if only he never wrote, or let me argue with him (because I always win) or looked at a bed. This cowardice terrified me; for it was that. I could not admit then, as I do now, the essential tragic fact: I love you with all my heart and soul and body; in your weakness as in your strength; and for me to love a man even in his weakness is something I have never all my life been able to do before. And if you can take that weakness in me which wrote my last cringing, begging-dog letter and admit that it belongs to the same woman who wrote the first letter in her strength and faith, and love the whole woman, you will know how I love you.

I was thinking of the few times in my life[3] I have felt I was all alive, tensed, using everything in me: mind and body, instead of giving away little crumbs, lest the audience be glutted with too much plum-cake.

Once, I was on the top of the ski slope, having to go down to a small figure below, and not knowing how to steer; I plunged; I flew, screaming with joy that my body braced and mastered this speed; and then a man stepped carelessly in my path and I broke my leg. Then there was the time with Wertz when the horse galloped into the street-crossing and the stirrups came off leaving me hanging around his neck, jarred breathless, thinking in an ecstasy: is this the way the end will be? And then there

1 – 'For, ~~my Richard,~~ I am committed to you' appears in the original.
2 – 'the flesh, ~~of Gordon~~ whom I was going to marry' appears in the original.
3 – 'I was thinking, ~~my darling,~~ of the few times in my life' appears in the original.

are the many many times I have given myself to that fury and that death which is loving you, and I am, to my own knifing hurt, more faithful than is kind to my peace and my wholeness. I live in two worlds and as long as we are apart, I always shall.

Now that this sudden articulate awareness of my most terrible eternal predicament has come to me, I must know that you understand this and why I had to write you then and now: if you do not ever want to write to me again, send me a blank, unsigned postcard, something, anything, to let me know that you did not tear my words and burn them before knowing that I am both worse and better than you thought. I am human enough to want to be talking to the only other human who matters in this world.

I suppose I was most appalled that you should bind me to you (so that neither of us have the power to break this, through all hate, venom, disgust and all the mistresses in the world) and that you could leave me thus cut open, my heart utterly gone, without anesthetic or stitching; my vital blood was spilling on the barren table, and nothing could grow. Well, it still is spilling. And I wonder why you fear seeing me even in the time we have: for I have faith in you, and cannot believe (as I once wanted to) that it's merely for convenience, so I won't overlap with other women. Why must you be so much like Brand:[1] so utterly intransigeant?

I could see it, if you thought your being with me would bind me to you more, or give me less freedom to find someone else, but knowing now, as I do and you must, that I am so far bled white that no mere abstinance of knives can cure me, why do you forbid our making the small, limited world we have. Why so tabu? I ask you to ask yourself this. And if you have the courage or understanding in you, to tell me.

When I was weak, there was a reason; now I see none. I see not why I should not live in Paris with you and go to your classes and read French with you. I am not any more perilous, outside myself. Why do you make our case (which is hell enough, and we have enough to test us in these coming cruel years) so utterly and absolutely rigid? I can take the even harder horror of letting myself melt into feeling again, and knowing it must freeze again, if only I can believe it is making a minute part of time and space better than it would have been by stubbornly staying always apart when we have so little time to be near.

I ask you to turn these things in your heart and mind, for I see a sudden deep question now: why do you flee me, if you know I would rather make life rich under shadow of the sword? You said before that I wanted

1–A reference to Henrik Ibsen's play *Brand* (1865).

something of you you couldn't give. Well, so I do. But now I understand what must be (which I didn't then) and understand also that my faith and love for you cannot be blunted or blinded by drinking or hurling myself into other men's beds. I found this, and know this, and what do I have?

Understanding. Love. Two worlds. I am simple enough to love the spring and think it foolish and terrible that you can deny it to us when it is the wonder of it that is uniquely ours. With that strange knowing that comes over me, like a clairvoyance, I know that I am sure of myself and my enormous and alarmingly timeless love for you; which will always be. But in a way, it is harder for me, for my body is bound to faith and love, and I feel I cannot really ever live with another man; which means I must become (since I could not be a nun) a consecrated single woman. Now if I were inclined to a career as a lawyer or journalist that would be all right.

But I am not. I am inclined to babies and bed and brilliant friends and a magnificent stimulating home where geniuses drink gin in the kitchen after a delectable dinner and read their own novels and tell about why the stock market is the way it will be and discuss scientific mysticism (which, by the way, is intriguing: in all forms: several tremendous men in botany, chemistry, math and physics, etc. here are all mystics in various ways)---well, anyhow, this is what I was meant to make for a man, and to give him this colossal reservoir of faith and love for him to swim in daily, and to give him children; lots of them, in great pain and pride. And I hated you most, in my unreason, for making me woman, to want this, and making me your woman alone, and then making me face the very real and terribly immediate possibility that I would have to live my life chastely as a schoolteacher who sublimated by influencing other women's children. More than anything else in the world I want to bear you a son and I go about full with the darkness of my flame, like Phedre, forbidden by what auster pudeur, what fierté?

In a way, I suppose, I felt you were like Signor Rappacini who bred his only daughter to exist solely on perilous poisonous food and atmosphere exhaled by a poisonous exotic plant:[1] she became fatally unable to live in the normal world, and a death-menace to those who wanted to approach her from this world.

Well, that is what I became, for a while. I really cruelly wounded several people here, desperately, because I wanted to get back to that normal world and live and love in it. Well, I couldn't, and I hated them for showing me that.

1 – A reference to Nathaniel Hawthorne's short story 'Rappacini's Daughter' (1844).

Now this is all, and you must know it. But you must also let me know by some means that you know it. If you are not too scrupulous and why, now, are you? You might write me a letter and tell me honestly why, if you do not fear my childish pleadings, which are far far away and dead after today, why you refuse to let me make a few days of spring with you in Paris? I am coming, and I feel it is somehow now honestly superfluous and much too abstract and stringent of you to pretend there is left any important reason why you do not wish to see me.

I know if I were coming in a chaos, a turmoil of accusations, or even making it harder to leave you again (which it may well be, but it is possible to manage this)---I know then that you would have a right to forbid. But all I want is to see you, be with you, walk, talk, in a way which I imagine people past the age of love could do (although I am not pretending I would not passionately want to be with you) but we have come into the time and understanding where we could be most kind and good to each other. Even if those eternal years are upon us, why do you now refuse to see me?

I believe I can ask you this, and not have you feel that there is some disease of over-scrupulosity that makes letters reveal weakness or carry contagion. As a woman who know herself now, I ask you. And if you have courage, and look into yourself, you will answer. For I shall come, and respect your wish; but I shall also now ask why you so wish. Do not, o do not make an artificial stasis which is unbreakable; break and bend and grow again, as I have done only today.

TO *Elinor Friedman Klein*

Tues.–Thurs. 6–8 March 1956 TLS (aerogramme), Smith College

tuesday morning in march

dear dear elly . . .

by now it is thursday night which shows how time passes; I said "dear dear elly" and then a letter from sassoon came which sent me raving for two days, while running to supervisions and reading electras[1] and translating ronsard (o pick ye roses, roses, baby) and mourning faustus trying to leap up to his god: who pulls me down?

you have got to listen to this, because I am full of it, and I spent one whole day banging my head into rocks and indulging in those salt sprees

1 – SP was reading at this time both *Electra* by Euripides and *Electra* by Sophocles.

of crying, railing and saying: o my god. well, it's like this. after all that, that paris and riviera and vence, we came to a point where for the first time in my life I felt I actually could see giving my life to this one man; all the nagging conventional society doubts while there, didn't matter a damn. but, coming like rhett butler from his slambang hedonist life through love that is holy, sassoon, not saying "I don't give a damn" and leaving her on the stairs holding a piece of red dirt, but saying: "two years of army (it may kill him) and I must make a fortune and only then found a family, and always in the holy skies our love is and will be: someday; meanwhile, I must be noble and give you your freedom." so I went on a holy jag of vowing eternal faith and wrote a beautiful raging furiously inspired letter saying as how I was always here for him in this world, loving him, and being here making light and being here; on the stairs, with my little hunk of red dirt, coaxing it to grow, or at least sprout a few sonnets & give me enough to eat. but after two months I had that daily angel come wrestle with me: the kind that says: so okay, you are noble and holy, but why can't you see him, because it is spring and paris, and then there is italy; so the eternal years are swording it over your head, but why can't you just see him this spring, before he goes back to be killed in the army?

well, I wrote him a crude, materialistic letter, dictated by this pragmatic angel, and sent it off, asking him to tell me if he would not see me in paris, italy, etc., and also to say he had a mistress, or a wife, or something that would get this obssession out of me and let me enter the normal real daily sherry-&-cashew-nuts world where I had become as deadly poisonous as rappacini's daughter, hurting well-meaning people right and left simply because they were not richard sassoon. this letter disillusioned him terribly; he sent me a disquieting note, a dear postcard of him as a thinking gargoyle on notre-dame, and two letters he had written before and not sent: with the most fantastic holy reaction to my words of my first saintly letter, and a kind of promise to come crashing out of the aether in countless years hence and claim me amidst blood, thunder, and apotheosis as his woman and all the rest of it. well, I screamed, yelled, and kept finally calmer: I thought: so no one can free me from him, and I must face living in a world of midgets and parceling out my big huge crying love in little homeopathic doses, so no one will get sick, while he scrupulously won't let me see him until he conquers the stock-market and all the professions; then I thought: if I am ready to accept this and not beg, or plead or be impossible as I was in the 2nd wailing letter, why can't we be happy as hell in spring in paris anyway, if I choose to admit no absence will free me, because I am committed, until some big, brilliant combination of all the men I have ever met, plus jean marais[1] (alias orphée) comes and transforms me into the Woman I am with richard: writer, poet, reader, sleeper, eater, and all except skiier and like that. I wish to hell I would meet some other man who could break richard's image & free me, because I miss being of the world around me: a kind of schizophrenic, living in cambridge with her clocks and books and running naked on the bay of angels in her head with sassoon.

well, all this is so complicated, with all it's qualifying nuances, that I can only hint at the turmoil it threw me in: especially as I am reading d. h. lawrence's "the man who died" (god, you must must immediately read: it's very short: but, with reversal, I can know how the man who died felt, and all that about the sun; read it, please) and lawrence died in vence, which was our last place. and I am also writing a paper of "passion as destiny" in racine's plays and learning about the redemptive power of love in my moralist (!) lectures.

well, now I am suddenly happy, because the world here is getting richer, a bit, and it is getting to be spring, which in itself is holy, with snowdrops. and on the spur of the moment I called a guy in london and said I'd share expenses driving to paris with him at the end of march. I feel totally myself now, not desperate, or begging, but positive and seeing no honest reason to be so damn scrupulous; knowing about the honesty of that love is the hell: if he loved someone else it would be so simple; so "goodbye, it was just one of those things." now, it is hell; but I have from somewhere got the guts to go to paris, stand in his door, rouse him from whatever mistress it is now, and say, smiling "here I am darling. how about coffee?" we shall see. then to gordon in munich, who will be sweet and kind and friendly and big and strong with wide shoulders.

enough: I can't wait to see you in june! I dream all my nights: let's revel in spain & sun (portugal too) those 1st 4 weeks, & try just try to get across gibraltar to tangier! then, after my summer term, perhaps greece & maybe turkey . . . maybe maybe. write write. tell me you understand. just wrote some poems; must send you the black panther one. will send to mr. fisher too, in a week or so. understand about how I had to blather about sassoon; you know, so I tell you. it's mad and holy, like dostoevsky. write write, love.

SYL

1–French actor and director Jean Marais (1913–98). Marais was in Jean Cocteau, *Orphée* (1949).

TO *Aurelia Schober Plath*

Friday 9 March 1956

TLS with envelope,
Indiana University

Friday morning
March 9, 1956

Dearest of mothers . . .

It is a beauteous morning, and I have my windows thrown wide open to let the crisp, clear air and pale sunlight flood into my room; song sparrows are twirping and chirring in the gutters under my windows, and the orange-tile roof tops are all sparkling in the light, which reminds me so of the chilled champagne air of Vence, Nice and the January riviera. I felt especially desirous of just hugging you and sharing this lovely morning, so, in substitute, I am writing this letter before I set out to the laundromat and my weekly shopping, and also sending you my two most recent, and, I think, best poems which I have written in the last weeks. (Pardon the rather smutchy carbons!)

I'll be so eager to hear what you think of these: for myself, they show a rather encouraging growth: "Channel Crossing" is one of the first I've written in a "new line": turning away from the small, coy love lyric (I am most scornful of the small preciousness of much of my past work) and bringing the larger, social world of other people into my poems; I have been terribly limited hitherto, and my growing strong concepts of the universe have been excluded from my poetry (coming out, I think, most interestingly in my series of Seventeen stories about social problems: jewish question, sororities, etc., which I still admire!) Now, I am making a shift. The world and the problems of an individual in this particular civilization are going to be forged into my discipline, which is still there, but, if you will read the poem out-loud (it's meant to be) you will, I hope, not be conscious of rhymes and end-stopped lines, but of the conversational quality of the verse.

"The Pursuit" is more in my old style, but larger, influenced a bit by Blake, I think (tiger, tiger) and more powerful than any of my other "metaphysical" poems; read aloud also. It is, of course, a symbol of the terrible beauty of death, and the paradox that the more intensely one lives, the more one burns and consumes oneself; death, here, includes the concept of love, and is larger and richer than mere love, which is part of it. The quotation is from Racine's "Phèdre", where passion as destiny is magnificently expressed. I am hypnotized by this poem and wonder if the simple seductive beauty of the words will come across to you if you read it slowly and deliberately aloud. Another epigraph could have been from my beloved Yeats: "Whatever flames upon the night, Man's own resinous heart has fed."[1] The painter's brush consumes his dreams, and all that.

Oh, mother, if only you knew how I am forging a soul! How fortunate to have these two years! I am fighting, fighting, and I am making a self, in great pain, often, as for a birth, but it is right that it should be so, and I am being refined in the fires of pain and love. You know, I have loved Richard above and beyond all thought; that boy's soul is the most furious and saintly I have met in this world; all my conventional doubts about his health, his frail body, his lack of that "athletic" physique which I possess and admire, all pales to nothing at the voice of his soul, which speaks to me in such words as the gods would envy. I shall perhaps read you his last letter when you come; it is my entrance into the taj mahal of eternity.

Well, overcome as he is by an intense, almost Platonic scrupulosity, he feels he must conquer the phenomenal world, serve two years in the army, find a profession and become self-supporting and then and only then found a home and all the rest. So with all these large things, he leaves me, consecrated to silence, and a kind of abstract understanding in our own particular world of devils and angels; it would be a good thing if someone from this world could overcome his image and win me, but I seriously doubt that, however I seek, I will find someone that strong. And I will settle for nothing less than a great soul; it would be sinful to compromise, when I have known this. I feel like the princess on the glass hill; what possible knight could overcome this image? This dynamic holy soul which we share?

Well, the essence of my difficulty and torment this past term has been to realize that no matter how I wanted to escape the commitment, I cannot deny that I am captive to a powerful love which passes all the surface considerations of this world and reaches to what we can know of the eternal. I am also, now, deprived of this person (I can't even see him this spring in Paris, he is so obsessed with this ideal of conquering the world before returning to me; he won't compromise, which, being very practical, I would, sharing the present spring and making it lovely). With these circumstances faced, the situation, while torturing, becomes real enough to deal with:

I have changed in my attitudes: I parcel out the love I have, the enormous desire to give (which is my problem, not "being loved" so much: I just

1–W. B. Yeats, 'Two Songs from a Play' (1931). SP adds a comma after the word 'night'.

have to "Give out" and feel smothered when[1] there is no being strong enough for my intensity) in homeopathic doses to those around me: the little woman in the subway lavatory whom I changed from a machine into a person for a minute, and hugged her; the crooked man selling malt bread; the little boy running his black dog which urinated over a pool of white swans: and all those around me. I am, essentially, living in two worlds: one, where my love is gone with Richard; the other, this world of books, market, and nice people. If I could meet anyone this summer, or next year, or next, I would be most happy to learn to love again: I am always open to this. But until someone can create worlds with me the way Richard can, I am essentially unavailable.

I hope you understand that all this is very private, and I am sharing it with you as I would the deepest secrets of my soul, because I want you to understand that my battles are intricate and complex, and that I am, without despair, facing them, wrestling with angels, and learning to tolerate that inevitable conflict which is our portion as long as we are truly alive. I am growing strong by practice. All the growing visions of beauty and new worlds which I am experiencing are paid for by birth pangs. The idea of perfect happiness and adjustment was exploded in "Brave New World"; what I am fighting for is the strength to claim the "right to be unhappy" together with the joy of creative affirmation.

More practically: please reassure me about the money which you said you sent. It was not in your letter which said it was, ambiguously "enclosed" and "coming." Do let me know how you sent it, for it hasn't come yet. Also, more seriously, how is grammy? I heard she was in the hospital again this week and am most concerned to hear how she is coming along. Please do let me count on your coming this June, unless she is in a critical state: in a sense, you have a debt to the young, to the living, and the future, you know. I'd love to be able to think you'd do everything possible to come; I've gotten to look so extremely forward to your sharing England with me!

More immediately still: will you please write to the Eugene Saxton fellowship fund (cf. that book in our library at home on scholarships) and ask for information about applications: I want very seriously to apply for a grant for the years 1957-1958 for either writing a book of poems or a novel; I believe that my background of poetry prizes is a rather fine statement of promise: The Academy of American Poets, Lyric Young Poet's, sharing the Irene Glascock, Smith prizes and publications; if, as

1 – 'feel smothered ~~which~~ when' appears in the original.

I hope I can write a good deal this spring & publish, I should be the "young writer" they seem to favor; also, I feel the sproutings of a novel in me, which would have to be started in the form of short stories; but I am going to revolt from this critical world (which can dry one's blood, if one isn't careful: I see it in all the women around me) and want desperately to try spending a year writing, preferably in southern france, Italy or Spain, where the climate is "my air" all year round. I know I probably will have to apply sometime next fall early, and want to be prepared with documents, etc. Please, please, ask them about this in a letter, saying, perhaps that your daughter is on a Fulbright. Better still, send me their adress & a copy of their paragraph of purpose in the book, & I'll write: that would be best. I've had a new vision, partly because of this brilliant analytical critical boy I've met from Yale whose mind has clarified certain purposes in me which see dangers in the academic continuity: he's going back to be a professor at Yale and knows all the brilliant critics: Cleanth Brooks, E. M. Forster, David Daiches, C. S. Lewis, and so on. But the pedestrian, analytic mind, while tonic, appalls me: I fly to the saintly, religious, intuitive: the blend of both: Ivan Karamazov!

Love from a very happy
sivvy

Sylvia Plath
4 Barton Road
Cambridge, England

Channel Crossing

On storm-struck deck, wind sirens caterwaul;
With each tilt, shock and shudder, our blunt ship
Cleaves forward into fury; dark as anger,
Waves wallop, assaulting the stubborn hull.
Flayed by spary, we take the challenge up,
Grip the rail, squint ahead, and wonder how much longer

Such force can last; but beyond, the neutral view
Shows, rank on rank, the hungry seas advancing.
Below, rocked havoc-sick, voyagers lie
Retching in bright orange basins; a refugee
Sprawls, hunched in black, among baggage, wincing
Under the strict mask of his agony.

Far from the sweet stench of that perilous air
In which our comrades are betrayed, we freeze
And marvel at the smashing nonchalance
Of nature: what better way to test taut fiber
Than against this onslaught, these casual blasts of ice
That wrestle with us like angels; the mere chance

Of making harbor through this racketing flux
Taunts us to valor. Blue sailors sang that our journey
Would be full of sun, white gulls, and waters drenched
With radiance, peacock-colored; instead, bleak rocks
Jutted early to mark our going, while sky
Curded over with clouds and chalk cliffs blanched

In sullen light of the inauspicious day.
Now, free, by hazard's quirk, from the common ill
Knocking our brothers down, we strike a stance
Most mock-heroic, to cloak our waking awe
At this rare rumpus which no man can control:
Meek and proud both fall; stark violence

Lays all walls waste; private estates are torn,
Ransacked in the public eye. We forsake
Our lone luck now, compelled by bond, by blood,
To keep some unsaid pact; perhaps concern
Is helpless here, quite extra, yet we must make
The gesture, bend and hold the prone man's head.

And so we sail toward cities, streets and homes
Of other men, where statues celebrate
Brave acts played out in peace, in war; all dangers
End: green shores appear; we assume our names,
Our luggage, as docks halt our brief epic; no debt
Survives arrival; we walk the plank with strangers.

Pursuit

"Dans le fond des forêts votre image me suit."[1]
Racine

There is a panther stalks me down:
One day I'll have my death of him;
His greed has set the woods aflame,
He prowls more lordly than the sun.
Most soft, most suavely glides that step,
Advancing always at my back;
From gaunt hemlock, rooks croak havoc:
The hunt is on, and sprung the trap.
Flayed by thorns I trek the rocks,
Haggard through the hot white noon.
Along red network of his veins
What fires run, what craving wakes?

Insatiate, he ransacks the land
Condemned by our ancestral fault,
Crying: blood, let blood be spilt;
Meat must glut his mouth's raw wound.
Keen the rending teeth and sweet
The singeing fury of his fur;
His kisses parch, each paw's a briar,
Doom consummates that appetite.
In the wake of this fierce cat,
Kindled like torches for his joy,
Charred and ravened women lie,
Become his starving body's bait.

Now hills hatch menace, spawning shade;
Midnight cloaks the sultry grove;
The black marauder, hauled by love
On fluent haunches, keeps my speed.
Behind snarled thickets of my eyes
Lurks the lithe one; in dreams' ambush

1 – 'In the depths of the forests your image pursues me.'

Bright those claws that mar the flesh
And hungry, hungry, those taut thighs.
His ardor snares me, lights the trees,
And I run flaring in my skin;
What lull, what cool can lap me in
When burns and brands that yellow gaze?

I hurl my heart to halt his pace,
To quench his thirst I squander blood;
He eats, and still his need seeks food,
Compels a total sacrifice.
His voice waylays me, spells a trance,
The gutted forest falls to ash;
Appalled by secret want, I rush
From such assault of radiance.
Entering the tower of my fears,
I shut my doors on that dark guilt,
I bolt the door, each door I bolt.
Blood quickens, gonging in my ears:

The panther's tread is on the stairs,
Coming up and up the stairs.

TO *Aurelia Schober Plath*

Tuesday 13 March 1956 — TLS (aerogramme), Indiana University

Tuesday morning
March 13, 1956

Dearest darling beautiful saintly mother!!!

Hold on to your hat and brace yourself for a whistling hurricane of happiness! Spring has sprouted early this year, and all the cold doubts and dark fears of winter exploded in a mass of magnificent mail this morning:

MY FULBRIGHT HAS BEEN RENEWED! Joy, bliss, and how wonderful it comes before my vacation! You must imagine what this does to my peace of mind: I've weighed myself and found wanting so often this hectic term (I've really slaved this term, and often felt no matter how hard I read, I still would never make the grade) that this kind of consecration from the powers that be make me feel that needed surge of strength to dare and drive through this next and last week of term; tired and discouraged as I've been, fighting for a stoic and creative attitude in spite of all frustrations and rejections and conflicts on every side: they are giving me a 12 month allowance to cover as much of the summer as I'm in England, so when you're here, I hope to be your hostess from the 13th to the 22nd of June! What joy to show you my London, my lovely Cambridge! And not have that worry of money over my head! I am sure my acting and writing has something to do with it, for my academic letters surely weren't anything more than business like: also, my statement of purpose was rather eloquent, and I luckily have the gift of an angel's tongue when I want to be persuasive! Let me say it again in loud print: MY FULBRIGHT IS RENEWED!!!

There! Now I can write to Smith and cancel my application for aid with thanks and joy. Oh, I must send the Fulbright office here copies of my Cambridge articles and drawing: I think my love and joy of this place shows through there. I was so elated to hear that it "shared" Cambridge with so many at home. I am planning to go around sketching Cambridge this next week, when everybody will be gone, and the Backs and flowers will be shining in the strengthening sun. I cannot draw well, or write exceptionally, but I feel now so far beyond that perfectionist streak which would be flawless or nothing: now I go on in my most happy-go-lucky way, and make my little imperfect worlds in pen and on typewriter, and share them with those I love. You have no idea how fresh courage came to me through your last letter and those who appreciated my article and drawing: I look ever upward, and am in the midst of brilliant, beautiful, talented people. My accomplishments and abilities often seem so small in comparison: I often wonder "who am I to teach!" and must be helped to look back and see what a fine career I've really had, and how far I've come: in the academic world, I'm with real scholars, and of course, feel ignorant & untutored. But compared with highschool, even college, I'm really becoming well-read!

Other wonderful news came too: I am meeting Gordon somewhere in Germany at the beginning of April and we are renting a car and driving through Germany, Austria, Switzerland, to Italy (Venice, Rome in Spring, Capri!) Isn't it like a fairy tale! Mrs. Lameyer wrote me a dear letter, and I am happy, because Gordon & I are so compatible (in a friendly way) that it should be a fine trip! Then he may come to England to visit, too! My vacation plans had depressed me, for I didn't want to go to Italy alone, and now, I can be truly "alone" when I want, and Gordon, too, because of being together. (Single girls are always having to fight off men in Europe, and it is a bother to travel alone).

Also, I have the brilliant, attractive woman supervisor I wanted for the moralists next term, and, if she likes, next year! The one woman I admire at Cambridge! I should grow amazingly by fighting her logically through Aristotle, Plato, through the British philosophers, up to D. H. Lawrence! I always wanted to take philosophy, and here's my chance! She is a fine woman, young and much admired by the most brilliant dons here. Also, I am probably going to be tutored in German beginning next term, through the summer here (I plan to be in Cambridge a month from July 20 to August 20 to read and write) and Gary Haupt,[1] my most analytical and intelligent friend from Yale has offered to do an hour of Rilke a week with me! (He studied German under the best men in the world for 3 years!) Also, we are going to hear the Vienna choir boys in King's Chapel this Wednesday! Saw the best performance ever of "Troilus and Cressida" (Shakespeare) last night: felt delighted: most professional, compared favorably with Old Vic: such a place this is!

Another thing I must mention: you know I am very much in love with Richard. Well, we are both this way. And, knowing this, I can live through much sorrow and pain. I have never felt so celestially holy, for the fury which I have, and the power, is, for the first time, met with an equal soul. In a way, I must tell you that our community life in Wellesley, which I love and admire like an "Our Town", has bothered me a bit in this regard, for I feel they could well accept and admire a Gordon, who is physically beautiful & really my match outwardly, I think. But I still feel dubious about my Richard, because I see now through the boyish weakness of his frame, & the delicate health & unathletic nature, to a soul which is kingly and beautiful and strong; I see it so powerfully, that I fear to expose him to the "conventional" world of judgment which I am so much a part of; he is a solitary soul, and I have given him life & faith. Do you understand my dilemma? Gordon has the body but Richard has the soul. And I live in both worlds. It is hard; both fight now, and the perfectionist in me wants to combine them, but that seems impossible. Do write.

Love to ALL.
YOUR HAPPY SIVVY!

1–Garry Eugene Haupt (1933–79), American; B.A. 1955, Yale College; B.A. 1957, English, Pembroke College, Cambridge; dated SP in 1956.

TO *Aurelia Schober Plath*

Sunday 18 March 1956 TLS (aerogramme), Indiana University

Sunday afternoon
March 18. 1956

Dearest mother . . .

It has been a lovely cool spring day, and I walked slowly through green meadows and herds of grazing cows to Granchester for coffee with Gary Haupt, a sweet, if pedantic, Fulbright student from Yale whom I no doubt mentioned before, and who saw me through a rather traumatic experience yesterday at the casualty ward of Addenbrooks Hospital, where I seem to be spending a good deal of time lately. I'd gotten some cinder or splinter in my eye Monday,[1] and tried to bathe it out, but the itch and hurt got worse and worse; in the midst of the rush of last week's classes and final supervisions I chalked it up to a cold in my eye, and let it go till yesterday, when I couldn't eat or sleep because of the irritation, so Gary took me to the doctor. I spent a difficult hour waiting in the casualty ward for my turn, listening to screams and seeing blood-stained people being wheeled by on stretchers. Finally the doctor examined me and said gravely: "Why didn't you come in before?" and announced they would have to operate on my eye. Well, you can imagine my horror. Fortunately I was in such pain that I would have let them cut it out if only the hurt would stop. The doctor was very kind and gentle, and gave me a local anesthesia via drops which made my eye hard as a rock, and then proceeded to take all sorts of gruesome knives and scrapers and cut the imbedded cinder out of the brown-part of my eye while I looked on (couldn't help it) and babbled about how Oedipus and Gloucester in King Lear got new vision through losing eyes, but how I would just as soon keep my sight and get new vision too. The operation was a success, and I went through the next 24 hours having to give myself eye-drops every hour to heal the hole, so couldn't sleep all night. Gary was a great help and consolation and stood by me through the long operation and fed me wine and sherry all day and read Thurber aloud while I went through a very painful time as the anesthetic wore off. I'm having a final checkup tomorrow at the hospital, but feel fine now, except for being tired, and the world looks shining as eden through my healed eyes. I certainly have learned not to "be stoic" like the English, and to bear pain; the minute I itch or hurt ever, I'm going to

1–See Sylvia Plath, 'The Eye-Mote'.

fly to be examined. Luckily, under "the system", this was all free! I have discovered that accidents are the best way to take advantage of socialized medecine! But hope this will be the last time I impose on their kindness. I really had a scare, and, knowing my imagination you can imagine how gruelling it was to be operated on fully conscious with both eyes open!

Now I feel I deserve Paris and pampering. I've really slaved this term! I'm so happy to have this brilliant, attractive young woman for supervisor in philosophy next term, and am cutting out all classes and other academic supervisions to devote my all to her: I'm supposed to read all Plato and Aristotle over vacation! and will go right through the British moralists to literary moralists, up to D. H. Lawrence (on whom she gave the most frank, brilliant lecture I've ever heard on the redemptive power of love). Friday, I'm going to London, and early Saturday morning I'm driving with Emmet Larkin,[1] a Fulbright student whom I haven't met yet, to Paris, where I shall stay about a week prior to meeting Gordon in Germany. Every time I think of the renewal of my Fulbright, I feel a blessed relief and joy. Only about 20 people out of about 200 get renewals, and most are doing research; both Gary and I got renewals in undergrad English, so I feel very lucky. Have already written Smith canceling application for aid there and thanking them.

I wonder, by the way, if you'd consider being a literary agent for me? It would be so much easier than spending a fortune on postage for heavy mss. over here. I'm thinking now of my story the "Christmas Heart" which you have at home and would be so grateful if you would start sending it off now (simply with stamped, self-addressed large manila envelope inside, no letters) to a series of magazines in the order mentioned: when it comes back, just quote me the rejection and send it to the next. I'm going to try writing commercially once again, and might as well try the rounds on that story, which is not too bad. Just send it flat, on a piece of bracing cardboard to: (I think it was the Journal that rejected it) (address all letters to "Short Story Editor")

McCALL'S: 230 Park Avenue, New York 17, N.Y
WOMAN'S HOME COMPANION: 640 Fifth Ave., NY 19, NY
GOOD HOUSEKEEPING: 57th St. & 8th Ave., NY 19,

1–Emmet J. Larkin (1927–2012); B.A. 1950, New York University; M.A. 1951, Ph.D. 1957, Columbia University; graduate student at London School of Economics and Political Science, 1955–6; author of *James Larkin: Irish Labour Leader, 1876–1947* (Boston: M.I.T. Press, 1965). In March 1956, Emmet Larkin gave SP and his British friend Janet Drake a ride to Paris.

WOMAN'S DAY: 19 West 44th St., Ny 36, NY.
EVERYWOMAN'S: 16 East 40th Street, N.Y. 17

After all these magazine reject it, send it to me, and I'll try my luck in England. I am just starting to feel out the markets here, but the slicks printed here are much too rose-colored and improbable to be published at home; I admire the slick market in NYC and find the stories muscular, pragmatic, fine technically and with a good sense of humor. This one is probably too feminine and serious, but please, if it isn't asking too much, try those five markets. This coming term, I'm going to write. I'd be happiest writing, I think, with a vital husband; if that doesnt happen for a while, I'll write while teaching. No more advanced degrees for me. I have no desire to be a critic or scholar. Amusingly enough, all the scholarly boys I know here think of me as a 2nd Virginia Woolf! Some of them are so idealistic! It's a wonderful world, and I want to live an active creative life, giving of my joy and love to others. My love to you, and do let me know how dear grammy is, and how Warren's plans are coming. His program sounds so esoteric!

Love from your bright-eyed
Sivvy

TO *Gordon Lameyer*

Sunday 18 March 1956 — TLS (aerogramme), Indiana University

sunday, march 18

dear gordon . . .

I have just come back from the casualty ward of the hospital here (where I seem to be spending most of my time) after a rather gruelling operation on my eye for a splinter of glass which got in it, and, being rather punchy from no sleep, may sound slightly shook; the blessing is, I can see perfectly now, and after a week of hell, the world looks shining and blessed as eden and I am in a "fern hill" mood.[1]

essentially, this letter will be bulletins: I'm staying in cambridge till the 23rd of march, when I have a ride from london to paris. I'll be in paris till you and I meet, and so you can send your final messages to me c/o the american express, 11 rue scribe, paris from this coming saturday, the 24th, on. I plan to sit at holiday tables, sketch, and read along the seine.

1–A reference to the poem 'Fern Hill' by Dylan Thomas.

I would be happy if you got the flight to london and came to pick me up in paris on your way to germany. on the other hand, if I met you in germany, the best place would be munich, I think, which might put the date off later for you, since you want to do such business about universities before heading south. as you probably leave the states late in march or early april, give me the best address for me to telegraph our final meeting time and place from paris. if you could write me a letter in paris telling me of your final flight plans and your preference for itinerary (meeting me either in munich, later, or paris, when you come), I shall be able to write back ultimate confirmation.

my time will be limited by the fact that I have to be back in cambridge on april 14th, ready to plunge into an arduous semester of study on the moralists in philosophy, starting with plato and ending up with d. h. lawrence under a brilliant, but demanding, supervisor. thus perhaps I could plan to fly to london from rome on the 13th or 14th, and you coming or not, as you wished. it might be best for you to see your relatives then, and then come back for a short stay with me in cambridge, after I had got my first week of term's work accomplished.

naturally, I hope that we can spend as much time as possible in my 3 favorite aimed cities Venice, Florence and Rome. somehow, it seems a little like sacrilege to "run through" them without having a few days at least in each, and if you're willing, I'd be pleased to drive right through central europe and concentrate on absorbing italian atmosphere for at least a week. how about that? I'd rather soak up these three places than just dash through on one-night stands. I do have a beautiful and enchanting friend in switzerland who has invited us to come visit her for a day or two,[1] but that will probably be impossible with our limited time. I just wish my vacation began and ended later, but we are so damn lucky anyway that even 2 weeks coincide!

about finances: I shall be fortunate if I get even a few pounds smuggled into france to keep me alive for the week or 10 days I'll be in paris, so shall probably be close to broke when I see you. however, if you could possibly help me with expenses while we travel, I'd be able to reimburse you in pounds (as much as we mutually decide upon) as soon as we get to england. I'll be happy to be your guest part of the time, if you feel desirous of this; I'm not all that rigidly scrupulous, if you feel endowed enough to host now and then, or often as you please. we'll talk about this when we get together.

1 – According to SP's calendar, this was Marianne Frisch in Arlesheim, Switzerland.

as for the "us" part of this: I am proud to think that we are both strong enough to be dear, good friends and am sure that the trip will be a fine one. we can "be alone" with each other, I mean, in our particular selves (I always feel more free when I'm traveling with someone, because it makes a whole unit, complete in itself, and then I'm not beset with pick-ups or unsought conversation) and both modulate our own plans to make a fruitful voyage. I feel so at ease with you, and will always be so interested in your ideas and experiences, that we shall probably have a most wonderful time making discoveries together and adventuring. I shall never get over the feeling that we "go together" in an important way, however the currents of our mutual lives may diverge in actuality; and so, will always want to be aware of a rich friendship with you. in this light, I think, we shall have a fine time together; we can enjoy each other thoroughly as highly congenial people.

ah well, I am not saying as well as I should, partly because I haven't slept for two days, and ergo am rather blurred after this most traumatic experience. write me in paris and tell me what day and time you'll meet me there or in munich (there is a day train getting into munich from paris at sometime around 9 or 10 in the evening). do let me know as soon as you can. also, whether you'd like to haste to italy as soon as possible, too. your mother wrote me a dear letter last week which I enjoyed so much. it will be nice, in a way, to be "taken care of" a bit again, or to have a protective man guard me: I seem to get into more drastic predicaments!

I am looking extremely forward to this trip and hope to hear from you very soon.

until april,
your fond sylvia

TO *Aurelia Schober Plath*

Tuesday 20 March 1956 — TLS (aerogramme), Indiana University

Tuesday noon
March 20, 1956

Dearest mother . . .

I received your lovely letter this morning with the note about the Saxton Fund, which I am coming to believe is exactly the chance I want to devote a year to nothing but writing while living in southern France and Italy. It is possible to write while studying or teaching, but I need an opportunity to concentrate on nothing but for a year to find my style, my voice. I do believe I have one! But the complex life here, and the academic demands of my Fulbright, make writing too incidental.

Do tell me what the doctor's verdict is on grammy's difficulty. She is such a dear, courageous woman, and I love her so! And I only hope you are not straining yourself too much with this double life of teacher and visiting nurse! When you come to England in June, I want you to worry about nothing, and I shall take complete charge of you for at least 10 days! Already so many lovely plans are sprouting in my head!

My eye is getting better every day: I am going tomorrow to the hospital for a final check-up. Your postal money order finally came, and I went out this morning for my pre-Europe shopping trip: had my hair trimmed (I feel so worldly when I tell the sweet hairdresser: "Yes, I'm spending the easter vacation in Paris and Rome!") and investigated a different bank, where I wheedled my way around currency regulations and bought francs with pounds (you have no idea how hard it is for me to maneuver between the legal pitfalls, but I signed a business man's form for travel-allowance abroad, and told them I was writing articles.)

I must admit that a smile and a helpless gentle air go a long way. I was charioted about the bank after hours, and given a marvelous exchange rate, and found that this bank would let me open an "American account", so that you can please send me any checks I get in dollars in America, and they will convert them into dollar traveler's checks. I'm living completely on my Fulbright, & do feel justified in working "deals" to travel abroad. Shh. I'm very careful.

In a splurge, I bought not one but <u>three</u> exquisite cashmere sweaters this morning! I haven't looked at clothes since I've been here, and felt rather dowdy: they are the most divine colors, and at least \$5 to \$7 cheaper than in America. I got two long-sleeved ones, in a luscious turquoise and cherry-red with blue in it, and a short-sleeved deep jade or forest green one! Now for the job of sewing in shields! Next fall I think I may well invest in a London tweed suit and coat which would be more practical for informal living than my charcoal gray cashmere coat; since I have to spend all my Fulbright money in England, I want to make the most of it! My sweaters were a kind of spring gift to myself for working so hard this term and being brave for my eye operation; I feel so happy with them!

I am just beginning to rest up again, and by the time I go to London Friday should feel like a new woman. Yesterday I spent with a very nice boy from Trinity College[1] whom I met in the casualty ward last week. He took me on a long liesurely walk along the Backs where the crocuses are a riot of purple and gold and already students are lounging on the brilliant green grass under the spires of King's Chapel reading poetry or just lazily watching the punts maneuver past. Such a sense of timeless peace. <u>You</u> will love this.

Where, by the way, is the money for grammy's hospital care coming from? I am so lucky here under "the system" for I have to pay nothing for doctor's or hospital fees while the British have to pay large weekly amounts insurance. I must say, too, I am happier every day to be an American! For all the golden "atmosphere" of England, there is an oppressive ugliness about even the upper middle class homes, an ancient, threadbare dirtiness which at first shocked me; our little white house is a gem of light and color compared to the dwellings here. On a low budget in America, one can have stylish clothes and mobility and health. And the "class-system" is really nonexistent. Someday maybe I'll have a home in the Conn. valley, lots of children, stories and Cape Cod summers!

I am so happy Warren is well and jumping again! I really miss him, and hope it will be possible to see him in Germany this summer! I think I may go out for the university weekly newspaper[2] next term as reporter, for I believe that my Fulbright renewal had something to do with my acting and writing and thus "mixing" with Britishers and giving something, instead of just grubbing in the library. I'd meet a lot of interesting people and keep my hand in the reporting line, which will be good practice, and also, be on "the inside" of Cambridge life. This summer I think I'll either take ballet or horseback riding lessons! I have so much energy, I'd like to put it to formal use, and want to be a Renaissance woman all my life long. Now that spring is here, and I can see, and am getting rested, all seems possible. Please give my dearest love to grammy; I think of her constantly, and wish for her health. She is a saintly woman. Keep a large amount of love for yourself, and take good care: I want a rosy fat mummy to meet me in June!

Love to all –
sivvy

1 – According to SP's calendar, this was George Gavin Blakey; B.A. 1957, economics, law, Trinity College, Cambridge.
2 – *Varsity*.

TO *Aurelia Greenwood Schober*

Wednesday 21 March 1956[1] ALS (picture postcard), Indiana University

<picture postcard caption>
Trinity Bridge, Cambridge.

4 Barton Road
Cambridge, Eng.

Dearest grammy . .

The leaves along the river aren't out like this yet, but it's warm enough to boat between banks of purple & gold crocuses! I do hope you'll feel much better with the returning spring and I wanted to send you Easter greetings together with all my love & hope for your getting better soon. If you only knew how much I think of you & miss you! My Love to dear grampy, too.

Your own roving granddaughter –
Sylvia

TO *Jane V. Anderson*

Wednesday 21 March 1956 TLS (photocopy), Smith College

Wednesday, March 21

Dear Jane . . .

It was so nice to hear from you and learn about your plans for coming to Europe this summer. I shall be in Cambridge till about June 10th, and would like so much to see you and Dot Wormser[2] when you come (I remember her vaguely from some art courses at Smith). Cambridge will probably be at its best then, with exams over, & the legendary May Balls in full swing, which last till dawn with breakfasts in the apple orchards in Granchester. Please do come up and let's plan to have lunch, and maybe I can consider myself expert enough on Cambridge by then to take you about: although you'll probably be able to tell me a good deal about the fine & complex architecture which has been surrounding me for the past year! Spring has already begun here, after the arduous siberian winter,

1–Date supplied from postmark.

2–Dorothea Wormser Stein (1930–88); B.A. 1952, art, Smith College; resident of Gillett House. While Wormser was an art major, she had no art classes with SP.

and crocuses are sprouting in yellow and purple along the Backs under the spires of King's Chapel, while a kind of gold haze gives an atmosphere of centuries of peace along the narrow river where punts are out already.

I was so interested to hear about your plans for med school and can't tell you how much I admire you; you certainly are working toward a difficult, most rewarding career. Let me know where you finally decide to go: you're right about the importance of being a doctor coming first, & the particular school being secondary. Harvard seems to give an especially hard time. I don't remember whether I told you about a gruelling interview I had there last winter (by four men, all at once!) when they spent almost an hour asking me difficult & mocking questions (on everything from philsophies of teaching to what I thought of marriage), & ended up by refusing me a scholarship. I can understand how difficult some of your interviews must have been.

I, too, have felt the handicap of having a record in a mental hospital, and probably was the only Fulbright student to have a letter of recommendation written by her psychiatrist! But I decided to be frank, although I feared it might cut me out; I can't say how I appreciate their accepting the risk (being as I was going abroad to a completely new situation made it even more risky for them) and I heard just this week that by some miracle I am one of the 20 "happy few" to get a renewal for this coming year, so I can finish my Honours B.A. degree. Each month of reliable living & growing, I think, is a solid step away from McLean. Do you remember Carol Pierson, my vital, talented friend at Smith? Well, she is in Belknap now! When I am wealthy, I am going to endow a fund to finance a group of bright, young psychiatrists to work at Smith on a visiting, part-time basis so they can keep up city practices!

Life here is so rich and complex that it is hard to remember the hard times (and there have been very dark days, however rosy a mere skimming summary may sound). I started out in amateur dramatics when I came, and met many fine creative people this way. In courses, I'm hearing lectures by men like Basil Willey, David Daiches & F. R. Leavis. Cultural life is better than NYC! This term alone, for example, I saw several surrealistic films (2 by my admired Cocteau: "Orphée", "La Belle et La Bête") O'Casey's "Juno & Paycock";[1] a student performance of "Troilus & Cressida" rivaling Old Vic; Euripides' "Bacchae" <u>in Greek</u> with student chorus, sets & original music; heard Vienna choirboys in King's Chapel, and on and

1–Sean O'Casey, *Juno and the Paycock* (1924); presented by the Comedy Theatre Club, SP saw the play with Luke Myers on 15 March 1956.

on. It is hardest to choose among the lives offered: politics, too, are most vital & controversial, with communist & fascist groups, arab & israeli disputes, etc. Next term, I'm cutting out all but one unit with a brilliant young woman don in the moralists (which will give me good discipline in philosophy) so I can spend mornings just writing.

Best of all though, is the continuous proximity of the continent in the three long vacations! Untraveled that I am, I luxuriate in this new mobility: I just take out a map of Europe & plan! I spent Christmas in Paris for 10 days with an artist-writer friend at the Sorbonne, going to plays, Louvre, Orangerie, cafes, & walking miles & miles; we took an express to the Mediterranean on New Year's & based ourselves in Nice, rented a motor-scooter, & rode along blazing blue Riviera through Villefranche, Menton, Monaco, to Italy in clear sunlight by violent green palms, olive trees, orange groves & frivolous pastel villas. I was so hungry for color, & find the southern temperament so congenial that I'm going to try somehow to get a year for writing in southern Europe after I graduate in June 1957. I just can't bear to put the Atlantic between me and Europe! Am leaving tomorrow for London, then April in Paris, and am meeting Gordon Lameyer in Germany for a drive to Rome through Venice & Florence for Easter. So you see, the world is coming alive. There is much fighting and inner struggling going on all the time, a kind of forging of the soul through conflict, and, often, pain, but behind it all, there is this Chaucerian affirmation which holds fast.

I look so forward to hearing from you, and want you to know how interested I am in what you are doing next year. I hope I'll have a chance to "really talk" to you when you come to Cambridge this June!

Good luck and best wishes!
Sincerely,
Sylvia

TO *Marcia B. Stern*

Wednesday 21 March 1956 TLS (aerogramme), Smith College

wednesday, march 21

dear marty . . .

miraculously the siberian winter is gone and my gable window opens out on a garden all blowing purple and yellow crocuses in the sun, while the air is full of birds twirping and voices of turtles. god, it is beautiful here, along the Backs, with a kind of golden, mellow, renaissance haze along the swanful river! I've been skipping around in this week after the end of a really tough term (lots of classes & supervisions) buying pussy-willows, hearing vienna choirboys sing in king's chapel, savoring a few very fine people at leisure over tea and sherry, and marshaling forces for the easter vacation: hold your hat and listen to this, because I still can't quite believe it: I'm heading for london friday (visiting two young erratic poets: one, allen tate's cousin, e. lucas meyers,[1] good friend of bert wyatt-brown[2] who is somehow very much aware of charlie gardner & mike--via st. james? and a british guy), driving to paris, via canterbury, right over channel, with a fulbright fellow at the london school of economics, spending easter and april in paris with holiday tables and all that, for a week, meeting gordon lameyer somewhere in germany (where he's flying over to look for a university for next year) and driving through austria, venice, & florence, to rome!

somehow, fairy-tale as it sounds, I feel I really deserve it after this long, packed arduous winter where I've been in the casualty ward twice: once for an emergency appendix which wasn't after all, and recently for a splinter which got in my eye & had to be operated on while I was fully conscious and staring up into the knives babbling frantically about oedipus and gloucester getting new vision by losing their eyes, but me wanting, so to speak, new vision and my eyes too. the doctor quoted housman[3] cheerfully: "if by chance your eye offend you, pluck it out lass and be sound." but I can see fine now, and all is well.

life here is so rich I can't begin to describe it: this term I've seen two superlative cocteau films (esp. "orphée"), sean o'casey's "juno & paycock", a production of shakespeare's "troilus & cressida" rivaling the old vic, a play <u>in greek</u>: euripides' "bacchae" complete with student chorus, sets, & original music; vaughan williams' opera "sir john in love" & much much more! student life here is fast, furious and creative. had sherry with stephen spender (most impressive build, snow-white hair & brilliant blue eyes) on his visit here & am simply loving this life. it's so hard to find fault, so much is good, but I had a dark time this winter with the flu, frigid cold, & over-crowded classes. but next term, I've got a fine

1–Elvis Lucas Myers (1930–), American; B.A. 1953, University of the South; B.A. 1956, archaeology and anthropology, Downing College, Cambridge; friend of TH and contributor to *Saint Botolph's Review*.

2–Bertram Wyatt-Brown (1932–2012), American; B.A. 1953, University of the South; B.A. 1957, history, King's College, Cambridge; dated SP's housemate Jane Baltzell.

3–English scholar and poet A. E. Housman (1859–1936); his 'XLV. If it chance your eye offend you'. The lines read 'If it chance your eye offend you, / Pluck it out, lad, and be sound'.

brilliant, beautiful young supervisor in philosophy, & have cut out all else so I can write mornings daily, while reading german & french on my own: this woman's lecture on d. h. lawrence's concept of the redemptive power of love in "the man who died" is the finest, frankest I've heard in my life: she'll be a blessed change from the majority of newnham grotesque dons who are relics from the victorian era when a woman had to sacrifice all claims to femininity & family to be a scholar!

by some joyous miracle my fulbright was renewed this week for next year, so I can get my honors BA in june 1957. I'll be reading here about a month this summer & hopefully seeing mother in england in june (my grandmother has cancer, so things are dubious & hard at home) & traveling in spain with elly friedman, later to greece. honestly, marty, this mobility, with all the countries in the world just over the channel is the most wonderful feeling! I can go out and live in the long vacations, and come back & write in this tranquil atmosphere. so far, I've only done a few poems, a story, & a news article & sketch on cambridge (for the monitor, which came out around march 5 or 6.)

I must admit I'm slightly concerned at my total lack of desire to come back home ever! the thought of the atlantic between me and europe literally makes me have claustrophobia! I'm seriously thinking of schemes which would let me live in southern europe (france, italy or spain) for a year just writing. this heavy critical atmosphere here (influenced badly by f. r. leavis, I'm afraid) can be deadly: I had 2 poems published in the "little mags" & the number of reviews they got was astounding: it seems there are 50 critics & dissectors ready to fasten like leeches to every poem ground out! I find myself loth to go on to any more grad work after this, & want very badly to "find my voice" writing before I teach.

cambridge is also intriguing from the point of view of politics: I am getting more and more aware: we have arabs & jews arguing here, south african communists who are going back to fight the totalitarian white government that keeps the colored people in appalling chains; indians, orientals (one man is translating greek literature into persian!) all is fluid, mobile: traveling in europe with the multilinguial signs, the chance to meet people from all different national backgrounds & professions, all that! I spent christmas in paris with richard sassoon (at sorbonne) going to plays, walking miles & miles along seine, through montmartre up hill to sacre coeur, listening to whores (fascinating) pickup & refuse, a whole day in tuileries playing with children & going to "grand guignol" puppetshow, endless escargots, wine, cognac sessions, louvre & orangerie with original cezannes. all this, then new year's morning seeing sun exploding up out of incredibly azure med: living in nice, motorscootered all along riviera to italy, matisse chapel in vence. oh marty, so much: the whole world coming alive, banging through my eyes and fibers! want so to write & write it all down. am very hungry for news from usa: esp. regarding production plans! also, more re carol et. al.! love to you & mike . . .

SYL

TO *Aurelia Schober Plath*

Mon.–Wed. 26–28 March 1956 — TLS[1] with envelope, Indiana University

Monday morning

Dearest mother . . .

Oh you would never believe it if you saw me now: I have the loveliest garret in Paris[2] over-looking the rooftops and gables and artists' skylight! I was marvelously lucky to find a place during the Easter week because everywhere is full and I moved to this room this morning: it costs 520 francs a night which is roughly one dollar fifty and not bad especially at this time. I hear music now rising up in the courtyard; the people here are lovely in the hotel and I am fortunate to have such genial characters running it: they gave me this cheapest room today because they knew I was a student.

I had a rather bumpy ride here with a Fulbright student from the London School of Economics and his girl, a beautiful flighty british thing. The crossing was wonderfully smooth however & I had a good dinner on shipboard Saturday. I was exhausted Saturday night and felt very much alone. Luckily, I met the nicest man in the hotel lobby who offered to loan me his map of Paris since I'd left mine in Emmet's car. He turned out to be an Italian journalist, Paris correspondent for the communist newspaper in Rome: Paese Sera; well, since he speaks no English, we both managed in French, and had a really fine conversation: he had read so much American lit. in translation (admires Melville, Poe, TS Eliot etc.) and it is his olivetti I'm borrowing now (some letters are differently placed, hence the mistakes); I was amazed at my ability to carry on

1–Pages numbered 1 and 2 by SP are from 26 March 1956. The 28 March 1956 letter continues this and is numbered by SP 3, 4, 5, and 6.

2–Per the return address on the envelope, SP stayed in room 26, Hôtel de Béarn, then at 38 rue de Lille, Paris.

conversation & learned new words fast. His name is Giovanni Perego[1] & he writes mainly political articles but also on artists & writers. He is without a doubt the nicest communist I've ever met and I've learned so much: he is very idealistic & has fine aesthetic appreciations: fought in the resistance during the war and has been a journalist for 11 years: yesterday he introduced me to his friend Lucio, also a journalist from Rome, and Lucio's most lovely blonde German sweetheart Margot who is studying french here: we had a good supper at a small cheap restaurant & fine conversation: Lucio was very proud of speaking English which he had learned as a British prisoner for 5 years in the African campaign and told me a good deal about the British & maumau in Africa, especially Kenya. I am learning more every day!

Perhaps the hardest & yet best thing for me is that Sassoon isn't here; he is still down south on vacation, so except for a possible Cambridge boy I know is coming, I am on my own. As you may imagine, this is very different from being escorted everywhere as I was at Christmas but I am getting most proud of my ability to maneuver alone! It is good for me and I am beginning to enjoy it thoroughly: the weather is heaven: warm enough to sit out in the sun, and all Sunday afternoon I sketched in pen & ink on the green park on the tip of the Ile de la Cité where dozens of tourists came to stare at my little sketch of the Pont Neuf; I felt happy to sketch for the first time since my Cambridge drawing and feel it is my best passport to paris! Ah well, I'm off to the American Express to see if there's any mail. Will write more soon. Love to all from your

Americaine à Paris!
Sylvia

Wednesday morning
March 28

Dearest of mothers . . . .

Eh bien, life gets better and better: I am sitting by my window with the fresh morning air blowing the starched white curtains and my own special vista of rooftops & chimney-pots which I draw daily, it has such good tilts and textures: to me it is simply beautiful; there is a large green-eyed cat at the window opposite, a tiger cat, who stares at me when I work and plays games of hiding. I am getting to love this city like no other in the world: it is so intimate & warm and kind with its lacy gray stone buildings, hundreds of black wroughtiron balconies, marvelous gardens & parks and little shops all pastels and even the peeling walls & colored

1–Giovanni Perego; Paris correspondent of *Paese Sera*; dated SP, spring 1956.

posters pasted over each other seem exquisite to me. My day begins early: I have breakfast in bed about 9: two big cups of cafe au lait, two moist fluffy croissons (which float above the plate, they're so light) with lots of delectable unsalted butter. Then I write a bit on Giovanni's typewriter (his day begins in the afternoon & he does his articles at night) which he comes every morning to lend me; it is so nice to have someone in the hotel who knows me, and Giovanni is like a kind father and so helpful. I walk about 5 to 10 miles a day and it is the best way: I can dawdle, look in windows (I live by the way in a wonderful district full of antique shops and small esoteric art galleries) and when a view pleases me, sit down to sketch. I have never felt so growingly proud of my increasing ability to take care of myself: I am so happy that I skip & sing in the parks. I wrote a note to Anthony Gray,[1] the British boy I just met before I left, & he surprised me by coming over that very night with his sister Sally:[2] I was napping (from about six to eight pm) because I'd walked over ten miles & was weary. It was so nice to wake up & find them: we went out to dinner together & had a good talk: Tony is tall, blond & blue-eyed, and an Oxford man (his father teaches Zoology at Cambridge[3]) and very debonair and confident, much the most self-assured fellow, good for fun but I am sure not for serious talk (so many Englishmen think women become unfeminine when they have ideas & opinions); Sally is small, terribly conventional & with bad feet & thick ankles so she can't walk far; I'm sure my gay joie de vivre & casualness shocks her! You see, I am developing the most happy-go-lucky attitude about details such as clothes, etc: I learned a lot from my last trip (where I loaded myself down with endless dresses pettitcoats & shoes) and am really traveling light: I bought the most wonderful light khaki mackintosh before leaving Cambridge which is cut in high-fashion, with princess lines like an evening coat, with shiny round gold buttons & a back-belt: it is just the thing for this divine warm weather. I can sit on the ground & sketch in it or wear it over my black velvet dress to the theater (which I did last night) and feel chic. I wear my cashmere sweaters with skirts, matching hair-bands and large simple earrings and feel very fine; my ballet shoes are ideal for walking & I only wear stockings at night. My room is dear pale yellow walls patterned with delicate rosebuds and dark green corduroy curtains & dark wood bookshelves!

1–Anthony James Gray (1936–), British; B.A. 1956, New College, Oxford; toured Paris with SP, spring 1956.
2–Anthony Gray's sister.
3–Professor Sir James Gray (1891–1975), Professor of Zoology and Comparative Anatomy 1937–59.

Yesterday was like a fairy-tale: I crossed the Seine about 10 am (I'm really on the Left Bank: just a street away!) and walked past the Louvre into the Tuileries: a kind of garden for children with rows of trees, countless white statues, ponds & fountains for sailing boats & swings & the dearest little pony carts which are always trotting around full of wide-eyed babies; I sniffed the fresh spring air, spotted a ginger-bready refreshment stand which had already opened to sell lemonade & cookies, so rented a chair & sat down to sketch the stand: I was just shading it when I heard my name called & looked up surprised to see Tony & Sally who happened to be walking by; we had lemonade & I joined them on a trip to the Eiffel Tower, which is really an ugly marvel of interlaced girders looking like some domestic Martian animal about to start walking off on all fours; we took the elevator up to the observation platform, and there lay Paris at our feet, with the crooked gray-green Seine, the spires of Notre Dame, the acres of quaint rooftops & chimneypots and red & yellow sunshades on the windows like squares in a Mondrian[1] painting. Sacré coeur rose like a white Byzantine wedding cake on its hill of Montmartre overlooking all. We had dinner in a restaurant up there, with the whole city spread out below through the plate glass windows. I parted from them then & walked along the Grands Boulevards windowshopping & staring at people: Browsed on the Rue de la Paix near the Opera, bought a ticket (balcony for about 250 francs---75 cents!) to Anouilh's new comedy: "Ornifle."[2] Delightful: could understand most of it (at least the plot & most words) & then home to bed. Will be glad when Tony's sister goes tomorrow because I think he will take me out for a little nightlife.

Stood sketching in sun by Seine yesterday & met Garry Haupt! The only two people I know in Paris (Tony & Gary) both have run into me this way! I am having such fun. Gary & I went to dinner & good surrealist movie Wednesday night.[3]

I'm hoping to hear from Gordon any day about when I'll meet him – Should be here through Easter –

Love from
Sylvia –

1–A reference to Dutch painter Piet Mondrian (1872–1944).

2–Jean Anouilh's *Ornifle* played at the Comédie Champs Elysées, 15 Avenue Montaigne, Paris.

3–According to SP's calendar, she saw *Rêves à vendre* at Studio Parnasse, 11 Rue Jules Chaplain, Paris.

TO *Aurelia Schober Plath*

Tuesday 3 April 1956 ALS (picture postcard), Indiana University

<picture postcard caption>
PARIS – Notre Dame.

April 3 – Tuesday

I

Dear mother . . .

I am sitting in a little café about to eat lunch with Gordon whom I met yesterday by a total accident – the American Express having scrupulously sent all mail & notes back to Whitstead (the address I left them last Xmas) so that I went every day for 10 days futilely – I feel terribly concerned & out-of-touch with you since I haven't heard a word since I wrote about my Fulbright & my eye operation. I am anxious to know how grammy is & how you weathered the blizzards – Please write me a kind of summary airmail to: American Express No. 38 Piazza di Spagna Rome, Italy – you can imagine that I am a bit desolate with all mail in England & no word from you

xxx
sivvy

TO *Aurelia Schober Plath*

Thursday 5 April 1956 ALS (picture postcard), Indiana

<picture postcard caption>
PARIS – La Seine au Quai d'Anjou.

Thursday – April 5:

2.

Dearest mother –

Here is one of the vistas in which I have wandered with my sketchbook – went up to Montmartre under domes of sacré coeur with Tony (a very sweet Oxford chap) & had delectable dinner, iced white wine & a silouhette cut as a present amid crowds of onlookers in the central square – saw two plays by Cocteau & Anouilh, and last night with Gordon, a fine ballet at the Opera – Cocteau's version of Racine's "Phèdre" – Am most brave & desolate without Richard – he being still on vacation in south – and hope that trip with Gordon via Munich, Venice, Florence &

Rome will help me forget my loneliness for a week – am flying back to London on April 13 (Friday!) – do write to me c/o Am. Express in Rome before then

xxx
Sivvy

TO *Aurelia Schober Plath*

Tuesday 17 April 1956 TLS (aerogramme), Indiana University

Tuesday afternoon, April 17

Dearest of mothers . . .

I am back at Whitstead at last, grateful to rest in peace, to see no more trains or hotel rooms, to stop running. I didn't get any of your letters all my vacation because of the imbecilic American Express, and so felt terribly cut off from all communication for that time and was glad to get back to my calm, daffodil-starred yet chilly Cambridge and find mail.

It hurts terribly in my heart not to be home with you all, helping you through this hard hard time with grammy; I cannot believe that I will never see her again, and wish that you would make as much effort as you can to give her some of the power of the love I have for her. I feel so cut off, and all my strength so futile here. I love that woman so, and all of you, and would give anything to share the sorrow and the adoration for dear grammy in the community of our family and our neighborhood.

Most of all, I am concerned for you. Will grampy live with Dot and Joe this summer? Because you must come to England. I know the mere prospect of injections or passport must seem insurmountable now, but that is all you must go through, and on the ship you can rest and read the pamphlets or guide books you wish, or just lie in the sun, and the food is good (remember to take seasick pills just in case). I shall meet you at Southampton and take complete charge of you for two weeks; I'll plan a slow relaxed time, and do all the arranging; only let me know definitely if you will arrive the 13th and how long you want to stay, and what places you would like to go most besides London and Cambridge; I shall arrange all the rest, and you can just give yourself into my hands.

Now your birthday is coming up this next week, and I know you will hardly think of it, with all your grieving and concern. However, I would like to order you to take at least from \$30 to \$50 from my money I sent and buy yourself the lightest and prettiest of weekend suitcases. I refuse to let you carry my large case which is heavy even for me, and a weekend case the size of the one I had would be just right. Ive learned that its most important to travel very very light and to take a few things one really loves to wear over and over. Another thing, it is most important to be warm: and in rainy weather, I imagine Austria, and surely England, can be frigid even in summer. So do bring one pair of flannel pajamas, a good warm thick wool sweater (more like a skisweater) and some sort of bathrobe, perhaps. Be sure you have warm stockings and shoes. Otherwise, your plans sound fine. Don't spend any of the money on clothes, because that is of least importance. One black suit or dress, for eve theater or churchgoing; a sweater and shirt, and nylon blouses for walking and daytime. Get a lovely suitcase (maybe Mrs. Cantor can help you) and be sure its light as a feather! Happy Birthday, and remember that I'll be thinking of you and planning to give you England as a delayed present!

I have been having a rather strenuous time, myself of late, and much to deal with. Richard went off to Spain for a month to think things over and was miserable alone and wrote long letters which I didn't receive till I got back here, too late, after feeling terribly deserted in Paris that last week: Giovanni Perego, the communist reporter, was like a kind father and I don't know what I'd have done without his comfort and hot milk and support. Gordon was also a mistake; I should know by now that there is always bound to be a hidden rankling between the rejector and rejected. In spite of this I managed to enjoy much, although fighting a great sorrow and preferring to be alone, rather than with him.

We left Paris for Munich where I froze in a blizzard and Gordon's utter lack of language ability & blundering horrified me, I must admit. We left the next morning (he'd vaguely wanted to see the university) through Austria and the Tyrolean Alps; I sat with my nose pressed to the window and almost cried as we went through Insbruck. Two days in Venice, in a gondola and exploring the little streets & bridges, then to Rome for 5 days where by utter accident we ran into Donald Cheney[1] (remember him: my 6th grade rival!) who'd gone to Choate with Gordon & was on a Fulbright in Rome! I saw much of him & it was heaven to be with someone who spoke the language: sat in sun eating dates in Roman forum, Colisseum, sunlit Spanish steps, lovely spurting fountains everywhere, art museums, Renaissance palaces, Sistine chapel & Vatican (I stared for hours in reverence at Michaelangelo's ceiling & last judgement); yet was happy to

1–Donald Cheney (1932–); B.A. 1954, Yale College.

fly to London Friday the 13th in 4 hours! Greeted by smudgy black rain & cold, but had wash in posh London club & steak dinner there with charming South African ex-Cambridge man[1] I met on plane. Now back to recuperate, write, work. I am writing for the college newspaper, & should have some sketches & an article on Paris[2] in this week; god, it's good to get back to newsprint & an office! I think I'll get along fine; all very nice, honest guys. The most shattering thing is that in the last two months I have fallen terribly in love, which can only lead to great hurt: I met the strongest man in the world, ex-Cambridge, brilliant poet whose work I loved before I met him,[3] a large hulking healthy Adam, half French, half Irish, with a voice like the thunder of God; a singer, story-teller, lion and world-wanderer & vagabond who will never stop. The times I am with him are a horror because I am then so strong & creative & happy, and his very power & brilliance & endless health & iron will to beat the world across is why I love him and never will be able to do more, for he'll blast off to Spain & then Australia & never stop conquering people & saying poems. It is very hard to have him here in Cambridge this week & I am terrified even to have known him, he makes all others mere puny fragments. Such a torment & pain to love him.

ah, well, Forgive my own talk of hurt & sorrow! I love you so & only wish I could be home to help you in yours.

All my love –

sivvy

1–According to SP's calendar, this was Michael Ross Butcher; B.A. 1952, economics, law, Jesus College, Cambridge.

2–Sylvia Plath, 'An American in Paris', *Varsity*, 21 April 1956, 6–7; with two sketches by SP captioned 'Kiosque by Louvre' and 'Tabac opposite the Palais de Justice'.

3–Ted Hughes.

TO *Edward Weeks*

Tuesday 17 April 1956 TLS (photocopy), Yale University

Whitstead
4 Barton Road
Cambridge, England
April 17, 1956

Editor Edward Weeks
THE ATLANTIC MONTHLY
8 Arlington Street
Boston 16, Massachusetts

Dear Editor Weeks:

I am writing from a gabled attic near the Backs of the River Cam where I'm studying for two years at Cambridge University on a Fulbright grant.

Enclosed please find a whole batch of new poems,[1] some of which I hope you may find suitable for publication in the Atlantic.

Thanking you, as always, for your time and consideration,

Sincerely yours,
Sylvia Plath

1–According to handwritten annotations made to the letter by an *Atlantic Monthly* employee, Plath submitted eleven poems. These include only two titles which elicited commentary by *Atlantic* staff: 'Pursuit' and 'Pigeon Post'.

TO *Karl Shapiro*

Tuesday 17 April 1956 TLS, University of Chicago

Whitstead
4 Barton Road
Cambridge, England
April 17, 1956

Editor Karl Shapiro[1]
POETRY
60 W. Walton Street
Chicago 10, Illinois

Dear Editor Shapiro:

Enclosed please find a batch of poems,[2] some of which I hope you may find suitable for publication in Poetry. I've had poems published previously in The Atlantic, Harper's, The Nation, Mademoiselle, and the New Orleans Poetry Journal.

Thanking your for your time and consideration.

Sincerely yours,
Sylvia Plath

TO *Richard Sassoon*

Wednesday 18 April 1956 TL (excerpt),[3] Smith College

April 18[4]

now the forces are gathering still against me, and my dearest grandmother who took care of me all my life while mother worked is dying very very slowly and bravely of cancer, and she has not even been able to have intravenous feeding for six weeks but is living on her body, which will be all sublimed away, and then only she may die. my mother is working, teaching, cooking, driving, shoveling snow from blizzards, growing thin in the terror of her slow sorrow. I had hoped to make her strong and healthy, and now she may be too weak herself after this slow death, like my father's slow long death, to come to me. and I am here, futile, cut off from the ritual of family love and neighborhood and from giving

1–American poet and editor Karl Shapiro (1913–2000).
2–A note on the letter indicates SP submitted seven poems.
3–SP excerpted this letter in her journals.
4–'~~To Sassoon:~~ April 18' appears in the original.

strength and love to my dear brave grandmother's dying whom I loved above thought. and my mother will go, and there is the terror of having no parents, no older seasoned beings, to advise and love me in this world.

something very terrifying too has happened to me, which started two months ago and which needed not to have happened, just as it needed not to have happened that you wrote that you did not want to see me in paris and would not go to italy with me. when I came back to london, there seemed only this one way of happening, and I am living now in a kind of present hell and god knows what ceremonies of life or love can patch the havoc wrought.[1] I took care, such care, and even that was not enough, for my being deserted utterly. you said that when you returned to paris, you said that you told me "brutally" your vacation would be spent. well, mine is spent too, brutally, and I am spent, giving with both hands, daily, and the blight and terror has been made in the choice and the superfluous unnecessary and howling void of your long absence. your handwriting has gone so wild and racked not all the devils could burn a meaning out of it.

TO *Aurelia Schober Plath*

Thursday 19 April 1956 — TLS (aerogramme), Indiana University

Thursday morning, April 19

Dearest mother . . .

I have not heard from you in several days and wish with all my heart that these times are not trying beyond endurance. Know I think of you momently, and grammy, and will with all the fierce force of willing I have to make my love cross the seas to you.

I shall tell you now about something most miraculous and thundering and terrifying and wish you to think on it and share some of it. It is this man, this poet, this Ted Hughes. I have never known anything like it: for the first time in my life I can use <u>all</u> my knowing and laughing and force and writing to the hilt all the time, everything, and you should see him, hear him:

He is tall, hulking, with a large-cut face, shocks of dark brown hair and blazing green & blue flecked eyes; he wears the same old clothes all the time: a thick black sweater & wine-stained khaki pants. His voice is richer and rarer than Dylan Thomas, booming through walls and doors: he stalks

1 – See 'Conversation Among the Ruins', *Collected Poems*, 21

into the room and yanks a book out of my cases: Chaucer, Shakespeare, Thomas, and begins to read. He reads his own poems which are better than Thomas and Hopkins many times, and better than all I know: fierce, disciplined with a straight honest saying. He tells me endless stories, in the Irish spinning way, dropping his voice to a hush and acting some out, and I am enchanted: such a yarn-spinner. He is 25 and from Yorkshire, and has done everything in the world: rose-grafting, plowing, reading for movie studios, hunting, fishing; he reads horoscopes, knows Joyce, so much much more than I, but all I love. He is a violent Adam, and his least gesture is like a derrick; unruly, yet creative as God speaking the world; he was a discus-thrower.

He has a health and hugeness so that the more he loves, the more he loves, the more he writes poems, the more he writes poems; he knows all about the habits of animals and takes me amid cows and coots; I am writing poems, & they are better and stronger than anything I have ever done: here is a small one about one night we went into the moonlight to find owls:

Metamorphosis[1]

Haunched like a faun, he hooed
from grove of moon-glint and fen-frost
until all owls in the twigged forest
flapped black to look and brood
on the call this man made.

No sound but a drunken coot
lurching home along river bank;
stars hung water-sunk, so a rank
of double star-eyes lit
boughs where those owls sat.

An arena of yellow eyes
watched the changing shape he cut,
saw hoof harden from foot, saw sprout
goat-horns; heard how god rose
and galloped woodward in that guise.

1–According to SP's calendar, she wrote 'Metamorphosis' (later 'Faun') on 18 April 1956.

Daily I am full of poems; my joy whirls in tongues of words. There is a price, always, and the price I can pay: he is arrogant, used to walking over women like a blast of Jove's lightning, but I am a match: I feel a growing strength, I do not merely idolize, I see right into the core of him, and he knows it, and knows that I am strong enough, and can make him grow. Strange, but all the women he has known and will know bother me not at all. I know myself, in vigor and prime and growing, and know I am strong enough to keep myself whole, no matter what. He is a breaker of things and people; I can teach him care, can use every fiber of wisdom I have to give him growing gentleness of others.

Living in this sick small insular inbred land he has gone wild and become a breaker: drinking and charging about with his glorious poet-friends: but this will change if he gets somewhere the land is big enough, free enough for his colossal gestures. In the midst of my knowing that there is no other man like this, no other man who could breed supermen, with all the vigor of mind and body in this world of cerebralism and with the primitive force too, which has split off in our pale white-collared race---in the midst of this, I accept these days and these livings for I am growing and shall be a woman beyond women for my strength. I have never be so exultant, the joy of using all my wit and womanly wisdom is a joy beyond words; what a huge humor we have, what running strength!

We had dinner last week at Luke Myer's, a fine American boy-poet whose poems are fine in their way as Ted's: no precocious hushed literary circles for us: we write, read, talk plain and straight and produce from the fiber of our hearts and bones. Luke's girl was an artist, and I fell in love with her right away. Ted knows music, so we listen to Beethoven & Bartok in record shops, for free, & I'm making dinner for Ted & a mutual Jewish friend Iko next week, & we'll go listen to Iko's Beethoven. I am happy, in the midst of all jeopardy, and this spring in Cambridge, with Ted here even for a little before he goes off to Spain, and then Australia, is utter joy. I am beyond jealousy, which I something I thought I'd never come to: because myself is fun enough & joy enough, even in sorrow, to make a life! Please think of me, accepting sorrow & pain, but living in the midst in a singing joy which is the best of Hopkins, Thomas, Chaucer, Shakespeare, Blake, Donne, and all the poets we love together.

Your own loving,
sivvy

TO *Aurelia Schober Plath*

Saturday 21 April 1956 — TLS with envelope, Indiana University

Saturday morning
April 21

Dearest of mothers . . .

I only hope the paradoxical joy of my being and intense sense of living as richly and deeply as ever in the world may shed some power and solace in the middle of your dark sad time. I shall tell you most amazing news:

The best thing is my joining Varsity! The Cambridge weekly paper! Here, enclosed,[1] is my first feature and the two upper sketches are mine! The Fulbright commission should go wild with delight. Already I am assigned interviews, fashion stories, sketching at a horse-race! I dearly love the boys on the paper, and as there are only two girl reporters,[2] I feel like Marguerite Higgins, only better!

Guess what: the feature editor[3] has invited me to drive to London on Tuesday with him to a large reception for Bulganin and Kruschev[4] at the Claridge hotel! I am drunk with amazement: shall go wrapped in bunting of stars & stripes! Your daughter drinking in the same room with the heads of Russia!

All gathers in incredible joy. I cannot stop writing poems! They come better and better. They come from the vocabulary of woods and animals and earth that Ted is teaching me: we walked 15 miles yesterday through wood, field and fen, and came home through moonlit granchester and fields of sleeping cows. I cook steaks, trout on my gas ring, and we eat well; we drink sherry in the garden and read poems; we quote on and on: he says a line of Thomas or Shakespeare and says: Finish! We romp through words: I learn new words and use them in poems. My god. Listen: here are two lyrics; they are meant to be said aloud, and they are from my joy in discovering a world I never knew: all nature.

1–Enclosure held by Lilly Library.
2–The other female reporter was Josephine Scarr.
3–Timothy Seton Green; B.A. 1957, history, Christ's College, Cambridge.
4–Soviet politicians Nikolai Bulganin (1895–1975) and Nikita Khrushchev (1894–1971).

Ode for Ted[1]

From under crunch of my man's boot
green oat-sprouts jut;
he names a lapwing, starts rabbits in a rout
legging it most nimble
to sprigged hedge of bramble,
stalks redfox, shrewd stoat.

Loam-humps, he says, moles shunt
up from delved worm-haunt;
blue fur, moles have; hefting chalk-hulled flint
he with rock splits open
knobbed quartz; flayed colors ripen
rich, brown, sudden in sunglint.

For his least look, scant acres yield:
each finger-furrowed field
heaves forth stalk, leaf, fruit-nubbed emerald;
bright grain sprung so rarely
he hauls to his will early;
at his hand's staunch hest, birds build.

Ringdoves roost well within his wood,
shirr songs to suit which mood
he saunters in; how but most glad
could be this adam's woman
when all earth his words do summon
leaps to laud such man's blood!

1–According to SP's calendar, she wrote 'Ode for Ted' on 21 April 1956; originally titled 'Poem for Pan'.

Song[1]

Through fen and farmland walking
with my high mighty love
I saw slow flocked cows move
white hulks on their day's cruising;
milk-sap sprang for their grazing.

Spruce air was bright for looking:
most far in blue, aloft,
clouds steered a burnished drift;
larks' nip and tuck arising
came in for my love's praising.

Sheen of the noon sun striking
took my heart as if
it were a green-tipped leaf
kindled by such rare seizing
into an ardent blazing.

In a nest of spiders plucking
silk of their frail trade
we made our proper bed;
under yellow willows' hazing
I lay for my love's pleasing.

No thought was there of tricking,
yet the artful spider spun
a web for my one man
till at the day's flawed closing
no call could work his rising.

Now far from that ransacking
I range in my unease
and my whole wonder is
that frost's felled all worth prizing
and the early year turned freezing
like the bleak shape of my losing.

1–According to SP's calendar, she finished this poem on 20 April 1956; poem later titled 'Song for a Summer's Day'.

And these are for you to say aloud on your birthday. And remember to buy a lovely suitcase! Please let me know you are coming so I can start making reservations. This is eden here, and the people are all shining and I must show it you!

All my love –
your singing girl –
sivvy

ps. If ever someone can get me several copies of CS Monitor articles, please send!

xxx
sivvy

TO *Aurelia Schober Plath*

Monday 23 April 1956

TLS (aerogramme),
Indiana University

Monday, April 23rd

Dearest mother . . .

Well, finally the blundering American Express sent me your letter from Rome telling about the suitcase you bought! Our minds certainly work on the same track! I am sorry to have gone on so about it, you must think I have a memory like water. Now, listen, bring all my money, in dollars, don't change a cent to pounds, and let yourself in for 10 days at my joyful expense here in England.

I have already planned to stay in London 3 nights, and have written to reserve a room for us: we'll just eat and talk the day you come, but for the next two I'll get some theater tickets and we'll plan jaunts to flowering parks, Picadilly, Trafalgar Square, all very easy, walking, strolling, feeding pigeons and sunning ourselves like happy clams. Then, to Cambridge, where I have already reserved a room for you for 2 nights; let me know if you wish to stay longer. I have made a contract with one of my husky men to teach me how to manage a punt before you come, so you shall step one afternoon from your room at the beautiful Garden House Hotel[1] right onto the Cam and be boated up to Granchester through weeping willows for tea in an orchard! Worry about nothing. Just let me know your predilections and it shall be accomplished.

1 – The Garden House Hotel was at Little Saint Mary's Lane, Cambridge.

After this hectic week I'll go to the English-speaking union to see about plans for the next 7 days of our trip: I'll be discovering things with you then and am revolving several plans which I'd like you to write me about, giving your preference: Am I right in thinking you'd rather be a "nature-woman" and wander in beautiful country in peace with your daughter than rush through tourist spots like Stratford? If so, I thought of discovering either the Lake Country, Cornwall, or Wales for a week of simple pleasure: my main joy will be giving you sun (if only England doesn't betray me after this green eden of a spring!) and food and all my love and care.

Then, if you plan to go to Paris, I really would like to get you settled there. I could only stay a day or two, but in that time, I'd see you in a central, reasonable hotel, do my best in my still rough-hewn french, loan you my beautiful Paris map, and take you at least to some of my favorite haunts. It will be tourist-crowded, and I want to show you how to manage and perhaps some very special places. I simply can't let you go there yourself, without a competent guide, and if you will accept my introduction (which as you may see from my article, isn't too bad) I'll be happy to write and reserve rooms there too, if you let me know how many days you want to stay, for it will be packed with tourists!

Me: I'm cherishing the idea of buying an Olivetti in London, under your guidance, if you will be so good (so I won't get cheated) and plan to go to Spain immediately after leaving you in Paris to write, sun and live as cheaply as possible for a month. I can really write now. I have never been so alive. You, too, owe the other end of your line your presence: Frank, Dot, even Grampy, you must remember, have had rich, full lives: they have their families (Frank and Dot have a partner to share whatever choices they must make, whatever troubles to bear; Grampy has had as good a life as a man his age could wish). You, alone, of all, have had crosses that would cause many a stronger woman to break under the never-ceasing load.

You have born daddy's long hard death, and taken on a man's portion in your work; you have fought your own ulcer-attacks, kept us children sheltered, happy, rich with art & music lessons, camp and play; you have seen me through that black night when the only word I knew was No and when I thought I could never write or think again; and, you have been brave through your own operation. Now, just as you begin to breathe, this terrible slow, dragging pain comes upon you, almost as if it would be too easy to free you so soon from the deepest, most exhausting care and giving of love.

Well, when grampy is silent, resentful, when Frank doesn't speak, or Dot is dubious, just think in your heart of the rich, full homes they live in now, with wife and husband; think of the countless years of joy grampy has had, of the home you have made him, which would not have been possible without you, and which he still shall share, and know with a certain knowing that you deserve, too, to be with the loved ones who can give you strength in your trouble: Warren and myself. Think of your trip here as a trip to the heart of strength in your daughter who loves you more dearly than words can say. I am waiting for you, and your trip shall be for your own soul's health and growing; you need, even as Frank and Dot now have, a context where all burdens are not on your shoulders, where some loving person comes to heft the hardest, to walk beside you. Know this, and know that it is right you should come. You need to imbibe power and health and serenity to return to your job, grampy, and whatever else our home has in store. I feel with all my joy and life that these are qualities I can give you, from the fulness and brimming of my heart. So come, and slowly we will walk through green gardens and marvel at this strange and sweet world.

your own loving
sivvy

<on the return address side of letter>

PS: Guess what! I'm going to London this Tuesday to attend a posh press reception for comrades Bulganin and Khruschev at the Claridge Hotel! As a Varsity reporter, with two other boys & a girl![1] I am overcome. Very tempted to capitalize on article material! Think I told you before. but forgive me!

xxx
sivvy

1–According to SP's calendar, she attended with Timothy Green, Barry Wagg, and Jo Scarr.

TO *Warren Plath*

Monday 23 April 1956 — TLS in greeting card[1] (photocopy), Indiana University

<printed greeting>

I feel / Gay as a Ferris / Wheel / As an Acrobat Troupe / As a / Loop the loop / As a pink / Lemonade / As a Penny / Arcade / And the reason I'm gay / As a carnival in May / Is because / It's Your Birthday

<signed>

best / love / from / your own sivvy / see inside →

Monday morning, April 23rd

Dearest Warren . . .

I realize this card may sound strange to you, coming as it does in the midst of this dark time which I am so grieved not so share, but it is the week of your birthday, and for this I rejoice, and am glad. And it is spring in Cambridge, with incredible fields of daffodils and cherry blossoms and rare colored birds singing and a peace of golden honey-air along the Cam, and for this I am glad: that in face of blackness and cruelty and unreason, Chaucer's world sprouts green in everlasting cycles of birth leaps like the corn-god out of the husks of death.

This letter is only for you: I am asking you some things to help me in. First, I have hacked through a hard vacation, shared really only the best parts with mother, not the racking ones (it is so easy to give merely the impression of rich joy here, and not the roots of sorrow and hurt from which it comes) and am now coming into the full of my power: I am writing poetry as I never have before, and it is the best, because I am strong in myself and in love with the only man in the world who is my match and whom I shall no doubt never see after this summer as he is going to Australia. He is worth you, the very first one, and worth me and all the strength and health I have; maybe mother will show you one or two poems I've sent her about him; his name is Ted Hughes: he is tall, hulking, with rough brown hair, a large-cut face, hands like derricks, a voice more thundering and rich than Dylan Thomas, a force that breaks windows when he stalks into a room, half-Irish and half-French with a gift of story-telling that spellbinds; he writes poetry that masters form, bangs and smashes through speech to go better than Yeats, better than Hopkins at its best: none of this pale niggling cerebralizing. We are both

1 – On Panda Prints birthday card designed by Rosalind Welcher.

strong and healthy as blazes. He throws the discus, hunts, shoots, plows, grafts roses, writes for film studios, knows the name of every bird and beast hopping over the moors: I am learning a new vocabulary from him. He hikes into the room, yanks out Chaucer or Shakespeare or Hopkins or Blake and begins to read in a voice that shakes the house. We walked 15 miles the other day, yelling poetry and words and stories at each other. He has done nothing but write, rave, work and desert women for 10 years (graduated from Cambridge two years ago) and is the most brilliant, creative, and violently strong man I have ever met. All this, because I had to tell someone; my poetry, my words, my eyes are sprouting like the bay tree; I am learning about coots and stoats and moles and Cuchulain and Snatchcraftington, one of his fairytale wizards with a face like rhubarb-leaf!

I cook trout and steak in my room, learn poems, read aloud, find owls and hares which come when he whistles; he is rough, rugged: has worn the same thick black sweater & khaki pants for the two months I've known him. What, you say, is the catch? The catch is that he has never thought about anything or anyone except himself and his will (but for a few men friends) and has done a kind of uncaring rip through every woman he's ever met. I am the first one, I think, who is as strong in herself (by this I mean, the sense of self which is inviolable & creative in spite of all) as he is, who can see the lack of care in him, and be independent: this gives me a kind of balance of power. I could make him kind, I think, and a little more caring of people; but I know what I shall never again find his like in the world. Such times we have. I would give everything if you could meet him; never have two people, too strong for most in one dose, lived so powerfully & creatively!

All this, by way of the joy I live in. Now, to business: I want mother to come to England for 10 green healing days at my expense. I shall plan all, shall give all my love and care to her: London, Cambridge, and some country place where she can rest, sun, heal, and be mended and grow strong in the world of nature, which I am learning is the solace of all grief and pain. I want you to work <u>daily</u> at her, emphasizing something she may not see in face of grampy's resentment & Frank & Dot's grudging: mother alone, of all of them, has has crosses to bear that would shatter a stronger soul: daddy's long hard death, her own ulcer, taking man's role of job, my black time when I thought I could never think or write again, her operation, and now, this. Grampy has had the best, richest life a man could want for his years with grammy as partner; Frank and Dot have husband and wife to bear choices, share sorrow, heft burdens. Mother alone has had to fight: now you and I are come of age and coming of strength: we can give her that power and renewed joy of living which the others have: She needs to be taken care of, and for this, I want you to convince her subtly that she not only deserves to come, but that it is morally the right thing: I shall plan all details, and she will have to do nothing but say her wishes, be guided about, and trust me to devote every fiber of my new strength & love to this end; I shall even see her on her first days in Paris, though I vowed never to return there. Do write. I hunger so to share some of my life with you, to learn of yours, even though the obligations of my philosophy course is now on my neck, I write: one has to make time. I love you beyond words. You and mother are my whole family, and now you and I must give of ourselves to make her life rich and radiant, in the midst of her great sorrow. I so hope you can come to Europe this summer.

My most proud love on your birthday & coming of age!

Sivvy

ps. – see back!

A small postscript, as I discovered this white space and can't let a speck go to waste! I am, as mother may tell, a reporter on Varsity, the Cambridge weekly paper, and just got a huge article & two sketches on Paris published this week which I sent her. Tuesday, I am going to London with 3 other reporters to a Press reception for comrades Bulganin and Krushchev! How's that for High! Maybe I'll interview stewards & Scotland yard for an article! What a chance! Am hoping to get scattered poems published this spring & get together a book for a contest in June at which Richard Wilbur & 4 other poets whose style is congenial to mine, will judge; won't know till October, but am determined to publish a book of 33 poems within next year. Then, apply for a Saxton fellowship to write for a year in Italy or Spain. I am living like mad, and would like to find my voice in writing: I'm sketching again, too: stilted, stiff, but fun. Oh, Warren, how I long to see you again; we can teach each other so much by our respective lives; I am finding a growing self and soul of which I am becoming proud in a good, honest sense. The one sin in this world is exploiting other people or cheating & fooling oneself; it's a lifelong fight to forge a vital life; I wish us both the guts and grace to do it on your birthday and my half-birthday. I'll get Ted to read your horoscope! He does that, too!

Love again,

Sivvy

ps. maybe you could share some of this with mother after all!

TO *Aurelia Schober Plath*

Thursday 26 April 1956 TLS (aerogramme), Indiana University

Thursday morning, April 26

Dearest mother . . .

Happy birthday! I am thinking of you at this very moment and hoping that in the midst of your present trial you can spare the energy and moment to be glad, most utterly, that you were born, to carry on grammy's spirit and flesh, and to spread the blood and being of our line to Warren and me: we have had such joys in our lives that it is only fitting somehow we be chastened and strengthened by bearing sorrow. If anyone asked me what time of my life was most invaluable, I would say those 6 terrible months at McLean: for by re-forging my soul, I am a woman now the like of which I could never have dreamed of.

Last night, at the posh Claridge Hotel, with the hammer & sickle waving over the door, your daughter shook hands with Bulganin! Oh, mother, such a time! Read the April 24th write-ups in the papers! The biggest diplomatic crush of all time! I stayed the full 2-hours from 6:30 to 8:30 and gorged on more black caviare than I've ever seen in my life, drank Russia's health in vodka, and met the most amazing people, all through my joy: rubbed elbows with Anthony Eden[1] and Clement Attlee,[2] was introduced as "Miss Plath" by red-clad major domo to Madame and Mr. Malik,[3] Soviet Ambassadors who threw the party. Met many mayors: by accident, mayor of Northampton, England,[4] who, by coincidence, was going to entertain the mayor from my Northampton[5] in a few weeks; had picture taken with the lovely, red-fezzed Commissioner of Nigeria and his beautiful, laughing negro wife:[6] both spoke perfect English and understood my childlike delight at the whole affair. Saw Khrushchev & Bulganin from inches in a press of people that would have crushed them to death had it not been for muscular Russian body-guards: Bulganin a dear white-bearded little man with clear blue eyes, went about like a small plump ship, waving two fingers, smiling, shaking hands and having his

1–British Conservative Party politician Robert Anthony Eden (1897–1977).

2–British Labour Party politician Clement Atlee (1883–1967).

3–Soviet diplomat Jacob Malik (1906–80) and his wife Valentina Malik.

4–The mayor of Northampton through April 1956 was Walter Lewis; in May Thomas H. Cockerill became the new mayor.

5–The mayor of Northampton, Mass., at this time was James Cahillane (1910–91).

6–Chief and Mrs Michael Okorodudu.

interpreters translate the good wishes of all who spoke to him: I found myself shaking his hand and begging "Please do come to visit Cambridge" which word was repeated by his interpreters. The crowd broke into "For he's a jolly good fellow" and one wise-cracking British radio man hissed in my ear: "They'll never let you back in the states if you sing that!" Had several short, good talks with Russian officers who were learning English, even mentioned Dostoevsky, and ended up toasting Russo-American relations in vodka with a charming blond chap working in commerce: both of us agreeing that if we could meet each other as simple people who wanted to have families and jobs and a good life, there would never be any wars, because we would make such friends.

Now, back in Cambridge, it seems impossible to settle down to work: had my first supervision Tuesday morning with my brilliant woman (who reminds me so much of Dr. Beuscher) and we had a fine spirited hour discussing Plato's Gorgias.[1] My mind is whetted; I have never been so keen, so eager to learn: I am in pure delight about this supervision. Am also working on a book of poems which I shall submit just before you come in June to a board of judges[2] (5) including the best poets and most congenial to my style: Louise Bogan, Richard Wilbur, Rolfe Humphries, May Sarton & one other.[3] If this does not pass, I shall write more in the summer and turn it in for the Yale Series of Younger Poets next winter. Ted is teaching me about horoscopes, how to cook herring roes, and we are going to the world's biggest circus tonight. God, such a life!

Now in the midst of all this I am working hard on arrangements for your 10 days in my fair country! I have reserved a luxurious room for us in London on Fleet Street (where all the newspapers are) which I stayed[4] in before going to Paris, courtesy of Emmet Larkin, Phd student and Fulbrighter from NYC: only members of the hotel can reserve this guest-room, so I got it through him. Also have you room in Cambridge hotel. Now for a matter of your choice: I have the unparalelled chance to get us tickets for a trip to Stratford-on-Avon for Friday and Saturday the 15th to 16th including seeing "Hamlet" & "Othello". Now this would mean our cutting London to a mere one day and coming almost right up to Cambridge, so we could leave early Friday morning. Would you like to do this, or would you rather spend all Friday and Saturday in London,

1–Plato, *Lysis, Symposium, Gorgias* (London: William Heinemann, 1953); SP's copy is held by Smith College.

2–This was for the Lamont Poetry Selection of the Academy of American Poets.

3–American poet John Holmes (1904–62).

4–SP stayed at Clifford's Inn, Fetter Lane, off Fleet Street, London.

walking about and seeing things and plays there? I thought you might want to take advantage of the Stratford jaunt, as it's a harder place to get to, and you'll probably have a chance to see as much London as you want in August when you come back with Mrs. Prouty. I'll tentatively reserve tickets to Stratford and do write quickly and let me know! For the rest of our week, I'm thinking of renting a car (after getting a British license if I can this May) and driving us to the most beautiful coast of Wales. I have a hankering for Wales, and Dylan-Thomas salt water and thought you might like a slow cruising drive there, stopped at leisure, not on a train. We'll see. Let me know if it sounds good to you! I am looking more forward to your coming than you can imagine. Also let met know what days you'd like me to reserve for you in Paris at a hotel! When and if you have a chance, could you send over my "Joy of Cooking"? It's the one book I really miss!

Love and joy from your Caviar-ful daughter,

sivvy

TO *Aurelia Schober Plath*

Sunday 29 April 1956 — TLS with envelope, Indiana University

April 29th
Sunday morning

Dearest most wonderful of mothers . . .

I'm so struck full of joy and love I can scarcely stop a minute from dancing, writing poems, cooking and living. I sleep a bare eight hours a night and wake springing up merry with the sun. Outside my window now is our green garden with a pink cherry tree right under my window in full bloom, thick with thrushes caroling.

Enclosed: article in <u>Varsity</u> by my two friends:[1] I'm trying a free-lance one for the New Yorker called "B. and K. at the Claridge." I met so many peculiar mayors and ministers that it's chock full of anecdotes. I can still hear the rich lovely Negro wife of the commissioner of Nigeria (in red fez) chuckling and saying in perfect English: "It's so nice to see someone excited." I have been so active and busy that I can't even remember if I wrote you about last weekend, or which poems I sent!

1–Jo Scarr and Timothy Green, '"Varsity" Goes to Meet B & K and has Vodka and Caviar', *Varsity*, 28 April 1956, 6. SP is mentioned in the article: 'Sylvia Plath, American undergraduate at Newnham, took the Marshal's hand – "You must come to Cambridge".'

I never have eaten and no doubt never shall eat again so much black caviar, flown especially from Russia; or drink so much vodka! I'm writing enough to make the Fulbright commission go mad with joy: am assigned a brief article on Smith College to appear in Varsity,[1] interview with my favorite South African girl, Margaret Roberts, fashion coverage of shops[2] in Cambridge. Am planning to try Monitor with Paris article, and sketches, after carefully deleting any references to wine or tobacco! Have also been asked to write a newsletter next week for an Oxford paper![3] I'm writing about America for the British, and vice versa for America! Am shipping poems off by the cartload: in two weeks I have written the seven best poems of my life[4] which make the rest look like baby-talk. I am learning and mastering new words each day, and drunker than Dylan, harder than Hopkins, younger than Yeats in my saying. Ted reads in his strong voice, is my best critic, as I am his.

My philosophy supervisor, Doctor Krook, is more than a miracle! She took me on an extra half hour last week, and I'm in medias res of Plato, marveling at the dialectic method, whetting my mind like a blue-bladed knife. Such joy.

Bodily, I've never been healthier: radiance and love just surge out of me like a sun: I can't wait to set you down in its rays: think, I shall devote two whole weeks of my life to taking utter care, and very special tendering, of you. I've already reserved London and Cambridge rooms, have decided against Stratford as It would be too much of a rush and I want to sip slowly the green healing of my paradise with you. We'll leave about the 22nd (I have to be out of Whitstead then) for Paris, where I'll see you through your first two or three days and get all set up for you so you'll know what you want there, and then I'll take off for a month of writing in Spain, on the south coast. Being tan, doing nothing but writing, sunning and cooking. Maybe even learning to catch fish!

Ted is up here this week, and I have become a woman to make you proud. It came over me while we were listening to Beethoven, the sudden shock and knowledge that although this is the one man in the world for me, although I am using every fiber of my being to love him, even so, I am

1 – Sylvia Plath, 'Smith College in Retrospect', *Varsity*, 12 May 1956, 6–7.

2 – Sylvia Plath, 'Sylvia Plath Tours the Stores and Forecasts May Week Fashions', *Varsity*, 26 May 1956, 6–7.

3 – Sylvia Plath, 'Cambridge Letter', *Isis*, 16 May 1956, 9.

4 – According to SP's calendar, in addition to writing 'Faun', 'Ode for Ted', and 'Song for a Summer's Day', she recently wrote: 'Mad Queen's Song' (probably 'The Queen's Complaint') on 18–19 April; 'Firesong' on 21–2 April; 'The Glutton' on 27 April; and 'Strumpet Song' on 29 April 1956.

true to the essence of myself, and I know who that self is, and like her, and will live with her through sorrow and pain, singing all the way, even in anguish and grief, the triumph of life over death and sickness and war and all the flaws of my dear world. And this woman I am stretching to be is one whom no man can send crying out of life. Ted knows this, and I know this, and my next months into the summer, before he goes to Australia, will be spent making him learn with every bit of his mind and heart that my like is not to be found the world over; nor is his, and in the sight of all the stars and planets and words and food and people in the world, there are only the two of us who are whole and strong enough to be a match, one for the other. If he grows to this, the whole world will flare for joy; if not, I shall write and love life all the same.

I know this with a sure strong knowing to the tips of my toes, and having been on the other side of life like Lazarus, I know that my whole being shall be one song of affirmation and love all my life long; I shall praise the lord and the crooked[1] creatures he has made. My life shall be a constant finding of new ways and words in which to do this.

Ted is incredible, mother. We went to the circus the other night and loved it to the hilt; he has not changed his clothes since I met him two months ago, but wears always the same black sweater and corduroy jacket with pockets full of poems, fresh trout and horoscopes. In his horoscope book, imagine, it says people born in scorpio have "squashed-out noses"![2] All the signs in the sky point to this man and me.

How I cook on one gas ring! Ted is the first man who really has a love of food, a clean, strong love: he stalked in the door yesterday with a packet of little pink shrimp and four fresh trout. I made a nectar of shrimp newberg with essence of butter, cream, sherry and cheese, had it on rice, with the trout. It took us 3 hours to peel all the little tiny shrimp, and Ted just lay groaning by the hearth after the meal with utter delight, like a huge Goliath.

His humor is the salt of the earth; I've never laughed so hard and long in my life; he tells me fairy stories, and stories of kings and green knights, and has made up a marvelous fable of his own about a little wizard named Snatchcraftington, who looks like a stalk of rhubarb. He tells me

1 – 'praise the lord and ~~and~~ the crooked' appears in the original.

2 – Possibly a reference to Colin Evans and Herbert T. Waite, *The New Waite's Compendium of Natal Astrology* (London: Routlege & Kegan Paul, 1953), which contains the following quote: 'Scorpio governs the secret parts . . . generally coarse, thick, and curling; bullet-shaped top part of head, prominent over eyes; square face, aquiline or sometimes ill-shapen "squashed-out" type of nose, the face often reminding one of an eagle' (30).

dreams, marvelous colored dreams, about certain red foxes and about his mad cousins. His health is phenomenal. The first man I've known who is brilliant, full of stories, poems (he memorizes all poems he likes, and we quote each other through all literature) and is big, healthy, humorous with the affirming humor of power and vigor. My poems sprout about him like shoots; even when he goes, I shall go on, for what I have learned in loving him is part of me, now, and not dependent on him; this is the core of my joy.

The reason why you must be at ease and not worry about my proud growing this time is because I have learned to make a life growing through toleration of conflict, sorrow, and hurt: I fear none of these things, and turn myself to whatever trial, with an utter faith that life is good, and a song of joy on my lips. I feel like Job, and will rejoice in the deadly blasts of whatever comes. I love others, the girls in the house, the boys on the newspaper, and I am flocked about by people who bask in my sun; I give and give; my whole life will be a saying of poems and a loving of people and giving of my best fiber to them.

This faith comes from the earth and sun; it is pagan in a way; it comes from the heart of man after the fall. I know that within a year I shall publish a book of 33 poems which will hit the critics violently in some way or another; my voice is taking shape, coming strong; Ted says he never read poems by a woman like mine: they are strong and full and rich, not quailing and whining like Teasdale, or simple lyrics like Millay: they are working sweating heaving poems born out of the way words should be said.

I want to get a Saxton grant after Cambridge (I hope to send off a manuscript of poems at the end of May where the best judges I could have would decide: Richard Wilbur, Rolfe Humphries, May Sarton, Louise Bogan: all in love with words and lyrics, not loose social statements!) and if this does not win, I shall try Auden next winter with my summer's harvest. I haven't time to write stories now, but this summer I shall. I have a growing voice: I must get a grant for a year, to write in Spain or Italy, a second book of poems together with either a novel or a book of short stories. Oh, mother, rejoice with me and fear not. I love you, and Warren, and my dear suffering grammy and dear loving grampy with all my heart and shall spend my life making you strong and proud of me!

Enclosed, a poem or two, I don't remember whether I sent you these.

your loving
sivvy

Strumpet Song

With white frost gone
and all green dreams not worth much,
after a lean day's work
time comes round for that foul slut:
mere bruit of her takes our street
until every man,
be he red, pale or dark,
veers to her slouch.

Mark, I cry, that mouth
made to do violence on,
that seamed face
askew with blotch, dint, scar
struck by each dour year;
stalks there not some such wild man
as can find ruth
to patch with brand of love this rank grimace
which out from black tarn, ditch and cup
into my most chaste own eyes
looks up.

Complaint of the Crazed Queen

In ruck and quibble of courtfolk
this giant hulked, I tell you, on my scene
with hands like derricks,
looks fierce and black as rooks;
why, all the windows broke when he stalked in.

My dainty acres he ramped through
and used my gentle doves with manners rude;
I do not know
what fury urged him slay
my antelope who meant him nought but good.

No one pale queen could quell a man
drunk so dire and puissant on his prowl,

yet lest he ruin
my whole choice terrain
I voluntary ran to halt his kill.

I spoke most chiding in his ear
till he some pity took upon my crying;
of rich attire
he made my shoulders bare
and solaced me, but quit me at cock's crowing.

A hundred heralds I sent out
to summon in my slight all doughty men
whose force might fit
shape of my sleep, my thought---
none of that greenhorn lot matched my bright crown.

So I am come to this rare pass
whereby I trek in blood through sun and squall
and sing you thus:
"How sore, alas, it is
to see my people shrunk so small, so small."

Firesong

Born green we were
to this flawed garden,
but in speckled thickets, warted as a toad,
spitefully skulks our warden,
fixing his snare
which hauls down buck, cock, trout, till all most fair
is tricked to falter in spilt blood.

Now our whole task's to hack
some angel-shape worth wearing
from his crabbed midden where all's wrought so awry
that no straight inquiring
could unlock
shrewd catch silting our each bright act back
to unmade mud cloaked by sour sky.

Sweet salts warped stem
of weeds we tackle towards way's rank ending;
scorched by red sun
we heft globed flint, racked in veins' barbed binding;
brave love, dream
not of staunching such strict flame, but come,
lean to my wound; burn on, burn on.

TO *Aurelia Schober Plath*

Thursday 3 May 1956 — TLS (aerogramme), Indiana University

May 3rd, 1956

Dearest of mothers.

No doubt this is the most difficult of times for you; know that I feel this; and that from the sorrow at one end of your scale, I want you to turn to the joy and love growing day by day at this young green end. I really must share with you the miracles of the last days.

I am coming into my own; I am becoming at one with myself, growing toward the best in me. The incredible thing is that I have passed through the husk, the mask of cruelty, ruthlessness, callousness, in Ted and come into the essence and truth of his best right being: he is the tenderest, kindest, most faithful man I have ever known in my life. I have, in a flash of clairvoyance, seen into him and into the colossal capacity he has for being strong and straight to the end of time, and he has seen into me, how best I can be for a woman, even with my past wastes and squanderings of energy. We are getting through, wrestling through, the unessential husks into the only real place in the world: that whistling desert where human beings stand naked before the sun and the earth and give in full honesty and faith of all their being: there is no question of other faces or figures turning us aside: once one passed beyond the mere look and shape of a being, into the essence of their spirit, their best powers for growing, there is only one kind of committment till the end of time, and this is what we are working to.

For the first time in my life, mother, I am at peace; never before, even with Richard, did I cease to have little opportunist lawcourts in session in my head whispering: look at this flaw, that weakness; how about a new man, a better man? For the first time I am free. I have, ironically, been exposed this term to the handsomest, most creative and intelligent men in

Cambridge (writers, artists, etc.) and in the midst of this, I am at peace, able to enjoy them as people, but utterly invulnerable. Even with Richard I had my eye out for a strong healthy man. This is gone, for the first time.

I feel that all my life, all my pain and work has been for this one thing. All the blood spilt, the words written, the people loved, have been a work to fit me for loving Ted. He has a voice, a trueness, which someday will be sought the world over; yet, even as he scorns Dylan Thomas for lack of discipline, for betraying his best self foully, he turns from adulation: his writing and his woman are the sole things. I am good for him; I see the power and voice in him that will shake the world alive. Even as he sees into my poems, and will work with me to make me a woman poet like the world will gape at; even as he sees into my character and will tolerate no fallings away from my best right self.

All I know is, that with Ted, the "necessities" of the world dwindle to nothing: we want food (and love to cook, eat, and will learn to catch our own), a roof, our books and typewriter and even these could be blown away in a high wind and we would hack out of ourselves a world like man never saw. It is not easy, but it is the most magnificent and godlike thing I have done to work to know this man, who works to know me; once we come to the point far enough on in this long lifetime work, we will say it to the whole world, and that will be the main good there is. I have no fear, only a faith; I am calm, joyous, and peaceful as I have never known peace. And, fantastically, I am keen mentally as I have never been; my supervisor is delighted, I can tell: I told her this week, at the best supervision yet, on Plato, that I was not taking this as a "course" but as a fight to earn my humanism through the centuries of philosophy and religion in this world. It is a voyage of the mind; to true knowledge and not just opinion and belief.

She, in turn, said she had been so stimulated by my questions last week that she had revised some lecture notes. Oh, mother, on Mayday, Ted and I went up a green river in a punt and miraculously, there was not another boat on the river! I learned to punt, so I can take you the same way, and saw baby owls, cows and even a water-rat. We had tea, honey & sandwiches under the apple tree in Granchester. While Ted has written many virile deep banging poems, I have a small one I like which I shall quote to you:

<poem text not included for copyright reasons>[1]

1–Ted Hughes, 'Soliloquy of a Misanthrope', *The Hawk in the Rain* (London: Faber & Faber, 1957); later retitled 'Soliloquy'.

And that, by Ted. He has a stright voice; here it is a lyric speech; but it is the least bit of his finger; the might of his arm is to be most wondered at. All smallness, all warping and vanity falls away with this man; he is big as I only thought a dream or a god could be; there were giants in the earth, and I think we come from another age to this world; we love the flesh of the earth and the spirit of that thin, exacting air which blows beyond the farthest planets; all is learning, discovering, and speaking in a strong voice out of the heart of sorrow and joy; oh, mother, I shall be so happy to have you come. I have never had so much love to give before. Do be strong, bear what is to be born at home, and come to me to be loved and cared for.

your own loving
sivvy

TO *Aurelia Schober Plath*

Friday 4 May 1956 — TLS (aerogramme), Indiana University

Friday morning, May 4

Dearest mother . . .

It was with a sense of rest and peace at last that I received your letter yesterday telling me of grammy; strangely enough, I have been living in tense wait long distance, and often every day talked with Ted about grammy and grampy and my home. He was with me when I read your letter, and we felt we sort of consecrated our Mayday to grammy. Before I got your letter yesterday, we were shopping together for mushrooms and steak and wine for dinner and had the impulse to go into a cool lovely little 15th century church in the heart of Cambridge and just sit together in peace and silence and love. I gave a prayer in my heart then for grammy, and for my own family, and for my dear Ted. We are so very happy together.

I can't tell you with what joy I read of Warren's Experiment fellowship to Austria! I am proud as proud; if any boy deserves it, he does. I want very much for Ted to meet him, as Ted at last is a man worthy of my brother, and I want Warren to know Ted. I hope you will have the chance to meet Ted in Paris where his older sister[1] is living and working.

Yesterday, it was gray and brilliant; Ted & I had salmon sandwiches, sausages and a glass of red wine on the outdoor punt docks of the Cam,

1–Olwyn Marguerite Hughes (1928–2016); SP's sister-in-law.

throwing crumbs to swans and basking in the sun and our projects which sprout merry and many as stars in the sky. I have the most blazing idea of all, now: out of the many vital, funny, and profound experiences as an American girl in Cambridge, I am going to write a series of tight, packed, perfect short stories which I shall make into a novel, and this is what I shall apply to the Saxton fund for money to do. I shall begin it in Spain this summer, and hope to finish it at the end of the year following graduation.

All the notes I've taken on socialized medecine, British men, characters, will come in. Ted is with me all the way, and we are rather excited about this; it is "my own corner" and his criticism as it is in progress, from the British slant, with his infallible eye, will be invaluable. What a product of the Fulbright! My work on Varsity next year will take me into the heart of Cambridge, and I can really make a fine thing of this: starting with the voyage over, and having about a year's time covered. Will try to sell the stories separately in the New Yorker and Mademoiselle.

Yesterday I discovered another wonderful thing about Ted and me together: he sat on the couch all afternoon and read my copy of Salinger's "Catcher in the Rye" while I wrote a bright, witty 10-page article on the Bulganin reception which I'm sending, on a long chance, to the New Yorker, and I re-wrote my Paris article and sent it with sketches to the Monitor. Never before have I composed and worked with a man around, and I felt so at one with Ted, so happy and better able to work than ever before in my life. Every aspect of my personality is growing vivid, shaped, and creative about him.

You will definitely meet him this summer. He may shock you at first, unless you imagine a big unruly Huckleberry Finn: he hasn't even a suit of clothes, he is so poor, and wears new dungarees and an old black sweater which I must mend at the elbows this week; he has his rugged handsomeness, his godlike voice, his brilliant mind (we are going to learn anatomy & zoology together), his huge unquenchable want to write which pours poems and stories out of him like Niagra: once he starts to publish, the world will be a different place. Our mutual feelings for how to live is simply to be honest, straight, grow every day to new learning & joy; to eat well, write always and work hard in the sweat of god's sun.

The hardest thing for me now is not to share all this with a rich community of friends; I hope Sue will be able to help me take a little the the pressure off next year; it is like having discovered the one only biggest diamond mine in the world and having to sit inside alone full of radiance, and not tell anyone. But I can tell you, if you will sit tight on it, that within a year, after I graduate, I can think of nothing I'd rather do than be married to Ted; I know he would want this, too, and we are doing all we can just to look ahead to the summer, before he has to go to Australia next fall. He is signed up to go on a kind of British program which pays the way of the men who will work over there; I can let him go, knowing as I do that he will stalk back over the world to claim me when the proper time is come. There is no question, just a case of waiting till that time is come.

Statistically, by the way, he will be 26 this August; served in the RAF as radio mechanic 2 years before Cambridge, graduated from Cambridge in 1954, and has worked at everything from grafting roses to reading for a movie studio. Now, this summer, he will be writing and waiting for his ship to leave for Australia.

All the social questions about money, family position, bank accounts, blow off like chittering irrelevancies in a cyclone before two people who depend solely on their native talent and love of honesty, frankness, and the beauty of this various world; we will work and hack out the best of lives. Oh, mother, take this to your own secret heart and share it with me; you will I hope be able to understand how this is the only real basis of lifetime love: the feeling that another being's soul and health without adornment of wealth or prestige, is enough to carry the world on it's shoulders.

much love from your own
sivvy

TO *Aurelia Schober Plath*

Sunday 6 May 1956 — TLS (aerogramme), Indiana University

Sunday noon, May 6

Dearest mother . . .

A small happy note before I go out in the Whitstead gardens to sit under a full-bloom cherry tree and read Plato in halter & shorts. The Aldriches came about 3 yesterday afternoon and we had the most idyllic day! I just hope they had half as good a time as I had.

Weather was warm and blue, and after a little talk in my room here, Ted and I took them punting up the most beautiful part of the "Backs" under willows and by the colleges; Duane took some snapshots and Ted looked like a colossal Huck Finn, or Charon piloting us over the River of Paradise instead of Styx. Duane even took over the punt for a short way and did fine! All my friends were out boating, saying hello, and I felt so intensely happy at being able to share my dear Cambridge.

Then all four of us drove over to Granchester to have a full tea---sandwiches, scones, pancakes and honey---in the apple orchard among twittering birds. Then Ted & I dropped off to wash up and met Betty and Duane at the hotel[1] we'd found them for the night and we went out to the most sumptuous dinner[2] I've had since coming back from Europe. Roast duck and orange sauce, the most delicious Chablis wine, hundreds of assorted cheeses & cognac. Duane and Ted seemed to get on fine, and we had a lovely easy laughing meal which lasted till about 10. All the waiters, who knew me already, made little jokes and were very sweet. I can't tell you how touching Ted was: he has just his dungarees and he borrowed a new black and white checked shirt from his poet friend Luke and I polished his shoes: I could walk into the Royal Palace and feel proud of him, just as he is, and I felt Duane and Betty would accept him for that, too.

Then I thought over to myself about how my friends would accept this man of mine: with nothing to his name but the shirt on his back and the most magnificent soul and voice and body that ever were: all the couples I know and love---Marty and Mike Plumer, Claiborne and Avrom Handleman, Louise & Eddie White, Betsy and Bob MacArthur, the Crocketts, Patsy---all would love him and listen to him and take him for the fine man he is. And this is all I could ever ask for.

Ted has changed so in the two months I've known him that it is incredible, just as I've changed too: from being bitter, selfish, despairing of ever being able to use our whole selves, our whole strengths, without terrifying other people, we have turned into the most happy magnanimous creative pair in the world: Ted says himself that I have saved him from being ruthless, cynical, cruel and a warped hermit because he never thought there could be a girl like me and I feel that I too have new power by pouring all my love and care in one direction to someone strong enough to take me in my fullest joy (it is interesting to know that most Cambridge boys preferred me when I was sick with sinus and they could take care of me, because that was the only time they were stronger). I know how straight and good Ted can grow and will not have anything less; he wants this, and likes the kind of self he is with me, as I am utterly at peace and joyously my best when with him. I do hope you can meet him in Paris, mother; he is the dearest, kindest, most honest man that ever lived, and if, for my faith and

1–According to SP's calendar, this was the Red Lion Hotel.

2–According to SP's calendar, this was at Miller's.

work and fighting to re-make him daily according to his best potential, I can at the end of my course here live with him the rest of my life, I can think of no better way to sing my songs in the world: creating stories, babies and poems and delectable meals. On the most limited financial budget and the biggest potential capital of talent & native ability I've ever met.

much much love,
sivvy

PS: a few random jottings: am ecstatic about Warren's Experiment fellowship! Congratulate him a hundred times for me, and let me know when and where he'll be there! Ted might hitch-hike to Austria with me to meet Warren, I'd just love the two of them to meet!

About your trip: do bring as many wash'n'dri packs as possible: they are godsends: put a few into handbag while traveling, whip one out when you feel grimy, and your old makeup comes off and your skin feels braced and fresh, and you can begin all over.

If it isn't too much, in passing, could you get a couple of those Christian Science Monitor sets & send them over with my Joy of Cooking: cooking is certainly my happiest domestic joy! I love it utterly & was made to cook!

Also, I'd love one or two of those lovely simple white nylon slips (without lace, just borders of nylon) for the summer: the styles here are lousy.

And tell me whether you'll be coming morning noon or night of June 13th so I can make plans: roughly, even, what time! I'll be there doing jigs of joy on the docks at Southampton: am writing Paris about reservations this week! We will have such fun together! Will also try to hitch-hike up from Spain to make you and Mrs. Prouty on August 6th: Spain is my base for writing & I'm beginning my novel this summer. Am not going to Cambridge summer school after all. Hope you'll help me choose my Olivetti Letteretta 22[1] this June in London!

love again, your happy
sivvy

<on the return address side of letter>

PS: at last received package: shirt is lovely, slippers like angel's garb; am not bothering with thyroid anymore and feel fine.

xxxx
sivvy

1 – ASP bought SP an Olivetti Lettera 22, #C8850.

TO *Aurelia Schober Plath*

Wednesday 9 May 1956 TLS (aerogramme), Indiana University

Wednesday morning, May 9

Dear mother . . .

It is a lovely gray day, with the wet smell of cherry blossoms and lilacs in the air; outside Whitstead, the white lilac bush is coming into full bloom, and there is in the hedge a nest of four blackbirds which I have been following on their progress from mottled blue eggs to large, blinking, feathered children.

Do you realize that in about a month from the time you receive this, I'll be meeting you at Southampton? I am so excited: I am going to start this week finding out about cars and licences; is my red wallet with my licence in it at home? I wish you'd just look to make sure I didn't leave it there. I cant seem to locate it here.

Had a wonderful supervision with dear shining Doctor Krook yesterday morning on Plato again: I do a paper every week, read it and discuss violently; I know she has fun, and feel that by the time I am through with this course in the middle of next year, we will be good friends; already we are communicating about our own private feelings & opinions: everything relates. Had the most moving discussion of the idea of the Trinity with her, a revelation to me of the blind stupid ignorance I had in not even "listening" to such conceptions: I am standing at the juncture of Greek and Christian thought, now, and it is magnificent to see what the mind of man has made, the significance of the development from the dialectical inquiries of Socrates to the Epistles of St. Paul, which will be my next port after Aristotle. Never has my mind been so eager, so keen, so able to make leaps and sallies into new understanding!

In a very real sense, all this fresh directive power and creativity is due to my growing love for Ted. He has changed so in the time I have known him from a boy afraid of being vulnerable and committed (and therefore cruel and destructive) to the most loving, tender, careful, dear man in the world. His goal is not a particular job, or a particular place, narrowly, in the world, but a "way of life" with one right woman, and I know that this is the way I want to live, and it is the only way for me. Together, as he said, our lives would be worth living out even if we never set foot out of a shack in the ugly sooty midst of Birmingham; meaning, of course, that no matter what comes, however little, the least is better together than the worldly "most" with anyone else.

Both of us want to live in the world, mastering each country, writing and giving to the people, until we re-create the whole world in our words. Ted is probably the most brilliant boy I know: I am constantly amazed at his vast fund of knowledge and understanding: not facts or quotes of second-hand knowledge, but an organic, digested comprehension which enriches his every word. He has a phenomenal ability to learn languages, & I have, by some miracle, drawn up from inside him the desire not to go to Australia next year but to find a job teaching English in Spain, so I can see him during vacations and make the next year, no doubt the hardest in both our lives, having to be apart so much, bearable. My most cherished dream, which you must think of only as a dream so far, is to bring him home with me next June for a sort of enormous barbeque in Wellesley to which I will invite all the neighbors, young couples, and dear people like Mrs. Prouty & Dr. Beuscher, et al. just to meet him before we set out on our world-wandering; not really wandering, but living & teaching English in country after country, writing, mastering languages and having many many babies.

Oh, mummy, I have never been so calm and peaceful and happy in my life; if it is this way, with all the awkward limitations of our separate positions now, me studying, he having to work, it will be incredible to fight out a life side by side. We are both ripe and mature, sure, because of so much experience in the world, so much waste of our true energies, of our wish to have one undeviating faith and love our lives long and to commit every fiber & dream to forging this life: always growing straight in the light of each other. I am so glad you and Warren are coming this summer, so you can meet him. If only you both will just take him for what he is, in his whole self, without wealth, or a slick 10-year guarantee for a secure job, or a house & car---just for his native dearness, story-telling, poem-making, nature-loving, humorous, rugged self---I am sure you will be as drawn to him as I could wish. To find such a man, to make him into the best man the world has seen: such a life work! I know I was not meant to be a single woman, a career woman, and this is my reward for waiting and waiting and not accepting all the lesser tempting offers which would have betrayed my capacity for growing beyond thought into the fulness of my middle and late years.

I am beginning my novel in Spain this summer, working on it next year, and using <u>Varsity</u> to get in every nook & cranny of Cambridge: it is my corner, and such a salable subject! I'll try to sell the stories to Mlle & the NYorker, & get some grant to finish it & rewrite it to unity the year following graduation, along with a book of poems. Honestly, my whole being just sings straight with purpose and projects: you must come and share this joy! You'll be a proud grandmother yet! Probably quadruplets when the time comes: statesmen, scientists, artists and discus-throwers!

Much love from your own,
sivvy

TO *Aurelia Schober Plath*

Thursday 10 May 1956 — TLS (aerogramme), Indiana University

Thursday morning, May 10

Dearest mother . . .

You will no doubt think I have gone utterly potty to be writing you so many letters, but I am at that time when a girl wants to share all her joys and wonders at her one man with those who will understand and be happy about it, and I miss your presence more now than I did in all the hard times during the winter then I was unhappy, uncreative and discouraged about the course my life was to take. Please bear with my volubility at this point! I have no girl here like Sue or Marty with whom I can share my happiness (without their feeling secretly jealous, as do all girls who do not have that strong singleness of purpose which love brings) and I really long for a woman confidante.

I hope so much you will be able to get to know Ted; one look in his eyes will tell you what marvelous care I shall have at his hands: I have never felt so protected and at one in my life. He is the one boy with whom I can be perfectly "alone" with myself, utterly creative, working and at peace, while he is in the same room, partly because we have such an "I-thou" feeling that we are never outside the medium of our mutual presence; I can't consider him objectively as a "thing" as I could every other man I've ever known; I <u>can</u> be critical of him, truly, but only because I know the best he can be and wish to work with him always so he will grow toward this, as he feels about me. Yesterday, a gray rainy day, I sat and wrote an article for an Oxford magazine while he read DeQuincey and worked on a poem; we have such a completely at-ease time of it: my stopping to ask his advice about a metaphor, he telling me about anthropology. We got two enormous books of Siberian fairy-tales & Magyar folk-tales out of the University library and are reading them aloud every evening. His imagination has brought to life all the goblin and fairy and witch lore I ever loved as a child, and I shall slowly return to that magic state: we spent a whole afternoon looking at Arthur Rackham drawings for Rip Van Winkle and Peter Pan. Ted can draw, too, and once wanted to do just that; he has a brother Gerald,[1] 10 years older than he, with a family in Australia, and Gerald sells all his paintings (which he only does for fun: he hunts & fishes most) and is an aircraft mechanic; he has an older sister, Olwyn, in Paris, and Ted is the youngest. I have never enjoyed drawing so much, and will get a sketch-book of stylized drawings slowly together over our travels; the whole world is our country, and we shall travel and live everywhere, teaching English and learning the languages of each country, writing and drawing and me cooking and learning international dishes. With Ted, and his natural inborn talents, I need nothing but himself: we'll spin the rest in our words and drawings and actions, and be the truest simplest loving people under the sun.

Tomorrow I am suiting my actions to my words and taking Ted to meet the Duke of Edinburgh at the Fulbright reception in London; he has one old suit, which I haven't seen, and will resurrect it for the occasion: I don't care what it's like, for I feel my love and faith in Ted will make what he wears or has like the emperor's new clothes: I look at him and he is dressed in purple and gold cloth and crowned with laurel: and the world will come to see him in the light of my look, even as I shall be the most beautiful woman in the blazing sun of his belief in me. So there it is, the two of us, and each morning I wake incredulous with a song in my heart and say: "Ted" to myself, and the day jumps up straight and creative as solomon's metaphors.

Later Thursday: I've just come from the most marvelous 2-hour coffee session with dear Mary Ellen Chase who came to Cambridge last weekend with her brilliant classical scholar companion, Eleanor Shipley Duckett (both of them making fabulous money on new books and articles & radio broadcasts!) It was absolute heaven to tell her all about my year, my writing and to hear about my beloved Smith and all the people there; she strongly suggested that I would be asked back there to teach as soon as I graduate from Newnham; I would really like the chance to teach & get the experience of Smith, but could never imagine going back without a husband. Imagine living in that atmosphere of 2000 young attractive girls, without any social life of my own! I wouldn't want "social life" either, as I've known it. I just want my home and my one man. I feel most honored at this prospect of their asking me, though, and if Ted and I need

1–Gerald Hughes (1920–2016), TH's brother, married to Joan (Whelan), 1950; father of Ashley (1954–) and Brendon (1956–).

money, maybe he could get a job at Amherst for a year, and we could write and teach and have a home: some time: it's a thing to think of. But I'm so pleased about his not going to Australia but teaching in Spain next year, and his apparent willingness to book passage back to America with me next June that I'm going to live the summer out before getting any more previous. If we got married (I don't know just where or when right now, but probably sometime after I graduate next year) do you suppose it would be possible for us both to get part- or full-time summer jobs & a cottage down the Cape for the summer as Perry & Shirley and Marty & Mike did, so we could travel & write all over America the next year? This is just one of the little pots cooking in my head, but you might talk to the Cantors or anyone who has an "in" at the big hotels where we can make lots & lots of money: I'd waitress or work part-time & he could be a bartender or chauffeur with a millionaire family or something: do think about it! What a gala year with Warren graduating & me bringing my man home! Cross your fingers.

Much love,
sivvy

TO *Aurelia Schober Plath*

Friday 18 May 1956

TLS (aerogramme),
Indiana University

Friday morning, May 18

Dearest mother . . .

It was so wonderful to get your last happy letter and to think that in less than a month I shall be welcoming you at Waterloo Station! Just let me know whether it is morning, noon, or night, and I'll take my station in the waiting room with sandwiches & a camp stool! Our hotel, by the way, is Clifford's Inn, Fleet Street, London. In case you want to know.

I know you're fantastically busy, but have two small desperate requests: could you please possibly send my "Joy of Cooking" and lots more 3¢ stamps: I'm starting to send batches of Ted's poems out to American magazines because I want the editors to be crying for him when we come to America next June; he has commissioned me his official agent and writes prolifically as shooting stars in August. I have great faith in his promise; we are coming into our era of richness, both of us, late maturing, reaching beginning ripeness after 25 & going to be fabulous old people! Ted, by the way, is Ted Hughes (Edward James Hughes, by the book). We are going to do pen & ink portraits of each other for the frontispieces of our first books. You should see Ted draw! He is like Arthur Rackham, only better! All sorts of gnarled witches, wolves frightened by ghosts, and will start some portraits of me! A combination of both witch and ghost, perhaps.

I forget whether I wrote you or someone else[1] about the Fulbright blast in London:[2] I took Ted in his ancient gray 8-year old suit & introduced him to the American Ambassador; then, after the Duke of Edinburgh spoke, he came down to chat, asking me where I was studying & what I was doing. When he asked Ted the same, Ted grinned & said he was "Chaperoning Sylvia." "Ah," the Duke smiled & sighed, "the idle rich." So international protocol is taken care of.

Had a wonderful tea for Mary Ellen Chase and brilliant dear Miss Duckett (whose new book on King Arthur[3] is coming out in both England & America) in my room at Whitstead Wednesday with Jane Baltzell (the other beautiful blonde English major) and Isabel Murray, a charming girl studying Celtic and ancient literature & anthropology. I spent the whole day shopping for flowers, fruit and tea things: my room looked exquisite, and we had the most hysterical hour and a half! Miss Chase & Miss Duckett are like a comedy team, love a young audience, and so kept us in stitches with their tales of old Newnham days and students & professor characters. I could see everybody had a fine time and felt most joyous at being able to give love and hospitality to those two women who are largely responsible for my being here.

I am really longing for this summer in which to concentrate on writing; I feel such new power coming on me: I've been working up all kinds of things: poems, articles on everything from the women-situation at Cambridge (my short witty article on this came out verbatim today in the esoteric Isis magazine at Oxford: I'm going inter-collegiate! as this week's Cambridge newsletter) and spring and summer fashions for Varsity (I'm doing a survey of the dress shops tomorrow morning). The New Yorker rejected my Bulganin article as too late which of course crushed me as it was a damn good, neat funny article. My biggest projects now are, of course, a book of poems which I want to send to the Yale Series of Younger Poets next winter, and my short story series which will be a novel: after next year on Varsity, where I'll invent assignments to take

1–According to SP's calendar, she wrote to Elinor Friedman Klein on 15 May 1956.

2–Held at Draper's Hall, Throgmorton Street, London, on 11 May 1956.

3–Eleanor Shipley Duckett, *Alfred the Great: The King and His England* (Chicago: University of Chicago Press, 1956).

me into every nook and cranny and mind in Cambridge, I should be able to write a perfect locale story, and the American-British contact is very salable. I was awfully pleased to get the Oxford assignment, as you may guess, for it is an honor to contribute, especially as representative of the women at Cambridge!

In your letter you didn't say where and from when to when Warren will be in Austria. I am dying of curiosity, for I want Ted to meet him very much; I think those two will get along fine. Oh, mother, I only want you to have time to get to know Ted; in a few years the world will be marveling at us; we both have such strength & creativity and productive discipline (Ted's poems are like controlled explosions of dynamite when he really writes full tilt) and practicality. We are capable of the most scrupulous and utter faithfulness in the world, demanding the most from each other, caring intensely for bringing each other to full capacity & production. We can rest & laze in the sun, or after a meal in a colossal peace, too. Our energy is something amazing. I only want you to come into the light of this and share our humor and love of life, which is almost impossible to convey the least speck of in words. We definitely want to get married in Wellesley next June after I graduate, and naturally I am just dying to talk over plans: I've already started pairing up bridesmaids & trying to figure how I can have both Libby[1] & Nancy[2] for flowergirls! By the way, if you think it might help grampy to fix on something special for him, tell him specially & very privately as a secret that I want him to know he should begin preparing for his granddaughter's wedding where there will be at least one bottle of champagne and one small dish of caviar! I want it to be a town festival, small & intimate, of all those I love & who know what life means to me: Cantors, Crocketts, Prouty, neighbors, Marty, Patsy, everyone I love. I was so happy to hear about your plans to come to Italy in 1958; hope Ted & I might be working there that year! What fun to have you come visit us! We plan on 7 children, after each of us has published a book & traveled some, so the 7th child of that child might be a rare white witch! Cambridge is a lovely green eden, & to have an English spring & the dearest, most brilliant, strong tender man in the world is too much to keep alone: do come share with us!

Much much love,
sivvy

1 – Probably Elizabeth 'Libby' Aldrich, daughter of SP's neighbours in Wellesley.
2 – Probably SP's cousin Nancy Benotti (1947–).

TO *Aurelia Schober Plath*

Saturday 26 May 1956 TLS with envelope, Indiana University

Saturday, May 26

Dearest mother . . .

May has turned chill and grey these last days, and I am writing from the midst of a wet, snuffly spring cold, but very happy. I'm enclosing the clippings from my latest article in Varsity on which I appeared as a cover-girl (!),[1] showing how hard-up they are! and my article inside, with more pictures. At least I look healthy, don't I?

This article was the hardest I've ever done, and really took a lot out of me. I made arrangements with three store managers to choose clothes & come round with a photographer; of course, the details of price and description had to be perfectly accurate, and the bathing-suit store gave us all the help in the world and no trouble, because it is a big cheap department store, and the people simple and lovely. Met a charming woman salesmanager who had toured the U.S.A in a Shakespeare company and offered to send me an invitation to the Cambridge Arts & Sculpture exhibit[2] opening next week. Well, the bathing suit photos went fine, there, and I sauntered off with my very kind, slow Varsity photographer to posh Joshua Taylor's,[3] where I have my only charge account, for snapshots in the most bouffant lovely cocktail dress ever.

I had spent a half-hour several days before sweet-talking the negative manager out of an old remembered Varsity feud two years old in which Varsity had printed a facetious article with pictures of their young model: "Who'd be caught dead wearing this?" etc. Well, I got him to agree to try to patch it up, and made the stupid mistake of assuming he'd made a mistake in the appointment which was on a Bank Holiday (all stores closed). Turned out he'd been there, and the day I came with photographer had left town with an emphatic "No, it's all off." I came back later, and he had come back, said No again and gone off. Well, I was crushed at my own carelessness (I always learn the hard way) and at the thought of all my mending work going down the drain, and tears started to my eyes.

1 – Enclosures held by Lilly Library. On one, next to a photograph of SP modelling a bathing suit, SP typed 'From front page of Varsity! with love, from Betty Grable.'

2 – The Cambridge Society of Painters and Sculptors exhibition, featuring works by Betty Rea, Shelley Fausset, John Smith, Cecil Collins, and Christopher Cornford was held at the Cambridge Arts Council gallery, All Saint's Passage, Cambridge.

3 – Joshua Taylor's was a department store then on Market Street, Cambridge.

I stood there red-eyed asking the buyer to at least read the dress-descriptions I'd written because it was probably the best free advertising they'd had yet: my words were so laudatory, that she whisked off to the store director, who came down and OKed the pictures over the absent manager's head, and so, red-eyed and puffy faced, I put on the dress, and suddenly felt all right. Today I'm taking the paper with my personal apologies for wasting the manager's time, to the store. As my photographer & I left, who should walk out but Mr. Joshua Taylor, owner of the store himself, to ask if we'd send over a Varsity cartoonist to discuss possible publicity ads. So all is once again sweetness & light due to my sheer stubbornness & refusal to give up.

The elegant store of formals also betrayed us, being busier than they thought and telling us it was impossible to take pictures or choose dresses on that day, as they had promised. In sheer desperation of ingenuity, I insisted on looking at dresses on my own for possible May Ball wear, as a customer (potential), which they couldn't refuse, figuring I could at least write them up. While I was trying on the white one, the chastened store-owner, thinking better of it, came in to tell me to go out in the garden & take the pictures.

I was shot after all this arguing sweetly and quick thinking, just to get my story & pictures, having spent from 9 a.m. to 3 p.m. in personal relations. But I got the desired results, and the editor and shop people are happy, which is what I wanted. As the sweet photographer said: "I could have stood all day and argued, and they would have still said no." I really am getting to be a determined newspaper woman. All this experience will be wonderful for my Cambridge novel. Varsity is my key to the town and all the people in it. Needless to say, Ted is very proud of me, especially the poems I'm doing now.[1] He just wants me to develop every talent I have, to do well in exams, and is very helpful and encouraging, and my best critic.

Most amazing is the way all my faculties are flourishing in my daily happiness & joy. I had the best philosophy supervision yesterday and neither Dr. Krook or I could believe it when the bell rang for her next pupil; she told me to come again this morning for an extra hour as we "hadn't finished talking", and I am just blazing with intellectual joy and keenness; she is very very pleased with my work, especially my last papers on Plato, and she is going to become my mentor in the poetic and philosophic realm just as Dr. Beuscher is in the personal and psychological. At last I have discovered a woman on the Cambridge faculty for whom I would sweat

1–According to SP's calendar, her recent poems were: 'Bucolics' on 5 May; 'Wreath for a Bridal' on 17–18 May, and 'Two Sisters of Persephone' on 24 May 1956.

my brains out. This philosophic discipline will be invaluable for me, and I'm so happy I can continue it next year with her; she has become the most beautiful woman to me, is just alight, and we are temperamentally most compatible.

Ted is staying with his poet-friend,[1] E. Lucas Meyers (my next favorite poet after Ted) through May Ball week, and I generally meet him after lunch for an afternoon of study while he writes, and cook dinner here (Cambridge food in restaurants is probably the worst in the world) and talk and read aloud; our minds are just enraptured with words, ideas, languages. I took out my Rilke poems and my dear Märchen der Brüder Grimm[2] to read aloud my favorite German pieces to him (he doesn't know German) and translated on the spot, getting very excited; I've definitely decided to take German all next year, concentrating on Rilke and Kafka, and some Thomas Mann. Ted likes hearing it, gets intrigued by my rough, impromptu translations. He is now applying for a job teaching English in Madrid, Spain, to earn us some money for next year. We spent a whole day out in the Whitstead gardens in the sun, me typing first copies and carbons of about 25 of his best poems & he editing, to send off to the New Yorker, Atlantic, Harper's & Poetry magazines. He has just never bothered to try to publish (outside the Cambridge magazines) and I can't wait to see how he is received in America. He is going to be a brilliant poet; I know it with every critical fiber in me. His imagination is unbelievably fertile; our children will have such fun: last night while I peeled mushrooms to go with our dinner of sweetbreads, he read me aloud from a book of Celtic tales[3] we just bought, and from Dylan Thomas' story-book, "Portrait of the Artist as a Young Dog." I can't tell you how wonderful it is to share so completely my greatest loves of words and poems and fairy-tales and languages; so completely, also, the world of nature and birds and animals and plants. I shall be one of the few women poets in the world who is fully a rejoicing woman, not a bitter or frustrated or warped man-imitator, which ruins most of them in the end. I am a woman, and glad of it, and my songs will be of fertility of the earth and the people in it through waste, sorrow and death. I shall be a woman singer, and Ted and I shall make a fine life together. This year of work and discipline away from each

1–At the time, Myers lived at 12 Tenison Avenue, Cambridge.
2–Jacob Grimm, *Märchen der Brüder Grimm* (Munich: Droemersche Verlagsanstalt, 1937); SP's copy is now held by Emory University; presented to SP from her mother on Christmas Day 1954,
3–Probably Kenneth Hurlstone Jackson, *A Celtic Miscellany* (London: Routledge & Kegan Paul, 1951); SP's copy is now held by Emory University and includes the ownership inscription 'Sylvia Plath, Cambridge, 1956'.

other will probably be the hardest ever, but we can both be ascetics while we are working for something so magnificent as our whole creative lives; we plan to live for at least a hundred years.

You should see how Ted is changing under my love and cooking and daily care! Gone is the tortured black cruel look, the ruthless banging gestures; he is mellowing, growing rich and kind and dear and tender and caring of me as he would be of a delicate bird. I was so lucky to meet him at this age, this time; I have saved him to be the best man he can be. As he says himself, in two more years he would have grown to be a hard, knotty nut to crack, bitter & cynical, and destructive. Now he is responding, re-forming, even as I am. Both of us are old enough to have our own identities and self-knowledge quite firmly shaped, but, thank god, young enough to grow and change under the love and guidance of each other, so that we will become truly one person in the world's eyes. I am hoping that you and I will have a good deal of time walking about and talking with him in London and in Paris (where his sister lives, whom I hope to meet). I want you to know him well, in all his talent and dearness; he will make us both really proud of him some day, not far off. Warren will be able to help me very subtly, I think, into weaning Ted into shopping for clothes for himself and giving him "man information" about America. Realize that my work is only begun, and if he seems to look rough, that is just the outside, which is shaping to match the lovely person he is growing to be within.

Much much love,
sivvy

TO *Patricia O'Neil Pratson*

Sunday 27 May 1956 TLS (aerogramme), Private owner

May 27th,

Dearest Pat . . .

You must think I'm the world's worst correspondent! I've so loved your letters and the card from Smith, and all your news, most especially the marvelous new job teaching in NYC! And so near Louise and Eddie, too! Please do give them both my love when you see them: already, amazingly enough, I'm thinking with quite some joy of returning home next June. I thought for a while that I never would want to come back, because of the magnificent feeling of closeness here to all the peoples, politics and languages in the world, but the tide has turned, and I plan to come home for at least a year before returning to Europe.

Do let me know how Julie's[1] applications to college turn out---there's a lovely Bryn Mawr graduate on a Fulbright[2] in Whitstead this year and, although of course it's not Smith, it sounds like the finest place! Warren, as mother has probably said, got his Experiment Fellowship, and I hope to hitchhike to see him in Europe this summer; we are, suddenly, an international family. I've spent much time this last month getting reservations for mother & me in London, Cambridge and Paris for the first two weeks of her visit. After the long hard dark months of my dear grammy's sickness & death, I want to do all I can to heal mother & make her grow strong in this green eden of peace and beauty, taking care of all details so she only has to let herself be charioted about. I look so forward to her coming! Right now I am sitting in the green garden outside Whitstead trying to bake a wet spring cold out of my head, surrounded by poppies, fragrant lilacs and golden cascades of laburnum; I don't know a more beautiful place in the world than this; the air is like honey, the calm and loveliness of birds, flowers and white cows incredible.

Academically, I have at last left the antique grotesque Victorian dons at Newnham and found a brilliant, attractive young woman whom I can admire as a <u>whole person</u>, not just a dry ticking brain (a problem with women dons here, not so much the men). I am taking philosophy with her, this year and next, and we get so intense and impassioned about Plato that she fits in extra hours in the week for our discussions; poetically & philosophically, she is for me what my dear psychiatrist Dr. Beuscher was personally & psychologically: a brilliant, lovely woman whom I can admire as mentor & friend both mentally & personally (the way our professors all were at Smith).

Mary Ellen Chase, by the way, has arrived with dear Miss Duckett, who has been asked to give a series of lectures here this next winter; such a pair! In spite of a long illness this winter, Miss Chase is hardy & spare & humorous as ever. I invited the two of them for tea to which I also asked Jane Baltzell, a lovely blonde American studying English on a Marshall grant, and Isabel Murray, a charming Aberdden girl studying Celtic language & lit. Well, Miss Chase and Miss Duckett had us rolling on the floor with laughter at their tales, like an expert comedy team. I do so love them both. It was so heavenly to get all the recent news of the Smith English faculty and life back home.

1–Patricia O'Neil's younger sister Julie O'Neil. She attended Bryn Mawr.
2–Lois Marshall.

I've been specially happy this term getting my fingers back into printer's ink: perhaps mother told you of this fabulous jaunt to London with 3 other Varsity reporters to a big champagne, vodka and caviar blast at the Claridge Hotel for Bulganin and Khrushchev at which I rubbed elbows with Anthony Eden, Clement Attlee, myriads of mayors, and was ultimately able to shake hands with Bulganin himself & talk with many fine, friendly Russian officers & businessmen, toasting American-Russian relations <illegible> cola![1]

Best news of all, and very new & secret, which I can't resist sharing with you, is that next June I'll be bringing home a brilliant, rugged Yorkshire poet by the name of Ted Hughes for what we plan to be a Wellesley wedding in late June; we've had such a time struggling out our plans for the next year (I met him most uniquely this February just after he'd given up his job as reader for a London movie studio and was preparing to leave immediately for Australia. & is now teaching in Europe instead next year.), that we can hardly believe next June will ever come! I am hoping to introduce him to mother and Warren this summer, and, if all goes well, would love you to consider being "en attendance" at what I hope will be a small, intimate festival of friends and relations some Saturday in late June. With your having shared so much of our life and hard times, I'd be so happy if you'd participate in this joyous celebration!

I fell in love with Ted's poems before I met him, at a very bohemian party given for a new literary review. He is big, athletic (a discus-thrower, archer, plowman, etc.) with a voice that out-roars Dylan Thomas, knows all Shakespeare & Donne & Blake & Yeats & all my favorite writers by heart (most Un-British, half Irish, half French, with a dash of Spanish); can draw magnificently, witches & animals, portraits; can tell fairytales, ghost stories, legends about Irish heroes till the birds are struck dumb on the trees; has one pair of dungarees to his name, is utterly penniless, honest, dear and brilliant. We'll earn bread & butter by teaching English in all the countries in Europe, living simply on next-to-nothing, learning languages & living with the people & writing and writing, which is the main love for both of us. Oh, Pat, I simply can't wait till you meet him! Do say you'll think, even if it's all very tentative about dates, etc., of being in a wedding next June 1957. I know it's a year off, but it would be so perfect to have you standing by!

Do write . . . much much love,
syl

1–This part of the letter is handwritten and illegible due to damage and water staining.

TO *Aurelia Schober Plath*

Monday 28 May 1956 TLS (aerogramme), Indiana University

Monday morning
May 28th

Dearest mother . . .

It was so lovely to get your letter today telling of the "Bon Voyage" party and Mrs. Prouty's garden party and all. I'm also very happy that Betty had such nice things to say about my dear Ted, because the two of us had such a fine time showing them about that we hoped it was all reciprocal; Ted wants them to have some seat of honor at our wedding because they're really the first of my close friends he's met. I do love that whole Aldrich family so much. Imagine, yesterday I started even making out lists of people to invite! I so long to share some of these plans with you and have your help; it is so difficult for me here without anybody knowing how I feel and no girl confidante to talk to. Sometimes I think I will just explode with plans and anticipation: there are so many families and neighbors and handsome, talented young couples I want to invite. Not really many, but a good number: people like Mrs. Prouty, Mary Ellen Chase (if she's home), and Dr. Beuscher etc. And all the Aldriches, McGowans, Cruikshanks & Gary's.[1] I want there to be a very good reason for everybody asked, so it's a small tight group of people who really know what this means to me; sort of an apocryphal dedication to a tough, honest, creative life full of love and giving to the world of books and babies.

I have, recently, more or less cut down on our travel plans in England, and, I hope you will agree, for the best. With the few days left for the Wales trip, all became rushed and crowded, and I don't know about you, but I'm getting old, and like to just rest and drink in scenery in languid peace. So I cut out the Wales trip, giving us 4 days and 3 nights in London; I've left the first night perfectly free, as I thought you'd be maybe a bit tired, and anyway, I selfishly just want to talk to you over a long, leisurely dinner. Thursday I've reserved seats for a new Anouilh play "Waltz of the Toreadors",[2] and Friday I thought I'd go over the entertainment page with you to pick something you fancied; of course the days will be full

1–Probably Rex. I and Mary R. Geary.

2–Jean Anouilh's *Waltz of the Toreadors* (1952) played at the Criterion Theatre, Piccadilly Circus, London.

with parks and Thames and Trafalgar Square, etc. Saturday we leave for Cambridge, where I've reserved you rooms at the Garden House Hotel, where Mary Ellen Chase is staying now, so you may be sure it's the finest; I've signed up for bed & breakfast, but would enjoy coming over to take several other meals there with you; had lovely dinner there with M. E. Chase and two couples:[1] British father, American mother, of sweet young American girl who had followed family pattern & married a young British doctor. Charming company, most auspicious for my own international marriage!

Then I've just planned us to stay in Cambridge from Saturday the 16th to Thursday the 21st, on which I want to leave for London early, meet Elly Friedman, take her out with us and leave for Paris the next day, 22nd. I thought you'd love to stay in Cambridge, punt up the river, go to evensong at King's chapel, to a play or so perhaps, depending what's on, and to read and talk leisurely with me at Whitstead where I'll even cook a sample dinner for you on my one gas-ring. I figured you'd probably welcome four or five days to learn about currency, French phrases (I have a phrase book I'll give you) and to plot out details on your trip with such a seasoned traveler as your daughter. I also do hope Ted will join us for as much of our trip as possible, for I'd like you to get to know him well. He is the dearest, sweetest man alive, and when I walk down the streets beside him, I feel if the whole sky caved in in a blast of thunder & lightning, he'd simply hold it up with one arm to keep the least bit from falling on my head!

In Paris, I'm planning to reserve a room for you for a week from the 22nd on, and one for me from the 22nd to the 26th, when I'll be leaving for Spain, having shared a full 2 weeks with you; I plan to hitchhike up to London in August for our rendez-vous with Mrs. Prouty, then to wherever my dear darling brother is in Germany, because, please tell him, I want to spend a good week with him, living where he is, or traveling, or whatever. Do please let me know where he'll be! He must meet Ted, and I think they'll be great friends; they are my two favorite men in the world. I feel so happy to bring such a grand man into our family, such a great surge of strength to our line. He is penniless, and all the considerations of cars & clothes become meaningless to me; I hope that in the 2 weeks or 10 days we are home before our wedding (can he stay in Warren's room?) that we'll manage to gather enough wedding gifts to start us on a home, but

1–According to SP's calendar, these were Mr and Mrs Forbes and Diana and Humphrey Lloyd.

I'll probably have to store most of them in Wellesley for some while, until we are earning enough to move about on a little larger scale; I want to talk much of this over with you: even down to the stainless steel patterns! I've got about a hundred candidates for bridesmaids: Marcia Brown Plumer for maid matron!-of-honor, and then definitely Patsy (whom I couldn't resist writing) & Ruth Freeman Geissler (if she can make it) and Joan Cantor & Elly Friedman as runners-up. Oh, do forgive me for going on & on, but this is the most wonderful plan in my whole life, and I'm just skipping about in it and want to share it with the neighbors & all & have it as right and warm & hearty as can be; do hope Bill Rice will officiate, as he & Ted should get along fine. Yesterday Ted & I went outdoor sketching in the sun in the Cambridge garden allotments where I did a chicken-coop & detailed grass & plant line drawings & he drew a good sketch of my head and lots of little weasels & cows smiling. We both can't wait to see you when you come! Tell me when & where in Waterloo to meet you. I'll be in London from Sat. 9th so send any last minute note to me c/o American Express, 6 Haymarket, London.

xxx
sivvy

TO *Elinor Friedman Klein*

Monday 18 June 1956 TLS, Smith College

Monday night

Dear dear Elly!

welcomewelcomewelcome! to green isle set in silver sea and all that. to rain, custard sauce and yorkshire pudding.

mother, ted hughes and I will be waiting for you at 5 p.m. to go to dinner at mother's hotel: CLIFFORD'S INN, FETTER LANE, just off Fleet Street where are all the printersink smelling newspapers. very very London.

we all love you.

room 140, sixth floor. we have phone, but I don't know number. just come.

ted is now my financé,[1] as we say in france, and mother is very happy, and we are all very happy. wellesley wedding planned for next june.

1–In fact Sylvia Plath and Ted Hughes married on Saturday 16 June 1956, at St George-the-Martyr, Queen Square, Holborn, London.

we all love you and are dying for you to come and have dinner and good talk.

much much love
sylvia

TO *Warren Plath*

Monday 18 June 1956 — TLS (aerogramme, photocopy), Indiana University

Monday, June 18th

Dearest Warren . . .

It was so wonderful to hear from you about your marvelous summer plans. Suddenly the world has shrunk to travelable size and all becomes possible. My fingers are so full of amazing news to type that I hardly know where to begin. First of all, you better stop what you are doing and be very quiet and sit down with a tall glass of cool lager and be ready to keep a huge and miraculous secret: your sister, as of 1:30 p.m. June 16th in London at the 250 year old church of St. George the Martyr is now a married woman! Mrs. Sylvia Hughes, Mrs. Ted Hughes, Mrs. Edward James Hughes, Mrs. E. J. Hughes (wife of the internationally-known poet and genius): take your pick. It is really true. And it is a dead secret between you and mummy and Ted and me. Because I am going to have another wedding at the Unitarian Church in Wellesley next June with you (I hope, if you're willing) as Ted's best man, and Frankie giving me away, and a huge reception for all our friends and relations who will be informed by mother this fall that Ted and I are engaged.

This all seems so logical and inevitable to me that I can hardly begin to answer the questions which I know will be flocking to your mind: why two weddings? why a secret wedding? why anyhow? Well, it so happens that I have at last found the one man in the world for me, which mother saw immediately (she and Ted get along beautifully, and he loves her and cares for her very much) and after three months of seeing each other every day, doing everything from writing to reading aloud to hiking and cooking together, there was absolutely no shred of doubt in our minds. We are both poverty-stricken now, have no money, and are in no position to have people know we are married. Me at Newnham, where the Victorian virgins wouldn't see how I could concentrate on my studies with being married to such a handsome virile man, the Fulbright, etc. etc. Also, he is getting a job teaching English in Spain next year, to earn money to come to America with me next June, so we'll have to be apart while I finish my degree for 3 long 8-week periods (I must do very well on my exams). I'll fly to be with him for the 5-week-long vacations at Christmas and Easter. So this marriage is in keeping with our situation: private, personal, legal, true, but limited in its way. Neither of us will think of giving up the fullest ceremony, which will be a kind of folk festival in Wellesley when we proclaim our decision to the world in another ceremony, very simple, but with a wonderful reception: then, too, we can really start our life of living together forever. So this seems the best way. I have never been through such fantastic strenuous living in my life! Mother and I are here in Cambridge now for 5 days, Ted having gone off to his home in Yorkshire for 2 days to take all his stuff from the condemned London slum where he lived (and, thank God, will never return to). The three of us leave for London early Thursday, the 21st, fly to Paris (I wouldn't risk mother on a channel crossing) the 22nd where we will stay for a week, Ted and I seeing mother off, after showing her Paris for a week, on her flight. Ted has been simply heavenly: mother came Wednesday (I haven't been able to eat or sleep for excitement at her coming) and Ted took us to supper at Schmidt's,[1] a good cheap German restaurant that night, and we decided to get married while mother was in London. Our only sorrow was that you weren't there. When Ted & I see you in Europe this summer we'll tell you all the fantastic details of our struggle to get a license, (from the Archbishop of Canterbury,[2] no less), searching for the parish church where Ted belonged & had, by law, to be married, spotting a priest on the street, Ted pointing: "That's him!" following him home & finding he was the right one.

We rushed about London, buying dear Ted shoes & trousers, two gold wedding rings (I never wanted an engagement ring) with the last of our money, and mummy supplying a lovely pink knitted suit dress she brought (intuitively never having worn) and me in that & a pink hairribbon and a pink rose from Ted, standing with rain pouring outside in the dim little church, saying the most beautiful words in the world as our vows, with the curate as second witness and the dear Reverend,[3] an old, bright-eyed man (who lives right opposite Charles Dickens' house!) kissing my cheek,

1–Schmidt's, a German restaurant then, according to SP's address book, at 33–43 Charlotte Street, London.

2–In 1956, the Archbishop of Canterbury was Geoffrey Francis Fisher, Baron Fisher of Lambeth (1887–1972).

3–SP and TH were married by Reverend R. Mercer Wilson (b. 1887). Wilson lived at 13 Doughty Street, London; Dickens's house was number 48.

and the tears just falling down from my eyes like rain I was so happy with my dear lovely Ted. Oh, you will love him, too. He wants so to meet you. So to the world, we are engaged, and you must help us keep this an utter secret. After mother goes on June 29th we will be alone together for the first time, and go to Spain for the summer, to rent a little house by the sea and write and learn Spanish. We are meeting mother in London around August 5th & Ted is taking her (& me) to his home in Yorkshire (he wants her to rest & is very concerned about her packed tour, trying to get her to stay longer in one place, Austria, for she was very sick in London the first days, still shaky from the boat). We'll no doubt see her off August 14th. THEN, we'd like to see you, joining you whereever would be best (we'd love to see Vienna, but would have to hitchhike, so maybe nearer, Italy, France or Rotterdam, whereever you'd be then.) We'll travel, or stay put. We MUST be with you at least a week. Preferably more. Tell us what day to meet where anytime after the 14th & we'll try to arrange: write me c/O Whitstead here till I write you our Spain address. Tell us when you'll be free, where, & we'll come. I want you so to get to know my dear new husband. By the way, his first poem[1] (about us in an allegorical way!) has been accepted by POETRY mag in Chicago (should bring $34 when published). Hope we'll both be teaching Eng. at some college in New England in 1957!

Much love –
SYLVIA HUGHES

(ps – write c/o my maiden name!)

TO *Elinor Friedman Klein*

Wednesday 27 June 1956 — ALS (picture postcard), Smith College

<picture postcard caption covered by stamps; image shows Pont au Change, the River Seine, La Conciergerie, and in the distance the Eiffel Tower; printed by Editions Chantal>

Paris, June 27

Dear Ellie . . .

Where o where are you! Ted & I waited with Yorkshire one-armed artist all Thursday, hoping for reunion dinner – got worried with all these

1 – Ted Hughes, 'Bawdry Embraced', *Poetry* 88 (August 1956), 295–7.

plane crashes – am at 25 Rue Jacob, Hotel des Deux Continents till Wed, July 4 – write or come, but do either soon –

Much Love,
Sylvia

TO *Aurelia Schober Plath*

Wednesday 4 July 1956 — TLS with envelope, Indiana University

July 4, 1956

Dearest mother . . .

It was lovely to get the beautiful card from Amsterdam and Ted and I wer so pleased to hear what a time you're having. I think the rest of your trip should be a total joy; now that you've mastered one city, you can master them all.

We've been delayed here because Ted couldn't get his visa for Spain until tomorrow morning, and so we're leaving on the 9 p.m. train Thursday for Madrid, a 24-hour trip which should be rather exhausting (the longest I've ever taken is half that). We've been learning the hard way about making reservations early and doing things ahead of time: the official world simply does not run to suit private schedules.

Both of us are just slowly coming out of our great fatigue from the whirlwind plans and events of last month, and after meandering about Paris, sitting writing and reading in the Tuileries, have produced a good poem apiece[1] which is a necessity to our personal self-esteem---not so much a good poem or story, but at least several hours work of solid writing a day. Something in both of us needs to write for a large period daily, or we get cold on paper, cross, or nervous. Ted is doing a large detailed story of "O'Kelley's Angel" which he will soon whittle down to about 10 pages of a simply told fable. It is a marvelous tale, and he has also another one called "The Callum Makers" which is a take-off of a civilization completely run by TV. I have never been so entertained in my life, and if by faith and criticism and giving him the opportunity to write and write I can help bring these stories into perfect being, I shall be completely happy. I really think, that with Ted's ideas someday we'll have best-selling novels or illustrated fables on the market. My commercial flair has been much stimulated by reading the McCall's you left, and

1 – According to SP's calendar, she wrote 'The Shrike' on 3 July 1956.

I have several ideas which I hope to write out in the next month. We are really happiest keeping to ourselves, and writing, writing, writing. I never thought I should grow so fast so far in my life; the whole secret for both of us, I think, is being utterly in love with each other, which frees our writing from being a merely egoistic mirror, but rather a powerful canvas on which other people live and move.

Our funds will just cover Spain, and we hope to persuade Warren to meet us in Paris: all plans to cross England or go to Vienna are out, and we will be lucky if we make it to Paris to see Warrie at the end of August. Our hotel here treats us beautifully, and we have found a marvelous cheap restaurant[1] where we can get a full meal of tender Chateaubriand steak, vegetables, bread and wine for only about 250 francs apiece (less than a dollar!) and so can eat there daily. Do try to get your travel agent to plan that week in England for you; I am crushed that I won't be able to see you off, for I so loved being with you those last days in Paris. But in less than a year, I shall be home.

You have no idea how forward I look to that cottage on Cape Cod! To have a laundromat handy to keep clothes clean (which will be impossible in lukewarm water and facesoap this summer) and to have an icechest with food on hand! Such a dream. I'd like any advice you can give me early next fall about applying for jobs for both of us. Should he write to say "my wife and I", or me saying "My husband", or both separately? I suppose I should write "my-husband-to-be", technically! How I long to settle in Spain next week with our blessed Olivetti and write uninterrupted for a month! I am really weary of making practical travel arrangements and will be glad when we find a place down there. I'll try to write again from Madrid, where we'll stop to reconnoiter before heading to the southern coast; have written Mrs. Prouty about being engaged & unable to make England.

Am very very happy with my wonderful husband,

much love,
sivvy

1 – According to SP's calendar, this was called Chez Jean.

TO *Aurelia Schober Plath*

Saturday 7 July 1956 — TLS with envelope, Indiana University

Madrid
July 7, 1956

Dearest of mothers!

If only you could see me now, sitting in haltar and shorts seven stories high above the modern tooting city of Madrid on our large private balcony with gay blue-and-yellow tiles on floor and wall-shelves, pots of geranium and ivy, and across, baroque towers and a blazing blue sky even now, going on eight p.m. Ted is inside writing on another fable and I just finished a detailed design sketch of my sky-view. Both of us, although still tired from our gruelling 24-hour train trip which got us here at 9 p.m. last night, are just beginning to feel deeply what an incredibly rich, creative life is opening up before us.

We are staying here till next tuesday to gather forces, enjoy the city: our hotel was recommended by the railway station, and we've had a much easier time getting around and discovering places and making practical arrangements than in either London or Paris! Our hotel-room which is spacious, comfortable, cool, with a high cross-ventilated breeze, costs roughly $2.75 a night, the most we've ever paid, but we were so exhausted from our 40-hour stretch of Paris business and the train ride that we felt this three-day interim deserved comfort. For this price we have a divine balcony, where I lie and tan in the early morning sun, and type in the cool shade of the afternoon; a private bathroom complete with tub, shower, etc. Dear Ted has never been in a place with a shower before (the last bath he took being in a public hole in London, the day of our wedding!) He is like an excited small boy about it, just reveling in a daily shower, yipping like Frankie used to.

Our train trip was fantastic. The first half of it (Paris to Bordeaux and the French border) was definitely the worst: we were, at night, just as we were ready to sleep, sitting straight up in a crowded compartment of 8. Worst of all, the 4 people on one side got into one of those interminable impassioned conversations (three old ladies and an old man) which was fun to watch and listen to at first, in which they treated their case histories of horrible deaths, the disquieting troubles of life after the happy days of the twenties, and their favorite beverages with equal passion and opinionated vehemence. However, about one in the morning, and I thought I'd scream. I was glad when the smutty gray dawn came, and we disembarked at the border for an hour of going through customs and a saving mug of coffee on the Spanish side. Ted and I felt increasingly grubby; the wash'n'dry cloths helped, and the coffee really sustained us.

The change of atmosphere in the Spanish 3rd-class train was incredible and very wonderful. The French people have a calculating, mean, intellectual critcalness about them which I really do not care for; the Italians are too soft and plump and childlike, with an even slimier commercial bent. But the Spaniards! They are utterly magnificent. I have never been treated so marvelously in my life.

Ted and I looked pretty dirty, with his rucksack and my shopping bag into which I'd packed, in Paris, milk, butter, bread (mile-long loaves), cheese, peaches and cherries, according to the train fashion, which is to eat continually from large bottomless sacks. Well, Ted accidentally put the bottle of milk on top of the butter during one snack, and the butter squushed and went all over everything. Then, by the time we got on the Italian train, the milk had curdled and it spilt all over the floor as we went over some bumps. Well, we learned. And the bread and cheese and fruit tasted marvelous.

As I was saying, on the Spanish train, we had a compartment with two dear Spanish soldiers, rifle-men, tremendously fierce looking, with big guns, queer black hats with a back-flap, and many bullet pockets. They began to talk to us immediately, and Ted and I made do with his minute Spanish-English dictionary which soon became the pet article of the compartment, everyone looking through the dictionary for the spanish word they wanted to convey, finding it, and then showing it to us and doing the rest with their hands and inflection. We both actually felt perfect rapport with them all. There were the two soldiers, a handsome gay dandy with a moustache, a dark tan peasant, a charming young boy, and a very helpful and friendly working-man. The first thing that knit us together was that the workman had brought a leather wine-flask from which one squirts a jet of wine into the mouth. Well, this was passed around and around during the 12-hour train trip to Madrid, a different man getting out at each station to refill it. The jet only squirted about a mouthful, so it takes a long time to make up the glass. The sharing, utterly heartfelt and unselfconscious, delighted me. Ted and I had some salami, tomato and wine from the rest, and divided up our immense store of bread and cheese and cherries among them. Everybody took a piece of everything, and we looked up words, discussed where Ted and I thought we might go to live in South spain, discussed clothes, everything.

The trip felt twice as short as the night ride through Paris. You should have seen me learning to use the wine-flask! I was the Little Buttercup of the car, and everybody went into hysterics when I'd squint my eyes and get wine up my nose or something. Eventually I learned just how to tilt the flask, point back down into the throat swallow while drinking and spraying, and tip and stop without spilling.

It is so wonderful that wherever Ted and I go people seem to love us. We are fantastically matched; both of us need the same amount of sleep and food and time for writing; both are inner-directed, almost anti-social in that we don't like functional parties and are happiest with simple, unpretentious working people, who adopt us immediately. Before we left Paris, we discovered a tiny, ugly cheap restaurant where negroes & workpeople flocked for platters of good simple food. We went there daily for the specialty of the house: a thick, tender, rare Chateaubriand steak smothered in parsley butter, plenty of bread to sop up sauce, a pile of delicious string beans, red wine and Yoghurt, the whole meal mounting up to about $1.60 for the two of us!!! Can you imagine. Both of us would have been perfectly happy to have gone on eating the same dish all day for the summer.

Anyway, I have never felt so native to a country as I do to Spain. First of all, the colors we saw from the train window all the way down were brighter than I thought possible in the world: blazing yellow, tan and light green fields under a blue-white sky, green-black pine trees, white adobe houses with orange tile roofs, and all, bless it, utterly agricultural or sheep and bull country. We saw endless miles of grass pampas on which grazed flocks of black and white sheep, black bulls, spotted cows, guarded by shepherds with crooks & sheep dogs, seemingly in the middle of nowhere. Then after miles of rocky outcropping hills and resin-pines, a pink walled village would spring up, with burros circling wells to draw water, storks nesting on the church steeple, chickens and children riding donkey carts. Sparsely populated and ruggedly, vividly beautiful. Everything here seems so clean, compared to Italy: all is white, and violent colors. Now, at 9 p.m. it is still light enough to type outside, perfectly comfortable in haltar and shorts.

Perhaps what is most "mine" about the climate is the blessed <u>dry</u> heat. One simply doesn't sweat at all; there is no sense of that heavy wet oppression that comes on our "dog-days" at home. Clean dry hot air strikes one, invigorating, even though I can well understand the siesta habit where everything is closed from 1 to 4. It is impossible to hurry. Best of all, I have a light clear head that I never knew was possible. I never knew what a load of weight I was carrying in my sinuses! For the first time in my life I feel clear-headed, vigorous and energetic in my own fashion: bright sun, dry heat, good cheap food (Ted and I bought delicious nectarines & a small watermelon to eat at home today). Laundry, hair, everything is bone dry after about 15 minutes![1] I am utterly delighted at the thought of coming back here for two 5-week periods during the year. Plan to learn Spanish cold this summer & study it on my own at Cambridge. It is so much faster here, in the center of Spain, where everyone is only too eager to teach us words and pronunciation.

We plan to go to a bullfight tomorrow night, buy Ted some light summer jerseys and a summer suit Monday (it was only after today and the blazing dry heat that I persuaded him he needed a light-weight suit--the dear stubborn boy had planned to wear his heavy winter sweater or heavy black corduroy jacket all summer!) His almost blind unwillingness to spend money for necessities to health (like the teeth) or comfort (like proper outfits for summer & winter climates) is a carry-over from his impoverished years in London, his sight of a spendthrift spoilt sister (which makes it an impossibility, in his eyes, to ask for money from home, which she, older as she is, does successfully & selfishly very often). I hope that slowly I'll be able to reecucate him to be more generous to himself, although I am very glad he is economical. I'm going to try to slip off alone Monday to get him a tie or a toilet kit for his birthday (which is August 17, in case you'd like to send him a card). We plan to take a day bus-trip to get to the large city of Alicante, down from Valencia on the coast, Tuesday, rent a small cottage, furnished (the man at the American Express today was very encouraging) in which I hope to cook, very near the beach. Spain is utter heaven.

Our best idea came today, when I asked Ted if he wouldn't rather teach Spanish at an American university than English, it being a more specialized subject, and a year teaching in Madrid would be excellent recommendation. He would much rather teach a language than English lit. since he doesn't like the false, narrow critical approach to English lit. (having a very original mind and opinions himself, being really too big and demanding for a freshman English course, I think, which I am not). We'd probably have more chance of being appointed together then, and language is really easier to teach than English lit., it being more definite and less demanding on time. He also hopes to make a sideline of translating and selling, maybe anthologizing, Spanish poetry. We'd also like to spend

1–SP handwrote this sentence in the left margin.

some time in South America, maybe in the summer following our year teaching in New England. By then, both of us should be almost bilingual with Spanish and get on fine. With Ted and me together, all is possible. We have such fun, and both agree that we don't feel we're living with "another" person, but only the perfect male and female counterparts of our own selves, very whole and happy.

We both send best love to you, hoping your trip is as wonderful as it sounded from the first card. Will be writing toward the end of the week with our permanent address.

Much much love, your own
sivvy[1]

TO *Aurelia Schober Plath*

Sunday 8 July 1956[2] — ALS (picture postcard), Indiana University

<picture postcard caption>
EL TORO SALTA LA BARRERA.

Dearest mother –

at last I have found my native country – dry blazing heat – violent colors – strong dear wonderful people – have never felt so well or been so happy – on train ride saw only vivid yellow pampas, sheep, storks, burros – it is like a primitive unspoilt dreamland.

xxx
sivvy[3]

1–The postscript appended to this letter and printed in *Letters Home* was taken from page 3 of SP to ASP, 10 August 1956.

2–Date supplied from postmark; postmarked Madrid, 8 July 1956.

3–A postscript by TH has not been transcribed

TO *Aurelia Schober Plath*

Saturday 14 July 1956 TLS with envelope, Indiana University

Write us till Sept. 20 c/o Enriqueta Luhoz Ortiz
Avenida de Alcoy, Benidorm, Province of Alicante Spain

Saturday morning
July 14th

Dearest, dearest mother!

At last we have found our place, our home, after a hectic month of living out of suitcases and searching for cheap restaurants. You would hardly believe it if you saw where I am sitting now! What has happened in the last two days is like a fairy-tale, and I can hardly believe myself that our summer dwelling has surpassed my wildest, most exotic dreams. I feel that our real honeymoon has at last begun, with our plan for simple living, writing and studying.

First, let me say that we left Madrid Tuesday morning on an 8 hour bus trip through dry, deserty Spanish country, relieved by olive trees, vineyards and blazing yellow wheat fields, eating from a watermelon I'd brought, drinking cold beer at the little stops, staring at the vivid reddish-purple earth, the workers taking siestas in the shade of hay wains. Alicante, our big stop-off from which we planned to find our place, was a terrible honky-tonk port, and we spent a nightmarish two nights there, utterly exhausted, miserable, disgusted by the cheap resort blare, worse than any Coney Island. The first day, we asked for information of little villas in near-by small towns, and were given dubious looks & talk about the height of the season. Well, we just managed to board a bus going to Benidorm, supposed to have a good beach, an hour's ride off, to walk and look about in person. It was then our luck started.

As soon as I saw the tiny village ahead, after an hour of driving through the red sand desert hills, dusty olive orchards & scrub grass that is so typical around here, and saw the blaze of blue sea, clean curve of beach, immaculate white houses and streets, like a small sparkling dream town, I felt instinctively with Ted that this was our place. On the bus-ride we'd become more and more skeptical about the feasibility of getting a furnished house, with linens, etc. & cooking utensils and had almost regretfully decided a hotel room would be more likely a place for good plumbing, light, air etc., when a little lively black-eyed woman on the bus seat in front of us turned to ask if we understood French. Whereupon she informed us that she had a lovely house on the sea-front with a garden, and big kitchen, where she was letting rooms for the summer. It sounded almost too good to be true, combining the advantages of a private house which we couldn't afford with the comfort of a hotel.

Well, she led us through the bright white streets where there were burro carts, open market with fresh fruit and vegetables, gay shops, a strange mixture of clean colorful poverty with large pastel hotels, everything apparently just finished being built before we came, utterly new, with the modern styles blending with the simple native architecture. Very strange, because while Benidorm is just being discovered by tourists, except for the hotels, it is utterly uncommercial, built along a mile curve of perfect beach, with glassy clear waves breaking on shore, a large rock island out in the bay, and the most incredible azure sea, prussian blue toward the horizon and brilliant aqua nearer shore.

Her house was a large brown café-au-lait-colored stucco closer to the sea than grammy's place in Winthrop, with a palm and a pine tree growing in the front yard, a back and side garden full of red geraniums, white daisies, roses, a fig tree and tree with bright red flowers, with a backdrop of purple mountainous hills, incredibly lovely. She also had a huge cool kitchen with all the cooking utensils one could wish. Of the four rooms for rent upstairs, Ted and I fell in love utterly with the one we are living in now: a small pink-washed room just big enough for two new maple beds which we pushed together facing the sea, a little dressing shelf & mirror, & a half-bookcase, half-wardrobe. The real glory, though, are the large French window-doors opening onto our balcony-terrace! That's where I'm sitting now, drying my newly washed hair, facing the whole expanse of blazing blue Mediterranean, the palm-tree rustling in the continuous salt sea-breeze, the sun tanning me at last, freshly laundered clothes, flapping dry over the deck-chair beside me. Ted is in the inner room on the bed studying Spanish, utterly happy. Our life is incredibly wonderful, and we will stay here solidly till September 29th, when we'll head back to leave me in Cambridge. There is so much to tell about our wonderful place here!

The Señora is Spanish, a widow, very stylish and a kind of town character. Not only has she taught French, and offered to exchange Spanish lessons for English lessons with us, but she is also a writer of romance stories and poems (Ted and I are dying to learn enough Spanish so we can read them). So far we are the only lodgers and plan to get established comfortably in a routine before any new people move in; we have every advantage on our side. Our balcony-terrace also adjoins another room, much larger than ours, which naturally the Señora hoped to use as a selling-point for the other room. Ted and I were horrified, for it would mean we'd have absolutely no privacy, so we explained to her that for people on vacation the beach and garden were fine, but for us, wanting to write, we needed a quiet place, and since our room was too small, the terrace was the only spot. She was perfectly understanding, being a writer herself, and so the terrace-balcony is completely ours!

In the morning, early, I wake about 6 with the sunrise coming over the sea through the palms, go down into the kitchen to make Ted and me big mugs of café-con-leche (coffee made completely with hot milk) and bring it up with muffins to eat on our balcony overlooking the breakers. Day and night we hear the blessed roar of the waves on shore and get the sea breeze which makes even the blazing Spanish sun cool!

Then we go early to market, and, miraculously, have figured that we can eat perfectly well on $1 for the two of us a day! We are very low on money, having spent more than we budgeted in Madrid; Ted needed a summer suit, so we went to a big sale and got him a nice café-au-lait brownish linen and a stylish black tie which he is very happy with; he really needs it when he applies for his teaching later in the summer, but it knocked our budget way off. As it is, we are putting train fare home aside and Ted is writing to Olwyn for more of the money she owes him, as we need at least $50 to cover the rest of the summer food expenses. We are paying $2.50 a night for our room, which at first sounds like a lot, but isn't when you consider we have actually two rooms: the bedroom & balcony-study,-dining-room-&-solarium! use of a modern bathroom (with shower and tub) right outside, and the marvelous kitchen which enables us to save so much on food. All the tourists eat in expensive restaurants here, and Ted and I are about the only foreigners who buy food with the natives at the early-morning markets.

I wish you could see them! We've gotten shrewd & go all about pricing things, before we buy, to find the lowest stand. Everything is very cheap. A kilo of potatoes, about 2 pounds, is 5 cents, a pound of sardines about 10 cents, etc. The fish-market is Ted's favorite place, for the fishermen here go out all night (we can see the lights of the sardine boats bobbing from our balcony as we eat dinner there at twilight) and the fish is literally still wet from the sea! We have a very simple but good diet, and Ted likes what I make. We have two litres of milk a day (bigger than quarts), drinking milk for breakfast in coffee and lots at lunch, which is a cold lunch, usually a picnic on the beach, of bread, butter, cheese, tomatoes & onions, deviled eggs & fruit. Supper I cook, and we have it with wine at twilight when the stars and moon are out over our balcony and the evening sea breeze- blows in the palm leaves.

We are in bed before ten p.m., going asleep to the sound of the breakers. As I write, I can see children scampering along the shore; a white donkey wagon just went by. Ted and I hope to learn Spanish well by the end of the month, to get friendly with the natives & maybe go out fishing with them. I am going to do a series of sketches with a local color article which may be sent to the Monitor. This is The Place to write. We have just been resting the last two days, getting rid of the last months' tension & exhaustion; both of us got sunstroke our first day, Ted burning an excruciating red, which he is just recovering from, and me getting that terrible siege of diarreaha (sp?) which leaves one utterly weak. Last night, however, he hypnotized me to sleep, and I woke up completely cured and feeling wonderful. It is quite marvelous to have a husband like this! If I have a headache or am tired, he can hypnotize me and I wake up refreshed and fine and relaxed. We are utterly happy together, and I can't imagine how I ever lived without him. I think he is the handsomest, most brilliant, creative, dear man in the world. My whole thought is for him, how to please him, to make a comfortable place for him, and I am free, as is he, from that dread narrowness which comes from growing self-centeredness. He is kind and thoughtful, with a wonderful sense of humor and we shall have a wonderful rich life. We'd love to come back here and buy a house before the prices soar. If we were drawing an American salary from writing, we could live on the Spanish shore fantastically cheaply. Good wine is only about 7 cents a bottle!

I naturally have very limited supplies on which to cook, none of the seasonings, mushrooms, spices etc. which I hope to use in America next year, but with the blessed cookbook I can make really tasty things with what I have: made a delicious cold potato salad last night with onions, French dressing, hard boiled eggs and mayonnaise, which we had with fried ham. Ted also loves deviled eggs the way I make them with onions & mayonnaise. The Señora showed me how to make a wonderful tortilla with potatoes, onions & eggs which I'll make for us tomorrow night, with ripe tomato salad.

In about a week, Villajoyosa, next door, is having a big all-week festival in which they are re-enacting the invasion of the Moors on the Spanish coast. Ted and I will hitchhike over, & maybe write it up. Ted is now working on the best idea yet, which is utterly enchanting: a children's book of short stories of "How the Animals Became"![1] he told me the beginning introduction of how God's Creatures were at first all the same, and the stories will be how each one became what he now is: "How the Donkey Became" is exquisite, and the same with the Hyena. It is much better than kipling's "How the Leopard Got its Spots",[2] etc. because each animal forms itself from some inner moral condition, really original and excellent. I have great faith in him as a writer of children's books; he can make up a story like no one I've every heard!

We have figured that it would be good for me to write a series of stories for the Women's magazines about Americans-abroad, because I am very good at local color and also can write dramatic contrast plots where the native scene gives rise to a parallel in psychological conflict. I'm going to begin one on the Madrid bullfights[3] this week. We went last Sunday evening,[4] and I am glad that Ted and I both feel the same way: full of sympathy for the bull. I'd imagined that the matador danced around with the dangerous bull, then killed him neatly. Not so. The bull is utterly innocent, peaceful, taunted to run about by the many cape-wavers. Then a horrid picador on a horse with a straw-mat guard about it stabs a huge hole in the bull's neck with a pike, from which gushed blood, and men run to stick little colored picks in it. The killing isn't even neat, and with all the chances against it, we felt disgusted and sickened by such brutality. The most satisfying moment for us was when one of the six beautiful doomed bulls managed to gore a fat cruel picador lift him off the horse, and, I hope, make him eventually bleed to death; he was carried out spurting blood from his thigh. My last bull-fight. But I'll now write a story with it as a background. We plan to write a good four to six hours a day in a rigid routine for the next two months. At last. Bliss.

<u>Wish</u> you could try to arrange your last week here instead of England. We're down the coast from Valencia, right above Alicante. <u>Do</u> try, even if only for a few days. You'd love it & could swim & sun & I'd cook here. You could take a train to Madrid, fly from there to London.

xxx
sivvy

Ted says to take it easy, gaze at greenery & sends love.

1 – Ted Hughes, *How the Whale Became* (London: Faber & Faber, 1963).

2 – Rudyard Kipling, *Just So Stories* (London: Macmillan, 1902).

3 – Sylvia Plath, 'The Black Bull'; an incomplete typescript of the story is held by Emory University.

4 – According to SP's calendar, they saw the bullfight at 'Ventas': Plaza de Toros de Las Ventas in Madrid.

TO *Warren Plath*

Saturday 14 July 1956[1]

TLS (photocopy),
Indiana University

c/o Enriqueta Luhoz Ortiz
Avenida de Alcoy
Benidorm
Province of Alicante
Spain

Dearest Warren . . .

You would never believe it if you saw where I am sitting now, finally, in our summer town in Spain: by utter luck: of a Spanish woman (who speaks French, fortunately) overhearing us talk on the bus and saying she had just the place for us, her large summer home where she was renting out rooms for the summer. After a very exhausting month of living out of suitcases and hot dusty almost nightmare traveling on bus and train, Ted and I finally came from Paris through Madrid to Alicante on the Spanish coast (an awful honkey-tonk sea-port resort) to this exquisite small village, Benidorm, an hour up the coast from Alicante, and a bit more down from Valencia (it's probably too small to be on your map). Essentially, we wanted a quiet place, right on the sea, where we could write and cook. It looked pretty impossible to find a small house, furnished with linen, cooking utensils, etc. at the height of the season, and we were sick of hotels, and the search and expense of eating out. Well, listen to what we have now, with this fantastic character Señora (a widow) who is also a writer of poems and romance stories (in Spanish) and a teacher of languages (she has offered to give us Spanish conversation lessons in exchange for English; meanwhile, we get along famously in French; she loves Ted, and has already taught me how to make a Spanish potato-and-onion tortilla).

Ted and I live in her beautiful house which is right on the beach in the middle of a fabulous brilliant azure Mediterranean bay and our little room has just enough space for beds, bookcase-wardrobe & a dressing-table shelf. The miracle is our balcony-terrace on which I am sitting now, which adjoins our room by two French doors which we always keep open. A palm and a pine tree are waving over my head. Below is a colorful garden full of fig trees, red geraniums, daisies and roses. Across the street, as far as eye can see is the open ocean, with an island in the bay, Prussian

1–Date supplied from postmark by Warren Plath.

blue toward the horizon, bright azure nearer shore. Even as we sat on the Cape and looked toward Spain, now Ted and I sit in Spain and look toward Africa! Since the Señora is also a writer, she understood when we said we'd like a balcony for ourselves to write on (it also adjoins another room) as the other vacationing guests (there aren't any more yet) can use the garden & beach.

It is utter heaven here. The little village is a queer combination of modern tourist elegant hotels (but completely uncommercial) and colorful poverty-stricken white pueblos, blending perfectly. Donkey and burro carts fill the streets; milk is delivered by bicycle, and one carries bottles to market to fill with oil, wine and vinegar. I have the use of the big kitchen here with all kinds of pots and pans, and the two of us can eat well on $1 a day! Wine for example is only about 8 cents a bottle; sardine, 10 cents a pound.

We wake up in the early morning about 6, with the sun coming over the bay through the palms, and I go down to make two big cups of café-con-leche which I serve with muffins on the balcony; all day and night we watch and listen to the breakers along the shore opposite; a continuous salt sea breeze keeps us always cool, even in the hot direct Spanish sun. Then we go early to market (we have no refrigerator) and buy really fresh fish (all night we can see the lights of the sardine boats bobbing out in the ocean) and fruit and vegetables & bread made in dark cave-like ovens. We have a picnic lunch; bread, butter, cheese, deviled eggs, tomatoes & onions & lots of milk. Then swim in the clear glassy water, study Spanish, translate French, write. I cook supper at twilight which we eat in the moon-light on our balcony! We're in bed and asleep by ten. It is the sort of life I've dreamed of all my existence, & which I thought was only for millionaires. The use of the whole house, kitchen, modern bathroom (only there's no hot water), garden, terrace, is only $2.50 a night for the two of us!

We are staying here for two months and more, till September 29th, as we can live more cheaply here with all the natural beauty of the Riviera and none of flashy commerciality, write, sun, swim, study languages. We bought Ted a light brown linen summer suit in Madrid at a sale for $12 as he had to have something more than dungarees in applying for a job next year down here teaching English (which he hopes to do next month, after intensive Spanish study this month), and so are literally down to the minimum in budget, having had to spend also more in Madrid eating out than we thought. So it looks like we won't be able to move from Benidorm all summer.

Which brings me to the hope nearest my heart: that if you have anything close to a week or even 5 days free at the end of your Experiment trip, that you could take the train from northern Italy (you said you were going to Venice) and come straight along the Riviera through Marseilles, Valencia, to Benidorm to stay with us for a few days, swim, sun and get to know my dear wonderful handsome brilliant husband! We'd reserve a room for you, and you could eat & swim with us if you'd just let us know ahead when you could come. It would not be very expensive for you to travel here, where it would be formidable for the two of us on our scanty budget of $1 a day for food to get train tickets anywhere. Along the coast, too, it is not hard to hitchhike if you don't have too much baggage. It breaks my heart that we can't afford to travel up near where you are, but I hope you will put all your resources & ingenuity to planning on a couple of days with us here. The surroundings are as beautiful as any I've ever seen, with purple mountainous hills as a backdrop for the sparkling white adobe villas. Please, please, write that you can come in the last week of your trip. You could get the train up here through Paris to Rotterdam. I am so longing to see you and can't bear to wait two whole years when we are comparatively so close! I have just forwarded my mailing address to Whitstead, so hope to be hearing from you soon about your summer in Germany. – but of course write me here now

It seems so natural for me now to write about Ted and me without describing him, for I can't imagine how I ever lived without him. We are utterly made for each other, and marrying a fine writer is the best thing I could have ever done. We are perfectly congenial, enjoying communicating with the natives, disliking parties and superficial cocktail affairs, loving the simple rich inward life, devoting most time to writing, loving good simple cooking, reading & learning languages. Ted is the only man I've ever met whom I'd rather be with than alone; it is like living with the male counterpart of myself: he knows all about so many things: fishing, hunting birds, animals, and is utterly dear. We finished typing a manuscript of about 30 of his best poems[1] & sent them off from Paris to a contest in America. He is now working on a series of wonderful children's stories on "How the Animals Became": each chapter tells how a particular animal turned to what he was, because in the beginning, all God's creatures were exactly the same; you would love the one "How the Hyena Became." He is also writing a magnificent fable called "O'Kelly's

1–According to SP's calendar, she sent TH's poems to *Virginia Quarterly Review* on 4 July 1956.

Angel" about an enterprising Irishman who caught an angel, and what happened; hysterically funny and profound, carrying in it the whole problem of demonstrable miracles, etc. Also, Ted is a good hypnotist. I had sunstroke and an upset stomach our first day here after much dusty travel & weary nights, and he hypnotized me so I slept all night to wake up completely refreshed and cured. What a husband! You Must come meet him. Write me, Mrs. Sylvia Hughes or Mrs. Ted Hughes, c/o the address on the letter-head. PLEASE COME.

Though we are very poor now, and will be for a year (I literally don't have a cent left till I get my next Fulbright check in September, & Ted won't be getting money till he starts teaching) I feel we will be lucky as anything in our writing, & we have the daring to live the way most people dream of living when they are fifty: to sacrifice all for <u>our</u> ideal of a good life, not other people's cars & securities & 10-year leases: we hope to learn languages, live in foreign countries all over the world, write & draw them, publish, teach & have babies as soon as we can afford them. We have fingers cross that you'll come –

Love,
Sivvy

TO *Warren Plath*

Wednesday 18 July 1956 — AL (picture postcard, photocopy), Indiana University

<picture postcard caption>
N. 15 Alicante / Muelle de Poniente / Quai de l'ouest / Pier facing west

July 18
Wednesday

Dearest Warren –

Our fickle Señora had decided to let her whole house to one family for the whole summer, so after a day of feeling like DP's, Ted & I found a huge place with our own kitchen bath, etc – one whole floor, quiet for writing, among the natives. We'd have <u>plenty</u> of room there for you & could feed you for less than $1. a day – so <u>please</u> do your darndest to come for a week – as long as you can – could you turn the end of your Experiment trip here? Wonderful salt water swimming. Write soon to: Mrs. Sylvia Hughes – Tomas Ortunio – 59, Benidorm, SPAiN

TO *Aurelia Schober Plath*

Wednesday 25 July 1956 TLS[1] with envelope, Indiana University

July 25, 1956

Dearest mother . . .

I haven't received any new forwarding address from you, so I'll just write out a few installments and wait till you tell me where to send them. I was so happy to get your wonderful letters about your trip and only wish that you could manage to turn the last week of it toward us in Spain. If only we could have foreseen the kind of establishment we'd be in! I wish you could see us now.

A week ago, we moved from the Widow Mangada's house, where conditions were driving us literally mad, to this large, spacious, cool airy first floor in the native part of the village which is completely ours, no bothers, no interruptions, for the whole summer till the last week in September, at exactly the same price the Widow's tiny room and noisy balcony cost us! During the course of the week, the emotional,[2] flighty, fussy temperament of the widow (always boasting of her high-born family and her dead doctor husband and her education) was on the verge of driving me to murder her: I couldn't cook a thing in the kitchen, but she was mincing about peering under the lids of my frying pans, snatching potatoes out of my hand to show me her way of peeling them, rearranging my cupboard shelf, which I re-arranged back again. And flying into an actressy temper. She had never rented her house out as rooms before this way, having rented the whole thing to one family for the summer (obviously she thought she was going to get more money this way) and got more and more irritable as she saw inconveniences rise: her dream of nine roomers cooking in one kitchen and using one bathroom with lousy plumbing soon collapsed. Five Spaniards lived on our floor, left sand silting shower and bowl, and we discovered that our beautiful balcony with the view hung over the main boulevard promenade of the town, crowded with gaping pedestrians from 10 in the morning till ten at night. Ted was driven to write in the bedroom on the beds and neither of us was accomplishing any work except the exhausting task of coping with Widow Mangada and her ceaseless changing whims. She didn't like

1–This letter is in two parts: 25 July 1956 comprises the first four pages; and the 2 August 1956 instalment pages numbered 5 and 6, respectively. The entire letter was probably sent on 3 August 1956, the date on which the envelope was postmarked.

2–'~~in which~~ the emotional' appears in the original.

me, because I understood her French perfectly and could immediately interpret all the things she said in plain practical English which bothered her fancy hypocrisy, so she turned to Ted, whose ability to speak French is most elementary. One day as I was cooking, she sweetly announced that she'd decided (or, rather, was forced by the government) to let the house out to one family for the summer instead of worrying about getting new roomers all the time; but not to be concerned, she wouldn't really try to get anyone and we could just live on till she did. Then, two days notice if we were lucky. Ted and I were just sick. The gall of her assuming we could live under the shadow of that uncertainty, just so she could get our rent until it suited her convenience, made us furious. We had just figured that we could live out the whole summer by a frugal cooking budget of $1.25 a day for the two of us, and the prospect of being on the road again made us both exhausted. We'd lived such an utterly business-like, exterior life the last month, on trains, looking for cheap restaurants, buying more tickets, finding cheap hotels, that all we wanted was peace & quiet and a place to cook. So we dressed up that night, planning to see the mayor, who is evidently the head real-estate agent in town. He was not coming back home till late, so we went walking about. I saw a street that I intuitively liked, on a hill going up toward the mountains in a native quarter. Little old brown wizened women, clad in rusty black from head to toe, were sitting in their white pueblo doorways weaving fish nets. Ted wanted to go in the other direction to look for a cheap place, but my intuition pulled me forcibly up the road. We saw, set in a cornfield, a lovely large white stucco house with a sign which we translated as "One floor for rent." That seemed to mean a kitchen, our biggest concern for the fantastic economy it meant. The nice woman upstairs threw open the doors of the first floor on what struck us at first as a grand mansion: three huge bedrooms, a large diningroom and livingroom and big kitchen and pantry and bathroom and garage. We were awed, and said of course it was too big. Whereupon she asked us how much we could pay for the summer. We settled on 7000 pesetas (about $175 for two and a half months), and walked away in an utter daze of joy, with a summer contract.

The widow was furious at first, obviously wishing she hadn't told us until she actually got someone for the rent, never thinking we were clever enough to act immediately and so decisively (she evidently figured she could take advantage of us at her place by calling us "friends", and treating the other lodgers as paying customers). Finally, when she realized we were still in the same town and it would be to her advantage to be nice & uphold her reputation, she was all sweetness & light. We moved the next day, exhausted from the emotional strain of packing & traveling. How can I tell you how wonderful it is here?

For the first time in a year, I have come to rest. Two rich, potential summer months still lie ahead. All the change and furor of this past year, in which I don't think I've really ever rested, going from a tiring term to even more tiring traveling vacations---are melting into one. Our house is cool as a well, stone tiled, quiet, with a view of blue mountains and even a corner of the sea. Our front porch is shaded by a grape arbor, pungent with geraniums. Our furniture is dark heavy walnut which is pleasant against the white plaster walls. We don't see a tourist from morning till night.

Ted and I are just coming into our own. We have figured out a rigorous schedule which is at last beginning to be realized: here is a day in the life of the writing Hughes': We wake about seven in the morning, with a cool breeze blowing in the grape leaves outside our window. I get up, take the two litres of milk left daily on our doorstep in a can and heat it for my cafe con leche and Ted's brandy-milk which we have with delectable wild bananas and sugar. Then we go early to market, first for fish, which must begin about six: it is fascinating, because every day brings a different catch: there are mussels, crabs, shrimp, little baby octopusses, and sometimes a huge fish which they sell in steaks. I generally make egg & lemon mixture, dip them in that and flour and fry them to a golden brown. Then we price vegetables, buying our staples of eggs, potatoes, tomatoes and onions (I see we each have an egg and a good portion of meat a day). If only you could see how fantastically we economize: we go to the one potato stand that sells a kilo for 1.50 instead of 1.75 pesetas and have found a place that charges a peseta less (about 2½ cents) for butter! I hope never again in my life I will have to be so tight with money. We will one day have a great deal, I am sure of it, but this summer's flock of unexpected expenses with the wedding and all our un-budgetable travels has knocked us down so that neither of us will have a shilling or a cent when we return to England at the end of September. I so appreciated your generous help this spring, and only hope you have enough to get about with comfortably now!

Any advice you have about what to do with summer squash and zucchini (is that the purple squash-looking thing that seems a cross between an eggplant look and a cucumber shape?) and carrots, etc. would be appreciated. I have one frying pan, and a large boiling pan, and fry most everything in olive oil. Ted is quite pleased with the tasty little tortillas and battered things I make, out of my Rombauer book, but almost every recipe has a few crucial ingredients I don't have, or the tantalizing end: "bake or broil," which, of course, I can't do. I have a one-ring petrol burner on which I cook everything, no hot water, and straw tangles to clean dishes; no icebox, so milk must be boiled if it is kept a full day. Yet no modern bride was as happy with her modern kitchen as I am with my first own place; even the Longueways in Maine wasn't so primitive: my main dishes are potato salad, mashed potato cakes, fried potatoes & onions, deviled eggs, tomato & egg tortilla, string beans & tomatoes, string bean salad; fish hot & fish cold with mayonnaise. You see there is a limit to the permutations & combinations. But we do eat healthily. Bread, butter & cheese, plenty of milk & eggs. But how I long for a good american kitchen. I almost cry with longing when I read the beautiful recipes in Rombauer, my favorite book now.

Ted and I write, he at the big oak table, me at the typewriter table by the window in the diningroom (our writing room) from about 8:30 till 12. Then I make lunch and we go to the beach for two hours for a siesta and swim when the crowds are all gone home and have it completely to ourselves. Then two more hours of writing from 4 to 6, when I make supper. From 8 to 10 we study languages, me translating "Le Rouge at Le Noire" and planning to do all the French for my exams this summer, Ted working on Spanish. Then, if there is time, we walk through the moonlit almond groves toward the still purple mountains where we can see the Mediterranean sparkling silver far below.

I am just beginning to get the feel of prose again, going through that very painful period of writing much bad uneven prose to get back in story form as I was when I was doing the Mintons and those for Seventeen. I am working on the bullfight one now, and have a terrific idea for a humorous Ladies Home Journal story called "The Hypnotizing Husband" which, alas, I won't be able to finish till this fall at Cambridge, because I want to read up on a lot of hypnotism stunts to make it ring true. It is a great idea, and keeps coming at me while I'm cutting beans, etc. Ted is now doing the last chapter of the most enchanting children's book ever! Every day he reads me a new chapter or two. It is 10 chapters long, about how different animals became, and just marvelous: clear, lucid, with that pure fable style which is uniquely his. He has absolutely enchanting tales about the Donkey, Owl, Whale, Tortoise, Bee, Hyena, Fox and Dog, Elephant---you would love them. They are so beautiful I just laugh and cry. I am sure it will become a children's classic.

My greatest hope is that in spite of the distance, Warren will come for a couple of days. I'd give anything to see him. We could put him up and feed him for about 75 cents a day, which is a fraction of what board and room would be in any city. I await eagerly to hear from him.

Ted and I have decided to go stay with his family[1] for the week before I go back to Cambridge, and tell them we are married. I have been feeling very badly about his writing them as if he were alone, and he was sorry he hadn't told them when we were married, if I wanted to tell them now, so he is writing them, and I will go meet my new parents-in-law in September. In spite of the discouraging rejections which arrive daily (we can't afford stamps to send stuff out Spanish airmail to America now, so are piling up manuscripts till this fall), Ted has had one more piece of good news: The Nation has enthusiastically accepted his poem "The Hag",[2] so that is two poems, and we share one magazine! Next year will be most fruitful, I feel; I should write 10 stories this summer, & Ted, two short books at least: the animals and O'Kelley and a few more. We are very happy even in these lean times. How I look forward to America and my friends and the Cape next year! My life has been like the plot of a movie these past years: a psychological, romance & travel thriller. Such a plot. Do write & take care of yourself.

Love from us both –
sivvy

TO *Warren Plath*

Monday 30 July 1956

TLS (photocopy),
Indiana University

July 30: Monday

Dearest Warren . . .

It was wonderful to get your letter and card and hear what a fine time you're having in Feldbach; you will probably have equally marvellous fun in Italy; I loved Venice, with the queer water streets & barber-shop striped poles at the mossy green entrances to the houses, even though it was frigid cold when Gordon and I stayed there in April. Also, I envy you Florence, which I missed because I was so tired of traveling that I wanted to stay longer & rest in Rome. What a traveled family we have become! Between us, we'll have covered about nine countries this summer!

Your letter was a good thing, in quite an unexpected way. It made Ted & me sit down having a realistic discussion about finances which had

1 – Edith Farrar Hughes (1898–1969) and William Henry Hughes (1894–1981); SP's mother- and father-in-law; lived at the Beacon, Heptonstall Slack, Yorkshire.
2 – Ted Hughes, 'The Hag', *The Nation*, 18 August 1956, 144.

been bothering us more and more without our talking about it: when you feel you have to look around endlessly for 1 peseta differences in the price of butter (about 2½ cents), and feel hungry all the time, in spite of regular meals, it gets constricting. Ted's older sister Olwyn, who works in Paris, owes him about $150 which we had counted on to feed us for the rest of the summer. Well, a letter from her, arriving in the same mail, made us realize we couldn't go on expecting her to come through in time: she is evidently extravagant, always overspending, and extracting money from her is a painful job of nagging. Which Ted will have to do during this year so he can get the money for his ship passage over.

Well, the upshot of all this is that we see perfectly how absurd it would be for you to make such a long, arduous trip down for only one day, and have decided to cut our stay in Benidorm to August 23rd or 24th when we shall pack bag and baggage to join you for your four days in Paris, then proceeding to the home of Ted's parents in Yorkshire, on the wild Bronte moors, where we shall write and study for the month of September---Ted has just written his parents about our being married secretely, so I hope they take it well. I look really forward, in spite of losing this blessed azure ocean, palm & almond trees, an d white Spanish sun---to living with Ted's folks in his boyhood home.

We discovered that the train-trip up for both of us will come to about $50 (making our return here & trip up again impossible, since we'd be paying double for lodging while we were away)---so IF you could please send that much to us by money order, it would be much much appreciated. When we are wealthy with published novels, you can come vacation with us in our Spanish villa!

I am <u>so</u> happy and excited about seeing you in Paris and having you meet Ted! We'll have enough time to cover the city (and can get you a good simple steak dinner for under a dollar---we are forced to eat always at the same place because of our continued near broke-ness). You must make Ted read you some of his animal stories about the whale, owl, polar bear, etc. I have great faith that they will sell as a classic children's book in America. We have not yet got Ted's checks from Poetry magazine and The Nation, but the Poetry proofs for "Bawdry Embraced" have arrived (most impressive, long sheet) and we hope that the checks will come early this fall. We have several large bills outstanding: About $60 for Ted's teeth---I sent him to an American-trained dentist who really saved his mouth---the English dentists on the socialized medecine just pull out teeth---it's less work, & cheaper, so Ted already had two gone and hadn't been for ages. Almost every English boy your age has his appearance ruined by missing teeth; it's simply scandalous neglect, which is all over England: they let things decay, and then grudgingly try to repair or get rid of them. How I miss our American hygiene, preventative and wise. And also, bills for his new gray flannel suit, in progress, and a tweed sports jacket being made at a Cambridge tailors: much cheaper in England, to have a tailor & a perfect fit, and dear Ted had absolutely nothing to wear. And I mean nothing. All of which we hope to pay for with these coming poetry checks.

Now, for business. We'll greatly appreciate the money-order for $50 to get us up to Paris. NB[1] Let me know immediately what day you'll arrive in Paris and I'll write reserving you a room at our hotel, which you must remember the address of:

HOTEL DES DEUX CONTINENTS[2]
25 Rue Jacob
Paris 6

We'll reserve the room in your name, under aegis of Mr. & Mrs. Ted Hughes, so you can go right to it as soon as you come. We'll plan to get up on the same day. We'll wait, or you wait, in the hotel till the others (you or us) arrive. I simply can't wait to see you! We'll be able to show you around Paris for next to nothing: you decide what you want most to see and we'll walk around the Seine, Notre Dame, Sainte Chapelle stained-glass, Tuileries park and see the puppet show, Place de la Concorde, Champs-Elysees & Arc de Triomphe at night; Sacre Coeur & Monmartre (now rather spoiled by tourists). and so on. You speak, we'll take you.

I do feel sorry you can't see our palatial mansion, the palms, the view of purple hills, white pueblos, donkey carts, azure sea which we bathe in daily; it's utter heaven, and for two poverty-stricken (but brilliantly promising!) writers to have their own white house, complete with fig tree, grape arbor, & kitchen & studio on the Spanish riviera is a freak mark of fortune: we have all the wealth of life, spiritual, intellectual, love, etc. ---except money. Oh, well, that'll come too. Just wait. WRITE SOON. HAVE FUN.

Till Paris –
Much love
from Ted & Sivvy

1 – Added in pen by SP in the left margin.
2 – SP has encircled the address in pen.

TO *Aurelia Schober Plath*

Thursday 2 August 1956

TLS with envelope, Indiana University

August 2, Thursday

Dearest mother . . .

Another installment. It was so fine to get your long letter and lovely cards! I envy you the mountainous scenes and only hope that some day Ted and I may visit our relatives in Austria, too.

We have come to another change in plans, this week. Warren wrote a nice long letter (dated the 23rd of July) in which he sounded very happy. I quote: "I'm having a great time swimming, playing tennis, drinking great wine and getting heavier with black bread and dark beer." What stories we shall have to exchange next year, the three of us; or, rather, the four, because my dear Ted is as close to me as any blood relation ever could be, now. Warren would only be able to stay here one day, if he came, and would be exhausted from the long train trip, so we did a detailed and disquieting survey of our finances, Ted & I. He'll be lucky if he gets the $150 his sister owes him throughout next year, and we are planning to use it for his ship fare, so we simply don't have enough to stay on here. Warren, bless his heart, has offered to send us the $50 he has saved as a wedding present so we can come up to Paris to see him. We have decided to do this, as we could have four wonderful days with him there. Then we shall go immediately to Ted's home in Yorkshire and live and write there for the month of September on the Bronte moors. I really look forward to living with him in his boyhood home and wandering about on the wuthering moors.

So you can write us here till about August 14th. We shall leave Benidorm about the 21st, meet Warren in Paris about the 24th till 28th, and get to Ted's home about August 30th. So write to us, after August 14th:

c/o The Beacon
Heptonstall Slack
Hebden Bridge
Yorkshire, England

I was so sorry you caught cold; I hope it didn't ruin much of your trip. I myself am just recovering today from the most devastating case of fever & diarrhea I've ever had; Ted & I think it's food poisoning from a queer red sausage we ate the other night. I was racked by fever so that my skin actually burned, my joints ached, & I felt peeled raw. I couldn't sleep, or even have the energy to open my mouth & drink water, I was so utterly wasted. Ted was an absolute angel, making me vegetable broth & eggnog & feeding me watermelon & holding my head so I could drink water. The siege lasted about 24 hours, which seemed eternity. Today I am cool, & slowly regaining strength & by tomorrow should be my old self again.

Probably you will feel really grateful to get home. There is actually nothing so exhausting as traveling, and one only learns by experience. Notice that in my vacations now, I only want to be in one place, and that for at least a month. I am at home now in Benidorm, as I am in Paris, and Cambridge; but these are the only three places in all my travels which aren't a strain on me. It is a blessing here not to have to go out to eat, but to cook when and what we feel like. Eating out is the biggest tedium when you have no money; if you have money, travel & eating out can be a joy.

I am dreaming so about the Cape next summer, & refrigerators, & pasteurized milk and drinkable tap water (we have to draw our drinking water from a well). Now that I have lived without icebox or variety of food or any convenience whatsoever, any place in America will seem like luxury to me. There is nowhere in the world like it, and I only hope that subtly I can convince Ted to love it as much as I do, so he will eventually want to come back there after our travels. But these next years shall probably be voyaging ones for us; he has a great longing to go to Australia to visit his brother, who is really the most important person in his family to him.

Do let me know when you plan to announce my engagement. Perhaps early in October would be best, when I have been back in Cambridge & had time to write the Cantors, Marty Plumer, and a few other people personally. In order of preference, for bridesmaid, I'd like Pat O'Neil, Ruthie, or Marcia. If Uncle Frank gives me away & Warren is best man (I do hope dear Patsy can be the bridesmaid), all strain should be lifted, since everyone's in the family. I look more forward to this wedding than I can say, for it is the beginning of our real life always together, with the burdens of the present lifted. I do hope we can get good teaching jobs at the same college! With Ted's poems in the <u>Nation</u> & <u>Poetry</u> (I hope the New Yorker may accept O'Kelley's Angel & his TV-satire, the Callum Makers), he should be helped a good deal. He is the most brilliant man I've ever met, and so unassuming about his knowledge that I'll have to help his applications by making him put all his assets down. He literally knows shakespeare by heart & is shocked that I have read only 13 plays. He is going to help me on dating literature (part of the Cambridge exams) at his home, and is making me really think, & write deeply. I could never get to be such a good person without his help; he is educating me daily, setting me exercises of concentration & observation. This bull fight story is the most difficult thing I've ever written, with the action descriptions; it made me realize that his vision is really photographic, while mine is inclined to be an impressionist blur, which I am gradually clarifying by exercise & practice. We are completely happy together, & as long as we are together, I can bear anything in the world.

Do write soon –
much love –
sivvy

TO *Aurelia Schober Plath*

Friday 10 August 1956[1]

TLS with envelope,
Indiana University

59 Tomas Ortunio
Provincia de Alicante
SPAIN

Dearest of mothers . . .

What a life you are leading! Each new postcard and letter sounds like a fairytale. I do hope this reaches you before you sail: did I tell you a letter from Mrs. Prouty came for you in charge of me? The addresses covered the envelope & it was just routine, so I didn't send it on. About the money: both Ted & I agree you shouldn't have taken it from your funds to send. We being frugal and managing, now that we've decided to leave Spain for good when we go to meet Warren in Paris, and then spend a month at Ted's home in Yorkshire so I can meet all his mad aunts and crooked uncles (he does actually have one millionaire uncle! with a mad daughter and hypochondriac wife[2]---probably will leave us thousands just as Walt Disney buys Ted's animal fables and I sell my novel to the movies!) Just finished a 2nd 25-page story, very funny in a way, about "That Widow Mangada",[3] the queer witchy woman whom we lived with for our first wild week in Benidorm. I think you'd like it. I'm at last coming into my own, writing about 5 hours daily. We work perfectly together. My "Black

1–Date supplied from postmark.

2–TH's uncle Walter Farrar (1893–1976); married to Alice Horfsall Thomas Farrar (1896–1968). Their children were Barbara Farrar (1928–91), Edwin T. Farrar (1931–52), and James M. Farrar (1932–43).

3–According to SP's calendar, she worked on 'That Widow Mangada' 3–9 August 1956.

Bull" story[1] while the most difficult description I've ever done, was stilted & awkward compared to the fast-moving incidents of this last. Am now beginning one called "The Fabulous Roommate",[2] a kind of Double story about Nancy Hunter. Ted is a master at thinking up plots, my hardest task, and a perfect critic. O'Kelley is coming on magnificently and Ted reads me Shakespeare aloud while I prepare meals so I won't waste any time.

He is an absolute angel. I have never been so happy in my life. Whatever uncertainty we have about jobs & where money will come from in the immediate future, we are golden with work & love; our lives just blend perfectly. I never felt so at ease with anyone in my life; both of us are so fluent with writing and ideas, and criticize each other's output every day, stimulating each other and exchanging ideas. We are getting healthy and rested at last.

This summer, full of tests, new situations, money problems, uprootings, searchings for homes, has certainly been a fine proof of our ability to grow and learn together. We are both eager and pliable enough to help each other grow to a better, richer, more disciplined, self-demanding person. Ted is so tender and loving, I find I can express my enthusiasm and affection fully for the first time in years and years--since I was a little girl. All my fancies and whimsical imaginings and fairy-tale thoughts are awakened by his marvelous mind. Every morning he tells me the wonderful brilliant dreams he has about animals and Blake and all sorts of vivid queer plots. It is like living in a fairy-tale with the dearest, kindest, handsomest, most lovable man in the world.

I'm rambling on so I haven't said what I started to: Ted and I don't want to touch the $100 you so dearly sent. We can manage without, I think. Shall keep it by us till Paris, just in case. But then, wish to give it to Warren (do I have to cash & sign it) for you to put toward our wedding reception next year. My big ambition in the next year is to sell an $850 story to the women's magazines to pay for our Cape cottage for the summer. I've got great ideas for this "Hypnotizing Husband" story, but have to wait till I'm back at the Cambridge library to read up on it.

Hope you are well & happy. What a lovely family we are now! All of us opening wide new horizons, and you right up with us! I can't wait to cook in our little home kitchen again, make chicken sandwiches for picnics on Nauset Beach, revisit our dear neighbors & have everybody

1–According to SP's calendar, she finished typing 'The Black Bull' on 2 August 1956.

2–According to SP's calendar, she got the idea for 'The Fabulous Roommate' on 10 August 1956.

meet Ted. We look so forward to our second wedding. Life should be easier next summer, if we can manage good jobs. I really should apply to at least 5 or 6 colleges. We'd like a New England country college if possible; the big Women's colleges take both men & women. Smith of course would be ideal, but I don't know if they'd take Ted in English unless--and this would help--he published more poems & a story or two. That would take the place of degrees for a start. Tell me more about such pairs as Tufts, Smith-Amherst, Radcliffe-Harvard, or whatever else you can think of. The State & City colleges probably only take Teacher's certificate people.

Every now and then I have to pinch myself to make sure my life has catapulted into such joy and good fortune; I was not meant to live for myself alone and would have turned sour and selfish if I'd tried to be a "career woman", with even my career going acid in my mouth. Now I can have my cake and eat it: my writing will prosper in my full love (I'm not a Sara-Teasdale type unhappy writer---I'm only able to write when I'm living a rich, full life & have an objective sense of humor) and I have the best husband in the world: we are so close, with our dearest work: like, I imagine, the Beuschers, or Perry & Shirley---there is nothing quite like sharing the same life-work. Our children will really be lucky: they'll be bred on original fables!

If one has courage and conviction and thinks and acts straight, all comes. I feel this daily in my daring and difficult conviction that I would love Ted, whatever fears and doubts I had. By boldness and faith, I have discovered the dearest tender person who wanted to get out of the destructive black whirlwind he was warping in; I have worked hard & given my all to bring him to his proper self, and he has given me that rare lovely ability to love beyond myself, and care for him more than myself, and want to make myself fine and creative, for his sake. I feel freed for the first time. What a blessing this Fulbright has brought; I'm sure there was no other man in the world but Ted for me; physically strong and vital and dynamic; whimsical, humorous, creative, loving, brilliant, practical. Everything. My address from August 17th on – The Beacon, Heptonstall Slack, Hebden Bridge, Yorkshire ENG.

xxx
Sivvy

TO *Elinor Friedman Klein*

Friday 10 August 1956 TLS, Smith College

Friday, August 10

Dear wandering one . . .

Please, please get this. Your letter caught up with me in my vine-grown white stucco villa from whose window (I am now sitting at) I see a blue corner of the Mediterranean. I hang my laundry on a fig tree in the back yard; steal almonds from the groves with Ted at night; swim, cook on a fickle one-ring petrol burner, and write and write. We are happy as hell, writing stories, poems, books, fables. Much has occurred. Madrid, bullfights, wild mad Spanish widows, movings. Did I tell you Ted's had two poems accepted: by Poetry (Chicago) and the blessed Nation (at least we share one magazine). Our projects are legendary.

I hardly can speak of my frustration about the London mess; I had a similar time in Paris trying to get together with the-old-man-of-the-sea Gordon last spring. The American Express is a blackguard ring of foreign agents designing to undermine & overthrow the individual American morale. They use airmail letters for toilet paper, its so soft, so gentle.

I MUST SEE YOU: please please come to Paris to see us. You can, you will, you must. Ted is meeting my brother, I'm meeting Ted's sister, there from ☆ AUGUST 23rd to August 28th, no doubt at the HOTEL DES DEUX CONTINENTS: 25 Rue Jacob, Paris 6e. ☆ Left Bank, that is. Please write me quick anytime before August 17th here at:

E. J. Hughes
59 Tomas Ortunio
Benidorm
Provincia de Alicante
SPAIN

or have a letter waiting for us at the Hotel des Deux Continents (with our arrival date: August 23rd on it) telling when if, how where, etc. you can meet us in Paris. Plane from Athens, mayhap? It's right on your way. Please, please. Have you ever met my young blond brother? He's just written some mathematical thesis on the Russian vowels and is quite a dear. He's been living in Austria on an Experiment in International Living fellowship this summer and will be fresh from Venice.

All will be manifest when you come. Please come. After our 6 day sojourn in Paris, I go with Ted to Yorkshire for a month to meet his parents and clan of mad aunts and crooked uncles. We're having a wedding in Wellesley next June. All is like some miracle. We write like mad all morning, both of us in this immense room with hundreds of mahogany chairs around a huge dark polished table. Black goats keep jangling by, and bread ladies, and donkey taxis to the railway station. You are expected to kill your own rabbits at the peasant market. I love you and want to see you and Have you meet my brilliant writer man. COME TO PARIS –

much love –
sylvia

TO *Aurelia Schober Plath*

Mon.–Sat. 20–25 August 1956 TLS, Indiana University

59 Tomas Ortunio
Benidorm
Provincia de Alicante
Spain
August 20: Monday

Dearest of mothers . . .

Between the heading and this sentence about five days have passed: it is now Saturday the 25th and Warren is sitting on our bed reading your letter while Ted is at the bowl scrubbing the last dirt out of his shirt, which only his hands are strong enough to get clean. Our trip up was really wearying, but much of it fun: I enjoyed the last week in Benidorm more than any yet, as if I were just coming awake to the town, and went about with Ted doing detailed pen-and-ink sketches while he sat at my side and read, wrote or just meditated. He loves to go with me while I sketch and is very pleased with my drawings and sudden return to sketching: wait till you see these few of Benidorm: the best I've ever done in my life, very heavy stylized shading and lines: very difficult subjects too: the peasant market (the peasants crowded around like curious children, and one little man who wanted me to get his stand in too, hung a wreath of garlic over it artistically so I would draw that); a composition of three sardine boats on the bay side, with their elaborate lights; and a good one of the cliff-headland with the houses over the sea.[1] I'm going to write an article for them and send them to the Monitor; I feel I'm really developing a kind of primitive style of my own which I am very fond of. Wait till you see; the

1 – Many of SP's sketches from Spain and other locations mentioned in these letters appeared in *Sylvia Plath: Drawings* (2013).

Cambridge sketch was nothing compared to these. Ted wants me to do more and more.

I made a huge picnic the night we left: hard-boiled eggs, tuna and onion sandwiches, tomato and cheese, chocolate and grapes: the first day was much enlivened by continual munching of little snacks while on the bus from Benidorm to Valencia, where we found a little park to eat lunch and took the train to Barcelona where we spent a gruelling night at a filthy fly-ridden hotel, the only one, it appears within a mile of the station. Wednesday morning in Barcelona was lovely: I made a picnic in the park on a bench, mixing tuna and mayonnaise and onions in bits in their jars and stuffing a huge loaf of bread; we spent a marvelous morning at the outdoor zoo staring at a blue-nosed, black-looking mandrils, hundreds of curly little yellow monkeys small as humming birds; porcupines, a playful otter, crocodiles and baby lions and eagles; then the first really fine dinner at an elaborate empty inn near a cascade full of swans: steak and wine and icecream, red meat at last.

The trip to Paris was exhausting, leaving at 3 in the afternoon and getting in at nine the next morning; we were stiff and cramped, but revived over breakfast on the train, and had a delightful gray morning sitting by the early Seine watching the fishermen on the bank and the women on the barges hanging out washing; such a joy to have subtle gray weather after the blank blazing sun; life is so much heightened by contrasts; I am actually looking extremely forward to going up to Ted's wuthering-heights home next week; for all my love of the blazing sun, there is a lack of intellectual stimulus in countries as hot as spain.

Warren arrived early yesterday morning, and we fed him breakfast and made him take a nap all afternoon. Had a nice supper and saw two excellent movies: an hysterical old Harold Lloyd film and Eisenstein's magnificent 1925 version in Russian of the Battleship Potemkin,[1] which struck us all with tremendous power; took a brief walk in the rain and talked about it. Had not the least trouble in writing ahead and reserving rooms at the Hotel des Deux continents for the three of us, although they are more expensive at the height of the tourist season. Paris is not French Paris; the only language you hear is English, and I am glad that Ted and I can give Warren the atmosphere as we know it, not as the tourists find it. Hope we can live here a year some day (but not in July and August), because of the continuous fine movies and plays and art exhibits; I really love this city above any I've ever been in; it is dear and graceful and

1 – Sergei Eisenstein, *Battleship Potemkin* (1925).

elegant and what one makes it. I could never live in London or New York or Madrid, or even Rome, but here, yes.

Now we are all going to get our reservations at the American express; I love being with my two favorite men. Warren looks handsome and fine, and told us yesterday at lunch about his thesis paper and language work, most fascinating, a juncture of several fields, and an intriguing possibility of pioneer work; see that he gets his Fulbright & other applications off like clockwork in October, emphasizes his extra-work: from polio ward to mental hospital, stresses his eventual hope to help people. He should get a fellowship to study psychology in a German university, none finer; make him write them about their programs, find names of special men; he could combine math, language and psychology degree, and have rich life. Hope your trip back was not full of mal de mer; rest before school. We all love you dearly.

Much love,
sivvy

TO *Aurelia Schober Plath*

Sunday 2 September 1956 — TLS (aerogramme), Indiana University

September 2, 1956
Sunday morning

Dearest mother . . .

I wish you could see your daughter now, a veritable convert to the Brontë clan, in warm woolen sweaters, slacks, knee socks, with a steaming mug of coffee, sitting upstairs in Ted's room looking out of three huge windows over an incredible wild green landscape of bare hills, crisscrossed by innumerable black stone walls like a spider's web, in which gray woolly sheep graze, and chickens and dappled brown-and-white cows; a wicked north wind is whipping a blowing rain against the little house and coal fires are glowing; this is the most magnificent landscape in the world: incredible hills, bare grass and vivid green, with amazing deep creviced valleys, feathered with trees, at the bottom of which clear peat-flavored streams run. Climbing along the ridges of the hills, one has an airplane view of the towns in the valleys; up here, it is like sitting on top of the world, and in the distance the purple moors curve away; I have never been so happy in my life; it is wild and lonely and a perfect place to work and read. I am basically, I think, a nature-loving recluse. Ted and I are at last "home." And what a trip to get here!

We saw Warren off on the train to Rotterdam early on the rainy morning of the 28th, Ted had caught a miserable cold, and we were tired and numb as we took the boat train that evening for the night crossing; how glad I am you didn't take the channel boat! Both of us were deadly sick, vomiting by turns on the freezing deck and sharing a basin, in utter misery; a whole gruelling day's trip ahead, lugging suitcase & sacks and changing busses, and finally, after all that, peace.

Ted's parents are dear, simple Yorkshire folk, and I love them both; we live upstairs in Ted's old room, which I have for my workroom, and he writes in the parlor downstairs; his father, a white-haired, spare, wiry fellow, has a little tobbaconist's shop downtown, and his mother is plumpish, humorous, with marvelous funny tales of neighbors and a vivid way of describing things; she has a tiny kitchen, and I cook for Ted & me, and she loves pottering about making us starchy little pottages and meat pies. (I'll be so happy to have an American kitchen at last, though, with orange juice and egg beater and all my lovely supplies for light cookies and cakes!) I think they both like me, and seem to find me more congenial than Gerald's wife who visited them once, a blonde flighty glamor girl from Australia, evidently very giddy and always wanting to go to parties and dances. I've borrowed a duffle coat and knee boots from Ted's cousin Vicky,[1] a quiet, attractive girl who has won a two-year art scholarship, and hike around the country comfortably. Ted's marvelous millionaire Uncle Walt (married to a hypochondriac hag, with two sons dead, one an idiot, and only an idiot daughter left) took us over to Wuthering Heights Friday in his car. He is a powerful heavy man with a terrific sense of dramatic humor, and we got along fine. We had a picnic in a field of purple heather, and the sun, by a miracle, was out among white luminous clouds in a blue sky; there is no way to Wuthering Heights but for several miles by foot over the moors: how can I tell you how wonderful it is: imagine yourself on top of the world, with all the purplish hills curving away, and gray sheep grazing, with horns curling and black demonic faces and yellow eyes, like ancient druids; black walls of stone, clear streams from which we drank; and at last, a lonely, deserted black stone house, broken down, clinging to the windy edge of a hill. I began a sketch of the sagging roof and stone walls; will hike back the first nice day to finish. Last night Ted and I hiked out at sunset to stalk rabbits in a fairy-tale

1–TH's cousin Victoria Farrar (1938–).

wood falling almost perpendicularly to a river valley below; I swung over cascading brooks on tree-branches, stared at the gold sky and clear light, stopped in a farm to pet three black new-born kittens, admired cows & chickens; Ted, a dead-eye marksman shot a beautiful silken rabbit, but it was a doe with children, and I didn't have the heart to take it home to make a stew of it. You should see Ted. He is the handsomest man in the world; if possible, we are a happy Heathcliffe and Cathy! Striding about in the woods and over the moors. Please, if the pictures come out, send two copies, no matter what the expense; I'd love Mrs. Hughes sr. to have some. Best news came yesterday morning: guess what, at last! A marvelous letter[1] and check for $50 from Editor Weeks of the Atlantic for my poem "Pursuit"[2] which I sent you. And such a letter. I must quote: "We all think your poem "Pursuit" a fine and handsome thing and look forward to the opportunity of publishing it on a page by itself in the Atlantic. Could you tell me about another poem of yours, not in this sheaf, "Two lovers and a beachcomber by the real sea," a copy of which was shown me by a mutual friend? It is really quite striking." And more about Cambridge. Too bad Mlle has already published the latter poem; but I was delirious with joy at such a lovely letter; I've been badly needing some acceptance this year, and this will keep me going for another year; keep an eye out for the issue, and buy up lots of copies: a whole page to myself! Like Dylan Thomas, and for the same price! It is the first poem I wrote after meeting Ted, and his "Bawdry Embraced" in Poetry was dedicated to me, so our future should be great; we are so happy working and planning together and I have never loved anybody so much in my life. I adore you and my love to Warren. Do write and say you survived your crossing.

Much, much love –
Sivvy

<on the return address side of letter>

PS: Have sent Warren home with your kind check for $100 which, thank heavens, we didn't have to use; do put it toward our wedding fund. Also want to send you my $50 Atlantic check for deposit in my bank account. How shall I make it out? "For deposit only by Mrs. A. S. Plath?"

xxxx
sivvy

1–Edward Weeks to Sylvia Plath, 27 August 1956; held by Lilly Library.
2–Sylvia Plath, 'Pursuit', *Atlantic Monthly*, January 1957, 65.

TO *Aurelia Schober Plath*

Tuesday 11 September 1956 TLS (aerogramme), Indiana University

Tuesday afternoon
September 11, 1956

Dearest mother . . .

It was so good to get your wonderful fat letter with the snapshots of you looking so lovely, and all the news: I am so glad dear Frankie is better and feel much more relieved about him anyway now that he is leading a quieter life. Your quaint green map of Boston is now hanging up in our room as I write, and I spent a time going over the landmarks with Ted. He is in London for the day and night on some errands, so I got up early at six this morning and made him a hearty breakfast; rain and wind are howling outside, and I sit cosy upstairs before the picture windows, writing at poems and stories.[1] After the first week of adjustment, I am as happy here as I have ever been in my life: Ted and I take a long walk each day up over the moors (It's generally rainy, or at least overcast) and never have I loved country so! All you can see is dark hills of heather stretching toward the horizon, as if you were striding on top of the world; last night at sunset the horizontal light turned us both luminous pink as we hiked in waterproof boots in the wuthering free wind, starting up rabbits that flicked away with a white flag of tail, staring back at the black-faced, gray furred moor sheep that graze, apparently wild, and with their curling horns looking like primeval yellow-eyed druid monsters. I never thought I could like any country as well as the ocean, but these moors are really even better, with the great luminous emerald lights changing always, and the animals and wildness. Read "Wuthering Heights" again here, and really <u>felt</u> it this time more than ever.

Ted is the most wonderful man in the world; I am constantly incredulous with joy at how much I love him and how magnificently well we work together, writing all morning, me typing out his stories from dictation in the afternoon for a few hours each day (just finished triplicate 20-page version of lovely "O'Kelley's Angel" which we'll send to New Yorker when I've typed two other fables to go with it---"The Callum Makers" and one about the life of a boy-boar: "Bartholomew Pig")[2] Ted is so

1–According to SP's calendar, she worked on 'two slight poems re golden Midas & Firesong' on 5 September; a story called 'Hardcastle Crags' on 7–10 September; and the poem 'November Graveyard' on 9 September 1956.

2–Ted Hughes, 'Bartholomew Pygge, Esq.'

dear, and handsome and loving and brilliant, every minute with him is a rare delight; our lives will be very highly disciplined, rough-clothed and casual, and I'm sure some day we both shall be close to wealthy. We are so close to each other in our writing, and both need much rest and leisure, and are perfectly happy and self-contained alone. I can hardly believe I have such a perfect magnificent husband; I can't for a minute think of him as someone "other" than the male counterpart of myself, always just that many steps ahead of me intellectually and creatively so that I feel very feminine and admiring. There is an animal farm across the street where we've been seeing baby pigs, calves, kittens and puppies; I really want my children to be brought up in the country, so you must get a little place too somewhere in the country or by the sea (we'll buy it when we're rich) where we can alternate leaving our countless children with you and Mrs. Hughes while we take vacations or travel. Our life will be a constant adventure and we'll have a fine old age; this year will be a tough discipline but I need it, and so does Ted. We've talked much about our wedding in June and both of us are determined to have it; we both long for a kind of symbolic "town" ceremony, and it may be the last time I see my friends and relatives together for many many years. So plan on it definitely. Any money we earn will be put toward our summer on the Cape---do let me know how to make out my $50 check from the blessed <u>Atlantic</u> so you can deposit in my bankrupt account as a first drop in the bucket. We've decided to cross in separate cabins on the ship as fiancées, so you have <u>nothing</u> to worry about there; I'll write to the ship company for reservations early this fall; hope to make Sat. the 29th of June our wedding day, but <u>may</u> have to wait till the next Saturday, depending on ship. Why not make engagement announcement some time, any time, in October: use happy ¾ picture of me: copy form of others in paper: Me: Smith B.A. summa cum laude 1955; Fulbright to study for Honours B.A. in Eng. Lit. at Cambridge. 1956-7 Ted: Graduated from Pembroke College, Cambridge University in 1954 with Honours B.A. in English and in Archaeology and Anthropology; served two years in RAF before that; worked for J. Arthur Rank studios at Pinewood after. Do send me a copy. Tell those silly ones who think I should get married here that a ship is a hell of a place for a honeymoon, no privacy, no peace; I have no one here to give me away and naturally want my lifelong friends standing by it; it should be easy to shut them up, there are so many arguments against being married here. Why don't I make out a list of names and addresses for announcements over Christmas . . . doubt if I'll have time till then; want simple ceremony with gala reception for all, lots of food & plenty of drink; Ted wants that too very much. Your daughter is married to a genius and a great hercules and the most darling man that ever walked. Cant wait to get to America and cook for him. Am sending three stories to Mlle[1] with fingers crossed: my stories. We are full of projects, plans and love. Want to see and hold our stainless steel before we choose; where can I go in London to do so & see samples? Do write. VIVE THE 1957 WEDDING OF THE WRITING HUGHES! All is perfectly quiet on the British front. Ted's family's dear. We both love you; can't wait to share our life & times with you in America. Life is work and joy.

Much much love to you & Warrie –
Sivvy

TO *Aurelia Schober Plath*

Friday 21 September 1956 — TLS (aerogramme), Indiana University

Friday morning
September 21, 1956

Deareast lovely mother . . .

How we have loved your long, newsy pink letters! So much is happening, hanging fire, that I now, these last 10 days before I return to Cambridge, feel rather torn; I am actually almost eager to be back and plunged in work, for as you know, I generally leave places a week early, and am going through my worst homesickness for Ted now. Elly Friedman, the dear, is up here now, and Ted and I got her an exquisite room at the most magnificent quaint old stone inn, low beamed, lined with books: Ted and I would love to buy it. She is the best visitor: perfectly independent and leaves us to work until late afternoon, and I've had some good long talks with her which have caught me up on Smith. Imagine, there was a rumor among the seniors that I was coming back to teach there this year! Probably one of my teachers confided to a student, and this got around. I should think, if I do well at Cambridge this year, I should have no worry of a job there. But I have decided very definitely against applying for a job for Ted there too for many important reasons: first, I would have the responsibility for him, proving him, in a way, and my ties there are very emotional and deep, with place and professors both; in my first year of marriage and

1–According to SP's calendar, she sent 'That Widow Mangada', 'The Black Bull', and 'Hardcastle Crags' to *Mademoiselle* on 17 September 1956.

teaching I don't want to stack the odds against me; and the girls at Smith are unscrupulous (witness the two professors, still on the faculty, who have married three Smith girls in succession). From the things Elly told me this year about the intolerable gossip and intense, irresponsible flirting with a new young one-legged (!) creative writing professor[1] (who decided to leave even though he was asked back), I would be absurd to throw Ted into such hysterical, girlish adulation; I wouldn't have a minute's peace, because I know how college girls talk and romanticize endlessly and how they throw themselves at men professors, be they ancient or one-legged. So I shall apply for Ted at Amherst; possibly Harvard-Radcliffe; or even Middlebury. But, Ideally, I'd like to be near a big city while living in the country, and Smith (also Radcliffe, of course) would be ideal; I really feel they must want me; so if Ted doesn't get in Amherst, he's perfectly willing to take another kind of job on radio or TV station or whatever, and, if he is successful writing TV scripts, he could do that at home. But I refuse to give my married life and independence completely to Smith; I don't want <u>both</u> of us to have to be tied to the same faculty meetings, social-life and Smith-girl gossip. Just got a really nice letter from the editor of the Smith Alumnae Quarterly,[2] telling me they're publishing my funny article on the Bulganin-Khrushchev party[3] at the Claridges (I don't get paid, of course, but it's too late for any other place, and I feel a certain loyalty to them; do tell Mrs. Prouty to look out for it; she'll love it). Mrs. Prouty sent me a lovely letter[4] about my Atlantic poem, too, after I'd written her a long letter about it, Ted, etc. About Mr. Rice, naturally I'd like to have him know <u>if</u> he can keep a secret and if he's sure not to object or suggest a mere reception instead of wedding; we want no risks about the wedding and are determined to have it; so if there is any chance he object, don't tell him. I'd love a shell pink dress, or white with pink slip or something. Also, would be delighted to have reception at Mrs. Cantor's place. Want to have delectable drinks (<u>with</u> alcohol in spite of her Christian science!) and much much food both meats and sweets. I'd like all stainless steel kitchenware, brown-and-aqua baking dishes; and, if possible, a white and forest-green bathroom towel set (the color of warren's bedroom

1–American screenwriter and theatre producer David Shaber (1929–99); instructor in the Theatre Department at Smith College, 1955–6. Shaber taught Playwriting (37a and 37b), Play Analysis (38), and Writing for Radio and Television (43a and 43b). During her senior year, Klein took Playwriting. Due to an accident at age seven, one of Shaber's legs had been amputated.

2–Frances Reed Robinson (1907–83); B.A. 1928, Smith College.

3–Sylvia Plath, 'B. and K. at the Claridge', *Smith Alumnae Quarterly*, Fall 1956, 16–17.

4–Olive Higgins Prouty to SP, 12 September 1956; held by Lilly Library.

wallpaper; we hate pastels, except aqua, around the house. Like striking lovely modern. also like black & white diamond-patterned towels Mrs. Cantor has – very striking –

You can imagine how weary I am of living off Other People's kitchens and houses; Mrs. Hughes is a messy pottering kitchen-keeper and atrocious cook: burnt tough meat, starchy leaden pies and biscuits, and it is all I can do not to rearrange her sloppy cupboards etc. I long for my own privacy and pantry more than anything and will go just wild with joy over kitchen strainers, pans, egg beaters, etc. I cook for Ted and me and manage all right, but it is not the same. If I get through this hard year, I feel I deserve a wedding and gifts and reception and honeymoon for a summer the worst way; it has not always been easy; we will really begin our proper married life with our wedding next June. About the date: I'll have to write the Fulbright, then the ship, to find if I can get allowance to go back earlier than their return-ship schedule begins and if Ted & I can get reservations, before I know if we can make the 29th or will have to put it off till the next Saturday. Ted has not a definite job yet in Spain but will leave with his millionaire uncle on October 1st or thereabout and be settled, I hope, by the time I come down the second week in December; his uncle is so queer, with his devil wife and mad daughter: fifty pounds gift to Ted would not touch him, yet Ted must struggle on without any help; if I ever have money, I shall want my immediate family to have a share in my good fortune. Ted, by the way, has an audition for reading modern poetry at the BBC in London next week (they heard a tape-recording of his reading of Gawain & the Green Knight which he made at a friend's[1] and liked it); I am going down with him, fingers crossed that they'll want to make a program recording of him reading and broadcast it. I have great hopes for Ted in T-V scripts, too. If only Amherst would accept him, it would be so great. Advise me about how to apply for applications. Much much love to you and Warren.

Love,
sivvy

1 – The tape recorder was owned by British poet Peter Redgrove (1932–2003).

TO *Aurelia Schober Plath*

Friday 28 September 1956 TLS (aerogramme), Indiana University

Friday afternoon
September 28, 1956

Dearest mummy . . .

Received your kindly sent batch of snapshots with the dear letter---grieve that I didn't have my hair down and don't think they do Ted or me justice, although Warren is great--be careful of showing one with Ted & me--he has ring on left hand for sharp eyes. Love overshoes you sent; quiet and comfortable. So glad you aren't renting room. DON'T! I know from repeated experience that for sensitive persons--like you and me--for whom the home is the last refuge of rest, peace and privacy, it is impossible to live and share kitchens with strangers: one is always wondering "Are they through with the bathroom now? Can I shove their stuff over in the icebox to make room for mine?" Even if you got a quiet old maid who stuck to her room, it would be a constant bother. But a couple---no, no. Even with inlaws, I find housekeeping a trial---living in Mrs. Hughes' small messy kitchen is such a bother, with her being such a bad cook, too---can't wait till I'm home and in the brief days Ted & I are in Wellesley, I'd love you to give me recipes of our favorite thing you make so well---corn & fish chowders, apple pie, apricot-jam halfmoons, etc. I long to make Ted's daily menus a treat and surprise with orange juice for breakfast, chicken livers, homemade cookies--molasses, toll house oatmeal, etc. Tell potential gift-givers by the way that neither Ted or I smoke or eat candy! I dream of toasters, pressure cookers, strainers, a blender, gay aprons, rough modern linen or woven mats, kitchen utensils, towels, sheets, blankets, one sturdy set of pottery for every day and better china for dinners--I'll pick out patters early this fall on a shopping Saturday in London.

Am sure I'll have earned enough money by spring to help considerably with wedding expenses---never felt so creative, so many projects out: this year, I'm concentrating on my novel of Cambridge life and a book of poems for the Yale Younger Poets Series; Ted has a book of poems & children's animal stories waiting to be typed & sent out, and is working on a book of adult fables. We wait the news from 6 stories and 60 poems (half each) sent out. I'll be back in Cambridge hard at work Monday October 1st---have passed "blues" period and am now dying to get there & plunge into a stoic year of study. Will try like fury to get Ted a teaching job at Amherst---they like young writer-teachers & I'll wait a month or two to see what he gets published. I shouldn't have much trouble at Smith, I think, if I get a good degree here. We spent two days in London & just got back---very auspicious, Ted having audition reading modern poetry for the B.B.C. I was thrilled---I made him read one of his own poems stuck between Yeats & Hopkins. The dear man judging---a Mr. Carne-Ross,[1] sat with me in the listening room, saying "perfect", "superb". Ted was fine. The man wants him to do a broadcast of Yeats, if the Committee approves, and perhaps they'll also approve his reading his own poems---over the erudite 3rd Program, this would be! The pay is excellent for this, and we wait word of the committee's decision eagerly---it would be another feather to his letter of application for a teaching job. When we're famous enough, we want to make reading tours in America. My mind seethes with ideas for stories---my novel preoccupies me, and I am spending this year, daily, doing a detailed notebook of cambridge with sketches, trying to sell chapters as stories, finish writing of it next summer. I need this year badly to read, study & write. What bliss not to have to consider any social life! I am really a recluse at heart!

Elly Friedman has come and gone---she promised to call you up & give you latest word of Ted & I---thinks we're engaged (I didn't bring up what the doorman at the hotel told her about our being married nor did she). We spent one athletic day hiking ten miles back over moors & swamps from Wuthering Heights where I did a sketch in freezing wind & saw musem of Brontes things in old Parsonage---incredible miniature childhood books of a magic kingdom they made up in tiny print with exquisite luminous watercolors---what creative children! Charlotte did the loveliest little watercolors. Will write article about it this week. Have received proof for poem "Pursuit" from Atlantic so it should come out soon---looks terrific, with French quote from Racine and all, from "Phèdre", meaning, in case anyone asks you: "In the depths of the forests your image pursues me." Hope I can get novel out within next two years: I'd like best to dedicate the novel to Mrs. Prouty, but wish to dedicate my first book to her, and it may be poems, which I'd rather dedicate to Dr. Beuscher---those two women have been the greatest helps in my life and both I think deserve a book dedication. I shall write Peg Cantor, Marty, Patsy and others as soon as I get back to Cambridge. Shall I tell Peg I'm delighted and touched and accept with joy her offering of the house for the reception? I want to invite everybody to that. Am going to put all my money earned toward my wedding dress, small trousseau, wedding

1–BBC producer in the Talks Department, D. S. Carne-Ross (1921–2010).

and reception, while Ted will put what he earns toward the rent for our cottage and summer food. If only we can teach at Amherst and Smith! I'd love to live in Amherst and commute to Smith, and pray that it works out. I'll write Mary Ellen Chase for advice in applying as soon as Ted has his job settled & some things published. She might be able to help me with names. All goes well, Ted and I thrive and plan to work like mad this year to secure a writing Cape summer after a gala wedding & reception and get good twin teaching jobs. Wish us luck & write often –

Love –
sivvy

TO *Peter Davison*

Sunday 30 September 1956 TLS (photocopy), Yale University

Whitstead
4 Barton Road
Cambridge, England
September 30, 1956

Dear Peter,

It was so good to hear from you today.[1] This letter may sound rather like an explosion of facts, projects and mere jottings, because I have been planning to write you to beg all kinds of advice which I need more with each day; I am sitting, as it were, on a stockpile of publishable material---stories, poems and incipient books---and would greatly appreciate your guidance at this point.

First, let me say that my year at Cambridge was a magnificent madhouse; it took me the whole year to hack out an idea of what I was doing there, and now I know, and the blessed Fulbright has renewed my grant for this year so I can get my Honours B.A. come this June. I spent last year in an incredible whirl---acting all the first term for the A.D.C., ravening through the pathetically pompous uncreative literary set & publishing in their Deltas, Chequers, etc., and, finally, becoming a feature and news reporter for Varsity and covering the gala wild caviar-and-vodka reception for Bulganin and unspellable Khrushchev at the Claridge with a Cambridge photographer, shaking hands with Bulganin, begging him to come to Cambridge, meeting countless mayors, Russians, Nigerian

1–Peter Davison to SP, 25 September 1956; held by Lilly Library.

potentates, and tripping over Attlee and Eden. All of which I wrote up in a kind of "Talk of the Town" article which, alas, the New Yorker said was "too late" for them; Mollie Panter-Downes[1] did a long scoop on that one. Anyway, after a grim dark winter, I came into the Cambridge spring and started living from the center, and writing.

Paris is now my second home---I've lived there over two months in winter, spring and fall; Riviera and Matisse chapel at Christmas on a motor-scooter; Venice and Rome so briefly in spring I want to live a year in Italy after a long stay in America; Spanish coast in a native fishing village most of the summer, and the Bronte moors and Wuthering Heights (sat out in a frigid wuthering wind to do a pen drawing of the latter to illustrate travel article---the C. S. Monitor publishes drawings and articles of mine off and on) this past month. This year at Cambridge, I am working like a stoic; its like having a second chance to have cake after gorging on it last year---or something equivalent.

Anyway, I am spending the year reading like fury, and writing four hours a day: chief projects: getting a volume of poems together to submit to the Yale Younger Poets series this winter, in hope; and, writing a novel, very detailed, on an American girl in Cambridge from September to June, called, tentatively, "Hill of Leopards"; I always believe in titles. I've got a rich background for this novel, and am casing Cambridge this year, doing drawings and a notebook, and writing the rough novel in story-chapters which, if all goes well, I'll try to sell as stories first. Then, next summer (I'm taking the first boat home after exams in June) I want to spend two months on Cape Cod trying to finish it. We'll see. I'll let you know how it's getting on this year, and if it works out as I plan, perhaps you'd be willing to advise me about the first draft next summer. I'd like best to submit it for one of those big publishing house prizes---am I right in thinking the Atlantic Company runs one? I'm also writing short stories again---my favorite medium really, so far: will let you know the results of these, both serious (Mademoiselle and so forth) and funny (New Yorker kind of thing) and then the Ladies' Home Journal sort. All I am doing this year is writing and studying and drawing; it is like being free of an albatross. So that's about my projects---the novel, the Yale Poet's contest, and stories.

My main need for advice concerns my discovery of the year. A new Review got published at Cambridge this year by a rebellious rough uncombed group of ballad singers, Celtic fanatics and refreshingly honest

1 – Mollie Panter-Downes, 'Letter from London', *New Yorker*, 5 May 1956, 113–14, 116–17.

writers, only two of which were good, one of whom I looked up, in deepest admiration, on account of several poems which made Thom Gunn[1] look sick---his reputation is far over-rated, I think. Although, compared to the ruck of bad bad young British writers, he seems good in contrast. Well, anyway, this writer I found is named Ted Hughes, graduated from Cambridge in 1954 (Pembroke). Unpublished professionally. I became his agent, as it were, in America, and so far, he's received enthusiastic acceptances of poems from Poetry and the Nation, and still has about thirty excellent poems out---the Atlantic, by the way, has had some of his poems for four months, in case you want to look them up, wherever they hide such things; I'll be interested to know if Editor Weeks has seen them. The poems he's had accepted so far came out in the August Poetry and about August 17 Nation. He is a brilliant writer and London and England are too small for him (I have never been so disappointed and disgusted by anything as the London literati, with their outposts in Oxford and Cambridge---writing in England is sick, sick, sick . . . Spender is a soft flabby over-rated conceited man; the young poets are incredibly malicious, vain, and with no sense of music, readable-ness, or, for that matter, deep honest meaning). I shall be glad to get home; bless America; bless the American editor. How I miss it all!

Well, Ted Hughes has written a delightful book of children's fables, nine chapters, about 70 to 100 typed pages---I'm working on typing it out now, called "How the Donkey Became" and Other Fables---about how nine animals became---Whale, Elephant, Bee, Polar Bear, Owl, etc. I don't want to rave about it, because I'd like you to see it and become a convert. Now where should I send this? I could look up children's publishers in NYC and send it around, but the air mail postage of back-and-forth manuscripts will reduce me to eating bean sprout pilaus at the Taj Mahal if I'm not careful. Do you know any good children's publishers that will do one proud regarding pay, illustrations, royalties etc.? I feel I'm beginning to need a lawyer. (I haven't sent anything to that agent, because I want to get confidence by publishing a story first and then saying to him: "Look, how much money I can earn you." I am very shy of committing myself before I've got a lot of manuscripts in back of me, and I'm just beginning to get there, writing every day in the mornings). If you'd be interested in seeing a copy of this children's book, let me know. Otherwise, I'll ferret out the names of some publishers and try my blind luck.

1–Anglo-American poet Thom Gunn (1929–2004).

Next, Ted writes excellent adult fables---three of which are now at the New Yorker (the day either Ted or I get into that glittering rag will be the occasion of a colossal duck and orange sauce dinner with seven different wines for each course; Sorry, Please Try Us Again.) The best fable, I think, is a 20 page one, "O'Kelly's Angel"---about an Irish guy who catches an angel and what happens: you know, the breaking in of the angelic order on this world; perfect simple flawless style of telling; sort of a cross between Hemingway, Thurber and Saki.[1] Then, a 10-page satire of TV "The Callum-Makers", and one about the same length on the college and business life of a pig, born to an English crass society and industrial family, "Bartholomew Pygge, Esq." I'm going on about these, so in case you have enough interest, I could send you copies. Ted wants to make up a book of these adult fables, and I hope many will find hospitable editors at the various magazines during the coming year. We've had readings of them, and the audience, British and American, is, gratifyingly, very happy with them.

Well, whew, there it is: I'm going fine, and the novel is my big project, about which I'd eventually like your kind advice, but it'll be months yet, before it takes shape. The short stories are seething in my head, over the typewriter, like hot-cakes; or boiling oil. Do help me, if you can, about a place for Ted's children's book, or even, magazines for the adult fables. The satire on TV is excruciatingly funny.

Another thing: I'm desperate to know more about copyright laws: both Ted & I will want to publish our stories in book form, and, naturally want to keep the TV and movie rights (don't laugh, it may come to this in a few years!) How to keep avaricious magazine editors from wanting to keep all rights and make a fortune? This is the most pressing question.

Thanks for listening to all this. I would like to keep in close touch with you this coming year, until I'll be home to fight in person with editors and copyrights next June. You really can be a terrific help, knowing about all the practical problems, as you do. I don't want to muck about with professional agents until I've satisfied myself that our stuff can get in on its own; after that nightmare month as guest managing ed. of Mademoiselle, I realize only too clearly how disastrous it is to have too many contacts with hungry editors and not half enough manuscripts backing one up. This year should result in a huge pile.

I'm really eager to know the details about your job. Please tell how the change came about, and how all is with you. I heard the most enthusiastic

1–British writer Hector Hugh Munro (1870–1916); Munro wrote under the name Saki.

reports about your acting in the Misanthrope, Alceste? and have the copy of Wilbur's translation. Wish I could have seen it. Please tell me how all is. Met Nathaniel LaMar---dear, warm young Negro writer from Harvard, published twice by Atlantic,[1] at Pembroke this year. Fine fellow.

I'll be bringing Ted Hughes home in June, too, to be married in Wellesley; we're hoping to get teaching jobs in New England at twin colleges and go on writing like fury. When the time draws nigh (only nine months) I'd like very much to plan a kind of reunion meeting. You have no idea how hungry I am for home; British writing is dead; so are the magazines. I find myself no literary exile, but a staunch American girl. Such a fate.

My very best to you, with much gratitude for letting me blast off about all this. Hoping to hear from you soon . . . .

Sincerely,
Sylvia Plath

Mr. Peter Davison
Office of the Associate Editor
The Atlantic Monthly Press
8 Arlington Street
Boston 16, Massachusetts
U.S.A.

TO *Ted Hughes*

Monday 1 October 1956

TLS on RMS *Queen Elizabeth* letterhead, family owned

Monday night about eight-thirty . . .

Dearest Teddy:

I am back. The gas fire wheezes and dehydrates my right side, the rain blowing in the open window hydrates the left; I am codeine-numb, dazed, and utterly blissfully insensible. The trip back was hell; I found by picking up my suitcase and letting a noble agonized expression pass immediately over my face, I needed no porter until Cambridge. I stared at the wet landscape en route; it was flat and gray-green. That was that. If there were buildings they were ugly.

Something wonderful and incredible has happened; I restrained myself and didn't phone you; I restrained myself and put it in the second paragraph.

1–In addition to 'Creole Love Song', Lamar published two additional stories: 'Miss Carlo', *Atlantic Monthly*, January 1957, 61–4; and 'The Music Teacher', May 1957, 57–60.

I came back to several sad things: a sweetly pencilled New Yorker rejection of Ella Mason, etc., begging me, too, to try again; also, Mrs. Guinea, the charwoman, smashed to smithereens my lovely big imported pottery fruit platter; there was, however, a new green rug covering the Indian girl's ink blots---Jean somebody, the dull Southafrican girl, just wasted the last half-hour, hemming and blithering about Her Summer Abroad. Hell. Also suffered Mrs. Milne and tea and much meandering about her doubts concerning going to Australia with the Nasser crisis, and how everybody she knows or is related to is sheep farmers in Australia, and how nice Indian girls are, they come in and out of her room all day and send her such lovely presents: gold-embroidered purple saris; Salome Milne. Brushed through the fifteen odd New Yorkers which had stacked up; will read slowly week by week: colossal amount of fables by Thurber[1] about Grizzly Bears and Gadgets, Oysters and Philosophers, etc.; haven't had time or eyesight to read yet; also multitudes of poems by Theodore Roethke[2]---very lyric sentimental, all about fire, birds, tree and love o love. Also poems by John Malcolm Brinnin[3] (one huge long funny type fake poem; probably picked a word from a published poem here, there, and pasted them together$(), Adrienne Ceceile Rich,[4] getting richer but duller; Ogden Nash,[5] the lucre-monger. They'll be begging for us yet. The latest serious poems are all about plants: orange milkweed,[6] St.-John's wort,[7] and a Robert Graves[8] coy one about rose gardeners; also about birds: gulls,[9] peewits,[10] and very sweet detailed nature descriptions. Stories all begin either: "One of my greatest problems when young . . ."[11] or

1–James Thurber, 'Further Fables For Our Time', *New Yorker*, 23 June 1956, 24–5. Additional fables published under this collective title appeared in the following issues: 7 July 1956, 18–19; 28 July 1956, 23–4; 11 August 1956, 19; 1 September 1956, 22–3; 22 September 1956, 45–6. The 'Fables' in the 7 July 1956 issue were: 'The Grizzly and the Gadgets', 'The Goose that Laid the Gilded Egg', and 'The Philosopher and the Oyster'.
2–Theodore Roethke, 'They Sing', *New Yorker*, 18 August 1956, 22; and 'The Small', *New Yorker*, 8 September 1956, 32.
3–John Malcolm Brinnin, 'Ich am of Irlaunde', *New Yorker*, 25 August 1956, 30.
4–Adrienne Rich, 'At the Jewish New Year', *New Yorker*, 1 September 1956, 28.
5–Ogden Nash, 'The Strange Case of the Lucrative Compromise', *New Yorker*, 11 August 1956, 24; 'It Would Have Been Quicker to Walk', *New Yorker*, 8 September 1956, 36; 'Ms. Found Under a Serviette in a Lovely Home', *New Yorker*, 22 September 1956, 49.
6–Luke Zilles, 'Bunch of Wildflowers', *New Yorker*, 7 July 1956, 67.
7–Louis O. Coxe, 'From the Window Down', *New Yorker*, 14 July 1956, 20.
8–Robert Graves, 'A Bouquet From a Fellow-Roseman', *New Yorker*, 30 June 1956, 30.
9–May Swenson, 'The Promontory Moment', *New Yorker*, 28 July 1956, 21.
10–Possibly a reference to Theodore Roethke's 'The Small' cited above with the line: 'A towhee pecks the ground' (32).
11–Jean Stafford, 'A Reading Problem', *New Yorker*, 30 June 1956, 24–32; begins, 'One of the great hardships of my childhood . . .'

"Eating bhindi ghust on a 19th century morocco carpet with Sahib X . . ." A duck dinner with seven courses the day we get in . . .

AND NOW FOR THE GREAT NEWS: sit down, take a long sip of beer and bless Henry Rago.[1] POETRY has accepted SIX of my poems!!!!!!!!!![2] Like we dreamed of. Didn't I say the Fulbright would start the trigger? Strange, isn't it, that the day I come back last June, it's you; this time, it's me. Tutored by your most mercenary self, I ran to count lines: Teddy, it should be about $76 (seventy-six dollars!) One line was only two words: "Looks up": that's 25 cents for looks, and 25 cents for up;

Lovely Henry Rago said: "We think these poems admirable, and we will be delighted to keep six of them for Poetry . . . . With all good wishes for your work."

AND THEY BOUGHT ALL MY NEW POEMS (I can just hear Leftover Cravenson's[3] pitying lisp: "I don't think you'll sell much of such poetry . . . I wish I could help you, poor wayward girl")

They rejected three ("In ruck and quibble of court folk",[4] The Glutton (alas) and The Shrike) BUT: they bought (bless, ah bless them): Wreath for a Bridal, Dream With Clam-Diggers, Two Sisters of Persephone, Strumpet Song, Metamorphosis ("Haunched like a faun he hooed") AND Epitaph for Fire and Flower!!!

So there is a god afterall; and it isn't, praise be, Stephen Spender. I am so happy. It is the consecration of my new writing, which properly, began with you and "Pursuit" and ramped on through spring and summer. "Epitaph for Fire and Flower" was begun on Benidorm beach;[5] bless it. Bless it all. You, if only you were here. I don't know how I can keep still without exploding; I want to share everything with you---rain, rejections, wine, money, acceptances, reading. God. They will be flocking to the dock in hundreds when we arrive: children, begging you to autograph fables, Tv and movie producers; everybody. I am very numb and very insensible though. I have been unpacking, making huge piles for laundry, cleaners, rubbish, throwing away stacks of letters & scrap, during which I lacerated my thumb on a broken wine bottle; the cream crackers are

1–Henry Rago to SP, 24 September 1956; held by Lilly Library.

2–Sylvia Plath, 'Two Sisters of Persephone', 'Metamorphosis', 'Wreath for a Bridal', 'Strumpet Song', 'Dream with Clam-Diggers', and 'Epitaph for Fire and Flower', *Poetry* 89 (January 1957), 231–7.

3–Christopher Levenson.

4–First line of SP's, 'The Queen's Complaint'. In the poem's final form, the first line reads, 'In ruck and quibble of courtfolk'.

5–According to SP's calendar, she began 'Epitaph for Fire and Flower' on 18 August 1956; she completed the poem the following day.

soggy; the nescafe is a hard cake; the strawberry jam is rancid. I drank the last of the vinagery chilean burgundy and I love you. I will live in you and with every thought for you, however I must smile and be politic with my supervisor and the odd girls here, none of whom, thank heaven, are back yet. But I am all for you, and you are that world in which I walk. I am still eating your dear lovely sandwiches; I felt too lousy on the train to eat, except for the bananas like you said; so I am having hot milk and loving you over those sandwiches now. Thank heaven I will be seeing you before you go; it is about the only way I can assuage my present resentment of everybody that blocks my vision and jabbers on my hearing, because they aren't you; you are the only face my eyes know how to see; you are the dearest love and crinkle-eyed smiler and darling Teddy. I miss you like hell, because somehow I can't bear being with people who aren't you and I just want to be alone now, and not be sociable; I won't be; I must cut off all those little girls and boys who will want to wear down the spirals of my ear; I shall be so noncommital and cold it's death.

Oh, I must get all this in: the camp bed is here, angled tautly and neurotically in one corner; and, amaze of amaze, your huge colossal leather coat is here, hanging blandly and god knows how in my closet. Your poems are here;[1] the Macaw, Bayonet Charge, Two Wise Generals, the new version of Hawk in Rain. Shall type all over many times. Am sending copies of pictures of us for your dear parents on condition none go to Australia. Please send that book-stack when you can; and any shots of us that came out well on the little film.

Tomorrow is a formidable looming day: to laundry, cleaners, bank, po, libe, shopping, everywhere everywhere Christmas tonight. But after that one seige of practicality, all shall be merely the typewriter or the hushed whisper of turning pages and batting eyelashes—

Please, now, tell your dear mother and dad I love them and am thinking of them, and thank them from the bottom of my heart for making such a lovely comfortable warm home for me during my stay---how I miss the coal fires, the sherry and stories, the apple pies, the great green meadows stretching outside the windows, the black bandit-faced sheep and all the moors and valleys I tramped through. Give them both a kiss for me, and my dearest best love.

1–Ted Hughes, 'Macaw and Little Miss', 'Bayonet Charge', 'Two Wise Generals', and 'The Hawk in the Rain'.

Oh, Teddy, I am now for a hot bath, and hot milk, and perhaps tomorrow it will not rain. I dont think I want to eat until I taste your lovely mouth again my very very enormous dear teddy how I love you . . .

your own wife,
sylvia
with her love

TO *Aurelia Schober Plath*

Tuesday 2 October 1956 TLS, Indiana University

Whitstead
Tuesday morning
October 2, 1956

Dearest darling mother . . .

Enclosed please find the exquisite Atlantic check endorsed for deposit to me. I would appreciate it if you would keep it, and subsequent checks, in a separate account for me, so I can see how it grows in my simple childlike way, toward my lovely coming wedding.

Something very wonderful has happened: On my return to Whitstead in rain, weariness and general numb sadness yesterday, I received a lovely letter from poetry magazine (Chicago) saying they found my poems admirable and are buying SIX (!) for publication! Do you know what this means! First, about $76 (they pay 50 cents a line); then, Ted's long poem "Bawdry Embraced" was published there in August so we "share" another magazine; then, they are all my new poems, written after "Pursuit" and glorifying love and Ted!---they are obviously in the market for a new lyrical woman! And they are happy poems. This also means that my manuscript of poetry which I am going to get ready to submit to the Yale Series of Younger Poet's Contest this January will have a terrific list of introductory credits---already, nine of my poems were published; add seven, this fall, and perhaps more this winter, and its rather impressing. My manuscript should have much more chance; and, bless it, Poetry is a magazine of poets (I wish I could get Mrs. Prouty to help endow it subtly---it's always got pleas for funds in the front by T. S. Eliot, Auden, Sitwell, etc.) and not commercial! That, combined with my commercial publications, is also fine. I am very happy. They are publishing: "Two Sisters of Persephone", "Metamorphosis", "Wreath for a Bridal", "Strumpet Song", "Dream with Clam-Diggers" and "Epitaph for Fire and Flower", a longish one which I began on the beach in Benidorm, Spain! I'll enclose a copy.

Also got a lovely letter from Peter Davison, who is now associate editor of the Atlantic Monthly Press, saying he wants to encourage me from his new position, and wouldn't it be nice if they could publish a novel by me some day? I wrote him a colossal letter,[1] telling him of Ted's stuff, and my novel plans, asking advice, etc. He can be a most valuable friend. Your little daughter will be a writer yet! When I listed the prizes I'd won for the Poetry biography, I was rather surprised at myself; from Seventeen, through Mademoiselle (story and guest ed); Irene Glascock tie, Lyric Young Poets Prize; Acad. Of American Poets Prize at Smith---all that help. My life is, praise be, going to be crammed daily with writing and my darling Ted.

So much to ask you, too. Will go to London some Saturday late this fall to shop for silver (stainless steel) patterns, perhaps china; want to buy Ted a leather brief-case for Christmas; we both need one; our manuscripts are the most valuable part of our luggage; the darling one needs so much, gifts are no problem; want to get him a leather shaving kit; also, that Viyella bathrobe (as unbulky, but as warm as possible---could you possibly try to send it? Or shall I try to shop for one here?) By the way, a huge favor to ask you:

Please, please, shop for two small nice presents to send M. B. Derr[2] and Nancy Hunter as wedding gifts; and mail them; I want to ask them to my wedding, and would like to establish a precedent for gift-giving: the suavest modern present to Nancy; a silver candy dish (hoho) to M.B.---no, but something sweet and simpery and cute; she's like that. Nan's home address is 302[3] Noah Avenue, Akron, Ohio. (302 that is); Mary Bailey Derr (now Mrs. David Knox) should be 260 Quinobequin Road, Waban. I was invited to wedding and reception at both, it seems.

Now, some time at your convenience, could you send me my two German grammars---I believe the one from Summer School (the most necessary) is a big thinnish gray one, the Smith one, a red squat review;[4] I want to start German next term, after I get through Chaucer and Philosophy. Also: bless you, could we have a few packets, at least three, of corrasable bond?[5] You have no idea the horror of getting type paper here: it's not our standard ms. size, and I have to have it cut, which is expensive, and there

1–See SP to Peter Davison, 30 September 1956.

2–Mary Bailey Derr Knox (1932–   ), B.A. 1954, art, Smith College.

3–SP typed a forward slash over the 3 of 302, thus her parenthetical correction.

4–Robert O. Röseler, *German in Review* (New York: H. Holt, rev. edn 1953); SP's copy held by Smith College.

5–A brand of erasable typing paper.

is no corrasable. Ted has the children's book of about 70 to 100 pages which I want to type and send off this month (could you investigate about addresses of children's book publishers---I have no addresses here; you could just look in the bookstores, perhaps; or ask about): also, I want to type up a poem-book ms. for each of us. Ted is producing terrifically---the Atlantic has had his poems for four months; I have fingers crossed. You would be so touched---he wants to get his fables printed especially for you, so you would not worry that he can support me! He thinks you would be pleased. The dear one.

Naturally, it will be hard work here, but I am happy alone, want to see no one, but live in the spirit of Ted, writing daily; I'll see him in London before he leaves for Spain, so there is that to look forward to; he waits now, word from the BBC. You must tell Mrs. Prouty about my new poem acceptances! It shows what true love can produce!

If only you knew how happy I am with Ted! I have been with him every minute for over four months, and every day I love him more and more; we share everything, and never run out of growing conversation: we talked one whole day on our bus-trip to London, and it is so exciting, both of us writing, producing something new every day, criticizing, dreaming, encouraging, mulling over common experiences; I am walking on air; I love him more than the world and would do anything for him: he is the dearest, kindest, gentlest, most loving darling person alive! We want to work and work, and are both recluses at heart; success will never spoil either of us; we are not dependent on the social arty world, but scorn it, for those that are drinking and calling themselves "writers" at parties, should be home writing and writing; everyday, one has to earn the name of "writer" over again, with much wrestling.

Our last days at Ted's were lovely, even under the strain of coming parting; we listened to Beethoven after dinner, by the light of the coal fire, the stars shining outside the big windows, and read in bed together quietly and happily; I finished my drawing of Wuthering Heights and will do a little article on it. By the way, I'd love red geraniums around the front of our house! I always thought petunias straggly and messy, and geranium are so sturdy, and My Color! I don't know what records you have of Beethoven, but would be overjoyed if you would stock up before our coming: esp. "The Grosse Fugue", The Emperor Concerto; and the 4th and 7th Symphonies, etc. Beethoven is the only music big enough for Ted. He can whistle all the themes by heart.

Both of us yearn so for our wedding in Wellesley, which we work to now, for it will mean that we are never apart again, but together all our lives; I will try to get the ship date set, and pray for the 29th of June; all money I earn goes toward wedding, dress, reception; Ted's will go to rent and food for two months on Cape. We are hard, disciplined workers, and he wants me do do very well on my exams, and is always giving me peptalks about them. He is the dearest person there is; I never thought I could feel so holy and exalted from day to day, doing dishes, making his meals; it is so wonderful to love someone incalculably more than oneself; such freedom: everything I do now, is for him, to please him and make him proud . . . do write a lot this year . . .

much love, your happy
sivvy

One of the poems Poetry accepted:

Epitaph for Fire and Flower

You might as well string up
This wave's green peak on wire
To prevent fall, or anchor the fluent air
In quartz, as crack your skull to keep
These two most perishable lovers from the touch
That will kindle angels' envy, scorch and drop
Their fond hearts charred as any match.

Seek no stony camera-eye to fix
The passing dazzle of each face
In black and white, or put on ice
Mouth's instant flare for future looks;
Stars shoot their petals, and suns run to seed,
However you may sweat to hold such darling wrecks
Hived like honey in your head.

Now in the crux of their vows, hang your ear
Still as a shell: hear what an age of glass
These lovers prophesy to lock embrace
Secure in museum diamond for the stare
Of astounded generations; they wrestle
To conquer cinder's kingdom in the stroke of an hour
And hoard faith safe in a fossil.

But though they'd rivet sinews in rock
And have every weathercock kiss hang fire
As if to outflame a phoenix, the moment's spur
Drives nimble blood too quick
For a wish to tether: they ride nightlong
In their heartbeats' blazing wake until red cock
Plucks bare that comet's flowering.

Dawn snuffs out star's spent wick
Even as love's dear fools cry evergreen,
And a languor of wax congeals the vein
No matter how fiercely lit; staunch contracts break
And recoil in the altering light: the radiant limb
Blows ash in each lover's eye; the ardent look
Blackens flesh to bone and devours them.

Sylvia Plath

TO *Edward Weeks*

Wednesday 3 October 1956 TLS (photocopy), Yale University

Whitstead
4 Barton Road
Cambridge, England
October 3, 1956

Mr. Edward Weeks
Editor
THE ATLANTIC MONTHLY
8 Arlington Street
Boston 16, Massachusetts
U.S.A.

Dear Editor Weeks,

It was with great pleasure recently that I received your kind letter accepting my poem "Pursuit"; I am very happy that it will appear in the Atlantic. About the other poem you mentioned---"Two Lovers and a Beachcomber By The Real Sea"---that was bought by Mademoiselle and printed as part of an article on the Irene Glascock Poetry Contest, "Poets On College Time", in their August 1955 issue. I am, however, enclosing a sheaf of recent poems,[1] among which I hope you may find something which interests you as well.

I have just returned to Cambridge for my second and last year on the renewed Fulbright grant to complete work for my Honours B.A. in English Literature. It is one of those rare, cloudless delicate blue days, with the glossy chestnuts breaking from green pods, the rooks clacking like scraped metal, and that unique mellowed gold light over the Backs where I like to walk and sketch. Best of all, here there is the leisure to write for quiet, uninterrupted mornings (as there would never be, at an American graduate school, I think, with the crammed class schedule and frequent exams). I am working daily on poems, articles with little pen sketches which the Monitor publishes from time to time, and a pack of short stories about Spain, bull-fights, quirky widows, Yorkshire moor people, and so on. This year I'm beginning a longish fiction piece on Cambridge itself, of the impact of an American on this particular Cambridge University society, part humorous, part serious: having this second year is ideal: whereas I participated furiously last year, discovering and tasting experience, this year I feel seasoned and objective enough to write about it all.

I've also taken advantage of the long vacations to satisfy much of the eager wanderlust which has been accumulating these past twenty-three years of being a steadfast New Englander---have lived much in Paris, Spain, and Yorkshire, writing and sketching everywhere. But now I am looking most forward to returning to my home in Wellesley next June, for a summer of writing on the Cape, followed by teaching English at some New England college.

Thanking you again for your kind interest,

Sincerely yours,
Sylvia Plath

1–According to documents in the Peter Davison papers at Yale University, the poems enclosed were: 'The Dying Witch Addresses Her Young Apprentice', 'November Graveyard', 'Aerialist', 'Tinker Jack and the Tidy Wives', 'Panegyric', 'Firesong', 'On the Difficulty of Conjuring Up a Dryad', 'Complaint of the Crazed Queen', and 'Ella Mason and Her Eleven Cats'.

TO *Ted Hughes*

Wednesday 3 October 1956 TLS on RMS *Queen Elizabeth* letterhead, family owned

Wednesday morning: Oct.3

Dearest Teddy . . .

It is early yet, a clear miraculous guileless blue day with heather-colored asters, shining chestnuts breaking from green pods (I wait till after dark to collect these) and rooks clacking like bright scraped metal; I find myself walking straight, talking incessantly to you and myself, and painfully abrased by the crowds of people---the motion, chatter and nip and tuck of cars and throngs in Petty Cury nearly drove me home screaming yesterday; I've been, for four months, conscious really of only living in and with you, with the great sense of complete contained safe aloneness and protection that grew to mean in my deepest bone and marrow. Now the voices in the desert assail me; but, somewhat like your "egg-head"[1] (which, by the way, peter-pumpkin-eater[2] sent me with a sweet letter saying how very happy they were to have us and we're very welcome any time) I am already "walling myself in", and the part of me really operating in the world of people and commerce is so small, so merely politic, that it's like a grain of sand in my holy nun-eye. I smiled at the bank man who greeted me with enthusiasm, told me how Lloyd's had missed me, grieved over his his miserable rainy summer and said how lucky I was. He also said, n.b., that I can keep a dollar account for you there (I said you're <u>American</u> to avoid complication) if you endorse the checks you get: "For deposit to the account of Miss Sylvia Plath" and sign your name to that. Then no one can cash it, and I'll deposit it to our next summer.

I am writing this in my bathrobe after a lousy little breakfast of queer-tasting honey on white (ugh) toast and nescafe---regular breakfasts don't start here till tomorrow; the way I miss you makes that hissing small anemic word look ridiculous. I have very simply never felt this way before, and what I and we must do is fight and live with these floods of strange feeling; my whole life, being, breathing, thinking, sleeping, and eating, has somehow, in the course of these last months, become indissolubly welded to you; it is difficult to describe---sort of as if I had innumerable tender, sensitive tentacles joined to you, and suddenly, except for those in my mind, all were cut off, left wavering loose; now people affect me like

1 – Ted Hughes, 'Egg-Head'.

2 – Possibly a reference to Peter Redgrove; the letter does not appear to survive.

vinager does our lovely poached eggs; I contract, concentrate, withdraw, and not a tentacle is left out; I marvel at how well I can get along without giving anything of myself to anyone. I sat at supper at Newnham for the first meal last night amid the seven girls returned, one of whom I knew, and ate rapidly listening to the most incredibly pained conversation: "I always thought they expected girls to do worse than boys at things, you know." "What?" "Worse than boys." "Oh." "Really?" "But here, you know, it's quite the opposite; there's such competition for girls to get in the boys are quite terrified of them."

Whereupon I tore my long white hair, clawed my wrinkles, rejected the pale bilious green dessert (dyed custard) poured over a lady-finger biscuit and left for the college library.

You would be amazed at what I did yesterday; I felt like hell, the numbness of Monday leaving, with a sick, rather mad feeling; in a daze, I tromped through most of my colossal errands; everything needed to be repaired: my bike had to get a new tire & tube, my watch is gone for a good three weeks to an invisible force of tick-tacking jewelers upstairs in the glittering suave Samuel's, whose clock we told time by in Alexandra House;[1] my clothes to the cleaner's (I discovered my pleated skirt must be taken apart[2] and put together again; very depressing thought; the woman said I should order coffee without milk for breakfast because coffee-with-milks-stains don't, alas, come out; I learn so much merely by being civil and listening; somehow, every tradesperson, from banker to cleaner to wine-merchant decides to explain the quirks of their trade to me; I will write a Quirks of the Trade Book).

I banked, got a postal order for the Dinner Dress Contest, mailed innumerable letters---my demand for a new book allowance backed by the itemized and receipts for last term.

A plea for an early sailing date---the earlier we go, the longer writing summer we have; a warning note to the ignorant passport office who still have my damn passport, but sent a small official slip here to "Mrs. S. Hughes" which looked opened and peered-into when I found it on return, saying "Née Plath" inside; I wrote begging them to return it in my maiden name; If, however, Miss Abbott or snotty snooper Milne ask about it, they can have not the face to admit they opened it; I shall say blandly and

1–TH had a room at Alexandra House, a soup kitchen on Petty Cury, Cambridge, across the street from a branch of the jeweller's H. Samuel (now demolished), in the spring of 1956 during his courtship of SP. For more information, see Ted Hughes's *Birthday Letters* poem 'Fidelity'.

2–'must be ~~taking~~ apart' appears in the original.

blithely---"Oh, a silly confusion" and smile snakily into their eyes. Saw my dear pretty tutor MissMorris[1] who is so vague and really sweet; made her sign my University Library slip and she congratulated me on getting poems published (the grapevine---Mrs. Milne was there when I opened the letter from Poetry and screamed; so fast, so far it goes). All was gray yesterday; it was dead; it stuck in my craw. I have a way of glaring at people now; they quail and look the other way.

Sent check to Dr. Kaplan[2] after calling up about address; just got a bill for same from him this morning; with compliments; well, he's taken care of: DO see him when you go to London no matter what; I am all-American[3] (what a misprint that was going to be) in my hygienic mania for prevention etc. Will go see tailor soon and try to have him send suit and jacket to you; please wear them to London, so I and Mr. Carne-Ross can admire you. I live for seeing you there. I shall live with this loneliness, in myself, and must begin to find solace in turning my force on reading, drawing and writing; it will be good, but this first week or two will be hardest---with the joy of living with you so vivid and present by the dour contrast of your absence; but I am in a queer way, capable of being happy completely alone; living with my god, which is you; like a nun; I talk to you each night before I go to bed, opening the window wide, leaning out, looking at clouds of stars, smelling the wet earth and concentrating hard and completely on you, whatever you're doing, wherever you are. It will be best if I see you the weekend just before you go; by then, I'll have made the happiest sort of routine of work here, and seeing you won't be escape from establishing work then, but a right thing, because I'll be settled to this queer ascetic way of life.

Got six Chaucer critical books from college libe; will not get another thing till I've finished these and philosophy books---St. Augustine and St. Paul. Ridiculously enough, I've had trouble finding the right translation of the Epistles; bookdealers look at me like I'm crazy. Well.

Today, a finishing of business and then work: laundry, odds and ends of shopping; etc. Read several Nations at Newnham libe---couldn't resist finding your poem; it was there. Also several terrible pseudo-poems by wiseguy John Ciardi,[4] who I can't really criticize as a person for he wrote

1–Irene Victoria Morris (1913–2007); lecturer in German, Newnham College, Cambridge, 1947–66; SP's tutor while on Fulbright at the University of Cambridge.

2–According to SP's address book, Dr Lewis Kaplan, 85 Harley Street, London W1.

3–'I am all$American' appears in the original.

4–John Ciardi, 'Washington, D.C.', *The Nation*, 28 July 1956, 84; 'Of History, Fiction, Language', *The Nation*, 1 September 1956, 184; and 'Memory of Paris', *The Nation*, 15 September 1956, 226.

many eulogic things after he heard me poetry-read at that contest last year and helped me get two published by sending editors names; the Nation is in very bad need of good poetry; a nice Robert Hillyer[1]---no, that was in the New Yorker, again about a bird, humming-bird, flying into glass window after bright illusion flowers and "hit nothingness, and hit it hard."[2] The New Yorker poetry editor is a psychiatric case; they are split between the most appallingly sentimental nature and love poetry, very still in movement, unrhymed often as not, and this jig-jogging pirouetting funny-wit stuff, usually take-offs on some quoted news item of the moment. Read the story on Spain--"Road to Barcelona",[3] and was furious; will write "Discontented Mayor"[4] and see if they take it; much room for vignette stories; short revealing episodes. To get a Story in there! No other news as yet; am sending severalpoems with letter to Editor Weeks[5] in answer to his---Dryad, November Graveyard, etc. Feel like Poetry lifted an albatross from my neck with those six blessed poems gone---all about love and you; they must be in the market for a female lyricist who sings the glory of love and joins herself with the green sprouted world instead of going psuedo-male intellectual Platonist like Kathleen Raine,[6] or bitter-sour lovelorn like Teasdale, Parker, or even Millay. Joy, joy. A woman's place is in her husband's bed. We shall be living proof that great writing comes from a pure, faithfull, joyous creative bed. I love you; I will live like an intellectual nun without you; I need noone but you and look forward in a queer way to the concentrated work loneliness will crush out of me this year. Loved your letter[7] and will use much of it, I think – the article is gestating; I feel it kick on occasion – will wait it out – I love you like fury –

your own,
sylvia

1 – Robert Hillyer, 'The Victim', *New Yorker*, 16 June 1956, 105.

2 – The last line of Hillyer's poem; '~~hitting~~ nothingness, and hit it hard' appears in the original.

3 – Frederick L. Keefe, 'Road to Barcelona', *New Yorker*, 5 May 1956, 102, 104–7.

4 – SP planned to write a story titled 'Discontented Mayor'; SP mentions it twice in her journals: by name on 19 May 1959 and with a brief plot on 31 May 1959.

5 – See SP to Edward Weeks, 3 October 1956.

6 – British poet and critic Kathleen Raine (1908–2003).

7 – Probably TH to SP, [1–2 October 1956]; held by Lilly Library.

TO *Ted Hughes*

Thursday 4 October 1956 TLS on RMS *Queen Elizabeth* letterhead, family owned

Thursday, October 4

Dearest Teddy-ponk . . .

it is early, almost, and raw and gray; a huge many-legged green grasshopper has got in; mail over bitter acrid turkishy coffee quite uneventful, meaning no acceptances, rejections or large checks. Sweet note from Elly, back home, who is about to send book of TV script-writer Paddy Chayevsky's plays;[1] should be fine guide to how America wants them; he's The Fair Haired Boy; all his plays get on Broadway or in movies. A dear handwritten note from your dentist Kaplan, in answer to mine which I sent with check---thanking him for the care of that most precious orifice; he said he'd be glad to see you any time you're in London for further attention---"further attention"---there's something so discreetly hushed and mortuary about that, isn't there? Also a note in feminine handwriting from someone named Terry[2] on a card showing giraffes, elephants and negroes bearing letters and mailboxes; this really put me off; this Terry-person has been advised by somebody or other in America that I can answer "her million questions" over tea, sherry, coffee---she gives me choice. I shall put it off and off; I shall ignore it. A new American Fulbright girl, Dina Ferran[3]---the Other, arrived yesterday; very sweet, more quiet blonde type doing archaeology and engaged to be married next August; took her to supper last night, asked her to explain flint to me, this morning am taking her shopping, leaving her in market hill after a few necessary purchases, and running home to write. I can't wait till the other Old Guard comes---I'm damned if I'm going to play hostess to sundry Indians, South Africans, etc. Mrs. Milne brings them up to my den, where I growl welcome, as if I were supposed to be Perle Mesta[4]---god, I hate people; they are nice, but that isn't it. I don't want any of it.

1–Paddy Chayefsky, *Television Plays* (New York: Simon and Schuster, 1955); SP's copy held by Lilly Library.

2–According to SP's calendar, she met Terry, a friend of Dick Wertz, on 9 October 1956.

3–Dr Dena Ferran Dincauze (1934–2016); Fulbright scholar, pre-historic archaeology 1956–7; Newnham College, Cambridge; Ph.D. 1967, Harvard University. See *Memories of Whitstead* (18–19).

4–American socialite and political hostess Perle Mesta (1889–1975).

Yesterday, O Listen, I went to the tailor, fingered the beautiful cloth of your suit and jacket with tears; they just emphasized your absence by being empty, and paid the man the unprecedented sum of £37.13s! He is sending them off to Yorkshire today. I have now, in three days, spent the incredible sum of £70. But our bills are paid; I am left with £10 in the bank, and same in cash to last till November 20 (my next check must pay Newnham in October). So there it is. The £10 making up the £70 after paying your two bills went largely on postage stamps, bike repairs and things like soap. Was welcomed with open arms by the Lady of the Laundromat: "Well you're a stranger---where have you been?" I told her; seems she will always remember me as the little girl who by accident dyed her clothes orange and purple last year because something wasn't color-fast.

I have the queerest feeling the New Yorker will buy some of Luke's poems; let me know, they're addressed to Yorkshire. The New Yorker makes me rather scared, and just a little sick; there are these great long articles, bristling scrupulously with facts, history and incredible Naming of Names: a long letter from Jaipur[1] (the secret is to go where noone's ever been and write for "Our Far-Flung Correspondents") and a tender piece explaining why the cedars in Bermuda[2] are all dead; a sestina by Elizabeth Bishop,[3] whom I formerly admired for her "Fish" and "Roosters" poems, using the end words: child, house, almanac, grandmother, tears and stove; guess what <u>that</u> sestina's like. Teddy, the poems, I have cold-eyedly discovered, are all <u>weak</u>; that is it; write delicate weak poems; I wasn't being funny, either, about the birds; this latest issue had orioles, thrushes[4] and "vulgar starlings"[5] in it getting drunk on choke-cherries. They are featuring tales about heads in the cartoons, of which I send you a sample;[6] rather lovely. A queer story, almost like your exercises in description wholly, about a little boy watching the sea[7] the last day of summer; very minutely and accurately described. I feel I can get in if only I write with care. Thurber's fables are <u>awful</u>. They have a false ring, sort of singsong rhymed prose; I can only figure he is dying and they are buying at fabulous prices to pay the hospital bills.

1–Christopher Rand, 'Letter from Jaipur', *New Yorker*, 15 September 1956, 118–32.
2–E. J. Khan, 'Letter from Bermuda', *New Yorker*, 16 June 1956, 117–20.
3–Elizabeth Bishop, 'Sestina', *New Yorker*, 15 September 1956, 46.
4–SP refers to John Hall Wheelock, 'Aubade', *New Yorker*, 30 June 1962, 23.
5–James L. Montague, 'Chokecherries', *New Yorker*, 15 September 1956, 152.
6–The enclosure is no longer with the letter.
7–William Wertenbaker, 'The Last Day of Summer', *New Yorker*, 15 September 1956, 111–12, 115–17.

Last night was hell; I feel completely paralysed, away from you; I'm not hungry; I can't sleep; can't read; can't think. I'll be all right, but not by recovering from missing you; only by learning, and it must take a good deal of learning, how to live with this huge whistling hole in my guts and heart. God, I miss sharing thoughts and food and bed and all the warm lovely little things; I read Crowe Ransom last night and felt better---the "ten poor idiot fingers"[1] one, especially. I was awake and awake until 3 a.m. I'll have to start taking night walks before bed; I dread going to bed now something awful. I feel terribly miserable and noble; like learning to live without legs and arms and with mechanical intestines after some colossal operation which nobody really thought I'd come out of; I'll never stop this incredibly overpowering sense of absence; I'll just learn to wall it up in a series of bare enormous rooms, which I don't enter except when I'm alone; all the rest is rot. The reading will take a while before every other sentence doesn't make me want to run and hackle over it with you; I still will want to, but will save it. I have got to learn to live this way, I know, but oh. Wrote a bad fourteen line poem last night; will probably write many such, bad because they are naked and do not have the sophistication of technique which cares how it says more than what it says; you must criticize coldly, even if you know it is all about you and done in such simple love:

Monologue at 3 A.M.[2] it is called:

> Better that every fiber crack
> And fury make head,
> Blood drenching vivid
> Couch, carpet, floor
> And the snake-figured almanac
> Vouching you are
> A million green counties from here,
>
> Than to sit mute, twitching so
> Under prickling stars,
> With stare, with curse
> Blackening the time
> Goodbyes were said, trains let go,

1–John Crowe Ransom, 'Winter Remembered'.

2–In SP's *Collected Poems*, the first letters of each line after the first are lowercase.

And I, great magnanimous fool, thus wrenched from
My one kingdom.

I love you, love you, love you,
your own sylvia

TO *Ted Hughes*

Friday 5 October 1956 — TLS on RMS *Queen Elizabeth* letterhead, family owned

Friday morn, Oct. 5

Dearest love Teddy . . .

This Cunard ship must keep sailing until it's burned itself out; I believe in writing on everything including toilet paper. It is another ringing blue morning and bless it, it's mine, now practicalia is done. Traitors Baltzell and Isabel, only old guard left, don't arrive till Monday, leaving me with a growing houseful of sweet new green creaking aliens which Miss Abbott bestows on me to lead flocking across to meals like some mother duck, answering questions; la.

They are nice, reserved; I will get to know not one; getting to know people takes time and energy; I don't have any for them. One is from S. Africa (Natal),[1] one Eurasian Malayan,[2] several sari-ed Indians[3] to come, for whom Mrs. Milne no doubt waits with dreams of sugared saris dancing in her mean spectacled head. Oh how sweet I am. Miss Abbott deigned to visit me last night, which was to pot, since after supper I'd given the Malayan a map, on loan, much free advice, especially about warm clothes and dispatched her; Miss Abbott took longer; I told her about poems, you, family, summer, and when she said "It's wonderful to see someone who's life is so happy", I murmured darkly about passing through the forge of sorrow, the valley of tears. She promised to find out the earliest legal date I can leave Newnham next June.

1–Jess Ivy Brown Bishop (1934–); from Durban, South Africa. B.A. 1954, University of Natal; 1956–8, English, Newnham College, Cambridge.

2–Marie Thérèse Consigliere Fernando (1932–2013); B.A. 1955, University of Malaya, Singapore; B.A. 1958, English, Newnham College, Cambridge.

3–The *Newnham College Report* for January 1957 lists the following Whitstead residents from India: Lakshmi Burra Krishnamurty, Lotika Purkayastha Varadarajan, and Zahida Zaidi.

I am just barely breaking into my old fields of concentration; I really haven't concentrated since my Plato papers last spring on reading-thinking, albeit I've done a hell of a lot of concentrating on my own writing and private thinking. I found myself near hysteria at the sight of books piled on the floor; like having to eat one and only one dish at a smorgasbord while all the other cates and dainties obtruded with painful distraction on the sense. I'm learning. I'm really not a bad thinker. Have patience through this first week or two, Ted, while I finger my way back through the stacks of Augustine, St. Paul and Chaucer, man and critics. I'll slack on all else till I get this conglomerate albatross off my conscience. Once I catch up, all will be eased.

Began the epistles of St. Paul last night, going to sweet Bowes and Bowes for a change to get the proper modern translation cheap second hand, appealing in my childlike way, for them to tell me what were the epistles; hushed conference among the ones who knew; I was told; I went, gratified. I am standing at the crack, the hinge, the abyss, the suspension bridge between Greek and Christian thought. It awes me. I find the Christian writings of Augustine and Paul almost intolerable: the mystic workings of God's plan, can, alas, be "known" (in the rich rounded sense of that word, distinguishing it from the mere "thinking knowledge" we use it to mean today) only by faith. That blind leap which so appalls me. And the whole tone of the Christian writings is so full of assurance---one can see the appeal here, the assurance of immortal life, reward and redemption, in contrast to the wistful hazardings of my dear Socrates who presented his view and hope of immortal life as a fable to the skeptical worldling rhetoricians around him.

Also, I find God hideously conceited; every time you want to argue with the apostles, the saints, about the origin of evil (my favorite black sheep which even drove Augustine almost wild), they blind you with some hocus-pocus about God's inscrutability; having cake of doctrine but refusing to impart heavenly recipe for lesser cooks. God seems so often a rat---that same distaste I felt in reading Paradise Lost where God is such an egomaniac, spelling his objective pronoun Mee; "I do this in glorification of Mee . . ." Also, Paul is ridiculously smug about his celibate state; the flesh always embarasses them so; they divide it completely from the soul; flesh means sin, nothing else; all men, because of Adam are born in sin, conceived in sin, etc.

Paul writes: "It is an excellent thing for a man to have no intercourse with a woman (the married man is anxious about world affairs, how best to satisfy his wife---so he is torn in two directions) but there is so much immorality that every man had better have a wife of his own---Better marry than be aflame with passion!" Now this low view of the body, the senses, the flesh, is intolerable to me: "The interests of the flesh are hostile to God." They speak of marriage as a regrettable necessity, allowing it as a kind of lesser evil, but smugly asserting: "He who does not marry will be found to have done better . . . I would like," says pretty Paul, "all men to be as I am." Now I, in my pagan earth-mother way, glorify my God through the flesh; through your flesh; and through our multitudes of unborn children. I find it horrible to cut the flesh from the soul and starve it, for thus it loses its roots in the earth and in turn starves the soul; this is my own private doctrine, and will come in many poems; it is my answer to the Christians and Kathleen Raine. I feel it my place as a singing woman; God how these writings stimulate my thinking, though; and I'm just humbly beginning. Tell me if you object to my tentative philosophizing rant, darling one. It helps no end to write it out to you.

All while I was reading Paul, and Augustine's confessions[1] about the sweets of sin in early youth, I heard the assurance of the Holy Spirit whose function is to sustain the faith of man through trouble; now I have a private holy spirit in small letters, an earth-faith which flickers, at times, in my need for stoicism away from you, but I cannot make the leap of faith to God, who seems so unreasonable to me and won't let me argue with Him but announces that the world's wisdom shall be confounded, and that man must become a "fool" if he is to be properly wise: meaning, I suppose, humble and full of faith and no sophistical arguments; but the riddle in Eden's apple core remains: If God made man "free to fall", wasn't He glad man fell by "choice" so he could generously bend down and redeem him through Christ, grace, etc. and thus reveal his own Glory? Oh well.

All through my reading I heard blessed Yeats:

> "Odour of Blood when Christ was slain
> Made all Platonic tolerance vain
> And vain all Doric discipline . . ."[2]

I understand that more perfectly now, in the midst of this terrifying strong blood-faith.

1–Saint Augustine, *The Confessions of St. Augustine* (London: J. M. Dent, 1953); SP's copy held by Smith College.
2–W. B. Yeats, 'Two Songs from a Play'.

I loved your letter[1] this morning; barged down in midst of a painful still correct breakfast and read it over three cups of coffee while Malayan asked South African "Do you have four seasons?" and such like. Laughed richly over Graves-nightmare story, read it to South African. "How does he know so much?" she asked. I thought, "He is," I replied sweetly, "a kind of genius." And so he is.

Found your story-plot Terrific. I was very attracted by it and think it's full of potential. The motives are the most important; I must learn enough about how Inns work to make conversion of farm probable; details, details. Maybe Sutcliffes[2] could help. It could be a great story. I leapt into the characters psychological problems right off, and they took sudden shape, still hazy about edges, and began to move about place resembling Sutcliffe's.

I liked your poem[3] very much; will ruminate on it, and write about it in a little while . . .

Later: 6 p.m. The time of day I like least; I resent going to meals; people wound me; I shut up like a clam. Just finished St. Paul's Epistles; this evening, further in Augustine.

I miss you like hell. Certain words in the bible are like lovely clear sustaining water; you should cleave to me, it says; I honestly believe that by some mystic uniting we have become one flesh; I am simply sick, physically sick, without you. I cry; I lay my head on the floor; I choke, hate eating; hate sleeping, or going to bed; and am perpetually freezing cold (you can imagine from mere icy meetings with my chill hands what an ice age has come on me now away from you). I am living in a kind of death-in-life; when will the Word, these words I cram my eye with, assuage this hunger for your sweet incredibly dear flesh; I never knew before what a newborn ghost must feel---I have somehow lost my most darling one; it is so strange to me---never before in my life have I been parted from one I love so immeasurably more than myself; my god, do let me be with you soon—

Could I be a glutton and see you more than just once before you go? If I were good and slaved till then, could you come and I come to London the weekend of the 13th? (there's that number again) Money's no object, now I've got the Fulbright, and you could reserve a room at some hotel

1–TH to SP, [3 October 1956]; held by Lilly Library.

2–Sutcliffe's Inn, then in Colden, approximately 2 miles from the Hughes family home.

3–Possibly Ted Hughes, 'Phaetons'; in his [3 October 1956] letter Hughes mentions writing 'The Horses of the Sun, or the Mark of a Modern Apollo' (55). See also SP to TH, 6 October 1956.

when you got there---I couldn't bear being sociable with Jim[1] or anybody. I don't know what you'll be hearing from Carne-Ross, but I would give anything to see you---it is, today being Friday, next weekend. I simply don't believe in killing myself with meaningless stoicism when you're in the same country. Even if the BBC is during the week, or not settled then, will you come? I'll probably have had a supervision in each class and will bring a book for the train. Teddy I love you so it is simply murdering me. And I am no baby really; but you are my own self for which I exist, somehow being father, brother, husband, son, in all one, the whole male principle of the world, in you, and without you how barren that world is, and sterile.

Your books came, and the dear letter,[2] and the sweet note from your mother[3]---thank her for me. I will work some livable existence out of this, but only by freezing my most vital parts.

The New Yorker is really like I said, crazy for nature life: peewits and towhees: the enclosed poem[4] is by a boy who knows the trade and strings his line short and sweet. "Virtue" probably netted him $10 all by itself; they want no blood and guts, just goldenrod[5] and wistful crayfish (same man had long crayfish poem[6] in couplets!)

Must stop ranting or you will weary and flag each time you get a fat envelope. Wrote a poem yesterday,[7] and another today,[8] very slight, probably---I lose perspective away from our tennis-partnered volleyings of opinion; here's the shorter: will send the other tomorrow with talk of your fine one:

1–Jim Downer, who lived with TH for a period at 18 Rugby Street, London.

2–Probably TH to SP, [4 October 1956]; held by Lilly Library.

3–Probably Edith Hughes to SP, undated [*c.* 3 October 1956]; held by Lilly Library.

4–The enclosure is no longer with the letter. Robert Wallace, 'The Garden Snail', *New Yorker*, 8 September 1956, 98. 'Virtue' appears as the lone word and last line of the tenth stanza.

5–A reference to the line 'loosestrife, orange milkweed, and goldenrod' from Luke Zilles, 'Bunch of Wildflowers' cited above.

6–Robert Wallace, 'The Crayfish', *New Yorker*, 21 July 1956, 29.

7–According to her calendar, SP wrote 'Street Song' on 4 October 1956.

8–Sylvia Plath, 'Touch-and-Go'; included in the letter. 'Touch-and-Go' erroneously placed in the 'Juvenilia' section of SP's *Collected Poems*.

Sing praise for statuary:
For those anchored attitudes
And staunch stone eyes that look[1]
Through lichen-lid and passing bird-foot
At some steadfast mark
Beyond the inconstant green
Gallop and flick of light
In this precarious park

Where vivid children twirl
Like colored tops through time
Nor stop to understand
How all their play is touch-and-go:
But, Go! they cry, and the swing
Arcs up to the tall tree tip;
Go! and the merry-go-round
Hauls them round with it.

And I, like the children, caught
In the mortal active verb,
Let break an elegiac tear
For each fierce, flaring game
Of quick child, leaf and cloud,
While on this same fugue, unmoved,
Those stonier eyes stare[2]
Safe-socketed in rock.

The other poem's for you and probably, like most plaints, keepable only because it is done in love; my darling darling Teddy. Tell me how soon I may see you –

your own wife
sylvia

1–In SP's *Collected Poems*, this line reads 'And staunch stone eyes that stare'.
2–In SP's *Collected Poems*, there are several textual differences in these lines: 'Let my transient eye break a tear / For each quick, flaring game / Of child, leaf and cloud, / While on this same fugue, unmoved, / Those stonier eyes look,'.

TO *Ted Hughes*

Saturday 6 October 1956 TLS, family owned

saturday morning, oct. 6

dearest darling teddy . . .

two lovely letters this morning and that's that, from you,[1] from the one who easily sounds like our best angel, peter davison.[2] now don't get too optimistic (I say this, for it's hard for me not to, and <u>one</u> of us must keep that icy head if all things we handle are fire-and-icily).

peter's letter was like a plum-cake of helps, hints and interest for both of us. first things first, says he, and congratulates us on our engagement. next, to business: he investigated about your poems, says: "the magazine is definitely interested in his poems, although they have not yet definitely decided for or against them. Edward Weeks will be seeing them soon; but I am afraid I cannot predict just when the decision will be made. These things depend so much on the magazine's schedule and on how much room there is expected for poetry."[3]

obviously, there is hope. if they keep your manuscript four months it always means the head editor sees it and decides, which is a Good Thing anyway. only I wish they'd hurry. the blessed London Magazine hasn't sent word yet and they've had your terrific batch over a month, which must mean Lehmann is ruminating. also, Nation and Poetry are off, both good prospects. whatever batch comes off back here first, I'll add egg-head too (like some rich recipe) and send off.

now listen, darling, this is nicest of all for you, us, etc. going on: HEARKEN: "About Ted's other work, we would be extremely interested in considering the children's fable."(That's the lovely animals o my dear ponk) "We have a small but effective children's department here with a new young juvenile editor and we have done particularly well of late with a volume of children's poems by W. J. Smith entitled "The Laughing Time".[4] He also says you can ask publishers to forward manuscripts to other publishers and avoid this criss-crossing of the Atlantic ocean & bankrupting postage-charges. SO. After this strict week till the 13th, in which I am merely doing Chaucer and Augustine, I take out two whole days and type your fables and then Off To Mr. Davison. I am very

1–Probably TH to SP, [5 October 1956]; held by Lilly Library.

2–Peter Davison to SP, 2 October 1956; held by Lilly Library. The 'Novel Contest brochure' SP mentions is with the letter.

3–SP slightly misquotes Davison's letter, 'there is expected to be for poetry'.

4–William Jay Smith, *Laughing Time* (Boston: Little, Brown, 1955).

confident, but we must brace ourselves for every slight or hitch in our fortunes and not go black if everything doesn't immediately find a richly-paying-accepting-kudoing audience. THEY WILL.

NOW: they say when you have enough for a book of adult fables they would also be very interested although, for adults, he says, fables "are extremely difficult things to sell,[1] and they would have to be quite extraordinary and original to be at all successful." Of course, I think they are just that, but this should wait a year until you've written and sold enough to have created the audience and interest for a book.

Peter is reassuring about copyright laws. Advises agent, who should handle all such matters when we get big enough for serial rights, movie rights, TV rights, technical details being workable, but very preoccupying. So, passing through New York, perhaps next spring, we'll both wed agents for our stories; we should both have sold <u>something</u> by then. Peter also enclosed the Atlantic Press Novel Contest brochure. $5000 outright---$2500 of it as prize, $2500 as advance toward first royalties. Due date is June 30, so probably I better wait till a year from now in 1958, but What An Incentive! Peter will be terrific help. He tells me not to hurry, and "whether you have finished the novel in time for our contest or not,[2] I will be delighted and eager to read the manuscript and talk to you about it when you get back here." Peter, my darling Teddy, is that rare rare good editor type person who is utterly unselfish and eager to work with creative writers for publication. It would be so nice, all of us being so young, if he could help us, and, we, in turn, could give him a reputation among the publishers and editors of New Discoveries. La, what prospects. Work Work Work. Crooked Aunts And Uncles, Please. Now, why not write fable-style stories in the Frank O'Connor manner (or Dylan Thomas, for that matter), meaning, putting yourself as a young-boy observer, thus giving a particular limited lens through which the reader sees the whole appalling or funny scene: instead of a separate book, short stories merely, to go with your fables? You've got terrific story material there, and if you wrote a good one or two, I'd send them off to Peter. We must see that a good half of his time this year is spent reading our manuscripts.

I love you love you love you.

Began "The Book of The Duchess" out loud to myself last night and broke the Chaucer paralysis.

1–SP slightly misquotes Davison's letter: 'an extremely difficult thing to sell'.

2–SP slightly misquotes Davison's letter: 'whether you will have finished the novel in time for our contest or not'.

I must keep a hard head, not panicking at the seemingly endless stacks of reading. I will read all Chaucer, old and new, aloud in the evenings, saving my favorite reading for evening and doing drudgery in the afternoon, writing in morning. O the lovely sweetmeanderings on sleeplessness, the elaborate feather-bed, the dear story of Seys and Alcione:

"And farewell, swete, my worldes blysse!
I preye God youre sorwe lysse.
To lytel while oure blysse lasteth!"[1]

And the marvelous cave of sleeping gods and the water running down the cliff walls making a "dedly slepynge soun." For every critical page, it must be two of Chaucer. Bless the day I can ignore this scholastic bicker and stick to sources.

But a peace spread over me. All afternoon I'd read about: "To Carthage I came"[2] and about the cauldron of unholy loves singing. Bless Chaucer; bless the Wife of Bath. Bless the strong loving body.

I think I'd like to change the title on my book of poems to "Firesong." What think you. I've outgrown circuses, and flames of love, death, time and sun crackle everywhere in my book. I'd use Yeats as epigraph: "Everything that flames upon the night, Man's own resinous heart has fed."[3]

I love your poem on the changeling.[4] But please leave off at: "Fondly I smile/Into your hideous eyes." Have I your permission? If so, I'll type it up. It's too good a poem-as-poem to get slick and commercial-ironic about the baby-contest. Also, how about another word for "hideous"? I'd like better something that <u>showed</u> the eyes hideous, as in the fine "Snake's twisted eye."

What's title? "The Changeling"?

Darling, you're the wildest loveliest piece of flesh walking. If little girls scream, it is only in a kind of Bacchic ecstasy; the police are just jealous and want to convict such exceptional Samsonian excellence. I love you so.

1 – Geoffrey Chaucer, *The Canterbury Tales*.
2 – From St Augustine, *The Confessions of Saint Augustine*.
3 – W. B. Yeats, 'Two Songs from a Play'; SP slightly misquotes the poem: 'Whatever flames upon the night / Man's own resinous heart has fed'.
4 – Ted Hughes, 'Dolly Topplebull mourns her ascendant Vanity' (first line: 'Old wives in their day') enclosed in TH to SP, [5 October 1956]; published for the first time in *Letters of Ted Hughes* (59–60). SP quotes additional lines from this poem in this paragraph. The Lilly Library holds two versions of the poem, one typed and one in manuscript. The one in manuscript bears the title 'Dolly Topplebull mourns her ascendant Vanity'. On the verso are continued lines from a long poem entitled 'Bluebeard's Last Bride', unattributed.

Went for walk after dinner last night; my old habit coming back---not waiting for dessert, but, sick, fed-up, ramping out of the chattering hall into the night to stride and stride ranting at what unlucky stars gimlet-eyed the clouds. Walked over bridges by our island, our benches, musing how many of our unborn children were squandered in love on earth, grass, carpets, couches, floorboards; all Cambridge hisses with your absence still keeping all those luminous meandering ghosts of who and where we were last spring.

Darling, be scrupulous and date your letters. When we are old and spent, they will come asking for our letters; and we will have them dove-tail-able.

Your new plot[1] is eminently worthy of True Confessions; the woman, however, is a fool. Obviously she doesn't love her husband. She should delight to be raped on the floor.

Don't be silly about your TV play; nothing you write should Ever Be Torn Up or Mangled. Save it, bring it to London for me to read.

I love the "Horses of the Sun." The close is terrific: "Read, wanted your dream-green countryside . . . . to "A thundering tossing upside-down team drags you on fire / Among the monsters of the zodiac."

I'll send back this copy as you said---do you have another? Send it back, revised, and I'll type out final copy. To go through piece by piece: again, I don't think "horrible void" is the best you can do; I'm eternally suspicious of editorializing with horribles, terribles, awfuls and hideouses; make the void horrible; let your reader have the sweet joy of exclaiming: "ah! horrible!" Like "bland grain of air." Does this line read right?: "You clock your progress, you garments your man:"? the last four words sound like a misprint slang: "You takes your choice," that sort of thing. Don't think, here, its good. Explicate this please. Don't like garments in any case. How should it read from "O hold now"? Love the last two lines of the first verse.

Like very much "steadfast saints of window and table and chair administer fresh faiths of light." Like that kind of athletic inwoven metaphor which makes description both realistic, psychologically valid and musical. Again: "inert vegetative immensity" somehow sticks. "Sunlight pools green fields" is limpid and lovely; couldn't you do better for either "vegetative" or "immensity"? Try like you showed me in Shakespeare, some monosyllabic concrete word to wed one or the other of those four-syllabled colossi.

1–See second plot in TH to SP, [3 October 1956]; held by Lilly Library.

Please, to my denseness and satisfaction, explain the meaning of the first five lines of the last verse. I can't criticize it properly till I'm sure: Is it really "you bouncing head"? If so, don't approve of addressing it "Smile", somehow sounds mock-heroic. Would like better: "Smile, with your heels in the reins, your bouncing head." Or is it: "You bouncing head, read . . ." No, because then the wandering is conjuring up a most peculiar image. Do not let me go astray because of typing-error or lack of proper punctuation; you <u>must</u>, wicked one, help the reader (probably I will be your most niggling demanding one) to read, because you know, your syntax is very difficult; as you admit yourself, your poems are damn hard to read, they are so complex, and so you must be careful to the death not to let any mere mechanical complexity---punctuation, grammar---obstruct.

As I said, the last four lines are perfect.

I am enclosing my sentimental one; be strict in criticizing, for you are my one proper lens; even if you know I am blithering on about how I love you, it is a poem, and, as such, can be attacked brutally.

You brute. I love you. Please come to London next weekend in spite of Carne-Ross or because of. I can work amazingly hard if I have something specific to live for. You. Next weekend.

I love you like fury . . .
your own sylvia

(over for poem)

Street Song:

By a mad miracle I go intact
Among the common rout
Thronging sidewalk, street,
And bickering shops;
Nobody blinks a lid, gapes,
Or cries that this raw flesh
Reeks of the butcher's cleaver,
Its heart and guts hung hooked
And bloodied as a cow's split frame
Parceled out by white-jacketed assassins.

Oh no, for I strut it clever
As a greenly escaped idiot,
Buying wine, bread,

Yellow-casqued chrysanthemums---
Arming myself with the most reasonable items
To ward off, at all cost, suspicions
Roused by thorned hands, feet, head,
And that great wound
Squandering red
From the pierced side.[1]

Even as my each mangled nerve-end
Trills its hurt out
Above pitch of pedestrian ear,
So perhaps I, knelled dumb by your absence,
Alone am cursed to hear
Sun's parched phoenix-scream,
Every downfall and crash
Of gutted star,
And world's hinges' incessant hiss
Like some daft goose.[2]

(I have copies of my ones, so just write about them and rip apart in your letters)

Love,
S.

TO *Ted Hughes*

Sun.–Mon. 7–8 October 1956 TLS, family owned

Sunday morning
October 7, 1956

Dearest love Teddy . . .

A brilliant gray morning . . . sweet gift of an extra hour last night---why can't they do that every day? All the new little girls including Janeen,[3] Dina, Jess, Marie, left for church this morning after breakfast armed with bibles

1–In SP's *Collected Poems*, this line reads 'From the flayed side'.
2–In SP's *Collected Poems*, there are several textual differences in the last seven lines: 'So, perhaps I, knelled dumb by your absence, / Alone can hear / Sun's parched scream, / Every downfall and crash / Of gutted star, / And, more daft than any goose, / This cracked world's incessant gabble and hiss.'
3–Possibly Edna Janean Walsh; affiliated student 1956–7, Newnham College, Cambridge.

talking about catching the service as if it were a bus. I beamed benevolently at them over my third atheistic cup of coffee and ate my existentialist egg; they really are very sweet, but, my god, so young, so young. In twenty days I shall have completed my 24th year and begun my 25th---I am cruel in putting it this way, but it is true; a quarter of a century gone to pot; and please the lord let there be three more quarter centuries all blessed by your presence, come day, come night, come hurricane and holocaust . . .

O Teddy, how I repent for scoffing in my green and unchastened youth at the legend of Eve's being plucked from Adam's left rib; because the damn story's true; I ache and ache to return to my proper place, which is curled up right there, sheltered and cherished; I am sure you, as a man, will hack out some sort of self-sufficience in this year, missing only one rib; but I; my whole sense of being is blasted by your absence; and I am again having the most terrible of nightmares, no matter how stoically I go about in the day; it all catches up at night; last night it was you and you---terribly realistic, and then this gruesome series of Ethiopian tribal ceremonies all centering about totems, purifying rituals, and most terrible; perhaps over all was the epigraph of Augustine's I read yesterday---"Verily some have become eunuchs for Thy sake." God, it's terrible; the daily world I can wrest, amid great hurt and void, more and more to my will, but I get to dread the night so; before supper I can feel it coming on me, and I get cloyed at supper and don't want to eat, and rush out into the dark, and walk blindly; and then read, putting off bed and putting it off; and then those damn nightmares.

I will, actually, be glad when classes begin; it will give me a rooted sense of obligation which I need; of speaking with my tutors or dons and on a level in which this howling loss I feel can not yell out; but it gets even and rides me to foam and gnashing of teeth all night.

Yesterday, right after lunch, I took my sketch-paper and strode out to the Granchester Meadows where I sat in the long green grass amid cow dung and drew two cows; my first cows. They sat obligingly while I drew the first, couchant, its head very cowish, but its body, more like a horsehair sofa, very flat and unmodeled; then, suddenly, they all got hungry and got up in a drove; I think they were bulls; they seemed to have no udders. So I forged ahead, sat down on the river brink, and did a quick sketch of one grazing, or, rather, of several put into one, as they all moved continually, so the side muscles are all wrong, but most decorative; I got a kind of peace from the cows; what curious broody looks they gave me; what marvelous colossal shits and pissings. I shall go back soon; I shall do a volume of cow-drawings.

Various people biking past or strolling to Granchester stared at me, way out there, drawing the cows; it is so strange, this feeling of abnormality I get away from you---like your experience with police and little girls; I feel, in my singular passions and furies, that I become a gargoyle, and that people will point. One thing, I certainly prefer being alone; I shun people like poison; I simply don't want them; I sit and answer the countless questions of the new girls at table; I find myself being funny and making them laugh with descriptions of people & events, and wonder that I can operate so mechanically, with such little feeling, still retaining the habits of a sane person, without being discovered. There are very dear girls here; sweet, pretty, serious; but I feel like some eon-old matriarch who has been through ice age and 40-day flood; they chirp like new-hatched sparrows. They know I write---the Fulbright commission saw they knew that; I am always rather amazed that, according to Janeen, the commission knows me so well; they must have spied; also, they know I am engaged. Jess endeared herself incredibly to me by asking about what you wrote; "What does your Ted write?" she said. I told her briefly, restraining myself only with great effort from imparting my apocalyptic vision of your blazing, radiant future in which all the Wasters and Spenders of this world stand confounded.

You will perish laughing: I was glancing through the new Varsity handbook[1] last night and discovered a new society on campus: THE CAMBRIDGE MAKERS![2] O love, guess what, guess founded by whom! Yes, sweet Leftover is providing, hush-hush, the Creative Sounding Board for "secret writers",[3] for those shy undiscovered ones who can get doctored, who can get their plaints heard; master-surgeons will be invited to speak from time to time; you can be a member through submitting

1–Tony Reeve, ed., *Varsity Handbook, 1956–1957*, 10th edn (Cambridge: Varsity Publications, 1956). Anthony Wallace Alan Reeve; B.A. 1957, history, St John's College, Cambridge.

2–The description of the Cambridge Makers in *Varsity* reads, 'Founded as an essentially small and informal group of Cambridge writers who meet and read and discuss any form of creative writing produced by its members, its aim is partly to provide detailed technical criticism and partly to bring individual writers together. From time to time established writers will be invited to talk to the group. Membership is open to all members of the university on the basis of Mss. or published work submitted. Those interested should contact Christopher Levenson (Downing)' (85).

3–SP quotes from the previous page in *Varsity Handbook*: 'The most hopeful development in this direction is the founding of the Cambridge Makers, who, while attached to no one magazine have the editorial support of *Chequer*, *Delta* and *Granta*, and will incidentally provide a sounding-board for Cambridge magazines . . . If it is to succeed in this, "secret writers" must stop thinking in terms of "rackets" and "cliques" and come forward' (84).

an ms. or (o holy of holies) published work; the impeccable infallible stainless Mr. Levenson will judge whether one shall "sell much of such work". God, how free I feel, leaping such lisping mispronouncings and having direct commerce with the best editors in the world---America, America, God Shed His Grace On Thee.

I brought, from my walk yesterday, a purple thistle and a dandelion cluster home with me, and drew them both in great and loving detail; I also did a rather bad drawing of a teapot and some chestnuts, but will improve with practice; it gives me such a sense of peace to draw; more than prayer, walks, anything. I can close myself completely in the line, lose myself in it; shall I tell you my latest ambition? It is to make a sheaf of detailed stylized small drawings of plants, mail-boxes, little scenes, and send them to the New Yorker which is full of these black-and-white things---if I could establish a style, which would be a kind of child-like simplifying of each object into design, peasantish decorative motifs, perhaps I could become one of the little people who draws a rose here, a snowflake there, to stick in the middle of a story to break the continuous mat of print; they print everything from wastebaskets to city-street scenes.

It is as if, by concentrating on the "inscape", as Hopkins says,[1] of leaf and plant and animal, I can know the world a new and special way; and make up my own versions of it. I must do some in London and of Cambridge scenes, and perhaps the NY would take them for their British letters from damn-her-hide Mollie-Panter-Downes. O Panter Panter.

I hate Sundays – no mail. How I miss your written voice – read Sartre's thin simple book on existentialism[2] – That's what I am; damn good little book – please say I can come to London Friday to Sunday & be with you come Carne-Ross or no C-R.

my love & more love
sylvia

A Monday Morning P.S.

Dearest darling Teddy . . .

How proud I am How proud I am---the Carne-Ross acceptance seems the loveliest thing yet; I read your letter[3] over breakfast (I have gone into a strange decline over eating---just aren't hungry; the food here doesn't lure me to gorge much, either)---and fought and conquered a huge urge to rudely interrupt Miss Abbott & sweet numberous Co.'S discussion

1–A reference to the journals of Gerard Manley Hopkins.
2–Jean-Paul Sartre, *Existentialism and Humanism* (1946).
3–The date assigned to this letter in the *Letters of Ted Hughes*, [9 or 10 October 1956], is incorrect. The date should be 6 October 1956.

about gowns and bicycle numbers, leap up in the center of the table and shout: MY HUSBAND IS GOING TO READ OVER THE BBC! With appropriate whoopdedos. I AM SO PROUD. I think it will make applying for a teaching job infinitely easier; SO: don't tell them definitely your going to Spain when, but WAIT, cast about for future readings even if you must stay here a month---this is more important to your career (and, probably, finances,) than Spain ever thought of being. Ask shyly about your own poems; whatever day you are giving the reading, write ahead and ☆ let me come. I refuse to sit here while you are recording Yeats. I have a week of extra nights at the beginning of this term, and I can thus come to London a bit while being able to leave for you wherever you are about Dec. 7. So try to get more readings. I must come every time; if it's not soon, let me come this weekend. The Fulbright can pay for these things; I am---just---beginning to fill my days with proper work; it has taken me a whole stricken week to be able to even read; I don't like this life; but I do it. Like a good girl.

What you wrote about writing stories to one's own strict taste and joy really hit home. I'm doing, really, that; you would be proud, perhaps, a little; every morning I am breakfasted by 8:30, write letters till 9, write and write till noon or one. Then parcel out the day among my howling obligations; met my Director of Studies by accident yesterday and found, to my immense relief that my Chaucer supervisor[1] is obligingly having a baby this term in good Wife-of-Bath fashion, so I won't have her till next, and thus can without panic, Read On. Dr. Krook and Philosophy (the reading here is beyond belief---must cover all British moralists, plus the literary ones, including Swift and about 15 others!). Such a wise one your little girl will be---it'll give me a rich excuse to buy Books. Thus this term I can get our Big Mss. typed (your fable book, my NY stories, and whatever else you send), draw, and get the writing under a rigid powerful schedule which will take the added Chaucer and German next term without too much of a flinch.

Yesterday I drew a good umbrella and chianti bottle, better chestnuts, bad shoes and beaujolais bottle. Soon I will go about fanatically doing exact and painstaking landscapes of grass-blades---but I bet if I covered a page of grass-blades it would sell; I keep seeing Infinity in a grain of sand.[2]

1–Middle English scholar and university professor Elizabeth Zeeman (later Salter, 1925–80). According to SP's calendar, the Zeemans lived at 7 Grange Road, Cambridge.

2–A reference to William Blake, 'Auguries of Innocence': 'To see a World in a Grain of Sand / And a Heaven in a Wild Flower / Hold Infinity in the palm of your hand'.

Read in this terrific Modern Abnormal Psychology[1] book last night (mine) about Schizophrenia---marvelous case-histories, lucidly written; collection of essays by psychiatrists; about manic-depressive geniuses (Beethoven---what do you think of Romain Rolland's "Beethoven the Creator"[2]---referred to; Dickens, Tolstoi & others; also one on hypnotism which I begin today---excellent bibliographies). Finished a rather good 8-page NY story about the dreamless woman[3] yesterday; strange how competent I get to feel with each new story, even if the story, as such, mightn't sell – I begin "The Invisible Man" today[4] – write o write when I can come to London – for two days?? –

with love, your admiring
SYLVIA

TO *Aurelia Schober Plath*

Monday 8 October 1956 — TLS (aerogramme), Indiana University

Monday morn, Oct. 8

Dearest of mothers . . .

Loved your letter this morning; love all your letters; so much to say. First good news: the erudite 3rd program of the BBC has accepted Ted's program of Yeats reading and will make a recording! I am just exploding with pride; it was all I could do not to leap up at breakfast today and shout: MY HUSBAND IS A GENIUS AND WILL READ YEATS ON THE BBC! As soon as he finds the date they want him to make the recording, he'll let me know and we'll meet in London; we hope more readings may come out of this. It means Ted has a certified enunciation & should be a big help in getting a teaching job, don't you think? I'm praying for Amherst, but will wait out this month or so before applying, to see what is published. Will also write to ME Chase for advice in applying procedures. Do tell Mrs. Prouty about my 6 poems accepted by Poetry (Chicago)---will let you know when they're coming out, so you can buy me a few copies---should really shoot up my poetic reputation; all written for my dear Ted.

1–William Henry Mikesell, ed., *Modern Abnormal Psychology* (New York: Philosophical Library, 1950). SP's copy sold at auction in 1982.

2–Romain Rolland, *Beethoven the Creator* (New York: Harper & Brothers, 1929).

3–Sylvia Plath, 'The Wishing Box'.

4–Incomplete drafts of 'The Invisible Man' are held by Emory University (pp. 2–8) and Smith College (p. 15).

I can't help but think it would be most discreet to dedicate my novel to Mrs. P. and my poems to Ted; they are mostly all violent love-and-praise poems and all for my darling Ted.

Have been back here exactly a week and am going through the most terrible state, but stoically, and will somehow manage---it is the longest I have ever been away from Ted and somehow, in the course of this working and vital summer, we have mystically become one; I can appreciate the legend of Eve coming from Adam's rib as I never did before; the damn story's true! That's where I belong. Away from Ted, I feel as if I were living with one eyelash of myself only; it is really agony; we <u>are</u> different from most couples; for we share our selves perhaps more intensely at every moment (every thing I do with and for Ted has a celestial radiance, be it only ironing or cooking, and this <u>increases</u> with custom, instead of growing less) and, perhaps most important, our writing is founded in the inspiration of the other, and grows by the proper, inimitable criticism of the other, and publications are made with joy of the other; what wife shares her husband's dearest career as I do? except maybe Marie Curie? Actually, I never could stand Ted to have a nine to five job because I love being with him and working in his presence so much; this summer has knit us in rock; our faith and love will astonish the vain fickle world yet. I hope you will forgive me for blasting off about this, but you must understand, as you have only Warren to talk to, that I have only you. I am living like a nun, sequestered completely in my study (it took me a whole week to be able to read: am reading Paul's Epistles and Augustine for philosophy; also Chaucer; bless Chaucer). Writing every morning, all morning. Will type Ted's children's book MS. this month. It is a gift of God, or Fortuna, but Ted and I can write best and fullest in the joy and love of each other's happiness; I need no sorrow to write; I have had and no doubt will have enough; my poems and stories I want to be the strongest female paean yet for the creative forces of nature, the joy of being a loved and loving woman; that is my song. I believe it is destructive to try to be an abstractionist man-imitator, or a bitter sarcastic Dorothy Parker or Teasdale. Ted and I are both recluses; we want to work and read and raise a big family (he admires the Aldrich clan as much as I do) and stay out of NY circles and ego-flattering fan parties; Ve Vant to be Alone.

Whew! Now about practicalia: am delighted that you haven't told Bill Rice; I was worried about him---somehow I can never quite completely trust him, there's a touch of almost garrulous sensationalism there; also, he'll probably feel different himself about the ceremony if he thinks we're not married; so we'll willingly go through all extra inconveniences. We will deserve this wedding as few people have! Did you get the Atlantic check??? Have written Fulbright to beg for early sailing; must settle with Newnham too. will let you know the minute I hear. Have paid huge dentist bill for dear Ted (£22) with note thanking man for saving the most important mouth in the world; also paid the huge clothing bill at tailor's (£38) for Ted's new suit (charcoal gray) and brown & black tweed sports jacket so he can go to London in style; he is so happy with these things; I love that dear boy so and would lay down my life for him. He hasn't lived in anything except rags for so long.

About Mrs. Cantor---by all means, with this situation come up, DON'T use her house for reception; say it wouldn't be big enough as I want everybody at the wedding to come to the reception. Why not invite Joan over for dinner during Thanksgiving vacation---for a homey evening; doesn't Warren usually bring friends home then? my heart bleeds for them; if only you could tell her how unpopular I was, etc. And Look At Me Now. But don't take any of their hospitality you think isn't just given in itself; I must say, I do not think they, or anyone, has the right to other people's lives, just because they choose to lavish hospitality, money, or food on them; That should be done out of love with no thought of return . . . there, your little moralizing daughter will close for now – do investigate the Wellesley College place for reception –

love & more love to you & dear Warrie –

your own sivvy

<on the return address side of letter>

P.S. Got Terrific lovely letter from Peter Davison in his new influential position as Associate Editor of the Atlantic Press: he is very interested in Ted & me; wants me to send Ted's children's fables to their small but receptive children's dept; wants me to enter their novel contest – probably in 1958; will read all manuscripts gladly; what a wonderful help & friend he can be; he looked up Ted's poems still at the Monthly offices; says no decision has yet been made, but they are definitely interested & Ed. Weeks will see them soon – cross your fingers –

xx

s.

TO *Ted Hughes*

Tuesday 9 October 1956 TLS, family owned

Tuesday morning

O my darling Teddy . . .

How I live for your letters; such queer things are happening to me; I feel that in myself I am observing the progress of a deadly disease never before recorded: when I listen to the other girls casually talking about their fiancés, going out in a platonic way with lots of boys anyhow, etc., I wonder if I am of such a different species. I can't stand anyone; especially men; I walk out in town when I have to for fruit and cheese with a glowering scowl; I talk only to cows and swans; yesterday in a lovely wet mist I walked to market and passed several nasty fellows from the ADC and Varsity; they stared, with various grimaces of recognition; I snubbed, feeling very much like vomiting on them all; I do not think I will go out for Varsity at all this year, somehow. I have got this queer untouchable pride; I think if anything ever happened to you, I would really kill myself; I count on fingers: it is eight months till the 9th of June which I hold in front of me like some shining grail: I shall never leave your side a day in my life after exams.

Yesterday, in my fond delusion, I thought was going better; yes, I was wicked and wrote all day instead of studying, but felt happy that I could work on anything at all. I finished the 8-page story about the dreamless woman ("The Wishing-Box"), a kind of story on the same subject as my Shrike-poem; I must say that I have a growing feeling, perhaps also delusive, of a new prowess in knowing what I want to say and, miraculously, getting closer to saying it than ever I have before.

But, alas, away from you my own judgments are all out of kilter, or to cock, and I can't tell if I've been typing over and over on the same line immortal folderol or what; these new stories have got a kind of humorous objectivity I've never gotten before, I think, though; I do have hopes, such hopes, for the New Yorker's liking them: when I finished the new one I also began yesterday---the one about the invisible man, I shall send "Remember The Stick Man" (20pp.)[1] "The Wishing-Box"(8p.), "All the Dead Dears"(10pp.) and the "Invisible Man"(?pp. but short) off in a batch; about 50 pages of prose to knock their eyes in. I feel incredulous when I read the previous 50 pages I wrote---the three stories now at Mlle. They seem to me now incredibly dull. I am excited about these new short

1–An incomplete draft, p. 11 only, is held by Emory University.

packed ones; you must have a look (I'll bring them and my little drawings to London Friday---god, can I live that long!) and be wise. Your words[1] on my poems are so right, as ever; you know.

In the dreamless woman story, her husband is a complete escapist who accepts his vivid dreams as reality; she reviews her own private sordid and sparse dream-life, gets worried about her powers of imagination (also its like the Dryad poem) and goes from bad to worse, trying to fill her mind by reading (finally can't make out words), then by movies, then TV combined with sherry, finally (being totally sleepless) commits suicide by an overdose of sleeping pills; her day-dreaming husband comes home (having lulled himself with a particularly elaborate dream on the train) and finds her dressed for a fancy ball, dead, with a beatific smile on her face. All in 8 pages. I shamelessly plagiarized some of your magnificent dreams---notably the fox and pike and American poets? Are you angry? It's actually a very humorous terrible little story.

It is amazing how the "Invisible Man" story has my love now I am in the midst of it; I see that I best like doing completely realistic detailed descriptions of psychological states, giving them symbolic form; kind of "psychological fables for our time": this guy, Oswald McQuail, is invisible to himself, but to no one else---his shadows and reflections appear properly, etc. He goes invisible (to his shock) at the peak of a very successful all-round college career; is liked by everyone---in short, is the versatile American dream-guy, with no rough edges, just beautifully all-round. Now his own identity, obviously, must depend on the verdicts of those around him; hence his sudden invisibility to himself---it is as if he must seek his own true image, the proof of his corporeal existence, in the eyes and reflections about him, which give himself back to himself with varying degrees of distortion. How to get out of this is the problem---he is a happy family man, successful in the law office---I think I will have his most promising eldest son (following in father's footsteps) become invisible at college, but, of a more artistic nature, commit suicide by drowning. That Narcississtic leap. It must be funny, but terribly serious. Now Teddy, I want you to help me: think how it would be if you were invisible yourself---you could see your clothes, of course, but wouldn't have the sense of looking down your nose or up at your hair, and your hands would be missing; bathing would be a struggle, because of only the suit being present; undressing before your wife always a risk (until the

1–See *Letters of Ted Hughes*, TH to SP, [9 or 10 October 1956]. The original is dated [8 October 1956]; held by Lilly Library.

lights were out); you feel exactly the same; you appear in mirrors, so can shave, dress, etc., just as before; you can see yourself in others eyes; what I want is for you to check this thing when I'm done to see if I've made the most of reflecting mediums etc.--go around looking for your shadow or reflection in everything at home and help me add to my list, describing distortions in each: I can't help but think the story has great possibilities; it won't be over 10 pages---my new length. After I get this story done, and the 150 odd pages I have to type typed (between us, we have written colossal amounts!), I shall start on your terrific plots am terrifically drawn to this new recluse-woman & murderer one – ![1] (for women's magazines and Money) and my novel; the Idea Of Novel scares me. I must pick up several, see how simply they begin. I will have no idea of what tone I want until I get the whole first draft done. I'll try to put everything in, and then sleek it to a silvery greyhound of a thing. Don't let it scare me: it's really only 25 stories of 10 pages each, I keep telling myself; or 10 stories of 25 pages each; with the same daft girl doing different daft things.

I love you I love you I love you. At breakfast I wrap myself up in your letters; Jane and Isabel are back and I am glad; someone to be ancient with; the responsibility of those baby-dolls is at last forever gone; I shall get the reputation among them for a queer unsociable recluse who does nothing but type from morning to night; I am, at least, and this should shut you up about clever knaves, utterly incapable and undesirous of seeking to assuage my hideous loneliness in other people: other people only serve to sicken me further of the general impotence and meanness and laziness of the human race. I work; you work; we work. I have no desire, above my typewriter and my cows, to do anything except work for you, slave for you, make myself an always richening woman for you; and that is that. Queer, but loneliness serves only to shut me up more, this wrenched horror of being from you; I am more miserable among people than alone.

Last night was the worst; I was so pleased, as I said, that I had finished one little story and begun another & then my misery hit me and dashed all this sense of industry: I read till midnight and then, with that wide-eyed wakeful tiredness, went to bed; owls hooed and hooted in some witchy congregation outside my window; I tossed, tossed, dry-eyed, aching, with a terrible feeling that I needed to hit myself on the head with a hammer to knock myself out; my body seemed incredibly thistledowny and light, as if I needed weight after weight to hold it down from flying up; at two a.m.

1–SP added this by hand in the margin.

I had a sudden wild craving for ten buttered crackers with cheese and a glass of sherry; I leapt up, buttered myself ten crackers, with cheese, and poured a glass of sherry; I drink a glass a day now; it is my one luxury; it will stay one glass; unlike my dreamless woman; but she, poor thing, is certainly an aspect of one of my selves now, god rest her soul. I have a terror that I will not sleep until you lay me to sleep again. Please, please tell me the time I should arrive in London Friday???

I shall get an exeat for Friday and Saturday even if you only told me Friday; please stay; two nights. Tell me, roughly, what time you can meet me at the station, and I'll look up a train and say which station; my god, I have never spent such an intolerable numbed two weeks. Two---it is still only one; my god, I hope Carne-Ross will make you come to London every weekend to read; how well I could live if I could look forward to each weekend. Dreamer I am. Loved your Willie Crib poem;[1] you must explain the fairy & nut one to me. Think Willie should be in your book, like Auden's ballads on virgin-cancer,[2] etc. Write me about what time Friday – I love you more than the whole gibbering world which owes its existence & worth – if it has any – to your being in it –

your loving wife
sylvia

TO *Ted Hughes*

Wednesday 10 October 1956 TLS, family owned

Wednesday morning
October 10

O dear darling Teddy-one . . .

The eyes and ears of the world are upon me: just got an exeat for Friday and Saturday night, lied straight in the clouded lapis lazuli eyes of my tutor ("I'm having a reunion with a girlfriend of mine from Oxford on a fellowship"---she really does exist, is there, Jane reports, on her Marshall, but I haven't heard a word from her, probably won't; I am supposedly staying in the YW on Great Russell street but left a loophole by saying Sue might get a place at a friend's apartment. I feel cold and unscrupulous as a cobra. Mrs. Milne, when I told her I'd be gone, a few moments ago,

1–See TH to SP, [6–8 October 1956]; held by Lilly Library. The first line reads, 'Very pleased with himself was littke [*sic*] Willie Crib'.

2–W. H. Auden, 'Miss Gee', *Another Time* (London: Faber & Faber, 1940).

coyly and sillily pulled my scarf---whereupon I almost bashed her one at her familiarity, touching the hem of my most untouchable garments---and giggled "And what would you be doing in London?" I gave her a basilisk glare; being had by my husband, what else?) Now I sit after one faculty appointment, before another, feeling like hell.

O Teddy, I am so sick; literally sick to my stomach. Why do I have this terrible revulsion at the words and gestures of everybody who is not you? While listening to my Director of Studies, Miss Burton, meander on about classes, papers, etc. for our Part II group, I held my hand over my mouth and froze; I could very horribly hear myself screaming at all the prim scholarly little British bitches, knocking over desks, and strangling as many as I could get my hands on; God I was glad I'm taking part II in two years when I heard their crammed schedules---no time to brood-muse-meditate or do anything but grind it out. I'll have Dr. Krook and moralists this term (I'm going to try and get her to continue next term, too); I'll call this woman up about German reading, which will be a help, & get started there. Next term is Chaucer, although we have a meeting with the Pregnant Woman this afternoon. I am, to my horror, assigned to a Practical Crit. class (as is everyone) with a fat vampirish monster Miss Pitt[1] whom I'd thought to escape; I have a morbid desire to cut open her fat white flesh each time I see her and see if its onion juice or what that keeps her going; I shall try, desperately, to get out of it by pleading I have to do the reading in order to criticise and wouldn't it be Better Miss Burton if I used that precious hour to read in? I can just hear her soft snaky voice: "Do both."

Teddy Teddy Teddy: I have the feeling that if only I see you, just curl up warmly with you, all this tension, the gorging of fury which I eat again and again until it crams my throat, all this will flow gently away and there will be peace peace peace. You must scold me, beat me, help me. This gift of creative passion I've somehow been blessed with is now ironically turning in on itself and blighting me; away from you, it is as if my hair were shorn, my tongue cut out, and my whole body reduced to some cold ungainly clay that plods about not knowing what the hell it was made for. You say your bus Friday gets in at seven. Well I'll take a train getting me into <u>King's Cross at 7:35</u>. Meet me there? If there's a waiting room, I'll go to it; the day after tomorrow; I can't conceptualize it; I am dying some

1–English scholar Valerie Joan Pitt (1925–99); lecturer in English and Fellow of Newnham College, 1952–8.

death. I'll stay till Sunday; there's a Braque exhibit at the Tate[1] I think; I am quite mad.

Later: managed to persuade Miss Burton to postpone the Practical Crit. till next term by telling her I would be no addition to any class until I'd finished my rigorous private reading program covering the periods I know nothing of; it's true, too, unlike most of the things I've been telling official people lately; I find, alarmingly, that I am just the kind of person who can lie successfully: I have a direct honest look; I am plausive as the devil with my reasons; my actress-side is sensitive to mood and situation and, without calculation on my part, responds as the occasion demands. The secret of perfect lying is to believe to your heart and guts that you are right and that they are all silly-rule-mongers and deserve no confidence or obedience; I am so rock-firm in my conscience about our marriage that I feel, of course, no guilt; only a cold pragmatic intellectual sequence of reasoning how I can best keep them blind to my marriage and my living with my husband every second I can. I must be always prepared, by some quirk or other, to be discovered; and be prepared to quell them nobly.

Yesterday afternoon it was miraculous and sunny; I went on a long solitary walk along the Backs, stared at the incredible color and splendor of Clare gardens; sat down under the tent of a Clare willow and wrote a description[2] of the gardens and ducks; squelched coolly and with great efficiency two fresh little first year boys who hung about; walked over to green promontory by Mill Bridge braving the raised-wing attack and hiss of two terrifyingly militant swans, and did the outlines of a rather potential drawing of the Anchor & Boat House which I shall fill in on the next good day. ("Nice to see you again," the British girl says to someone outside my door; "Nice to see you." the someone replies.) Oh, God, why is everybody so banal? The two new British girls[3] in the house take over the breakfast table conversation (there never was any before they came) with all the professional suavity of a hired hostess: "Yes, our mornings are misty, don't you think?" Gone are the lax easy blissfully grumpy breakfasts of last year, broken only by Jane or me or Margaret guffawing over letter

1–G. Braque: An exhibition of paintings arranged by the Arts Council of Great Britain in association with the Edinburgh Festival Society, Tate Gallery, 28 September–11 November 1956.

2–See Appendix 10, *The Journals of Sylvia Plath* (2000).

3–Rosemary Nesta Yale (1929–); B.A. 1957, modern languages, Newnham College, Cambridge. Grace Marjorie Allen (1927–); B.A. 1957, modern languages, Newnham College, Cambridge.

or New Yorkers. I rudely and silently read my mail; which means you; not one editorial correspondence yet---rejection or acceptance. To satisfy my continual checkings, I made a list of what we both have out on what dates: there is much:

May 22:	Atlantic: your poems.
Sept 3:	London Magazine: your poems.
Sept 6:	CS Monitor: my Benidorm article & drawings.
Sept 17:	New Yorker: your 3 fables.
	Mademoiselle: my 3 stories.
Sept 29:	Nation & Poetry: your poems.
Oct. 3:	Atlantic & Nation: my poems.

As of this month, the Atlantic press will have your book and the New Yorker my 4 stories; I am in the middle of the invisible man. I practice going around feeling invisible.

I must write my tutors for appointments. I have now only two classes I'll go to: Krook and Holloway,[1] from 9 to 11 Tuesday. And two supervisions. Will read Chaucer, French and all Oxford books of poetry on my own. Can't wait to try Women's Magazine stories. The murderer one is great; I'd love to try a New Yorker version of this hysterical couple one, with the crying child; (two helicopters just burred by very low; like fish spinning tops in the celestial sea).

I really think your new version of "Secret Phaetons" is fine; I like it very very much; I also, and am very serious, thought the leprechaun parody possible; I know you were being funny, but the idea is small and nice; why don't you, as a finger-limbering exercise, try several of these innocent poems, (this could be condensed) that meet a certain simple criterion for light amusement, and we'll send them to the New Yorker; I wish you'd revise the Pecos Bill[2] one; make them short and sweet and we'll probably earn fantastic amounts of money. Bring whatever you've done on the TV play to London; I'll bring Chaucer & the little I've oozed out.

Teddy, I feel I'm walking in my grave cerements. My flesh is colder than wet sod. Do you know that you have the most delicious quirked lovely mouth and your eyes crink up and you are all warm and smooth and elegantly muscled and long-striding and my god I go mad when I let myself think of you; the thinking assaults me and I either cry or pound my

1–Poet and professor John Holloway (1920–99); fellow and lecturer of Queens' College, Cambridge.

2–A reference to the American cowboy Pecos Bill.

head, or go out on a long blind wild walk or pretend pretend you are there and talk out loud to you at night before bed I kneel on the couch in the pitch black and throw all my force and love in the direction, as nearly as I can discern, of your bed in Yorkshire. I am living until Friday in a kind of chill controlled hysteria; when I wash my hair, now, it will be for you; when I drink water, it is for you; when I get dressed it is for you. I can't believe any body ever loved like this; nobody will again. We will burn love to death all our long lives; I shall never let you have a day-long job, for I couldn't live that long without kissing and kissing your dear special particular mouth.

Last night I read a long involved Jean Stafford story[1] in the New Yorker and had one of my apocalyptic visions: someday, I will be a rather damn good woman writer. Suddenly, I feel this queer sense that, in time, I can surpass her; and Even Eudora. If I live "in-myself" this way, all the quirks and queer musings in my head can bear fruit, without being blurred and blunted by constant prosaic contacts with exterior people; this year will set me deeper than ever in the dark secret well of my own fancies, dreams and visions; living with you will save me from being suffocated with no outlet (except these interminable letters, please forgive their length & tediums) as I am now.

Do get in touch with Carne-Ross when you come to London; and promise me that the weekend before you go to Spain we may again spend together in London; I hope we can find a good unobtrusive hotel where we'll see no one we know. I'll bring my sketch-paper and maybe you'll see me through a drawing or two in medias res. It's such a protection, having you at my side. I feel really vulnerable as a Victorian maiden away from you: geese attack me, cows stampede on me; people stare until I tell them to go to hell. I keep telling myself I have more right to be here than they do; I am really a very shy person. With a kind of brazen cocky sheath like the armor of a turtle or armadillo or porcupine prickles.

Thurber's fables, I am sure, are the work of senility; the singsong rhyming and painful punning and moralizing is strangely disquieting to me. I love you and think and know you are the most brilliant writer and will be more and astound the green babbling world and are the only man and husband and giant walking; please write you will meet me at Kings Cross then – I love you to hell and back and to every last cell of my being & thought –

1 – Either 'A Reading Problem' cited above or 'The Mountain Day', *New Yorker*, 18 August 1956, 24–32.

love to my darling lovely ponky own ted –

your
Sylvia

TO *Aurelia Schober Plath*

Tuesday 16 October 1956 — TLS (aerogramme), Indiana University

Tuesday noon, October 16

Dearest mother . . .

It was with joy that I received your dear letter from Hartford with all the news about your active life; I'm so happy you are getting about and seeing your friends; it is amazing how necessary a car is in our vast country simply to keep up with people in the same town! I am just through with the colossal job of typing Ted's children's book manuscript: "How The Donkey Became And Other Fables" (9 fables in all, 61 pages). I spent two solid days at it (he is going to try to get a reading of some sort for it on the BBC Children's Program) and this week I send it off to Peter Davison and the Atlantic Press. It is a classic, I think; I know it almost by heart now, having listened during the writing in Spain this summer, suggested the revising, listened again, and, finally typed the whole work up in 3 copies (two carbons). The Olivetti has got constant use since purchase; in the lull of the next weeks, I'll go have the action tuned up---it's a bit sticky; can I have it done free at that place where you bought it? I want to sell my other type-writer and, for Ted & me next summer & next year, get a sturdy, table model with a type-face just like Warren's which I love. I dislike the crooked badly lettered type-face on my Corona after this neat Olivetti, and like Warren's bold squarish print. Should I advertise to sell it here, so I won't have to lug it home, or bring it home for a trade-in; that might be best. No word yet from Fulbright re sailing dates; shall I write and ask Patsy to be my maid-of-honor anyway? If her religion means she can't (will you ask Betty Aldrich about this first), I'd ask Ruthie, and 3rd choice, Marty Plumer or even Elly Friedman (I'm a bit dubious about Marty's height is all). I'll try to send Nancy and MB gifts of some sort soon, after this first packed week; I would love to have you send the brief-case to me (when you said you preferred "seasoned" leather, did you mean this briefcase was seasoned?) We need to save money, and it will help; did I tell you that along with Ted's charcoal gray suit I have made him get a lovely brown-and-black tweed jacket made (of his own choice tweed) which he wore to London last weekend and looked handsome as a Duke. He could do with another, though. I'd postpone shirts till America, when I can take proper care of them; I'll try to get him a bathrobe; what he needs very badly is a kind of leather shaving kit & I thought Warren might help you select one for him, with hairbrush, nail-file, shaving soap & brush (he uses a regular razor); how about that from both of you? He also needs luggage; but that would be too much to send; he needs just about everything; let me choose his ties, he is very particular & only likes one or two.

Our London weekend has given me a new calm & dispelled that first hectic suffocating wild depression I had away from my husband for the first time in our married life; it almost began with a nightmare: I'd arranged to have Ted meet me at King's Cross station about 7:30, but when I found he was getting in to the bus station at 7, decided to take an early train to Liverpool St. and meet him; I wrote a letter to this effect which, if he didn't receive, I figured would be all right as I'd be at the bus terminal from 6 on and would have no chance of missing him; well, I waited from 6 to 8 at the terminal and the bus he was supposed to take came, and he wasn't on it; the bus terminal inspectors were all callous cretins, and the most I could get out of them was that all busses were in, and no accidents reported; I was really frantic, unable to understand why Ted wasn't on one of them; he'd bought reservations; so, in a fury of tears, I fell sobbing into a taxi & for 20 minutes begged him to hurry to King's Cross to see if by some miracle Ted might be there; I was sick, not knowing what to do but yell raving through the streets of London; well, to shorten the trauma, I walked into King's Cross into Ted's arms---he'd made the bus driver drop him off early so he could get to me sooner and had been worried about my not arriving on the train, not having got my later letter. He looked like the most beautiful dear person in the world; everything began to shine, and the taxi driver sprouted wings, and all was fine. For two blessed days we wandered about together, sitting in parks, browsing in book shops, reading aloud, eating fruit, and just basking in each other's presence; for the first time, now, I feel I can work and concentrate and manage this stoic year. Ted makes his BBC recording on Oct. 24, so I'll manage to get down on the 27th to celebrate my birthday with him, one more reunion before he goes off to Spain; I have never dreamed that love could be so incredibly transforming; I am no longer, miraculously, a self-concerned individual, but part of a miniature cosmos all of which revolves around my dear darling Ted; have written several of my best short stories this week, which he criticized in London; my best: "The Invisible Man", I have great hopes for---about this charming extroverted versatile chap who is invisible to himself alone and no one else, & what happens. Maybe it'll be a classic too, to add to Peter Schlemiel[1] & Hoffmann's mirror-imageless man;[2] I can't wait to send it off. Love your letters---only 8 months till we're Home---bless Warren for me; love to Grampy---

your own
sivvy

TO *Ted Hughes*

Tuesday 16 October 1956 TLS, family owned

Tuesday noon: October 16

Dearest Teddy . . .

The Great Calm has descended; I just got back from mailing your copy of "How the Donkey Became And Other Fables" (registered) to Peter Redgrove; a letter enclosed with it tells all corrections and questions I have about it. It is strange, but now, after this weekend of savouring and plunging deep deep into the presence of you, I feel a new peace, a new calm, and that hectic stifled desperation is gone; I am obviously taking my place among the Stoic Orders. I feel now that I am walking on a place totally different and apart from anyone else, and the presence of the mobs and yattering misses around me no longer distracts and obsesses; for the first time, deep in me (and not just pasted on top of a seething mass of circumstance by a wishful intellect) I know I can do this year; and do it with an intensity and concentration that will make you proud of me. Being vulnerable and fallible, I suppose, I may have lapses into loneliness from your being away, where my will urges me to pack up and find you; but my reason, or whatever induces this strange wonderful inner calm and deep, introverted love, will keep me together.

Enough; or I shall be talking only to myself; I could do your great and awe-inspiring ms. only because dear lovely Dr. Krook put my supervision on Thursday at 11 (for which I must yet read parts of the "City of God"[3] and write, alas, and already, a paper;[4] today and tomorrow I have,

1–Adelbert von Chamisso, *Peter Schlemihls wundersame Geschichte* (1814).

2–E. T. A. Hoffmann; wrote Schlemihl into his 1815 story 'Die Abenteuer der Silvester-Nacht'.

3–Saint Augustine,*The City of God* (London: J. M. Dent, 1950); SP's copy held by Smith College.

4–Sylvia Plath, 'Some Observations on The City Of God'; held by Lilly Library.

though). Went to lecture today; she is incredibly lucid; I would like to be her disciple this year; shall go to all her lectures: they are clear and cadenced as a piece of exquisite music; I can grow by her. Holloway was very disappointing a tall, pale, quick-eyed dark-haired chap with horn-rimmed spectacles and a fluid meandering talk which implies it's much more important than it is. He proposes to talk on Ideas In English Literature ("Some Major Themes") which he outlined today as Reason; Unreason; Progress; Circe's Garden; Evolution; History etc. I began to feel like rising and shouting "Fraud fraud", as Mr. Huys once cried at me (oh Danny-boy) as Holloway generously offered to allow an hour for each of these subjects. We got Reason this morning---a most spurious kind of skip-skimming with specific footnoted (book, paragraph, line) references to Antony & Cleo, Hamlet, Hooker, Milton---mere jump references to the use of the word "reason" which I found highly obvious and useless. I may give him one more chance, as I can't imagine what he would say on Circe's Garden. But if this is the kind of cotton-stuffing Cambridge pays her young genii to give, no, no. His kind of versatility (as revealed in these lectures, at least) seems only that impressive "mass knowledge" jumped over by grasshopper minds who find by picking a "theme", or rather, wringing a theme out of a conglomeration of works, they can dream up some large coherent elucidation of the world's thought in 8 hours. I become more and more reassured about my own ability to give Freshman lectures in America. A pox on surveys; I shall stick to specific texts until they know a few of my favorite men by heart, as well as their own dreams. Holloway drops specific references like crown-jewels---it's supposed to impress and convince of a richness which I simply can't find. Well, that's one lecture only a week now; I may try Lewis[1] on Chaucer background; shall see.

no teas, sherries or bothers. I like life like this; for the first time, have no conscience pangs about leading it full scale, which I always did when I depended on friends and admirers, having no one I was completely realized with. I love the plot about the party;[2] please don't apologize for drawing on my own experience---you will do best doing that, I think: showing me, in a way, what and how I can draw from my own life: like the "invisible man" might never (or at least, never so soon) have become a story if you didn't pick up the metaphor I used and suggest story. all

1–British novelist and academic C. S. Lewis (1898–1963). According to SP's calendar, she attended lectures by Lewis on 25 October and 2 November 1956.

2–TH to SP, [16 October 1956]; held by Lilly Library. The assigned date of the letter, which was excluded from *Letters of Ted Hughes*, is likely incorrect.

these plots are in my head, gestating. it is the most terrific way; each time I write, now, I'll pluck the ripest.

I like your idea for the play;[1] could be a terrific character study; also, do work on snatchcraftington. I'm sure your children's fables will find an audience (publishing) in the course of a year and it would be good to have snatchcraftington ready to offer up after your first success.

am pleased about the nimbus editor[2] asking for you: it is a beautifully set-up magazine (I, too, read auden's poems[3] and was appalled---there was such an unpleasant nastiness to them; like grinding metal; if someone would print these poems in paragraph form, I think it might embarrass hell out of the "poet", because it's atrocious prose; how can editors be so blind?) let's wait till the next batch of poems comes back (you've got them out still at the atlantic, london magazine, nation and poetry)---and make up a group from whatever rejects the others send back and mail it to nimbus. all those 4 magazines should send them back by the end of this month. if only one of my 4 stories and your children's fables would be accepted now. I get much sadder about prose return than poetry, somehow.

off and on have had the strangest dreams---as if my story about dreams in part exorcised my worry about bad dreams. sunday night, had a lovely rich one, brightly colored, about finding a patch of huge green four-leaf clovers with you and picking three (somebody must have accepted something this monday!); also sat by water, writing, looking into dazzling sea-gull crammed sky; as they landed, they became ducks, very white (that damn poem of wain's,[4] wasn't it?); anyhow, I was writing an immortal sonnet about it, correcting etc., and with the casual cocksureness of dreams, didn't bother to memorize it when I was writing, but knew it had the words "luminous vein" in it and was indeed a very luminous poem. Last night, I was sitting on a resort beach clad oddly enough in my paisley velvet jersey with matching slippers and wearing leopard pants---which had turned, I remember thinking, orange (with black spots), orange with age---I compared them to a leopard kitten playing nearby on the sand and my pants were very definitely more orange with age; I was lolled in a deck chair, talking with eva gabor and a south american princess (looking much like one of our indian girls) who showed me a map of south america and a tiny principality around where brazil should be called rigi or something where she ruled; a motor-boat all shining and

1–See TH to SP, [16 October 1956], cited above.

2–David Wright; mentioned in the [16 October 1956] letter.

3–W. H. Auden, 'The Epigoni' and 'Merax and Mullin', *Nimbus* 3 (Summer 1956), 3–4.

4–British poet and critic John Wain (1925–94).

speeding loomed over the horizon and dragged all the people swimming, water-skiing, and sail-boating in the sea up on the sand; if this keeps up, I shouldn't worry about my nights anymore. I think it shows my powers of observations must be improving. I love you, every bit of you, and kiss your damn london-gone mouth and love you – please go on writing – I love your letters –

your own
sylvia

Why not ask Carne-Ross if you can read some Crow Ransom – CR for CR?[1]

Have just sent Luke's poems off to Poetry – felt Atlantic would wait too long if they liked them – Poetry seems most quick & accepting of your genius.[2]

TO *Ted Hughes*

Wednesday 17 October 1956 TLS, family owned

Wednesday morning early
october 17

dearest love ted . . .

it is a black day: warm, humid, heavy with unshed rain; your letter[3] came, so did a large battered envelope from mademoiselle rejecting my 3 stories. I knew it would come, but some small foolhardy little part of me didn't know it for sure and was sorry and depressed. it is good, I suppose, in a queer way, for both of us to have got our first triple prose offerings back; it will make us (at least me) build up a kind of defiant high-pressure resentment and maybe fight harder; better than getting a too-easy acceptance and then relaxing and getting rejections. you see how the paltry mind tries to rationalize away its disillusion---it's all for the best, said god, as he turned out one misshapen pot after another. do cheer me up. that day in manchester certainly was infuriatingly wasted; but that is not the way to think. who knows what glories lie ahead. what mademoiselle and new yorker editors will, in years to come, be writing us coy notes begging us to send "something for Them." they will, too, if we work constantly and hard enough. that I know. we're really only scraping

1 – This sentence added by SP by hand in the left margin of the page.
2 – This sentence added by SP by hand in the left margin on the first page.
3 – Probably TH to SP, [16 October 1956]; held by Lilly Library.

off the first scum, as you said; only, only, I do not think I will feel much worse if these last 4 stories are rejected. I have only sent the "stick man" out,[1] and am saving the other 3 till it's come back and I've rewritten the "invisible man". that should sell. it honestly should. somewhere.

how I love your letters. picture me sitting at the head of the long table in whitstead dining room, immersed in reading and re-reading your words (except for one or two of the latter, I can read your writing fine; it is beautiful writing; it is the writing of a genius and a teddy-ponk), letter propped up against butter dish, eyes cutting through the charcoal smoke arising from the toaster which the 3 indian girls don't know how to use yet---"they say the burnt part is good for you," one indian observed philosophically this morning; I speak not; I had fried potatoes and bacon and buttered brown toast and two cups of coffee this morning; my favorite breakfast, to make up for the huge rejection and the subtraction of just one more dream from the batch flittering rainbows in my head.

today: to finish the parts necessary of the "city of god" and write a paper for tomorrow morning; I shall probably be compelled to write a poem in the old procrastinator's tradition. I don't like today; not at all; I felt depressed, too, last night for some reason: bought a bottle of sherry and couldn't get the cork out all day, which became a looming Thing: I realized, in time, that I couldn't run hectically downstairs in the late evening, begging someone to open the damn thing, as if I were some sort of unspeakable addict; finally, at night, I got it open piece by piece and drank a glass to wash down the more ascetic rant of augustine. I am probably the strongest fiend in this house anyway.

after my supervision tomorrow (and I think it will be good & make me feel better to get back into thinking form with dr. krook), I begain again to write 4 hours each morning; it is such a blessing, as I look ahead, to have completely spacious days.

Your dear letter came this morning along with one from mother---all aglow about next year; she's being, for the first time in her life, blessedly "social"---she even had a "date"; my god; I am proud of her. She's driving about the country (she never could drive before last year, a necessity for being able to see friends in our vast country) visiting her favorite people, going to plays, and, I gather, everybody is trying to draw her out, so she won't brood about the echoing house and my grammy's absence, which must be terrifically oppressing, after a lifetime of her living with us. She is overjoyed that Beethoven is Your Man and no doubt will be stocked

1–SP sent 'Remember the Stick Man' to the *New Yorker* on 12 October 1956.

with his lps when we come (she is much relieved it's not Hindemith or those twelve-tone scale guys; my records of them were a trial to her). Her planning about our wedding really saves her from depression; I'm so glad we can give her that. If you want to write her, the address is:

26 Elmwood Road, Wellesley, Massachusetts: USA

No future word of our mss. I am surprised. I feel they will all pile up (acceptance) around the end of the month; have large hopes. Very quiet on Cambridge front; not a single invitation or pestering; I like very much. My room is a green haven; feel like writing (will have to wait till end of week after supervision, since I threw proportion off so by these last two days on your ms.) But I feel I can bring a focus of powers to bear that I never knew I had; like I began to do on the "Invisible Man." Must write many letters to people, contests, etc.

Still, green day today; I observe all clearly now, from a deep seat way back, taking notes in my head; sat in wet still yard yesterday and drew an anemone; before bed last night, over hot milk and hair-drying, as a treat for going through the Big Typing, I began reading my "Painted Caravan"[1] book; it is my favorite book; I have the queerest love for holding it, staring at the pictures; read the introduction in which the author claims the Gypsies have incorporated all the ritualistic rites of all religions and cults in their Tarot pack (a sort of World-Book) and that the Initiate can penetrate beyond the surface denotative meaning of the symbols, through the veils, etc. to the Alone. I meditated on the Fool and the Juggler, staring at the pictures, reading and re-reading the lucid, pleasantly written descriptions of them and their significance. I shall go through the whole book slowly this way, so that I shall come upon the difficulties of setting out the Pack with a basic sense, at least, of the cards, which will flow and re-cross and blend, I think, by great concentration and much practice. I really look forward to giving this my deepest love and attention; I feel very "kin" to the cards, sort of.

This weekend with you was so fine; I feel it was best, just browsing among books and sitting open to the evening in that blue-green park;[2] you are the creative force in my world and cosmos which gives my own force direction and meaning; all I do and concentrate on now, is in the deep unalterable sense of my living in your presence which is here, although invisible. I love you and love you.

1–Basil Ivan Rákóczi, *The Painted Caravan* (The Hague: L. J. C. Boucher, 1954). According to SP's calendar, she bought *The Painted Caravan* on 13 October 1956, probably from Watkins Books at 19–21 Cecil Court, London. SP's copy held by Smith College.

2–According to SP's calendar, this was Russell Square, London.

Get all you can, judiciously, out of Carne-Ross; will send some of my poems which maybe you can leave with him next week after your reading; I don't envy you London, but milk it dry; eat steak; know how I love you; bless my Birthday <drawing of radio microphone>

my love to my own husband & Teddy-ponk –

SYLVIA

TO *Ted Hughes*

Thursday 18 October 1956[1] TLS on Newnham College letterhead, family owned

thursday afternoon 2:30
october 17

forgive this <arrow pointing to Newnham crest on letterhead> am using up old scraps in my rag & bone shop

dearest darling ted . . .

I am in my usual post-supervision thursday coma; having miraculously, as usual, completed in the small hours of 2 am or so a 13 page paper outlining the uniqueness & chief tenets of the christian gospel, contrasting their tone & assurance with platonic writing, and bringing up my questions and objections to the christian view of the origin, nature and continuance of evil; god's foreknowledge and man's free will, and the low, debased view of physical love between man and women even in "blameless wedlock."[2] for an hour and a half this morning, rain falling outside, I read this, argued, discussed, and was illuminated by my lovely dr. krook; I feel at last, as if I am not working in a vacuum. she is willing to take me all this term on the british moralists, and even the next on whatever literary moralists I choose; my reading is damn thorough, a paper every week, and my review of exams should be familiar ground.

but now though I feel free,[3] momently, of pressure (hooker & the cambridge platonists[4] for next week), I'm too tired to do anything creative; maybe I'll try a nap this afternoon; I'm going to an english-

1–Letter misdated by SP.

2–Augustine, *The City of God*.

3–'but now I feel though free' appears in the original. SP encircled 'though' and drew an arrow to move it.

4–Sylvia Plath, 'On the Elevation of Reason: Some Notes Concerning the Cambridge Platonists, Whichcote and Smith', dated 24 October 1956; held by Lilly Library.

speaking union[1] sherry to meet new overseas students and the countess of tunis late this afternoon with dina and janean; I am going to the english club tonight to hear kenneth muir[2]---they have enough good speakers coming for me to join. I am very much alone. Jenean typifies vividly all I dislike most in extrovert, surface, blithering america: sorority president, silly conventional patter all the time, enthusiastic about everything continually without the slightest vestige of reserve or discrimination. all the rest of the girls are vehement catholics; narrow, secure, and incredibly pious. I really think of dr. krook as my one woman friend, here; she is the kind of teacher I would slave to be and these next two terms should be deeply rewarding just for what I can learn of lecturing and discussion-leading from her; jane baltzell is another extrovert and her life is spent continually in company of people I find intolerably artificial, like that oswald-theater set I tried to avoid so last spring. so I walk alone. and I really am all right.

granta writes that they are printing an old story I turned in last year, "the day mr. prescott died",[3] which I believe I read to you. it seems slight to me now, but I'll probably proof-read it tomorrow and try to palm of my dream story or oswald story on them, although both are rather long. all else is quiet as death; in a week from the day after tomorrow I'll be seeing you again. dr. krook thinks it is too bad for me you aren't working in london or in nearby area: she suggests trying the american army base english schools which pay fabulous sums, something like £15 a week for only two full evenings of lecturing; they have bases everywhere. I wonder if they employ britishers; I should think they might. but spain is probably best. I would almost rather be either fully with you for a long period and fully away while I must work, than be torn when with you by knowing I must leave in a day, and torn when away by counting the days till I return. but I'll miss you terribly when you go to spain. at least, if you don't go till the end of october it will mean only 5 weeks before I am with you for 5 weeks altogether.

tomorrow I start writing in the mornings again. I will change[4] the donkey-story elephant to ant. I don't think there are any other inconsistencies beside this and I am probably over-sticky, but I read the thing as a whole; I still wish you would change the polar-bear story

1–Located above Matthew's Restaurant in Trinity Street, the English-Speaking Union brought together people of every English-speaking nation.

2–English Shakespeare scholar Kenneth Muir (1907–96).

3–Sylvia Plath, 'The Day Mr Prescott Died', *Granta*, 20 October 1956, 20–3.

4–See TH to SP, [17 October 1956]; held by Lilly Library.

elephant to some other strong useful tree-uprooting creature, though. I can see your point keeping the ear-fanning.

I am terrifically happy you got the stories to the children's program girl with such dispatch; even if they eschew familiar sweating fallible finger-burning vegetable-cooking gods, there are other fine stories in it that don't mention god; alas, of course, my favorites do: torto, whale-wort, and demon---which I think are exquisite and charming. when I send the stuff to peter, I shall ask him to take god as in marc connelly's play "green pastures"[5] which was a great success in america where god was a negro, the whole thing the negro's concept of the bible; I think god smoked a cigar. anyway, there is certainly a precedent for your familiar way of presenting god; a kind of childlike innocence of fear and trembling, making it all very concrete poetic story without I think any "danger" of overthrowing the young reader's faith in an omniscient invulnerable abstract god---but the lord alone knows what are the editorial scruples about offending Religion.

I am blithering; I am very tired. I wish I could curl up in your lap. let me know immediately if anything happens re fables & also what poems of yours carne-ross has you read. please please send me the copy of "egg-head" along with the rest when you're through, so I can make copies of them to keep on eternal file. I'll send you some of mine to leave him in time for your reading.

no news of manuscripts after the mlle rejection; we each have four things out. probably good news will all come at once. I would fly up with joy if your children's fables---any or all---get accepted by the BBC.

will write better tomorrow. am appalled at mr. redgrove's following of c-r---the latter must get ulcers every time he goes into a bar and sees the gleaming machiavellian advances of the former; also, am glad he can brag of his poems (is their any chance of their publication?) but am appalled at the taste of the praisers. I'll stick to yeats and you, thanks. I love you and love you---take care, eat steak, and I kiss and kiss your mouth and all over in crannies & nooks my dear lovely own Teddy –

your
sylvia

5–Marc Connelly, *The Green Pastures* (New York: Farrar & Rinehart, 1930).

TO *Ted Hughes*

Friday 19 October 1956 — TLS on Newnham College letterhead, family owned

friday morning
october 19

dearest love teddy . . .

you will get two letters together because of a strange missing to mail one at dinner last night because of an occurence I'll tell you that seems to me good omened, and probably what I was destined to follow up . . .

spent a miserable dull tedious afternoon before the fire in the midst of which I wrote you yesterday, unable to read or write, being very tired; shall not let lateness happen again; I got last year's late hour from 4 am to 2 am; next week shall be 12, next 10pm etc. I can't afford to waste afternoons. anyhow, in spite of a headache, I walked out into the sultry wet with jabbering janean & went for the first time to the english speaking union which was an experience in itself.

that old house on trinity street, right, with white plaster & dark beams, very fine inner room, same way; it was a reception, I found out, for the new americans; god knows how I got invited, being an old one. anyway, I drank sherry, devoured canapes, and conversed with various vintage toothy englishwomen; suddenly hundreds of strange americans converged on me, calling me, disquietingly enough, by my name, and begging didn't I remember them. I managed my usual story of being a cretin about remembering names and places, so they told: one little sweet quiet girl was from smith and married to a husband here on a marshall grant; a striking handsome couple[1]---big tall dark though sort of open-faced shiny boy and his stalwart vivid red-haired wife reminded me I'd been at their wedding (at which, I remembered, I distinguished myself by drinking at least several gallons of champagne); yet another was a young minister, friend of a married couple I know at the new york theological seminary; still another was the most mixed-up little girl I've ever seen with big batting eyelashes whose parents have been sending her around, for about the last 10 years from one university to another which she's never

1–Julia 'Judy' Gamble Kahrl and Stanley J. Kahrl. Judy Kahrl (1934–); B.A. 1955, English literature and history, Radcliffe College. Stanley J. Kahrl (1931–89); B.A. 1953, English, Harvard College; B.A. English, 1958, St Catharine's College, Cambridge. Kahrl served on the USS *Perry* with Gordon Lameyer. Lameyer and SP attended the Gamble–Kahrl wedding on 20 June 1954 in Milton, Mass. Stan Kahrl studied at Cambridge on the GI Bill, not a Marshall scholarship.

finished; she, I found to my dismay, was the girl who sent the letter of elephants, giraffes and black natives carrying mailboxes, which I'd never bothered to answer; she is breathily interested in liturgical art . . . .

well, I felt like mothercary; they clucked, crowded, and I made them laugh, and all the time some machiavellian little part of me was sitting in a corner scribbling notes and laughing and laughing; it is so strange now, to me---my social self is no longer all of me thrown out on a long leash and sniffing about enthusiastically---it is seated way deep down and doesn't give itself or commit itself, but watches and notes, and manages this other part which talks and gestures & so on . . .

for some reason, now, I seem to attract married couples. I was invited to dinner after this affair by the queerish british couple[1] yet---a little oddly shaped man with staring gog eyes thinning hair, on the british council who knew louis macneice in greece, has had a book of criticism published[2] by geoffrey cumberledge or some such spelling, and a book of 100 poems[3] coming out this month, and has appeared in the london magazine[4] & writes for time etc. all of which he modestly informed me immediately upon my introduction to him & his strange big soft towering wife who looks like his mother and wears no ring and has graying hair. we all, or rather the little man & I, quoted enough lines in chorus of crowe ransom, wallace stevens, etc. etc. to realize we had common talking ground, while the wife bent, smiled, crooned, and made herself generally pleasant. they promised to give me a list of all the magazines & addresses in england, information about a poetry book contest, and a cheese souflee served up by their "german girl" if I came home to dinner with them . . .

it was already too late for all, so I went. I have never heard such talk: they knew, with the accuracy of history, the marital affairs of spender, macneice, kathleen raine, hugh sykes-davis[5] (whom I met at johns last year) and natasha and hedley[6] (louise macneice's wife) and auden and erica mann.[7] I never heard such a fascinating and disgusting story: they are all, linked by some first, second or third wife and have simply traded off wives

1–English writer John Press (1920–2007) and Janet Crompton Press (1920–2009).

2–John Press, *The Fire and the Fountain* (London: Geoffrey Cumberlege, 1955).

3–John Press, *Uncertainties, and Other Poems* (London: Oxford University Press, 1956).

4–John Press, 'Farewell', *London Magazine* 3 (April 1956), 20; and John Press, untitled review of *The Chatto Book of Modern Poetry, 1915–1955*, *New Lines: An Anthology*, and *New Poems 1956*, *London Magazine* 3, October 1956, 71–7.

5–English poet Hugh Sykes Davies (1909–84).

6–English singer and actress Hedli Anderson (1907–90), second wife (1942–60) of the poet Louis MacNeice (1907–63).

7–Erika Hedwig Mann (1905–69); wife of W. H. Auden, 1935–69.

in the most incredible and burlesque fashion; now, teddy, I'm sure this would make a terrific play---very dramatic, say three of the young poets in the 30's and, over the years (much could have happened previously and come out in the story---like have the first or second round of marriages already happened) because of intellectual novelty, fashion, etc. have them trade about & divorce, and new women come on. this could be a terrific thing, I think---say, a new young innocent woman marries, in innocence, one of the old warhorse poets, is invited to dinner by his first or second wife and all the others, etc. am I giving you plots? but it's rich . . .

Spender whose first wife[1] ran away with someone of the others as the other's 2nd or 3rd, married a russian pianist Natasha by whom he now has offspring; louis macneice whose wife[2] also ran away or something, married this hedley for whom auden wrote many cabaret songs; hedley is not liked by many in the london circle because at the anniversary of dylan thomas's death when they all got together to read his poems---macneice was reading some, she insisted on getting up and singing something; the london wives think she wants to be a prima donna. oh, god, how I chortled inside and begged them to go on. roy campbell,[3] evidently, is the only virile, honest man going.

anyway, this couple (mr. and mr. john press) had some (2) children upstairs, the souflee and dark bread was good; I entertained them with stories of american poets and editors, admired the lyric mr. press had in the london magazine.

I told them about you, and they were very interested. they seemed quite sympathetic, in spite of a queer over-niceness about most things. over indulgent, I mean, not over-precise.

well, now, this is the thing: I sat on the white fur greek rug on the couch, admired the stylized black white and red print covers, and took down the address of this contest which, without my going to the sherry & to their dinner, I never would have run across in time; so I am sure your book will win. I'll write the borestone, but have no faith in them whatever.

this contest is american-sponsered by harper's and as a prize offers only publication of the book, which is the usual prize for such things and would be good auspices to get your book out under. it must be by a poet who has not yet published a book (anything in the english language is eligible) and is due by november 30. it must be double spaced and about

1–Spender was married to Agnes Maria (Inez) Pearn, 1936–9.
2–MacNeice was married to Mary Ezra MacNeice, 1930–6; she left him for an American.
3–South African poet Roy Campbell (1901–57).

60 pages. now, I ran right home and counted, estimating your poems double-spaced. 55 pages. almost exact. let me do this typing (it will give me the excuse of having a carbon of all your stuff to keep eternally, which I wanted anyhow). I'm sure you'll win this; I feel very queer about it.

the hitch, if such there be, is that the judges are: wh auden, marianne moore and, o god, stephen spender. what queer bed-fellows. but I trust miss moore's exactness & love of form; and you certainly have enough wit to win auden and social war consciousness to please spender. I'll bring your poetry ms. again to london for you to title and arrange it in order, checking each copy of each poem to see if it's the final form you want it. how about it? I'm strangely sure that the whole purpose I went to this dull gathering was to find out about this contest. I feel our luck coming.

your letter[1] this morning was lovely. your voice is like the spirit of god on the waters. I really move in it and with it. I love you to tell me things about reading. I loved the american indians and their tails. I am hoping and hoping about your dear fables. I wish to hell I could see you every two weeks at least during the year; I could live on you for a week after, look forward for a week before; a week from tomorrow now.

I love you and perish to be with you and lying in bed with you and kissing you all over and go just wild with thinking & wishing & remembering of your dear lovely mouth & incredibly lovely made flesh and oh how warm you are. I love you teddy teddy teddy and how I wish I could be with you, living with you, and you writing in granchester or something.

all my love ever
your own lone wife
sylvia

TO *Ted Hughes*

Saturday 20 October 1956 — TLS on Newnham College letterhead, family owned

Saturday morning
october 20

dearest love teddy . . .

in a week from today I shall be taking a very early train to meet you in london and commence living my 25th year. it is a rainy, blowy, gray ten thirtyish time; I am still in pajamas, having spent this hour after

1–TH to SP, [18 October 1956]; held by Lilly Library.

breakfast reading the latest new yorker stories---a moving one by william maxwell,[1] one of the editors, whom I heard speak eloquently and shyly at a college symposium[2]---a most "inward" man; story called "the french scarecrow", very tenderly, slowly told unfolding the fear of a man whose second wife is 3 months pregnant & who hasn't yet any children. dreams & the psychoanalyst play too much; but it's an honest thing; "something small",[3] another story set in rome about the haunting yearnings for lost youth; it makes me feel, that as soon as my poor dear "remember the stick man" comes back, I'll send them the "wishing box," "all the dead dears" and "the invisible man" (which I sat up last night typing the final copy, revised, of---such dangling prepositions!) they are all very wistful stories; heard rumors yesterday that j. d. salinger is supposed to be in a mental hospital. I feel very strangely about him for some reason; I am sure insanity is the most necessary state for a fine artist---that "divine madness" where the terror & piercing insights he has daily are not locked in retreat or raving but made into works of art; a kind of flickering wild light of susceptibility playing over psychic states which, if frozen, would become intolerable and result in madness. I wish I knew about j. d. salinger.

your news[4] about the children's hour which came this morning is just another documentary to my vivid conviction that england is not your place. people have the right of judging your life and work here who are narrow, bigoted, and just plain ignorant; worse, there is no higher court of appeal than this monolithic london. any mind which is quirked and limited enough to write "abstract and nebulous in conception and execution" is close to pathetically poverty-stricken. I am not saying this because they are your stories and I love them. it is a flannely false excuse---conception and execution are both jargon words; the stories are exactly the opposite of abstract and nebulous; they are as concrete and symbolic as the old fox-and-grapes aesop. every detail is vividly concrete---from fox renting deck-chairs to god burning his fingers. you say in your letter "they are abstract in conception"---well, what, for god' sake, isn't? conception is the "power of the mind to form ideas";[5] ideas themselves, however concrete they may

1–William Maxwell, 'The French Scarecrow', *New Yorker*, 6 October 1956, 38–44.

2–William Maxwell, 'The Writer as Illusionist', given at the symposium 'The American Novel at Mid-Century', Smith College, 4 March 1955.

3–Patricia Collinge, 'Something Small', *New Yorker*, 6 October 1956, 45–7.

4–TH to SP, [19 October 1956]; held by Lilly Library.

5–The definition stated in SP's dictionary, Noah Webster, *Webster's New Collegiate Dictionary* (Springfield, Mass.: G. & C. Merriam & Co, 1949), 171.

be (ideas of bricks & markets) are abstract until made vivid in stories, paintings or the objects themselves. so the conception being abstract, as an accusation, is ridiculously irrelevant---and "nebulous"---cloudy, hazy, misty, is simply false: what more conc<u>eptu</u>ally clear than vanity, as in polar bear (concretely realized throughout the story in her staying home on muddy days, preening & prinking, etc.) or sly deceitfulness in fox & dog story---"concrete" as any detective story plot. "Execution", it seems, means how they're written and embodied in form. there is nothing abstract or nebulous about this---torto's skin (one could make this a symbol for so much---discrimination, the smugness of the individualist who is "different"---all those human foibles which can, but don't have to be, read into each one of your tales). what is more concrete and clear than races, beauty contests, the demon making the bee, bumbo's rescue of the animals in the fire. teddy, these words of rejection were written by a very ignorant, pretentious person; they are, quite simply, arrant lies. they are not true.

I am going to send the stories off to peter davison[1] this week. even if they do not accept them, he will have a valuable point-of-view; he is a very imaginative man, and I remember he told me some stories, impromptu, that he made up about spotted dogs and children swinging and talking to the sun. alice in wonderland, the little prince, tolkien's "hobbit"---all the classic, best loved fairy tales are loved by grownups and children alike: why? because the adult mind, accustomed as it is in dealing with "abstract" ideas---about love, vanity, etc. (how about the bible stories---that is "fable" style, realizing an abstract concept in symbolic terms) finds rich food in, for example, the problems of alice and the mirror; the fox & the little prince discussing "friendship," etc., while the child loves the simple story, with, I am sure, an instinctive apprehension of the deeper levels of meaning. your fables are of this order. I know this with my head, and with my simple, childlike love of such fairy-tales, the uncritical, instinctive power of just "feeling" what is good.

I only wish I were with you. the thought of your work being at the mercy of such jargon-slinging idiots (their verdict, worded as it is is patent evidence that they liked them somehow, or felt they had some certain excellence "imaginative and well-written", but were disturbed, and afraid, and didn't know how to explain this but in impressive and utterly absurd rigmarole words).

1 – According to SP's calendar, she mailed 'How the Donkey Became' to the Atlantic Monthly Press on 23 October 1956.

I feel, in taking you to america, I am bringing, as it were, the grail to a place where it will be reverenced properly. time it may take; but in america, your voice will, increasingly, be heard. and loved.

carne-ross is taking two poems. that is something very good. realize, you haven't published in england yet (I wish lehmann would hurry up with a verdict), so here, at least, you are unknown; even though our international consciousness is sure, and rightly, that poetry and the nation are seething in wait for your next batch, which, by mail, should be there now. so sweet c-r is taking a risk, as it were. although he no doubt in a year or two or three will be famous and, by proxy, immortal for being the first british organization to spread your work. be glad of this. we are new, green yet, in their tremulous eyes; you are reading two; that is in itself wonderful. forget about the money, for god's sake.

I got my october fulbright check today for £70, meaning my book allowance is on it. of this, about £60 must go for college term bill. but there will be hotel money for next week, and food money out of it. november, I'll have to deduct the £18 for books out of £52, which should leave £34 clear; for you, for me, for getting me to spain. so forget about money. we are eating, sleeping. and will do.

NOW: with my incorrigible american weather-eye cocked for windfalls & contests I have a project for you to work on this year, for the next 5 or 6 months, and I want you to give it all you've got. you have enough "rightness" in your writing already to make this a real possibility. the observer, as you may already have heard, is running a competition[1] for a full-length play with three prizes of £500, £200 and £100 respectively, and a promise to put the winner on at the arts' theater (with royalties in addition) If the winner's good enough. the due date is not till next april 14th! exactly a year from when I came back from rome and our life together began.

judges are alec guinness, peter ustinov, michael barry, peter hall and kenneth tynan. action must take place in the period since the last war. must be submitted under psuedonym. and that is that. now, dear ponk, I want you to revolve several play ideas and work on a couple this year. write them or It to your own true standards. your integrity is the most magnificent I've ever known in this lousy corrupt world. the judges would appreciate this; your technique is essentially and naturally dramatic. even third prize would be wonderful. how about it?

1–'The Observer Play Competition £800 in Prizes', *The Observer*, 14 October 1956, 14. Errol John, *Moon on a Rainbow Shawl*, won the competition.

I loved your last story plot about country girl and city boy; is very potential.

I am about to brave weather to go to market, tailor and all the practical extroverted places I've been putting off all week; I hate doing errands for some reason. wrote small slight poem[1] yesterday morning, all morning: on reverse side:

please, please, though, darling, do not start thinking of writing first "to sell." I was very angry to hear the stupid children's hour verdict give you such pause. I'm sending the stories as is to peter davison; your next book of 10 is another thing. write for you, for me, and for our unborn children. and that is that is that is that.

separate page for poem now. since I had to get so righteously indignant.

and how I love you – I want you to <u>feel</u> it, to think of me, sitting here in the flesh & quick & loving you with all my mind, heart & body. it is so hard for me to be deprived of doing all the woman-things for you – cooking & bedding & listening & telling you how fine you are & how all my faith is in you. I walk in the thought & love of you as in a sheath of radiance which keeps me. in spite of the nightmares, the strange instinctive <u>guilt</u> I feel at being your wife, and cut off from all the symbolic, rich gestures and acts of a wife. (read schopenhauer's ridiculous essay "on women"[2] last night – according to him, we <u>are</u> the indian's vain lying tails! what poverty of experience he must have had to deny us minds & souls – & make us mere procreating animal machines!) I am living only for next saturday – birthday, day of being born again with you – my love – all of it & let it burn your mouth –

sylvia

1–According to SP's calendar, she wrote 'Spinster' on 19 October 1956. The poem, if it was included, is no longer with the letter.

2–German philosopher Arthur Schopenhauer (1788–1860); his 'On Women' (1851).

TO *Ted Hughes*

Sunday 21 October 1956 TLS, family owned

Sunday noon
October 21

dearest ted . . .

it is just before noon, and now clouds are covering a sheeny clear morning; I took my little notebook and walked along the river for an hour, making my way through mud and a quag of wet decayed leaves along by where you called the owls that night; I saw a strange animal that looked at first like a squirrel but wasn't, climbing up by the mud bank; was it a muskrat? an otter? passing three quiet fisherman, I went and sat up on the bank, writing a page of very simple description[1] of the scene, watching a translucent amber spider stitch his shiny thread from grass blade to stinging nettle, listening to the fall of yellow willow leaves, and breathing it all in.

when I came back to the house, zahida,[2] the little brown birdlike indian girl on my floor was ironing all her saris; they were hung along the stair railing like butterfly wings and peacock feathers; I have never seen such vivid jeweled colors, shining in gossamery silk---yellows, scarlets, purples, and all the spectrum of greens and blues like the head of a mallard duck; it was an incredibly joyous sight.

yesterday, granta came out with my story I wrote last year, very nicely illustrated (a guitar and a girl) by ben nash,[3] the editor, with whom I left the wishing-box and the invisible man. I shall bring a copy to london for you to look at. I wish they'd print these latest ones.

yesterday in late afternoon I saw two good films at the arts---a short incident about the civil war, "time out of war", very fine, and jean gabin in the french versionoof "le jour se lève." both of which I enjoyed. I had got a ticket to go see michael marland's[4] production of "deirdre of the sorrows"[5] with jess & the malayan girl, but was so full up at the end of the movies, that I extravagantly didn't go; the play got lousy reviews[6] &

1–See Appendix 10, *The Journals of Sylvia Plath* (2000).
2–Zahida Zaidi (1929–2011); B.A. 1948, Women's College, Aligarh Muslim University; 1958, English, Newnham College, Cambridge.
3–Benjamin Joliffe Nash (1935–), British; B.A. 1958, modern and medieval languages, King's College, Cambridge.
4–Educator Michael Marland (1934–2008), British, B.A. 1957, Sidney Sussex College, Cambridge; president of the ADC. Married Eileen Lim (1934–68) in 1955.
5–J. M Synge, *Deirdre of the Sorrows* (1910); performed at the ADC.
6–One such review is 'Cambridge Amateur Dramatic Club: "Deirdre of the Sorrows"', *The Times*, 17 October 1956, 3.

sounded terrible anyway---marland starred his pregnant wife who was his mistress and wardrobe mistress last year, and evidently she just was peasanty and munched apples through the whole thing. I got into one of my bad times, missing you terribly, biking through sheep's green under the dark poplars past all the kissing couples feeling hellish; I walked about in the blue frost of moonlight in the park, staring at all the empty benches upon which we'd sat and loved, wearing my black gown still stained white with relics of unborn children. I get these electric shocks of knowing how I miss you, which my general numbness protects me from during the day, unless, I masochistically let myself brood and brood on you. which I do often enough.

must read hooker & cambridge platonists today. I had queer dreams last night, about than minton[1] (after your letter,[2] I'm sure) and mother publishing a book called "above the rooftops of boston university" dated 1003 (I'm sure it was meant to be 2003) in which she described a landscape like a cloudy venice all done in darks moody greens, browns and blacks; I remember being very proud of her. I can't wait till next saturday.

now darling love ponk I took the swatch of green corduroy[3] down to roper tailors and they told me to drop by at the beginning of this next week & see about a convenient time for your fitting. how about, if it suits your plans, coming back to cambridge for a fitting monday october 29---you could ride back with me on the train and stay over the next day, & I could cook for you and you could go back to yorkshire or to london from there. write me right away what you'd like for a fitting day and I'll wait till I hear from you to make it with them. they said about £9 with lining & all and may need another piece for collar, etc. is that too much? I didn't know, but figured you could settle price when you have fitting. it will make your eyes green, this jacket. your damn lovely green eyes.

I hate sunday for no mail. I'm enclosing a contest[4] which appeared in granta. I'm sure no one hardly will try for it; why don't you? the main thing is the words & layout. look around at their other ads & what their main appeal is. even £5 would be nice. this olivetti has a £ key. I never had one before ££££££££££. I £ike it; it is the £ov£iest £yric £ithe shape. £a£a£a.

1–Nathaniel David Minton (1935–2012), British; B.A. 1956, natural sciences, Trinity College, Cambridge; friend of TH and contributor to *Saint Botolph's Review*.

2–TH to SP, [20–2 October 1956]; held by Lilly Library. Date assigned in *Letters of Ted Hughes* may be questionable.

3–The swatch is held by Lilly Library.

4–The enclosure is no longer with the letter.

I £ove you. I can't think of much else; I wait and wait for news of manuscripts. I think I will take the early Saturday morning train getting me in to Liverpool Street at 10 am. I will bring your poetry ms. to arrange in order for the Harper's contest. I will bring a birthday dress to wear. Will you meet me at the track? If you're late, I'll go into the main waiting room. Let's get this set and never change it.

Now, Teddy, could you get a hotel reserved ahead of time so we could just go right to it? We could come back to Cambridge (if you wanted your fitting Monday) Sunday afternoon, have shish kebabs and you stay till 10 in the evening at Whitstead. you write and tell me what.

I keep saying by myself: I am married I am married. I feel so mere and fractional without you. I look about at the petty simple weak people around me; I am amazed you live, that I didn't just make up your being warm and talking and being my husband.

The week turns now toward you, and climbs & climbs till Saturday – do fine on those readings Wednesday, tell me all about them; know I will be thinking & thinking of you & wishing you so well –

all my love –
your own
sylvia

TO *Ted Hughes*

Sunday 21 October 1956[1] ALS, family owned

dearest darling teddy . . .

it is sunday night right after dinner and I am terribly lonely for you – I think I have been writing you off & on for the whole day. but in spite of all my spasmodic calm & resolve I feel horrid & very black & wicked. it is simply a sin not to live with you. I could cry. I stalked alone to buffet supper in hall, ate in silence among strangers until the food stuck in my throat, threw the rest of it away and walked out into the mild night. I stared in the little intimate safe lighted rooms on clare road and felt like some queer alien not right in her head. every night I should go to bed with you & every day break I should rise with you. I begin to think how even if I cooked 3 meals (for us) a day & marketed, still I would save the time I now waste brooding & stalking tense through the mud wanting to cry out for you to come. if only I cooked for you.

1 – Date supplied from internal evidence.

I feel too, – very strongly, that I could work better if I were living properly with you – contrary to what I first supposed; i.e. that I could concentrate more spartanly on intellectual study if cut off from the constant sense of your presence. well, it's not so – I can probe & root most deeply & well when planted every minute in the rich, almost unconscious feeling of your presence. whatever time I so rightly would squander in nibbling your ear would not equal half the time I sit raging & frustrate here, wishing & imagining nibbling your ear. – I wish I was more clairvoyant – as it is, I am terribly torn: being apart from you six months, knowing I can spend vacations with you for a total of over 2½ months, our projected wedding – the present peace with authority (Newnham & Fulbright) – the stoic sense of sacrifice for a worthy end – all this opposed & troubled by the other side – the constant, deep – (so deep it is forming into vivid terrible nightmares) sense of terror, lack, superstition (symbolised by that traumatic last meeting in London which almost drove me wild, a kind of confirmation of my feeling of wrongness about our being apart – a judgment on that wrongness) – a sense that I could work <u>better</u> with you, which undercuts my whole former sureness about the wisdom of separation – of course, you hate cambridge & wouldn't want to come here again; I know. it is easier not to worry about persuading authorities – (yet even now some opportunistic devil in me is arguing for our case: tell them you were going to keep your marriage secret because you thought he'd have to be in spain all year, & now he's not). oh teddy, I need you so badly to talk to now, just to be with you. if we could live together in cambridge I could study all during the long vacations at christmas & easter, use the libraries, not worry about lugging books – we'd save fabulously in travel expenses & I wouldn't care if it rained all winter or if we got a nasty little place to live & I gave up whitstead. I could then combine love & writing & study much better then splitting them this abnormal way – wasting time when away from you in wishing you were here & wasting time with you by cursing the swiftness of that time & dreading fresh separation and wedding, official problems – all pales before the fact that I am rightfully sylvia hughes & I feed sad, sick & disinherited. my first purpose is not just a wedding – it is you; I am married to you & I would work & write best in living with you. I waste so much strength in simply fighting my tears for you – please understand about this & help me work it out –

love & more love –

sylvia

some more, still – just bear with me through this; I've got to get it out. if you ever even vaguely would consider living this year out with me in cambridge, the one difficult act would be telling newnham (there are married students here, though few; & dr. Krook, I'm sure, would back me up) & the fulbright (they also have many married students, though mostly male) & getting a place to live & moving me – it would cause a stir, but so what. we could do it all at the end of this term & maybe you try for a job teaching english at one of the many american air bases around here – the aesthetic beauty of whitstead, the peace & quiet of my room – all is as nothing without you, without constantly expressing my love for you. I do not want to be away from you for 6 of the best months of our lives!

I do not think we would be "making things easy" by living together – it would be a different kind of sacrifice (the wedding presents, etc) & also work & hard. I would ask dr. Krook's advice first, then the fulbright's permission, then newnham's. I am sure that the only difficulty would be the mere physical "bother" of going about it. I know you will discount all this – that you hate cambridge – but would living apart from the university with me be so awful to you? maybe we could live in granchester – you could write, teach part time & go to london for occasional BBC broadcasts – dr. Krook was right, you know – it is not good to be deprived of the rich seat of all power – the loved one – please please think about this –

I love you so –
your own
Sylvia

TO *Aurelia Schober Plath*

Monday 22 October 1956 — TLS (aerogramme), Indiana University

monday afternoon
October 22, 1956

dearest mother . . .

it is a rare blue and gold day; very rare; walked out this afternoon to sit by the delicate yellow willows in a golden haze by the cam, brooding over white swans, bobbing black water hens, and much else. I'm sending regular mail under separate cover a copy of granta (the "new yorker" of cambridge undergraduate life) which contains a story I believe you might have read as I wrote it for mr. kazin; in any case, don't let it get near the freeman's; you will recognize the characters. ben nash, the nice editor, has done fine illustrations, I think.

just received word that the nation had accepted another one of ted's poems,[1] a fine one about the violence of wind. I am with great difficulty saving this to tell him when I go to london on my birthday, as I can't bear not seeing his joy and being present at it, the "new yorker" rejected his fables (yet we will try it till we're bloody) so I hope this will cheer him up: if only the atlantic would buy one of the poems they've kept for 5 months now. ted makes his recordings of yeats & two of his own poems this wednesday.

which brings me to this great enormous problem I must discuss with you or explode. more and more I doubt the wisdom of being apart from ted in this tense, crucial year of our lives. at first, I thought I could study better away from him & domestic cares and that the fulbright might cancel my grant if I were married and newnham disown me. also, I wanted a wedding, a gala social ceremony. however, one by one these motives are exploding in front of my eyes: both of us work and write immeasurably better when with each other; I, for one, waste more time away from ted in dreaming about him, writing him, brooding on my absence from him, than I'd ever use up cooking us 3 meals a day; I looked up the fulbright lists, and they have three married women on grants; dr. krook, my philosophy professor, is most sympathetic about ted's & my work together & I am sure would testify to newnham that I could do my work better while living & studying with my husband. all of which revolves around the question: to reveal my secret marriage & live with ted in cambridge for the next two terms or Not? now even he doesn't know of my increasing desperation over this, although he certainly feels the same way about being apart from me. if we decided to reveal our marriage, we would decide it, of necessity this week. (of course ted hates much about cambridge & I don't know if he'd consider living & trying for a teaching job here or not; it would certainly be better qualification for teaching than in spain---I mean teaching children or at an american air force base) and we would save greatly if I didn't have to travel back & forth to spain twice. not to mention how much more time & energy I would have to work at the library here during term and the long vacations.

it would not be easy; it would be almost more difficult than not challenging the authorities & going on with wedding plans. but I feel a great guilt and sorrow at not living with ted. I waste more energy fighting tears & loneliness than I would cooking meals for him; if I could persuade him to live here, you could simply announce my wedding in england

1–Ted Hughes, 'Wind', *The Nation*, 10 November 1956, 408.

sometime in december (even if you've already announced my engagement, it wouldn't matter).

then we could cross on the ship together without subterfuge; we could still invite everybody to a big welcoming reception and all the tension of planning the actual wedding ceremony & wasting money on a dress would be gone---we could just all easily enjoy ourselves; cost all round would be less. I have perfect reasons for both fulbright & newnham authorities---I can say we thought ted would be working in spain & the job fell through (which is true) and that he can't support me but must earn ship-fare, so I should still keep grant; dr. krook can testify, I'm sure, to my keeping up & increasing the quality of my work. I feel I am not living to put on a ceremony before mrs. prouty, mary ellen chase, etc, although I love them dearly. I am living for ted, and ted before all else, and if he would think it good to reveal our marriage & go through the official red-tape, I would move out of whitstead into no-matter-what lodgings to work & write & study with him. I feel it is wrong to live apart for six of the best months of our lives; we are very miserable apart, and waste so much time and energy longing to be together; also, even when together, the need for separation subtly blights our joy.

now I would like to know how you feel about this. I will decide things with ted this weekend; he may well still want to go to spain with his uncle & not live in england, but I hope he will change his mind; I do not think this will make explanations difficult for you. in our engagement announcement this month you could put wedding "unannounced" & then in december engrave announcements of our wedding (what about dec. 16th--half a year from our actual wedding date?) and say to friends, ted got a job in cambridge or london & we felt it ridiculous not to get married here & now & will reune with all of them next june. do help me through this by advice & opinions; I feel sure I could go through the difficulty of red-tape here if you back me up –

all my love –
sivvy

TO *Ted Hughes*

Monday 22 October 1956 TLS, family owned

monday noon
october 22

dearest teddy . . .

it's not sunday, but it might as well be with no mail from you and all dead quiet; if the noon post doesn't bring any I shall be sad. I wrote you a letter last night which will no doubt arrive with this one; all is calm, now, and it is a fresh day; but the feelings I wrote about occur and recur, in spite of lulls and resolute plodding on; so I sent it.

I wrote two very very slight poems this morning and in penalty must read solidly from now till 10 tonight. one, "evergreens"[1] is particularly written to send to the new yorker; the other,[2] which I'll write on the back of this, describes my walk yesterday morning; that's that.

I had the queerest dreams last night; rather eerie & yet somehow pleasant. probably because I ate 6 cheese crackers before bed. I dreamt much of mrs. cantor & joan, her daughter, for whom I worked several summers ago; I thought I was working for them again, very vividly, at some beach. and strangely, this morning I got the first letter from mrs. cantor I've had in 6 months, about joan, etc.

the next part was weirdest---you and I were living with dr. krook, both of us being a kind of sorcerer's apprentice; she was, we decided, a magic, dangerous witch, and we would discover her power, but hide our intention, as she kept us working mercilessly and always appearing just as we thought we were alone. now, in the cantor dream, we were all seated around a big banquet table on the street of my first home-town by the ocean, about to begin a sort of wedding feast, when it started to pour, and clouds lowered in the stormy sky. Let's, mrs. cantor suggested, try levitation; whereupon we shut our eyes, put our hands on the table, jerked, rose, us with it, above the clouds and we felt sun warm on our bodies and ate in peace above the storm in the upper air. while at dr. krook's, you and I wanted to experiment with this newly discovered power: we sat, over a picnic, trying to concentrate and escape her continuous forays to see if we were working (how my philosophy reading must weigh on me!)

1–This poem does not appear to survive. TH comments on 'Evergreens' in his letter to SP, [23 October 1956]; held by Lilly Library.

2–According to SP's calendar, the second poem was 'Sheen & Speck'. This poem does not appear to survive. TH comments on 'Sheen & Speck' in his letter to SP, [23 October 1956]; held by Lilly Library.

and we found a very vivid green lawn, with a dark willow, squat dark trunk, smack in the middle, and I was showing this to you, with our manuscripts laid out under the tree, as the place of peace where at last we could practice rising together to this world above dr. krook's power and power of storm and vicissitudes. that was that. it came as close to any dream I've had for years in giving me the delight and breathless soaring I used to have in my flying dreams. I must eat more cheese.

I looked up the fulbright lists and found three married women on it; so singleness is not a condition of a fulbright for ladies.

I count the days till saturday: if I try my old trick of mixing my work & paper (which I don't want to come) with you & saturday, which I do want, then malicious time will hurry the work & deadline up & inadvertently catapult me into being with you again –

I love you & love you
sylvia

TO *Aurelia Schober Plath*

Tuesday 23 October 1956 — TLS (aerogramme), Indiana University

october 23
tuesday morning

dearest mother . . .

this will be an installment letter . . . coming so soon after the last; it is chiefly to tell you another bit of good news after ted's nation acceptance (which will only mean about $10 but nonetheless very lovely). I got a beautiful check for over £9 this morning (that's about $26) from guess who! The Christian Science Monitor!!!!

at their pay-rates, this seems like a rather glorious sum; you will be awe-struck, I think when you see what they bought: a short little article on benidorm[1] (that lovely little spanish town where we spent 5 weeks on our honeymoon) and 4 (four) of the best sketches in pen-and-ink I've ever done. I think that these drawings will also amaze you; it shows what I've done since going out with ted; every drawing has in my mind and

1–Sylvia Plath, 'Sketchbook of a Spanish Summer', *Christian Science Monitor*, 5 November 1956, 15, with drawings captioned 'Sardine boats and lights patterned the beach during daylight hours' and 'At sunup, the banana stand at the peasant market in Benidorm opened for business'; and 6 November 1956, 19, with drawings captioned 'Palms and pueblos on the sea cliffs at Benidorm, Spain' and 'Arched stairway to Castillo, in Benidorm'.

heart a beautiful association of our sitting together in the hot sun, ted reading, writing poems, or just talking with me; please get lots and lots of copies of each article; the sketches are very important to me: the one of the sardine boats is the most difficult & unusual I've ever done; the spanish market was wonderful fun (the little man at the stand on the right wanted to get in, & so put his garlic string over to make his place extra decorative) & hot & difficult; the castle rock & houses for design is a favorite; the stairway is my least favorite, but not too bad; I hope you love them; send them to mrs. prouty please; show her how creative ted's made me! got a lovely letter from mrs. cantor yesterday all about how happy she is about joan's harvard date! the queerest thing---I had the most vivid dream about mrs. cantor & joan the early morning before I got the letter: I dreamt I was back working for them, and we were having a wedding feast on the streets in winthrop right off somerset terrace & it started to storm & rain: "well," mrs. cantor suggested philosophically, "let's try levitation." so we all---you, warren, ted me & the cantors, put our hands on the table & shut our eyes; jerk, tilt, the table rose & soon we could feel the sun on our bodies, opened our eyes, & continued our feast in the air above the vicissitudes of the earthly storm! I must eat more cheese before bed! anyway, the letter came that morning, the 1st I've had from her for months, & the dream it seems, was somehow sent to me by this letter in my mailbox; when ted & I begin living together we shall become a team better than mr. & mrs. yeats[1]---he being a competent astrologist, reading horoscopes, & me being a tarot-pack reader and, when we have enough money, a crystal-gazer. will let you know of our decision after this weekend. I hope ted will go through all this with me; it is ridiculous for us to separate our forces when it is such a magnificently aspected year---I'm typing a book of his poems (an impressive 50 pages) for a contest at the end of november; he will spend the year writing a verse play for a contest in the spring at which alec guinness, kenneth tynan & others will judge; I know he can't work in spain, or in london; he needs my daily love & care as much as I need his; we will fight this out; I'd love cambridge so if he were here; the fulbright has other married women---there's no question of his supporting me, either, since all he'll earn will have to go for ship fare to america. I can't rest till I get this settled. I write & think & study perfectly when with him; apart, I'm split & only can work properly in brief stoic spells.

1–Georgie Yeats, née Hyde-Lees (1892–1968), wife of W. B Yeats.

got your darling card & the $10 this morning; you are wonderful! already you know what makes me happiest---those wonderful records which ted and I can share together! I can't wait to tell him. I'd honestly rather have <u>him</u> get something than myself, and if it's something we both can listen to together that's just perfect!

---

later tuesday night: WELL: HERE IS THE LATEST BULLETIN: ted came up from london tonight at my urgent request, going back just now after a delectable steak & mushroom dinner, peas, strawberries AND your delectable birthday date-nut bars. both of us have been literally sick to death being apart, wasting all our time & force trying to cope with the huge fierce sense of absence. SO: spain is out; ted is coming to live & work in cambridge for the rest of the year; in the next two weeks we are going on a rigorous campaign of making our marriage public to first my philosophy supervisor, next the fulbright, next newnham; we are married and it is ridiculous and impossible for either of us to be whole or healthy apart. the year could be so fine, with us studying & writing together & much more advantageous financially without those silly 3 round trips to spain & no certain job there. in 10 days the proper people should know; it will be a fight, but I feel this is the only right thing, as does ted; why don't you just announce our engagement now, wedding unscheduled; then announce by engraving our wedding on december 16th & the new home address we'll hope to have by then; then for a gala party on our return; no wedding expense (we'll need every bit of money for cape summer) & relatively no strain on you to keep up pretenses any more; we can live openly at home, come home married on ship, & I can write & do good exams if my teddy is with me – do write & stand by. we will be so happy together from dec. 7th on – wish us luck with the authorities

your own loving
sivvy

TO *Peter Davison*

Tuesday 23 October 1956 TLS (photocopy), Yale University

Whitstead
4 Barton Road
Cambridge, England
October 23, 1956

Mr. Peter Davison
Office of the Associate Editor
The Atlantic Monthly Press
8 Arlington Street
Boston 16, Massachusetts
U.S.A.

Dear Peter,

I was so pleased to get your fine letter.[1] Life here is divided between writing and studying and, with Ted in London, not too stoic.

I am enclosing, as you suggested, the manuscript of Ted's book of children's fables in case the children's department at the Atlantic Press might be at all interested. Perhaps they might want to shorten it to fewer fables, or present them in different order; let me know if they even consider it any sort of possibility. Now, if they don't think it's suitable for them, would you be so good as to have them send it on to one of the larger children's publishers in New York---probably you would know which were most potential---Macmillan, Grosset & Dunlap, Reynal Hitchcock, or what. I don't even know if these places still exist, having only my few children's books here to go by. I hope the familiar treatment of God won't be against these stories: I don't know how rigidly careful children's editors have to be about religion. God here is presented in a very concrete childlike way (not omniscient, but deceivable & burnable) and, I think, something like that play "Green Pastures" (by Marc Connelly or some such?) where it's a case of colloquial folk-god. Needless to say, I'd greatly appreciate any words you yourself have of opinion and advice about these fables.

Ted is at present doing a series of free-lance readings for the BBC third program---a recording of Yeats' "Tower" and some of the short Crazy Jane poems: also, two of his own poems for one of their "Poets' Voice" features. The Nation likes his poems as does Poetry, Chicago (what a difference in standard, though!) and keep buying. Much is out, has been out ages; we wait.

1–Peter Davison to SP, 2 October 1956; held by Lilly Library.

As for me: I write short stories & poems daily, work on rough stories around the central idea of this novel, feel awed enough by the Idea of A Novel to say probably I'll have a rough draft ready for you to look at sometime toward the end of next summer. I probably should postpone all thoughts of Atlantic Contests till 1958; or at least not think about them, but work steadily.

I have several recent stories out which I'm waiting to hear from. Poetry (Chicago, of course; it's just habit, writing it after) gratifyingly just bought six (6!) of my latest poems in one lovely fell swoop with a very nice letter. I am convinced that there will be a market for a woman lyric poet who is not a man-imitating neo-platonist intellectual (e.g. Kathleen Raine) nor a bitter-sweet coy feminine one, like the weaker Millay, sarcastic Dorothy Parker, or miserable Teasdale; such tremulousness; such frustration. So here comes a burgeoning Wife of Bath hand in glove with Marie Curie; or some such. My.

Anyhow, the Christian Science Monitor has just bought a little article I wrote on Benidorm, Spain, with four of the best pen-and-ink sketches I think I've ever done---sardine boats, market place, castle hill, spanish staircase. They have raised my rate most pleasantly since I first started doing scrubby little free-lance articles and sketches for them. And their pay standards are notoriously low. Spiritual compensation, I suppose, is intended to remunerate the truly righteous.

Let me know about these fables. And if they do not work out with your press, do send them on to New York at your discretion. Be really frank in your criticism: it will help a lot.

I look most forward to coming back home next June. I feel somehow like a feminine Samson with hair cut, if such is possible---being so far away from editors & publishing houses!

Very best wishes.
Sincerely,
Sylvia Plath

INDEX